Lady Boss

&

The

Bitch

JACKIE COLLINS

Jackie Collins brings the wild and sexy world of superstardom alive. Her phenomenally successful novels have made her as famous as the movers and shakers, power-brokers and superstars she writes about with an insider's knowledge. With 200 million copies of her books sold in more than forty countries, Jackie Collins is one of the world's top-selling writers. In a series of sensational bestsellers, she has blown the lid off Hollywood life and loves. 'It's all true,' she says. 'I write about real people in disguise. If anything, my characters are toned down – the real thing is much more bizarre.'

There have been many imitators, but only Jackie Collins can tell you what *really* goes on in the fastest lane of all. From Beverly Hills bedrooms to a raunchy prowl along the streets of Hollywood. From glittering rock parties and concerts to stretch limos and the mansions of the power-brokers – Jackie Collins chronicles the *real* truth.

JACKIE COLLINS

Lady Boss

& The Bitch

PAN BOOKS

Lady Boss first published 1990 by Willian Heinemann Ltd.
First published by Pan Books 1991
The Bitch first published 1979 by Pan Books

This omnibus edition published 2004 by Pan Books
an imprint of Pan Macmillan Ltd
Pan Macmillan, 20 New Wharf Road, London N1 9RR
Basingstoke and Oxford
Associated companies throughout the world
www.panmacmillan.com

ISBN 0 330 43930 8

1 3 5 7 9 8 6 4 2

A CIP catalogue record for this book is available from
the British Library.

Phototypeset by Input Typesetting Ltd, London
Printed and bound in Great Britain by
Mackays of Chatham plc, Chatham Kent

Lady Boss

For Tracy, Tiffany and Rory.
Girls can do anything!

Chapter 1

From the very beginning they were destined to be a lethal combination – Lucky Santangelo and Lennie Golden. Two stubborn, crazy, smart people.

Lennie was tall and lanky, with dirty-blond hair and ocean-green eyes. He was good-looking in an edgy offhand way. Women loved his looks. At thirty-seven, he'd finally made it as a movie star. He was the new breed – a comedian of the Eddie Murphy/Chevy Chase school. Cynical and funny, his films made big bucks – the bottom line in Hollywood.

Lucky Santangelo Richmond Stanislopoulos Golden was the thrice-married daughter of the infamous Gino Santangelo. In her early thirties, she was darkly, exotically beautiful, with a tangle of wild jet curls, dangerous black eyes, smooth olive skin, a full sensual mouth, and a slim body. She was a fiercely independent, strong-willed woman who never compromised and always took chances.

Together they were like charged electricity.

They'd been married for nearly a year, and both looked forward to their wedding anniversary in September with a mixture of delight and amazement. Delight, because they loved each other very much. Amazement, because who would ever have thought it would last?

Currently Lennie was in Los Angeles shooting *Macho Man* for Panther Studios. The film was a comedy take-off on all the Hollywood super-heroes – Eastwood, Stallone, and Schwarzenegger.

They'd rented a beach house in Malibu, but while Lennie was filming, Lucky chose to stay in New York where she headed a billion-dollar shipping company – left to her by her second husband, Dimitri Stanislopoulos. She also wanted Bobby, her six-and-a-half-year-old son by Dimitri, to be educated in England, and being in New York meant she was closer to his English school.

On most weekends she either visited Bobby in London or Lennie in Los Angeles. "My life is one long plane ride," she joked ruefully to friends. But everyone knew Lucky thrived on activity, and to sit by Lennie's side playing movie star's wife would have bored her. As it was they had a volatile and passionate marriage.

Macho Man was causing Lennie nothing but problems. Every night he called Lucky with a litany of complaints. She listened patiently while he told her the producer was a jerk, the director a has-been lush, his leading lady was sharing her bed with the producer, and Panther Studios was run by money-mad grafters; he wanted out.

Lucky listened, smiling to herself. She was working on a deal that, if all went according to plan, would free him from the restrictions of answering to a director he didn't respect, a producer he loathed, and a studio run by people he never planned to do business with again – even though he'd foolishly, against her advice, signed a three-picture contract with Panther.

"I'm about ready to walk," he threatened for the hundredth time.

"Don't," she said, attempting to soothe him.

"I can't make it with these assholes," he groaned.

"Those *assholes* can sue you for a fortune. *And* stop you working elsewhere," she added, the perfect voice of reason.

"Fuck 'em!" he replied recklessly.

"Don't do anything until I get out there," she warned. "Promise me that."

"*When*, for chrissakes? I'm beginning to feel like a virgin."

A throaty chuckle. "Hmm . . . I didn't know you had that good a memory!"

"Hurry it up, Lucky. I really miss you."

"Maybe I'll be there sooner than you think," she said mysteriously.

8

"I'm sure you'll recognize me," he said dryly. "I'm the guy with the permanent hard-on."

"Very funny." Still smiling, she replaced the receiver.

Lennie Golden would be shocked and delighted when he found out her surprise. And when he did, she planned to be right there next to him, ready to enjoy the expression on his face.

Once he had put the phone down Lennie felt restless. His wife was the most exciting woman in the world, but – damn it – she pissed him off. Why couldn't she say – *Lennie, if things are tough I'll be right there?* Why couldn't she forget everything else and be with him?

Lucky Santangelo. Drop-dead gorgeous. Strong. Determined. Enormously rich. And too independent.

Lucky Santangelo. His wife.

Sometimes it all seemed like a fantasy – their marriage, his career, everything. Six years ago he'd been just another comedian looking to score a gig, a few bucks, anything going.

Lennie Golden. Son of crusty old Jack Golden, a stand-up Vegas hack, and the unstoppable Alice – or "Alice the Swizzle" as his mother was known in her heyday as a "now you see 'em – now you don't" Las Vegas stripper. He'd split from New York when he was seventeen and made it all the way without any help from his folks. His father was long dead, but Alice was still around. Sixty-five years old and frisky as an overbleached starlet, Alice Golden was caught in a time warp. She had never come to terms with getting older, and the only reason she acknowledged Lennie as her son was that he was famous. "I was a child bride," she'd simper to anyone who'd listen, batting her fake lashes, and curling her overpainted lips in a lascivious leer. "I gave birth to Lennie when I was twelve!"

Lennie had bought her a small house in Sherman Oaks. She wasn't thrilled at being shunted out to the Valley, but what could she do? Alice Golden lived with the dream that one day she'd be a star herself, and then – as far as she was concerned – they could all watch out.

"You're wanted on the set, Mr Golden," said Cristi, the second assistant, appearing at the door of his trailer.

Cristi was a natural California blonde, with an earnest expression, and extra-long legs encased in patched dungarees. Lennie knew she was a natural blonde because Joey Firello, his friend and cohort in *Macho Man*, had been there, and when it came to women Joey had a notoriously big mouth. Not to mention a notoriously big dick – which he'd affectionately christened Joey Senior.

Lennie never double-taked anyone anymore. Since Lucky had entered his life he couldn't even be bothered to look, and he really didn't appreciate Joey giving him a rundown of the sexual habits of every female on the set. "You're just jealous, man," Joey had laughed when he'd complained. "Out of action an' gettin' no action, huh?"

Lennie had merely shaken his head with a "Why don't you grow up" expression. Once he'd been a serious cocksman. *If it's blonde and it moves – nail it* had been his motto. For years he'd explored every possibility, managing to avoid any lasting commitments.

Along the way there'd been a few women who'd left their mark. Eden Antonio for one.

Ah, Eden, he thought ruefully. She was something else, a real operator.

Poor Eden. In spite of all her dreams she'd ended up living with a vicious mobster who'd used her in a series of porno movies. Not exactly the future she'd planned for herself.

And then there was Olympia. He'd married the plump, spoilt shipping heiress because he felt sorry for her – and stayed because it never got any easier. Unfortunately, even he was unable to save Olympia from her own excesses. Eventually she and spaced-out rock star Flash overdosed in a sleazy New York hotel, and Lennie was a free man.

Now he had Lucky, and life didn't get any better.

Grabbing a pack of cigarettes from the dresser, he said, "OK, Cristi, I'm on my way."

10

The girl nodded thankfully, earnest expression firmly in place. This was not an easy movie to work on, and any co-operation at all was a definite plus.

On the set Joey Firello was arguing with the old-time director, Grudge Freeport, about the next scene. Grudge wore a bad rug and chewed tobacco – spitting great gobs of it indiscriminately wherever he pleased. As usual he was almost drunk.

Marisa Birch, Lennie's leading lady, who doubled as the producer's girlfriend, leaned against a slant board idly picking her cuticles. She was a startling-looking woman, six feet tall with spiky silver hair and frighteningly huge silicone breasts – a present from her former husband, who hadn't considered thirty-six inches enough. Marisa was a terrible actress, and as far as Lennie was concerned she was helping to ruin the movie in a big way.

Macho Man, he thought sourly, a comedy destined to be dead on arrival at the box-office – in spite of his presence. His other movies had been hits; now he was stuck in a real disaster waiting to happen, and there was nothing he could do about it. The trouble was he'd been dazzled by the astronomical amount of money Mickey Stolli, the head of Panther Studios, had offered him – and like a greedy fool he'd gone ahead and made another three-picture commitment.

"Don't do it," Lucky had warned him. "The lawyers only just got you out of your other deal, and now you're tying yourself up again. When are you going to learn? I'm telling you – keep your options open, it's more of a challenge."

Sure, his wife loved a challenge. The trouble was *he* couldn't resist the lure of mega-bucks – and mega-bucks put him one step nearer to his wife's unbeatable fortune.

Oh yeah, he knew he should have listened to Lucky – she had the Santangelo knack of knowing all the right moves and when to make them. Her father, Gino, had parlayed himself up from nothing. The old guy had style, and Lennie admired him. But what the hell – big bucks were big bucks, and he never wanted to be the poor relation.

Fortunately, they were back in the studio shooting interiors. The week before, they'd been on location in the rugged Santa Monica mountains – a real pain. And coming right up was a five-week location shoot in Acapulco.

With a sigh he entered the fray.

Marisa puckered up luscious, swollen lips and blew him a kiss. She'd been after him from their first meeting. He'd managed to remain totally uninterested. Even if he hadn't had Lucky, he'd never been turned on by silicone.

"Hi, Lennie, cookie," she crooned, erect nipples straining in his direction.

Shit! Another fun day at the studio.

Lucky hurried from the tall chrome and glass building on Park Avenue that still bore the Stanislopoulos name. She had no desire to change it. One day everything would belong to her son Bobby, and Dimitri's granddaughter, Brigitte, so the name stayed.

Lucky was extremely fond of Brigitte. The seventeen-year-old reminded her of Olympia, the girl's mother, at the same age. Olympia and Lucky had once been close friends; but that was long ago and far away, and a lot had happened since their out-of-control teenage years when they'd been at boarding school in Switzerland and ended up getting expelled.

When Olympia had died so tragically young, Lucky was sad, even though Olympia's death had finally released Lennie – who was married to her at the time – from a lifetime of unwanted responsibility.

Occasionally she'd felt guilty that everything had worked out so well – but what the hell, that was life, and hers hadn't exactly been a day at the beach. At the age of five she'd discovered her mother's body floating in the family swimming pool. Then years later, Marco, her first love, was gunned down in the parking lot of the Magiriano Hotel. Shortly after, Dario, her brother, was shot to death. Three tragic murders.

Lucky had taken her revenge. She was a Santangelo, after all. *Don't fuck with a Santangelo*. The family motto.

As soon as she walked out of the building she spotted Boogie lounging against the side of the dark green Mercedes. He leapt to attention when he saw his boss striding purposefully towards him and quickly threw open the passenger door.

Boogie was her driver, bodyguard, and friend. They'd been together for many years and his loyalty was unquestioning. He was long-haired, tall, and skinny, with an uncanny ability to be there whenever she needed him. Boogie knew her better than almost anyone.

"The airport," she said, sliding onto the front seat.

"Are we in a hurry?" he asked.

Lucky's black eyes flickered with amusement. "We're *always* in a hurry," she replied. "Isn't that what life's all about?"

Chapter 2

When Gino Santangelo took his morning constitutional he invariably followed the same route. Straight out of his apartment building on Sixty-fourth Street. Across Park to Lexington. And then a brisk walk along Lexington for several blocks.

He enjoyed his routine. At seven a.m. the streets of New York were not crowded, and in the early hours the weather was usually bearable.

He always stopped for a Danish at his favourite coffee shop, then picked up a newspaper from the corner vendor.

As far as Gino was concerned this was the most pleasurable hour of his day – except when Paige Wheeler visited from Los Angeles, which was not as often as he would have liked.

When Paige came into town his morning stroll was put on hold while he spent lazy mornings with her rolling around on his comfortable double bed. Not bad for an old man in his seventies. Suffice it to say, Paige brought out the best in him.

God damn it, he loved the woman, even though she still steadfastly refused to leave her producer husband of twenty years.

For a long time he'd been asking her to get a divorce. For some unknown reason she wouldn't do it. "It would destroy Ryder if I wasn't around," she'd said simply, as if that was explanation enough.

"Bullshit," Gino had exploded. "What about me?"

"You're strong," Paige had replied. "You can survive without me. Ryder would crumble."

My ass he'd crumble, Gino thought to himself as he walked along the street. Ryder Wheeler was one of the most successful independent producers in Hollywood. If Paige dumped him, he'd jump the nearest bimbo and that would be that.

What made Paige think she was so goddamn indispensable? To Gino she *was* indispensable. To Ryder she was just a wife he'd had for twenty years. The guy would probably *pay* for his freedom.

Gino had seriously thought about sending in a third party to plead his case. Offer Ryder a million bucks and goodbye schmuck.

Unfortunately, in the last eighteen months Ryder Wheeler had fathered two movie mega-hits and had no need of anyone's money. The jerk was shovelling it in.

"Screw the son of a bitch," Gino muttered aloud, well aware of the fact that he was not getting any younger, and he wanted Paige by his side permanently.

There was a crisp breeze as he stopped at his usual news-stand and schmoozed for a moment with Mick, the dour Welshman with one glass eye and a bad set of yellowing false teeth. Mick ran his little kingdom with unfailing gloom and bad humour.

"What's goin' on in the neighbourhood?" Gino asked casually, pulling up the collar of his windbreaker.

"Hookers an' cab drivers. They should bloody shoot the

lot of 'em," Mick replied, a malevolent gleam in his one good eye. "A couple of 'em bastards nearly got me t'other day. It's a good thing I got me wits about me – I paid 'em back good."

Gino knew better than to question further – Mick was given to telling long imaginative stories. Throwing down change, he picked up a *New York Post* and hurried on his way.

The headlines were lurid. Mob boss Vincenzio Strobbinno gunned down outside his own home. There was a picture of Vincenzio face down in a pool of his own blood.

The jerk had it coming, Gino thought with hardly a flicker of surprise. Young Turks. Hotheads. The assholes never waited to see if they could work things out, they just blew each other away as if that was the answer to everything. Today Vincenzio – tomorrow another one. The violence now was relentless.

Gino was relieved he was out of it. Many years ago he would have been right in the middle, loving every minute.

Not now. Now he was an old man. A *rich* old man. A *powerful* old man. He could afford to say nothing – merely observe.

Gino did not look seventy-nine years old. He was amazing – easily able to pass for a man in his mid-sixties with his energetic gait, thick mop of grey hair, and penetrating black eyes. His doctors were constantly surprised at his energy and enthusiasm for life, not to mention his remarkable physical appearance.

"What about this AIDS problem I keep hearin' about?" he'd recently asked his personal physician.

"You don't have to worry about that, Gino," his doctor had replied with a hearty laugh.

"Yeah? Says who?"

"Well . . ." The doctor had cleared his throat. "You're not still . . . active . . . are you?"

"Active?" Gino had roared with laughter. "Are you shittin' me, doc? The day I can't get it up is the day I lie down an' die. *Capisce?*"

"What's your secret?" the doctor had asked enviously.

15

He was fifty-six and a tired man. He was also full of admiration for his feisty patient.

"Don't take no crap from no one." Gino grinned, most of his strong white teeth still intact. "Hey – 'scuse me, doc – correct that. Do not suffer fools. I read that somewhere. Sounds more like it, huh?"

Gino Santangelo had obviously led a fascinating life full of adventure. The doctor thought gloomily of his own five years in medical school, followed by over twenty years of private practice. The only adventure *he'd* experienced was when one of his patients fell in lust with him and they'd enjoyed a furtive six-week affair. Not much to get excited about.

"Your blood pressure is perfect," he'd assured Gino. "The cholesterol test turned out fine. Uh . . . about your sex life. Maybe you might consider investing in some condoms."

"Condoms, doc?" Gino began to laugh. "We used to call 'em rubber joy-killers. Y'know – like takin' a swim in your boots."

"They're much improved today. Thin latex, a smooth feel. You can even get them in different colours if you're so inclined."

"No kiddin'?" Gino had laughed again. He could just imagine Paige's face if he slipped a black johnny over his cock.

Oh boy, not such a bad idea – Paige loved variety. Maybe he'd try it. Maybe . . .

The airport was a mob scene as usual. Lucky was met by an efficient young man in a three-piece business suit who escorted her from her car to the private TWA lounge.

"Your flight's running fifteen minutes late, Ms Santangelo," he said apologetically, as if he were personally responsible. "Can I get you a drink?"

Automatically she glanced at her watch. It was past noon. "I'll have a J & B on the rocks," she decided.

"Coming right up, Ms Santangelo."

Leaning back she closed her eyes. Another lightning trip

16

to LA she couldn't tell Lennie about. Only this time she hoped to close the deal that would make her husband a free man again.

This journey west was the final clincher.

Chapter 3

Abedon Panercrimski — or as he'd been known to a world that had all but forgotten him, Abe Panther — was eighty-eight years old and looked it, even though he didn't act it. Abe still had his balls, although many — including two ex-wives and countless lovers — had tried to cut them off.

Abe rose every morning promptly at six. First he showered, then he put in his new set of brilliant white teeth, combed his few remaining strands of silver hair, swam the length of his pool ten times, and feasted on a hearty breakfast of steak, eggs, and three cups of bitter black Turkish coffee.

Next he lit up a formidable Havana cigar and proceeded to read the daily newspapers.

Abe loved reading anything. He devoured the *Wall Street Journal* and the English *Financial Times*. With equal enthusiasm he scanned the gossip rags, enjoyed every juicy item. It pleased him to have knowledge, however useless. From world affairs to idle chitchat, he absorbed it all.

After his marathon reading session it was time for Inga Irving, his long-time companion, to join him on the terrace of his Miller Drive home.

Inga was a big-boned, straight-backed Swedish woman in her early fifties. She never used makeup and had allowed her shoulder-length club-cut hair to grey naturally. Inga always wore loose-fitting slacks and a shapeless sweater. In spite of her lack of decoration she was still a striking-looking woman who had obviously once been a great beauty.

Long ago, when Abe was *the* Hollywood tycoon to

17

beat all Hollywood tycoons – including Messrs Goldwyn, Mayer, Zanuck, and Cohn – he'd attempted to make Inga into a star. He had not succeeded. The camera didn't like Inga Irving, the public didn't like Inga Irving, and after several tries in three big Panther Studios productions Abe had finally given up. Every contract producer, director, and leading man on the lot had breathed freely again. Inga Irving was not destined to be the new Greta Garbo, in spite of Abe's valiant efforts.

When she so desired, Inga could be a prize bitch, moody, rude, and insulting. Those qualities might have been acceptable if she'd possessed talent and star potential. Alas, she didn't. And during her rise to nowhere she'd made many enemies.

Inga had never forgiven Abe for not persevering on her career. She'd stayed with him anyway: being the companion of the once great Abe Panther was better than anything else she could think of.

When his last divorce had taken place he didn't marry her. Inga refused to blackmail or beg. She was a proud woman. Besides, as far as she was concerned, she was his common-law wife, and when Abe died she had every intention of claiming what was rightfully and legally hers.

Every day around noon, Abe partook of a light snack. He favoured oysters when they were in season, accompanied by a glass of dry white wine. After lunch he had a nap, awaking refreshed after an hour to watch two of his favourite soaps on television, followed by a solid dose of Phil Donahue.

Abe Panther never left his house. He hadn't done so for ten years – ever since his stroke.

Six weeks in the hospital and he allowed them to wrest the studio from his grasp. Although technically he never lost control – and was indeed still President and owner of Panther Studios – he had not had any inclination to return. Making movies wasn't the same as it once was. Abe had been in the picture business since he was eighteen, and at seventy-eight he'd decided taking a break was no big deal.

18

The break had lasted ten years, and nobody expected him to return.

What they did expect, Abe realized, was for him to drop dead and leave everything to them.

His living relatives consisted of two granddaughters – Abigaile and Primrose – and their offspring.

Abigaile and Primrose were as unalike as two sisters could be. They couldn't stand each other. Sisterly love and affection failed to exist between them.

Abigaile was pushy and grasping. She loved entertaining and big parties. She lived for shopping and glitzy social events. A true Hollywood princess.

Primrose – the younger and prettier of the two – had opted for a different kind of life in England, where she was able to raise her two children in what she considered a more real atmosphere.

And then there were his granddaughters' husbands. Abigaile's husband, Mickey Stolli, ran the studio, while Primrose's spouse, Ben Harrison, took care of Panther Studio's overseas operation.

Mickey and Ben also loathed each other. For the sake of business they had formed an uneasy truce. It helped that they lived on different sides of the Atlantic.

Abe had christened them the scum-in-laws. He considered them both cheating connivers who would steal everything they could.

It amused him to discuss the scum-in-laws with Inga. She hardly ever cracked a smile, although she was certainly an avid listener, missing no detail of what he imagined were the scum-in-laws' latest nefarious activities.

Abe had a loyal employee firmly ensconced on the studio lot. This was Herman Stone, an unassuming man with the useless title of Personal Assistant to Mr Panther. Herman visited Abe once a month and gave him a rundown of studio activities. Everyone knew he was Abe's spy, therefore he was left alone and was never privy to any important information. He had a comfortable office, and an elderly secretary, Sheila. Herman and Sheila were both relics of

Abe Panther's reign, perfectly harmless and absolutely unfirable until the day Abe Panther dropped dead.

Soon, Mickey Stolli hoped. For then he would have complete control and could set about getting rid of his brother-in-law, Ben Harrison.

Soon, Ben Harrison hoped. For then he was going to move back to Hollywood and grab the studio from his conniving brother-in-law's grasp.

When Abe Panther dropped, Abigaile Stolli and Primrose Harrison knew they were destined to become two of the most powerful women in Hollywood. Abe had never gone public with Panther Studios. He owned it — all one hundred and twenty glorious acres of prime land. So the girls would inherit everything.

Mickey Stolli planned to rule his inherited kingdom like the studio heads of the old days.

Ben Harrison planned to sell off parcels of the valuable land just as Twentieth Century-Fox had done, and become a multi-billionaire.

The scum-in-laws. They couldn't wait, and old Abe Panther knew it.

That's why he had other ideas. Ideas that if Abigaile and Mickey, Primrose and Ben knew about, they would have committed hara-kiri in the middle of Chasens on a Sunday night.

Abe planned to sell the studio.

And the buyer he had in mind was Lucky Santangelo.

Chapter 4

In New York Steven Berkeley kissed Mary-Lou, patted her lovingly on the stomach, and headed for the door, pausing only to ask, "Are we in or out tonight?"

"Out," she replied.

Steven groaned. "Why?" he asked plaintively.

"'Cause when the baby starts to bulge, I ain't goin' nowhere, man."

They both laughed. Mary-Lou was a glowingly pretty black woman, a few months away from her twenty-third birthday, and two and half months away from giving birth to their first child. They'd been married nearly three years.

Steven Berkeley had skin the colour of rich milk chocolate, black curly hair, and unfathomable green eyes. Six feet three inches tall, and forty-seven years of age, he kept himself in great shape — visiting the gym three times a week, and swimming at an indoor pool every other day.

Mary-Lou was the star of a popular television sitcom, and Steven was a highly successful defence attorney. They'd met when her managers had approached his firm to represent her while she sued a low-life magazine for publishing nude photos of her taken when she was sixteen. Steven had accepted the case, won her an award of sixteen million dollars — since appealed and reduced — and married the girl. In spite of a twenty-four-year age difference, both of them had never been happier.

"And what kind of incredibly exciting evening do you have planned for us tonight?" he asked sarcastically.

Mary-Lou grinned. Whatever it was, she knew Steven would sooner stay home. He loved to cook, watch television, and make love — not necessarily in that order.

"We were supposed to see Lucky," she said. "But her secretary phoned to say she had to go out of town. So . . . I called my mother and asked her to join us."

"Your mother!"

Mary-Lou shook her head in exasperation. "You *looove* my mother. Quit giving me a hard time."

"Sure I *looove* your mother," he mimicked, "only I *looove* my wife even better. Why can't we spend a quiet evening at home, just you and me?"

Mary-Lou stuck out her tongue and wiggled it at him. "That's all you ever want to do."

"Anything wrong with that?"

"Get outta here, Steven. Go to work. You're *such* a nag."

21

"Who, me?"

"Good*bye*, Steven."

He continued to defend himself. "Is it a criminal offence to want to be alone with my wife?"

"Out!" Mary-Lou said firmly.

"One kiss and I'm history," he promised.

"*One* kiss only," she said sternly.

One kiss turned into two, then three, and before either of them could help it they were back in the bedroom pulling off each other's clothes and falling breathlessly on the bed.

Making love to Mary-Lou was a sweet wild ride of mutual passion. Steven tried to be gentle with her, he was frightened of hurting the baby. Mary-Lou didn't seem to care, she was full of exuberant love, pulling him close, wrapping her legs around his waist, rocking and rolling until she climaxed with a series of little screams.

By the time they were finished he was ready for another shower and late for an appointment.

"Not my fault," Mary-Lou said primly as he raced from the house.

"Not your fault!" he yelled, running for his car. "Face it! You're an uncontrollable sex machine! How am I ever expected to get any work done?"

"Will you shut *up*!" Mary-Lou hissed, standing at the door wrapped in a silk kimono, her pretty face alive with pleasure. "People will *hear* you!"

At the office, Jerry Myerson, his closest friend and partner in the law firm of Myerson, Laker, Brandon, and Berkeley, waited impatiently in the reception area. "You're late," Jerry reprimanded him sharply, tapping his watch as if he were anticipating an argument.

"I know," Steve replied, straight-faced. "Had to make love to my wife."

"Very funny," Jerry snorted. He was a forty-eight-year-old playboy bachelor with the unshakable belief that once you got married your hard-on shrivelled up and died forever. "Let's go," he said impatiently.

It wasn't often that Jerry Myerson and Steven Berkeley

made house calls, though sometimes there were exceptions. The client they were on their way to see was an extremely rich woman called Deena Swanson. Deena was married to billionaire Martin Z. Swanson, President and owner of Swanson Industries – an all-powerful organization that owned major New York real estate, hotels, cosmetic companies, and publishing firms.

Martin Z. Swanson was Mister New York, a charismatic man of forty-five with unlimited power and an insatiable thirst for even more. Deena had parlayed her position as his wife into one of importance. Early on she had hired a press agent to make sure she was known as much more than just the wife. From social butterfly and fashion plate, she had risen to fame, lending her name to everything from perfume to her own line of designer jeans. She figureheaded Swanson Style, one of her husband's many companies. For five million bucks a year Deena made sure the name Swanson was always in the columns.

The Swansons had been married ten years. They suited each other. Deena's appetite for even more fame, money, and power was just as voracious as her husband's.

When Deena Swanson had called and requested their presence, Jerry was delighted. The firm had been representing her for several months on minor matters, but Jerry figured being summoned to her home meant things were definitely looking up: maybe they were going to get her husband's account. He liked that idea a lot.

"Why do I have to come along?" Steven grumbled as they sat in the back of Jerry's chauffeured town car on their way to Deena's Park Avenue apartment, one of the Swansons' three permanent residences.

"Because we don't know what she wants," Jerry replied patiently. "It could be simple. Maybe it's complicated. Two minds are better than one." A pause, and then a sly, "Besides, the rumour is she likes her coffee black."

Steven narrowed his eyes. "What?" he said sharply.

Jerry was unperturbed. "You heard."

Shaking his head, Steven said, "You're an asshole, Jerry. Sometimes I don't think you ever took it out of college."

23

"Took what out of college?" Jerry inquired innocently.

"Your fucking brains."

"Thank *you*."

The car stopped at a red light. Jerry studied two girls crossing the street. One, a bouncy redhead, really got his attention. "Do you think she sucks c–"

"Don't even say it," interrupted Steven grimly. "Y'know, Jerry, you should get married and stop behaving like a dirty old lawyer."

"Married?" Jerry's voice filled with undisguised horror. "What makes you think I'd ever be that stupid?"

Every so often Steven wondered how their friendship had endured since college. They were so different, and yet he couldn't imagine a more loyal and supportive friend than Jerry Myerson. Jerry had seen him through so much – including a disastrous marriage to a wild Puerto Rican dancer named Zizi, his many years as a crusading assistant DA, and finally the long years painstakingly trying to find out the identity of his father. When he'd finally discovered his father was the infamous Gino Santangelo, Jerry had congratulated him.

"Hey – now you've got one white ball and one black," he'd joked. "The man can play in both courts. Not bad, Steven. There's a little larceny in you after all."

The discovery was a shock, but life went on, and Steven weathered the revelation. With Jerry's help he threw himself into his work, deciding to specialize in criminal law. He'd discovered his vocation and loved it. Soon he developed quite a reputation as one of the best defence attorneys in New York. He was the first to admit that without Jerry he certainly wouldn't be a partner in one of the most successful law firms in New York. Jerry had supported him all the way. So what if he conducted his personal life like the ideal *Playboy* subscriber? Underneath his sexist front the man had heart, and that's what really counted.

Deena Swanson was a coolly attractive woman with chiselled features, dead blue eyes, and very pale red hair cropped in a thirties bob. She was one of those women of indeterminate age – white pulled skin without a line in sight, perfect makeup, and a slim figure clad in a tailored grey skirt and an expensive silk shirt. Steven figured her to be anywhere between thirty and forty, it was impossible to tell. What he could tell was that she didn't look happy.

She greeted them with a limp handshake, receiving them in a spacious living room filled with African artefacts, sculpture, and fine paintings. Above the mantel hung an impressive oil painting of Mr and Mrs Swanson, she clad in a pink ball gown, and Martin Swanson sporting a white tuxedo. Both faces wore the same expression – bland indifference.

A Lebanese houseman hovered, waiting to take their order for coffee before backing respectfully from the room.

Deena indicated they should sit on an overstuffed couch, and when they were settled she said in her slightly accented voice, "The meeting we are about to have must be absolutely confidential. Am I assured of this?"

"Of course," Jerry replied quickly, offended she might think otherwise.

"My husband is not to know of this conversation either."

"Mrs Swanson, you are a valued client. Whatever you say to us is strictly for our ears only."

"Good." She crossed impressive silk-clad legs and reached for a thin black cigarette from a silver box.

Jerry leaped to attention with his lighter.

Deena drew deeply on her cigarette, stared first at Jerry then at Steven, and said, "I don't believe in wasting time. Do you?"

"Couldn't agree more," replied Jerry, ever obliging, and quite attracted to this cool, expensive-looking woman, even though she wasn't his usual type.

Deena silenced him with a look. "Kindly hear me out," she said imperiously. "No interruptions."

Jerry's back stiffened. He wasn't used to being spoken to as if he were hired help.

Deena began to speak again, oblivious to his hurt feelings. "Gentlemen," she said calmly, "it has recently come to my attention that one of these days I might be obliged to commit the perfect murder."

A heavy silence hung over the room while Deena paused for a long moment, allowing her words to register. When she was satisfied they had, she continued. "If this situation ever arose, and I failed in my attempt to make it perfect, I would naturally expect you, as my attorneys, to do everything in your power to defend me." A long white finger, decorated with a huge diamond ring, pointed straight at Steven. "*You*. I would want you to defend me. I understand you're the best."

"Now *wait* a minute," Steven interrupted heatedly. "I can't–"

"No, *you* wait a minute," she snapped, a woman used to getting her own way. "Allow me to finish." She glared at them both, dead blue eyes daring either of them to interrupt again. "A retainer of one million dollars was transferred into your company's account today. All you have to do, Mr Myerson, Mr Berkeley, is to be there *when* and *if* – and I emphasize the *if* – I need you." She gave a brittle laugh, before adding with slow deliberation, "For all our sakes, we should hope that day never comes."

Chapter 5

Abe Panther sat behind his large walnut desk, a fierce Inga positioned in the background.

Lucky Santangelo entered the room, accompanied by Morton Sharkey, her West Coast lawyer.

Abe greeted Lucky with a friendly nod. They had met only once before and he's warmed to her instantly – recognizing in her a true maverick and adventurer. She reminded him of himself when he was young.

"You're looking well, Mr Panther," Morton Sharkey said politely, still in a mild state of shock that Lucky had been able to get this far. When she'd first come to him with her wild proposition he'd almost laughed in her face. "Don't you know you're asking the impossible," he'd warned her. "Panther Studios is controlled by Mickey Stolli and Ben Harrison. And let me tell you, I know for a fact they'd never even consider selling."

"Aren't you forgetting they merely run it?" Lucky had replied coolly. "And from what I hear, they're mostly in business for themselves. Don't worry, Morton, I've had every detail checked out. Abe Panther owns the studio one hundred per cent. He can do whatever he likes. And I want him to sell it to me."

"The man is a hundred and six," Morton had joked.

"The man is eighty-eight, and in full possession of all his faculties," she replied, full of confidence.

Morton Sharkey had never thought it possible. But then Morton Sharkey had never dealt with a Santangelo before. When Lucky put something in motion she was behind it all the way, and instinct had immediately told her Abe Panther would love to dump on his granddaughters' two thieving husbands and pull the studio – *his* studio – out from under them.

Secret negotiations had taken place. At first Abe hadn't seemed interested, until Lucky had insisted on flying out to Los Angeles for a face-to-face confrontation.

Abe Panther might be an old man, but she had known they were kindred spirits the moment her black Santangelo eyes met his canny faded blue ones at their first meeting.

"What the hell you know 'bout runnin' a studio an' makin' movies?" he'd snapped at her.

"Not much," she replied honestly. "But I *can* smell garbage when I'm near it, and that's what your studio is turning out. Cheap, exploitive garbage." Her eyes glowed. "So. I reckon I can only do a better job, right?"

"The studio's turnin' a profit," Abe had pointed out.

"Yes, but you're still makin' shit movies. I want to make Panther great again, as it once was. And let me tell you something – I *can* do it. That, I assure you, is a Santangelo promise. And the Santangelos do not break promises."

She'd paused and stared at him, mesmerizing him with her dangerous black eyes before adding, "Bet on it."

He'd warmed to her immediately. She had spirit and ballsiness, refreshing qualities in a woman.

And Lucky had guessed right: Abe would enjoy nothing more than to screw Mickey Stolli and Ben Harrison out of what they took for granted as their rightful inheritance.

A deal was put in motion. All that was needed now was Abe's signature.

"Let me talk to Lucky alone," Abe said, shifting in his chair.

They were almost there, but Morton sensed a curve ball coming. "Certainly," he said, far more easily than he felt. He glanced over at Lucky.

Imperceptibly she nodded, indicating he should leave.

Morton walked out of the room.

Inga didn't budge. She remained behind the old man's desk, a stoic Swedish monument.

"Out!" Abe commanded sharply.

A twitch of her thin lips was the only indication that she minded being dismissed. As she left the room she slammed the door behind her to show her displeasure.

Abe cackled. "Inga don't like me telling her what to do. Still blames me for never makin' her a star." He shook his head. "Not my fault. No screen presence. Movie stars gotta have two qualities – without 'em they're dead." He cocked his head on one side. "Know what they are?"

Lucky nodded. She knew Abe Panther's credo by heart. "Likability and fuckability," she recited without hesitation.

He was impressed. "How'd you know that?" he demanded.

"Because I've read everything about you. Every press clip, studio release, three unauthorized biographies. Oh, and a few personal biographies by some *very* beautiful female stars who couldn't help but mention you." She grinned. "You sure got around in your time, didn't you? You're a very famous man, Mr Panther."

He nodded, pleased at her assessment of his standing.

"Yup. I'm the last of 'em," he said proudly. "The last of the movie dinosaurs."

"I wouldn't call you a dinosaur."

"Don't need your flattery, girlie. You've almost got your deal."

"I know." Her black eyes shone. "I'm ready to meet your price. You're ready to sell to me. So come on, Mr P. What exactly is holding us up?"

"Just a little something I need from you."

She tried to suppress the impatience in her voice. When Lucky wanted something she wanted it immediately. "What?" she asked edgily.

"Retribution."

"Huh?"

"The scum-in-laws, an' all the bloodsuckers around 'em."

"Yes?"

"I want you to nail 'em, girlie. Nail 'em good."

"I plan to."

"My way."

She continued to curb her impatience. "What's your way?"

"Before you gain control, you take a job at the studio. You'll be assistant to Herman Stone – he's my man." Abe sparkled as he felt excitement creeping back into his life. "An' when you're there, right in the thick of it, you'll catch 'em all doin' what they shouldn't be doin'." He cackled with delight. "Six weeks on the inside, an' then whammo, girlie, you're the new boss, an' you can dump 'em all. Some good plan, huh?"

Lucky could hardly believe what she was hearing. It was an insane idea. How could she vanish for six weeks and assume another identity? She headed an empire, there was no way she could just disappear. What about Lennie? And Bobby and Brigette? Not to mention all her numerous business commitments?

"Impossible," she said, shaking her head regretfully.

"If you want my studio you'll do it," Abe retorted, clicking his false teeth. "If you *really* want it."

She brushed a hand through her dark hair, stood up, and began pacing agitatedly around the room.

Sure she wanted the studio, but she wasn't about to jump through hoops to satisfy the whims of a demanding old man. Or was she?

Hmm . . . Maybe it wasn't such an insane idea after all . . . Maybe it was quite a tempting proposition . . . a challenge. And there was nothing Lucky enjoyed more than a challenge.

Undercover she could catch everyone doing what they weren't supposed to be doing.

It was kind of a wild scam, an adventure.

Hmm . . .

Abe watched her carefully, crinkling his shrewd eyes as he reached for a glass of prune juice on his desk. "No undercover . . . no sale," he said, just to make quite sure she understood his rules.

Lucky spun around and stared at him. "You mean you'd blow this deal?" she asked incredulously. 'All that money?"

Abe smiled, clicking his teeth into a neat porcelain row. They didn't fit his leathery, lined old face. They looked too new. "I'm eighty-eight years old, girlie, what am I gonna do with the money? It ain't gonna buy me a hard-on, huh? Huh? It ain't gonna raise my schnickel."

Lucky grinned, "Who knows?"

"*I* know, girlie, that's for sure."

"Nothing in life is a certainty."

Abe clicked his false teeth in and out of his mouth one more time, not exactly an endearing habit. "Six weeks," he said with surprising firmness. "Or we got no deal."

Chapter 6

Brigette Stanislopoulos was seventeen years old and undeniably pretty. She had long, naturally blonde hair, and a rounded, well-developed figure. She was also a heiress, due to inherit half the Stanislopoulos fortune left to her by her grandfather, Dimitri. She already had her mother's vast estate in trust, and when she reached twenty-one she was destined to become one of the richest women in the world. A sobering thought, for Brigette, although just a teenager, had already lived a life filled with pain and confusion, and instinctively she knew her huge inheritance was only going to add further complications.

Money had failed to bring her mother happiness. Poor Olympia – discovered in a seedy New York hotel with the famous rock star Flash, both of them drugged out and dead. Not a very fitting end for Olympia – the girl who should have had everything.

Brigette was determined *her* life would be different. She had no intention of following her mother's treacherous path to unhappiness: three husbands, and an excess of selfish pleasures.

Brigette was thirteen when Olympia died. She'd never known her real father – an Italian businessman whom her grandfather had always referred to as "the fortune-hunter". Olympia had divorced him shortly after Brigette was born, and several months later he'd been blown to pieces by a terrorist car-bomb in Paris. Losing her mother and natural father at such an early age was bad enough, but more tragedies loomed ahead. Several months later she and Lucky's son, Bobby, became involved in a kidnapping. Santino Bonnatti, a known crime czar and lifetime enemy of the Santangelo family, had the two children trapped in the house of his girlfriend, Eden Antonio, and was intent on sexually molesting them. Before he was able to succeed,

Brigette had managed to grab his gun and fire three times, just as Lucky came to their rescue. Almost immediately the police were at the front door, but by that time Lucky had made sure Brigette and Bobby were hustled out the back, and taken safely home. Lucky had then proceeded to accept responsibility for Santino's death.

Months later at Lucky's trial, Brigette had gathered all her courage and jumped to her feet, publicly confessing. It was a brave thing to do, but she was unable to sit back any longer and allow Lucky to take the blame. Fortunately, there was a videotape proving Bonnatti's shooting to be a clear case of self-defence.

Brigette was placed on probation for a year and sent to live with her grandmother, Charlotte, Dimitri's first wife.

Charlotte was no comfortable grandmother figure. She was an elegant society matron, now married to her fourth husband, an English stage actor ten years her junior. They divided their time between a house in London's Eaton Square and a New York brownstone.

Looking after Brigette's welfare was not exactly Charlotte's dream come true. She had immediately enrolled her granddaughter in a strict private boarding school an hour's drive from New York.

All Brigette wanted was to be left alone. She felt like the original poor little rich girl with a scandalous past.

She kept to herself, shunning any offers of friendship, for above all Brigette had learned the true secret of survival – and that was never to trust anyone.

"Hey – Stanislob – it's the phone for you."

Stanislob was one of the better names they called her. Brigette didn't care. She knew who she was. She was Brigette Stanislopoulos. Person. Human being. Not the spoiled brat some of the tabloids liked to make her out to be.

They never left her in peace, the gutter press. There was always someone lurking around, spying. A photographer hiding in the bushes, an insolent reporter tracking her every move. They watched her relentlessly.

The tabloids had their favourites. Lisa Marie Presley,

32

Princess Stephanie of Monaco, and Brigette Stanislopoulos – three young heiresses, always good for a story.

Ignoring the stupid nickname, Brigette took the phone from a tall girl with frizzed hair and an abundance of freckles. Maybe they could have been friends. Another time – another life.

"Yes?" She spoke hesitantly into the receiver. Her calls were supposed to be monitored, but nobody ever bothered.

"Hey – pretty girl – it's Lennie. As usual I've come up with a sensational idea. What are your plans for the summer?"

"No plans."

"I like it. I'm gonna speak to Lucky about you coming out here and spending time with us in Malibu. We've rented a sensational house. How about it?"

Brigette was delighted. Lennie Golden and Lucky were the only two people she really cared about. Lennie, her ex-stepfather now married to Lucky, who had once been married to her grandfather. What a tangled web of relationships! The Stanislopoulos clan made the Onassis family tree seem simple.

"I'd love that," she said eagerly.

"Great. I'll have Lucky persuade Charlotte to let you go for a few weeks."

"God! The last thing Charlotte needs is persuading. Just tell her, she'll be thrilled to get rid of me."

"Now, now, don't be nasty, little girl," he teased.

"It's true, Lennie!"

"And then, when I finish the movie, maybe we'll all take off for Europe."

"Brilliant!"

"Tough. No enthusiasm, huh?"

"C'mon! I'd kill for this trip."

"You don't have to. It's almost settled."

"I can't wait!"

"Good."

"How come you're not working? Isn't it the middle of the day in LA?"

"What about you?" he countered.

33

"It's five-thirty. I'm a free person."

"So get out an' run riot."

She giggled. "I can't. It's a weekday. We're not allowed out on weekdays."

"Break a rule or two, live dangerously."

"*You're* not supposed to tell me to do things like that," she said, remembering the one time she had broken the rules and suffered the consequences.

"No shit? If I were you I'd go for it."

Go for what? She had no friends, no one to cut school with. Besides, she was not like her mother, she had no desire to break loose. The price, she'd discovered, was far too high.

"How's the movie going?" she asked, hurriedly changing the subject.

He groaned. "Don't ruin my day."

"Is Lucky in LA with you?"

He feigned exasperation. "What is it with the questions? Are you needlin' me because you've nothing better to do, or what?"

She smiled. "Don't you know — I live to piss you off."

Laughing, he said, "Well, keep on livin', and I'll call you next week with more plans. OK, bait?"

"OK, dirty old man."

Lennie always made her feel terrific, especially when he called her "bait", an abbreviation of "jail bait" — his pet name for her. She always retaliated with "dirty old man". It was their private game, their way of saying the past meant nothing. "You gotta laugh about something an' it'll go away," Lennie had often told her.

Maybe he was right, but it didn't mean she had to let her guard down. She was Brigette Stanislopoulos. Person. Heiress. Always an heiress. No getting away from *that*.

With a deep sigh she returned to the dormitory — a prison shared with three other girls. There was a stack of homework piled on the table next to her bed, and on her side of the wall hung a single poster of Boy George smiling shyly in full makeup and ringlets. She liked his music, and she liked the fact that he didn't seem to give a damn. Her kind of person.

The other girls had posters and pictures of everyone from Rob Lowe to an almost naked Richard Gere. So what? Romantic involvements were something Brigette never wanted to experience again.

For a moment she allowed her mind to drift back in time. First there was Santino Bonnatti's face – always there – that evil, sneering face. And then there was Tim Wealth. Handsome and young. A would-be famous actor who'd had the bad luck to try and pull a scam with Bobby and herself as the central characters. The newspapers had never connected the murder of the young actor with the Bonnatti events.

Thank goodness, Brigette thought with a shudder. She'd loved Tim, and he'd tricked her. Unfortunately he had paid with his life. No fault of hers. Bonnatti's men had done what they were told, and they were told Tim Wealth was in the way.

Don't think about it, she scolded herself silently. For two months they'd made her see psychiatrists. *Don't think about it*, the last one had told her – the only good advice she'd received. All that talk about her real father being dead and then her mother leaving her, causing her to feel like an abandoned child, meant nothing.

She wasn't abandoned – she was strong. A survivor. Brigette Stanislopoulos didn't need anyone.

Chapter 7

Sitting still for an interview had never been Lennie's favourite pastime. Especially when the interviewer insisted on intruding on the set, watching everything, eavesdropping, and making copious notes.

Shorty Rawlings, the PR on the movie, had talked Lennie into it against his better judgement. It was a cover story for *People* or *Us*, he couldn't remember which, and the interviewer was a horse-faced woman who kept on skirting dangerously near his private life — a subject he *never* discussed, a fact always made very clear up front.

Not that his private life was a secret. Marrying Olympia Stanislopoulos, and then Lucky Santangelo, did not exactly help him maintain a low profile. What the hell — he refused to fuel the gossip — better to keep quiet.

Lucky was paranoid about staying out of the press. She refused to give interviews, and like her father, Gino, she went to a great deal of trouble to avoid being photographed "I'm not a public person," she'd warned Lennie before they were married. "And I intend to keep it that way."

Not that easy when you marry a movie star — he'd wanted to say. Especially when your previous husband was one of the richest men in the world and your father made plenty of headlines in his day.

Somehow Lucky had succeeded in holding on to a certain amount of anonymity. Not many people knew what she looked like — her name was better known than her face.

"How's your wife?" the horse-faced reporter threw in casually, tracking his thoughts. "Is it true you're separated?"

Lennie fixed her with his disconcertingly green eyes. "I gotta get back to work," he said, rising from his canvas chair. He'd had enough.

Undaunted, the reporter pressed on. "Lucky Santangelo. Quite a woman. Is she in LA?"

"Ever thought of getting a tongue job?" Lennie asked sharply.

The woman was startled. "I *beg* your pardon?"

"Y'know, a little snip at the end? Just to stop you asking those personal questions you've been told not to ask."

Before she could respond, Shorty Rawlings appeared, and Lennie stalked off without saying another word.

"Well, really!" the woman said, her face flushed. "Did I hit a nerve?"

36

"I sure hope not," Shorty replied anxiously. This movie was giving him ulcers – what with Joey Firello laying everything in sight, Grudge Freeport drinking himself into oblivion, Marisa Birch shacking up with her female stand-in as well as the producer, and Lennie Golden behaving like he didn't have to do publicity. And this was on home ground – Christ knows what they'd all be like on a five-week location in Acapulco.

Shorty frowned. Lennie Golden wasn't Nicholson or Redford, for crissake. He was just the new schmuck on the lot with a couple of money-making movies behind him and no solid track record.

Shorty Rawlings was fifty-two years old, he'd seen them come and he'd seen them fade – real fast. Plenty of publicity kept you up there, and Lennie Golden better wise up.

Shorty threw his arm around the journalist's shoulders. She was a tall woman with greasy hair and a bad nose job. Probably a failed actress – Hollywood was full of 'em, and they all ended up doing something else. "C'mon, honey," he said expansively, "I'll buy you a drink." *An' maybe you'll give me a blow-job*, he added silently. After all, this was Hollywood, and the perks of the job were many.

"What's going on, man?" Joey Firello caught him on the way back to his trailer.

Lennie shrugged non-committally. "Some stupid cow of a reporter."

"Fuck 'er," Joey said, cavalier as ever.

"No, *you* fuck her," Lennie retorted.

Joey was not averse to the idea. "What does she look like?" he asked.

Lennie couldn't help laughing. Joey would screw a table if it eyeballed him nicely. "I'm going home," he said. "See you tomorrow."

"Home." Joey repeated *home* as if it were a dirty word. "How about my party?"

"I told you, I can't make it."

37

"You're missin' out on a wild time."

Lennie was not into Joey's bad behaviour. "I've had enough wild times to last me several lifetimes, thank you," he said.

"You don't know what you're missin!"

"That's just it, Joey. I do."

He bumped into Cristi on the way to his car. She certainly was a prime California girl. All bronzed limbs, pale hair, and white gleaming teeth. He couldn't help noticing that her legs ended at her neck.

"Good night, Mr Golden," she said politely.

Mr Golden! Was he that old?

Climbing into his Ferrari he realized he not only missed Lucky, he needed her. She'd promised to spend a couple of weeks at the Acapulco location, and he couldn't wait.

Being together – wasn't that what marriage was supposed to be all about? For eighteen months they'd spent most of their time apart. OK, so he'd known up front that Lucky wasn't the kind of woman to drop everything just to be with him. She had a multi-billion-dollar business to watch over, and a son and a father she liked to spend time with. But somehow he'd always imagined he could handle it, that it didn't bother him. Lately he'd been realizing this wasn't exactly turning out to be true. He'd been missing her plenty. And a more traditional marriage didn't seem like such a bad idea. He enjoyed being married. It gave him security and balance, made him feel centred for once in his life. And after *his* crazy childhood he needed a stabilizing influence. He certainly hadn't found it with Olympia. Lucky was supposed to be it.

Maybe the time had come to think about having a kid of their own. A Golden kid – with Lucky's looks and his humour. He'd mentioned it a couple of times and Lucky had changed the subject before they'd really had a chance to get into it.

Yes, he decided, Acapulco was the time and the place. The more he thought about it the more sure he was. Fun times in the Mexican sun, talk her into a baby, and after the movie was finished they'd spend a couple of weeks in

38

Malibu with Brigette and Bobby, and then take the summer off and drift around Europe doing nothing.

He remembered the first time he and Lucky had made love. What a memory! It was a late afternoon in St Tropez. Calm sea, deserted beach, balmy weather. Some great trip!

God damn it! The memory was making him horny.

He screeched the Ferrari to a stop at a red light and craved a cold shower.

"Hi!" A girl in a white convertible pulled alongside him. She wore a purple tank top and matching visor.

Before he could decide whether he knew her or not, she solved his problem. "I *looove* your movies," she purred. "You're *sooo* funny and *sooo* sexy."

If he'd wanted to he could have hit on her with no trouble. She was certainly pretty enough. But those days were over. He was a happily married man with an incredible wife and a baby on the way. Well . . . almost.

Flashing her a smile, he muttered a quick "Thanks," and without a second thought floored the Ferrari, making a fast and clean getaway.

Chapter 8

Back in New York, Lucky made her decision. She would do it! God damn it, if that was the only way she could get Panther Studios, she would do it! Go in undercover and find out everything Abe Panther wanted to know. She wasn't about to tell Abe, but she was beginning to think it was a great idea! This way, when she took over the studio she'd know everything. What an advantage!

Immediately after the meeting with Abe, she'd caught a plane back to New York. Morton Sharkey had accompanied her in the limousine on the drive to LAX. He'd talked all the way – telling her how ridiculous Abe's idea was, how it would never work, how it was quite obvious that Abe Panther was getting senile.

Morton couldn't help but notice her silence. "You're not actually thinking of doing it?" he'd demanded incredulously.

She'd smiled a slow, inscrutable smile. "I'll let you know, Morton."

Now she was ready to tell him "Yes, we're going for it."

Naturally Mr Morton Sharkey would throw a fit: lawyers were always creating problems, studying every legal angle, pointing out the pitfalls.

So what? Lucky Santangelo did what she wanted. And this caper was just the kind of adventure she craved. She was already thinking of ways to change her appearance so no one would recognize her. As Gino's daughter, the widow of Dimitri Stanislopoulos, and Lennie Golden's wife, she'd had her photograph in the newspapers from time to time. But not that often. And she'd never cooperated with the press — there were no official posed pictures, only random paparazzi shots.

A wig would take care of her hair. And glasses for her eyes. Dowdy clothes and a subservient attitude. This was going to be fun! Six weeks of play-acting and then Panther Studios would be hers.

There was only one catch. How was she supposed to take six weeks off from normal life? How was she going to explain it to Lennie?

First she decided to confide in Gino.

The Santangelos. Black-eyed Gino, and his wild daughter. They'd been through a lot together — more than most families in ten lifetimes. Lucky loved him with a fierce and enduring passion.

She called him, saying she had to see him urgently. They usually dined together several times a month. Unfortunately she'd had to cancel their last dinner because she'd been in LA.

"Paige is in town," Gino said, over the phone. "Can it wait?"

Lucky was insistent. "Urgent means urgent."

"And Paige in town means an old man's feelin' pretty damn good."

"So feel good later. This can't wait."

"Lucky, Lucky, you're a difficult woman."

"So what else is new?"

"Hey — how about I bring Paige with me?" he suggested.

Lucky stood firm. "Absolutely not."

She wasn't being possessive, but the last thing she needed was Paige Wheeler knowing what she planned. Who could guess what kind of mouth the woman had? She was after all, married to a Hollywood producer. One word in the wrong direction could blow the whole setup.

Lucky was determined to make sure nothing went wrong. Acquiring Panther Studios was all important to her. There could be no tripping up along the way.

They met at a small Italian restaurant on Lexington. Father and daughter. Lucky so dark-haired, black-eyed, and exotically beautiful. Gino still walking with a swagger, a certain energy and cockiness about him that belied his years.

The man's still got it, Lucky thought admiringly as he approached their table. *He really must have been something when he was young.*

She'd heard enough stories about him from Uncle Costa, her father's dearest and oldest friend. Costa Zennocotti, who'd once been Gino's lawyer, was now a retired and respectable old gentleman living in Miami.

Ah . . . when Costa got to talking about the old days it was a treat. To hear Costa tell it there'd never been anyone quite like Gino the Ram. What a nickname! Lucky couldn't help smiling.

"What are *you* grinnin' at?" Gino demanded, sitting down and winking at their regular waitress — a big, surly woman who saved all her good moods for Gino.

"I was reflecting on your lurid past."

"Sweetheart, you don't know nothin'."

"Bullshit."

"My daughter the lady."

41

"Just what you wanted, huh?"

Their eyes met, full of warmth. Gino summoned the waitress and ordered his favourite red wine and hot crusty bread to be brought to their table immediately.

"It's on the way," the waitress said triumphantly.

He pinched her big ass, making her day. "What a girl!" he said, and then he turned his full attention to Lucky. "How's Bobby — an' more important, when am I gonna see him?"

Gino was crazy about his grandchild, and never stopped complaining about the boy being educated in England.

"Bobby is fine," Lucky replied, "I speak to him every day. Naturally he sends you his love. You're his favourite, as if you didn't know."

"The kid would be better off in New York," Gino grumbled. "He's an American, he should be here. What's he gonna learn in one of them fancy schmancy English schools?"

She did not feel the time was right to remind her father that Bobby was half Greek. "Manners," she said.

"Ha!" Gino snorted his amusement. "I sent you to Switzerland to learn manners, an' look what happened to you!"

"Yeah, look what happened to me. I *really* bummed out, didn't I?"-

The waitress poured a drop of wine for Gino to taste. He sipped, nodded. "You're one hell of a Santangelo," he said, facing his daughter. "You got my street smarts, your mother's class, *and* you're a looker on top of it all. We did OK by you, kiddo, huh?"

"Thanks a lot. Don't *I* get any credit?" Lucky asked good-naturedly.

"It's all in the genes, kid."

"*Sure.*"

Gino's eyes scanned the restaurant as he drank his favourite wine and tore into the freshly baked bread. "So," he said slowly, "tell me, what's so important that I had to leave Paige? She thinks I got another broad stashed away."

"At your age?" Lucky asked, raising a sceptical eyebrow.

"Listen, kid, age has nothin' t'do with nothin'. Just remember that. In your head you're always whatever age you wanna be – and *I'm* stickin' to forty-five. *Capisce?*"

My father is a remarkable man, Lucky thought. *He's probably going to die on the job – humping his way to heaven!*

"You're grinnin' again," Gino said. "What's up? Are you pregnant? You an' Lennie hit the old jackpot, huh? Is that what you got to tell me?"

"No *way!*"

"OK, OK, so don't get excited. It's about time Bobby had a brother or sister, I'm only askin'."

"Why is it that whenever a woman has a secret, every man in the world naturally assumes she's pregnant?"

"So stab me in the back. I came up with a bad guess."

Taking a deep breath she made her announcement. "I'm going to buy a movie studio."

"You're gonna do *what?*"

"I'm buying Panther Studios," Lucky went on excitedly. "The studio that has Lennie tied to a three picture deal." Her eyes glowed. "You see, the truth is he's hating every minute of the movie he's shooting now. He wants out, and *I'm* going to arrange it. Not out – but control. All the control he wants! Isn't it a sensational idea? *I* own the studio, and *he* gets his freedom."

"Slow down, kid – an' correct me if I'm readin' you wrong. But the thought here seems to be that you're gonna buy a film studio just 'cause your old man is not havin' a day at the beach. Am I hittin' it straight on?"

"You got it!" Lucky was on a roll. She felt the adrenaline coursing through her body. Telling Gino was a kick. When she'd financed and built the Magiriano Hotel in Vegas by herself, and her father had seen the results, it had been a real triumph. Somehow, purchasing a movie studio was even more of a thrill.

Gino laughed derisively. "What the hell do *you* know about makin' movies?" he asked.

"What did *you* know about running a hotel when you put up the Mirage in 1902?" Lucky countered.

43

"It was 1951, smart ass, an' I knew plenty."

"Like what?" she challenged.

"Like more than *you* know about the goddamn picture business."

"What I don't know, I'll find out. I plan to surround myself with professionals. If you look around at some of the jerks in charge of major studios you can see it's no big challenge. Panther is coasting along on cheap exploitation flicks and stars' ego trips. I'm going to turn the studio around and make it hot again."

Gino shrugged, sipped more wine, and shook his head. "Yeah, you're my daughter all right. You're a Santangelo."

With a smile she charmed him. "Was there ever any question?"

Three hours later they'd finished two bottles of wine, eaten a mound of spaghetti and clam sauce, dallied with a dishful of home-made pastries, and were now on hot, whisky-soaked Irish coffees.

"Cholesterol heaven!" Lucky murmured happily. "Are you *sure* you're supposed to do this at your age?"

He winked. "I'm forty-five, remember?"

She leaned forward to kiss him on the cheek. "I do love you, Gino . . . uh . . . Daddy." It was only on very special occasions that she called him daddy.

Basking in her affection, he said, "It's mutual, kid. You never doubted it, didja?"

Yes, lots of times, she wanted to say. *When Mommy was murdered and you withdrew from your children. And how about the time you paid to marry me off to Senator Richmond's dumb son when I was only sixteen? And shutting me out of the family business. And treating me like women were an inferior species. And marrying that Beverly Hills bitch, Susan Martino, and almost adopting her scuzzy, fully grown children . . .*

Oh yes, there were plenty of bad memories. But now things couldn't be better. They were a team. And somehow she knew it would never change.

Chapter 9

"You've been edgy for the last three days," Mary-Lou said, massaging Steven's left foot. "What is it, honey? Are you ever going to tell me, or have I just got to carry on tiptoeing around your bad mood like a zombie?"

Steven roused himself from Johnny Carson's television monologue. "What bad mood are you talking about?"

Mary-Lou dropped his foot and let out an exasperated sigh. "Either you're going to tell me, or you're not. Obviously you're not, so quit with the short answers and long silences, otherwise *I* am out of here." She raised her voice. "You hear me, Steven? O-U-T."

He looked faintly amused. "Where would you go?"

"Go? Me? I'm a star, honey, I can go where I want. So there!"

Lazily he reached for her. "With that big belly?"

She pulled away. "Don't try an' sweet-talk me now. You're too late."

His hands found their way to her swollen breasts, where they lingered.

She didn't move. A good sign. Maybe he could short-stop a fight and get lost in her warmness. He needed comforting and nurturing – not a damned argument.

"Steven," she murmured in a low voice that was neither denial nor acceptance.

With practised ease he continued to fondle her breasts, springing one of them free from the confines of a lacy nightgown, and bending his head to play small circling games with his tongue.

"Steven Berkeley," she sighed breathlessly, "I *really* hate you."

There was no more talking after that. Three years of marriage and they were both still hopelessly turned on by each other.

On television Johnny Carson continued to entertain.

In the Berkeley household no one was watching.

The next morning Mary-Lou was up first. She showered, dressed in a sensible track suit, and sat on the side of the bed waiting for Steven to wake up.

He rolled into consciousness, foggily aware it was Saturday, his favourite day.

As soon as he opened his eyes Mary-Lou pounced. "About time, lover boy," she said matter-of-factly. "Now let's continue that conversation we never finished last night."

Piece by piece she dragged it out of him until eventually he confided the whole story to her. What else could he do? She was relentless when it came to extracting information.

He told her about Deena Swanson and their bizarre meeting. And then he told her about Jerry — the fool — who'd laughed the whole thing off and claimed they were dealing with a crazy woman, and no way was he handing back a million bucks' retainer, no damn way.

"Perhaps she *is* crazy," Mary-Lou mused. "She must be, to even tell you she's considering murdering someone. I'm sure she's putting you on."

"Great. Just great. *You're* sure she's putting us on," Steven replied sarcastically, jumping out of bed. "That solves everything. Now I can go about my business with a clear conscience." He stalked into the bathroom. "Let's not worry about the poor victim, huh?" he called over his shoulder.

"There *is* no victim," Mary-Lou pointed out.

"Yet," Steven replied ominously.

"And there won't be."

He was annoyed. "For crissakes, Mary-Lou. Don't come off as if you know what the hell you're talking about."

Slamming the bathroom door he stared at himself in the mirror. *Satisfied?* his inner voice lectured, *you've betrayed a client-lawyer confidence, and hurt your pregnant wife's feelings. All in one morning too. How clever can you get?*

By the time he emerged, Mary-Lou had left the house,

leaving behind a terse note saying she would not be back until late.

Steven was really pissed off. They always spent Saturdays together, shopping for food, catching a movie, dropping by Bloomingdales, and finally, when they came home and she began to do things around the house, he was able to collapse on the couch in front of the television and watch sport.

Now their day was ruined thanks to Mrs Deena Swanson.

He considered calling Jerry and telling him exactly what he could do with Deena Swanson's million bucks. But then again, maybe Jerry was right: maybe they should keep the money and wait for nothing to happen. Deena Swanson was no dangerous killer. She was a very rich woman with a grudge against someone – and there was no way she was ever going to go through with her plan to commit the perfect murder.

Besides, what could either he or Jerry do? Talk was talk, and lawyer–client privilege was supposed to be sacrosanct.

So why had he spilled the goods to Mary-Lou and spoiled a perfect day?

Because it bothered him. He didn't like it. He felt caught in a trap.

On the other hand, there was absolutely nothing he could do about it.

Impulsively he picked up the phone and dialled Lucky's number. He hadn't seen her in a few weeks and he wouldn't mind talking to her. She was something else, his half-sister – a really incredible woman who'd added so much to his life, especially since the death of Carrie, his mother, who'd died peacefully in her sleep of a heart attack.

He really missed Carrie. She'd raised him alone, and in spite of terrible beginnings had managed to give him a sense of values, a great education, and a chance to succeed.

For many years she'd lied to him about his father – claimed that he'd died when Steven was a small boy. One day he'd found out the truth. His real father was Gino

47

Santangelo, a man Carrie had slept with only once, and never told the result of that union.

The truth was difficult to accept, for Gino too, but gradually, over the last eighteen months, they'd forged a relationship. Hardly father and son, but a strong bond of mutual respect.

Lucky was different. She'd accepted him as her half-brother with immediate warmth. And when Carrie was alive she'd embraced her into the family too. He would always love Lucky for that. She was a very special woman.

The answering machine picked up at her apartment. Steven left a message and then tried Gino. "How about lunch?" he asked.

"What is it with my kids this week?" Gino demanded gruffly. "I got Paige in town. Don't that mean nothin' to any of you?"

Steven was delighted to be called one of Gino's kids. It was taking time but he was getting there. "How about I buy you *both* lunch?" he suggested.

"When Paige is here I don't eat," Gino replied. "Y'know how it is."

"Hey, sorry I asked."

"Don't be sorry, call me Monday."

Paige Wheeler wore a lacy brown garter belt, silk stockings, very high heels, a push-up bra, and nothing else. Although nearing fifty, she was still a very attractive woman with her pocket Venus figure, abundance of copper-coloured frizzy hair, husky voice, and sensual smile.

Gino, who'd had more women in his life than most rock stars, couldn't get enough of her. To him she was the perfect companion to grow old with – a smart, sassy broad who appreciated Frank Sinatra, enjoyed sex, and could hold a more than decent conversation.

"Who was that?" Paige asked as soon as he put the phone down.

"Steven. He wanted to take us to lunch. I told him to forget it."

48

"Why?" She paraded in front of him, spreading her legs in a dancer's stance.

"Why the hell d'you think?" he replied, grabbing her. "Has anyone ever told you you're one hot number?"

She smiled. "Yes, you, Gino. Constantly. And I love it."

He put his hand down the top of her stocking. "Get on your knees an' say that."

"If you insist. However, let me remind you – a lady *never* speaks with her mouth full!"

When they were done, Gino collapsed on the bed, his heart pounding at a roaring pace.

Better take it easy, old man, he warned himself. *You're not as young as you used to be.*

No shit?

When his heart resumed its normal rhythm he remembered Steven, and regretted being so abrupt with him. Reaching for the phone he called him back. There was no reply.

Paige slept face down on his rumpled bed. The woman was an original. No shadows of the past to haunt him when she was around.

He got up and went to his dresser, unlocked the top right-hand drawer, and took out a Harry Winston box. Opening it, he gazed at an Elizabeth Taylor sized diamond ring.

He'd bought Paige gifts before – usually from Forty-seventh Street, where he had connections and could get a deal. But this ring was different. This ring he'd gotten retail.

If Paige wanted it she could have it. There was only one small catch. *If* she wanted it, she had to divorce Wheeler – no more excuses – and marry him.

Gino Santangelo had waited long enough.

Brigette was counting the weeks until vacation. June 15 and she was a free person for the rest of the summer. What a relief to escape the daily grind of suffocating, boring school. She'd already spoken to her grandmother about spending a good chunk of her vacation with Lennie and Lucky.

Charlotte had not objected. "Whatever you like, dear," she'd said vaguely, probably thrilled to be rid of her.

Sitting in English class Brigette daydreamed about all the fun she'd have. There had to be more than getting up in the morning, mingling with a bunch of stupid, unfriendly girls, and listening to a succession of uninspiring teachers drone on about nothing that interested her. Malibu with Lennie and Lucky was sure to be a major blast.

"Stanislopoulos!" Mr Louthe, her English teacher, interrupted her reverie. He was a grey-haired man with ferret teeth and a droopy moustache. "What did I just say?" he asked sharply.

Brigette looked at him blankly. "Huh?"

Two of her classmates whispered an exaggerated *huh* at each other and giggled.

"Silence!" Mr Louthe said sternly. "See me after class, Stanislopoulos."

She groaned inwardly. She'd be late for tennis practice – her one pleasure. And Mr Louthe was notorious for his sanctimonious lectures.

After the class was over she went and stood by his desk. He was attending to paperwork and made her wait for fifteen minutes. Finally he looked up. "Stanislopoulos," he said, "I'll make this brief."

Thank goodness, she thought.

"You are an intelligent girl. A pretty girl–"

Oh, no! Was he coming on to her? After Santino Bonnatti she was never going to allow anybody to do anything to her again – unless she wanted them to.

"And you are also an extremely isolated and unsociable girl."

Thanks a lot! she thought sourly.

"In life," Mr Louthe continued in a sonorous tone, "there is always a price to pay. And I do not mean a monetary price. You must realize, young lady, that with all your money and connections, you will not end up a

50

very happy person if you go through your days and weeks and months living in your own cocooned little space. Learning, sharing, reading, mixing with other people, giving of yourself — these are all growth experiences. Learn to grow, Miss Stanislopoulos, and your life may have some meaning. Thank you. You are dismissed." He bent his head and resumed work.

Brigette was stunned. How dare he talk to her like that! She knew how to learn — only it wasn't something she cared to do. She knew how to share — but why should she? And as for mixing with other people — well, it was they who didn't want to mix with her . . . wasn't it?

Returning to the dormitory she continued to fume. What did he know about her life anyway? What did he care?

Dumb man.

Dumb *old* man.

Dumb *old* man with a stupid moustache!

Inexplicably she began to cry, and suddenly it was a deluge of tears, as if all the pain and frustration and hurt of the last few years came pouring out.

It occurred to her that this was the first time she'd cried since Tim Wealth's death and the ensuing nightmare events.

When the tears were over she felt better, until she noticed Nona, one of her more recent roommates, standing inside the door. God! On top of everything else she would now have a reputation as a crybaby.

"Are you OK?" Nona asked, sounding sympathetic.

Brigette rubbed her eyes. "Just a choking fit — nothing terminal."

"I know what you mean," Nona said çasually. "I get 'em all the time. Especially when I have to endure one of Louthe's lectures."

"It wasn't too bad."

Suddenly they were having a conversation, something Brigette had managed to avoid until now.

"OK," Nona said brightly, "I'm out of here. I've got a pass for town." She picked up her purse and hesitated a moment. "You wouldn't like to come, would you?"

Normally Brigette would have said no and that would have been that. But today was different. Today was the start of something new – making friends.

"I'd love to," she answered shyly.

Nona was surprised. The other girls would kill her for dragging along the poor little rich kid – but she couldn't help it, Brigette looked so lost and lonely.

"Come on," she said warmly, grabbing her by the arm. "I don't know about you, but the sooner I'm out of this prison the better."

Chapter 10

It was a go situation and Lucky felt incredibly elated. First she made a short trip to London by Concorde to visit Bobby. He was in fine shape, small and handsome with an endearing British accent. Gino would have a shit fit!

After visiting Bobby, she flew out to Los Angeles to spend a couple of days with Lennie before embarking on her adventure. If she was to vanish successfully for six weeks everything had to be carefully co-ordinated.

Arriving at their rented house in Malibu, she was met by Miko, their diminutive Japanese houseboy. Miko informed her he was expecting Mr Golden home at seven.

She was pleased. She'd told Lennie she wasn't flying out until Sunday, figuring a surprise would enhance the mood nicely. Now she'd have time to relax for a few hours.

"OK, Miko," she said, handing him a wad of bills. "Here's five hundred bucks to do a vanishing act. This'll pay for your hotel and expenses. I don't want to see you for forty-eight hours. Do we understand each other?"

Miko accepted the money with a small, formal bow. "I am gone, Madame," he said in perfect English.

With Miko out the way, she threw open the doors to the beach, plumped up the cushions on the large rattan couches, put Luther Vandross on the stereo, called Trader

Vic's and requested Lennie's favourite Indonesian lamb roast to be delivered at nine p.m., and prepared a mean margarita mix.

When that was all done she indulged in a leisurely shower and slipped white shorts and T-shirt over nothing. Lucky rarely bothered with underclothes, she didn't see the point. Piling her long dark hair atop her head, she added a touch more gloss to her lips, and tawny blusher to accentuate her sharply defined cheekbones.

In her mid-thirties Lucky Santangelo had only grown more beautiful — a beauty she treated very casually, for ego was not her thing.

The beach looked inviting. It was almost dusk and several people jogged along the shoreline with their dogs while a single swimmer braved the cool Pacific Ocean.

She'd only spent a few weekends at the house, but there was something about it she was beginning to get attached to. It was so peaceful and quiet. You couldn't hear the cars racing by on the nearby Pacific Coast Highway, only the soothing rhythm of the waves hitting the beach.

Maybe they should buy it, she mused. Not that she was crazy about California, but once she owned Panther Studios they would obviously be spending more time here.

Mental note: call the real estate agent and find out if the house was for sale.

It was nearing seven. She blended the margaritas, poured hers into a tall frosted glass, and sat outside on the deck overlooking the beach.

Luther serenaded her with "Superstar".

Leaning back, she closed her eyes and drifted off into a jet-lagged sleep.

Cristi was definitely coming on to him in her all-California-girl way. She'd been doing it throughout the day. Nothing too overwhelming, but Lennie was more than aware of her interest.

"I'm takin' the twist to Spago, why don't you come with us?" Joey suggested, enjoying the possibilities. He referred to all women as twists or grunts. The twists were the delectable ones, and Cristi was certainly edible.

Lennie said no.

"You prefer drivin' back to an empty beach house rather than a fine pizza with two of your best friends?" Joey tried to look hurt. The expression did not take.

Joey Firello was short and wiry, with rubbery lips, an ethnic face, and lots of nervous energy. Not traditionally good-looking, he was seemingly irresistible to women. "They want to mother me," he deadpanned. "Hey – the day I say no to tit is the day it's over, man."

Joey had been very supportive of Lennie when he'd first arrived in LA fresh from being fired out of a gig in Vegas and stone-cold broke. Joey, who at that time was just beginning to make it himself, had gotten Lennie a job at the legendary Foxie's club on Hollywood Boulevard, and been there for him all the way.

Lennie did not forget favours, so when his own career began to surpass Joey's by a long streak, and Joey's was on a downward spiral due to a serious cocaine problem, he'd always made sure there was a role for his friend in everything he did. Right now Joey's career was on an upswing.

"You comin' for dinner or what?" Joey demanded.

"Maybe I'll let you buy me a pizza," Lennie said relenting. After all, the house in Malibu was distinctly lonely with just Miko and himself for company. And he was tired of trying to make improvements on a script that was going nowhere.

Joey seemed pleased: he'd been trying to get Lennie out for weeks. "We'll go back to my place, you can grab a shower, an' then we'll *paaarty* all night long! Yeah!"

"Dinner, Joey. That's it."

Joey pulled a disappointed face. "Dinner, Joey," he mimicked. "Hey – hey – hey – Whatever happened to the wild guy I used to know? Whatever happened to the king of the party scene?"

"He got married," Lennie said.

"Yeah, he got married – not dead."

*

The doorbell woke Lucky. Asleep on the outside deck she came to with a start and shivered. A brisk wind whipped along the beach and now the ocean was black and the waves sounded thunderous.

A quick glance at her watch revealed that it was nine o'clock.

She hurried through the dark house to the front door and let in the waiter from Trader Vic's. The food was sealed in cardboard cartons. She had him place them on a counter in the kitchen and leave.

Nine o'clock and where was Lennie? Miko had told her he was expecting him at seven, and like an idiot she hadn't thought of checking because she'd wanted to surprise him. Obviously not so smart. Lennie was out and about, and she had no idea where to start looking.

It's your own fault, Santangelo, she scolded herself sternly. *That'll teach you to go for the unexpected.*

She wondered if Abe Panther was awake, or did the fierce Inga put him down to sleep at eight o'clock? She wouldn't mind talking to the old guy. He was sharp and canny. She liked him.

Morton Sharkey had insisted that two separate psychiatrists and an independent doctor examine Abe before allowing Lucky to go ahead with the idea. "What if he drops dead?" Morton had asked. "Or even worse — what if *when* he dies the family steps forward and challenges his state of mind? We need to have this covered."

Abe had not objected. Like Lucky, he was enjoying the game. He brought his own lawyer into play, and every intricate detail was worked out.

Now they had a deal set in concrete. Starting Monday Lucky was going in undercover. She couldn't wait!

Joey knew almost everyone in the restaurant, so what started out as a quiet dinner for three gradually grew into chaos.

"I'm getting out of here," Lennie announced at ten-fifteen. He'd had enough.

Joey grimaced. He was surrounded by women of all

shapes, hues, and sizes. "I may be talented but I need help," he complained. "You can't leave me, man."

"Watch me." Lennie was already on his feet.

"Can you drop me off at my car?" Cristi asked hopefully. "I never was one for group auditions."

How could he say no to Miss California? "Aren't you staying with Joey?" he asked half-heartedly.

She eyed the seven other girls hanging on to Joey Firello's every breath. "Give me a break, Lennie." With that she pushed her chair away from the table and stood up, allowing him no choice but to take her with him.

"Bye, Joey," they both said in unison, although not intentionally.

Joey signalled a thumbs-up. After four vodkas and several lines of cocaine (surreptitiously snorted because after numerous dry-out periods he was supposed to be reformed) he was flying on a solo journey.

Instinctively Lennie steered Cristi towards the back entrance which led directly to the parking lot. Sometimes fans and photographers nested outside the front, and he didn't want to get caught. Even though this was a perfectly innocent situation, being photographed with Cristi wouldn't look right, and he had no wish to put Lucky's understanding to the test.

Once in the passenger seat of his Ferrari, Cristi let out a little sigh and said – all Miss California Clean-Cut – "I'd *really* enjoy having sex with you, Lennie."

She made it sound so matter-of-fact he almost didn't get it. But when she accompanied the words with a silky hand on his crotch, cleverly missing the gear shift by inches, he had no doubt of her intentions.

Pulling on a thick sweater and a pair of faded Levis, Lucky walked along the beach. It was deserted, windy, and dark. She stuck close to the shoreline, listening to the waves hitting the sand.

The solitude was enjoyable, giving her a great feeling of peace.

Being alone had never bothered her. Apart from her

brother, Dario, she'd spent most of her childhood by herself and had gotten quite used to it.

Thinking about Dario made her shiver. Once they'd been each other's lifelines, sharing every secret until she was sent away to boarding school. And then, after she was expelled, Gino had forced her into a marriage with Senator Peter Richmond's dumb son, Craven.

Gino had thought he was doing her a big favour.

Ha! Some big favour. She'd shown *him*.

She remembered the first love of her life – Marco. Gorgeous Marco, with his dark curly hair, Mediterranean features, muscular build, and brooding good looks.

Ah, Marco . . . She'd loved him when she was fifteen, and bedded him when she was twenty-two. He'd first worked for Gino as a bodyguard and risen to casino manager.

When Marco was brutally gunned down she'd held him in her arms and felt his life slip away.

Taking revenge was satisfying. Above all she was a Santangelo. She was Gino's daughter.

Gino had always labelled her a wild child. Now she was all grown up and had everything she'd ever wanted. Including Lennie. He made her laugh. He was her rock, her steadying influence. He was funny and warm and loving. She felt safe and protected when they were together. Lennie gave her more strength than she'd ever believed possible, and she loved him for it. That's why she wanted to give him something back – and what better prize than a movie studio?

The wind whipped the pins from her hair and it flew around her face.

Time to head back.

There was that split-second almost automatic masculine reaction. *Why not? Who's going to know?* Then Lennie removed Cristi's enthusiastic hand, changed gears and said, "Thanks, but no thanks. I'm not interested."

Obviously this was the first time in her young and delectable life that Cristi had been turned down. To her credit she took it bravely. "My car's at Joey's," she said without taking a beat.

Lennie swung the Ferrari left on Sunset, and again at Nichols Canyon. They rode in silence.

Joey owned a large house halfway up the hill – a ramshackle place with a breathtaking view and hidden snakes slithering around in the bushes.

When they drew into the driveway Lennie leaned across and opened the door. "Don't take it personally," he said, feeling some acknowledgement of her move was necessary. "I'm a very happily married man."

Cristi was not at all put out. "Why should I? You'll change your mind," she replied, confident and pretty as she climbed out of his car and walked towards the front door, turning for a final wave, her pale hair catching the light on the porch.

Hey, before Lucky things might have been different . . . Now he couldn't wait to get home and call his beautiful wife in New York.

Lucky turned around and began the long jog back. The beach was still deserted. The waves continued to hit the sand with monotonous regularity.

With a shudder she wondered what was out there hiding in the vast dark ocean. A recent news report had mentioned sharks venturing closer inland. Not that they were going to come sliding out of the sea onto the beach, but suddenly she felt an overwhelming desire to hurry back to the safety of the house.

The Ferrari made a noise that expensive Italian sports cars are never supposed to make and spluttered to a standstill in the middle of Sunset – opposite the Roxy, where groups of stoned, long-haired rock fans waited for the next heavy-metal concert.

"Shit!" Lennie muttered. He needed this like he needed the clap.

A patrol car cruised by and pulled up in front of him. The policeman who emerged was better-looking than Tom

Selleck and wore his uniform well. He exhibited plenty of attitude as he sashayed towards Lennie. Big cock with a big gun. An unbeatable combination.

"We got a little problem here?" the cop drawled, a Southern import.

"Nothing that a new engine won't fix," Lennie replied.

"Aren't you—" The cop hesitated for a moment, determined to get it right. "Lennie Golden!" he announced, triumphantly. "You're some funny guy."

Happiness is finding a policeman who's a fan, Lennie thought. Sometimes it was just the opposite, and they broke your balls because of your celebrity.

"I guess we gotta get you outta here before the crowds discover you," the cop said, doing nothing except standing by the stalled car while a traffic jam built up in the lane behind them and impatient horns began to blast.

"That would be nice," Lennie agreed.

"I came out to LA ten years ago," the cop continued conversationally. "Wanted to be an actor. I guess it didn't work out." He fingered his holstered gun. "Being a cop ain't all that bad. Sometimes I *feel* like an actor. Women really get off on the uniform." He smiled, pleased with himself. "Y'know what I mean?"

"I know," Lennie said amicably, wishing this schmuck would get his shit together.

"I bet you got a lotta women chasin' you," the cop said with a lewd wink. "Famous ones, huh?"

Lennie ignored the comment. "Do we phone the Automobile Club or what?" he asked, trying not to sound too irritable.

The policeman ran a stubby finger along the shiny paint of the Ferrari. "Anytime you got a part for a real live cop y'can call on Marian Wolff," he said casually.

Lennie frowned. "Who?"

"Marian Wolff. That's me. That's my name. Y'see, my mom figured if they could give the name of Marian to John Wayne when he was born, then it was OK enough for me. An' y'know something? My old mom was right. I

59

kinda like the name Marian. It's got character. What d'you think?'

Lennie shook his head, already working this whole routine into some future comedy schtick. Not that he did stand-up anymore – he'd passed on that a long time ago. But this could be a funny set piece for Letterman or Carson.

An older policeman emerged from the patrol car, a grizzled guy with a mean stomp to his walk. "Marian," he yelled gruffly, "what the fuck is goin' on here? Ya want the whole of Sunset to grind to a fuckin' stop or fuckin' what? Get this Italian piece-a-shit tin outta here."

"Wally," the first cop announced proudly, "this here's Lennie Golden."

The old cop spat on the ground in disgust, completely unimpressed. "Marian," he said wearily, "who gives a flying fuck?"

It occurred to Lucky that Lennie might be out screwing around. The thought had never entered her mind before, because she knew they had something very special, and it was not to be put at risk by either of them. Jealousy was an emotion she wasn't comfortable with. However, she couldn't ignore the fact that Lennie was a very attractive man, a very *famous* man, a very *fuckable* man, and she'd been neglecting him for the last few weeks because she'd been so involved in putting the Panther Studios deal in place.

What if thoughts kept creeping into her mind.

What if Lennie was with another woman . . . ?

What if there was more than one woman . . . ?

What if . . . ?

The telephone interrupted her reverie. "Yes?" she answered sharply.

"Who's this?"

"Who's *this*?"

"Lucky?"

"Lennie?"

And together they both yelled, "WHERE ARE YOU?"

*

It was almost an hour before his cab pulled up in front of the house.

Lucky raced out of the front door to greet him, throwing herself into his arms.

He hugged her tight and kissed her, a long lingering soul kiss that excited the entranced cab driver no end.

"Pay the man," Lucky said at last, extracting herself from his arms. "Then come in the house, lock the door, activate the answering machine, and *do not* speak to another human being for twenty-four hours."

The cab driver leered. "Sounds good t'me."

"Goodbye," Lennie said, seeing the leering man on his way.

And so they fell into bed immediately, both craving the touch and sound and smell of the other.

No conversation. First sex. Fast, pure, exciting lust took over as he remembered her smooth body, silky skin, the tangle of her black hair, and the wildness of her lips.

She lost herself in his rhythm, luxuriating in the passion of his arms and legs and body language. Holding him in every way, a captive to her strong desire.

"I love you, lady," he said as they rode the crest.

"And I love you, husband," she managed, before losing herself in an orgasm that seemed to last an hour.

Later, in bed, there was warmed-up Indonesian lamb roast with thick peanut butter sauce and Chinese pea pods.

They ate with their fingers from paper plates, tearing at the meat, dipping it into the creamy sauce, feeding each other and giggling like a couple of wired teenagers.

"I *never* want to leave this bed," Lennie said happily. "This is it, lady. This is *it*."

"We waited a long time to get here," Lucky murmured softly.

"We sure did. A lot of time wasted, huh?"

"Not wasted, Lennie. We're together now, and we'll be together for ever. We both know that, don't we?"

Taking her face in his hands, he kissed her slowly and passionately.

61

She stroked his chest, delicate fingers touching his nipples, drifting down towards her real objective.

To her delight he responded immediately.

"I'd hate to have met you when you were nineteen," she teased. "I bet you were the horniest guy in the neighbourhood!"

"Don't give me that story. You'd *love* to have met me when I was nineteen. Your life's greatest wish – right?"

She laughed. "Right!"

"I love you, beautiful lady."

"Yeah?"

"Yeah."

They held a long look. "Pass me the peanut butter sauce," she said with a wicked smile. "I've got plans."

He feigned alarm. "What plans?"

"Lie back, Lennie, and don't ask so many questions."

In the morning they surfaced just before noon, automatically reaching for each other as if it were the most natural move in the world.

Outside, the sun attempted to break through the closed shades, and a dog barked incessantly.

They made love again, slowly, languorously, and when they were finally finished Lennie said, "What would the love of my life like to do today?"

Lucky stretched and smiled. "Take a shower with you. Take a walk along the beach with you. And then come straight back to bed without passing go."

"It sounds like the perfect day to me," he replied with a grin. "Only how about we cut out the shower and the walk?"

"Don't you think we need the exercise?" she asked innocently.

"I have exercises for you even Jane Fonda doesn't know!"

"You do?"

"I'll be your personal instructor."

"Sounds good to me."

It wasn't until later that they began to talk. Lennie had

his usual list of complaints about the movie, and Lucky listened quietly, hugging to herself the knowledge that soon she was going to make everything OK.

"I write new dialogue, the asshole director says great — fantastic stuff, Lennie. And then he doesn't want to shoot it. I go to the dailies — I give my suggestions — they ignore 'em. Jesus H. Christ, they're getting my input for free — you'd think they'd run with it, right?"

She nodded her agreement, stroking his back, lightly massaging his neck.

He lay face down on the bed, completely relaxed for the first time in weeks. Lucky was the only woman in the world who was able to draw every bit of tension out of him and make him feel this good.

"We've got to think of a way to get you out of this contract," she said.

He admitted defeat. "As usual you were right. I'm gonna talk to my lawyer."

"Hold off until *Macho Man* is finished. *That's* the time to make a move."

"Yeah, I guess so. How come you're always right?"

She laughed. "'cause I'm Gino's daughter an' he taught me good."

"Pretty damn good."

"*Very* good — and don't you forget it, husband."

He rolled over and grabbed her in a hug. "So — the big question. When are you coming to Acapulco? I need you there like immediately."

Now came the crunch. She took a deep breath. "Uh, Lennie, I've been meaning to talk to you about Acapulco."

"What?" he asked suspiciously.

"Don't get mad," she warned.

"What?" he repeated more forcefully.

She began the carefully rehearsed speech she'd planned. "There's a huge business deal in Japan I have to take care of. If all goes as it should I'll be out of there in a couple of weeks, and then I'll stop off and see Bobby in London, maybe spend a few days at the office in New York. After that, I'm all yours."

His tone was bleak. "You've *got* to be kidding."

"I'm not."

"Lucky," he exclaimed vehemently, "you promised me Acapulco."

"I'll be there," she lied.

"When?" he asked accusingly.

"As soon as I can."

Angrily he sat up. "I don't fucking believe this."

"I'm not exactly thrilled myself. But the Japanese are very particular when it comes to deal-making." She reached for a cigarette. "Oh, sure, I could send one of the heads of the company – but it's me they want. Something to do with honour. The owner of their company will only deal with the owner of *our* company – and until Bobby and Brigette reach a legal age, that's me. This is an enormous deal we've all been working on for over a year. I can't risk blowing it."

Fortunately Lennie knew nothing about what went on at Stanislopoulos Shipping – he'd never shown any interest, and she'd never volunteered information. Her story sounded plausible.

"Shit!" he grumbled. "Why did I have to marry a business tycoon? I never fucking see you." He leaped off the bed and stalked into the bathroom.

"Because I excite the hell out of you," she yelled after him. "And with anyone else you'd be bored. C'mon Lennie, admit it."

The sound of the shower drowned her out. God damn it, he wasn't taking this well.

Stubbing out her cigarette, she followed him into the bathroom and into the shower, wrapping her arms around his waist from behind.

"Quit," he said sternly, attempting to shake her off.

"Don't be a pain in the ass," she replied, hanging on. "This is only a delay. I'll be there. After all, it's not like you're going to be a free person. You'll be working every day, and you know I hate to sit around playing the wife role."

"I had other plans," he said, reaching for the soap.

"What other plans?" she demanded, sneaking her hands around to the front of his body, cupping his balls and going for the main event.

"Listen, lady, sex ain't gonna get you out of this one," he warned, turning to face her as the luke-warm water cascaded over both of them.

"*What* other plans?" Lucky demanded a second time, sinking to her knees.

"No you don't." Weakly he attempted to push her away. "You can torture me all you want, but I'm not telling."

She flicked his growing hard-on with her tongue. "Tell!" she insisted. "Give me the information or you're in big trouble!"

"No . . . way," he managed to groan.

Her tongue teased him lightly, causing him to change his mind. He began to thrust against her.

Now it was her turn to back away. "Tell," she repeated sternly. "Or suffer."

They were both beginning to break up. The crisis was over.

Urgently he grabbed the back of her wet hair, pressing her head towards him.

She wriggled free and slipped out of the shower.

"Jesus! Now I *really* know what prick-tease means!" he muttered through clenched teeth, following her from the shower.

With a quick lunge he caught her in the bathroom. They both fell to the floor, naked, slippery, and laughing.

"Gotcha!" he muttered triumphantly, spread-eagling her arms, and pinning her legs with his body as he manoeuvred into position.

And then he was pounding into her and the words came out, surprising both of them.

"I . . . want . . . you . . . to . . . have . . . our . . . baby. And . . . I . . . don't . . . want . . . any . . . excuses. OK, Lucky, OK?"

Chapter 11

Under the guiding hand of Mickey Stolli, Panther Studios was a changed place from the days when Abe Panther was in charge. Once it had been one of the great old studios making tasteful, stylish films, but Mickey had made sure that Panther moved with the times. As he was so fond of saying at meetings, "It's the frigging eighties, for crissake. Let's give the dumb unwashed what they *really* wanna see."

What Mickey wanted the public to see was multiple violence with an avalanche of tits and ass. Not harmless tits and ass, but the pornographic kind. Girls being stripped, terrified, mutilated, raped, and murdered. On film, of course. In fact, whatever he and his willing team of writers, directors, and producers could get away with.

These were not big movies star-wise, but they were huge money-makers all over the world — every one of them. They were cheap to shoot, cost nothing to put out, and were easy to produce.

America the great. They could kick the hell out of women up there on the screen any way they wanted, and as long as the sex wasn't too graphic they could get away with murder. Literally.

Panther Studios had begun to specialize in these low-bucks, soft-core exploitation films, thanks to Mickey Stolli, who liked the big bucks they generated. But as powerful as he was, even Mickey had to cover his ass, bolster his ego, *and* shut up his brother-in-law, Ben Harrison — who was always bitching and complaining about the cheapos. So, aside from the exploitation cheapos, Panther Studios made deals with major stars — paying them more money than anyone else, and also giving them sweet development deals that included their own production companies and a suite of offices on the studio lot.

Every year Panther made three or four legitimate big-time movies. One of these was *Macho Man*, the film currently shooting with Lennie Golden, Joey Firello and Marisa Birch. Then there was *Strut*, a dramatic movie about a charming con man and a street-smart woman, starring Venus Maria – *the* hot property of the year – with Cooper Turner co-starring and directing. Quite a coup.

In post-production they had the new Johnny Romano action comedy, *Motherfaker*.

Abigaile Strolli insisted that Mickey make movies with big stars. It was good for her social life.

Quite frankly, Mickey didn't give a rat's ass. Movie stars were trouble – always causing problems, holding things up, and expecting more money and attention than they were worth. Their egos were beyond enormous.

Mickey preferred shooting his cheapos. A nice fast production with a guaranteed box-office bonanza at the end of it.

Of course, he had to take into account Abigaile's feelings. She was, after all, Abe Panther's granddaughter, *and* the reason Mickey Stolli was where he was today.

And where was he?

He was in an air-conditioned office bigger than the house he'd grown up in. He was forty-eight years old. He was five feet nine inches tall. He was bald and didn't wear a rug. He had a deep permanent suntan, flashing white teeth (all his own – the teeth compensated for the hair), a hard body (thanks to daily tennis, his passion), and a rough-edged voice tinged with memories of the Bronx only when he was angry.

Mickey had lived in Hollywood for thirty years, first coming out as an eighteen-year-old would-be actor. Giving that up when he lost his hair at twenty and becoming an agent. Giving that up when he married Abigaile eighteen years ago and becoming Abe's right-hand man. Giving that up ten years ago when Abe had his stroke and Mickey took over.

Mickey Stolli was a happy man. He had a wife, a thirteen-year-old daughter, Tabitha (nobody knew about the illegitimate son he'd fathered when he was twenty-nine, just before meeting and marrying Abigaile), a black mistress, two houses (Bel Air and Trancas), three cars (a Rolls, a Porsche, and a jeep), and a studio.

What more could any man ask for?

Olive, his English personal secretary, entered the office. Olive was a slim woman of forty cast in the Deborah Kerr mould. "Good morning, Mr Stolli," she said crisply.

Mickey grunted. On Monday mornings Olive presented him with a private and confidential report of all the studio activities from the previous week. She handed it to him as usual. It never bothered him that she had to work all weekend to get it ready for their eight a.m. meeting.

He skimmed through it quickly, jotting notes in the margin with a thick red pen. When he was finished he handed it back to her to be retyped with his notes included. After this was done, she filed it in a locked cabinet in his office.

"Juice," Mickey snapped. "Carrot."

Olive hurried into the small gleaming kitchen adjoining his office, and prepared freshly blended carrot juice for her boss. Mickey Stolli had a health and cleanliness fetish. He allowed nobody but the fastidious Olive to fix his fruit and vegetable drinks.

While Olive busied herself at the blender, Mickey called his head of production, Ford Werne, at home. He told Ford he wanted a private discussion before the regular Monday morning meeting of all the department heads.

Ford agreed, although he wasn't happy about having to leave his house in the Palisades an hour earlier than usual.

Mickey sipped his fresh carrot juice and studied the list of stars with current production deals at Panther. It was quite a list. There were six of them. Six superstars. And Mickey Stolli had them all tied up.

At one time Virginia Venus Maria Sierra was nothing more than a scrawny American-born Italian kid who lived in Brooklyn with her widowed father and four older brothers. She worked like a modern-day Cinderella looking after them: cooking, cleaning, shopping, washing, and ironing – whatever there was to do, it was her job.

Virginia Venus Maria Sierra was a conscientious girl. She devoted her young life to her family of males, and in return they took her totally for granted. As far as they were concerned she was a woman, and it was her mission to attend to their every need. So naturally, it came as a nasty surprise and quite a shock for all of them when one day she left home and ran off with Ron Machio, the long-haired gay son of a neighbour, who danced for a living in Broadway shows.

"What kind of a whore slut have I raised?" shouted her father in an almighty rage.

"We'll beat the fag punk's brains out!" screamed her brothers, equally angry.

Virginia Venus Maria Sierra was no fool. She heard of their threats and she and Ron took to the road, hitching their way across country until they reached California, the promised land – and eventually, after many adventures, Hollywood.

Ah . . . Hollywood. Nirvana. Paradise. Palm trees, sunshine, and agents. Virginia Venus Maria Sierra and Ron were at peace, they knew they'd found heaven. Destiny hovered overhead, and all they had to do was reach up and touch.

Actually they had to do a lot more than that. They had to scrape the bottom and rise slowly – Ron as a choreographer, and Venus Maria (the adaptation of her name she decided on) as a movie extra who performed in underground clubs as a singer/dancer/actress.

Between gigs they sampled a variety of jobs. Ron attempted waitering, messengering, and chauffeuring, while Venus Maria worked in a supermarket, a bank, and finally as a nude model for an art class.

"Surely all those strange people staring at your naked body makes your flesh *shrivel*?" Ron shuddered.

"No way. I get off on it," Venus Maria replied confidently, shaking her newly dyed platinum-blonde curls, while pursing freshly glossed lips. "I *looove* to watch 'em drool! It's a real kick."

At that precise moment Ron Machio knew for certain that Virginia Venus Maria Sierra was going to be an enormous star.

It took several years, but sure enough it happened. Eventually Venus Maria was discovered by a small-time record producer who hung out at the same all-night clubs that she and Ron frequented. With some heavy persuasion she got him to cut a record with her, and then she and Ron put together an outrageous, sexy, and controversial video to go with it. Venus Maria planned the look and the style, while Ron came up with all the right moves.

Overnight she scored — a lightning strike, for within six weeks the record was number one and Venus Maria was launched.

Now, three years later, at the age of twenty-five, she was a superstar, a cult figure, an icon.

Venus Maria had it made.

Caught in a seventies time warp, Charlie Dollar was permanently stoned, a joint never far from his reach.

Charlie was hardly your average matinee idol. He was overweight with a comfortable gut, fifty years old, and balding. But when Charlie Dollar smiled, the world lit up, and every female around got itchy pants, for Charlie possessed a particular wild, stoned charm that was irresistible to both men and women.

A Charlie Dollar movie was a guaranteed box-office smash, thanks to his quirky presence and brilliant offbeat performances. Charlie had a way of taking on a role, and bending the character until it fitted him to perfection.

Some said that Charlie Dollar was a genius. Others claimed it was just old Charlie up there on the screen jerking off over anyone who'd pay attention.

Nobody knew the real story about Charlie. He'd kind of burst upon the scene as a burnt-out, thirty-five-year-old in an underground rock and roll movie, playing the crazed manager of a heavy-metal group. After that one brilliant, insane performance he'd never looked back. And he'd never wanted to.

Charlie Dollar – the hero of stoned America. He enjoyed fame, but pretended to hate it. Life was simpler that way. After all, a guy had to look like he had some ethics.

Susie Rush came up through television. Sweetly pretty, with a neurotic girl-next-door quality, she'd parlayed two hit television series into an important big-screen career as a light comedienne.

Susie was an intensely competitive, driven woman who allowed no one to get in her way. She admitted to being thirty-two years old, although she was actually nearer to forty, a fact that petrified her.

Susie was into good causes, ecology, and channelling. She believed she'd lived many previous lives, and was not shy about telling people.

The public considered her to be above reproach.

The folks who worked with her had christened her the bitch of the lot and loathed her. Her nickname around the studio was Rent-a-Cunt.

On screen, Susie was sugary sweet with delicate looks and a helpless demeanour.

Off screen she was a tyrant. Her husband – poor soul – had long ago hung up his balls and lived meekly in her shadow. It suited him. He was an unsuccessful actor – where else was he going?

Susie Rush was known as America's sweetheart.

Poor America.

Johnny Romano was Hispanic, six feet tall, and of slender build, although he'd developed his upper body enough to boast a powerful set of muscles. He had thick sensual lips, a sly smile, and deep-set brown eyes – mocking eyes, challenging eyes, but most of all, sexually inviting eyes. Women couldn't get enough.

Johnny Romano was twenty-eight years old. He had starred in three extraordinarily successful films: *Hollywood Dick*, *Lover Boy*, and *Hollywood Dick* 2. These

71

blockbuster movies had made him a very valuable property, and also extremely famous. In case anyone was in doubt, he travelled with an ever-present entourage consisting of two sassy female assistants – one white, one black; two formidable bodyguards whose main function was to proposition women for Johnny; a yes-man uncle; and a best friend/stand-in/chief procurer of any young lady who caught Johnny Romano's fancy.

One sweet, nubile female a day was not unusual. Ever aware of the perils of AIDS, Johnny Romano protected himself with two condoms and a cavalier attitude. After all, AIDS could never happen to him. He was a mega-star, for God's sake – and what's more, he was a *straight* mega-star. The condoms were merely a gesture in the right direction, a nod to the good Lord.

Yes, Johnny Romano was a responsible human being who liked to get laid a lot. And why not? He'd worked hard for the privilege of bedding any piece he wanted.

Right now he wanted Venus Maria. But the woman didn't want him. Unheard of! Ridiculous! Nobody turned down Johnny Romano.

Oh, sure, she was riding way up there, certainly the most successful young female star around. Venus Maria left Madonna, Pfeiffer, and Basinger trailing in her wake. There was no doubt she was in demand. But to turn Johnny Romano down. Ha!

Ha! Ha!

The woman had to be crazy!

And then there was Cooper Turner – the handsome, mysterious, insomniac Cooper Turner, who lived in a Wilshire high-rise penthouse and had only made a few movies over the years, but was still regarded as a major player.

Cooper's looks belied his forty-five years. He was boyishly handsome with brownish hair, penetrating ice-blue eyes, and a well-preserved body.

Cooper refused to give interviews. He kept his private life very private indeed, although there was always one special woman in residence, usually a breathtaking beauty or great talent. Cooper enjoyed discovering the woman of the moment. His sexual prowess was legendary.

In spite of his attachment to women, Cooper had never married, although there'd been a few close calls. He definitely preferred the perennial bachelor life. Cooper Turner was not the marrying kind.

Currently the tabloids were alive with news of his supposed affair with Venus Maria. He was directing and co-starring with the young superstar in *Strut*, and tongues were busy all over town. The latest rumour concerned a very public fight they'd had on the set, and the way they'd supposedly made up. According to *Truth and Fact*, one of the more scurrilous tabloids, Venus Maria had apparently quieted his anger with a somewhat public blow-job on the set in front of everyone. Enough to deflate anyone's temper tantrum.

Cooper would neither deny nor confirm the scandalous story. He liked to keep a low profile.

Also tied to Panther with a three-picture deal – the first of which he was currently shooting – was Lennie Golden, Tabitha's favourite. She nagged Mickey constantly. "I wanna meet him, Daddy. All my friends love him. What's he like? Can I marry him some day?"

Mickey couldn't understand the attraction. As far as he was concerned Lennie Golden was just another comedian going through a hot streak, part of the Billy Crystal/Robin Williams syndrome.

But since he *was* so hot, Mickey had signed him. It was good business – and if there was one thing Mickey excelled at, it was business.

Six superstars. And as far as he was concerned all six of them belonged to Mickey Stolli. He had them tied to Panther Studios with the best deals in town. They were his. All the way.

Panther Studios. Mickey Stolli. What a team!

His brother-in-law, Ben Harrison, hardly counted. And

73

as soon as old Abe Panther died, Mickey Stolli planned to buy Ben out whether he wished to sell or not.

Panther Studios. Mickey Stolli. A winning combination. And woe betide anyone who got in his way.

Chapter 12

Panther Studios was one of the last of the great landmark Hollywood studios. Over the forty-five years since it was originally built, occasional modernization had taken place. There was a brand new six-storey gleaming steel and chrome office building that was Mickey Stolli's pride. He regarded it as an architectural statement. Naturally it housed his sumptuous suite of offices, as well as those of Ford Werne, his chief of production, and the offices of the heads of marketing, distribution, and international production. Mickey Stolli's team – his A-team as he liked to call them. Sometimes the A stood for Ace Achievers, other times for Asinine Assholes. The title depended on Mickey Stolli's mood and his "team's" performance.

Hidden behind Mickey's building was the old publicity structure, complete with photographic studios and rabbit-hole office spaces. And a long way behind that, right at the back of the lot, stood the oldest building of all – the main administrative block, nicknamed Alcatraz, because it was gloomy and depressing, and did indeed remind one of a prison. Alcatraz was sandwiched between two of the largest sound stages – massive towers that cut off all light. It was a building due for demolition. It was also the building that housed Herman Stone's office. Herman Stone was Abe's faithful man on the lot. Sheila, his secretary, had been sent off on a six-week cruise. The story was – if anyone asked or even cared – that Sheila was visiting a sick relative, and that Lucky (rechristened Luce for the gig), her niece, was helping out on a temporary basis.

On Monday morning Lucky reported for work at the

gates of Panther Studios at exactly ten o'clock. She wore a long shapeless dress, loose cardigan, and flat shoes. Her jet hair was hidden beneath a badly styled mousy-brown wig with heavy bangs, and very thick pebble glasses covered her eyes, causing her to squint.

She was driving Sheila's car, of which she had temporary possession – along with Sheila's apartment, a depressing two rooms in West Hollywood that she'd used to change in after she'd left Lennie early in the morning, supposedly to fly to New York and then on to Japan.

Lennie had kissed her long and hard. "Don't forget what you promised me, sweetheart," he'd said.

How could she forget? She'd promised him a baby, but she hadn't said when. A couple of years down the line – maybe. Right now she had a studio to think about.

Entering Panther Studios was a Hollywood historian's dream. The huge arched gates were intricately carved in stone, with fancy art deco iron railings, and on top of the gates perched a sleek black granite panther, just about to take flight. MGM had its lion – but Panther Studios had the *real* power symbol.

Lucky gave a shiver of delight as she stopped Sheila's modest Chevrolet by the security guard's window and stated her business.

One of these days all of this was going to be hers – an exciting and stimulating thought.

The guard was rude. He questioned her brusquely, giving her vague directions about where to park her car.

"Well, buddy, we know what's going to happen to *you* in six weeks," she muttered under her breath when, after driving around the vast studio twice, she realized she was completely lost.

Stopping the car on what seemed to be the main street, she asked a slim woman in a floral print dress where the parking for Herman Stone's office was.

"Isn't this Sheila's car?" the woman asked. She spoke with a strong English accent.

Test number one. "Yes," Lucky replied without taking

a beat. "Sheila had to go and care for a sick relative. I'm Luce, her niece. I'm helping out for a couple of weeks."

"I do hope it's nothing serious," the woman in the floral print dress said, looking concerned.

"I don't think so."

"Good." The woman then proceeded to give her directions before entering a nearby building.

Lucky found the parking lot, left the car, and walked quite a distance. It seemed that secretaries were not allowed the privilege of parking their cars close to their bosses' offices.

Hm . . . better start making notes, Santangelo.

Trekking briskly past a group of bare-chested workmen, she couldn't help noticing that none of them whistled or cat-called. There were no anguished cries of "Give it to me, baby. C'mon, sweet sweet stuff, *give it up*! I *waaant* your fine ass!! I *neeed* to taste pussy!"

This was a first. Her disguise was better than she'd anticipated. She really had managed to turn herself into a dowdy, nondescript drone. Even Lennie would fail to recognize her if they came face to face. Not that it was likely, for he was due to leave for the Acapulco location that very afternoon and would be away for five weeks. At least her timing was impeccable.

She quickened her step and headed for adventure.

Herman Stone was a nervous wreck. He hustled Lucky into his dark office, arms flailing, muttering to himself, practically pushing her into a chair in front of his desk. "You're late," he fussed.

"I had to walk ten miles to get here," she complained. "Why can't I park outside the office?"

"Executive parking only," Herman explained.

"My ass," Lucky muttered.

"Excuse me?"

Herman Stone was in on the scam and Lucky wondered if he'd last the six weeks. A small, wizened man, he looked older than Abe, and frightened out of his shiny blue suit.

She wanted to give him a shot of brandy and tell him

to calm down. Instead she leaned back in her chair and spoke slowly and reassuringly. "Mr Stone. All I need from you is information. Everything you have on everyone who works here. And then, after I familiarize myself with the players, you're to send me out into the field to play. OK?"

Herman breathed sharply. Short, jerky gasps, as if at any moment someone was going to shut off his air supply.

"Don't worry," Lucky went on reassuringly. "This entire exercise is going to be easy. And since your job is totally secure, let's just relax. OK?"

Herman gasped another breath. "Whatever Mr Panther requires," he said sourly, glaring balefully at her.

Lucky nodded. "Yeah." And for the first time she realized that maybe it wasn't going to be as easy as she'd imagined.

The morning passed slowly while Herman repeated everything she'd already learned about the key executives. Mickey Stolli was Number One, followed by Ford Werne, his Head of Production; Teddy T. Lauden, Chief of Business Affairs; Zev Lorenzo, Head of the Television Division; and three Senior Vice Presidents – Buck Graham, Marketing, Eddie Kane, Distribution, and Grant Wendell, Worldwide Production.

These were the most important players, but other influential figures on the lot included several producers with multi-picture deals, the two most important being Frankie Lombardo and Arnie Blackwood.

And then, of course, there were Mickey Stolli's six resident stars.

"C'mon, I'm after the *real* dirt," Lucky pressed. "I can get all this stuff you're telling me from their studio bios."

"What real dirt?" Herman asked blankly, fiddling with his heavy horn-rimmed spectacles. "I've told you everything I know."

Some spy Abe had stashed on the lot. Herman was either too old or too out of touch. Probably a combination of both. Lucky realized she was going to have to figure out who was doing what to whom all by herself.

"What do you usually *do* all day?" she asked. She'd

77

been sitting in his office for two and a half hours and the phone hadn't rung once.

"I look over papers."

"What kind of papers?"

"Deal memos."

"And whose deal memos would these be?"

"Various."

"I don't see any today."

"They're usually sent over at the end of the week."

"Can I look at last week's?"

"If you wish."

Herman Stone was a tired old man. It was quite obvious that he considered his nice ordered life was being threatened. She could understand his discomfort, but she couldn't accept it. He had to know where at least *one* body was buried.

The deal memos turned out to be a stack of duplicates dealing with mundane everyday affairs at the studio. None of them meant anything.

Lucky decided it was time to get started. "Call Mickey Stolli and tell him you want to see copies of the budgets for *Motherfaker*, *Strut*, and *Macho Man*," she said briskly.

"Why would I do that?" Herman asked, blinking nervously.

"Because you're supposed to be looking after Abe Panther's interests at the studio, and you're entitled to see anything you want. Tell him you're sending your secretary over for the papers. OK?"

Herman Stone visibly blanched. Reluctantly he did as she requested.

Marching across the studio lot was no fun, especially at midday. By the time Lucky reached the outer limits of Mickey Stolli's quarters she was exhausted. The dowdy clothes clung to her body, and the heavy wig didn't help. Sweat moistened every inch of her, and she could hardly stop the thick pebble glasses from sliding off her nose. Playing dressing-up was not exactly dinner with Al Pacino.

"Oh," said Olive, the woman with the English accent

and floral print dress who'd given her directions earlier. "It's you again."

Lucky attempted a pleasant expression. "'Fraid so. Mr Stone sent me over to collect some papers."

"Yes." Olive appeared flustered. "Mr Stolli will get them to Mr Stone later in the week."

Why? Lucky wanted to ask. What's wrong with now? Instead she mock-groaned. "Don't tell me I've come all the way over here for nothing?"

Olive put on a suitably sympathetic face. "It is hot, isn't it."

Noticing a water-cooler in the corner, Lucky asked if she might have a drink.

"Certainly," Olive said crisply, although her eyes darted towards the door to the inner sanctum, as if she needed Mickey Stolli's approval.

Lucky approached the water-cooler and took a long refreshing drink, using the time to check out her surroundings. The outer office was painted a cool light beige, with matching wall-to-wall carpet, and a large modern window overlooked fancy landscaping. Quite a difference from Herman Stone's dreary space. On the walls were permaplaqued pictures of Mickey Stolli with various celebrities and politicians.

A sudden commotion took place as a woman swept through the door, paused dramatically, and said, "Olive, dear, is he here?"

Olive jumped to her feet. "Miss Rush. He's expecting you."

A tinkling, phony laugh. "Of *course* he is."

Susie Rush was petite and slim, with straggly yellow hair artfully arranged in neat curls, wide pale blue eyes, porcelain skin, and thin lips. She was almost pretty, certainly petulant. She did not have the presence of a movie star. More girl-next-door than Marilyn Monroe.

Olive buzzed her boss, who apparently didn't hesitate once he got the news. Throwing open the door to his office, along with his arms, he exclaimed, "Susie, my *pet*! Come in."

Susie my pet ran straight into his welcoming arms and nuzzled for a moment or two. Small mewing sounds could be heard. Then the two of them, still in full embrace, entered his office and slammed the door shut.

Olive's nostrils flared. A sign of disapproval? Lucky couldn't be sure. "Wasn't that Susie Rush?" she asked brightly.

"You must *never* ask for autographs," Olive admonished sternly. "It's a studio rule."

"I wasn't planning on doing so," Lucky couldn't help responding.

Olive ignored her, busying herself with a pile of papers on her desk. Susie Rush being in her boss's office was obviously not a thrilling happening.

"Is there somewhere around here for lunch?" Lucky asked in her best polite voice, hoping to win Olive over.

"The commissary," Olive replied, without looking up.

"Maybe we can lunch together," Lucky ventured.

"I rarely eat lunch," Olive replied brusquely. "The commissary is halfway between here and your office. Do give my regards to your aunt." It was a dismissal, firm and proper.

So . . . English Olive had a thing about her boss, who was very obviously kissing Susie Rush's ass — if not other parts of her anatomy.

Veree interesting.

And Mickey Stolli did not want to hand over the budget sheets on his three big movies in production. Even more interesting.

These weren't important discoveries, but it was a start. And at least she'd got a look at the first "scum-in-law", Mickey Stolli, a bronzed bullet of a man with cobra eyes and a phony whiter-than-white smile.

Outside the gleaming structure there was a pleasant walkway lined with shady trees, banks of flowers, and in the middle an elaborate fountain. There was also a bench where Lucky stationed herself, all the better to catch the action as people hurried in and out of the main building.

A few secretaries came and went. A couple of executives

– recognizable because of their California Casual attire. A tall woman in a tightly belted yellow Donna Karan suit. And finally Susie Rush emerged, hiding behind large white-rimmed sunglasses.

Susie stood on the steps for only a minute before a sleek chocolate-brown limousine slid into position, and she vanished inside.

Five minutes later Mickey Stolli appeared, accompanied by two other men. The three of them set off at a brisk pace.

Lucky trailed them all the way to the commissary, where they were ushered into the private dining room. She found herself a table for two in the crowded main restaurant and sat down.

Now that she looked like a drudge she felt almost invisible. People didn't seem to notice she existed – a good way to get a massive inferiority complex. Fortunately she knew that if she took off the disguise, things would change instantly. The power of appearance was potent indeed. Luce and Lucky – two different people inhabiting two different worlds.

What have I got myself into? she thought. *One morning and I'm ready to rip off this stupid disguise and run back to real life. How am I going to last six goddamn weeks?*

Because it's a challenge.

Right.

"You're sitting at my table."

A man. Slight, bespectacled, undernourished. He spoke in an agitated voice.

Lucky checked him out. She judged him to be somewhere in his fifties. "I didn't see a reserved sign," she replied coolly.

He was clearly irritated. "Everyone knows this is my table."

"Then why don't you sit here, there *is* another chair," she suggested quite reasonably.

He hesitated for a moment, then, realizing he had no alternative, pulled out a clean handkerchief, dusted off the vacant chair, and sat down. His close-set brown eyes, covered by wire-rimmed spectacles, darted around the room looking everywhere except at her.

A plump waitress appeared at their table. "The usual, Harry?" she asked cheerfully, adjusting her diamanté-tipped wing glasses.

"Yes, thank you, Myrtle," he replied, rubbing a spot on the brightly checked tablecloth.

Myrtle turned her attention to Lucky, pad poised. "Yes, dear? Have you decided?"

"Can I try a Susie Rush salad?"

"Why not? Everyone else has." Myrtle guffawed at her own joke. Harry didn't crack a smile. "Beverage?" Myrtle asked.

"Fresh orange juice," Lucky replied.

"Canned or frozen? Take your pick."

"I'll just have water."

Myrtle glanced from Lucky to Harry. "You two make a fine pair. The last of the big spenders!"

"She's friendly," Lucky remarked as Myrtle departed.

"Myrtle's not the best waitress here," Harry confided. "Leona is. She would never have let my table go. Unfortunately she's in the hospital at this time attending to her varicose veins. I hope she'll return soon."

He was definitely a strange one, Lucky thought. "Can't wait," she said flippantly.

He peered across the table, finally looking at her. "I beg your pardon?" he said.

Stop being smart, Santangelo. Shape up and act the way you look.

"Do you work here?" she asked nicely.

Harry considered her question before answering. "I have been at Panther Studios for thirty-three years," he announced at last. "Panther Studios is my home."

"Your home?"

"It seems I have spent more time here than in my own house. My wife left me because of it."

"Really?" She tried to look interested. "And what do you do around here?"

If Harry had been standing he would have pulled himself

up to his full height. As it was he squared his shoulders and answered proudly, "I am the Chief Projectionist."

"How interesting."

"I worked for Mr Abe Panther himself when he was here," Harry continued with dignity. "This studio was different then, I can tell you." Realizing that this might sound like a complaint, he stopped himself from saying more.

"I bet you miss the good old days, huh?" Lucky asked encouragingly.

Harry found a new spot on the tablecloth and began to rub it vigorously. "Things change. I understand," he said in a noncommittal voice. "Are you visiting? Or are you employed here?"

"Sort of both," Lucky replied. "I'm Luce, Sheila Hervey's niece. Y'know, Sheila, Mr Stone's secretary? Well, she's off sick, and I'm kind of filling in for her."

"Sheila doesn't have a niece," Harry said, blinking rapidly several times.

Son of a bitch! "You're looking at her," Lucky replied without taking a beat.

"She has one sister, childless, and no other living relatives," Harry said, adjusting his spectacles. "I make it my business to find out about people."

What was *his* problem? "I guess Shèila kept secrets," she said lightly.

Harry shook his head as if he still didn't believe her, but he didn't question further. In fact he lapsed into silence.

Myrtle brought two glasses of ice water, placed them on the table, and pointed out Johnny Romano as the flamboyant star made his way into the private dining room, flanked by his ever-attentive entourage.

"Isn't he a big hunk of real man? And *sooo* sexy," Myrtle gushed, nudging Lucky. "I can tell you this, honey – I wouldn't mind crawling into *his* tent one long dark night. How about *you*?"

"Where's my fish?" Harry demanded testily.

"Still swimming." Cackling heartily, Myrtle hurried off.

An hour later, Lucky sat in front of Herman's desk

again. "Why doesn't Mickey want to send you over the budgets?" she asked.

Herman tapped a heavy glass paperweight. "I have no idea," he admitted.

She reached for a cigarette and lit up. "You'll just have to keep on pressuring them."

Herman didn't like her tone, but he said nothing.

"Oh, and by the way, who's this projectionist guy, Harry something or other?"

Herman thought for a moment and then said, "Do you mean Harry Browning?"

"I guess so." She exhaled a thin stream of smoke. "Skinny man in his fifties – maybe heading full tilt for sixty. Finicky little guy."

Herman coughed, letting her know the smoke bothered him. "Yes, that's Harry Browning. He's one of the oldest employees on the lot. Why do you ask?"

"Because when I told him who I was, he couldn't wait to tell *me* that Sheila doesn't *have* a niece."

Herman clucked nervously. "Harry thinks he knows everything. Ignore him, he's a little strange."

"Shit, Herman – if Harry knows everything, maybe *he* can give me some info on Mickey Stolli. What do you think?"

"I'm not sure exactly what you're looking for," Herman said frostily, offended not only by her smoking, but also by her unladylike language.

"All the things *you* missed," she replied pointedly.

In six weeks she was going to have to put this old guy out to gaze at the stars. His days as a studio executive were definitely numbered.

"OK, Herman, I'll tell you what to do. Call Harry what-sit. If he asks you, assure him I'm Sheila's niece – make up a 'long-lost' story or something. And while you're at it, arrange for a screening of all the dailies on *Macho Man*. I want to see what it's like."

"But–"

She stubbed out her cigarette. Smoking was a bad habit she had to give up. "Don't even fight it, Herman. You're supposed to have clout, so use it for once. Let us not forget you are Abe Panther's representative, and it's about time you started kicking ass, because if you don't, I'm going to be awfully tempted."

Herman twitched.

"Right now I'm out of here," she continued. "I am hot. I am tired. And tomorrow I'll start again. I'll see you in the morning."

Sheila's car broke down on Hollywood Boulevard. Lucky got out, gave it a vicious kick – hurting her foot in the process – and strode into the porno theatre the car had chosen to die in front of.

"Can I use your phone?" she asked the gum-chewing blonde behind the counter.

"Out on the street," lisped Blondie. "Two blocks down."

"You don't have a phone here?"

"S'private."

Lucky pulled off the hideous glasses that were driving her crazy and stared at the woman with her deadly black eyes. "Will ten bucks make it public?"

The woman didn't hesitate. "Gimme the money."

Lucky waved a ten in the air. The woman grabbed, stuffed it down her mottled cleavage, and produced a filthy white phone hidden on the floor.

A customer buying a ticket for *Hot Tight Lust*, the current movie on show, nudged closer to Lucky as she punched out a number. "Wanna come in with me?" he offered suggestively. "I'll spring fer ya ticket, cutie."

She smiled, a cold smile. "Take your ticket *and* mine. Roll them tightly, then shove them up your dumb ass. OK, *cutie*?"

He snatched his ticket and ran.

Lucky spoke into the receiver, a plaintive cry for help. "Boogie? Come get me. School's out and I've *had* it."

Chapter 13

"Where *is* Lucky?" Steven asked impatiently. "I've been trying to reach her for days and nobody seems able to give me an intelligent answer."

"Japan," Gino lied with a straight face. "You know how she likes to make the big deals herself. And I understand this is some killer."

The two men sat companionably next to each other in a steak house with sawdust on the floor and autographed photographs of boxers on the walls.

The more time Gino spent with Steven the more he enjoyed his company. Steven was a no-bullshit guy, like himself. They didn't share the same set of morals, but that was OK too.

When Gino had first learned of Steven's existence it had been a tremendous shock. Not only did he get the news *you have a son*, but *your son is black* really sent him reeling.

Lucky couldn't have been more thrilled. "I always wanted another brother," she said. "And now I've got a *black* brother. Hey – thank you, Gino. You really come up with wild surprises. You're the best!"

He'd searched his memory for the one time he'd slept with Steven's mother, Carrie, and had finally remembered. A few hours of pleasure, and forty-five years later a son.

The revelation had come two years earlier, and he was over the shock now. Steven had arranged a reunion with him and Carrie before she died. She'd turned out to be an elegant woman in her sixties who bore no resemblance to the young teenage girl he'd once made love to. They'd gotten along just fine.

Gino had reconciled himself to the fact that while Steven could never replace Dario – the son he'd lost to the Bonnatti family's murdering hands – he was certainly a true

86

comfort to have around. Not to mention Mary-Lou, his pretty and talented wife, who made the best pasta this side of Little Italy.

"Why do you need to reach Lucky?" Gino asked.

"Nothing important. I like to talk to her every so often. Usually she calls me back."

"I may be speaking to her in the next few days. Shall I give her a message from you?"

Steven shook his head. "It can wait. When *is* she expected back?"

"A week. Maybe longer, maybe sooner." Gino attacked his steak. "So, tell me, how's the pregnancy going? Is Mary-Lou bad-tempered? Good-tempered? What?"

Steven grinned. "It ain't easy," he said.

Gino nodded knowingly. "When my Maria was pregnant with Lucky she drove me insane! All the time it was somethin' – I could hardly keep up. And *that's* when I was young and strong!"

"C'mon, you'll always be young and strong," Steven said affectionately. "And by the way, isn't it about time you handed over the family secret of your sex life? From what I hear, you're unbelievable!"

"Words of advice," Gino said sagely. "A hard-on keeps you young, an' I don't *ever* intend to get old!"

Mary-Lou was in bed when Steven arrived home. She was propped up against several lace pillows watching a *Taxi* rerun while devouring a box of Reece's Peanut Butter Cups.

"What are you *doing*?" he demanded.

"Watching gorgeous Tony Danza and having a *great* time," she replied, happily munching chocolate. "How was Gino? Did you give him my love?"

"I sure did. He was sorry you couldn't make it. I told him if you left the house you'd frighten women and horses! He understood."

She pulled a pillow from behind her and threw it at him. "I don't look *that* bad."

"You look sensational, babe."

"*Babe?*" she echoed, smiling. "Has Gino been teaching you a new vocabulary?"

He loosened his tie as he approached the bed. "Gino's been teaching me that the secret of staying young is maintaining a constant hard-on. How about *that*?"

"Steven! You're beginning to sound like Jerry!"

"Wanna feel what I got for you?"

Mary-Lou began to giggle. "I love it when you talk dirty! It's so un-you."

"Hey, who's talking dirty? I'm just trying to get you horny."

"Try some butter pecan ice cream and mucho chocolate. That's my big turn-on. Sorry, sweetheart. I promise I'll make it up to you the day I leave the hospital."

"Yeah, yeah." He strolled into the bathroom, dropping his clothes on the way. "You know, I almost told Gino about the Deena Swanson deal," he called out.

"I hope you didn't," Mary-Lou replied disapprovingly.

"No. I kept it to myself."

"Good thing. You're a lawyer, Steven. You're *supposed* to be able to keep your client's secrets. Remember?"

"Yes, ma'am."

Sometimes Mary-Lou felt twenty years older than Steven instead of it being the other way around. She knew the Deena Swanson situation was worrying him, but why couldn't he relax about it like Jerry? It was no big deal. It was just some rich woman showing off and paying for the privilege.

Steven had to learn to lighten up. When they had the baby she would teach him. Oh, how she would teach him!

Paige Wheeler had not turned Gino down. She had not said yes to his proposal either.

"Your kids are grown, the time has come," he'd told her. "This once-in-a-while shit don't work for me no more."

Paige had studied the huge diamond ring he'd presented her with. She'd tried it on and admired the way it sparkled on her finger. Then she'd said, "I can't live in New York."

"No problem. We'll live wherever you want. Tahiti, Tokyo — you name it."

She'd returned the ring to its box and reluctantly handed it back to him. "Give me some time and I'll give you an answer."

"Do I pay for the ring?" he'd joked.

"Make a deposit," she'd joked back.

Now two weeks had passed and no word. Gino tried to pretend he didn't care, but he did. Getting old did nothing to diminish the strength of his feelings. He might be seventy-something, but he certainly wasn't dead yet. True, he had a few aches and pains, more than a few, but complaining had never been his style.

He'd had some life. Yeah! A real adventure. And God damn it, he had no regrets. Gino Santangelo had managed to live every minute of it. Now all he wanted to do was settle down with Paige and live quietly ever after.

Lucky had called him the night before. She was his daughter all right. Ready to try anything. He recognized so much of himself in her.

"What have I let myself in for?" she'd wailed over the phone. "I'm finding out nothing. I need ACTION!"

They'd talked awhile. She'd told him about Olive, Mickey Stolli's English secretary, Harry, the projectionist, and No-balls Stone — her nickname for Herman.

"Get friendly with the projectionist," Gino had advised. "He'll know a lot more than you think."

"How come?"

"'Cause he's always around, y'know? He's in that small dark room where nobody sees him. And I can bet you *he* sees everything."

"You may be right," Lucky had replied slowly.

"Sure I'm right, kid. When I was datin' that movie star — Marabelle Blue — she made it her business to get friendly with the little guys. That way she always had a bead on what the big guys were gonna do next. *Capisce?*"

"*Capisco.*"

He wondered how Lucky was making out her second day on the job. Maybe he'd fly out to California and see for himself. Or maybe the real reason he wanted to visit LA was to force an answer out of Paige.

Whatever . . . A trip to the Coast wasn't such a bad idea. He had his routine, but routines could become boring. Sometimes it was healthy to shake things up. There was nothing wrong with surprising Paige on her own territory.

Reaching for the phone he called his travel agent. Gino never had been good at sitting still and waiting.

"Didja score?"

"Did I *what*?"

Joey leaned closer. "Didja score with Cristi? Miss Legs-up-to-her-eyeballs."

"*C'mon*, Joey."

"I'm serious, man."

"Get real. I went home to my wife."

"Lucky ain't here."

"She flew in for the weekend."

"Yeah?"

"Yeah."

"Ya missed out."

"On what?"

"Cristi's a trip."

Lennie gave a weary sigh. "Let's get this straight. I am not in the ball park for any trips. I'm married *and* I like it. Can that fact penetrate what I laughingly refer to as your brain?"

Joey shrugged. "What the cow don't know, the bull don't tell her."

Lennie shook his head in amazement. "You have no idea what being with one woman is all about, do you?"

Joey mock-shuddered. "Don't ever let me in on it, it's too frightening!"

They were on the private Panther plane en route to Acapulco. Attractive flight attendants served drinks while Marisa Birch sucked up the attention of her producer boyfriend, Ned Magnus. Grudge Freeport and Shorty Rawlings also formed an admiring audience. The three men all had a hot nut for her.

"You want to talk frightening – how about shacking up with that?" Lennie nodded down the aisle towards the amazonian Marisa. "She could crush Schwarzenegger with those knockers!"

"Maybe I should go for it," Joey mused.

"Maybe you wouldn't have a chance. She's screwing for a part, and the part she's screwing for is definitely not yours, Romeo."

"If she saw it, she'd want it," Joey boasted. "They all do. Joey Senior gets 'em every time!"

Lennie sighed. "You got anything else to talk about?"

"Not really," Joey said, with a casual shrug.

There were press waiting at Acapulco airport, and more at the hotel. Lennie hated it. He couldn't get off on the attention anymore, although in the early days it had been a kick. He didn't enjoy smiling for photographers and making nice for the assorted journalists. In his next contract he was going to insist on a no-publicity clause.

What did it all mean anyway, this celebrity crap? Sometimes he thought about taking all this stardom shit and shoving it. So he was having a terrible time on *Macho Man* – so fucking what? It was only a movie.

Marisa Birch revelled in the attention. She gave herself to the photographers. She gave them her eyes and her teeth and her hair. She gave them her forty-inch silicone breasts barely covered by a thin silk top, nipples erect, thrusting their way into the public's consciousness.

On the side Ned Magnus gazed lustfully on. Mister Producer. Mister Married Man. Mister Asshole.

Lennie had met his wife, Anna, a tight-lipped WASP with an anorexic body and a penchant for good causes.

Thankfully Lennie thought about Lucky. He couldn't imagine being with anyone else. She was the best, everything he'd ever wanted. And soon she would be pregnant with his baby and they'd be a real family.

He made a decision. After this film he was going to take a year off. Relax and do nothing except be with Lucky. And if Panther Studios sued him, let them. He deserved the time with his wife. Since their marriage they'd both done nothing but work. It was getting to be too much.

As soon as Lucky arrived in Acapulco he planned to tell her. He could convince her. He knew she'd understand.

One year. No responsibilities. No work. No nothing. Yeah!

Chapter 14

Deena Swanson and her husband, Martin, were one of the most sought-after couples in New York. They had what everyone else seemed to lust after – money, position, power, good looks, and invitations to every major event and party in town.

Deena, with her ice-cold appearance, trademark pale red bobbed hair, frosty blue eyes, and famous-for-being-famous demeanour, aroused envy in other women, and a certain kind of desire in men. She was so cool she was hot. The Grace Kelly syndrome. Rip off the Chanel suit, the lace teddy, the silk panties, and crack the zero-temperature façade.

Everyone thought Martin must be a fortunate man, for surely, between the satin sheets, Deena was an untamed tigress, enough to make any man crazy with her passion? And Martin must be something too. The manly profile, ready smile, toned body, and charismatic charm.

Were the truth to be made public, sad to say, a different story lay beneath the glossy exterior of the very visible Swansons. Deena loved her handsome husband, and was prepared to do anything he wanted. But Martin only enjoyed sleeping with star achievers, and famous as his wife might be, she was only famous because of him, as far as he was concerned that didn't count. Besides, everyone knew Deena was merely a figurehead. She didn't design the jeans she lent her name to, or create the perfume that bore her signature.

When Martin married her he'd thought she showed terrific potential. Deena had arrived in New York from her native Holland a few years previously, and soon became a partner in a small interior design firm which seemed to be going places. She was beautiful, smart, and appeared to be everything Martin was looking for in the woman who was going to be his wife. His own career was taking off, lifting him above the wildest expectations, and it was time to connect with the perfect partner.

On their honeymoon in a selected villa in Barbados, Deena had told him that as soon as they got back to New York she was leaving her job.

Martin had objected strongly. "You can't do that, you're a full partner. they need you there."

"Well, actually," she'd confessed, "I'm more an employee. They used my image as one of the partners because it seemed to be good for business. You don't mind if I leave, do you?"

Yes, he did mind. Deena was not the woman he'd thought she was. And discreet inquiries revealed she didn't come from one of the wealthiest families in Amsterdam. Her father, it turned out, was an innkeeper, and her mother worked at the American Embassy as a translator. Furthermore, Deena was six years older than she'd told him, making her only two years younger than him, instead of the eight years he'd believed.

Martin Z. Swanson was not a happy man when he discovered all this information. He'd angrily confronted his bride. She'd nodded, perfectly composed. "Yes, it's true. But what does it matter? Besides, if I can fool a smart man like you, then I can certainly fool the rest of the world, making me the perfect wife for you, don't you think?"

She happened to be right. The image was there, why bother about the past?

So the Swansons embarked on married life, both determined to reach the top. Deena became pregnant twice, and miscarried on both occasions. After the second time, Martin took his first mistress, a Tony award-winning stage actress with a jutting lower lip and an insatiable sexual appetite. The important thing was she was famous, extremely talented, and her achievements really turned Martin on in a big way.

After the actress came a prima ballerina. Then came a voluptuous blonde author who wrote about sex and had topped the *New York Times* bestseller list several times. The author was followed by a female racing-car driver, and then a particularly skilled lawyer.

By this time, Deena had grown used to Martin's indiscretions. She didn't like it, but what could she do? Divorce was not even a consideration. She was Mrs Martin Z. Swanson for life and let no one forget it. Especially her erring husband.

When Deena decided to parlay her social celebrity into real bucks, Martin was unimpressed. After she showed him how much money her various products were making, he was still unmoved. "Money is not talent," he'd said flatly.

"Ah, but that's *all* you've got — money," she'd answered triumphantly.

"The truth is, I'm closer to real talent than you'll ever be," he'd replied.

"If you think sleeping with sluts is being close to real talent, then you're deluding yourself."

Martin had given his infuriating, self-satisfied smirk. "Try it. You'll see," he'd said.

She tried it. She had an affair with a sleek black soul singer. Naked, he was the most magnificent man she'd ever seen. But he wasn't Martin, and although the affair satisfied her physically, it wasn't enough, so she dropped him.

Just in time, for when Martin found out, he was furious. "If you wish to stay married to me, you'll *never* sleep around again." he'd warned her. "You are my wife, Deena. Do you understand me? *My wife*. And you will *not* make me out to be a fool."

She'd stared at him angrily. "And you're my husband. Yet you expect me to accept your screwing around without

94

question. I'm only doing what you do all the time. Why do you object?"

"Because you're a woman. And for a woman it's not the same. No more affairs."

"What am I *supposed* to do? *You* never sleep with me," she'd cried. "I'm hardly going to become a nun."

So they'd struck a bargain. Every Sunday night Martin would take care of his husbandly duties. And in return Deena would remain the faithful wife.

She welcomed him back into her bed with every trick she could think of. Not that Martin was such a great lover. He did not believe in foreplay unless it was for himself. And his action was short, sharp, and clinical.

Deena comforted herself with the thought that at least he was in *her* bed again, and wasn't that what really mattered?

Although Deena had no love for the women her husband slept with, she couldn't help feeling the tiniest bit sorry for them. Anyone who knew Martin at all was fully aware that his work came first. The man had an insatiable lust for more money and power. He also enjoyed the headlines on the financial pages.

Over the last few years the name Swanson was everywhere. There was a Swanson Sports Stadium, a chain of Swanson shopping malls, Swanson Publishing, and in development there was a new luxury automobile to be named the Swanson.

Yes, Martin got off on seeing his name in print, but only if he was shown in a positive light. He abhorred scandal and gossip, regarding it as a major embarrassment. When the newspaper column hinted at some of his affairs he was furious, and since they couldn't prove anything he immediately threatened legal action.

The press had learned to leave the great Martin Swanson alone unless they had something favourable to write or could prove his infidelities.

One of these days, Deena was sure, Martin would tire of being unfaithful, and then he would be all hers. No more talented whores. No more super-achievers. She couldn't wait.

And then along came The Bitch, and Deena knew her almost perfect existence was seriously threatened.

At first she didn't take the intrusion of another mistress as anything more than a passing fling. They came, they went, and usually a month or two was enough to rid Martin of his new-found passion.

But this latest one was different. This one was here to stay, and Deena recognized her as putting the great Swanson marriage at risk.

She'd thought of many ways to handle it. Perhaps pay her off. No good, because The Bitch made mega-bucks and had no need of anyone's money.

Threaten her with physical violence. No good either, because she'd merely run to Martin for protection.

Kill her. Extreme, but if she became too much of a threat – the only answer.

Deena had thought about this solution for many months. At first the idea of hiring a professional had seemed best. There were men for hire, and she knew of acquaintances who could probably arrange a contact. But the risks were enormous. And how convoluted did the trail have to be before it led back to her?

She was also opening herself up to life-long blackmail, and that would never do. There was no way she could allow her position to be jeopardized.

There was only one answer. If she wanted The Bitch dead, she was going to have to do it herself.

Once she reached that momentous conclusion she felt secure.

But there remained three big questions.

How?

Where?

When?

How was easy: Growing up in Holland, she'd always been exceptionally close to her father, a handsome man, with two passions in life – hunting and fishing. He'd taught his only daughter to do both, and she'd learned well.

Very well. Deena was a crack shot. She knew about guns. Disposing of The Bitch with a single bullet through the head would be simple.

Where was another matter. It all depended on timing.

And *when* was entirely in Martin's hands, for if he stopped seeing The Bitch none of the above would apply.

Unfortunately, Deena did not think this would happen. Her instincts told her that eventually Martin was going to come to her for a divorce, and if and when that day ever arrived she was ready to put her plan into operation.

She had already taken out insurance. Jerry Myerson's firm was one of the best. But the real reason she'd chosen them was because of Steven Berkeley and his reputation as being the finest defence attorney in town. If and when she was ever forced to act, she had a plan. Of course, she had no intention of getting caught. But events took strange turns, and Deena wished to be fully prepared.

She knew one thing for sure, and one thing only. Nobody was going to take Martin away from her. Absolutely nobody.

Chapter 15

For some time Harry Browning had been considering inviting Olive Watson, Mr Stolli's English secretary – or personal assistant as she referred to herself – out. Not exactly on a date, more an evening of shared companionship, although he certainly had every intention of picking up the cheque should they go to a restaurant. He'd been thinking about this for eight months – ever since Olive had wished him a happy birthday on his big day. However, these things could not be rushed, so it was quite a disappointment when she'd announced – calmly and coolly – that she was engaged.

"Engaged?" Harry had echoed blankly. They were on

the phone at the time, arranging the hours Mr Stolli would require the screening room that week.

"Yes," Olive confirmed happily. "My fiancé proposed long distance from England last night. It's quite a surprise."

It was quite a surprise for Harry too, for he'd always imagined Olive was there for the taking whenever he decided to take.

Now this ruffle. It annoyed Harry. All those wasted hours thinking about Olive, only to discover she was no longer available.

When Lucky Santangelo – whom Harry knew only as Luce – sat herself down at his table in the commissary for the third consecutive day, Harry impulsively blurted out, "Would you like to go out one night?"

Lucky stared at the small, bespectacled man who'd so far told her nothing, in spite of the fact that Gino seemed to think Harry Browning held the knowledge to all of Panther Studios' secrets. Did he actually imagine she'd go out with him? Wow – her disguise must *really* be terrific.

"Where?" she answered carefully, not wishing to offend him.

Harry hadn't expected a "Where?" He'd expected a "Yes", or a "No". Certainly not "Where?"

"I don't know," he confessed.

"Perhaps," Lucky replied, giving him hope.

Harry peered at her. She was certainly no Olive. In fact she was rather strange looking with her frumpy clothes, dowdy hairstyle, and impenetrable glasses. But still, had she been more attractive he would not have dared to invite her out, nor even wanted to. Harry knew his limitations. Once he'd dated a pretty, red-headed extra – a date that had ended in disaster when she'd turned on him publicly, screaming in a banshee-like voice: "If you can't get me in to see Mickey Stolli, what the fuck am I doing out with a dumb creep like you anyway?"

That nasty and humiliating incident had taken place five years ago. Harry had never forgotten it.

He was wary of women. Most of the secretaries and

female staff around the studio were what he termed loose. They wore revealing clothes and slept with anybody. On four separate occasions during the last year he'd discovered couples "at it" in the screening rooms when they thought they were not in use. Each time he'd got rid of them with the same ominous words: "Mr Stolli is due here in five minutes."

He could get away with telling that to the minor players. With the majors it was another game. They could do what they liked, and they did. Frequently.

Gino Santangelo was right. There was not much Harry hadn't seen in his years of standing in the projection booth looking out over the moguls and producers, directors and movie stars who always seemed to forget his very existence and do exactly as they pleased in the darkened screening rooms.

Harry often mused that one day he might write a book. A pleasant dream, it made his secrets very valuable. He'd never told anyone of the goings-on he'd witnessed.

Lucky drew a deep breath. She was getting nowhere. If she met with Harry away from the studio maybe he *would* have stories to reveal. It was worth a shot.

Leaning across her Johnny Romano steak and french fries, she fixed him with a friendly stare. "As a matter of fact, I'm making . . . uh . . . fish pie tonight. Why don't you come by Sheila's apartment? I know you like fish."

Sure she knew he liked fish, he'd eaten it three days in a row.

Harry considered the invitation. There was something about her he found slightly odd. However, a night away from his Sony television and three cats was a tempting prospect. And fish pie . . . his favourite. "Yes," he said, nodding decisively.

"Good," Lucky replied, thinking to herself – *What the hell am I doing?* "Shall we say seven-thirty?"

Harry looked almost eager. "Yes," he repeated, blinking rapidly.

A man of not many words. Lucky forced a smile and stood up. How the fuck was she going to get hold of a fish pie? Why hadn't she said pizza or pasta or something sane?

Her glasses rolled down her nose and she pushed them up in exasperation.

"Later, Harry," she said, going for the fast getaway. "I'll be expecting you."

Herman Stone was horrified. "Seeing someone away from the studio is dangerous," he said.

Lucky raised a cynical eyebrow. "Dangerous, Herman? I'm not cocaine-busting, I'm just trying to get a little insight into what's really going on around here."

"You're leading Harry Browning on. He's a decent man."

Lucky was outraged. Herman was such a stuffed asshole. "I'm not planning to fuck him," she said coolly. "Merely pump his tongue a little."

Herman stood up. He was red in the face. "I can't be a party to this folly. I'm phoning Abe. You talk like a . . . a . . ."

"Man?" she offered helpfully.

Herman sat down again. He picked up a pen and banged it on the table. For ten years he'd led a quiet life. Two hours in the office, four hours on the golf course. No pressures. No headaches. No foul-mouthed woman to harass him.

"Call Abe if you want," Lucky said. "Remember, though, it's *me* you're going to be working for."

They both knew this wasn't true. Lucky would retire him the moment she took control. And he wouldn't work for Lucky Santangelo if she trebled his salary.

"Do what you wish," Herman muttered.

"Thank you *sooo* much. Your permission has made my day."

"Sherry?"

"I don't drink," Harry Browning replied.

"Never?" Lucky asked.

He hesitated. "Only if it's an occasion."

100

She poured him a glass of sherry and handed it to him. "This *is* an occasion," she said firmly.

The occasion of Olive's engagement, Harry thought dourly as he drank the pale brown liquid. He deserved one drink.

Lucky decided Sheila Hervey's tiny apartment was the most depressing place she'd ever had to spend time in. The walls were painted a particularly dreary shade of maroon, and the oppressive furniture was a mixture of heavy oak combined with cheap plastic modern, all of it too big for the small apartment. Voluminous velvet drapes completed the claustrophobic effect. And an ancient record player offered only Julio Iglesias for entertainment. Lucky was fed up.

While Julio crooned something indecipherable in broken English, Harry Browning gulped two glasses of sherry in quick succession and waited patiently for his fish pie.

Boogie had delivered the pie fifteen minutes before deadline. "Now I *know* you can do anything," Lucky had complimented him. "It better be good."

Boogie had merely shaken his head in exasperation. Like Herman Stone, but for different reasons, he did not approve of his boss's adventures. But then working for Lucky had never been dull.

"Did you bake it yourself, Boog?" she'd asked with a sly grin.

"Try the best fish restaurant in LA. You'll get the bill," he'd replied laconically. "Call me in the car when you're ready to go home."

She was ready to go home the moment Harry Browning arrived. But she'd gone this far, and she couldn't back out without giving him a chance to tell all.

Somewhere real life was going on while she was busy play-acting with a mild little projectionist called Harry Browning, who probably couldn't tell her anything she needed to know anyway.

Damn! And on top of everything else she was now going to have to eat fish pie — which she hated. What a night!

Eventually Harry Browning started to talk. Like a

101

hooker revealing how she first got into the business, it all came rushing out.

For two hours Lucky had babied him along, flattering and feeding, plying him with a good white wine Boogie had thoughtfully provided, and after that, brandy. Now it was paying-off time.

After his first sip of Courvoisier, quiet little Harry Browning turned into Harry the Mouth. Lucky could hardly believe it. This was going to turn out to be worthwhile after all.

"When Abe Panther was in charge we had a decent studio," Harry said vehemently, sounding proud. "Mr Panther was a *real* boss. People respected him."

"Don't people respect Mickey Stolli?" Lucky murmured.

"Him!" Harry spat in disgust. "He doesn't care about making movies. All *he* cares about is money."

"At least he's honest. Mickey is looking after Abe Panther's interests, isn't he?" Lucky asked innocently.

"The only interests Mickey Stolli cares about are his own."

"How do *you* know that?"

"I see plenty," Harry said, reaching for the bottle of brandy. "I *hear* plenty."

"Like what?"

Fuzzily Harry realized he might be saying too much. So what? He could talk if he wanted to. He felt pretty damned good. This woman was fascinated by everything that came out of his mouth, and it was a long time since he'd had a woman spellbound. Maybe he would impress her even more with his knowledge. "Do you know who Lionel Fricke is?"

Lucky tried to sound suitably impressed. "The big agent?" she asked.

"Yes, that's right." He peered at her through his wire-rimmed spectacles. Her image swam before his eyes. She wasn't Olive, but she was a woman, and if she got rid of those god-awful glasses . . .

"What about Lionel Fricke?" Lucky pressed.

Harry wondered how far he could go. He took another

gulp of brandy and placed his hand on her knee. "I saw the two of them together . . . Lionel Fricke and Mr Stolli. I heard 'em make a deal for Johnny Romano. A *big* deal."

"Yes?" Lucky leaned towards him, her eyes gleaming.

"A five-million-dollar price for Johnny Romano — only *he* never sees the full pay-out. Lionel Fricke sells Johnny to Panther for four million. Then he sells a script to a shell company for one hundred thousand. A month later Panther purchases the same script for one million."

"And Lionel and Mickey split the million minus the hundred thousand, and put it in their own pockets. Right?" Lucky finished.

Harry nodded. "I heard 'em. No mistaking what I heard."

"I'm sure you did," Lucky said matter-of-factly, removing his hand from her knee. "So tell me," she added casually. "Who else is stealing?"

"Everyone. Eddie Kane, Ford Werne, most of the producers on the lot. They all have their ways, you know."

"I bet," she said, topping his glass up with more brandy.

Suddenly he sat up straighter. "Why are you so interested?" he asked suspiciously.

"Wouldn't anyone be? You've seen so much. You should write a book."

Harry was flattered. She had touched his secret dream, this odd-looking woman. He nodded. "Maybe . . . one day." Reaching for his glass he took a healthy swig. "I could tell you about drugs, sex . . . the loose women and the things they do."

"What sort of things, Harry?"

"They lean on women for sex. They use them."

"Who uses them?"

"Everyone," Harry said darkly. "They promise a girl a part in their movie if she'll perform certain disgusting acts."

"How do you know?"

"Because they do it in my screening room. In plain sight."

"I guess you *have* seen it all."

He mumbled on some more, complaining about the quality of the films Panther produced, and the low level of management. He particularly loathed Arnie Blackwood and Frankie Lombardo. The two producers were apparently the worst offenders when it came to sex in the screening room. After a while his eyes began to roll.

"Do you feel all right, Harry?" she asked anxiously.

"Not so good."

Helping him to his feet she said, "Maybe it's time to put you in a cab. There's no way you can drive your car."

"They sit in my screening room an' I see everything," Harry repeated. "Some people have no shame."

Putting her arm around him, she steered him towards the door.

"Drugs," he mumbled, "an' sex. That's all they think about." He hiccuped loudly. "Don't feel so good."

"Can we talk another time?"

"We'll see." He hiccuped again, and stumbled.

She managed to get him outside, hail a passing cab, and bundle him in. There was no point in letting him pass out on her floor. If he did, she'd have to stay the night and look after him – and that was the last thing she needed.

Harry Browning had given her enough for one session. At least it was a promising beginning.

Chapter 16

Two more weeks and she'd be out of school! Brigette was marking the days. Two weeks ago she'd been counting seconds. Now it was OK, she had a friend, and what a difference it made.

Her new-found friend, Nona Webster, was the funny, vivacious daughter of a New York publisher and his fashion designer wife. Nona had long natural red hair, slanted eyes, and an interesting face covered in freckles. She was slender and quite tall. Like Brigette, she'd seen plenty of the fast life, and once they got to talking they soon found out they had lots in common. Nona had lived in Europe, met many famous people, slept with a man ten years older than herself, and tried cocaine on more than one occasion.

Brigette confided about her own troubled past, including the kidnapping and her mother's death from a drug overdose. They'd both decided drugs were useless, causing nothing but heartache and trouble.

"We're cosmic twins," Nona explained eagerly when she found out their birthdays fell in the same month. "It's amazing we didn't get to talking before. I never bothered, because everyone told me you were such an unbearable snob. And let's face it — you don't exactly encourage friendships, do you?"

"Right," Brigette admitted. "It's not easy being who I am." She looked embarrassed. "Y'know, with the money thing and all."

"God! I wish *I* was going to inherit a fortune," Nona said enviously.

"Your family has money," Brigette pointed out.

"Compared to you we're bloody paupers!" Nona complained. "And my parents don't believe in passing it on to their kids. They spend everything they make. It's not fair. My brother is furious. He's threatened to murder them both before they get rid of it all!"

Brigette giggled. "How old is your brother?"

"Twenty-three and much too cool-looking for his own good. He's into rich older women and money. In that order. I'm trying to save his soul. Trust me, it's a losing battle."

Brigette was immediately intrigued. "Save his soul from what?"

"Booze, coke, and women. He's a real loser, but I love him."

"I wish *I* had a brother," Brigette sighed wistfully.

"I'll let you share mine if you promise to help me save him," Nona offered.

"How can I do that?"

"Marry him. All your money will surely make him a very happy man!"

They both giggled. Ridiculous conversations could be fun.

The other girls did not change their attitude towards Brigette. "You gotta ignore them, they're just jealous," Nona said one afternoon as they took off for town.

"Why?" Brigette asked. She couldn't understand how anyone could possibly be jealous of her.

"'Cause you're pretty, *and* you've got big boobs!" Nona joked. "That's quite a combination."

Brigette was glad Nona thought she was pretty. But they both knew it wasn't that. It was the money. The money was an impenetrable barrier separating her from the rest of the world.

"What are you doing this summer?" Nona asked as they trudged along the country lane on their way to the bus stop.

"Some of the time I have to spend with my grandmother. Then I'm joining my ex-stepfather and his wife in California. They're renting a house in Malibu. How about you?"

Nona kicked a pebble. "Montauk some of the time. We've got a place there. It's really boring. Malibu sounds more like it."

"Hey – I've got a sensational idea. Why don't you come with me?" Brigette suggested impulsively. "Lennie and Lucky won't mind – really – they're terrific."

"Lennie, as in Lennie Golden?" Nona asked, raising her eyebrows. "Lucky, as in Lucky Santangelo?"

"She's Lucky Golden now," Brigette pointed out.

"Wow! That makes all the difference."

Brigette laughed. "Well?"

"Well, how can I possibly turn down an invitation to meet a real live movie star," Nona said. "Lennie Golden is gorgeous."

Brigette smiled. "He's OK."

Nona looked pleased. "It sounds like a cool idea. But only if you come stay with us first. You'll meet Paul, my

106

brother. What a thrill! Maybe even marry him. Can you do me that small favour? Get him off my case for ever."

Brigette went along with the joke. "Yeah, sure. Why not? Anything to oblige a friend."

They both laughed.

"I'll call Lennie tomorrow," she promised.

And for the first time in ages she felt she really had something to look forward to.

"*Ooh*, Lennie, you're *sooo* cold. Why are you so icy to me? What have I done to upset you?"

Marisa was all over him and she was big. Long legs and arms, huge breasts, thick gooey lips, and an overly active tongue that slid into his mouth every time they had to kiss for the camera.

Love scenes were the worst, especially with someone you didn't like, and there was a Berlin wall between Marisa Birch and Lennie Golden. He didn't respect what he considered she represented — the phony glitz and so-called glamour of show business. He also thought she was an abysmal actress. Not to mention that she was screwing Ned Magnus, *and* managing to put in time with her stand-in, Hylda, another Amazon with large knockers.

The crew were in pussy heaven. Marisa wore nothing except a flesh-coloured G-string as she thrashed around under a sheet with Lennie. She got off on giving the boys a show, and it annoyed her that she couldn't turn Lennie on too. Marisa was used to instant drool. She felt insecure when a man didn't react to her all too obvious charms.

"We've got a scene to do, Marisa," Lennie said patiently, trying not to notice an erect nipple thrust dangerously close to his face. "It's called acting. Isn't that what you are — an actress? Remember?"

They were on location in the bedroom of a spectacular villa perched high on a cliff top.

"Darling, when I'm making love I'm *never* acting," Marisa confessed, waving away her dresser, who wished to cover her undulating flesh between takes.

"Let's roll another one," Grudge Freeport said, striding

over to confer with his stars. "Lennie, you're supposed to be enjoying yourself. The broad is naked. Go for it, for crissakes." He turned to spit a great gob of tobacco into a yellow dish, handily carried by his young female assistant.

"Don't call me a broad," Marisa scolded. "Call me a star." She stretched languidly, and spotted Ned Magnus, who'd just arrived. "Hi, honey." She waved and blew him a few kisses.

Ned looked pleased.

"Does Honey's wife know about you?" Lennie asked.

Marisa smiled. Her teeth were big and white. Lethal teeth. Man-biting teeth. "Wives are always the last to know," she said sweetly. "And if it's the wife who's fooling around, then it's the husband who finds out last. Didn't you know that?" Another stretch. Another treat for the crew. "By the way, Lennie, where is *your* wife? I'd heard she was joining us on location. Did something exciting come up?"

"Action!" Grudge Freeport yelled.

Gino Santangelo checked into the Beverly Wilshire Hotel and called Paige.

"Mrs Wheeler, she out," a maid informed him. "You lika Mister?"

No. He would not like Mister. He hung up.

The Beverly Wilshire held all sorts of good memories. Afternoon trysts with Paige. Non-stop champagne and sex. Long, throbbing marathon sessions.

Gino grinned, and fingered the faded scar on his cheek, a souvenir of his youth. Ah, if Paige had known him in those days she would not have hesitated. Gino the Ram was his nickname then.

Gina Santangelo . . . the first boy in the neighbourhood to discover the secret of pleasing women . . .

He was twenty-two and horny when he met the incredible Clementine Duke, wife of an elderly senator. What a lady! She'd taken raw street material and moulded him into something. She'd taught him how to dress, what to drink, how to make polite conversation. She'd *really* taught him how to make love. And he'd allowed her to tutor him willingly, because he'd wanted to learn. More than anything else he'd had a strong desire to succeed, and Clementine and the senator had helped him achieve every one of his goals.

Now, all these years later, he could still remember her sensuous silk underclothes, the smoothness of her firm white thighs, and the musky scent of her hair.

There'd been many women, but only a few he remembered. His first love was Leonora, who turned out to be a bitch on wheels. Next came Cindy, his first wife, another winner. Followed by Bee, a woman he almost married. And then Carrie – a short one-nighter resulting in Steven. And then his second wife, Maria, the true love of his life, innocent and beautiful mother of his other two children.

When he thought about Maria and the tragic way she'd been taken from him it was almost too much to bear. But he'd carried on without her, although there was always a deep sadness buried in his soul.

After Maria there were countless women. A fling with Marabelle Blue, the movie star, had kept him busy. The widow Rosaline had looked after him in Israel. Finally he'd married for the third time, to Susan Martino, a perfect Hollywood Wife.

The only good thing about Susan was that she'd introduced him to Paige. Actually he'd caught them together, enjoying each other in bed. Paige had never offered an explanation or an apology, although at the time they'd already embarked on their affair. He understood that Paige had a voracious sexual appetite. It didn't faze him. He was no slouch himself.

Now he wanted to marry her – and the sooner the better.

Grabbing the phone he tried her number gain.

This time Ryder Wheeler picked up.

"Is Paige around?" Gino demanded, deciding he'd had enough game-playing. If *she* wasn't going to get it out in the open, *he* would.

"Who wants her?" Ryder asked abruptly.

"I want her, Ryder. This is Gino Santangelo. Remember me?"

Chapter 17

Lucky Santangelo knew how to kick ass – she'd had enough experience over the years. First the hotels in Vegas, then Dimitri's business empire which she ran with steely confidence, never depending on management, always going on her own instincts, which were rarely wrong. Now, to sit back in her little corner of Panther Studios, to merely watch and have no power, was driving her crazy.

Herman was hardly any help. If she gave him a chicken he couldn't make soup, the man was that incompetent. No wonder Mickey Stolli didn't mind having him around as Abe's spy – he knew Herman was incapable of doing any harm.

She'd told Herman to get copies of the budgets on the three big movies Panther was shooting. So far – nothing. She'd asked him to arrange screenings of the *Macho Man* dailies. He hadn't even done that. They fed him an excuse and he bought it.

Mister Ineffectual.

Arriving for her second Monday of work at Panther Studios, she was determined that this week things would be different.

Since her dinner with Harry Browning – the famous fish pie night – he'd hardly spoken to her. A mumbled, embarrassed hello was all she could get out of him. He'd changed his lunch hour, and fled whenever he saw her coming. So much for Harry.

In the meantime she'd put in serious work on Olive. Congratulating her on her engagement with a bottle of mediocre champagne. Popping in whenever she could to see if the budgets were ready for Mr Stone. Staying to chat idly about inconsequential matters.

110

Olive had gradually warmed to her. "You're different from the other secretaries around here," she'd confided. "Most of them are only interested in men, money, and makeup."

They'd had a laugh at that. "What are *you* interested in?" Lucky had asked, trying to gain her confidence.

"I pride myself on being the best personal assistant Mr Stolli has ever had. Us English girls are very dedicated, you know."

"How long have you worked for him?"

"Five years," Olive had replied proudly. "And he appreciates me. He gave me a car for Christmas."

"A car! How wonderful!"

"Yes. Mr Stolli is a fine boss."

Any probing as to what Mickey Stolli was like as a person got her nowhere. Olive was close-mouthed and loyal – a particularly annoying English trait.

Lucky had managed to have an interesting if somewhat exhausting weekend. On Friday afternoon she'd flown to London, arriving at noon on Saturday. She'd spent the rest of the day and Sunday morning with Bobby. And then she'd taken the Concorde to New York, where she'd made a fast connection back to LA.

She'd needed the break, and Bobby was thrilled to see her. They'd taken a boat out in Hyde Park, eaten hamburgers at the Hard Rock Café, visited Harrods' toy department, and seen a movie.

Bobby was an incredible kid. At six and a half he looked just like a small Gino. Same black eyes and hair, with a jaunty little walk and sharp, inquisitive personality.

"I miss you, Mommy," he'd told her, just before she left.

"You'll be with me all summer," she'd promised, hugging him. "You're coming out to California, and we'll all be together in a big house right on the beach. You, Lennie, Brigette, and me. OK, baby? Does that sound like fun?"

He'd nodded solemnly, and she'd left him with his nanny and two permanent bodyguards. It was sad that Bobby had to lead such a protected life, but after his kidnapping she couldn't take chances. Anyway, it wasn't so bad. He enjoyed his school, and he adored Cee Cee, his pretty Jamaican nanny who'd been with him since he was a baby.

Back in LA Lucky felt invigorated. She'd called Lennie in Acapulco on Sunday night and covered herself there.

"How's the deal going?" he'd asked.

"Slowly," she'd replied, setting him up for a delay. "You know what the Japanese are like."

"Are you having a good time?"

"Without you? No way."

"This movie sucks."

"You've told me that seven thousand times."

"Make way for seven thousand and one."

"I love you, Lennie," she said wistfully, aching to be with him.

"Prove it."

"How?"

"Dump your deal and get on the next plane."

"Have you ever heard of the word *patience*?"

"I'm trying."

"Keep trying."

When he eventually found out she'd bought the studio it was all going to be worth it. Oh boy, would *he* regret his relentless nagging!

Now it was Monday morning, and Herman was staring at her, and she was ready for action.

"Mr Panther wishes to speak to you," he announced as soon as she arrived.

"He does? Why?"

Herman fidgeted in his seat. "I don't know."

It was a particularly hot day. Lucky pulled at her awful wig in disgust. After two days of freedom, being back in disguise was a burden. She flopped into a chair and called Abe.

Inga answered the phone, asking, "Who's this?" in a clipped, unfriendly tone.

"Lucky Santangelo."

"I'll see if Mr Panther is available."

"*He* called *me*, Inga. I'm sure you'll find he's available."

"I'll see."

Tight-assed dragon lady!

A short wait, and then Abe on the phone, talkative, excited. "What's goin' on, Lucky? What's happening? How come you haven't phoned me? Did you forget about keeping in touch?"

"Our deal is six weeks, Abe. I didn't realize you expected me to check in."

"I'm anxious for a report, girlie. I want to hear it all."

"Nothing much yet."

"Come for dinner tonight. Six o'clock."

"Just you, me, and Inga?"

"Yes, yes," he said impatiently.

"I wouldn't miss it," she drawled sarcastically.

As soon as she hung up, Herman couldn't wait to ask what Abe wanted.

"My body," Lucky replied dryly.

Her humour was lost on poor Herman. He gazed at her blankly.

She reached for a cigarette and lit up. "Have they sent the budgets over?"

He shook his head.

"Pick up the phone and tell Mickey Stolli personally you want them today or else."

"Or else what?" Herman asked, wheezing.

"Good point." Thoughtfully she sucked on a pencil. "Or else you tell Mickey you're going to have to inform Abe Panther you can't get any co-operation, and that maybe Abe had better put a younger guy in your position. Mickey won't like that."

Herman loosened his tie. He had a chicken neck etched with wrinkles. "It's so warm today," he grumbled.

"Tell me about it," Lucky sighed, tugging at her wig again. "It's only going to get hotter. Let's make the call, Herman. Are you ready?"

He nodded reluctantly.

Lucky reached Olive, who told her that Mr Stolli was in conference and could not be disturbed.

"Mr Stone needs to talk to him about the copies of the

budgets he asked for a week ago. I *have* reminded you, Olive. When can we expect them?"

"Doesn't he have them? I was under the impression they were sent over," Olive said, sounding quite put out.

"Not yet."

"Oh, dear."

"I can drop by and collect them," Lucky offered helpfully.

"Let me check with Mr Stolli when he leaves his meeting. I'll get back to you."

Lucky put down the phone. "You are getting what is commonly known as the royal runaround," she informed Herman. "Or, as my daddy used to say — fucked."

Herman winced.

"But I," Lucky announced grandly, "will take care of it." She leaped to her feet, full of sudden energy. "Today we will have the budgets in our possession. Sit tight, Herman, and trust me. I'll see you later."

Over at the main building there was the usual activity. People coming and going. Executives in tight jeans with open shirts. A sprinkling of gold chains. A ton of hairspray. Tennis tans and toned bodies. And that was just the men.

The women were divided into two categories — business and pleasure. The business ones wore suits with no-nonsense jackets, silk shirts, and determined expressions. The pleasure-seekers let it all hang out in clinging tops, and miniskirts with no visible panty line.

It was difficult figuring out who did what. One of the secretaries — conservatively dressed — was so drop-dead gorgeous you would have sworn she was a movie star. And an expensive-looking young man, featuring all the right gold accoutrements, worked in the mail room as a runner.

The two hottest producers on the lot — specializing in the sex/horror mega-bucks movies so dear to Mickey Stolli's heart — resembled a couple of bums off the street. Lucky recognized them from a recent photograph in *Variety* as they made their way into the building.

Frankie Lombardo and Arnie Blackwood were partners. Arnie was lean and lanky, with greasy hair pulled back in a ponytail, and mirrored shades covering watery eyes. Frankie had freaked-out brown hair, an unruly beard, small eyes, bushy eyebrows, and a rolling gut.

Their nickname was the Sleazy Singles, and most female employees went out of their way to avoid them. "Sexist pigs" was a kind of description.

Lucky kept her distance as she followed them all the way to Mickey Stolli's office, where Olive promptly stopped them at her desk.

"Gentlemen," Olive said crisply, "kindly take a seat. Mr Stolli will be with you in a moment."

"What an accent!" Frankie exclaimed, perching on the corner of her desk, his big bulk dislodging a framed photo of her fiancé.

"What class!" What an ass!" Arnie joined in. "*I* want a limey broad to do *my* dirty work, Frankie. How about it?"

"Whatever Arnie wants — Arnie gets," Frankie promised, and then he noticed Lucky lurking in the doorway. "Hello, gorgeous," he said in a loud, arrogant voice. "You ever given any thought to changing your hairdresser?"

Arnie guffawed. "Looks like a wig t'me. Gives a whole new meaning to the word *head*, huh?"

This broke Frankie up.

Lucky had to bite her tongue to prevent herself from zapping these dumb assholes into the ground. She recalled Harry Browning's reports of their scandalous activities in the screening room.

Olive jumped to her feet, two bright red spots highlighting her very English complexion. "Mr Stolli will see you now," she said in a strained voice. "Please go in."

Frankie moved himself from her desk and ambled towards Mickey's office, closely followed by Arnie. When they opened the door, Mickey Stolli could be spotted behind his enormous desk, leaning back in an oversized leather chair speaking on the phone. He waved a greeting to the two producers, and then Arnie kicked the door closed with an unpolished cowboy boot.

Olive turned to face Lucky. "I'm so sorry," she said, clearly embarrassed. "They don't mean any harm. They're like two big, naughty schoolboys."

Lucky found it hard keeping her mouth shut. She'd heard about Frankie and Arnie from Lennie. "A couple of major zeros," he'd told her. "They run around the lot with T-shirts emblazoned I EAT PUSSY IF IT DON'T EAT ME FIRST."

"They sound like real charmers," she'd replied.

"Put it like this — I'd have to be dead to do a movie for 'em," Lennie had laughed. "They make Ned Magnus look classy."

Olive was staring at her, waiting for a response. "You're upset, aren't you? Please don't be. Your hair looks very nice," she said.

Oh, Olive, Olive. You are full of shit. Speak out. My hair — wig — is a disaster. Arnie called it like he saw it.

"That's all right," Lucky managed in a low voice, hoping she sounded suitably hurt.

"How about lunch?" Olive said brightly. "One o'clock. My treat."

"You said you didn't eat lunch."

"Certainly not every day. I don't get engaged every week either. We'll call it a celebration. Yes?"

Lucky agreed, deciding not to bother Olive about the budgets. If she didn't mention them now it would give her an excuse to come back tomorrow. They arranged to meet in the commissary and Lucky departed.

Outside she observed the tall, striking woman she'd seen entering the building the week before. Last Monday the woman had been wearing Dona Karan. This Monday it was Yves Saint Laurent. There was something about her that didn't quite jell.

Instinct made Lucky turn around and follow her back inside. The woman walked fast and knew exactly where she was going. High heels clicked their way down the marble hallway, stopping in front of a door marked EDDIE

116

KANE, SENIOR VICE PRESIDENT OF DISTRIBUTION. She entered and vanished.

Lucky waited a few minutes before pushing open the door. Two secretaries were carrying on a conversation about Tom Selleck. One of them glanced up. She had blood-red talon nails and lips to match. "Can I help you?" she asked tartly.

"I think I'm in the wrong place. I'm looking for Mr Stolli's office."

"One floor up," Talon Nails said, generously adding, "You can take the elevator if you like."

Just as she spoke, the tall woman emerged from Eddie Kane's private office. Close up she had a face carved in granite, decorated with perfect makeup. Her eyes were hard and unrelenting. Lucky recognized the look — she'd seen it on hookers and gamblers and druggies. Vegas was full of expensive whores; Lucky had grown up observing them.

"Thanks," she said to the secretary, and followed the woman outside.

Johnny Romano was on his way towards the building. He walked with a pelvic thrust, cock first, everything else trailing behind, including his entourage.

The woman didn't even glance in his direction. She hurried over to a grey Cadillac Seville, climbed inside, and took off.

Feeling like a detective, Lucky made a note of the licence plate before hurrying back to Eddie's office.

Talon Nails was now on the phone, while the other secretary, a pretty, black girl, flicked through a copy of *Rolling Stone*.

"Excuse me," Lucky said. This playing meek and mild was getting her down, and the fucking wig stuck on top of her head was driving her insane, especially on this exceptionally hot and humid Monday morning.

The girl reading *Rolling Stone* lowered the magazine and managed a desultory "Yes?"

"The woman who was just in here, does she work at the studio?"

117

"No. Why?"

"Uh, because I just saw someone damage her car and I thought I ought to tell her."

Talon Nails got off the phone and said, "What's up, Brenda?" to the other girl.

Brenda shrugged. "Something about a car accident."

"I need to reach the woman who was just in here," Lucky said assertively. "Do you have a number I can call?"

Now it was Talon Nails' turn to shrug. "Dunno. Maybe Eddie does."

"*Mr* Kane," Brenda interrupted with a warning look.

Talon Nails pulled a face. "I hate calling anyone *Mister* anything," she snapped. "It's so demeaning. Like we're inferior or something. I'll call him Eddie if I want."

"Do what you like. I'm just reminding you what he said."

"Yeah, like he's going to fire me if I forget," Talon Nails sneered. "Sure. He's lucky to *have* a secretary the way *he* carries on with his horny hands. They're everywhere. Bending *down* is a hazard in this office!"

Brenda couldn't help giggling.

They both suddenly remembered Lucky was standing there.

"I seem to remember her name is Smith," Talon Nails said, all business. "Let me check the Rolodex."

"If you can't reach her she'll be here next Monday," Brenda chimed in helpfully. "She comes in once a week to look after his fish."

"I'm sorry?"

"Tropical fish. He keeps them in a tank in his office."

"Really? And what exactly does she do to them?"

"Who knows?" Brenda yawned. "Feeds 'em, I guess. He *is* kind of obsessive about it, though. One Monday she didn't turn up, and he just about threw a fit. Screaming and yelling like Stallone on a rampage."

"Very good, Brenda," Talon Nails said admiringly. "You should be writing scripts."

Brenda giggled and picked up *Rolling Stone* again. She'd had enough conversation for one day. She was more interested in whether David Lee Roth bleached his hair or not.

"Here we are," Talon Nails said. "J. Smith, Tropical Fish." She scribbled on a piece of paper and handed Lucky the number. "Do you work here?"

"I'm Mr Stone's temporary assistant."

"Who's he?"

"An executive."

"Of what?"

"He was around in Mr Panther's day."

"Yeah?" Talon Nails was bored.

Lucky made her escape. *Tropical fish, my ass*, she thought, trudging back to Herman's quarters.

So far it had been an interesting morning. She'd observed the Sleazy Singles in action, elicited Olive's sympathy, and come across a woman who – if her gut instinct was anything to go on – was quite obviously Eddie Kane's drug supplier.

Not bad. Not bad at all.

And now she had lunch with Olive to look forward to, and dinner with Abe and Inga. How exciting could one day get?

Chapter 18

Abigaile Stolli was entertaining, or at least preparing to. She marched around her Bel Air mansion checking every little detail, closely followed by her two Spanish maids, Consuela and Firella.

Abigaile was a short woman with thick, shoulder-length auburn hair, snub features, and an abundance of designer clothes. She was not a beauty, but as Abe Panther's grand-daughter she had no need to be. Abigaile was true Holly-wood royalty.

At the age of forty she had managed to keep a girlish figure (thanks to Jane Fonda), a smooth complexion (thanks to Aida Thibiant), and a keen sense of competitiveness with every other Hollywood wife in town.

When Abigaile did something it had to be the best. She strove to give the best big parties, the best charity premières, and the best intimate little dinners. The food was always wonderful, the service impeccable, but her true secret was putting together the right mix of guests.

Tonight was a perfect example. A simple dinner party for twelve people and the mix was dynamite. One black politician – male. One famous feminist – female. A legendary rock singer with his darkly exotic wife, who happened to be a successful model – an added plus. Two movie stars – Cooper Turner and Venus Maria. A hot young director and his girlfriend. And to round out the group, fast-talking, newly appointed head of Orpheus Studios, Zeppo White, and his mildly stoned wife, Ida.

Zeppo (a former top agent) and Ida (a so-called producer who never produced anything) were mainstays of any good dinner party. Zeppo, with his snobbish ways and acid conversation. Ida, chicly turned out, with all the latest outrageous gossip. Abigaile always tried to include them. They were insurance against boredom.

Abigaile was especially pleased Cooper Turner had accepted her invitation. He was notorious for never appearing anywhere, so it was a coup to get him. And Venus Maria was another hard-to-get guest.

Abigaile was satisfied this was going to be a talked-about evening. She would call George Christy personally to inform him of the guest list. Let the town read and weep.

'Hmmm . . .' Abigaile spotted a Lalique wine glass with a tiny chip in the rim. She picked it up and turned to her two maids, glaring at them accusingly. Words were not necessary.

"So sorry, Madame," gasped Consuela, immediately accepting responsibility along with the offending glass. "I will take care of it, Madame," she promised.

"Yes, and perhaps you can find out who is responsible," Abigaile said testily. "These glasses cost over one hundred and fifty dollars each. *Somebody* should pay. And that somebody is certainly *not* going to be me."

Consuela and Firella exchanged glances. One hundred and fifty dollars! For a glass! American women were surely crazy.

Abigaile finished her inspection without further incident, and set off for the beauty salon in her cream-coloured Mercedes.

Speeding down Sunset, she used her cellular car phone to catch Mickey at the studio.

"I'm on my way to lunch," Mickey said, sounding harassed. "What is it?"

"You were supposed to send over three dozen bottles of Cristal from your office. Where are they?"

Here he was, running a major studio, and his wife spoke to him like he was a goddamn liquor salesman. Wonderful! "Talk to Olive," he snapped.

"No, *you* talk to Olive," Abigaile snapped back.

In most Hollywood marriages the men sat in the power seat and the women danced carefully around their delicate egos. In the Stolli household, Abigaile held the real chair of authority. She was Abe Panther's granddaughter and let no one forget it, especially Mickey.

"And while you're speaking to Olive," she added, "make sure she confirms the time and place with Cooper Turner *and* Venus Maria for tonight. I don't want any no-shows."

"Yeah, yeah," Mickey said impatiently, tagging on a sarcastic "Anything else? Maybe you'd like me to pick up your dry cleaning, or stop by the market?"

"Goodbye, Mickey dear." The way Abigaile said goodbye spoke volumes.

She pulled up to the valet parker in front of Ivana's — the hot new beauty salon — and hurried briskly inside.

Abigaile Stolli was giving one of her famous intimate dinners. She had no time to waste.

Chapter 19

Olive Watson spoke glowingly of her fiancé – a computer expert. She'd met him on her annual vacation trip to England a year ago, and they'd corresponded ever since.

"How much time have you actually spent with him?" Lucky asked curiously.

"Ten days," Olive replied. "It was quite the whirlwind courtship."

I bet, Lucky thought. She was dying to ask if they'd slept together. But there was no way demure Luce would go for an intimate question like that, so she discreetly shut up and settled for "What's his name?"

"George," Olive sounded in love. "He's an older man. Very distinguished looking."

"How old is older?" Lucky ventured.

Olive pursed her lips. "Fifty-something," she disclosed.

"There's nothing wrong with an older man," Lucky said reassuringly, thinking of her own marriage to Dimitri Stanislopoulos when she was twenty-something and he was in his sixties.

"You're very understanding," Olive replied, picking at a light salad. She hesitated a moment and then said, "I hope you don't mind me saying this, but actually your hairstyle could be improved, and I'd be willing to take you to my hairdresser. That's if you want me to," she added hastily, anxious not to offend.

"Thanks, I like it this way," Lucky said quickly, automatically touching the hideous wig.

"Oh. I don't mean that it's not very nice. It is. Very nice," Olive said, obviously flustered, and lying as best she could.

For the first time Lucky felt like a fraud. Olive was genuinely concerned, and maybe it wasn't fair to be playing games with her.

No problem, she decided. When she took over the studio she'd give Olive a hefty raise and a promotion; the woman deserved it after working for Mickey Stolli all these years.

Changing the subject she asked, "When are you planning to get married?"

"George wants to do it at once," Olive said with a worried frown, thinking of the difficulties. "I told him it's impossible. There's so much to discuss, and I have no desire to leave my job. I'm not sure if George is prepared to live in California."

"Shouldn't you find out?"

"Yes." Olive nodded vigorously. "George is going to be in Boston for two days next week on business. It would be a perfect time to talk things over." She sighed. "He wants me to join him. Unfortunately it's impossible."

Lucky sensed an opportunity. "Why?"

"Because Mr Stolli can't do without me. He's a very particular man. Everything has to be just so."

"Really? He won't accept a temp?"

"Certainly not."

"Or one of the girls in your building?"

"Absolutely out of the question."

"How about me?"

"You?"

This was a hard sell, but she could do it. "Yes, me. I can take over for a couple of days. You'll show me what to do, and I promise you he'll have no complaints."

"You work for Mr Stone," Olive pointed out.

"He's off on vacation next week. Besides, even when he's around I have nothing to do. It's a boring job. To tell you the truth, I was thinking of leaving."

Olive was silent for a moment. It was tempting offer. Luce certainly seemed competent enough. "I'll have to ask Mr Stolli," she said doubtfully. "After all, it's his decision, and as I said before, he's a very particular man with cast-iron habits."

"OK," Lucky said, willing Olive to go for the idea. "I understand."

Olive nodded. "I *shall* ask him," she decided. "This is

such an important trip for me, and it's best to get things settled as soon as possible."

"Quite," agreed Lucky.

Olive nodded again. "I'll let you know," she said.

Lucky had Boogie run a trace on Eddie Kane's tropical fish lady's car. It was registered to one Kathleen Le Paul. J. Smith never even entered the picture. Well, anyone with half a brain would have guessed that.

She instructed Boogie to check Ms Le Paul out, and to get her the information as soon as possible.

"It's done," Boogie assured her.

Herman immediately wanted to know what was going on. The air-conditioning in his office had broken down and he was feeling the heat in more ways than one. He was red in the face and stressed out.

Lucky felt sorry for him. "You're taking a vacation," she said firmly.

He became agitated. "What?"

"A vacation. You need it. You deserve it. A week in Palm Springs. You're to get out of here so I'm free to fill in for Olive. OK?"

Herman wasn't about to argue. Any excuse to stay away was welcome. "When shall I leave?" he asked stiffly.

"Stick around until Thursday. Maybe we can get to see the dailies you requested. In fact," – she grabbed the phone – "I'm going to arrange that right now."

The screening room was comfortably decorated in plush green leather with thick carpeting and blow-up pictures of some of Panther's biggest stars on the walls. There was Venus Maria, clad in black leather, with a mocking expression. A full close-up of the very handsome Cooper Turner. Susie Rush, pert and coy, hiding beneath a pink parasol. Charlie Dollar, maniacal grin in place. Johnny Romano, surrounded by girls in low-cut dresses. Marisa Birch, standing tall with her crew-cut hair and enormous bosom. And Lennie Golden, laid-back and quirky, with his longish dirty-blond hair, penetrating green eyes, and cynical smile.

Lucky lingered in front of his photograph. He looked great. As always. She missed him with a vengeance.

Harry Browning came out of the projection booth to greet Herman Stone personally. Ignoring Lucky, he shook Herman by the hand, and said, "How very nice to see you Mr Stone. It's been a long time."

"What do you have I can look at?" Herman asked gruffly, playing his part just as Lucky had instructed him to.

"I've got the latest dailies on *Macho Man*. And a rough cut of *Motherfaker*," Harry offered.

"That'll do," Herman said, making his way to the centre of the back row of seats, where there was a telephone to issue orders to the projection booth, and a small cooler containing a selection of soft drinks.

"What would you like to see first?" Harry asked.

"The dailies on *Macho Man*," Lucky replied, adding quickly, "Mr Stone would like to see the *Macho Man* dailies first."

"That's right," agreed Herman, playing his part for once.

"Certainly," said Harry stiffly, avoiding eye contact with Lucky.

When Lennie's presence took over the screen, Lucky was filled with pride. Apart from being funny and intelligent – he was so goddamn horny-looking! And he was her husband!

The first scene was a brief setup between Lennie and Joey Firello. They worked well together. Their dialogue played fast and snappy. Lucky recognized Lennie's beat on the material. Why was he complaining? This was good stuff.

And then Marisa Birch dominated the screen in more ways than one, and Lucky knew exactly what Lennie was bitching about. Marisa's physical appearance was overpowering, but there was not an ounce of talent to back it up. Her acting — such as it was — seemed to be a giant put-on.

The scene where she was in bed with Lennie was a joke. Grudge Freeport had obviously got his rocks off directing it. Marisa's huge tits were the only focus he was interested in. They managed to take over every shot — great big bouncy things, large enough to do serious damage.

Lennie was not happy and it showed. Talk about no chemistry! Marisa and Lennie did not create sparks. There was no sizzle — merely fizzle.

Watching the five takes Grudge had ordered printed, Lucky began to feel acutely embarrassed. No wonder Lennie was complaining all the time — this was worse than she'd imagined.

She knew exactly what she would do when she took over. Halt production, get rid of the director *and* Marisa, save the good stuff, recast, rewrite, and reshoot. Whatever the cost it had to be worth it.

Maybe Lennie could direct. A great idea! He'd always talked about wanting to.

This running-a-studio business was going to be a real trip. She hadn't felt this excited since she'd built her two hotels, the Magiriano and the Santangelo. Lucky loved a challenge, and this was definitely it!

"What kind of films are they making now?" Herman complained, looking distressed. "I'm watching por-nography."

"When did you last see one of Panther's movies?" Lucky asked curiously.

Herman failed to reply.

He probably hasn't seen a movie since Gone With the Wind, *she thought. Poor old Herman. What a shock he's in for if he ever gets out into the real world.*

The rough cut of *Motherfaker* hit the screen with an opening shot of a tough, leather-jacketed Johnny Romano strutting down a rain-slicked street — practising the old familiar cock-thrust swagger.

Suddenly, a man steps in his path, blocking him.

"Whattaya want, motherfucker?" Johnny Romano asks.

126

"I want what's mine, shithead," the other actor replies.

"Man, whyn't you take your dick an' shove it up your ass, 'cause you ain't gettin' shit from me, prick-face."

"What ya call me, fuckhead?"

"Prick-face, motherfucker. You want I spell it out for you?"

"You're fuckin' with the wrong dude, spic."

"Yeah?"

"Yeah, ya dumb cocksucker."

A tight close-up on Johnny Romano. His eyes hold the screen. Deep-set and brown, they draw you into the character. His eyes register anger and a lurking danger. His eyes are lethal weapons.

The camera pans back to show the other character reaching for a gun.

Johnny kicks the gun from the man's hand, produces a weapon of his own, and blows him away.

Loud rap music blares and the credits begin to roll.

"This is appalling!" Herman gasped.

"Welcome to the eighties," Lucky said dryly.

Chapter 20

Ivana's was a hotbed of gossip. Everyone knew something that nobody else knew. "I can tell you this only if you *promise* not to tell anyone else" was the battle cry.

Naturally everyone promised and everyone told.

The story about Venus Maria giving Cooper Turner a blow-job on the set was still circulating, only now the tale was embellished. It wasn't just Cooper she'd attended to, it was half the crew she'd obliged at the same time.

"Nonsense!" snapped Abigaile when the skinny black girl who shampooed her hair recounted the story.

"Oh, it's true, Abigaile," the girl assured her, nodding solemnly.

"Kindly address me as Mrs Stolli," Abigaile said

grandly. "And dear, please be aware that my husband is the head of Panther Studios where this event is *supposed* to have taken place. And, if you continue to spread malicious gossip, you will be sued."

Wide-eyed, the girl wrapped a towel around Abigaile's wet hair and fled.

When Saxon, the owner of Ivana's, came over to style her hair, Abigaile complained.

Saxon did not kiss ass. Saxon was tall and muscular with shoulder-length blond curls. He had the body of a weight-lifter and the look of a heavy-metal rock star. At thirty he was the most popular hair-stylist in town, having arrived from New York and opened his salon a mere ten months ago.

"Stop bitching, Abby, I hate it when you whine," Saxon said in a deep, gruff voice. Nobody had managed to figure out whether he was gay or straight – and nobody dared ask.

"I'm not whining," Abigaile replied tartly. "And I don't think it's too much to ask for your transient staff to address me with some respect. I am Mrs Stolli to them. *Mrs.*"

"Yes, dear," Saxon said, with a notable lack of respect.

"Thank you." Her eyes dropped to his crotch. Saxon wore the tightest jeans known to man.

He caught her checking him out. She quickly glanced away.

"So, and how does *Mrs* Stolli want to look today?" he asked, tossing back his mane of enviable blond hair.

"Do your best," she replied shortly.

"I always do, dear, I always do."

Boogie was a whiz at getting fast information. By the time Lucky returned from the screening there was a message waiting for her to call him.

Herman was slumped behind his desk. He had left the screening twenty minutes into the picture muttering to himself.

Lucky was certainly no prude, and she abhorred any

kind of censorship, but *Motherfaker* managed to offend almost everyone. Every other word was *motherfucker*, the violence was relentless and mostly pointless, and women were portrayed as either whores or dumb victims.

Johnny Romano had written, executive-produced, and starred in it. Some message he was putting out there.

"Does Abe know what kind of sexist, violent junk this studio is making?" Lucky demanded.

Herman shrugged hopelessly. "A Johnny Romano film makes money," he said.

"So does a thousand-dollar-a-night hooker, but that doesn't mean you have to fuck her, does it?"

Herman pushed his chair away from the desk and stood up. "I'm leaving," he said.

And don't bother coming back, she wanted to say. *Stay at home, Herman. Grow roses and play golf. Home is where you belong.*

"Don't forget you'll be taking a vacation next week," she reminded him.

He nodded, and walked slowly from the office. A tired old man being dragged reluctantly into the present.

For a moment Lucky almost felt sorry for him. But then she thought what the hell – he was being paid a fat salary to sit on his can and do precisely nothing. The least he could have done was view the product once in a while.

Boogie answered her call immediately. "What's up?" she asked. "Can it wait, or should I hear it now?"

"You're right, as usual," Boogie said admiringly. "You should be at the racetrack picking horses."

"Give me the story," Lucky said impatiently, cradling the phone under her chin while she reached for a cigarette.

"Kathleen Le Paul," Boogie announced. "Alias Cathy Paulson, alias Candy Ganini. Thirty-four years old. She started out as a sixteen-year-old stripper, married a hood, became a call girl, then started to run dope across borders for anyone who'd pay enough. Arrested in 1980 for transporting drugs. She had three bags of cocaine stuffed up her snatch."

"That's pleasant!"

"Did time, came out, married a small-time agent, had a child, then went back to her old ways. She's now the Los Angeles girlfriend of Colombian drug lord Umberto Castelli, and one of the chief suppliers of the showbiz community. They trust her. She dresses in designer clothes."

"I noticed," Lucky said dryly.

"Anything else?" Boogie asked.

"What colour panties does she wear?"

"Blue. Pink on Tuesdays."

"Fun-nee."

"Incidentally, your father is here."

Lucky was surprised. "Gino's in LA?"

"At the Wilshire. He wants you to have dinner with him tonight."

"I can't do that, Boog. Tonight is Abe Panther time, I'm going up to his house. Call Gino and tell him I'll be in touch tomorrow. Oh, and run a fast check on Eddie Kane, he's Senior Vice President of Distribution at Panther. I want to know it all."

"You got it."

She thought about Bobby and missed him like crazy. "Did you call London?" she asked anxiously.

"Bobby's fine," he assured her.

"And my office?"

"Running smoothly."

She sighed. "I guess I'm not missed."

"You're always missed."

"Thanks, Boog."

She hung up the phone and contemplated this latest information. So Eddie Kane was a coke-head, and who else had the same little habit?

A cocaine high was expensive to support. Just what other scams was Eddie Kane into?

In the executive dining room Susie Rush laid her delicate white hand over Mickey Stolli's not so delicate hairy fist, and said, "Next time we lunch, we should do it at my place."

She fluttered her eyelids at him, a flirtatious gesture he did not appreciate. The broad had been coming on to him for weeks and he couldn't quite figure out how to handle it. She was a major Panther star, and a major pain in the ass. He had no desire to fuck her. But the problem was – how to get out of it gracefully? Because as each day passed, Ms Rush was making her intentions undeniably clearer.

"Susie, my pet," he said clearing his throat. "If I ever had lunch at your place it would be all over."

"What do you mean, Mickey?" she asked, girlishly innocent, knowing perfectly well what he meant.

"I mean I couldn't stop myself from jumpin' your gorgeous bones, an' that wouldn't be right, would it?"

Susie giggled. "Why not?" she asked, tilting her head coquettishly.

He couldn't help noticing the fine network of lines around her watery blue eyes, and the two deeper furrows between her brows. This broad was no longer in the first flush – it was miraculous what a great lighting cameraman could do.

"We're both married, Susie. Gotta remember that," Mickey said, trying to sound sincere.

She rubbed her fingers lightly across his clenched fist. "You're tense, Mickey. Relax, it's only little me."

This had gone far enough – better snap this back onto a business level. "I'm very married, Susie," he reminded her. And then, just to keep her in a good mood, "If I wasn't, who knows . . ."

Susie patted his fist and withdrew her hand. "Do you know something, Mickey?"

"What?"

"In spite of your *fierce* reputation, you really are a very sweet and loyal man." She honoured him with a sugary smile.

Mickey Stolli had been called a lot of things in his life, but "sweet and loyal" was a definite first. He sincerely hoped nobody was eavesdropping. "Sweet and loyal" could blow his entire reputation.

"Let's talk about the script," he said, firmly changing the subject.

"Which script?" Susie replied, delicately picking the leaves off an artichoke and dipping them in a buttery sauce.

"*Sunshine.*"

"I don't want to do *Sunshine*," Susie replied, getting quite snappish. "If you ever listened to me, you'd be aware I have no intention of doing *Sunshine*." She paused for dramatic effect. "I wish to play the lead in *Bombshell*."

Mickey laughed. A mistake.

Susie glared. "What's so funny?"

He recovered quickly. "Nothin's funny. Venus Maria is set for *Bombshell*."

"She hasn't signed."

"She will."

Susie's eyes hardened. "I want a shot at that role, Mickey. And I will not be happy if I don't get it."

He put on his best jerk-off voice. "C'mon, pet. What are we talkin' here? *Bombshell* is all wrong for you, it's not your image. The public wouldn't want to see you in it. You're Susie Rush, America's sweetheart. Stick to type. Right now you're queen of the box-office."

Not strictly true. Her last film had been a disappointment, making a mere sixty million as opposed to breaking the one hundred million mark – a goal her movies usually achieved.

"I need a change of pace," Susie said, all business.

Where was the hand-holding of ten minutes ago? Mickey thought sourly, realizing this whole come-on for the last few weeks didn't mean shit. She had no wish to get into his pants, she merely wanted to get into his movie.

He sighed wearily. They were all the same, these actresses. Big star or minor player, they'd all drop their lace panties for the right role.

Everyone knew *Bombshell* was his special project – a script developed and written from an idea he'd suggested, a movie he was going to produce personally. *Bombshell* – the true, shocking story of a Hollywood sex symbol. He

132

could see the billboard on Sunset now — preferably the one overlooking Spago. And with Venus Maria in the lead role it was a movie that couldn't miss. Venus Maria was the hottest actress in America. She had a fascinating chameleon quality, a new open sexuality that seemed to turn everyone on. Little girls copied what she wore. Big girls admired her feisty style of sticking her tongue out at convention. And all the males — whether sixteen or sixty — felt the musky heat she exuded. Most of all she was now — a true woman of the moment.

"Well?" demanded a purse-lipped Susie, obviously waiting for some comment on her desire to star in his movie.

"You're not right for it," Mickey repeated.

"I'm prepared to test," Susie said stubbornly.

Mickey shook his head.

She glared at him. Hell hath no fury like an actress scorned. "*I'm* willing to test and *you're* saying no?"

"Honey, I wouldn't put you through it. Venus Maria is set. It's a done deal."

"She's too cheap-looking — too obvious."

Mickey was smart enough to make no comment when one woman was putting down another. Dealing with Abigaile had taught him that. He shrugged non-committally.

Susie sighed, a deeply put-upon type of sigh, and played her trump card. "Zeppo White has a script he wants me to read for Orpheus. I hardly wish to be disloyal, but I guess I'll take a little peek. What do *you* think?"

I think you're a blackmailing cunt.

"Go ahead if it makes you happy, Susie. But I'd still like you to think about doing *Sunshine*."

A phony smile. "Thank you, darling, I knew you wouldn't mind."

Olive called Lucky three times during the afternoon. The first time she thanked her for listening to her problems over lunch. The second time she informed her she'd made a decision, she was definitely going to broach the subject of Luce taking over for her a couple of days the following week while she visited her fiancé in Boston. The third time she sounded dispirited. "Mr Stolli's in a dreadful mood," she said. "I daren't mention my plans until he calms down."

"What's the matter with him?" Lucky asked curiously.

"It's Susie Rush," Olive confided in a low voice. "She's refusing to commit to the film Mr Stolli wants her to do next." Olive's voice got even lower. "And she's threatening to move over to Orpheus."

"Really?"

"He's very upset. Not a word to anyone, Luce."

"Wouldn't dream of it."

"I must go now. I have to send champagne to his wife."

"Can't she call the liquor store?"

Olive snorted derisively. "Three dozen bottles. If she gets it from the studio she doesn't have to pay."

Another petty scam. "Really?"

"Oh, dear," Olive fretted. "I shouldn't have told you that."

"Don't worry. Who am I going to tell?"

"Thank you, Luce. You're a good friend for putting up with all my carrying on. Perhaps we can lunch again tomorrow."

"I'd like that," Lucky said agreeably.

Shortly after Olive's final call, she took off. The heat was unbearable in the stuffy little office, and she couldn't wait to strip off her dreary clothes, dump the wig and glasses, and return to her real self.

Harry Browning was in the parking lot.

Harry Browning was watching her.

Chapter 21

Virginia Venus Maria Sierra stared at her reflection in the mirrored wall of her all-white gym next to her all-white bedroom in her Hollywood Hills home. She was on her Precor Stairmaster, a lethal machine that simulated climbing stairs. Clad in pale blue sweats, a headband holding back her platinum-blonde hair, she worked diligently.

Stereo speakers cleverly concealed in the ceiling entertained her with the latest Eurythmics. Much as she admired Annie Lennox, she wasn't really listening: she had other things on her mind.

Like Ron.

Like Emilio – one of her brothers.

Like Cooper.

And like this stupid dinner party at the Stollis' she'd rashly agreed to attend tonight.

Oh, God! How she hated Hollywood dinner parties. They were such pretentious affairs. And she'd have to make nice to the Stollis – especially Mickey – Mister Mogul himself.

She and Ron had christened Mickey Stolli Mister Mogul the moment they'd met him. He was the perfect Hollywood studio head prototype. Central Casting couldn't do better. He had the mogul look, the mogul voice, and the mogul bullshit charm.

She suspected the charm only lasted as long as one was hot.

Venus Maria was no fool. She was savvy and street smart. She even kept a watchful eye on her money – no smooth-talking "I'll just take twenty per cent of your income" business manager for her. She knew where every dollar went, and signed all her own cheques, along with Ron. Early on she and Ron had formed a company together. They'd called it Maro Productions, and they were fifty-fifty partners. At the time it had seemed like a wonderful idea. Two best friends, joined for ever. Now Ron had acquired a new busybody boyfriend, and Ken – that was his name – was pissing Venus Maria off.

Not that she was jealous. Lord knows Ron had gone through enough different boyfriends since they'd arrived in Hollywood three years ago. But this one was definitely a pumped up pain in the butt. A handsome – if you enjoyed the "I've got a hot poker up my ass" look – know-all male model. Behind his back she called him the Ken Doll. He was twenty-eight, and acted as if he were fifty.

Ron was in love. Ron was buying the Ken Doll suits and jackets and paintings and sculptures and jewellery, and finally – a Mercedes. A fucking Mercedes, for Christ's sake!! *She* didn't even have a Mercedes.

Angrily her legs worked the Stairmaster. She'd made up her mind she had to split the partnership, and although she realized it was the only sane thing to do, it still hurt. Ron was her family, her spiritual brother, and she loved him. But she couldn't sit back and allow him to spend her money on some loser he had a hot nut for.

She'd turned to Cooper Turner for advice. "Do it," he'd advised her. "It's a foolish arrangement anyway. He makes plenty, it's not like you're leaving him with nothing."

This was true. Ron was an extremely successful choreographer, very much in demand since he'd done all the dance routines for *Danceflash*, a smash hit sleeper movie. And he always choreographed the top videos, including all of hers. So it wasn't like he was broke. He'd have plenty of money, and if he wanted to spend it on the Ken Doll that was his prerogative. As long as it was *his* money buying the presents there was no need for her to be angry.

Now all she had to do was tell him.

Next problem. Her brother Emilio had turned up at her front door uninvited and unannounced. "I've come out to Hollywood t'be a star, just like you, little sis," he said.

Little sis!! Was this the same Emilio who used to scream at her all the time? The brother who used to whack her across the face if his Saturday-night-date shirt wasn't pressed exactly the way he liked? The very Emilio who'd called her "rat face" in front of his friends, and repeatedly told her she was the ugliest, shittiest little turd he'd ever seen?

Yes, it was the same Emilio. Thirty years old and too fat to be anything but a slob.

"Get out of my face," she'd told him. "Go home. I can't help you."

He'd shoved his way inside her house, checked it out,

settled down in front of the big-screen TV and said, "I'll only stay a few days, just till I get a job, little sis."

Big chance of that. Five weeks later he was still comfortably ensconced in front of her television with no intention of ever moving.

Another situation she was going to have to deal with.

One thing Venus Maria hated was confrontations. She wasn't good when it came to a showdown. Ever since she was a little girl she'd wanted to run away and not face up to conflict. It was a weakness she was working on.

Fortunately the movie with Cooper was going well. She liked herself in the dailies, she looked better than she had in her other two films. The acting classes she'd taken had helped, and her new worked-out worked-on body was a definite improvement.

It was a challenge to be up there on the screen with Cooper Turner. She clearly remembered – although she hadn't told Cooper, because he was sensitive about his age – the first time she'd ever seen him. Her mother was alive then, and Venus Maria had been about eleven. Her mother was a big fan, and had taken her to see Cooper in one of his early movies.

Venus had thought he was sexy. That night she'd ended up playing doctor with herself under the bedclothes.

Cooper would enjoy that part, but she wasn't about to give him the pleasure.

Right now Cooper was being too dictatorial for his own good. He thought he knew everything, but professionally Venus Maria had an instinctive knack of sensing exactly what move to make next – and nobody could alter that, not even Cooper Turner.

"Tone it down," he kept advising her about her performance. "You're too stylized. Wear less makeup. Darken your hair. Don't come on so strong."

She had the savvy not to listen. She knew the way she was playing the role was right. And if all went according to plan – her plan – she would steal the film.

Cooper was not happy. They fought a lot. Venus Maria was wise for her years, and she understood him very well.

He was an ageing matinée idol who didn't enjoy getting older. At forty-five he was twenty years older than her, and on screen it showed. Consciously or subconsciously he was trying to dilute her impact.

Too bad. She knew the Venus Maria her fans were expecting to see, and she refused to let them down. Not at this stage of her career.

Finishing her workout she jumped off the machine, stripped off her sweaty exercise clothes, and stood under an icy shower for a good ten minutes. Cold water toned the skin. And after it was toned she lathered on a Clarins body lotion, making sure she covered every inch of valuable flesh.

As she was doing this the door to her private bathroom was flung open, and there stood Emilio.

She was stark naked, with one leg up on a stool as she diligently applied the creamy lotion.

"Oh, wow. 'Scuse *me*!" exclaimed Emilio, eyes taking in every inch of little sis.

Venus Maria did not move. She refused to give him the satisfaction of grabbing for a towel and covering herself. Instead she glared at him, a put-down menacing glare. "Get the fuck out," she said coldly.

He thought about a smart reply, decided against it, checked out pussy and tits and everything else he could lay his eyes on, then backed slowly from the doorway.

She was furious. This intrusion was too much. Emilio was out.

Once, a long time ago, another of her brothers had come to her bed in the middle of the night drunk and amorous. She'd kicked him in the balls so hard he'd walked with a limp for several days. A week later she'd fled the family home with Ron, her saviour. Without Ron she'd never have had the courage to hitch across the country all the way to Hollywood. She owed Ron a lot. She didn't owe him half her money.

With Emilio out of the room she walked over to the door, slammed and locked it. Burning with anger she decided five weeks was long enough. Emilio had to go, no more putting up with his shit.

The phone rang. She snatched it up quickly. Emilio had developed a habit of picking up the phone before either she or her housekeeper could get to it, and chatting to her friends. She'd overheard him speaking to her agent one day. "Hi, I'm Emilio, Venus's brother." Pause, while her agent probably said something polite. Then Emilio again. "Yeah, I'm good-lookin'. Sure, I'm talented. Hey, man, I got more talent than she got in her—"

She'd removed the phone from his big fat fist and snapped, "Don't you *dare* pick up my calls!"

It had not deterred him.

"Who's this?" she asked in her best disguise voice.

"Hi, babe. It's Johnny. What's with the funny accent?"

Ha! *He* could talk!

Why did she have to be put in this position? Johnny Romano was a pest. He seemed incapable of accepting the fact that she had no desire to go out with him. "Johnny, I'll have to call you back, I'm on the other line," she lied.

"Don't give me that, babe. Hang up your other call. It's me. In person."

She tried to sound reverent. "I'm talking to Michael Jackson."

A touch of respect. "Michael, huh? How is the home boy?"

"I'll find out and get back to you."

"When?"

"Soon."

"How soon?"

"Sooner than you think."

"Hey, babe. You an' I — we gotta take this further."

"We will."

"When?"

"Goodbye, Johnny."

She knew it destroyed him that she didn't jump. And why should she? Johnny Romano was not for her. He was a stud factory, nailing everything that breathed.

She wished he'd get the message and leave her alone.

There were too many guys like him in Hollywood – Johnny was just a bigger star than most of them.

It was time to get ready for the Stollis' dinner party. After applying an alabaster-white makeup with darkened eyes and bright red lips, she pinned her platinum hair on top of her head and marched into her walk-in closet to survey the possibilities. Abigaile Stolli's secretary had said ties for the men and pretty for the women. What the fuck did *that* mean?

Venus Maria selected a black suit with a thin pinstripe – cut masculine style. Under it she chose a matching vest which only just covered her breasts. On her feet she wore white stockings and granny-style lace-up black boots.

She chose her jewellery carefully – deciding on silver hoop earrings accompanied by three small diamond studs embedded in each ear, and eight thin silver and gold bangles on both wrists. The Venus Maria look was complete.

A star was ready to face the world.

Chapter 22

The driveway leading to Abe Panther's house was shrouded in darkness. Talk about creepy! Lucky wasn't frightened of the dark, but surely the old guy could afford a few lights?

She'd decided against bringing Boogie, he'd only have to sit outside in the car all night.

From the studio she'd driven straight back to her rented house, bypassing Sheila Hervey's depressing apartment where Boogie had installed an answering machine with a remote so if anyone from the studio called her – such as Olive or Harry Browning – she would know about it.

Once at the house she'd thrown off the hated wig, dumped the heavy glasses, stripped off the disgusting clothes, and dived into the pool for a welcome and invigorating swim.

She'd swum twenty lengths before quitting, and then she'd hurried to get ready for an evening with good old Abe. There wasn't even time to call Gino.

Inga answered the door of Abe's Miller Drive house. Big-boned Inga with her cropped hair and sour expression.

"Hello," Lucky said pleasantly.

Inga merely gave a curt nod and stomped off, obviously expecting Lucky to follow, which she did.

Abe was in the dining room sitting at one end of an elaborate oak table. "You're late," he snapped impatiently, indicating she should occupy the chair next to him.

"I wasn't aware we were running on a strict timetable," Lucky remarked.

Gnarled fingers beat out a rhythm on the table. "I always eat at six o'clock."

She glanced at her watch. "It's only twelve past."

"That means I've been sitting here for twelve minutes," he said crossly.

"C'mon, Abe, lighten up," Lucky said, attempting to put him in a better mood. "Eating dinner a few minutes late is hardly a disaster. And frankly, I wouldn't mind being offered a drink."

"What do you drink, girlie?"

"Jack Daniels. What do *you* drink?" she replied, challenging him.

He admired her attitude. "Whatever I goddamn feel like."

"And what do you feel like tonight?"

"I'll join you. Two Jack Daniels, on the rocks. Pronto! Pronto!" He issued these instructions to an uptight Inga, who stormed off without saying a word.

"Used to have a houseful of servants," Abe offered. "Hated it! Couldn't take a crap without somebody smellin' it."

Lucky laughed. It felt good to laugh. She realized she'd been taking the whole Panther Studios deal too seriously. It was time to lie back and relax. Not too much, just enough to let it all go for a night.

"Y'know, my father, Gino, is in town. I'd love to bring

him up here one day," she said, thinking to herself how well the two old men would get along.

"Why?" Abe snapped. "He and I acquainted or somethin'?"

"Maybe. He built one of the first hotels in Las Vegas, the Mirage."

"I remember the Mirage," Abe said gruffly. "Lost ten thousand big ones at the crap tables. That was way back when ten thousand meant somethin'. Today you can't buy nothin' for ten thousand bucks."

"You wouldn't want to buy anything anyway, you never leave the house."

"Why should I?" he demanded testily. "You think I'm crazy? I know all about what goes on out on the streets today. You think I want t'get mugged an' shot at? No, thank you, girlie. No, thank you very much."

Inga appeared, carrying the drinks. She placed them on the table with a disapproving thump.

Abe cackled. "She don't like me to drink," he said, taking a hearty swig. "Thinks I'm too old. Thinks the old tick-tock can't take it. Ain't that right, Inga?"

"You do whatever pleases you," Inga replied dourly. "I can't stop you."

"Don't even try," he warned, shaking a bony finger in her direction.

"You're only as old as you feel," Lucky said cheerfully. "That's what my father says. He's decided to stick at forty-five — he's actually seventy-nine, though you'd never believe it. The man is amazing."

"Seventy-nine's not old," Abe scoffed. "I was still runnin' the studio in my seventies." Realizing Inga had remained standing beside him, he waved her away with his bird-like arms. "Shoo! Shoo! Go get the food. I'm a hungry old dinosaur, an' I want to eat *now*! Hurry, woman."

Once more Inga departed to do his bidding.

"Uh . . . how does she feel about our deal?" Lucky asked curiously.

Abe shrugged. "What do I care?"

"You must care," Lucky insisted. "Inga's been with you a long time. She looks after you. Surely you depend on her? I don't see anyone else around taking care of your needs."

"I employ two gardeners, a pool man who comes in twice a week, an' two maids," Abe said grandly. "Inga sits on her big Swedish bottom all day doin' nothin'. She should kiss my ass to have such a life."

Lucky got to the point. "I'm sure. But can you trust her? I mean we don't want her blowing my cover. She's not exactly friendly towards me, you know."

Abe began to laugh. "Inga does what's good for her," he cackled. "She's a smart one. She's thought it out, an' she knows it's better for her if I sell the studio *before* I die, that way she gets a stash of cash. If I *don't* sell the studio, she's going to have a fight on her hands with my granddaughters. Those two'll tie her up in court for ever."

"Why?"

"Because they're greedy. It runs in the family. They'll want everything I've got. No sharing."

"But they'll still inherit all your money."

He cocked his head on one side, a canny old man with a plan. "Maybe. Maybe not. I could move to Bora Bora an' give it all away to a cats' home before I go."

"Then you'd *really* have a fight on your hands."

"Not me, girlie. I'll be ten foot under. I could care less." He tapped his gnarled fingers on the table. "Now, let's get down to business. I want to hear everything you've got. Every goddamn detail."

Mickey Stolli prepared to leave the studio early. "If my wife calls, tell her I'm in an important meeting and cannot be disturbed," he instructed Olive. "Whatever you do, don't let her know I've left."

"Yes, Mr Stolli."

Mickey was not in a good mood, and he was wise enough to realize he had to do something about it before going home to Abigaile's perfect little dinner party. Christ!

How he hated her parties. Phony conversations. Too much rich food. And everyone as secretly bored as he was.

Why did she have to do it to him? Just so she could see her name in George Christy's column? Big deal. He worked like a slave at the studio all week – wouldn't it be nice to come home to some much-needed rest and relaxation?

Tonight Cooper Turner would corner him about the movie. Venus Maria would do the same. They both wanted to complain about something or other.

How did he know?

Movie stars. They were all the same. Their part was never big enough. Their percentage didn't satisfy. And their close-ups were too few and far between

Zeppo White would also want to talk business. Fucking social-climbing ex-agent snob. Zeppo thought he was running Orpheus Studios. He couldn't run an errand! Mickey missed the days when Howard Soloman was in charge. Howard was a goer – a little whacked out, especially when he had the coke problem, but a real studio man. Howard *knew* what it was all about. And it was about making money, not hosting lousy dinner parties.

Just as he was about to leave the building, Eddie Kane grabbed him.

"Gotta talk to you, Mickey," Eddie said urgently, hanging onto his arm. "It's important."

"Not now," Mickey replied, freeing himself with a quick shake. He didn't like being touched unless he instigated it.

"When?" Eddie demanded. He was a sandy-haired, attractive man in his early forties, with a Don Johnson stubble, transparent blue eyes, and a penchant for crumpled sports clothes. A former child star, the innocence he'd once been famous for had settled into a kind of bemused adulthood.

Eddie and Mickey went way back – almost twenty-five years. For a while Mickey had been his agent, nailing his once hot career right into the ground. When Eddie had given up acting – or rather when acting had given up him – Mickey had found him a job at his agency. Too mundane for Eddie – after a while he got bored and took off for

Hawaii, where he became a production manager on a private-eye television series. The drugs were plentiful and good, but eventually they got him into trouble, and once again he was on the move. Back in LA Mickey helped him out. He used a little influence, and fixed Eddie up with a job at Panther.

As Mickey rose to power, so he took Eddie along with him. Mickey knew the wisdom of surrounding himself with grateful people.

Now Eddie Kane had plenty of clout; a gorgeous wife; a simple little two-million-dollar Malibu beach house; and an out-of-control cocaine habit.

"Speak to Olive. She'll set it up," Mickey said, already on his way.

"Tomorrow?" Eddie asked anxiously. "'Cause we gotta talk, man. This is serious shit."

"Check with Olive."

Mickey ducked out of the building and hurried to his car. He could, if he so desired, have a limousine and chauffeur on twenty-four-hour call. But there were occasions for formality and times for privacy. Today he needed privacy. What he didn't need was Eddie Kane driving him crazy. Eddie was an asset who at any moment could turn into a major liability. Drug users were bad news. Mickey had given quite a lot of thought to cutting him loose.

A dream. Eddie knew too much.

Mickey made a mental note to call Leslie, Eddie's wife, and talk to her about getting her husband into drug rehab. Lately he looked stoned all the time, and that wasn't good for business.

Behind the wheel of his Porsche, Mickey felt in complete control. He had his stereo equipment, a CD player, a telephone, and emergency supplies in the trunk should he ever get caught in an earthquake.

Mickey thought about earthquakes quite a lot. He fantasized all sorts of scenarios. His favourite was the one where Abigaile was shopping in Magnins or Saks – buying just another little five-thousand-dollar evening purse – when the big one hit, and poor Abby was buried beneath a mountain of designer goods and suffocated by a rare two-hundred-thousand-dollar sable coat.

Fortunately, in his fantasy, the earthquake bypassed the studio and both his houses. Tabitha was safe, and so were his cars. Only Abby got it.

Naturally he arranged a magnificent funeral. Abe Panther would have attended, but the shock of the earthquake was too much for him, and the feisty son of a bitch finally expired.

At last Mickey Stolli was a free man – and Panther Studios was legally his. When Primrose and Ben Harrison arrived in LA to claim their share, a freeway overpass collapsed on their limo and crushed them out of his life.

What a fantasy! The best!

Mickey waved to the studio guard as he shot out of the gates.

The man saluted him. They all loved him at the studio, he was their king – their ruler! He was Mickey Stolli, and they all wanted to be him.

Everything was in place – the china, the glassware, the finest linens and silver.

Clad in a sweeping silk robe, Abigaile prowled around her pristine mansion checking details.

An army of servants were all present. Her permanent staff – Jeffries, her English butler, and Mrs Jeffries, his plump wife who acted as housekeeper. Jacko, a young Australian who cleaned the cars and did driving duties for Tabitha – tonight he would be assisting Jeffries. And Consuela and Firella, her two Spanish maids.

Hired for the evening were three valet parkers, two bartenders, a cook with two assistants, and a special dessert chef.

The total was a staff of fourteen to look after twelve guests. Abigaile liked to do things right. She was Hollywood royalty, after all. She was Abe Panther's granddaughter, and people expected a certain level of style. Her own mother, long dead – killed along with her father in a boating accident – had been a fine hostess, entertaining lavishly. When Abigaile and Primrose were children they'd been allowed to peek in at some of the extravagant parties. Grandfather Abe was always present – surrounded by the great movie stars of the time, often with a dazzling beauty on each arm.

Abigaile had always been in awe of her grandfather. It wasn't until after his stroke that she'd been able to deal with him at all. Now she visited him as little as possible, and secretly wished he would fade quietly away so she could take centre stage.

She loathed Inga, and Inga loathed her. They barely spoke when Abigaile arrived at the house with Abe's grandchild, Tabitha, a precocious thirteen-year-old. It was difficult for Abigaile to persuade Tabitha to accompany her, but a touch of bribery usually did it, for she refused to go alone.

"Why do I have to come every time?" Tabitha whined.

"Because one of these days you're going to be a very rich little girl indeed. And you'd better remember where the money is coming from."

"Daddy's got money, I'll take his."

Daddy couldn't take a piss in the moonlight if it wasn't for your great-grandfather, Abigaile wanted to say – but she always stopped herself just in time.

"Is everything to your satisfaction, Mrs Stolli?"

Jeffries was dogging her footsteps, the old fool. The fact that he was English was a plus. He was also unutterably nosy, and so was his wife. Abigaile suspected that if the opportunity ever arose they would sell her secrets to the gossip rags without so much as a twinge of regret.

Not that they knew any of her secrets.

Not that she had any.

Well . . . maybe a few . . .

"No, Jeffries," she said tartly, spying a dead branch on a prominent orchid arrangement. She plucked at the offending twig – pulling it out, scattering earth on the expensive Chinese rug. "What exactly is *this*?" she asked accusingly.

Jeffries had been waiting for this moment. "If you will recall, Mrs Stolli, you gave the entire staff instructions we were *never* to touch the house plants or floral arrangements."

"Why would I do that?" she asked testily.

A small moment of triumph. "Because, Mrs Stolli, you said that only the plant man was to tend them."

Aggravation. "I did?"

"Yes, Mrs Stolli."

"And where *is* the plant man?"

"He only comes on Fridays."

God! Servants! Especially English ones. "Thank you, Jeffries. In the meantime have someone clean up the mess before Mr Stolli gets home."

When he gets home, she added silently. For Mickey had this bad habit of always being late for his own dinner parties.

It drove Abigaile crazy.

Mickey Stolli wore his socks – pale grey Italian silk – and nothing else. He had a thing about his feet: he thought they were ugly and never allowed anyone to see them.

Surprisingly enough, even though he was devoid of hair on his head, his body was covered in tufts of black hair. A patch here, a patch there – strange little outbreaks of hairiness.

"You're gorgeous," Warner, his black mistress, assured him. She was tall and skinny with huge black nipples on generous breasts, and cropped black hair.

She straddled him, riding his erect penis as if she were taking an afternoon trot on a horse.

"You're gorgeous," she repeated, as the action heated up.

Nobody had ever told Mickey Stolli he was gorgeous before. Only Warner – who'd been his mistress for eighteen months. She was a cop. One day she'd pulled him over for a traffic ticket, and the rest was the stuff wet dreams are made of.

The thing he liked about Warner was her uniqueness.

148

The first time they'd slept together she'd had no idea who he was or what he did. It simply didn't matter to her.

Mickey felt the moment of truth was going to be upon him at any moment. He let out a long strangulated sigh.

Warner contracted the muscles that really mattered and gave him the ride of his life.

He felt the come from the tip of his toes to the back of his head – which he thought might explode one of these days if Warner kept doing what she obviously loved to do. With him. Only him. Mickey Stolli was the only man in Warner Franklin's sex life. She had told him so many times and he believed her.

"Was that a trip to heaven or what?" Warner demanded, climbing off. "You get better every time, Mickey. You're the greatest lover in the world."

Nobody had ever told Mickey Stolli he was the greatest lover in the world before – only Warner. She knew how to make him feel like he could climb the Empire State Building from the outside and jump off without breaking a bone.

Warner Franklin was thirty-five years old and not particularly pretty. She lived alone in a small West Hollywood apartment with a skinny mongrel dog, and much to Mickey's relief she had no aspirations to be an actress.

She didn't want his money. She didn't want his favours. She'd turned down his offer of a Wilshire condo and a white Mercedes. The only gifts she'd accepted were a giant-screen colour television, and a video recorder. She'd only taken those presents because she was partial to *Hill Street Blues* repeats and *Hunter*. "Gotta do *something* when I'm not working and I'm not with you," she'd explained.

He thought he might love her. But the dreaded thought – lurking at the back of his mind – was so scary that he'd never taken it out to inspect.

"Abby's having one of her dinner parties tonight," he said, stifling a satisfied yawn.

"I know how you *looove* them," Warner drawled, rolling her eyes. "Don't worry, honey – you're always the smartest man in any room."

149

By the time Mickey Stolli left Warner Franklin's apartment he was walking ten feet tall. He was the most gorgeous, the best lover, the smartest man in the whole fucking world!

Screw you, Abby.

You never told me shit.

Lucky was fascinated watching Abe eat. He picked at his food like a ravenous monkey, rarely using a knife or fork if his fingers could do the job. For a man of eighty-eight his appetite was quite extraordinary.

Inga did not eat. She did not sit. But she was around enough to eavesdrop on exactly what was said.

Lucky was curious to know if they discussed things later. In fact, what exactly *was* their relationship now? Failed movie star and former studio head. Was there a lot to talk about?

During her research on Abe, Lucky had come across quite a few photos of Inga. There were many studio shots, and a few casual photographs of Abe and Inga together.

Twenty-five years ago when Abe was a mere sixty-three and Inga twenty-something, she'd been a ravishing beauty – luminous skin, wide grey eyes, a lithe body, and bewitching smile.

What happens to people? Lucky wondered. *How come some – like Gino and Abe – are born survivors, and others – like Inga – wither away into a miserable shell?*

It's just the way the crap-shoot goes, she thought.

She'd told Abe everything she knew to date. He'd been disappointed. He wanted more. So did she.

A few petty scams were not worth getting heated over. So Mickey charged the studio for his personal supply of Cristal. Big deal. And Eddie Kane was probably a cocaine freak. So what?

Mickey pulling a phony script scam with the agent Lionel Fricke – that was the only information worth getting excited about.

How many times had Mickey pulled that particular stunt? She'd have to look into it.

"Enjoyin' yourself, girlie?" Abe asked, cocking his head on one side. "You like the movie business?"

"I think I'm going to love it," she replied honestly. "When I'm in control."

Abe cackled. He liked a woman who knew what she wanted.

Chapter 23

There was not much Cooper Turner didn't know about women. He'd had the best, he'd had the worst, and anything he could get his hands on in between.

Growing up in Ardmore, a small town outside Philadelphia, Cooper had started experimenting with girls when he was thirteen. Not for Cooper the paper cutouts and other girlie magazines. Oh no – one sniff of snatch and it became his life's pursuit. Girls, girls, girls.

"You should have been a gynaecologist," his older sister joked when he was nineteen. "At least get paid for what you do."

If he hadn't become an actor he would have made a great male hooker – the kind that services only the female sex.

He moved to New York when he was twenty, living in the Village and hanging out at the Actors' Studio. His contemporaries got themselves jobs waiting tables, and pumping gas while preparing for the big break.

Cooper never had to do any of that. There was always a hot meal and a warm bed begging for his attention. Not to mention a woman.

When he finally got out to Hollywood he met a beautiful young screen actress his first week in town. Within days he became her live-in lover. The relationship led to his picture in the papers, and his picture led him to a female agent who secured him the second lead in a small-budget teen film.

At the age of twenty-four, Cooper Turner became a heart-throb. Over the years his career just got better and better, culminating in an Oscar nomination when he was thirty-two.

He didn't win and it soured him. He stopped doing publicity and shied away from the press. The films he decided to appear in were few and far between.

The less Cooper made himself available the more he was wanted. He tried to lead a private life – it was impossible. Women came and went. Some stayed around almost long enough to drag a commitment out of him. He would have liked children, but the price of being with one woman wasn't worth it.

And then he met Venus Maria and things changed. With Venus Maria anything was possible. She was young and incredibly sexy. She had knowing eyes and a maneating mouth. She was sharp and street smart. She had a body made to tango and the mind of an accountant. She was sensual, startling, and above all vitally alive.

One drawback. Contrary to popular belief and the headlines in the supermarket tabloids, he was not fucking her and she was not fucking him. Not even the famous blowjob story was true, although he'd heard it from various sources – including Mickey Stolli, who'd laughed, punched him slyly in the ribs, and said, "I like to see my stars getting along. Makes for a happy set."

What Venus Maria *was* doing was fucking one of Cooper Turner's best friends. A married man. A *very* married man. And Cooper found himself in the ridiculous position of being the beard.

Cooper Turner!

The beard!

What a laugh!

He looked at himself in the mirror and shook his head. He was dressed for the Stolli dinner party in a dark blue Armani suit, white shirt, and loosely knotted silk tie. The well-cut suit got 'em every time. Women loved a man they thought they could rumple.

Cooper ran a hand through his brownish hair. There

152

were traces of grey along the sides — but nothing a talented hairdresser couldn't disguise. His eyes remained an intense blue. His skin was lightly sunkissed.

Cooper knew he looked good. He wasn't twenty-five, but he was still a killer.

Venus Maria had no idea what she was missing.

Chapter 24

Steven Berkeley took it upon himself to visit Deena Swanson. He didn't tell Jerry. He didn't even confide in Mary-Lou. He phoned Deena and told her they had to meet. She almost objected, changed her mind, and asked him to be at her house at ten o'clock the next morning.

He was there.

She greeted him in a lime-green track suit, a matching headband holding back her pale red hair, running shoes on her feet. She looked thin and attractive and not at all athletic.

She proffered a delicate hand.

He shook it.

Limp handshake. No character.

"I found our last meeting very disturbing," he informed her, getting right down to business.

She raised a thinly pencilled eyebrow. "Why?"

"We're talking about murder."

"Survival, Mr Berkeley."

"Murder, Mrs Swanson."

She clasped her hands together and lowered her eyes. "You defend people all the time. What's the difference if you get a little warning up front?"

Her attitude was bizarre. The woman was strange. "Are you kidding me??" he asked.

"Would it make you happy to know that I *didn't* mean it?"

"Did you?" he persisted.

She looked up at him. Dead blue eyes in a pale face. "I'm considering writing a book, Mr Berkeley. I needed a genuine reaction. I'm sorry if it disturbed you."

"So you're not planning to kill someone?"

A low, throaty laugh. "Do I seem like the kind of woman who would plan such a thing?"

"How about the million bucks you deposited in our company account?"

"Now that the game is over, I'll expect it back. Naturally I'll pay a handsome fee for your time and trouble."

Steven was angry. "Your game is not funny, Mrs Swanson. I don't appreciate being used for research."

He got up to leave.

She watched him go. A lawyer with principles, quite unusual. No wonder he was so good.

She waited a few minutes then picked up the phone.

"Jerry?"

"Who else?"

How sensible of Jerry Myerson to have a direct line.

"I said what you told me to."

"Did he believe you?"

"I think so."

"Sorry about this, Mrs Swanson. The trouble with Steven is that he has a conscience."

"And you don't?"

"I abide by a rule I never break."

"And that is?"

"The client always comes first."

"I'm delighted to hear it." She paused for a moment, and then added casually, "Oh, and by the way, if anything *was* to happen . . ."

"Steven *will* defend you."

"Can I count on that . . . Jerry?"

"Absolutely."

Jerry Myerson replaced the receiver of his private line and considered what he'd just done. He'd jollied along an eccentric woman and saved the firm a million bucks. Not bad for a morning's work.

*

Later that night Steven regaled Mary-Lou with the story of his visit to Deena Swanson.

Mary-Lou was engrossed in a television movie starring Ted Danson. She was eating a Häagan Daz ice-cream bar. She was contented and pregnant and getting larger every week.

"One of these days you'll learn to listen to me, Steven Berkeley," she scolded. "I told you that woman was putting you on all along. And you've been worrying about it. What a stiff!"

He felt relieved, and yet . . .

"Yeah," he said, not fully convinced.

"Did you tell Jerry?"

"I sure did."

"And what was his comment?"

"He hated to lose a million big ones. You know Jerry."

Mary-Lou licked her ice-cream bar. "Sure, who *doesn't* know Jerry. He must have been *very* disappointed."

Steven walked to the bedroom door. "I'm hungry," he said, lingering, hoping she'd offer to make him something to eat.

"That's a good sign," she replied, not taking the hint.

He came right out with it. "Make me a sandwich?"

"Honey," she said patiently. "We ate dinner two hours ago. You had steak and fries. You had cake. You had ice cream. I'll make you a sandwich when I've had the baby!"

"I have to fly out to the Coast for a few days."

Martin Swanson walked into the bedroom to make the announcement. Deena stared at her husband. Mister Handsome if you were partial to weak chins and watery eyes. Mister New York if you could stomach the self-promoting charm. Mister unfaithful, lying, cheating son of a bitch. But he was *her* son of a bitch, and she loved him. She had no intention of losing him.

Deena smiled. She had very nice even teeth – all her own – no Hollywood movie-star caps for Deena.

"Perhaps I'll come with you," she suggested.

"Too hectic," Martin replied, cool and controlled. "I've

155

got meetings on that studio takeover deal I told you about."

Oh yes, the studio deal. The studio Martin wished to control so he could make movies starring his little tramp.

Martin didn't think she knew. It was better this way. Keep him in a fog. Confuse him with kindness.

"When will you go?" she asked.

"Thought I'd fly out tomorrow."

"Are you sure you don't want me to come?"

"I'll manage."

Oh yes, he'd manage all right, with a hard cock and The Bitch waiting for him with her legs spread.

"You're going to throw half the hostesses in New York into a panic. There's the opera tomorrow night. A lunch for the mayor on Thursday. Gloria's party. Diana's dinner."

Martin could care less. "You'll go without me. They love you."

They love you better, Deena thought. *How many of them have you slept with? Only the famous ones, or do money and position count too?*

"I suppose so. If I feel like it."

He walked over and kissed her. More a peck really, an unaffectionate peck on the cheek to say goodbye. "I'll be leaving early in the morning."

Deena stood up and with one fluid movement unzipped her dress. Underneath she wore a black lace garter belt, silk stockings, and a half-bra.

Martin took a step back.

Deena could remember their early days together. Once upon a time she'd always been able to excite him.

"You won't be here on Sunday," she said pointedly, walking slowly towards him.

156

Chapter 25

The dinner table conversation was going nicely. Abigaile glanced around at her guests. They all seemed to be enjoying themselves. The black politician was deep in conversation with the famous feminist. The hot young director had zeroed in on Venus Maria, while his girlfriend enjoyed the attention of Cooper Turner. Ida White chatted in her stoned way to the rock star and his exotic-looking wife, while Zeppo and Mickey were head to head.

Abigaile breathed deeply. She could relax.

"CUNT!"

The forbidden word, said loudly and with great venom, shocked the entire table into silence.

"What did you call me, you black prick?" screamed the feminist, clearly in a fury.

"I called you a cunt, and that's what you are," the black politician yelled back.

It was quite obvious that neither of them gave a damn about the rest of the guests, let alone their host and hostess.

Witnessing a calamity about to happen, and a speechless Mickey sitting there with his mouth hanging open, Abigaile leaped to her feet. "Now, now," she said, in what she hoped was a conciliatory tone. "Let's quiet our tempers down."

"Fuck you!" from the feminist, shoving her chair away from the table. She had alabaster skin, sixties straight hair, and a direct gaze. She was fifty, but looked ten years younger. "I've had it with this phony full-of-shit skirt-chasing bum!"

Mickey forced himself into action. "Mona," he said, taking the feminist's arm. "If you've got a problem here, let's go in the other room and discuss it."

Mona Sykes withered him with a look. "A problem, Mickey?" she said sarcastically. "Why would *I* have a

157

problem? I *love* being called a cunt by this womanizing piece of excrement." She pointed accusingly at the black politician, whose name was Andrew J. Burnley.

Andrew J. did not take her last remark well. He too rose to his feet. He was six feet three with a semi-Afro hairstyle, a round face, protruding eyes, and honeyed voice. He was fifty-two years old and had a wife and five children who resided in Chicago and never came with him on his frequent trips to LA.

"You *girls* are all the same, baby. If you're not gettin' fucked you're lookin' to fuck everyone around you."

That did it. Mona picked up a full glass of red wine and hurled it across the table at him, glass and all. The glass fell to the Italian limestone floor and shattered. Unfortunately most of the wine landed on Ida White, sitting there, pleasantly stoned, minding her own business as she waited to be taken home.

Now it was Zeppo's turn to jump to his feet, all five feet four inches of him. "Can't you people behave like human beings?" he snapped, waving his short arms in the air. He directed his scolding at Andrew J., who immediately took it as some sort of hidden racial slur and retaliated accordingly.

"I don't need this crap," he shouted, stalking towards the door.

"Neither do I," hissed an angry Mona, following him.

And before anyone could say another word they were both out the door.

Abigaile rose to the occasion magnificently. "Civilians!" she sniffed. "Never did like 'em!"

Venus Maria felt as if she'd been watching a particularly fast tennis match. It was certainly more entertaining than the rest of the evening, although the young director on her left *was* kind of cute, and she'd been leaning towards him as opposed to her host, Mickey Stolli, who bored her into cross-eyedom.

"What was *that* all about?" the rock star asked, quizzically, as Firella and Consuela mopped Ida White down.

"Peasants!" snapped Zeppo. "Hollywood used t'be a

place where people had manners and knew how to entertain."

Abigaile wasn't going to take that kind of typical Zeppo White remark without a fight. The man was the most appalling snob. "My grandfather told me you started your career selling fish from a cart in Brooklyn," she said sweetly. "Is that true? I find it a most fascinating story, Zeppo. *Do* tell us all about it. I'm sure we'd *love* to hear."

Zeppo glared at her. He could make a good story out of almost anything except his humble beginnings, which he preferred to forget.

Cooper Turner saved the moment. "The two of 'em are in bed together, y'know," he announced with a nod of his head and a slight smile.

"What?" cried Abigaile and the rock star's wife in unison.

"Really?" said Venus Maria, intrigued. Now that she thought about it Cooper was probably right. He knew about such things.

"Who?" demanded Mickey.

"Andrew J. and Mona," Cooper said, grinning.

"Don't be ridiculous!" exclaimed Abigaile.

"Abby, would *I* put you on?" Cooper teased. "They're making out. It's obvious."

Everybody started to talk at once.

Abigaile's dinner party was a success after all.

Lucky drove home slowly – home being the rented hideout in the hills where she had only Boogie for company.

She missed Lennie. She missed Bobby. She missed Gino. She missed her life.

And then she remembered that Gino was in town, and it wasn't too late to call him. Maybe he'd come over. She couldn't risk being seen out anywhere in case she ran into someone who knew her and would report to Lennie that she'd been spotted hanging out in LA. Too bad. She felt like visiting a club and listening to some good soul music – one of her passions.

What if she put on her disguise and sneaked into a club?

No way. She wasn't going to wear that god-awful disguise any more than she had to. When all this was over — burn, baby, burn!

The house Boogie had rented for her was discreetly tucked away at the top of Doheny Drive. There was a drive-in garage with a door leading directly into the house. As she turned left and drew into the garage she had a sense of another car right behind her on the street, slowing down. Probably because she was making a left. Unless Abe had had someone follow her home.

Why would he do a thing like that? Was she getting paranoid? Been reading too much Ed McBain, she thought with a laugh.

Boogie was in the kitchen flicking through car catalogues.

"Do me a favour, Boog. Drive down to Tower Records and buy me some sounds. I'm getting withdrawal symptoms!"

Boogie raised his lanky frame. "Sure. What do you want?"

"I'm in the mood for Luther, Bobby Womack, Teddy P., Marvin, and Isaac."

Boogie knew exactly who she meant. "No Billie Holiday?" he asked.

"Only when Lennie's around," she replied with a wry grin.

Boogie hurried off. Lucky picked up the phone and called Gino. There was no answer from his suite. She didn't leave a message.

Harry Browning sat in his car outside Lucky's rented house and waited. He didn't know what he was waiting for. In fact he didn't know what he was doing at all. But whatever it was, he had a full charge of excitement coursing through his body. This was the best he'd felt in years.

He'd been following Luce all night. On impulse he'd trailed her from the studio. He'd always thought there was something odd about her, and he was determined to find out more. Was he the only one to notice that she wore a wig? And when he'd screened the movie, she'd taken off her glasses and not replaced them with another pair. Also, her clothes were worth noting. They hung on her as if she was trying to hide beneath them. And who – in 1986 – wore clothes like that? Especially at her age, because she was quite a young woman, and if you looked closely – a good-looking woman.

Harry Browning had not sat in a projection booth for thirty-three years screening every movie Panther had ever made without learning plenty about women's beauty.

And then there was the Sheila Hervey connection to consider. Luce claimed to be Sheila Hervey's niece – but Sheila had no living relatives other than her childless sister. She'd told him enough times when she'd been after him to take her out on a date. Of course, that had been quite a few years back, but Harry Browning did not forget. He had an excellent memory.

If Luce had left him alone he probably would have left her alone. But no. She'd invited him to dinner, and out of curiosity he'd gone, and that's about all he remembered. He'd woken up in his own bed the next morning with a dry, parched mouth, a throbbing head, and an urge to wreak some kind of punishment on the woman who had lured him to start drinking again.

Harry Browning had been dry for nineteen years. But he was an alcoholic all the same. You never stopped being an alcoholic.

He thought about having a drink now. A cold beer, or a glass of wine, maybe even a shot of scotch.

The thought tempted him, but he was determined never to give in to temptation again. Never.

Following Luce had turned out to be quite an evening. First he'd trailed her to this house – the same house he was parked outside now. And when her car emerged, he'd followed her to Abe Panther's mansion on Miller Drive. He knew it was Abe's residence, for he'd spent numerous evenings there screening movies in Abe's private theatre. That had been many years ago, but he was sure Abe Panther still lived there. Harry knew, because every year

he sent the great Mr Panther a Christmas card signed
HARRY BROWNING — YOUR LOYAL EMPLOYEE.

And he *was* loyal, for it was old Abe himself who'd
stopped them from firing him when he was caught drunk
on the job one day. "Get yourself over to AA, Harry,"
Abe had told him. "Take a couple of weeks off and come
back a new man."

Harry Browning would never forget Abe Panther's kindness.

Luce stayed inside the Panther residence for two hours.
Harry had waited patiently on the street outside the fancy
gates. When she left, he'd managed to catch a glimpse of
her as she drove past his parked car.

Luce looked different, although he was sure it was her.
The wig was gone. No glasses. Her mousy hair was now
jet black and glossy.

That's all he could see.

He followed her back to the first house, and now he
waited, patiently — for Harry Browning was a patient man,
and he knew he was onto something.

The only problem was — what?

Cooper Turner drove Venus Maria home. They laughed
all the way.

Venus Maria: Did you see Abby's face when Andrew J.
yelled the C word?

Cooper: Didja get a look at Ida when the wine hit?

Venus Maria: I thought she was going to come!

Cooper: First time in twenty years!

Venus Maria: Thirty!

Cooper: Forty!

Venus Maria: Fifty!

Cooper: A hundred!

Venus Maria: And Zeppo, when Abby threw the Brooklyn fish cart shit at him?

Cooper: He turned red.

Venus Maria: Purple!

Cooper: Orange!

They were laughing so much he had to pull his black Mercedes over to the side of the street.

They were alone in the car. No entourage, no crew, no acquaintances, no paparazzi.

He was drawn to her, even though he knew instinctively she would turn him down.

Leaning across the seat he kissed her, and for a moment she responded. Soft lips, wet lips, and a sweet pointed tongue that darted into his mouth for a second, and then withdrew as if she suddenly realized what she was doing.

"Cooper!" she scolded, cross with him and filled with guilt because she'd almost settled back to enjoy it.

"Can I help it?" he said, feeling an immediate hard-on in spite of her withdrawal.

"We're friends, remember?" she reminded him.

"Everybody *thinks* we're in bed together," he reasoned.

"Martin doesn't."

Oh yeah, Martin. Why oh why had he ever introduced her to Martin Swanson?

Chapter 26

On Wednesday Olive called and said, "The job is yours."

"Fantastic!" exclaimed Lucky. "He's approved your trip?"

"He certainly has," Olive replied, sounding delighted. "Come over to our office after lunch and I'll introduce you to Mr Stolli. After you've met him I can go over his daily routine with you. He's *very* particular."

"What did you tell him about me?"

"That you're discreet, trustworthy, and a fine worker. He says he'll take my word on it, so don't let me down, Luce."

"I won't, Olive."

"Are you *sure* this is going to be all right with Mr Stone?" Olive fussed, hoping she was doing the right thing.

"Positive. He leaves on vacation tomorrow," Lucky assured her.

"Very well. You'll watch me all day tomorrow and take over on Friday. Does that suit you?"

"Yes, it suits me fine."

And indeed it did. In the heart of Mickey's office she would be able to find out everything there was to know.

"Herman, you're out of here," she said as soon as she put the phone down. "I just got promoted!"

Herman was impressed. He was also relieved. Now he could play golf without any interruptions and forget about Panther Studios for a while.

"I'll call you when it's time for you to come back," she told him. "In the meantime, why don't you put in an order to have this office painted? It's an absolute dump."

"You do it," he said. "You're my secretary."

A show of balls – albeit tired and old – but refreshing.

"I will," she said. "And I'll order a new air-conditioning unit. You're living in the Middle Ages over here. Have you *seen* Mickey Stolli's office?"

Herman shook his head. "No."

"You'd have a shit fit. It's a palace."

It bothered Herman that he was getting used to her language.

Olive greeted Lucky excitedly. "You'll use my desk. I'll explain the phone system to you. And then we'll have to go over Mr Stolli's personal requirements."

Personal requirements? A blow-job every hour, or two blondes for breakfast? Lucky couldn't help smiling.

Olive took this to be enthusiasm for the job. "Don't be *too* good at taking care of Mr Stolli," she admonished, wagging a warning finger. "It's only for a few days and then I'll be back."

Meeting Mickey Stolli for the first time was interesting. He sat behind his desk, king of his kingdom, bald, tanned, and rude.

Proudly Olive led Lucky into his domain. "This is Luce, the assistant I told you about," she said in a reverent voice.

Mickey was going over some papers. He didn't bother

164

looking up, merely waved a hand in the air. "Yeah, yeah," he said.

Lucky noticed that an unruly clump of black hair was growing wild on the back of his hand. If only it could be transplanted to the top of his head it might be the start of something big.

"She'll be taking over on Friday," Olive said.

His private line rang and he picked it up. "Willya get *outta* here," he said, covering the mouthpiece of the phone.

"Thank you, Mr Stolli." Olive almost curtsied.

Get outta here and she gave him a *thank you* and a bob? Something was wrong somewhere. Olive needed a refresher course in self-respect.

"Sometimes Mr Stolli has too much work to cope with," Olive explained. "You'll get used to his moods. He doesn't mean any harm."

That night Lucky dined with Gino. She went to his hotel in full disguise and broke him up. "You're unbelievable, kid," he said, starting to laugh. "You shoulda been an actress."

"Would you have recognized me?" she challenged.

"I'm your father."

"That wasn't the question." She flopped into a chair, pulling her wig off and throwing it across the room.

He looked at her quizzically. "I guess I'd have to say no."

She laughed. "There's something very potent about changing one's identity. I'd probably have made an excellent spy."

"You'd have made an excellent whatever you wanted to."

"Thanks," she said, pleased.

They ordered room service. Thick juicy steaks, old-fashioned mashed potatoes, and buttery corn on the cob.

While they ate they talked. Gino told her all about his run-in with Paige's husband.

"I went over to the house an' met him. Funny thing — turns out he knows all about me and Paige."

Lucky leaned forward anxiously. "Yes? Does that mean I'm going to be a bridesmaid?"

"It don't mean nothin', kid. He tells me Paige can do what she wants. If she fancies a divorce – he'll give it to her. Only there's one problem."

"What's that?"

"She's never asked."

"Oh. Not so good."

"Then Paige comes home, sees me in her house, an' nearly passes out. By this time Ryder an' me – we're gettin' along like old pals. The lady ain't thrilled."

"What happened then?"

"Ryder asks me to stay for dinner. I say no. Paige looks uncomfortable an' I split. Since then I haven't heard a whisper from either of 'em." He chewed on a husk of corn. "I'm on my way back to New York tomorrow. I'm gonna start datin' again."

"Dating! C'mon, Gino, I know you're a miracle – but you're also seventy-nine years old!"

"Do I look it?" he demanded.

"No."

"Do I act it?"

"Well . . . no," she admitted.

"So what the hell, kid. I wanna find me a wife."

They grinned at each other, Lucky and her old man. They were a matched pair.

Leslie Kane was too pretty and too fresh-looking to be an ex-hooker – but that's exactly what she was.

Leslie had long, wavy red hair which hung below her creamy white shoulders, widely spaced eyes, a pert nose, and full luscious lips. She was tall and willowy with rounded breasts, a tiny waist, and extra-long legs.

She and Eddie had been married for one year. Before that she'd been a call girl for eleven months.

Leslie was crazy about Eddie, and Eddie was crazy about Leslie. They'd met at the car wash on Santa Monica Boulevard, and by the time they'd both followed the progress of their cars through the system they'd decided it was love.

Leslie had told Eddie she was a secretary, which was true in a way because she'd started out as a secretary, and some of the men she serviced liked her to dress up as one, although black leather and schoolgirl outfits were much more popular.

Eddie had told her he was Head of Distribution at Panther Studios, and Leslie, who had no ambition to be an actress, thought, "Hmmm, this is the guy for me."

And so true love blossomed.

Eddie gave up seeing a well-known television actress, who was not pleased.

Leslie gave up her apartment and her profession.

They were married in Marina Del Rey on a friend's boat.

Married life was good. They both enjoyed being in a formal relationship. It made a change. Eddie had always been a chaser. He liked women, they liked him. And being in the film business he'd found there was never a shortage of new talent. After meeting Leslie he had no desire to chase any more. Not only was she gorgeous, she kept him more than busy in the bedroom. "Where'd you learn all this stuff?" he'd asked her with a quizzical grin.

"*Cosmopolitan*," she'd replied straight-faced. And he'd believed her.

Leslie had never been a street hooker. She'd arrived in LA at eighteen, found a job on Rodeo Drive in one of the fancy dress-stores, and there she'd been discovered by a certain Madame Loretta, who'd set her up in an apartment.

Madame Loretta was a short, squat woman who'd come to America from her native Czechoslovakia many years earlier. She specialized in discovering beautiful, fresh young girls. She specialized in supplying top-of-the-line beauties to the Hollywood stars, executives, and moguls who came her way. She made her girls feel special and at all times beautiful, and they, in turn, made her clients very satisfied indeed. Leslie was no exception.

When Leslie told Madame Loretta she wished to get married, nobody could have been happier. The old madam invited her to tea in her hillside house and regaled her with a few facts of life. "There are three ways to keep a man," she informed Leslie, wagging a chubby finger in her face. "Three golden rules you must always remember. Rule one, Find something about your man that you think is the most wonderful thing in the world and tell him about it constantly. Maybe it's his eyes, his hair, his ass. Whatever it is — make sure he knows you love it. Rule two: When you're in bed together, tell him he's the most sensational lover you've ever had. And rule three: Whatever he says, be amazed at his knowledge. Look at him with adoration and assure him it's the cleverest thing you've ever heard anybody say." Madame Loretta nodded knowingly. "With these three rules," she said, "you'll never go wrong."

Leslie listened and learned good. She knew how to please in more ways than one, and Eddie was very receptive to her charms.

Leslie was happy, but the one fear she did have was that some day they would come across one of her previous clients and she would be exposed. She knew Eddie would never accept her past if he found out the truth, and it frightened her. At parties her wide eyes scanned the room, ever watchful. In restaurants she was always on the look out. How many clients had she serviced in eleven months? It was impossible to remember.

Leslie knew her husband had a cocaine habit. She chose to ignore it. If a little snort of white powder made him feel good, who was she to argue?

She'd tried it once and hadn't liked it. Too comfortable. Too dangerous. She had a past to watch out for; it wouldn't do to put it at risk.

Lately, Eddie had been jumpy and nervous. He snapped at her for no reason. He got up at four o'clock in the morning and wandered around the house. He took a double shot of vodka with his morning orange juice.

Leslie couldn't help worrying. Maybe he'd found out, and was getting ready to tell her it was all over.

What would she do? What *could* she do? She had no desire to return to hooking. She couldn't go home to Florida, because she'd skipped with a thousand bucks of her stepfather's money. If Eddie wanted out of their marriage her life was finished.

"Honey, is something bothering you?" she asked him one day, touching the back of his neck, ruffling his longish hair just the way she knew he liked it.

"Nothin', baby," he said, jumping up and pacing around the room. "Nothin' that a million bucks an' a little co-operation from Mickey Stolli can't fix."

Lucky started her position as Mickey Stolli's temporary assistant at seven-thirty on Friday morning. She knew he arrived in his office punctually at seven-forty-five, and she wanted to be there waiting for him.

The faint smell of Olive lingered in the air. A crisp English toilet water, peppermint lozenges, and a small azalea plant.

Sitting behind Olive's desk, Lucky took a deep breath. She was prepared for action. Any action. She was not prepared for the first phone call to be from Lennie! She recognized his voice immediately.

"Olive," he said snappishly, "put me through to Mr Stolli. This is an emergency."

Lennie! An emergency! She panicked – something she rarely did – and hung up. Whereupon Mickey Stolli made his entrance. Clad in tennis clothes. Sweating.

"Be in my office in ten minutes," Mickey said, and slammed the door to his private domain.

She acted fast, buzzed Mickey, and said, "Lennie Golden is on the line. He says it's an emergency."

God was on her side. Just as Mickey grumbled a sharp "Put him through," the phone rang again and she quickly connected the call, hoping it was Lennie ringing back.

Lennie was a problem she had not considered. She could disguise herself physically, but she hadn't thought about her voice. Fortunately he had not called on Mickey's private line, so she was able to press a button and listen in on the conversation.

"I've had enough of this shit, Mickey. Either Grudge

goes, or I do," Lennie said angrily. "The man is an amateur."

Mickey stated a fact: "The man has been in the business longer than either of us."

"Perhaps that's his problem. He thinks he knows it all. And maybe he did twenty-five years ago. Things change, let's move with the times."

Mickey's soothing voice: "Don't worry. I'll deal with it."

"Your promises are crowding my ass. If nothing happens, I'm gonna walk."

"You wouldn't be threatening me, would you?"

"You can bet your wife's jewellery on it."

"I hate to remind you about something called a contract."

"Tell you what," said Lennie, sounding quite reasonable. "Take your contract, put it through a shredder, mix it with a bagful of cement, an' shove it up your ass. There'll still be room for a decent human being."

Bang! He hung up.

Bang! Mickey was out of his office bouncing with fury.

"Get me Lennie Golden's contract," he screamed. "I've had it with fuckin' actors." He threw a key at her and pointed to a file cabinet.

She kept her voice low and subservient, figuring it was what Mickey required from his staff. "Yes, Mr Stolli."

"And don't put any fuckin' actors through to me in the mornin'. You got it?"

Shades of his native Brooklyn. Stay calm, don't call him a rude prick – plenty of time for that when she took control.

"Yes, Mr Stolli."

"An' get hold of Eddie Kane – cancel my ten o'clock appointment."

"Shall I give an excuse?"

"Fuck excuses. I'm head of this studio. No excuses – remember that."

"Yes, Mr Stolli."

170

He marched back into his office, slamming the door again.

Obviously working for Mickey was not going to be dull.

She went over to the contract file cabinet, opened it with the key, and began investigating.

Chapter 27

Martin Z. Swanson had his own private jet, modestly named Swanson. He had a crew of seven and, on his trip from New York to the West Coast, no other passengers.

Two flight attendants took care of his every need. They were pretty girls – a brunette and a redhead. Both twenty-five, five feet seven inches, and one hundred and twenty-five pounds.

The Swanson uniform was a short white skirt, fitted white jacket, and a navy blue T-shirt with SWANSON stencilled in white across their busts. Their breasts measured thirty-six inches B-cup. Martin was a stickler for detail.

The flight attendants called him "Mr Swanson", and smiled a lot. Good teeth was another job requirement.

Martin never messed with the help, however attractive. In fact he hardly even noticed them. They were hired for a purpose, and that was to keep up the Swanson image. Martin did a lot of business entertaining, and if his guests cared to make time with his employees that was their prerogative.

Martin demanded three things from the people who worked for him – loyalty, brains, and a decent appearance. If they didn't shape up, they were fired.

On the other hand, if they did things the Swanson way they were richly rewarded.

At forty-five Martin had thought his life was more or less settled. From fairly modest beginnings he'd achieved more than he'd ever imagined. He was publicly known as a charismatic, dynamic wheeler-dealer who could make any dream come true. He had powerful, famous friends in politics, show business, sports, and the social scene. Connections were his for the asking. And he had a beautiful wife who was obviously smart and intelligent.

But until four months ago Martin had never truly known passion.

"Another glass of Evian, Mr Swanson?" the redhead flight attendant inquired solicitously.

He nodded, and a cut crystal glass was in front of him in seconds. Pure Evian water, one slice of fresh lime, and two ice cubes. Just the way he liked it.

"Are you ready to eat, Mr Swanson?" asked the other flight attendant.

He noticed a dark spot on her tight white skirt and stared until she was forced to look down.

"Oops!" she exclaimed in an embarrassed voice.

He hated women who said things like *oops* – it made them sound as if they'd quit trying to better themselves after the sixth grade.

"Fix it," he said shortly.

"Yes, *sir*."

Deena had designed their uniforms. "Make them up-to-date, sexy, not too obvious," had been his instructions. Deena knew exactly what would please him.

Deena. His wife. A woman of steel. Not unlike him when it came to getting what she wanted.

When he'd first met her it was like looking in a mirror and seeing the female version of himself. A sharp woman, a worker. A woman who knew what she wanted and would do anything to get it.

Deena. He'd liked her a lot. He'd married her.

When he'd found out she'd lied to him about her age and background something had clicked off. Martin did not appreciate being lied to.

Their marriage was one of convenience. From the outside it appeared that the Swansons had it all. The truth was that Martin worked eighteen hours a day, while Deena tried to keep up. Perhaps children would have helped, but after two miscarriages Deena was informed she shouldn't

172

try for more babies, and her tubes were tied to make sure it never happened.

Although he had gallantly told Deena it didn't matter, Martin was a disappointed man. He would love to have had a son, a small image of himself whom he could mould and shape. Martin Z. Swanson, Junior. A boy he could take to ball games and teach the intricacies of real business.

Who was going to carry on the great Swanson name?

Who was going to inherit all his money?

Deena had let him down.

Sex was not particularly important to Martin. He'd been a virgin until he was seventeen, and his first experience was with a forty-three-year-old prostitute who'd sulkily told him to hurry up. She'd cost him ten dollars and an unfortunate dose of the clap.

An early lesson to be learned – you pay for what you get.

His second experience was with a five-hundred-dollar-a-night call girl who resided in a Park Avenue apartment. He'd used his Christmas present money, and disappointingly found the second time almost as unexciting as the first.

After that he settled for a series of young ladies who gave it away for free. He didn't exactly fuck his way through college, but he did OK.

After college, business came first. Then came Deena. Then the miscarriages. Then the mistresses.

Martin was not interested in mere physical beauty. He only pursued women who'd achieved something.

The chase excited him. Targeting a woman he wanted, and then seeing how long it took to nail her, that was the best game. Sometimes he even stayed around for a month or two.

What he'd found out was that they all had their price.

What he'd found out was that he could pay it.

Then along came Venus Maria, and finally, at forty-five, Martin Z. Swanson discovered love and lust and living. And the passion engulfed him.

He leaned back in his seat and relived their first encounter.

Venus Maria.

Martin Z. Swanson.

A volcano waiting to erupt.

"Hi." *Venus Maria smiled at him. She had small white teeth and a provocative smile.*

"I'm an admirer," he replied, with the charming Swanson smooth look and a cavalier wink.

The smile did not leave her face. "You're full of shit. I bet you've never even seen anything I've done."

"Not true," he protested.

"So tell me."

"Tell you what exactly?"

"What've you seen me do?"

He paused. "You were on the cover of Time."

"That's not doing anything. That's publicity."

"I know that."

"So?"

"You're a singer."

"Wow! How astute."

"And an actress."

"But you've never actually seen me in anything, have you?"

He shrugged. "You've got me."

Still smiling she said, "You see, I was right, you're full of shit."

Martin was not used to people telling him he was full of shit. Especially not a young woman — however famous she might be — with platinum hair, challenging eyes, and the strangest outfit he'd ever seen. She looked like some kind of travelling gypsy, strung with silver ethnic jewellery, worn over a long multi-coloured skirt and midriff-exposing gold blouse.

They were at a dinner party in New York given by the Websters. Effie Webster was an avant-garde *fashion* designer, and Yul, her husband, published books. Both of them were well known for their weird assortment of *friends and their drug-taking proclivities. Although Deena was good friends with the Websters, Martin was only there because the party was for his old friend and former roommate, Cooper Turner. Deena had stayed home with a migraine. Her first mistake.*

"Now we've established you're full of shit," Venus Maria said, enjoying herself as she plucked a shrimp cake from a passing waiter's tray and popped it between disturbingly full ruby-red lips, "what are we going to do about it?"

The "we" got his attention. He'd recently called it off with the feminist lawyer he was sleeping with — she was too demanding. So he was available for the next adventure. But this girl was something else — too young — too wild — too much. Warning signals told him to stay away.

"Do you know who I am?" he asked, fully confident she did.

"Nope," she replied nonchalantly. "Although I have to admit you do look a little familiar. Are you a politician? Like a senator or something?"

"I'm Martin Swanson," he said, the way someone would say "This is the Empire State Building" or "Here stands the Eiffel Tower."

Venus Maria cocked her head on one side. He noticed her earrings did not match.

"No ringing bells," she said. "Zap me with a clue."

Now she was beginning to irritate him, this strange-looking creature. Her eyebrows were too dark for her hair, and her eyes had a hooded quality — far too knowledgeable for the rest of her face. "Read Time, January 1984," he said abruptly. "You're not the only one who's been on the cover."

Cooper Turner walked over then — the handsome Cooper himself. Cooper, who was probably nailing this famous-for-fifteen-minutes bimbo into the ground. He had a reputation to maintain.

"I see you've met Venus," Cooper said with a grin. "Has she insulted you yet?"

"I'm not sure," Martin replied.

"Hang onto your balls, fellas. One day you might need 'em." Venus Maria laughed gaily and honoured them with a jaunty wave. "I gotta go. Nice meeting you – uh . . ."

"Martin."

"My memory stinks, but I give great head."

She left them with that line, sashaying across the room attracting attention every step of the way.

"Ah, but I wish I knew," Cooper said wistfully. "Young Venus Maria is what we used to call a prick-tease. Remember them? Back in the good old sixties."

"You mean you're not in bed with her?" Martin asked curiously.

"Difficult to believe, isn't it?" Cooper said with a wry grin. "I finally seem to have struck out. She laughed when I suggested it. Do you think we're getting old, Martin?" Cooper said this last line with the confidence of a man who knew he'd never be too old for anyone.

Martin kept a watchful eye on Venus Maria for the rest of the night. She fluttered around the room like an inquisitive bird, never staying long in one place, all platinum hair and full red lips – her heady perfume trailing her wherever she went.

At one point their eyes met. Just once. She held his gaze like a cat, forcing him to look away first. Another small triumph for her. Martin was intrigued.

The next day he sent for her press file. His secretary handed him an avalanche of magazine and newspaper clippings. She was more famous than he'd thought.

He then asked for copies of her videos, and the two movies she'd made. On screen she had a dynamic presence. A sexual siren with a solid dose of street smarts. She could dance, she could sing, she could even act.

By the end of the day Martin was in lust. He found out she was staying at the Chelsea Hotel and sent over three dozen sterling silver roses with a note. The note read: SO DO I – MARTIN SWANSON.

Not strictly true. He'd never given head to a woman in his life. Never had to.

She neither acknowledged nor thanked him for his

flowers. He wondered if she'd even received them, for he discovered she'd returned to LA the next day.

Venus Maria.

Unfinished business.

Martin liked every deal sewn up tight.

Six weeks later Deena decided there was a party she wished to attend in LA. It was for a big charity, and she quite fancied wearing her new sapphire and diamond necklace which set off her pale blue eyes and translucent skin.

"Let's go," Martin said agreeably, surprising Deena because she knew he hated LA.

He must have had an instinct about it. Venus Maria was at the event, standing out in black leather, while all around her there was a sea of Valentinos, Ungaros, and Adolfos. Her hair was dyed a harsh black – all the better to match her eyebrows – and her full lips were painted a strident purple. Under her black leather motorcycle jacket she wore a softer black leather bustier, studded with silver nails. Her breasts were creamy invitations to whatever else lay hidden beneath the leather.

"My God! That Venus Maria girl is just awful! Did you see her?" Deena asked.

Could he miss her?

No.

And this time he had no intention of doing so.

Cooper Turner was not anxious to part with her phone number. "She's not for you, Martin," he warned. "This girl dances to a whole new step. Forget it."

"Frightened of the competition?" Martin asked.

"I'm just trying to warn you. Venus is different. Say you did make out with her – which I can tell you now you won't – she's not the kind of woman who's going to sit at home while you run back and forth to Deena. Forget it, Martin. This is a tough kid."

"Do I get the number or do I go elsewhere?"

He got the number and called, prepared for anything.

"I took my roses back to LA," she said casually. "Oh, and I had my assistant get me Time *magazine. I don't like*

the picture — you look like a self-satisfied asshole. I do a little photography myself — wanna pose in front of my lens?"

He made an excuse to Deena and left her in the hotel while he hurried over to Venus Maria's house in the Hollywood Hills.

She made him a cup of herb tea and touched his face with long silky fingers. "I won't sleep with you until I know you," she said softly. "That might take a couple of years. Right?"

Wrong.

It took five weeks. During which time he made six trips to the Coast and she visited New York twice.

It happened in a friend's house overlooking Big Sur in a four-poster bed with an incredible view of the ocean.

And Martin Z. Swanson — tycoon, sophisticate, billionaire, man-of-the-world, forty-five years old — finally learned about love and sex and passion.

It was a revelation.

The first thing Martin did upon arriving in LA was to call Venus Maria from his limo. She was on the set, but he got through anyway, using their private code-name — Mr Whacko. He felt like a fool using such a name, but Venus Maria had insisted. "Only a stupid name like that will work," she assured him. And she was probably right. So Mr Whacko it was.

"What time shall I come over?" he asked.

"You can't. My brother's still at my house."

"God damn it! I thought you were getting rid of him."

"I am. It takes time. I'd really prefer he doesn't go running to the *National Enquirer* to sell my secrets."

"He'll do that anyway."

"You think?"

"I know."

"I'll rent him an apartment."

"When?"

"Today."

"I've missed you."

"Good."

"Well?"

"What?"

"You *know* what. Have you missed me?"

"Martin, when you're here, you're here. When you're away, that's your other life. Missing you is negative energy. I don't have time for it."

She could be infuriating. Didn't she have any idea how much it took for him to say "I miss you"? He'd never said it to anyone in his life. And she dismissed it like it was nothing.

"I'm out here to do a takeover deal on a studio," he said, as if that would impress her.

"You told me on your last trip."

"That particular deal fell through."

"So what now?"

"New negotiations."

"I've gotta go, they're yelling for me."

"Make 'em wait."

"Martin! I'm surprised at you. I'm a professional."

"Get rid of your brother. I want to come to the house."

"I'll try."

"Don't try. Do."

"Later."

Later he would have her in his arms. That young, vibrant body pulsating with energy. Pulsating all over him. Giving him the best hard-on he'd ever had.

And so to work. Martin Z. Swanson wanted to achieve a takeover. And when Martin Z. Swanson wanted something he always succeeded.

Chapter 28

Lucky lit a cigarette. Once, long ago, she'd promised herself she'd give up smoking. Impossible. The habit was too deeply ingrained. And besides, she enjoyed the process.

Lighting up, inhaling, allowing the smoke to drift lazily away.

Boogie didn't smoke. Boogie was into wheat bran and whole flakes and brown rice and grains. He'd discovered health with a vengeance and kept on shooting her disapproving looks when she gulped her coffee black, strong, and certainly not De-caf, and settled into a thick juicy steak for dinner.

It was Saturday morning and there was lots to do. No time to run off to London – maybe a day trip to Acapulco if she wasn't supposed to be in Japan.

Goddammit! She needed to be with Lennie.

She called him tentatively. From the sound of his voice on the phone to Mickey yesterday he was not likely to be in the best of moods. She was right.

"Where are you?" was his first question, asked in a belligerent tone.

"Bowing a lot and drinking tea," she replied calmly.

He was getting more annoyed by the minute. "Are you aware you have moronic idiots working for you?"

"Don't we all?"

"C'mon, Lucky, I'm not screwing around. The people in your office are either slow-witted or totally obtuse."

Who had he spoken to? "Why do you say that?" she asked anxiously. It wouldn't do to blow it now.

"Because for the last twenty-four hours I've been trying to find out exactly where you are. A phone number. An address. Anything. 'We have no idea, Mr Golden,' they tell me – like I'm some kind of schmuck."

Two weeks and she was already in deep shit.

"They don't know where I am," she answered blankly. "*I* don't know where I am. Mr Tagasaki is a strange and wonderful man who conducts his business in a somewhat eccentric way."

Lennie sounded disgusted. "What the *fuck* are you talking about?"

"It's difficult to explain," she answered quickly. "It's that kind of a deal. He's a little crazy. I'll be out of here soon."

180

Lennie was not to be placated. "Are you sleeping with this Japanese prick?" he asked accusingly.

"Don't be ridiculous."

"No, Lucky, *you're* being ridiculous."

Now it was her turn to get angry. "*I'm* making a deal. Do I interfere with the way *you* do things?"

"All the time."

Oh, God! She didn't want this to develop into a fully fledged fight. "Please understand, Lennie," she said softly. "Just this once."

"I *don't* understand. Get your ass back here."

His accusing tone was beginning to grate. "Lennie," she said carefully, "I do what *I* want."

"Well, keep on doing it, honey, an' you'll be doing it on your own."

Honey! He was *really* mad.

"This deal is important to me. Why don't you just let me pull it off my way, and then I'm all yours. We won't move for the entire summer. We'll sit in Malibu and build sand castles." Her voice softened again. "OK, baby?"

He calmed down. "I was going to surprise you this weekend. Just turn up. That's if there'd been anywhere to turn up at."

"What about the movie?"

"Screw the movie. I told Mickey Stolli if they're not prepared to dump Grudge, I'm walking."

"I'll have a big surprise for you soon."

"What?"

"Be patient."

He wasn't giving up. "Since when was I patient? What's your phone number?"

"There isn't one."

"Where are you speaking from, the street?"

"A hotel."

He sounded exasperated. "I don't know what game you're playing, Lucky, but do me and yourself a favour and get back here. I need you."

"I'll be with you sooner than you think."

Not the ideal phone conversation. How long was he going to believe her lightweight excuses?

She tried Bobby in London next. He'd been to a James Bond movie and insisted on telling her the entire plot. She listened patiently, told her son she loved him, and hung up.

You're fucking up your life, Santangelo.
Only temporarily.

Monday morning back at the studio she knew a lot more than she'd known when she'd left on Friday carrying a briefcase full of papers and contracts from Mickey's locked file cabinet. She'd had plenty of time to study them over the weekend. It seemed Mickey was creaming money all over the place. The head of business affairs had to be in on it. Major collusion.

Mickey came running in late snapping his fingers. "Get me Zeppo White on the phone. Cancel my nine o'clock with Eddie Kane. Tell Teddy Lauden to stay after the meeting. An' fix me fresh juice — grapefruit. Get your ass in here. Fast."

The man was unbelievable. Whatever happened to "Good morning" and a little common courtesy?

She followed him into his office. He was already throwing off his tennis shirt, revealing an extremely hairy chest. If the shorts came next she was out of there.

He trotted into his private bathroom, took a loud pee with the door open, and dictated a terse fax to Grudge Freeport.

The fax read:

> Unhappy actors are a pain in
> the ass. A pain there makes
> me unhappy. You are
> replaceable. The stars are
> not. Do something nice and
> make everyone happy.

He then dictated a similar fax to Ned Magnus, the producer of Lennie's movie. Lucky added a terse

> Accommodate Lennie Golden in
> every way. Allow him to
> make any changes he wants.

Mickey then disappeared under the shower while she hurried to make his phone calls.

He emerged screaming for his fresh juice.

Lucky darted into the stainless-steel kitchen, sliced a grapefruit in half – nearly taking her finger along with it – and threw it on top of the juicer.

A fit of laughter almost overcame her. This was insane! What the hell was she doing this for?

Adventure.

A studio.

Lennie.

Eddie Kane was nervous. He had urgent matters to discuss with Mickey, and the prick was giving him a runaround.

Eddie Kane smoked a joint in the men's room ten minutes before the Monday morning meeting of the major players. He would have preferred a hit of coke, but he was all out, and Kathleen Le Paul never made her weekly visit until after lunch.

A joint took the edge off. Just about. Not really.

Fuck! He was wired to the hilt. He needed to sit down with Mickey and straighten out business.

Staring in the men's room mirror he noticed he'd developed a twitch. Almost imperceptible, but it was there – if you were looking.

Who's looking, for crissake?

Eddie "The Twitch" Kane. Former child star. Still hot with his *Miami Vice* attitude.

This is what Eddie was into:

Porno flicks.

Distributing them.

Hiding them along with Panther's legit products.

Making a tidy pile.

Scooping it in.

He stared at himself for a long while. *Who else has a*

183

wife like Leslie? he thought. She was prettier than any movie star. Sexier, too.

Ah, what wouldn't he give to see her thigh high in diamonds. She deserved every single one. Thigh-high and bare-assed. What a sight!

"Good morning, Eddie."

Zev Lorenzo, head of the recently formed Television Division, snuck up on him. Zev was an elegant man in his late forties, with a pencil moustache, thinning hair, and a trim build. If he'd had to make a guess, Eddie would have said that Zev was the only executive at Panther who wasn't in business for himself in some way or other.

"Hiya, Zev."

The older man nodded, and stood in front of the urinals.

A closet queen zipped through Eddie's mind. Someone had told Eddie that Zev was a closet queen – although why, in 1986, anybody would bother staying in the closet was beyond Eddie.

"How's everything?" he mumbled, running a hand through his long hair.

"Excellent," replied Zev. He was into words like *supreme* and *primacy* and *surpass*. Eddie had never heard him swear, not even a simple *fuck*.

"That's good, that's very good," Eddie said. "Hey – one of these days ya gotta meet my wife."

"I've heard she's a stunner." Zev zipped up and exited. Didn't even stay to wash his hands.

Eddie twitched again. He didn't feel good. He felt like shit. He looked like shit. He'd frightened Zev off.

"Do I accompany you to the meeting, Mr Stolli?" Lucky asked.

"Yeah, yeah, yeah. Take notes. Get it all down. You do fast shorthand, right?"

She nodded.

"What's wrong with your hair?"

"Uh . . ."

"Forget it. Follow me an' don't open your mouth."

184

She trailed him into the conference room. Three steps behind, like an obedient geisha.

The boys were gathered. No girls.

Shame.

That's Hollywood.

Quietly taking a back seat, notepad poised (shorthand was the one useful skill she'd learned at school in Switzerland), she looked around, silently identifying the players, matching them up to their photographs in the glossy Panther end-of-year financial report.

Ford Werne, Head of Production. Killer sharp in an Armani suit and five-hundred-dollar tinted aviator shades. He was around fifty, but he'd kept his act very much together.

Teddy T. Lauden, Head of Business Affairs, was exactly the opposite – thin, nondescript, precise.

Zev Lorenzo, the man who ran the Television Division, impeccable and charming.

Eddie Kane, Mister Distribution, Mister Coke-Head, looked like he was ready to fall apart. *Seedy* was too kind a description. He was handsome in a smarmy way – but definitely in trouble.

That left only two other senior executives:

Grant Wendell, Jr, Vice President of Worldwide Production – young and sharp-eyed in baggy pants with a button-down Gap shirt.

And Buck Graham – Marketing. A plump, jovial man, with ruddy cheeks and an "I'm here to please" smile.

Average age of the group – early forties.

That's why there were no women execs. These guys had not experienced feminist mothers. What did they know?

Lucky grinned to herself. In her dowdy wig and glasses, concealed by her baggy clothes, she was invisible to this group of probable chauvinists.

Two women appeared, ready to serve coffee and tea. One of them was Eddie Kane's black secretary, Brenda. She'd dressed for the occasion in a tight pink leather dress that ended somewhere mid-thigh. On her long legs she wore outrageous fishnet tights – more suitable for a lady

185

of the night than an office meeting – and very high red patent heels.

Brenda fussed over the men, calling every one of them by name as she poured their coffee, gold-painted nails curling around the coffee pot handle.

The other woman was a ponytailed blonde, also in a miniskirt. She apparently belonged to Grant Wendell.

The men ignored the two females, although Lucky observed Eddie giving Grant's secretary a quick feel under her skimpy skirt as she passed by.

"Okay, girls – outta here," said Mickey Stolli, Mister Charm. "We're not runnin' a restaurant."

Brenda shot Lucky a mean look as if to say – *What the hell are you doing here?* Obviously this was a fill-in job most of the other secretaries would have been only too delighted to do.

And so the meeting started.

Mickey had a mind like a machine-gun, firing questions, talking fast. He wanted to know every detail of what was happening around the studio, and round the world – if it was anything to do with Panther.

Ford Werne adjusted his aviator shades and talked about a million-dollar script he thought they should buy.

Grant Wendell discussed his desire to sign Madonna or Cher to a multi-pic deal.

Zev Lorenzo boasted about ratings on two of his television shows, and claimed to be negotiating for the television rights to a Norman Mailer book. "We'll do it as a long-form mini-series – similar to Irwin Shaw's *Rich Man, Poor Man*."

"Too classy," Mickey interjected. "We need somethin' with jiggle. An' talkin' of jiggle – we gotta develop a property for that seventeen-year-old ex-porn star who's goin' straight. She's a natural."

"Natural what, Mickey?" asked Buck Graham, with a bar-room chuckle.

"I saw her in *Under Glass*," Teddy Lauden chimed in, suddenly coming to life. "She was sixteen at the time. What a body!"

"Never mind the body, can she act?" asked Grant.

"Who gives a shit?" demanded Mickey. "She's gonna make us a fuckin' fortune. Fresh young snatch. It brings 'em into the box-office every time. Cooper's givin' her a coupla lines in his movie."

Ah, to be in the company of real men, Lucky thought. *What a delightful bunch.*

Eddie cornered her after the meeting. He was a jumping time bomb. "Hey – hey – lady – *you*."

"The name is Luce."

"OK, Luce. Ya gotta do me a big one."

"Yes?"

"Don't keep on cancelling my goddamn appointments with Mickey. I havta see him – like today. Urgent biz."

She noticed he had a twitch. It was fascinating.

"*I'm* not cancelling your appointments, Mr Kane. Mr Stolli does so himself. *I* merely do as I'm told."

Holy shit! She was beginning to sound like Olive!

"Sure. So when he tells you to cancel the next one – just forget. An' then, I'm there. Like in. Y'know what I'm sayin?"

"Why would I do that, Mr Kane?"

"You'll catch on. It's the only way to operate with Mickey. He flakes on everyone. Olive'll tell you. When's she comin' back?"

"Tomorrow."

"I gotta see him today. Arrange it."

"I'll try."

"Good girl."

"The name is Luce."

"I'd change it if I was you."

Back in the office there was a stack of messages. Mickey Stolli was a popular man.

She flicked through his appointment book. It was full for a month. Olive's neat script had jotted down every detail.

Knocking on the door to his office, she waited for him to call out his customary "Yeah" and went in.

"Mr Kane would like to reschedule," she said, all business.

"I can't stand the sight of that bum," Mickey said.

"When shall I reschedule it for? He says it's urgent."

"Taking a dump is urgent. Eddie can wait."

"Are you sure?"

"Don't give me grief. Who's on next?"

"You have lunch with Frankie Lombardo and Arnie Blackwood, and then a three o'clock meeting at the Beverly Hills Hotel with Martin Swanson."

"Cancel lunch. I gotta go somewhere."

"May I ask where?"

"No."

"Thank you, Mr Stolli."

Alerted by Lucky, Boogie was in place when Mickey Stolli left the studio. He followed him all the way to a modest West Hollywood apartment house, where he observed Mickey park his Porsche in an underground space reserved for Apartment 4.

Checking the listings on the front entrance. Boogie discovered Apartment 4 belonged to a Warner Franklin.

Did Mickey Stolli have an afternoon boyfriend?

Obviously.

Boogie called Lucky from the car and gave her the information.

"Are you *sure*?" she asked.

"It certainly looks that way."

"Hang around. Maybe they'll come out together."

"I doubt it. They're not likely to be seen in public, are they?"

"Who knows? Mickey's hardly the smartest guy in the world."

"I'll see what I can find out."

"Nobody does it better."

Spurred by Lucky's praise, Boogie found out plenty. The mailman, an inquisitive neighbour, and a bored nine-year-old off school with the flu supplied the story.

The facts. Warner Franklin. Black. Female. A cop.

Boogie smelled graft.

Chapter 29

Martin Swanson had an army of lawyers. He called. They ran.

His lawyers had an army of top connections. They'd put the word out that Martin Swanson was interested in acquiring a controlling interest in a major studio, and all possibilities fell into position.

Martin had examined every option, reading confidential reports on United Artists, Columbia, Fox, *et cetera*, and finally coming to the conclusion that Orpheus and Panther were the two most viable propositions.

Orpheus was ripe for a takeover. Panther, still privately owned by the reclusive Abe Panther, was possibly available if the price was right, or so his lawyers had led him to believe.

"If I want Panther, who do I talk to?" Martin had asked.

Mickey Stolli, he was told.

Martin had his people run an immediate check on Mickey, and while he might be Chairman and Chief Executive Officer of Panther, he was certainly not in a position to sell without Abe Panther's say-so.

Interesting — for Mickey had done an excellent job at Panther since taking over. The studio was turning a healthy profit.

Martin had been pursuing the idea of acquiring a large stake in a film studio long before Venus Maria entered his life. Hollywood was the lure. Money was the merry-go-round. And the film business as a potential money-maker was irresistible.

Orpheus Studios was in trouble. Owned by a parent company whose main concern was making airplane parts, it had been consistently losing money for the past three years. With Zeppo White – the former agent – in charge, things had gotten worse.

Right now they had five movies in production. Four of them were already millions of dollars over budget and had very little chance of showing a profit unless a miracle occurred.

Martin Swanson did not believe in miracles.

Orpheus could be bought. At a price.

Maybe Panther could, maybe not, but Martin was certain that Mickey Stolli was buyable. And if his purchase turned out to be Orpheus, why not bring Mickey over to run things? He certainly had the right track record.

Hence Martin's planned meeting with Mickey. One way or the other they could do business.

Mickey had no idea what Martin Swanson wanted. He'd heard rumours that Martin was looking to gain control of a studio, but surely the guy was savvy enough to investigate? And if he did, he'd find out what everybody in town knew, that Mickey Stolli was just a paid employee, and could no more sell him Panther than take a flying dive in Macy's window.

It pissed Mickey off. It pissed Mickey off enough to trigger a twice-a-year furious fight with Abigaile, who didn't understand at all. She looked down at him like a mother who'd just caught her son jacking off over a naked picture of Hitler.

"My grandfather has been very good to you," she usually said, or words to that effect. "And when he goes, we'll get everything we deserve."

"Why do we have to wait?" was Mickey's argument. "How about the lawyers going in and declaring him senile?"

Abigaile would have none of it. She knew for a fact that her grandfather had constructed an extremely complicated and iron-clad will – and any messing with it was going to cause nothing but unwanted complications.

She also knew that Abe Panther, in spite of his age, was certainly not senile. He was as smart as Mickey any day, and Mickey should think himself more than fortunate that Abe had not returned to run the studio, but had allowed Mickey to do it his way.

Of course, there were financial restrictions put into place by Abe's lawyers. These restrictions infuriated Mickey. They meant that his salary could not exceed one million dollars a year. It sounded a lot, but when some asshole actor could receive five or six million, plus gross points of a potential hit movie, it was hardly satisfactory.

Abigaile had her own trust fund of money inherited from her parents, but Mickey had to make do on a lousy million – and when tax was taken off . . .

It didn't bear thinking about.

Mickey in fact thought about it quite a lot – though not usually when he was humping Warner. But today was hot, and there was a fly buzzing in her apartment, and she'd just informed him that she'd been promoted to Vice (*that* was a promotion?), and he was altogether not in the mood for their usual steamy sex session.

"What seems to be the matter, lover?" Warner asked.

He was on top of her at the time, exhibiting his lack of desire. It was hardly something he could hide.

"There's a fly in here," he said lamely.

Her voice rose in surprise. "A fly?"

"Maybe a wasp." That sounded better.

Warner couldn't help herself – after all, she'd grown up in a house where rats were in everyday occurrence. "Frightened it's gonna sting you on the ass, Mickey?" she teased, laughter in her voice.

That did it. No hiding the hot dog today. Lurching off her, he reached for his pants.

"Stop!" said Warner.

He continued to pull on his pants.

She sat up. "Stop! Or I'm gonna havta arrest and hand-cuff you."

His cock, searching for a life of its own, sprang to attention.

Mickey dropped his pants.

Warner reached for her handcuffs.

They were back in business.

The Polo Lounge was the perfect meeting place. At three o'clock in the afternoon, it was relatively quiet, fairly discreet, and pleasantly air-conditioned.

Martin Z. Swanson and Mickey Stolli had never met before, although they were certainly well aware of each other.

They shook hands in front of the dimly lit number one red leather booth.

"We could've done this in my bungalow," Martin said.

"Or at the studio," Mickey offered.

"It's better here," they both agreed.

Mickey Stolli felt fucked. Literally.

Martin wondered what time he'd be able to meet with Venus Maria. "Let's talk business," he said.

"Show business," Mickey corrected with a sly smile.

"I want you to go," Venus Maria said in a not-to-be-argued with voice. "I've rented you an apartment on Fountain Avenue. It has a swimming pool, television, and maid service. It's furnished nicely. I'll pay your rent for six months, and after that you're on your own. I'm sure you'll be able to manage."

Her brother Emilio stared at her. They had the same eyes, big and brown and soulful. Apart from that they did not look at all alike.

"Why?" Emilio asked plaintively.

"Because . . . because I need my privacy."

"We're family," Emilio said, fixing her with a hurt expression, as if she'd let him down.

She was determined not to give in. "That's why I'm paying your rent for six months."

He sighed. A big sigh. A put-upon sigh. "I'll go," he said reluctantly. As if he had a choice.

Venus Maria nodded. "Good."

"When I'm ready," Emilio added.

He was pushing her. It was infuriating. But she had a temper too and she refused to be pushed any further. "You

192

go today," she said. "Within the hour. Or the deal is off and you can hustle your lazy ass on Santa Monica Boulevard for all I care."

"*Putain!*" he muttered.

Her eyes narrowed. "What?"

"Do I get a car?"

She decided to ignore his insult. "You can borrow the station wagon," she said, wearily.

Emilio scowled. Why should he drive a lowly station wagon while his sister sat in limos and Porsches? It wasn't the way things should be, but it looked like it was inevitable. Venus Maria meant business.

He slouched off to pack his belongings.

Venus Maria experienced a frisson of triumph, small but satisfying. She sent her housekeeper out to buy fresh flowers, and then hurried to her huge walk-in closet and tried to decide on the perfect outfit.

Martin liked her in white, he'd told her so. She preferred black. It was more sophisticated and raunchy. It made her feel sexy.

How about white on the outside and black against her flesh?

How about nothing against her flesh?

Martin was not the greatest lover in the world. He was inhibited, fast, not into any real sensual pleasure.

She was teaching him.

Slowly . . .

Very, very slowly . . .

Venus Maria was twenty-five, and she'd had four lovers – Martin being the fourth. The press would have a field day if they ever found out she'd only had four men. After all, she was a liberated woman – a high priestess of the sexual come-on. Everything she did radiated pure sex, from her videos to her acting performances. She touched herself in secret places publicly. And even with AIDS casting its giant shadow, she should have experienced more than four men.

Lover number one: Manuel. A killer in the sack. Black

193

hair, black eyes, dark olive skin. A cock to die for, and a dancer's flair for exquisite movement.

She met him a week after arriving in LA and he took her virginity with a sticky, hard passion she found breathtaking.

For three months they made love every day, and then he left her for a California beach bunny.

When she became famous he tried to insinuate himself back into her world.

Forget it.

Lover number two: Ryan. A sensualist. Rumpled blond hair, puppy-dog eyes, sun-kissed skin. A cock to die for, and the best ass she'd ever seen.

He accompanied her on the ride, and got off when he fell in love with the bearded manager of an English rock group.

They'd remained friends.

Lover number three: Innes. A killer in the sack *and* a sensualist. What a lethal combination.

They stayed together nearly a year until her career became more than a threat.

Manuel, Ryan, and Innes were all in their twenties.

Martin was forty-five. He could have been their father. He could have been *her* father.

She loved him.

She didn't know why.

Choosing a virginal white dress, all layers, and lace, she paired it with a short, tight brocade jacket, seventeen silver bracelets, dangling earrings — not a matched pair — and skating boots without the blades. Then she called Martin at his hotel and left a message. *The Whacko family will be at home after six.*

When Mickey entered his house he was buzzing.

Thirteen-year-old Tabitha greeted him with a sulky glare. "Mommy says I can't go to Vegas with Lulu and her dad. I wanna go. Why can't I go?"

Tabitha had straight brown hair, a just developing

figure, and frightening braces on her teeth. She was hardly going to be jumped on by every guy in sight.

"If your mother says so – " he began.

"I *wanna* go, Daddy," Tabitha wailed. "*You* talk to her. You fix it. You're so smart you can fix anything!"

Had she been taking lessons from Warner?

"I'll try," he promised, without much enthusiasm.

Tabitha threw her arms around him, gnarling his cheek with her braces.

As if sensing collusion, Abigaile appeared in the front hallway. "Were you meeting with Martin Swanson in the Polo Lounge today?" she asked peevishly, ignoring her daughter, who was busy signalling to Mickey behind her mother's back, urging him to say something.

Was nothing secret? The Beverly Hills bush telegraph worked like lightning, or maybe the new girl (what was her name? Lucy, Luce – something stupid) had too big a mouth. Olive was smart enough to be aware that if he wanted Abigaile to know anything, he'd tell her himself.

"Who told you that?" he asked, automatically on the defensive.

"Daddy!" complained Tabitha, panting for action.

"Does it matter who told me?" bristled Abigaile. "What *matters* is that you never let me *know* you were seeing Martin Swanson. I would have liked to have had a dinner party for the Swansons."

Ah, another cosy little dinner for fifty.

"Why? You don't even know them."

"I most certainly do," Abigaile countered indignantly. "I've met Deena on more than one occasion."

"She's not with him."

"Vegas, Daddy!" interjected Tabitha, hopping anxiously up and down.

"Uh . . . why can't Tabitha go to Vegas?"

Abigaile withered him with a look. She was good at reducing grown men to ashes. Raising an imperious eyebrow she said, "Are you *serious*?"

"Yes, I'm serious. She wants to go with her friend Lulu and her father. That sounds all right to me."

"Are you aware who Lulu's father *is*?"

"Uh . . . he's a singer, right?"

"He's a *rock* singer." Abigaile spat the words out. "And not a very famous one at that — unless you count his time spent in AA and drug rehab. My daughter is not going anywhere with *that* family."

My daughter. It was always *my* this and *my* that. Sometimes Mickey thought Abigaile went out of her way to prove he didn't exist.

He was still buzzing, but now he decided to keep the buzz to himself.

Screw Abby. If things went the way he hoped they'd go, she'd find out soon enough.

Chapter 30

Olive Watson broke her leg. As far as Lucky was concerned it was great news. She felt guilty about being so pleased, although she commiserated with Olive over the phone.

Mickey did not take it well. He summoned Lucky into his office, screaming and yelling as if it was her fault.

"We'll manage, Mr Stolli," she said calmly, the perfect secretary.

"*You'll* manage," he screamed. "My life is a fuck-up!"

It certainly is, she replied silently.

Eddie Kane arrived for his newly scheduled appointment. Mickey had attempted to cancel it, but Lucky told him she hadn't been able to reach Mr Kane.

Eddie looked like a good night's sleep might be a fine idea. He winked at Lucky, whispered, "You're a good girl," patted her on the ass, and entered Mickey Stolli's lair.

Sitting outside, Lucky pressed the office intercom so that she could listen in.

"What's going on, Eddie? I warned you if we went into this I wasn't to be bothered." Mickey sounded weary.

"Yeah," Eddie said. "Only I didn't reckon on a couple bent-nose fuckheads breathin' down my pants for a bigger piece of the action."

"Whaddya mean?"

"It's simple. We take their porno product, bury it all the way outta the country with the legit Panther stuff, split the proceeds, an' there ya go — they've got clean money. We've got us a nice healthy score with no problems."

"So?"

"So they're claimin' we ain't splittin' fair."

"And are we?" Mickey's tone was ominous.

The lie was in Eddie's voice, plain to hear. "Would I try t'fuck the big boys?"

"You'd try to fuck a skunk if it pissed in the right direction."

Lucky heard someone approaching. She slammed off the intercom, hastily picking up a pile of letters.

"Workin' hard, doll?"

It was the Sleazy Singles themselves. If they were a singing group Eddie Kane would have made a perfect third partner.

"Mr Lombardo. Mr Blackwood," she said primly, emulating Olive. "Can I help you?"

Arnie leaned across the desk, and before she could stop him he flicked off her thick glasses. "Ya got nice eyes, babe. Get yourself contacts."

She attempted to grab her glasses. He waved them at her, keeping them just out of reach.

"Mr Blackwood, I can't see," she said sternly.

"I get off on babes who can't see," leered Frankie.

"Yeah, all the better not to notice your one-and-a-half-inch dick!" said Arnie.

This remark broke them both up. Lucky took the opportunity to snatch her glasses and put them back on. What a couple of major jerks!

"What's he doin'?" asked Frankie, gesturing towards Mickey's office.

"Mr Stolli is in a meeting with Mr Kane."

"Then I guess he's ready for the light relief brigade," Arnie said with a hearty chuckle.

"You can't — "

Before she could finish they were on their way into Mickey's office.

She quickly buzzed Mickey. "Mr Stolli. I'm sorry, they just barged past me. I — "

Mickey's familiar "Yeah, yeah, yeah. Order up coffee."

"And banana cake," yelled Frankie in the background.

All the better to enlarge your fat ass, Lucky thought.

The boys are having a meeting.

Let them eat cake.

Acapulco sunshine could be boring Every day the same thing — blue skies, blazing sun, and a picture-postcard setting.

Two friends of Lennie's arrived to stay for a few days — Jess and Matt Traynor. Jess was Lennie's oldest friend: they'd grown up together in Las Vegas, attended the same high school, and remained close ever since.

At only five feet tall and very pretty, Jess was a super-charged package. She had wide eyes, a mop of orange hair, freckles, and a great body.

Matt, her second husband (the first was a drugged-out bum who'd run out on her), was, at sixty-something, almost thirty years older. He didn't look it with his close-cropped silver hair and well-dressed, foxy appearance.

Lennie was happy to have visitors. How many nights could he spend with Joey Firello? Joey's continual pursuit of the female form was exhausting.

Nights spent alone were not much fun either, and he had no intention of socializing with either Grudge, Marisa, or Ned — the fun trio as he'd christened them.

Jess and Matt were a welcome relief. They arrived armed with photos of their sixteen-month-old twins — a boy and a girl.

"Your godchildren," Jess told Lennie proudly. "When are you going to have a few of your own?"

Trust Jess to come right out with it. She sounded like Gino, who was always dropping not-so-subtle hints.

"When Lucky decides to fit me in between deals," he said wryly.

"What does *that* mean?"

"She's busy."

"Ah, that's what happens when you marry a working woman."

"Tell me about it."

Jess had stopped work several months before her twins were born. She'd once been Lennie's personal manager. In fact, it was Jess who'd been responsible for getting his career off the ground in the first place. He owed her plenty. They'd certainly come a long way together.

"I miss you, monkey face," he said dejectedly.

"Don't call me that!" she shrieked, hating her pet name from their school days.

"Why not?"

"Because you know I hate it."

"But it suits you."

"Get fucked."

"I wish I could!"

"Very funny."

He flopped into a chair and stared at her. "Well, are you coming back to work with me or what? If you were still my manager I wouldn't be stuck in this piece-of-shit movie."

"When Matt divorces me," Jess replied matter-of-factly.

"When will that be?"

She grinned. "Never! I'm a very happy person!"

"Nice to know somebody is," he said ruefully.

Jess sat on the arm of his chair. "I may be slow, but do I detect a note of dissatisfaction here?"

He mugged for her. "Are you kidding? Why would *I* be dissatisfied? I'm making a movie I hate. I'm stuck in Mexico. And my wife is probably shacked up with Mr Japan so she can add another million or four to her bank account. Things couldn't be better, Jess. Tell me about *your* life."

Jess ruffled the back of his hair. "Oooh, baby, baby. You want me to talk to Lucky?"

"If you can find her."

"Give me her number."

He sounded disgusted. "If I had it, I would."

"Where is she?"

"Who the fuck knows?"

Jess didn't question further. With Lennie you could only push so far.

Later she said to Matt, "A marriage counsellor I'm not, but I have a feeling I should give this one a whirl. Lennie's about ready to blow."

"Don't interfere," warned Matt.

What did he know?

Mickey spent the week on the run, expecting Lucky to keep up with him at all times. He dodged from meeting to screening, and in between he stopped for another shower or fresh juice or a screaming fit about something or other.

Occasionally he had Lucky accompany him to the dailies on what he called his bread and soup movies, instructing her to take notes of everything he said while sitting in the darkened screening room. His comments ran from "Nice tits" to "Fat ass" to "She's too old" to "Get a close-up on her face when he sticks her with the knife."

He rarely had anything to say about the male actors, who all managed to stay fully dressed in spite of the gore and sex all around them.

Lucky discovered the Hollywood difference between hard-core pornography and so-called soft. In hard-core the men took their clothes off too. In soft – as far as the women were concerned – anything seemed to go. They were forever stripping off their clothes, simulating orgasm, or getting their throats slit. Real classy stuff, with plenty of rape thrown in for good measure.

It was a sorry situation, and one that Lucky had no intention of allowing to continue once she took control.

The three cheapo movies currently in production were

all produced by the exciting team of Blackwood and Lombardo. *It figures*, Lucky thought grimly.

On perusing the books, to which she had free access now she was ensconced in Mickey's quarters, she found out that the cheapo movies were the biggest money-makers Panther had. Mostly abroad, where they scored on every level – theatres, cable, home video, and pay-as-you-view TV.

The cheapos kept Panther in the black.

The big movies with the star names sometimes made money too – but only sometimes.

Any idiot knew the film business was a gamble. Sometimes you scored, and sometimes you crapped out. With his cheapos, Mickey had loaded the dice in his favour.

Lucky decided she had an interesting challenge ahead of her: how to make movies without exploiting women.

Hmmm . . . Maybe she'd exploit men for a change . . . Not such a bad idea.

By the time she got home at night she was wiped out. Boogie was waiting for her with a strong drink. She ordered pizza or Chinese, made a few notes, and immediately fell asleep.

She'd called Lennie twice. His reception got cooler and cooler. Finally he informed her in an exasperated tone that he didn't care to hear from her unless she told him exactly where she was.

Fine. If that's the way he wanted it.

When he found out the truth he was going to be very sorry indeed.

Grudge Freeport's idea of doing something nice and making everyone happy was not to fart in public. Apart from that little concession to human dignity he kept right on going.

Lennie took another week of it. He had Jess and Matt around to keep him calm. When they left, he blew.

"You know something, Grudge? You're an ass-licking, no-talent, drunken slob – and I'm out of here." He yelled this one day after Grudge had screwed up yet another scene.

Grudge took it like a true old-timer. "Fuck off," he said grandly. "All actors never should have left their mother's tit!"

Lennie didn't think about the consequences. He packed and flew back to LA, spent two days alone at the Malibu house, and then took off for New York.

He did not go to the apartment he and Lucky shared. He vanished. She knew this because Mickey Stolli threw a fit searching for him.

"I'll sue the fucking son of a bitch for everything he's got. Everything! He's not getting away with this. I've got a crew and actors sitting in Acapulco slapping their dicks! It's costing this studio dearly, and that dumb cocksucker's gonna pay. Oh, is he gonna pay!"

Lucky was assigned the awkward task of tracking Lennie Golden down. She perfected a new voice and duly called his current agent and manager. Through secretaries she learned that nobody knew where he was.

"How about his wife?" Mickey screamed. "Isn't he married to some rich broad with a gangster father?"

So that's what it got down to. *Some rich broad with a gangster father.*

Not Lucky Santangelo, businesswoman supreme.

Not Lucky Santangelo, wife and mother.

Some rich broad with a gangster father. Charming!

"I don't know, Mr Stolli," she said, attempting to remain cool.

"Find out an' tell 'em we're gonna sue."

Later in the day, Lucky took great pleasure in informing Mickey that she had indeed reached Lennie Golden's wife.

"And?" Mickey demanded.

"I can't repeat what she said, Mr Stolli."

"What'd she say?"

"Uh . . . she said . . . uh . . ."

"Spit it out, for crissake."

"She said to tell you you're a pathetic asshole with cotton wool balls and a black heart."

Mickey was outraged. "Are you *shittin'* me?"

"I'm sorry, Mr Stolli."

Mickey made a solemn vow. "As long as I'm here," he said. "Lennie Golden'll never work for this friggin' studio again."

"Quite right," Lucky agreed sympathetically.

That night she had Boogie install a sophisticated bugging system in Mickey's office. All the better to know exactly what was going on.

Chapter 31

Venus Maria had rock-hard thighs on account of her daily workouts with a personal trainer. Her stomach was flat and firm, her arms and shoulders lightly muscled since she'd been regularly using weights. She jogged every day, and swam fifty lengths in her private pool. She treated her body as if it were a finely tuned instrument, never letting up on her vigorous schedule.

Martin Swanson appreciated every glowing inch. In bed with Venus Maria he felt as if the sex they enjoyed together couldn't get any better – except that every time it did.

Venus Maria had learned plenty from Manuel, Ryan, and Innes. She'd made it her business to find out the details that turned them on. Ryan had liked taking showers together. Manual had wanted her to massage his balls with a very expensive, highly scented body lotion. Innes was into being tied up with the lightest of silk scarves. The trick was, he'd told her, never to tear your bindings.

Venus Maria had soon discovered what he meant. The exquisite torture of not breaking the silken bonds was excruciating ecstasy. She had saved that particular experience for Martin until she knew the moment was exactly right.

The night before he returned to New York she took him on a trip to heaven and back. First they dined on sushi and champagne. Then they frolicked in her open-air hot tub overlooking the spectacular Hollywood view. And finally, she led him into her bedroom, flicked off the towel around his waist, and instructed him to lie naked on her four-poster bed while she bound him with fine silk scarves.

She knotted the scarves lightly around his wrists, tying them to the bedposts. Then she did the same to his ankles.

"What are you doing?" he asked, putting up the semblance of a fight.

"Relax," she smiled. "Lie back and dream your favourite fantasy."

"I don't have fantasies."

"Unlucky you."

She sat back and admired her work. He was completely helpless as long as he didn't struggle, his excitement already evident.

Venus Maria smiled. What a turn-on! Martin Swanson – Mister New York – at her mercy.

"This is a challenge," she announced. "A game. You break the scarves and the game is over. If you're a good boy we'll play all night."

He fell right into it. "What's the penalty?"

"Ten thousand bucks a scarf," she said boldly.

"High stakes."

"Can you afford it?"

He laughed. "Can you?"

"I'm just the games-mistress. I don't have to bet."

"Oh yes, you do. Give me a time limit. If I don't break the ties – say in one hour – I win and you pay."

"Two hours an' you got a deal."

"One and a half."

"We're not negotiating on a building, Martin."

His hard-on stayed steady. Bartering was obviously another favourite sport.

"One hour and three quarters," he said.

"A deal," she replied. "Goodbye."

"Goodbye who?"

"Goodbye you. I'll be back when I feel like it."

"Are you serious?"

"Never more."

"C'mon, Venus. What kind of a game is this?"

"A challenge. I told you that before. Let's see if you're up to it, Martin." She left the room.

Talk about a power trip! Little Virginia Venus Maria Sierra from Brooklyn had Martin Swanson — Mister New York — trussed up and at her mercy.

With a secret smile she remembered the first time she'd set eyes on him. Ten years ago. 1977. She'd been fifteen years old.

Occasionally Virginia Venus Maria Sierra was able to get out of the house. It wasn't often, because with four brothers to look after and a demanding father, there was always work to be done. Oh yeah, she got out of the house to attend school, but that wasn't the same as recreational fun. Ron, her next-door neighbour and confidant, was all for encouraging her to escape and accompany him on his many trips to Broadway and Times Square.

Ron was a few years older than her. She thought he was incredibly exciting and daring. He was tall and gangly and a laugh to be with, totally unlike her burly brothers, who were macho men, full of their own strength and only interested in scoring with any neighbourhood girl they could get their hands on. Venus always had a strong suspicion they would try to score with her given half a chance. She never gave them that chance.

Whenever she was able, she and Ron would wander around New York having fun. Sometimes they would lurk outside the stage door of one of the big Broadway shows waiting for the stars to emerge. Ron kept an autograph book and persuaded her to do the same. It was interesting to see which stars would stop and sign their names, and which celebrities would sweep past, climb into their limousines, and ride off into the night.

"Glamorous, isn't it?" Ron would say with a smile.

And Virginia Venus Maria would nod in total agreement.

"I'm going to be a dancer," Ron confided.

"How are you going to train for that?" she asked. "Who's going to put up the money?"

Ron said he was going to try for an audition at the School of Performing Arts.

"How do you get to do that?" Virginia Venus Maria asked curiously.

"Talent," Ron replied.

One Saturday afternoon they were walking down Park Avenue when they saw a crowd gathered outside a church.

"It's a wedding!" Ron said excitedly. "I love weddings, don't you?"

Virginia Venus Maria nodded vigorously.

"Brides always look so gorgeous," Ron exclaimed.

Virginia Venus Maria nodded again, thinking that she never looked gorgeous. She had straight brown hair and a pretty face, but there was nothing special about her, much to her chagrin.

They joined the crowd outside the church, watched, and waited. And when the happy couple emerged, Virginia Venus Maria set eyes on Martin Swanson for the first time.

She stood back in awe and watched him. He was handsome in a way she didn't believe. He was handsome straight off the pages of a glossy magazine. He had sandy-coloured hair, full lips, and a ready smile for the photographers. He wore a morning suit and a bright red carnation.

Virginia Venus Maria glanced quickly at his bride, a pale and willowy redhead in an expensive white lace gown. They looked like a fairy-tale couple. They looked as if they came from another world.

"Who are they?" Virginia Venus Maria asked Ron.

"Rich," Ron replied. "And that's what we're gonna be some day."

The next morning she saw the bridegroom's picture in the paper, along with his new wife. His name was Martin Swanson. Property tycoon. Now married to the beautiful Deena Akveld, a Dutch society woman.

For some unknown reason Virgina Venus Maria clipped the newspaper photograph, stashing it beneath her underwear in her dresser drawer. The picture seemed to rep-

206

resent a fantasy world, and yet it was a world that one day she wanted to be part of. And why not? Virginia Venus Maria had ambition.

Martin Swanson's image stayed with her over the years. She read about him, followed his activities, watched him on television, and read even more about him in the gossip columns. Then one day she finally met him.

Of course, by the time she met him she was Venus Maria, the Venus Maria, and she pretended she had no idea who he was. Cooper Turner introduced him. The Cooper Turner.

Martin smiled that special bullshit smile of his and flirted outrageously. She looked around to see if his wife was present, but the coolly beautiful Deena appeared to have taken the night off.

When Martin sent her flowers the next day she was delighted — and when he turned up in Los Angeles a few weeks later, even more so.

By this time she'd found out more about him, having questioned Cooper into the ground.

Cooper was amused. "Have you got a hot spot for Martin?" he asked, raising a quizzical eyebrow.

"Why? Would it bother you if I did?" she retorted.

"I don't know," Cooper said. "I thought I was going to be your golden boy."

Venus Maria laughed. "Cooper, you're everyone's golden boy!"

"And you think Martin is a virgin?"

"I just think he's . . . fascinating."

Cooper looked at her for a long moment. "I may as well tell you," he said, "Martin's had a lot of girlfriends. A lot of beautiful, talented girlfriends. And he always goes back to Deena. No question. Deena is in his life to stay."

"Only as long as he wants her to," Venus Maria pointed out.

"You're a determined little thing, huh?"

"Nobody ever accused me of being shy."

When Martin called, Venus was not surprised. She invited him over to her house. He arrived within the hour.

207

"I'm not going to sleep with you until I know you," she warned him. *"That might take a couple of years. Right?"*

"I feel I know you now," he said. *"I've read every press clipping I could find. Why don't you look at my press file? Maybe we can save time that way."*

"Are you interested in saving time?"

"I'm interested in being with a woman like you."

Five weeks later they consummated the deal. In the meantime he'd made three trips to the Coast and she'd visited New York twice.

The flirtation was hot, the anticipation almost better than the act. But the act wasn't bad either. Venus Maria staged a long weekend at a friend's house in Big Sur. She made it a weekend to remember. Scented candles, the best champagne, music, a four-poster bed, and raunchy unabandoned sex.

Their affair had been going on for several months and now she wanted it to be more.

All she had to do was wait for Martin to leave his wife, get a divorce, and marry her.

Venus Maria had the uncanny knack of tapping into other people's fantasies, hence the enormous success of her videos. She went for the forbidden and dressed it up as entertainment. She could play any role — from little girl lost to voracious sexual superwoman. Her strut was every bit as good as her soft gentle side. She could kick ass or cuddle up with equal aplomb.

She could — if she so desired — tailor her act to fit any man's fantasy.

Martin Swanson said he didn't have fantasies.

Bull —

Shit.

Martin Swanson was a man. He had fantasies all right. And Venus Maria had figured out the one that would really turn him on — that all-time favourite, two girls together.

Only Venus Maria had no plans to appear as one of the girls. Group sex did not interest her. She liked her sexual

208

experiences to be between two people – private and personal and wildly sensuous.

Martin needed shaking up. He was too stiff-assed, more concerned about his next deal than his sensual pleasure. Although Venus Maria had to admit she'd loosened him up considerably.

Late at night, alone in her bed, alone in Los Angeles, she often wondered if Deena was receiving the benefit of Martin's new experience. He swore he never slept with his wife any more, but he was a man, and all men lied about sex. Especially married men.

Venus Maria loved Martin. She didn't know why. But did know she had to have him.

It wasn't his money, because she had plenty of her own.

It wasn't his looks, because although he was an attractive man he was no Mel Gibson.

It wasn't his personality, because even when he turned on the charm he was not exactly Mister Nice.

Love's a bitch, Venus Maria thought bitterly, and hurried to rendezvous with Ron, who had brought two expensive hookers to her house, supplied by his friend Madame Loretta. (Ron collected weird friends – useful on this occasion.)

The girls did not look like whores. One of them resembled a college cheerleader – in fact she'd dressed the part. And the other was a five-feet-tall Oriental girl with shiny jet hair hanging below her ass.

Ron grinned. He adored intrigue. "Meet Tai and Lemon."

Venus Maria raised an eyebrow. "Lemon?"

"That's me!" squeaked the cheerleader. "My real name too! I love your records!"

That was the trouble with being famous. Everyone knew your business.

Trying to remain cool and uninvolved, Venus Maria told the girls exactly what she wished them to do, adding, somewhat apologetically, "It's for a friend's birthday, y'know. A special treat."

"*Veree* special," interjected Ron with a sly grin.

209

"Shut up!" hissed Venus Maria.

The girls were true professionals. They knew exactly what was expected of them. Stripping down to silky undergarments, they produced a lethal-looking vibrator and a bottle of scented oil, then entered the bedroom where Martin Swanson lay waiting.

Venus Maria estimated he'd been alone for twenty minutes. Long enough to drive him a little bit crazy.

She hurried to the two-way mirror she'd had specially installed.

"Can I watch too?" Ron begged, following her.

"No, you can't," she replied sternly. "Just wait and get these two girls out of here when I'm ready."

"Spoilsport!"

"Since when did *you* like watching girls?"

"Oh, I don't care about *them*. It's himself I wouldn't mind taking a peek at."

"Ron! Behave yourself."

Martin was still tied up when the girls entered the bedroom. Determined not to lose the bet, he didn't move.

Tai and Lemon ignored him as they started in on each other. First they kissed. And then they touched nipples, delicately brushing silk against silk.

Breathlessly Venus Maria watched as Martin rose to the occasion.

Tai undid Lemon's bra, and the pretty blonde's breasts tumbled free, surprisingly large and firm.

Martin groaned.

Tai fixed her mouth onto a welcoming nipple.

Martin groaned louder.

Lemon divested herself of her panties. She had shaved her pubic area, and the skin there was very white.

Tai's long dark hair swept downwards as she bent to kiss between Lemon's legs. Obligingly Lemon spread wide.

"Oh God, Venus!" Martin managed, desperately trying not to move.

Tai stopped attending to Lemon, and unclipped her own bra before stepping out of her panties. Her black bush was forest thick — all the better for Lemon to return the favour and bury her blonde curls.

Venus Maria could see Martin was desperate for release. His penis stood erect and ready. But still he didn't break the bonds.

Tai stepped back from Lemon, took the bottle of oil, and squeezed it over both their breasts.

Then Lemon reached for the vibrator, switched it on, and held it to Tai's pubic mound.

Martin reached orgasm, spurting all over himself.

"God damn it!" he muttered. "God *damn*!"

Time to do away with the entertainment. Venus Maria entered the room, waving the girls out.

They picked up their things and exited quickly.

"Hmmm . . ." Venus Maria stared mesmerizingly at her prisoner. "You've been a bad boy. Look at the mess you've made."

"Come here," he said desperately.

"Wait!" she commanded.

"Come *here*!" he insisted.

She walked slowly into the bathroom, came back with a fluffy white towel, and wiped him clean.

"Not such a big shot on campus, after all," she sighed.

"You're unbelievable!"

"I try to please."

"I want to fuck you."

"What else is new?"

"I want to — "

"What?"

"Spend more time with you."

"That's nice. How about your wife?"

"She's in New York."

"I know."

"Come here, Venus. Untie me. All bets are off."

She glanced at her Cartier tank watch, a present from Martin last time he was in town. "You have another thirty-five minutes to go."

"I want out."

"Pay me."

211

"No way."

"Then . . . stay where you are and keep quiet. A bet is a bet is a bet is a – "

"I *know* what a bet is."

She had on denim cut-offs and a white T-shirt. Standing at the end of the bed she did a slow strip. Underneath she wore crotchless red lace panties and a cut-out black leather bra. Hooker gear designed to excite.

Stretching her arms into the air she grinned provocatively. "I think I'll go see Cooper," she said.

Martin broke the silk scarves with one bound and was on her like a randy New York tycoon.

"You're something else," he said.

"And so are you," she whispered softly. "So are you."

Chapter 32

Harry Browning took his time deciding what he should do about Luce. He brooded about it on and off for a couple of weeks before approaching her. He couldn't help noticing her promotion. All of a sudden this strange woman who'd entered the studio as Sheila Hervey's niece was suddenly ensconced as Mickey Stolli's personal secretary. And where was Olive? The rumour was she'd broken her leg and was not coming back for a while. How convenient.

Harry waited until Luce was sitting alone in the commissary one lunchtime and then he approached her.

She glanced up at him. "Hello, Harry."

He sat down at her table without being invited. "What are you up to?" he demanded accusingly.

She stared straight at him. Two more weeks to go and she was out of this charade. "I beg your pardon?" she said calmly.

He fiddled with his spectacles, took them off, cleaned them with a napkin, and put them on again. "What exactly

212

are you up to?" he repeated excitedly. "I know it's something."

Lucky remained cool. "I'm not getting your drift."

"I'm no fool," Harry Browning said agitatedly. "You lured me to your apartment, got me drunk, and tried to wheedle information out of me."

This was unexpected. Lucky wasn't sure how to play it. "I've no idea what you're talking about," she said at last. "I never lured you anywhere. You asked me out and I offered to cook you dinner. It's not my fault you hit the booze."

Harry narrowed his eyes beneath his wire-rimmed spectacles. He was unhappy with the way this was going. He'd expected her to be more unsettled, not quite so in control. Determined to get to the point, he pressed on. "I *know* what you're up to," he said.

"If you know," she replied coolly, "how come you're asking *me*?"

This stumped Harry for a moment. He didn't like her attitude. He didn't like her. And he certainly didn't like the fact that she'd made him turn to the bottle again. "Does Mickey Stolli know who you are?" he demanded hotly.

"Who am I?" she replied, staring him down.

"Who are you?" he persisted. "Why don't *you* tell *me*? Or do I have to ask Mr Stolli myself?"

"What would you ask him exactly?"

"To investigate your background. I know that's a wig you're wearing. And you don't need glasses. I also know you visited Abe Panther the other night."

She stared him down. "Then perhaps you should ask Mr Panther what this is all about."

Harry lapsed into silence. Spotting a mark on the tablecloth he went to work, rubbing vigorously with his napkin.

Lucky took a low beat. "Whose side are you on, Harry?" she asked, keeping an even tone.

"What do you mean?" he asked suspiciously.

"You're well aware of the kind of product this studio is turning out. You know how it used to be."

213

"It used to be great," he said vehemently.

Lucky nodded. "It can be great again, Harry. Just trust me."

He was indignant. "Why should I trust somebody who tried to get me drunk?"

"I had no idea you had a . . . problem."

He jumped on that one. "Did Mr Panther tell you?"

"Abe Panther never mentioned you."

She wasn't sure whether he believed her or not, but she decided she wasn't hanging around to find out. She got up from the table and prepared to leave. "Harry," she said, "you'd be doing me an enormous favour if you didn't tell anybody what's going on."

"I'll do what I like," he said curtly.

"In two weeks' time," she said slowly, "everything will be clear."

"I'll do what I like," he repeated. "You'd better be careful. I'm watching you."

Hurrying back to the office she thought about things. Another week working for Mickey Stolli. Another week closer to the end of this charade. And what had she discovered? That most people were stealing. That there were a lot of petty scams gong on. And that men in the film business used women as commodities.

When she took over, Mickey Stolli was out, and so were most of his little band of merry men. She already had her lawyer, Morton Sharkey, preparing a list of suitable replacements.

"Let's bring some women executives aboard," she'd suggested, and Morton had agreed. Already he was coming up with suggestions, although there weren't that many women executives to choose from.

In the meantime, Lennie was still on the missing list. Nobody seemed to know his whereabouts.

She knew why he was doing it. Lennie had this childish habit of retaliating with more of the same. She'd done it to him, so he figured he'd pay her back.

She really couldn't blame him, because if the situation

were reversed she'd probably behave in exactly the same way.

Her conversation with Harry Browning was disturbing. What exactly *did* he know? Maybe she should have stayed and talked to him some more. But the quickest way out of a difficult situation seemed to be retreat.

She made it back to the office five minutes before Mickey. He returned from his lunch early and shut himself away, telling Lucky that when Leslie Kane arrived she was to keep her waiting. "And if Eddie calls," he added, "don't let him know his wife's here."

Lucky had realized from Mickey's previous conversation and meeting with Eddie that they were indeed into some distribution scam with certain underworld figures. She'd instructed Boogie to investigate, and Boogie had come up with the news that Eddie Kane was dealing with Carlos Bonnatti.

It was a strange and unwelcome coincidence. Carlos, the scumbag brother of Santino and son of Enzio. The Bonnattis had always been enemies of the Santangelos. Their feud went back to the good old Vegas days. And now that Santino and Enzio were deceased, it was Carlos who controlled the family drug and porno empire.

It was weird, Lucky thought, how the Bonnattis stayed connected to her life. She would be more than happy if she never had to hear the name again.

From what Boogie was able to find out, Eddie Kane had made an arrangement with the Bonnatti organization to distribute their porno films in Europe, hiding them along with legitimate Panther product. If Lucky read Mickey correctly, he was anxious to get out of the deal, and wisely so, for Lucky knew it was a big mistake to fuck with the Bonnattis.

Leslie Kane turned up promptly at three o'clock. She gave Lucky a friendly smile. "I'm here to see Mr Stolli," she said brightly. "My name is Leslie Kane. I have an appointment."

Lucky was surprised. She hadn't realized Eddie was married to such a fresh-looking beauty. "He's expecting you. Take a seat, I'll let him know you're here."

Leslie sat down, picked up a copy of *People* magazine, and leafed through it. After a moment she put the magazine down. "I'm not too early, am I?" she asked anxiously.

Lucky glanced up. "You're exactly on time. Your appointment is for three."

Leslie nodded thankfully. "That's right."

Mickey kept her waiting twenty-five minutes. He didn't come to his office door to greet her. Lucky had noticed he only made that meaningful move for major stars. As soon as Leslie entered his office, Lucky put on her miniature headphones, activated the tape machine, and began picking up every word.

"Sit down, sit down," Mickey said, gesturing at Leslie.

She sat in a chair opposite him, full of rapt attention. "You wanted to see me, Mr Stolli?"

He cleared his throat and shuffled some papers around his desk. "Uh . . . y'can call me Mickey."

Leslie, the wide-eyed beauty, gazed at him. "Thank you."

Mickey wondered where Eddie had stumbled upon this Iowa beauty queen. She still had corn in her hair. "Honey," he said, "we got ourselves a problem."

"What's that, Mr Stolli?" she asked, full of concern. "I mean . . . Mickey."

Oh God! He'd found out about her past!

"Your husband is a jerk," Mickey said flatly. "I've tried to help him – God knows I've tried. Over the years I've given him jobs an' he's screwed up. I've given him help an' he's thrown it back in my face. And now he's got us into a mess I refuse to take responsibility for."

Leslie lowered her eyes. She had long, sweeping lashes. "I'm sorry," she whispered, overwhelmed with relief that this meeting wasn't about her.

"It's not your fault," said Mickey, wondering what she was like in bed.

"Then why am I here?" she asked, frowning slightly.

Mickey chewed the end of his pen. "You're here because

216

Eddie's in trouble," he said. "And this time *I* can't help him."

"What kind of trouble?" she asked, sweeping lashes going into overdrive.

"A million big ones."

Leslie felt a flutter in the pit of her stomach. She hadn't taken Eddie seriously when a couple of weeks ago she'd asked him if something was bothering him and he'd replied, "Nothing that a million bucks and a little co-operation from Mickey Stolli can't fix."

"What can I do?" she asked earnestly, leaning forward.

"You'd better get Eddie to dig into his pockets and come up with the money," Mickey said harshly. "'Cause if he doesn't, he's gonna find himself wearing cement boots on the wrong end of Santa Monica pier."

"Mr Stolli . . . uh, Mickey . . . Eddie did mention this to me a couple of weeks ago. I thought he was joking."

"You go into business, you take the consequences. Eddie put together a deal. He brought it to me. And then he cheated me *and* his other partners, and now he's got to pay the price. He tells me he has no money. What's he done with it, Leslie, spent it on you?"

She sat up straighter in her chair. "No, certainly not."

"That's good, because he's going to need it and I can't help him. If he thinks I'm bailing him out yet again — I ain't doing it. He's on his way and he'd better pay up or he's in over the top." Mickey picked up a script and began to flip through it. "That's all," he said brusquely.

The meeting was over.

Leslie got up to leave. "I'll do what I can," she murmured.

She had a pair of legs on her that could strangle a giraffe! "You'd better," he said gruffly.

"I will," she assured him earnestly.

"Oh," Mickey added, "and do yourself another favour. Get that asshole husband of yours into drug rehab. He's snorting his life away. I hope he hasn't got you doing the same thing."

She was indignant. "I don't touch drugs."

217

"Make sure you stick to that."

Leslie rushed out of the office.

Lucky watched her on her way. Mickey Stolli was a mean bastard. What did he expect a young girl like Leslie to do about the mess Eddie had gotten them into?

Mickey left his office soon after. "I'm going out," he said on his way to the door.

Lucky knew better than to ask where. When he wanted to reveal his destination he did so. She figured another visit to Warner was about to take place.

"What time can I expect you back, Mr Stolli?" she asked politely. This perfect-secretary shit was driving her nuts!

"Expect me when you see me."

"And how shall I handle your afternoon appointments?"

"Cancel 'em."

Fuck you, asshole. "Yes, Mr Stolli."

It was amazing that people were prepared to do business with Mickey at all. He cared about nobody except himself.

Twenty minutes after he left the building, Venus Maria appeared in the office. She wandered in wearing torn jeans, an oversize T-shirt, sneakers, and a Lakers baseball cap.

At first Lucky thought she was a teenager. "Can I help you?" she asked.

"I need five minutes of Mickey's time," Venus Maria said. "A mere five minutes so I can tell him what I think, an' then I'm outta here."

Lucky recognized her voice. "I'm sorry, he's not in his office."

"Shit!" Venus Maria exclaimed. "I really needed to talk to him today."

"Is there something I can tell him?"

Venus Maria threw a script onto Lucky's desk. "Yeah. Tell Mr S. this script stinks. He promised me a strong woman, and naturally he's come up with the usual dumb bimbo victim. There's no way I'm playing this sexist crap."

Lucky picked up the offending script. It was *Bombshell*, Mickey's pet project.

"I'll be happy to tell him," she said.

Venus Maria threw herself into a chair. "It's not your fault. Jesus! When are these dumb jerks ever gonna learn?"

Here was a woman after Lucky's own heart. "Are you not doing it because of the way it's written?" she ventured.

"You can bet your ass I'm not," Venus Maria replied vehemently. "I only do things I believe in."

"That's the right attitude," Lucky said approvingly, forgetting her role for a moment.

Venus Maria glanced at her. "It's nice to know you agree. All girls together, huh?"

"It's about time somebody stood up to these . . . producers."

"Hey, you'd better not let your boss hear you talk that way." She looked around. "Where's the English angel?"

"Olive's on sick leave. She broke her leg."

Venus Maria stifled a laugh. "What did Mickey do, kick her out of the office?"

Not wanting to blow her cover, Lucky didn't respond, although she realized this was a woman she could get along with just fine.

Venus Maria stood up, yawned, and stretched. "Well, I guess it's back to the grind. I'm on the set if he dares talk to me. He can call me in my dressing room or at home later. Just tell him – this is *not* the story line we discussed. The woman in this script is a victim, and this baby ain't playing no victims."

Lucky was delighted. Venus Maria had a big future at Panther. She would make sure of that.

Chapter 33

Eddie was pacing restlessly around the house when Leslie arrived home. He hadn't been to the studio for three days. He looked haggard, there were bags under his eyes and the beginnings of a full beard. "Where have you been?" he demanded, staring at her accusingly.

Leslie wasn't sure whether she was supposed to tell him she'd been summoned to visit Mickey or not. She decided honesty was the best way to handle this. "Um . . . I went to see Mickey Stolli," she said, taking off her jacket.

Eddie immediately exploded. "What the *fuck* did you go see him for?"

"Because he asked me to," she explained patiently.

"And if he asked you to give him a blow-job, you'd do that, too, huh?"

She walked into the kitchen. "Eddie, don't be silly."

"Quit talkin' to me like I'm a schmuck, OK? You go see Mickey an' you don't even *tell* me about it. Then you come back here an' try to put me down. What's the game, Leslie?"

She looked at him with wide eyes. "We're in trouble, Eddie, aren't we?"

"Trouble?" he snorted. "What kind of *trouble* are we in, honey?"

She picked up the kettle and began filling it with water. "Mickey says we're in trouble. He says you owe a lot of money."

Eddie paced up and down. "Oh, he says *I* owe money, does he? Well, let me tell you this, baby. The studio owes money. They're responsible. He's in this as much as I am, and there's no way he's getting out."

"Mickey says you owe a million dollars."

"Why is he bringing *you* into it?" Eddie snapped.

Leslie shook her head. "Maybe he thinks I can help."

Eddie laughed mirthlessly. "Help? *You?* Who the fuck is he kidding?"

Leslie looked at him with a hurt expression. "Maybe I can," she said defensively.

"Come on, baby, it's a million bucks we're talkin' here, not ten cents. Wise up."

"What are you going to do?"

Eddie shook his head. "I haven't figured it out yet. But whatever it is, Mickey's gonna to be on for the ride. Panther can pay without blinkin' – why should *I* take the fall?"

"Eddie," Leslie said tentatively. "Mickey says you've got a drug problem. He says you should do something about it."

Eddie exploded. "What's his friggin' game? It's none of his goddamn business *what* I've got. So I do a little coke occasionally. Big fucking deal."

"More than occasionally."

"Hey, hey, hey, who am I married to, Mother Teresa?"

"I only want to help you."

"I'll tell you how to help me, baby. Just shut the fuck up and leave me alone, OK?"

Leslie nodded miserably. "OK."

Warner was not at home. Mickey couldn't believe he'd driven all the way to her apartment and she wasn't there. They'd arranged the rendezvous on the phone the previous day, and it wasn't like Warner to break a date. He rang the doorbell, and then in frustration kicked the door a few times before angrily making his way down to the underground garage. Climbing into his Porsche, he revved the engine.

Mickey Stolli liked to get laid on a regular basis. Warner satisfied him, but she had to be there when he needed her.

Sitting in his car he made a call to Ford Werne. Ford had often mentioned in passing that he did not believe in having affairs, he believed in paying for it. Mickey had laughed in his face. "Paying for pussy? In *this* town!" he'd exclaimed. "LA is a free pussy heaven!"

Ford had responded in a calm and sensible way. "You pay for it, Mickey, you know exactly what you're getting. They don't want a part in your movie. They don't want a piece of your life. They don't want you to take them to Hawaii, give them head, and buy them dresses. They do what *you* want. It's the perfect situation. Sex without guilt, served up *exactly* as you like it."

Mickey had visions of a Chicano hooker on the corner of Vermont and Sunset in a fake-leather miniskirt, fluorescent tube-top, and ten-inch heels.

As if reading his mind Ford had said, "And let me tell

221

you something else. The girls I sleep with are far more beautiful than any transient date."

"Where do you find them?" Mickey had asked curiously.

"That's the great thing," Ford had replied. "*I* don't find them, Loretta does."

"Who's Loretta?"

"She's the greatest little madam in town. She has a house in the hills and she hand-picks all her girls. They're only in action for a few months, and let me tell you this, they're gorgeous."

It sounded like a great deal for those who were interested. After Ford had told him about it, Mickey heard the name Madame Loretta from a couple of other guys. He'd never given it a whirl because he'd always had Warner standing by. But today he needed action, and he needed it immediately.

When Ford came on the line he requested Madame Loretta's number.

Ford chuckled softly. "Coming around to my way of thinking?" he asked.

Mickey lowered his voice, even though he was sitting in his car where nobody could possibly hear him. "Is this woman discreet?"

Ford reassured him. "She gives the word *discreet* a whole new meaning. I'll call her and tell her you're on your way."

"Do that," Mickey said. He didn't like asking anybody for a favour, but today he had no choice.

Madame Loretta greeted him like an over-solicitous Jewish mother. She was a plump woman with glowing skin and a warm smile. "Welcome, welcome," she beamed, leading him into a large living room overlooking the city view. "Can I get you a refreshment – coffee, tea, a drink?"

"You know what I'm here for," Mickey said, getting right to the point.

Loretta smiled warmly. "Oh yes, and you won't be disappointed. Now tell me, what are your preferences?"

222

Mickey cleared his throat. "Do you have any black girls?"

"I have a lovely black girl," Madame Loretta replied. "She's a college graduate, clean, works hard. You'll be very happy."

"Can I see her now?" Mickey asked.

Madame Loretta was not put out. "Give me five minutes," she said and left the room.

Mickey gazed out over the view. How simple it would be if he could have great sex with his wife. But there were too many hurdles to overcome with Abigaile, too many conversations to survive before one could even think about sex, and in the end it was too much of a hassle.

Madame Loretta returned to the room and smiled reassuringly. "Yvette will be here shortly."

"I'd like to see her first," Mickey said. "Before I make a decision."

Madame Loretta nodded knowingly. "I can assure you you'll be very happy. I *never* make a mistake."

Every evening Lucky tried to work out the tangled web of business deals going down at Panther Studios. She knew about the scam with the distribution overseas of the porno movies, but apparently Mickey had decided to make this Eddie's problem not the studio's. His position was that Eddie had got them in and it was up to him to get them out.

It was quite obvious Eddie had been stealing all over, and that Mickey didn't care to bail him out.

Then there was Harry Browning to deal with. What was he going to do? Was he planning to blow her cover before she was ready? She would just have to wait and see.

Boogie had hired a secretary to come to the house each night, sit in a room, and type out the transcripts of Mickey's recorded conversations. They made interesting reading.

Working nine to five was an exhausting business. Spending every day kissing Mickey Stolli's ass for hours on end was depressing, to say the least. Lucky wasn't used to being in a subservient position and it didn't suit her.

It was also depressing not knowing where Lennie was. Boogie was working on tracking him down.

In London, Bobby whined on the phone. It was unlike him. "Mommy, Mommy, when are you coming? I haven't seen you for ages. Where are you?" he asked.

"Don't worry, we'll all be together soon, sweetheart," she assured him, feeling full of guilt.

And then she remembered she hadn't called Brigette since she'd started this caper. Quickly she placed a call to the private boarding school Brigette attended.

A secretary informed her the school was closed for the summer and Brigette had returned to New York and her grandmother.

"Freedom," Lucky whispered to herself. "I need my freedom."

Chapter 34

Nona Webster belonged to a crazy family. Brigette had never met anybody quite like them before. Effie Webster was an extraordinary-looking woman. No more than five feet tall and bone thin, she had hair even redder than her daughter's, worn in a strange cockatoo style with a renegade clump of brilliant green at the front. Her makeup was bright and unusual, and her clothes reflected the image of a woman who'd never bowed to convention.

On the other hand, Yul Webster, her husband, was a very proper-looking man. Tall and imposing, he wore Savile Row suits, silk shirts, hand-made shoes, and his only concession to his wife's outlandish taste was his ties, which were designed by Effie and made up specially for him. Yul sported ties with hand-painted naked women, birds in flight, airplanes landing – any subject that took Effie's fancy – and he wore them with panache.

"My parents are slightly weird," Nona warned her friend before they arrived in New York — an understatement, to say the least.

Weird they might be, but warm and friendly they certainly were. They welcomed Brigette into their home as if she were a member of the family.

"They take drugs," Nona confessed rather sheepishly. "I've learned to ignore it. Actually, it's only a little snort of recreational coke here and there, and they're into grass. You know what it is, they're kind of bogged down in that whole sixties thing. Just pretend you don't notice, and if they offer you anything say no."

Brigette understood. "I went through my drug stage when I was fourteen," she explained.

Nona nodded. "Another coincidence. So did I."

"Karma."

"Definitely." Warmly Nona took her friend's arm. "Y'know, I really feel comfortable with you," she said. "We're so alike."

"Alike — but different."

"You *know* what I mean," Nona said.

The Websters' New York penthouse was a splash of colour from the moment you entered. They'd settled on a startling array of modern furniture. The walls were painted black and covered in contemporary art. Their paintings made a striking statement.

Every week they threw an enormous party attended by an army of beautiful and talented people.

"A few months ago Venus Maria was here," Nona confided. "She's the best. I got to stare at her all night!"

Brigette was impressed. "Amazing!" she said.

"Absolutely," agreed Nona. "I love meeting interesting people, don't you?"

"Where's your brother?" Brigette asked curiously.

"Don't worry, he'll turn up. Whenever he needs money he's here." Nona nodded sagely. "That's his thing — getting money out of anyone he can."

"What's his name?"

"Paul," Nona replied. "They must have been having a normal day when they named him."

Brigette picked up a framed photo from the piano and studied it. "Is this him?" she asked.

"Handsome, isn't he?" Nona said.

"Not bad," Brigette lied. She thought he was gorgeous. "What does he do?"

"He's an artist. Unsuccessful. Paints bloody great canvases of naked people. If he asks you to pose for him, say no."

"Right – like I'd say yes!"

"We're going to have a terrific summer." Nona sighed happily. "I have a feeling, don't you?"

Brigette nodded.

Deena Swanson and Effie Webster were best friends. An odd coupling, but one that seemed to work. They'd actually been friends for many years since Deena first came to America. They'd met when Effie had visited the showroom where Deena worked and picked out several pieces of furniture.

When Deena began dating Martin Swanson, Effie had immediately suggested she should think seriously about marrying him. "Darling, the man is going places," Effie had assured her. "And methinks you should go right along with him."

Deena didn't need much persuading. She found Martin attractive and killer sharp. Definitely a man on his way to the top.

Martin and Yul did not get along quite so well. Yul found Martin boring. "The man has an ego the size of the Empire State Building," he'd told Effie.

"As long as it's only his ego, darling!" she'd replied, laughing gaily.

When Martin started to sleep around, the first person Deena confided in was Effie. "What shall I do?" she'd wailed.

"Ignore it," Effie had advised. "Most men play – it's their damn libido! If you take no notice they soon get

bored and come home to Momma. After all, a lay is a lay
— but a wife is a lifetime commitment. The very thought
of the alimony involved drives them straight back into
your arms."

"How about Yul?" Deena wanted to know.

"I couldn't care less," Effie had replied briskly. "As long
as he comes home."

"But you *would* care if it interfered with your marriage."

Quite firmly Effie had said, "*Nothing* will ever interfere
with *my* marriage."

Effie Webster obviously adored her only daughter. She
took both Brigette and Nona to Saks, and then on to
Trump Tower, where they shopped until they couldn't
carry any more bags.

Anything Nona asked for, her mother bought her. "I
told you," she whispered to Brigette. "They spend everything they make. My parents are crazy!"

After shopping Effie took them to lunch at the Russian
Tea Room, where they spotted Rudolph Nureyev and Paul
Newman lunching at different tables.

"What do you get up to when you're in town with your
grandmother?" Nona asked, wolfing delicious blinis.

Brigette grimaced. "Charlotte's really boring. She never
takes me anywhere."

"What was your mother like when she was alive?"

"Well," Brigette replied slowly, thinking about it, "she
was kind of fun. At least we *did* things. We were always
flying off to stay with my grandfather on his Greek island.
Or to the fashion shows in Paris. We used to travel all
over the world, it was exciting."

"You must miss her," Nona said sympathetically, touching her friend's arm.

Brigette nodded sadly. "Yes, I do," she replied, realizing
for the first time that she did indeed miss Olympia very
much indeed.

Nona's brother, Paul, turned up on Sunday wearing dirty
jeans, scuffed cowboy boots, a black T-shirt, and a distressed leather motorcycle jacket. He was thin and intense

looking, and he did not have the family red hair. His hair was long and dark and worn in a tight ponytail. His eyes were covered by dark shades.

Nona greeted him brightly.

"I'm here for money," he announced.

"The story of your life." Nona sighed. "Don't I at least get a greeting? A kiss? A hug? Anything?"

"You got bucks, you get a greeting."

"Thanks a lot! It's *so* nice to find all this brotherly love flowing in my direction."

Paul threw himself into a chair, removed his dark shades, and stared straight at Brigette. "Who's this?" he asked.

"The one girl you can't resist," Nona replied.

"Too young," said Paul.

"Uh-uh." Nona shook her head. "Wait until you hear what she's got that you want."

"Too young," Paul repeated.

Brigette was not sure she was enjoying this conversation. Who did this idiot think he was?

"This is my new best friend, Brigette," Nona said, introducing her at last.

"Hi ya, Brigette," Paul said casually.

"Stanislopoulos," Nona added.

Paul raised an eyebrow. "As in *the*?" he questioned, brightening considerably.

Nona grinned triumphantly. "You've got it."

Paul's stare intensified. "I'd like to ask for your hand in marriage," he said, staring at Brigette.

She went along with the game. "Too late. You're much too old for me."

Nona laughed delightedly.

"How about a second chance?" Paul begged.

"I told you, didn't I?" Nona said. "Money – that's all this stinker cares about. He doesn't have a heart, he has a cash register!"

"*Is* there anything else?" Paul asked, checking Brigette out.

Effie entered the room dressed from head to toe in flaming orange.

"You look like a minah bird who just got a nasty shock," Paul remarked. "What *is* that outfit."

Effie smiled. Obviously the Websters were used to Paul and took no notice of his rudeness. "That's no way to ask for money," she admonished, shaking a finger at him. "Naughty, naughty."

"How come everybody is under the impression I only come here for money?" Paul complained.

"Because it's true," Nona said.

Watching this family scene, Brigette decided that even though he was exceptionally rude, Paul Webster was perhaps the best-looking man she'd ever seen.

But Brigette knew what handsome meant. It meant danger, excitement, and then even more danger.

She was wise enough to steer clear.

There were times in life to get away and this was one of them. Lennie rented a loft in the Village and holed up. As long as he had instant coffee, a bottle of Scotch, and plenty of yellow legal pads, he was happy.

Walking out on the movie was the best move he'd ever made. Compromise and Lennie Golden did not mix. He needed to be creative, and sometimes the pressures of stardom stifled the creative spirit.

Not to mention Lucky pissing off to Japan.

He'd had the "movie star in a bad film" trip and now it was time to get back to work.

It occurred to him that if he wanted a successful movie he'd better sit down and write it himself. Being alone was exactly what he needed.

He was well aware that his agent and manager were probably frantically searching for him. But he also knew he was not in the mood to be bothered, so he covered his tracks, making a large cash withdrawal at his bank and not writing any further cheques.

The only person he phoned was Jess.

"Listen," he told her, "I've got to be by myself for a

while. If Lucky calls, tell her you've heard from me and I'm fine — nothing else."

Jess had said they were both playing games and should grow up.

"This isn't a revenge move," he'd explained patiently. "Lucky's in Japan. When she gets back, I'll see her. Right now she doesn't want me to contact her. So I won't. That's not playing games."

"Oh, c'mon," Jess had said disgustedly. "You're worse than a couple of kids."

"Whatever," he'd replied, getting off the phone. "I'll call you in a week."

He enjoyed solitary confinement. It gave him the freedom he required. From early in the morning until late at night he sat at a large table by the window and wrote. Writing made him feel good. It released the pressure.

When he wasn't writing he thought about Lucky and tried to figure out what was really going on between them. She worked in New York. He worked in LA. And in between they saw each other for brief spells.

Oh, yes. The sex was great. Sure. Why not? But great sex wasn't enough. He wanted more.

The thoughts he'd had about taking a year off were getting stronger. If they didn't do it, he had a bad feeling their marriage was going to fall apart. It wasn't what he wanted.

He kept on writing and found his script turning into the story of their life together.

Right now he didn't know the ending. He only hoped it was a happy one.

Chapter 35

When Martin Swanson arrived back in New York from the coast, Deena greeted him like a dutiful wife even though she feared the worst. Every time he went away she feared the worst. Was Martin getting ready to tell her their marriage was over?

"How was LA?" she asked as soon as he walked into their bedroom.

"Hot," he replied, loosening his tie.

"And business? Did we get a studio?"

Using the word *we* was an important part of the strategy she'd decided to employ. Martin wasn't getting any help from her. If he wanted a divorce he was going to have to tell her himself.

"Still negotiating," he said. "But it looks like we're going to take over Orpheus."

"Weren't you interested in Panther?"

Martin sat down on the edge of the bed. "I met with Mickey Stolli. He doesn't seem to have any say in the matter. The studio still belongs to Abe Panther, and apparently he doesn't want to sell. But Mickey promised he'd have his wife talk to the old man — she's Abe's grand-daughter."

"What's Mickey Stolli like?" Deena asked, moving on to the interested wife role.

"A Hollywood type," Martin replied, yawning. "Full of ideas. He's made Panther into a money-making machine. They produce a lot of movies nobody's ever heard of."

"What kind of movies?"

"You know the sort of thing," Martin replied off-hand-edly. "Tits and ass."

"That's nice," Deena said, thinking to herself — *Your girlfriend would fit nicely into those kind of films.* "Who else did you see while you were out there?"

"The usual."

Deena imagined The Bitch must be putting on the pressure by now. Martin didn't give a hint of trouble.

"The Websters are giving a party in your honour next week," she said,

"Why?" he asked, shrugging off his jacket.

"Because it's your birthday," she said. "Had you forgotten?"

As a matter of fact he had forgotten. There was so much

on his mind that the last thing he wanted to think about was getting a year older. He got off the bed and walked over to the mirror, peering at himself. "I guess I don't look too bad for nearly forty-six," he said, waiting for the compliment.

"You're a handsome man, Martin," Deena replied, coming up behind him. He'd always thrived on flattery.

He turned around and kissed her lightly on the cheek. "I've a few calls to make," he said. "I'll be in my study."

He left their bedroom and went downstairs. It was quite clear Deena had no idea that anything was amiss. She obviously did not suspect this latest infidelity. He wondered how he was going to broach the subject of divorce if it ever came to that. Venus Maria had told him that if he wanted to be with her, he was going to have to think about being with her permanently. Otherwise it was goodbye.

Martin hadn't made up his mind yet. But it was a thought.

"One, two, three, four. One, two, three, four."

Venus Maria's personal trainer was a son of a bitch. He worked her like a dog.

"One, two, three, four. One, two, three, four."

Sweat was pouring off her, yet he didn't quit. He made her do the excruciating exercises. Arms, legs, buttocks, stomach – everything had to be toned.

"I've had enough!" she gasped.

"You've had enough when *I* say you've had enough," replied her trainer. He was young and vigorous, with sleek muscles and an enthusiastic attitude. Had she not been involved with Martin she might have considered a fling.

At last he allowed her to stop. "You'll thank me when you're in the middle of your tour," he said.

"Thanks," she replied breathlessly.

As soon as he left she threw herself into the shower, washing her hair, watching the water trickle down her body. Her firm, hard body. The famous Venus Maria body that turned so many people on.

232

Martin had flown off to New York the night before. She knew she had him hooked. All she had to do now was reel him in.

Ron appeared at her house for lunch. Her business manager had taken care of separating their financial interests, and Ron had taken it quite well. Now he could buy his boyfriend Rodeo Drive if he so desired, and it wouldn't bother her one bit.

"Where's the Ken Doll?" she asked mockingly. "I was under the distinct impression he never let you out of his sight."

"Now, now. Don't get bitchy," Ron retorted, heading straight for the kitchen. "Has Mister Major Mogul returned to New York?"

"Yes, he has," she said, dancing along behind him, humming her latest recording.

"Did we have fun while he was here?" Ron asked, opening up the fridge and removing a bowl of tuna salad.

"We had a great time," Venus Maria replied, reaching for the lettuce and tomatoes, while Ron grabbed a fresh loaf of bread. Companionably they began to put together large sandwiches filled with tuna mix, lettuce, tomato, and avocado.

"This is a riot," Ron said, slicing tomatoes like an expert. "We don't get to do this enough. I adore behaving like a normal person!"

Venus Maria agreed. "I sent the maid to the market. I wanted to thank you for helping me out the other night."

"My pleasure," Ron replied. "I enjoyed every delicious minute. Oh, and I have *the* most scandalous gossip."

"What?" she asked, stuffing a wedge of lettuce into her mouth.

"Your boss."

"I don't have a boss."

"Does the name Mickey Stolli mean anything to you?" She laughed. "I don't regard Mickey as my boss."

"Well, anyway, my dear, Mr Stolli himself turned up at the house of a certain very close friend of mine. All bushy-tailed and eager for action."

"Who would that be?"

"Who do you *think*?"

Venus Maria almost choked. "Not Loretta?" she gasped.

"The very same. And guess what his preference is?"

"I can't wait to hear!"

"Ladies of a darker hue."

"Oh, come *on*, you're kidding me."

"Would *I* kid the greatest kidder of all time?"

Venus Maria grinned. She loved gossip as long as it wasn't about her. "How do you know this?" she asked.

"Madame Loretta tells me everything," Ron said proudly. "I am her confidant and friend."

"Obviously she doesn't know about your big mouth," Venus Maria teased.

"Mmm . . . look who's talking about a big mouth."

"Abigaile would skin Mickey if she ever found out."

"Can you *imagine* what Abigaile must be like between the sheets?" Ron mused. "A laugh a minute no doubt. The poor man probably has to get his R and R elsewhere. Not to mention a blow-job." He strolled over to the fridge and took out a can of 7-Up. "By the way, have you heard from Emilio since you chucked him out?"

"Why?" Venus Maria frowned. "Should I have?"

"He wasn't exactly thrilled about your forcing him to leave. I have a feeling we might be reading your secrets somewhere."

Venus didn't care to be reminded of her brother. He was a big boy. He could look after himself. She refused to feel responsible for him. "Don't start that again," she groaned. "Emilio wouldn't do that to me. I'm paying his rent, for God's sake."

"Hmm . . . If they offered him enough money Emilio would probably do anything."

Venus Maria placed her hands on her hips. "What could he possibly tell them that the great unwashed doesn't already know?"

"About Major Mogul."

"He doesn't *know* about Martin."

234

"Are you sure?"

"Positive." She grinned confidently. "Anyway, I'm not exactly shivering waiting to find out what Emilio has to say about me. He's a deadhead. A loser."

"Emilio is your brother, dear. Speak kindly."

"He's still a loser, *and* you know it."

"Is Mister New York hooked?" Ron inquired, raising an eyebrow.

She smiled, "Martin's a *very* special man, and we have a *very* special relationship."

"Ah, yes," Ron agreed. "And thank God the newspapers don't know about it, or even Emilio. Because if they did, you'd really be in deep shit."

"I was very careful when Emilio was around," she assured him. "He knows nothing."

Ron nodded sagely. "Keep it that way."

Emilio Sierra and one of the editors of *Truth and Fact* met at Café Roma on Canon Drive. Emilio had dressed for the part. He wore an off-white jacket, white chinos, a cream shirt, and several heavy fake gold chains around his thick neck. His hair was slicked back. Unfortunately he was thirty pounds overweight, which rather spoiled the effect.

Dennis Walla, the Australian reporter sent to meet him slumped at a corner table slurping beer. He was a big man, also overweight, in his early forties, with bloodshot eyes, bags under them, and a ruddy complexion.

Emilio stood at the door to the restaurant and surveyed the room.

Dennis spotted him, thought it might be the so-called brother, and waved a copy of *Truth and Fact* in the air.

accent.

Emilio sat down. "*Truth and Fact?*" he asked.

"The very same," Dennis replied, thinking to himself that this guy must be a real dolt if he had to ask. "And you're Emilio Sierra?"

Emilio's brown eyes darted around the restaurant. He

spotted two women he fancied. They were expensively dressed and obviously out on a shopping spree. Dennis caught him watching. "Nice class of tarts in here," he said. "Wouldn't mind zipping up the back skirt of that one, eh?"

Emilio licked his lips. "I got a hot story to sell," he announced.

"Well, mate, that's exactly why we're here," Dennis said cheerfully, downing another healthy slug of beer. He peered across the table at Emilio. "You don't look like your sister, do you?"

"There's a certain family resemblance," Emilio replied proudly, almost preening, but managing to control himself.

"Are the two of you friendly?" Dennis probed.

"Of course we are," Emilio snapped. He hadn't planned on enduring a third degree. "Why wouldn't we be?"

"Don't get shirty with me, mate. You're here to sell her dirty little secrets, aren't you?"

"I'm here to make money," Emilio corrected, as if that made everything all right.

"Aren't we all," replied Dennis sagely.

One of the expensive-looking women got up and walked outside.

Emilio whistled softly as she passed his table. "These Beverly Hills women," he mumbled under his breath.

"I know what y'mean, mate," agreed Dennis. "They'll get you hotter than a hamburger on a barbecue."

Two bikers swaggered into the restaurant. Emilio thought he recognized one of them as a famous actor. He decided he should get himself some biker gear, it would look good on him. He should also lose a few pounds. But who had the time? And who could make the effort? Venus Maria had her own personal trainer – it was all right for her, she could afford those kinds of luxuries. Besides, she had an investment in her body. She made money from it.

In a way, he decided, she wasn't so different from a hooker. They were both hawking sex.

There was nothing wrong with him selling her secrets, he thought self-righteously. Why shouldn't he? He was her

236

brother, after all, and she treated him like a leper. Putting him out of her house. Sticking him in some crummy apartment while she lived in luxury. Giving him a station wagon to drive. A station wagon! He should be sitting proud in the latest Porsche, or a Ferrari at least. As her brother he had a certain standard to adhere to. People expected things.

"Well," Dennis said, leaning back and belching not so discreetly. "What have you got to tell me about your sister that we don't already know?"

Emilio glanced around. He wasn't sure he liked this man with the exceptionally loud mouth. Couldn't he be a little more discreet and talk in a quieter tone?

Emilio leaned close. "I don't think this is the place."

"Listen, we're not taking it any further than this until you tell me what you got for me," Dennis said loudly. "How do I even know you're her brother? Do you have any proof?"

Emilio had been expecting questions. He fished out his driving licence and handed it over.

Dennis checked it out. "OK, OK, so your name is Sierra. Big pickings. What does that prove?"

Emilio dived into his pocket again and came up with a picture of him and Venus Maria taken in Brooklyn. The early days. He thrust it at Dennis. "See?"

Dennis glanced at the photo and then at Emilio. "OK, OK, I believe you."

"If I tell you what I know," Emilio said craftily, "how much will you pay me?"

Dennis sighed wearily. It always got down to money.

different, and he'd get his bucks as long as he had something worthwhile to sell.

"It depends on what you got," Dennis said.

"She's sleeping with a married man," Emilio blurted out. "How much is *that* worth?"

"Who?" Dennis asked.

"Big time," Emilio said, lowering his voice. "Real big

237

time. When I tell you it'll blow you away. You'll sell more copies of your magazine than you've ever sold before."

"Sounds good t'me," Dennis said, picking his teeth with the corner of a book of matches.

Emilio was getting into it. "More than good," he promised.

Dennis was intrigued. "So who is it?"

Emilio backed off. "I'm not givin' out his name, not until we fix a price an' I get a cheque."

"We'll have to work this one out," Dennis said. "No name, no loot."

Emilio scowled.

"Come up with a name that means something, an' if it's worth anything to us we'll give you a fair amount of moola. But you have to substantiate whatever you tell us. Do you understand what that means?"

Emilio glared at him. "What do you think I am, an idiot?"

Yes, Dennis wanted to reply, but he kept quiet. This had the smell of a good story. And there was nothing *Truth and Fact* liked better than a headline-busting sex-filled superstar and married man good story.

Scandal. That was the name of the game. And nobody capitalized on scandal better than *Truth and Fact*.

Chapter 36

Lucky called Abe and told him that Harry Browning had been to see her and had his suspicions.

Abe was silent for a moment before saying, "Sure, I remember Harry. The man's a drunk. You be careful of him."

"Thanks a lot. What shall I do? We don't want the news of our deal leaking, do we?"

"You're not throwin' him out of a job when you take over, are you?" Abe asked.

"There's a lot of people I'll fire," she replied. "So far he's not one of them."

"Good," Abe said. "Leave it to me, girlie. I'll handle it."

"Thanks."

"I've got t'go now. My granddaughter's payin' me a duty visit."

Lucky knew what the visit was all about. Listening in on Mickey's conversations she'd discovered the reason he'd met with Martin Swanson. The New York tycoon was interested in buying or gaining control of a movie studio, and from Mickey's conversation with Ford Werne, whom he'd later confided in, it seemed one of the studios Martin was interested in was Panther.

"I'm gonna get Abigaile to sit down with her grandfather. See if the old man shows any interest in selling out," Mickey had said to Ford. "When she speaks to him, she won't tell him what they're willing to pay. She'll suggest he makes an agreement with me, then *I'll* sell the studio. That way I can get myself a cushy management deal and I'll be here for ever. And so will you, Ford. You and I work well together."

"What if he doesn't want to sell?" Ford had asked.

"Then I got a new plan. There's another studio my connection is considering. If he buys, I'm there."

"What about Panther? You'd walk away?"

"Hey," Mickey had said. "A deal is a deal is a deal. I treat the old man as good as he treats me, an' he's not treating me so good."

"You'd really go?"

"Do rabbits fuck? But only if the deal is right, Ford. It all comes down to the deal."

~~consisted that there was a man with no conscience. This life~~ consisted of business, his mistress, and brief trips home, although in the last couple of days he seemed to have added Madame Loretta to that list.

Boogie had found out Madame Loretta was the biggest madam in town, running a high-class brothel high in the

Hollywood Hills, supplying only beautiful young girls to the rich executives who could afford the exorbitant prices. Obviously Warner was not doing her job. Mickey was restless.

Olive returned to Los Angeles and managed to hobble into the studio on crutches.

Mickey, ever sympathetic, emerged from his office, glared at her, and said accusingly, "How could you do this to me?"

"I'm so sorry, Mr Stolli," Olive apologized, as if she could have helped it. She would have kissed his feet if she'd felt it would do any good.

Mickey merely glared at her and stomped back into his office.

"What happened with your fiancé? Did everything work out?" Lucky felt obliged to ask.

Sadly Olive shook her head. "It was not to be," she said, crestfallen. "I shouldn't have gone."

"Bad break," Lucky said, trying to look suitably sympathetic.

"These things happen," Olive glanced around the office, checking to make sure everything was in place. "How are *you* managing?"

"Fine," Lucky said carefully.

"Hmmm . . ." Olive didn't seem pleased. She'd rather hoped things would fall to pieces without her conscientious touch. "Mr Stolli isn't an easy man."

"I'm glad to say you taught me well. I seem to be making him happy."

Olive looked even more displeased. "I should be back in about six weeks," she said waspishly. "When my cast is off."

"Excellent." Lucky tried to make her feel good. "Everyone misses you."

Olive brightened. "What about your Mr Stone? Aren't you supposed to be working for him again?"

"I discussed it with Mr Stolli. He thought it best if I stayed here. Mr Stone doesn't mind. He's extending his vacation."

After more small-talk, Olive finally left the office. Later, Lucky observed her having lunch in the commissary with Harry Browning. She hoped Abe had already talked to Harry and warned him not to open his mouth.

With only one more week to go, Lucky felt she was coming to the end of a long prison sentence. It seemed amazing to her that some people actually led their lives like this. Day in, day out, being bossed around by a crude, irascible boss. Taking shit from all the people who visited his office. Putting up with rude sexist comments from the men. And this was while she'd made herself look as unattractive as possible. God knows what the other girls had to put up with, the secretaries in their miniskirts and low-cut blouses and long blonde hair.

Hmm . . . Maybe they loved it. Maybe they'd been brainwashed into thinking getting hit on by randy married men was a compliment.

Eddie Kane hadn't been in for over a week. Lucky decided to pay a visit to Brenda and Talon Nails, his two faithful secretaries who stood guard downstairs, and find out what was going on.

Now that she was officially known as Mickey Stolli's personal assistant, most of the other secretaries in the building knew who she was.

Brenda, as usual, was perusing magazines, while Talon Nails sat in the corner making personal phone calls.

"Is Mr Kane around?" Lucky asked. "We haven't seen him in a while. Mr Stolli was asking."

"He's sick," Brenda volunteered.

"Flu," Talon Nails added, covering the mouthpiece of the phone with her hand.

Lucky wondered if Eddie had the crap beaten out of him by Carlos Bonnatti's boys, or if this was merely an interim period while he struggled to get his act together and come up with a million bucks.

"Perhaps you can let our office know when he returns," Lucky said, all business.

Brenda put down her magazine. She had a snippy expression on her face. "May I ask you something?"

Talon Nails hung up the phone and shot Brenda a warning look.

"What?" asked Lucky.

"We were wondering," said Brenda belligerently.

"*She* was wondering," interjected Talon Nails.

"Bull!" Brenda said sharply. "*You* were wondering just as much as *I* was."

"Can we get to the point?" Lucky asked politely.

"How come you snuck in out of nowhere an' grabbed the key job around here?" Brenda stared at her accusingly.

What the hell, Lucky thought, would it hurt if she jumped out of character – just this once? The temptation was too much. "I slept with the boss," she answered, straight-faced – and made her exit.

Brenda and Talon Nails were speechless.

As usual Abigaile insisted Tabitha accompany her when she went to visit her grandfather. Naturally Tabitha complained, but Abigaile was having none of it. "You'll come with me and like it," she insisted firmly.

"I'll come with you, but I won't like it," Tabitha retorted with a sulky glare.

"Young lady," Abigaile said grandly, "it's about time you learned to treat me with respect. I do not appreciate your attitude."

"Please!" Tabitha said in disgust. "Don't start playing mommy with me now. It's a little late."

Abigaile glared at the girl. Thirteen years old and with a smarter mouth than her father.

Inga was as pleased to see them as they were to be there. "Come in," she said haughtily and stalked away, leaving them to fend for themselves.

They found old Abe out on the patio surrounded by newspapers, magazines, and a blaring television.

Dutifully Abigaile kissed him on the cheek. Dutifully Tabitha followed suit.

"Another month zip by already?" Abe asked against the bright sun.

"I beg your pardon?" said Abigaile.

242

"Another month," repeated Abe. "You only come every four weeks. I bet Mickey says the same thing!" He cackled at his own ribald joke.

Tabitha sneaked a smile. The thought of her mother coming was ludicrous. In fact, the thought of either of her parents having sex was the funniest notion she'd ever heard of.

Abigaile dusted off a patio chair with a tissue and sat down. "How are you feeling, Grandpa?" she asked solicitously.

Abe's canny old eyes crinkled. "Why? Whattaya care?" he asked suspiciously.

"Don't be silly, Grandpa. How come you're always so abrasive with me?"

"'Cause I calls it the way I sees it, girlie."

"I'm sorry you feel that way," Abigaile replied, primly, smoothing down the skirt of her Adolfo suit. "Now, Grandfather, there's something I wish to discuss with you."

"Go on," Abe said. "Shoot." He winked at Tabitha, who giggled.

"Well." Abigaile plunged ahead, deciding to ignore his irascible attitude. "You're not getting any younger."

Abe chortled. "Zippo – the girl's developin' brains. I'm not gettin' any younger. Eighty-eight years old and she finally realizes it!"

Abigaile took a deep breath. This was going to be difficult. She'd told Mickey he should come with her. Selfish as usual, he'd refused. Gamely she pressed on. "Um, what would you say if I told you that Mickey could possibly sell the studio?"

Tabitha picked up on that. "What do you wanna sell the studio for, it's Daddy's," she said sulkily. "He's gotta keep it. I wanna have my sweet sixteen there."

"Shhhhh," hissed Abigaile.

"I'm not gonna shhhh," Tabitha retorted. "You told me I had to come with you, so why do I have to shhhh?"

Abigaile fixed her daughter with a look. "Will you

243

kindly be quiet." Her tone would have quieted the Russian army.

Abe cackled. "Why would I wanna sell my studio?"

"Because," Abigaile replied in a cool, reasonable voice, "we can get an excellent price for it."

"Who's the 'we'?"

"Inga and you," Abigaile replied quickly. "And me. And of course, Tabitha."

Abe rose from his chair. "Big fat news," he said. "I could've had a hundred buyers for Panther if I'd've wanted to sell it."

"Then why didn't you?" Abigaile asked tartly.

"'Cause I didn't want to. An' if I did, it'd be none of *your* business, girlie." Without a backward glance he marched into the house.

Abigaile didn't feel like following him. She'd always been in awe of her grandfather, and now that he was a very old man she still felt uncomfortable in his presence.

"Can we go home now?" whined Tabitha.

Abigaile stood up. "Yes," she said, tight-lipped. "Let's do that."

Venus Maria strolled into Mickey's office at four o'clock. As she passed by Lucky's desk, she smiled and said, "Hi, howya doing?"

As soon as Mickey's door closed Lucky put on her earphones to listen in.

Venus Maria didn't play polite games. She got straight to the point. "I hate this script, Mickey," she said. "I hate it with a passion, and there's no way I'm doing it unless it's completely rewritten. Right now the script tells the story from a man's point of view. You promised me this was about a strong woman. A survivor. In this piece of crap she's just another victim. And I'm *not* playing victims."

"Aw, c'mon, baby, this is a great role for an actress," Mickey said in his most charming voice. "An Oscar winning role."

"Don't snow me with that tired old bullshit you hand

to all the other actresses around here, and I use the word loosely," Venus Maria said sharply. "A rewrite or I'm out of this project. And another thing—"

Cunt! "What?"

"The only way I'll take my clothes off is when the actor playing opposite me strips off too."

Mickey sounded disgusted. "Wake up, baby. Broads don't want to see naked guys on the screen. They're not interested in some poor schmuck with his schnickle hanging out."

"That's where you're wrong," Venus Maria declared. "That's *exactly* what they want to see."

He looked offended. "Maybe *you* do."

"No, not just me. Women get off on seeing guys with it all hanging out. And the reason we *don't* see it is because men run the film industry, and men can't handle the competition, so they don't want us getting an eyeful. I'm telling you, Mickey, I'm not walking around the screen bare-assed if my leading man is clothed. No fucking way."

"You're a demanding broad," Mickey griped.

"Yeah," Venus Maria agreed. "And I'm in the fortunate position of being able to demand whatever I want. Are we making contact here?"

He stood up from behind his desk. "You need a rewrite, you got a rewrite, OK?"

"Good. And if I *do* decide to sign for this movie, I also want co-star and director approval."

This broad was driving him crazy with her demands. "You got it. It's in your contract already."

"I haven't signed a contract for this film yet."

"It's in your old contract."

"That doesn't mean anything, and you know it. It has to be in *this* contract. In writing. And I'm not signing until I've seen the rewrite. Am I coming across loud and clear?"

"Yeah, yeah, yeah," he said disgustedly.

Venus Maria left his office without another word. She stopped at Lucky's desk. "Tell me," she said, "how can you work for such a jerk and stay sane?"

Lucky laughed. "It's not easy."

245

As soon as Venus Maria left, Mickey came running out, screaming and yelling.

"Who the *fuck* does that dumb broad think she is? Actresses! They're all the same. You make 'em a star an' they think they did it on their own without any goddamn help. If that bimbo didn't have a studio behind her, *and* a good director, *and* a great lighting cameraman, she'd be checking out dog meat in Safeway. Actresses!"

He didn't like actresses. He didn't like actors. Who did he like?

"I'm out of here," he said gruffly.

She knew better than to ask where he was going.

Ten minutes after he left, Johnny Romano made an unscheduled entrance, swaggering his way into the office, macho to the core.

"Hello, beautiful," he said. "Is the big man around?"

Johnny's faithful entourage hovered two steps behind him.

"Mr Stolli had to go out," Lucky said.

"Shame," exclaimed Johnny. "I thought I'd visit him. Celebrate."

"What are you celebrating, Mr Romano?" she asked politely.

"My movie, sweet stuff. It opens this week. Don't you keep up around here? *Motherfaker*'s gonna make this studio the biggest bucks it's ever seen." He leaned across her desk, his handsome, arrogant face insolently close to hers. "You know what a motherfaker is, beautiful?"

Yeah, you, asshole, she replied silently.

"Well, do you?"

She shook her head.

Johnny Romano laughed.

His entourage laughed.

They waited for her to laugh.

Lucky stared at him blankly.

"Hey, lady," Johnny said, leaning even closer. "Lighten up. You're way too serious. Working for Mickey is a tough business, huh? You want my autograph?"

On my butt, thought Lucky.

246

Without waiting for a reply, Johnny snapped his fingers. One of his entourage stepped forward with a signed photo.

"Hey, I'm gonna make your day an' personalize it," Johnny said magnanimously. "Gimme your name, baby."

"Luce," she muttered.

"Lucy. To Lucy. I'm gonna write To Lucy," Johnny said, scrawling an illegible *To Lucy* on the picture, *Love and heart, Johnny Romano* was already stamped on.

He handed her the signed picture with a flourish. "Tell the man I was here," he said. "An' enjoy yourself, you hear? Johnny Romano, he say so."

Big fucking deal!

Suddenly Lucky knew what Mickey meant. Actors! You could have 'em!

When she took over, things were going to be different around here.

Chapter 37

The telephone woke Gino at three in the morning.

"We're having a baby," Steven said urgently. "Can you get over to the hospital?"

Gino groped for his clothes. "We're having a baby," he repeated delightedly.

"Mary-Lou's in the delivery room now," Steven said, sounding stressed.

"I'm on my way," Gino assured him.

"Where's Lucky?"

"I'll try and contact her."

"She should be here with us," Steven said. "Mary-Lou's asking for her."

Gino was elated. Much to his annoyance Bobby lived in England and he hardly ever saw him. Now Steven and Mary-Lou were presenting him with another grandchild. It was an exciting moment.

Hurriedly pulling on his clothes, he called down to the

doorman and ordered a cab. Then he rushed out of his apartment.

Steven was pacing the floor of the hospital when he arrived.

Gino patted him on the shoulder. "You gotta calm down. Take a beat. This happens every day, y'know."

"Not to me," Steven said grimly.

"Shouldn't you be in there with her?"

"She doesn't want me," Steven said with a shrug. "Threw me out."

"How come?"

"Her mother's with her. You know what mothers are like. She's an old-fashioned lady, doesn't want the husband there. Hey – I don't mind. Who *wants* to be there? It's a frightening business."

Gino laughed. "I went through it twice," he said. "When Lucky was born. And Dario. I wish I'd been there for you, Steven."

It was a moment. Their eyes met and then they moved on.

"Did you get hold of Lucky?" Steven asked.

"I'm trying," Gino replied. "Don't worry. She's not gonna miss being an aunt."

Mary-Lou gave birth to a seven-pound ten-ounce little girl at eight o'clock in the morning. They named her Carioca Jade.

When Gino got back to his apartment he called Lucky in California and told her.

"Oh, no!" she exclaimed. "The baby was early and I missed it! Are they both all right?"

"They're fine," he assured her. "Mary-Lou came through it like a veteran."

"I'll send flowers. I'm so sorry I wasn't there. The good news is I'll be back next week."

"What makes you think that?" he said. "You're takin' over the studio. That's when you're really gonna have to spend time in LA."

"I guess you're right. But at least I'll be free to do what I want. I can fly into New York every weekend. I'll get

Panther running smoothly and then . . ." Realization sunk in. "Oh God, it'll take me a while, won't it?"

"Yup."

"Lennie will help me. He'll be ecstatic when he hears!"

Gino wasn't so sure. "Where is he?" he asked.

"I'll worry about that when I take over."

"If you're certain," Gino said.

"I'm certain," she replied.

Warner was trembling by the time Mickey finished making love to her. It gave him a great sense of power to have a six-foot black Vice cop trembling because he made love to her with such finesse. "Mickey, you're truly the best lover I ever had," she told him ecstatically.

Funny, one of Madame Loretta's hookers had said the very same thing to him two days earlier. A man couldn't ask for any further proof than that. First the hooker, now Warner. He really must be something between the sheets. It was a shame Abigaile never told him.

He tried to remember the last time he and Abigaile had made love. It had something to do with her birthday and a diamond bracelet. And it wasn't making love, it was a blow-job. But don't knock a blow-job when you're married. Actually, in a town where blow-jobs had been elevated to a fine art, Abigaile was way up there.

He wondered where she'd learned. They'd really never discussed their past lives. To this day, Abigaile had no idea about his illegitimate son who lived with his ex-girlfriend just outside of Chicago.

Abigaile would not be pleased if she found out.

Mickey had no intention of ever telling her, although, to his credit, over the years he'd supported his son with a healthy monthly cheque. He'd promised his ex-girlfriend that the money would keep on flowing as long as she kept her mouth shut.

He'd never seen his son. It was a part of his past he kept locked away. He never wanted it to interfere with his future.

When he got up to take a shower, Warner remained

spread-eagled on the bed like an impressive ebony carving. "I can't move," she gasped. "You're too much man for me."

If he was smothering her with furs and jewels he would have been suspicious of her words of praise. But Warner wanted nothing from him, so he was inclined to believe her.

He hurried into her small bathroom to take a shower. Unfortunately she didn't have a shower, just an attachment above the tub, which really pissed him off.

"You know somethin', honey," he yelled. "I gotta get you a new bathroom, I don't care what you say."

"No way, Mickey. You're not spending that kind of money on me."

She walked into the bathroom stark naked. She had breasts the like of which he'd never seen before. They were jutting and angular, with enormous black nipples. Edible tits.

The black girl at Madame Loretta's had small breasts, nothing like this. Warner's were straight out of a proud African tribe.

"Did your parents come from Africa?" he asked.

Warner laughed. "No, downtown LA! Why?"

He reached out to touch one more time before struggling with the shower, nearly tripping and breaking his neck. Then he wrapped himself in a too small bathsheet, pummelled himself dry, dressed, and left.

At home Abigaile was on red alert. She glared at him. "Why do *I* have to do all the dirty work?"

He sighed. "What's the matter now?"

"I saw my grandfather today. He's definitely not interested in selling. What made you think he would be? He's perfectly happy the way he is, and quite frankly, Mickey, we should be happy too. Because when he dies, Panther is ours, and we can do exactly as we please."

"Says you," Mickey said sourly.

Abigaile was ready for battle. "What's *that* supposed to mean?"

"Who knows *what* the old guy's gonna do?"

"Well, exactly. That's why I have to talk to you about it. You mentioned the other day you were considering accepting a job elsewhere. If you do, who's going to run Panther? And more important – who will inherit Panther?"

"*You'll* inherit, there's no question. You and your charming sister."

"Yes, I know, Mickey, but if somebody else is running the studio, it could create problems." She shook her head, making the decision for both of them. "You're going to have to turn Martin Swanson down."

"Abigaile, I am *not* saying no to Martin Swanson if it means more money."

"Why? You're making a million dollars a year, plus whatever you can steal. Isn't that enough?"

He looked at her in disgust. "Thanks a lot. It's great to have a really supportive wife. I thrive on the support you give me, Abigaile."

She took his sarcasm and swallowed it. "Thank you, Mickey. I aim to please."

Chapter 38

Effie Webster loved giving parties. They were an important part of her life. She couldn't imagine not giving them. After all, Effie and Yul Webster were famous for their parties.

Half the fun was putting together an eclectic mix. Anyone from starving actors and artists to successful Broadway producers. Or maybe not-so-starving artists.

Effie knew everyone. Planning a party for Martin Swanson's birthday was not difficult, because Martin and Deena knew everyone, too. The hard part was who not to invite.

Effie decided a theme party would be fun. She sent out black invitations with gold printing: COME AS YOUR FAVOURITE FANTASY. What a charming way to delve into the psyches of the rich and famous. "Come as your favourite fantasy" was an invitation to reveal your very secret self – an invitation most people couldn't resist.

Effie decided she was going to dress up as Queen Nefertiti. "Darling," she informed Deena on the phone, "I've always wanted to be a queen, and this is a perfect opportunity. What are *you* coming as?"

Deena had given it a lot of consideration. "I've decided on Marlene Dietrich. The way she looked in *The Blue Angel*."

"Wonderful idea!" Effie exclaimed, wishing she'd thought of it. "With *your* legs you'll be a sensation! But I suppose that's the whole point, isn't it?"

"Yes," Deena agreed. "I suppose it is."

She put down the phone and thought about Martin. He hadn't said a word about divorce. In fact, since he'd come back from LA, he'd thrown himself into business, concentrating on his Swanson sports stadium, where he planned to stage the next world heavyweight fight if he could arrange it. And the new luxury automobile soon to be launched. The Swanson.

Martin was very excited about the Swanson. It was a sleek and powerful car – a car that represented everything he wanted the public to know about him.

Martin planned to present the Swanson at a big media publicity launch in Detroit.

Deena felt sure her errant husband wasn't going to jeopardize the anticipated publicity on the Swanson for a tawdry little slut like Venus Maria.

She tried to imagine what hold the girl had over him. It was sexual, of course.

But why? Martin wasn't particularly interested in sex.

Deena shook her head; she couldn't figure it out. She could only stand by, wait, and see what happened.

If the worst happened she had her solution.

Brigette was excited about the party, although she didn't let on to Nona, who appeared to take it all very casually. To Brigette it was a return to the real world. She'd been shut up in boarding school for so long, and when she *was*

252

allowed out it was always with Charlotte, who never took her anywhere. Now here she was, part of an exciting life again, back in the big city.

"I can't make up my mind whether we should go or not," Nona vacillated. "How about taking in a movie instead and skipping the party?"

"I vote for the party." Brigette was full of enthusiasm and dying to go. "It'll be a blast."

"My idea of a blast is *not* attending my parents' crazy parties." Finally Brigette got her to agree that it might be a laugh. The next question was, who would they go as?

"I'll be Janet Jackson," Nona decided.

"That's not exactly easy to put together," Brigette pointed out.

Nona thought about it. "Why not? I'll put on an incredible black makeup. And I'll wear a Janet Jackson wig, tight jeans, and a motorcycle jacket. I can borrow Paul's. He's coming to the party you know."

"What's *his* favourite fantasy?" Brigette inquired, trying not to sound too interested.

"Probably Picasso mixed with Donald Trump's money." Nona replied dryly.

Eventually they decided it would be fun if they both dressed up as Venus Maria.

Nona giggled. "We'll blow everybody's mind!"

"She's not going to be there, is she?" Brigette asked anxiously, thinking it wouldn't be too cool if she was.

"You never know *who's* going to turn up at my parents' parties," Nona answered.

They went on a wild shopping spree in the Village, running into places Effie would never dream of visiting. They arrived home with a selection of outlandish clothes, everything from long, army surplus overcoats to frilled miniskirts, leather bustiers, and midriff-exposing tops.

"Venus Maria always puts together such a fantastic look," Nona said, poring over an interview with Venus in one of the latest magazines. "I think she's great. It's obvious she doesn't give a damn about anybody."

Brigette laughed. "Just like you, huh?"

"What's so bad about that? *My* opinion is that women do what men *think* they should do. I'm not going to be like that when I'm old."

"What's old?"

"It says here Venus Maria is twenty-five. I guess she's sort of old."

Brigette laughed again. "Don't let your mother hear you say that!"

"Effie is forever young," Nona said with a wicked grin. "She'll be young when she's eighty. I bet she'll still have that crazy streak of green hair, and wear outlandish clothes. Mom's quite a character."

"You're fortunate to have her," Brigette said wistfully.

"I know," Nona agreed. "Oh, and by the way, have you spoken to your stepfather? When are we going to Malibu? Effie needs to know. It's not that she's dying to get rid of us, but she's got this little side trip planned to Bangkok and she doesn't want us tagging along."

"I've left a message with Lennie's agent to call me here," Brigette said. "I heard he walked off the movie, and nobody seems to know where he is. He'll come through. Lennie won't let me down. He promised me Malibu, and Lennie always keeps his promises."

"Great!" exclaimed Nona. "I don't know about you, but *I* can't wait."

Emilio Sierra and Dennis Walla formed an alliance. It was not a relationship based on trust, more on greed. They had a couple of meetings bickering about money back and forth. Emilio flatly refused to say who Venus Maria's married lover was until a price was settled. Dennis, on the other hand, insisted there could be no price until Emilio revealed his information.

After their initial meeting in Café Roma, they got together in a seedy coffee shop on Pico and tried to hammer it out. Finally they met at the offices of *Truth and Fact* in Hollywood.

Emilio said he wanted fifty thousand dollars. *Truth and*

Fact agreed to pay it if the name he gave them was worth it. Now they were meeting to finalize the deal.

"'Morning, mate," Dennis greeted him, sitting behind a littered desk, smoking a foul-smelling cheap cigar. "Today's the day, huh?" A mangy cat strolled by.

Emilio nodded uneasily. He wasn't sure if he should be here. Appearing at the offices of *Truth and Fact* was really blowing his cover. When he'd walked through the main room he'd noticed people at desks, behind typewriters, glancing in his direction. He felt like a traitor! And yet why shouldn't he do what he had to if it made him money?

Dennis introduced him to one of his colleagues, a short, squat Englishman with a rat face, scraggly eyebrows, and a droopy little moustache.

"Who's he?" Emilio asked suspiciously.

"We gotta have a witness," Dennis explained. "Can't hand over a cheque without a witness. You gotta give us the facts, Emilio. Times, places, names. The lot."

Emilio nodded. "I know all that," he said rather crossly. God, you would think it would be easier than this. Why couldn't he just tell them who she was sleeping with, take his money, and go?

"Sit down," said Dennis. "Want a beer?"

Emilio shook his head. For the last week he'd been working on his gut. This had meant cutting out beer – a real drag.

When he had his fifty thousand dollars he wanted to be in better shape. He'd buy a decent car, new clothes, and move to a luxurious apartment. Emilio Sierra was going places.

"Let's get this show on the road," Dennis said, switching on a tape recorder.

"Why are you doing that?" Emilio asked, alarmed.

"I keep on telling you," Dennis replied patiently. "We need the proof. We don't plan on getting sued, do we?"

Emilio thought about that one. "How can you be sued if it all happened?" he asked.

"You'd be surprised who tries it on. Sinatra, Romano, Reynolds, the biggies. They're stupid, 'cause they never

255

win. It ends up costing them big money. But we don't want to be dragged through the courts for years, do we?"

"No," agreed Emilio, wondering if Venus Maria would sue.

"OK, shoot," said Dennis, releasing the pause button.

Emilio felt hot. A thin trickle of sweat ran down his neck. He had an ache in his gut. He didn't feel well. "It's like this," he said, sitting down. "Uh . . . where's my cheque?"

Dennis opened his desk drawer and took out a cheque for five thousand dollars. He waved it under Emilio's nose. "You get this now, the rest when the story's ready for press."

Emilio tried to grab it.

Dennis snatched it out of reach. "Not so fast. I'm only showing it to you. Before you get it we need the name. If it's worth something to us an' you've got proof, it's yours, an' plenty more to come."

Shit, Emilio thought, *better get this over and done with*, "The boyfriend's name is Martin Swanson." He blurted it quickly, savouring the shock and amazement on both men's faces.

Dennis let out a long, low whistle. "Martin Swanson! The New York biggie?"

"Martin Swanson?" repeated the Englishman. "This is juicy stuff."

"Shit!" exclaimed Dennis happily. "If you can back this one up, you've given us a good one, mate."

"Oh, I can back it up," Emilio boasted cockily. "I even have a picture of them together." His trump card.

"A picture?" Dennis said, getting more excited. "You never mentioned you had photos."

Emilio thought quickly. "Yeah, well, if you want the picture, it's extra."

"Oh," said Dennis. "The picture is extra?"

"If you want it," Emilio said.

"We want it," Dennis said.

Martin Swanson stood in his dressing room and examined

his face in a magnifying mirror. He reached for the tweezers and plucked a few offending hairs from beneath his eyebrows. Then he stood back and admired himself in a full-length mirror. He was dressed as a Confederate soldier. Deena had thought it an original costume. He had to admit the outfit suited him.

Birthdays usually sunk him into a deep depression, but today he felt particularly good. It seemed he had a lot of friends. Presents had been arriving at the house all day, along with flowers, balloons, and greeting telegrams.

Deena had presented him with a solid gold picture frame. In it she had placed their wedding picture. There they were, Deena and Martin Swanson, standing outside the church, the happy couple.

Was it only ten years ago? It seemed like a lifetime. When he'd married Deena he had been ready to settle down. Who'd have thought he'd ever find a woman like Venus Maria?

Venus had called him at his office earlier. "Happy birthday, Martin," she'd said long-distance. "I'm disappointed you couldn't get out here to celebrate with me."

"It's been difficult," he'd replied. "Business."

"You shouldn't let business run your life," she'd chided. "All work and no play makes Martin a very dull boy indeed."

He'd laughed. "I'm never dull when I'm around you, am I?"

"Baby, *I* make sure of that."

They'd talked for a few minutes more. She hadn't said, "When am I going to see you?" She didn't have to. He knew it was on her mind. It was on his mind, too. Their relationship had reached the point where she required more than promises.

It wasn't easy. Sure he could divorce Deena. It would probably cost him a bundle, even though he'd made her sign a prenuptial agreement, and they'd suffer through a wave of bad publicity. But after that he'd be free to do whatever he wanted.

OK, so right now they were the Swansons. They owned

New York. But Martin Swanson on his own could still own New York.

It was a difficult decision, and one he wasn't quite ready to make. At the end of the phone conversation with Venus Maria he'd promised to fly to LA the following week. The thought excited him. She really knew how to turn him on. Her little tricks and surprises were something else. For a moment he allowed his thoughts to linger on the two hookers and the silk scarves. Quite an event. Venus Maria knew how to keep a man interested.

One final glance and he strolled out of his dressing room, satisfied with his appearance.

Deena was downstairs, her full-length sable coat covering her outfit for the evening.

"Let's have a look at you," Martin said easily.

She swung around, dropping her coat.

"Wow!" Martin was impressed. He'd married a beautiful woman.

Deena had on some outfit. Her long legs were encased in sleek black stockings, and the rest of her get-up was a carbon copy of the famous Marlene Dietrich costume in *The Blue Angel*. Deena, when she wanted to, could turn herself into a real stunner.

"You're very handsome tonight, Martin," she said, reaching out to smooth the back of his hair.

"And you – well, what can I tell you? You've really done it, haven't you?" He laughed. "Effie will be a jealous wreck."

Deena smiled triumphantly. "Why is that?" she inquired.

"Because, my dear" – he held out his arm – "tonight, *everyone* is going to be looking at you. Including me," he added.

Deena felt her triumph grow. She raised an eyebrow. "Really?"

"Really," he said.

Chapter 39

There was not much spare time in Venus Maria's life. From the moment she got up in the morning until the moment she went to bed at night, she was always busy doing something. If it wasn't her workouts, it was rehearsals for her videos. If it wasn't rehearsals, she was in the studio recording. Or she was sitting with the two songwriters she liked to work with, making suggestions as far as lyrics were concerned. Several times a week she worked with Ron. He still choreographed all her routines, and they were still best friends – in spite of the Ken Doll.

Then there was her acting. She tried to read every script sent to her. And if she didn't have time, she depended on a reader she employed.

Frankly, she was annoyed that Martin hadn't flown back for his birthday as he'd promised. She confided in Ron while they sweated their way through a new dance routine in his rehearsal room.

"What do you want from the man?" Ron asked, straight to the point as usual.

"To be with me all the time," she said.

"That's a ridiculous suggestion," Ron exclaimed truthfully. "Martin Swanson is based in New York. You're here. What kind of life would the two of you have together? He'd be out screwing around and so would you. I *know* you, Venus."

"Maybe you don't know me as well as you think you do," she replied indignantly.

"Come off it," Ron said. "I know you better than anybody. I knew you when – before all the big-deal star stuff. I knew you when Venus Maria was just a twitch in your fanny."

"And don't *you* forget, Ron," she reiterated. "I knew *you* before you were the gay prince of Hollywood."

"The what?"

"You heard," she replied tartly.

"Oh, thank you *so* much, Madame. I always wanted to be a gay prince."

"And may I be the first to tell you you're doing a marvellous job. You and the Ken Doll are the talk of boys' town."

Ron was annoyed. "Don't call him the Ken Doll. I've told you a million times."

She brushed a hand through her platinum hair. "That's what he is."

"Listen, honey, don't talk about *my* lover and I won't talk about *yours*, OK?"

They glared at each other and continued the rehearsal.

Ron was a hard taskmaster. When he choreographed a routine it had to be perfect. And he made sure Venus Maria practised every move before he put her with the other dancers. She was his star pupil.

Secretly she knew that Ron believed he was totally responsible for her success. It didn't bother her. If he wished to take the credit, let him do so. She knew she would have gotten to the top with or without Ron. He'd been a great help, especially in the early days, but now she didn't need him.

She didn't need anybody.

Except Martin.

Effie greeted all her guests personally. Not for her an army of servants, although there were plenty around. Effie considered the personal touch important to make any party successful.

When Deena and Martin arrived, Effie was at the door to welcome them.

Deena slid her sable coat off her shoulders.

"My God!" Yul said, hovering behind Effie. "I never realized you had such incredible legs."

Deena smiled her cool smile. Tonight she was going to make every man in the room hot, and she knew it.

"You look divine, darling," enthused Effie. "And

Martin, the handsome soldier look suits you. You should do it more often. I simply adore a uniform."

"I feel like a fool," Martin said, perfectly at ease.

Yul, who was dressed as a caveman, said, "*You* feel like a fool? Try this outfit for ten minutes."

Martin laughed and got lost in a sea of greetings. Everyone wanted to wish him a happy birthday. He was Mister Popular.

Gathered in a corner, Brigette, Nona, and Paul watched the activities.

"Martin Swanson is such a corny old smoothie," Nona proclaimed. "Just watch him work a room. What an operator!"

"Wow," Paul said. "Get a load of his old lady's legs."

"She's too ancient for you *and* she's married," Nona said snappishly.

"But she's rich," Paul remarked.

"Will you get off it? She's not as rich as Brigette."

"Oh well, we all know it's impossible for anyone to be as rich as Brigette. And while we're on the subject, since she's so rich, how come you two didn't come up with decent outfits? You look like a couple of tarts."

Nona narrowed her eyes. "We're supposed to be Venus Maria, can't you tell?"

"Nope," replied Paul. "You still look like two little tramps."

"Honestly!" Nona said crossly. "You're so full of bullshit."

"Takes one to know one."

"Do you two fight all the time?" Brigette asked curiously.

"This isn't fighting," said Paul.

"Oh, no!" agreed Nona. "You should see us when we *really* go at it!"

Paul had decided not to play dress-up, refusing to change his all-black outfit. Nobody seemed to notice except Brigette, who couldn't keep her eyes off him, much as she tried.

She remembered the first time she'd spotted her first

boyfriend, Tim Wealth. It seemed such a long time ago, and yet it couldn't be more than two years. Tim had been tall and gangly with a thin face, nice smile, and longish hair. The first time she'd spotted him at the opening of Lucky's hotel, it had been love at first sight. Later that same night he'd invited her to his hotel suite, made her snort coke, and instructed her to undress. He'd had no idea who she was or that she was not quite fifteen. And then he'd made love to her. Fast and furious.

Memories of Tim were making her uncomfortably warm. She took off her short brocade jacket. Underneath she wore a skimpy white bra and minuscule skirt.

Paul second-glanced her. "Not bad," he said. "It's a shame you're still a baby."

I was even more of a baby when I met Tim Wealth, she thought. *It didn't bother him.*

Paul's eyes followed Deena's seductive legs across the room. "She sure looks good tonight," he sighed lustfuly.

"She's old enough to be your mother," Nona said disapprovingly.

"Not quite."

"Almost," Nona countered.

He got up. "I'm leaving you two nymphets to fend for yourselves. I'll be back in a minute."

"I don't believe it!" Nona exclaimed. "He's planning to hit on Deena Swanson. Can you imagine? He's going to hit on Mommy's best friend!"

Brigette forced a laugh. She was jealous. But she was determined not to let anybody see it, because falling in love meant heartbreak, and Brigette knew heartbreak only too well.

"Howya doin', Mrs S.?"

Deena turned to look at the thin young man with the intense stare. "Have we met?" she asked coolly.

His eyes clashed with hers. He had a very direct gaze. "It's me – Paul. Effie's son."

She was genuinely surprised. "Oh my God, Paul. How you've changed. It's been so long since I've seen you."

"It has been a while," he agreed. "I was travelling around Europe. Backpacking. Not quite your style, huh?"

"You were a little boy last time we . . . uh . . . we were together," she said.

He gave her the intense stare. "That sounds sexy, Deena."

Was he coming on to her? No. Impossible. He was just a kid . . . albeit a very attractive one. "I beg your pardon?"

"Well, y'know . . . like 'when we were together' sounds sort of sexy. Don'tcha think?"

"Paul, are you flirting with me?"

Now came the charming smile. "I hope so. If not, I'm doing a lousy job."

Deena couldn't help smiling back. "It's nice to see you, dear," she said. "And I can tell you've inherited your mother's sense of fun."

He moved on to the brooding look. "Enough with the *dear*. Don't try and put me down, Deena."

"I wouldn't dream of it."

Time to challenge her. "You wouldn't dream of what?"

"I wouldn't dream of trying to put you down, Paul. Where *is* your mother?"

"She's around. Why? Do you need her to get you out of this?"

Deena shook her head.

Paul switched moods and grinned. "Feeling threatened?"

"By you? I don't think so, dear." She turned her back and walked briskly away.

"Nice legs," he said to her retreating back.

He felt it was a victory. Satisfied, he returned to Nona and Brigette.

"She totally wants my body," he said. "I had to say no."

"Really," said Nona sarcastically. "How nice for you. I always knew you were the biggest liar in the world."

"Don't believe me. See if I care." Nonchalantly he turned his attention to Brigette. "Can I bug you for a loan?

Like maybe a hundred thousand big ones? I'll pay you back when I'm rich and famous."

"Ha!" snorted Nona.

"I don't control my money," Brigette muttered. "It's all in various trusts."

"And even if she did," Nona interrupted, "you'd be the last person to get any. *I'd* be the first, wouldn't I?"

Brigette would never admit it, but she thought Paul was even more attractive than Tim Wealth.

Emilio signed the contract. He probably should have taken it to some high-powered Hollywood lawyer and had him look it over – but Emilio knew what he was doing. His business instincts were good. After all, he'd negotiated himself a fat fifty thousand dollars without any help from some sharp lawyer. Now all he had to do was give them the exclusive story of Venus Maria and her married lover.

The first thing he did was open up a bank account. Then he promptly withdrew five thousand dollars in cash, and hit the town, taking in all the clubs.

Everyone who knew him was surprised. "Where'd you score the bucks, man?" they asked. They were all aware that Emilio was an expert at using his sister's name, joining people's tables, and getting his drinks put on other people's tabs.

"My sister gave it to me," Emilio replied with a jaunty wink.

In a way it was true. Without Venus Maria, he certainly wouldn't have fifty thousand stashed away. Well, only five for now, but he'd get the balance when the story was written and checked out.

Several margaritas later he picked up a hooker at one of the bars. He didn't realize she was a hooker. She said she was an actress. They all said they were actresses or models. It was the Hollywood game.

She had long dyed blonde hair and even longer skinny legs. She wore a very short red dress cut low in the back and even lower in the front. There was not much left to anybody's imagination.

Emilio wasn't into imagining, he was into celebrating.

He took the girl back to his apartment and made love to her for a fast five minutes.

"Is that it?" she asked indignantly when he was through. "I came here for a good time. I coulda had more action with a jack-rabbit!"

"I gave you a good time," Emilio mumbled, wishing she'd get the hell out.

She demanded fifty bucks for a cab home.

He was outraged. "Fifty bucks for a cab?"

"Honey, I didn't come here for your smile."

Grumbling, Emilio gave her a twenty and shoved her out.

When she was gone he switched on the television and fantasized over Gloria Estafan. Now she was a *real* woman. He bet Gloria Estafan wouldn't start asking him for fifty bucks.

Eventually he fell asleep. Tomorrow he had another session with Dennis and his tape recorder. They were progressing on the story.

Soon he would be headline news. It was some kind of kick.

Emilio Sierra was going to be famous too.

Chapter 40

Eddie Kane thought he might be going crazy, totally freaking out. And nobody wanted to help him, there wasn't one person he could trust.

He roamed around his house like a man possessed. God damn it! Ten days ago he'd had everything – plenty of money, a gorgeous wife – things were running smoothly. And he'd had his coke to keep him warm. A little snort of cocaine and everything looked rosy. Now it took more than a little snort to get him out of bed in the morning.

He'd known he was in trouble when Mickey stopped

talking to him. Mickey, whom he'd depended on over the years and always turned to.

So he'd got them into a jam. Jesus Christ, it wasn't like they were standing at gunpoint in front of the fucking Mexican army. It was a mess a million bucks could solve. And Mickey Stolli and Panther Studios were going to have to come up with the money. Fast.

But no, Mickey was trying to act like a big man and pretend it wasn't his responsibility. Mickey was full of crap.

The calls had started nicely enough. "Hey, Eddie, you owe us money. When's it coming?" Then they'd progressed to "Hey, Eddie, ya better get the bucks soon. Mr Bonnatti ain't a patient man." And now it was "Eddie, your time is up. Mr Bonnatti don't appreciate bein' kept waiting."

At first it had seemed like such a sweet irresistible deal. Eddie had been introduced to Carlos Bonnatti in New York at Le Club. Actually he'd known one of the women Bonnatti was with, his LA cocaine connection, Kathleen Le Paul.

After Kathleen introduced him to Carlos they'd got to talking. "Panther Pictures, huh?" Carlos had said. "I'm in the picture business myself."

"You are?" Eddie had asked, surprised, thinking that he'd never heard of him.

"Yeah," Carlos had laughed. "We don't quite make your style of movies."

Eddie had been accused of a lot of things in his time, but being slow was not one of them. "You're into the other side of the tennis net, huh?" he'd said smoothly.

"There's plenty of money in it," Bonnatti had replied. "Plenty. My brother, Santino, started the business. When he, uh, unfortunately passed away, I took over. I got a guy running it out on the West Coast, an' my own people in New York. Our only real problem is abroad."

It went on from there. Bonnatti was looking for a way to get his porno product into Europe. There were certain countries such as Spain and Italy that had a block on importing pornographic material.

Eddie came up with the perfect solution: smuggle it in with legitimate product. Who was going to question Panther Studios when they shipped in their big movies?

Bonnatti was easy to convince. When Eddie smelled a deal he went all the way. "Maybe I can help you," he'd said. And they'd worked out a tentative arrangement.

All Eddie had to do was run it by Mickey, guaranteeing him a big chunk of the action.

He'd thought about it long and hard before going to him. First he'd formed his own shell company in Liechtenstein, reckoning he could shift the European funds through the company without becoming personally involved.

Mickey was immediately receptive to the idea. "Just money, no risk?" he'd asked.

"That's the deal," Eddie had said. "A fifty-fifty split with Bonnatti, an' I hand you half my action. It's as easy as that."

Mickey had agreed.

Screw Mickey. For three years he'd been happy to take the money when things were running smoothly. Now there was trouble, he didn't want to know.

Eddie wondered how everybody had found out he was creaming off the top. Fuck it, he was the one doing all the work, setting up the deals in the various countries, funnelling the money through. If anybody was going to get busted, it was him. So why shouldn't he take more than his fair share?

A million bucks was far more than his fair share, and he was busted. Carlos Bonnatti had discovered he was stealing, and Bonnatti wanted what was his.

Leslie followed Eddie around the house looking mournful. "How can I help?" she asked for the tenth time.

He was in no mood for the caring-wife bit. "By shutting up," he snapped.

It occurred to him that the only way he could raise the money in a hurry was by selling their only real asset.

"We gotta put the house on the market," he announced,

"Call a realtor an' tell 'em we need a cash sale an' we need it like yesterday."

Leslie looked dismayed, but she did as he told her, even though they both knew it wasn't going to be fast enough.

Now that he had the threat of Bonnatti breathing in his face he didn't know what else to do.

Eddie had sensed it was going to be a bad day the moment he'd woken up. It was Friday. There was a thick smog hanging over the beach. There was a thick smog hanging over his head. He felt more than depressed. Rolling across the bed he reached for the phone and called Kathleen Le Paul. "Come by my house," he ordered. "I need medication."

"I don't make house calls," she replied tersely, not exactly thrilled to hear from him.

His head was exploding. "I'm out of the office."

"I noticed. If you'd let me know I could have saved myself a trip."

"Listen, honey, I've got the flu. Whaddaya want from me? Come to my house. Bring the goods."

"Cash?"

"Yeah."

"You're into me for fifteen hundred from last week."

"It's waitin' for you."

Reluctantly she agreed, and they arranged a noon rendezvous.

Leslie was in the kitchen frying eggs and bacon. The smell made him sick. "I'm cooking breakfast for you," she sang out, too goddamn cheerful for her own good.

"Take off your clothes," he said.

She spun around, startled. "What?"

"Take off your clothes," he repeated. "How about cooking my breakfast bare-assed naked?"

"Eddie, don't be like this," she pleaded. There was pain in her voice but he failed to hear it.

"Aw, forget it." He stomped back into the bedroom. And then he felt bad. Poor kid, he was taking it out on her, but who else did he have to take it out on?

Five minutes later Leslie surprised him. She walked into

the bedroom wearing nothing but high heels and a frilly bib apron.

What a body! For the first time in weeks he felt the old juices begin to flow. "Hey," he said, "come to Poppa!"

"It's what you wanted, isn't it?" she asked stiffly.

"I wasn't serious," he said, tweaking her breasts. "Only now that you're here . . ."

He lay back and let her do all the work. She was very good at performing. For a girl from Iowa she sure knew plenty . . .

Later he wolfed breakfast, downed a couple of vodkas, smoked a joint, and went for a walk along the beach.

When he got back to his house, Carlos Bonnatti was sitting in his living room.

A white-faced Leslie said, "I didn't know you were expecting company."

Eddie stared at Carlos. He felt his skin crawl. "Neither did I."

Carlos Bonnatti was a stockily built man in his mid-forties with tightly curled hair, drooping eyelids, sallow skin, and an indolent expression.

"I was in the neighbourhood," he said easily. "Thought I'd drop by."

"Since when was your neighbourhood the beach?" Eddie asked, glaring at him.

Carlos waved a vague hand in the air. "Since you owe me a million bucks," he said, "an' since I don't seem to be getting no answers to my questions, I figured I'd make a side trip, see what's goin' on. You have anythin' to say for yourself, Eddie?"

Leslie hovered at the back of the room, paralysed with fear. She'd known something was up the moment the long black limousine had deposited Carlos Bonnatti at her door with two heavies stationed right behind him. When she'd opened the door he hadn't even asked if he could come in, merely pushed past her, saying a terse "I'm here to see Eddie," as if that was explanation enough.

"You shouldn't have come here," Eddie muttered. "I

don't need this shit. You'll get your money, I told you that last week."

"Last week was then," Carlos said. "Now is now. I want my money by Monday morning or you know what you can expect."

"Are you threatening me?" Eddie demanded, full of false bravado.

"Call it a threat if you want," Carlos replied mildly. "You should know one thing – Carlos Bonnatti don't make threats. He makes things happen. Either I get what's owed me by Monday, or you an' I are outta business. In fact" – Carlos rose to his feet – "you're likely to find you won't be doing business with nobody." He walked towards the door, stopping to touch Leslie on her bare shoulder. "Pretty wife," he said. "Very pretty." And then he was gone.

Eddie rushed into the bathroom and threw up. When he emerged, Leslie was waiting, gazing at him expectantly, those damn big eyes staring at him, trusting him to come up with an answer to all of this.

"I'll go see Mickey," he said quickly. "Don't worry, babe, I'll have this worked out today."

"You will?"

"This is a promise."

He hugged her and hurried outside to his car.

Now it was Leslie's turn to pace around the house. She didn't know what to do. She only knew Eddie was in trouble, and there had to be some way she could help.

Picking up the phone she dialled Madame Loretta's number.

When the older woman got on the line, Leslie sobbed out her story. "Can you help me?" she begged.

"Leave him," Madame Loretta advised. "You're still young and beautiful. There's plenty of other men. Come back to work. I'll find you another one."

Leslie was shocked. "But I don't want anyone else," she protested. "I love Eddie."

"Love's no good," Madame Loretta warned her. "He'll

bring you down with him. I've seen this happen before. Leave him, Leslie, before it's too late."

"No," Leslie replied. "I could never leave Eddie. I love him."

"Then I can't help you," Madame Loretta said brusquely, and put the phone down.

Chapter 41

Eddie Kane allowed his white Maserati to rip on the Pacific Coast Highway. When he hit the freeway he really let loose.

Five minutes later he was pulled over by a motorcycle cop.

The cop was movie-star handsome as he swaggered towards Eddie's window. "Hey, bud, you going for a world record or what?" the cop said, pulling out his notebook.

Eddie sensed this was somebody he could deal with. "Listen, uh, I got a hot date, you know how it is."

The cop grinned. He certainly knew how it was.

"Nice car," he remarked, pen poised for action.

"I worked hard to get it," Eddie said, trying to sound humble.

"You been drinking?" the cop asked.

Eddie laughed mirthlessly. He knew he looked like a bum. Only the car gave him credibility. "Who me?" he said. "Are you serious?"

The cop rocked back and forth on the heels of his boots. "Yes, I'm serious. Have you been drinking?"

Eddie forced a friendly smile. "Let me introduce myself. Eddie Kane. Head of Distribution at Panther Studios. Hey – did you ever think about being an actor?"

"Yeah, I've thought about it," the cop said. "Who hasn't, in this town?"

"Tell you what," Eddie said in his persuasive voice. "I'll

271

give you my card an' you can call me at the studio. I'll see if I can get you an audition."

The cop laughed.

Eddie fished out one of his cards and handed it over. "I'm serious. What are you laughing at?"

The cop laughed again. "I've heard of being discovered, but this is ridiculous!"

"You've got charisma," Eddie said, rising to the occasion. "You've got the look. And a sense of humour. So come on, I'll try to help you, an' you can help me. Let me go, huh? I'm late for an appointment."

It was the one good thing that happened to Eddie that day. The cop pocketed his card and waved him on his way.

Undaunted, Eddie did not slow down. He hit the gas all the way to Panther.

Mickey was in a meeting with a writer on one of his special projects. When Eddie burst into his office he was taken by surprise.

Lucky let him through without question. This was her last day at the studio and she didn't care what happened.

The writer, an earnest young man, leaped to his feet as soon as Eddie entered. Eddie looked like a madman with his ten days' growth of beard, crumpled clothes, and wild bloodshot eyes.

"I'm through takin' shit," Eddie yelled, placing both hands on Mickey's desk and glaring at him. "Carlos Bonnatti came to my house. My fucking *house*, for crissakes! No more, Mickey. You're in this with me, an' there's no way you're backin' out. Panther's gotta pay him."

Mickey's eyes narrowed. This was what happened when you tried to assist a friend? "Luce," he shouted.

No acknowledgement.

"Get the guards up here," he screamed.

"You get the fucking guards an' you got more trouble than you ever believed possible," Eddie yelled, grabbing Mickey by the lapels of his sports jacket. "I'll go to Abe Panther. I'll spill the works. Your fat ass won't be worth a dime."

The writer slowly and carefully backed his way towards the door. He'd heard about these scenes where unhinged maniacs went on a rampage. Sometimes they had a gun. This could get nasty. "I'll come back later, Mr Stolli," he said.

"Get your hands off my jacket," Mickey growled at Eddie.

"Fuck you," replied Eddie.

They began to scuffle.

The writer scuttled out of the office, slamming the door behind him.

Lucky glanced up from her desk.

"Did you call the guards?" the writer asked urgently.

"I think they'll be able to work it out between them, don't you?" she said sweetly.

Shaking his head, the writer ran out of there. He was paid to write, not get involved in grudge battles.

Just as she was recovering from Madame Loretta's callous attitude, the doorbell rang.

Tentatively Leslie peered through the peephole. A woman stood on the other side of the door. A well-dressed, heavily made up woman. "Yes?" Leslie called out. "Can I help you?"

"Where's Eddie?" the woman said irritably.

"He's not here."

"Shit! We had an appointment."

"I'm Mrs Kane," Leslie said, attempting to assert herself. "And who are *you*?"

"Kathleen Le Paul. Open up this goddamn door."

Tentatively Leslie opened it an inch, keeping the security chain firmly in place. "What do you want?" she asked.

"Eddie told me to meet him at noon," Kathleen said. "I haven't driven all the way here for nothing. Did he leave me the money?"

"What money?"

"The money for his . . . delivery. I have a package for him."

"How much does he owe you?" Leslie asked curiously.

"Fifteen hundred dollars, cash," Kathleen replied, thinking to herself she was getting too old for this kind of thing. If Umberto Castelli would only divorce his fat Colombian wife and move to Los Angeles, she could live in luxury instead of being a runner.

"He didn't mention you or any money," Leslie said.

Kathleen impatiently tapped a Chanel-clad toe on the sidewalk. "Take a look," she said abruptly. "Maybe you'll find he left something for me."

Leslie shut the door in her face and scurried into the bedroom. Sure enough there was a pile of cash on top of Eddie's dresser.

For a moment she was unsure about what to do. If she refused to accept this package, Eddie could be mad. And yet if she took it and gave the woman money, he could also be angry. Thinking fast, she tried to reach him on his car phone. There was no reply.

By this time Kathleen Le Paul was banging on the door again.

Leslie hurried back to the door.

"I'm not standing out here all day," Kathleen Le Paul complained. "Do you have the money or don't you?"

Leslie took a deep breath and decided to pay. She went back to his dresser, counted out fifteen hundred dollars, and took it out to the woman.

In return Kathleen handed over the package and left.

When she had gone, Leslie carried the small, wrapped package into the kitchen, put it on the table, and opened it up with a kitchen knife.

Inside there was a small glassine bag filled with white powder.

Carefully Leslie slit the bag and tipped the powder onto the table.

Cocaine.

It was ruining their lives.

It was taking all their money and screwing up their marriage.

She knew what she had to do.

Chapter 42

It was incredibly great knowing this was her last day of purgatory. After today she was a free person. No longer Luce — quiet, obedient little secretary. Within hours she was returning to her true identity. Lucky Santangelo. Winner takes all.

It was Friday noon, and at the end of the day she was out of there.

She knew the first thing she'd do. Burn the goddamn wig and dreadful clothes. Smash the vile glasses. And dance around a bonfire chanting thanks like a crazy woman.

After that she'd get on the next plane to New York, and be with Lennie.

Ah . . . she couldn't wait. A long weekend with her husband was just what they both needed. A very long weekend in bed catching up on all the time they'd been apart. And during the weekend she'd give him the news.

Dear husband, I've brought you a present. I hope you like it.

Naturally they'd run Panther Studios together. What a trip!

Soon, Bobby would be out of school for summer break. He'd travel with his nanny straight to California. And Lennie had mentioned something about Brigette joining them. It was going to be the most wonderful summer. A real family affair. Maybe she'd even persuade Gino to come out for a week or two.

When Eddie Kane came racing through her office like a deranged maniac, she didn't take much notice. Eddie Kane was Mickey's problem, not hers. In fact, Mickey was going to have a lot of problems to deal with after today — not the least being that on Monday morning he was going to find himself out of a job.

This was the plan. Today, she was out of there. At six

o'clock there was a meeting at Abe's house to sign the final papers with both sets of lawyers present. And when all was signed, sealed, and delivered, Panther Studios would be officially hers.

Monday morning Abe had requested the pleasure of announcing the sale himself. He'd already sent an urgent telegram to his other granddaughter, Primrose, and her husband, Ben Harrison, in London, summoning them to the meeting.

Abe had decided to visit the studio in person for the first time in ten years. "Can't wait to see their faces," he'd told Lucky excitedly. "Can't wait to present 'em with you, girlie."

As long as she had the weekend to spend with Lennie, she was ready for anything.

The noises coming from Mickey Stolli's office were becoming violent. Idly she wondered who was getting beat up. In a fight she would put her money on Mickey. He was shorter than Eddie, and older, but he had the real strength. Mickey was a street fighter. She'd recognized that quality in him the first time she'd seen him.

Mickey's writer ran from the office with a panicked expression on his face.

Her intercom was buzzing out of control. "Call security," yelled Mickey. "Get 'em up here *now*."

She could hear Eddie's raised voice. "Don't fuck with me, Mickey, 'cause you're fucking with the wrong guy."

"*I'm* fucking with the wrong guy?" screamed Mickey. "*Me*? Clean up your act, shithead, and get the fuck out of my sight."

Lucky called the front gate. "Can you send a security guard to Mr Stolli's office please?" she requested.

"Sure, ma'am," one of the guards replied. "Is it urgent?"

"It depends what you call urgent," she said calmly.

"Life-threatening?"

"Hardly."

Before the guard had a chance to arrive, Eddie stormed out of there with a bloodied nose.

Hmmm, Lucky thought, she was right. In a fight it was

always the street fighter who came out on top. Eddie was a little too weak around the edges. Too many late nights and too much cocaine.

Mickey emerged from his office in a black fury. "You dumb cunt!" he yelled. "Don't you ever let anybody in here unless I tell you to. Even if you have to throw yourself in front of my office door and they have to trample over your body, you *do not* let anybody in here. Am I makin' myself clear?"

"No," she said blankly, trying to ignore the fact that he'd screamed "dumb cunt" at her. Nobody called Lucky Santangelo a dumb cunt and lived.

"What?" he bellowed.

"No, I don't understand you," she said evenly. "I'm not allowing people to trample over my body. And I'm certainly not putting myself at risk for you."

He stared at her in disbelief. A secretary – answering back?

"Are you tryin' to get yourself fired?" he asked angrily, practically hopping up and down.

She shrugged. "Whatever you want to do. It's up to you."

He could hardly believe what he was hearing. Until now this one had been the perfect secretary. She'd fended off his calls, taken care of his appointments, made him coffee, squeezed his juice. She'd even squeeze his balls if he told her to. Now she was developing lip. Jesus Christ!

He stormed back into his office and slammed the door. When the fuck was Olive coming back?

Lucky took a final leisurely lunch in the commissary as Luce.

When she was finished she strolled over to Harry Browning's table and said, "Do you mind if I join you?"

He glanced up, not pleased to see her. "Yes, I do," he said shortly.

"I'd like to explain something," she said. She felt ever so slightly guilty about Harry. If she'd known he was an alcoholic she'd never have plied him with liquor that fateful night of the fish pie. She sat down. "Harry—" she began.

"Mr Browning to you," he interrupted.

"I'm sure you imagine I'm playing some kind of strange game."

"I *know* what you're doing," Harry said. "The whole studio knows what you are."

She raised an eyebrow. "What am I?"

"You're Abe Panther's spy. He sent you in to sleep with Mickey Stolli."

She began to laugh. "Huh?"

"You told Brenda in Eddie Kane's office you were sleeping with Mickey Stolli," Harry said furiously. "Now the whole studio knows."

Lucky almost choked. The thought of shacking up with Mickey did that to a person. "Are you kidding me? I was *joking* when I said that to Brenda."

Harry drummed his fingers on the table. "A sick joke," he said grimly.

"Oh, you bet it is," she agreed. "And anyway, what do you mean – the whole studio knows?"

"Brenda told everybody. All the secretaries, messengers, assistants. And they in turn told everybody else."

Oh, wonderful! She sighed. *What a reputation to have. Sleeping with Mickey Stolli, the man of my dreams!* "And does everybody at the studio think I'm Abe's spy?" she asked.

"No," Harry replied shortly. "Only *I* know. I suppose that's why you're sleeping with Mickey Stolli. Mr Panther told you to."

Now she was getting irritated. "Cut it out, Harry. I am *not* sleeping with Mickey. Everything's going to become clear on Monday."

"Yes?" He looked at her suspiciously.

"Yes." She nodded her head and got up from the table. "Don't forget. Monday morning. Things are going to happen around here."

Abigaile Stolli called at three o'clock. She had an annoying voice, sharp and imperious, as if everybody should jump the moment they heard it. "Who's this?" she asked.

"Luce," Lucky replied. "And who's this?"

"Mrs Stolli," Abigaile said haughtily. "Are you the new girl?"

"I've been here a few weeks," Lucky answered.

"When is Olive coming back?" Abigaile demanded, as if it was a great imposition for her to have to talk to Lucky at all.

"Soon," Lucky replied.

"Have you ordered our car?"

"What car is that, Mrs Stolli?"

"Our limousine for the première tonight. Surely you know?"

"I wasn't aware you needed a car."

Abigaile exploded. "My God! Do I have to take care of *everything* myself? Didn't Mr Stolli tell you? We need a studio limousine. My usual driver. And the car must be stocked with Cristal champagne and Perrier water. Oh, and have it at my house at six-thirty. Not six-twenty-five, or six-thirty-five. Six-thirty. Arrange it."

Lucky decided Abigaile and Mickey made the perfect couple. Both of them dripping with charm.

"I'll see to it, Mrs Stolli," she said, the perfect secretary.

"Where's my husband?" Abigaile asked crossly.

For a moment Lucky was tempted to say, "Why don't you try Warner's apartment? You know, the black Vice cop he's been screwing twice a week for God knows how long." Instead she replied, "I've no idea, Mrs Stolli. But I'll be sure to leave a message that you phoned."

"Do that," snapped Abigaile, banging the phone down.

Lucky called up Dispatch. "Marty," she said, "Mrs Stolli needs a car for tonight. Not her usual limousine. She's requested one of the small sedans. OK? Have it at her house at six-forty-five. Thank you."

While Mickey was safely out of the office she then called Boogie. "Did you charter a plane for tonight?"

"All set," he replied.

"And you've found out where Lennie is?"

279

"Yes."

"What would I do without you, Boogie?"

"You'd get into a lot of trouble."

She smiled to herself. He was probably right.

Chapter 43

"Mickey," Warner asked, "are you seeing other women?"

Mickey looked at her in surprise. "What kind of a stupid remark is that? Why would I want to see other women?"

"I'm just asking," Warner said. "I can ask, can't I?"

He didn't like her tone. "You can do what you want, but it's a goddamn stupid question."

Warner stared at him. He'd been in a bad mood all day. Usually she respected his moods and tiptoed around them, but today she'd heard some disturbing gossip and it was on her mind. Some of the cops in Vice had a sting going on concerning a brothel in the Hollywood Hills. The high-class whorehouse was run by a woman called Madame Loretta, and according to the word around the locker room, many important and influential people in the film industry frequented this place. One of the names she'd heard mentioned today was Mickey Stolli.

Mickey got up from Warner's bed. The sex had not been good. Maybe it was time to move on.

"It really pisses me off when you ask questions like that," he said, annoyed. "For those kind of questions I may as well stay home with my wife. What do I need to come here for?"

Warner wondered if Mickey's guilt was making him even angrier. She clenched her teeth and didn't say anything. Instead she walked briskly into her tiny kitchen and plugged in the kettle.

"How about a cup of coffee?" she called out. *Bastard!* If he was playing games with other women – especially hookers – she wasn't going to take it. No way.

"What are you trying to do, kill me?" he complained, following her into the kitchen. "All that caffeine they put in coffee. I have to watch my diet."

She bit back a sharp retort. Mickey only watched his diet when it suited him. Who was he kidding? "Did you remember to get my tickets for tonight?" she asked, tight-lipped.

"Huh?" Mickey looked guilty.

She strode out of the kitchen. "You promised me four tickets for the première of *Motherfaker*, remember?"

"Oh, Christ," he mumbled, right behind her. Naturally he'd forgotten, and she'd made the request months ago, Johnny Romano being one of her favourite movie stars and all. Shit! He'd gotten her an autographed picture of Johnny – wasn't that enough? Now she had to have tickets for the goddamn première too.

He reached for the phone. "Luce," he said, when his dumb secretary picked up. First thing Monday morning he was firing her. He'd bring in Brenda, the pretty black girl from Eddie Kane's office. At least he'd have someone decent to look at.

"Yes, Mr Stolli?"

"Get me four extra tickets for the première tonight. They don't have to be great seats. And I want them . . . uh . . . shit, you'd better messenger them to . . . uh . . ." He held his hand over the mouthpiece. "Warner, I can't give them your address. Where shall I have the tickets sent?"

"Why can't you give them my address?" Warner demanded belligerently.

"'Cause it's not a smart thing to do." She was definitely beginning to needle him.

"I'll pick them up," she said. "I'm going to be out that way today."

The thought of Warner appearing at his office to pick up tickets for *Motherfaker* was one he didn't even wish to contemplate. "The best thing is to have them left at the box-office," he said quickly, "under your name."

"If that suits you."

"Leave 'em at the box-office under the name of Franklin," he mumbled into the phone, hanging up and turning back to her.

"Who are you taking anyway?"

She glared at him. "Don't worry, Mickey. I won't come near you or your wife."

He didn't like the way she said that, or the way their relationship was going. He'd thought Warner was different, making no demands. But all women turned out to be the same. They all ended up nagging and wanting more than any sane man was prepared to give.

"OK, OK," he said, reaching for his clothes. "I've got to get dressed an' out of here."

The scene with Eddie had unsettled him. He hated scenes, let alone a fist fight. God knows what Eddie would do next, he was hardly a stable character. If Leslie wasn't such a stupid piece of ass she'd have gotten him into drug rehab long before now.

Driving back to the studio Mickey felt dissatisfied and restless. Making a sudden detour he headed for Madame Loretta's. He'd finally realized Ford Werne spoke the truth. *Pay for it and you don't get any grief. Pay for it and your life is your own.*

Madame Loretta greeted him warmly. No hassles. No ticket requests. No questions.

"Who've you got for me today?" he asked, as if he was chatting to a butcher in the supermarket selecting a better cut of meat.

"A beautiful Oriental girl," Madame Loretta offered soothingly. "Very nice. Very sweet. Very talented. You'll like her."

"Yes," Mickey said, looking forward to being pampered. "I will."

Eddie called Kathleen Le Paul from his car phone. "I'm sorry," he mumbled. "I forgot."

"Perfectly all right," Kathleen replied calmly. "Your wife gave me the money."

Eddie was shocked. "She did?"

282

"You left it for me, didn't you?"

"Yeah, yeah, sure. I had to run to the studio. Unexpected."

Kathleen gave a deep sigh. "One of these days you'll clean your life up, Eddie."

"No thanks to you."

"What do you mean by that?"

"You introduced me to Carlos Bonnatti. Now I'm in deep trouble."

"What kind of trouble?"

"Don't give me the you-haven't-heard bit. It's all over town."

Kathleen's voice had a steely edge. "What did you do, steal from him?"

"I tried to make a living. That's all, a living," he said defensively. "What is it, a crime? The studio'll pay."

"Eddie, Eddie, you'll never learn, will you? You don't fuck with a man like Carlos. If you do, you could end up dead."

Jesus Christ! Eddie Kane had no desire to end up dead. Maybe the only answer was to get out of town. He'd thought about running to Hawaii, where he'd once had such a good time. Plenty of cheap dope and gorgeous girlfriends.

But wait a minute, wasn't he forgetting about Leslie? What was he going to do about her?

Christ! Why had he allowed himself to get into this mess?

Why had he allowed his perfect existence to fall apart?

The call from her sister took Abigaile by surprise.

"What's this all about?" Primrose shrieked all the way from London.

Abigaile quivered with suppressed fury. Primrose managed to make everything seem like it was her fault. Whatever happened to the niceties of life such as — "How are you? Are your children well?" No, Primrose jumped right to it as though Abigaile owed her an explanation.

"I have no idea what you're talking about," she snapped.

"The telegram," Primrose replied impatiently.

"*What* telegram?"

"Oh, for God's sake! Don't tell me you're going to pretend you don't know anything about it. Ben's furious."

Abigaile spoke slowly and evenly to make sure her sister understood every word. "Primrose, I have absolutely no clue what your problem is."

"Ben and I received a telegram from Grandfather today," Primrose said in an accusing voice, as if Abigaile should know.

Abigaile was surprised. "You did? Saying what?"

"Saying that he wishes us to be at the studio for an urgent meeting on Monday morning."

Abigaile frowned. Did this have something to do with her recent visit to old Abe? Was he readying himself to inform Primrose and Ben that Mickey was trying to sell the studio without his knowledge?

She sighed. "I really don't know what it's about."

"Inconvenient, that's all I can say," Primrose snorted. "Do you realize we've got to get on a plane tomorrow morning? That hardly gives me time to pack. *And* I have to make arrangements for the children. It's simply disgraceful."

"Why don't I get back to you?" Abigaile suggested, anxious to get off the phone. "I'll call Mickey and see what he knows."

"Fine," Primrose snapped.

Abigaile put down the phone. The easiest thing would have been to contact her grandfather immediately. Unfortunately she didn't have the courage. Abe, in his feisty old way, would say something rude and insulting like "Butt out, girlie, it's none of your goddamn business."

She placed another call to Mickey and got his new secretary again. "Is he back yet?" she asked impatiently.

"He's not, Mrs Stolli."

"Are you *sure* you don't know where he is? This is urgent."

Irresistible, thought Lucky. "Well ... I do have a number you might try ... "

"Give it to me," Abigaile said, brooking no argument.

"One moment, please."

Lucky scooted into Mickey's office, dashed over to his private phone book, and looked up Warner's number.

You're being a real bitch, Santangelo.

So what? The guy called me a cunt. This is his punishment.

She returned to the phone and gave Abigaile Warner Franklin's number.

Abigaile called, expecting to reach an office. "Is Mr Stolli there?" she demanded imperiously when a female answered.

"Who's this?" asked Warner.

"This is his wife."

"Are you calling *me*?" said Warner.

"I beg your pardon?" said Abigaile.

"Is it me you're calling?"

Abigaile was having the most confusing day. "No, I'm not calling you," she said crossly. "Whose secretary are you?"

"I'm nobody's secretary. I'm Warner Franklin." She said her name as if Abigaile was supposed to know who she was.

"Are you an actress?" Abigaile asked, sniffing instant danger.

"No, I'm not an actress, I'm a cop."

"A cop?"

"That's right."

Abigaile was confused.

Warner took a slow beat. "I'm also your husband's mistress," she added, thinking it was about time Mickey's wife realized she existed.

285

Chapter 44

Twenty thousand dollars' worth of IBM stock made out in her name was delivered to Venus Maria's house on Friday afternoon. She arrived home from the studio early to find a large, hand-delivered envelope waiting for her. Inside there was a Tiffany card from Martin. His name was hand-engraved on the top, and on it he had written *Don't say I never pay my bets!*

Venus Maria grinned. Obviously Martin could afford it, but it was nice to know he'd remembered. It was also a clever way to settle his bet without involving cash.

How should she respond? It had to be something original. Ron was always full of great ideas, so she called him.

Naturally he was out. He and the Ken Doll had gone shopping to Fred Segal on Melrose. They were not expected back for a couple of hours.

Hmmmm. Ron was probably making more purchases for his live-in lover. He certainly knew how to spend it.

She thought about who else she could call. Unfortunately she didn't have any close women friends. It was difficult in her position. She was rich, young, and famous. She had everything most other females in Hollywood wanted. The envy factor was high.

Oh, of course there were the executives' wives, but she was hardly going to become bosom buddies with Abigaile Stolli and the like. All they seemed to be interested in was giving great charity, buying designer dresses, and having long, leisurely lunches where they trashed everybody in town.

It would have been nice to have one special close girl-friend to confide in. Growing up in Brooklyn, she'd always been different from the other girls. While they were hanging out at the corner drugstore, going to movies, rock concerts, and sitting around drinking sodas and flirting with boys, Venus Maria had always been obliged to rush home from school to take care of her many chores. Looking after her father and four brothers was extremely demanding. Sometimes she'd felt like a modern-day Cinderella.

None of them appreciated it. They took her completely for granted.

And then she'd met Ron, the boy next door. *The fag next door*, she thought with a hysterical giggle.

They'd hit it off right from the beginning. Two soul mates, finding each other in Brooklyn of all places.

Ron had encouraged her to cut loose, taking her on wild trips to Times Square, and then down Broadway where they'd enjoyed hanging out. She and Ron spoke each other's language. Showbiz. They both knew exactly what they wanted, and were determined to get it.

Stardom and fame. Staying in Brooklyn was not going to do it for them, so eventually they'd taken off.

Both were prepared to work hard. Venus Maria's big turn-on had always been singing, dancing, and acting. It was a thrill, a major charge. She strove to do everything to the best of her ability and usually succeeded.

Ron loved dancing and putting together fantastic routines. Hard work and tenacity brought them both the recognition they craved.

Venus Maria's father and three other brothers still lived in the same house in Brooklyn. She'd offered to buy them something better. They hadn't accepted, although her father had said he wouldn't mind a new car, and her brothers had mentioned they could do with some extra cash. Two of them were married. Venus Maria imagined the wives were doing all the work now.

She'd bought her father a brand new Chevrolet, and given her brothers ten thousand dollars each. Nobody bothered to thank her. Nice family.

And then there was Emilio – following her out to Hollywood, installing himself in her house, moaning when she'd asked him to leave. Since he'd left she hadn't heard a word from him. Not so much as a "Thanks, it's nice of you to pay my rent. It's nice of you to lend me a car."

OK, so she was rich, but she'd worked hard to get where she was. Nobody had ever given her anything for nothing.

She took the envelope containing the share certificates up to her bedroom – a bright, spacious room overlooking the obligatory Hollywood swimming pool. Off to one side there was her bathroom, and on the other her mirrored gym.

On the wall in her closet hung a giant blow-up photograph of her taken by Helmut Newton. It was an interesting photo. She was sitting on a stool, wearing a flesh-coloured leotard. Her legs were bent under her, while her body arched, and her head was thrown back in profile. She looked sexy, and innocent, wanton and prim all at the same time. It was her favourite photograph – taken before Martin.

With a wry grimace she realized her life fell into two categories. Before Martin. And after.

Maybe she'd been better off before. Who needed a man to obsess on?

She pressed a hidden button and the photograph slid aside to reveal a medium-sized safe. Clicking the knob, she hit the right combination and the safe opened. In it she kept her passport, share certificates, letters from old lovers, and a photograph of her with Martin. Cooper had taken the photo one night at her house. It was the only picture she had of them together and she loved it. They were sitting on the couch in her living room. Martin had his arm around her, while she gazed up at him. It was definitely an intimate photograph. Anyone seeing it would know immediately they were lovers. Which is why she couldn't put it in a frame and display it. Too risky. It would be like telling the world, "Hey, this is my boy-friend." And she didn't want to be the one to reveal their relationship. Martin had to make his own decision.

Johnny Romano's voice was on her private answering machine. "Hey, baby," he crooned. "You promised to call me back. This is Johnny. You were s'posed to let me know if you were comin' to my première with me tonight." A plaintive cry from a superstar.

Oh, sure Johnny would love her to arrive on his arm. Let the media salivate over Johnny Romano and Venus Maria together at last. What a picture! What a break! Not to mention sensational publicity for his movie.

Word around the studio was that the film was a bomb. But this was Hollywood – land of hype. The movie would make a fortune whatever it was like. Johnny Romano could take a piss on Rodeo Drive and still make money!

Why was he calling her anyway? She'd never said she would even consider going with him.

The man obviously got off on rejection. He was always calling her, and she was always saying no. Why did he bother? He could have any girl he wanted. How come he was so intent on having her?

She put away her IBM stock certificates and closed the safe. Then, feeling just a tad guilty, although she didn't know why, she picked up the phone and dialled Emilio's apartment.

He'd moved with the times and bought himself an answering machine. "Emilio Sierra is out," his message said. "But Emilio Sierra would love to know who is calling him, so you call back and I'll call back. Don't forget now – leave your number."

She waited for the beep and said a crisp "Emilio, this is Venus. Just checking in to see if you're settled."

Duty call. It was done. Not that she owed him anything. But still . . .

While she was on a family kick she decided to call her father in New York. He'd never acknowledged her success. He was happy to accept the monthly cheque she sent him, but he wouldn't give her one word of praise. To her chagrin she couldn't help herself from still seeking his approval. It was a losing battle.

She was sure he was home, sitting in front of the television with his beer belly, a can of Heineken, a large pepperoni pizza, and two bags of salted potato chips.

"Hi, Dad, it's Venus," she said when he picked up.

"Virginia?" He refused to use her professional name.

"Yeah. How ya doin', Dad? Just thought I'd check in."

"Can't complain," her father replied gruffly. "Why're you calling?"

Why *was* she calling? He had her number, but he'd never bothered to use it, except once, when he'd wanted to complain about one of her videos. "Ya look like a cheap little whore," he'd exploded. "Whaddaya think it's like for me at work? I got guys ribbin' me all over."

That was at the beginning. When the money started to pour in, the ribbing hadn't seemed to matter so much.

"I'm calling to see how you all are," she said flatly, feeling rejected as usual. "Nothing important."

"We're OK," he said shortly. "Could do with some extra money."

So what else was new? "I'll talk to my business manager," she said with a sigh. And that was the extent of their conversation.

If Martin Swanson left Deena and married her, the wedding would be a riot! She could just see her father and brothers mixing with New York high society and the cream of Hollywood.

God, she was hungry. Sometimes fame was a drag. If she wasn't so famous she could jump in her jeep, race down to Fred Segal, find Ron and the Ken Doll, and they could sit in the restaurant and pig out on delicious club sandwiches. But God forbid she wasn't looking her best, didn't have makeup on and her hair primped. People would say, "Oh, look, there's Venus Maria. She doesn't look as good as she does on her videos or in the movies, does she?" And then others would come over and start asking for her autograph. She was always polite to them, but it soon became too much of a hassle. And she lived in fear of that one maniac fan coming at her from out of nowhere, screaming "Whore!" and stabbing her to death.

Only another famous person could understand her fears. Cooper, for instance. Cooper understood everything. In fact, he was the only one she could really talk to.

Strut was winding down. She'd finished all her scenes.

It was funny, because when they were in the midst of shooting she and Cooper had fought all the time. Now she found that she missed him.

The end of the filming was always difficult. During the shoot everyone became part of a large family – all working towards the same goal. And when it was over, you were suddenly cast adrift and no longer had that family to depend on. It was a wrench.

She decided to call him.

He was in his office at the studio. "What's up?" he said cheerfully.

"I was wondering, will you be going to the première tonight?"

"Are you certifiable?" He laughed. "I wouldn't see *Motherfaker* if you paid me. Mucho bucks."

"Then why don't we get a bite to eat?"

He sounded amused. "Are we talking Spago here?"

"If you like."

"That means we'll be photographed together," he warned. "What will Martin have to say about that?"

"I don't tell him everything I do," she replied defensively.

"I'm glad to hear it. We'll dine at Spago and enjoy ourselves."

She was pleased, but she hoped he wouldn't get the wrong impression. "Cooper, I need somebody to talk to. I'm not calling so you can jump my bones."

"When did I ever try to jump your bones?" he asked indignantly.

"You know . . ."

"Sweetheart," he said firmly, "don't worry. We'll have a quiet dinner. We'll talk. I'll take you to your house, leave you at the door, and then I'll go home and jerk off. Does that suit you?"

She couldn't help laughing. "The day *you* have to jerk off is a day indeed."

"Don't be too sure. With AIDS creeping around every corner I'm not interested any more."

She didn't believe a word. "Oh, Cooper, *please*! It's *me* you're talking to."

He laughed ruefully. "Yeah, I suppose so. You don't buy my lines, do you?"

She smiled. "No."

"What time shall I pick you up?"

"Eight o'clock."

"I'll be there."

She put down the phone and felt quite pleased. An evening with Cooper. He was a friend. He was also Martin's friend, which meant that if she wanted to she could talk about Martin all night long.

And that was just what she felt like doing.

Chapter 45

Eddie wiped the back of his hand across his nose. There was dried blood there, he could feel it. The humiliation of allowing Mickey Stolli to beat up on him was too much. He'd gone in expecting action, but certainly not the violent kind. Mickey Stolli was a son of a bitch.

The Maserati got him home in record time. He barged into the house, wound up and ready to kick ass.

Leslie was waiting for him. "I was worried about you," she said, full of wifely concern.

He knew he was treating her badly but he couldn't help himself. "Where's my delivery?" were the first words out of his mouth.

Leslie faced him, wide-eyed and sincere. "I paid the woman who came here," she said tremulously. "Your debt is clear."

"OK, OK, where's the stuff?" He wasn't in the mood for a lecture. He needed to get high. And fast.

She faced him. His lovely wife.

"I threw it away, Eddie," she said quietly. "We're starting a new life."

*

Abigaile hyperventilated all the way to Warner Franklin's apartment. When she reached the street she drove around the block twice, unsure about where to park. Abigaile had used valet parking for so many years she didn't know how to manage without it. Finally, she left her Mercedes on a red line, walked up to the front of the building, and pressed the buzzer marked Franklin.

A disembodied voice instructed her to come to the third floor.

Heart beating, Abigaile took the elevator. What was she *doing* here? This was madness.

One look at Warner and her heart almost stopped altogether. *This* was Mickey's girlfriend. *This* was the woman he was having an affair with? This six-foot black giant of a female?

Abigaile experienced serious palpitations. Was this a sick joke?

"Come in," Warner said, facing Mickey's wife for the first time.

Abigaile was sure she'd made some kind of insane mistake. Clearly she was about to be kidnapped, bundled into the trunk of a Ford Taurus, and driven to a lonely and deserted spot. They would call Mickey for the ransom and he'd refuse to pay. She'd be raped, shot, and thrown over the edge of Mulholland.

"I don't think so," she said, shrinking away. "I've made a mistake."

"What mistake?" asked Warner, towering over her.

"You and my husband. It's not possible."

"Oh, honey, it's possible all right."

Abigaile took two steps backwards. "No."

"Trust me."

Abigaile never trusted anybody when they said "trust me". Quickly she turned around and scurried back to the elevator. Pressing the call button she prayed for its imminent arrival before she was brutally attacked.

"We should talk," Warner called out after her.

"No," Abigaile repeated, controlling hysteria. "No, we shouldn't."

She got in the elevator and pressed the button. When Mickey heard about this he was going to be furious. Anything could have happened.

Reaching the safety of her Mercedes, she slumped weakly over the wheel. Oh God! At least she was safe.

After a few moments of deep breaths she remembered she had to go to the beauty shop. It was the première of *Motherfaker* that night, followed by a big charity dinner.

In her panic she forgot about phoning Primrose back. She forgot about Abe summoning her sister and brother-in-law to an urgent meeting on Monday morning. She drove straight to Ivana's and surrendered herself into Saxon's tender loving hands.

"You look a little pale, Mrs S.," Saxon commented, tossing his mane of blond hair, strutting around, snug in indecently tight white chinos.

"I had a nasty experience," she confessed.

He caught his reflection in the mirror and checked himself out. "Yeah?"

"*Very* nasty."

"You've got to watch yourself, Mrs S.," he said vaguely.

"I know."

She did look upset. "You want me to call your husband for you?" he asked casually.

That's the last thing she wanted. "No, no, I'll be fine," she assured him.

He stepped back and narrowed his eyes, viewing her in the mirror. "So, how do we want to look tonight?"

"I don't care."

Saxon went to work.

When Mickey arrived back at the studio refreshed after a relaxing session with a Chinese hooker, Lucky couldn't wait to give him the good news. "Mr Panther has called a meeting for ten o'clock on Monday morning," she informed him. "He'll be here personally, and he's requested that you and Mrs Stolli attend. He's also contacted your brother-in-law, Ben Harrison, and his wife.

They'll be flying in from England. Oh, and a Miss Franklin has called twice. She says it's urgent."

Mickey stared at his secretary, Luce. This mousy woman. This harridan.

"Fuck!" he snarled, before slamming his way into his office.

Mickey Stolli was not having a good day.

Chapter 46

The photographers gathered outside Spago went into a feeding frenzy when they spotted Cooper Turner arriving with Venus Maria. This was the break they'd been waiting for. The magic couple. A picture capable of making them thousands of dollars.

Venus and Cooper refused to pose. On the other hand they didn't duck in the back way. They walked down the little hill to the entrance, holding hands, giving the photographers plenty of excellent photo opportunities.

At the front desk Bernard greeted them with a friendly handshake, and Jannis ushered them to a window table.

Venus immediately ordered a frozen margarita and one of Wolfgang's famous smoked salmon pizzas with cream cheese.

Cooper was amused. "I thought you were one of those strong-willed women. Y'know, the kind who never puts anything between her lips if it's fattening."

"Tonight, I'm doing exactly what pleases me," she replied recklessly.

He nodded agreeably. "Does that mean we'll have sex?"

She burst out laughing. "Cooper! You're Martin's best friend. Behave like it. Anyway, you promised."

"You know I'm only joking," he said, waving at Ida and Zeppo White, who were dining with Susie Rush and her husband.

She smiled. "Yeah, sure."

Cooper was forty-five years old, the same age as Martin, and yet he had a little-boy quality she loved. He might be the famous Cooper Turner, but to her he was a friend, and a good one.

"How well do you know Martin's wife?" she asked, trying to sound casual.

"Deena? I've known her as long as Martin has. I met her before they were married."

"What's she like?"

"Deena's an interesting woman."

"In what way?"

"She's got balls."

"Like me?"

"Nobody's got your balls."

The pizza arrived and Venus Maria dug in. "Does she know about me?" she asked, chewing ravenously.

"Look, Martin's never been the faithful husband type. I told you before. A lot of beautiful women have passed through his life. I'm sure Deena knows what goes on. She chooses to ignore it."

"I'm not just another woman," Venus Maria said vehemently.

"I know that."

"Are you sure you know it? Has he told you?" she pressed, gulping her margarita.

"No. But you couldn't be just another woman in anybody's life. You're special, kiddo."

Cooper made her feel good. "You think so, huh?"

"I know so." He picked up his glass and toasted her. "You're an original."

"Thank you, Cooper. Coming from you I appreciate it."

Their waiter interrupted to recite the specials. Venus Maria ordered duck with a rich plum sauce, while Cooper settled for thinly sliced steak.

"By the way," he said, once they'd both ordered, "I've been meaning to tell you."

"What?" she asked eagerly.

"I have to admit it – you're really something in the dailies. I know I tried to tone down your performance, but whatever you were doing up there, it works. You've got it, kiddo. Whatever *it* might be."

His praise delighted her. "That's because I was in the hands of a good director."

"You sure know how to flatter a guy, huh?"

"I know how to do a lot of things," she replied provocatively.

He nodded knowingly. "Yup."

She leaned across the table, an intent expression on her face. "Cooper?"

"What?"

"Do you think Martin will ever leave Deena?"

He looked at her quizzically. "Are we back to that?"

"Sorry!"

He sighed. "Do you want him to?"

She looked unsure. "Sometimes I think it's what I want more than anything else in the world, and other times I'm not so sure."

"You'd better make up your mind, because whatever *he* does depends on what *you* do."

He was telling her what she already knew. "I guess you're right."

"But I'll tell you this," he added. "If he *does* decide to leave Deena, it won't be easy. She's a tough lady."

Venus Maria sat up straighter. "I'm tough, too."

"Sweetheart, next to Deena you're a cupcake."

Across town, Emilio sat in a small, cramped office with Dennis Walla putting the finishing touches to his tape-recorded story. He'd come up with everything he could think of. Everything from what colour panties Venus Maria wore, to how she looked when she got up in the morning.

Dennis was satisfied they had a good story, but he still pushed for more. "When are you going to show me the photo you talked about?" he asked. "We need it on the double."

"I'm getting it."

"I thought you already had it," Dennis countered.

"Yes, I do, it's somewhere safe." Emilio replied, slouching in his chair. "You don't expect me to keep a valuable picture like that hanging around, do you? My apartment could be broken into. Anyone could get hold of it. Besides, we haven't agreed a price."

Dennis picked up a can of beer and took a hearty swig. "The price depends on the photo. If it's worth it, you'll get your money."

Emilio scratched his head. "I'll have it for you soon," he promised.

Dennis rocked back and forth impatiently. "Yeah, well *soon* better be within the next twenty-four hours if we're gonna run it."

"Don't worry, I'll have it for you tomorrow," Emilio replied, thinking to himself, what the hell was he promising here? He knew there was a photograph, he'd seen it one day when Venus Maria had left her house in a hurry, forgetting to close her safe. When he was staying with her he'd enjoyed taking little exploration trips around the house while she was out. This had been a bonus day. He'd inspected the safe's contents and spotted the picture of Venus with Martin Swanson. What he should have done was taken it then and there and had it copied. But he hadn't thought about it at the time.

Now it was a question of getting back into her house, opening the safe, and stealing the photograph.

Clever as he was, Emilio wasn't quite sure how he was going to manage such a feat.

Dennis stood up, yawned, and stretched. "That's me for tonight, mate. I've had it," he said, scrunching his empty beer can and tossing it into a trash basket.

Thankfully Emilio nodded. He had a hot date. It was amazing how women's attitudes changed towards him once they discovered he had money. He'd already leased a decent car and bought himself some new clothes.

His date was a hot little dancer who wouldn't have second-glanced him two weeks ago. Now she'd purred, "Sure, Emilio honey. Love to," when he'd called and asked her out. Her name was Rita and she was a bundle of dynamite. Half Puerto Rican, half American, she was the girl of Emilio's dreams. She looked a little like Venus Maria, but so did half the other would-be video stars in LA.

Dennis and he shook hands. "Tomorrow, mate," Dennis said, slapping him on the shoulder. "I'll be waiting for your call."

"Right," agreed Emilio, and they parted company.

Cooper Turner was a good listener. Better than Ron, because Ron was always too ready with his bitchy little comments. Cooper's advice was constructive.

"I understand what you're going through," he said sympathetically. "You're in love with the guy. There's no way to explain why we fall in love with certain people. You and Martin make a strange couple. You must admit the two of you have absolutely nothing in common. But you love him, and I understand."

Venus Maria nodded wistfully. "I wish I knew why."

Cooper looked wise. "Maybe you're searching for a father figure. He *is* twenty years older than you."

"So are you, Cooper. And I wouldn't regard *you* as a father figure."

He reached across the table and took her hand. "What *would* you regard me as?"

She smiled. "A very attractive man who, if I wasn't involved, I could quite easily think about being with. Even though your reputation goes before you."

"What reputation?" he asked casually.

She began to laugh. "There's no way you can hide it, Coop, you're a real tomcat. You've been around this town so long there's not a woman over thirty-five you haven't had, *including* the married ones."

Cooper had a glint in his eyes. "That was when I was young and didn't know any better."

"What are you now, senile?"

"Do you want me to talk to Martin?" he asked, briskly changing the subject. "Find out how he really feels?"

Venus tossed her platinum curls. "I know he's crazy

about me. But I guess I wouldn't mind knowing if he sees a future for us."

"OK, I'll do it."

"You will?"

"For you — anything."

"Not a hint that we've spoken about him, OK? Can you be cool?" she asked anxiously.

"Can *I* be cool?"

"Well, can you?" she demanded.

"Sweetheart, I can do whatever you want me to."

She was suddenly very serious. "I trust you, Cooper."

He returned her big-brown-eyed gaze. "And so you should."

They drove back to her house. She couldn't help thinking how simple it would be if it was Cooper she was in love with. But no, it had to be Martin. It had to be Mister New York himself.

"Am I coming in?" Cooper asked when they pulled up outside.

"It depends on what you expect."

He gave her a wry smile. "I expect a cup of coffee."

"Then you'd better come in."

Inside the house she activated her answering machine. There were several messages. Two were business-related, and the third was from Martin. "Did you get my payoff?" his voice said. "I always settle my debts."

The fourth message was from Emilio. "Hey, little sis, nice of you to call me, I 'preciate it. I bin workin' pretty hard. Scored myself some cash. Is it OK if I come by in the morning and put it in your safe? Thanks. I don't like to leave it lying around the apartment. See you tomorrow."

"Who was that?" Cooper asked.

"My brother," she replied. "God knows what he's done to get himself a stash of cash. And why does he have to bring it here? Why can't he rent a safe-deposit box?" She sighed. "I tell you, family."

Cooper nodded sympathetically. "I know what you mean." He watched her as she flitted around the room. She was making him uncomfortably hot.

"How about a brandy?" she asked. "I can't be bothered making coffee."

Abruptly he stood up. "I've changed my mind. I'm going home. Early call in the morning."

"Are you sure?"

"Listen, if I stay I'm likely to attack you. So I may as well get out of here while we're still on good terms. Agreed?"

She laughed. "The man is honest."

"The man is horny!"

"I'm sorry I can't do anything about it."

He looked at her ruefully. "No you're not."

"You're right."

She walked him to the door, stood on tiptoe, and kissed him on the cheek. "Thanks, Cooper. You've been a real friend tonight."

When she was alone she thought about Martin. The trouble with sleeping with a married man was that you couldn't pick up the phone and call him when you felt like it.

Restlessly she opened the freezer, helped herself to a carton of chocolate chip ice cream, and curled up in front of the television.

Soon she fell asleep.

The hottest young superstar in America slept alone.

Chapter 47

Abe Panther had dressed up for the meeting. He looked quite dapper for an eighty-eight-year-old man in white pants and shirt, a blue blazer, and a jaunty red scarf tossed casually around his scrawny neck.

Lucky arrived with Morton Sharkey. She'd rushed back to her rented house from the studio, showered, washed her hair, put on makeup, and piled the wig, glasses, and clothes in a bundle on the bathroom floor ready for the burning ceremony she planned to perform before leaving for New York.

Abe greeted her with a hug and a rascally wink. "This is it, girlie! This is it!" he said exuberantly.

She grinned back at him. "It sure is, Abe. You look wonderful."

"I'm lookin' forward to Monday mornin'," he said. "It's gonna be a real killer!"

Inga appeared. There was actually a pleasant expression on her face. "Good evening, Lucky," she said.

Good evening, Lucky! Inga acknowledged her existence! Abe must have promised her a bundle!

"Well, girlie, you ready to take over?" Abe asked. "You got all your plans in place?"

"I can tell you this, Abe. I'm going to be changing the way Panther does things. No more exploitation films. No more using women. Panther Studios is about to become the equal opportunity studio."

He cackled. "An' you really think you'll make money that way?"

She took a beat. "Sometimes," she replied slowly. "standing up for principles is more important than making money."

Abe cocked his head to one side. "You know somethin', girlie? I wouldn't mind meetin' that father of yours. He taught you good."

She nodded. "He certainly did. We'll all have dinner next time he's out here."

"If I'm around."

"Don't give me that. You're going to be around for ever."

The lawyers were lined up and waiting. Morton had two assistants with him, while Abe's lawyers consisted of two business-like men in three-piece suits.

Abe made quite a ceremony over signing the final papers. He'd had Inga put out the best glassware, all the better to serve vintage champagne.

Just before signing he handed Lucky a Cartier box. "Got

you this, girlie," he said proudly. "Wanted you to have a souvenir of today."

Lucky was quite touched. She opened the box. Inside was an exquisite gold panther pin. On the inside was inscribed *To Lucky, from Abe Panther. Kill 'em girlie!*

She leaned over and kissed him. "This is beautiful, Abe. I'll wear it proudly. And I'll look after your studio." Her black eyes gleamed. "Bet on it!"

Abe signed the papers with a flourish, and the champagne flowed. "Here's to the end of an era," he said, toasting her. "The start of somethin' new."

"It'll be something new all right," Lucky said. "I made you a promise and I'll keep it. Panther Studios will be great again."

They locked eyes. Lucky Santangelo and Abe Panther. Nearly sixty years separated them, but they were perfectly in tune.

An hour later Boogie drove her to the airport. She was elated beyond her wildest expectations. Lucky Santangelo. Owner and President of Panther Studios. God damn it! Who would ever have believed it? She couldn't wait to see Lennie's face. *And* the rest of him.

Triumphantly she boarded the chartered plane.

Boogie made sure the luggage was aboard, and joined her.

It was a clear LA night. Lucky gazed out of the window as the smooth jet zoomed down the runway and took off into the star-studded night sky.

She ordered champagne from the steward and toasted the sea of lights spread out like a shimmering blanket beneath her.

"Here's to you, LA," she said. "And here's to Panther."

A new adventure was just beginning.

303

Chapter 48

The white treble stretch limo snaked its way through the crowds to the front of Grauman's Chinese Theater on Hollywood Boulevard. A red carpet led from the sidewalk into the theatre. Lining the sides of the carpet were various members of the press and camera crews from many different countries. The huge crowds spilled over into the road. When they saw the white limo approaching a chant went up from the crowd. "JOHNNY! JOHNNY! JOHNNY!" screamed the masses "WE WANT JOHNNY! WE WANT JOHNNY ROMANO!"

Safely ensconced in his limo, Johnny Romano could hear the tribal yell. He grinned at his date, a pretty young actress with large breasts and a twinkling smile. He'd called her at the last moment. The woman he'd really wanted on his arm was Venus Maria, but since Venus wouldn't honour him with her presence he'd settled for this one.

Also in the car were his two faithful bodyguards and his manager.

When the limo pulled to a halt, they all stayed put for a couple of minutes, allowing the excitement to build outside on the sidewalk.

"What's going on?" the actress asked. "Why are we waiting?"

"Foreplay," Johnny replied with a suggestive wink.

The manager got out of the car first, followed by the bodyguards, followed by Johnny's date, and finally the great Johnny Romano himself.

A hysterical scream went up from the crowd.

Johnny acknowledged his fans with a kingly wave, pausing by the limo for a few seconds before strutting down the red carpet, his bodyguard flanking him on either side, his date trailing behind, his manager bringing up the rear.

Reporters and camera crews pleaded for a moment of his time.

He ignored them all until he reached *Entertainment Tonight*. *ET* was his favourite TV program. He watched it every night.

Jeannie Wolf was there with a microphone and a welcoming smile. "Johnny, are you pleased about the movie?" she asked.

"Hey, Jeannie. Good to see you. Howya doin'?" he said, playing Mister Humble Movie Star to the hilt. "Yeah, I guess I'm kinda pleased. *Motherfaker*'s gonna surprise a lot of people. I put mucho heavy work into it. My fans are gonna like it. My mother's gonna like it. My father's gonna be ecstatic!"

The crowd roared its approval. They wanted Johnny to be a hit. They rooted for him.

Jeannie laughed politely.

Johnny threw a long, lingering look straight to camera. "All you folks out there, go buy your tickets for *Motherfaker*. You'll have a good time. Johnny — he promises you that."

"Thank you, Johnny," said Jeannie.

"Thank *you*, Jeannie," said Johnny, waving to his fans as he strode manfully into the theatre.

Crawling along Hollywood Boulevard, caught in a horrendous traffic jam, trapped in a small sedan, were Abigaile and Mickey Stolli. They'd bickered all the way from their house. First of all the car had arrived late, and when it finally did get there Abigaile had freaked out when she'd realized she was expected to ride to the première in a small sedan. She'd thrown an absolute fit, screaming at the driver, an out-of-work actor who almost walked off the job.

"I never ordered a car like this," she'd yelled. "I've never been in a car like this in my life. Where's my stretch limo?"

"It's down on the sheet, ma'am," the driver replied politely. "This is the car you requested."

Abigaile had narrowed her eyes, naturally blaming

305

Mickey. "I'll murder that secretary of yours. She's an idiot. And it's *your* fault."

"Don't worry about it," Mickey had replied calmly. "I'm firing her first thing Monday."

"Monday isn't soon enough," Abigaile said ominously, before turning her attention back to the driver. "Why are you so late?"

"Six-forty-five, ma'am. That's the time I was told to be here."

"I expected the car to be here at six-thirty," Abigaile had said through clenched teeth. "This is simply not good enough."

Mickey had shrugged. There were enough things on his mind. He didn't need Abigaile screaming too.

She'd wanted him to send the car back and get a limousine, but he'd pointed out there wasn't time. "I'll have the driver arrange everything while we're in the theatre," he'd assured her. "There'll be a limousine to meet us when we leave."

She'd finally agreed and got in the car reluctantly. Image was all-important to Abigaile and this just wouldn't do.

Even earlier than that, when Mickey had arrived home from the studio, they'd discussed Abe-Panther calling a Monday morning meeting without consulting either of them.

"I don't understand what's going on," Abigaile fretted. "Why would he contact Primrose and Ben without first telling me? I saw him this week. It would have been easy for him to mention something."

"Why is he coming to the studio at all?" Mickey had growled. "There's something out of line going on."

Abigaile had muttered her agreement, wondering if now was the right moment to tell him about Warner.

Eventually she'd decided against it. Mickey would accuse her of being insane if she admitted she'd called a number and gone to see a woman who claimed to be having an affair with him.

Mickey had not returned Warner's urgent phone calls. Why should he? He'd finally decided it was time to ease out of the relationship, and the fact that she'd called his office twice really annoyed him.

They were the last to arrive at the theatre. The television camera crews were packing up. Only the stragglers remained. Mickey hustled Abigaile inside.

"Sorry," said an officious usher. "The doors are closed."

"Do you know who I am?" demanded Mickey in a rage.

"I'm sorry, the doors are closed," the usher repeated firmly.

"I'm Mickey Stolli, President of Panther Studios. You'd better let us in right now if you plan to keep your job."

The usher snapped to attention. "Certainly, sir," he said, changing his tune in a hurry.

To get to their seats they had to squeeze past Johnny Romano, who was not pleased. "You're late," he hissed at Mickey. As if they didn't already know.

Finally they were settled. Abigaile gazed at the screen, her mind elsewhere.

Mickey settled back and tried to concentrate on the film.

"You motherfuckers," sneered Johnny Romano in full closeup, his handsome face filling the screen.

"Who you callin' motherfucker?" answered the actor playing opposite him.

"Don't fuck with me, man," said Johnny menacingly. "Don't do it."

"Listen, motherfucker, I fuck with anyone I want," replied the other actor.

Oh, nice, Abigaile thought to herself. *Another one of Mickey's classy productions.* She leaned over to her husband and whispered sarcastically in his ear, "Are there going to be any normal words in this picture?"

Mickey grunted. "It's a money-maker," he replied gruffly.

At the party afterwards, everybody told Johnny Romano he was wonderful, the movie was a sure-fire hit, and how creative and clever he was to have starred, written, and directed.

Johnny Romano accepted their praise modestly, with a shrug here, a smile there.

Privately the buzz was – *How come this asshole gets away with making a piece of shit like this? And how come it's going to score a fucking fortune?*

Johnny strutted around the party giving interviews, greeting friends, playing superstar to the hilt.

Some of the early reviews on the movie had been less than positive, in fact there'd been some killers. Johnny didn't care. He knew he could do whatever he wanted to and the public would accept it. He was Johnny Romano and they loved him, and they'd take anything he cared to dish out.

Abigaile and Mickey sat at a table with several Panther executives. Mickey knew something deadly was up when Ford Werne leaned across the table and said, "What's all this about a meeting on Monday morning?"

"Huh?" Mickey feigned ignorance.

"I received a communiqué from Abe Panther," Ford said. "Apparently he's coming to the studio on Monday, and has requested a meeting with all the senior executives at noon."

"Really?" Mickey was aware of a sinking feeling in the pit of his stomach. Crafty old Abe Panther was finally emerging, and he was up to something serious. Maybe he was coming back to take over.

Mickey decided he'd better call Martin Swanson and find out what was happening with the other deal, because if Abe Panther came back to work, Mickey Stolli was getting the hell out. There was no way he was answering to a decrepit, senile old man. No way at all.

As he was thinking all this, he happened to glance up, and there was Warner, all six feet of her, wearing a short spangly dress, talking to Johnny Romano. Jesus Christ! She was actually talking to Johnny Romano!

Mickey double-taked. What the hell was Warner doing here? He'd gotten her tickets to the movie, certainly not an invitation to the party.

No doubt that stupid secretary of his had fucked up again and left a party invitation along with the tickets.

308

From the perfect replacement, Luce had turned into dumb cunt of the year. He couldn't wait to fire her.

"Oh my God!" exclaimed Abigaile, spotting Warner a few moments after her husband. "It's that dreadful woman."

"What woman? Where?" spat Mickey, knowing Abigaile couldn't possibly mean Warner.

"Over there," Abigaile hissed, pointing straight at Warner. "Talking to Johnny Romano. It's her."

Mickey looked blank. "She's just another one of Johnny's dates," he said. "What are you getting so bothered about?"

"I should have told you what happened today," Abigaile said excitedly, her face flushing.

"What?" Mickey was in no mood to hear about Abigaile's day.

"I . . . I called your office," she said, "to find out where you were so I could tell you about Primrose and Ben and the telegram."

He had a dull feeling he wasn't going to like what came next. "Yes?"

"And your secretary gave me a phone number. I called and this woman answered."

"What woman?"

"The one talking to Johnny."

"Get to the point, Abigaile. Make sense, for crissakes."

"A woman answered the phone and told me she was a cop, and she was your girlfriend. Can you believe such nonsense? Anyway, I didn't know what to do." Abigaile hesitated before plunging on. "You're going to kill me for this, Mickey, but I was so confused, I got in my car and I went to see her. She lives in a tacky little apartment. She tried to threaten me. I'm sure it was some sort of kidnapping plan. Of course, I got out of there as fast as I could."

Mickey scratched his head. "I don't fucking believe what I'm hearing. Some woman says on the phone she's my girlfriend, and you buy that? And you go over to a strange apartment?" He shook his head wearily, "Abby, Abby, you've gone too far this time."

309

Abigaile lowered her eyes. "I know, Mickey, it was a foolish thing to do. I'm fortunate to have escaped."

While Abigaile was talking, Mickey was thinking fast. Once Abigaile got to consider what had taken place she would realize all was not as it seemed. He had to come up with some explanation as to why his stupid secretary had given her Warner's number. And then he had to explain who Warner was.

"Listen," he said quickly. "I didn't want you involved in this, but now I guess I'll have to tell you what it's all about."

Abigaile looked alarmed. "What, Mickey?"

"Johnny Romano is heavily into drugs."

"Oh, dear," cried Abigaile.

"Uh . . . I've had this uh . . . private cop following him and uh . . . obviously Luce got confused and gave you the wrong number. The woman must have thought it was Johnny's girlfriend calling him."

"Why would she think that?" asked Abigaile. "I told her my name."

"What am I, a thought-reader?" he snapped. "All I know is you should never have gone over there. Don't you realize your position?"

"Why is that woman here tonight? Is she watching Johnny?"

"Yeah, yeah, that's it. She's an undercover drug cop. I have to protect Johnny."

"I didn't realize you got involved in these kind of things."

"Honey, when you run a studio, you get to watch over everybody and everything."

Mickey figured he'd covered his tracks, for now anyway. He shot a quick glance at Warner. She was still all over Johnny Romano, and was it his imagination or did Johnny seem to be responding?

In all the time they'd been together Mickey had never seen Warner dressed up before. She didn't look bad. She certainly had the longest legs in town, and although she wasn't pretty she had a certain style of her own. Come to think of it he'd only ever seen her in her cop's uniform or in the nude. This was a new exciting Warner. He experienced a sharp twinge of jealousy.

"When can we go home?" Abigaiie whispered. "I hated the movie. I hate this party. I hate the fact we don't know what's going to happen at the meeting on Monday morning. Let's go now."

"You're right," Mickey agreed. "Give me five minutes and we're out of here."

"Where are you going?"

"I gotta go stroke ego, tell Johnny he's the greatest thing since banana yogurt. It'll take me two seconds."

"Shall I come with you?"

"No, stay here. You'll send him over a gift from Cartier's tomorrow."

Mickey walked over just in time to hear Johnny Romano say to Warner, "Hey, baby, baby, you got the longest legs I ever put my eyes on. They about measure up to the height of my date. Bet you can do things with those legs I've never even imagined."

Warner, the six-feet seen-everything, done-everything hard-knuckled cop, gazed at Johnny Romano as if he was God.

"How about you an' me gettin' together later?" Johnny suggested, bored with his actress girlfriend, who was busy scanning the room.

Mickey made his presence felt. "Hey, Johnny, we've got another big money-maker here. Congratulations," he enthused.

"The biggest," Johnny replied modestly.

Mickey kissed ass. He knew how to do it when he had to. "No doubt about it."

Johnny stroked Warner's arm. "Have you met . . . um . . . What did you say your name was, babe?"

Warner threw Mickey a filthy look.

He was infuriated. What had *he* done? *She* was the one at fault, talking to Abigaile on the phone and telling her to come to her apartment. He couldn't wait to have it out with her. But not now, not while Abigaile was present and probably tracking his every move.

"Warner Franklin," she said, cool as you like.

"That's a pretty name, baby," said Johnny with a sexy leer. "Warner, huh?"

Mickey shook her hand.

She squeezed too hard, favouring him with a real bone-crusher.

"Hey, baby, this here's Micky Stolli, the head of the studio." Johnny nudged her and winked. "This guy's an important man to know. What do you do, honey? You an actress?"

"No." Warner loved to shock. "I'm a cop."

Johnny thought this was the funniest thing he'd ever heard. "A *cop? You?* Oh, baby, baby, I wouldn't mind gettin' myself arrested by you."

She shot Mickey a triumphant look. "Maybe you will be. Later."

Seething, Mickey returned to Abigaile, yanked her by the arm, and said, "Let's go."

The Stollis made their exit – head of studio and his Hollywood princess wife.

Who knew what Monday morning would bring?

Chapter 49

It was three o'clock in the morning when Lucky, accompanied by Boogie, finally arrived on the sidewalk outside Lennie's rented New York loft. She looked around. "God, Boogie, this is a real dump. Why didn't he stay at our apartment?"

Boogie shook his head. "Beats me. I suppose he felt he could hide away here."

"He did a pretty good job," she replied, feeling nervous and excited at the same time. Tracking Lennie was an adventure, and this little caper had her adrenalin pumping.

She took a deep breath. "OK, Boog, exhibit your skills and let's break in here without anybody knowing."

"You're going to surprise him in bed?" Boogie asked.

"That's exactly what I plan to do."

It was unlike Boogie to offer a comment, but he did so anyway. "You're pretty confident."

"Oh, you *know* I'm confident."

Boogie shot her a look.

Hmmmm, she thought. Did he honestly imagine she was going to find Lennie shacked up with a woman? Her husband might be mad at her, but he certainly wasn't that mad. Their relationship was based on trust, and the last thing she expected was for Lennie to break that trust. Not that she imagined he wasn't attracted to other women. But being attracted and doing something about it were two different things.

The loft he'd chosen was on the eighth floor of a run-down building. Boogie sprang the street door with ease, and the two of them entered the lobby, where they were confronted by a row of mailboxes. Lennie's was marked with a cryptic L.G.

The elevator didn't appear to be in great shape. "We'll take the fire stairs," Lucky decided.

"You feeling energetic?" Boogie said. "It's eight floors up."

"You're full of questions tonight, Boog. What's with you?"

"I don't approve of this," he said dourly.

She sighed. All she needed was an uptight Boogie. Why couldn't he get into the spirit of the adventure and enjoy it? "How come?" she asked lightly.

"It's not your style."

"That's where you're wrong. It's exactly my style." And it was. Vanish for six weeks. Come back with a bang. What was wrong with that?

They traipsed upstairs, Lucky making better time than Boogie. When they reached the top and let themselves through the fire door to Lennie's floor, they were faced with a steel front door.

313

Boogie frowned. "I can get through a lot of things, but this looks like a no-go."

"How about the back door?" Lucky suggested brightly. "There must be an easier way to get in."

"I don't know." Boogie shook his head uncertainly. "What if he's not living here? What if a new tenant's moved in – a new tenant with a gun?"

"Are you frightened?" Lucky teased. "I always considered you such a macho man."

"I'm protecting your ass," Boogie reminded her pointedly.

"*I'll* worry about *my* ass, *you* worry about *yours*."

The back door turned out to be an easier proposition. It took Boogie about five minutes, but eventually he clicked it open.

"Shhhh." Lucky held a finger on her lips as they made their way stealthily into a small, dark kitchen.

Once inside she turned around and whispered to Boogie, "You can go now. I'm OK."

"I can't leave you here," he objected.

"Sure you can," she whispered. "Wait downstairs in the car. If I'm not out in ten minutes, take off."

"I shouldn't go," he repeated stubbornly.

"Will you get out of here?" she said impatiently. "You'll spoil the surprise."

He didn't budge.

"Split," she hissed, "or you're fired."

Reluctantly he departed.

She closed the kitchen door behind him and made her way into a huge studio. In the middle of the open space was a winding flight of stairs leading to a gallery. Since this appeared to be the extent of the apartment she imagined the bedroom must be at the top of the stairs. Pulling off her sneakers, she crept stealthily upstairs.

In the centre of the gallery there was an enormous circular bed, and in the middle of the bed was Lennie, fast asleep on his stomach, a sheet half covering him.

Lucky couldn't remove the smile from her face. She

stood there for a moment just staring at him. Her husband! Her gorgeous husband!

Quietly she began to remove her clothes until she was naked. And then, without a sound, she edged her way into bed next to him.

Lennie groaned in his sleep and threw an arm across her.

She snaked closer, wrapping her body around him.

In his sleep he started to become aroused.

She smiled, trying to decide whether to be insulted or pleased. Was he getting hard because he knew it was her? Or was he merely in the middle of a wonderful dream?

It didn't matter, because she was just as horny as he was. "Lennie," she whispered, rubbing against his back. "Wake up."

He let out a groan and slowly opened his eyes. "What the—" he began.

"Shhh." She held her finger to his lips, attempting to silence him.

"Hey — I don't believe this," he mumbled, still half asleep.

"Believe it, baby. It's me. I'm back!" she exclaimed delightedly.

He rolled over. "How the hell did you find me?"

She laughed softly. "Who did you think you were dealing with here, a wife?"

He propped himself up on one elbow. "You're too much, you know that?"

"Uh huh."

"Jess told you where to find me, huh? I always knew she had a big mouth."

"My sources are secret. I'm here — isn't that enough?" As she spoke her hands caressed his body.

He attempted to push her away with very little real intent. He was mad, but losing the battle. "Jesus, Lucky. What happens next? Another great sex scene so you can take off again when it's over?"

"No way," she replied indignantly. "I never repeat myself. You should know that by now."

"The only thing I know about you is that you're crazy."

"I know I'm crazy too. Six weeks away from you is the longest I can take."

He sat up, brushing his hands through his hair. "Was it worth it? Did you make your deal?"

She put her arms around him from behind. "I'll tell you all about it tomorrow."

He shook his head. "How did you get in here?"

She grinned. "I used to be a burglar. Didn't I tell you?"

"Oh, baby, you're something else, you really are. I should be mad at you."

She scratched the back of his neck, a place she knew he loved to be touched. "Are you, Lennie?"

He shook his head again. "What am I supposed to do?"

"You're supposed to kiss me – make love to me. And we're supposed to have incredible sex." She took a beat, continuing to stroke the nape of his neck. "I'm ready," she whispered tantalizingly. "How about you?"

He didn't fight it. What could he do? He loved her.

He turned her over until she was flat on her back. And then he bent to kiss her. Slow, burning kisses – his lips scorching hers – making up for six weeks of pent-up passion.

She sighed voluptuously. It was like the first time she'd ever been kissed. It was like going on a diet and having chocolate for the first time in months. It was like a hot summer day after rain. It was like the time they'd made out on a raft in the South of France with nobody around to bother them.

He kissed her long and hard until they both fell into the slow fast build-up to the wild roller-coaster trip they knew awaited them.

His hands moved ravenously down her body, touching her as only he could. "Oh, Christ," he groaned. "I still love you. You know that, don't you?"

"Did you think it was over?" she murmured, winding her body around his, touching him wherever she could.

"I never know what to think when it comes to you."

"You've got to learn to trust me, Lennie."

And so they made love, long and leisurely, slow and even slower, their bodies fusing together as if nothing else in the world mattered. And at that very moment nothing else did.

She gave herself up to ecstasy, luxuriating in the thought of a wild throbbing release. And as it drew close she whispered in his ear. "I want to come with you. I want us to come together."

"You got it, lady. There's no way I'm goin' anywhere without you."

"I love you, Lennie," she sighed happily. "I love you so much."

And they made it happen.

And they made it last.

And they ended up wrapped into each other's arms, sleeping soundly until the morning light.

Chapter 50

Eddie Kane paced up and down Kathleen Le Paul's living room talking fast. "My life's a fuck-up. I got no idea what I'm gonna do. You can't help me. Leslie can't. And Mickey doesn't give a damn. I'm a failure. An' on top of everything else I hit my wife." He slapped his forehead with the palm of his hand — a gesture of self-hatred. "I've never hit a woman before. Do you understand what I'm saying? I've never hit a woman, and I hit Leslie, who's the sweetest person in the world."

Kathleen was really not interested in hearing Eddie's stream of consciousness. She was interested in getting him out of her house. "How did you get my address?" she asked edgily, her calculator brain figuring out how much he owed her.

"You think I've dealt with you all this time and haven't found out a thing or two?" Eddie replied heatedly. "I tried to call you from my car, but I couldn't get through." His facial twitch went into overdrive. "I gotta have some stuff, an' I gotta have it like now."

"Eddie," Kathleen said patiently, although she didn't feel patient at all – she felt like throwing the bum out. "I made a delivery to you today. Another fifteen hundred dollars' worth, which, I might remind you, is currently on your tab."

"Yeah, well, you wanna know why I laid one on my wife? You wanna know?" Now he smashed his fist into the palm of his hand. "She threw my stash down the friggin' garbage disposal."

Other people's problems bored Kathleen. She had enough of her own. What Leslie did was not her concern.

Eddie was on a roll. "How was I supposed to handle that? Say 'Thank you, dear, for saving my soul?' No way. I'll get fuckin' straight when *I* wanna get straight." He walked over to the window and stared out. "I can stop any time. Right now I don't need crap." He turned back to her. "So you're gonna help me out."

"If you think I keep a supply in my house you're not as smart as I imagined," she said, hoping to get rid of him.

There was no getting rid of Eddie. "Kathleen, don't talk to me like I'm a schmuck. Go to the safe or wherever the fuck you keep it an' get me somethin'."

"Eddie, I can't encourage this kind of behaviour. If you ever come to my house again I'll be forced to put a bullet through your ass. I can always say I thought you were an intruder."

Now he was getting really edgy. "Fine, fine, whatever makes your day. Do I get the stuff or not?"

"Cash only."

This broad was getting on his nerves. "I gave you cash this morning."

"You owed me. Now you owe me more. You haven't even paid for the stuff your wife dumped."

He was truly surprised. "Shit! Am I supposed to pay for that?"

"Am *I*?" she answered coldly.

"OK, OK, so I owe you. Don't get your balls in an uproar."

It was quite obvious there was only one way to get him to leave. "Wait here," she said brusquely. "Don't touch anything."

While she was away he rifled his pockets. All he could find was a few credit cards, his driver's licence, and maybe two hundred and fifty bucks. That was it.

Painfully he relived the scene with Leslie.

"I threw it away, Eddie," she'd said, all sweetness and light. "We're going to start a new life."

"You did what?" he'd shouted, unable to believe anyone could be that stupid.

"I threw it away, Eddie," she'd repeated. "You're addicted."

What was she all of a sudden, a nurse? "I hope you're kidding me," he'd said ominously.

"No," she'd replied, as if it was her right to do what she liked.

He'd slapped her so suddenly it surprised even him. One good whack across the face and Leslie went down like a bowling pin. Oh Christ, he hadn't even felt bad about it then. He'd gone on a rampage through the house, searching everywhere, throwing clothes out of drawers, dishes from kitchen cabinets. And then he'd walked back into the room where she still lay on the floor. "Tell me where the fuck it is," he'd screamed.

By that time she was crying, above her eye already beginning to puff up where his pinkie ring had caught her.

"I threw it away," she sobbed.

"Bitch!" he'd yelled. "You *know* what I'm suffering. A little coke helps get me through the day. You're nothin' but a blood-sucking bitch! All you want is my money, an' now I don't have any you're drivin' me nuts."

"Eddie, I'm only trying to help you," she said miserably, tears running down her cheeks.

"If this is the kind of help you give, get out of here. This is *my* house, an' I want you gone when I get back."

He'd stormed out, climbed in his Maserati, and now he was at Kathleen's.

When she came back into the room he handed her four fifty-dollar bills. "This'll hold you, unless you'd sooner have a cheque."

"I don't take cheques," she said icily.

He hunched his shoulders. "What's the matter, you're not into trustin' me?"

"I don't trust anybody," Kathleen Le Paul replied flatly. "And what am I supposed to do with a lousy two hundred dollars?"

She could stuff it up her snatch for all he cared. He needed a snort more than he needed anything. "Come on, baby," he wheedled. "I'm good for the money." Maybe he should throw a fuck into her. Kathleen looked like the kind of woman who could do with it.

"What are you doing about your debt to Bonnatti?" she asked curiously.

He picked up a gold table lighter and studied it. This broad must be doing pretty well for herself. "I put my house on the market. Monday I'll get a bank loan. He'll get paid, don't worry about it, and so will you."

She tried to control her underlying anger. "Eddie, I'm strictly a cash business. This is the last time." She handed him the package. "I mean it."

"You want to do some together, be sociable?" he suggested.

Was he crazy? She wouldn't touch the stuff. "No, just get out of my house."

Outside in the car he snorted the white powder from the back of his hand. And once the effect took hold, he immediately felt like a calmer, saner man.

In fact, he felt as if he could accomplish anything.

Leslie was stunned. Never in her wildest dreams had she imagined Eddie would ever strike her. It brought back every bad memory. When she was a little girl, her step-father had knocked the hell out of her. When she was a big girl, her first boyfriend had done the same thing. And when she'd run away to California with a thousand dollars of her stepfather's money which she reckoned he owed her, she'd vowed that no man was ever going to get away with hitting her again. Now this.

Leslie had really thought she loved Eddie. But Leslie was no victim. One blow and he didn't have to tell her to go, she was out of there.

Hurrying into the bedroom she threw some clothes into a suitcase. Then she went outside to her jeep, got in, and drove directly to Madame Loretta's.

When the friendly old madam saw her, she was immediately sympathetic and took her upstairs.

"Can I stay here until I figure out what to do?" Leslie asked mournfully.

Madame Loretta nodded. "Are you coming back to work?"

Leslie shook her head. "It's not what I want to do."

"No pressure," replied Madame Loretta. "We'll talk tomorrow. Why don't you take a hot bath and get a good night's sleep?"

Leslie nodded. At least she'd had somewhere to run to.

Chapter 51

Saturday morning in New York dawned crisp and clear. The sun filtered through the flimsy blinds in Lennie's loft and woke Lucky. For a moment she was disoriented, and then she remembered where she was and smiled to herself. Lennie was asleep next to her, exactly where he should be.

Trying not to disturb him, she crept from bed, dashed into the bathroom, and switched on the shower. It was old and rusty and didn't have much pressure, but she stood under it anyway, allowing the warm water to sting her into awareness.

Emerging from the shower she wrapped herself in Lennie's white terry-cloth robe. It swamped her. Barefoot, she padded downstairs to the kitchen and inspected the contents of the fridge. There wasn't much there. A couple of eggs, some mouldy tomatoes, a stale loaf of bread, and half a pint of sour milk. Hardly ingredients for a feast.

Cooking was not one of her greatest talents, but she could rustle up scrambled eggs and French toast if the mood took her. "Hmmm," she murmured, surveying what was available. It didn't look very promising.

Quietly she padded upstairs, slipped into her clothes, grabbed her purse, found the keys to the loft lying on a table next to the bed, and let herself out.

Down on the street it was New York crazy, hustle and bustle, and the smells, sights, and sounds she'd missed being in California for six weeks.

In the neighbourhood grocery store she picked up fresh rolls, juice, eggs, fruit, butter, and milk. Then she had the old man behind the counter slice her half a pound of fresh ham.

Satisfied, she hurried back. Lennie was still asleep, and who could blame him? It had been some wonderful night.!

Busying herself in the kitchen she began scrambling eggs and heating the rolls. Then she squeezed fresh orange juice, made coffee, and set everything out on the kitchen table.

When it was all ready she yelled out, "Hey, Lennie, get your sexy ass down here for breakfast."

No response.

Noticing a stereo, she slotted in a Stevie Wonder tape and "Isn't She Lovely" blasted out.

Finally Lennie staggered downstairs with rumpled hair and a half-asleep look.

"Good morning," she sang out cheerfully.

"I had this wild dream," he mumbled. "Who're you?"

"Your wife. Remember?"

"A wife who cooks?" he said blankly, shaking his head. "I don't have a wife who cooks."

She offered him a spoonful of eggs. "Try it and live!"

Gingerly he tasted the eggs. "Hmm . . . Not bad."

"Not bad my ass. They're fuckin' great! Admit it."

"You're back."

"Oh yeah!"

"Still as crazy as ever, huh?" he said, sitting at the table. She grinned. "Would you have it any other way?"

"It'd be nice if you stayed home occasionally."

"Stop nagging!" She stood back and surveyed him. "Hey – look at you in the daylight. Is that the very same beard that was scratching the hell out of me all night long?"

"The very same."

"Hmm . . ."

"You like?"

"I hate."

"It's gone."

She put her arms around his shoulders – anticipating the surprise she had for him, but not wanting to reveal it yet. "I'm really back."

"I noticed. For how long this time?"

"No more trips, Lennie. We'll be together all summer long. That's a Santangelo promise."

"A Golden promise," he corrected.

She smiled. "Right!"

He surveyed the table. "So . . . what made you turn into Housewife of the Year?"

"I thought you might be hungry." She bent down and kissed his neck. "Did I make you hungry, Lennie?"

"Ravenous!"

"Really?"

He twisted around and his hands began to stray beneath her T-shirt.

She backed away. "Later. I want to see you eat."

He ate like a starving man, grabbing everything in sight. "This is great," he said with his mouth full. "Best meal you've ever cooked me."

She laughed. "The *only* meal I've ever cooked you, right?"

"You made me soup once."

"Was it good?"

"Passable."

"Thanks a lot!" She glanced around the loft. "This place is a mess. Who's been looking after you?"

"Nobody."

"I can see that. What have you been doing?"

"What I should have done a long time ago. Writing a script. A movie I might direct."

"Oh, we're a director now, are we?" she teased.

"Why not? If Grudge Freeport can do it, anyone can."

"You're talking to the right person," she said. "Will you star in it too?"

He laughed. "Hey – you think I'd let anyone else do it? It's a terrific role."

"When can I read it?"

"Not until it's finished." He paused. "So, I guess you heard I walked off the film?"

"It's not exactly a secret."

"I warned everyone it had to happen. They'll probably sue, but who cares? It was something I had to do."

She almost told him about Panther, but held back just in time. It was too important to blurt out.

"Don't worry, they won't sue," she said reassuringly.

"What makes you say that? I hear Mickey Stolli is so crazed he nearly blew a blood vessel."

"Listen to me, Lennie. I *know* they won't sue."

"Why?" he joked. "Are you getting Gino to put a hit on them?"

She laughed. "Gino doesn't do that kind of thing."

"But he could arrange it if he wanted to, huh?"

"Gino was never into putting hits on people. Why do you always imagine my father was such a major gangster?"

"Wasn't he?"

"He shipped booze in during Prohibition. And then he ran a speakeasy. After that he got into Vegas and became respectable."

"Sure."

"Really. Have you seen him?"

"I haven't seen anybody. I've been holed up here."

"We must call him."

"Later." He pushed his chair away from the table and

got up. Then he reached out his arms for her. "C'mere, cook."

"Why?"

"Because I want to try and knock you up. OK?"

"Sweet-talker."

"And don't you love it!"

Chapter 52

Saturday morning in Los Angeles was smoggy. Emilio Sierra couldn't help but notice that Rita had stayed the night. Her clothes made a trail from the living room to the bedroom, and she herself was asleep in his bed. Score one for Emilio. He was some stud!

Nudging her roughly, he urged her to wake up.

"What time is it?" Rita mumbled, hugging the pillow.

"I told you – it's late, an' I gotta go out."

Rita buried her face in the pillow. "I'll stay here."

"You won't stay anywhere," Emilio replied, agitated. "I gotta lock the apartment."

"Whaddaya think – I'm gonna rip you off?" Rita asked accusingly.

"Naw. My mother's comin' over," he lied. "I better drop you off."

She dressed, unabashed about strutting naked in front of him. She was a hot little number all right – although not quite so hot in the harsh light of morning with the sun streaming through the windows, hitting her un-made-up face.

"Come on," Emilio urged, forcing her to dress in a hurry.

She did so, complaining all the way.

Then he hustled her out to his car, drove her to her apartment, and said a fast goodbye.

"When am I gonna see you again?" she asked, stalling.

"Soon." He winked. "I'll call you."

She wasn't thrilled with his reply, but she sashayed into the entrance of her apartment building as if she didn't have a care in the world.

Women, Emilio thought to himself. *The worse you treat 'em, the more they like it.*

Once rid of Rita, he drove directly to Venus Maria's house. He knew it was too early for her to be up, and it being a weekend the housekeeper had the day off, which was exactly what he was counting on. Her housekeeper was too protective by far, always spying on him. With just himself and Venus Maria in the house he'd have a better chance of getting what he needed from her safe.

He didn't bother ringing the doorbell. There was a window at the back that allowed him easy access. Why disturb her if she was asleep? All the better to surprise little sis.

Venus Maria was asleep all right, curled up in front of the television, an empty ice-cream carton on the floor beside her, a jacket thrown casually across her body.

This was too good to be true.

Stealthily Emilio made his way through the living room, up the stairs to her bedroom, straight to her hidden safe. He knew where she'd jotted down the combination in some kind of a code. Quickly he found her private phone book, located the coded combination, hurried to the safe, opened it, slid out the picture of Venus Maria with Martin Swanson, and placed it safely in his pocket.

All this took only a few minutes. It was far easier than he'd expected. Now he could skip, and she wouldn't even know he'd been there.

Unknown to Emilio, when he'd opened the window he'd triggered a silent alarm connected directly to the police. As he started to make his way downstairs he was shocked to hear the screaming siren of a police car. It sounded like it was right outside the house.

Venus Maria awoke with a start. "Oh, God!" she exclaimed, realizing she'd fallen asleep in front of the television. The police were already urgently pressing her front door buzzer.

Groggily she rushed to the door.

Two uniformed cops stood at attention. One of them had a hand hovering near his gun. "Your alarm went off, miss," he said. "You all right?" And then realization hit. He nudged his partner. "Excuse me, aren't you—?"

She nodded. "Yes, I am, and I'm not looking my best. What do you mean, my alarm went off?"

"There's an intruder in your home."

Oh, God! The crazed fan she'd always dreaded was somewhere in her house. She shivered. "I'm here by myself."

"Don't worry. We'll check everything out. Do you mind if we come in?"

"Mind? I'd be delighted."

Emilio lurked at the top of the stairs, listening. How was he going to get out of this one?

His mind raced over the possibilities. He could always say the back door was open and he'd gone up to her bedroom to see if she was awake. Venus Maria wouldn't be pleased, but what could she do? He *was* her brother.

Before he could make any move at all, the two cops were crouched at the bottom of the stairs, guns drawn. "Hit the floor, sucker," one of them yelled. "Don't even think about going for a weapon."

Dennis Walla groped for the ringing phone. "Yeah?" he muttered into the receiver. "Wassa matter?"

"Dennis?"

"Who's this?"

"'Ere, Dennis, it's yer New York connection, Bert. You got a short memory or wot?"

With a weary sigh Dennis recognized the rough Cockney accent of Bert Slocombe, one of his colleagues in New York. Just for a lark they'd put a man on Swanson watch.

Dennis yawned and scratched his balls. "Find anything out, mate?"

"Only that they go out a lot," replied Bert sourly. "Bleedin' 'ell, they're never at 'ome."

"Yeah? Where'd they go?"

"Try just about every party in town. An' every club. It's bloody well not easy following 'em."

"Do they seem like a happy, loving couple?"

"'Ere, you ever seen a husband and wife out in public who don't seem lovey-dovey? They're all over each other. It's bleedin' sickenin'."

"Hmmm." Dennis groped for a cigarette, lit up, and inhaled deeply. "I don't suppose he'll be so cheerful come Monday."

"Yer think the bugger'll sue us?"

"Talk sense, mate. Nobody's that stupid. Four or five years with lawyers swarmin' all over you, an' then finally sloggin' it out in court. No. He won't sue."

"Yeah, but Martin Swanson's a tough one."

"Don't worry about him being so tough. Today I'm getting my hands on a photograph of him with Venus Maria. A very telling photograph. When our story runs we'll have plenty to back it up."

"OK. Am I off duty now?"

"Stick with 'em another twenty-four hours."

"It's-a useless waste of time," Bert complained.

"Waste it. You're gettin' paid," Dennis said. He took another drag of his cigarette, stubbed it out in an over-flowing ashtray, turned over, and went back to sleep.

At seven o'clock on Saturday morning Martin Swanson played racquetball for two hours. He got off on the challenge of beating the hell out of his opponent, and since most of his opponents usually worked for him he managed to win every time.

Afterwards he took a shower, towelled himself dry, dressed, and jogged up the stairs to the top floor of the Swanson Building, where his penthouse office gave him a panoramic view of the city.

It was too early to call Venus Maria in California. He wondered what her reaction was to his gift. Well, it wasn't a gift really. He'd lost a bet. And what a beautiful way to lose!

Gertrude, his personal assistant, greeted him with a triumphant smile. She'd been with him eleven years and knew more about his business than anyone. "Good morning, Mr Swanson, and how are we today?"

He nodded.

"I'm sure you'll be delighted with these," she said, handing him a sheaf of faxes. "Yes, Mr Swanson, it looks as if we'll be taking over the studio. Shall I alert your pilot and have him ready the plane?"

He read the first fax quickly. And the second one. And the third.

A smile played around his lips. "Do that," he said. "I'll leave first thing tomorrow."

Mickey was awoken by a troop of Mexican gardeners using their illegal leaf-blowers right outside his bedroom window. The smell of gas assailed his nostrils. Furiously he turned over to prod Abigaile, but she was already up and gone.

"God dammit," he muttered under his breath. How many times had he told her that under no circumstances were the gardeners to come anywhere near his house on a Saturday? He groped for his watch. Was is ten o'clock already?

Rolling from his comfortable bed he stalked into his bathroom, glared at himself in the mirror, filled his sink with ice-cold water, and plunged his face into the icy bowl. It woke him in a hurry.

When his head cleared he called Warner. "What kind of game are you playing?" he demanded in a low voice, just in case Abigaile was listening.

"It's over, Mickey," hissed Warner, not pleased to hear from him.

"What do you mean, it's over?"

"I've had enough."

"Enough of what?"

"Your bad moods, your wife, and the way you use me for sex. Besides, I'm in love with somebody else now."

He nearly choked. "You're *what*?"

"Yes, I'm in love with somebody else," she said, repeating the ego-busting news.

"And who might that be?" he demanded.

"Johnny Romano," she replied, and promptly hung up on him.

Leslie Kane awoke in LA and shivered when she realized where she was and what she'd done. She'd run out on Eddie, straight back to her old life. On reflection it probably wasn't the smartest move in the world.

Tearfully she thought about her husband. Eddie wasn't so bad. He had his problems – didn't everyone? And she'd deserted him just when he'd needed her most. What kind of wife did that make her?

Madame Loretta's house was very still. Saturday mornings and sex for sale did not mix. Most men were busy with their children.

She lay in bed and tried to decide what to do. One thing was sure, and that was she had to teach Eddie some kind of lesson. He had to be made aware that he could not treat her like dirt.

Twenty-four hours should do it.

Twenty-four hours and then she'd go home.

In New York Deena opened her eyes at ten o'clock, removed her black satin sleep mask, and summoned her maid, who served her tea in bed and brought her the morning papers. She skipped straight to the gossip columns, anxious to know who was doing what to whom and if there were any parties she might have missed. Satisfied that there weren't, she immediately turned to the fashion pages. Not for Deena world events and crime news. She wasn't interested.

Her houseman buzzed the bedroom to tell her there was a call for her.

"Who is it?" she asked.

"Mr Paul Webster," he replied.

Hmm . . . what was Effie's son calling her for?

She picked up the phone. "Paul? *Little* Paul?"

"Do you get your kicks trying to make me feel small?" he asked.

Nice voice. Very low. Very sexy. In spite of herself Deena felt a tingle. "I don't think your mother would enjoy it if she knew you were flirting with me," she said.

He came right back to her. "What makes you think I'm flirting?"

"Either that or you're calling to ask after my health. Which is it, Paul?"

"You're a turn-on, Deena."

She couldn't help being amused. "Paul, I'm old enough to be your . . . your . . ."

"Older sister?" he offered.

"Something like that."

"Can I take you to lunch?"

Why not? she thought to herself. Effie would have a thousand fits — but Effie didn't have to find out, did she? "Where did you have in mind?"

"The park," he said easily.

She thought he meant Tavern on the Green. "What time?"

"I'll pick you up at noon." He paused, waiting for her response.

"I'm not sure I—"

"Twelve o'clock," he interjected. "See you."

She smiled. There'd been nobody since the soul singer. Just because Martin said she wasn't supposed to . . .

Why should she listen to Martin when he did exactly as he pleased?

But Paul Webster . . . a boy . . . Effie's son . . .

Deena Swanson, she scolded herself. *You ought to be ashamed . . .*

Eddie Kane didn't sleep at all. He went to a party at the beach house shared by Arnie Blackwood and Frankie Lombardo. He got good and truly bombed. He snorted as much cocaine as he could manage because he knew Arnie and Frankie kept a generous supply for their friends, and it would cost him nothing. At one point he'd asked Arnie for a loan. Arnie had laughed in his face.

There were plenty of girls around, but Eddie didn't feel

331

like getting laid. He knew how badly he'd treated Leslie. He'd hurt her, and he didn't know how she'd react. What was he going to do about it?

First of all he had no idea where she'd gone. And secondly he wasn't sure how long it would take her to return.

Talk about fucking up a perfect relationship. The story of his life.

On Saturday morning he came to, only to find himself slumped on the living room floor of Arnie and Frankie's house in Trancas along with half a dozen other bums who'd spent the night.

Fortunately, he'd managed to score enough coke at the party to give himself a jump start. After visiting the bathroom and doing just that, he felt considerably better. He made his way outside to his car.

Home sweet home.

He could only hope Leslie was waiting.

Chapter 53

"Don't shoot! I'm her brother," Emilio shrieked, his voice filled with panic.

"Hit the ground *now*, or you ain't gonna be nobody's brother," one of the cops yelled.

Venus Maria hovered behind them.

"Get back, miss," said the other cop.

She'd recognized Emilio's voice. Damn! What the hell was he doing sneaking around her house without permission?

Warily one of the cops climbed the stairs, while the other one stayed behind and covered him.

Cop number one reached Emilio, twisted his arms behind him, and roughly handcuffed his wrists.

"You're making a big mistake," Emilio managed. "I'm tellin' you, man, I'm Venus Maria's brother. I'm no trespasser."

"We'll see about that," said the first cop. "On your feet."

"You bet we'll see about it," Emilio shouted, gaining confidence. "I'll sue you."

"You'll sue us, huh?" said the cop in a bored voice. He'd heard it many times before. It was the Beverly Hills battle cry.

Once downstairs, they frog-marched him outside to the police car.

"Get her to identify me," Emilio screamed, suddenly panicking. "I'm telling you, I'm her brother."

One of the cops walked back to the house. "Can I have your autograph?" he asked. "For my little girl. It'd really make her day."

"Sure," Venus Maria said agreeably, signing the piece of paper he thrust at her.

"Uh, I don't know if we've got a deranged fan or what, but this guy claims he's your brother. You have a brother?"

She nodded. "Four of 'em. All bums."

"How about takin' a look before we haul him in an' book him."

For a moment she was tempted to say no, but then she thought about the headlines and reluctantly agreed.

Outside, Emilio slouched against the side of the police car looking guilty.

Shit! It *was* him. "I'm sorry, guys," she said. "This is my brother. I have no idea what he's doing in my house – he doesn't live here."

The cops exchanged glances. "Should we let him go?"

She had no choice. Locking Emilio up for being a pain in the ass was just not on.

Reluctantly she nodded. "I guess so."

A night in jail would have done Emilio a world of good. Paid him back for all the bullying he'd inflicted on her when she was growing up.

They removed the handcuffs. Emilio rubbed his wrists, glaring at both the cops. "There'll be a court case about this," he said, puffing himself up. "Count on it, man."

"Shut up and get inside," Venus Maria interrupted. "Why were you breaking into my house anyway?"

"Breaking in?" replied Emilio, aghast. "You think *I* would break in? Your own brother! I came to bring the money you said I could leave in your safe. I was looking for you in the bedroom when the cops arrived."

"How did you get in?" she asked suspiciously.

"Through the back window. It's always open."

"You set off the silent alarm. There's a beam across it."

He tried to look contrite. "Sorry, little sis, didn't mean to cause no trouble."

Venus Maria glanced helplessly at the officers and ran a hand through her platinum hair. "I'm sorry you've been bothered, guys. Seems like it was a mistake."

"No bother," they both agreed. "Any time. Love your records. Love your videos."

She smiled. "Thanks. Hey, why don't you leave me your names? I'll see you get tickets for my next concert."

The cops looked pleased.

Emilio slunk back into the house. All he had to do now was get out. He didn't want Venus opening her safe and finding her precious photo missing. He had the photograph safely stashed inside his jacket. Best to make a speedy getaway.

Venus Maria followed him in. "When you come to my house," she said clearly, "you will ring the front doorbell. Can you do that?"

He nodded sulkily.

"Give me the money you want me to put away. And Emilio, next time, telephone before you come here."

He hit his forehead. "I'm stupid!" he exclaimed. "I rushed over here so fast I forgot the money. Left it in my apartment. Y'know, maybe I should put it in a bank anyway."

"Yes, maybe you should," she agreed, wondering what he was up to.

He prepared for a fast exist. "I'll see you, little sis."

Of all her brothers, Emilio was the most devious. She

didn't trust him, she never had — and he was far too anxious to get out of there. He ran like a rat.

Maybe the police had unnerved him.

Or maybe not.

Venus Maria's gut instinct told her Emilio was up to something.

The trouble was, she couldn't figure out what that something was.

Chapter 54

"What do you want to do today?"

"I don't know. What do you want to do today?"

"*I* dunno, Marty. What do *you* wanna do today?"

Lennie laughed. "Hey, you're too young to have seen that movie."

"So are you," she retorted affectionately, happy to be in her husband's company.

"I'm not as young as I used to be."

"Who is?"

They bantered back and forth, delighted to be together. It was a hot New York day. They'd had breakfast, made love again, and now it was time for decisions.

"What I'd *really* like to do," Lucky decided, "is visit Mary-Lou and the baby. How does that grab you?"

"It would grab me great if I even knew she'd given birth. What am I — the poor relation?"

"No. You're the rich movie star relation who — if you hadn't vanished out of everyone's life — would certainly have been told."

"Enlighten me — is it a boy or a girl?"

"A girl," she said excitedly. "I haven't spoken to Steven yet. He must be out of his mind!"

"Let's call 'em."

"Yes, and then I've got a great idea. We'll raid Zabars,

pick up a whole load of food, and go over to see the baby."

"Is that all you have on your mind, food?" he chided. "What *is* it with you lately?"

"I'm building up my strength."

"For what?"

"A surprise."

He groaned. "Not another one."

"*This* one you're going to like."

"Does it involve travel?"

"Not without you by my side."

"Does it involve sex?"

She looked at him quizzically. "Hmm . . . do you find power sexy?"

"It depends who's got it."

"You'll see," she answered mysteriously.

He shook his head. "You're a tough act to handle, kid."

She laughed. "And you're beginning to sound just like Gino."

"Poor old Gino. It must have been some struggle bringing you up."

"Yeah, that's why he married me off at sixteen."

"He really did that, huh?"

"You'd better believe it. I was the perfect little Washington wife. Craven and I lived with the Richmonds in their tasteful mansion while I played good little wifey-pie at all the fancy functions. And guess what? Peter Richmond is going to run for President one of these days. Ain't *that* the laugh of the century?"

"Whatever happened to husband number one?"

"Ah, Craven. He met a girl who liked horses. And I can assure you – a horse is about the only thing she'll ever find between *her* legs!"

Lennie burst out laughing. "Hey – lady – I love it when you talk dirty."

She grinned. "Why do you think I do it?"

"To turn me on."

"You got it!"

He pulled her to him. "Come here, wife."

She pushed him gently away. "Not now."

"How come?"

"'Cause we gotta go out like normal people. We can't make out the entire weekend."

"Why not?"

"*No, Lennie*," she said firmly, trying not to give in.

He sighed with disappointment. "OK, so what are we going to do?"

"Visit my brother. Unless you want to work. That, I'll understand."

"I've been locked up here so long I'm stir crazy."

"Can I read the script soon?" she asked eagerly.

"I told you – not until it's finished."

"When will that be?"

"I'm heading towards a rough draft."

"I can read it then, huh?"

"We'll see."

"Bullshit! I'm reading it, Lennie!"

"That's what I love about you – Little Miss Reticent!"

She called Gino, who sounded pleased to hear from her. "So you're back. It's about time," he said good-naturedly.

"I sure am."

"Everything go according to plan?"

"It sure did."

"Hey – you broken the news to Lennie?"

"I sure haven't." She changed the subject quickly. "How about lunch today? I'd like to see Steven and Mary-Lou. Is she at home? How's the baby?"

"Hey, hey, one question at a time. Yeah, they're all at home. It's a good idea. Steven's been missing you."

"We thought we'd pick up lunch and come over. Will you call Steven and warn him?"

"You got it, kid. Family reunion, huh?"

"Can't wait, Gino."

Boogie drove them to Zabars, and then Lucky decided she needed to pick up gifts at Bloomingdales, where she ran riot in the baby department, selecting hundreds of dollars' worth of toys and clothes.

337

"What's Mary-Lou going to do with all this stuff?" Lennie asked, exasperated.

"Use it."

"Very funny. Can we leave?"

"Let's go."

Loaded down with packages they made it to the elevator, where Lennie was recognized and a crowd began to surround him. They had to run to get out of there.

Laughing and giggling they piled into the car.

"I'm glad to see you're still a star," Lucky joked. "I thought you might have lost it."

"Yeah. I really get off on being mobbed in good old Bloomies," he said wryly.

"I love you." Gently she touched the side of his face. "And I missed you more than you can imagine."

"Don't get sloppy on me, I can't take the pressure."

Giggling, she stuck her tongue out.

"Nice tongue!" he said admiringly.

"Keep this up an' you ain't *never* gonna know just how nice!"

Boogie sat impassively in the driving seat. "Where to?" he asked.

"Steven's house," Lucky said. "And fast." She turned to Lennie. "Have you spoken to Brigette?"

"Not lately. I promised she could stay with us in Malibu."

"Great. Maybe we'll all fly back together on Sunday night."

"What's your hurry?"

"We don't want to hang around here, do we? It's hot and muggy, and we've got that great beach house sitting empty."

He shrugged. "Whatever you like. I can pack in five minutes."

"So . . . what are we waiting for? You'll finish your script at the beach. It'll be sensational. A real family summer, right?"

"Yeah, all the better to deal with the lawyers," he said grimly

"I keep telling you, relax. They're not going to sue."

"Don't bet on it, Lucky."

"Oh, I'm betting. And I'm right."

Steven greeted her with a big hug and kiss. "*Where* have you been?" he asked.

"Japan," she lied. "I learned to give a great back rub. Can I see the baby?"

Mary-Lou smiled proudly. "Come on, we'll take you up to her room."

"What did you name her?" Lucky asked.

"Carioca Jade," Steven replied.

Lennie nodded wisely. "That'll get her through school with no problems."

"It's a beautiful name," Lucky enthused.

Carioca Jade was a cute little bundle, small, helpless, and appealing.

Steven picked her up and handed her to Lucky. "Say hello to Auntie," he said.

"Auntie?" Lucky exclaimed. "That makes me feel ancient!"

"Well, you're not exactly a kid any more," Lennie pointed out.

"Thanks!" She peered at the baby. "I'll be picking up my old age pension next week! Steven, Mary-Lou – this child is *gorgeous*!"

"I did my best," Steven said modestly.

"You did *your* best!" Mary-Lou objected.

"It wasn't easy," Steven joked.

Mary-Lou picked up a cushion and threw it at him. "Get outta here!"

Gino turned up shortly after. Once more he asked Lucky if she'd told Lennie about Panther.

"I will," she said. "Quit bugging me."

"When?"

"What's the big deal. I'll tell him tonight. I want to savour the moment."

"Are you sure he likes surprises?"

"Don't worry about it, Gino. He'll be delighted."

They spent a couple of hours at the house and then

wandered off on their own. She'd given Boogie the rest of the weekend free.

"What do you want to do?" Lennie said as they strolled along the street hand in hand.

Lucky smiled. "You're always asking me that. More important, what do *you* want to do?"

"Whatever makes you happy."

"Can we walk around like normal people or will you be recognized again?"

"We can walk around like normal people. I'll avoid eye contact. I've discovered being recognized is a state of mind. If you want them to recognize you they do, and if you don't, they don't. It's that simple."

"OK, this is what I'd like to do," she decided. "Go to a movie. Eat popcorn and spill it all over myself. Feel sick, have one of those horrible fizzy orange drinks. And then I want to go home and make love all night long. Can we do that?"

"You know something? That's why I'm crazy about you. We have exactly the same tastes." He took a beat. "Woody Allen?"

She answered instantly. "But of course."

They lined up for a Woody Allen film. Saw it. Loved it. And talked about it all the way home.

It wasn't until they were back in his rented loft that Lucky looked at him, started to laugh, and said, "Hey, wait a minute, we own a luxury apartment in New York. What are we doing in this dump?"

"It's romantic," Lennie replied. "Nobody knows we're here. No phone calls. No nothing. We'll stay tonight and take off for LA tomorrow."

"Suits me."

"And now what do you want?"

She couldn't help thinking to herself how much she loved him. And how much she'd missed him. "I want Chinese food, Marvin Gaye music, and great sex. What do *you* want?"

"Indian food, Billie Holliday, and great sex."

"I guess if we can't make up our mind about the food, it'll have to wait."

"I guess so."

She shrugged. "And if we can't make up our mind about Marvin or Billie, same thing, huh?"

He shrugged too.

"Well . . ." she said slowly, "it looks like there's nothing else left to do except . . ."

Together they shouted it out: "Great sex!"

And then, laughing, they fell into each other's arms.

Chapter 55

Paul Webster's idea of the park was certainly not Tavern on the Green. Deena, clad from head to toe in Chanel, discovered this when he arrived to pick her up.

"We're going on a picnic," he informed her.

She raised an imperious eyebrow. "Really?"

"Why not?" he asked. "It'll be a blast."

She didn't want to reveal that grown women dressed in Chanel, with rich husbands, did not picnic in the park. "I'm hardly dressed for it," she pointed out.

"Go change."

"I don't think so," she said.

He stared at her with his intense eyes. "Do I make you nervous?"

She gave an amused laugh. "How could *you* possibly make *me* nervous? I've known you since you were a baby."

"Go change, Deena," he said.

He seemed determined, so she capitulated. She hurried upstairs, took off Chanel, and put on a Christian Dior track suit and jogging shoes.

Paul waited in the front hall. Deena wondered what her houseman thought. What *could* he think? After all, Paul was young enough to be her . . . younger brother.

Martin was safely at the office. He always left early on

Saturday mornings, never returning until six or seven at night. He did the same on Sundays. Sometimes they spent the weekend at their Connecticut house. When they did, Martin usually spent his entire time on the phone or receiving faxes. Martin was a true workaholic. He found it difficult to relax.

Did The Bitch make him relax?

Did The Bitch make him forget business for more than five minutes at a time?

Deena tried to put the thought from her mind. It wasn't healthy to ponder about Martin and Venus Maria. If she shut it out maybe their relationship would fade away and Martin would be all hers again.

And if that failed to happen . . . if The Bitch tried to take it further . . .

Deena sighed. She had her solution.

Paul greeted her when she reappeared. "You're a real sport," he said, looking her up and down. "Now we can relax and enjoy ourselves."

"How are we going to get there?" she asked when they hit the street, already regretting her decision to go with him.

He took her hand. "We're walking."

She pulled her hand away. "I don't walk."

He stared at her quizzically. "You don't walk? That's funny — seems to me your legs *look* like they're moving one in front of the other."

"Don't be facetious, Paul. We'll take a cab."

He was intent on asserting his manhood. "We'll walk."

Deena hid behind a pair of large black sunglasses and hoped she wouldn't bump into any of her friends. Not that there was anything wrong with strolling through the city with Effie's young son — but still . . .

She entered Central Park as if she was taking a trip on the wild side. She couldn't remember the last time she'd been in such close proximity to so many people. Deena led her life in a rarefied atmosphere, and she wasn't comfortable getting down amongst the people. But she had to admit it made a change. And the attentive Paul Webster was certainly an intriguing young man. Besides, she needed someone to tell her she was beautiful, intelligent, and attractive. All the things Martin usually forgot to mention.

"Guess where Paul's gone today," Nona said, struggling into a pair of too-tight jeans.

"Where?" replied Brigette, biting into an apple.

"He's taking old lady Deena Swanson to lunch. Are you ready for that?"

Brigette almost choked. No, she was not ready for that. Swallowing her hurt feelings she said, "Why?" Then added, "How do you know?"

"*I* know everything," Nona replied confidently, finally closing the zipper on her jeans. "I listened in on the phone when he called her."

"Does he like her?" Brigette asked casually.

"Do *you* like him?" Nona asked, not so casually.

"Don't be crazy," Brigette replied, trying to look cool.

"I think you do," Nona said, very sure of herself.

Before Brigette could reply, Effie swept into the room. "There's a phone call for you Brigette, dear. It's your stepfather, Lennie Golden. We'd love to meet him sometime. Ask him over for drinks."

Brigette was pleased. She'd thought Lennie had forgotten her. "What shall I tell him?" she asked Nona.

"Tell him he's got us whenever he wants," Nona said. "You *have* mentioned *I'm* coming, haven't you?"

Brigette looked vague. "Sure."

Nona pulled a face. "Bet you haven't – do so now."

"I will," replied Brigette, rushing to the phone.

Lennie sounded like his old self. He said the Malibu trip was on, and yes, she could bring a friend. They agreed that she and Nona would fly out in a week.

Nona was delighted. "Can't wait to meet your stepfather," she said excitedly. "Is he as hot as he looks on the screen?"

"Lennie? Hot?" Brigette almost laughed aloud. She'd never thought of him in that way, although, of course, he did have quite a following.

On reflection she considered he probably was hot. "You don't fancy him, do you?" she teased Nona.

"Not as much as I fancy Tom Cruise," Nona replied, grabbing her jacket. "Come on, let's go shopping. I can't wait to buy the smallest bikini anybody's ever seen in their entire life!"

Bert Slocombe figured he was the smartest reporter in town. Well, reporter-photographer really, because he never went anywhere without his little camera cleverly concealed on his person. Bert was known to be the best at getting the goods on the rich and famous, which was exactly why they'd put him on Swanson watch.

That morning he'd considered following Martin Swanson, but a hunch had made him decide to concentrate on Deena instead. And sure enough his hunch paid off. The stylish Mrs Swanson emerged from her house just after noon, all togged out in a fancy jogging outfit. She was accompanied by some young geezer who kept on giving her lustful looks. Bert recognized a lustful look from five hundred yards.

Happily he settled in behind them as they made their way to the park. He'd known something good was up the moment she left her house and didn't immediately climb into a chauffered limousine.

Deena Swanson walking to the park was picture enough, but add some young stud and it really made a front-page scandal shot. Nothing like a well-known married woman playing around to sell magazines. Especially with a younger man.

Bert wondered who the kid was. He was good-looking enough with his long hair and one small gold earring in his earlobe. Maybe he was a rock star. Those rock and rollers managed to get in everywhere.

No, Bert decided. He didn't recognize him, and he was familiar with most of the long-haired brigade.

When they arrived at the park, the young guy pulled out a blanket from the bag he carried and laid it out on the grass.

Bert thought he'd died and gone to heaven.

He could see Deena arguing – she obviously wasn't used to this kind of outing – but she sat on the grass anyway, making it an easy job for Bert to scoot around behind a tree and shoot some great pictures.

The two of them stayed in the park for over an hour. Bert was hoping the guy would make a move on her, but no such luck. A lot of talk and that was it.

He wished he could hear what they were saying. Impossible, couldn't make himself too obvious. As it was he was flitting around behind trees like a secret wanker.

He managed to get one picture he knew was going to be special. Deena had a wasp or something trapped in her hair and the kid leaned forward to brush it out. Of course, the gullible public wouldn't know what he was doing. It looked like he was about to give her a hot wet one full on the lips.

Bert followed them back to Deena's house and lingered for a moment. Sure enough the young guy emerged almost immediately and Bert fell into step a discreet distance behind him. Might as well put a name to the kid.

He chuckled to himself. This story, combined with the Venus Maria stuff, was going to be bigger than ever. He couldn't wait to give Dennis the good news in LA.

Chapter 56

Once she was rid of Emilio, Venus Maria spoke to Ron on the phone.

"And where were *you* last night?" he asked crisply. Ron always liked to know everyone's business.

"At Spago."

"Hitting the town, are we? Who was your fortunate escort?"

"Cooper."

"Hmm . . ." Ron was intrigued. "And did we finally do the deed?"

She sighed. "No, Ron. We did *not* do the deed. Cooper and I are just friends. Why even ask a question like that?"

"Because I know you. You're not exactly a patient wench, and if you can't have Martin all the way you're hardly going to wait for ever."

She twirled the cord of the phone. "What makes you so certain I can't have Martin all the way?"

"He's not gettable," Ron said firmly. "He's taken."

"I can get any man I want," Venus Maria replied, full of bravado.

"Show me," Ron taunted.

It infuriated her that Ron always thought he had to challenge her. "I'll show you all right," she snapped, hoping to shut him up. "Talk to you later." She hung up without giving him a chance to say another word.

In a couple of weeks they were supposed to begin serious rehearsals for her upcoming "Soft Seduction" tour. She planned to hit twenty-two cities – a gruelling prospect, but one she looked forward to. The "Soft Seduction" album would be released at the same time, along with her video of the title track. She was filming the video next week. It was to be directed by the famous Italian photographer Antonio, a good friend of hers.

Ron was pissed off because he'd wanted to direct it. She'd tried to explain that she felt like a change, but Ron was in a sulk about it, even though he'd done all the choreography.

In the video she was to play three roles: a beautiful, seductive woman; a handsome gigolo-type man; and a half-woman, half-man creature. As usual it would arouse controversy and criticism. That was the whole point. Her fans would love it, they'd go "Soft Seduction" crazy. She was going to give them the Venus Maria they *really* craved.

As far as her fans were concerned Venus Maria could do no wrong. She was their video queen. Their princess. She was everything they aspired to be. Dangerous. Stylish.

A woman unafraid in a world run by men. A "fuck you" woman.

The thought of the upcoming tour excited her. She'd only been out on the road once before, and that was right before her career took off, just after her first hit record. At the time she'd been too inexperienced to understand the intricate interaction between audience and artist. Now she knew it was going to be a sensational blast, some kind of heady exchange of energy and power between star and fans. And after the tour, if the script was changed to her liking, she was to star in Mickey Stolli's big movie, *Bombshell* – a role coveted by every young actress in Hollywood.

First the video, then the tour, next the movie. The rest of her year was well taken care of.

She'd heard that all tickets were sold out in record time as soon as the box-offices opened.

Maybe she shouldn't even worry about Martin until she got back, but she knew that if she didn't cement their relationship with a definite commitment from him before she went, by the time the tour was finished it would be over.

His phone call came at just the right moment.

"I'm going to be in LA tomorrow," he informed her, all business. "I'm planning a takeover at one of the studios. I'll pick you up at noon and we'll fly to San Francisco for the day."

She didn't like it when he took her for granted. "What if I'm busy?" she said.

"Are you?" he asked abruptly.

She took a moment before replying. "No."

"Why do you always try to give me a hard time?"

"Because nobody else does."

He laughed. "Good reason. Did you get the shares?"

"Oh, those little things," she said casually. "I added them to my collection."

"That's what I like about you."

She held the phone tightly to her ear. "What?"

"You're totally independent."

Sure, Martin. But not when it comes to you. "Isn't everyone?" she said coolly.

"No. Definitely not."

As soon as she hung up she couldn't wait to call Ron back. "We'll have to cancel the video rehearsal tomorrow. I'm flying to San Francisco for the day," she told him.

"With whom?"

"Martin."

"Mmm . . ." Ron said in his usual bitchy tone. "Mister Big calls — little Virginia runs."

"*Don't* call me that."

"Why not?"

"'Cause you *know* it pisses me off."

"Well, now, I'm *so* sorry, miss. However, some of us do feel we can still talk to you as if you're a mere mortal."

Ron was in his definite pain-in-the-ass mood. "Cut it out," she said crossly.

He changed his tune, suddenly becoming overly solicitous. "Shall I pop over and help you select outfits for tomorrow? You have to look your best."

"I can manage."

"How about Madame Loretta's girls? I could arrange to have them waiting at the hotel."

Trust him to bring up the hookers. She should never have let Ron in on that little game. "The girls were a one-time experience. OK?"

"Just checking. What are you doing the rest of the day?"

She relented. After all, he was her best friend. "Nothing. Come over if you want."

"Can I bring Ken?" he asked anxiously, still dying for her and the Ken Doll to become close buddies.

No way, José. "Another time, Ron."

"You're such a bitch."

"Thank you. I love you, too."

"Have fun tomorrow."

"I plan to."

After putting the phone down on Ron she immediately called Cooper.

"What are you doing tonight?" she asked, getting straight to the point.

He sounded cautious. "I have a date with a seventeen-year-old ex-porn queen. Why?"

"Can I come too?"

Now he sounded amused. "Are you suggesting a three-some?"

"No! I am not! I'd like to go out for dinner. Martin's arriving tomorrow and I don't feel like being alone tonight. Can I join you or not?"

"I'm sure my date will be thrilled," Cooper said dryly. "We're going to a Mexican restaurant."

"Will you pick me up?"

He sighed. "Venus, I'll do anything you want."

"Just pick me up. That'll be fine."

Martin arrived home from the office early because they were attending a dinner party. Since he planned to tell Deena he was leaving the next morning for Los Angeles, he didn't care to experience her wrath by walking in late.

Deena seemed particularly restless.

"I'm off to LA in the morning," he announced. "That studio deal is coming through."

She didn't hesitate. "I'll come with you."

"No," he said quickly.

"Why not?" she asked, narrowing her eyes.

"Because this is a complicated takeover. And when I'm this involved I can't have outside influences."

She glared at him. "Is that what I am — an outside influence? I was under the impression I was your wife."

"You know what I mean," he said.

She felt a sickness in the pit of her stomach. This was it. He was going back to Los Angeles sooner than antici-pated. All this talk about the studio takeover coming to fruition was merely a smokescreen. The Bitch beckoned and he came running.

Deena knew the time was drawing near to put her master plan into operation.

Chapter 57

Eventually the moment of truth had to come and Lucky was excited beyond belief. She waited until late Saturday night. They'd made love again, sent out for pizza, and now Lennie was settling down to watch *Saturday Night Live*.

"Hey – you coming in?" he called out to her.

She was in the bathroom brushing her long dark hair. Clad in one of Lennie's oversized shirts and nothing else she wandered back into the bedroom.

"Are you *really* going to watch TV?" she teased.

He was stretched out on the bed. "Sweetheart, I don't have the strength to do anything else."

"Doesn't take much to tire you out, huh?"

"Right!" he joked. "Non-stop sex'll do it every time!"

She curled up beside him. "Complaining?"

"Are you kidding? C'mere, wife."

He kissed her, putting his tongue in her mouth and sliding it across her teeth.

She shivered. "Don't do that unless you mean it."

"Oh, I mean it, lady." His hands began to explore beneath her shirt.

She felt herself responding; Lennie always had that effect on her.

"I thought you were tired."

"I made a rapid recovery."

"You're turning into Superman, Lennie."

He smiled lazily. "Hey – give me a break – I've been seriously deprived!"

Gently she pushed him away. She wanted to make love again, but not until after she'd told him her news.

"It's time to break open the champagne," she said softly.

"How come?"

She took a deep breath. "Remember that surprise I mentioned?"

"Yeah."

"Now's the time."

He stared at his wildly beautiful wife and it came to him in a flash. She was about to tell him she was pregnant. *That* was her surprise. And he was going to be the happiest expectant father in the world!

"Hold everything," he said. "Don't move. I'll get the champagne, you light the candles, and I'll be right back. Then you can give me the good news."

"You'll be crazy with happiness," she promised him, kneeling on the bed.

He couldn't stop himself from grinning like an idiot. "You're probably right. You're always right."

She grinned back. "Oh yeah, I'm *always* right!"

He rushed downstairs, grabbed the bottle of champagne she'd put in the fridge earlier, balanced two glasses, and raced back upstairs.

Lucky sat cross-legged in the centre of the bed.

He popped the cork on the champagne, poured the golden liquid into two glasses, and handed her one.

Solemnly she toasted him. "Lennie Golden," she said, controlling her exhilaration. "I know it's not your birthday, but . . . I have something for you."

He reached out and touched her face. "Did I ever tell you how much I–"

"Quiet!" she interrupted. "This is *my* surprise."

He settled back on the bed. "OK, go for it."

In his mind he thought about a name for the baby. Maria for a girl, after Lucky's mother. And if it was a boy, how about Lennie Junior? Or was it too difficult for a kid to grow up with junior attached to his name? Yeah, it probably was. Hmm . . . How about Nick – real gangster's name. Nick Golden – sounded good. A killer name for a killer kid.

"Lennie," Lucky said quietly, savouring every word, "I bought you Panther Studios."

He stared at her blankly. "Huh?"

351

She repeated the words as slowly as she could. "I said I bought you Panther Studios."

There was a long moment of silence while he digested this incredible information. "You've done what?" he managed at last.

"How many times do I have to tell you?" she yelled happily. "*I* bought Panther Studios. *We* bought Panther Studios. It's ours, Lennie, it's ours!"

"What about the baby?" he couldn't help blurting out.

She looked puzzled. "What baby?"

Her news sank in. "Jesus, you're serious, aren't you?"

"Of *course* I'm serious. Where do you think I've been for the last six weeks? I made a deal to buy the studio from old Abe Panther, and he wouldn't sell to me unless I went in undercover for six weeks. What a trip! Can you believe it? Me – undercover – pretending to be Luce, the obedient little secretary. And Lennie, get this. I've been kissing Mickey Stolli's ass! In fact, I even talked to you on the phone one day."

He was in a state of severe shock. "You talked to me on the phone one day," he repeated, dazed.

"That's right." She grinned. "Isn't it incredible? We're movie moguls. We're gonna kick butt and make great movies!"

This wasn't exactly the news he'd imagined. This was a bombshell. "You're serious, aren't you? You've bought a goddamn studio."

"You bet your ass I have," she said excitedly. "That's why we have to fly back to LA tomorrow. I've arranged a meeting on Monday morning I think you should come too. It'll be great. The lawyers will be there, and old Abe Panther himself. He's quite a character. I can't wait to see Mickey's face when they tell him. Not to mention his wife – the delightful Abigaile."

"How much did it cost you?" he asked blankly.

"A lot. Trust me, *a lot.* But you know me when it comes to business, and Panther is worth every penny. There's land to be sold off, and a wonderful library of old films. Plus the Television Department really has a shot. Of course, when we stop making these dumb tits-and-ass films the revenues will go down. But only temporarily." Her black eyes gleamed with excitement. "I plan to make really good movies, Lennie. I want to show women as real people. I mean, come on, what do we see on the screen today? We see women as men's fantasies. The guys making movies are a bunch of jerks — and it seems to me they all hate women. They've either got some slasher chasing them around cutting their heads off, or they've got them taking off their clothes while adolescent boys jerk off through holes in the wall. I mean, movies don't celebrate the human condition — they degrade it."

He stood up, shaking his head. "Lucky, you don't know the first thing about film-making."

"You hardly have to be a fucking genius to put together a movie," she pointed out. "Have you *seen* the guys running the industry? Anyway — " she raced on at full tilt. "Let's discuss what we can do about *your* movie. I've taken a look at the dailies and there's some terrific stuff in there. If we leave Marisa on the cutting room floor, recast, reshoot, and you'll rewrite, then we can hire a new director and put it together again. It's salvageable if we take control." She paused for breath. "Hey — maybe you'd even like to direct it yourself? How about that for a great idea?"

"Would I be working for you?"

She missed the tightness in his voice. "Lennie, aren't you listening to me? I bought the studio for *us*. We're in this together."

Distractedly he ran a hand through his hair. "Did you use my money?"

"I don't have your money, do I?" she replied patiently. "I used *my* money."

"The money you inherited from Dimitri?"

Was his problem whose money she'd used? "OK, so I had a rich husband, I inherited part of the Stanislopoulos fortune. But now it's my money, and I can spend it any way I like."

He began pacing up and down the room. "So you weren't in Japan?"

Was Lennie being obtuse on purpose? "Hardly."

"Let me get this straight. You were in LA impersonating a secretary at Panther Studios, while I was getting my balls busted in Acapulco. Is that right?"

"I was securing our future," she corrected. "You want to be a movie star – let's be in control. It's the only way."

"*You'll* be in control, Lucky. I'll be working for *you*."

She was exasperated. "Will you quit saying that. How many times do I have to tell you? It's our studio. *Ours*. Hey – Lennie – I'm beginning to feel like a broken record."

"Why didn't you at least mention what you planned to do?"

She reached for a cigarette. "Because it would have spoiled the surprise."

"You know what I thought, Lucky?"

"No, what?"

"I thought you were going to tell me we were having a baby."

She stared at him. His negative reaction was so totally unexpected and hurtful that she struck back. "I'm so sorry," she said sarcastically. "Maybe you'd be happier if I was in the kitchen, barefoot and pregnant."

"Is that such a terrible thing?" he retorted angrily.

She leaped off the bed. "I don't *believe* this. I've been stuck at the studio imitating a stupid secretary for six weeks for *us*. And now I tell you, thinking you'll be knocked out, and what do you do? God damn it, you start nagging."

He glared at her. "Nagging? Oh, so that's what I'm doing, is it? You blatantly lied to me for six weeks. Then you break into my apartment, we have non-stop sex for twenty-four hours, and finally you spring this on me. And *I'm* nagging. Do you really think the world has to revolve around you, Lucky?"

She couldn't understand his attitude. "What have I done that's so terrible?" she demanded. "Tell me that."

"You did it without me," he said flatly. "We should have discussed it. I do not appreciate being shut out."

"And I don't appreciate being told what to do. I'm not a child, Lennie."

"Sometimes you act like one."

"Fuck you!" she exploded. "If this situation was reversed you'd expect *me* to be jumping up and down with delight."

"And would you?"

"Yes."

He stared at her for a long moment before saying, "You know what I feel like?"

She dragged on her cigarette. "What?"

"Like a kept man. It's as if you said to yourself. 'Oh, poor Lennie's not happy at the studio, I'll buy it for him.' You've made me feel like nothing."

"That's the most ridiculous thing I've ever heard," she said abruptly.

"It's how I feel."

"You're not being fair."

"I'm not, huh? Can't you *see* what you've done?"

"I can see very clearly what's going on around here. I'm not pregnant, so you're pissed off. That's what it really gets down to, isn't it?"

He didn't reply.

She stubbed out her cigarette and walked into the bathroom. From sheer exhilaration she was reduced to frustrated anger. Men! They pretended they liked women with balls, and when they found one they just couldn't handle it. She'd thought Lennie was different. It seemed she was wrong.

Quickly she threw on some clothes and emerged. "I'm getting out of here," she said curtly. "There's no need for this to escalate into a bigger fight that it already is."

Her words made him even more furious. "What are you saying? That you're going to walk?" he asked.

"I don't want to be around you any more tonight."

Now it was his turn to explode. "*You* don't want to be

355

around *me*? Hey, Lucky – you walk out of here and you walk out of my life."

Her black eyes were deadly as she turned to him. "Are you threatening me?"

"Can't you listen to what I have to say?" he yelled. "Has it always got to be your way?"

She felt tears sting the back of her eyelids and quickly turned away. "Like you said, Lennie, I'm not the little woman at home. I never will be and I never pretended to be. I've got nothing against having a baby one of these days, but right now there's so much I want to do."

"Then maybe you'd better do it by yourself," he said bitterly.

She couldn't believe how wrong this was all going. This was supposed to have been the most wonderful moment for both of them, but it was turning out to be the worst. Maybe he was right, maybe they weren't destined to be together. After all, what did they really have in common? A sense of humour, great sex, Chinese food, and walking on the beach – it wasn't enough.

She picked up the phone and called a cab. "I'm going to the apartment," she said. "We both need time apart. Think about it, Lennie. And remember – I did this for you. I didn't do it for selfish reasons."

He couldn't look at her. "You can't buy me, Lucky," he said tightly. "There's no sales tag."

"That wasn't my intention. I'm flying back to LA tomorrow. If you decide to come I'll be delighted. Let me know."

With a sick feeling she walked to the front door, waiting for him to call her back – longing for him to say he was only joking, that everything was OK and he was thrilled.

He didn't say any of those things.

Outside on the street she was accosted by a stoned teenage girl, eyes as big as saucers, long matted hair. "Spare a coupla bucks?" the girl whined.

Lucky handed her a fifty. "Get yourself a life. Throw away the drugs and straighten out."

"Hey, man – what else is there?" the girl said blankly as she wandered off down the street.

Lucky's cab zoomed up to the doorway. The Puerto Rican driver was busy muttering to himself.

She opened the door and climbed in. Leaning from the window she could see the lights of Lennie's apartment. He hadn't even bothered to follow her down.

"Goodbye," she whispered. "Don't write, don't call. I can make it without you."

"Huh?" the cab driver said.

"Just drive," she replied dully. "And while you're at it, try not to kill us both."

Chapter 58

Emilio Sierra delivered the goods much to Dennis Walla's satisfaction. The photograph of Venus Maria with Martin Swanson was worth every penny they'd had to pay. It was sexy and intimate. Two people entwined. A real front-pager.

Dennis congratulated Emilio. "You really came through mate," he said, clapping him on the shoulder.

Emilio was pleased. He'd decided to spend a week in Hawaii, and take his new-found love, Rita the firecracker. She was a wildcat between the sheets, and pretty too. It was best to get out of town before the shit hit. And that was exactly what would happen when *Truth and Fact* arrived on the stands. Venus Maria was going to freak out.

Too bad. He didn't need little sis anymore. With his new-found notoriety he would soon become a famous actor. Now he'd be able to call important agents and producers and say, "Hey — this is Emilio Sierra." And they'd reply, "Emilio, good of you to call, my friend — come in and see us."

Yes, it was all going to happen for him. It was about time he was discovered.

Shortly after Dennis received the photograph from Emilio, Bert Slocombe telephoned from New York.

"Hold the front page," Bert crowed triumphantly. "We're about t'make a bloody great splash."

"What's up?" Dennis asked.

"Sit still an' listen."

When Dennis heard the story Bert had to relate, he was only too happy to hold the front page.

This issue of *Truth and Fact* was going to be a total sellout.

And Dennis Walla was planning on taking full credit.

Warner had been in his life too long for Mickey to allow her to walk when she felt like it. The fact that he was visiting Madame Loretta's on a regular basis had nothing to do with their relationship. Warner couldn't break up with him. *He* had to be the one to say it was over.

On Saturday morning he played a vicious game of tennis with an ambitious director, and instead of staying for lunch at the club he drove directly to Warner's apartment. She was not home. Deflated, he continued on to his house. Abigaile was also out.

"Where's Mrs Stolli?" he asked Consuela.

"She's shopping, Mister," Consuela replied, rolling her eyes as if she too disapproved of Abigaile's shopping mania.

Shopping, Mickey thought. Not at the market, that was for sure. To Abigaile shopping meant Saks and Neiman Marcus, with a side trip down Rodeo Drive.

Tabitha, his daughter, appeared. "Daddy, can I have a Porsche when I'm sixteen?"

Why was it that every time he came into contact with Tabitha she wanted something? "We'll talk about it when you reach that age," he replied as calmly as he could manage.

"Why can't we talk now?" she nagged. "Why can't you promise me?"

The girl was just like her mother. Relentless.

"Because now is not the time," he said patiently.

"Mommy said I could."

Trust Abigaile. "She did?"

"Yes," Tabitha said triumphantly. "She promised me if I got good grades and if she never caught me doing dope or sleeping with boys – then I could have a Porsche. So I've decided not to smoke any more."

He stared at his thirteen-year-old daughter. "You smoke?"

"Everybody at school does," she answered defensively.

He wondered what else she did. She was turning into a well-developed girl. Too well developed for her age.

"We'll see," he said vaguely, bored with all this father–daughter crap. He had other things on his mind.

"Some man phoned you," Tabitha announced. "He asked for our address."

Mickey was immediately alarmed. "What do you mean – he asked for our address?"

"What is it, a state secret or something?"

"I don't like people having our home address, Tabitha. You know that," he said sternly.

"Like I *don't* know that, Daddy," she replied smartly. "Like you *never* told me."

"Yes, I did."

"I can't do anything right in this house," Tabitha said. "Maybe I'll run away," she added, flouncing from the room.

Ha! Mickey thought. *Chance would be a fine thing*.

Saturday was supposed to be a day of rest, and all he was getting was stress. Stress at his age was no good.

Not that he was old. He was in perfect physical shape, and his bedroom prowess only improved with age.

But still, stress was the enemy. And if he had to contend with Abe Panther on Monday morning *and* his brother-in-law, there was plenty of added stress headed in his direction. Plenty.

Across town in Johnny Romano's Hancock Park mansion, Warner thought she'd died and gone to movie star heaven.

Warner Franklin, Vice cop, cavorting with Johnny Romano – too much!

He'd called her that morning right after she'd put the phone down on Mickey.

"Come on over, baby," Johnny had crooned. "We'll read my reviews together."

And that's exactly what they'd done.

It would have helped if the reviews had been good. As it was they were terrible.

It didn't seem to bother Johnny. He'd shrugged nonchalantly. "So what, baby," he'd said. "My public loves me. I belong to 'em. They don't give no friggin' power to nothin' these uptight critics gotta say. You think they got knowledge what's goin' on in the world today? No way, baby. *Johnny* knows what's goin' on in the world. *Johnny*'s givin' the people exactly what they wanna see."

It was slightly disconcerting when Johnny referred to himself in the third person, but Warner went along with it. She wasn't too sure about his confidence in the movie. After all, she'd seen *Motherfaker* the previous evening, and while Johnny was tall and sexy and certainly handsome, he was not a great actor. He was everything she'd ever dreamed of in a man, but he was also a sexist pig, and his movie celebrated that fact. The Romano entourage milled around the house. There were bodyguards, managers, agents, friends, wellwishers. And yet he'd chosen to be with her. She was immensely flattered.

"Come on, baby, let's go get us some private time," he'd finally said. And they'd retired to his bedroom where at last they were alone.

Sexually he was a raging bull. He made Mickey Stolli seem like a non-starter.

Being with a younger man was a revelation. Warner had forgotten how energetic and fun sex could be. With Mickey, sex was not fun. He never really relaxed. He approached the sexual act as if it was a game of strenuous tennis and he had to perform well or there would be a punishment.

Sex with Johnny Romano was exactly the opposite. He

laughed a lot and crooned "baby, baby, baby" non-stop in her ear.

As far as she was concerned he could call her anything he wanted. He was her favourite movie star, and this was her fantasy come true. Skinny Warner Franklin from Watts was just about to get it for the second time with Johnny Romano. She loved Hollywood!

Johnny lay spread-eagled on the bed, erect and ready.

"You really a cop, baby?" he asked, absent-mindedly stroking his own erection.

"I really am," she replied, admiring every inch of him.

"Well, baby, baby, cop this," he drawled, pushing his hard-on towards her.

She mounted him because he obviously liked it that way. And then she squeezed him all the way to heaven.

When they were through she began to dress, ready to go to work.

"Come back soon, baby, baby," Johnny mumbled before falling into a deep sleep.

Oh, he could count on that.

Cooper was alone when he arrived to pick up Venus Maria for dinner.

"Where's your seventeen-year-old ex-porn star?" she asked, looking around.

He shrugged. "Why share you?"

"If we dine by ourselves again, people will talk."

He watched her carefully. "Does it bother you?"

She shook her head. "Nope. I'm used to it. Does it bother *you*?"

"Not at all." He didn't want to mention that he'd had to put up with the press longer than she could remember.

"Let's go," she sang out. "I'm starving!"

On the way to the restaurant she told him about Martin flying in and their plans to spend the day in San Francisco. "I've got a great idea. Why don't you come with us?" she suggested brightly.

Cooper burst out laughing. "Oh, yeah. That would really go down well with Martin. He'd be thrilled."

"*I'm* inviting you," she insisted. "You're one of Martin's best friends. Why shouldn't you come? It'll be great. And if we're spotted or anything, people will think *we're* the big romance. You don't mind people thinking that, do you?"

"Ah, if only it was true," he said wistfully.

There was a challenge in her big brown eyes. "Come on, Cooper. Live dangerously."

"What'll Martin say?"

"He'll say what I tell him to."

"Oh, Miss Ballsy."

"You bet. It'll be great, and it'll give you a chance to talk to Martin. You know I really want you to do that for me."

He nodded. "If it pleases you, I'll come."

She smiled and took his hand. "You're the best."

By late Saturday afternoon, bored and almost addicted, Mickey decided he wasn't in the mood to hang around the house waiting for Abigaile to get home or Warner to contact him. So he called up his addiction, Madame Loretta, and informed her he was on his way over and that she should have the Chinese girl ready for him.

When he arrived, he was discreetly taken upstairs and ushered into a private bedroom.

Tai, the beautiful Oriental girl he'd had before, greeted him with a shy smile, her long black hair flowing down her back. "And how may I pleasure you today?" she asked dutifully.

There was nothing like an obedient woman. He unzipped his pants and flopped down on the bed. "Gimme a blow-job."

The nice thing about going to a whorehouse was that you could actually come right out with it. No flowers. No sweet talk. Just action. Every man's dream.

Tai nodded and reached for a bottle of aromatic oil.

Mickey allowed his mind to go blank and she began to gently massage his balls, her delicate fingers doing marvellous things.

Forget everything. Go with the moment. Relax.
He closed his eyes.

When he felt the insistent tip of her talented tongue he couldn't help groaning aloud. The pleasure was overwhelming.

Unfortunately for Mickey, just as he was about to reach ecstasy, the door was flung open and Warner and another plain-clothes Vice cop burst into the room.

"OK, buddy, get your pants on. This is a raid. We're Vice," said the male cop.

"Mickey?" cried a surprised Warner.

Mickey's hard-on deflated like a pricked balloon.

Chapter 59

"What the fuck is going on?" demanded Carlos Bonnatti.

"Whaddya mean, Big C?" asked Link, his bodyguard and right-hand man.

"I mean, what the fuck is going on?" repeated Carlos flatly.

Link shrugged. He was a tall, thin-faced man with slit eyes and a lethal scar curving down his left cheek. "Ya talked to Eddie Kane yourself," Link pointed out.

"I know that," Carlos said impatiently. "And I also know he don't have the money. The asshole snorted it. All my goddamn money up his goddamn nose."

Link came up with a good suggestion. "Do ya want me to break his legs?"

"If I thought broken legs would get me my money, I'd go for the idea. But let's get realistic here. The prick don't have the money. So I gotta go to the studio. Panther Studios, Mickey Stolli. Set me up a meet."

Link nodded. "It's arranged. When d'ya want it?"

"Monday," Carlos said broodingly. "Set it up."

He walked to the window of the Century City penthouse he used when he was in Los Angeles and stared at the view. He liked visiting LA. Maybe he should think about spending more time on the Coast. Get out of New York with the dirt and the crime and the homeless roaming the streets.

Now that he was a free man it didn't seem like such a bad idea. After ten years of marriage his wife had left him. Her loss. The dumb broad had run off with some fag interior designer.

He'd decided to let her learn her lesson the hard way. After a few months she'd come crawling back, begging for what she was missing. When she did, he'd take great pleasure in slamming the door in her face.

Fortunately there were no kids to consider. Carlos had always wanted a son, but his wife had never delivered. He was not fond of people who didn't deliver.

He was not fond of Eddie Kane.

Nobody stole from Carlos Bonnatti and got away with it.

Chapter 60

"I've got to make a phone call," Mickey said urgently, zipping up his pants.

"I told you, bud, you make your phone call down at the station," replied the male cop, who couldn't care less.

Warner stood back and stared at him in disgust, shaking her head as if he was the lowest of the low.

"Do you know who I am?" Mickey persisted, concentrating on the male cop because he knew he was getting no help from Warner.

"Yeah, we know who you are," replied Warner sharply, joining in for both of them. "Just another pathetic john."

He was hustled downstairs along with everybody else. Madame Loretta was trying to put on a good front as she assured customers and girls alike that everything would be all right. Surrounding her were the girls in various stages of undress. Mickey thought he saw Leslie Kane among them, but it was just a glimpse and he knew he must be mistaken.

Mickey was in shock. He could not afford to be arrested in a whorehouse and carted off to jail like a common criminal. This was somebody's idea of a bad joke.

"Who's in charge here?" he demanded, looking around for an authority figure.

Although there were police everywhere, plain-clothes and otherwise, he couldn't seem to find the captain of this operation.

Warner threw him another filthy glare. "Do yourself a favour and shut up," she said, vitriol accompanying every word. "*Mr* Stolli."

He glared back. "Why don't *you* get me out of this stinkin' mess?"

"You got yourself into it, work it out," she retorted sharply, adding under her breath, "Asshole." If looks could kill he'd be ten foot under.

This was the woman he'd been sleeping with for over a year? The woman who'd gone out of her way to constantly tell him how wonderful he was? Whatever they'd had together, it was definitely over.

Eventually everybody was herded outside and bundled into a police van.

Mickey shielded his face and huddled by the window, wondering if he could sue. He'd certainly like to. Sue the sons of bitches for harassment.

By the time they reached the holding jail, there were television news crews and photographers milling around waiting to greet them.

Charming! A fucking circus! How could this be happening to him?

He considered Abigaile's reaction and knew he was a dead man.

Locked in the police van, Leslie Kane shivered at the injustice of it all. In vain she'd tried to explain to the cops that she was merely an overnight guest. "Right, honey," they'd said, ignoring her protestations of innocence, and bundled her into the van along with everyone else.

Her heart was beating wildly. When Eddie found out he would surely investigate further and her past would be revealed.

Oh, the shame! Eddie was going to discover he'd married a prostitute.

She tried to calm herself. It wasn't so bad really. After all, *she'd* married a cocaine addict. Maybe it was time they both cleaned up their acts.

She spotted Mickey Stolli outside. Mickey Stolli, head of Panther Studios, pillar of Hollywood society. Married to Abigaile, the Hollywood princess. What was *he* doing there?

Men! When she'd been a working girl she'd always been surprised at the types that came in for a little action. Why should Mickey Stolli surprise her? He was typical.

Men went to whores for two things – conversation and sex. The conversation always came first.

Hoping he hadn't seen her, she turned away.

Arriving from London, Primrose and Ben Harrison checked into the Beverly Hills Hotel. Abigaile felt obliged to invite them over for dinner on Saturday night.

"We're tired," Primrose warned her over the phone, agreeing to come anyway.

It was most inconvenient. Jeffries, the butler, and his wife usually had Saturdays off. Now Abigaile realized she would have to try and find them and summon them back. They would not be pleased – and neither was she.

"Where's Mr Stolli?" Abigaile asked Consuela, after instructing the cook to prepare lightly grilled chicken with broccoli and fresh corn on the cob.

Consuela shrugged. Why did the Stollis always imagine *she* knew where everybody was? "Don't know, Missus," she answered vaguely. "Mr Stolli, he out. You shopping."

"I know, I know," Abigaile said irritably. "I went shopping and now I'm back. Did Mr Stolli leave me a message?"

"No," Consuela shook her head and wondered why she couldn't have weekends off like most of the other maids in Beverly Hills.

After locating Jeffries, Abigaile went to find Tabitha. Flinging open the door to her daughter's room she was assailed by the ear-splitting sounds of Van Halen blaring from the stereo.

"Tabitha," she shouted above the din.

Tabitha, lying in the middle of a messy bed surrounded by teen magazines, did not hear her. She was too busy speaking on her pink princess phone.

"Tabitha," Abigaile yelled crossly, marching across the room and switching off the stereo.

Tabitha sprang to attention as though she'd been mortally wounded. "Watcha do that for?"

"Because I wish to speak to you," Abigaile replied haughtily. "How can you hear yourself? How can you speak with all this noise going on? You'll damage your hearing."

"Don't be so old-fashioned." Tabitha muttered something into the phone and hung up. "By the way, did Daddy tell you? He said I can have a Porsche when I'm sixteen."

"Don't be ridiculous," snorted Abigaile.

"He did. He said so."

"Where *is* your father?"

"Dunno."

"Didn't he say where he was going?"

"Dunno."

Getting information out of her daughter was like persuading the Pope to have sex.

Abigaile stalked from the room.

Before she was one step out of the door, Van Halen blasted from the stereo, twice as loud as before.

Down at the station Mickey made a lot of noise and was finally allowed his one phone call. He called Ford Werne.

Unfortunately Ford was not at home.

Leslie used her one call to telephone the beach house, hoping Eddie was there. Indeed he was.

"Eddie," she exclaimed thankfully.

"Sweetheart! Where are you? I'm glad you phoned. I want you to come home, baby. I'm sorry, I'm so sorry. I'll never hit you again. I don't know what came over me."

"I'm in trouble," Leslie whispered.

"Just tell me where you are and I'll come and get you," he promised.

"I'm in jail, Eddie. I've been arrested. You need to bail me out."

He was shocked. "What?"

"It's a mistake. I'll explain everything when I see you."

"What've you been arrested for?"

"It doesn't matter. Just come and get me."

"I'm on my way."

Chapter 61

Abigaile and Primrose greeted each other with a stiff embrace. Primrose was taller than her sister, with fine golden hair and china-blue eyes. Her husband, Ben Harrison, was a heavily built man, youthful-looking for his fifty years, in spite of crinkled grey hair and a stern expression. He treated Primrose with a certain amount of deference.

"Where's Mickey?" was his first question.

"He'll be home soon," Abigaile replied agitatedly. "He's out on a business meeting."

"We have to talk," Ben said curtly. "I have no clue what this is about. I only know we're not happy being summoned here at the last moment. Has anybody contacted Abe?"

"I saw him last week," Abigaile said. "He never mentioned anything. I've tried to call him. Inga insists he can't be disturbed."

"Can't be disturbed?" Ben repeated, frowning darkly. "What kind of excuse is that?"

"We'll find out on Monday morning," Abigaile replied stiffly, wondering where Mickey was.

They were in the middle of dinner by the time Mickey finally showed up. Abigaile heard him sneaking into the house trying to slide past the dining room and vanish upstairs.

"Excuse me a minute," she said with a sweet smile to Ben and Primrose. She rushed into the hall. "Mickey! Where the *hell* have you been?"

He looked dishevelled. "I was in a car accident," he lied.

"A car accident? Is the car all right?"

Is the car all right? A typical Abigaile question.

"Yeah," he said sourly. "The car is fine. I'm dead, but the car is fine."

"Primrose and Ben are here," she hissed, ignoring his sarcasm. "Hurry up and join us. I am *not* entertaining them on my own."

"Gimme a break," he protested. "I nearly got myself killed."

"Mickey." Her warning tone spoke volumes.

What did she care? "OK, OK, five minutes."

He hurried upstairs. Jesus! This was his worst nightmare come true. Arrested while a Chinese hooker gave him a blow-job. Was nothing sacred any more? Thank God Madame Loretta had gathered her wits about her and contacted her lawyer. The man had arrived in record time and bailed everyone out.

Now Mickey had a date to appear in court.

If Abigaile ever found out he was visiting a whorehouse . . .

The ride back to the beach seemed longer than usual. Eddie was silent for a while, driving with one hand on the steering wheel and drumming the fingers of his other hand on the dashboard.

Finally he spoke. "What were you doing in a whore-house, Leslie?"

"I met Madame Loretta when I first came to Los Angeles," Leslie explained, telling him the story she'd decided to use. "She seemed like a nice woman. In fact she helped me out. I used to go up to her house for tea."

"Tea?" Eddie yelled. "What did you think she was running — an English tea parlour?" He paused to make a point. "She runs a whorehouse, Leslie. You were sleeping there last night. What's goin' on here? *How* did she help you out?"

Leslie stared straight ahead. "I can explain."

The Maserati roared down the highway. "The facts speak for themselves, huh?" Eddie said edgily.

"How many times do I have to tell you? I was sleeping over. By myself. I had nowhere else to go."

Eddie slapped the side of his head. "Jesus!" he said sarcastically. "I can't figure out why I'm suspicious, can you?"

"Will I have to appear in court?" she asked anxiously.

"Naw," he replied. "I'll havta fix it."

"Can you?"

"If I say I can do it, I can do it."

"Thank you, Eddie." Her voice was almost a whisper.

The car swerved along the highway. Eddie's driving was erratic to say the least.

He pressed on. "How come you never told me about Madame Loretta before?"

"You never asked," she replied quietly.

He glanced in his rear-view mirror. "Oh, I'm supposed to ask, am I? Hey, Leslie, babe, you friendly with a whore-monger? Is that what I'm supposed to ask — that kind of shit?"

Her eyes filled with tears. She hadn't done anything wrong. She was just sleeping over. It was his fault in the first place. This wasn't fair. "Eddie, please. Don't be mad at me. I'm very tired," she pleaded.

"*You're* tired," he said, outraged by her selfishness. "What the fuck do you think *I* am? I've got this hood

370

Bonnatti breathing all over me. It's a responsibility I don't need."

She sighed. "How did you find yourself in this position? If you and Mickey are partners why doesn't the studio pay?"

"It's not exactly Mickey who owes the money," he grumbled. "The fact is we had an arrangement, and, uh, I guess I sliced a little too much off the end. I didn't think anybody would notice. Trouble is, they did."

She was relieved to have steered the conversation away from Madame Loretta. "We're talking about a million dollars, Eddie."

"I know, I know. I had some debts to pay. Gotta face it, cocaine ain't cheap."

"What you should do," she said firmly, "is forget about the debt and check yourself into a detox centre. I'll support you, Eddie. I'll be by your side."

"You don't seem to understand," he said urgently. "Carlos Bonnatti is threatening to break more than my balls if I don't pay."

"That's ridiculous," Leslie gasped. "Things like that only happen in gangster movies."

"Honey," he said dryly, "welcome to the real world."

Mickey joined his sister- and brother-in-law for dinner, his mind in fast forward. He had so much to take care of and yet he had to sit there and suffer through polite bullshit. The main topic of conversation concerned Abe Panther. What could the meeting on Monday morning possibly be about?

Mickey shrugged. "I got no idea. We're making money, the studio's doing well. The old man should stay home an' stay happy. We don't need his interference."

Ben Harrison didn't seem to agree. "You know, Mickey," he said thoughtfully, "maybe Abe doesn't like the films the studio is producing. I have to tell you, I saw *Motherfaker* and it's a disaster. It's a movie I wouldn't want my mother to see – or, come to think of it, my sisters either."

371

"Yeah, well, everybody else in the country's going to love it," Mickey said defensively. "This is the kind of movie they're clamouring for today."

"I don't know." Ben shook his head doubtfully. "It'll do a big weekend gross and then fall down. There'll be no word of mouth. In fact the word of mouth will be – stay away."

"Johnny Romano's a big star," Mickey pointed out. "The public is crazy about him."

"He loves himself," Ben replied evenly. "That much is obvious. Who had control over him? Didn't anybody try to pull in the reins?" He lowered his voice. "You know how many times he says 'motherfucker'? Not to mention the other actors."

Primrose heard him anyway. "Ben!" she admonished. "Kindly don't use language like that."

Mickey raised an eyebrow. Primrose lived in England for a few years and suddenly she became the Queen Mother!

Jeffries, the butler, entered the room. "There's a phone call for you, Mr Stolli," he said, looking down his long thin nose.

"Who is it?" Mickey asked rudely. "I'm eating dinner."

"He said it was most important. A Mr Bonnatti."

"Bonnatti?"

"That is correct, sir."

This was not turning out to be a good day.

Chapter 62

Sitting on the Swanson private jet, Venus Maria felt a million miles away from the scrawny little kid who'd lingered on Fifth Avenue and watched from afar as Martin Swanson married Deena Akveld. It was unbelievable really. Here she was with Cooper Turner, famous movie star, on one side, and Martin Swanson, billionaire, on the other. And she had them both under her spell.

Venus Maria smiled. It was kind of a kick. In a way she wished Ron was there to witness it. He'd love every minute.

Martin leaned over to speak to her. "Why did you ask Cooper?" he said in a low voice. "What do we need him for?"

"Cooper's your best friend," she replied guilelessly. "I thought you'd be pleased."

"I'm not pleased," he said irritably. "A romantic day for two in San Francisco hardly works when it's for three."

She laughed softly. Was Martin jealous? "Don't be silly. Cooper's hardly a drag. He'll find plenty to do."

"He'll go off and leave us alone, will he?" Martin asked sarcastically.

"No," she replied firmly. "The three of us are going to have a fantastic time together." She kissed him on the cheek, flicking her tongue into his ear just to give him a little taste of things to come. "I'm going to freshen up," she added, excusing herself.

As she wandered off down the plane she winked at Cooper. Now was the time for him to have a serious talk with Martin and find out his intentions.

The Swanson jet was luxurious, to say the least. It was set up like an amazing apartment, with a living room, functional stainless-steel Space Age kitchen, glamorous bedroom, and two marble bathrooms.

She shut herself in the bedroom, closed the door, and threw herself on the circular bed. *Hey, this is great*, she thought. *Maybe he'll lend it to me for the tour.*

Not exactly subtle. They still had to keep the relationship quiet.

In San Francisco they were met by a limousine and taken straight to the penthouse suite of the Fairmont Hotel to freshen up. Martin had a short business meeting to attend, so Venus Maria and Cooper admired the panoramic view and ordered a bottle of champagne.

"So?" she demanded anxiously. "Did you talk to him? What did he have to say?"

Cooper considered his reply. In his opinion Martin

didn't have the balls to leave Deena. He was enjoying his affair with Venus – and indeed who wouldn't – but he wasn't prepared to screw up his perfect marriage. Deena represented stability. She was his wife and they'd achieved a certain social standing that Martin was not ready to give up.

But *his* opinion was not what Venus wanted to hear.

"Hey," he said, "you know Martin – Mister Closed Mouth."

She was disappointed. "Do you mean to tell me you couldn't get *anything* out of him?"

"He thinks you're fantastic."

"Yes?"

"Oh, yes."

"Is that all?"

"Just that I agree with him."

She laughed, not taking him seriously at all. "You would!"

Later the three of them dined at Stars, causing quite a sensation.

"You see," Venus Maria whispered to Martin. "It's good that Cooper's with us. Now everybody will think he and I are an item. Can you imagine if we were spotted in San Francisco alone together?"

"It was a wise decision," he agreed.

She hammered the point home. "There's only one way we can be seen out in public, and that's if you split with your wife."

It was not the first time she'd said something like that to him.

He didn't reply.

After dinner they drove down to the bay and drank strong capucinos in a small, crowded café. Women appeared from nowhere, strutting their stuff in the hope of getting noticed. Cooper Turner and Martin Swanson in the same place at the same time – what an irresistible challenge! Men eyed Venus Maria up and down. And so did the women. Martin and Cooper gave her their full attention.

"Don't you feel like getting laid?" Venus teased, flirting with Cooper, a mischievous twinkle in her eye.

"Getting laid today is a perilous business," he replied, perfectly serious. "I need to know their sexual history for the past seven years. It takes time and energy. Not like the old days. I'm too tired."

Martin shot him a look. "I never thought I'd hear *you* say that."

Venus Maria shook her platinum curls. "Oh, he's *always* saying that. Take no notice."

Cooper smiled. "I'm saving myself."

"Who for?" she asked curiously.

"I'll let you know when she comes along."

He held her gaze.

She looked away.

Later they boarded Martin's plane and flew back to LA.

"Do you want to stay at my house?" she asked Martin.

"I'm desperate to stay at your house," he replied. "I didn't fly in early for my health."

"Just the two of us this time," she promised.

"No more games?"

Was it her imagination, or did he sound just the tiniest bit disappointed?

"Yes, Martin. Just the two of us."

They said goodbye to Cooper in the limo.

"I'll call you tomorrow," she said. Cooper was rapidly turning into her best friend.

"Tomorrow," he said.

"Goodnight." She kissed him lightly on the cheek.

And then she was alone with Martin.

Dennis Walla stared at the current edition of *Truth and Fact*. At this very moment it was being delivered all over the country. The front page was the strongest layout he'd seen in a long time. It made the latest headlines in the *Enquirer* and *Star* look sick.

First of all there were the headings in blazing red letters:

Surrounding these headings were five photographs. In the centre was the large picture of Venus Maria with Martin Swanson. On the left, a small shot of Venus entering Spago with Cooper Turner. Beneath that, another photo of Venus and Cooper, taken on the set. And the two smaller photographs on the right were of Deena Swanson and Paul Webster in Central Park, and Paul strolling along the street with Brigette Stanislopoulos.

Dennis was more than delighted. He'd never expected this to turn out to be such an important story. At first it was merely going to be Emilio's revelations about Venus Maria. Now they'd held that part of the story for the following week, and this week they'd concentrated on the various romantic entanglements of the main players. Excellent coverage!

Bert Slocombe had really come up trumps when he'd discovered Deena stepping out. But he'd doubled Dennis's pleasure when he'd managed to catch a photo of Deena's toy boy with Brigette Stanislopoulos, the teenage shipping heiress. What a coup!

There was more copy above the photographs:

BILLIONAIRE'S MISTRESS IS VENUS MARIA!
BROKEN WIFE DEENA SEES YOUNGER MAN!
DOES COOPER KNOW SHE'S CHEATING?

Dennis Walla threw the magazine down on his coffee table. He was well pleased. As far as he was concerned every editor in town was going to be after him.

Dennis Walla was about to become the hottest tabloid journalist in the world.

Without the silken bindings and the two exotic hookers to excite him, sex with Martin seemed a little pedestrian. He was too fast in every way.

Much to Venus Maria's chagrin, foreplay seemed to

376

have gone by the board, and all he could give her was a cursory going-over. Sex by numbers. Touch the breasts for twenty-five seconds, move the hands down, spread the legs, and go for it.

Venus Maria was disappointed. This wasn't the way she liked to make love at all. He had no stamina either. It was all over in minutes.

"What's the matter with you tonight?" she asked edgily, feeling totally unsatisfied.

Obviously he wasn't aware anything was amiss. "Aren't you happy?" he said.

She frowned. "No, I'm not particularly happy. It was so quick."

Martin seemed unconcerned. "What did you expect?" he said, yawning. "It seems like I've been on planes for the last twenty-four hours. I'm not Superman."

You can say that again, she thought bitterly.

Venus Maria hated bad sex. It made her feel dirty and used. Sex was supposed to be long and leisurely and satisfying.

Bad sex reminded her of the sort of behaviour her brothers used to dish out to the neighbourhood girls who would come to the old house in Brooklyn whining and crying about their treatment.

It was quite obvious her brothers considered women were put on the earth to clean, cook, fuck, and shut up.

Charming monsters.

Observing them had given Venus Maria a great deal of determination to make it as a strong woman, capable of anything. And she'd done it. She'd really done it!

Now that she was a modern-day sex symbol it had to drive her brothers crazy.

She jumped out of bed and marched into her bathroom, slamming the door behind her. Damn Martin. Did he expect silken ties and two hookers every time they did it?

She imagined that Cooper Turner didn't need any props. He was probably a master between the sheets. Well, he'd had enough experience over the years, hadn't he? Mister Casanova – the Don Juan of Hollywood.

She wouldn't care to go to bed with him. God, no! The

comparisons! He'd had some of the most beautiful women in the world.

Ah . . . the Cooper Turner Hall of Fame. Venus Maria planned *never* to be part of *that* long parade.

Martin was asleep when she returned to the bedroom. He lay on his side, snoring loudly.

Maybe she wasn't being fair. He'd had a long journey and was probably exhausted.

She snuggled into bed beside him and closed her eyes. It took forty-five minutes before she was able to fall asleep.

Chapter 63

Lucky flew back to Los Angeles with only Boogie for company. Lennie hadn't called, and she had too much pride to call him. If this was the way he wanted things to end – so be it.

Face facts, she told herself. She'd bought the studio for Lennie and he didn't give a damn. He'd felt it was a blow to his ego or some such masculine crap. Why the hell couldn't he just relax and enjoy it?

When she'd arrived back at her apartment in New York, she'd phoned Gino and told him of Lennie's reaction.

"I tried to warn you, kid," he'd sighed. "I had an idea this was the way he'd feel."

"Why do you say that?"

"'Cause it's a man's thing. You can buy him a sweater or a tie, but a studio . . . Jeez! What can I tell you?"

"His attitude is totally old-fashioned. I'm not putting up with it," she'd said stubbornly. "I'm excited about owning Panther. He should be too."

"So what are you gonna do, kid?"

"Leave Lennie in New York until he gets over his sulks."

"Big solution."

"What else *can* I do?"

"How about tryin' to work it out?" he'd suggested.

"Too late. The next move is his."

The truth was that she felt hurt and frustrated by Lennie's macho attitude. He, above all people, should understand her. She'd never pretended to be the perfect wife prepared to sit home and have babies. He'd always known she was a woman who liked to take chances. That's why he'd fallen in love with her.

Now he was acting like "You – woman. Me – man." It was almost as if he was saying. "Get knocked up or it's over." They had Bobby and Brigette. Wasn't that enough of a family for now?

Screw Lennie Golden.

She had a life to live.

From LAX, Boogie drove her straight to the Malibu house.

Miko greeted her with a polite bow. "So good to have you back, Madame."

It was good to be back. She felt strong. She felt invincible. She was ready to accomplish anything.

On Sunday evening Morton Sharkey came over and they spent the evening going over Panther business. She had so many plans to put into operation: new people to hire, decisions on all the various productions, who stayed and who did she dump?

Later, when Morton had left, she walked out onto the deck and stared at the sea. *Everything's going to be all right, Santangelo*, she promised herself, breathing in the crisp night air.

All her life she'd had to make it on her own, prove she could do it. And Panther Studios was no different from anything else. She'd show everyone. And if Lennie didn't want to come along for the ride, she'd do it by herself.

Lucky Santangelo was a true survivor.

Nothing and nobody stopped her.

Abe Panther had decided they should all arrive at the studio together, so on Monday morning Lucky reported to Abe's Miller Drive home along with Morton Starkey.

Abe greeted her with a feisty smile. "Morning, girlie. Are we ready to kick us some ass?"

"I'm always ready to kick ass," she replied, confirming what he'd suspected.

She looked particularly beautiful with her mass of wild jet hair, olive skin, and dark eyes full of drama.

She wore a cream leather Claude Montana suit and very high heels, diamond hoops in her ears, and a large diamond ring on her finger. She was all business in a classy, sexy, stylish way.

What a difference from drab little Luce! That was the whole idea.

Abe seemed full of high spirits, and so did Inga for once. He'd promised she could come to the meeting, and she'd dressed up for the occasion.

Lucky wondered what the old man was planning to do with all his money. Probably sit on it until he dropped!

"Are we meeting in Mickey's office?" she asked.

"Naw, we'll settle in the conference room," Abe decided. "I want to be there before any of 'em arrive."

"Mickey usually gets in early," Lucky pointed out.

"Maybe not today," Abe replied with a wicked laugh. "Here's a little something for you to feast your eyes on, girlie."

He handed her a copy of the *Los Angeles Times*. On the bottom of the front page there was a picture of Mickey being led out of a police van. The caption read:

STUDIO HEAD ARRESTED IN RAID ON HOLLYWOOD HOUSE OF SHAME

"Oh my God!" she exclaimed. "He's getting it from all sides today. Do you think he'll turn up?"

"Of course he will," snapped Abe.

They set off in convoy, Abe and Lucky in the first car, Inga following behind with Morton Sharkey and Abe's lawyer.

All the way Lucky could feel Abe's excitement building. When they approached the studio gates he really started to buzz.

"This is like coming home, girlie," he said rubbing his hands together. "Can't think why I ever left."

"Why *did* you leave?" she asked curiously.

He shrugged. "Don't know. We were entering a new decade. I didn't like what was goin' on in the movies any more. The public wanted to see things I wasn't prepared to show 'em."

She could understand that. Abe came from a different era. A kinder, gentler time. "How does it feel to be coming back?" she asked.

He bobbed his head happily. "Pretty damned good!"

Up in the conference room there were nervous secretaries flitting all over the place.

"Good morning, Mr Panther."

"Welcome back, Mr Panther."

"Is there anything I can get you, Mr Panther?"

Abe took his place at the head of the table and indicated to Lucky that she should sit on his right.

She did so. Although the studio was officially hers, she wouldn't dream of cheating him out of his moment of glory.

At ten o'clock precisely Mickey Stolli marched in. He was followed by Abigaile, Primrose, and Ben.

Abe waved his hand in the air. "Take a seat everybody. Make yourselves at home."

Mickey glanced around the room. His eyes passed over Lucky without a flicker of recognition.

"You're looking well, Grandfather," said Primrose, rushing over to kiss him.

"How come you never write or call?" Abe demanded, clicking his false teeth in and out.

Primrose sighed as if he had no right to ask such a question. "We're all so busy, Grandfather. The children send you their love."

"Sit down," instructed Mickey sharply. He didn't need Primrose kissing the old man's ass.

When everybody was settled, Abe got right to it. "I've been outta here ten years," he said roughly, "an' I let you all do whatever the hell you wanted. Now I've made other arrangements. I've sold the studio."

There was a stunned silence. And four shocked faces.

Mickey was the first on his feet. "You've done *what*?" he asked incredulously.

"I've sold the studio," Abe repeated with a crafty cackle. "It's mine to sell, eh?"

"Grandfather, you can't do that without consulting us," Abigaile protested, a flush spreading across her face.

"Certainly not," agreed a distressed Primrose.

"Girlies, I can do what I damn well please. I'm old enough and ugly enough."

"What you're saying is you've sold the studio, is that it?" Mickey said harshly.

"This is good," joked Abe. "The man understands English."

Ben joined in. "Who've you sold it to?"

"Ladies and gentlemen." Abe savoured the words. "I'd like you to meet the *new* owner of Panther Studios." He turned to Lucky. "Allow me to introduce Lucky Santangelo."

There was another long silence. Once again Mickey was the first to break it. "What is this? Some kind of joke?"

"You can't do this, Grandfather," shrieked Abigaile.

Morton Sharkey rose to his feet. "Miss Santangelo will be taking over, effective today," he said. "In the future you will report to her."

"If you think I'm staying to be told what to do by some dumb broad – you're wrong," spat Mickey. "I'm out of here."

Good, Lucky thought.

"Now wait a minute," interrupted Ben. He knew who Lucky Santangelo was. He was well aware of her reputation. She'd taken over the Stanislopoulos shipping empire when Dimitri Stanislopoulos passed away, and today – under her management – it was more successful than ever. Lucky Santangelo knew what she was doing. "We're going to have to discuss this unexpected situation."

"Who gets the money?" asked Abigaile furiously, unable to control herself. "It's *our* money."

"Grandfather," Primrose said, the voice of reason, "we have to sit down and talk privately. Not in front of all these people."

"I feel like I'm at my own funeral," Abe cackled, enjoying every minute. "What? You think I'm dead already? I can do what I want with my money. It's not *your* money. It's *my* money."

Lucky spoke at last. "Gentlemen, there'll be a meeting of all department heads at noon today. Right here."

"What do *you* know about the movie business?" Mickey asked rudely, turning to glare at her.

"Let's just say as much as you," she replied coolly.

He recognized something in her voice. Had he met her before? Lucky Santangelo. Lucky Santangelo . . . Christ! Wasn't she the broad with the gangster father? Wasn't she the one married to Lennie Golden?

Of course! Now it began to make sense. Her husband got pissed off with the studio and the broad bought it to keep him happy. Son of a bitch!

He couldn't look at Abigaile. His dear wife wasn't speaking to him on account of the story of his arrest making the front page of *LA Times*. When Abigaile had seen it she'd turned into a hysterical shrew. "Out of this house," she'd screamed. "Out of my life. I'll sue you for every penny you've got. How *dare* you disgrace me and Tabitha! This is the biggest humiliation of my life."

"It was a mistake," he'd replied lamely. "I was visiting the place with a director. The guy was researching a movie. I told him a scene he wanted to shoot wouldn't work. He took me up there to prove it would. It was business, Abby."

"Mickey Stolli, you've lied to me for the last time." Abigaile had shouted, narrowing he eyes. "We'll meet with my grandfather and behave like human beings. And then you'll pack your bags and get out of *my* house. We're through."

He wondered how she felt now. Abigaile wasn't going

to continue to ignore him after *this* little shocker. He shot her a look.

She was destroyed.

He glanced over at Ben and Primrose. Ben was foaming at the mouth, and Primrose seemed about to burst into tears.

Abe was loving every minute of the confusion he'd caused. Crafty little shithead.

Mickey stood up. He didn't have to take this crap. He'd made Panther the success it was today – he could get a job anywhere in town.

"I resign," he said sharply. "Find yourself another schmuck."

Chapter 64

Venus Maria slept in the nude. When she was a little girl she'd read an article about Marilyn Monroe.

> *What do you wear in bed, Miss Monroe?*
> *Chanel Number Five.*

Venus Maria wore nothing except her favourite scent, Poison, and a delicate tattoo of two white doves on the inside of her left thigh – souvenir of a two-day visit to Bangkok.

She awoke early, stretched languidly, and reached out for Martin.

He was not there.

She jumped out of bed and checked the bathroom. No note. No nothing.

Who the hell did he think he was dealing with here? Some Hollywood bimbo he could visit when he came into town, bang, and then take off? No way. She was Venus Maria. She deserved better than this. God damn it! Martin Swanson had to be taught a lesson.

Jumping under a cold shower she thought things over.

Martin Swanson . . . Martin Swanson . . . Why this obsession? What was wrong with her, for God's sake? He was just another man, after all.

Once out of the shower, she wrapped herself in a terry-cloth robe and vigorously shook out her wet hair. Today she was supposed to rehearse for the video. She loved it when she had nothing else to do except rehearse. It meant she didn't have to bother with makeup and putting on the Venus Maria persona. She could just be herself, bundle her hair into a ponytail, wear exercise clothes, and relax.

Ron made sure it was hard work – but he also made it fun. Long ago she'd decided she was a gypsy at heart. Her work was everything, the recognition an added bonus.

She decided Martin Swanson wasn't going to spoil her day. Screw him.

Downstairs, Hannah, her housekeeper, greeted her with the usual large glass of freshly squeezed orange juice, and a dish filled with chopped apples, melon, bananas, and oranges, covered with a healthful sprinkling of bran.

"Good morning," Venus sang out, feeling surprisingly good in spite of mediocre sex and Martin's early exit. "How was your weekend?"

Hannah didn't mention that her two days of rest were non-stop drudgery while she caught up on household chores in her two-room apartment downtown. With four children and a husband to look after it wasn't easy. "Fine, Miss Venus," she said, clearing up the dishes.

After the juice and fruit, Venus Maria indulged in a couple of pieces of toast liberally spread with chunky English marmalade.

Just as she was in the middle of the second piece, Ron arrived.

She looked up, pleased to see him. "What are you doing here? Aren't we supposed to meet at rehearsal in an hour?"

He carried a magazine which he placed carefully on the table. "I thought you should hear it from me first," he announced dramatically. Ron always liked to make the most of everything.

"Hear what?" she asked brightly.

His voice rose. "You mean nobody's told you? You haven't *seen* it?"

"What are you talking about?"

He was making a three-course meal out of this one. "Remember I warned you about Emilio when you chucked him out?"

She had a nasty feeling she wasn't going to like what she was about to hear. "Yes?" she said slowly.

Ron picked up a piece of toast and took a bite. "I never trusted him."

"Ha!" she said. "You think *I* trusted him? He broke into my house on Saturday."

"Yeah? I wonder what he was after? Take a look at this." He picked up the copy of *Truth and Fact* and waved it in front of her face.

She stared at it in horror. There, on the front page, was a photograph of her with Martin. It was *her* photograph – the two of them together taken by Cooper.

"Oh, no!" she cried.

"Oh, yes!" stated Ron firmly. "He probably dropped by to rip off the photo. Where did you keep it?"

She jumped up. "In my safe."

He sighed. "Let's go check it out."

"I can't believe he'd do this to me," she said angrily. "I'm paying his goddamn rent. I let him stay here for months! Ron, oh, God! Look what it says – *Next week Venus Maria's brother is going to reveal all.* What the *hell* is all?"

"When you're famous you can't even take a crap in peace," Ron said succinctly.

Venus headed upstairs, with Ron close behind her.

She stormed over to her safe, opened it, and searched frantically for her picture.

It wasn't there.

"He stole it!" she yelled. "That lousy, low-life rat-faced piece of shit!"

"Don't hold back," encouraged Ron.

"Oh my God," she wailed. "What does the story say? Martin's going to have a fit. Oh, Jesus!"

"It's not such a bad thing," Ron said, trying to calm her. "At least Deena will know you exist now. You won't have to creep around in hiding every time you get together with Martin."

Venus Maria snatched the magazine from him, eyes racing over the story:

> Billionaire Martin Swanson's phone calls and secret visits to ravishing superstar Venus Maria are driving his beautiful society wife, Deena, into the arms of young Paul Webster, son of Deena's best friend, interior designer to the rich and famous, Effie Webster.
>
> Sexy superstar Venus Maria can teach billionaire tycoon Martin Swanson a thing or two about getting to the top. Heart-broken Deena moved in on Paul after hearing about her husband's fascination with video superstar, Venus Maria. Deena is making a last-ditch effort to get Martin back. In the meantime, Martin Swanson has been showering Venus Maria with gifts. According to a close friend, Venus Maria and Martin Swanson met casually at a party in New York several months ago. But after a chance second meeting in Los Angeles, they couldn't resist each other any longer. All of Venus Maria's close friends were soon telling Swanson, "She likes you, she wants you." Within a week the two got together at a hideaway in Big Sur. According to another close friend, Martin told Venus he was not happy in his marriage. "From the beginning," an acquaintance said, "Venus Maria and Martin Swanson were magic together. Martin finds her extremely erotic, and Venus Maria is fascinated with his power and wealth.

Venus threw the magazine down in a fury. "Where do they got this garbage?" she yelled.

"Let's call Emilio," Ron suggested. "It's quite obvious he's been paid for this."

She pulled a face. "How can people *do* these things? If he needed money so desperately I would have given it to him. Doesn't he have any pride?"

"Emilio, pride?" Ron said, raising a sceptical eyebrow.

She was determined. "Gimme the phone."

Ron did so, and she dialled Emilio's number. His answering machine picked up.

"Fuck you!" she screamed into the receiver and slammed the phone down.

"That'll do you a lot of good, dear," remarked Ron.

Venus snatched up the magazine again. "Oh, and get this bit – Cooper's going to be *really* thrilled." She read aloud from the magazine. " '*While Venus Maria plays house with Martin Swanson, Cooper Turner thinks he's her only lover.*' Can you believe this crap? I'm calling my lawyer."

"What can *he* do?"

"I'll sue 'em."

"How can you? Most of it's true."

She hadn't thought about that. "I'd better warn Martin."

"Where is he?"

"He left early. He's involved in some kind of takeover bid. He's gaining control of a studio."

"Oh, just like that. The very rich *are* different."

"Ron, do me a favour. Call his office in New York and find out where I can reach him."

"What do you think he'll say?"

She shrugged. "I don't know. He's not used to this kind of publicity. At least *I* know what to expect. I've been everything from a lesbian alien to a woman with three breasts – and that's just this year! The shit comes with the territory."

"Don't kid yourself, dear," Ron said mildly. "Martin will probably love every minute of it."

Martin Swanson was in a board meeting when a secretary discreetly entered the room, tapped him on the shoulder, and said, "Your assistant in New York has to speak to you urgently, Mr Swanson."

Martin couldn't imagine what was so urgent that they

had to interrupt him in the middle of a meeting. "Excuse me, gentlemen," he said, standing up.

He walked outside. The secretary hovered behind him. "I'm sorry to disturb you, Mr Swanson," she apologized. "However, your assistant *did* say it was imperative that she speak to you at once."

"Don't worry about it." He waved a vague hand in her direction and picked up the phone. "What is it, Gertrude?" he asked abruptly.

"Mr Swanson, Venus Maria is trying to reach you. She says it's extremely urgent and that she must talk to you immediately."

"OK, Gertrude."

"Mr Swanson?"

"Yes? What now?"

"I believe I know what it's about."

"Do you want to tell me? Or would you prefer to keep it a secret?" he said sarcastically, not feeling particularly patient.

Gertrude plunged right in. "There's a magazine called *Truth and Fact*. It's similar to the *Enquirer*."

"So?"

"On the cover of the issue out today there's a front-page story concerning you and Venus Maria. Of course, I'm certain it's all lies." She hesitated, and then rushed on. "Mr Swanson, it's not a very nice story. Mrs Swanson will not be pleased."

Martin turned to the secretary hovering nearby. "Is there a news-stand downstairs?"

"Yes." She nodded.

"Be a good girl — run down and get me a copy of *Truth and Fact*."

"Certainly, Mr Swanson, at once."

He replaced the receiver and immediately phoned Venus Maria.

"Have you seen *Truth and Fact*?" he demanded.

"I just read it," she replied.

"Do you want to tell me about it?" he said curtly.

"What have they got? San Francisco? Is Cooper in the picture?"

"It's worse than that, Martin. Remember that photo Cooper took of us one night at my house? Well, I had it in my safe, and I suspect my brother must have stolen it and sold it to *Truth and Fact*."

"Your brother?"

"Emilio. He was staying with me. A real loser."

"So what you're telling me is that they've printed this picture of us together?"

"Yes, and it's pretty intimate. We're kind of sitting on the couch with our arms all over each other."

"Didn't you destroy it?"

She resented his tone. "Obviously not. I had it in my safe. That seemed like a pretty secure place to me."

"Christ!" he exclaimed, thinking of Deena's reaction.

"Don't get pissed with *me*, it's not my fault."

"Whose fault is it?" he asked coldly.

"I don't know, and quite frankly I don't give a fuck." She slammed the phone down. It was about time Martin learned to treat her with a little respect.

"Trouble in lifestyles-of-the-rich-and-famous land?" Ron ventured, pretending not to be enjoying every minute.

"Let's go rehearse," she said. "I've had it with that ego-inflated asshole."

Chapter 65

The news spread like an out-of-control brush fire. This was Hollywood, after all, capital of innuendo, gossip, and scandal. Already everyone was talking about Mickey Stolli's arrest at Madame Loretta's. What a delicious item to start the day! Now the rumour was that Lucky Santangelo had purchased Panther Studios with Abe Panther's full cooperation.

The word was out of the room before they finished the

meeting. The word spread from person to person. Phones were picked up. Calls were made. The news was passed on. The news spread across Hollywood.

At Panther everyone was abuzz with Mickey Stolli's arrest. Ford Werne couldn't understand it. The rule was, if you go to a prostitute, never get caught. Mickey had spoiled it for all of them.

This was no ordinary Monday morning at the studio.

When Arnie Blackwood and Frankie Lombardo had finished sniggering about Mickey's misfortune, they heard about Lucky Santangelo's purchase of the studio and her call for a noon meeting with all the department heads. They immediately placed a call to Eddie Kane.

Eddie picked up his own phone. "Yeah?"

"Don't you come in any more?" Arnie demanded.

Eddie was in no mood to be harassed. "Only when it suits me."

"So I guess you've got no idea what's going on," Frankie said, speaking on a conference call so Arnie could join in.

"You got something to tell me?" Eddie asked impatiently, knowing that Arnie and Frankie would never call just to inquire after his health. Maybe they were about to complain he'd scored too much coke at their party. Well, fuck 'em. Don't have the party if you can't part with the goods.

"Yeah," Arnie replied, drawing the words out slowly. "Some rich broad from New York walked in with Abe this morning and bought the fuckin' studio."

"What?" Eddie wasn't sure he'd heard correctly.

"Yeah, old Abe sold the studio from right under Mickey. Didn't you know?"

"If I knew, do you think I'd be sitting here?" Eddie replied agitatedly. "I got problems of my own."

"Get your stoned ass down here," ordered Frankie sharply. "There's a meeting of all department heads at noon. We need someone in there."

Eddie's mind was racing. He wondered if Mickey had known about this beforehand. Maybe that's why he'd been so cold and uptight.

Christ! Yes, Arnie and Frankie were right, he should be there. "I'm on my way," he said.

Leslie was pottering around in the kitchen. She looked beautiful. He still hadn't figured out what she was doing in a whorehouse. Eventually he was going to have to investigate.

"Gotta go to the studio, babe," he said, like this was the start of another normal day.

She looked dismayed. "Oh, no, Eddie. I thought we were going to find a counsellor and talk about getting you into a detox centre. Do you have to go?"

"Yeah," Eddie said, his twitching in full swing. "Too bad about that counsellor thing. We'll do it next week. OK, babe?"

It wasn't OK, but Leslie didn't say a word.

Lucky had an advantage. She knew who the players were and they didn't know her.

At twelve o'clock precisely they all trooped into the conference room.

Abe had taken off, followed by Inga, followed by Abigaile, followed by Primrose and Ben — both complaining bitterly. No doubt she would hear from them later.

The contingent of department heads was led by Ford Werne, still looking as if he'd stepped from the front page of G.Q. magazine, impeccable in another Armani suit, the same five-hundred-dollar tinted aviator shades covering his eyes. He was an attractive man — if you liked killers.

Zev Lorenzo followed Ford into the room and walked straight over to her, offering his hand. "Welcome aboard," he said in a friendly fashion.

Then came Grant Wendell, Junior, Vice President of Worldwide Production, looking like a reject from the mailroom in his baggy pants and Dodgers baseball cap. He gave her a casual sort of half-wave. "Hiya."

Lucky wondered if Mickey was going to put in a final appearance, or if his resignation was it. He must be in shock. Good. Mickey deserved a little shock in his life.

Teddy T. Lauden hurried into the room — a thin, precise

man, constantly glancing at his watch. "Good afternoon, Miss Santangelo," he said, opting for a more formal relationship. "A pleasure to meet you. I do hope I'm not late. I had another meeting to attend. Unfortunately I wasn't allowed enough time to cancel it. As you must understand, this has been a big shock for all of us."

Lucky nodded. "Yes, I do understand," she said quietly. "I'm sure it has been."

"You could say that," Ford Werne agreed, taking off his aviator shades and immediately putting them on again.

"I *am* saying it, Mr Werne."

He was clearly surprised she knew who he was, since he hadn't bothered to introduce himself. "Where's Mickey?" he asked.

"He won't be joining us," Morton Sharkey said, from his position beside Lucky.

Glancing around, she observed that Buck Graham and Eddie Kane were the only two still missing. "Will Mr Graham and Mr Kane be joining us?"

Grant Wendell shrugged. "Ummm, I talked to Eddie this morning. He's on his way in. And, uh, Buck had another meeting he's trying to break out of."

Lucky was cool and in control. "Why don't we give it ten minutes," she said pleasantly.

"Suits me." Ford adjusted his expensive shades yet again and stood up. "I have a phone call to make. Will you excuse me?"

"What a group!" Lucky murmured to Morton.

"They all want to keep their jobs," he answered in a low voice. "Unless a better offer comes along."

"I understand what goes on in this town very well," she replied. "It's no different than any other business. Naturally, if there's something better around the corner — go for it. If not, stand firm. The rules of the game."

"I hardly think any of them are thrilled to find themselves working for a woman."

"I guess not. After all, this is Hollywood, and women are not exactly power figures here. Ford is probably on the phone right now trying to get another job. Right?"

Morton agreed. "I wouldn't be surprised."

Buck Graham burst into the room, red in the face. Buck was Head of Marketing. His speciality was getting right down to the common denominator. Whatever the content of the film, Buck sold it with a strong dose of tits and ass. As far as he was concerned, America had a permanent hard-on.

He'd used a body double on the poster for Susie Rush's last movie – Susie's face atop an outrageously overdeveloped body. She was furious, and threatened to sue unless the poster was immediately withdrawn. Buck had given in – reluctantly.

Finally Eddie Kane came bouncing in, making the meeting complete.

Eddie looked like he'd slept in his clothes. His growing beard was a serious mistake, and his eyes were blood-shot and more spacey than ever.

"Where's Mickey?" were the first words out of his mouth.

"Not here," Buck said, shaking his head.

Eddie twitched. "Is he coming?"

"Didja see the *LA Times*?" Grant asked. "'Cause if you did, you know there's no way he'll be in today."

"What happened?"

"He got caught buyin' pussy."

Before Eddie could get into it, Ford returned from his phone call and Lucky got straight down to business.

"Well, gentlemen," she said, rising to her feet. "I'm sure you've all heard the news. My name is Lucky Santangelo and I'm the new owner of Panther Studios." She paused while a buzz went around the room. "I'm also new to the film industry. But I do know what I want. And that is to make good movies. Films Panther can be proud of. I'm interested in hearing what you feel hasn't been accomplished here in the last few years." She paused again. At least they were listening. When she'd first taken over Stanislopoulos Shipping it had taken months to get the male executives' attention. "Trust me when I say this, Panther's been putting out garbage, and those days are over. I'm leading this studio on to great things." She stared at them, black eyes ablaze. "Gentlemen," she said forcefully, "you can bet on it."

Chapter 66

Deena Swanson did not enjoy exercise. She was not some crazed Californian who thought an hour's aerobics and two hours of Jane Fonda was exciting stuff. No, Deena hated exerting herself. However, the trend was to do it — and nobody had ever accused Deena of being behind the trends. So eventually, like all chic New Yorkers, she'd hired her own personal trainer who came to the house. His name was Sven, and fortunately he didn't speak much English, which suited Deena fine because it was not conversation she was after.

Sven certainly knew how to get the best out of her in fifteen minutes of pure torture. Three times a week she started her day with him. When he left she usually luxuriated in the tub for fifteen minutes before dressing to go to her office for an hour or so before lunch.

Lunch was the most important part of Deena's day. She dressed for lunch. She accessorized for lunch. She made sure her makeup, nails, and hair were always perfect. Deena knew maintenance was a woman's best defence.

Most of Deena's women friends worked for their husbands. It was the new chic thing to do. They gave their opinions on style, fabrics, perfumes, cosmetics, and in return they were paid a fat director's fee for their input. But all of them found time to lunch.

Deena belonged to that exclusive group of rich New York women who wore only designer clothes, real jewellery, and fur coats if they were sure they weren't going to get a can of paint thrown over them.

Today, Deena was lunching at Le Cirque. Effie and she had a standing appointment for Mondays.

Deena dressed carefully in a pale lime green Adolfo suit with Chanel shoes and bag. She then added Bulgari earrings and choker, plus a huge diamond ring Martin had presented her with last Christmas.

Outside her apartment on Park Avenue, her car and driver waited to take her the few blocks to her office in the Swanson Building – a gleaming tower of modern architecture.

She loved her office. Effie had decorated it in cool pastels to make it a tranquil haven away from home.

Deena was proud of the fact that her fashion and perfume business was successful. When she'd embarked on it, she'd surrounded herself with the best executives money could buy. Martin had advised her. But that couldn't change the fact that it was *her* name on the products the public bought. Deena Swanson. Her name sold.

One of her secretaries greeted her with the news that Effie Webster had called and cancelled lunch.

"Why?" Deena asked, disappointed.

The girl shrugged. "I don't know, Mrs Swanson."

"Get her on the phone for me," Deena said, quite put out. For as long as she could remember, Effie and she had always lunched on Mondays.

"Mrs Webster is not at her office," the secretary informed her.

"Try her at home," Deena ordered.

"I already did. An answering machine picks up," the girl said.

Deena frowned. Was Effie sick?

She sat behind her bleached-wood desk and counted ten perfect sharply pointed pencils in a lucite holder. The pristine legal-sized pad of white paper with *Deena Swanson* written in pink on the top awaited her attention. A silver-framed photograph of herself and Martin faced her. There was really nothing for Deena to do at the office: everything was taken care of.

She called Martin in California. He was not at the hotel. Then she called another friend of hers, a sleek redhead who made exorbitantly priced belts and other fine accessories.

"Lunch, darling?" she asked.

"Isn't Monday your day with Effie?" her friend replied.

"She's sick," Deena explained.

"Ah, well, so I'm the substitute?"

"If you like. Le Cirque at one o'clock?"

"Why not?" her friend said.

It was arranged. Deena replaced the phone.

"Send Mrs Webster some flowers," she told her secretary. "A hundred dollars' worth. Make sure it's a beautiful arrangement."

"I can't wait to get out of here," Nona whispered. "My mother is in an absolute fury. I warned Paul."

Brigette wasn't exactly delighted herself. She'd managed to stay out of the supermarket rags for quite some time, and now they'd sneaked a picture of her and Paul taken with a hidden camera. Not so bad, but above that picture there was Paul, practically kissing Mrs Swanson. It was disgusting!

Effie Webster had taken it personally. Her son photographed in what looked like a compromising position with her best friend. This just wasn't on.

She summoned Paul to the house immediately. "What's this?" she demanded, thrusting a copy of *Truth and Fact* at him.

"Oh, that," he said casually, as if it didn't matter. "I took Deena out to lunch, big deal."

"It doesn't look like you're lunching here," replied Effie furiously. "You're all over her."

"So?" Paul said. "What's wrong with that? She's a woman. I'm a man."

"You're a *child*," Effie exclaimed. "And how *dare* you take one of my friends out! Deena is married."

"I told you, we were lunching — not fucking," Paul retorted sharply. "And may I remind you — I'm nearly twenty-four years old. I'm hardly a child."

Effie didn't take this well. "Stop asking us for money and get out of here," she hissed. "How dare you speak to me like that!"

Paul slouched from the room.

Nona caught him by the front door. "Where are you going?" she asked.

"I don't have to put up with her talking to me like I'm nothing. It's not like I live here. There's no way I have to answer to anyone."

"Stop asking for money and maybe she'll leave you alone," Nona said, wise beyond her years.

"Butt out. You've no idea what's going on."

"Oh yes I do. You're trying to score with her best friend. No wonder she's pissed with you."

"I can do what I like."

"Do you want to see Brigette while you're here?"

"She's a kid. Quit pushing her at me."

Brigette overheard. Her stomach knotted. Why had she ever set eyes on Nona's stupid brother?

Casually Nona tried to gloss over things. "Take no notice of Paul," she said airily when her brother had departed. "He's a jerk. All men are. That should be our new credo. All men are pigs – don't you agree?"

Brigette couldn't help laughing. "You're right."

"Let's get the hell out of here," Nona decided. "Call Lennie and see if we can fly to Malibu tomorrow."

Deena was sitting at her desk wondering what to do next, when her secretary informed her that Adam Bobo Grant was on the line.

Deena was always delighted to hear from Adam Bobo Grant. Apart from being entertaining, gay, and independently rich, he was also one of the premier gossip columnists in New York.

She grabbed the phone. "Bobo, darling! What can I do for you?"

"You can call me Adam for a start – it's so much more macho, don't you think?"

"But darling," Deena protested, "everyone calls you Bobo."

"Not during business hours, Deena."

"Is this a business call?"

398

"I need your confirmation on something."

"My confirmation about what, darling?"

"About the story."

"What story?"

Bobo paused for a moment, sucking on a silver Cartier pen. "You *have* seen it, haven't you?" he asked at last.

Deena didn't want to appear slow. She racked her brains going over all the items she'd read in the papers that morning. Nothing of great interest. "Clue me in, Bobo, um . . . Adam, and I'll give you a quote."

On the other end of the line, Adam Bobo Grant came to the swift conclusion that Deena Swanson had no idea what he was talking about. The woman had not seen *Truth and Fact*. Nobody had dared show it to her.

He made a quick decision. "Are you free for lunch, Deena?"

Lunch with Adam Bobo Grant was considerably better than lunch with another woman. "Why, yes, as a matter of fact I am." Deena said, mentally cancelling her other date.

"We'll have an early lunch," he decided. "I'll meet you there. Does half an hour suit you?"

"Wonderful," she replied. "Shall I keep my table at Le Cirque?"

"Unless you prefer Mortimers?"

She considered where she wanted to be seen with Bobo, and decided Le Cirque was the most visible. "On a Monday? I don't think so."

"Then Le Cirque it is."

Deena was happy. She'd hear all the latest gossip. Everything he couldn't write about because it was too outrageous and scandalous. The real dirt.

She buzzed her secretary. "Cancel my other lunch," she said coolly. "I shall be lunching with Adam Bobo Grant today."

As soon as Adam Bobo Grant put the phone down on Deena Swanson he checked with one of his minions. "Did you manage to locate Martin Swanson?" he asked brusquely.

"He's in Los Angeles. Right now he's in a meeting at Orpheus Studios. The rumour is there's a takeover going on."

"And Venus Maria?" asked Bobo.

"I spoke to her publicist. She's in rehearsal for the 'Soft Seduction' video."

Adam Bobo Grant nodded knowingly. "Place calls to both of them. Leave my name and home phone number. Tell them I'd like them to call me back as soon as possible. And warn Mack in the news room to make space for me on the front page. If I judge people correctly, we're going to have the exclusive on the Swanson–Venus Maria affair."

Chapter 67

While Lucky Santangelo was presiding over a gathering of department heads at Panther Studios, Mickey Stolli was meeting with Carlos Bonnatti in a high-rise Century City penthouse.

Mickey would have been only too delighted to see what the dumb broad had to say. What did Lucky Santangelo know about running a studio and making movies? Absolutely nothing.

The morning announcement had taken him by surprise. He'd imagined Abe Panther was coming to tell everybody he was returning to work. No way. The crafty old fart had sold the goddamn studio!

Abigaile's face! It was almost worth it to observe her stunned expression.

When they'd left the meeting, Mickey had given her a brusque "Gotta go to another meeting."

"We have things to discuss," Ben had objected, pushing his long nose in where it wasn't wanted.

"Impossible," Mickey had replied with a certain amount of satisfaction.

"Your resignation was premature," Ben said.

"But satisfying," Mickey replied.

Abigaile had glared at him. Not content with being arrested with a hooker, now he was walking away from the most important moment of their lives.

"We must consult our lawyers immediately," she'd said grimly, turning to her brother-in-law for support. "Isn't that right, Ben?"

Ben and Primrose both agreed.

Mickey had shrugged. "Sorry," he'd said, not sorry at all.

Abigaile had continued to glare at him.

Ben had taken her arm. "I'm sure Mickey will catch up with us later," he said soothingly.

Abigaile's voice had reached a high, feverish pitch. "Later is not good enough," she'd cried. "Mickey, why are you doing this to me?"

Abigaile Stolli – queen of the "me" generation. Mickey didn't care. He'd spent eighteen years worrying what Abby would think. Now it was over.

Once he was rid of them he'd stopped by his office. No Olive. No Luce. Where was his stupid temporary secretary? He was in the mood to fire her before he did anything else.

His office was strangely quiet. He picked up the phone to call Warner so he could tell her exactly what he thought of her. Then he changed his mind and banged it down.

He'd had it with Warner. As far as he was concerned she'd never hear from him again.

He'd already placed a call to his lawyer, who'd assured him they would find some way to get around him having to appear in court.

Carlos Bonnatti had reached him at home and requested his presence. Mickey didn't usually jump, but he knew enough about the ways of the world to realize that if Carlos Bonnatti called, he'd better be there. Eddie Kane had really fucked up. Now it was up to Mickey to straighten things out. As usual.

Driving over to the Century City he'd arrived at a smart conclusion. Maybe the million dollars was Panther's problem after all . . .

Maybe it was Lucky Santangelo's inheritance . . .

He tried to reach Eddie on the car phone.

A subdued Leslie told him he wasn't there.

For a moment Mickey was tempted to say, "Didn't I see you at Madame Loretta's?" But then he thought better of it and hung up.

Carlos Bonnatti greeted him with an oily smile and a limp handshake. He had a low, grating voice. A dangerous voice. "Mr Stolli," he said slowly, "nice of you to come. It's about time we talked. I don't seem to be getting anywhere with your associate, Mr Kane, and it's good that you and I are meeting like this."

Mickey decided the setting was exactly right. Flashy apartment, a couple of goons hanging around in the front hall. Where was the obligatory blonde?

"You're right, Mr Bonnatti," he said smoothly. "How can I help you?"

"I got a little problem," Carlos said, rubbing his fingers together. "You may have heard 'bout it. You run a big studio, maybe you don't hear everything."

"What's your problem?" asked Mickey, knowing perfectly well what it was.

Carlos's oily hair glistened. His permanent smile was snake-like. "Well, we entered into a business deal, no contracts, but a handshake is a handshake," he said in a low, dangerous voice. "I mostly dealt with your colleague Eddie Kane. We put our product in with your product. It was sent over to Europe an' the money came through. This all went fluently for a time." He paused.

Mickey stared at him. Carlos was wearing a dark blue suit, black silk shirt, and white tie. The hood look. You could spot New Yorkers a mile away. They always overdressed in California.

"So . . ." Carlos continued, "the money flowed good for

402

a while, and then the amounts comin' to us got smaller and smaller, and I knew somethin' wasn't right." He threw his arms up in a gesture of surrender. "But what am I gonna do? Panther's a big outfit – so I trusted you."

"I'm getting the message," Mickey said. "You didn't receive all the money you were expecting."

"Let's just say there's a shortfall of a million bucks," Carlos said, nodding to himself. "Yeah, an' who owes the money? That's the question. The big question."

"You want to know whose pocket it ended up in," Mickey said.

"I refuse to point a finger." Carlos smoothed the cuffs of his silk shirt. "But Eddie Kane is the name that comes to mind."

"And he's not paying. Right?"

"No way a bum like Eddie's gonna give back a million bucks." A short pause. "So . . . Mickey, you can understand my dilemma."

Mickey understood it only too well. "You'd like Panther Studios to reimburse you." He made it a statement, not a question.

"That's correct. An' if you see a way to do that, then you'll save Mr Kane a lot of grief. Maybe you'll take it out of his salary for the next twenty, thirty years."

"Sounds workable," Mickey agreed amicably.

Carlos was obviously surprised at Mickey's immediate co-operation. "How we gonna handle this? A handshake don't do it for me. I'd like a note drawn up sayin' Panther owes my company a million bucks. We can put it down for services."

Mickey nodded. "Good idea. Call in your lawyers. I have the authority to sign on behalf of Panther. One stipulation – it has to be pre-dated. And I have to sign the papers today."

"Done," said Carlos. "My lawyer'll take care of it. No questions asked."

They shook hands – Carlos Bonnatti and Mickey Stolli.

"Be back around two, I'll have everythin' ready," Carlos said. He paused and gave Mickey a long, penetrating look.

"You're a very obliging man, Mr Stolli. A very smart man. Any time you need a favour . . ."

Mickey nodded modestly. "Thank you."

When Mickey had left, Carlos walked around his apartment considering the action. He pressed his fingers to his temples. Sometimes he wished his father was around. Enzio Bonnatti had always had a way of knowing exactly what was going on. He could immediately assess any situation and explain the whys and wherefores. Santino, his brother, had been a schmuck. All Santino cared about was pussy. He'd been in the right business – porno movies and drugs.

Carlos knew he was smarter than Santino. Shit, anybody was smarter than Santino. But he wouldn't have minded having Enzio around to talk to.

Mickey Stolli had complied too willingly, without so much as a struggle.

Something was going on here and Carlos wasn't sure what. But as long as the papers were drawn up and he got his money, what did he care?

Chapter 68

Sitting in a private office at Orpheus Studios, Martin Swanson read about himself like a voyeur. His eyes scanned the page of the cheap magazine. He couldn't believe some of the things he was reading:

BILLIONAIRE MARTIN SWANSON!
RAVISHING SUPERSTAR VENUS MARIA!
BEAUTIFUL SOCIETY WIFE DEENA!

And there were all these quotes from supposed best friends and close acquaintances.

Martin had controlled his press for so long that the sheer effrontery of this really shocked him. The ramifications were many. What was Deena going to say? She would be furious when she saw the photograph of himself with Venus. How was he going to explain it? It wasn't taken at a function, nor in a restaurant. It was obviously an intimate photo taken on somebody's couch.

At least they weren't naked. They hadn't been caught in bed. But you only had to look at the photograph to know they were sleeping with each other.

Thinking about the photographs reminded him of the one of Deena with Effie's kid. What the hell was Deena doing in Central Park with Paul Webster?

Not that Martin considered such a callow youth a threat, but it made Deena look foolish — like she was desperate or something.

He continued to read the story:

Sexy superstar Venus Maria could teach
billionaire tycoon Martin Swanson a thing or
two about getting to the top.

Oh yeah? What did they know? Who owned this cheap magazine anyway? He placed a call to his secretary in New York to have her find out.

"Have you heard from Mrs Swanson?" he asked.

"I do believe she's in her office," Gertrude replied.

"Has anybody shown this to her?"

Gertrude sounded embarrassed. "I really have no idea, Mr Swanson."

"If she tries to reach me, tell her I'm in non-stop meetings and that you can't get to me."

"Certainly, sir."

Now that his affair with Venus was out in the open he was going to have to be very careful. Was it worth it? Did he wish to continue seeing her?

She'd been more than aggravating this weekend, dragging Cooper along to San Francisco and then complaining about his sexual prowess when they got back. God damn it! One moment she was plying him with hookers, and the next she expected him to put on a record-breaking performance when he was tired and had a lot on his mind.

At least when you were married a wife understood these kind of things.

On the other hand, Venus Maria was special. She was universally desired. Cooper was after her – that was obvious. And *he* had her, Martin Swanson – Billionaire Lover. Billionaire Stud!

He couldn't help smiling. It was kind of funny in a way.

It wouldn't be so funny when he had to explain the photograph to Deena.

A buzzer sounded in the office. "Mr Swanson," one of the secretaries said, "Mr White would like to know when you are returning to the meeting."

"I'll be right there," he said, folding the magazine in half.

No more worrying about some low-down supermarket scandal-sheet. He'd put his lawyers onto them. He'd kill 'em. He'd break their balls as only Martin Swanson could.

He walked back into the meeting. He was taking over Orpheus Studios. A far more important task.

Side by side on Cooper Turner's desk lay the front page of the *LA Times* with the story about Mickey Stolli circled, and alongside it a copy of *Truth and Fact*.

Cooper read about Mickey first. He was amused. It had to have been the funniest scene going – Mickey Stolli arrested with a hooker. Cooper was acquainted with Madame Loretta. Not in a professional sense, but an actress he'd been dating at one time had been playing the role of a prostitute on screen and had wanted to research the part. Forde Werne had arranged an introduction, and Cooper and his lady friend had spent many a pleasant afternoon having tea with the madam and listening to her outlandish stories.

Cooper wondered how Venus Maria was going to feel when she saw *Truth and Fact*. It would certainly bring her affair with Martin out into the open.

Maybe that's what she wanted. Martin would be forced into making a decision.

Cooper couldn't help but raise a cynical eyebrow when

he read about Deena with a younger man. Martin wouldn't like that. A blow to his enormous ego.

But all this wasn't his problem. He called the florist and sent Venus Maria two dozen red roses. It was the least he could do.

It soon became obvious that everybody in the rehearsal room had seen the stupid magazine. Venus Maria could tell by the covert little glances coming her way, and a certain amount of nervous giggling here and there.

Ah, well, if you can't fight it, lie back and enjoy it. Her new philosophy. Vigorously she launched herself into Ron's latest torture routine.

The Ken Doll wandered in around noon, washed and scrubbed, tall and bland-faced, wearing a muscle boy T-shirt and tight blue jeans outlining his outstanding crotch – obviously the main attraction. She'd been thinking of saying to Ron, "*What* do you see in him?" But after observing the jeans she knew exactly what the crowd-puller was.

"Why don't we all have lunch?" Ron suggested, deciding it was about time his best friend and his live-in lover got friendly. "You can at least try and be nice to Ken. After all, *I* put up with Martin."

Ha! Ron hardly knew Martin. But just to please him, she agreed.

"I booked us a table at the Ivy." Ron was obviously delighted.

Venus Maria frowned. "Isn't that a little visible? Especially today?"

"We'll get a table in the back room. In and out before anyone realizes you're there."

At twelve-thirty they set off for the restaurant in the Ken Doll's gleaming Mercedes. Venus Maria hid beneath huge black shades and sat in the back.

"I probably smell like a camel," she remarked. "You too, Ron."

"Count *me* out," said the very pristine Ken.

Anytime, Venus Maria thought.

Lunch turned out to be a drag. Ron changed from his usual acerbic self into a love-sick jerk. Ken was pompous. Ken knew everything. Ken tried to tell her everything. When they got out of the restaurant she was regretting the whole deal.

By the time they arrived back at the rehearsal studios there was a rapidly escalating group of photographers waiting outside. They began snapping the moment the car drew up.

"Where do they all come from?" Venus Maria sighed, making a wild dash from the car.

"You're front-page news today, darling. They're after the real scoop," Ron explained, chugging after her, quite happy to pose.

Ken adored every minute of the attention. "Don't worry, I'll protect you," he said, smiling for the cameras.

Macho Ken Doll.

Stupid Ken Doll.

"What's your comment on the story, Venus?"

"Got anything to say about Martin Swanson?"

"Is it true?"

"Do you love him?"

"Is Martin leaving his wife?"

She ignored all the reporters' questions and, hidden behind her dark glass, made it into the rehearsal room.

Chapter 69

Lennie brooded his way through the weekend. He spoke to Jess and she told him he was an asshole.

"You always take Lucky's side," he complained. "*I'm* your friend. What the hell is going on?"

"Lighten up, Lennie. You married an unusual woman — stop fighting her."

Stop fighting, indeed! What did Jess know? She hadn't had her balls cut off for all the world to see.

Oh, dear. Poor Lennie, he's unhappy. Let's buy him a studio.

Well, fuck that crap.

And yet . . . he missed Lucky already. And throwing himself back into the script didn't seem to do it for him this time.

He contacted Brigette, and she met him at Serendipity for lunch.

"You're looking great, kiddo," he said, kissing her on both cheeks. "School agrees with you."

"School does not agree with me," she objected. "I hate it. I can't wait to get out."

"You *are* out," he said, ruffling her hair.

"Only for the summer," she groaned. "I gotta go back again, huh?"

"If you want to grow up to be smart."

"And then college?"

"Yup."

"Why, Lennie? It's not as though I need to get a job or anything. "I'm going to be inheriting all that money."

"Hey – you want to turn out like your mother?" he asked sternly. "Getting married and spending money? What kind of life is that? You ought to think about your future."

"I know," she agreed reluctantly.

They sat at a corner table. Brigette ordered a foot-long hot dog and a double chocolate malted milk.

"No appetite, huh?" he said with a grin.

"It's terrific to see you, Lennie. I'm really excited about Malibu."

"Yeah, well . . ." He stared at the menu. "I got something to tell you."

She gazed at him expectantly.

He hated to disappoint her. "Uh . . . things aren't working out exactly as we planned."

"What's the matter?" she asked, looking concerned.

"Lucky and I . . . well, we've been having some problems, and . . . uh, we haven't exactly worked them out. I'm not sure if we'll spend the summer together."

"Oh, no," Brigette cried. "You and Lucky are so great with each other. Please don't have any problems. *Please*."

"If life were only that simple." He took her hand. "Listen, I promised you the summer. You'll bring your girlfriend and we'll go to the South of France or Spain or Greece — somewhere. We'll put it together."

"But I was looking forward to being with you and Lucky," Brigette said in a sad little voice. "And Bobby. I *really* miss Bobby. I haven't seen him in ages."

Lennie ignored a blonde at the next table who'd decided to fixate on him, and groped in his pocket for a cigarette. "Yeah, well, life's a bitch, huh?"

"Can I call Lucky?" Brigette asked, staring at the checkered tablecloth, wondering why everything always had to go wrong.

"If she's got time for you," Lennie replied. "She's busy buying a studio."

"A movie studio?"

"Yeah. You'll read about it in the papers. She's bought Panther Studios." He dragged on his cigarette. "My wife the mogul. Not content with running the biggest shipping empire in the world, she now wants to own Hollywood."

"Is that why you're mad?" Brigette ventured.

"Hey — it's a long story. If that's what she wants to do . . . But I wish she'd told me about it. Where do you think she was for the last six weeks while she was supposed to be in Japan?"

"Where?"

"In Hollywood, playing secretary. She went in undercover."

Brigette's eyes widened. "Really? Sounds exciting to me."

"Yeah, if you don't have any other responsibilities. But Lucky is my wife. I'd like to see her once in a while. I'd like to have her support." He stubbed out his cigarette after two puffs. "Ah, hell. Why am I boring *you* with this?"

"Because I'm a good listener?"

He laughed. "Yeah, you sure are. Let's change the subject — what's going on with you?"

"Nothing," she said vaguely. "Actually I was going to ask if we could come to LA like tomorrow or the day after. Nona's mother is throwing a fit. There's this stupid magazine with a picture of Nona's brother Paul in it with Deena Swanson. She's the wife of that billionaire?"

"Oh, yeah."

"Anyway, Paul was photographed with her, and Deena is Effie's best friend — that's Paul's mother. So, as Nona puts it, we've *got* to get out of here. But since you're obviously not going to LA, I suppose we can't either."

She looked so deflated that Lennie decided he had to cheer her up. "Tell you what," he said. "We'll eat lunch, we'll talk, and then we'll stop by a travel agent and plan a trip. How's that? You, me, and what's this girl's name?"

"Nona."

"OK. You got it, kiddo."

"What about Lucky and Bobby?"

Lennie shook his head. "Another time, another life."

Chapter 70

There were photographers outside the gleaming Swanson Building when Deena left. Usually they were only around when she and Martin attended an event. But she smiled anyway and climbed into her chauffeur-driven car.

At Le Cirque she got her usual ebullient greeting from the proprietor, Sirio Maccioni, and was led to a table where Adam Bobo Grant sat waiting.

"Darling!"

"Darling!"

They had the Hollywood kiss down pat. New York version.

"You look delightful, as usual," Bobo said. "Lime green is your colour."

Deena smiled. "Thank you, darling. Martin thinks so too."

"Does he?" said Bobo, waving to people at every table. "And how *is* the big man?"

"Fine," Deena said. "In fact, very soon we're going to have an exciting story for you."

Bobo raised an eyebrow. "You are? And what might that be, my sweet?"

"Martin would kill me if he knew I was going to tell you, and you have to *promise* not to print anything until I give you the OK."

"If you can't trust me, who can you trust?" Bobo said in his best sincere voice.

"Martin is taking over Orpheus Studios in Hollywood," Deena announced. "What do you think of that?"

All the better to star Venus Maria in movies, Bobo thought to himself. Was *this* the reason for the romance? "How very interesting," he said, eyes darting around the room, checking everyone out.

"Isn't it just?" Deena smiled, she had lovely teeth. "We'll have to spend more time in LA of course. But I think it will be fun. Don't you?"

Bobo nodded. Trust Deena – queen of the understatement. "Great fun, my dear," he agreed.

The wine waiter came by the table and they ordered drinks. Deena decided on a martini. Bobo ordered straight vodka.

"It makes such a refreshing change to lunch with somebody who actually drinks hard liquor," Deena said with a tinkling laugh. "When I lunch with the ladies nobody touches anything except Perrier or Evian. It's incredibly boring. I rather enjoy a martini before lunch."

Bobo nodded and leaned towards her, speaking confidentially. "Now, Deena," he said, lowering his voice, "tell me the situation."

"What situation, Bobo?"

Surely she wasn't trying to hide it from him? "Why you and Martin, of course."

She looked at him blankly.

412

"You have seen *Truth and Fact* haven't you?" He moved closer, daring her to lie.

Deena continued to look blank. "*Truth and Fact*? What's that?"

Bobo was rapidly losing patience. "It's one of those magazines. The kind they sell in supermarkets."

"Oh, you mean like the *Star*, or the *Globe*. I simply adore the *Globe*. Headless woman gives birth to triplets — marvellous stuff. My maid brings it in."

"Then I'm surprised your maid hasn't presented you with *Truth and Fact*."

She gazed at him, perfectly innocent. "Is there something in it I should know about?"

"Yes, Deena, there certainly is." He took her manicured delicate hand in his pudgy little fist. On his pinky there was an enormous sapphire ring surrounded by diamonds.

She stared at the glittering ring and sensed she was about to hear something she wouldn't like. "What, Bobo?" she asked, her tone even and well modulated, her slight accent thickening.

"There's a story about your husband and Venus Maria," Bobo said, getting right to it.

Her stomach tightened, but she managed to remain in complete control. "There is?" she asked carefully. "Everybody's always trying to link Martin with some little popsy or other. Surely not another one?"

"There's a photograph of them together," Bobo said. "And the story goes into quite a few details."

"What kind of details?" Deena asked, withdrawing her hand.

"Oh, that they've been seeing each other for several months. And that Martin is supposed to be crazy about her, and that she loves him." He paused, then zeroed in. "I wouldn't bring this up, Deena, but I hardly wish to see you eaten alive by the press. The magazine only came out today, and I'm trying to protect you." He paused again, waiting for her reaction. She remained cool, so he continued. "I'm ready to hear your side of the story. And to report it any way you like."

413

"There's no story to hear," Deena said through clenched teeth. "I'll have to look at this magazine, Bobo. When I've seen it, perhaps I'll be able to comment."

He reached for the manila envelope he had with him and handed it to her. "It's in here, Deena. Go to the powder room, read it, come back, and talk to me."

She took the magazine and, head held high, walked towards the ladies' room.

When she read the story the colour drained from her face.

When she stared at the picture of Martin with Venus Maria she knew she had to act.

Venus Maria had signed her own death warrant.

Deena Swanson was about to make sure of that.

Chapter 71

After getting together with all the department heads, Lucky decided she should meet with the various stars who had deals at the studio. She'd set up her office in the conference room as a temporary measure, giving Mickey Stolli a couple of days to get out. He'd robbed her of the pleasure of firing him. Too bad.

Morton Sharkey had found an experienced assistant and promptly stolen him from another studio on her behalf. Otis Lindcrest was an efficient black man in his late twenties. He certainly seemed to know his way around, and worked hard setting appointments and making Lucky feel as comfortable and secure as possible.

There was so much to do that she couldn't quite decide where to start. The most important thing of all was overseeing the projects the studio had in post- and pre-production, and then deciding the direction Panther should take in the future.

Out of the executives she'd met with she wasn't sure

whom she could trust. It would take a while to get to know them as individuals and assess their loyalty.

Her immediate plan was to sit down with them one by one over the next few weeks. In the meantime, she'd sent for Lennie's contract and told Morton she wanted it rescinded.

"Send him a letter," she'd instructed, "saying he's out of his deal with Panther. We're releasing him — unless he wants to stay."

"Why are you doing this?" Morton had asked.

"I don't want him thinking he has any obligation to Panther just because I own it. If he decides to come and work here, that'll be great. But if he doesn't, he's free to go elsewhere."

"Lucky, he's an asset," Morton pointed out. "A big one."

"He's also my husband," she replied firmly. "And I can't have him feeling he's tied here."

Flowers began to pour in from various people she didn't know. They were accompanied by warm and welcoming notes. They were from agents, producers, and managers. The stars didn't bother. Being a star meant never having to send flowers — merely receive them.

Otis gave her a rundown of all the players. For a young man he certainly knew plenty.

"How long have you been in this business?" she asked curiously.

"Started as a set PR. Moved on to the mailroom at CAA. Almost got into producing. And I've been personal assisting for five years."

She noted that he'd like to produce. Somewhere down the line she'd take care of it. Right now Otis was invaluable.

She didn't leave the studio until nine o'clock. Boogie handed her a copy of *Truth and Fact* in the car. "I thought you'd want to see this," he said as he drove her home.

She glanced at the magazine, skipping over the stuff about Martin Swanson and Venus Maria. Who cared? She never believed anything she read in these papers anyway.

But when she saw the picture of Brigette, she was immediately concerned. After Brigette's bad experience with Tim Wealth, Lucky knew she was far too young and vulnerable to get involved with another renegade. And that's exactly what Paul Webster looked like, with his long hair and intense eyes.

"Remind me to phone Brigette first thing in the morning," she said. "And call London and alert Mike Baverstock at British Airways to watch out for Bobby and nanny. They're flying in on Friday. Oh, and tell Otis to clear Friday afternoon for me, I'll meet them at the airport."

By the time they got back to the beach it was past ten.

"Any messages for me, Miko?" she asked hopefully.

Miko bowed. "No, Madame, no messages."

Apparently Lennie didn't feel like calling.

She was too tired to eat, too tired to do anything except fall into bed and drop off into a deep sleep.

She awoke refreshed and invigorated, showered, dressed, sat down for breakfast. The trades were full of news:

LUCKY SANTANGELO TAKES OVER PANTHER
MARTIN SWANSON MOVES IN ON ORPHEUS

She couldn't wait to get to the studio. There was a lot of hard work ahead, but one thing she knew for sure: running a studio was becoming an addiction.

Johnny Romano was her first appointment. He swaggered into the conference room, entourage hovering close behind.

As soon as he walked in the room he did a double-take. This woman was beautiful.

"Can we talk by ourselves, Mr Romano?" she asked.

"Hey, baby, my pleasure." He signalled his entourage to leave.

Lucky got up from behind the conference table and walked over to shake hands. "The name is Lucky Santangelo," she said. "*Baby* doesn't cut it."

416

He took her hand and pulled her towards him. "You're a very beautiful lady," he said in a husky voice. "Welcome to my life."

She removed her hand from his. "That's about the corniest line I've ever heard. How many times have you used it?"

He laughed. "It usually goes down pretty good."

"Not with me."

"OK, OK, so you're a beautiful woman and I – Johnny Romano – am coming on to you. Such a terrible thing?"

She decided to ignore the obvious come-on. "You know, Johnny, your movie grossed big this weekend."

"Sure, baby," he said confidently.

"But I think we'll see a substantial drop next weekend."

He lifted his chin, displaying a great movie-star jawline. "What you sayin', baby?"

She didn't hold back. "I'm saying *Motherfaker* is a sexist piece of crap."

Johnny's face darkened. Nobody ever spoke to him like that. "Are you crazy, woman?" he growled.

She shook her head. "Not crazy, just giving you some useful advice."

"What's that?" he said arrogantly.

"You *can* take criticism, can't you?"

"You think I can't?" he countered.

"Johnny, you're a sensational-looking guy. Everyone loves you. You're macho, handsome, and sexy. But this movie cancels out a huge audience for you. Kids can't see it, old people won't want to. I don't understand it – for some crazy reason you make yourself into an anti-hero. The result is that everyone ends up hating the character you play. And every other word is motherfucker. You wrote the film, Johnny. Surely you have a larger vocabulary than that?"

He glared at her. "This movie's gonna make a fuckin' fortune for Panther and *you're* criticizing it?"

"I'm saying I know you're capable of so much more. And I'd love you to do another movie for Panther. But I'm willing to tear up your contract and let you walk, because I'm not prepared to make another *Motherfaker*. If you're after a lasting career you have to build it, not tear it down. What you're saying to your audience is 'Fuck you. I can do what I like and get away with it.' It doesn't work any more, Johnny."

"You're a crazy woman." He laughed. "I can go anywhere in this town an' get any deal I want."

"Then maybe that's what you should do," she said evenly.

He couldn't believe what he was hearing. Was this broad insane? "OK. OK, lady, if that's what you want, maybe that's what I'll do."

"Go ahead," she said, challenging him. "But if you're smart you'll listen to me. Don't make an instant decision. Think it over, and we'll talk next week."

When Johnny Romano left the room he was not a happy man.

Venus Maria was Lucky's second appointment.

The blond superstar breezed into her office with a big grin on her face. "This is *really* great," she said enthusiastically. "A woman in charge! My wildest dream come true. Howdja do it?"

Lucky grinned back. "I thought it was about time. My plan is to kick a little ass. Are you on for the ride?"

Venus Maria's grin widened. "Oh, have you picked the right star here!"

"I hope so," Lucky said. "I need all the support I can get."

"You *know* so," Venus Maria replied, flopping into a chair and sticking her legs out. She wore cut-off jeans, a Save the World T-shirt, and a long vest covered with pins. Her platinum hair was bunched on top of her head, and on her feet she wore short white socks and Reeboks. "I'm rehearsing," she announced, "for my upcoming video. It's gonna be a trip!"

"I'm delighted you're with Panther," Lucky said warmly. "I know you're committed to do *Bombshell*, and I also know you're not happy with the script."

"How do you know that."

"Because you told me."

Venus Maria looked puzzled. "*I* told you. Have we met before?"

Lucky reached for a cigarette. "Oh, yeah, we've met. Only you don't remember, do you?"

"In New York?"

"No. Right here at this studio. You bitched to me about the script – and now that I've read it, I couldn't agree more. There's a rewrite in the works. In fact I met with the writer before you came in. He knows what we want."

"He does?"

"Oh yes."

"Fast worker."

"No point in sitting around. I know the kind of movie you're after. *Bombshell* should be a statement about women and the way they're used. Am I right?"

"Absolutely." Venus Maria looked puzzled. "I still can't figure out where we met."

"Mickey Stolli's secretary."

"Huh?"

"Remember Mickey Stolli's secretary? The one with the pebbled glasses, bad hairstyle, and terrible clothes. You were really sweet to her."

Venus looked perplexed. "Yes, so?"

"It was me."

Venus Maria jumped out of her chair. "You?" she said in amazement. "Oh, come *on*. You've *got* to be kidding. You!"

Lucky burst out laughing. "Yes, me. I was in disguise."

"No!"

"Yes!"

"Wow!"

"Well, I didn't want to buy the place and not know what was happening, so I worked at the studio for six weeks to find out a thing or two."

"And did you?"

Lucky drew on her cigarette and smiled. "You could say that."

"I bet!"

"I'm telling you because I feel I can trust you. But I don't want the suits knowing. Perhaps I'll tell 'em. Perhaps I won't. Let 'em wonder how I know so much."

"Holy shit!" Venus exclaimed. "This is the greatest. I fucking love it!"

"Anyway," Lucky continued, "the plan is this. We'll get the *Bombshell* script exactly right, and then we're going to make a terrific movie. I've been thinking about directors. How about a female?"

"I love women directors," Venus said. "Only every time I mention it around here they look at me like I'm a zombie!"

"It seems to me a woman director is the only way to go. I have several in mind. Have you heard of Montana Grey?"

"I sure have. She wrote and directed that amazing little movie *Street People*. I think she's great, very talented."

"Good. She's coming in to see me tomorrow. As far as I'm concerned she'd be perfect. Are you happy with that?"

"Happy? I'm ecstatic!"

"If she likes the idea I'll set up a meeting for all three of us."

"Anytime."

"And I want to see a screening of *Strut*. I understand there's a rough cut. I'm meeting with Cooper Turner, so I'll discuss that with him."

Venus Maria nodded. "You'll like Cooper, he's a good guy. Don't believe all the stuff you've read about him. Oh—" she added jauntily, "and don't believe all the stuff you've read about me either."

Lucky laughed. "I've had a few headlines of my own. Believe me, I understand."

"So . . . how are the *boys* taking your arrival?"

Lucky took a drag of her cigarette. "I guess they're not used to having a woman walk in and take over."

"No way."

Lucky blew a smoke ring or two. "I always did love a challenge."

Chapter 72

Emilio Sierra had booked a double room at a fancy hotel in Hawaii overlooking the sea. What he and Rita actually got when they arrived was a room overlooking the vast outdoor parking lot. A far from spectacular sight.

"This is not good enough," Emilio yelled angrily.

"It's OK, honey," Rita soothed. "At least we can see the ocean in the distance."

Dumb broad. Why did he always manage to pick the dumb ones?

"It's not OK at all," Emilio fumed. "I'm kickin' up a stink."

He swaggered down to the reception desk and demanded to see the manager.

Ten minutes later the manager appeared, a tall, thin man with a congenial manner and constipated smile. "Yes, sir, how may I help you?" he asked.

"I requested a room with an ocean view," Emilio said, trying to drag his eyes away from the busty redhead in shorts and a clinging T-shirt as she sashayed on by.

"You're not happy with your room?" asked the manager, sounding hurt, as if Emilio's complaint was a personal affront.

The redhead swayed out of sight, allowing Emilio to concentrate. "No way, man. It stinks."

"I'm sure it doesn't stink, Mr . . . ?"

"Sierra." Emilio obliged. "S-I-E-R-R-A," he spelled it out. "You've no doubt heard of my sister, Venus Maria."

The manager wasn't sure if he believed him or not, but he looked impressed anyway. "Venus Maria?" he said, with just the right note of reverence in his voice. "The singer?"

"And movie star," Emilio boasted. "I'm from Los Angeles. Well, Hollywood really. I'm an actor too."

421

The manager nodded. They'd had bigger celebrities than Venus Maria's brother staying at the hotel. Try the President of the United States.

"Well," the manager said, "Right now, Mr Sierra, we don't seem to have anything else. But I can promise you that as soon as something becomes available you will be the first to know."

"Not satisfactory," growled Emilio, deciding he loved having money. It gave him a certain amount of power for the first time in his life.

"It's the best I can do," said the manager, wishing this uncouth-looking person would elect to stay elsewhere.

"Get me somethin' else or I'm campin' out in the lobby," Emilio threatened, continuing to complain until they moved him into a bungalow on the beach. It cost more, but for once Emilio figured he'd go for the big bucks. Now that he had them he might as well live it up. Not that Rita appreciated it. She was hot. She was also stupid.

No sooner were they settled in the bungalow than Rita thought she spotted a sand-mouse running across the floor.

"Oh my *God!*" she screamed hysterically, jumping on top of the bed. "Emilio! Emilio! There's a *mouse!*"

"So what?" he said, completely unconcerned. "It ain't gonna eat you."

"I'm frightened," she squealed, refusing to get off the bed.

Emilio remembered New York back in the good old days when Venus Maria was just a kid and he could boss her around. She'd been frightened of mice too. He and his brothers had caught three one day and stuffed them in her bed under the sheets. When she'd discovered their grisly surprise she'd screamed for an hour. But he had to admit she'd gotten her revenge. Two nights later she'd cooked a thick and juicy stew with what appeared to be chunks of chicken in it. Only it turned out it wasn't chicken. She'd cooked the goddamn mice and served them up for dinner!

Rita was not to be placated, so Emilio had to march back to the manager and complain again.

Finally, probably to get rid of him and his bitching, they

were ushered into the suite of his dreams. Two rooms consisting of a luxurious bedroom complete with vibrating bed, and a well-appointed living room leading out to a large terrace overlooking a blanket of white sand and a gorgeous blue ocean. This was more like it -- even if it was probably going to cost an arm and two legs.

"Satisfied?" he said to Rita.

She nodded.

Later he stood on the terrace while she unzipped his jeans and showed him exactly how satisfied she really was.

Sometimes it paid to be extravagant.

The next morning he sent her down to the news stand instructing her to buy a copy of *Truth and Fact*.

When she brought it back to the room and he read it he was outraged. Where was his story? There wasn't even a picture of him. What kind of deal was this?

In a fury he telephoned Dennis Walla in Los Angeles. "Where's my story?" he screamed over the phone. "It was supposed to be in this week."

"Next week," Dennis said. "Read the blurb."

"You told me this week, and you've used the picture I gave you," said a disgruntled Emilio. "Listen, man, I've only gotten paid for one week. This is a swindle."

"Hang on a moment, mate," said Dennis, thinking -- *Here we go again.* Why were the relatives of the stars so bloody greedy? "You're making plenty of moola outta this. Your story runs when *we* decide to run it. You can't tell *us* what to do."

Emilio slammed down the phone in a rage. Now it would be awkward returning to LA. Venus Maria had advance warning his story was going to appear. She'd be furious and would certainly be tracking him.

"What's the matter, sweetie?" asked Rita, pirouetting in front of the mirror, admiring her short but perfect legs.

"Nothing." He wasn't about to confide in her. "Come here."

They made the bed vibrate for ten minutes before going outside to sample the Hawaiian sunshine.

Emilio was disappointed to discover there wasn't much

Hawaiian sunshine to sample. It was a cloudy day with strong gusty winds.

He chose two prime positions by the pool and they settled down – Rita in a bikini that attracted the attention of every man within fifty yards.

Emilio was pleased. Maybe she wasn't so stupid after all. He enjoyed being with a woman who scored so much attention.

At lunchtime Rita suggested that perhaps they should go inside. "It may be cloudy," she said wisely, "but there's still a real strong sun coming through. You'd better be careful."

"Me?" he boasted, "I never burn, I tan."

"I don't," she said, pulling up her bikini top, which was just about to slip and reveal a perky nipple. "Do you mind if I go in?"

He didn't mind. He was too busy enjoying the parade of beautiful women in various small bikinis and great tans.

Come five o'clock Emilio was burnt to a crisp.

"Jesus! Why didn't you warn me?" he complained when he finally got back to the suite.

"Honey, I did," Rita pointed out, busily slathering scented cream all over his naked body.

"I don't understand," he whined, feeling sorry for himself. "It was cloudy – how could I burn?"

"It doesn't matter in Hawaii," she explained. "The sun burns right through the clouds. I tried to tell you."

"Were you here before?" he asked suspiciously.

"Once or twice," she said, deciding not to mention her last trip with two stuntmen and a bewigged director with a penchant for discipline.

Emilio was in serious pain. Rita rushed down to the pharmacy and came back with soothing lotions. They didn't help. He suffered all through the night. And not silently.

The next morning when he regarded his lobster complexion in the mirror he decided they were going back to LA.

"I'm not spending all this money to lie around in bed," he complained. "We're gettin' outta here."

Rita shrugged. "Whatever you want."

She'd already decided Emilio was only good for a short ride. While he had the bucks, she was there. Who knew how long it would last?

Chapter 73

"There's a Harry Browning to see you," Otis said. "No appointment. He looks kind of agitated."

Lucky nodded. "It's OK, show him in."

Harry took a few steps into the room and stopped. He waited until the secretary had shut the door behind her and then he stared at Lucky accusingly. "You're Luce, aren't you?"

Finally! Somebody had busted her disguise. "You're the only person who's recognized me," she said. "Pretty sharp of you."

"I thought you were working for Abe Panther."

"In a way, I was. We both thought it was a good idea for me to come in undercover. An interesting exercise. I found out plenty."

"You weren't honest with me," Harry said stiffly, obviously uncomfortable with this confrontation.

She wasn't about to explain things further. "I'd be happy for you to stay at the studio, Harry. We're changing things around here. And I'd also like you to report to me personally."

"Why?" he asked suspiciously.

"Because *you* want what *I* want. We're both into making Panther great again. No more exploitation flicks. No more executives playing casting couch with every actress who walks through the door. Are you with me?"

He nodded slowly.

Shortly after Lucky's meeting with Harry, Susie Rush

425

arrived. Susie was used to dealing with male executives. She appeared wearing frills and flounces and a pink ribbon in her hair. Privately Lucky thought she looked like a kewpie doll.

Susie pursed her lips in a girlish way and said, "Well, this is quite a shock to the system."

"What can I offer you?" Lucky said, playing it nice and friendly. "A drink? Coffee? Tea?"

"An explanation would be nice. After all, when I signed with this studio Mickey Stolli was in charge. A change is something I hadn't considered."

"The first thing you should know," Lucky said easily, "is that although you have a development deal at the studio, you're free to do anything you want. I'm not holding anybody at Panther against their will."

"Oh," Susie said. She hadn't expected that.

"However, I also know," Lucky continued, "that you're one of this studio's great assets – and as I've told everyone else, my goal is to bring Panther back to the forefront again. And I love your kind of movies. You make films the whole family can see. You're really a wonderful actress."

Susie looked at her suspiciously. She wasn't used to receiving compliments from other women. She also wasn't used to seeing women who looked like Lucky Santangelo in positions of power.

"Here's what I'd like you to do," Lucky said, all business. "Tell me the kind of movie you want to do. I know you're developing a couple of projects at the moment, and if you're happy with those then we'll certainly consider them."

"Actually," Susie said, "I feel like a change of pace. My career is in a rut. I have the desire to play a different kind of role."

"What kind of role is that?" Lucky asked.

"I want to play the lead in *Bombshell*," Susie said. "As a matter of fact Mickey promised me I could."

This was a surprise. "*Bombshell* is a Venus Maria project," Lucky pointed out.

"Oh yes, Mickey mentioned Venus might be interested.

426

But when I told him *I* liked the script, he immediately said I could test. I should remind you that normally I wouldn't dream of testing for anything. But I know I can capture this role. She's me."

"I'll tell you what," Lucky suggested. "Venus Maria is definitely set for *Bombshell*. But if you have another script, we'll see what we can work out."

Susie's lips tightened into a thin line. "I want to do *Bombshell*," she said. "I've been offered another film at Orpheus."

Lucky smiled pleasantly. She wasn't about to be black-mailed by any stars and their egos. "Susie, if the role is what you want, then I suggest you take it. As I said before, I'm not holding anybody back."

Susie departed, not quite sure where she was at.

So far so good. Lucky's last meeting of the day was with Cooper Turner. He was over in the editing rooms, and instead of asking him to come to her she decided to run over there.

Lucky was not impressed by movie stars. She'd observed them all her life. When Gino opened his Vegas hotels they'd come down for special gambling junkets, openings, and all the big parties. And when she was married to Senator Richmond's son, Craven, big celebrities had often made the trek to Washington.

Movie stars equalled fragile egos – she was well aware of that. Now dealing with them on a one-to-one basis was interesting and a definite challenge.

Cooper Turner was better-looking than on the screen, with his boyishly handsome face, rumpled hair, and pen-etrating ice-blue eyes. He had a devastating smile which he put into immediate action. "So you're my new boss, huh?"

"Yes," she said, going for a handshake.

He took her hand and gave it an extra squeeze. Behind his horn-rimmed glasses he favoured her with a penetrating look. "You're a surprise," he said. "I was expecting a dragon lady."

"Looks don't matter," she replied.

"Sure they do," he said casually, removing his glasses. "Beautiful women always get more attention. Not that I'm saying you're not smart, but looks help. And honey — you've got 'em."

She threw it right back at him. "And honey, so have you."

He laughed. "*Touché*, Ms Santangelo."

"I'm looking forward to viewing a rough cut of *Strut*. When can I?" she asked, getting down to the purpose of her visit.

"How about next week sometime?"

"Sounds good. Was this your directorial debut?"

His eyes without the glasses were lethal weapons. "You mean you haven't been following my career?"

She returned his stare, matching his gaze with her black Santangelo eyes. "Let's put it this way, your career has not been the centre of my universe."

He laughed again. "No, as a matter of fact I've directed one dog before, but this one's going to be better. Venus Maria gives a very special performance."

"So I've heard."

"Ah, the rumour is around the studio. That's good."

"It appears your movie is the only decent one we've got going for us. Have you seen *Motherfaker*?"

"My time is valuable. I don't believe in self-punishment."

Now it was her turn to laugh. "I know what you mean. Can we have lunch together next week? There's a lot I feel we need to discuss. The marketing of *Strut* is crucial."

"Why don't I take you to dinner?" he suggested.

She put the meeting back on track. "Have you met my husband, Lennie Golden?"

"You're married to Lennie?" he said, surprised.

"You didn't know?"

"Hey — I've followed your career about as closely as you've followed mine."

"My turn to say *touché*, huh?"

He dazzled he with a movie-star smile. "I guess so. Lunch then. I'd like that."

The only star she had left was Charlie Dollar, and he was out of the country, due back in a couple of weeks. Charlie had nothing in pre-production. She put out the word — "Find a property suitable for Charlie Dollar. Something sensational."

Her final meeting of the day was with the Sleazy Singles, Arnie Blackwood and Frankie Lombardo.

Arnie, the lean and lanky one with the greasy hair pulled back in a ponytail and mirrored shades covering watery eyes, was the first to speak. "Congrats, sweetie. This is gonna be a piece of pie," he said.

Frankie, with the freaked-out brown hair and unruly beard, joined in. "Yeah, cutie, we're all gonna work together like we bin in bed all our lives."

"Fortunately," said Lucky with a pleasant smile, "we haven't."

They both guffawed.

"She's got a sense of humour," Arnie said.

"What's a good-looking broad like you doing in a job like this anyway?" Frankie asked, collapsing his bulky frame into a chair.

"Probably the same as a handsome man like yourself," Lucky replied sarcastically. "And may I remind you it's not a job — I own Panther."

Frankie didn't like that.

Arnie walked over to the conference table, put his hands on it, and leaned across. "Are you here to stay?" he demanded. "Or is this a temporary measure? What's the deal, Lucky? Have you bought the studio to sell out the land and then get out, or what?"

"I'm here to stay," she replied with a cold smile. "How about you?"

"Oh, we're here to stay all right." Arnie replied, taking off his mirrored shades, polishing them on a corner of his shirt, and putting them back on again.

Frankie brushed his hands through his unruly long hair and pulled on his scruffy beard. Both of them appeared to be stoned.

"I'm cancelling your two current projects," Lucky said.

"I may as well get straight to it — I don't like 'em. They're not the kind of films Panther is going to continue to make."

"You're doing *what*, baby?" Arnie asked in disbelief.

"Aren't I making myself clear?" she replied, cool and in control. "If you need an interpreter I'll be happy to supply one."

"Where have I seen you before?" Frankie got to his feet.

"Let's just say I've been around the studio for some time. I know everything that's going on."

"Everything, huh?" Arnie sneered.

"That's right," she replied, trying to stay calm, although these two assholes could really send her out of control.

"OK, sweetie, we're gonna give you a break. We won't take you seriously. We got two movies shooting now, an' three in pre-production. Our movies keep Panther in the black. You know what I mean? Our movies score all the profit around here, while your so-called superstars make all the flops."

"Yes," Lucky said calmly. "But I'm here to tell you the system just changed. I don't care for the kind of movies you make. I don't appreciate seeing girls having their clothes ripped off and heads bashed in. Rape and mutilation doesn't do it for me. Am I making myself clear?"

"Wake up and join the real world," said Arnie, with an insulting leer. "It's what's goin' on out there."

"Ah, but there lies the difference," Lucky said. "I'm *not* everybody else."

Frankie scratched his beard. "Are you telling us to get out?"

"Wow!" Lucky said. "You're beginning to understand me. This is fun."

"You fucking bitch," Arnie said, finally getting the message. "You can't treat us like shit. We're two of the biggest producers in Hollywood. An' what's more, we have a deal with Panther."

"You know something, Mr Blackwood, Mr Lombardo? I don't give a rat's ass."

And so ended Lucky's first day on the job. How to make friends and influence people it wasn't, but it was satisfying.

And her next project was to put together a team of people who could work together and create the kind of movies she wished to make.

Lucky Santangelo was on a roll.

Chapter 74

Swanson fever hit like a hurricane – fast, furious, and all-encompassing. It seemed every newspaper and television programme in America wanted in on this story. Adam Bobo Grant led the pack. He took everything Deena said and built it into front-page news.

I'LL NEVER DIVORCE HIM! screamed the headlines. I LOVE MY HUSBAND!

Dennis Walla may have started it, but Adam Bobo Grant was launching it in a big way. An important way. The front page of the *New York Runner* was no *Truth and Fact*. People believed the stories they read in the *New York Runner*.

Bert Slocombe faxed the story to Dennis Walla in Los Angeles.

Sitting in his Hollywood office, Dennis read it with mounting disbelief. He recognized some of his own quotes. Adam Bobo Grant, the faggot hack, was stealing from him! And there was absolutely nothing he could do. It never occurred to Dennis to get angry. What did occur to him was that he might be able to make money out of this.

He picked up the phone and placed a call to Adam Bobo Grant at his newspaper.

An officious assistant informed him that Mr Grant was unavailable.

"Tell him it's important," Dennis insisted.

"I'm sorry," the assistant said, full of his own importance. "If you have an item for Mr Grant, I can take it."

"Listen," Dennis said with heavy authority, his Australian accent thickening, "I'm not saying this twice. Just go

431

'tell him I'm the one who wrote the story in *Truth and Fact* about the Swanson divorce. And comin' up, I have an exclusive story by Venus Maria's brother. We're runnin' it next week. Now I thought he might be interested in some of this information. If he isn't, that's fine by me. Go run it by him, mate."

The assistant left him hanging on the line for a good five minutes before Adam Bobo Grant, gossip columnist supreme, came on the line.

"Mr Walla," Adam Bobo Grant said.

"Saw your story," Dennis replied. "A nice crib."

Adam Bobo Grant was offended. "I *beg* your pardon?"

"I said a nice crib. You stole half the stuff from *Truth and Fact*. My stuff — I wrote it."

"Did you phone to complain?" Bobo asked with a deeply put-upon sigh.

"Nah, I'm takin' a shot we can do business."

"Business?" Bobo perked up.

"Yeah, well, you've got items I find interesting, an' you'll find my next story very juicy indeed. It's this exclusive piece running next week, an' I thought — since you're making such a meal out of the Swansons — that you might want to take a peek at my upcomin' story before it runs."

"For a price, of course?" Bobo said crisply.

"Yeah, mate. Whattaya think I am — a charity?"

Bobo thought fast. As successful as his daily column was, it was always nice to make the front pages. "How much?" he asked tartly.

"A bargain price," Dennis replied.

Sure, Adam Bobo Grant thought. But he went for it anyway.

"Photographers are camped outside my house," Venus Maria complained to Martin on the phone.

"Don't think they're not trailing me everywhere, too," he said.

Was it her imagination, or did he sound quite pleased?

They'd talked a couple of times since *Truth and Fact*

432

appeared, but they hadn't seen each other. Now they were attempting to set up a rendezvous.

"We'd better forget about my house, and I'm sure your hotel is a definite no," she said. "But I have an idea. If I can get out without being followed, I can make it to the Bel Air Hotel. What do you think?"

He thought it was an excellent idea and told her that he would book a suite under an assumed name and they could spend the night together.

"Have you spoken to Deena?" she ventured tentatively.

"No. I haven't called her."

"She must have seen it."

"I don't intend to speak to her on the phone. I'll discuss it when I get back. I *am* taking over the studio, you know, I've been kind of busy."

"Oh, yeah. And I'm just lying around doing nothing," she snapped back.

His tone softened. "I can't wait to see you."

After she put the phone down she planned her escape. In a way it was a kick trying to fool the hovering paparazzi.

She summoned Ron, who dashed over to her house dying to be in on the game. They dressed one of her secretaries in a platinum wig, dark shades, and one of Venus Maria's outfits.

When they decided she was ready, the girl ran from the house, jumped into a car, and roared off down the hill. Sure enough the photographers followed.

Meanwhile, Venus Maria slipped out the back into Ron's car. They giggled all the way as he drove her to the Bel Air Hotel.

Clad in a long coat, floppy hat, and dark glasses she went straight to the suite Martin had booked.

He was waiting for her.

The moment she was inside he jumped on her like a randy schoolboy.

She was taken aback. "Martin!" she began to object, but he was having none of it. He kissed her frantically, pawing at her clothes.

433

She threw off her hat, and her platinum hair tumbled around her face.

He buried his hands in her curls. "God, I've missed you," he mumbled, unbuttoning her coat and groping under her sweater.

She'd never known him to be this passionate. Headlines obviously turned him on.

They ended up making love on the floor. It was the wildest she'd ever known Martin.

"Wow! You're hot tonight. What happened to you?" she laughed, when they were finished.

"Are you saying I was cool before?"

She wasn't saying it, but she was certainly thinking it.

"A girlfriend called me from New York today," she said casually. "We're on the front of the New York papers. And last night there was a story on that TV show — *Entertainment Tonight*. Why all this coverage?"

"You're a popular lady."

"It's not just me, Martin. It's *you* that's captured the imagination of the public. Billionaire this and billionaire that. Hey, you're getting a real stud reputation!"

"Don't be ridiculous," he said. But he didn't sound at all mad.

She bent down and began picking up her crumpled clothes. "I'm going to soak in a hot tub. Shall we order room service? I'm starving!"

"I've already ordered caviar, steak and ice cream. Does that sound like a feast?"

"This is an adventure! Here we are, just the two of us, and nobody knows where we are. Exciting, huh?"

"It works for me."

She couldn't help smiling. "So I noticed."

She drew herself a long hot tub filled with bubbles and luxuriated in it.

Martin strolled into the bathroom carrying two glasses of champagne. He perched on the side of the tub and handed her one.

She lay back. "So . . ." she said dreamily. "What's going

434

to happen? Now that Deena knows, it's a whole different game, huh?"

Martin wasn't about to be drawn into conversation. "We'll have to see what she says."

"How about what *you* say?"

"I've been married to Deena for ten years. It's impossible for me to pick up and go."

"Isn't that what we wanted?"

"It is, but there are ways of doing things. It'll be better if Deena asks me to leave."

"If she has any pride she will."

He nodded.

"Martin," Venus said, "you *are* going to make a decision, aren't you?"

He nodded again.

"'Cause if you don't," she added, "I'm not staying in this relationship. Especially now it's out in the open."

He trailed his hand in the bubbles, touching the tip of her breast. "You wouldn't be threatening me, would you?"

She smiled seductively. "Would *I* do a thing like that? Come here, billionaire stud. Get in the tub with me."

He couldn't help laughing. "I'm not nineteen."

She sat up, wrapping her wet arms around him. "Pretend," she said. "Let's play pretend."

In New York, Deena raged around her apartment, angry and humiliated. It seemed she'd been deserted — which wasn't exactly true, because her phone was ringing off the hook. Everyone had phoned except for Martin, and she couldn't reach him. When she'd called him in California, various secretaries and assistants had told her he was in important meetings and could not be disturbed.

Meetings, she thought to herself. *Ha!* He was with The Bitch.

Deena had already put her plans into action. She'd activated the private detective she'd hired several months earlier in Los Angeles. His instructions were to give her a complete dossier on Venus Maria, tracking all her movements. The detective had no idea who he was dealing with. She'd set it up by phone, and he reported to a box number.

Deena knew exactly what she had to do. However, she hadn't anticipated the amount of publicity Martin's affair with Venus Maria would generate.

She stared at her list of incoming phone calls. Every married woman in New York had called her. They all wanted the inside dish. Adam Bobo Grant had telephoned three times. Did he want more from her? Hadn't he taken enough?

She picked up the *New York Runner* and reread the front-page story. It was different from *Truth and Fact*. Everyone knew *Truth and Fact* was a cheap rag. The story in the *New York Runner* gave it credence.

Her eyes scanned the page.

Deena Swanson, wanly beautiful in a lime-green Adolfo suit, refuses to discuss her rival, Venus Maria. Her only comment, "I'm sure Venus Maria is quite talented."

And then further down:

For a moment Deena is silent as she gazes across the crowded restaurant. A fragile woman. A beautiful woman. A woman about to lose her husband?

At least Bobo had had the good grace to put a question mark after that.

She was not about to lose her husband. She was not about to lose anything.

She'd planned what she had to do for the last six months, and now the inevitable was in motion.

Chapter 75

Nobody could operate like Mickey Stolli. He was a master at the game. He'd exceeded even his own expectations.

First of all he'd outsmarted Abe Panther and Lucky

Santangelo by signing a pre-dated note giving Panther the full responsibility of owing Carlos Bonnatti a million dollars. Supposedly legally. And then he'd had the document filed neatly away — buried in business affairs.

Secondly, he'd sat down with Martin Swanson and clinched himself a fine deal with Orpheus at double the salary he made at Panther, plus profit-sharing.

Martin Swanson was a straight-talker. "I'm only interested in making money," he'd said. "You can bring with you whomever you want. We're turning Orpheus into a money-making machine."

Business taken care of, Mickey had then returned home to Abigaile. Dear sweet Abigaile.

She was stewing — but what did he care? He had a whole new life ahead of him.

One of the good things about Hollywood was that when you failed, you failed up. And being caught in a whorehouse was no big deal. He wasn't committing some heinous crime, he was merely getting laid. Abe Panther's sale of the studio had completely deflated Abigaile. She was almost prepared to forgive him for being arrested.

But not quite. When he'd arrived back at the house after the meeting with Lucky Santangelo, she'd greeted him with a miserable expression and Ben and Primrose. They were all waiting in the library.

"We have to sit down and discuss everything," Abigaile said very matter-of-factly. "Ben has kindly offered to deal with the lawyers."

"What's to deal with?" Mickey had fixed himself a drink. By this time he was a happy man. And he was about to be a free man.

"Mickey," Ben said, with a long, serious face, "we can't let Abe get away with this."

"It seems to me there's nothing we can do," Mickey replied, downing a hefty shot of Scotch.

"Oh yes there is," said Ben, the upright family man, who Mickey knew for a fact had been screwing a buxom blonde starlet who'd worked on one of Panther's movies shooting in London last summer.

"What, Ben?" Mickey asked wearily.

"First of all Abigaile has told me of your problems, and you can't walk out on her now," Ben said pompously, pacing up and down. "We're in a crisis situation. We have to present a united front. I've already spoken to my lawyer. He suggests we might be able to have Abe declared incompetent."

"No way," Mickey said. "What's incompetent about Abe? He's walking and talking. This is Hollywood, for chrissakes! So he's old – big deal. Look at George Burns, Bob Hope."

"At least we should discuss it," Ben insisted.

"Discuss what? My wife *wants* me out – so I'm out."

Ben put his hand on Mickey's shoulder. "Think about your Tabitha."

"Listen, I didn't *ask* to go. Get this straight – Abby threw me out. Remember that."

"And now she's asking you to stay."

"Too late."

"We'll have to work this out, Mickey," Abigaile said, her no-nonsense expression firmly in place.

"There's nothing to work out," he shrugged. "I screwed around. I got caught. Now I have to take the consequences. I suggest you see a lawyer."

"Mickey, you don't seem to understand," Primrose chimed in, speaking firmly. "Abe has sold the studio. Things are different."

"Stay out of it, Primrose," he warned. "What goes on between me and my wife has nothing to do with you."

"We're all involved." Ben was determined to make his presence felt.

"Not in my private affairs," Mickey declared. "What we do about our marriage concerns me and Abby. It's nobody else's business." He wanted to add, "Get fucked," but didn't deem it appropriate.

Without further discussion he went upstairs to his dressing room and packed a small suitcase. Then he got in his Porsche and drove straight to the Beverly Hills Hotel, where he checked into a bungalow.

Mickey Stolli was back in action.

Forty-eight hours later the news of Mickey's new appointment was all over town. It hadn't actually hit the trade press – after all, the deal wasn't even signed – but everybody in the know was aware of it.

Eddie tracked him down at the studio, where Mickey was packing up his personal papers and effects.

"What's happening, Mickey?" he asked feverishly. "Did you hear from Bonnatti?"

"I've taken care of it," Mickey said. "Like I take care of all your fuck-ups."

"Hey." Eddie refused to feel guilty. "It was just one of those things."

"Yeah. One of those things you always seem to get involved in."

"So . . . how did you take care of it?" Eddie asked, trying to sound casual.

"Never mind, and keep your mouth closed. It's no longer your responsibility – there's a deal memo says it's the studio's."

"Really? You fixed it?"

"Forget about it, Eddie. All right?"

"I heard about you and Orpheus." Eddie hesitated before making a pitch. "How about bringing me along for the ride? Am I your good luck charm or what?"

"Are you shitting me, Eddie?"

"No, Mickey. I need a job."

"You've already got a job."

"Word is Lucky Santangelo is cleaning house." He picked up a script, stared at it blankly, then put it down again. "Take me with you, huh?"

Mickey sighed. When was Eddie going to stop with the favours. "Get clean and I'll see what I can do," he said.

"Clean?" Eddie looked hurt. "I got no problem."

Sure. "I'm *telling* you, Eddie – you're hooked. Check yourself into some kind of drug rehab and then we'll talk." He took a beat. "By the way, was that your wife I saw at Madame Loretta's?"

439

Eddie glowered. "Are you crazy?"

"And if it was her, what was she doing there?"

Now he was really furious. "You need glasses, Mickey."

"And you need to straighten out."

"Bullshit."

"Panther's going down when I leave," Mickey boasted. "Everybody's gonna follow me. Johnny Romano, Arnie and Frankie, Susie – they'll all come over to Orpheus."

Eddie scowled. "Yeah. You'll take everybody except me. Right?"

"I told you – clean up your act and you're in."

Clean up his act. Easier said than put into operation. When he was high he felt like he owned the world. And when he was straight he felt like the world wasn't even worth living in.

Why couldn't he carry on the way he was? Why was everyone on his case?

He left Mickey and drove home.

Leslie was showing a realtor around their house. He stared edgily at the two women.

Leslie attempted to introduce him.

"Forget it," he said rudely. "We're not selling."

The realtor looked shocked. "What do you mean, Mr Kane? I was under the impression we had an arrangement."

"No deal, baby. We've decided not to sell."

"Eddie?" Leslie said, her face flushing.

The realtor saw her fat commission fading away. "I feel you should reconsider your decision, Mr Kane," she said anxiously. "Once you've decided to sell a house, it's never a good idea to stay."

"Scram," Eddie said.

"Mr Kane—"

"Out!"

The realtor departed.

"What happened, Eddie?" Leslie asked.

"Things got taken care of. I'm off the dime."

"Yes?"

"That's right. C'mon, baby, we're goin' out."

"Where?"

"I'm about to surprise you."

Mickey was emptying out his desk drawers into a briefcase when Lucky entered the office. He glanced up and their eyes met. She leaned against the door and stared at him.

"Well, Mr Stolli," she said. "So you're moving on."

"That's right," he replied shortly. What was this – visiting day?

"I'm glad for you," she said. "Saves me the trouble of firing you, huh?"

He looked at her like she was crazy. "You were going to fire me?"

"Does that seem like such a strange idea?"

"Yeah. As a matter of fact it does."

"How come?"

"A New York broad like you – what do *you* know about the movie business? You need me desperately."

"Is that all you have to say?"

"What do you want me to say? I've spent the last ten years building this studio up, and Abe goes behind my back and sells it to you. I wouldn't work for you, sweetheart, if you were the last broad in town."

She stayed cool. "Really? You weren't a laugh a minute to work for yourself."

He laughed derisively. "Your husband's been telling you stories, huh? Well, let *me* give you the facts. Lennie Golden ain't such a hotshot. Take a look at the dailies."

"I wasn't talking about Lennie."

Brenda, one of Eddie Kane's secretaries, entered the room. She'd corn-rowed her hair and it looked good. "I shredded all those papers you asked me to take care of, Mr Stolli," she said, glancing at Lucky – checking her out so she could report to the rest of the girls what the new boss looked like.

Mickey shot her a filthy look.

"What papers?" Lucky interjected.

"Personal files," Mickey replied quickly. "Nothing to do with you."

441

"If it's studio business, I'd prefer you didn't shred any-thing," Lucky said.

"A little late for that." Mickey smiled triumphantly. Fuck her. Who did she think she was dealing with? "I'm outta here," he said, waving Brenda out of the room.

Lucky walked over and sat in the chair in front of his desk.

Brenda hovered by the door, dying to listen in.

"How's . . . Warner?" Lucky asked casually.

Mickey snapped to attention. "Huh?"

"Warner Franklin? The black cop you were servicing twice a week. Oh, and that kid of yours in Chicago, the one you send a cheque to every month. Did you ever marry his mother? Or was she only another girlfriend?"

Mickey's skin flushed a dark red. He glared at Lucky and waved a frantic hand at Brenda, indicating she should get the hell out. Brenda exited.

Mickey was furious. "Where did you get all this infor-mation?" he asked gruffly.

She lapsed into her best Luce voice. "Working for you, Mr Stolli. Kissing your ass, Mr Stolli. You were such a *charming* boss. A real pleasure to work for."

He glared at her as if he couldn't quite believe his eyes. She wasn't . . . couldn't be . . .

"Yes." She nodded, confirming the bad news. "I was Luce. Little Luce who you kicked around pretty good. It's amazing what a good disguise can do, huh?"

His flush deepened, sweeping upwards until even his bald head was covered. "You spying *bitch*. What did you do that for?"

"Abe and I figured it was a fun thing to do. Y'know, see what his favourite scum-in-law was up to. That's what he affectionately calls you and Ben — the scum-in-laws."

"I'll tell you something," Mickey said angrily. "You may be a rich broad with a lot of money, but you're going to lose every penny in this business, 'cause this studio's going down. Right to the bottom. I'm taking everybody with me. You'll be left with nothing but shit."

Calmly she walked outside to where Brenda pretended not to be eavesdropping.

"Brenda, dear," she said coolly, "call in the exterminators. I want this office fumigated before I move in."

"Where are we going, Eddie?" Leslie asked for the sixth time.

"It's a surprise. You'll see babe," he said, leaning across and patting her knee. "Just relax."

She wasn't relaxed. She wasn't relaxed at all. Eddie had something on his mind, and she didn't know what to expect.

Chapter 76

Deena was appalled at the press coverage. She was even more appalled when Martin made no attempt to contact her.

As the days passed, her anger grew until she was finally reduced to leaving a cryptic message with Gertrude: "Tell Mr Swanson if he does not call me back within the next hour, I am making a statement to Adam Bobo Grant which he will regret."

It worked. Within an hour Martin was on the phone.

"How nice to hear from you," Deena said coldly.

"My God," he replied. "You have no idea what it's been like here."

"*I* have no idea?" Deena said, her voice like ice.

"I *am* trying to take over a studio," Martin said testily. "I'm in meetings twenty-six hours a day And it seems every time I get to a phone it's the wrong time to call you."

"Really, Martin?"

"Besides, isn't it best if we talk when I get back?"

"When are you coming back?"

He thought swiftly. "I'll be in New York by the weekend."

"We have a party to go to on Saturday night. Can I depend on you? It would be nice to be seen together in public. Don't you agree?"

He hesitated, reluctant to bring the subject up, but it couldn't be ignored any longer. "You're not mad at me, are you?" he asked. "That picture in the magazine was a fake. A pasted-together job. My lawyers are looking into it. We're going to sue 'em."

"We are?"

"Don't you think we should?"

"Whatever you want, Martin. As you say, we'll discuss it when you get back."

Did Martin honestly imagine he was fooling her? Did he think she would believe the photograph was a fake?

She was dying to talk to Effie about it – but unfortunately Effie was taking no calls. Obviously she was still upset about the picture with Paul.

Deena decided to set things straight. She sent her a short note requesting a chance to explain. If Effie was any kind of friend she would call back.

Paul Webster had telephoned the house three times. Deena had not returned his calls. She had enough on her mind.

Her latest aggravation was Adam Bobo Grant. She was quite upset that he'd betrayed every confidence she'd whispered to him. Now her confidences were spread daily across the front of the *New York Runner*.

Deena Swanson loves her husband, and refuses to give him up. "Whatever happens," she said today, "Martin and I refuse to give credence to these ugly rumours."

There were many conversations to have – and when Martin returned they would have them.

In the meantime, her plans regarding Venus Maria were progressing smoothly.

Soon she would be ready to make her move.

Abigaile was not Abe Panther's granddaughter for nothing. She had a certain amount of larceny in her, and she soon decided that Mickey Stolli deserved to be taught a lesson. He'd humiliated her and Tabitha. He'd publicly disgraced them and nobody seemed to care except herself.

Her girlfriends dismissed the news that Mickey had been caught in a whorehouse as nothing more than an irritation. "Just ignore it," they'd advised her. "Most men play around. What difference does it make as long as they don't bring it home?"

Ah, but Mickey *had* brought it home. He could hardly bring it any closer to home than the front page of the *LA Times*.

While Primrose and Ben dealt with lawyers, she sat and brooded. It soon became clear why Mickey did not wish to become embroiled in a fight over Panther Studios. He had a new job. He was taking over as head of Orpheus Studios.

Abigaile frowned. He'd be Martin Swanson's boy, that's all. Didn't he realize? Mickey had no idea what it was like to work for somebody else. He'd never had to answer to Abe, but he'd certainly have to answer to Martin Swanson.

While she was sitting and brooding, Abigaile began to think about Mickey's secretary at the studio, Luce, the one who'd given her Warner Franklin's number. And then she thought about Warner Franklin, the six-foot black cop. Why had Luce given her the number? And why had Mickey made such a lame excuse?

None of it made sense. And yet, if she thought about it long enough . . .

Abigaile picked up the *LA Times* and reread the story on Mickey. It stated that he'd been arrested while in the company of an Oriental lady of the night.

Oriental . . . Black . . . Warner Franklin's words began to come back to Abigaile.

"I'm also your husband's mistress," the woman had said over the phone.

Your husband's mistress . . .

Abigaile searched her desk to see if she had jotted down

445

Warner Franklin's phone number. No. However, she did remember where she lived.

Abigaile was anxious to find out more. If Mickey planned to leave her she wasn't about to let him get away unpunished. He was going to have to pay. Oh, was he going to have to pay!

Abigaile climbed in her Mercedes and headed for Hollywood.

Chapter 77

Lucky's first week at the studio passed quickly. There were meetings, meetings, and more meetings. There were decisions to be made, films to be halted, films to be continued with, distribution discussions, pre-production, post-production, editing, business affairs. Suddenly Lucky found herself immersed in the creative process. She attended script meetings, looked at dailies, viewed rough cuts, went over budgets, and at night, quite exhausted, she read scripts.

"You don't have to do *everything*," Morton Sharkey told her, amused at the idea that she would want to. "There are employees to take care of the everyday affairs. You're supposed to only make the big decisions."

Lucky was into it. "I *want* to be hands on," she said, full of enthusiasm. "These are *my* decisions."

On Friday she and Boogie drove out to the airport to meet Bobby and Cee Cee, his Jamaican nanny. It was a joyful moment. Her son bounded off the plane straight into her arms.

Bobby was six and a half years old and gorgeous.

Lucky swept him up and swung him around.

After a moment he got embarrassed. "Hey – Mom, put me down, I'm too big," he objected, struggling like crazy.

She crushed him with a kiss. "You're mine," she sang out, wildly happy. "Mine! Mine! Mine!"

Bobby chattered all the way to the house, while Cee Cee just smiled.

"Where's Lennie, Mommy?" he asked as soon as they arrived.

"He's working, sweetheart."

Bobby was persistent. "Will he be here soon?"

"Sure," she said, although she still hadn't heard from him — not one word.

It was disappointing. She'd hoped that by this time he'd have gotten over his anger and would have called to make things all right.

"Where's Brigette?" was Bobby's next question.

Lucky had tried to reach Brigette on several occasions, but missed her each time.

"I'll try her again now," she promised. "Maybe we can persuade her to come out here soon. Would you like that?"

Bobby liked it a lot.

Lucky placed another call to the Websters. "You're in luck this time," said Effie Webster. "She's right here. Hang on a second."

Brigette sounded full of high spirits. "Lucky! I'm sorry we keep on missing each other. How *are* you?"

"Fine," Lucky replied. "More important — how are *you*? Enjoying New York?"

"Yes, it's terrific. Is Bobby with you?"

"That's exactly why I'm calling. I met him at the airport today, and he's disappointed you're not here. I hope you're coming."

Brigette hesitated. "I wasn't sure you still wanted us."

Did *us* mean she was bringing Lennie? "Of course I still want you. Lennie told me we're all spending the summer together."

"Yes, I know," Brigette said awkwardly. "But Lennie told *me* that you and he were having some sort of um . . . disagreement . . . and so we've made other plans."

"Who's made other plans?"

"Well, Lennie actually. He's taking me and my girlfriend to the South of France."

Lucky felt a cold chill. Lennie had made plans to go

447

away without telling her. He was taking off without a word. Was that how much their relationship meant to him? *Christ!* He really *didn't* care.

"How long are you going for?"

Brigette sounded vague. "Lennie said maybe ten days or a couple of weeks."

She took a long deep breath. It wasn't fair to involve Brigette. "Well, that sounds wonderful. Perhaps when you get back you'll come to Malibu."

"I'd love to," Brigette said happily. "Can I bring my girlfriend?"

"Sure." Lucky paused, and then added carefully, "By the way, I saw *Truth and Fact*. Who was that boy you were pictured with?"

"Oh, Paul. He's nobody," Brigette said casually. "Just Nona's brother. You know how these stupid photographers trail me whenever they find out where I am."

"I was just wondering," Lucky said. "I don't want to see you get into any more difficult situations."

"Lucky, I was a kid when all that happened with Tim Wealth. I'm grown up now."

"Hardly grown up!"

"I'm seventeen. That's old. You were running wild in the South of France with Mommy when *you* were my age. And then you were married a few months after that."

True. She couldn't deny it. She and Olympia. Out of control. Until Gino and Dimitri had come to collect their errant daughters. And then a forced marriage to Craven Richmond — Mister Personality!

"OK, sweetheart. It's just that I worry about you."

"You don't have to, Lucky. I *can* look after myself."

"Good. Call me when you get back."

"Yes, I promise."

Lucky put the phone down and went to find Bobby. He was on the beach and into everything — running, swimming, playing with a neighbour's dog.

He was having the best time. Later, he fell asleep watching television.

She picked him up, carried him to his bed, and tucked

him in. Then she brushed the soft dark hair off his fore-head. He looked so like Gino. Olive skin, black eyes, curling lashes – a miniature Gino. God! She loved him.

She kissed him and left the room.

The nights were the loneliest. She couldn't stand the thought that it might be over with Lennie. It was just too painful.

After a while she went to her bedroom and called him – something she'd promised herself she wouldn't do. He was the angry one. It was up to him to make the first move. But so what?

He answered on the third ring. "Yeah?"

She didn't know what to say. It was so unlike her to be at a loss for words. After a long and painful silence she hung up.

If Lennie really loved her he would pursue her. He'd fly out to California and make everything all right.

Sadly she realized he wasn't going to make that move.

She went to bed and slept restlessly. Sleep was not easy. She missed Lennie so very much.

Chapter 78

Martin Swanson flew back to New York. He'd left the city a well-known businessman and returned a media superstar. Somehow, Martin Swanson had attracted the attention of a celebrity-hungry public. He was fairly young. He was extraordinarily rich. And sex was involved. What better headline for the eighties?

Deena greeted him as if everything was normal.

"We can't ignore what's going on," he said, getting straight to it. "We're going to have to face it."

"It's you who has to face it," Deena said, trying to keep her fury under control. "Do you want to be with that . . . that . . . woman?"

Was Deena saying he *could* be with Venus Maria *and*

keep their marriage intact? That's what he'd like. Maybe it wasn't necessary for things to change.

"I haven't thought about it," he lied, because apart from the successful takeover of Orpheus, he hadn't thought about anything else. "Venus Maria *is* special," he added carefully.

Deena raised a sceptical eyebrow, "Special?" she sneered. "As special as the ballet dancer, or the author, or the lawyer? How *special* is she, Martin? Is she special enough for you to give up half your money?"

"What are you talking about?"

"If you ever considered divorce, that's exactly what you'd have to do."

"Do you want a divorce? Is that what you're saying?"

"I'm *saying* I do not enjoy being followed by the media and having my personal life written about in the press. It's an embarrassment. I feel foolish and humiliated."

"Yes, well, might I mention that one of the reasons we're all over the newspapers is because you keep giving exclusive interviews to Adam Bobo Grant. Why can't you tell the little fag to back off?"

"Bobo has been a true friend to me. I couldn't even get you on the phone in Los Angeles. That's hardly loyalty, Martin."

"You know what I'm like when I'm closing a deal," he said.

"Didn't you feel this was important enough to take the time to speak to me?"

"Deena, I'm here now. What more do you want?"

"I want you to stop seeing her."

There! She'd said it. Her words were out in the open. It was the first time she'd challenged Martin about a woman. Now all he had to do was agree, and everything would be all right.

Deena held her breath. This was a crucial moment.

"Give me time to make a decision," Martin said, not looking her in the eye.

Deena sighed. As far as she was concerned Venus Maria was dead.

*

Dennis Walla turned out to be right. When Emilio Sierra's revelations about his famous sister hit the stands, *Truth and Fact* was another sellout. Two weeks in a row – not bad. He was on a winning streak. It seemed the public couldn't get enough of mega-money, power, and lustful sex. They loved the combination.

Dennis Walla was now in daily contact with Adam Bobo Grant. He fed the New York gossip columnist tit-bits, and Bobo used them in his column.

Dennis had two men watching Venus Maria around the clock – a photographer and Bert Slocombe. They reported everything she did. In fact, they were even getting pretty good at figuring out her various disguises. Sometimes she wore a long black wig. Other times she hid under a floppy Garbo hat and big dark glasses. Sometimes she rushed out with a ponytail and no makeup hoping they wouldn't recognize her. Other times she dressed up as the maid.

It was a game. They were winning. Usually she just attempted to ignore them and rushed to her car. When she was particularly irritated she gave them the finger.

They had her house, the studio, and the video rehearsal hall staked out. She couldn't make a move without them knowing it.

Martin Swanson wasn't such an easy deal. There were two more reporters assigned to him.

A stray paparazzo had managed to snatch a shot of Martin and Venus Maria strolling in the grounds of the Bel Air Hotel. *Truth and Fact* bought it, and planned to run it front page in the next issue with the lurid headlines:

LOVE NEST DISCOVERED!
THE BILLIONAIRE AND THE SHOWGIRL!

A third week's bonanza coming up.

Did Dennis ever have any regrets about invading people's privacy?

No way. He knew he was onto a good thing, and felt no guilt whatsoever.

When he got back from Hawaii Emilio called up to whine. "There's a message from my sister on my machine telling me to fuck off. She's furious with me," Emilio nagged. "And that's before my story has even appeared."

"It's out on the stands now," Dennis said. "Read it. All good juicy. You'll be proud, mate."

The Hawaii trip had cost Emilio more than expected. He wouldn't mind making a further killing out of this story. After all, it was unlikely Venus would ever speak to him again.

"Uh, I've got more stuff for you," he told an insatiable Dennis.

"Yes? What?" Dennis asked eagerly.

"Oh, just some more bits and pieces about Venus I remembered. Friends she went to school with. Her first boyfriend, that kind of thing."

Dennis was interested. "You have?"

"Yeah. How much can I get for it?"

"Why don't you tell me exactly what you got an' we'll see," Dennis said.

"I just told you. School friends, boyfriends – whatever you're after."

"Give me 'the day she lost her virginity' story and I'll find out what it's worth."

Emilio decided to get his ass back to New York. With a little intelligent digging he could come up with anything Dennis wanted.

Chapter 79

Cooper greeted Lucky at the door to the screening room, dressed casually and looking as good as ever. There was a showing of *Strut*, and Lucky was anxious to see it. She studied Cooper and idly wondered if she'd ever feel the desire to go to bed with another man again. She'd done as she pleased before Lennie. Now, if their relationship was over, what next? Going to bed with somebody in the eighties was a whole new thing. A dangerous commitment.

"Venus is joining us," Cooper said, taking her arm and leading her inside.

"I was hoping she could come."

"How's everything going? Are you enjoying running a studio?"

"It's time-consuming," she said, taking a seat at the back.

"I hear you bumped the Sleazy Singles," he remarked, sitting down beside her.

"That was Lennie's nickname for them."

"Yeah, it's everybody's nickname for them. Are they hitting you with a law suit?"

She shrugged casually. "Who knows? Who cares? We're in good shape. I told them I was willing to honour their contract, it's just that I won't make any of their dumb movies. If they want to make sexist crap, they can make it elsewhere."

"I understand," he said. "Pretty smart move."

"I don't imagine they've got much of a case, do you? Besides, the rumour is they'll follow Mickey to Orpheus."

He smiled. "Ah . . . Mickey, Arnie, and Frankie. The perfect team."

Venus Maria rushed in late. "The paparazzi are driving me insane!" she complained. "They're camped outside my house like a band of gypsies. I nearly knocked a couple of 'em down this morning."

Cooper kissed her on the cheek. "Maybe you should have."

"Oh, yeah, great. I can see the headlines now – *Venus Maria – the paparazzi killer!* Very tasteful!"

Lucky picked up the phone and instructed Harry to roll the film. They settled down to watch.

From the moment Venus Maria appeared on the screen everybody knew the film was hers. She looked sensational and her acting was captivating. Even Cooper was aware of it, and yet he didn't seem to mind because it made *him* look good as the director.

"Oh, God! I hate watching myself!" Venus Maria cried,

453

half covering her eyes. "It's so painful. God! Do you see how big my teeth look? And my hair – I *hate* my hair!"

Cooper groped for her hand in the dark and squeezed it. "Shut up," he said firmly. "You're a star. Face it."

Cooper wasn't so bad himself. On screen he came across with exactly the right amount of charm and self-deprecating humour. It was a skilful performance.

When the lights went up, Lucky said confidently, "We've got a winner. In spite of the fact it was made under Mickey Stolli's regime."

"I did have *something* to do with it," Cooper chided gently. "Mickey requested seventeen bare-breasted girls in the opening credits, but I told him no, let's cool it."

"What does everybody think?" Venus Maria asked anxiously. "Am I OK?"

It amazed Lucky that Venus Maria had to seek reassurance. Couldn't she see? "You're a natural," she told her. "You light up the screen. You really do."

"Yes?"

"*Yes*. You're going to be a mega-movie star. And *I'm* going to make sure this film is handled in exactly the right way."

"Yeah," Cooper interjected dryly. "Bud Graham is designing the poster now. A naked Amazon surrounded by a dozen nymphets with their tits on fire!"

Everyone laughed. But Graham's reputation went before him.

Lucky suggested the three of them lunch together. They went to the Columbia Bar and Grill, where they pigged out on pasta and spent the entire time discussing everyone at the studio.

By the time they emerged the paparazzi were gathered in force. Word travelled fast.

"Jesus!" Venus Maria exclaimed. "We can't go anywhere any more. Hey – come on, Cooper, let's give 'em a picture they won't forget. Lucky, grab his other arm."

They held onto Cooper and smiled for the cameras. The photographers went wild.

Venus Maria giggled. "That's gonna give them something to think about."

"I can't believe the amount of publicity Martin's getting." Cooper shook his head in amazement. "From a conservative unknown businessman in New York he's become a super-stud."

"Not exactly unknown," Venus Maria interjected.

"Yeah, but not exactly Warren Beatty either," Cooper corrected. "Now he's on the cover of every magazine and newspaper across the country. The Battling Swansons. What's going on with them anyway?"

Venus Maria shrugged. "You think *I* know? One night in the Bel Air Hotel does not a relationship make!"

"One night?" Cooper asked.

"He was too busy with the Orpheus deal."

"That figures. Business first."

"Anyway, he's flying back to New York tomorrow. I guess we'll all find out together. I start shooting my new video soon, and that's all I'm in to for the next couple of weeks. What Martin decides is up to him."

Lucky found herself liking Venus Maria more and more. The girl had spirit. She did what she wanted, and she did it her way. She reminded Lucky of herself.

Bobby and his nanny settled nicely into Malibu, but Bobby wouldn't stop asking about Lennie and Brigette and when they were coming. To keep him occupied Lucky sent for one of his school friends from England.

Finally Lennie called.

"Hi," Lucky said, holding her breath, hoping he was going to say – *I'm sorry, I've behaved like a jerk, I'm on my way out there, and we'll get through this together.*

"Lucky, what the hell is all this about my contract?" he asked bluntly.

"I thought you'd be pleased," she replied. "Panther is releasing you from all future commitments. You can tear your contract up."

He didn't sound as pleased as she'd hoped. "Oh, really," he said.

"It's what you wanted, isn't it?"

"Sure."

"Now you don't have to worry about anyone suing you."

"Oh, you were thinking of suing me, huh?"

"Not me, Lennie. Mickey's out now and I'm in." She hesitated for a moment. "If you wanted to, you could be here beside me."

"Hey — Lucky — we've had that conversation."

When Lennie was impossible he was *really* impossible. Her voice hardened. "Why are you calling? To thank me for releasing you from your contract? Is that it?"

"I wanted to say . . . uh . . . Jesus, I don't know. What's going on with us?"

He'd given her an opening and she went for it. "If you flew out this weekend, maybe we could talk it out. That's what we need to do, Lennie. And I'm prepared to listen to your point of view if you're ready to listen to mine."

There was a long silence, then, "No, it's not going to work. I'm taking Brigette to France. We're leaving tomorrow."

Pleading wasn't her style, but Lennie was worth it. "We could all be here together. Isn't that what you wanted?"

"No, Lucky," he said resolutely, as if he'd given it a great deal of thought. "I can't fly in because it suits you."

"What do you mean by that?"

"You're running Panther. You're in LA. So now it's convenient, huh. You can fit us all into your busy schedule. But what about next time? How about when you decide to buy a hotel in Hong Kong or India? Am I supposed to sit around and wait? Hey, Lucky, remember this — I'm not the waiting kind."

The words almost stuck in her throat. "Do you want a divorce?"

He came right back at her. "Do you?"

"If we're not together . . ."

"Hey — if it's what you want . . ."

"I didn't say that."

"Yeah, well, we'll talk later." He hung up on her.

She couldn't believe he was taking it this far.

456

At first she was hurt, then angry. What did he want from her?

A baby.

Barefoot and knocked up.

A proper wife.

Well, damn him! She had things to do first, and if he didn't like it – too bad.

She phoned Mary-Lou and asked if she and Steven would like to come out and stay for a couple of weeks with the baby.

"A fine idea," Mary-Lou said enthusiastically. "I'll ask Baby first, and *then* I'll run it by Steven."

"How *is* Carioca Jade?"

"Adorable!"

"When does your series start reshooting?"

"You're not going to believe this, but we just got cancelled. I go away and have a baby, and look what happens!"

"Are you upset?"

"Sure I am. But Steven's delighted. He wants me at home changing diapers."

"Of course he does," Lucky said dryly.

"Steven's so traditional," Mary-Lou explained. "But I go along with it – makes him feel good."

Lucky thought about Steven for a moment. She missed him. It seemed like she never had time to spend with the people she really cared about.

"Hey – maybe when you come out here, we'll put you in a movie. How about it?"

Mary-Lou laughed. "A movie?"

"You're a big television star. Why not?"

"Suits me," said Mary-Lou happily. "I'll tell Steven. He'll kill himself. He thinks I should never work again!"

"Men!" Lucky said.

"Yeah!" Mary-Lou agreed.

Next Lucky called Gino and invited him. He was easy to persuade. "I'm feeling tired, kid," he said, sounding weary.

"Have you spoken to Paige?" she asked, knowing that Paige always perked him up.

"Nope. She knows how I feel. If she don't leave Ryder, I ain't seein' her again."

"Oh, come on, Gino. You and Paige have been sneaking into hotel bedrooms for years. What difference does it make if she has a husband?"

"Hey, maybe in my old age I'm findin' out I got ethics. How about that, kid?"

"I'll believe it when I see it!"

"You'll see it."

"Sure."

He promised he'd fly out soon. She couldn't wait for everyone to arrive. Maybe filling the house with people would take her mind off Lennie.

Meanwhile, business at the studio went on. Out of the Panther executives, she decided Zev Lorenzo, Ford Werne, and Teddy T. Lauden were the best of the bunch. She knew she was going to have to let Eddie Kane go. And Bud Graham wasn't about to dance to her tune. She hadn't decided about Grant Wendell, Jr.

The Sleazy Singles were definitely out. Naturally they'd threatened to sue.

"On what grounds?" Lucky had asked. "You have a three-year deal that says you make the movies and Panther pays. But the studio has to approve them. Listen, I don't mind paying you the money while you sit here and play with yourselves for three years. How about it, huh?"

They'd told her to shove it and duly departed.

Ben Harrison requested a meeting. He came in and told her he'd be willing to stay and take over Mickey's job.

"*I've* taken over Mickey's job," she pointed out. What did they all think this was? A game?

She decided to keep Ben running the European side of things until she had the time to investigate his skills. Abe had called them both the "scum-in-laws". Maybe he was wrong about Ben.

The important thing was to get the studio headed in the

right direction. No more mindless violence against women. No more tits-and-ass specials.

The word soon spread around Hollywood that Panther was the place to take any interesting and exciting new projects and ideas. The scripts began pouring in.

And so business went on while Hollywood watched and waited.

Lucky Santangelo was in charge. It felt good.

Chapter 80

The second time around Abigaile knew exactly where to park. She didn't bother driving around the block. She dumped her car on the red zone, walked up the front of the building and pressed the buzzer marked Franklin.

"Warner Franklin?" she said imperiously when a woman's voice answered.

"Who's this?"

"Abigaile Stolli. I'd like to come up and talk to you."

There was a long pause while Warner decided what to do. Finally she said, "Third floor — watch the elevator door, sometimes it sticks."

"Thank you," replied Abigaile politely, keeping a hold on herself. This time her heart wasn't beating fast at all. She willed herself to remain in control. Mickey Stolli had lied to her for the last time.

Once on the third floor she marched resolutely towards the apartment.

Warner flung open the door and stared at her.

Abigaile stared back. "Can I come in?" she asked, feeling uncomfortable, but determined to follow through.

"You sure you're not gonna run away this time?" Warner said caustically. "Seems to me you take one look at a black face an' shit your pants."

"I beg your pardon?" said Abigaile, putting on her best Beverly Hills Bitch face.

459

"Ah, forget it." Warner was anxious to know what Mickey's wife wanted. "Come in."

Abigaile followed Warner into her small apartment.

"Drink?" offered Warner.

Abigaile noticed a holstered gun thrown casually on a chair and shuddered. "No, thank you."

"Sit down," said Warner.

Abigaile did so, folding her hands in her lap. Her perfect Beverly Hills manicure glistened. Warner's nails were cut short and unpolished.

"You told me something before," Abigaile began. "On the phone, do you remember?"

"No, what was that?" asked Warner. She wasn't in a good mood on account of the fact that Johnny Romano – the new love of her life – was not returning her calls. Warner was not used to fuck and run. She didn't appreciate it.

"You said you were my husband's mistress," Abigaile rushed on. "Is that true?"

"*Was* is the operative word," said Warner.

"Was?" echoed Abigaile. "Does that mean it's over?"

"Hey – you think when I find my man making out with hookers it's going to continue?" Warner asked, surprised, "*You* might put up with it, but *I* certainly won't."

"I see you read about it too," sighed Abigaile.

"No, I didn't read about it," corrected Warner. "*I* was the arresting officer."

Abigaile felt quite faint. "How long have you been seeing Mickey?"

"About eighteen months."

Abigaile was horrified. "Eighteen months!"

"You may as well make yourself comfortable," said Warner, thinking to herself that most men deserved everything they got. "And if you like – I'll tell you all about it."

Leslie was used to Eddie's erratic driving. She buckled her seat belt and hoped for the best.

It wasn't his driving that was causing anxiety to sweep

over her in great waves. It was when she began to suspect where they were heading.

Sure enough, Eddie finally pulled up outside Madame Loretta's house.

Leslie didn't unbuckle her seat belt. She sat perfectly still and waited.

He didn't say a word.

After a few minutes Leslie asked quietly, "Eddie? What are we doing here?"

"Hey," he said, "we're gonna have tea. Isn't that what you said you used to do here? Tea and a chat."

"Yes, that's right. But I always called first."

"That's OK, honey. I hear Madame Loretta is *very* accommodating, always ready to receive people. She'll be pleased to see us."

"Eddie." She looked at him imploringly. "Why are you doing this to me?"

"Why am I doing *what*, baby? I don't understand."

"You understand perfectly well."

"Somebody you don't want to see here?" he said, looking around innocently. "Come on, baby, get out of the car. We're visiting, just like you used to."

Slowly she unbuckled her seat belt and climbed out.

He took her hand and marched her up to the front door. One of the maids answered his ring.

"Is Madame Loretta around?" he asked.

"Who shall I say is calling?"

"Tell her . . . Leslie's here. Tell her . . . Leslie is ready to go back to work."

Leslie turned to him and her eyes filled with tears. "You bastard," she said in a low voice. "When did you find out?"

"Why didn't you tell me?" he demanded angrily.

"Because you wouldn't have understood."

"What makes you think that? You *knew* you should have told me. 'I'm a hooker, Eddie,' that's all you had to say. 'Guys have sex with me for money.' You think that would have made me run, huh? You think I wouldn't have married you?"

"You're a mean son of a bitch."

"What *I* am is honest. What *you* are is a fraud. Now I'm leaving you here, baby, 'cause it's where you belong. Don't bother coming back to the house."

"You can't do this," she said.

"Watch me."

"Don't you love me?" she asked sadly. "You always told me you did."

"Hey — I loved the pretty little girl from Iowa. I don't love the hooker who's probably had every guy in town." He turned to leave. "Goodbye, Leslie. Thanks for the free ride."

"Is this the way you want it, Eddie? Because if it is, don't expect me to come back."

He laughed aloud. "Who wants you back? I gotta be out of my head to take you back."

He walked away, swaggering over to his prized Maserati.

Stoned as usual, Eddie didn't really know what he was doing.

Chapter 81

"There's some guy to see you," Otis said. "Says he knows you. Informs me you're an old friend."

"Does he have an appointment?" Lucky asked.

"Nope. The man drove onto the lot in a limousine with a driver and two other guys in the car. I guess the limo impressed the guards. Nobody stopped him."

"What's his name?"

"Carlos Bonnatti," Otis said. "Sounds like an Italian hood. Looks like one too. Central Casting couldn't have done better."

"Bonnatti?" Lucky said. "What's Carlos doing here?"

"So you do know him. Shall I show the man in?"

Carlos Bonnatti. A name from her past. The Santangelos and the Bonnattis went way back. Too many years . . .

"Yes. Show him in," she said.

Carlos had the Bonnatti swagger and the same ominously hooded eyes. When he walked into her office Lucky felt as if she was in some crazy time machine. Suddenly all kinds of bad memories came flooding back. Her mother's murder . . . The time she'd gone to Enzio Bonnatti for money to help finance her Vegas hotel . . .

Enzio, Carlos's father, her godfather. A man so evil there'd been only one way to deal with him . . .

She'd known Carlos all her life, and yet she didn't know him at all. Was he like his sadistic brother, Santino? Or did he take after the truly vicious Enzio?

She didn't know. She didn't want to know.

What did it matter anyway? They were both dead – and good riddance.

"Well, well, well." Carlos strolled into her office as if he owned it. "Little Lucky Santangelo, we meet again."

She wasn't about to be polite. "What the hell do *you* want?" she snapped.

He grimaced. "Nice welcome. Childhood friends, an' that's all you have to say?" He paused. "Whaddaya think I want, Lucky?"

"I've no idea, Carlos. Why don't you tell me and get out."

His hooded eyes darted around the office. The Mickey Stolli chrome and leather look was still very much in evidence.

"Nice place," he said. "Word is you're the new owner around here. Seems like you did pretty good for Gino's dumb little kid."

"Give it up, Carlos, and get the fuck out."

"Still the perfect lady, huh?"

"You wouldn't know a lady from a ten-cent hooker."

He stared at her. "Right . . ."

She contemplated buzzing Otis to throw the asshole out – but why start trouble for no reason?

"Panther owes me a million bucks," Carlos said, sitting down. "It'll be a pleasure taking your money."

Lucky stood up. "Out," she said sharply. "I'm not in the mood for blackmail."

"I'm not sure you understand," he replied, making no attempt to move.

"Oh, yes, I understand perfectly well. I know all about what was going on here before I took over. You had a deal with Eddie Kane, and Eddie stole from you. Right?"

Carlos regarded her from under drooping eyelids. For a moment an image of Enzio flashed before her. Enzio's face, just before she shot him . . .

It was self-defence. The case never even came to trial.

But still . . . his face . . .

"Get out of my office," she repeated.

"Lucky, you got it all wrong. My company performed certain services for Panther, *legitimate* services, an' in return they signed a note. Your studio owes me a million bucks. I'm here to collect."

"Panther owes you nothing."

They locked stares.

He reached into his pocket and drew out a copy of an official deal memo which he placed on her desk. "Read it," he said, standing up. "I'll be back to collect."

Without another word he walked out of the office.

Otis put his head around the door. "Everything all right?"

"Yes, Otis. Thank you."

"Who was that guy?"

"It doesn't matter."

She picked up the document and began to read. It appeared to come from a legitimate firm of lawyers in Century City.

Her eyes scanned the page. It was a legal paper stating that Panther Studios owed Bonnatti Inc a million dollars for services rendered. And it was signed by Mickey Stolli.

What services? What kind of scam was this?

She looked at the date. It was dated a month earlier.

Impossible. It couldn't be true. As Luce, she'd sat in the

outer office listening in on every conversation. She knew Eddie Kane owed the money and that Mickey had refused to accept responsibility for Panther. If this deal memo existed, how come Mickey had backed off? He must have known about it.

Something was going on. The document had to be a phony.

She called up Business Affairs and reached Teddy P. Lauden.

"Teddy," she said, "can somebody check through the files on outstanding debts? Let me know if we've got anything on Bonnatti Incorporated. If so, send it over."

Sure enough Teddy sent over the original of Bonnatti's deal memo. He attached a note saying this was a Mickey Stolli deal he wasn't aware of.

So Mickey had paid old Abe Panther back and stuck it to her at the same time.

Son of a bitch!

She had no intention of giving Carlos Bonnatti one red cent. She knew what was right and what was wrong, and there was no way she was going to give in to this.

As far as Lucky was concerned it was a matter of principle.

Chapter 82

The media bombarded them. Everywhere they went, Deena and Martin Swanson were swamped with questions from intrusive journalists.

"I can't live my life like this," Deena said icily. "I'm going away to a health spa."

"The Golden Door?" Martin asked.

"No. There's a new place in Palm Springs I hear is excellent. I need to get away, Martin. You've been honest with me and I appreciate it. Now I must be alone."

He nodded. Deena was taking this better than anticipated. He hadn't actually come right out and said he wanted a divorce, merely asked for time to make a decision. But if he were truly honest he'd admit he was quite enjoying all the publicity. It was a real ego boost to be regarded as a Don Juan. And quite frankly, it wasn't so bad for business either. Orders for his new car, the Swanson, were pouring in – and that was before they'd even presented it to the public.

A divorce. He'd never thought about it seriously before. But if Deena was prepared to let him go . . .

Not that he'd pay her half his money. She must be crazy even to contemplate that. But the lawyers would work out a fair settlement.

"So you're not coming to Detroit for the launch of the Swanson?"

"Definitely not," she replied coolly. "I'm sure you'll manage on your own."

"How long do you plan to be away?"

"Ten days or so." She gave him a long cool look before adding, "And you'll be in Detroit?"

"Yes. And then I'll fly to Los Angeles to make arrangements at Orpheus. When I get rid of Zeppo I'm putting Mickey Stolli in to run it. I'll oversee appointing the other executives while I'm there."

"Martin," she said quietly. "Promise me one thing."

"What's that?"

"Don't make a decision until I return. Or any statements. If we're going to separate, then we have to announce it together in a dignified fashion. Agreed?"

He nodded. "I wouldn't embarrass you."

"It will certainly embarrass me if you see Venus Maria while you're on the Coast. So kindly don't. When we make our decision you'll be free to do whatever you want." She paused. "It's not much to ask, is it?"

He nodded again. "As you wish."

She fixed him with her dead blue eyes. "I'm asking for your promise."

"Isn't–"

"Your *promise*, Martin."

"Very well," he said reluctantly.

"Thank you."

Upstairs in her bedroom she instructed her personal maid which clothes to pack for her trip.

"Will you be away long, Mrs Swanson?" inquired her maid.

"Just long enough."

When the maid was gone she went to her safe and selected a few pieces of jewellery to take with her. Hidden in the back was the gun she'd purchased under an assumed name six months earlier – just in case. It was always good to be prepared, although she hadn't really expected the day would come when she'd be forced to use it.

Locking herself in her bathroom she expertly loaded the weapon, clicking on the safety catch, and hid it in the bottom of her carry-on bag.

When she re-entered the bedroom, Martin was preparing for bed. He wore blue silk pyjamas and a satisfied smirk.

She stared at her errant husband. What forced him into the arms of other women? Had she been such a terrible wife? She was attractive, perfectly groomed, beautifully dressed. She loved him, looked after him, she was available for him sexually when he wanted her. What was it?

"Did you see this?" He handed her a magazine in which he was profiled. "The photo's not so good. They caught my bad side."

Who did he think he was, a movie star?

Hollywood was going to Martin Swanson's head. His publicity was taking over.

In the morning, Martin had left for the office before Deena departed. She'd told him she wished to use the Swanson jet, and it was waiting at the airport. She boarded, nodded to the captain and crew, and sat quietly in a window seat. When this was all over she decided she would redecorate. First the plane, then their New York town house, followed by their summer retreat, and then their house in Connecticut.

The plane flew her directly to Palm Springs. It was a smooth flight. She read a few magazines and slept a little.

When they arrived, there was a car and chauffeur to meet her. It took her straight to the Final Resort Health Spa.

What an aptly named place, she thought to herself. The Final Resort . . .

Emilio strutted around his old neighbourhood like a king. He'd bought himself a camel-hair coat and a white fedora with a black band. He wore the fedora gangster style, the coat flung casually over his shoulders.

To really blow everyone's mind he'd brought Rita with him. Rita, the Hollywood starlet – red hair, fine ass, and a lot of attitude.

"Wear clothes that show it all off, honey," he'd encouraged her. "I want 'em to see what I got."

"I *know* what you got," she giggled, always the flatterer.

Emilio had booked them into a hotel. He didn't fancy staying at his father's house, knowing his brothers would all try to come on to Rita. It ran in the family. But what could he do? The Sierra men were a horny bunch.

When he and Rita appeared for Sunday lunch, relatives and friends filled the house.

"Where's Venus?" they all asked when he arrived. "Isn't she coming?" Disappointment was in the air. Wasn't it enough that they had the great Emilio, fresh from Hollywood, with his beautiful starlet girlfriend?

"Venus sent me instead," he said magnanimously, shrugging off his coat. "She's kind of busy right now, but I got a few days off before I start work on my first movie."

"A movie?" shrieked one of his second cousins. "You?"

"Yeah," boasted Emilio, "a Stallone movie. I'm playin' Sly's best friend."

Rita shot him a look. She'd heard of lying, but Emilio was an expert.

As expected, his brothers were all over her. When he checked out the women they'd married he could understand why. Thank God he'd made the decision to follow

Venus to Hollywood. Thank God he'd gotten out of Brooklyn.

"I've been readin' about you," his father said, patting his swollen beer belly.

"You have?" Emilio tried to appear casual, but he *loved* being the centre of attention.

"Yeah, that *Truth an'* . . . somethin' shit. Your picture's in it."

"It was taken special," Emilio said modestly, like his photo turned up in magazines all the time.

"They pay you?" his father asked, scratching his balls – a Sierra family habit.

Trust his father to ask about money.

"Sure they paid me, Pa," he boated. "They paid me pretty good."

"So, when ya gonna put some in *my* direction?"

Emilio hadn't been planning on doing so, but since he wanted to look like a big man he took out a couple of crumpled hundred-dollar bills and handed them over. "Here's cash, Pa. There's more where that came from."

His father looked at it, was about to make a derogatory remark, changed his mind, and stuffed it in his pocket. He knew he was in luck to get anything out of Emilio. The boy had always been a cheapskate.

One by one, Emilio took the old gang aside and questioned them. "*People* magazine have asked me to write a piece," he lied. "On Venus. What do you remember about her? Like when she was a kid. What was she doing? Who was she friendly with? That kind of stuff."

"She was a good girl," said Uncle Louie.

"She was a little slut," said his wife.

"She studied hard," said one of his cousins.

"She played hooky from school all the time," said another.

"I knew her well," said a friend from school who Emilio remembered was Venus's dreaded enemy.

"We were best friends," said a girl who hadn't even been in the same grade.

Emilio pumped his brothers for information. "Who was

that greasy guy she was seeing in school? Did she make out with him? Was he her first boyfriend?"

"Yeah, I remember him," said one of his brothers. "Scrawny little fucker. I caught them necking in the kitchen one night. Hadda throw him out."

"What was his name?"

"Vinnie somethin' or other . . ." said one brother.

"Nah," corrected his older brother. "It was Tony Maglioni. He's drivin' a cab now, hangs out at the pizza parlour every Saturday night."

Rita was bored. She didn't appreciate getting pinched by Emilio's father and three brothers. She wasn't enjoying the experience. At first it had been fun. She could act like a star and tell them all about Hollywood. But now it was a drag and she wanted to leave.

"Come on, Emilio, let's go," she whined.

"Come on, Emilio, let's go," imitated one of his brothers with a sly nudge to Emilio's ribs. "Hot stuff," he whispered, "I wouldn't mind a piece of that."

"You gotta wife an' kid," reminded Emilio.

"I can wish, can't I?" drooled his brother, making sucking noises with his lips.

Emilio took Rita back to the hotel.

If he could get hold of this Tony guy maybe he'd have a story.

Martin took his plane out of New York the next day, and flew straight to Detroit ready to launch the Swanson. It seemed all the publicity linking him with Venus Maria had only helped the enormous press coverage he was receiving. If it sold more cars, why object?

It occurred to him that if he'd persuaded Venus Maria to attend, the publicity would really explode.

That would be something, except that Deena would be furious. As it was she was talking about getting half his money.

No chance. He'd already spoken to his lawyers. Deena would get a reasonable settlement and that was all.

He contemplated what it would be like to be married

470

to Venus Maria. Exciting, that was for sure. Different . . .
Stimulating . . .

He'd be sorry to lose Deena. In a way she was an asset.
But he was forty-six years old and it was time for a more
exciting life.

Martin loved being headline news.

Settled into the health spa, Deena felt perfectly calm. She
had a simple solution, and soon she would put it into
action.

She was getting closer every day.

Chapter 83

Saxon was fixing Venus Maria's hair at her home in preparation for a major shoot with the great Antonio.

"I feel like a prisoner," she complained. "I can't take a
step out of here without being stalked. It's ridiculous."

"I know," Saxon agreed sympathetically.

How could he possibly know what it was like to be
emblazoned all over the supermarket rags? Let alone on
the cover.

God! If she ever got hold of Emilio again, she'd personally strangle the traitorous son of a bitch. How dare he!
HOW DARE HE!

She'd tried to find him, but it appeared he'd run off to
hide, for all she could get was his goddamn answering
machine.

The second instalment in *Truth and Fact* was a real put-
down. A lot of crap about how she wore curlers in her
hair, walked around without any makeup, admired herself
in the mirror for hours, sometimes wore men's underwear,
and liked to swim naked. She felt as if someone had broken
into her home. It was such an intrusion.

Saxon strutted around her — moussing and blow-drying,

tossing his own mane of thick hair, which was more impressive than any of his clients'.

"Are you gay?" she asked curiously.

"No, darling, just happy," he replied, without taking a beat.

"Seriously," she demanded.

He massaged the creamy mousse into her scalp. "That's a very personal question."

Ha! Did he want to talk personal? How would *he* like to be all over the papers?

The truth was he'd probably love it!

"Well, *are* you?" she persisted.

"I don't think it's any of your business," he replied, frothing her hair with his hands.

"Come on, Saxon, tell me," she teased. "Maybe we could get it on."

"You're such a bitch."

"And so are you."

"If you must know," he said, enjoying her attention, "I swing both ways."

"I *love* that expression," she squealed, "it's so old-fashioned. Swing both ways. You know, it kind of brings back memories of the playground. Playing on the swings and roundabouts – that choice – right? What exactly does it mean? And isn't it awfully dangerous right now?"

"You ask questions nobody else would dare."

"That's why I'm me. Anyway, what *is* your preference?"

He began to laugh. "None of your business."

"Aw, come *on*," she wheedled. "If you had a choice between, well, say me and Ron, who would you choose?"

"Both of you," he said, wielding his brush.

That shut her up. Grinning, she watched him in the mirror as he attended to her hair.

Saxon had a lot of admiration for Venus Maria. Not only was she a superstar with a full work schedule, but she also found time to support causes and charities she believed in. She worked hard for AIDS and also Mothers Against Drunk Driving and the Rape Crisis Center. She

472

preferred to keep her efforts quiet so they were not construed as publicity opportunities.

"Since we're on the personal-question kick," he ventured, "what's happening with you and Martin Swanson?"

"Now you sound like Ron," she groaned. "That's all he wants to know."

"You can confide in me. Who am *I* going to tell?"

"Oh, just about every woman in Beverly Hills. Your salon is gossip heaven. Isn't that what goes on there, Saxon? Everyone talks about everybody else? It's a hotbed of scurrilous rumour!"

"I can't control it."

"That's because you love it."

He brushed against her. She glanced at his jeans in the mirror. They were almost as tightly packed as the Ken Doll's, and that was saying something.

"I bet you hear some great scandals in the salon," she pressed.

"Let's put it this way – we hear it first." He smiled proudly.

"Was everybody talking about Mickey Stolli when he got himself arrested with the hooker?"

"You could say it was a hot topic of conversation."

She laughed. "But I'm more of a topic, huh?"

"Not so much *you* as Martin Swanson. They all love Martin Swanson."

"They love his money," she corrected.

"True. They love his money *and* they love his power. To be a Hollywood Wife you have to marry a man with both those things, and apparently Martin has more than anybody." He gave a wicked laugh. "*Does* he have more than anybody, darling?"

She laughed back. "I *never* screw and tell!"

Yves, her makeup artist, arrived next, followed by two stylists and Ron, dragging the Ken Doll behind him.

The Ken Doll had on his usual skin-tight jeans, and a white fifties T-shirt, all the better to show off his muscles. He flexed for the stylists.

"He's been shooting a beer commercial — doesn't he look divine?" Ron said, establishing ownership up front.

"Divine," Venus Maria said sarcastically. "You know Saxon, don't you?"

"Do *I* know Saxon?"

"We were just discussing his sex life," Venus Maria said wickedly.

"Really?" said Ron, all interested. "And how *are* all those little thirteen-year-old schoolboys, Saxon, dear?"

Saxon shook back his mane of hair and laughed. "You've got it all wrong. That's *your* territory, Ron."

"Oh, God, there's nothing worse than bantering fags," giggled Venus Maria.

At noon the great photographer Antonio arrived, accompanied by several hard-working assistants.

"Baby!" Venus greeted him.

"*Bellissima!*" gushed Antonio.

They hugged and kissed.

Antonio was extremely famous, extremely temperamental, and extremely tight when it came to spending money. Fortunately he rarely had to put his hand into his pocket, because the magazines who assigned him to photograph the various stars always paid. *Style Wars*, for whom this shoot was taking place, didn't pay as much as other publications, but that was because *Style Wars* was way ahead of the pack. It was the magazine of the moment — the avant-garde *must* read, a combination of *Vanity Fair* and *Interview*.

Antonio prowled around her house followed by his minions, deciding where he would shoot the cover picture. Usually Venus Maria did not allow photo sessions at her home, but for Antonio and *Style Wars* she'd made an exception.

"What do you think, darling?" Antonio asked, "the bedroom? Miss Venus Maria in the centre of her bed, naked with only the black silk sheet to cover her beauty."

Venus Maria quite got off on the idea of nothing except a thin silk sheet between her and her voracious public. "Yes," she said. "I like it."

"Why not, darling? You are the big star. Glamour is everything."

"What do *you* think, Ron?" she asked, turning to her closest advisor.

"Sounds good to me," he replied, busy thinking about the surprise birthday party he'd planned for her. She was going to be twenty-six in three days' time, and he'd been planning the surprise party for six weeks. It was going to be a fantastic affair if all went according to plan.

"Imagine," Antonio said, gesturing wildly as he spoke. "*Your* body, *bellissima*, one leg exposed. Your blonde hair piled up on top of your head. And black silk up to your chin. Maybe we go wild and one breast escapes."

"No nudity," Venus said firmly. "I've never done it in photographs, and I never will."

"For Antonio, you change your mind."

For Antonio she'd do a lot of things, but she'd decided right at the beginning of her career that she would never take her clothes off for media consumption.

Not that she couldn't if she wanted to. She had beautiful breasts. Not too big. Not too small. Just perfect.

Perfect Venus Maria breasts. She smiled to herself.

Antonio described to Saxon how he wanted her hair to look.

Saxon understood perfectly. A tumble of wild curls, the hair piled on top of the head, a few tantalising strands escaping on each side.

"You'll look great, Venus," he enthused.

"Naturally she look great," Antonio announced. "Antonio – he say so."

While her hair was up in rollers, the makeup artist went to work.

Antonio checked out the clothes the stylists had brought with them, just in case he decided she should wear anything at all. He discarded everything, obviously in love with the black silk sheet idea.

In the middle of it all Martin called. Her feelings were ambiguous. Since the rush of publicity he'd been particularly cagey towards her. They'd spent one night together in the Bel Air Hotel, and apart from that he'd told her he was too busy with the Orpheus takeover, and that he felt he was being followed and had to check with his lawyers because he didn't want to give Deena cause to take him for everything he had. And then he'd returned to New York.

Understandable, but still it pissed her off. Either Martin committed himself or he didn't. She wasn't going to be the Hollywood girlfriend any longer.

"I'm in Detroit," he said, like she was anxiously awaiting news of his whereabouts.

"Really," she replied coolly.

"You sound mad."

"I *am* mad, Martin. I refuse to sit around waiting for you any longer. When you were out here we saw each other once — it's not enough. Now you've been back in New York for almost a week and I've heard nothing from you. What's happening with you and Deena?"

"It's no good talking on the phone" he said, sounding very businesslike. "I need to be with you."

"In that case you'll have to make a choice."

"I've made a choice."

"You have?"

"Yes."

"Are you going to let me in on it?"

He took a deep breath and announced, "I'm leaving Deena."

She'd been waiting months to hear him say those words, and yet when she heard them she felt a cold chill. Did she really want to be with Martin all the time? Was this the relationship of her dreams?

"Well?" he demanded impatiently. "Don't you have anything to say?"

"I'm shocked," she managed.

"Why are you shocked?"

"Because I never thought you'd do it."

"I'm doing it for you. I'll launch the Swanson, and then I'm flying out to see you."

"Are you coming here for me, or Orpheus?"

476

He conveniently forgot about his promise to Deena. She'd never find out anyway. "You, Venus. We'll be together and discuss our future."

"Sounds serious."

"I *am* serious. Very serious."

"Hmm . . . we'll see."

"Who was that?" asked Ron when she returned to her dressing room.

"You're so goddamn nosy. You know perfectly well who it was. Martin, of course."

"Ah . . . And is Superstud flying to your side?"

"Good guess."

Ron's mind starting racing. If he could arrange to have Martin at the surprise party it would really make her evening.

While she'd been on the phone, Antonio had obviously fallen in love with the Ken Doll.

"We shall put him in the background," Antonio decided, pointing in the Ken Doll's direction. "You, Venus darling, on the bed. Ken, he lean against the headboard. It will look marvellous, so . . . how you say . . . macho. Ken, unbutton the top of your jeans." He clicked his fingers for one of the stylists. "And we tear the T-shirt. Very Marlon Brando, very sixties."

"I think you mean fifties," corrected Ron, eager to score points. "Of course I wasn't born then, but *you* would know, wouldn't you?"

Antonio ignored Ron.

"Mmm . . ." murmured Saxon. "I sense trouble in paradise."

Venus Maria was primed and painted. Her platinum hair was curled and pinned atop her head, her body was smoothly covered with makeup. Clad in a brief pair of bikini panties and with nothing else but her hands to cover her modesty, she arranged herself under the black silk sheets the stylist had draped on her bed.

She knew what Antonio was after. The classic pose. One leg provocatively snaking out, while she sat up, holding the sheet to her chin, her shoulders exposed, a seductive smile. The Venus Maria look. She'd perfected it. Over the years she'd studied carefully.

"*Bellissima*, darling," cooed Antonio, peering through his lens. "And now, Ken, you move a little closer."

As Ken slouched against the wall in the background, he and Antonio experienced serious eye contact.

Hovering on the sidelines, Ron could see what was going on. Venus Maria observed his mouth go into a thin tight line, a sign of deep trouble.

Somebody put Stevie Wonder on the stereo, and the house was flooded with music.

Venus Maria knew how to make love to a camera better than anyone. She licked her lips, somehow making them fuller and more seductive. Her eyes radiated sensuality. Her expression was pure sex.

She gazed at the camera, revelling in every minute.

Chapter 84

Gino arrived in LA before Steven and Mary-Lou. Lucky took the day off and met him at the airport, taking Bobby with her.

When Gino walked through the terminal she almost didn't recognize him. Where was the Gino strut? Where was that famous Santangelo grin? Where was Gino the Ram?

Oh, God, was it possible that Gino was getting old? Her father, her wonderful, vital father, who'd always been so much younger and stronger than everyone else?

She hugged him. "Hey, what's going on?"

He hugged her back. "I told you, kid. It's finally gettin' to me."

"What?" she asked anxiously.

"Old age, I guess. I'm wearin' out, kid. I'm wearin' out."

She was dismayed to hear Gino talk that way. "You, Gino. Never!" she said.

"Hey, Grandpa!" cried Bobby, clamouring for attention.

"Hey, Bobby!" cried Gino, hugging his grandson.

Boogie drove them to the beach house while Bobby chatted excitedly about his school in London and what he'd been doing.

"My friend is here, Grandpa," Bobby announced proudly. "I told him he couldn't come to the airport 'cause I had to see my grandpa first."

"That's *right*," agreed Gino, "and don't you forget it. I'm gonna teach you a thing or two this trip."

Bobby couldn't have been more thrilled. "Yes, Grandpa. What?"

"I'm gonna teach you how to be a Santangelo."

"He's not a Santangelo. He's a Stanislopoulos," Lucky pointed out.

"Bullshit," Gino retorted. "Bobby don't look like a Stanislopoulus, he looks exactly like a Santangelo."

She laughed. "You're right. Bullshit!"

"Thank you."

They grinned at each other.

"So . . . what have you been up to?" she asked.

"Aw, nothing," Gino said. "I sit around the apartment, take a walk. Sometimes I put a poker game together."

She hated to see her father inactive. Since he'd sold out the bulk of his companies he didn't seem to be interested in business any more.

"You know what we should do?" she suggested.

"Yeah. What?"

"Build another hotel. We did it with the Mirage and the Magiriano, but they don't belong to us any more. Why don't we build a new hotel and call it the Panther? We'll make it bigger than the Mirage, better than the Magiriano. What do you say?"

"I wouldn't build another hotel if you paid me," he said, shaking his head.

"Why not? You loved it. You were one of the first in Vegas."

"That was a long, long time ago. It's a different world today."

"It's not so different. We'd do it together. I'd *love* to build a new hotel."

"Yeah, you're gonna fit it in between doin' studio deals, huh?"

"I've got a lot of energy."

"Don't even talk about it. I'm too old."

Gino — admitting he was old. Something was wrong somewhere.

She waited until they were back at the house and Bobby had raced off to play with his school friend before mentioning Carlos Bonnatti.

"He came to see you?" Gino asked, concerned. "Did he threaten you in any way?"

"Are you *kidding*? I wouldn't allow that asshole to threaten me. I know this is a phony debt, and I'm not paying it."

"You know what, kid? Pay it, get him off your back. We don't need more trouble with the Bonnattis. There's been enough over the years."

She was surprised. "I can't believe this is *you* talking, Gino. Pay a debt we don't owe? Let the Bonnattis get the better of us? *No way*."

"Life's too short to worry about these things. You got the money — pay him."

She narrowed her black eyes and stared her father down. "I said no way."

Something had to be done about Gino. He was in a slump. She had to come up with a brilliant way to snap him out of it.

After playing with Bobby for a while Gino decided to take a nap. Lucky went straight to the phone and called Paige. A maid answered.

"Is Mrs Wheeler there?" Lucky asked, hoping she was.

"One moment please."

When Paige picked up the phone Lucky was delighted. "Hi, this is Lucky Santangelo. How *are* you?" she asked.

"Lucky," exclaimed Paige. "How nice to hear from you.

480

Congratulations. I'm thrilled about the Panther deal, although Ryder's not so thrilled. He loved doing business with the wonderful Mickey Stolli. But I hear you're planning good things."

"I hope so," Lucky said. "I want to make films that give women a chance to show their strength."

"You will," Paige said warmly. "You always manage to do whatever you set your heart on. When your father and I were together, Gino never stopped boasting about you."

Lucky was pleasantly surprised. "Really?"

"Always," Paige assured her.

"Can we meet?" Lucky asked. "I'm not into doing lunch, but maybe if it's convenient for you we could have a drink or something."

"Fine," said Paige. "I'd love to see you. When?"

"As soon as possible."

Chapter 85

The South of France was glorious, hot sunshine, beautiful women, wonderful restaurants, and a carefree atmosphere.

Lennie was miserable. All he could think about was Lucky. He sat around the pool at Eden Rock watching Brigette and Nona. The two girls were having a great time. They'd met plenty of friends and spent most of the day either in the pool or water-skiing. He only ever saw them for lunch, when they joined him and his friends, Jess and Matt Traynor, who'd flown out to keep him company.

Jess, his best friend, gave him a lot of good advice. "You're being very childish about this whole thing, Lennie," she scolded. "Lucky's *not* your average woman. You knew that when you married her. You love her. You want to be with her. And now you're playing hurt little boy because she bought a studio without asking your permission. Big deal!"

"She should have told me," he said stubbornly.

"Why?" Jess wrinkled her snub nose. "It was a surprise. For you."

Nobody understood. "Not for me, for her. She gets off on being in charge."

"No," Jess argued. "She did it to make you happy because you were always bitching about your contract, the movie, and the people you had to work with. She thought it would be fun. And let's face it – she can certainly afford it."

He tried to explain. "It's like she's buying me, Jess. You understand what I'm saying?"

"What kind of crap is that? You're her husband, for crissake – give the girl a break!"

"I'm trying."

"How?"

"By staying away."

Jess gave him a look. They knew each other too well to get away with lying.

"Lucky Santangelo is the best thing that ever happened to you," she said firmly. "Wake up and realize it before it's too late."

He grimaced. "Hey – you and Matt make it work pretty good. Howdja do it?"

"When you get married you commit yourself," Jess answered seriously. "I failed once – so did you. When you do it a second time you know exactly what you're getting into. I *want* to be with Matt because I love him. Don't you love Lucky?"

Yeah, he loved Lucky. He loved her more than anything in the world.

But could he live with her? That was another question.

"There's one thing about you, Lennie," Jess said, sighing with exasperation.

"What?"

"You're pretty damn good at screwing up your life."

"Thanks!"

"Think about what I'm saying. Did Lucky do such a terrible thing? It wasn't like she ran off and slept with another guy, for God's sake!"

482

"She lied to me."

Jess was getting impatient. "She lied to you for *you*, asshole. Why don't you at least go see her, and maybe the two of you can work it out. I hate to see it end like this. You're both too stubborn – that's the problem."

Later, alone in his hotel room, Lennie thought about what Jess had said. Yeah, he was stubborn. And so was Lucky. But it didn't mean they couldn't talk.

Jess was right. He loved Lucky – and he wasn't about to give up on their relationship. It was about time he did something about it.

"You're fired," Lucky said.

Eddie twitched. "Why?"

"Because I don't approve of the way you do business."

Eddie couldn't believe he was getting canned by a woman. "Oh, you've been here five minutes and you don't approve of the way *I* do business, huh?" he said nastily.

"Eddie, I *know* what's been going on around here."

"Hey, hey, hey, no big deal. I've been offered a job at Orpheus."

"Then I suggest you take it."

"I'm packing up today."

"Oh, and do me a favour."

"What's that?"

"When your drug dealer arrives, the lovely Miss Le Paul, give her a message from me, will you? Tell her if she ever sets foot on this lot again she's gonna find her ass in jail."

Eddie glared and twitched and left her office.

Later Lucky met with Paige. She was such a vibrant woman, full of life and fun. Lucky could certainly understand why Gino missed her.

Paige ordered a Campari and soda before settling back. "You look wonderful, Lucky," she said. "Hollywood agrees with you."

"Thanks. You never change, Paige."

Paige fluffed out her copper-coloured hair. "I try to keep it all together. How's little Bobby?"

"Absolutely great."

"And Lennie?"

"The same." She wasn't about to spread the word on their separation. "By the way, guess who's out here?"

"Who?" said Paige, knowing full well.

"Gino. He's staying at the beach with me and Bobby."

Paige sipped her Campari. "He is?"

"He's getting older, Paige."

"Ah, Gino, he'll never be old," Paige said, smiling warmly.

"Without you he's *definitely* getting older."

Paige fiddled with a heavy gold bracelet. "It wasn't me that stopped seeing him," she said. "It was the other way around."

"I guess he had to have you to himself. *You* know Gino."

Paige continued to smile. "He always *was* greedy."

Lucky got right to it. "So, are you leaving Ryder or what?"

"Is that what you're here to find out?"

"It's a pretty good reason, isn't it?"

Paige attracted the waiter's attention and ordered a second drink. "Did Gino send you?"

"He doesn't know I'm here. He'd kill me if he thought I was interfering."

"Ah yes, he would indeed."

"So?"

"You Santangelos are so pushy . . ."

"Think about it, Paige. Will you do me that favour?"

"I'll think about it, Lucky."

"That's all I need to hear."

Chapter 86

Deena hired the car a couple of days before she needed it. It was a sedan. A Ford. Dark brown. Ordinary.

The girl behind the rental desk would never remember

her. Deena wore a long black wig, dark glasses, jeans, and a denim jacket. Her own mother would not have recognized her.

She produced a phony driver's licence with the appropriate pictures attached, and hired the car.

"How long will you need it?" the girl asked, chewing gum and daydreaming about her truck driver boyfriend.

"A week or so," Deena said, trying to disguise her accent.

"OK." The girl behind the desk couldn't have cared less. "Sign here."

Deena wondered if it was necessary to bother with the disguise. Probably not. But she had every detail of her plan worked out, and there would be no trails leading back to her.

Once the car was hired she drove to an underground parking lot, collected a ticket, and left it there. Also parked in the lot was the silver Cadillac she was using supplied by the Last Resort.

Getting into the Cadillac, she drove to Saks, entered the ladies' room, removed her wig, dark glasses, and denim jacket, and emerged as Deena Swanson.

After making a few minor purchases, she headed back to the health spa in the Cadillac.

The Ford could take her anywhere she wished to go, and nobody could ever connect it to her.

Her next step was to use it.

Chapter 87

When Ron so desired he could be incredibly organized. His plans for Venus Maria's surprise twenty-sixth birthday party were proceeding full tilt. The trick was keeping it a surprise. But he'd personally invited every guest and sworn them to secrecy. And then, to be absolutely sure, he'd sent them a discreet little follow-up card, beautifully printed on Tiffany stationery with *Be There. Keep your mouth shut!* engraved on it.

He'd invited three hundred guests. Everyone from Cooper Turner and the other Panther stars to Mickey Stolli and his merry band of executives. Of course he'd invited them before he knew of the upheaval about to take place at Panther.

Now he'd also invited Lucky Santangelo, who said she'd be delighted to attend.

The cake had been ordered, a huge three-tiered affair with Venus Maria's image on the top tier, and fake records hanging from the sides with the names of her hits.

The icing on the cake was to be Martin Swanson. If he produced Martin for her, it would make her evening.

Ron was throwing the party in the tented back garden of his home. He'd arranged to have exotic flowers, soul food, three different live groups, and a discotheque. All of Venus Maria's favourite things. Mixed up in the guest list would be her dancers, personal staff, friends, and people she didn't know that well but might like to know better.

Unfortunately, he'd made the mistake of inviting Emilio. He'd issued the invitation long before her brother's scummy revelations.

Surely the dumb brother wouldn't have the nerve to turn up?

No. Ron didn't even consider it a possibility.

To make sure everybody had a good time he'd also invited twenty beautiful girls, and twenty good-looking boys to keep the husbands and wives of Hollywood happy.

The boys had been rounded up by Ken. He'd invited young actors, friends, and the best-looking male models in town.

"Try and make sure half of them are straight," Ron had instructed.

"You want I should personally test them?" Ken had replied.

Bitch! Ron had shaken his head in exasperation. "Never mind."

The girls he'd taken care of himself. He'd contacted

Madame Loretta, who without a doubt had the most beautiful supply of girls in town. "For once they won't have to put out," he'd told the dear madam. "Just dance, have a good time and look utterly gorgeous."

There was nothing like beautiful people to make a party go with a bang. And Venus Maria would adore the underlying humour of having the hookers mixing with the wives.

Ron had elected Cooper Turner as his co-conspirator as far as getting Venus Maria to the party was concerned.

"At least if she thinks she's going out with you she'll look fabulous," Ron had explained. "I wouldn't care to put up with the wrath of Madame if she walked in here not looking her best. As it is, I've bought her a divine new Gaultier outfit as a birthday present. She can change when she arrives."

The party was on Monday. Only two days to go. It was difficult keeping the secret – but he'd kept it this long, what difference did another two days make?

Warner Franklin marched up to the front door of Johnny Romano's Hancock Park mansion and rang the bell.

One of his entourage answered. He didn't recognize Warner as the six-foot black woman Johnny had been frolicking around with recently. All he saw was a very tall uniformed cop.

"Mr Romano," she said, all business.

"He's not available," replied the gofer.

Warner could be very stern when the occasion called for it. "Do I have to come back with a warrant?"

The gofer shifted uncomfortably. "What's it about?"

"That's for Mr Romano to know. If you value your job you'd better bring him down here."

The gofer hurried off, muttering under his breath. Five minutes later he returned with Johnny. Handsome Johnny. Sloe-eyed Johnny. Sexy, macho, and son of a bitch Johnny.

To Warner's annoyance, he didn't recognize her.

"Yeah?" he said. He was clad in a terry-cloth robe, with several gold chains jostling for position around his neck.

His long hair curled over his collar. Two bodyguards hovered in the background.

She remembered what he was like in bed and she wanted him.

Removing her large black sunglasses she stared at him. "I've been trying to reach you," she said. "You're impossible to get hold of."

Recognition dawned. "Holy shit!" he exclaimed. "It's you! Get an eyeful of the uniform!"

Warner knew there was something about a uniform that turned some men on. That's why she kept hers. Obviously Johnny was one of them.

"Why haven't you returned my calls?" she demanded.

"Honey, who knew you called?" He waved his arms vaguely in the air. "Hey, Chuck – did Warner call me?"

"Dunno, Johnny. I'll take a peek at your messages."

Johnny couldn't help grinning. He admired her balls, coming to his front door like it was her right. "I'd ask you in, but I'm . . . entertaining," he said.

She wanted to let him know she wasn't just another pass-in-the-night groupie. "When *can* I see you?" she pressed. "I'm through trying to reach you on the phone."

He thought quickly. There wasn't much going on in his life. Upstairs he had blonde twins rolling around on his bed. They would do for tonight, but after that . . .

"Tell you what, babe – I'm goin' to a big party Monday night. I'll take you with me. How's that?"

"Yes," said Warner.

"You got it," said Johnny, remembering her incredible tits.

Warner was satisfied.

He stretched out his hand and fingered the front of her uniform. "Whaddya say – maybe next time we stay in you'll bring the uniform, huh?"

She nodded. "Maybe."

Johnny was satisfied.

"Gimme your address. I'll have a limo pick you up. Eight o'clock Monday night. Put on something sexy."

"Yes," Warner said.

"Yes," Johnny agreed.

Chapter 88

In his Century City penthouse Carlos Bonnatti began to brood. Lucky Santangelo . . . treating him like shit . . . making him wait for money that was rightfully his. Fuck her, and fuck her father, Gino. The Santangelos had always thought they were better than everybody else. If it wasn't for that goddamn family . . .

He remembered growing up and Enzio complaining about Gino. *That lousy son of a bitch. Thinks he's smarter than everybody else. Doesn't want to get into drugs and hooking. Thinks just 'cause he takes money for loan-sharking and skims the casinos clean, he's a good guy. Fuck him. I'm gonna show him a thing or two.*

When Enzio was murdered by the Santangelo bitch, Carlos had backed off. He didn't care to get involved in the family grudges. He wanted to run his business his own way. And when Santino vowed revenge, Carlos said to himself – *Fuck Santino, he's a moron.* And Carlos, had distanced himself from his brother. Eventually Santino had gotten himself killed too – but Santino was always a dumb schmuck, more interested in pussy than anything else.

Carlos had his priorities straight. Money came first. Money came before everything. And now the Santangelo bitch was going head-to-head with him.

It was time he laid down the rules.

Twenty-four hours, bitch. And if you don't pay . . .

Chapter 89

Although the Beverly Hills Hotel was one of the most luxurious hotels in the world, it was not quite the same as living in one's own mansion. Mickey Stolli soon discovered that.

He'd installed himself in a bungalow. But what was the use of having a kitchen, when there was nobody to cook your meals?

Room service and he soon became very close indeed.

On Saturday, Tabitha insisted on visiting him.

"I wanna go out by the pool, Daddy. There's a lot of cute boys by the pool," she whined.

"There's no cute boys at the Beverly Hills Hotel," Mickey said flatly. "Just old producers."

"Like you, Daddy?"

"I'm not a producer."

Tabitha wore baggy shorts and a floppy shirt. Once they got out by the pool she removed both items of clothing, revealing a much too small bikini for such a young girl. He hadn't realized his daughter was developing so fast. If it wasn't for the glint of steel around her teeth you would never know she was only thirteen.

"Put your shirt on," he scolded.

"I wanna sunbathe, Daddy."

"I *said* cover yourself."

Tabitha made a face and reached for her shirt. "When are you coming home?"

"Who says I'm coming home?"

"Mommy says you are."

"She did, did she?"

"Yes, Mommy says you'll never stick it on your own."

"Does she want me back?"

"I dunno."

He waved to a few acquaintances as he and Tabitha

walked to the restaurant by the pool and settled at an outdoor table.

Tabitha decided to order everything on the menu. Mickey made her settle on a club sandwich and chocolate malt, while he ordered Eggs Benedict.

"Can I have my Sweet Sixteen at Orpheus?" Tabitha asked, eyes lustfully following a Mexican busboy.

"Who knows?" Mickey said irritably. "Jesus, what are you asking me now for? Your sixteenth birthday isn't for another three years."

"I'm planning ahead," his daughter announced. "Mommy says we always should. She taught me to do that."

Tabitha stared at the busboy.

He stared back.

This was Beverly Hills: there was no chance of them ever getting together.

"Did you know that when Grandfather dies he's leaving me a whole lot of money?" Tabitha asked.

Mickey perked up. "Really?"

"All the money he got for the studio he's divided between me, Aunt Primrose's kids, and Inga. When Grandfather dies, we get everything. *Everything*, Daddy. I'm gonna be like *really* rich."

"Good. You can keep me in your old age."

"You can keep yourself. You're rich."

Not as rich as he'd like to be. "What about your mother?" he asked curiously.

"I dunno. She gets interest or something until I'm twenty-one, and then *I* get everything. I'm gonna buy a Porsche, a Corvette, and a red Thunderbird. Whaddya think, Dad?"

Just like her mother, spending it before she had it.

Tabitha grabbed a bread roll and stuffed it into her mouth. "What's Orpheus like? Is it as nice as Panther? What movie stars work there? Tom Cruise? How about Matt Dillon? Can I meet Rob Lowe?"

"I haven't even signed the contract yet," he said irritably. "Gotta wait till Zeppo gets out. He's making noises."

"What noises?"

Was it his imagination, or did the busboy wink at her? "Threatening to sue, contract disputes. As soon as it's all sorted out I'll be there."

Tabitha fidgeted in her seat. "Can I come visit? What movies will you make?"

"Leave me alone," Mickey said gloomily. "I'm not in the mood."

"You've gotta be nice to me," Tabitha said, chewing on a hangnail. "I'm a deprived child now my parents are separated." She slurped her milkshake. "Can we go to a movie? Can we go to Westwood? Can we go to Tower Records?"

"Can *you* shut up?"

Was this what it would be like every Saturday?

Mickey had a feeling he was going to learn to dread weekends.

Warner phoned Abigaile. "I did as you suggested," she said excitedly.

"I told you it would work," replied Abigaile.

Warner giggled. "He was *really* surprised to see me."

"I'm sure he was."

"He's invited me to a party on Monday."

"How nice."

"You know, Abby," Warner said warmly, "I really misjudged you. The things Mickey told me. He made me think you were the bitch of Beverly Hills! God knows, when I was a traffic cop I met enough of them. If only I'd known the truth about you — I would *never* have had an affair with your husband."

"I understand, dear," said Abigaile soothingly. "After all, Mickey can be very persuasive. Perhaps we'll lunch one day. The Bistro Gardens, wouldn't that be nice?"

"The Bistro Gardens? I've never been there," said Warner. "What a treat!"

"Good," said Abigaile. "Call me anytime."

She put down the phone and nodded to herself. Better

to be friends with the enemy. It was an advantage. And Abigaile always enjoyed having an advantage.

"We're going to a party," Madame Loretta informed a select group of her special girls.

"For entertaining purposes?" asked Texas, a delicate blonde twenty-two-year-old.

"No, you don't have to entertain," replied Madame Loretta. "This is strictly a pleasure trip." She turned to Leslie. "The perfect opportunity for you, my dear."

"What kind of opportunity?" Leslie asked listlessly. Since Eddie had left her, she'd had no desire to do anything.

"The perfect opportunity to find you a husband," said Madame Loretta. "The place will be overflowing with rich successful men, and, Leslie, dear, much as I'd like you to resume working for me, I'd sooner see you settled. You're what I call the marrying kind."

Leslie nodded and wondered how Eddie was managing without her. He'd been so mean to her and yet she couldn't help thinking about him.

"Monday night," Madame Loretta told the assembled girls. "Make sure we all look our very best. We're going to the hottest party in town!"

Chapter 90

Being surrounded by her family – Gino and Bobby, Steven and Mary-Lou with Carioca Jade – made Lucky feel good, although it wasn't the same as Lennie being there. Having everyone around only made her miss him more.

She wondered where he was, what he was doing, if he was happy.

Things at the studio seemed to be falling into place. *Bombshell* had already been rewritten and the new script was excellent. Venus Maria had read it and loved it. Montana Grey visited the studio and met with both of them. She was an interesting woman, tall, smart, and most of all extremely talented. Lucky had hired her to direct the film.

She'd read two other scripts she liked and put them into development. And she'd also come across a black comedy which would take Susie Rush away from the sweet-little-thing roles she was so tired of playing.

Susie was interested, but she'd already made a commitment on another project at Orpheus.

"Is the deal signed?" Lucky had asked, and finding out it wasn't had offered Susie more money and extra points in the picture.

There was nothing like the mention of extra money to change an actress's mind. Besides, this was the opportunity Susie had been waiting for. She said yes.

In the short time she'd been at Panther Lucky felt she'd accomplished plenty.

One of the things she'd attended to was reviewing the footage of *Macho Man*. If Lennie was prepared to work on it again, it was certainly salvageable.

Maybe she should call him.

No.

Maybe *he* should call her.

Just as she'd predicted, *Motherfaker* was failing dismally at the box-office. Although there'd been a rush of business the first weekend, word of mouth soon killed it stone dead.

Johnny Romano was not a happy superstar.

The weekend came as a welcome break. After lunch on Saturday, Steven suggested they take a walk along the beach.

"I wanna come too," announced Bobby.

"No. I want to be with your mommy alone," Steven explained. "I never get to see her. This is our one opportunity."

Lucky grabbed his arm. "That's not true, big brother."

"Oh yes it is!"

"I'm here now."

"That's why we're taking a walk."

They set off along the beach.

"I'm so glad you and Mary-Lou could make it. Not to mention Carioca Jade — she's totally gorgeous!" Lucky squeezed his arm. "You're right, Steven, we don't get to see enough of each other."

"She's admitting it!"

"OK, Father of the Year, what else have you been up to?"

"More to the point, what have *you* been up to?" He studied her for a moment. "I heard about your undercover scam. You're really something, Lucky."

"Yeah," she said ruefully. "And look where it got me. I gained a studio and lost a husband."

Steven stopped walking. "What does *that* mean?"

"Haven't you head? Lennie went berserk when he found out what I'd done. He's not thrilled about my owning Panther. In fact . . ." She hesitated. "We're talking divorce."

Steven shook his head. "No way."

"I'm afraid so."

"Your problem is you always expect to get your own way. No roadblocks."

"Oh, like you've known me all my life, right?"

"Hey — it hasn't been that long, but I feel real close to you. Having you as a half-sister is an experience."

"Yeah. You too. Remember when we first met? The elevator?"

He couldn't help grinning. "Ah, the famous elevator. When we were trapped during the big New York blackout. Two strangers with nothing in common — little did we know . . ."

"I was pissed off about Gino coming back into the country from his tax exile. And you were *really* uptight!"

"Yeah, and you were a crazy one. There we were, stuck in the dark, didn't even know each other, and all you could talk about was sex — and I'm thinking to myself — who is this insane woman I'm trapped with?"

She laughed ruefully. "That was when I was wild and young."

"Hey, Lucky — nothing's changed — you're still the same pain in the ass!"

She gazed at him earnestly. "Is it such a terrible thing I've done to Lennie?"

"Well . . . it's not exactly sharing a relationship, is it? Mary-Lou taught me that to make a marriage work you have to do things together. Confide in each other. Don't hold back."

"So you're saying I shouldn't have surprised Lennie with Panther? I should have told him, and let him be part of it."

"That's it, kid."

"Steven! You're beginning to sound just like Gino!"

"Not such a bad thing."

"Can you imagine growing up with Gino as a father? Do you realize how dull and boring most people's lives are? And I had Gino — the most exciting father in the world."

"Sorry I missed out."

"You've got him now. He loves you, Steven." She reached up and kissed him. "And so do I."

"Mutual, kid."

"*Stop* calling me kid!"

They resumed their walk.

"Do you think Lennie will come back?" she asked wistfully.

"For sure."

"How do you know?"

"Because you're you — and no guy's gonna walk away from you."

She grinned. "Thank you, Steven. Just what I wanted to hear."

"I'm a lawyer. I give good advice."

"Am I about to get some?"

"Not that you'll listen."

"What?"

"When Lennie comes back, tell him you'll sell the goddamn studio if that's what he wants."

"Hey, hey, hey — hold on — I'm not about to become the little woman at home."

"Lucky — give marriage a chance. There's nothing *wrong* with sharing. Remember that."

"I'll try."

Back at the house Carioca Jade gurgled in her cot, Mary-Lou sunbathed, and Gino slept, while Bobby dragged buckets full of sand up from the beach and dumped them on the deck.

Miko gave Lucky a pained look.

"I told Mr Bobby not to bring the sand up, but he informed me you gave him permission."

"No big deal, Miko," she replied casually. "It's a weekend. Let him have fun."

"If you say so, Madame."

Miko certainly wasn't enjoying this influx of house guests. But she was loving every minute.

"We're flying back to America," Lennie said.

"What?" Brigette jumped with surprise. "We've only been here a short while. Why are we leaving?"

"Don't you want to see Lucky and Bobby?"

"Wow, I'd love to, but I thought you and Lucky weren't talking."

"You know something?" Lennie said. "Life's too short. It's about time we tried to work it out."

Brigette nodded happily.

"OK, so you and Nona get packed, and I'll take care of the arrangements. Not a word. I want to surprise Lucky, OK?"

The call came at noon on Sunday. Lucky picked up the phone as she sat by the pool. Carlos Bonnatti's low, grating voice was unmistakable.

"Pay up, bitch," he said. "I'm tired of waiting. I'm giving you twenty-four hours. If I don't get my money by then — you're in deep trouble. The Santangelos have fucked with the Bonnattis long enough, an' now it's time for retribution. So pay, bitch, or you *know* what's gonna happen."

She didn't say a word. She replaced the receiver and glanced over at Gino. He seemed so relaxed lying in a beach chair, his head back catching the sun, Bobby playing nearby.

Screw Carlos Bonnatti and his threats.

Lucky Santangelo wasn't intimidated by him or anyone else.

She could handle it. She'd think of a way.

Chapter 91

Tony Maglioni was a handsome, slick-haired, big-nosed hood who sat in the neighbourhood pizza parlour and held court. Emilio made his entrance dragging Rita behind him.

"What are we doing in this piss palace?" Rita asked in disgust.

"Securing my future," Emilio replied, wondering where she'd learned such a colourful turn of phrase. "So try and be nice to everybody, 'cause we're gonna score big."

Rita scowled. She was fed up with being nice to everybody. She'd thought that when she'd finally arrived in Hollywood she'd left all the old neighbourhoods behind. Especially Brooklyn.

Vaguely Emilio remembered Tony, even though the guy was younger than him.

"Yo, Tony!" he called out. "Emilio Sierra."

Tony was no slouch in the remembering-names department. He leaped up from the table. "Emilio, my man. How ya doin'?"

"Found myself in town. Didn't wanna miss seein' ya," said Emilio.

Getting a first-hand look at Tony was bringing it all back to him. Venus Maria had liked this guy a lot. She'd had a real schoolgirl crush, trailed him for months, and eventually nailed him in the kitchen one evening when everyone was out.

"I hear you're drivin' a cab now," said Emilio. "Takin' over Manhattan, huh?"

Tony laughed. "Yeah, I drive a cab. I part own it, y'know? An' I got a few other things goin' on the side. I do OK. An' you, Emilio — what's happenin' with you?"

Emilio shrugged modestly. "I live out in Hollywood, an' like I'm doin' a movie. Playin' Sly Stallone's best friend."

Tony was duly impressed. So was his girlfriend, a frizzy-haired miniskirted bimbo with cross-eyes and nice tits.

Rita gave a disgusted sigh. What was with Emilio and this Sly shit he kept coming out with?

"Mind if we join you?" said Emilio.

"Sit down, sit down," replied Tony, anxious to impress. "This is *the* pizza place. I gotta piece of the action." He thrust a greasy slice of pizza at Emilio. "Eat. Enjoy."

Emilio sat down, pulling a reluctant Rita into the chair next to him.

"Yeah, well, I always knew you was gonna be a bigshot," Emilio replied, gingerly biting into a stale piece of pepperoni. "No way Tony Maglioni wasn't goin' places."

Tony nodded. This Emilio was a smart guy. "So," he smirked, "how's your sister?"

Emilio smirked back — it was all-guys-together time.

"She's doin' pretty damn good."

"Yeah, little Virginia . . ." mused Tony.

"You two used to go together, right?"

"Well." Tony gestured expansively. "I took her out a few times. She was a wild kid."

"Bet you didn't think she was gonna become a big friggin' movie star, huh?"

Tony threw back his head and laughed. "Who would have guessed?"

"Ya know, if ya ever come out to Hollywood," Emilio said, laying the bait, "Venus an' me — we got a big house there. You could come visit us, she'd love to see ya. Talks about you a lot."

Tony looked eager. "Yeah?"

His girlfriend leaned forward. "He ain't goin' nowhere without me," she announced.

"Ya wanna shut up?" said Tony, turning on her viciously. "You wanna keep your mouth tightly closed? We're havin' man talk here."

Rita wasn't about to take that. "Emilio," she said. "Let's get out of here."

Emilio didn't say a word. He kicked her under the table, warning her to be quiet.

"You know," he continued, speaking to Tony, "Venus never married. I gotta feelin' she's still hankerin' after you. In fact I know."

"Me?" Tony grinned, exhibiting two crooked front teeth — the only flaw on his handsome face.

"Well, you gotta admit — you two were pretty tight for a while."

Tony gave a dirty laugh. "Nobody tighter!"

His girlfriend frowned. "Tony!" she complained. "Tell the man we're gettin' married. Go on, tell him!"

Tony turned on her again. This was his opportunity, and he was taking it. "You know what, baby? I just broke the engagement."

Chapter 92

What did you do with the million dollars, Eddie Kane?

He asked himself that question every morning when he awoke. It was a difficult one to answer. All he knew was that he was broke. No money in the bank. No money in his pocket.

Surely he couldn't have snorted the whole bankroll?

No. He'd had expenses. There was the house, a closet

full of designer clothes, marrying Leslie, his prized Maserati. A man had to spend to make it big.

What did you do with the million dollars, Eddie Kane?

The question haunted him. Since he'd dumped Leslie he'd been on a downward spiral. Most nights he spent over at Arnie and Frankie's house, where there was always a party going on. The drugs were plentiful and so were the girls.

And yet . . . none of them compared with Leslie.

He thought about her a lot. Her wide eyes, luscious body, open friendly smile.

Shit, man. She was a goddamn hooker. He'd been right to dump her.

Maybe.

But now he wanted her back, only he couldn't figure out a way to go about it and still save face.

Maybe cocaine would help him find an answer.

Snort enough and he could come up with an answer to almost anything.

Deena established a routine at the health spa. She was svelte and slim, her body pampered with the most expensive lotions and creams. In fact, she was in peak condition and really didn't need to be at the health spa at all. But that wasn't the point.

Every morning she would swim a few lengths in the outdoor pool, have a leisurely massage, and then partake of a light lunch in the dining room. After that she made sure she disappeared into her private suite until the next morning.

A routine. Establish a routine. That was the most important thing of all. She avoided contact with the other women staying there, barely spoke to the staff, and kept herself to herself.

Naturally, everyone knew who she was.

Monday morning the new edition of *Truth and Fact* hit the stands. On the front page there was a giant colour photograph of Venus Maria and Martin strolling in the grounds of the Bel Air Hotel, gazing at each other and holding hands.

SECRET RENDEZVOUS FOR LOVERS! blazoned the headlines.

Deena stared at the photograph for a while, and knew for sure she'd waited long enough.

"Hey, yo, Dennis! It's your friend Emilio, back in town."

Hang out the flags, Dennis thought sourly. Was there no getting rid of the guy?

"What you got for me?" he asked.

"What *haven't* I got for you?" Emilio replied arrogantly. "I got the real goods this time. I got her first make-out with a guy an' *all* the details."

"Who's the boyfriend?"

"Fuck you!"

"We can't print the story if we don't know his name."

"I'll give you the story an' *then* I'll give you the name. After I've gotten my money, of course." Emilio was getting smart in his old age.

"What's the matter? Don't you trust us by now?" Dennis complained.

"I don't trust nobody," Emilio said contemptuously.

"How do I know this is genuine?"

"Am I selling magazines for you, or what?" Emilio demanded in disgust. "Do I have to go through a third degree every time I give you somethin'?"

"Your *sister* is selling us magazines," Dennis pointed out. "Without her you got nothin', mate."

"Shit!" Emilio said, "maybe I should go to the *Enquirer*. Could be they'll treat me better."

Dennis sighed wearily. "OK, let's meet," he said. "I'll listen to the details and we'll arrange a price."

Triumphantly Emilio hung up.

Rita was primping in the bathroom mirror. She appeared to have moved into his apartment – her stuff was everywhere. He hadn't noticed how it happened, but it *had* happened.

Emilio didn't really mind. He'd never had a girl live with him before, and Rita was pretty.

"Your sister's mad as hell," she said, walking into the bedroom.

"How do *you* know?"

"'Cause I played your answering machine. I heard her. She's steaming."

"She'll get over it. In fact . . . You know something? I got a little treat for you tonight, baby."

"What's that?" she asked, hoping it wasn't his body.

"I'm gonna take you to meet Venus. Her fag friend Ron is throwing a surprise birthday party for her."

"Oh, yeah?" Rita sneered sarcastically. "She'll *surely* want to see *you*."

"I was invited," Emilio said cockily.

"When?" Rita asked, full of suspicion.

"A while ago. You gotta remember I'm her brother. Of course she'll expect me there."

"So? All the more reason for her to be mad."

He hated it when a woman had something to say. His father had been right. Women were put on earth for three reasons — cooking, cleaning and fucking. End of story.

"Whadda I care? I wanna go to the party, don't you?"

Rita's eyes gleamed. "Is it a big party?"

"Big enough."

Rita nodded. Try and keep her away! "Whatever you say, Emilio."

On Monday Deena followed her usual routine. After lunch she vanished to her room. Once there, she made her preparations. She took out her long black wig, the denim outfit, and finally she removed her gun from its hiding place.

Very soon she would slip out – unnoticed – get into the Cadillac, drive to the parking lot where she'd left the Ford, transfer into it, and drive straight to Los Angeles.

Tonight she was going to kill Venus Maria.

Chapter 93

Ron surveyed the scene at his house. There were people running around everywhere. It was total chaos.

He turned to Ken. "I hope she's going to appreciate it," he wailed. "They're wrecking my bougainvillaea!"

"She will," Ken assured him. "It'll be wonderful."

"It can't be just wonderful," Ron fretted. "It has to be *the* party of the year."

"It will be."

"Do you really think so?" Ron was a nervous wreck. It had taken so much planning and time. The good news was that he'd located Martin Swanson in Detroit, and Martin had promised to fly in a day early to surprise Venus at her party.

"Will there be any photographers present?" Martin had asked, remembering his promise to Deena.

"Absolutely not!" Ron had said. "This is a private affair. We might have one of our own photographers, but I'll make sure he has instructions not to photograph you and Venus together."

"Excellent," Martin said. He'd just been shown the new edition of *Truth and Fact*. When Deena saw it, there was going to be even more trouble. But still . . . He wasn't going to have to answer to Deena for much longer . . .

Ron was having a terrible time trying to decide on his seating arrangement. He wasn't place-carding the tables — that would be too difficult — but he was giving people table numbers so they'd know exactly which table they were at.

He placed himself, Ken, Lucky Santangelo, Cooper Turner, and of course Martin, at Venus Maria's table. Maybe he'd add another major star or two.

Nervously he went outside to inspect the tent once again. Everything looked marvellous. The tent was black with a sea of fairy lights strung around it. At night they'd look like a thousand tiny stars. The rest of the decor was black and silver – a dramatic theme Venus Maria would love. And the flower arrangements were exotic blooms imported from Hawaii.

Huge screens were erected on the sides of the tent. Hidden projectors would flash giant blow-up photographs of Venus Maria all night long.

"You must relax." Ken put a soothing hand on his arm.

Ron shook it off. He was not pleased with Ken since the eye incident with Antonio. "No more flirting," he'd warned him.

"As if I would," Ken had replied, quite affronted that Ron even imagined he was doing so.

"I've never given a party like this before," sighed Ron. "What a responsibility!"

"It will be successful," Ken said. "I can promise you that."

"I don't care about successful," Ron said irritably. "I already told you – it has to be the most talked-about party of the year."

"Same thing," said Ken.

Ron shot him a look. What did he know?

Abigaile had no intention of hiding herself from public life just because Mickey had done something most other men in town probably did all the time but were smart enough not to get caught doing. She had every intention of attending the surprise party for Venus Maria. Her problem was, who could she get to escort her? Abigaile had no male friends: all the men she knew belonged to Mickey.

Sitting in Ivana's, having her hair attended to by Saxon, she came up with a brilliant idea.

"Saxon, dear," she said, slightly condescendingly. "How would you like to attend a glamorous Hollywood party?"

Saxon couldn't believe Abigaile Stolli was about to invite him out. It certainly wasn't the first time a client had come on to him, but he'd never expected it from her.

"Well?" Abigaile said impatiently, waiting for his reply.

He stalled for time while he thought it over. "Well what, Mrs S.?"

"Do you want to come to a Hollywood party with me or not?"

Like he hadn't been to ten thousand of them. "Uh, I . . ." He didn't know what to say. Maybe he should say yes. She looked desperate. "Sure, what party did you have in mind?"

"A birthday party for Venus Maria."

"I'm already invited to that, Mrs S."

"You are?" She was surprised. Hairdressers weren't supposed to get invitations to important events.

"Yeah, I do her hair. She's a good friend."

"She is? I didn't know that. You've never mentioned her."

He grinned. "I'm discreet."

"Well, then, if you're already going, perhaps you can escort me."

Saxon saw no way out. This was really going to blow everyone's mind! He couldn't wait to see Venus Maria's face when she realized he was with Abigaile Stolli! It might be worth it for a laugh.

"It'll be a pleasure, Mrs S.," he said. "Shall I pick you up?"

Abigaile suffered from car anxiety. "What car do you drive?"

"A Jaguar."

She thought a moment before deciding a Jaguar was acceptable. "Hmm . . . very well."

"About what time?"

"What time does it start?"

"Ron wants everybody there by seven-thirty. He's planning the full surprise bit. So I'll pick you up around seven-fifteen. You'd better jot down your address for me."

Abigaile did so and left the salon feeling quite light-headed. If Mickey could have an affair with a six-foot-tall black policewoman, she could certainly appear at Venus Maria's party with an exceptionally good-looking hairdresser.

Why not? All was fair in love and marriage.

After mulling it over Mickey decided he'd go to the party for Venus Maria. He had nothing else to do. Sitting in a hotel room night after night, as luxurious as it was, had not turned out to be a laugh a minute. At home he had his Olympic-size swimming pool, his sauna, his steam bath, his gym, and his magnificent private study leading into his screening room.

Ah, the comforts of home. How he missed them.

If he was going to divorce Abigaile, he'd better think about buying himself a house – and fast. Hotel living was not for him.

Martin Swanson was screwing him around. He couldn't reach him. Every time he called he got one of Martin's many assistants, who gave him the Zeppo White story. Apparently they had to handle Zeppo carefully. Zeppo had an extremely lucrative contract with Orpheus, and he had no intention of leaving. At least not voluntarily.

"How long is this going to take?" Mickey had asked.

"Soon," was the reply he received.

Soon was getting to be a word he hated.

He didn't even have the energy to return to Madame Loretta's. Every time he thought about getting laid he remembered a hand clamping him on the shoulder and a voice saying, "You're under arrest."

Talk about putting a man off sex!

And as for Warner – he missed the sex, the compliments, and the uncomplicated pleasure of being with her.

But it was over. Of that he was sure.

Chapter 94

Rita had a red dress that emphasised every curve of her quite spectacular body. She pirouetted for Emilio, showing off. "You like, honey?"

507

He whistled. "Hot!"

Pleased with his reaction she twirled a couple more times. "What are *you* going to wear?" she asked.

Emilio had a new pair of brown leather pants and a matching leather jacket. He planned to wear the outfit with a dusty-pink frilled shirt.

When he put it on, the leather pants clung unflatteringly to his thighs, making him look plumper than he already was.

Rita didn't care to point this out, because Emilio was a vain one, and she wasn't about to piss him off.

"Do *I* look hot too?" he asked, strutting peacock-like in front of her.

"*Veree* hot," she replied. Not such a lie, because he'd already started to sweat. "Are you sure your sister's going to be pleased to see you?" Rita worried. "She screamed 'Fuck you' on the answering machine. It doesn't exactly sound like you're the person she wants to be with — especially with the new issue of *Truth and Fact* out today."

"Will you quit? She loves me," Emilio boasted. "The Sierras stick together."

"OK." Rita wasn't about to argue. This was going to be an amazing party and she didn't want to miss it. She'd get there somehow. With or without Emilio.

Warner went out and splurged on a gold spangled dress. If her idol — Eddie Murphy — ever saw her in it, he would die for her. She added a matching jacket.

Parading in front of the mirror, she decided Johnny Romano was definitely going to like what he saw. But just in case he didn't . . . she folded her old uniform and stuffed it in an overnight bag, along with her handcuffs and gun.

When the limo arrived to pick her up, she had the driver place her bag in the trunk.

"When we get to Mr Romano's at the end of the evening," she said with a pleasant smile, "make sure I don't forget it."

"Certainly, ma'am," replied the driver, looking her over and deciding she had the best tits he'd ever seen.

508

"Thank you." Warner climbed in the car, exhibiting plenty of leg. "Are we picking Mr Romano up?"

"We're on our way," said the driver, happy with his view.

"I'm a movie star," recited Johnny Romano, admiring himself in the mirror. "Hey, man, I'm a movie star."

There was nobody else in the room, but Johnny liked to hear the sound of his own voice. It turned him on, gave him a charge. "Hey, man, I'm a movie star." He repeated the words a third time and grinned at his reflection. Cool. He was looking cool.

A model he'd dated a couple of times had turned him on to Armani, and the Italian look really suited him. Sharp tailoring. A black suit, black shirt, white tie. And with his black hair, olive skin, and dark eyes, he certainly looked like a movie star.

The entourage waited downstairs. The entourage did everything for him.

Being a movie star meant never having to lift a finger.

He could remember when it wasn't that way. Oh, could he remember! Johnny's first job in Hollywood had been parking cars. Big, sleek, expensive automobiles.

Most people whose cars he parked treated him as if he didn't exist. Some of the nicer ones gave a decent tip, but most of the time he was fortunate to make the two-dollar parking fee.

Sometimes, at parties, he saw the very same people whose Rolls and Porsches he'd used to park. What a kick it would be to tell them, "Hey, man – I pissed in your trunk. I ripped off your radio. I stole your cassettes."

They wouldn't appreciate the joke, but he liked it a lot.

That was before stardom. Before he was Johnny Romano. Before he was a movie star.

One last look in the mirror. The man was hot. The man was gonna kill 'em! In spite of abysmal reviews of his movie and an ominous drop at the box-office.

What did he care? People loved him. They'd be back.

He flung open the door to his bedroom. "Hey, Johnny Romano is ready," he yelled out. "Let's go!"

The entourage snapped to attention.

The Sleazy Singles had sort of adopted Eddie Kane. He was their kind of guy.

"You going to that party?" Arnie asked him. "It's like a surprise thing for Venus Maria. We may as well pick up broads. Best place in town to do it."

"Sure," agreed Frankie. "You'll come with us."

Vaguely Eddie remembered he'd been invited several weeks ago. God! Several weeks ago seemed like a lifetime. "Yeah, why not?" he decided. "I'll take a ride to my house and change. I feel like a shower."

"Why don't you shower here?" said Frankie, ever the generous host.

"Yeah, why don't you fuckin' move in?" guffawed Arnie.

They all laughed.

"Hey, guys, I'll see you there. Gimme the address."

Frankie scribbled it on a piece of paper and handed it over.

Eddie drove back to his house. On the way he called Kathleen Le Paul. "I need to make a buy," he said. "Can you come by my house?"

She was short with him. "What do you think I am, your runner? I happen to be busy tonight."

"And I happen to be one of your best customers," he reminded her.

"Yeah, one of my best non-paying customers. You still owe, and until I get paid – no more deliveries."

He slammed the phone down in a fury. Bitch!

The Maserati ripped up the highway. God, he loved his car. He'd sell his house, he'd sell his clothes, but he'd never sell his goddamn car.

"We're going to a party," Lucky informed Gino.

"Aw, come on, I'm partied out," he said, groaning.

"Don't be such an old grouch. We're going to a real Hollywood bash, and having a great time."

"A great time, huh?" He looked at her like she was nuts. "You know how many of those things I went to when I was with Marabelle Blue? And how about when I was married to Susan? She dragged me to three a night! Christ. A great time – you gotta be kiddin'."

"Will you quit with the bitching? I want you to meet Venus Maria. She's a fabulous woman."

"Hey, kid, when you reach my age you've seen everythin', you've done everythin', an' you know something? You don't wanna see nothin' else."

"Stop talking like that. You're getting on my nerves. We're going, OK?"

Gino shook his head. "You're a tough broad."

"Yeah, yeah, yeah, I know, and I got a smart mouth. So you've always told me. I'm just like my daddy!"

They both laughed.

"Lucky, you really turned out to be somethin'."

"And so did you, Gino. So did you. Now go change – I want to see you in a suit."

Mary-Lou and Steven had taken little Carioca Jade, Cee Cee, Bobby, and his school friend to Santa Barbara to visit one of Mary-Lou's aunts. They were staying overnight.

Lucky had given Miko a few days off before he had a nervous breakdown. The place was a mess, but she didn't mind as long as everyone was having a good time.

Prowling through her closet, she decided on a white tuxedo with nothing underneath. When she was dressed she looked strikingly beautiful with her unruly mass of jet curls, black gypsy eyes, wide sensual mouth, and weekend suntan.

"Hey, kid," Gino said when he saw her. "What am I gonna tell you? You make me proud."

"Thanks, Gino . . . Daddy."

Their eyes met, father and daughter. They were truly united.

"Let's go party," Lucky said, smiling.

Chapter 95

"Kill her," Carlos Bonnatti said.

"Who?" asked Link.

Carlos Bonnatti paced around his Century City penthouse. "Lucky Santangelo, that's who."

"It's as good as done."

"I hope so."

"Don't worry, the lady is already dead."

"She's no lady, she's a Santangelo. It's to be done within the next twenty-four hours. And it better look like an accident."

"You got it, boss."

Carlos nodded. The time had come to take revenge.

Chapter 96

Cooper arrived on time to pick up Venus Maria.

"What's so important that we have to go out to dinner?" she asked. "I'd really like to stay home. It's my birthday tomorrow and Martin's coming in. I need an early night."

Cooper shrugged. "I'll bring you home by midnight — just in time to wish you a happy birthday. How's that?"

"Very funny, Cooper."

"My aim is to amuse."

"So, what's the big secret? Why were you so insistent we get together tonight?"

"When I explain it, you'll understand."

"Is it something about Martin?"

"In a way. Remember when you asked me to talk to him?"

"That was a while ago. Everything's changed since then."

"So I noticed. But I still think we should discuss some of the things he said."

She sighed. "OK, Cooper, if that's what turns you on."

He didn't crack a smile. "Yes, it is."

She reached for her purse. "We're awfully serious tonight."

"I'm practising for when you announce your wedding."

"Would it bother you?"

They exchanged a long, silent look before Cooper changed the subject and said, "Is that what you're wearing?"

She was clad in a ripped-at-the-knee jeans, a tight white T-shirt, and an oversized man's jacket. So much for Ron's theory that if she was seeing him she'd wear some incredible outfit.

"Oh, I'm so sorry," she said sarcastically. "Doesn't this cut it for Hamburger Hamlet?"

"I booked a table at Spago."

"Not again! I can't be photographed with you every time we go out. Once or twice is a laugh, but this is ridiculous. Martin's going to get pissed off."

"Martin couldn't care less about you and me. We're just friends, remember?"

"I'm not changing," she said stubbornly.

"Have it your own way. Don't say I didn't warn you."

She looked perplexed. "Warn me about *what*?"

"Not to worry."

"You're acting strange tonight, Cooper."

"Yeah?" He stared at her. She was the most desirable and stimulating woman he'd come across in a long time and she belonged to somebody else. "Why do you think that?"

"You're just like, uh . . . jumpy."

He glanced at his watch. "Come on. The sooner we go, the sooner I'll get you home."

"Charming! Maybe we *should* stay out until midnight."

"Why the change?"

"I told you — it's my birthday at midnight."

"You should have told me before, I would have bought you a present."

"That's OK, you can send me flowers tomorrow. Orchids. I'm crazy for orchids." She took his arm. "Let's hit the road. I'm starving."

Lennie booked the girls into the Beverly Hilton. He didn't deem it appropriate to turn up for a reunion with Lucky dragging Brigette and Nona along.

They loved the idea of staying in a hotel. Room service and cable television. They were perfectly happy.

"You're sure you're going to be OK?" he asked them for the fifth time.

"Will you get out of here, Lennie," Brigette said, giving him a little shove towards the door. "We're not kids, you know."

"OK," he said. "But you've got to promise me – no boys in the room."

Nona giggled. "What makes you think we'd bring boys up here?" she asked innocently.

"I was your age once. The memory doesn't go – just the body. Know what I'm saying?"

Both girls nodded and laughingly escorted him to the door. "Yeah, yeah, Lennie, now get the hell *out*. Good*bye*!"

He felt really good, like a weight had been lifted. It was all going to work out. He knew it.

Downstairs he had the doorman get him a cab, then he set off for the beach. He tried to think of a great opening line. How about *I'm home*? That should do it.

Martin Swanson was met at the airport by Ken, proud to be assigned such an important task.

"Venus Maria has no idea you're going to be at the party," Ken offered. "In fact, she has no idea about the party."

"No photographers. You're sure about that?"

"Absolutely sure," replied Ken, guiding Martin to a waiting limousine.

"I can't be photographed," Martin repeated his fears. "I've had it with the press. Publicity is exactly what I don't need. It's becoming ridiculous."

"Oh, yes," agreed Ken, wishing the press would hound *him* for a change. "We understand perfectly."

"Good," said Martin. He was not in a talkative mood.

"The surprise will be worth it," Ken said, putting on his Ray-Bans, even though it was after dark.

"I'm sure," replied Martin, less than modest.

Although neither of them was aware of it, they passed on the highway – Lucky and Gino heading for Beverly Hills, Lennie in a cab on his way to Malibu.

When Lennie arrived at the house he was disappointed to find it empty. After letting himself in with his key he looked around. The place was a mess. Had Lucky been entertaining?

He yelled for Miko a few times and then realized that even he wasn't home.

Shit! He should have told her he was coming. What made him think she was sitting around every night hoping he'd appear?

God damn it! Well . . . she'd be home eventually and he'd be waiting.

On another highway, a short distance outside Los Angeles, Deena sat behind the wheel of her rented Ford and headed towards her destination.

Chapter 97

The throbbing rhythms of a half-naked bongo player welcomed the guests into Ron's somewhat eclectic home. He had a passion for high ceilings, black granite, mirrors, and hug expanses of glass. His home was dramatic, to say the least.

The guests had been instructed to arrive before eight, giving Ron plenty of time to see that they were served drinks and a wonderful array of hors d'oeuvres.

An army of servants worked flat out while a parade of Hollywood luminaries arrived at the door. Ron didn't know everybody, but Venus Maria's name was enough to get them all out.

Among the first to arrive were several married couples – the Tony Danzas, Roger Moores, and Michael Caine with his dazzlingly beautiful wife, Shakira. They were followed by a smiling Susie Rush in the company of her husband. Singing star Al King entered next with his exotic-looking wife, Dallas. And then came a few studio executives, including Zeppo and Ida White, Mickey Stolli, and a rough-looking Eddie Kane, whom Ron couldn't remember inviting.

The vibrations were good. There was a definite buzz in the air.

Ron personally greeted legendary film director Billy Wilder with his elegant wife, Audrey, unquestionably the chicest woman in town. He waved at the Jourdans, Poitiers, and Davises. The evening was shaping up.

Johnny Romano's silver limo snaked its way along the driveway. Warner sat beside him, knees firmly together, skirt riding high somewhere near the top of her thighs.

"Hey, baby, how about a little feel?" Johnny encouraged, trying to wriggle his hand between her tightly closed knees.

"Not now," she objected. "Later."

"*Now*, baby," Johnny said, fingers fighting their way towards his goal. "Johnny says so. C'mon, baby, open up for Daddy."

She slapped his hand away.

"Oh boy, you got a sharp slap."

"I've been practising."

He grinned. "Yeah?"

His bodyguards travelled in the car behind. At private

functions they attempted to make themselves unobtrusive. Not easy – but insisted upon by most of the hosts.

"You ever fucked in the back of a limo?" Johnny asked, leering all over her.

She didn't want to tell him that this was the first time she'd been in a limousine, although she'd given out a few tickets in her time. "No," she said.

"Hey – baby – Johnny says your education is not complete. Johnny's gonna help you out!"

"Not now," she repeated vehemently.

"When?" he demanded. "Tomorrow? You want I should send the car for you in the morning?"

She was planning to spend the night. "I'll be with *you* in the morning, won't I?"

"Oh, yeah, sure, baby, if that's what you'd like."

"That's exactly what I'd like, Johnny." Warner Franklin was not about to get fucked in the back of his car and sent home.

"OK, I'll tell you what, baby. We'll drop by the party, stay an hour, an' when we leave I'll fuck you in the back of the limo. Hey – I'm gonna fuck you all the way home. How about *that*?"

Warner couldn't help getting excited at the thought,. As long as it was *his* home.

There was something about Johnny Romano that turned her to jelly.

Adam Bobo Grant wouldn't have missed this party for the world. He'd got word of it in New York, telephoned Ron personally, and requested an invitation.

Ron had been only too delighted to oblige. Bobo had hopped a plane and flown right out. He was certainly not regretting it. There were stars everywhere. Enough to fill his column for a month.

He cruised the room with a happy little smile and a retentive memory.

"Amazing house," he complimented Ron. "Simply . . . different."

Ron was pleased. "Do you really like it?"

"I just said so, didn't I?" Bobo said tartly, spotting Lionel Richie and his pretty wife, along with Luther Vandross and the Bacharachs.

"Then maybe you'd consider being my house guest, perhaps sometime in the future?"

Bobo didn't commit himself either way. He waved at Tita and Sammy Cahn, who were just coming through the front door, and took off in pursuit of Clint Eastwood.

Eddie wandered around looking for people he knew. Anyone who would talk to him, in fact. Word spread fast, and it was general knowledge that he was out at Panther.

He bumped into an actor friend.

"Hey, man, how you doin'?" said his friend.

"Good." He nodded, managing to control his twitch.

His friend glanced around before asking, "Got any blow?"

What was he? A fucking dealer? Why was this schmuck asking *him*? As a matter of fact he didn't, and if he did he certainly wouldn't share it with this asshole.

He tried to spot Arnie or Frankie, but they were nowhere to be seen.

Mickey was at the bar talking to Zeppo White. Eddie was surprised they were still talking. He'd heard that Zeppo had no intention of quitting Orpheus without a battle. Right now Mickey was out of a job – unless Martin was paying him for doing nothing.

But this was Hollywood, and in Hollywood you put on a good face and hoped for the best. Mickey was a survivor – just like the rest of them.

A long line of cars approached the driveway.

"Are you sure we're invited?" Rita asked yet again, anxiously checking her reflection in her compact mirror. "What if we're thrown out? I mean, I couldn't stand it, Emilio. I've never been thrown out of anywhere in my life." Which wasn't strictly true, because Rita had been fired from three jobs and thrown out of a topless bar for refusing to sleep with the owner. This, of course, was in her past, long forgotten. After all, she'd had three speaking roles in movies. She was an actress now.

"What's the matter, don't you trust me or something?" Emilio snapped. "I'm telling you, me and Venus are real tight."

"Did she give you her permission to write all those things about her?"

Emilio wished Rita would quit with the nagging. "I don't have to ask. She understands. When I get the money I'll probably share it with her."

"Oh, like she needs it. Right," said Rita sarcastically.

"So I won't give her any. It don't matter. We're family. Will you shut up?"

Rita sighed. "If you say so. But what about the new story? All that sex stuff Tony told you? Like how she is in bed, and the first time she did it — all of that?"

Christ! What did he have to do — gag her? "Who cares? She won't."

"I don't see how they're going to print it anyway," Rita added, clicking her compact shut.

Emilio wished he could click her mouth shut. She talked too much.

Their car reached the front of the house and valet parkers leaped to attention opening both doors.

Rita slid from her seat, stood still for a moment, and pulled her dress down over her hips. Two of the valet parkers nearly collided. And then — head held high — she took Emilio's arm and entered the house.

"Who the fuck is that?" Ron muttered, watching Rita sashay into his front hall. She looked like a Hollywood Boulevard hooker. At least Madame Loretta's hookers presented themselves like ladies.

Ron groaned inwardly when he noticed Emilio on her arm. This kind of a move took balls — and Emilio didn't have any.

As Ron began to head towards them he was cut off by Antonio. "Ah," said the diminutive photographer, "where is your friend? I talk to him about the photo."

519

Ron was enraged. Was this midget Italian creep still after Ken? "He's not here," he said disdainfully.

"Not here? I don't understand," replied Antonio, confused.

"Do you have a message?" Ron said. "I'll see he gets it."

Antonio was not to be fobbed off. "Ah, no, I promised to talk with him personally."

Lecherous little brute. Ron stalked off, forgetting that his purpose had been to throw Emilio and his trampy girlfriend out.

By the time he remembered, they'd vanished into the crowd.

Rita was hot to cruise. They'd actually gotten into the party, and she wasn't about to hang around with Emilio in his cheap leather outfit. He resembled a Hollywood Boulevard pimp!

"Get me a drink, honey. I'm going to the powder room," she purred. "I'll meet you at the bar."

Before he could object she wiggled off.

Heads turned as she passed. She knew she looked outstanding. Why else were they staring? Tonight was the night to make a very big impression. A career impression. Rita was all set to knock 'em on their Hollywood asses!

Chapter 98

When Saxon arrived to collect Abigaile Stolli he was faced with a truculent thirteen-year-old girl.

"Who are *you*?" Tabitha demanded, staring him down.

What a precocious child. "Saxon," he replied.

"You don't look like any of my mother's friends," Tabitha said rudely.

Thank God for that, Saxon thought to himself. "Is your

mother around?" he asked. "I'm supposed to be taking her to a party."

Tabitha laughed aloud. "*You're* taking Mommy to a party? Huh! Wait till Daddy hears about *this*."

"Aren't your parents separated?" Saxon remarked.

"None of your business," Tabitha sneered.

Fortunately Abigaile chose that moment to appear, quickly waving Tabitha away.

But Tabitha was having none of it. She glared at her mother. "You look stupid," she said. "Why've you got all that makeup on? It doesn't suit you. It's gross. Ugh!"

"Goodnight, dear," Abigaile said through clenched teeth.

In the car she apologized for her daughter's behaviour. "Tabitha's upset. It's been a most embarrassing time for all of us. I'm sure you heard about my husband's ... indiscretion."

Heard! The entire salon had talked of nothing else for days! He shrugged. "These things happen."

Abigaile was wearing a chic Valentino suit, lots of real jewellery, and an abundance of Joy.

"You smell good, Mrs S.," Saxon said, sniffing the air.

"Thank you." She stared straight ahead. It wouldn't do to encourage him too much. After all, he was merely her escort for the evening, nothing more.

When they arrived she noticed a few heads turn. Saxon was tall, good-looking, and hardly the man anybody would have expected to replace Mickey.

Abigaile revelled in the attention.

Spotting Zeppo and Ida White, she took Saxon by the hand and dragged him over.

Ida's lecherous eyes checked him out. Then she drew Abigaile to one side and whispered in her ear, "You came with your *hairdresser*? It's not on, darling, don't do it again. I know you must be desperate to get back at Mickey – but this kind of behaviour is not acceptable."

Abigaile bristled. How dare Ida White give her advice? The permanently stoned old cow!

"He's not my hairdresser, he's my lover," she spat.

Ida's eyebrows shot up. She was shocked. "I'm sorry, I . . . I didn't realize," she stuttered.

Abigaile smiled. "Why do you think Mickey had to go to a whorehouse? *I* haven't slept with him in months. Saxon and I are *very* close." She leaned towards Saxon and gave him an intimate squeeze.

Saxon was as surprised as Ida.

"Come along, darling." Clinging to his arm she led him away, leaving an open-mouthed Ida behind.

It was almost time for Venus Maria to arrive. Ron checked out the guests. Everybody appeared to be having a good time, and most people seemed to have arrived. The only person missing was Martin, but Ken would be bringing him from the airport in time to surprise Venus Maria.

Ron knew Cooper had the plan down pat. He was to collect Venus Maria, make out they were going to dinner, and in the car, say, "I have a surprise for you," blindfold her, and bring her straight to the house.

Venus Maria would go for it. She loved intrigue.

Ron had instructed everyone to be quiet when she arrived. He planned to take her into the middle of the room, whip off the blindfold, and have everybody scream, "Surprise!"

He made a little announcement to that effect. There was a smattering of applause and some laughter. But they would go along with it. This was Hollywood, after all. And Venus Maria was a superstar.

Warner held tightly onto Johnny Romano's arm as he made his usual flamboyant entrance. Heads turned. What a couple!

Warner wished her family in Watts could see her now, strolling into a big Hollywood party on the arm of a movie star. And not just any old movie star. Johnny Romano! The King!

She wondered how many people in the room she'd given parking tickets to when she was a traffic cop. This was something. This was *really* something.

Warner Franklin and Johnny Romano!

Johnny had a big smile on his face. Tonight was an important night for him. It was the first time he'd been out in public since the *Motherfaker* receipts had dropped so disastrously at the box-office.

Gotta put on a face.

Gotta show them that he didn't give a flying fuck.

And with Warner by his side he felt pretty damn good. She wasn't just another Hollywood bimbo. She was a woman. All woman. Six foot of woman.

The first person they ran into after Ron greeted them was Mickey Stolli.

Mickey was shocked.

Warner was delighted.

After saying hello, Mickey was about to make an excuse and escape, when who should come up behind them but Abigaile, dragging some long-haired hunk behind her.

She ignored Mickey altogether. "Warner, dear!" she exclaimed, as if they were the oldest of friends. "How *are* you? And Johnny, you're looking handsome as usual."

Mickey could hardly believe this little scene. When had this group gotten all pally?

He threw Abigaile a low aside: "What are *you* doing here? And who's that creep?"

"Creep?" She looked puzzled. "I've no idea *what* you are talking about."

"The jerk with the heavy-metal hairstyle?"

"Oh, do you mean Saxon? Haven't I ever mentioned him to you before? Saxon owns that wonderful salon on Sunset. Ivana's. Are you *sure* I haven't mentioned him, Mickey?" At which point she grabbed Saxon's hand and squeezed it. "Darling, meet my soon-to-be ex-husband, Mickey Stolli."

Saxon towered over Mickey, as did Warner. "Hey, man, nice to meet you," he said. "Heard a lot of things about you."

"Come on, Saxon," Abigaile said gaily. "We have to circulate." She favoured Mickey with a triumphant smile and swept off.

He didn't believe what was going on. Abigaile? Enjoying a party? Smiling? Dragging some guy around?

Abigaile was supposed to be sitting in her Hollywood mansion sulking.

Mickey Stolli decided this wasn't his night.

Rita caught Mickey on the rebound. "I know you," she said, excitedly pouncing. "I saw your picture in the paper. You're . . . you're Mickey Sully. Yes?"

"Stolli." He stared at the cheap-looking girl in the red dress. Too tight. Too much makeup. Too much hair. "Who are you?"

"I'm Rita."

"Rita who?"

"Rita, the girl who's gonna be the next Venus Maria," she said, taking a random shot. "I dance, I sing. In fact" – she moved in a little closer – "anything you want I do." In case he didn't get the message she added, "And I mean *anything*."

Before Mickey could reply, Emilio marched over and yanked her away. "I was waitin' for you at the bar," he said accusingly. "Where were you?"

Rita looked at Mickey apologetically. "My friend – he's a little uptight," she tried to explain.

"Who the fuck's uptight?" exploded Emilio.

"Please excuse me, Mr Scully." She hesitated. "Uh . . . are you casting? 'Cause if you are I'd appreciate it if you'd think about me. Rita. I sing, I dance, I–"

Emilio dragged her off.

In the car heading towards Ron's house, Cooper suddenly pulled over to the side of the road.

"Oh, no!" Venus Maria mocked. "Remember what happened last time we pulled over?"

He began to laugh. "This is different."

She put on her businesslike voice. "OK, what is it this time?"

"I want you to do something for me."

524

Now she was back to teasing him. "A blow-job is out of the question, Cooper."

"Will you shut up?"

"Why?"

"Just shut up and put on this blindfold. I've got a surprise for you."

"*Ooooh*," she squealed with delight. "I get *off* on surprises."

"I know. So be a good girl and do as you're told."

"I love it when you're firm with me, Cooper."

He took a silk scarf from the glove compartment and tied it over her eyes.

"This is sexy," she said. "I'll have to remember this one. Where will I end up, Cooper? Naked in your bed?"

"You're such a flirt, you really are. And another thing — you're all mouth."

She was amused. "Hmmm, don't you wish?"

"Can I concentrate on my driving?"

"Can you?" she teased. "Just thinking about me naked in your bed—"

"Enough," he said sternly.

"Tell me where we're going."

"And spoil the surprise? Forget it."

Deena drove down Sunset. The doors of her car were locked. She'd studied a street map of LA and Beverly Hills and knew exactly where she was going.

When she reached Doheny Road she turned left and drove up into the hills.

Very soon she would be outside Venus Maria's house.

Chapter 99

Lucky thought about telling Gino of Carlos Bonnatti's threat, then decided against it. Why worry him? She could handle Carlos. She could handle anything that came her way.

In her evening purse she carried a small gun for protection. It was a habit she'd acquired, and it certainly made her feel more secure. Especially now.

"God damn it," Gino groaned. "I hate these parties. Why'd I let you talk me into it?"

"Maybe you'll meet a beautiful movie star and she'll whisk you away from New York and you'll come out here to live," Lucky teased.

"Big deal," he snorted. "You've seen one movie star, you've seen 'em all."

"Whatever happened to Marabelle Blue?"

"She married a bullfighter, and then she married a singer, and after that I don't know."

"Is she still around?"

"Who cares?"

"If you like I'll find out."

Gino burst out laughing. "What for? I'm lookin' forward to a quiet life. I'm an old man."

"Will you *stop* saying that? It's really pissing me off. One moment you're telling me you're forty-five for ever, and the next you're an old man. What happened in between?"

"Nothin' happened, kid. I faced up to reality."

They made it into the party five minutes before Venus Maria arrived, and settled by the bar.

Lucky was a born voyeur. She loved watching the action as the stars jostled for position.

"Isn't this fun?" she whispered to Gino as Al King walked by.

"About as much fun as root canal in a heat wave."

"Surprise!" the yell went up.

Venus Maria snatched off her blindfold and gasped. "I don't believe this! Who arranged it?"

"Who do you think?" said a proud Ron, by her side.

"Oh my God! What a wonderful surprise. *Everybody's* here."

"Naturally, my princess. And you should *see* the presents. Oh, are we going to have fun opening them!"

"Thank you, Ron." She turned and kissed him. "You're the best friend a girl could possibly have."

"I've got another birthday present for you. It's a fab outfit. You might want to change," Ron suggested.

Ruefully she glanced down at her ripped jeans and oversized jacket. "Shit! Cooper — why didn't you *tell* me?"

"Come along, sweet. I'll take you to my bedroom."

"Oooh, Ron," she joked, "you *really* know how to turn a girl on."

They walked upstairs to Ron's bedroom, receiving a chorus of "Happy Birthday!" on the way. Standing in the middle of the room waiting for her was Martin.

She stopped short.

"Surprise, surprise!" said Ron, delighted. "Just the way we planned it."

"Happy birthday," said Martin.

She smiled. "Are you my gift?"

"One of them," interjected Ron. "Now I'll leave you two alone — but only for a minute. Hurry up and join the party. Here's another present." He indicated a large gift-wrapped box on the bed.

"Thank you, Ron."

"My pleasure."

He left them alone together.

Venus Maria sauntered slowly over to Martin, entwined her hands around his neck, pressed her body against his, and gave him a long, deep soul kiss. "Mmmmm," she said. "Welcome back."

They kissed for a few moments, until Venus asked him in a breathy voice — reminiscent of the young Marilyn Monroe — "Have you missed me?"

"Oh yes," he said.

"Prove it."

He thrust himself towards her. "Here's your proof."

She laughed softly. "*Oooh*, Martin, you've *really* been saving up."

And then she slid to her knees, unzipped his pants, and, before he knew what was happening, had him in her mouth.

That's what he liked about Venus Maria. It was her birthday and he got the present.

Downstairs Ron caught Antonio and Ken deep in conversation. He hurried over and grabbed Ken's arm possessively.

"Antonio says my photos came out great," Ken said enthusiastically. "It's going to be a big career boost to be in photographs with Venus Maria. Don't you agree?"

Ron sighed. Why did he always have to find the ambitious ones? Wouldn't it be nice if Ken was happy to stay home and just look handsome?

"Very nice," he said resignedly.

Ken leaned anxiously towards Antonio. "When can I see them?" he asked. "I can't wait."

"Tomorrow. You come to my studio." Antonio said, shooting Ron a triumphant look. "My house is my studio. We have a light lunch and I show you the pictures."

"Great," said Ken.

Ha! Ron thought, glaring at Antonio. *Why don't you unzip your pants and show it to him now?*

Madame Loretta's girls mingled easily. They were certainly among the most beautiful women in the room. Madame Loretta had an eye. She picked them fresh off the train or plane. They came to Hollywood to be stars. A little hooking on the way did nothing to harm their careers.

Madame Loretta's stable was famous. Several of her girls had already married movie stars and producers, and another was engaged to an Arab billionaire. It gave her a great sense of satisfaction.

Leslie was certainly one of the most special girls she'd ever had, and she wanted to see her well looked after.

Tonight Leslie was paired up with Tom, one of Ken's male model friends. They'd been told to circulate and charm everyone in sight.

"Are you getting paid for this?" Tom said.

"Why would I be getting paid?" Leslie replied defensively.

"There's a rumour going around that some of the girls here are. Look, I'm not saying *you* are, but some of the girls work for Madame Loretta."

"There's also a rumour that some of the guys are gay," Leslie retorted. "Are *you* gay?"

Tom blushed. "I'm an actor."

"Are you trying to say there's no gay actors?"

"I'm bisexual," he explained.

"I guess that covers a multitude of sins," she murmured.

When Venus reappeared with Martin by her side, a buzz travelled around the room. She'd transformed herself from a waif in blue jeans into the Venus Maria everyone knew and loved – the sexy, strutting, outrageous video queen – challenging, vampy, unafraid. Now she had on her birthday present from Ron, a Jean-Paul Gaultier tunic dress, over which she wore a jewelled vest and several red and black enamelled bangles.

"Everyone's staring at us," she whispered to Martin. "I guess they're surprised to see you."

"No photographs," he warned.

"Don't be so paranoid. Ron wouldn't allow photographers at a party like this."

A waiter handed them champagne. Martin squeezed her hand. "I'm here to stay."

She sipped the champagne and wrinkled her nose. "Really?"

"It's what you want, isn't it?"

She smiled. "Oh, yes, Martin, it's what I want. It really is."

But even as she said it, she knew she wasn't sure.

Chapter 100

"Are we having fun?" Cooper asked dryly.

Lucky smiled at him. "I always make the best of everything. It's an interesting party."

"If you like parties," Cooper said restlessly.

"And you don't?"

"I'd sooner be home reading a good book."

"From what I hear the *last* thing you do in your bedroom is read a good book."

He gave her a perplexed look. "Why is it that everyone thinks I'm this insatiable stud?"

"Because you are!"

"You know that for a fact, do you?"

"I've read plenty about you."

"And you believe everything you read, of course?"

She grinned. "Naturally. Don't you?"

He moved on. "How come I never see you with your husband? Where is Lennie anyway?"

"He's in Europe right now."

"What do you two have? One of those marriages where he goes his way and you go yours?"

"It's really none of your business."

"I see. It's perfectly OK for you to discuss *my* love life, but when it comes to yours – hands off, right?"

She sighed. "Right now we're having a . . . problem or two."

That's all Cooper needed to hear. He'd been attracted to Lucky from the first time he'd set eyes on her. "I'm very good at solving problems. It's my speciality," he said.

"I'm sure it is. But I can solve my own, thank you."

They locked eyes. If it wasn't for Lennie she would find Cooper Turner irresistibly attractive, in spite of his lethal reputation.

So what? In her time she'd had a reputation too.

"You're a very intriguing woman," Cooper said, refusing to break the stare.

Lucky did it for him. "Tell me," she said, "do you have an all-purpose line? Or do you come up with something new for every occasion?"

Gino was over at the bar getting a refill.

"Hello, Gino."

He turned around and discovered himself facing Paige. "Hey — what're you doin' here?" he asked.

"The same as you, having a lousy time."

"Are you with Ryder?"

"No."

He noticed she was not wearing her wedding ring and began to wonder. "Who *are* you with?"

She put a perfectly manicured hand over his. "There's something I've been meaning to ask you, Gino."

He could smell her musky scent. "Yeah?"

"Did you keep that ring?"

"What ring?"

She rolled her eyes. "What ring, he says. The big diamond ring, remember? The one you handed me when you asked me to leave Ryder."

He took a slug of Scotch. She was making him hot. "No, I took it back. Why do you wanna know?"

"Pity," she said quietly.

"What's goin' on here, Paige?"

She licked her full lips. "What do *you* think?"

"I got a feeling you're—"

She finished the sentence for him: "Ready to go home with you, Gino."

"Permanently?"

"Yes."

He burst out laughing. "About time!"

"Martin, perhaps I can get a quote from you."

Martin recoiled in horror. What the hell was Adam Bobo Grant doing here? Ron had said there was to be no press, absolutely none.

"Good evening, Bobo," he said amiably, smart enough not to let his displeasure show.

"I'm *so* sorry to hear about you and Deena," Bob gushed, placing a sympathetic hand on his arm. "But what must be, must be."

Martin glanced around the room, desperately searching for Ron. When he found him, he was going to strangle him. If Bobo wrote anything about tonight, Deena would try to take everything he had.

Hovering near the fireplace, Mickey and Abigaile came face to face.

"You're disgusting," Mickey hissed.

"*I'm* disgusting," Abigaile replied. "What about you and that . . . that whore?"

"It's better than being with a hairdresser. He's younger than you. How can you put yourself in this ridiculous position?"

"Don't tell *me* what to do, Mickey Stolli. You walked out, and when you walked you closed the door behind you. My life is my own now."

"I want to walk back in again," Mickey blurted, surprising himself.

"You do?"

"Yes, I do. How about it, Abby?"

Dinner was served. There was a long buffet table loaded with everything from fresh lobster to Southern fried chicken, barbecued spare-ribs, pan-fried potatoes, creamed corn, hot crusty garlic bread, and huge salads.

"All my favourite foods!" Venus Maria said excitedly. "Ron, you really pulled out all the stops. I'm so happy. This is a *sensational* evening. How did you ever keep it a secret?"

"It wasn't easy," he replied. "But you're worth it."

She sat between Ron and Martin, revelling in all the attention. Nobody had ever thrown a birthday party for her before and she was touched.

Lucky came over and sat down with a plate piled high with food. "Soul food — my favourite," she said.

Venus Maria grinned. "Mine too. By the way, have you met Martin Swanson?"

Lucky extended her hand. He returned her firm grip with a limp handshake. Hmmm. When she was at school the girls used to joke about guys with limp handshakes. "Limp handshake, limp dick," they'd all said. If it was true, what was Venus Maria doing with him?

Lucky kept her thoughts in check. "I've heard lots about you," she said.

"I knew your late husband," Martin replied. "Dimitri was an interesting man."

"Did you ever do business with him?" she asked.

"We talked, but never got around to it."

"Just as well. Dimitri was a killer."

Martin raised an eyebrow. "I'm not exactly a pussycat."

"I didn't say you were, but Dimitri was a *real* killer in business."

"I understand we're going head to head," Martin remarked.

"What do you mean?"

"You've bought Panther. I'm taking over Orpheus. In fact, Mickey Stolli is going to run it for me."

"If you ever get rid of Zeppo."

"Oh, I'll get rid of him." He waited a beat. "You must be sorry to lose Mickey."

"Yes," she said sadly. "We'll really miss him at Panther."

"And I expect you'll be even sorrier to lose Venus."

"Who said she's losing me?" Venus interrupted.

"We haven't discussed it yet," Martin said smoothly, "but I have wonderful plans for you at Orpheus."

"I'm very happy at Panther," Venus replied, waving to Angel and Buddy Hudson. "Lucky has had *Bombshell* rewritten for me. And *Strut* is terrific. Wait until you see it. I'm not moving anywhere."

Martin smiled politely. "Now is not the time to discuss

533

.it," he said. "I'll tell you what we have planned for you at another time."

Venus began to back up. "Martin, I don't care *what* you've got planned. I'm with Panther, period. OK?"

He didn't pursue the subject. Once he got Venus Maria alone he would educate her on the facts of life. If they were to be married, she would be an Orpheus star. No argument.

A waiter tapped Lucky on the shoulder. "Ms Santangelo?"

"Yes?"

"I have a message from your father."

She accepted a scrawled note from Gino.

You're on your own, kid. Paige and I have gone off to the Beverly Wilshire. Don't hold your breath. Maybe I'll be back tomorrow! P.S. You were right. I'm not as old as I thought!

Lucky grinned. Gino was back in action. Just where he belonged.

The cake was tremendous — so big it had to be wheeled in on its own special trolley.

As Venus blew out the candles, a naked boy burst through the top.

"Oh my God!" she exclaimed. "Just what I always wanted!"

Hundreds of balloons fell from the ceiling as twenty Brazilian dancers formed a conga line through the room.

Venus turned to Ron. "This is really amazing," she said, hugging him.

"A party to remember," he replied. "From one old friend to another."

They looked at each other, remembering the early days.

"Thanks, Ron," she said warmly. "I love you so much."

And nobody noticed the man called Link slip in amongst the guests.

Chapter 101

For all our sakes, we should hope that day never comes.
Deena thought about her words to Steven Berkeley and
Jerry Myerson. How many months ago had she said them?
And deep down had she ever imagined that the day would
come?

Probably not. But it was here, and Deena wouldn't shirk
the task that lay ahead of her.

She sat in the Ford outside Venus Maria's house, parked
a few yards away. She knew the house was empty except
for the housekeeper, who slept in the back. And she also
knew what kind of alarm system there was, where the
beams were located, and exactly what it took to trigger it
off. The information she'd paid for had been very thor-
ough.

Venus Maria . . . The girl's image danced in front of her
eyes. A tramp. A little tramp. A bitch. *The* Bitch.

What did Martin see in her? He didn't love her, she
merely represented sex. And Deena knew she had to save
him from Venus Maria's venal clutches. When The Bitch
arrived home she was going to take care of the problem
for ever. And nobody would ever suspect her. Deena was
far too smart for that. Besides, as far as everyone was
concerned she was asleep in her room at the health spa in
Palm Springs. How could they possibly track her to Los
Angeles?

Deena allowed her mind to drift back in time.

Fourteen . . . she'd been fourteen when she'd caught her
father in bed with another woman . . .

*Deena Akveld was a coltish-looking girl. She had a serious,
pale face, long red hair, and lived for the weekends with
her father. The two of them always went off together. Her
father liked to hunt and fish, and since Deena was an only*

child and he'd never had a son, Rione Akveld took her everywhere with him. She could run like a boy. She could fish like a boy. She could shoot like a boy. Her father was proud of her.

Deena had even managed to remain flat-chested. Quite a feat when all the girls around her were sprouting breasts. She was proud of the fact that she was as strong and sure-footed as any boy.

Rione Akveld ran a small inn outside of Amsterdam. It was a kick-off point for people who desired to go hunting and fishing. He gave his guests room and board, and supplied them with camping facilities.

When she wasn't in school, Deena helped around the inn. She made beds, did washing up, generally cleaned. It was not hard work. And as long as she had the weekends with her father to look forward to she was perfectly content.

On this particular weekend she'd been fourteen for just a month.

Her mother, who worked during the week as a translator at the American Embassy, arrived home tired. "You can't go with your father today," she said. "You're to stay here and help me."

Deena was crushed. It was a Sunday, their best day together. "But Daddy expects me to join him," she cried.

"Not today," her mother repeated. "You will help me. There is plenty to do here."

Deena was furious, but as the day progressed her mother began to feel a little better, and seeing that her daughter was so upset she finally gave permission for Deena to join her father in their one-room hunting lodge an hour away.

Deena thanked her mother, kissed her, hopped on her bicycle, and set off. She had several new jokes to tell her father. She'd heard them at school the previous week and remembered them for him. It was so nice when they were out in his boat – the sun shining and the breeze blowing – just the two of them alone together.

Deena was happy. Whistling to herself she rode her bicycle as fast as she could.

When she arrived at the lodge she was delighted to see her father's small black car parked outside. Good, he wasn't down at the lake without her.

She entered happily, ready to surprise him.

He was surprised, all right. He was naked in the centre of the bed, crouched over, his bare behind rutting up and down like a wild pig, and he was making horrible groaning noises.

For a moment Deena didn't understand. What was the matter with him? Was he sick?

And then she saw the woman spread out under him. A naked woman with huge breasts and a massive amount of pubic hair, her mouth wide open, making little sighing noises. "Oh, I love it. Give me more – more – more!"

Deena was perfectly calm. She picked up her father's hunting rifle which was propped next to the door.

Her father seemed to sense her presence, and moved off the woman just in time.

Deena fired the gun.

A bullet smashed into the woman's chest, killing her instantly. Deena scored a direct hit just as her father had taught her.

"Oh, Jesus!" her father screamed, rushing towards her and knocking the rifle out of her grip. "What have you done? What in God's name have you done?"

Deena stared at him blankly. It had all happened so fast she wasn't sure what she'd done.

"You killed her! You killed her!" her father yelled.

"Can we go fishing?" she asked very quietly, very calm.

A while later when he got over his shock, her father sat her down and talked to her in a low, quiet voice. "You will tell nobody what happened here today, do you understand me? You will tell nobody, because if you do, they will put you in prison and throw away the key and you will never be free again." He took her by the shoulders and shook her vigorously. "Deena, are you listening to me? Do you understand what I'm saying?"

Blankly she nodded. "Yes, Father. Can we go fishing?"

He shook his head in despair.

The woman in his bed was a hitchhiker he'd picked up earlier that day. Nobody had seen him with her. There was nothing to connect the two of them. He made Deena help him wrap her in the sheets until she was nothing more than a bundle of blood-soaked linen, then they wrapped the sheets in plastic, and placed the body in the trunk of his car.

When it was dark they took her down to the river. Her father weighted the body down with bricks, and finally they threw it in the cold, dark water.

"This never happened," her father said fiercely. "Do you understand me, Deena? This never happened."

"Very well, Father," she replied. "Can we go fishing tomorrow?"

"Yes," he said.

Neither of them had ever mentioned the incident again.

Deena could afford to be patient. She knew Venus Maria had to come home eventually.

And when she did, it would all be over.

Nobody crossed Deena Akveld.

Chapter 102

Lennie prowled around the house a few times. He had no idea where Lucky was, nor where anybody else was for that matter. Even Miko had failed to appear. Some reunion!

He raided the fridge, discovering cold roast beef and potato salad which he wolfed down.

Now that he was back he couldn't wait to talk to Lucky. But it seemed he was going to have to.

He should have called and warned her he was on his way.

By eleven o'clock he was tired. He decided he'd do what she had done to him when she'd surprised him in New

York. He entered their bedroom, stripped off his clothes, and got into bed. Before doing so, he removed the light bulb so she wouldn't be able to spot him when she came home. This way he'd certainly surprise her. She'd get into bed, and there he'd be!

He figured he'd lie down and close his eyes for a few moments, but before long he fell into a deep sleep.

Eventually it had to happen — Venus Maria spotted Emilio before Ron had been able to have him and his loud girl-friend removed. She stared at the offending couple across the room and really began to steam. "Ron. What the hell is *he* doing here? Get him out. And fast. He's a snivelling sneak. I never want to set eyes on his fat face again!"

Ron summoned two security guards, and pointed out Emilio and Rita.

"Get rid of them discreetly," he instructed the guards, which would have been OK if Emilio had any intention of going discreetly.

But no — this was not to be. "Get your hands off me!" Emilio yelled, when, after trying to persuade him to leave politely the two guards shifted into action.

People turned to observe.

"Excuse me for a moment." Suddenly Venus Maria jumped up from her table and marched over. She glared at her brother.

Rita gave her a futile little wave. "Hi, my name's Rita. Emilio said it was OK for us to come here tonight. I'm a big fan. I'm—"

Venus silenced her with a steely glare. "Emilio," she said in a hard, cold voice. "Get the fuck out of my party. And do it now."

"Hey — little sis — what've I done?" he whined plain-tively. "Nothin' so terrible, huh?" He added a hurt expression. "I'm your brother. We're family. It's like we should be close. In fact I think we—"

She hauled back and slapped him across the face. "That's for selling me out," she said fiercely. "Goodbye, Emilio. Don't come back."

Emilio snapped. Public humiliation was not for him. "Who the fuck do you think you're talkin' to?" he yelled, red in the face. "You ain't no big star to me. I know all about you – an' I'm gonna spit it out to the highest fuckin' bidder. So watch out, little sis – I'll get your high an' mighty ass. An' I'll get it good!"

Venus Maria turned her back on him. "Take him away," she ordered the guards.

They attempted to grab Emilio, but he shook them off. "I can *walk* outta here," he said harshly. "But that don't mean I won't be back."

"Well," commented Ron, watching Emilio depart, a pathetic Rita trailing behind. "I guess that takes care of *him*." He gestured to the watching guests. "Let the party continue." Then he turned to Venus Maria. "Are you all right?"

She nodded. "Hey – one less brother to worry about. He's history."

Lucky, Cooper, Venus, and Martin all left the party at the same time. Ron escorted them to the door.

"You really pulled this off," Venus Maria said affectionately, throwing her arms around his neck. "And my presents – what an amazing haul. I can't wait to rip 'em open!"

"Come by in the morning and we'll do it together," Ron suggested, dying to take a look at her gifts.

"Don't you *dare* touch anything. I know you!"

"As if I would!"

"Honestly! It was the best night of my life, Ron. I had the greatest time!"

Lucky agreed. "Fantastic party."

"Apart from Emilio," Ron said with a grimace.

"Forget it," Venus Maria shook her head. "He's nothing."

"I notice it didn't take your father long to get connected," Cooper said dryly, looking at Lucky.

She smiled. "Ah . . . the great Gino. In the good old days his nickname was Gino the Ram! He's probably been connected more times than you, Cooper!"

Everyone laughed.

"I do believe he was coming on to me earlier," Venus Maria said. "He's got those sexy dark eyes. Wow! He sure must've been something when he was young."

"Oh yes," Lucky agreed, nodding.

"So, how are we doing this?" Cooper asked. "Maybe I'll take Martin. Lucky, you go with Venus. And Ron, you can end up with whomever you want."

They all laughed again.

"Seriously though." Cooper put his arm around Lucky's shoulders. "You're not driving back to the beach by yourself. I'll take you."

"I'm perfectly all right. I've got a car and driver somewhere."

"I *said* I'll take you," Cooper repeated.

She felt particularly vulnerable. And there was something about Cooper . . .

"Well . . . as long as you don't expect me to ask you in for coffee."

"What is it with all you women lately? I take Venus home, she tells me nothing's going to happen. Now I escort you, and before we're even in the car you're giving me the same speech! Have I lost my touch or what?"

"I'm a married woman."

"Yeah, I can really see your husband around all the time."

"That's not the way it is."

"So I'll drive you home. Nothing's going to happen."

Once upon a time plenty would have happened. Cooper was an incredibly attractive man. But Lennie was still on her mind.

"Where's Ken?" Ron looked around peevishly.

One of the parking valets offered the information that Ken had left with Antonio.

Ron's mouth drew into a thin, tight line. "Are you sure?"

"Yeah – I know Ken. They were in Antonio's Cadillac."

"Ron, just remember . . . he was never good enough for you," Venus Maria whispered.

Ron tried to hide the hurt he was feeling. "You're right," he said. "I spent far too much money on him. The next fortunate contender will have to be richer and older. *I* want to be taken care of for once."

"Quite right," Venus Maria concurred. "Go for it, Ron. You deserve the best."

Martin was waiting for her by the limousine.

She glanced over at him and then back at Ron. "Would you like me to stay?" she asked. "I will if you want."

"No. I'm a big boy. I can handle it," he said. "You run along, Mister New York is waiting."

"Let him wait," she said recklessly. "I don't care."

"Happy birthday," Ron said, kissing her on the mouth. "We've both come a long way."

"We certainly have."

She strolled off to join Martin. Meanwhile, Lucky got into Cooper's Mercedes.

Ron turned and walked slowly back into his house. As far as he was concerned the party was over.

When Johnny Romano was horny there was no stopping him. In his limo on the way home he was all over Warner.

She attempted to push him off, but he was having none of it. "Spread 'em, baby," he said, and then laughed at his own joke. "Isn't that what you say to all the criminals? Spread 'em."

"Johnny, don't." She attempted to keep her dignity, but her skirt was so short he had it up around her waist with no trouble.

With one hand he expertly removed her panties.

"What about the driver?" she objected.

"He ain't watching," Johnny said, thinking to himself he's seen it all before.

And then, with one quick lunge, he was on top of her, thrusting away as the limo proceeded down Sunset Boulevard.

On one hand Warner enjoyed it. On the other she kept thinking – *Oh God I hope we're not pulled over and stopped.* The embarrassment of being arrested for doing it in a car would be too much to bear.

"If that little rat writes anything I'll sue his ass," Martin muttered as the limousine sped down the hill.

"Who?" Venus Maria asked, snuggling up to him.

"That asshole Bobo Adam Grant, or whatever his name is."

"Bobo's harmless."

"He's about as harmless as Johnny Romano's cock!"

"Martin!" She broke up laughing. "I never knew you could be so funny."

"Neither did I," he said grimly. "Look, I may as well tell you, I made Deena a firm promise that I wouldn't see you this trip. If Bobo prints anything, she's going to be mad as hell."

"So what? You're leaving her, aren't you?"

"Yes, but I'd like it to be amicable. I don't intend to end up giving her half my money."

Was that all he ever thought about — money? "Legally you wouldn't have to do that, would you?"

"No, but once a woman gets mad she gives her lawyer incentive to kill. I made her a promise, and I suppose I should have kept it."

"A little late to be thinking of that now, Martin."

"You're right."

"I'll tell you what," she suggested. "I'll call Bobo in the morning and give him an exclusive on something else. I'm sure he'll listen to me if I ask him to lay off us. Does that please you?"

"Yes. But it still pisses me off. I warned Ron, no press."

"Nobody regards Bobo as press. He's like part of the scene."

"He's not part of my scene. What's he doing out here anyway? He's usually in New York."

"Show Bobo a party and he's there."

The limousine drew smoothly into her driveway.

"You should have a better place than this," Martin

remarked. "There's no electric gates. Anyone could follow you in."

"I have an alarm system."

"That's not enough protection for someone like you. And it's certainly not enough for me. Tomorrow you'll start looking for a new house. My birthday present to you."

Didn't he realize she was a working woman? "I don't have time. *You* find one."

"Why don't we look together? I'll have someone line up some suitable properties. We can do it next weekend."

She wasn't sure she wanted to move. She liked her house.

"You're staying tonight, aren't you?" she asked.

"Of course."

They dismissed the limo and entered the house.

"So, Mr Swanson." She turned to face him. "It's my birthday. What have you got for me?"

Martin smiled. "What *haven't* I got for you? Come here."

She walked slowly over to him, putting her arms around his neck and pulling him very close.

He managed to peel down the top of her dress, touching her breasts.

"Oooh, I love the way you do that." She shivered with anticipation. "Touch me like it's my birthday. And don't let it happen too soon. Let's take our time. Tonight I want to do it slowly. Very, very . . . slowly."

He began to kiss her in earnest.

She gasped softly and fell back onto the couch. "Unzip me."

He did as she asked. Underneath she wore nothing but minuscule black bikini panties.

Martin shrugged his way out of his jacket, loosened his tie and bent to kiss her again.

Neither of them heard Deena enter the room.

Venus Maria threw her arms back over her head and sighed voluptuously. "*Oooh*, Martin, I really get off on the way your mouth feels. I adore it when you touch me . . ."

Neither of them heard the click as Deena took the safety catch off the gun.

Venus Maria reached for his pants and pulled down the zipper. "Satisfaction . . . guaranteed . . ." she teased, releasing him.

"Oh, God, I love you," he groaned, as she began to please him with her tongue.

Martin's words struck Deena like a lethal blow.

He loved her?

Martin loved The Bitch?

Impossible.

Unthinkable.

The ultimate betrayal.

"I've been waiting to hear you say that," Venus Maria murmured softly. "Do you mean it, Martin? Do you *really* mean it?"

"Oh yes, baby, oh yes."

The sound of a gunshot drowned out any further conversation.

Chapter 103

"You're not driving fast enough," Lucky said.

"Are we in a hurry?" Cooper asked, glancing over at her, a quizzical expression on his handsome face.

"It's one o'clock in the morning. I have to be back at the studio in six hours."

"So do I. Wouldn't it be convenient if I stayed the night?"

She began to laugh. "Didn't I tell you? *No* staying the night. *No* coming in for coffee. *No* nothing. I'm a married lady."

He reached out and placed his hand lightly on her knee. "You're a very beautiful married lady."

"Let me ask you something," she said, deftly removing is hand.

"Go ahead."

"Do you always feel obliged to make a pass at every woman you find yourself alone with?"

He smiled. "Why not? When you've got my kind of reputation, women expect it. If I don't make a move women begin to wonder what's wrong with them. And the *last* thing I want is you thinking you're unattractive."

She burst out laughing again. "Cooper, I can assure you I'm a *very* secure person. You don't have to worry about me?"

"Oh, but I do."

"Such a gentleman!"

"Thank you."

"Anyway," she said, "I'm very intuitive."

"Yes?"

"And I know you like Venus."

"She's my friend," he said defensively.

"She's your friend and you like her a lot, right?"

"Venus is with Martin."

"Oh yeah, he's a real prize."

"They're very happy."

"Come *on*, Cooper. You and I know it's not a match made in heaven. How long before he starts screwing around again? That's his way of operating, isn't it? Make a conquest and on to the next. A lot of high-powered businessmen are like that. It's the chase that turns them on."

"Maybe," he said carefully.

"Listen, trust me, I *know* what I'm talking about. I used to be like that myself."

"Like what?"

"Oh, you know — the thrill of the conquest was everything, and then on to the next. My father was always telling me I conducted myself just like a guy! If a man came along I wanted, I'd have him. It was the 'don't call me, I'll call you' syndrome. I didn't want to get involved. Of course, that was in the good old seventies when it was safe to sleep around. Now not only do you have to get a Dunn & Bradstreet on them, you also have to know their

546

medical history for the last seven years. Not to mention keeping your favourite condom manufacturer in business!"

"You're a straight-talker, aren't you?"

"Sure, it's the only way."

"It's refreshing."

"Thanks."

"In fact—"

"Yes, Cooper?"

"Can I call you one of the boys?"

She laughed. "Sure. Call me anything you like. Me and Lennie will be your new best friends."

"I'd like that."

If he ever comes back, she thought with a deep sigh.

The Mercedes roared down the Pacific Coast Highway.

"Make a left here," she instructed. "The house is in the Colony."

Cooper made the turn and asked if Gino was returning home.

"I sincerely doubt it," she said. "When he and Paige get at it there's no telling when they'll stop."

"You mean . . . at his age?"

"*You* should be so fortunate."

"Hmmm."

"Thinking it over, you probably will be."

He pulled the car to a stop in front of her house.

"OK," she said firmly, "you *can* come in for a cup of coffee, but that's all you're getting."

He smiled. "I appreciate your generous offer, but I'm not taking you up on it."

She smiled back. "Goodnight, Cooper."

He leaned over and kissed her on the cheek. "Goodnight, Lucky."

She got out of the car, walked over to the front door, waved, and let herself in.

Cooper waved back, revved the engine, and took off.

Neither of them noticed the black sedan slide past and stop a few yards down the street.

She hadn't been inside the house two minutes when the

547

doorbell rang. Thinking it was Cooper, she flung open the door.

Link didn't give her a chance to defend herself. He grabbed her before she could scream, roughly covering her mouth with his arm.

Frantically she tried to bite him.

He hauled back and smashed her in the face with his other fist.

Lucky slumped into unconsciousness without a sound.

Chapter 104

Rita ranted and raved all the way home. "I've *never* been so embarrassed. How could you do this to me? There were important connections at that party, Emilio, and *you* got us thrown out. How could you?"

"Don't worry, you'll read all about the dumb party in *Truth and Fact*," Emilio said sourly. "I'm going to expose every one of those uptight assholes. Show 'em up for the phony bums they all are. Nobody throws Emilio Sierra out."

"What are you going to do when you run out of stories?" Rita jeered. "That's all you've got going, Emilio. You make enemies of these people, an' you're *never* going to work in this town."

"What do *you* know?" he snapped.

"Plenty."

Their argument escalated, and by the time they got back to his apartment, Rita was ready to move on. She got all her stuff together and called a cab.

"You'll never find another guy like me," Emilio screamed after her.

"And I never want to," she screamed back.

In the Beverly Wilshire Hotel, Paige kissed Gino on the lips and snuggled into his comforting embrace.

"Goodnight, Gino," she sighed contentedly.

"Hey – what's so good about it?"

She shook her copper-coloured curls. "We're together, aren't we?"

His hand reached down her leg, and travelled up it with his fingers. "For keeps?"

"I want my ring!"

"Sweetheart – you got it! Tomorrow we go shoppin'!"

They embraced again and settled down under the covers.

"What took you so long?" he asked curiously, stroking her thigh.

"I was frightened."

"Of me?"

"Of making another commitment."

"Well, this is it."

She smiled happily. "I know, Gino. I know."

"Get used to it, kid."

"I already am."

"It's good to be home," Mickey said.

"You're not home yet," Abigaile replied tartly. "You can keep your bungalow at the Beverly Hills Hotel until we're both quite sure. You're here on probation, Mickey."

"What is it with the probation bit? We've been married long enough to know we belong together."

"If we *do* decide to reconcile, it has to be different from before," Abigaile said. "No more mistresses. No more whores. I've been thinking, maybe we should see a marriage counsellor."

Mickey roared incredulously. "A marriage counsellor! You and me? We'd be laughed out of town."

Venus Maria had departed, but there were still plenty of guests left. Ron wished they'd all get the hell out. He was destroyed about Ken taking off with Antonio.

They'd been together almost a year. Loyalty. Ha! It didn't exist any more. Ken was a taker. Venus Maria had been right about him all along. The Ken Doll – what an apt description.

Adam Bobo Grant approached him. "Sensational party, Ron. You certainly do things with style."

"Thank you, Adam."

"Tell me, where's your . . . friend?"

"He's not my friend any more."

"Really?"

"Really."

"You have beautiful hair," Saxon said, reaching out to touch.

"Thank you," Leslie replied, backing away.

"In fact, you're a very beautiful girl. Are you an actress?"

She stared at him — wide-eyed and luscious. "No. Are you an actor?"

He tossed his mane of hair. "Do I look like one?"

"You're certainly handsome enough," she said shyly.

"Who did you come with?"

"Friends. Who are you with?"

"A married lady about to get a divorce who changed her mind and reconciled with her husband tonight."

"Do you always take out married ladies?"

"They're kind of . . . attracted to me." He stared at her fresh beauty. "Why, are *you* married?"

She lowered her eyes. "I'm not sure."

Frankie and Arnie had picked up four girls. "We're goin' back to the house to party," Arnie said, grabbing Eddie. "Get your ass in gear."

Eddie had been pacing around all night long. He'd spotted Leslie early on and kept an eye on her. Now she was talking to some long-haired asshole and it pissed him off. He hadn't spoken to her, because he didn't know what to say.

"Sure, sure, I'll be with you in a minute." He waved Arnie away.

"We're outta here now," Frankie said. "See you later."

Eddie went to the john one more time. He laid out the last of his coke on the mirrored top, neatly arranged it

550

into three thin lines, and snorted it through a hundred-dollar bill.

As the cocaine exploded in his brain he had a revelation. Eddie Kane was going straight.

Leslie was going to help him.

Fuck everybody else. He'd made his decision.

And so the party ended. One by one the staff finished off their duties and went home for the night. The musicians packed up and left. The valet parkers produced the last of the cars.

Eventually there was peace and quiet.

The party was over.

Chapter 105

In Venus Maria's house a shaking hand groped for the phone and dialled 911.

"Help," a frantic voice gasped. "Please help us. Someone's been shot. Come as fast as you can."

Something woke Lennie. He didn't know what it was. Still half asleep he reached out to see if Lucky was in bed beside him. She wasn't there. Shit!

Rolling out of bed, he wandered into the bathroom, glancing at his watch on the way. It was past one o'clock.

Something was wrong. He had a feeling. The kind of feeling you get when you wake up after a real bad nightmare.

He walked around the house. There was nobody home, but the waves breaking on the shoreline sounded awfully loud.

In the living room he found the doors leading out to the deck were open.

Strange, he couldn't remember them being open before.

He went over to close them, and it was then that he saw a sight he was never going to forget.

A man – illuminated by the moonlight – was dragging a body into the sea.

Instinctively Lennie yelled out, "Hey!"

The man turned around, dropped the body, and began to sprint off along the beach.

Lennie raced down the steps onto the sand and ran towards the raging surf, heading towards where the man had been standing.

By the time he got there, whoever it was had vanished into the darkness.

Lennie waded into the surf. He couldn't see anything, and yet he was sure he'd seen the guy hauling something into the sea.

Another wave crashed in and then subsided. Suddenly he spotted a body lying there, slowly being dragged out to sea. It was Lucky. Oh, Jesus Christ, it was Lucky!

Stumbling, he managed to grab her under the arms, and little by little – because she was like a dead weight – he dragged and pulled her up onto the sand.

Was she breathing? He couldn't tell. He tried to remember everything he'd ever learned about CPR. Drowning . . . drowning . . . what the hell were you supposed to do when somebody was drowning?

Get the water out, turn her upside down. Oh God! This was his worst nightmare come true.

And he had no idea if he was going to be able to save her.

Chapter 106

The funeral was a sombre affair. The mourners wore black. And the huge crowd overflowed the church.

Martin was there, ignoring the crazed paparazzi as he walked inside, head bowed.

Several illegal helicopters hovered overhead.

Ahh . . . the price of fame . . .

"I still feel I went ten rounds with Mike Tyson," Lucky said, speaking carefully. Her jaw was bruised where the unknown assailant had smashed into it with his fist, and her arm was broken. That was before he'd tried to drag her into the ocean and attempted to drown her.

"If anything ever happened to you—" Lennie began.

She silenced him with a finger to his lips. "I'm here, you're here. That's enough. Don't let's think about what could have been if you hadn't come back to me."

He looked at her and shook his head. "I guess we were meant to be, Mrs Golden."

Ruefully she smiled up at him and responded with a simple "Yes, Mr Golden, I guess we were."

"She was a fine woman," said the minister. "Fine and respected. And she will be missed."

Martin stared straight ahead as the minister continued with the eulogy.

Yes, she would be missed, and so would Venus Maria. She'd run off to Mexico City and married Cooper Turner three days after Deena had turned the gun on herself and blown her own brains out in front of them.

Fate.

Who could control it?

Not even Martin Swanson.

He'd been publicly disgraced and humiliated all within days. It reflected badly on his image.

But he would rise again.

Nothing could hold Martin Swanson back. A tarnished image could regain its lustre. He was working towards that goal.

They watched the funeral on television.

"Tough break," Lennie said quietly.

"For whom?" Lucky said.

"All of them."

"Yes."

"Listen," Lennie said. "I talked to the police again. They've still got no lead on who it was. Are you absolutely certain you don't know anything?"

"I have no idea," Lucky said, picking up a magazine and glancing through it.

"You're sure?"

Bobby raced into the room. "Grandpa's gettin' married," he yelled. "Grandpa's gettin' married." He leaped on the bed and began bouncing up and down.

"When?" asked Lucky, throwing down the magazine.

"Soon as he can," shouted Bobby. "And I'm his best man. He told me, he said so."

Brigette followed Bobby into the bedroom. "It's true," she said, full of giggles. "Gino says he and Paige are getting married the minute her divorce comes through and they're going to live in Palm Springs."

"Gino will hate Palm Springs," Lucky murmured, shaking her head.

"If he's with Paige – Alaska will do it for him," corrected Lennie.

Brigette jumped on the bed too. "Can Nona and I borrow your car, Lennie? We're meeting Paul at the airport."

"The Ferrari? No way, take the jeep."

Brigette pulled a face. "I *do* drive a stick shift, you know," she said haughtily.

"Good for you. Take the jeep."

"Can I come with you?" yelled Bobby.

"Keep the noise down, your mother's supposed to be resting," Lennie said.

"Can I?" screeched Bobby, jumping up and down.

"Come on, brat," replied Brigette. "Catch me if you can."

They raced noisily out of the room.

"Hmmm," Lucky said. "And you want more kids? Aren't these two enough?"

He smiled. "I thought I did, but now that I know what

554

it's like to almost lose you, we can do whatever you want. It's your call."

"And I made it."

"Huh?"

"We're pregnant, Lennie."

"We're *what*?"

"Yup. We're pregnant, and we own a studio, and we're going to make your screenplay, and we're still married, and hey, do you realize we've been married almost a year?"

He shook his head and grinned. "A year, huh? and they said it wouldn't last."

"Spring open the champagne, husband."

"You got it, wife."

Their eyes met and they smiled. Two stubborn, crazy, smart people.

A new adventure was just beginning.

EPILOGUE

Mickey and Abigaile Stolli reconciled.

Mickey eventually became the head of Orpheus Studios, although by that time it was owned by a Japanese conglomerate.

Abigaile continued to give tasteful dinner parties. Mickey continued to fool around.

Tabitha celebrated her fourteenth birthday by running away with an eighteen-year-old Hispanic waiter.

Abigaile and Mickey were unamused. They sent her off to L'Evier – a strict boarding school for young ladies in Switzerland – and hoped for the best.

Johnny Romano took Lucky's advice and made a simple, heart-warming comedy in which he played the hero. He did not say "motherfucker" once.

The film – a Panther production – went through the roof.

Johnny celebrated by asking Warner Franklin to marry him in the middle of a promotional tour of Europe. He'd taken her along for the company,.

On the eve of their wedding in Italy, she met a six foot ten American basketball player and fell madly in love.

Johnny was left waiting at the church.

Emilio Sierra sold as many stories about his sister as he could, until there was nothing left to say.

When his money ran out he returned to New York and got a job as a bartender in a hot discotheque – where he met an ageing Euro-trash Contessa, who took a shine to his somewhat sleazy charm.

Emilio accompanied her to Marbella and learned how to tango.

They made an odd couple.

*

Eddie Kane tried for a reunion with his lovely wife.

Leslie wanted to get back together with him – after all, he needed her, and he'd faithfully promised to clean up his act. But something held her back and she told him they had to wait.

On his way to the beach house – high on yet another final blast of cocaine – his prized Maserati ricocheted out of control and hit a solid concrete wall head on.

Eddie Kane did not survive.

On his eighty-ninth birthday, Abe Panther married his long-time companion, Inga Irving.

His granddaughters – Abigaile and Primrose – were heartbroken.

After a short, abortive affair with Adam Bobo Grant, and still upset over the loss of the Ken Doll to the thieving arms of Antonio, Ron was granted his wish and met an older, richer, and far wiser man. His new friend was the owner of a big record company and revelled in mega-bucks. For once in his life Ron found himself on the receiving end, and happily accepted a Rolls-Royce, solid gold Rolex, and small Picasso in quick succession.

Venus Maria was thrilled for him.

Leslie Kane went to work at Ivana's as a receptionist. This enabled Saxon to keep a watchful eye on her.

Unfortunately Eddie had left her nothing but debts.

One day Abigaile Stolli spotted her, and thought she was the most exquisite creature she'd ever seen. "Are you an actress, dear?" she asked.

Leslie said no, but Abigaile insisted Mickey test her for his latest epic.

On screen Leslie's beauty was incandescent.

Within a year she was a star.

Brigette Stanislopoulos met the grandson of one of her grandfather Dimitri's business rivals. He was tall and blond and destined to be even richer than she was.

When she announced her engagement, Paul Webster stepped into the picture and declared his love for her.

Brigette was becoming wiser every year. "Too late," she said. "Try someone not so close to your own age!"

When Steven first heard the news of Deena Swanson's bizarre suicide he felt almost responsible.

"You couldn't have done a thing," Mary-Lou said consolingly. "She was bent on self-destruction."

"But maybe I should have tried to talk to Martin or something."

"No," Mary-Lou said firmly.

To his partner Jerry Myerson's fury, Steven found out the firm still had her million-dollar retainer, and made Jerry donate the entire amount to charity.

After that he felt better.

Gino Santangelo took care of business by making one phone call. It was enough.

Carlos Bonnatti suffered an unfortunate fall from the nineteenth floor of his Century City penthouse.

Nobody could figure out how it happened.

Link, his former right-hand man, got shot in an apparent mugging.

The perpetrators were never found.

Gino and Paige finally made it legal.

She was his fourth wife.

He was seventy-nine years old.

And very very happy.

Martin Swanson slowly put his life together again after the scandal. He missed Deena – she'd been his true partner and a help in every way.

He did not miss Venus Maria – too much of a responsibility.

When his business empire began to crumble because of shady investments in junk bonds, he moved to Spain to avoid being arrested, and became involved with a voluptuous opera singer.

Gradually he began to plan his triumphant return to New York.

Venus Maria and Cooper Turner remained the darlings of the tabloids.

What an explosive mix!

Everything they did was chronicled in great detail.

Their marriage was happy. But the paparazzi kept up a constant vigil.

Waiting . . . watching . . . ready to pounce . . .

Lucky and Lennie became the proud parents of a dark-haired baby girl.

They named her Maria.

Together they ran Panther Studios – united in their quest to make interesting, entertaining, intelligent movies of all kinds. From comedies to gritty dramas they excelled – giving women new opportunities at every level.

And just as Lucky had promised – Panther Studios became great again.

A year after Maria's birth they had another child – this time a boy.

They called him Gino.

The
Bitch

For J. K.

1

Nico Constantine rose from the blackjack table, smiled all round, threw the pretty croupier a fifty-dollar tip, and pocketed twelve shiny gold five-hundred-dollar chips. A nice round six thousand dollars. Not bad for a fast half hour's work. Not good for someone who was already down two hundred thousand.

Nico surveyed the crowded Las Vegas Casino. His intense dark eyes flicked back and forth amongst the assembled company. Little old ladies in floral dresses exhibiting surprising strength as their skinny arms pulled firmly on the slot machines. Florid couples – weak with excitement and too much sun – picking up a fast eighty or ninety dollars at the roulette tables. Strolling hookers – blank eyes alert for the big spenders. The big spenders themselves, in polyester leisure suits, screeching away in middle-American accents at the crap tables.

Nico smiled. Las Vegas always amused him. The hustle and the bustle. The win and the lose. The total unreality.

A carousel town set in the middle of arid desert. A blazing set of neon signs housing all the vices known to man. And a few unknown ones. In Las Vegas – if you could pay for it – you could get it. Just name it.

He lit a long narrow Havana cigar with a wafer-thin gold Dunhill lighter, and smiled and nodded at the people who went out of their way to catch his eye. A pit boss here, a cigarette girl there, a security guard on his rounds. Nico Constantine was a well known man in Vegas. More important – Nico Constantine was a gentleman – and how many of those were there left in the world?

He looked good. For forty-nine years of age he looked exceptionally good. Black hair – thick, curly, with slight traces of grey that only enhanced the jet. Black eyes – unfairly surrounded with thick black lashes. A strong nose. Dark olive skin beautifully tanned. A wide-shouldered, thin-hipped body that would make many a younger man envious.

However, the most attractive thing about Nico was his style – his aura – his charisma.

Hand-finished, tailor-made three-piece suits in the very finest cloth. Silk shirts of exquisite quality. Italian-made shoes in glove-soft leather. Nothing but the best for Nico Constantine. It had been his motto since he was twenty years of age.

'Can I get you a drink, Mr Constantine?' A cocktail waitress was at his side, long legs in black cobweb stockings, a wide mouth smiling and full of Las Vegas promise.

He grinned. Naturally he had wonderful teeth, and all his own, with just one vagabond gypsy cap. 'Why not? I think vodka, on the rocks, be sure its 90° proof.' His black eyes flirted with her outrageously, and she loved every minute of it. Women always did. Women positively adored Nico Constantine – and he, in his turn, was certainly not averse to them. From a cocktail waitress, to a Princess, he treated them all the same. Flowers (always red roses); Champagne (always Krug); presents (small gold charms from Tiffany in New York, or, if they lasted more than a few weeks, little diamond trinkets from Cartier).

The cocktail waitress went off to get his drink.

Nico consulted his Patek Phillipe digital gold watch. It was eight o'clock. The evening was ahead of him. He would sip his drink, watch the action, and then he would step once again into the fray, and fate would decide his future.

Nico Constantine was born in 1930 in a poor suburb of Athens. He was the first brother to three sisters, and his childhood had been that of a small boy caught up in a sea of femininity. His sisters fussed, bullied, and smothered him. His mother spoiled him, and various female relatives

8

kissed, cuddled and catered to him at all times.

His father was away a lot, being a crewman on one of the fabulous Onassis yachts – so Nico became the little man of the family. He was a beautiful baby, a cute little toddler, a devastating young boy and by the time he left school at 14, every female in the vicinity loved him madly.

His three sisters, not to forget his mother, guarded him ferociously. To them he was a prince.

When his father decided to take him away on a trip as a cabin boy, the entire family rebelled. No way was Nico to be allowed out of their sight. Absolutely no way.

His poor father argued, but to no avail, and Nico was given a job in a nearby fishing port, on the small dock, not a hundred yards from where one of his sisters worked scraping fish. She watched him like a hawk. If he so much as even talked to a member of the female sex she would appear, bossy and predatory.

The Constantine family desired to keep young Nico as innocent and untouched as possible. They worked on it as a team.

Nico meanwhile was growing up. His body was developing, his balls were dropping, his penis was growing, and most of the time he felt as horny as hell. Well who wouldn't, living in close proximity to four women? His sexual senses were assailed on every level. Naked breasts. Body hair. Creamy female smells. Underclothes hanging up to dry every way he turned.

By the time he was sixteen he was desperate. To jerk off was his only relief, but even that had to be planned like a military operation. Female eyes watched him constantly.

He realised he must run away, although it was a difficult decision to make. After all, leaving behind all that love and adoration . . . It had to be done though. He was being smothered, and it was the only answer. The only way he could become a real man.

He left on a Sunday night in December 1947, and arrived in the City of Athens two days later, cold, tired, hungry, certain he had made a wrong move, and already anxious that his family would come chasing after him.

He had no idea what to do, how to get a job, or even what kind of job to look for.

He wandered around the city, freezing in his thin cotton trousers and shirt, and only an oilskin to keep out the biting ice and sleet.

Finally he took shelter in the entrance of a large apartment building, and stayed there until a chauffeured car pulled up, and two women in furs got out, chattering and laughing together.

Instinct told him to attract their attention. He coughed loudly, caught the eye of one of the women, smiled appealingly, winked, projected unthreatening vulnerability.

'Yes?' the woman asked. 'Do you want my autograph?'

He was always quick, and without hesitation said, 'I have travelled three days to get your autograph.'

He had no idea who she was, only that she was mysteriously beautiful, with soft pale curls, a slender figure beneath the open fur, and a sympathetic smile.

She walked over to him and he inhaled sweet perfume. It reminded him of the womanly smells of home.

'You look exhausted,' she said. Her voice was magical, vibrant, and comforting.

Nico didn't answer. He just looked at her with his black eyes until she took him by the arm and said, 'Come, you shall have a hot drink and some warm clothes.'

Her name was Lise Maria Androtti. She was a very famous opera singer, thirty-three years old, divorced, extremely rich, and the most wonderful person Nico had ever met.

Within days they were lovers. The seventeen-year-old boy, and the thirty-three-year-old woman. She taught him to love her exactly as she had always wanted. And he was a willing learner. Listening, practising, achieving.

'God, Nico!' she would exclaim in the throes of ecstacy. 'You are the cleverest lover I have ever had.' And of course, after her expert tuition – he was.

Her friends were scandalized, and warnings abounded. 'He's hardly more than a child.' 'There'll be an outcry!' 'Your public will never stand for it!'

Lise Maria smiled in the face of their objections. 'He makes me happy,' she explained. 'He's the best thing that ever happened to me.'

Nico wrote a short formal note to his family. He was fine. He had a job. He would write again soon. He enclosed some of Lise Maria's money. She had insisted; and every month she made sure he did the same again. She understood how painful losing Nico must have been to them. He was truly a wonderful boy.

On Nico's twentieth birthday they were married. A ceremony Lise Maria tried to keep private, but every photographer in Greece turned up, and the small ceremony became a mad circus. The result was that Nico's family finally found out where their precious boy was, and they rushed to Athens, and added to the scandal Lise Maria had tried so calmly to ignore.

Of course there was nothing they could do. It was too late. Besides which, Nico and Lise Maria seemed so unbelievably happy together.

For nineteen years they remained locked in a state of bliss. The age difference seeming to bother neither of them. Only the world press made much of it.

Nico grew from a gauche young male, into a sophisticated man of the world. He developed a taste for the very best in everything, and Lise Maria was well able to afford the millionaire life style they adopted together.

Nico never bothered to work, Lise Maria didn't want him to. He travelled everywhere with her, and taught himself fluent English, French, German, and Italian.

He dabbled on the world stock market, and occasionally did well.

He learned to snow ski, water ski, drive a racing car, ride horses, play polo.

He became expert at bridge, backgammon, and poker.

11

He acquired an expert knowledge of wine and cuisine.

He was a faithful and ever expanding lover to his beautiful, famous wife. He treated her like a Queen right up until the day she died of cancer in 1969 aged fifty-five.

Then he was lost. Set adrift in a world he did not wish to live in without his beloved Lise Maria.

He was thirty-nine years old and alone for the first time in his life. He had everything – Lise Maria had bequeathed him her fortune. But he had nothing.

He could no longer stand their Athens penthouse, their island retreat, their smart Paris house.

He sold everything. The four cars. The fabulous jewellery. The homes.

He said goodbye to his family, now ensconced in a house in the very centre of Athens, and he set off for America – the one place Lise Maria had never been accepted as the superstar she was all over Europe.

America. A place to forget. New beginnings.

'Here's your vodka Mr Constantine,' the cocktail waitress twinkled at him, '90° proof – not our regular cra . . . er stuff.' She met his eyes with a bold glance, then reluctantly retreated at a signal from a surly blackjack player.

Las Vegas. A truly unique place. Twenty-four-hour non-stop gambling. Lavish hotels and entertainments. Beautiful showgirls. Blazing sunshine.

Nico remembered with a smile his very first sight of the place. Driving from Los Angeles in the dead of night, and after hours of blackness suddenly hitting this neon-lit fantasy in the middle of nowhere. It was a memory that would always linger.

Was it only ten years ago? It seemed like for ever . . .

Nico had arrived in Los Angeles with twenty-five pieces of impeccable Gucci luggage in the summer of 1969.

He had rented a white Mercedes, taken up residence in

a bungalow attached to the famed Beverly Hills Hotel, and sat back to see if he liked it.

He liked it. Who wouldn't in his position?

He was rich, handsome, available.

He was jumped on within two minutes of settling himself in a private *cabaña* beside the pool.

The jumpee was Dorothy Dainty, a sometime-in-work starlet with a mass of red hair, thirty-eight-inch silicone tits, and an unfortunate habit of talking out of the corner of her mouth like a refugee from a George Raft movie. 'You a producer?' she asked conspiratorily.

Nico looked her over, treated her with respect, and allowed her to show him the town.

To her annoyance he didn't try to fuck her. Dorothy Dainty was amazed. *Everyone* tried to fuck her. Everyone succeeded. What was with this strange foreign creep?

She took him around. The Bistro. La Scala. The Daisy. The Factory. One visit and Nico and the *maître d'* were the best of friends.

After two weeks he didn't need Dorothy. He sent her a gold charm inscribed with a few kind words, a dozen red roses, and he never called her again.

'The guy has to be a fag!' Dorothy told all her friends, 'Has to be!'

The thought of a man who didn't actually want to fuck her threw her into a decline for weeks!

Nico had no intention of screwing the Dorothy Daintys of this world. His wife had been dead three months, and he certainly felt the physical need of a woman, but nothing would make him lower his standards. He had had the best, and while he accepted the fact that he would never find another Lise Maria – he certainly was looking for something better than Dorothy Dainty.

He decided young girls would be best for him. Fresh-faced beauties with no track record.

He had never been to bed with a woman other than his wife. During the next ten years he made up for lost time and made love to one hundred and twenty fresh-faced beauties. They lasted on an average four weeks each, and not one of them ever regretted having been made love to by Nico Constantine. He was an ace lover. The very best.

He bought himself a mansion in the Hollywood hills, and settled down to having a good time.

The bachelors of the Beverly Hills community flocked around to be his friend. He had everything they all wanted. Class. Style. Panache. The money wasn't so impressive, they all had money, but he had that indefinable quality – a charm that was inborn.

For ten idyllic years Nico lived the good life. He played tennis, swam, messed around on the stock market, gambled with his friends, invested in the occasional deal, made love to beautiful girls, sunbathed, saunaed, hot bathed, went to the best parties, movies, restaurants.

It was a grave shock to him when his money finally ran out.

Nico Constantine broke. Ridiculous. But true. His late wife's lawyers in Athens had been warning him for two years that the estate was running dry. They had wanted him to invest, diversify his capital. Nico had taken no notice – and gradually he had spent everything there was.

The thought of having no money appalled him. He decided something must be done immediately. He was a brilliant gambler, always had been – and the lure of Las Vegas was so very close.

He thought about his situation carefully. How much money did he need to maintain his present life style? He supported his entire family in Athens, but apart from them there was only himself to think about. If he sold his mansion, and rented instead, he would have a substantial lump sum of money, *and* cut his weekly expenditure immediately. It seemed like a wonderful idea. He could take the money from the sale of his house, and in Vegas – with his luck and skill – he would double it – treble it –

certainly build it into a substantial stake that he could invest and then live off the income.

Nico had been in Las Vegas exactly twenty-three hours. Already he was down one-hundred-and-ninety-four thousand dollars.

Fontaine Khaled woke alone in her New York apartment. She removed her black lace sleep-mask, and reached for the orange juice in her bedside fridge.

Gulping the deliciously cold liquid she groaned aloud. A mammoth hangover was threatening to engulf her entirely. Christ! Studio 54. Two fags. One black. One white. What an entertainment!

She attempted to step out of bed, but felt too weak, and collapsed back amongst her Porthault pillows.

She reached over to her bedside table and picked up a bottle of vitamin pills. E was washed down with the orange juice, then C, then a multi-vitamin, and lastly two massive yeast tablets.

Fontaine sighed, and stretched for a silver hand-mirror. She sat up in bed and studied her face. Yes. She still looked incredible – in spite of the terrible year she had suffered through.

Mrs Fontaine Khaled. Ex-wife of *the* Benjamin Al Khaled – multi billionaire Arab businessman. Actually Fontaine could describe him very accurately as an Arab Shit. I mean what kind of man got away with saying to his wife 'I divorce thee' three times, and then walked away totally and utterly free?

An Arab Shit, that's what kind of man.

Fontaine conveniently blanked out on the more gory details of why Benjamin had divorced her. He had compromised her with sneak photographs of her and a variety of young men making love. It just hadn't been fair. She was entitled to lovers. Benjamin – in his sixties – was hardly likely to satisfy her most demanding needs.

The divorce still upset Fontaine – one of the reasons she had spent the better part of the year in New York, rather than London, where everyone knew. It wasn't Benjamin she missed so much, it was the world-wide respect and security of being Mrs Benjamin Al Khaled.

Of course she still *was* Mrs Khaled, but she made up a neat set of two with his other ex-wife – the one he had left to marry *her*.

Now there was a new Mrs Khaled Mark One. A disgustingly young model by the name of Delores. A very tacky looking girl, Fontaine thought, who was making a complete fool of Benjamin and spending all his money even faster than she had!

To Fontaine's way of thinking the divorce settlement was not equitable to her needs. Her standard of living had taken a sharp dive. She was even reduced to wearing last year's Sable coat. Last year's! *Quelle* horror!

She climbed out of bed, naked as usual. A fine body, full of muscle tone and skin lotion. Firm skin, small breasts as high as a sixteen-year-old.

Fontaine had always looked after herself. Massage. Steam baths. Facials. Exercises. Head-to-toe conditioning.

The work she had put in paid off. Soon she would be forty years old, and she didn't look a day over twenty-nine. No face lifts either. Just classical English beauty and good bones.

She put on a silk housecoat and rang for her maid, a fat Puerto Rican girl she was thinking of firing if only help wasn't so difficult to find these days . . .

The girl walked into the room without knocking. 'I wish you'd knock, Ria,' Fontaine said irritably. 'I've told you a million and one times.'

Ria smirked at her reflection in the mirrored bedroom. Oh Jeeze – would she like to fuck her boyfriend, Martino, in *these* surroundings!

'Sure Mrs K.,' she said. 'You want I should run you a bath?'

'Yes,' replied Fontaine shortly. She really couldn't stand the girl.

Sarah Grant, Fontaine's closest friend in New York, waited patiently at the Four Seasons for Fontaine to turn up for lunch. She consulted her neat Cartier Tank watch and sighed with annoyance. Fontaine was *always* late, one of her less endearing little habits.

Sarah signalled to the waiter to bring her another martini. She was an extremely striking looking woman, with intense slavic features, and jet black hair starkly rolled into a bun. She was rich in her own right, having been through two millionaire husbands, and now she was married to a writer called Allan who joined in her tastes for rather bizarre sex. At the moment they were both enjoying an affair with a New England transvestite who wanted to become a folk singer.

Fontaine made her entrance. Heads still turned.

The two women kissed, mouths barely brushing each other's cheeks.

'How was Beverly Hills?' Fontaine demanded. 'Did you have a divine time?'

Sarah shrugged, 'You know how I feel about Los Angeles. Boring and hot. Allan enjoyed it though, someone has finally been fool enough to option his screenplay. They paid him twenty thousand dollars. You would think he had personally discovered gold!'

'How sweet.'

'Adorable. My man has money at last. It will just about cover one quarter's payment on my jewellery insurance!'

Fontaine laughed, 'Sarah, you're so mean . . . The poor man has balls, you know.'

'Oh yes? *Do* tell me where he keeps them. I'd simply *love* to know.'

Lunch passed by in a flurry of the latest gossip – both women were experts. By the time coffee arrived they had carved up everyone and anyone, and loved every minute of it.

Sarah sipped her Grand Marnier, 'I saw an old friend of yours on the Coast,' she said casually. 'Remember Tony?'

'Tony?' Fontaine feigned ignorance, but she knew immediately who Sarah was talking about. Tony Blake. Tony the stud.

'*He* remembers *you*,' Sarah mocked. 'And with a quite violent lack of affection. What *did* you do to him?'

Fontaine frowned, 'I took him from being a nothing little waiter, and built him into the best manager of the best discothèque in London.'

'Oh yes. Then you threw him out, didn't you?'

'I dispensed with *his services* before *he* dispensed with mine. The cocky little bastard was only trying to open up on his own, knock me out of business.'

Sarah laughed, 'So what happened?'

'I thought I told you all about it. *I* went partners with his money man before *he* could. Poetic justice. I haven't heard from him since. What *is* he doing in LA?'

'Sniffing, snorting, what everyone does in LA. By the way, whatever happened to your club, "Hobo" wasn't it?'

Fontaine extracted an art deco compact from her Vuitton purse and minutely studied her face. 'My club is still going strong, still *the* place.' She selected a small tube of lip gloss and smoothed it over her lips with her finger. 'As a matter of fact I had a letter from my lawyer this morning. He seems to feel I should be getting back, sort out my affairs.'

'And *what* affairs are those?' Sarah teased.

Fontaine snapped the compact shut. 'The monetary kind darling. They're the only kind that matter aren't they?'

After the lunch they parted and went their separate ways. Fontaine felt that she had to keep up a certain front, even with a close friend like Sarah. As she strolled along Fifth Avenue she thought about the letter from her lawyer and what it had *really* said. Financial difficulties . . . Unpaid bills . . . Spending too much money . . . 'Hobo' in trouble . . .

19

Yes, the time had certainly come to return to London and sort things out.

But how could 'Hobo' possibly be in trouble? From the moment Benjamin had bought the place for her it had made money. Tony – her manager – lover – and stud – had become the most wanted man in London when she had put him in charge. And when she had got rid of him – Ian Thaine, her new partner – had redecorated the place, put in a new manager, and then got pissed off because she was not prepared to extend the partnership on to a personal level. So she had bought him out, and when she had left London 'Hobo' had been flourishing. And it was all hers, and should be a substantial asset; not a goddamn drain on her finances.

It was starting to rain, and Fontaine looked around in vain for a cab. God! It was about time she found herself another millionaire – who needed this searching for cabs garbage – she should have a chauffeur-driven Rolls, as she had always had when she was Mrs Benjamin Khaled. As it was she could only afford to hire a limousine and chauffeur for the evenings. She needed it desperately then, as the escorts she chose barely owned more than a motorbike – if that. Fontaine liked the men in her life to keep their assets on show – right up front – in their trousers.

She had never really pursued money, because of her devastating beauty it had always managed to pursue her. Benjamin Al Khaled for instance had spotted her when she was modelling in a St Moritz fashion show and dumped his first wife quicker than a hooker gives head.

After life with Benjamin, money was a necessity. Fontaine had a taste for the best that was very hard to quench. But she had wanted a pause before searching out another billionaire husband. Billionaire equalled old (unless you counted the freaked-out rock stars who always seemed to tie themselves up with young blonde starlets anyway). And old was not what Fontaine needed. She needed youth – she enjoyed youth – she revelled in the male body beautiful and an eight- or nine-inch solid cock.

A drunk weaved across Fifth Avenue and planted himself swaying and dribbling in front of her, blocking her path. 'Ya wanna get laid?' he demanded, displaying a mouthful of leer.

Fontaine ignored him, attempted to pass.

'Hey,' he managed to obstruct her way. 'Wassamatter? You don' wanna fuck?'

Fontaine gave him a hard shove, saw a cab, ran for it, collapsed in the back and sighed.

It really was time to get out of New York.

The very moment Fontaine departed for her lunch date, Ria, her Puerto Rican maid, rushed for the phone. Ten minutes later her boyfriend arrived. Martino. The best looking black guy in the whole of fuckin' New York City.

'Whatcha say, babe?' He greeted her with a kiss and a goose, while his stoned eyes checked out every inch of the luxurious apartment.

'We got two hours,' Ria said quickly. 'The bitch won't be back before that.'

'Let's go then, babe, let's go.'

'Sure, hon. Only thing is . . . Well I got me a fantasy. Martino, can we waste five whole minutes? Can I show you her bedroom? Can we make it all over her crazy fuckin' bedroom?'

Martino grinned. He was already unzipping his shiny leather pants.

Fontaine spent the afternoon at the beauty parlour listening to more gossip. Some of it was a repeat of what Sarah had already told her, but it was interesting to have it confirmed.

'I'm going back to London,' Fontaine confided to Leslie, her hairdresser.

'Yeah?' Leslie grinned, he had nice teeth, a good face, a nice body, but he was minus where he should be plus – a fact that Fontaine had personally checked.

'It's about time I had a change of scenery,' Fontaine continued. 'I feel as though I'm getting too static here.'

'I know what you mean,' Leslie replied sympathetically. Christ! Fontaine Khaled getting static! That was a laugh. The old bitch must have balled everything under twenty-five that walked in New York City!

Leslie himself was twenty-six, and not pleased that the notorious Mrs Khaled had taken him to bed only once, and then abandoned him like a bad smell. Oh, he was still all right to do her hair – and why not – he was the best goddamn hairdresser in town. The most fashionable too.

'Will you miss me, Leslie?' Fontaine fixed him with her lethal kaleidoscope eyes.

She was flirting and Leslie knew it. *What's the matter Mrs Khaled? Got a few hours to fill?*

'Of course I'll miss you, every time I set a wig I'll remember you!'

Game set and match to Leslie. For a change.

Fontaine was not in a good humour when she returned to her apartment. The horrible man in the street. Leslie getting smart ass. And then a foul-smelling cab driver who insisted on discussing President Carter's piles – as though they were a serious part of political history. Cretin! Ass hole! And she had a headache too.

Going up in the elevator she didn't bother to search for her key. She rang the doorbell, and cursed when it took Ria forever to answer.

It finally occurred to her that the stupid girl wasn't going to come to the door at all. She was probably asleep, slouched over a soap opera on television.

Furious, Fontaine rifled through her bag for her Gucci keyring, found it, and let herself into the apartment with an angry commanding shout of – 'Ria! Where the *hell* are you!'

The sight that greeted her eyes was not a pretty one.

22

Her apartment had been stripped, and from what she could see at first glance, what had been left was wrecked.

Shocked, she took two steps inside, and then realizing that Ria might be lying mutilated and murdered amongst the debris, or even that the robbers might still be on the premises, she backed quickly out.

The police were very good. It only took them an hour and a half to arrive, and they discovered no murdered Ria, just 'Fockin' Beetch!' scrawled in lipstick all over the mirrored bedroom.

Fontaine recognized the scrawl as being Ria's illiterate scribble.

Everything that could be moved was gone. Her clothes, luggage, toiletries, sheets, towels, small items of furniture – even light fitments and all electrical gadgets including the vacuum that Ria had pushed so disdainfully around the apartment.

The bed, stripped of everything except the mattress, bore its own personal message – a congealing mess of sperm.

'God Almighty!' Fontaine was fuming. She glared at the two patrolmen. 'Where the hell's the detective that is going to investigate this case? I have *very* important friends you know, and I want some action – fast!'

The two cops exchanged glances. Let's hope to Christ they don't put Slamish on this case they both thought at the same time. But they both knew it was inevitable. Slamish and Fontaine were destined to meet.

Chief Detective Marvin H. Slamish had three unfortunate things going for him. One – an uncontrollable defect in his left eye that caused him to wink at the most inopportune moments. Two – a tendency to store wind, and never to be quite sure when it would emerge. Three – a strong body odour that no amount of deodorants could smother.

23

Chief Detective Marvin H. Slamish was not a happy man.

He used mouthwash, underarm roll-ons, powders and sprays, and female vaginal deodorants sprayed liberally over his private parts.

He still smelled lousy.

Fontaine sniffed the moment he entered her apartment, 'My God! What's that terrible smell?'

Chief Detective Marvin H. Slamish winked, farted and removed his raincoat.

Fontaine was unamused. She gestured around her looted apartment, 'What are you going to do about this?' Her voice zinged with English authority. She glared at Chief Detective Slamish as though it was his own personal fault. 'Well?' her kaleidoscope eyes regarded him with disdain. 'Have you found my maid yet?'

Chief Detective Slamish slumped into a remaining chair, the stuffing bulging from where it had been ripped open. He had not had a good day. In fact his day had been pure shit. A drug bust that hadn't stuck. A row with his one-armed Vietnam-war-veteran brother-in-law who was the biggest con artist in Manhattan. And now this stiff-assed English society broad. Wasn't it enough that his balls ached? Wasn't it enough that his strong odour was beginning to pervade even his insensitive nostrils?

'Everything's under control ma'am,' he mumbled unconvincingly.

'Under control?' Fontaine arched incredulous eyebrows. 'Have you recovered my property? Have you arrested my maid?'

The two cops exchanged glances.

Slamish tried to summon an air of confidence and authority. 'Just give us time, ma'am, just give us time. An investigation is getting under way right now. In fact there are a few questions I'd like to ask you.'

'Questions? Me? You have to be kidding. *I'm* not the criminal in the case.'

'Of course you're not, ma'am. But then again it hasn't been unheard of for people to er . . . arrange things. Insurance . . . You know what I mean?'

Fontaine's eyes blazed. 'Are you implying that I might have set this up myself?'

It was an unfortunate moment for Slamish to wink.

'You *horrible* little man!' Fontaine screamed. 'I'll have your badge for your . . . your impertinence!'

Wearily Slamish rose, farted, and attempted to apologise.

'Get out of here,' Fontaine stormed. 'I don't want you on my case. My husband is Benjamin Al Khaled and when I tell him of your accusations . . .'

Chief Detective Slamish headed for the door. Some days it just wasn't worth getting out of bed.

Five long hours later Fontaine was comfortably installed in a suite at the Pierre Hotel. Thank God the bastards hadn't taken her jewellery. It had been safely locked up at the bank – a precaution Benjamin had always insisted on, and one that she had followed through with.

As for the apartment – well it had needed decorating. And her clothes . . . A new wardrobe was never a problem, and fortunately she was adequately insured.

Yes. A couple of days at the Pierre while she got herself together and did some shopping.

Then home . . . London . . . 'Hobo' . . . And a sorting-out of her life.

3

Bernie Darrell had been divorced four months, two days and twelve hours exactly. He knew, because his ex-wife, Susanna, never tired of telephoning to let him know. Of course there were other reasons she telephoned. The pool was malfunctioning. Her Ferrari had broken down. Their child missed him. Was he really tasteless enough to be seen at 'Pips' – a Beverly Hills discothèque – with another woman? So soon? How did he think she felt?

God! He would never really understand women. Susanna and he had spent a miserable five years as a married couple – in spite of how the gossip columns and fan magazines built them up as love's young dream.

Susanna Brent, beautiful young actress daughter of Carlos Brent, the famed singer/movie star/rumoured mafioso. And Bernie Darrell – hot shot record company mogul.

Mogul! Him! That was a laugh! He had managed to keep Susanna in the style to which she was accustomed. Just. Only just. And she had never tired of throwing daddy in his face, and how much better he could do it.

One morning Bernie had packed a suitcase, stacked it in the back of his silver Porsche, and fled. Susanna had been begging him to come back ever since.

Bernie didn't have much sense, but with the counsel of his friends, he had realised that to go back was to present Susanna with his *balls* – on a plate – nicely garnished. The longer he stayed away, the more he knew this to be the truth.

He was lucky to have a friend like Nico Constantine. Nico had allowed him to move into his house with an invitation to stay as long as he wanted. So far he had stayed seven months, and enjoyed Nico's company so much that he had no desire to find a place of his own.

Nico was his idol. He was everything that Bernie aspired to be. Bernie copied him religiously, but the result was not yet perfect.

At twenty-nine years of age Bernie had youth on his side. He was slim and athletic, and did all the good things such as tennis, jogging, working out at a gym. He also smoked grass profusely, sniffed coke constantly, and drank like a new generation Dean Martin.

Nico didn't touch drugs, and Bernie vowed he would give them up. But it was always tomorrow as far as he was concerned . . . and he never seemed to get around to tomorrow. Anyway he *needed* drugs, it was a social politeness. I mean as boss of a West Coast record company, how could he sit around at a meeting with one of his groups and not indulge? Professional murder. They would move on faster than a fag at an Anita Bryant coffee clutch.

Bernie attempted to imitate Nico's style of dress, but the suits were never that immaculate fit that Nico so effortlessly achieved, the shirts never laid correctly around the collar – even the hand-made ones. He looked good, but only until he stood next to Nico.

Bernie had a handsome bland face, capped teeth, bad breath, permed hair, a scar on his stomach, a perfect permanent suntan, and a small penis.

One of the great things about Susanna was that in all their mud-slinging arguments she had *never* mentioned his little dick. Never. He loved her for that.

Now Bernie sat on a Las Vegas bound plane, staring out of the window, wondering how the *hell* he was going to explain Cherry to Nico.

Cherry sat beside him, elegant hands crossed primly on her lap. Beautiful face in repose. Long straight blonde hair hanging luxuriously down.

She was a knockout. Nico's knockout to be precise. He had dumped her a week ago with the roses, and the diamond trinket, and the usual speech about how he was only leaving her for her own good – and how much happier she would be without him.

What a bullshit artist Nico was. The absolute best. The original fuck-and-run merchant. He always left the girl thinking *she* had left him! Clever.

In seven months Bernie had seen him do it to six of them. All staggeringly beautiful in that newly-scrubbed, wholesome young way. They all left without a whimper. Nico was right, they *would* be better off without him, (quite why they never seemed to figure out) but they parted the best of friends, and wore his diamond trinket from Cartier (usually a mouse or a butterfly) and spoke about him in only the most glowing of terms.

Bernie had never had that kind of luck with women. Whenever he tried to dump a girl they had hysterics, called him a motherfucking son-of-a-bitch bastard, and badmouthed him all over town.

What was he doing wrong?

'How long before we land?' Cherry asked sweetly.

Oh Christ! Cherry. She had turned up at the house looking for Nico. And she had been there when Nico had phoned from Las Vegas telling Bernie to grab some money and get on the next plane out. Then, firmly, but of course with bags of innocent girlishness, she had insisted on coming too. 'I have to talk with Nico,' she explained. 'My life is at a crossroads, and only he can help me.'

'Can't you wait a coupla days?' Bernie had grumbled, 'He'll be back in LA before that.'

'No. I have to see him immediately.'

So he had been unable to shake Cherry. And what *really* bugged him was she had let *him* pay for her ticket. The nerve! Not one move towards her purse, just a sweet smile, a soft hand on his arm and a 'Thank you, Bernie.'

Of course everyone thought he was loaded. If he didn't know better he would think so himself.

The newspapers described him as Bernie Darrell, millionaire record boss. Well the company did OK. But millionaire? Forget it. He could barely scrape enough together to make Susanna's ludicrous alimony payments. And of course, being Carlos Brent's son-in-law – even though he was *ex*-son-in-law – meant always having to pick up the check.

He wondered what Nico had meant by 'grab some money'. It seemed like such a strange request coming from Nico. Nico was always very flush, always the big spender. And in Vegas surely he could get as much credit as he could use? Anyway, Bernie had stopped by his office and extracted six thousand cash from his safe. It occured to him that ever since moving in with Nico he had never made an attempt to pay one household account. Even the liquor he ordered at the corner store and had them bill it to the house. He felt a bit guilty now, but Nico was truly the perfect host, and never expected a guest to put his hand in his pocket – even a seven-month guest.

Somewhere in the back of his mind Bernie knew that maybe something was amiss financially for Nico. An occurrence of events pointed to this. Firstly, why had Nico suddenly sold his house two months previously? He had got a good price, but everyone knew that if you had Beverly Hills real estate the name of the game was to sit on it. Prices were escalating at an exciting rate.

Bernie had joked at the time, 'Trying to get rid of a difficult house guest, huh?'

Nico had smiled that enigmatic smile of his, and made all arrangements to move them over to the new house he had rented. No discomfort for anyone.

Then another thing Bernie had noticed, stacks of unpaid bills were starting to accumulate on Nico's desk, and Nico had always been meticulous at settling his accounts immediately.

Just little things, but enough to make Bernie wonder somewhere in the back of his mind – a place he didn't visit too often.

Cherry said, 'Ooops! I'm not too fond of landings.'

She looked a little green. Bernie handed her the paper bag to throw up in, and sat back to enjoy the descent.

Nico had no sense of time. He had been sitting at the baccarat table how long? Two, three, four hours? He just didn't know. He only knew that the losing streak he was on had no intention of quitting.

A thin film of sweat skirted his brow, but otherwise he was unaffected – his usual smiling charming self.

His plan had gone disastrously horribly wrong. What had started out as a fool-proof scheme to make a big killing – had turned into a joke. He had lost every single dollar he had made on his house – worse – he had gone beyond that – and was now into the Casino for five hundred thousand dollars.

So much for skill and talent and luck. If the cards and dice were against you there was simply nothing you could do. Except stop playing. And he hadn't done that. He had kept right on going like some schmuck from the sticks.

He was now in a far more difficult situation than merely being broke. He was in debt to people who were hardly likely to be thrilled when they found out he couldn't pay up.

It was like a bad dream. It seemed to have happened before he knew it.

Two days. That's all it had taken.

The woman sitting beside him was pushing the baccarat shoe towards him. She was winning, quite heavily, and flirting with Nico, although she must have been well on her way towards being sixty. Her chubby arms and fingers were garnished liberally with jewellery, quite incredible jewellery – tasteless but effective. On her left hand she wore a gigantic diamond. Nico was fascinated by the size of it. It had to be worth at the very least five hundred thousand dollars.

As the cab took him and Cherry from the airport, Bernie

30

was disgusted to see that Carlos Brent himself was head-lining at 'The Forum Hotel'. Why the hell had Nico picked there?

'I've never been here before,' Cherry remarked, smoothing down her skirt with delicate pale hands.

'Don't get too comfortable,' Bernie muttered, 'you may be on the next plane back.'

'I don't think so,' replied Cherry, primly.

Oh yeah? One thing Bernie knew about Nico was that once a broad was out she was out. No going back, how-ever golden the muff.

Bernie was greeted regally at the reception desk. As Carlos Brent's ex-son-in-law he was a well-known figure at the Forum. He and Susanna had spent part of their honeymoon there – they had had to, Carlos was appearing at the time and he had insisted that the whole goddamn wedding party flew back to Vegas with him to celebrate.

Shit! Making love to his new bride with her famous daddy in the adjoining penthouse suite had not been the greatest of experiences.

'I'd like to freshen up before I see Nico,' Cherry was saying.

'Yeah,' Bernie agreed. 'Give me the key to Nico Con-stantine's suite,' he told the girl behind the desk. 'It'll be fine, he's expecting us.'

'Certainly Mr Darrell,' she said, giving Cherry a quick once-over from head to toe. News would have filtered over to Carlos that Bernie had arrived in Vegas with a nineteen-year-old blonde within the hour.

'This is Miss Cherry Lotte,' Bernie said quickly. 'Mr Constantine's fiancée.' Fiancée! Sweet! What a lovely old-fashioned word! Nico would kill him. But it was better than having Carlos Brent pissed off.

The baccarat shoe was emptied of cards by the bejewelled woman. Pass after pass she won, until the shoe was finished. She sorted out her stacks and stacks of chips with fat hands, and Nico was once again mesmerized by the size of her diamond ring.

He stood up. The pit boss said, 'Staying for another shoe Mr Constantine?'

Nico forced a smile as he left the enclosure, 'I'll be back later.'

He felt sick to his stomach, and then he saw Bernie hurrying towards him, and his spirits lifted. Bernie would have a way to bail him out. Bernie was a sharp kid, and anyway – after seven months of free everything he owed him a favour.

On the very top floor of the Forum Hotel, Joseph Fonicetti kept his eye on the proceedings. He owned the Forum, and with the help of his two sons, Dino and David, he ran a tight ship. Not too much happened within the confines of the Forum that Joseph Fonicetti didn't know about.

For instance – the fourth girl on the right – back chorus line – had obtained an abortion the previous afternoon. She would be back at work tonight.

For instance – two waitresses in the Orgy Room were stealing – nickel-and-dime stuff. Joseph would keep them on, good waitresses were hard to find.

For instance – one of his pit bosses was planning to screw the Casino manager's wife. That would have to be stopped – immediately.

'What about Nico Constantine?' David asked his father.

'How much is he in to us for now?' Joseph replied, his eyes flicking across his four closed-circuit TV screens that showed him plenty of action.

David picked up a phone to get up-to-the-minute information.

'He's given us six hundred thousand of his money – and he's into us for five hundred and ten thousand. He just left the baccarat table and is meeting with Bernie Darrell.'

'I like Nico,' Joseph said softly. 'But no more than

another fifty thousand credit, and see that he pays us before he leaves Vegas. You take care of it, Dino.'

'Do we take a cheque?' Dino asked.

Joseph closed his eyes, 'From Nico? Sure. Nico has plenty of money. Besides, he's too smart to ever try to shaft us. Besides, Nico Constantine without his balls – what kind of a ladies' man would that be?'

4

Fontaine zipped through the New York stores at an alarming pace. When it came to shopping for clothes there was nobody better at spending money than she was – except perhaps Jackie Onassis.

She used her credit cards liberally, unworried by the fact that her lawyer in England had warned her to run up absolutely no more bills.

She had been robbed. Surely she was entitled to clothe herself for her imminent return to London?

Armani, Cerrutti, Chloe – name-designer clothes had always looked well on her.

She had lunch with Allan Grant, Sarah's husband. He amused her, wanted to take her to bed for the afternoon. She demurred. She had so much more shopping to do. And she was to depart for London the very next day. She really didn't want to hurt Allan's feelings, she had been to bed with him before, but he was simply not her style. At thirty-six he was too old for her. Why settle for an old model when you could have the very latest twenty-two-year-old actor with a body like a young Marlon Brando?

Fontaine had always been a puller supreme. Men could never resist the lure of her perfumed thighs. Besides which, she had that very rare commodity – good old-fashioned glamour – and men – especially young men – loved it.

She left Allan, and went shopping in Henri Bendels, where she bought two pairs of boots at a hundred and eighty five dollars apiece. A simple black crocodile shoulder bag – four hundred dollars. An art deco necklace and earrings – one hundred and fifty dollars. And three hundred dollars' worth of make-up and perfume.

She charged everything, and ordered it sent special delivery to her hotel. Then she decided that she really must get some rest before the evening's activities, and she took a taxi to the Pierre, where she had a long luxurious bubble bath, carefully applied a special cucumber face mask, and went to sleep for three and a half hours.

Jump Jennings checked out his appearance one more nervous time before leaving his seedy village apartment. He looked good, he knew *that*. But the question was – did he look good enough? Tonight was the night to find out.

Jump had been christened Arthur George Jennings, but he had been nicknamed Jump in high school because of his athletic prowess, and it had just sort of stuck. Jump wasn't a bad name to be stuck with either. Jump Jennings. It sounded pretty good. It would *look* pretty good one day – stuck up on a marquee in lights next to Streisand or Redford. Rock, Tab, Rip . . . The world would be ready for Jump. His time would come. He hoped desperately that his time would come that very night.

He hitched up his black leather trousers, and adjusted the collar of his black leather bomber jacket. Sylvester Stallone was the look. Yeah – and it suited him too.

Confident at last, he left the apartment.

Fontaine awoke an hour before her date was due to pick her up. There was an exciting evening ahead. An art gallery opening, two parties, then the inevitable Studio 54 – a wild huge discothèque where anything could happen, and usually did.

She dressed with care after applying an impeccable makeup. She wore a deeply V-necked brown satin wrap dress, tightly belted over narrow crêpe de chine trousers. Strappy high-heeled pewter sandals by Halston completed the look.

One of Leslie's juniors arrived to comb out her hair.

and by the time he was finished teasing and crimping, she looked a knockout.

Of course her diamonds and emeralds helped. They always did.

Jump Jennings turned up on time. Fontaine shuddered at his choice of outfit. He looked like a refugee from the Hells Angels. Would her friends laugh? After all there was such a thing as going too far.

'Don't you have a suit?' she asked rather testily.

'Wassamatter with the leather?' Jump questioned aggressively.

'It's very . . . macho. But a suit might be more . . . well *right*. Something Italian, double breasted . . .'

Jump narrowed his eyes, 'Lady – you wanted a suit you should've bought me one. I'm an actor, man, not a fuckin' fashion plate.'

And so their evening started. Jump, broody and discontented. Fontaine, ever so slightly embarrassed by her escort.

Several glasses of champagne later she couldn't have cared less. So what if he wore leather? He was six feet tall and had muscles in places other men didn't even have places. He would do very nicely to round off the evening with.

Jump was doing his best early Brando, and it was knocking everyone sideways. Boy, he could've laid every woman in the place – they all looked like they could do with a good seeing to. But he concentrated all of his energies on Fontaine. She was some lady.

They had met the previous week at a loft party in the village, and she had whisked him back to her apartment in a chauffeur-driven limo real quick. There, they had indulged in a four-hour sex marathon that had taxed even Jump's giant strength. Wow – some wild woman! And rich. And classy. And stylish. And he was sick of dumb twenty-year-olds anyway. And he wanted her to take him to London with her. He ached to go to Europe.

'Having fun?' Fontaine sneaked up behind him.

'Beats jackin' off.'

She smile, 'Oh my, you're *so* crude.'

'You like it.'

'Sometimes.'

'Always.' His hand slid around her backside.

She pushed it away, 'Not here.'

'You'd like it anywhere.'

'I knew there was something about you that I found irresistible – it's your perception and intelligence.'

He moved very close to her and grinned. 'Naw – it's my cock!'

They made love for hours. It seemed like hours. It probably was hours.

Fontaine lay in bed, her head propped against the pillows, a cigarette in her hand. She was covered by a sheet in the semi-dark hotel room. Outside she could hear the occasional bleat of police sirens, and the usual New York street noises.

Jump was curled around in the foetal position at the foot of the bed. He was asleep, his muscled body twitching with occasional nervous spasms. He snored lightly.

Fontaine wished he had gone home. She wasn't too sure that she liked them staying the night. Why couldn't they just get dressed and go? In all honesty the only man she had ever enjoyed spending the night with was her ex-husband Benjamin, and that was strictly a non-sexual thing. Oh yes – they had made love on occasion – but Benjamin's stamina was low. To put it crudely, a two-minute erection was about all he could manage. So she had looked elsewhere for sex. And who could blame her? But Benjamin had been a friendly all-night companion – in spite of the fact that business calls came through from all over the world all night and every night – and *that* hadn't been too much fun. But still, she missed the basic companionship. The fact that at one time Benjamin had *cared* about her.

37

What did this muscled lump lying at the bottom of her bed care about? Certainly not her, that was for sure.

Oh maybe he liked her, was in awe of her, thought she could do him some good. But care? Forget it.

Most of the sexual athletes of this world were users. They bargained with their bodies. She should know – she had done it herself.

With a sigh Fontaine got up and went into the bathroom. She gazed at her reflection in the mirror. Her hair was a mess, and her make-up smudged. Good. Maybe Jump – what a positively *ridiculous* name – would take one look at her and leave. I must be getting old, she thought, with a wry smile, if all I have in mind is getting rid of him.

She ran the shower, and stood beneath the icy needles of water.

Jump stirred and woke. He reached up for Fontaine's leg, groped around, and realized that she wasn't there. He was annoyed with himself for falling asleep. After the sex should have come the talk. He was all ready to hurry back to his apartment, throw some clothes in a bag, and jet off to London with Fontaine. What would an extra ticket matter to her? Anyway he would give her plenty of value for money.

He could hear the sound of the shower. He leapt off the bed and padded into the bathroom.

Fontaine's body was silhouetted through the shower curtain. Jump didn't hesitate, he climbed right in with her. His entrance was spoiled by the fact that he hadn't realized it was a *cold* shower, and it took exactly two seconds for his powerful erection to become a shrivelled inch and a half!

Fontaine couldn't help laughing, but Jump was mortified.

By the time he recovered, Fontaine was briskly towelling herself dry, and brushed him away with a curt, 'Not now, I have to pack.'

Whiningly Jump seized his last chance. 'Hows about taking me with you?' he suggested. 'We could have ourselves a real good time.'

Fontaine had a fleeting vision of returning to London with a twenty-year-old, leather clad, dumb actor. *Not* exactly the image she wished to project.

'Jump,' she said kindly, 'one of the first things an actor should learn how to do is to make a good exit. You played your part beautifully, but darling, this is the end of the New York run, and London is not exactly beckoning.'

Jump scowled. He didn't know what the hell she was talking about – but he recognized a no when he heard one.

5

'Cherry?' Nico's black eyes glared at Bernie, 'Why the *hell* did you bring her?'

They sat in the bar lounge together, and Bernie had never seen Nico so angry.

'I had no choice,' he explained weakly. 'She was there when you called, and she just sort of insisted.'

'There is always a choice in life,' Nico said bleakly, and he gazed off into space sipping his vodka.

Bernie coughed nervously. 'So?' he ventured, 'What's happening? Are we having fun?'

'We're having shit. How much money did you bring?'

Bernie patted his jacket pocket. 'Six thousand dollars – cash. Are we going to play it?'

Nico laughed mirthlessly. 'I have already played it my friend. I am indebted to this very fine Casino to the tune of five hundred and fifty thousand dollars. And that is not to mention the six hundred thousand of my own that I lost upfront.'

Bernie sniggered. 'What is this? Some kind of a joke . . .'

'No joke,' Nico snapped. 'The truth. Feel free to call me any kind of schmuck you like.'

They sat in uneasy silence for a few minutes, then Bernie said, 'Hey listen, Nico, since when did *you* become the last of the great gamblers? I mean I've seen you play enough times and you've never been into heavy stakes.'

Nico nodded. 'What can I tell you? I got greedy, and I guess when you get greedy your luck flies out of the window. Right, my friend?'

Bernie nodded. He had seen it happen before. When gambling fever hit, sometimes there was nothing you could do about it. It carried you along with a force that was breathtaking. Win or lose you couldn't stop.

'How are you going to pay them?' he asked.

'I can't,' Nico replied calmly.

'Jesus! Don't even kid around on the subject.'

'Who's kidding? I can't pay, it's as simple as that.'

'The Fonicettis would never have given you that kind of credit if they didn't know you were good for it.'

Nico nodded. 'I realize that now. But at the time I wasn't thinking straight, and nobody put a limit on my markers. I suppose they figured if I could lose six hundred grand of my own, then I didn't exactly have a cash flow problem. The six hundred was my house. My final stake. I'm broke, kid, busted out.'

The full enormity of Nico's dilemma was only just occurring to Bernie. To lose was bad enough. But not to be able to pay . . . Suicide . . . Pure undiluted suicide. Everybody knew what happened to bad debtors . . . Bernie personally knew a guy in LA who had owed the bookies seven thousand dollars. *Seven thousand measly dollars for crissakes*. He had been washed up on Malibu beach one morning, and the word had gone around that he was 'an example'. A lot of outstanding debts had got settled that week.

'You're in trouble,' Bernie said.

'An understatement,' Nico agreed.

'We'll figure something out,' Bernie replied, and as he spoke his mind was already checking out the limited possibilities.

Cherry explored Nico's suite with childish delight. She even jumped up and down on the huge bed, and blushed when she thought of the fun they could have on *that* later.

Cherry had been in Los Angeles a little over a year, but already she had decided that the hustle and grind of being an actress was not for her. She had been a successful model in Texas when the call of Hollywood had brought her to a modest apartment on Fountain Avenue. Twenty-five auditions, two bit parts, and a commercial later, she had met Nico. Love had entered Cherry's life for the first time.

Sex had already entered it. First in high school with the football pro. Secondly with a blue jeans manufacturer. Thirdly with a Hollywood agent who promised her big things. She saw big things, but they weren't exactly what she had had in mind.

Nico was something else. He was everything she had always imagined a man should be. He was Nicky Ornstein, from *Funny Girl*. Rhett Butler, from *Gone With the Wind*, and Gatsby from *The Great Gatsby*.

Cherry always looked at life through the movies, things seemed more real that way.

Nico had swept her off her feet, from the moment they met at a party, to the moment he gave her his famous farewell speech.

At first she had cried and realized how right he was. Then she had thought, 'Why is he right? Why will I be happier without him?'

Then the thought had occured that without him she was miserable – so it stood to reason why they should be together.

Immediately she had rushed over to his house to tell him this exciting news, but he was not there, and Bernie had been kind enough to invite her to Las Vegas to find him.

She washed her hands, brushed her long golden hair, and sat and waited patiently. But after two hours she wondered if maybe she should go and look for them.

She checked her perfect appearance one final time, and set off to the elevator.

Dino Fonicetti had often been told he was the absolute image of a young Tony Curtis. It was true. He was the best-looking goddamn guinea in the whole of goddamn Las Vegas, and as such he had the pick of the girls.

Not that appearance had that much to do with sexual success. His brother David had the misfortune to look like a mack truck, and he also scored with monotonous regularity.

Dino entered the elevator, and was stopped in his tracks by just about the most exquisite-looking female he had ever seen.

Of course it was the delectable and innocent-looking Cherry.

Dino said, 'Hello there.'

Cherry looked demurely at the floor.

Dino, master of the fast line racked his brains for something to say. He came up with, 'Are you staying at the hotel?'

Not a bad opening. Not particularly good.

Cherry looked at him with wide blue eyes, 'I'm just visiting,' she said primly.

Some answer. Everyone was just visiting in Las Vegas.

The elevator reached lobby level and stopped. They both stepped out. Cherry hesitated.

'Where are you going?' Dino asked.

'I'm meeting a friend.'

He decided that he couldn't just let this exquisite girl walk out of his life. He extended his hand, 'I'm Dino Fonicetti. My family owns this hotel and if there is anything at all I can do for you . . . anything . . .'

Her hand, as she gripped his, felt soft and small. He was in love. Pow! Just like that, he was getting a hard-on!

'I'm trying to locate Mr Nico Constantine. Do you know him?' Her voice was soft and small, almost as good as her hand!

Did he know Nico. Why, he was the very man he was looking for himself.

Did *she* know Nico? Shit!

Nico and Bernie were still in a huddle discussing the possibilities, when Bernie said, 'I don't believe what I'm seeing. Dino Fonicetti is heading our way hand in hand with Cherry.'

43

Nico glanced around, and then stood as they approached the table.

Dino was indeed leading Cherry by the hand, determined not to let go. She went with him meekly, heads turning as she passed.

She looked at Nico, her eyes brimming over with the emotion of the moment. 'I had to come,' she murmured softly.

Nico's eyes flicked quickly between her and Dino.

'I met Mr Fonicetti in the elevator. He was kind enough to help me look for you,' Cherry said quickly.

'Nico!' Dino exclaimed warmly.

'Dino!' Nico's greeting was equally warm.

'And Bernie,' Dino added, 'why didn't you let me know you were coming?'

Bernie grinned, 'I didn't know I *was* until today.'

'Are you comfortable? Is everything all right?' Dino asked.

Nico grinned easily, 'Perfect.'

'Let me know if there's anything you need at all,' Dino said. 'By the way – how long will you be staying?'

The question was casual enough, but Nico felt he knew why it was asked. 'Long enough to recover some of my money,' he joked.

'Sure, sure,' Dino flashed his best Tony Curtis smile. 'We like everyone to leave here winners. Now tonight I want you all to be my guests for dinner.' He looked at Cherry. 'We'll catch Carlos Brent's late supper show. You'd like that, wouldn't you?'

She glanced at Nico. He nodded.

As a parting shot Dino turned to Bernie, 'Susanna's here,' he said. 'She looks great.' Then he strolled off.

'Who gives a shit,' Bernie muttered angrily.

Cherry asked, 'Who is Susanna?'

'Nobody important. Just my ex-wife.'

Nico was busily counting out some money. He handed Cherry two hundred dollars, 'Be a good girl, run along

44

and play something. Bernie and I have things to discuss.'

'But, Nico. I want to talk to you. I have some very important things to say to you. I came all this way just to . . .'

'I didn't ask you to come,' he interrupted mildly.

Her eyes filled with tears. 'I thought you'd be pleased.'

'I am pleased, but right now I'm busy.'

Cherry pouted, 'I don't know how to gamble.'

Nico pointed out Dino talking to one of the pit bosses. 'You friend will teach you. I have a feeling he'll be only too delighted to show you how it's done.'

Cherry departed reluctantly, and Bernie and Nico exchanged glances.

'I think little Cherry is going to work in our favour,' Bernie said. 'I haven't seen Dino so excited since he got laid by the whole of the Forum chorus line on two consecutive nights!'

'Right,' Nico agreed. 'Now let's go over the plan one more time.'

Solicitously Dino offered Cherry more wine. She declined, holding a delicate hand over her glass to prevent him filling it. 'I never drink more than one glass,' she said solemnly.

'Never?' Dino chided.

'Never,' Cherry replied. 'Unless of course it's a wedding or a big event.'

'This *is* a big event,' Dino insisted, moving her hand and filling her glass to the brim. He felt extremely elated at the way things were turning out. Nico had practically handed over Cherry on a plate. The four of them had eaten together – then Nico had taken Dino to one side and explained that he had a late date, and that Cherry arriving in Vegas had been an embarrassment that he didn't need. Dino had assured him not to worry. He would be more than happy to take personal care of Cherry.

'She's a wonderful girl,' Nico had enthused. 'But no more

45

than a sister to me now, and yet . . . well, I wouldn't want to hurt her feelings. I'll probably spend the night with my date . . .'

'I'll make sure Cherry never even finds out,' Dino said. If she spent the night with him how could she find out?

So after dinner Nico had made an excuse and left, and then Bernie had been set upon by his ex-wife Susanna, and gone off in a huddle with her, and now it was just Cherry and Dino.

Cherry was confused, but determined to help Nico out. He had asked her to keep Dino busy . . . 'Do anything, but be sure he is totally absorbed by you until at least noon tomorrow.' Nico had kissed her softly, 'It's important to me, and one day I'll explain it to you.'

Cherry sipped her wine slowly, 'Dino?' she questioned softly. 'Do you actually *live* in the hotel, or do you have a house?'

'I live right here, babe,' Dino said proudly. 'There are five penthouses, and one of them is all mine. Best view of the strip you're ever likely to see – that's if you want to see it.'

'Ooh, I'd simply *love* to see it. Can I?'

Could she? Goddamn. Things were working out better than he had hoped.

Dino's full concentration was on Cherry. He forgot about everything else. Going to bed with this exquisite little doll was his prime concern. He quite forgot about the fact that he was supposed to quiz Nico about his markers and get his personal cheque to cover them. Five hundred thousand big ones was quite a debt by anyone's standards. But still . . . Getting to Cherry was enough to take any-one's mind off anything. And it wasn't like Nico was taking off anywhere . . . He was around. Dino would talk to him about it the following day.

As soon as he made his excuses at the dinner and was able to get away, Nico headed straight for the Casino. His black eyes scanned the room searching for the lady who was to be his date.

Mrs Dean Costello scooped in another stack of hundred-dollar chips. God it was fun! It's a shame Mr Dean Costello hadn't dropped off a few years earlier. He had been so stingy with his massive fortune. Hadn't he realized that money was to have fun with?

Whoops – here came another number. Thirty-five. She had five chips on the centre and a cheval all round it.

'You're very lucky tonight, madame,' Nico said.

She turned to see who was speaking, and there, right behind her, stood that handsome sonofabitch from the baccarat table. She *knew* he had been after her.

'Yeah, I'm lucky,' she giggled, raking in her chips.

Nico watched her giant diamond ring catch the lights and sparkle invitingly. It had to be worth enough to get him out of trouble.

He wondered vaguely how much she weighed. Two hundred or three hundred pounds? Somewhere between the two.

He wondered how old she was. Fifty, maybe even sixty.

'You're a beautiful woman,' he muttered in her ear, 'and beautiful women shouldn't waste a night like tonight at the gaming tables.'

'Are you foreign?' she asked, flattered by his compliment but not surprised. Mrs Dean Costello thought that she was indeed beautiful. A few pounds overweight perhaps, and a little old for some tastes. But this guy was no chicken, and he knew a good-looking, *mature, sexual* woman when he saw one. He was no fool.

Busily she began to cash in her chips. Opportunities like this did not happen every day.

A half hour later they were in her room. When Nico wanted something he did not waste time.

'I don't usually invite strange men up to my room,' Mrs Costello giggled.

'I'm not strange,' Nico replied, opening up champagne

47

and surreptitiously slipping two strong sleeping draughts into hers. 'What is so strange about wanting to be alone with a beautiful woman?'

Mrs Costello cackled with delight. This was the best one to come her way since the twenty-year-old black waiter in Detroit.

Susanna had not been part of the plan – but what could Bernie do? She grabbed a hold of him, bossy as ever, and now she lectured him in an increasingly whiney voice about what a sonofabitch his lawyer was.

Bernie sat and nodded, hardly able to get a word in. He watched Dino and Cherry at a nearby table, and *that* all seemed to be going well.

Susanna tapped him sharply on the arm. 'I said, what are you doing here? Aren't you listening to me?'

'Sure,' he snapped back to attention and focused on Susanna. She had her mother's sharp features softened by a very good nose job.

'Well?' she glared at him.

'I didn't think I needed your permission.'

Susanna sneered, 'That's right, give me one of your smart-ass answers – that's all you know.'

Bernie stood up. He didn't need this crap. 'You'll have to excuse me, Susanna. I have a hot date with a black jack dealer. The cards are calling, and *that's* why I came here.'

'Gambling!' Susanna spat. 'And I have to fight you for every stinking cent of my alimony.'

He threw her a cold look. He was paying her fifteen hundred dollars a month, and she was insisting on more. It really was a joke. Carlos Brent was worth millions, and Susanna was his only child. Out of the corner of his eye he saw Cherry and Dino rise from their table.

'Got to go,' he said quickly.

'Bernie,' Susanna restrained him with a hand on his arm, her voice softening. 'Why don't we get together for a drink later? I really am sick of all the arguments.'

Oh, Christ! More complications! Susanna had that 'I wanna get laid' look about her.

Bernie managed an encouraging look. 'I'd like that. Where will you be?'

'I'm spending some time with daddy after the show, then I'll be in my room. Come for a drink.'

'Right. I'll see you later.' He made his escape just in time to check Cherry and Dino getting into the elevator. The kid had really come up trumps – one word from Nico and she was prepared to do anything to help.

Bernie hurried outside. He had his part to do as well.

They all wanted to help Nico.

6

New York's Kennedy airport was as busy as ever. The weather hadn't been too good, and a lot of people were sitting around and complaining, waiting for their flights to take off.

Fontaine Khaled arrived at the airport in her usual style. She swept in, followed by two porters organizing her luggage.

An airport official rushed over immediately.

Jump hovered in the background thinking about the day *he* would get treated in such a fashion.

'Mrs Khaled. So good to see you again,' said the official.

'Will you check me in?'

'Of course, of course. Would you like to wait in the lounge?'

Fontaine was irritated. 'There's not a delay is there?'

'Only slight.'

'Oh, Christ!'

The airport official signalled to a ground hostess. 'Escort Mrs Khaled to the lounge, please.'

'Lets go,' Fontaine beckoned Jump imperiously.

Nico's flight from Los Angeles had arrived one hour previously. He was not delighted to discover that his ongoing flight to London was delayed. He sat in the VIP lounge sipping vodka and musing on the events that had led him to where he was. He felt strangely elated when he really should be scared shitless. Christ! Maybe he had been stagnating for the last ten years. What had seemed like a good time had certainly not sent the adrenaline coursing through his veins like it was now.

Bernie had been very helpful. It had been *his* suggestion that if Nico couldn't pay his markers he split.

'Don't stay around to explain,' Bernie had urged. 'Get the hell out – get the money – and don't let them find you 'til you have it.'

Good thinking. But Nico had no idea at all how he was going to get the money. Then it had come to him. An idea so out of character – and yet so obvious. He would steal the fat lady's ring – it must be worth at least as much as he had lost.

At first Bernie thought he was kidding. Then he saw that Nico was indeed serious, and his mind had started to work. Steal the ring. Get the hell out of Vegas without the Fonicettis knowing. Sell the ring. Pay off the markers – and then worry about compensating the fat lady – for Nico insisted that she must be paid back.

It was a bizarre plan, but they both decided it would work.

Dino's crush on Cherry took care of him watching Nico too closely, and she had entered into the spirit of the whole caper with great enthusiasm. Bernie hired a car – and once Nico had the ring, he took the car – drove back to Los Angeles – picked up some clothes – and headed straight for the airport.

Bernie had a friend – Hal – in London, who had connections, and would be able to get the right deal on the ring. London was far enough away for Nico to have time to operate. By the time the Fonicettis had even realized he had left Vegas, he would be back with the money.

Of course the plan had holes. The fat lady would start hollering the moment she woke from her drug-induced sleep. But Nico had given her a false name – and who would suspect him anyway? He had taken care to make sure that they had left the Casino separately, and their only connection was sitting next to each other at the baccarat table.

Bernie and Cherry would stay in Vegas, and make believe Nico was still there too.

Now Nico waited for his connecting flight, and fingered

the ring lying loosely in his pocket. He was worried about customs. What if they stopped him and found it? Not a good thought.

A woman swept into the room. She was sophisticated, assured, and beautiful. Late thirties, very expensive, totally in control. Almost a female version of himself. He couldn't help smiling at the thought.

She was accompanied by a muscle-bound young man, who hung on to her every word. And her every word was very audible, as she spoke in a piercing voice that didn't give a damn about who might be listening.

'God! This is all so boring!' she said loudly. 'Why can't the bloody plane take off when it's supposed to?' She threw herself dramatically into a chair, shrugged off her sable coat, and crossed silken legs. 'Do order some champagne, darling.'

'Who *is* that?' Nico asked the girl serving drinks.

She shrugged. 'Mrs Khaled. Some Arab millionaire's wife. We have orders to look after her. She's been through here before and she's an absolute bitch.'

Fontaine wanted Jump to leave. He was annoying her. He was so obvious it was pathetic. All those little hints about how he longed to go to Europe. How he would miss her desperately. How she was bound to miss him. And of course – hadn't their love-making been the most erotic and sensual experience ever.

'I don't think you should hang around here any longer,' Fontaine said abruptly, 'I think I might just try and have a sleep.'

'I can't leave you,' Jump replied anxiously. 'The flight might be cancelled. I don't mind staying.'

Of course he didn't mind staying. He was hoping she would change her mind and take him with her.

'No, darling, I insist. You're been here quite long enough.'

Jump stood his ground. 'I'll stay, Fontaine. You never know what might happen.'

Before she could reply a hostess appeared and announced that the flight was ready to board.

'About time,' Fontaine complained, standing up and allowing Jump to adjust her sable coat around her shoulders.

He moved as if to hold her in a passionate embrace. She responded deftly, offering him an informal cheek to kiss. 'Not in public,' she murmured. 'I do have a certain reputation.'

'When will you call me?' he inquired anxiously, more concerned about a trip to London than her reputation.

'Soon enough,' she replied succinctly.

Nico secured the seat next to Mrs Khaled for two reasons. One – who better than to unwittingly carry his diamond through British customs than an English woman who it would seem unlikely they would stop. Two – the flight ahead was long and boring, and while Mrs Khaled was slightly long in the tooth for his admittedly juvenile tastes, she at least looked like she could amuse him, and if his luck was in – perhaps play a passable game of backgammon.

He allowed Fontaine to settle into her window seat before taking his place.

She glanced at him, amazing kaleidoscope eyes summing him up.

He smiled, full Nico charm. 'Allow me to introduce myself, Nico Constantine.'

She raised a cynical eyebrow, he was attractive, much too old for her, and conversations she didn't need.

Nico was not to be brushed off, 'And you are . . .?'

'Mrs Khaled,' she replied shortly. 'And I may as well warn you, that even though we are travelling companions for the next few hours, I am totally exhausted, and certainly not in the mood for polite conversations. You do understand, Mr er . . .'

'Constantine. And of course I understand. But perhaps I can offer you some champagne?'

'You can offer away. But let us not forget that they serve it free in first class.'

'I meant when we arrive in London. Perhaps dinner at Annabels?'

Fontaine frowned. How crass to have to cope with a man on the make when all she wanted to do was sleep. She glanced across the aisle at a thirtyish blonde in a striped mink coat, 'Try her,' she said coldly. 'I think you'll have more success.'

Nico followed her glance. 'Dyed hair, too much make-up, please credit me with some taste.'

Oh, God! What had she done to be stuck next to a man on the make. She turned and stared out of the window. Perhaps she should have brought Jump if only to protect her from bores on planes.

'Your seat belt.'

'What?'

'The sign is on.'

She fiddled for the seat belt, couldn't find one half of it. Nico realized it, and attempted to help her buckle up.

'I can manage, thank you,' she snapped.

Nico was perplexed. A woman who did not respond to his charm? Impossible. Unheard of. For ten years he had taken his pick of the best that Hollywood had to offer. Ripe juicy young beauties – at his beck and call day and night. Never a turn down. Always adoration. And now this . . . this English woman. So full of herself, waspish, and frankly a pain in the ass.

But still . . . If he wanted to plant the diamond on her he had to develop *some* line of communication.

The jumbo-jet was taxiing down the runway preparing for take-off.

'Are you nervous?' Nico asked.

Fontaine shot him a scornful look. 'Hardly. I have been flying since I was sixteen years old. God knows how many flights I have taken.' She shut her eyes. How many flights *had* she taken? Plenty. The first year of her marriage to Benjamin she had accompanied him everywhere. The perfect wife. Trips all over the world, boring business trips that had driven her mad, until at last she had begged off and only taken the interesting ones. Paris. Rome. Rio. New York. Acapulco. Marvellous shopping. Exciting friends. And then the lovers . . . Well, Benjamin had driven her to the lovers . . .

She felt the thrust as the big plane became airborne, but she kept her eyes tightly shut, didn't want to encourage her travelling companion to indulge in any more inane conversation. He *was* an attractive man. Not her type of course, much too ancient. Probably appeal to her friend Vanessa, who liked them a little worn.

'You've been asleep for two hours,' Nico announced.

Fontaine opened her eyes slowly. She felt hot and creased, and the taste in her mouth was truly vile.

Nico handed her a glass of champagne. She sipped it gratefully.

'Do you play backgammon?' he asked.

'Oh God! So that's what you are.' She couldn't help smiling. 'A backgammon hustler! I should have known.'

Nico grinned. 'A backgammon player – yes. A back-gammon hustler – no. Sorry to disappoint you.'

'But you look the part – my God, you're almost better dressed than I am!'

'That would be impossible.'

Suddenly they were talking and laughing. The steward-ess served food and more champagne.

He wasn't so bad, Fontaine decided. Rather nice actually. And what a refreshing change to have a conversation with a man who was neither a fag nor a young stud. Idly she wondered if he had money. He was certainly dressed well enough – and the jewellery was expensive and in perfect taste.

'What business are you in?' she asked casually.

Nico smiled. 'Commodities.'

'That sounds like it could be anything.'

'It usually is, I don't like to be pinned down.'

'Hmm . . .' She fixed him with a quizzical look.

'And you? Where is Mr Khaled?'

'Benjamin Al Khaled no longer has the pleasure of being my husband. Ex is the word – but keep it to yourself – I get better service when the world doesn't know.'

Nico looked her over admiringly. 'I'm sure *you* would always get good service.'

'Thank you.'

Their eyes met and locked. There was that moment when nothing is said but everything is known.

Fointaine broke the look. God! Maybe it was the plane trip, maybe she was overtired, but suddenly she felt incredibly horny.

'Excuse me,' she got up and moved past him to visit the toilet. She wanted to check out her appearance. She probably looked a mess.

Nico watched her go, and sniffed at the cloud of 'Opium' perfume she left behind. Lise Maria had always worn 'Jolie Madame'. It was the first time he had thought of his late wife in a long time. Lise Maria belonged in the past, wrapped in a beautiful memory he did not care to disturb. Why was he thinking of her now?

'Will you be watching the movie, Mr Constantine?' the stewardess inquired.

'What is it?'

'*The Fury*. Starring Kirk Douglas.'

'Sure – leave the earphones.'

'And Mrs Khaled?'

'Yes. Mrs Khaled will watch it too.'

Making decisions for her already! And thinking about how it would be in bed with a woman like that . . . It had been so long since he had had a woman. Plenty of girls – gorgeous sweet creatures who enjoyed his expert tuition . . . But to have a real woman again . . . A sophisticated sensual female . . .

Idly he wondered if she had money, what a plus *that* would be.

7

Polly Brand stirred in her sleep and reached out. Her arm encountered flesh, and she woke with a start. Then she remembered, grinned, and reached for her glasses. 'All the better to see you with my dear!' she giggled, as she trailed her fingers down her companion's back.

'Get off . . .' he mumbled, still half asleep.

'Oh come on,' Polly responded, full of enthusiasm. 'We've just got time to do it before we go to the airport.'

'Do what?'

'*It*, of course.' Her hand reached for his slumbering penis.

He moved away. 'I gotta sleep. Ten more minutes . . .'

'Ricky. I've got you a very good job, and I do expect you to be grateful – *very* grateful.'

'I'll be fucking grateful tonight. Right now I need sleep.'

Polly squirmed all over him. 'You'll be working tonight, Ricky Tick. Our Mrs Khaled will have you hard at it ferrying her around 'til all hours. The bitch never sleeps. She has to be seen – constantly – and your chauffeur duties will not be over 'til dawn. And that's when *I* like to sleep. So come on – let's fuck!'

Reluctantly Ricky allowed the energetic Polly to go to work on him until he was in a ready state to do her bidding.

A six-minute thrash and it was over.

'Thanks a *lot*!' complained Polly.

'Morning is not my best time,' Ricky grumbled, reaching for his watch. '*Especially* not five-a-bleedin'-clock.'

'We have to be at the airport by seven. Mrs Khaled cannot be kept waiting, she'll throw a right mood if she is. Your new employer is *very* temperamental.'

'Can't wait. Are you sure this job isn't just one big drag?'

Polly giggled, 'You'll love it. You'll have a great time. If I know dear old Fontaine . . .'

'Yeah?'

Polly climbed out of bed still giggling. 'Just wait and see, you're in for a big surprise . . . If she likes you that is . . . And oh boy . . . I've got a feeling she'll like you.'

Fontaine Khaled and Ricky the chauffeur. The thought sent Polly off into gales of laughter.

Ricky followed her out of bed. 'Come on, share the joke.'

'You'll know soon enough.' Polly clicked a cassette into her tape deck and the sound of Rod Stewart filled the room. She proceeded to exercise to the sound of his voice – unconcernedly naked.

Ricky watched her for a minute, then he went into the bathroom. Funny little thing that one. She had chatted him up in his mini-cab two weeks earlier – and before he knew it he had quit his job to accept the position as Mrs Khaled's chauffeur. Well, driving a mini-cab was not for him. Too many bleedin' headaches. Now chauffeuring was another thing . . . If you had to drive around London day and night you may as well do it in a Roller.

Polly stretched to the ceiling, back to touch the floor. Twenty-four . . . twenty-five . . . Finished.

She couldn't be bothered to wash, a bad habit but no one had ever complained. She pulled on a fluffy angora sweater and tight jeans, knee-length boots, and pulled a comb through her short spiky hair. Make-up was lipgloss only. Her tinted glasses did the rest. Polly was not pretty – more unusual and certainly attractive. She was twenty-nine years old, and head of her own Public Relations outfit. Not bad for a girl who started out as a secretary at seventeen. Her firm represented Fontaine Khaled's discothèque 'Hobo', and Mrs Khaled called on her whenever she needed anything. Polly didn't mind. For each service she performed she added a little extra on the bill. Finding Ricky would be worth at least a couple of hundred.

He emerged from the bathroom clad in a pair of

jockey shorts decorated with a garish picture of a rhinoceros and a slogan saying – 'I feel horny.'

'Christmas! Where did you get *those*?' Polly fell about laughing.

'My kid sister.' Ricky walked over to the mirror to admire himself. 'They look all right, don't they?'

'All right? They're a fucking scream!'

Ricky frowned. 'It's only a joke, no need to wet your panties.'

Polly tried to stop laughing. 'I didn't know guys actually *wore* things like that.'

Ricky's dignity was affronted. He pulled on his trousers quickly.

Polly leaned back and studied him through narrowed eyes. Great body. Thin, wiry, rock-hard thighs and stomach, and a nice tight ass. Sexy, sexy face, dirty blond hair, and when he was in the mood – a natural enthusiasm for screwing. Nice and normal. Not into grass or coke or tying you to the bed. Probably didn't even know what bondage was.

Fontaine Khaled . . . if she wanted to . . . would absolutely adore him.

The interior of the plane was dark as the big jet winged its way towards England. The movie had finished, and now most of the passengers were asleep.

Fontaine wasn't.

Nico wasn't.

They were indulging in a necking session – teenage in its intensity.

Who could ever forget the excitement of one's first furtive gropings. The hands under the sweater, up the skirt. The lips, tongues, teeth. The eroticism of investigating a strange ear. The exquisite thrill of a clandestinely fondled nipple.

Fontaine felt as flushed as any fifteen-year-old. It was an amazing sensation. Nico, too, was filled with an unremembered excitement.

To touch but not to be really able to. To feel – but not properly.

Whoever said making love on a plane was easy was a fool. It was goddamn difficult. Especially when a stewardess flitted up and down the aisle every ten minutes.

So they contented themselves with the sticky fondlings of first experience. And it was erotic to say the least. It was also fun. And it was a long time since either of them could remember sex being fun.

'When I get you in London, Mrs Khaled, I want time, space, and the luxury of a bed,' Nico whispered. His fingers were on her thigh, travelling up, sneaking round the leg of her panties.

Fontaine's hand fiddled with the zipper on his trousers. She could feel his maleness through the silk of his undershorts, and it was turning her on with a vengeance. 'Oh, yes, Mr Constantine, I think that could be arranged.'

The stewardess passed by, brisk and efficient. Could she see what was going on? They both remained stock still.

'I want to see your body,' Nico whispered. 'I know you have a very beautiful body.'

Fontaine traced the line of his mouth with her tongue, 'None of your bullshit lines please, Nico. None of your stock phrases. You don't have to play the perfect gentleman with me.'

She had him figured out pretty quickly. He liked that. 'So I want to fuck you,' he muttered. 'I want to fuck your beautiful body.' Christ! He hadn't felt free enough to talk to a woman like that since Lise Maria. Fontaine was right – he did open his mouth and out poured the perfect gentleman bullshit.

'That's better,' Fontaine sighed. 'I want to feel you're talking to me, not doing your number.'

Their tongues played sensuous games. Then dawn and lightness started to filter through the windows, and it was time to stop playing and brush out clothes and adjust things.

The stewardess served them breakfast with a thin smile. She had seen what was going on – and frankly she was jealous. It wasn't like she hadn't seen it all before. But a man like Nico Constantine . . . Well – if he hadn't been stuck next to that Khaled bitch there might have been a chance for her.

Fontaine nibbled on some toast, sipped the awful coffee, and smiled at Nico. 'That was —'

He put a finger on her lips. 'Don't give me any of *your* bullshit lines.'

'But it was.'

'It was.'

They grinned at each other stupidly.

'I'd better go and get myself together,' Fontaine said at last. 'A little makeup job, and my hair needs mouth to mouth resuscitation!'

It wasn't until she had gone that Nico suddenly remembered the reason he had struck up an acquaintance in the first place. It didn't seem so important now. But he had the ring, and it was burning a hole in his pocket. If he asked Fontaine he was sure that she wouldn't mind taking it through customs for him. But why involve her? The best thing was to have her do it for him unknowingly.

She had taken her makeup case and left her purse. Easy. He glanced across the aisle. The dyed blonde in the striped mink coat was engrossed in conversation with a drunken writer who was en route to London to get married for the fifth time.

Nico opened the purse. Easy. A double zipped compartment into which he dropped the ring. Easy.

Fontaine returned, her hair pulled sleekly back, a subtle makeup emphasizing her perfect bones. She smiled at him. 'Have I got time for a cigarette before we come down to earth?'

Ricky drove the large silver Rolls-Royce much too fast. Polly, enjoying an early morning joint, admonished

61

him. 'Mrs K. sets the speed when you're driving her. Don't you forget it.'

'What's she like?' Ricky asked for the sixth time.

'Oh, you'll either like her or you'll hate her. She's a difficult lady. No in-betweens. Typical Gemini – only ever does what she wants to do – hears what she wants to hear.'

'Has she still got a lot of money?'

Polly shrugged. 'Who knows? "Hobo" ain't making it any more, but her old man was so loaded . . . Look out Ricky – you nearly hit that car. You're supposed to be a chauffeur, not a racing car driver. And don't forget – call me Miss Brand in front of her. Wouldn't do to let her know I'm screwing the hired help.'

'Mrs Khaled. Welcome back to London.' Fontaine was greeted by an airport lackey paid to smooth the way for VIPs. He took her makeup case. 'This way, Mrs Khaled. Everything's taken care of. If we can just have your passport . . .'

She glanced around, looking for Nico. He stood at the back of a long line for foreign passports.

She waved, blew him a kiss, and swept right through British passport control.

Nico was impressed. Still married to her Arab billionaire or not she knew how to do things in style. What a stroke of genius planting the ring on her. No way would customs dare to stop her.

He thought about where he would take her for dinner. It was many years since he had been in London. But Annabels was always safe, then maybe a little gambling at the Clermont, and then bed. He anticipated a stimulating evening in every way.

Fontaine feigned surprise at seeing Polly. 'So early, darling? You shouldn't have bothered.'

Polly knew that if she hadn't bothered, Fontaine would never have let her forget it.

They kissed, the usual insincere brushing of cheeks.

'You look gorgeous!' Polly exclaimed. 'Have you had a wonderful time?'

'Terrible actually. Didn't you hear about my robbery?'

They walked to the car where Ricky respectfully held the Rolls door open.

'No! How awful! What happened?'

'I was wiped out. They took everything, absolutely everything!'

'Your jewellery?'

'Not my jewellery. That – thank God – was in the bank.'

Ricky shut the door on them. So this was the famous Mrs Khaled. Really something. She made Polly look like a bit of old rope.

Nico stood in line patiently for twenty five minutes. It was annoying, but a fact of life when entering a foreign country.

Naturally he was detained at customs. 'You have the look of an expensive smuggler!' Lise Maria had once told him. 'Don't ever change, I love that look!'

The customs official was polite but insistent. Every one of his Vuitton suitcases was opened up and searched. For one horrible moment Nico thought they might also search him, but luck was on his side, and he did not have to suffer the indignity of a body search.

At last he was free. He hoped that Fontaine had waited for him – she had mentioned something about her car and chauffeur meeting her. But she was nowhere to be seen. Long gone. He should have known she was not the sort of woman who would wait around.

Damn. It was annoying. He wanted to recover the ring as soon as possible. What if she discovered it? The idea of that was not a welcome one, but he would just bluff it out – tell her the truth – not about actually stealing the ring – just about her helping him through customs with it. And a good job too, considering he had been stopped.

Fontaine would probably be amused by the whole incident.

Still . . . it would be better if she didn't find the ring . . . which meant he had to see her as soon as possible.

He signalled a cab and directed the driver to the Lamont Hotel. He had been warned that no one of any note stayed at the Dorchester since it had been bought by the Arabs. The Lamont was *the* place – quiet, very English, with an excellent restaurant comparable to the Connaught.

'Cor blimey, mate,' sneered the cabbie. 'Sure you got enough bleedin' suitcases?'

8

Cherry's first night with Dino was a mechanical affair. He took her to his penthouse apartment atop the Forum, showed her the view – which she admired. Fixed her an exotic liqueur – which she drank. Played her some sensual Barry White sounds – which she enjoyed. Then moved in for the kill.

'I don't make love on a first date,' Cherry said demurely, long brownish black eyelashes fluttering over huge blue eyes.

'What?' snapped Dino. He had a hard-on that was threatening to burst the zipper on his pants.

'I like you a lot,' Cherry continued in her sweet baby girl voice, 'and I admire you. But I can't make love to you, it's against my principles.'

'Principles!' exclaimed Dino. 'Forget your goddamn principles.'

'Don't get mad,' Cherry replied firmly. 'You have no right to expect me to do anything I don't want to.'

He looked her over, every gorgeous inch of her, and for the first time in his life realized he was getting a turn-down. He couldn't offer her a better part in the show. She didn't want to be a cocktail waitress. If he proffered money she would throw it back in his face. But his father had taught him well – every woman has her price – and every smart man should be able to find out what that price is.

'What do you want?' Dino asked thickly.

Cherry shook her long blonde curls. 'Nothing,' she replied. 'But I like being with you, and if you want I'll stay the night with you – but I won't do anything, and you must promise not to force me.'

In all his many experiences with women this was a first. Dino was perplexed. He was also fascinated. He was also in love.

They spent the night together. They kissed. They caressed. She stripped down to a skimpy lace chemise that would give any red-blooded male a heart attack. He put on a bathrobe over a pair of restrictive jockey shorts.

He just did not believe what was going on. He fell asleep with a wrecking gut-ache, and woke at seven in the morning with the same nagging pain.

Cherry lay asleep beside him, yellow hair fanned out around her face, legs slightly apart, the chemise revealing just a wisp of lacy panties.

Enough was enough. Dino rolled on top of her, ripping her panties with one hand, and freeing himself with the other. He was inside her before she even awoke.

'Dino! You promised!' She was not as outraged as she might have been.

'That was last night,' he husked. 'Our first date. Now it's our second date and it's my turn to call the shots.'

Cherry didn't argue. She wrapped her long and beautiful legs around him and gave a little sigh. Nico was a marvellous man – but as he had pointed out – what kind of a future did she have with him?

Now Dino was a different matter . . .

So far so good. Everything was going according to plan.

Bernie placed a stack of chips on red and watched black come up. Roulette. What a game. Why was he even bothering?

He glanced at his watch. Two o'clock in the morning. Nico should be well on his way.

He eyed one of the cocktail waitresses. It wasn't his imagination that she had been coming on to him all night.

He gestured for another scotch, and wondered if he should hit on her for a fast fuck. He decided against it. He had too much on his mind, and anyway sex drained his vital energies.

At that precise moment his name was paged, and he thought – Christ! The shit has hit.

He rushed to the phone. It was Susanna. She was

drunk. Just what he needed in his life, a drunken ex-wife.

'I thought you were coming up for a drinkie,' giggle giggle, 'or something . . .?'

'Hey,' How should he play *this* one? He was in enough trouble with Susanna as it was. 'I called you earlier, guess you weren't back,' he explained.

'Daddy had a party,' she hiccoughed. 'Fifteen gofers, twenty hookers, and half the mob.'

The only time she put daddy down was when she was drunk. Then she saw him for the egotistical mean sonofabitch he really was.

Bernie played for time. 'Sounds like fun.'

'It wasn't. It was awful,' she paused, then in a sexy whine. 'Come on up Bernie, for old times' sake. We can just – talk.'

Oh shit! What did he have to lose?

Besides which, Susanna gave the best head in Hollywood. Or if there was anyone better *he'd* never found them.

Cherry and Dino spent the morning in bed.

They talked. They investigated the possibilities of getting further involved. They would have stayed there all day if Dino's father hadn't called and demanded his presence.

'What I want you to do is go back to Nico's suite, collect your things, and tell him bye bye,' Dino told her.

At the mention of Nico's name Cherry felt a twinge of guilt. Surely if she was planning to stay with Dino her loyalties lay with him? Maybe she should tell him that Nico had already left . . . But then again she had promised Nico she would help . . . And of course she wouldn't want him to come to any harm.

Dino was dressing. White slacks, a black shirt, white sports jacket. Las Vegas casual.

Cherry sat up in bed, blonde hair tumbling around her shoulders. 'Dino,' she ventured shyly, 'have you ever been married?'

Dino grinned at himself admiringly in the mirror.

'Me? No, of course not.'

'Why of course not?'

'Well . . . gee . . . I don't know . . .' Why *hadn't* he ever got married? Never met anyone he would want to marry. He looked at Cherry lying in his bed. She was so . . . delectable . . . He wanted to eat her up. His grin widened, he would later.

She climbed out of bed innocently unaware of his scrutiny – or so he thought.

Now that was what he called a body. Streamlined and golden. Soft and firm.

She walked to the bathroom door, turned, and smiled sweetly. 'I'd *like* to get married,' she said softly. 'Wouldn't you?'

Bernie did not escape Susanna's clutches until six in the morning. He staggered from her room bleary-eyed and exhausted. They had run through the whole book of emotions – plus some very wild sex.

He hurried back to Nico's suite, and collapsed on the bed.

He had blown checking with Nico on the phone, but hopefully, by this time, he was on a plane to Europe.

Now if the pretence of Nico still being in Vegas could only be kept up . . .

Bernie fell into a fully clothed sleep.

As Bernie fell asleep Mrs Dean Costello woke up. She felt as if someone had hit her over the head with a hammer, and she was surprised to note that she was still fully dressed.

She struggled to recollect the events of the previous evening . . . But she just couldn't, her brain seemed to be all fogged up.

She vaguely remembered an extremely charming gentleman . . . Champagne . . . And hadn't she won a fair amount of money . . .?

Her winnings! She struggled to sit up, and switched on a light.

Her winnings were neatly stacked on the bedside table. Eighteen thousand dollars if her memory served her correctly. Propped beside them was a note—

'Madame. You are a charming and gracious lady – and I am sure you would help a gentleman out of trouble. I have borrowed your diamond ring – but the loan is temporary and you shall be repaid in full . . . I would appreciate your co-operation of not going to the police . . .'

Mrs Dean Costello started to laugh. Why that cocky son-of-a-bitch. The nerve. The goddamn bare-assed nerve.

The Chelsea house was looking a little tacky, Fontaine decided. It was part of the divorce settlement – Benjamin had kept their Belgravia mansion and she had been bought what she considered to be a rather unimpressive abode.

It was certainly not unimpressive. It was a five-bedroomed, three-receptioned-room elegant house with a large garden. However, it was not the Belgravia mansion with the indoor swimming-pool, sauna, private cinema, internal elevator, and landscaped roof-garden.

Fontaine had furnished her new house in a hurry before she had left for New York, and it did have style. The trouble was that nobody had been living there except Mrs Walters, her ancient and faithful housekeeper, and the rooms smelt musty and unused, and there was even the faint aroma of cat pee.

'Christ!' Fontaine exclaimed. 'Why the hell didn't someone air this place out? And why aren't there any fresh flowers?'

Polly shrugged. Fontaine's domestic arrangements really were not her affair.

'Mrs Walters!' Fontaine yelled.

The old woman came running out from the kitchen. 'Welcome home, Mrs Khaled—' she started to say.

Fontaine cut her short with a barrage of complaints.

Ricky came through the front door carrying some of the luggage.

Polly winked at him. He frowned.

'I never said she was easy to work for . . .' Polly murmured as he passed by.

Nico checked into the Lamont Hotel and requested a suite.

He was shown to a smallish suite overlooking the back.

He handed the porter a five-pound note, and said, 'Stay

here a minute.' Then he picked up the phone and asked to see the Manager immediately.

The Manager, Mr Graheme, was with him ten minutes later, a thin harassed man whose main concern at that moment in time was whether he could prevent the entire kitchen staff from walking out. Earlier in the day he had fired an assistant chef who had been caught stealing fillet steaks – handing them to an accomplice as he took out the garbage. This had resulted in a flat statement from the rest of the kitchen workers that either the thief stayed or they walked. What to do? Mr Graheme had still not decided.

'Yes, sir, what can I do for you?' he snapped at Nico, a little too harshly but he *was* under a strain.

Nico gestured at his surroundings, 'Nice,' he said warmly. 'Very comfortable.' Then he moved over to Mr Graheme and offered him a cigar, then he put his arm conspiratorially around his shoulders, 'Mr Graheme. I stay at your hotel for the first time. The place has been highly recommended to me by many of my friends in Beverly Hills. But really . . . a suite like this for a man like me . . . Perhaps I should try the Connaught . . .'

Fifteen minutes later Nico was ensconced in the best suite in the hotel.

Mr Graheme knew a big spender when he saw one.

Once rid of Polly, Fontaine couldn't wait to get on the phone to Vanessa Grant, her very best friend in London.

'I'm back,' she announced dramatically. 'Exhausted and destroyed. I can't wait to see you. How about dinner tonight?'

Vanessa hesitated, she and her husband Leonard already had dinner plans, but once Fontaine wanted something it really didn't do to argue.

'I think that will be fine,' she said.

'Fine!' Fontaine snorted. 'Bloody enthusiastic welcome that is!'

'We weren't expecting you until next week . . .'

'I know, I know. I had to change my plans because of my *robbery*.'

'What robbery?'

'Darling – haven't you heard? It's all over the papers in New York.'

They chatted some more, arranging where and when to meet, then casually Fontaine asked, 'By the way, do you and Leonard know a man called Nico Constantine? An Americanized Greek. Lives in Beverly Hills, I think.'

'No, I don't think that name rings any bells. Who is he? Another of your juvenile delinquents?'

'Hardly juvenile, rather more mature.'

Vanessa laughed. 'Doesn't sound like you at all. Is he rich?'

'I don't really know . . . Maybe.'

'Are you bringing him tonight?'

'Certainly not. I have a rather divine Italian Count who is flying in especially to see me.'

Vanessa sighed, she had been married for too many years and had too many children. 'Sometimes I envy you . . .'

'I know,' replied Fontaine crisply. 'If you're a good girl I'll throw him your way when I'm finished with him. He's twenty-six years old and horny as a rutting dog!'

It occured to Nico that he had no idea how to get in touch with Fontaine. He had been so sure that she would wait for him at the airport that he had not even bothered to find out her phone number. Stupid really. But usually women waited . . . And after their undeniably erotic encounter on the plane he had felt sure that Fontaine would not go rushing off. Well, hardly rushing . . . Between passport control and customs it had taken him an hour to emerge. But still . . . She could at least have left a message.

He called the reception desk, told the porter her name, and asked him to find out her phone number and address immediately.

Half an hour later the porter gave him Benjamin Al Khaled's London office number, and a frosty secretary there said she could not possibly reveal the previous Mrs Khaled's phone number or address, and if he wished to contact her he should write in and his communication would be forwarded on.

Nico turned on his telephone charm – not as potent as the real thing – but effective enough to get him the number with a little gentle persuasion.

He phoned Fontaine immediately. A housekeeper answered his call and said that Mrs Khaled was resting and could not be disturbed.

He left his name and number and a message for her to call him back. Then he contacted the hotel florist and sent her three dozen red roses with a card saying – 'The flight was memorable – when do come in for landing? Nico.'

Next he phoned Hal – Bernie's London friend, whom he had never met – but who apparently knew everyone and everything – and who would be able to take excellent care of the ring situation – once he had it back of course.

They arranged to meet in the bar later.

Nico then called for the valet. Time to get his personal grooming in order. It would never do to look anything but perfect.

Fontaine slept all day. At seven o'clock Mrs Walters woke her, and she got up and started her numerous preparations for the evening's activities.

'A Mr Constantine phoned,' Mrs Walters informed her. 'Also Count Paulo Rispollo. They would both like you to phone them back.' Mrs Walters busied herself with running Fontaine's bath. She had worked for her for over ten years and felt she understood her – although Fontaine was extremely difficult to work for, what with her sudden screaming fits and unreasonable demands.

'Call the Count back, tell him to collect me at nine o'clock.' Fontaine handed Mrs Walters a number. 'And if

Mr Constantine phones again you can say I'm out.'

'They both sent flowers,' Mrs Walters continued. 'Three dozen roses from Mr Constantine. A bowl of orchids from Count Rispollo. I told the new chauffeur to be back at eight sharp, shall I send him to pick the Count up?'

'I suppose so,' Fontaine stripped off her thin silk dressing gown and stretched. 'I don't think for one moment he has his own.'

Mrs Walters scurried off, and Fontaine climbed into a deliciously hot bath.

Count Paulo Rispollo. Young. Good-looking. Unfortunately didn't have a pot to piss in. But he adored her. Had met her in New York and declared undying love. Probably bi-sexual, but very passable in bed – and that's where it all mattered – wasn't it? Besides, it was so good for her image . . . A young good-looking escort . . . especially a titled one.

She thought briefly of Nico Constantine, then put him quickly from her mind. Trouble. She sensed it. And anyway – since when did she date men older than herself? What a positively boring idea. Who needed real conversations? All she needed was a fine young body – no complications – just sex. And if sometimes she had to pick up the bills . . . well, that was life, wasn't it?

Nico was irritated when Fontaine failed to return his call by the time he met with Hal. He was more than irritated, he needed to recover the ring urgently.

Hal turned out to be an amiable fortyish American promoter operating out of London. Attractive, if you liked the Dean Martin gone-to-seed type. Constantly stoned, and well dressed. His speciality was hustling elderly widow ladies.

He greeted Nico warmly, asked after Bernie, and mumbled, 'Where's the item? I have a good set up waiting to accept. I'm working on a split percentage – five per cent

74

'from you – five from them – does that suit you?'

'Sure, but I have a problem,' Nico explained. 'I met a woman on the plane. I thought it would be safer for her to bring it in. I don't have it back yet.'

Hal made a face, 'I was given to understand time was of the essence.'

'It is, it is. The woman . . . I'm trying to reach her. Her name is Fontaine Khaled.'

Hal let out a whistle. 'The ice queen herself! Is she back?'

'Do you know her?'

Hal laughed. 'Sure I know her. She owns "Hobo". My good friend Tony Blake used to run it for her – along with a few more personal services. He's living in LA now trying to recover from the experience! What the hell was she doing with *you*? You're a little over her age limit.'

'What the hell was *I* doing with *her*?' Nico retorted quickly. 'She's a little over mine.'

'Does she know about the ring?' Hal asked.

'No. I hid it in her purse. I've been trying to contact her.'

'Don't worry. We'll see her tonight. The first place Mrs Khaled will go is "Hobo". We'll be there to greet her.'

'What you need is another Tony,' Vanessa whispered. 'Franco just doesn't have it where it counts.'

Fontaine glanced around the half-empty restaurant at 'Hobo'. She didn't even know any of the people who were there – a dreary-looking bunch of bores.

'Do *you* know who any of these people are?' she asked Vanessa.

'Absolutely not,' Vanessa replied. 'It seems anyone can get in nowadays. Now when Tony was here . . .'

'For Christ's sake do shut up about Tony. I know you had the hots for him, but he's long gone. He got a little too big for his . . .boots.'

'Or something!' giggled Vanessa.

'Quite,' agreed Fontaine. She glanced around the restaurant again. It was a bore – but it was quite obviously true. 'Hobo' was no longer *the* place to be seen. Franco had let things run to rack and ruin.

Count Paulo seemed to be enjoying every minute. His boyish face glowed with the thrill of being out with the glorious Fontaine Khaled. He watched her admiringly. Leonard, Vanessa's husband, tried to indulge him in a business dialogue, but Paulo was more interested in gazing at his date.

Fontaine tapped impatient scarlet fingernails on the table. 'Why don't we move on,' she suggested. 'Where *is* everyone going now?'

'There's a divine new club called "Dickies",' Vanessa enthused. 'Gay, of course – well, more mixed really. The waiters wear satin shorts and roller skates and they serve the most decadent drinks, they make you drunk for a week!'

'Let's go,' said Fontaine. 'I think I should see where the real action is.'

She rose from the table and swept out of the restaurant.

Franco snapped to attention. 'Mrs Khaled, you 'ees leaving so early. Something the matter?'

'Yes, Franco,' her voice was cold. 'You, as it happens. You're fired.'

Hal produced two beautiful girls. A black croupier on a two-week vacation, and a streaked blonde who was into meditation. Nico got the blonde, although he insisted to Hal he didn't want a date.

'It'll look better,' Hal explained. 'Trust me, I know Fontaine. Besides, tonight is my night off. Once a week I treat myself to a broad under sixty.'

'So have two,' Nico suggested. 'I don't want one.'

They arrived at 'Hobo' ten minutes after Fontaine had left.

'Mrs Khaled around?' Hal asked Franco.

'She come, she go,' Franco replied, then he burst into a stream of Italian abuse about his soon-to-be-former employer.

'Nobody ever called Fontaine a pussycat,' Hal agreed.

'A beetch!' Franco shrieked. 'I work my ass to the bone – and like that – poof – she throw me out.'

'Yeah,' said Hal. 'Like Tony. Remember Tony? You took his job.'

Franco glared.

'Come on,' Hal said to Nico. 'Knowing our Fontaine, she's checking out the competition.'

Fontaine was indeed checking out the competition, and she could see immediately why 'Dickies' had taken over. The disco music was great, the waiters outrageous, and the whole ambience reminded her of 'Hobo' when it had first opened.

Her kaleidoscope eyes surveyed the scene. Yes – All the same old faces. Every *one* of the 'Hobo' regulars.

'Fun, isn't it?' Vanessa enthused.

'Hmmm . . . Not bad.' Fontaine turned to Count Paulo, 'Let's dance.'

The floor was crowded – unlike the barren expanse at 'Hobo'. As Fontaine moved her body expertly in time to the Bee Gees, her mind was racing. What 'Hobo' needed was a revamp. New lighting. A change of menu. Definitely a different disc jockey. And a manager with the charisma Tony had possessed.

The music changed to a horny Isaac Hayes singing 'Just the way you are.'

Count Paulo pulled her close. Funny, but she didn't fancy him one little bit. He just seemed . . . boring.

'Fontaine, gorgeous! When did you get back?' Suddenly she was the centre of attention – so-called friends greeting her on all sides.

She smiled and nodded and enjoyed the scrutiny. She was no fool. She knew what they were all thinking – Poor old Fontaine – no more millionaire husband – no more successful discothèque. What was she going to do?

Well, she bloody well wasn't going to do what they all wanted – fade away defeated. She was back with a vengeance, and they'd better all believe it.

'Hello darlin', what you doin' here? "Hobo" not the same since you threw Tony out?'

She turned to confront the owner of the raucous cockney accent. It was Sammy, a small wiry-haired dress manufacturer who only went out with girls under the age of sixteen.

Fontaine smiled coldly. 'I'll find another Tony. He was never an original.'

'Oh, yeah?' Sammy winked knowingly. 'What you need is a guy like me to run the place for you. I'd soon get it all back together – 'ave 'em raving in the aisles in no time. Want to give me a try?'

Fontaine looked him over with a mixture of amusement and contempt. 'You?' the one word said it all.

'All right, all right, I know when I'm not appreciated,' Sammy backed off.

Count Paulo rubbed thighs. 'Who was that?' he asked possessively.

'Do you have to hold me so tight?' Her voice was ice. 'You're creasing my dress.'

Nico noticed Fontaine immediately. Well, she could hardly be missed. She certainly was striking.

He watched her on the dance floor clutched in the arms of some young stud. She obviously had a predilection for young studs – just as he had for fresh-faced young beauties.

'Told you she'd be here,' Hal announced triumphantly.

'Can we dance, Nico?' The black croupier was pulling on his jacket sleeve. 'Hal won't mind – he doesn't dance.'

Nico gently removed her tugging hand and adjusted his sleeve. 'Not right now, dear.'

Hal spotted his friend Sammy, and moved over to join him and his teenage companion.

After introductions Hal explained to Sammy that Nico wanted to get together with Fontaine.

Sammy laughed. 'Are you kidding? No chance, her highness wouldn't sniff in your direction!'

'Oh, yes?' Nico headed confidently towards the dance floor. 'Just watch her sniff!'

10

In Las Vegas, Bernie Darrell began to realize that protecting Nico was not exactly going to do him any good. Okay – so he was on fairly friendly terms with Dino Fonicetti – and he knew the father and the brother to nod to. But they were hard people . . . They had their reputation to consider . . . And when the fact that Nico had skipped town owing five hundred and fifty thousand grand was revealed . . . And then it came out that he, Bernie, had helped in the deception . . . Well . . .

By Tuesday evening he was apprehensive. And when Cherry baby came knocking at the door to pick up her things he was even more so.

'I shall have to tell Dino that Nico has left,' Cherry announced. 'I refuse to lie.'

Bernie was startled. 'What the hell are you talking about?' he snapped. '*We're* helping Nico – remember?'

'I have a certain loyalty to Dino,' Cherry replied primly.

'Loyalty? To Dino?' Bernie was amazed. 'What the *fuck* are you talking about?'

Cherry was oblivious to his anger as she packed up the few things she had brought with her. 'Of course, I won't mention that Nico left last night, I'll just say he's gone—'

Bernie grabbed her wrist roughly. 'You'll do no such fucking thing!'

'You're hurting me,' Cherry's blue eyes filled with tears. 'I'll tell Dino.'

Bernie released her. 'I don't believe this! I just don't believe it!' He mimicked her voice – ' "I'll tell Dino . . ." What is this – love's young dream all of a sudden? A one-night screw and the blonde and the hood see stars?'

Cherry raised her voice for the first time since Bernie had known her. 'It is possible, you know, for two people to fall in love. Dino is a warm and kind human being . . .'

'Holy shit!'

'We're going to get married if you must know.'

'I need a drink,' Bernie fixed himself a large scotch. His mind was racing. This was a beautiful situation. It could only happen to him. One moment the dumb cunt was trailing Nico to Las Vegas determined to sort out their future together. The next – true love with a mafioso one-night stand. Unbelievable!

He tried to soften his voice. 'Hey, Cherry – I'm really pleased for you and Dino, really I am. But if you tell him Nico has split, we're all in trouble – you included.'

'Not me,' Cherry protested indignantly.

'Yes – you, baby. How do you think your future bride-groom is going to feel when I tell him last night was a set-up?'

'What do you mean?'

'You spent the night with Dino so that Nico could get out of town. Right?'

'I suppose so . . .'

'Don't suppose. It's a fact of life. Now if Dino finds that out he is not going to be exactly thrilled.' Bernie took a deep breath. 'So listen carefully. You know nothing. Nico was here today when you picked up your things. You told him goodbye – that's all you know. And as far as you're concerned he's still here.'

'But I still think—'

'Will you listen to me sweetheart. Listen and learn. If your future plans include being Mrs Fonicetti, play it my way. You tell Dino the truth, and who knows how he'll react. Personally I wouldn't want to risk it.'

Cherry frowned. Bernie did have a point. 'Well, all right,' she said hesitantly. 'But when will Dino find out that Nico has gone?'

Bernie poured himself another scotch. 'By the time he finds out, Nico will be back – so don't you worry your pretty little head about it.'

Cherry nodded. 'OK Bernie, if you say so.'

So far so good. But could she be trusted? She was such a fucking idiot. Bernie sighed. How the hell had he ever got involved in this whole caper? Here he was – stuck in Las Vegas. What about his business? He had meetings to attend, and it would be at least a couple of days before Nico returned. That was if all went according to plan.

Cherry was packed up and ready to go. She smiled sweetly at him and stuck out a small delicate hand.

'Goodbye Bernie, and thank you for everything.'

Christ! She sounded like she'd taken a course in good manners!

'Yeah . . . well . . . I won't be leaving yet, so I guess we'll be seeing each other around. Now don't forget what I told you. Be a smart girl and you'll go far.'

She departed.

Bernie made a few mental calculations. Nico should be arriving in London about now. Hal was alerted to the situation. If all went smoothly the ring would be sold and the money in Nico's pocket within twenty-four hours. He would get on a plane immediately and be back in the suite before anyone realized he was gone. Pay off his markers. Back to LA. Mission accomplished. No broken bones.

It sounded easy.

Bernie wished the whole goddamn caper was over and done with.

11

'Mrs Khaled,' Nico cut in on the dance floor, subtly elbowing Count Paulo aside. 'What a pleasure to see you again so soon.'

'What do you think you are doing!' Count Paulo exploded. 'You cannot—'

'It's all right, Paulo,' Fontaine waved him aside. 'Run along and sit down, I'll join you in a minute.'

The Count glared, then reluctantly departed.

Nico took her in his arms, even though the beat was strident disco.

'Nice-looking boy,' Nico remarked. 'Similar to the one with you at Kennedy airport.'

'Yes. I like them full of energy.'

Nico raised an eyebrow.

Fontaine laughed.

'Did you get my flowers?' he asked.

'Very nice. How did you find my address?'

'If I want something I usually manage to get it.'

'Oh, really? We're so alike.'

'Thank you for waiting at the airport.'

'I'm hardly a taxi service.'

'I thought we had a date.'

'A date? How delightfully old world of you.'

'Has anybody ever told you that you're a bitch?'

'Frequently.'

Nico pulled her in very close indeed. Count Paulo, skulking at the edge of the dance floor, glared.

'Well, Mrs Khaled,' Nico said softly, 'are we going to finish what we started on the aeroplane?'

Fontaine responded to his maleness. 'Why not, Mr Constantine. Why not indeed?'

'Bleedin' hell!' Sammy exclaimed, as they all watched

Nico and Fontaine exit. ' 'E's only done it! What's 'e got? Mink-lined balls!'

'Oh, Sammy, you are awful!' his teenage girlfriend squealed.

'The guy has a lot of charm,' Hal stated. 'Not to mention the best tailor I've ever seen.'

'Charm schmarm – all Fontaine wants to know about is the size of the bank balance or the cock!'

'Honestly Sammy!'

'It's all right darlin' – you'll be OK on both counts!'

'I do believe she's leaving,' Vanessa whispered to Leonard.

'I think you're right,' he replied.

'Absolutely charming – you'd think she'd have the manners to say goodnight.'

'Nobody ever accused Fontaine of having any manners. Who is that man anyway?'

Vanessa peered at the couple swiftly leaving the dance floor.

'I don't know, he doesn't look her style at all – slightly too mature . . . but rather attractive.'

'Rich, I suppose,' said Leonard brusquely.

'Yes, I suppose,' Vanessa agreed.

'Oh, God!' Leonard exclaimed, 'Don't tell me we're stuck with her Italian juvenile.'

'Looks like we are.' Vanessa watched a surly Count Paulo approach. Oh yes. There was certainly something to be said for the young ones . . .

Maybe if Fontaine had finished with him . . .

Vanessa wasn't proud. She had accepted seconds from her friend before.

Ricky tried to concentrate on his driving, but it wasn't easy. God Almighty – you would think he had a couple of teenage ravers in the back.

He attempted to keep his eye on what was happening in

the rear-view mirror. Naturally Mrs Khaled had pressed the button which sent the glass partition up cutting him off from their sounds.

He drove the Rolls-Royce slower than usual, until Fontaine lowered the glass partition an inch and snapped, 'Do hurry up, Ricky.'

Bitch!

He wondered if he was free after he dropped her at her house. He was feeling extremely randy, and wondered if Polly would be up . . . Better than sleeping the night in that pisshole of a room he had rented.

The Rolls glided up to Fontaine's house. Ricky jumped out and opened the car door for them. He gazed disinterestedly off into space.

'Will you be needing me again tonight, Mrs Khaled?' he ventured.

'No, Ricky,' her voice was light and full of excitement. 'Tonight I will not be needing you.'

'What time tomorrow, Mrs Khaled?'

'Ten o'clock – I'd like you here every morning at ten o'clock.'

'Yes, Mrs Khaled.'

He waited until they turned to walk in the house, then he glanced at his watch. It was already two in the morning. Some job. It was a good thing the wages were right.

He wondered what had happened to the Italian ice cream. Must have got himself dumped . . .

Ricky couldn't help smiling. He liked a woman who behaved like a man.

It was an erotic experience.

It was clothes off on the stairs.

It was hot tongues and warm bodies.

It was touch – feel – smell.

Fontaine felt herself out of control for once. Here was a man she didn't have to tell what she wanted. He knew everything. He was very . . . accomplished.

'You're like a dancer,' he breathed in her ear. 'You make love like a dancer who has been in training.'

'Hmmm . . . And you . . . you're like a stallion . . .'

He laughed. 'The Greek Stallion. It sounds like a bad movie! When I was twenty I was a stallion – now I *know* what I'm doing.'

'You certainly do!'

They made love endlessly – or so it seemed to both of them. And they were comfortable together – there was none of the awkwardness that sometimes happens the first time two people are in bed together.

The added bonus was that they could talk, not about anything special, just conversation.

Fontaine never had conversations with her transient studs – sometimes verbal skirmishes, but never conversations.

The same applied to Nico and his fresh-faced beauties. How boring and bland they all seemed once the initial thrill of a new body was over.

The thing that turned him on about Fontaine more than anything was her mind. She might be one tough lady – but she had wit and perception, and he wanted to dig deeper and find out more about the woman beneath the sophisticated veneer.

'I want to know all about you,' he said softly, 'who – why – how. From the beginning.'

Fontaine rolled over in bed. She felt delightfully satisfied. '*You're* the man of mystery. I meet you on a plane – the next minute we're in bed. But all I know about you is your name. You could be—'

'What?' He pinned her arms to the bed playfully. 'A mass murderer? A maniac?' He kissed her hard and released her. 'And don't tell me Mrs Khaled hasn't gone to bed with a man she met on a plane before.'

'Well . . . once or twice.'

'Oh, yes, once or twice I bet.' He smiled. 'How many men *have* you had?'

Fontaine stretched and got out of bed, 'Let's put it this way, Nico – a meal a day means you never go hungry.'

'Come back here, I want my dessert!'

'I'm going to take a shower, I need reviving. Why don't you go downstairs and bring up some Grand Marnier, I'll show you a delicious new way to drink it.' She went in the bathroom and closed the door.

Nico lay back still smiling. He felt fantastically relaxed. Then he remembered the ring. Wasn't that the reason he was here? Well, originally . . .

He could hear water running in the bathroom. He got off the bed and looked around the room for the purse Fontaine had carried on the plane. He couldn't see it around, but the mirrored door of a large walk-in closet stood invitingly open. He peered inside. Racks and racks of shoes stacked in neat rows. Shelves for sweaters, shirts, T-shirts, scarves, gloves. Belts and beads hanging in rows. Underclothes in perspex drawers. And handbags. All on a bottom shelf. About twenty-five of them.

He looked through them quickly, searching for the Gucci stripe. There were five with Gucci stripes, but none were the right one.

He swore softly under his breath, then suddenly saw the one he was looking for. It was hanging on the back of the door.

He grabbed it quickly, unzipped the side compartment, and there, nestled at the bottom, was his ring.

Fontaine appeared at the wrong moment, a pink towel wrapped around her sarong style. Her voice was icy, 'What exactly do you think you are doing?'

Nico jumped. He felt like a schoolboy caught with his hand inside the cookie jar. He wished he had put his pants on at least. There is nothing more daunting for a man than to be caught in an awkward situation with a limp dick hanging down.

'Well?' Fontaine could make one word a meal.

Nico smiled. Charm. His smile had got him through

many tricky situations. 'You're never going to believe this.'

'Try me.' Her glacial expression did not crack.

'Well . . .' he tried to edge past her back into the bedroom.

She blocked his way.

'It's a long story,' he said quickly. 'I'm sure it will amuse you. Let me put some clothes on . . .'

Patiently, calmly, Fontaine interrupted him. 'Just tell me what you were doing in my bag – and just show me what you have in your hand. Now, Nico, right now. I don't want to hear any amusing stories, I'm not really in the mood for a good laugh.'

Nico shrugged, 'I can assure you I'm not taking anything of yours.'

'I can assure you of that too.'

'I had this ring . . . I thought maybe I would have problems with customs . . .'

He opened his hand and showed her the diamond.

She looked at it briefly, then at him.

'I was going to ask you if you would mind bringing it through for me . . . but I didn't know you that well . . . Of course, I was going to tell you—'

'You bastard. You son-of-a-bitch nasty little hustler,' her words struck icily through his. 'You *used* me – on the plane, this evening. How *dare* you!'

'I only—'

She held up an imperious hand. 'I don't want to hear. I just want you out – of my house, my life.'

'But Fontaine . . .'

She wasn't listening. She was in the bedroom gathering his clothes together, and when he emerged from the closet she threw them at him. 'Out!' she snapped. 'Before I have you thrown out.'

'I think we should talk about it.'

'Why? What more do you want from me? You've fucked me every way you can – and I might add that the screwing I got in bed wasn't half as good as the screwing I *really* got from you.'

She walked into her bathroom and slammed the door.

Quickly Nico got dressed. There was no point in staying around to argue. After all – he had what he had come for.

'What?' Joseph Fonicetti regarded his youngest son through narrowed eyes. 'What the fuck did I just hear you say?'

Dino shuffled his feet uneasily. How come everywhere he was a king – and in front of his father – zero – nothing – a goddamned kid again.

'I . . . I . . . er . . . well . . . I'm gonna get married.'

Joseph threw him a long unnerving stare. 'Just like that. Out of the blue you've found yourself a girl fit to be your wife. In *Las Vegas* you've found a girl to take the Fonicetti name. What is this beauty? A showgirl? A cocktail waitress? A *hooker*?' Joseph spat with disgust into a handy ashtray.

'She's a very lovely girl,' Dino said quickly. 'Not from Las Vegas.'

'None of them are *from* here – they only come here to develop their cunts and their bankrolls!'

'She's a nice girl,' Dino said defensively. 'You'll love her.'

Joseph shut his eyes and mulled over the fact that Dino was a good-looking boy, but when it came to women he was dense. Now David, his elder son, was smart. He had a wife, a plain Italian girl who would never give him a moment's trouble, and he fucked around with Las Vegas gash on his terms only.

'When did you meet this girl?' Joseph asked. 'A month? Two months ago? How come I've never heard you mention her before?'

'Well, Cherry only got here this week . . . You know how it is . . . this is the girl I want to marry. It happened just like that.'

Yes. Joseph knew how it was. Some smart broad had hooked her little finger round Dino's cock and thought she was going to get lucky. Well, she could think again. When Joseph was ready for Dino to get married – *he personally* would arrange it. A selection of Italian virgins would be shipped in – just as they had been for David – and Dino could take his choice.

'So . . . this Cherry. Who did she come here with?'

Dino answered quickly. He wanted to lie, but his father would find out the truth anyway. 'She came here with Bernie Darrell, they're just friends.'

'Sure. Bernie Darrell brought a girl all the way to Vegas and they're just friends. I believe that. Who wouldn't?'

'She came to see Nico Constantine, then she met me. Neither of us expected this . . . it just happened.'

'And what did Nico do? Kiss you both and wish you luck?'

'She and Nico . . . It was over anyway.'

Joseph nodded. 'Of course, she wasn't influenced by th~ `act that Nico was losing his ass at the tables. By the way – have you made arrangements with him about paying?'

'I will, I will.'

'Sure – leave it go while you make wedding arrangements. Who cares about five hundred and fifty thousand dollars.'

'Nico's good for the money.'

'He'd better be.'

'He is. I'll deal with it today.' Dino coughed nervously. 'Now, about Cherry, when can I bring her to meet you?'

Jospeh nodded thoughtfully, he had an idea. 'Tonight,' he said, 'we'll have dinner. The whole family. We'll discuss your wedding plans.'

Dino was relieved. It seemed his father was accepting Cherry without too much of a fight. Well – he must have known it was no use fighting – after all – he, Dino, was not exactly David who could be forced into a dull marriage with a placid Italian lump.

Dino smiled. They would all love Cherry. From the moment Joseph met her it would be smooth sailing.

'We have an invitation,' Susanna said, sitting down and joining Bernie in the coffee shop.

'We do?' He was halfway through a prune danish – wondering if it would solve his bowel problem.

'Yup.' Susanna studied the menu. 'Daddy wants us to have dinner with him and the Fonicettis tonight. I accepted on our behalf.'

'You did?' Bernie wondered how they had become a pair again. Two nights of torrid love-making and was the divorce supposed to be a past memory?

'He's invited Nico Constantine too, will you tell him please – there's no answer from his suite.'

Bernie nearly choked on his danish. 'Why Nico?'

'Why not? Daddy likes Nico.'

Yes, and hates me, Bernie thought. The last time they had met had been just before the divorce. Carlos Brent had confronted him at the Beverly Hills Hotel in the Polo lounge.

'You kike bastard – all I need is the word from Susanna, and my boys' club will be playing catch with your balls. You're lucky she's not vindictive.'

Charming! They had not spoken nor met since.

'I don't know if Nico will want to make it,' Bernie hedged. 'He's gotten very involved with a girl here.'

'Who?' Susanna demanded.

'Some chick, I don't even know her name.'

'Well he can bring her, a date will be OK.'

'I'll try to reach him.'

Susanna yawned and giggled. 'Can you believe what's happened to us? Can you believe it, Bernie? My analyst will have a blue fit!'

To be truthful Bernie was finding it very hard to believe himself. One moment he and Susanna were the worst of enemies – the next – making love like randy soldiers on twenty-four-hour leave! He had to admit that for him she was the absolute greatest in bed, but a pain in the ass to live with. Carlos had spoiled the pants off her, that was why.

A chubby waitress came rushing over. 'Miss Brent,' she gushed. 'And what can I get for you today?'

Miss Brent. It had always been Miss Brent, never ever Mrs Darrell. And on a couple of memorable occasions – memorable because of the blazing fight that followed – he had even been addressed as Mr Brent.

'I dunno, Maggi,' she knew all of the elderly waitresses by name – she had been coming to the hotel her entire life. 'I think maybe a cheese danish, and a black coffee.'

Maggi beamed. 'Certainly, dear.'

'I was thinking,' Susanna said, turning to Bernie. 'Why don't you and Nico fly back to LA with me? I can use daddy's plane whenever I want. I thought maybe tomorrow . . . You could stay at the house, Starr would like that.'

Starr was their very beautiful four-year-old daughter. She was also Carlos Brent's only grandchild, and as such she was spoiled rotten, just like her mother.

'I don't know,' Bernie answered, his mind racing. 'I promised Nico I'd stay with him . . .'

Susanna shot him a dirty look. 'Whose hand would you sooner hold? Mine or Nico's?'

'Yours, of course.'

'Anyway, his new girlfriend seems to be doing a pretty good job of holding his. I haven't even seen him yet.'

'You know how it is.'

'I certainly do.' She pushed her tinted shades up into her hair and sighed, 'We must have been mad to have gotten divorced. Why did we do it?'

Did she really expect an answer?

Because you nagged the shit out of me, Susanna.

Because you required my balls to be your balls.

Because daddy daddy daddy is enough to drive anyone to divorce.

Bernie shrugged, 'I don't know.'

Susanna giggled, that 'I wanna get laid' look came into her eyes. 'Why don't we forget about lunch?' she suggested. 'Why don't we just toddle on upstairs and smoke a little tiny bit of grass.'

'Yeah, why not.'

He certainly had nothing else to do with his time while he waited for Nico to surface.

13

'Who *was* he?' asked Vanessa.

'Some boring little con artist,' snapped Fontaine.

'He didn't look little to me, rather Omar Sharif actually.'

'A poor imitation.'

'You certainly left in a hurry, Paulo was furious.'

'Look, darling, I have to go, got a million things to do. I'll call you later.'

'Don't forget the fashion lunch tomorrow.'

'I've written it in my book.' Fontaine put the phone down, and checked out her appearance in the mirror. Chic, but understated. Silk shirt, pleated skirt, checked blazer. Just the outfit to interview aspiring managers for 'Hobo'. She had phoned Polly first thing and given her a blast. 'Get me some young, attractive, would-be front men. Franco's the reason "Hobo" is down the drain. Find me another Tony. I'll be over to see what you have at four o'clock.'

Polly hung up the phone and snuggled up to Ricky. 'You'd better move it,' she said. 'Mrs K. is up early and raring to go.'

'She told me ten o'clock,' Ricky replied.

'In that case . . . we might just have time . . . Oh shit! I forgot. I'm the one with the early appointment.' She bounced out of bed. 'Any ideas on how I go about finding a tall sexy man with a big dick?'

Ricky laughed crudely. 'Don't I fit that bill?'

'Yes, you do. But you got the chauffeur's job, and Mrs K. would never understand a change of image midstream.'

'Why not? She seems like a pretty smart lady to me.'

'Oh, really?' Polly winked. 'Fancy her already, do you?'

He laughed. 'I wouldn't mind dipping my toe in.'

'She'd want more than your toe, sonny. Much more . . .'

'Why don't you come here and shut up.' Every time he thought about his employer he got quite randy.

With the ring back in his possession Nico felt more secure. The delay had not been planned, and he imagined that Bernie must be worried by his silence. They had arranged that they would not make contact until he had actually fenced the ring and was on his way back.

But still, maybe he should call. Put Bernie's mind at rest. And then again, maybe not. Didn't want to alarm him unnecessarily. If all went well, and Hal came across, he could be on a plane within hours.

He delivered the ring personally to Hal the morning after his scene with Fontaine.

Hal wasn't pleased as he groped his way to the front door of his Park Lane service flat clad in a pair of black silk pyjamas. 'Jesus Christ!' he exclaimed, 'what the frig's the time?'

Nico glanced at his watch. 'Nine forty-five. Too early for you?'

'Too right it is. I never get up before two or three.'

'This is an emergency.'

'Yeah. I understand.' He led the way into an unused kitchen, and set about making some coffee. 'What happened? Fontaine throw you out early? Or didn't you get to stay?'

'I didn't stay.'

'Very wise. She's a balls-breaker.'

'Do you know her well?'

'Well enough.'

'Did you ever . . .'

'Me? Are you kidding?' Hal began to laugh. 'Fontaine wouldn't glance in my direction – not that I would ever want her to. She likes 'em young. When she was married

96

to the Arab, she used his money to set them up in business.'

Nico produced the ring from his pocket and showed it to Hal.

Hal let out a long whistle. 'That's really something, absolutely bee-u-tiful.'

'When can I hear from you?' Nico asked. 'I have to be on my way as soon as possible.'

Hal poured water over instant coffee, already thinking of how he would spend his commission. 'A cash transaction like this . . . I should think some time tomorrow.'

'Christ!' Nico exclaimed, 'It has to be sooner than that.'

'I'll do my best, but there's a lot of money involved here. Just be patient and relax. Why don't you do some gambling? The London clubs are the best.'

Nico gave a hollow laugh. 'Why do you think I'm in trouble today?'

'Hmmm . . . Not bad,' Fontaine yawned. 'What did you think, Polly?'

'I think that the cockney accent was just a little passé.'

Fontaine picked a nut from the glass dish on the table and tossed it into her mouth. 'Yes. I suppose you're right. Cockney was in last year – now it seems to be chinless or gay, but I *still* say what we need is a macho front man.'

'I know, I know, just like the fabulous Tony.'

Fontaine smiled dreamily. 'You never met him, did you?'

'I wish I had. But I was in America the year of "Hobo's" ascent.'

'Tony – at the beginning – was the best. In every way I might add.'

'So why did you get rid of him?'

'His ambitions screwed up his head.'

Polly and Fontaine sat together in the empty discothèque at 'Hobo' interviewing would-be managers. So far they had seen six, none of them suitable.

97

Fontaine was irritated, and getting more so by the minute. Why was it so goddamn difficult to find an attractive, ambitious, sexy, ballsy, young man?

She thought briefly of Jump Jennings. Thought even more briefly of importing him. Changed her mind, and peered at the next young man in line for the job.

He was better than the others. Curly black hair, tight faded jeans, a certain confidence.

Polly consulted a businesslike clipboard. 'And you are . . .?'

'Steve Valentine.'

Fontaine and Polly exchanged quick amused looks.

'You're running a disco in Ealing?' Polly asked. 'Is that right?'

'I've been the manager there for eighteen months.'

'Do you enjoy it?' Fontaine husked, her kaleidoscope eyes inspecting every inch of him.

Steve stared at her. 'Yeah, well it's all right. But I want to get into the West End.'

'I'm sure you do.' Fontaine picked up a cigarette, and waited for him to light it.

He fumbled for a cheap lighter and did the honours.

'Hmmm . . .' said Fontaine, still inspecting him. 'Do you have a girlfriend?'

Steve's stare became bold. 'One wouldn't be enough for me, Mrs Khaled.'

'I bet it wouldn't.' She turned to Polly, 'I think we should give Mr Valentine a try, don't you, Polly?'

When Nico left Hal's apartment he decided to make the most of his last day in London. He had in his possession the six thousand dollars that Bernie had withdrawn from his office safe – and apart from his hotel bill he would have no other expenses in London. By the time Hal disposed of the ring he would have more than enough cash to pay his debts in Vegas, repay Bernie, and still have a few thousand dollars over.

Of course, then he would have to start thinking of his future. But he would worry about that when the time came. Also Mrs Dean Costello must be compensated, and that would be his responsibility if her insurance company had not already taken care of it. He had every intention of repaying her if she was not insured. How, he didn't quite know. But Nico had the quality of supreme confidence in his ability to deal with any situation. Plus the fact that no way would a ring like that be uninsured.

He thought about Fontaine Khaled. Flowers of course. Red roses naturally. Six dozen with a discreet note of apology. And a gift. Not the usual token trinket. But something nice and substantial. Something beautiful that she would love.

Even though he would be leaving London he had every intention of seeing her again. It was not inconceivable that he might return as soon as everything was settled.

Fontaine interested him like no other woman had since Lise Maria. He knew her, and yet he also knew that he had barely scratched the surface. She was a woman – arrogant, assured, tough. And underneath the veneer was the woman he really wanted to know. Vulnerable, soft, lovable. Searching for the right man – just as he – unknowingly – had been searching for the right woman.

He hailed a taxi and directed the driver to Boucheron, the Bond Street jewellery shop.

Ricky watched Fontaine in the rear-view mirror as the Rolls glided through heavy traffic. Her eyes were closed, legs crossed, skirt riding up to reveal stocking tops. She wore suspenders! Christmas! Bloody suspenders! The only place he had ever seen those were in girly magazines!

He immediately felt randy – in spite of fifteen hot sticky minutes with Polly in the morning.

'Ricky.'

He shifted his eyes quickly to her face. She had woken up.

'Yes, Mrs Khaled?'

'Did you collect my things from the cleaners?'

'Yes, Mrs Khaled.'

'And pick up my prescription?'

'Yes, Mrs Khaled.'

'Good. When we get home you can take some time off. I won't be needing you until ten o'clock tonight.'

'Thank you, Mrs Khaled.' He glanced at the clock on the dashboard. It was nearly five. He was rather bushed himself. He sneaked another look in the mirror. She had pulled her skirt down. Spoilsport.

'Oh, and Ricky.'

'Yes, Mrs Khaled?'

'Be a good boy and keep your eyes on the road.'

'Yes, Mrs Khaled.'

Bitch!

Nico enjoyed himself. He had always had a knack for spending money. Three thousand dollars went on a diamond-studded heart for Fontaine. Another thousand on a Cartier watch for Bernie. And twelve hundred on clothes for himself – cashmere sweaters and silk shirts from Turnbull & Asser.

Well pleased, he returned to his hotel.

Hal waited in the lobby. Things were progressing even faster than Nico had hoped.

'Good news?' he questioned.

'Let's go upstairs,' Hal replied.

They travelled up to Nico's suite in silence.

Once inside Hal produced the diamond ring and flung it down on the bed. 'Glass – fuckin' glass!' He spat in disgust. 'What the hell kind of game are you playin', Nico?'

14

Bernie was stoned. Nicely so. Just enough to be able to face Carlos Brent and the Fonicettis with a smile.

He prepared to leave Susanna at six o'clock with the promise to collect her at seven.

She lay in bed, also stoned, and suggested for the sixth time that they should get married again.

'Why?' Bernie asked. 'We're having such a good time together *not* being married.'

'I know,' agreed Susanna. 'But for Starr's sake it would be nice.'

Not to mention Carlos, Bernie thought. Big daddy would be furious if he knew what was going on.

'Don't forget to invite Nico,' Susanna called out after him.

'If he's around,' Bernie replied.

'He must be back by now. Who is the new girlfriend anyway?'

'I told you, I don't know. See you later.'

Bernie made his escape and returned to the suite.

Wouldn't it be nice if Nico was waiting to greet him.

He wasn't.

Bernie wondered if a phone call was in order. He certainly wanted to know what was happening. How much longer could he keep up the pretence that Nico was around? Of course he couldn't risk phoning from the Forum. He would have to stroll over to Caesars or Circus Circus and use an anonymous phone booth. He hoped to Christ that Nico had checked into the Lamont in London as he had told him to.

He took a shower and changed his clothes. Then he sprayed his mouth with a fresh breath spray, and set off to make the phone call.

*

Cherry twirled in front of the full-length mirror. 'Do you like it?' she asked Dino breathily.

'Pretty,' he replied, more concerned with how the evening would go, than Cherry's new dress.

'You don't like it,' she pouted.

'Honey, I do,' he caught her up in his arms and hugged her reassuringly. 'You look like a great big beautiful doll.'

'I'm your wife,' she said proudly. 'Mrs Dino Foncetti!'

His stomach turned over with fear. In the entire thirty-one years he had been alive he had never made one important decision without consulting his father. Now he had really done it. He had sneaked off that very afternoon and married Cherry before Joseph thought of some smart way of getting rid of her.

'Your father's going to like me,' Cherry said, as if reading his mind. 'You'll see, he really will. I can promise you that.'

'I know, I know. Just keep your pretty mouth closed about us being married. I'll tell him in my own way.'

'Tonight?'

'Yeah, sure, tonight.'

She smiled. 'What a surprise it'll be! Me and your father meeting for the first time to talk about you and me getting married – and then boom – you'll tell him!'

'Yeah – boom.' Dino tried to smile. It was a struggle.

Joseph Fonicetti arrived in the Magna Carter restaurant precisely at six forty-five. He inspected the dinner table, pronounced it suitable, and the head waiter sighed with relief.

Working for Joseph Fonicetti you learned to be meticulous.

'Bring me some Perrier water,' Joseph requested. 'And some of those little white cards.'

The waiter responded immediately, then stood at a respectful distance while Joseph scrawled in his atrocious handwriting on the placement cards.

At exactly two minutes to seven, David, the eldest son, arrived with his wife, Mia. They both embraced Joseph, and took their places at the table. They both ordered Perrier water to drink.

At exactly two minutes past seven Dino arrived with Cherry. He was holding her hand, but his palm was sweating so badly that her hand threatened to slip away.

'Cherry, I want you to meet my father, Joseph Fonicetti,' he said nervously.

Cherry stepped forward, wide-eyed. 'Mr Fonicetti, I have been *so* looking forward to this moment.'

Joseph beamed, 'So have I, my dear, so have I.' The girl was prettier than he had expected. Dino had always gone for the sour-faced big-boobed kind before. 'Sit right here, next to me. What'll you have to drink?'

Cherry's eyes didn't waver, but she had already noticed the Perrier bottles. 'Oh, Perrier water if I may – you don't mind, do you?'

'Mind? Of course not.' Smarter than he had expected.

Dino went to sit beside her.

Joseph waved him away. 'Down there, next to your sister-in-law.'

Dino moved obediently to the other end of the table and ordered a double scotch.

Susanna and Bernie arrived next. He did a double take when he saw Cherry. A part of the family? So soon?

Susanna rushed to kiss Joseph. 'Uncle Joe, you look younger every time I see you.' She blew kisses at David and Dino. They had been friends since childhood.

Then Carlos Brent made his entrance. A typical Carlos Brent entrance with noise and excitement and an entourage of six.

The dinner party was almost complete.

'Where's Nico Constantine?' asked Joseph. 'It's nearly a quarter after seven.'

Anyone who knew Joseph at all knew he was a stickler for punctuality.

Susanna looked at Bernie. 'Where *is* Nico?'

Bernie shrugged and tried to look suitably casual. 'He sent his apologies, hopes to make it later for coffee.'

'He's got a new girlfriend,' Susanna announced, 'I don't think she ever lets him out of bed!'

Joseph turned to Cherry. 'You're a friend of Nico's, aren't you?'

She smoothed down the front of her new pink dress. 'Nico's been like a father to me,' she said demurely.

I bet, thought Joseph. He was on to Cherry. Miss sweetness and light. She had dazzled Dino with the first clean pussy he had seen in years.

He wondered what it would take to get rid if her. Maybe Nico would know – after all he had brought her into Dino's life, and he could take her right on out again.

She was amazingly pretty. Bad wife material. She'd be screwing around before the ink was dry on the marriage licence.

Joseph glanced down the table at Mia. Now *that* was wife material.

'Mr Fonicetti,' Cherry gushed, 'You don't know how exciting this all is for me . . . Meeting Dino . . . you . . .'

'Where are you from, dear?' Joseph asked. May as well find out her version of her background before he put a private detective on to her.

As far as Bernie was concerned the dinner dragged on for ever.

He needed it like he needed piles.

Susanna playing girl wife again. Carlos throwing him fishy dago false smiles. Mia and David both as dull as each other. Dino a nervous wreck. And Cherry – little Miss Blue Eyes – all innocence and golden curls and not fooling crafty old Joseph Fonicetti one bit.

Bernie had been unable to contact Nico in London. No answer in his hotel room. So he had left a message relaying the fact that everything was fine – so far. But how long before it was noticed that Nico's handsome face was no longer in evidence? And how long could Bernie fool them with a mystery girlfriend who didn't even exist?

As if on cue, Joseph said, 'Hey, Bernie, where's Nico? I thought you said he'd be here for coffee.'

'I guess he got hung up . . .'

'I invite people for dinner, they usually come. I want to talk to Nico . . . Business . . . Have him come up to my suite later.'

Oh, sure. Just like that. Bernie was beginning to seriously consider the possibility of jetting back to LA the next day with Susanna. Get out while he was clean.

'If I see him,' he said lamely. 'Like he's taken off with this girl . . .'

'Taken off?' Joseph snapped. 'Dino, did you hear that?'

'What?' Dino jumped. His mind had been exploring the possibility of a honeymoon in Europe, far far away from his father.

'Nico Constantine has taken off,' Joseph said grimly.

'Not taken off,' Bernie attempted a weak laugh. 'I mean he's around, but this girl . . . Well, you know how it can be . . .'

'What girl?' Joseph inquired, his eyes suddenly steely.

'I don't know her name . . .'

'Does she work here?'

'No, I don't think so.'

'So who is she? What does she do?'

Susanna joined in, 'Yes, who is this woman of mystery?'

Bernie could have belted her. He didn't like the look in Joseph's eyes. He was one smart old man.

'I told you, I don't know. Some broad who's dragged him away from the tables all the way into her bed.'

'Everyone!' Cherry clapped her hands excitedly, 'I can't keep it to myself any longer! Today, this very afternoon! Dino and I got married!'

Bernie could have kissed her. It was one heck of a good way to take everyone's mind off of Nico.

15

'What?' Nico could not believe what Hal was telling him.

'Glass,' Hal stated flatly, 'one helluva chunk of beautifully cut glass – set in real platinum of course. A copy – a beaut – but the real thing it ain't.'

'I don't believe it!' Nico felt an insane desire to laugh. 'I just don't believe it!'

'Start believing, kid. It's not worth more than a few hundred.'

Nico shook his head in amazement. So – Mrs Dean Costello had fooled him. Or had she? The old dear had never claimed that her ring was real. She had never handed him papers to prove its authenticity. She probably had the real thing locked up in a bank vault. Of course. It was obvious. A diamond that size – all the rich women had copies made of their gems. And excellent copies too. Good enough to fool everyone except the experts.

Nico was embarrassed. 'Hal, what can I say? I had no idea . . .'

Hal was friendly. 'Of course you didn't. Even I thought it was the real thing, and I have an eye – I can spot the real stuff a mile off. Listen, it was nice nearly doing business with you.' He prepared to leave. 'Give my best to Bernie. Will you be leaving today?'

Nico shrugged, 'I don't know what I'm going to do.'

'You know what you really need? A rich, old broad.' Hal laughed, 'Rich, old, and grateful.' He warmed to his subject. 'Now I have a couple of hot ones flying in from Texas tomorrow. You want a million dollars – no problem. But you'll have to work for it . . .'

'How old?'

'Not spring chickens . . .'

'How old?'

'In their sixties, maybe creeping up to seventy . . . But

you'd never know, what with silicone tits and face jobs and . . .'

'Forget it.'

'Suit yourself, but it's a winning game.'

Yeah. A winning game. That's what he really needed.

Hal left, and Nico paced his hotel room wondering what his next move should be. Alert Bernie. That had to be first. Tell him to get out of Vegas and stop covering up for him.

Then what? How was he ever going to get half a million dollars?

How had he ever lost half a million dollars?

Gambling.

His bankroll was almost non-existent, but that didn't phase him. He picked up the phone and requested the Manager.

Full Nico charm. 'Mr Graheme, I have a slight problem, my bank in Switzerland is transferring funds – by tomorrow no problem. In the meantime if you could let me have – say – five hundred pounds cash – and charge it to my bill I would be most grateful . . .'

The six dozen red roses arrived late afternoon. They were waiting for Fontaine when she returned to her house after the auditions. Mrs Walters had set them out in matching cut glass vases.

'Christ!' Fontaine exclaimed irritably. 'The place is beginning to look like a funeral parlour! I know I asked for fresh flowers Mrs Walters, but this is ridiculous.'

Mrs Walters clucked her agreement, and handed her employer the card which had accompanied the roses.

Fontaine read it. The message was brief – just – 'Thank you. Nico.'

Thank you for what? For a great screw? For throwing him out? For what?

Fontaine tore the card into tiny pieces and let it flutter over the carpet.

Mrs Walters pursed her lips. Who would have to clear *that* up later.

107

'I don't want to be disturbed,' Fontaine sighed. 'I simply have to rest.'

'Your lawyer has telephoned three times, Mrs Khaled, he says it's urgent that he arrange an appointment with you immediately.'

'How boring.'

'And Count Rispollo telephoned.'

'Even more boring.'

'What shall I say if they phone again, Mrs Khaled?'

'Tell them I am resting, and to telephone tomorrow.'

'Oh, and this arrived.' Mrs Walters produced a small package.

Fontaine took it from her and balanced it in her hand. Boucheron. Was it a token of Count Paulo's esteem?

'Wake me at eight o'clock.' She walked upstairs.

The thought occurred that maybe she should have brought Steve Valentine home with her. Personally seen to it that he had what it takes in all the right places.

Once that would have been exciting. But somehow the thrill of just another horny body was beginning to pall.

Now Nico . . .

Screw Nico . . . She didn't even want to think about him. Lousy hustler. Using her to smuggle his stuff through customs. Sharing her bed only to recover his ring.

She ripped open the packet from Boucheron, and read the card that fell out.

Same card. Same message. 'Thank you. Nico.'

Thoughtfully she stared at the diamond-encrusted heart. It was very lovely. She took it out of the box and held it in her hand.

Nico . . . He *had* been a very special lover . . .

So far so good. Nico was winning. Nothing sensational – but a beginning.

He had started the evening with a stake of a thousand pounds – this he had managed to work up to twenty-five thousand pounds. A nice beginning.

For a change everything seemed to be going his way.

And if his luck kept right on . . . Who knew what could happen?

He was enjoying the ambience of a British gaming club. So different from the brashness of Vegas.

Delightful female croupiers in low-cut dresses. Discreet pit bosses. Respectful girls serving unobtrusive drinks.

The atmosphere was that of a rather elegant club.

Nico lit up a long thin cigar, and moved from a blackjack table to roulette. The limit was not as high as he would have wished, and he was unable to bet more than five hundred on black. It came up. Good. But certainly not good enough. He needed to get into a high stake poker game, and he looked around for someone who might be able to arrange it.

The manager seemed a likely prospect, and sure enough he was. He recommended another club which would be happy to accommodate Nico as far as poker, backgammon, whatever he wished.

Nico took a taxi there.

He had tried to telephone Bernie earlier, but had been unable to reach him. Now he just wanted to concentrate on making some sort of big score.

'Hmmm . . .' Fontaine stood in the doorway and surveyed the disco at 'Hobo'. 'Well I suppose I mustn't expect miracles. It *is* his first night.'

Polly nodded. 'He looks good though, don't you think?'

Fontaine watched Steve through narrowed kaleidoscope eyes. 'He doesn't have the walk.'

'What walk?'

'The John Travolta cock thrust. You know what I mean, Polly.'

Polly couldn't help giggling. Cock thrust. It sounded like something you did in an aeroplane!

Steve came towards them. He was clad in a rather cheap black pinstripe suit, shirt, and tie.

'Mrs Khaled. A table for how many?'

'The look is wrong, Steve,' she snapped. 'You're running a disco – not your uncle's wedding!'

'Sorry.'

'Don't worry, I should have told you. Obviously they're a touch more formal in Ealing. Now, let me see . . .'

She reached for his tie, undid and removed it. Then she unbuttoned his shirt three buttons. 'That's better. Tomorrow I'll take you out shopping.'

Oh God! Shades of Tony! How well she remembered their first meeting. A disaster. He had possessed an animal charm, a sexy walk, but that was about all. And in bed – nothing but raw ability.

She had seen his potential, and trained him to make full use of it in every way.

He had learned quickly. And then he had got far too big for his newly acquired Gucci loafers.

Now Steve stood before her. Raw material. Was it worth building him into a monster too?

Count Paulo, who was lucky enough to be escorting Polly and Fontaine, gave Steve a dirty look. 'Mrs Khaled's table?'

'Of course,' Steve jumped to attention.

Count Paulo ordered the obligatory champagne, and asked Fontaine to dance.

'You dance with him Polly,' Fontaine commanded. 'At least try and make the place look busy.'

Nico's run of luck continued to the tune of fifty thousand pounds. He was smart enough to quit as soon as the cards began to turn.

He felt elated . . . so elated that he risked a phone call to Fontaine.

A disgruntled housekeeper – obviously woken from a deep sleep – informed him that madam was out.

Then he spotted the girl again. A very tall blonde in a very stark dress. He had noticed her earlier in the evening at the other gaming club. She was certainly striking. Not a fresh-faced beauty nor a sophisticated Fontaine. But very very striking . . .

She smiled at him across the room, and he smiled back.

He thought no more about her.

He collected his coat from reception, tipped the man at the desk handsomely, and signalled the doorman for a cab.

She appeared just as he was climbing in. 'Can you give me a lift?' Her voice was soothingly husky. 'I am escaping from an over-amorous Arab, and if I don't vanish immediately I'm in trouble.'

Nico raised a quizzical eyebrow. 'You are?'

'Please?'

'Hop in. I always help beautiful women in trouble.'

She smiled. 'I knew you'd say that.'

'You did?'

'You look like Omar Sharif – so why shouldn't you sound like him.'

'I'm not an Arab, I'm Greek.'

'I know that. There's no way I would've shared a taxi with an Arab, thank you.'

'How did you know I was Greek?'

She opened her purse, took out a compact, and inspected her face. 'I didn't know *what* you were . . . I just knew you weren't an Arab.' She clicked the compact shut. 'Hi – I'm Lynn.' Formally she extended her hand. 'And you?'

'Nico Constantine.'

'Greek name, but you sound American.'

'Yes, I've lived in LA for the last ten years. Now – where can I drop you?'

Lynn mock pouted, 'Trying to get rid of me so soon . . .'

Nico laughed, 'Not at all.'

'Did I hear you tell the cab driver the Lamont?'

'That's where I'm staying.'

'They only do the best scrambled eggs in town, don't they.'

'They do?'

'If you don't know you must try.'

'The restaurant will be closed . . .'

'And room service will be open . . .'

*

111

Vanessa, Leonard, and a whole group of people arrived at 'Hobo' as Fontaine's guests.

She watched the women's reactions to Steve. Nothing special.

'Do you fancy him?' she whispered to Vanessa.

'He's not Tony.'

'*Fuck* Tony. I'm sick to death of hearing about Tony. He's not the only stud in the world you know.' Fontaine drained her champagne glass, and gestured for more.

'He *is* quite cute . . .' Vanessa ventured.

'Cute! Christ! That's hardly what I'm looking for.'

The evening sped by in a haze of champagne. Fontaine allowed herself to get delightfully, pleasantly bombed.

Count Paulo clutched her in his arms on the dance floor and declared undying love and lust. 'We must be in bed together soon,' he panted, 'my whole body screams for you.'

He rubbed embarrassingly against her, and she wished he'd take his juvenile Italian horniness back to Italy with him.

She danced with Leonard.

'How about a cosy lunch one day, just the two of us?' He suggested.

God save her from the middle-aged husbands who considered her fair game.

Goodbyes were said in the early hours of the morning on the pavement outside 'Hobo'.

Ricky stood obediently holding the door of the Rolls open while Fontaine, Polly, and Count Paulo piled in.

'Drop Miss Brand first,' Fontaine ordered. 'Then Count Rispollo.'

'Yes, Mrs Khaled.'

Polly managed a surreptitious wink as she was dropped off. 'Later?' she whispered.

'You bet,' Ricky replied, *sotto voce*.

Count Paulo was complaining loudly about being driven to his hotel. 'Tonight I thought we would be together,' he said bitterly. 'I come all the way to see you – and you treat me like . . . like dirt.'

'I'm tired,' Fontaine replied coolly. 'Maybe tomorrow. Call me.'

A disappointed Count Paulo was deposited outside his hotel.

'Home, Ricky,' instructed Fontaine.

He glanced at the clock. Four o'clock in the bleedin' morning. He hoped she wasn't expecting him bright and early at ten a.m. By the time he made it back to Polly's and gave her a good seeing to . . . Well, he'd need some sleep, wouldn't he?

They arrived at Fontaine's Pelham Crescent house. Ricky jumped out of the Rolls and held the door open for her.

She yawned openly and sighed. Dawn was beginning to break. Her kaleidoscope eyes swept over him. 'Coming in for an early morning cup of tea, Ricky?'

Nico and Lynn made love in his hotel suite. A room service trolley bearing two plates of congealed scrambled eggs stood forlornly in the centre of the living room.

Lynn was accomplished, striking, pleasant.

The sex was enjoyable.

Nico wished he hadn't.

She was just another female. A beautiful body – yes. But a stranger. And somehow sex with strangers was not the way he wanted to lead his life anymore. He was too old for one-night stands. And too smart. And he wished he was with Fontaine beneath her black silk sheets exchanging lives.

'That was good,' Lynn said, getting up from the bed.

'Very good,' Nico agreed, hoping she would dress and go.

She stretched, naked and cat-like. 'Are you into bondage?'

'What?'

'Bondage. You know, being tied up and beaten. The Arabs love it.'

113

'I told you, I'm not an Arab.'

'I know.' She arched her back, then touched her toes. Her body was somewhat sinewy. 'You're a Greek who talks American.' She picked up her dress from the floor and started to pull it on. 'And you're also a dumb son-of-a-bitch who had better pay back the money you owe the Fonicettis or you're going to find yourself an unrecognizable son-of-a-bitch. Am I making myself clear?'

'What did you say?' Nico sat up in bed, shocked.

Lynn fiddled with the zipper on her dress. Her smoky voice was very sensuous. 'You heard me. I'm a messenger, so you had better listen very very carefully.' She searched for her spike-heeled shoes and put them on. 'You have a week, seven days, no credit. Understand?' She picked up her purse and moved towards the door. She paused and smiled. 'Every cent, Nico, or . . . well . . . they're going to cut your balls off, and wouldn't that be a shame?'

She exited, closing the door quietly behind her.

'Isn't this fun?' Fontaine watched Ricky through slitted eyes as he poured the tea.

He wasn't sure whether to answer or not. In fact he didn't know how to act at all.

'You know,' Fontaine murmured thoughtfully, 'you're really rather sexy. Why didn't I think of using *you* for the club?'

'Sugar, Mrs Khaled?'

'No, thank you,' she turned her back on him. 'Bring the tea up to the bedroom, Ricky, yours as well.'

He stood in the kitchen and watched her go. Then quick as a flash he whipped out a tray and put the two cups of tea on it. 'Ricky m'boy,' he muttered to himself, 'I think you just got lucky.'

'Ricky,' her slightly drunken voice called from the top of the stairs, 'are you coming?'

Of course he was. Polly would just have to wait.

Bernie, Susanna, and Cherry sat in silence aboard Carlos Brent's private plane. Each one of them in deep thought.

Susanna smiled slightly. The shit had hit – Bernie's charming expression – but it hadn't flown in her direction.

Cherry sobbed quietly, occasionally dabbing at her baby-blue eyes with a silk monogrammed handkerchief taken from one of Dino's drawers.

Bernie sat stoically. Mr Fall Guy. Mr Schmuck. It was just good luck he was connected to Carlos Brent, even if it was only a fragile connection. If he hadn't been . . .

If Susanna had not intervened on his behalf . . .

Well, he didn't like to think what would have happened.

Bernie reflected on the previous evening's happenings. It all seemed like a bad fucking dream.

First it was pure shit-luck that Joseph Fonicetti had decided to throw a dinner party. Second, the fact that Nico was an invited guest. And third, that Cherry and Dino had sneaked off and gotten married.

What a joke *that* was.

The whole mix was disaster time.

Joseph Fonicetti was far too canny an old animal to let anything slide past him. And the fact that Nico owed – and owed big – was reason enough for him to be suspicious when Nico failed to show.

Of course, when Cherry announced the fact that she and Dino were married the party really took off.

Joseph Fonicetti did not like surprises – especially of that kind. And he had risen from the table, small mean eyes burning in his nut brown face. 'Is this fuckin' true?' he had screamed at Dino, down the table. 'Are you gonna tell me you've *married* the dumb cunt?'

Cherry had joined in then, blue eyes tearful but determined. 'How dare you call me that – *how dare you!*'

Appealingly she had looked to Dino for support.

Dino had slunk down in his chair. How could he argue with his father? The unfortunate truth was that she *was* a dumb cunt for opening up her mouth.

'Get me Nico Constantine, cut out the bullshit and find him,' Joseph demanded.

Bernie had visibly blanched. He did not know what to say.

Joseph sensed this immediately. 'He *is* still here, isn't he, Bernie?' The voice was menacing.

Susanna cut in quickly with – 'Of course he is, Uncle Joe.'

Joseph ignored her. 'Check it out, David. I want that son-of-a-bitch, Nico, and I want him now.' He indicated a by now sobbing Cherry. 'She's his – this . . . this Barbie doll! He can take her right on out of our lives.'

'Mr Fonicetti!' Cherry had gulped. 'Dino and I are *married*.'

'Find out where the stupid fuck did it, and take care of that too, David,' Joseph snapped. 'And get me Nico – pronto. There's also the matter of the money he owes us. Dino was supposed to take care of that – but he's been too busy taking care of his cock.' At this point Joseph had burst into a stream of angry Italian – a language that had stayed with him since childhood.

Carlos Brent had risen from the table, gone to Joseph, and put his arm around him.

The dinner party was over.

So was Cherry and Dino's marriage.

So was Nico when they found out he had split.

And so was Bernie when they found out he had aided and abetted.

Quickly he had put his arm around Susanna, 'Let's get married again,' he suggested. 'We've had such a great time this last couple of days.'

'Anything to save your ass, huh Bernie?' But she grinned when she said it.

116

Naturally it did not take them long to find out that Nico was gone.

Bernie had been hauled up to the Fonicetti penthouse for questioning. Susanna had insisted on accompanying him.

To save his own ass he was forced to tell them where Nico was.

'We'll take care of it,' Joseph had muttered ominously.

'He only went so he could raise the money to pay you,' Bernie insisted. 'He's probably on his way back now.'

'Sure, sure.' Joseph stared him down with his mean little eyes. 'Remember one thing in your life, Bernie. Loyalty. But don't fuck it up. Loyalty to the *right* people. When you knew Nico couldn't pay you should have come to me immediately. No hesitation. You understand?'

Bernie nodded vigorously.

'But . . . you're young . . . you have a lot to learn. And I myself have loyalty to Carlos Brent. So you are lucky. You understand?'

'He understands, Uncle Joe,' Susanna kissed the old man on the cheek. 'It won't happen again. And thank you.'

So Bernie's balls were intact. Only thing was, they now belonged to Susanna again.

Cherry shared an apartment in Hollywood with two other girls. They were both away. One on a fishing trip with a porno-movie star. The other on location in Oregon.

Cherry wandered around the empty apartment in a daze. It had all happened so quickly. One moment she was Mrs Dino Fonicetti. The next – just plain Cherry, unsuccessful actress.

It wasn't fair. What was wrong with her? What made her unsuitable material to be Dino's wife? Why did his father automatically hate her?

She stared at her exquisite reflection in the mirror. Blonde hair. Blue eyes. Perfect features. With Dino's

117

dark good looks, what beautiful babies they would have made together.

Dino. His behaviour had not been very nice. Allowing his father to call her horrible names.

She gave a long drawn-out sigh, walked in the tiny bathroom, removed a line of drying underclothes from across the bath, selected her favourite bubbles, and started to run the water.

Then she stripped off her clothes and stepped into the bath.

'Operator, try that number again please.' Bernie bounced his daughter Starr on his knee, and tried to locate Nico for the fifth time.

Susanna was busy unpacking his clothes. On the way from the airport she had insisted on picking up all his things from Nico's rented house.

'We can do it tomorrow,' Bernie had complained.

'Now. I want to feel you're really back. Not just sharing my bed for a night.'

As she unpacked she complained, 'Look at these shirts! My God what kind of a laundry did you send these to!'

'Bernie, these socks should have been thrown away, they're full of holes.'

'Oh no! This is my favourite sweater and you've got a cigarette burn in it. How could you?'

Bernie tuned out, and concentrated on reaching Nico. The least he could do was warn him.

'I think we should have a small wedding, nothing flashy, something tasteful, with Starr as a bridesmaid. What do you think, Bernie?'

'Good idea.'

'Daddy suggested his house in Palm Springs. We could fly everyone up. That would be fun, wouldn't it?'

'Sure.' Goddamn daddy again.

'And I'll wear blue – and how about you in a blue suit

118

so that we match?' And Starr in blue frills. Oh Bernie, it's all so exciting!'

There was nothing Susanna liked better than planning a party – or a wedding for that matter. Bernie remembered with a feeling of dread their famous Saturday night intimate dinner parties for fifty or sixty. Shit. This time he would have to put his foot down.

'We're ringing Mr Constantine's suite,' the hotel operator's voice said.

Three rings and Nico answered.

'I've been trying to reach you for days,' Bernie exclaimed. 'The shit has —

'Hit. I know.' Nico replied.

'How do you know? What's happened?' Bernie stuttered.

'They have given me a very generous seven days to come up with the money.'

'And the ring?'

'Glass, my friend.'

'What'll you do?'

'I'll think of something.'

'Listen, Nico. It wasn't my fault they found out. I tried. I kept it going for days. What happened is a long story.'

'Save it. I'll be back to hear it personally. In one piece, I hope.'

'I'm glad you can take it so calmly.'

'What other way is there?'

'If you need me I'm at Susanna's.'

'Reconciliation?'

'I'll explain.'

'Keep hold of your balls.'

'You too.'

Nico hung up the phone. He *was* calm. His energies could not be wasted on panicking. He had sat and thought from the moment of Lynn's departure.

There were two moves that he could make. One – take his fifty thousand pounds winnings and escape. South America, Athens . . . Change his name, start a new life. The snag was he had no particular desire to change his name and life.

Two – pay them the money he owed. If he could somehow raise it that was.

Two was the only answer of course. But how?

He fell asleep still trying to work it out.

Fontaine awoke to the smell and a taste of a hangover,

and a hammering on her locked bedroom door.

Oh God! She felt positively dreadful.

'Mrs Khaled,' the voice assaulted her, 'it's past twelve, I have your breakfast tray.'

'Leave it outside, Mrs Walters.'

Oh God! Her headache was lethal. She tried to remember fragments of the previous evening – and did.

Oh God! Ricky. He was still asleep in her bed. She sat up and surveyed the room. It looked like a party had taken place.

Oh God! It had. Just the two of them. Talk about shades of Lady Chatterley's lover!

She slid from the bed into a silk kimono, and thought about how to get rid of him.

Mrs Walters wouldn't be shocked that she had had a man spend the night, she was used to that. But the fact that it was her chauffeur! Oh God!

'Ricky,' she gave him a short sharp shove. 'Kindly get up and piss off.'

'What? What?' He opened his eyes. 'Where am I?' Then he remembered. 'Oh – yes, 'course. C'm here darlin', I'll give you a bit more of what you enjoyed last night.'

She withered him with a look. 'Forget about last night, Ricky. And I am not darling, I am Mrs Khaled, and don't you forget it. Now kindly dress and get the hell out of here.'

He sat up in bed. 'Are you giving me the old elbow?'

'If you mean am I firing you, the answer is no. But just remember, last night was a figment of your imagination.'

Bloody hell! Some figment. He had a very good recollection of Mrs Khaled sitting astride him in nothing but a mink coat and his chauffeur's cap yelling, 'First one to the gate is the winner!' Bloody hell!

Fontaine retired into the bathroom, and Ricky dressed quickly. He let himself out of the locked bedroom, nearly tripped over the breakfast tray, and sneaked downstairs.

Mrs Walters was busy dusting. She gave him a look of disdain and a disgusted sniff.

'Morning Mrs Walters.'

She turned her back on him.

Backgammon had always been a game Nico excelled at. He presented himself at a London club and exercised his skills. London had no lack of backgammon hustlers, but Nico was more than a match for them.

He spent the afternoon at play, and emerged in the early evening a few thousand pounds richer.

Not bad, but not nearly enough to even begin to help.

He needed advice. He called Hal.

They met in 'Trader Vics' for a drink, Hal resplendent in a new white suit.

Nico fingered the lapel. 'Looks good.'

'Gotta be my best for the ladies. They're here. If I play it right I could well own half of Detroit by tomorrow morning! Sure you wouldn't like to join us for dinner?'

'If they have five hundred thousand dollars to hand my way . . .'

Hal laughed. 'Five years solid fucking could probably get you that.'

Nico grimaced. 'I need it a little sooner.' His black eyes fixed on to Hal, almost hypnotic in their intensity. 'I am deadly serious about needing the money, Hal. I blew out of Vegas owing. Thought the ring would cover it. Now' – he made a gesture of hopelessness – 'they've found me. They sent a woman messenger. I thought she was a beautiful girl looking to get laid. She got laid all right – and then she delivered the message. Seven days. They mean business – you know it and I know it. Do you have any suggestions?'

Hal summoned the pretty Chinese waitress and ordered another Navy Grog. He was sympathetic. But not *that* sympathetic. He liked Nico very much. But if trouble was coming he wanted to be long gone.

'Let me get some details here,' he said, stalling for time while he thought of a fast excuse to be on his way. 'Who do you owe? And how much?'

'I wasn't kidding you. I owe the Fonicettis five hundred and fifty grand.'

Hal let out a long low whistle, 'Jeez! I know old Joe Fonicetti. Are you gonna tell me they let you run up markers for that much? It's impossible.'

'Not when you lose six hundred thou of your own money up front.'

Hal whistled again. 'You are in trouble, my friend. Big big trouble.'

The Chinese girl brought his drink, and smiled inscrutably at both of them.

'I've never fucked a Chinese,' Hal said absently as she walked away. 'Now tell me, Nico. Who was your lady messenger? Did they send somebody over?'

Nico shook his head. 'She was English. Said her name was Lynn.'

'Very tall? Good body?'

Nico nodded. 'You know her?'

'She used to be a dancer on TV. Never made it out of the back line until she met the man himself.'

'What man?'

'Feathers. Lynn's his right-hand woman. One tough lady – expert judo – the martial arts – you were lucky you only got fucked!'

'Thanks a lot.'

'I wish I could talk to Feathers,' Hal mused aloud. 'Maybe we could figure out something . . .'

'Why can't you?' Nico asked.

'We're not on the best of terms right now. A debt. It's dragged on.'

'How much?'

'Five thousand pounds. I keep him happy with a payment here a payment there. But he'd be a lot happier to see a lump sum.'

'Pay him the lump sum. I have it. Call it a fee for your help.'

'Hey, Nico. You don't have to do that.'

'I know I don't. But if you can work out some deal with Feathers – that *he* can work out with Fonicetti. Maybe an instalment plan like you had . . . What do you think?'

Hal nodded slowly. 'Whatever I can do, I'll do.'

Nico patted him on the shoulder. 'Thanks. I'll appreciate anything you can manage.'

Wild looking model girls in exotic underclothes undulated frantically down the catwalk.

Fontaine, at a ringside table, openly yawned.

'Aren't you enjoying it?' Vanessa asked anxiously. The fashion show was raising money for one of her charities and she desperately wanted it to be a success.

'I never did get turned on gaping at other women's bodies,' Fontaine replied. 'Aren't there any *male* models? You know – horny little nineteen-year-olds in nothing but their jockeys and a smile?'

'Oh Fontaine! Really! It's the clothes you're supposed to be looking at.'

'Hmmm . . .' Fontaine allowed her gaze to wander around the restaurant where the fashion show was taking place. Tables and tables of boring women, all dressed in the latest most expensive clothes. Just as she was.

God! Was this what her life was all about? Fashion and Getting Fucked. Both were beginning to pall.

'I have to leave soon,' she whispered to Vanessa. 'Got to meet with my lawyer. Boring old Arnold is threatening me with the workhouse if I don't come up with some money soon. That pittance Benjamin pays me hardly covers my weekly expenses. I simply *have* to get "Hobo" back in action.'

'You will,' Vanessa replied. 'When you put your mind to it nothing can stop you.'

'I know, I know. I always get what I want. But don't you see, Vanessa, that's just an impression I create.'

The Angel's Game

'The language and mood remain intricate and beguiling…
The language purrs along, while the plot twists and unravels
with languid grace…atmospheric, beguiling and
thoroughly readable.'
Observer

'Anyone who enjoys novels that are scary, erotic, touching,
tragic and thrilling should rush right out to the nearest
bookstore and pick up *The Shadow of the Wind*.
Really, you should.'
Washington Post

'Good old-fashioned narrative is back in fashion…his tale [has]
a dramatic tension that so many contemporary novels today
seem to lack. This is highly sophisticated, fun reading that keeps
you gripped and tests the brain cells all at the same time. What
more could you ask for?'
Scotsman

'Gabriel Garcia Marquez meets Umberto Eco meets Jorge Luis
Borges…Ruiz Zafón gives us a panoply of alluring and savage
personages and stories. His novel eddies in currents of passion,
revenge and mysteries whose layers peel away onion-like yet
persist in growing back…We are taken on a wild ride that
executes its hairpin bends with breathtaking lurches.'
New York Times

'This story is so expansive that to describe it as an epic
doesn't quite do it justice.'
Adelaide Advertiser

'You'll read it and you'll want more.'
Age

CARLOS RUIZ ZAFÓN, author of *The Shadow of the Wind* and other novels, is one of the world's most read and best-loved writers. His work has been translated into more than forty languages and published around the world, garnering numerous international prizes and reaching millions of readers. He divides his time between Barcelona and Los Angeles.

LUCIA GRAVES is an author and the translator of several works, including Spanish editions of the poetry and prose of her father, Robert Graves.

CARLOS RUIZ ZAFÓN

The Angel's Game

Translated by Lucia Graves

TEXT PUBLISHING MELBOURNE AUSTRALIA

The paper in this book is manufactured only from wood grown in sustainable regrowth forests.

The Text Publishing Company
Swann House
22 William Street
Melbourne Victoria 3000
Australia
www.textpublishing.com.au

First published in Spanish as *El Juego del Angel*
by Editorial Planeta, Barcelona, 2008
First published in Australia by The Text Publishing Company, 2009
Printed and bound in Australia by Griffin Press

National Library of Australia
Cataloguing-in-Publication data:

Ruiz Zafón, Carlos, 1964–

The angel's game / Carlos Ruiz Zafón.

ISBN: 9781921520525 (hbk.)
ISBN: 9781921520433 (pbk.)

863.64

For MariCarmen

'a nation of two'

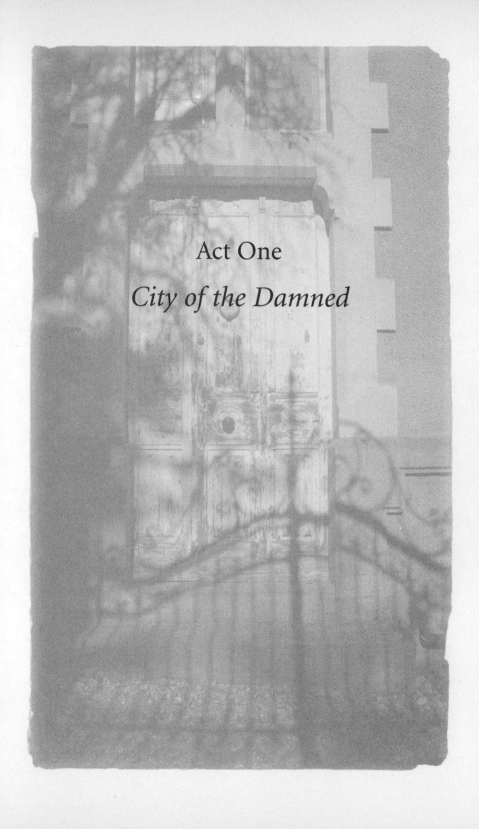

Act One

City of the Damned

1

A writer never forgets the first time he accepted a few coins or a word of praise in exchange for a story. He will never forget the sweet poison of vanity in his blood, and the belief that, if he succeeds in not letting anyone discover his lack of talent, the dream of literature will provide him with a roof over his head, a hot meal at the end of the day, and what he covets the most: his name printed on a miserable piece of paper that surely will outlive him. A writer is condemned to remember that moment, because from then on he is doomed and his soul has a price.

My first time came one faraway day in December 1917. I was seventeen and worked at *The Voice of Industry*, a newspaper which had seen better days and now languished in a barn of a building that had once housed a sulphuric acid factory. The walls still oozed the corrosive vapour that ate away at furniture and clothes, sapping the spirits, consuming even the soles of shoes. The newspaper's headquarters rose behind the forest of angels and crosses of the Pueblo Nuevo Cemetery; from afar, its outline merged with the mausoleums silhouetted against the horizon – a skyline stabbed by hundreds of chimneys and factories that wove a perpetual twilight of scarlet and black above Barcelona.

On the night that was about to change the course of my life, the newspaper's deputy editor, Don Basilio Moragas, saw fit to summon me, just before closing time, to the dark cubicle at the far end of the editorial staff room that doubled as his office and cigar den. Don Basilio was a forbidding-looking man with a bushy moustache who did not suffer fools and who subscribed to the theory that the liberal use of adverbs and adjectives was the mark of a pervert or someone with a vitamin deficiency. Any journalist prone to florid prose would be sent off to write funeral notices for three weeks. If, after this penance, the culprit relapsed, Don Basilio would ship him off permanently to the 'House and Home' pages. We were all terrified of him, and he knew it.

'Did you call me, Don Basilio?' I ventured timidly.

The deputy editor looked at me askance. I entered the office, which smelled of sweat and tobacco in that order. Ignoring my presence, Don Basilio continued to read through one of the articles lying on his table, a red pencil in hand. For a couple of minutes, he machine-gunned the text with corrections and amputations, muttering sharp comments as if I wasn't there. Not knowing what to do and noticing a chair placed against the wall, I slid into it.

'Who said you could sit down?' muttered Don Basilio without raising his eyes from the text.

I quickly stood up again and held my breath. The deputy editor sighed, let his red pencil fall and leaned back in his armchair, eyeing me as if I were some useless piece of junk.

'I've been told that you write, Martín.'

I gulped. When I opened my mouth only a ridiculous, reedy voice emerged.

'A little, well, I don't know, I mean, yes, I do write . . .'

'I hope you write better than you speak. And what do you write – if that's not too much to ask?'

'Crime stories. I mean . . .'

'I get the idea.'

The look Don Basilio gave me was priceless. If I'd said I devoted my time to sculpting figures for Nativity scenes out of fresh dung I would have drawn three times as much enthusiasm from him. He sighed again and shrugged his shoulders.

'Vidal says you're not altogether bad. He says you stand out. Of course, with the sort of competition in this neck of the woods, that's not saying much. Still, if Vidal says so.'

Pedro Vidal was the star writer at *The Voice of Industry*. He penned a weekly column on crime and lurid events – the only thing worth reading in the whole paper. He was also the author of a dozen thrillers about gangsters in the Raval quarter carrying out bedroom intrigues with ladies of high society, which had achieved a modest success. Invariably dressed in impeccable silk suits and shiny Italian moccasins, Vidal had the looks and the manner of a matinee idol: fair hair always well combed, a pencil moustache, and the easy, generous smile of someone who feels comfortable in his own skin and at ease with the world. He belonged to a family whose forebears had made their pile in the Americas in the sugar business and, on their return to Barcelona, had bitten off a large chunk of the city's electricity grid. His father, the patriarch of the clan, was one of the main shareholders of the newspaper, and Don Pedro used its offices as a playground to kill the tedium of never having worked out of necessity a single day in his life. It mattered little to him that the newspaper was losing money as quickly as the new automobiles that were beginning to run around Barcelona leaked oil: with its abundance of nobility, the Vidal dynasty was now busy collecting banks and plots of land the size of small principalities in the new part of town known as the Ensanche.

Pedro Vidal was the first person to whom I had dared show rough drafts of my writing when, barely a child, I carried coffee and cigarettes round the staff room. He always had time for me: he read what I had written and gave me good advice. Eventually, he made me his assistant and would allow me to type out his drafts. It was he who told me that if I wanted to bet my number on the Russian roulette of literature, he was willing to help me and set me on the right path. True to his word, he had now thrown me into the clutches of Don Basilio, the newspaper's Cerberus.

'Vidal is a sentimentalist who still believes in those profoundly un-Spanish myths such as meritocracy or giving opportunities to those who deserve them rather than to the current favourite. Loaded as he is, he can allow himself to go around being a free spirit. If I had one hundredth of the cash he doesn't even need I would have devoted my life to honing sonnets, and little twittering nightingales would come to eat from my hand, captivated by my kindness and charm.'

'Señor Vidal is a great man!' I protested.

'He's more than that. He's a saint, because although you may look like a ragamuffin he's been banging on at me for weeks about how talented and hard-working the office junior is. He knows that deep down I'm a softy, and besides he's assured me that if I give you this break he'll present me with a box of Cuban cigars. And if Vidal says so, it's as good as Moses coming down from the mountain with the lump of stone in his hand and the revealed truth shining from his forehead. So, to get to the point, because it's Christmas, and because

I want your friend to shut up once and for all, I'm offering you a head start, against wind and tide.'

'Thank you so much, Don Basilio. I promise you won't regret it . . .'

'Don't get too carried away, boy. Let's see, what do you think of the indiscriminate use of adjectives and adverbs?'

'I think it's a disgrace and should be set down in the penal code,' I replied with the conviction of a zealot.

Don Basilio nodded in approval.

'You're on the right track, Martín. Your priorities are clear. Those who make it in this business have priorities, not principles. This is the plan. Sit down and concentrate, because I'm not going to tell you twice.'

The plan was as follows. For reasons that Don Basilio thought best not to set out in detail, the back page of the Sunday edition, which was traditionally reserved for a short story or a travel feature, had fallen through at the last minute. The content was to have been a fiery narrative in patriotic vein about the exploits of Catalan medieval knights in which they saved Christianity and all that was decent under the sun, starting with the Holy Land and ending with the banks of our Llobregat delta. Unfortunately the text had not arrived in time or, I suspected, Don Basilio simply didn't want to publish it. This left us, only six hours before deadline, with no other substitute for the story than a whole-page advertisement for whalebone corsets that guaranteed perfect hips and full immunity from the effects of buttery by-products. Faced with such a dilemma, the editorial board had opted to take the bull by the horns and make the most of the literary excellence that permeated every corner of the newspaper. The problem would be overcome by bringing out a four-column human-interest piece for the entertainment and edification of our loyal family-orientated readership. The list of proven talent included ten names, none of which, needless to say, was mine.

'Martín, my friend, circumstances have conspired so that not one of the champions on our payroll is on the premises or can be contacted in due time. With disaster imminent, I have decided to give you your first crack at glory.'

'You can count on me.'

'I'm counting on five double-spaced pages in six hours' time, Don

Edgar Allan Poe. Bring me a story, not a speech. If I want a sermon, I'll go to Midnight Mass. Bring me a story I have not read before, and if I have read it, bring it to me so well written and narrated that I won't even notice.'

I was about to leave the room when Don Basilio got up, walked round his desk and rested a hand, heavy and large as an anvil, on my shoulder. Only then, when I saw him close up, did I notice a twinkle in his eyes.

'If the story is decent I'll pay you ten pesetas. And if it's better than decent and our readers like it, I'll publish more.'

'Any specific instructions, Don Basilio?' I asked.

'Yes: don't let me down.'

I spent the next six hours in a trance. I installed myself at a table that stood in the middle of the editorial room and was reserved for Vidal, on the days when he felt like dropping by. The room was deserted, submerged in a gloom thick with the smoke of a thousand cigarettes. Closing my eyes for a moment, I conjured up an image, a cloak of dark clouds spilling down over the city in the rain, a man walking under cover of shadows with blood on his hands and a secret in his eyes. I didn't know who he was or what he was fleeing from, but during the next six hours he was going to become my best friend. I slid a page into the typewriter and, without pausing, I proceeded to squeeze out everything I had inside me. I quarrelled with every word, every phrase and expression, every image and letter as if they were the last I was ever going to write. I wrote and rewrote every line as if my life depended on it, and then rewrote it again. My only company was the incessant clacking of the typewriter echoing in the darkened hall and the large clock on the wall exhausting the minutes left until dawn.

Shortly before six o'clock in the morning I pulled the last sheet out of the typewriter and sighed, utterly drained. My brain felt like a wasps' nest. I heard the slow, heavy footsteps of Don Basilio, who had emerged from one of his controlled naps and was approaching unhurriedly. I gathered up the pages and handed them to him, not daring to meet his gaze. Don Basilio sat down at the next table and turned on the lamp. His eyes skimmed the text, betraying no emotion. Then he rested his cigar on the end of the table for a moment, glared at me and read out the first line:

'Night falls on the city and the streets carry the scent of gunpowder like the breath of a curse.'

Don Basilio looked at me out of the corner of his eye and I hid behind a smile that didn't leave a single tooth uncovered. Without saying another word, he got up and left with my story in his hands. I saw him walking towards his office and closing the door behind him. I stood there, petrified, not knowing whether to run away or await the death sentence. Ten minutes later – it felt more like ten years to me – the door of the deputy editor's office opened and the voice of Don Basilio thundered right across the department.

'Martín. In here. Now.'

I dragged myself across as slowly as I could, shrinking a centimetre or two with every step, until I had no alternative but to show my face and look up. Don Basilio, the fearful red pencil in hand, was staring at me icily. I tried to swallow, but my mouth was dry. He picked up the pages and gave them back to me. I took them and turned to go as quickly as I could, telling myself that there would always be room for another shoeshine boy in the lobby of the Hotel Colón.

'Take this down to the composing room and have them set it,' said the voice behind me.

I turned round, thinking I was the object of some cruel joke. Don Basilio pulled open the drawer of his desk, counted ten pesetas and put them on the table.

'This belongs to you. I suggest you buy yourself a better suit with it – I've seen you wearing the same one for four years and it's still about six sizes too big. Why don't you pay a visit to Señor Pantaleoni at his shop in Calle Escudellers? Tell him I sent you. He'll look after you.'

'Thank you so much, Don Basilio. That's what I'll do.'

'And start thinking about another of these stories for me. I'll give you a week for the next one. But don't fall asleep. And let's see if we can have a lower body count this time – today's readers like a slushy ending in which the greatness of the human spirit triumphs over adversity, that sort of rubbish.'

'Yes, Don Basilio.'

The deputy editor nodded and held out his hand to me. I shook it.

'Good work, Martín. On Monday I want to see you at the desk that belonged to Junceda. It's yours now. I'm putting you on the crime beat.'

'I won't fail you, Don Basilio.'

'No, you won't fail me. You'll just cast me aside sooner or later. And you'll be right to do so, because you're not a journalist and you never will be. But you're not a crime novelist yet, even if you think you are. Stick around for a while and we'll teach you a thing or two that will always come in handy.'

At that moment, my guard down, I was so overwhelmed by a feeling of gratitude that I wanted to hug that great bulk of a man. Don Basilio, his fierce mask back in place, gave me a steely look and pointed towards the door.

'No scenes, please. Close the door. And happy Christmas.'

'Happy Christmas.'

The following Monday, when I arrived at the editorial room ready to sit at my own desk for the very first time, I found a coarse grey envelope with a ribbon and my name on it in the same recognisable font that I had been typing out for years. I opened it. Inside was a framed copy of my story from the back page of the Sunday edition, with a note saying:

'This is just the beginning. In ten years I'll be the apprentice and you'll be the teacher. Your friend and colleague, Pedro Vidal.'

2

My literary debut survived its baptism of fire, and Don Basilio, true to his word, offered me the opportunity to publish a few more stories in a similar style. Soon the management decided that my meteoric career would have a weekly outlet as long as I continued to perform my duties in the editorial room for the same price. Driven by vanity and exhaustion, I spent the days going over my colleagues' stories and churning out countless reports about local news and lurid horrors, so that later I could spend my nights alone in the office writing a serialised work that I had been toying with in my imagination for a long time. Entitled *The Mysteries of Barcelona,* this Byzantine melodrama was a farrago shamelessly borrowed from Dumas and Stoker, taking in Sue and Féval along the way. I slept about three hours a night and looked like I'd spent those inside a coffin. Vidal, who had never known that kind of hunger which has nothing to do with the stomach though it gnaws at one's insides, was of the opinion that I was burning up my brain and that, at the rate I was going, I would be celebrating my own funeral before I reached twenty. Don Basilio, who was unmoved by my diligence, had other reservations. He published each of my chapters reluctantly, annoyed by what he considered to be an excess of morbidity and an unfortunate waste of my talent at the service of plots and stories of dubious taste.

The Mysteries of Barcelona gave birth to a fictional starlet in instalments, a heroine I had imagined as one can only imagine a femme fatale at the ripe age of seventeen. Chloé Permanyer was the dark princess of all vamps. Beyond intelligent, and even more devious, always clad in fine lingerie, she was the lover and evil accomplice of the mysterious Baltasar Morel, king of the underworld, who lived in a subterranean mansion peopled by automatons and macabre relics with a secret entrance through tunnels buried under the catacombs of the Gothic quarter. Chloé's favourite way of finishing off her victims was to seduce them with a hypnotic dance during which she removed her clothes, then kiss them with a poisoned lipstick that paralysed all their muscles and made them die from silent suffocation as she looked into their eyes, having previously drunk an antidote mixed in a fine-vintage Dom Pérignon. Chloé and Baltasar had their own code of honour: they killed only the dregs of society, cleansing the globe of bullies, swines, fanatics and morons who made this world unnecessarily miserable for the rest of mankind in the name of flags, gods, tongues, races and other such rubbish in order to serve their own greed and meanness. For me Chloé and Baltasar were rebellious heroes, like all true heroes. For Don Basilio, whose literary tastes had settled in the

Spanish verse of the Golden Age, it was all a monstrous lunacy, but in view of the favourable reception my stories enjoyed and the affection which, despite himself, he felt towards me, he tolerated my extravagances and attributed them to an excess of youthful ardour.

'You have more zeal than good taste, Martín. The disease afflicting you has a name, and that is Grand Guignol: it does to drama what syphilis does to your privates. Getting it might be pleasurable, but from then on it's all downhill. You should read the classics, or at least Don Benito Pérez Galdós, to elevate your literary aspirations.'

'But the readers like my stories,' I argued.

'You don't deserve the credit. That belongs to your rivals: they are so bad and pedantic that they could render a donkey catatonic in less than a paragraph. When are you going to mature and stop munching the forbidden fruit once and for all?'

I would nod, full of contrition, but secretly I caressed those forbidden words, Grand Guignol, and I told myself that every cause, however frivolous, needed a champion to defend its honour.

I was beginning to feel like the most fortunate of creatures when I discovered that some of my colleagues at the paper were annoyed that the junior and official mascot of the editorial room had taken his first steps in the world of letters while their own literary ambitions had languished for years in a grey limbo of misery. The fact that the readers were lapping up these modest stories more than anything else published in the newspaper during the last twenty years only made matters worse. In just a few weeks I saw how the hurt pride of those whom, until recently, I had considered to be my only family now transformed them into a hostile jury. They stopped greeting me and ignored me, sharpening their malice by aiming phrases full of sarcasm and spite at me behind my back. My inexplicable good fortune was attributed to Pedro Vidal, to the ignorance and stupidity of our readers and to the widely held national belief that achieving any measure of success in any profession was irrefutable proof of one's lack of skill or merit.

In view of this unexpected and ominous turn of events, Vidal tried to encourage me, but I was beginning to suspect that my days at the newspaper were numbered.

'Envy is the religion of the mediocre. It comforts them, it responds to the worries that gnaw at them and finally it rots their souls, allowing them to justify their meanness and their greed until they believe these to be virtues. Such people are convinced that the doors of heaven will be opened only to poor wretches like themselves who go through life without leaving any trace but their threadbare attempts to belittle others and to exclude – and destroy if possible – those who, by the simple fact of their existence, show up their own poorness of spirit, mind and guts. Blessed be the one at whom the fools bark, because his soul will never belong to them.'

'Amen,' Don Basilio would agree. 'Had you not been born so rich you could have become a priest. Or a revolutionary. With sermons like that even a bishop would fall on his knees and repent.'

'You two can laugh,' I protested. 'But the one they can't stand the sight of is me.'

Despite the wide range of enmity and distrust that my efforts were generating, the sad truth was that, even though I gave myself the airs of a popular writer, my salary only allowed me to subsist, to buy more books than I had time to read and to rent a dingy room in a *pensión* buried in a narrow street near Calle Princesa. The *pensión* was run by a devout Galician woman who answered to the name of Doña Carmen. Doña Carmen demanded discretion and changed the sheets once a month: residents were advised to abstain from succumbing to onanism or getting into bed with dirty clothes. There was no need to forbid the presence of the fair sex in the rooms because there wasn't a single woman in all Barcelona who would have agreed to enter that miserable hole, even under pain of death. There I learned that one can forget almost everything in life, beginning with bad smells, and that if there was one thing I aspired to, it was not to die in a place like that. In the low hours – which were most hours – I told myself that if anything was going to get me out of there before an outbreak of tuberculosis did the job, it was literature, and if that pricked anyone's soul, or their balls, they could scratch them with a brick.

On Sundays, when it was time for Mass and Doña Carmen went out for her weekly meeting with the Almighty, the residents took advantage of her absence to gather in the room of the oldest person among us, a poor devil called Heliodoro whose ambition as a young man had been to become a matador, but who had ended up as a self-appointed expert and commentator on bullfighting, in charge of the urinals on the sunny side of the Monumental Bullring.

'The art of bullfighting is dead,' he would proclaim. 'Now it's just a business for greedy stockbreeders and bullfighters with no soul. The public cannot distinguish between bullfighting for the ignorant masses and an authentic *faena* only connoisseurs can appreciate.'

'If only you'd been allowed to show your skills as a bullfighter, Don Heliodoro, things would be very different.'

'Truth is, only the useless get to the top in this country.'

'Never better said.'

After Don Heliodoro's weekly sermon came the fun. Piled together like a load of sausages by the small window of his room, we residents could see and hear, across the inner well, the exertions of Marujita, a woman who lived in the next building and was nicknamed Hot Pepper because of her spicy language and the shape of her generous anatomy. Marujita earned her crust scrubbing floors in second-rate establishments, but she devoted her Sundays and feast days to a seminarist boyfriend who took the train down from Manresa and applied himself, body and soul, to the carnal knowledge of sin.

One Sunday, my *pensión* colleagues were crammed against the window hoping to catch a fleeting sight of Marujita's titanic buttocks in one of those undulations that pressed them like dough against the tiny window pane, when the doorbell rang. Since nobody volunteered to go and open the door, thereby losing their spot and a good view of the show, I gave up my attempts at joining the chorus and went to see who had come. When I opened the door I was confronted with a most unlikely sight inside that miserable frame: Don Pedro Vidal, cloaked in his panache and his Italian silk suit, stood smiling on the landing.

'And there was light,' he said, coming in without waiting for an invitation.

Vidal stopped to look at the sitting room that doubled as dining room and meeting place and gave a sigh of disgust.

'It might be better to go to my room,' I suggested.

I led the way. The shouts and cheers of my co-residents in honour of Marujita and her venereal acrobatics bored through the walls with jubilation.

'What a lively place,' Vidal commented.

'Please come into the presidential suite, Don Pedro,' I invited him.

We went in and I closed the door. After a very brief glance around my room he sat on the only chair and looked at me with little enthusiasm. It wasn't hard to imagine the impression my modest home had made on him.

'What do you think?'

'Charming. I'm thinking of moving here myself.'

Pedro Vidal lived in Villa Helius, a huge modernist mansion with three floors and a large tower, perched on the slopes that rose up to Pedralbes, at the crossing between Calle Abadesa Olzet and Calle Panamá. The house had been given to him by his father ten years earlier in the hope that he would settle down and start a family, an undertaking which Vidal had somewhat delayed. Life had blessed Don Pedro Vidal with many talents, chief among them that of disappointing and offending his father with every gesture he made and every step he took. To see him fraternising with undesirables like me did not help. I remember that once, when visiting my mentor to deliver some papers from the office, I bumped into the patriarch of the Vidal clan in one of the hallways of Villa Helius. When he saw me, Vidal's father told me to go and fetch him a glass of tonic water and a cloth to clean a stain off his lapel.

'I think you're confused, sir. I'm not a servant . . .'

He gave me a smile that clarified the order of things in the world without any need for words.

'You're the one who is confused, young lad. You're a servant, whether you know it or not. What's your name?'

'David Martín, sir.'

The patriarch considered my name.

'Take my advice, David Martín. Leave this house and go back to where you belong. You'll save yourself a lot of trouble, and you'll save me the trouble too.'

I never confessed this to Vidal, but I immediately went off to the kitchen in search of tonic water and a rag, and spent a quarter of an hour cleaning the great man's jacket. The shadow of the clan was a long one, and however much Don Pedro liked to affect a Bohemian air, his whole life was an extension of his family network. Villa Helius was conveniently situated five minutes away from the great paternal mansion that dominated the upper stretch of Avenida Pearson, a cathedral-like jumble of balustrades, staircases and dormer windows that looked out over the whole of Barcelona from a distance, like a child looking at the toys he has thrown away. Every day, an expedition of two servants and a cook left the big house, as the paternal home was known among the Vidal entourage, and went to Villa Helius to clean, shine, iron, cook and cosset my wealthy protector in a nest that comforted him and shielded him from the inconveniences of everyday life. Pedro Vidal moved around the city in a resplendent Hispano-Suiza, piloted by the family chauffeur, Manuel Sagnier, and he had probably never set foot in a tram in his life. The creature of an elite environment and good breeding, Vidal could not comprehend the dismal, faded charm of the cheap Barcelona *pensiones* of the time.

'Don't hold back, Don Pedro.'

'This place looks like a dungeon,' he finally proclaimed. 'I don't know how you can live here.'

'With my salary, only just.'

'If necessary, I could pay you whatever you need to live somewhere that doesn't smell of sulphur and urine.'

'I wouldn't dream of it.'

Vidal sighed.

'He died of suffocation and pride. There you are, a free epitaph.'

For a few moments Vidal wandered around the room without saying a word, stopping to inspect my meagre wardrobe, stare out of the window with a look of revulsion, touch the greenish paint that covered the walls and gently tap the naked bulb that hung from the ceiling with his index finger, as if he wanted to verify the wretched quality of each thing.

'What brings you here, Don Pedro? Too much fresh air in Pedralbes?'

'I haven't come from home. I've come from the newspaper.'

'Why?'

'I was curious to see where you lived and besides, I've brought something for you.'

He pulled a white parchment envelope from his jacket and handed it to me.

'This arrived today at the office, with your name.'

I took the envelope and examined it. It was closed with a wax seal on which I could make out a winged silhouette. An angel. Apart from that, the only other thing visible was my name, neatly written in scarlet ink, in a fine hand.

'Who sent this?' I asked, intrigued.

Vidal shrugged his shoulders.

'An admirer. Or admiress. I don't know. Open it.'

I opened the envelope with care and pulled out a folded sheet of paper on which, in the same writing, was the following:

Dear friend,

I'm taking the liberty of writing to you to express my admiration and congratulate you on the success you have obtained this season with *The Mysteries of Barcelona* in the pages of *The Voice of Industry*. As a reader and lover of good literature, it has given me great pleasure to discover a new voice brimming with talent, youth and promise. Allow me, then, as proof of my gratitude for the hours of pleasure provided by your stories, to invite you to a little surprise which I trust you will enjoy, tonight at midnight in El Ensueño del Raval. You are expected.

Affectionately

A.C.

Vidal, who had been reading over my shoulder, raised his eyebrows, intrigued.

'Interesting,' he mumbled.

'What do you mean, interesting?' I asked. 'What sort of a place is this El Ensueño?'

Vidal pulled a cigarette out of his platinum case.

'Doña Carmen doesn't allow smoking in the *pensión*,' I warned him.

'Why? Does it ruin the perfume from the sewers?'

Vidal lit the cigarette with twice the enjoyment, as one relishes all forbidden things.

'Have you ever known a woman, David?'

'Of course I have. Dozens of them.'

'I mean in the biblical sense.'

'As in Mass?'

'No, as in bed.'

'Ah.'

'And?'

The truth is that I had nothing much to tell that would impress someone like Vidal. My adventures and romances had been characterised until then by their modesty and a consistent lack of originality. Nothing in my brief catalogue of pinches, cuddles and kisses stolen in doorways or the back row of the picture house could aspire to deserve the consideration of Pedro Vidal – Barcelona's acclaimed master of the art and science of bedroom games.

'What does this have to do with anything?' I protested.

Vidal adopted a patronising air and launched into one of his speeches.

'In my younger days the normal thing, at least among my sort, was to be initiated in these matters with the help of a professional. When I was your age my father, who was and still is a regular of the most refined establishments in town, took me to a place called El Ensueño, just a few metres away from that macabre palace that our dear Count Güell insisted Gaudí should build for him near the Ramblas. Don't tell me you've never heard the name.'

'The name of the count or the brothel?'

'Very funny. El Ensueño used to be an elegant establishment for a select and discerning clientele. In fact, I thought it had closed down years ago, but I must be wrong. Unlike literature, some businesses are always on an upward trend.'

'I see. Is this your idea? Some sort of joke?'

Vidal shook his head.

'One of the idiots at the newspaper, then?'

'I detect a certain hostility in your words, but I doubt that anyone who devotes his life to the noble profession of the press, especially those at the bottom of the ranks, could afford a place like El Ensueño, if it's the same place I remember.'

I snorted.

'It doesn't really matter, because I'm not planning to go.'

Vidal raised his eyebrows.

'Don't tell me you're not a sceptic like I am and that you want to

17

reach the marriage bed pure of heart and loins; that you're an immaculate soul eagerly awaiting that magic moment when true love will lead you to the discovery of a joint ecstasy of flesh and inner being, blessed by the Holy Spirit, thus enabling you to populate the world with creatures who bear your family name and their mother's eyes – that saintly woman, a paragon of virtue and modesty in whose company you will enter the doors of heaven under the benevolent gaze of the Baby Jesus.'

'I was not going to say that.'

'I'm glad, because it's possible, and I stress possible, that such a moment may never come: you may not fall in love, you may not be able to or you may not wish to give your whole life to anyone and, like me, you may turn forty-five one day and realise that you're no longer young and you have never found a choir of cupids with lyres, or a bed of white roses leading towards the altar. The only revenge left for you then will be to steal from life the pleasure of firm and passionate flesh – a pleasure that evaporates faster than good intentions and is the nearest thing to heaven you will find in this stinking world, where everything decays, beginning with beauty and ending with memory.'

I allowed a solemn pause by way of silent ovation. Vidal was a keen opera-goer and had picked up the tempo and style of the great arias. He never missed his appointment with Puccini in the Liceo family box. He was one of the few – not counting the poor souls crammed together in the gods – who went there to listen to the music he loved so much, a music that tended to inspire the grandiloquent speeches with which at times he regaled me, as he was doing on that day.

'What?' asked Vidal defiantly.

'That last paragraph rings a bell.'

I had caught him red-handed. He sighed and nodded.

'It's from *Murder in the Liceo*,' admitted Vidal. 'The final scene where Miranda LaFleur shoots the wicked marquis who has broken her heart, by betraying her during one night of passion in the nuptial suite of the Hotel Colón, in the arms of the Tsar's spy Svetlana Ivanova.'

'That's what I thought. You couldn't have made a better choice. It's your most outstanding novel, Don Pedro.'

Vidal smiled at the compliment and considered whether or not to light another cigarette.

'Which doesn't mean there isn't some truth in what I say,' he concluded.

Vidal sat on the windowsill, but not without first placing a handkerchief on it so as to avoid soiling his classy trousers. I saw that his Hispano-Suiza was parked below, on the corner of Calle Princesa. The chauffeur, Manuel, was polishing the chrome with a rag as if it were a sculpture by Rodin. Manuel had always reminded me of my father, men of the same generation who had suffered too much misfortune and whose memories were written on their faces. I had heard some of the servants at Villa Helius say that Manuel Sagnier had done a long stretch in prison and that when he'd come out he had suffered hardship for years because nobody would offer him a job except as a stevedore, unloading sacks and crates on the docks, a job for which by then he no longer had the requisite youth or health. Rumour had it that one day, Manuel, risking his own life, had saved Vidal from being run over by a tram. In gratitude, when Pedro Vidal heard of the poor man's dire situation, he decided to offer him a job and the possibility of moving, with his wife and daughter, into a small apartment above the Villa Helius coach house. He assured him that little Cristina would study with the same tutors who came every day to his father's house on Avenida Pearson to teach the cubs of the Vidal dynasty, and his wife could work as seamstress to the family. He had been thinking of buying one of the first automobiles that were soon to appear on sale in Barcelona and if Manuel would agree to take instruction in the art of driving and forget the trap and the wagon, Vidal would be needing a chauffeur, because in those days gentlemen didn't lay their hands on combustion machines nor any device with a gaseous exhaust. Manuel, naturally, accepted. Following his rescue from penury, the official version assured us all that Manuel Sagnier and his family felt a blind devotion for Vidal, eternal champion of the dispossessed. I didn't know whether to believe this story or to attribute it to the long string of legends woven around the image of the benevolent aristocrat that Vidal cultivated. Sometimes it seemed as if all that remained for him to do was to appear wrapped in a halo before some orphaned shepherdess.

'You've got that rascally look about you, the one you get when you're harbouring wicked thoughts,' Vidal remarked. 'What are you scheming?'

'Nothing. I was thinking about how kind you are, Don Pedro.'

'At your age and in your position, cynicism opens no doors.'

'That explains everything.'

'Go on, say hello to good old Manuel. He's always asking after you.'

I looked out of the window, and when he saw me, the driver, who always treated me like a gentleman and not the bumpkin I was, waved up at me. I returned the greeting. Sitting on the passenger seat was his daughter, Cristina, a creature of pale skin and well-defined lips who was a couple of years older than me and had taken my breath away ever since I saw her the first time Vidal invited me to visit Villa Helius.

'Don't stare at her so much; you'll break her,' mumbled Vidal behind my back.

I turned round and met with the Machiavellian face that Vidal reserved for matters of the heart and other noble parts of the body.

'I don't know what you're talking about.'

'Never a truer word spoken,' replied Vidal. 'So, what are you going to do about tonight?'

I read the note once again and hesitated.

'Do you frequent this type of venue, Don Pedro?'

'I haven't paid for a woman since I was fifteen years old and then, technically, it was my father who paid,' replied Vidal without bragging. 'But don't look a gift horse in the mouth . . .'

'I don't know, Don Pedro . . .'

'Of course you know.'

Vidal patted me on the back as he walked towards the door.

'There are seven hours left to midnight,' he said. 'You might like to have a nap and gather your strength.'

I looked out of the window and saw him approach the car. Manuel opened the door and Vidal flopped onto the back seat. I heard the engine of the Hispano-Suiza deploy its symphony of pistons. At that moment Cristina looked up towards my window. I smiled at her, but realised that she didn't remember who I was. A moment later she looked away and Vidal's grand carriage sped off towards its own world.

3

In those days, the street lamps and illuminated signs of Calle Nou
de la Rambla projected a corridor of light through the shadows of
the Raval quarter. On either pavement, cabarets, dance halls and
other ill-defined venues jostled cheek by jowl with all-night
establishments that specialised in arcane remedies for venereal
diseases, condoms and douches, while a motley crew, from
gentlemen of some cachet to sailors from ships docked in the port,
mixed with all sorts of extravagant characters who lived only for the
night. On either side of the street, narrow alleyways, buried in mist,
housed a string of brothels of ever-decreasing quality.

El Ensueño occupied the top storey of a building. On the ground
floor was a music hall with large posters depicting a dancer clad in a
diaphanous toga that did nothing to hide her charms, holding in her
arms a black snake whose forked tongue seemed to be kissing her
lips.

'Eva Montenegro and the Tango of Death', the poster announced
in bold letters. 'The Queen of the Night, for six evenings only – no
further performances. With the guest appearance of Mesmero, the
mind reader who will reveal your most intimate secrets.'

Next to the main entrance was a narrow door behind which rose
a long staircase with its walls painted red. I went up the stairs and
stood in front of a large carved oak door adorned with a brass
knocker in the shape of a nymph wearing a modest clover leaf over
her pubis. I knocked a couple of times and waited, shying away from
my reflection in the tinted mirror that covered most of the
adjoining wall. I was debating the possibility of hotfooting it out of
the place when the door opened and a middle-aged woman, her hair
completely white and tied neatly in a bun, smiled at me calmly.

'You must be Señor David Martín.'

Nobody had ever called me 'señor' in all my life, and the formality
caught me by surprise.

'That's me.'

'Please be kind enough to follow me.'

I followed her down a short corridor that led into a spacious round room, the walls of which were covered in red velvet dimly lit by lamps. The ceiling was formed of an enamelled crystal dome from which hung a glass chandelier. Under the chandelier stood a mahogany table holding an enormous gramophone that whispered an operatic aria.

'Would you like anything to drink, sir?'

'A glass of water would be very nice, thank you.'

The lady with the white hair smiled without blinking, her kindly countenance unperturbed.

'Perhaps the gentleman would rather a glass of champagne? Or a fine sherry?'

My palate did not go beyond the subtleties of the different vintages of tap water, so I shrugged my shoulders.

'You choose.'

The lady nodded without losing her smile and pointed to one of the sumptuous armchairs that were dotted round the room.

'If you'd care to sit down, sir. Chloé will be with you presently.'

I thought I was going to choke.

'Chloé?'

Ignoring my perplexity, the lady with the white hair disappeared behind a door that I could just make out through a black bead-curtain, leaving me alone with my nerves and unmentionable desires. I wandered around the room to cast out the trembling that had taken hold of me. Apart from the faint music and the heartbeat throbbing in my temples, the place was as silent as a tomb. Six corridors led out of the sitting room, each one flanked by openings that were covered with blue curtains, and each corridor leading to a closed white double door. I fell into one of the armchairs, one of those pieces of furniture designed to cradle the backsides of princes and generalissimos with a certain weakness for *coups d'état*. Soon the lady with the white hair returned, carrying a glass of champagne on a silver tray. I accepted it and saw her disappear once again through the same door. I gulped down the champagne and loosened my shirt collar. I was starting to suspect that perhaps all this was just a joke devised by Vidal to make fun of me. At that moment I

22

noticed a figure advancing towards me down one of the corridors. It looked like a little girl. She was walking with her head down, so that I couldn't see her eyes. I stood up.

The girl made a respectful curtsy and beckoned me to follow her. Only then did I realise that one of her hands was false, like the hand of a mannequin. The girl led me to the end of the corridor, opened the door with a key that hung round her neck, and showed me in. The room was in almost complete darkness. I took a few steps, straining my eyes. Then I heard the door closing behind me and when I turned round, the girl had vanished. Hearing the key turn, I knew I had been locked in. For almost a minute I stood there, without moving. My eyes slowly grew used to the darkness and the outline of the room materialised around me. It was lined from floor to ceiling with black cloth. On one side I could just about make out a number of strange contraptions – I couldn't decide whether they looked sinister or tempting. A large round bed rested beneath a headboard that looked to me like a huge spider's web from which hung two candle holders with two black candles burning, giving off that waxy perfume that nests in chapels and at wakes. On one side of the bed stood a latticework screen with a sinuous design. I shuddered. The place was identical to the fictional bedroom I had created for my ineffable femme fatale Chloé, in her adventures in *The Mysteries of Barcelona*. I was about to try to force the door open when I realised I was not alone. I froze. I could see the outline of a silhouette through the screen. Two shining eyes were watching me and long white fingers with nails painted black peeped through the holes in the latticework. I swallowed hard.

'Chloé?' I whispered.

It was her. *My Chloé*. The operatic and insuperable femme fatale of my stories, made flesh – and lingerie. She had the palest skin I had ever seen and her short hair was cut at right angles, framing her face. Her lips were the colour of fresh blood and her green eyes were surrounded by a halo of dark shadow. She moved like a cat, as if her body, hugged by a corset that shone like scales, were made of water and had learned to defy gravity. Her slender, endless neck was circled by a scarlet velvet ribbon from which hung an upside-down crucifix. Unable to breathe, I watched her as she slowly approached,

23

my eyes glued to those lusciously shaped legs under silk stockings that probably cost more than I earned in a year, ending in shoes with points like daggers, tied round her ankles with silk ribbons. I had never, in my whole life, seen anything as beautiful, or as frightening.

I let that creature lead me to the bed, where I fell for her, literally, on my backside. The candlelight hugged the outline of her body. My face and my lips were level with her naked belly and without even realising what I was doing I kissed her under her navel and stroked her skin with my cheek. By then I had forgotten who I was or where I was. She knelt down in front of me and took my right hand. Languorously, like a cat, she licked my fingers one by one and then fixed her eyes on mine and began to remove my clothes. When I tried to help her she smiled and moved my hands away.

'Shhh.'

When she had finished, she leaned towards me and licked my lips.

'Now you do it. Undress me. Slowly. Very slowly.'

I then understood that I had survived my sickly and unfortunate childhood just to experience that instant. I undressed her slowly, as if I were pulling petals off her skin, until all that was left on her body was the velvet ribbon round her throat and those black stockings – the memory of which could keep a poor wretch like me going for a hundred years.

'Touch me,' she whispered in my ear. 'Play with me.'

I caressed and kissed every bit of her skin as if I wanted to memorise it forever. Chloé was in no hurry and responded to the touch of my hands and my lips with gentle moans that guided me. Then she made me lie on the bed and covered my body with hers until I felt as if every pore was on fire. I placed my hands on her back and followed the exquisite line of her spine. Her impenetrable eyes were just a few centimetres from my face, watching me. I felt as if I had to say something.

'My name is—'

'Shhhhh.'

Before I could make any other foolish comment, Chloé placed her lips on mine and, for the space of an hour, spirited me away from the world. Aware of my clumsiness but making me believe that she hadn't noticed, she anticipated each movement and directed my hands over her body without haste, and with no modesty either. I saw no boredom or absence in her eyes. She let herself be touched and enjoyed the sensations with infinite patience and a tenderness that made me forget how I had come to be there. That night, for the brief space of an hour, I learned every line of her skin as others learn their prayers or their fate. Later, when I had barely any breath left in me, Chloé let me rest my head on her breast, stroking my hair for a long time, in silence, until I fell asleep in her arms with my hand between her thighs.

When I awoke, the room was still in darkness and Chloé had left. I could no longer feel the touch of her skin on my hands. Instead I was holding a business card printed on the same white parchment as the envelope in which my invitation had arrived. Under the emblem of the angel, it read:

ANDREAS CORELLI

Éditeur

Éditions de la Lumière

Boulevard St.-Germain, 69, Paris

On the back was a handwritten note:

Dear David, life is filled with great expectations. When you are ready to make yours come true, get in touch with me. I'll be waiting. Your friend and reader,

A.C.

I gathered my clothes from the floor and got dressed. The door was not locked now. I walked down the corridor to the sitting room, where the gramophone had gone silent. No trace of the girl or the woman with white hair who had greeted me. Complete silence. As I made my way towards the exit I had the feeling that the lights behind me were going out, the corridors and rooms slowly growing dark. I stepped out onto the landing and went down the stairs, returning, unwillingly, to the world. Back on the street, I made my way towards the Ramblas, leaving behind me all the hubbub and the nocturnal crowds. A warm, thin mist floated up from the port and the glow from the large windows of the Hotel Oriente tinged it with a dirty, dusty yellow in which passers-by disappeared like wisps of smoke. I set off as Chloé's perfume began to fade from my mind, and I wondered whether the lips of Cristina Sagnier, the daughter of Vidal's chauffeur, might taste the same.

4

You don't know what thirst is until you drink for the first time. Three days after my visit to El Ensueño, the memory of Chloé's skin still burned my very thoughts. Without a word to anyone – especially not to Vidal – I decided to gather up what little savings I had and go back there, hoping it would be enough to buy even just one moment in her arms. It was past midnight when I reached the stairs with the red walls that led up to El Ensueño. The light was out in the stairway and I climbed cautiously, leaving behind the noisy citadel of cabarets, bars, music halls and random establishments which the years of the Great War had strewn along Calle Nou de la Rambla. Only the flickering light from the main door below outlined each stair as I ascended. When I reached the landing I stopped and groped about for the door knocker. My fingers touched the heavy metal ring and, when I lifted it, the door gave way slightly and I realised that it was open. I pushed it gently. A deathly silence caressed my face and a bluish darkness stretched before me. Disconcerted, I advanced a few steps. The echo of the street lights fluttered in the air, revealing fleeting visions of bare walls and broken wooden flooring. I came to the room that I remembered, decorated with velvet and lavish furniture. It was empty. The blanket of dust covering the floor shone like sand in the glimmer from the illuminated signs in the street. I walked on, leaving a trail of footsteps in the dust. No sign of the gramophone, of the armchairs or the pictures. The ceiling had burst open, revealing blackened beams. The paint hung from the walls in strips. I walked over to the corridor that led to the room where I had met Chloé, crossing through a tunnel of darkness until I reached the double door, which was no longer white. There was no handle on it, only a hole in the wood, as if the mechanism had been yanked out. I pushed open the door and went in.

Chloé's bedroom was a shadowy cell. The walls were charred and most of the ceiling had collapsed. I could see a canvas of black clouds crossing the sky and the moon projected a silver halo over the metal skeleton of what had once been a bed. It was then that I heard the floor creak behind me and turned round quickly, aware that I was not alone in that place. The dark, defined figure of a man was outlined against the entrance to the corridor. I couldn't distinguish his face, but I was sure he was watching me. He stood there for a few seconds, still as a spider, time enough for me to react and take a step towards him. In an instant the figure withdrew into the shadows, and by the time I reached the sitting room there was nobody there. A breath of light from a sign on the other side of the street flooded the room for a second, revealing a small pile of rubble heaped against the wall. I went over and knelt down by the remnants that had been devoured by fire. Something protruded from the pile. Fingers. I brushed away the ashes that covered them and slowly the shape of a hand emerged. I grasped it, and when I tried to pull it out I realised that it had been severed at the wrist. I recognised it instantly and saw that the girl's hand, which I had thought was wooden, was in fact made of porcelain. I let it fall back on the pile of debris and left.

I wondered whether I had imagined that stranger, because there were no other footprints in the dust. I went downstairs and stood outside the building, inspecting the first-floor windows from the pavement, utterly confused. People passed by laughing, unaware of my presence. I tried to spot the outline of the stranger among the crowd. I knew he was there, maybe a few metres away, watching me. After a while I crossed the street and went into a narrow café, packed with people. I managed to elbow out a space at the bar and signalled to the waiter.

'What would you like?'

My mouth was as dry as sandpaper.

'A beer,' I said, improvising.

While the waiter poured me my drink, I leaned forward.

'Excuse me, do you know whether the place opposite, El Ensueño, has closed down?'

The waiter put the glass on the bar and looked at me as if I were stupid.

'It closed fifteen years ago,' he said.

'Are you sure?'

'Of course I'm sure. After the fire it never reopened. Anything else?'

I shook my head.

'That will be four céntimos.'

I paid for my drink and left without touching the glass.

The following day I arrived at the newspaper offices before my usual time and went straight to the archives in the basement. With the help of Matías, the person in charge, and going on what the waiter had told me, I began to check through the front pages of *The Voice of Industry* from fifteen years back. It took me about forty minutes to find the story, just a short item. The fire had started in the early hours of Corpus Christi Day, 1903. Six people had died, trapped in the flames: a client, four of the girls on the payroll and a small child who worked there. The police and firemen believed that the cause of the tragedy was a faulty oil lamp, although the council of a nearby church alluded to divine retribution and the intervention of the Holy Spirit.

When I returned to the *pensión* I lay on my bed and tried in vain to fall asleep. I put my hand in my pocket and pulled out the business card from my strange benefactor – the card I was holding when I awoke in Chloé's bed – and in the dark I reread the words written on the back. '*Great expectations*'.

5

In my world, expectations – great or small – rarely came true. Until a few months previously, the only thing I longed for when I went to bed every night was to be able to muster enough courage to speak to Cristina, the daughter of my mentor's chauffeur, and for the hours that separated me from dawn to pass so that I could return to the newspaper offices. Now, even that refuge had begun to slip away from me. Perhaps, if one of my literary efforts were a resounding failure, I might be able to recover my colleagues' affection, I told myself. Perhaps if I wrote something so mediocre and despicable that no reader could get beyond the first paragraph, my youthful sins would be forgiven. Perhaps that was not too high a price to pay to feel at home again. Perhaps.

I had arrived at *The Voice of Industry* many years before, with my father, a tormented, penniless man who, on his return from the war in the Philippines, had found a city that preferred not to recognise him and a wife who had already forgotten him. Two years later she decided to abandon him altogether, leaving him with a broken heart and a son he had never wanted. He did not know what to do with a child. My father, who could barely read or write his own name, had no fixed job. All he had learned during the war was how to kill other men before they killed him – in the name of great and empty-sounding causes that seemed more absurd and repellent the closer he came to the fighting.

When he returned from the war, my father – who looked twenty years older than the man who had left – searched for work in various factories in the Pueblo Nuevo and Sant Martí districts. The jobs only lasted a few days, and sooner or later I would see him arrive home, his eyes blazing with resentment. As time went by, for want of anything better, he accepted a post as nightwatchman at *The Voice of Industry*. The pay was modest, but the months passed by and for the first time since he came back from the war it seemed he was not getting into trouble. But the peace was short-lived. Soon some of his old comrades in arms, living corpses who had come home maimed in body and soul only to discover that those who had sent them off to die in the name of God and the Fatherland were now spitting in their faces, got him involved in shady affairs that were too much for him and which he never really understood.

My father would often disappear for a couple of days, and when he returned his hands and clothes smelled of gunpowder, and his pockets of money. Then he would retreat to his room and, although he thought I didn't notice, he would inject himself with whatever he had been able to get. At first he never closed his door, but one day he caught me spying on him and slapped me so hard that he split my lip. He then hugged me until there was no strength left in his arms and lay down, stretched out on the floor with the hypodermic needle still stuck in his skin. I pulled out the needle and covered him with a blanket. After that, he began to lock himself in.

We lived in a small attic suspended over the building site of the new auditorium, the Palau de la Música. It was a cold, narrow place in which wind and humidity seemed to mock the walls. I used to sit on the tiny balcony with my legs dangling out, watching people pass by and gazing at the battlement of weird sculptures and columns that was growing on the other side of the street. Sometimes I felt I could almost touch the building with my fingertips, at others – most of them – it seemed as far away as the moon. I was a weak and sickly child, prone to fevers and infections that dragged me to the edge of the grave, although, at the last minute, death always repented and went off in search of larger prey. When I fell ill, my father would end up losing his patience and after the second sleepless night would leave me in the care of one of the neighbours and then disappear. As time went by I began to suspect that he hoped to find me dead on his return, and so free himself of the burden of a child with brittle health who was no use for anything.

More than once I too hoped that would happen, but my father always came back and found me alive and kicking, and a bit taller. Mother Nature didn't hold back: she punished me with her extensive range of germs and miseries, but never found a way of successfully finishing the job. Against all prognoses, I survived those first years on the tightrope of a childhood before penicillin. In those days death was not yet anonymous and one could see and smell it everywhere, devouring souls that had not even had time enough to sin.

Even at that time, my only friends were made of paper and ink. At school I had learned to read and write long before the other children. Where my school friends saw notches of ink on incomprehensible pages, I saw light, streets, and people. Words and the mystery of their hidden science fascinated me, and I saw in them a key with which I could unlock a boundless world, a safe haven from that home, those streets and those troubled days in which even I could sense that only a limited fortune awaited me. My father didn't like to see books in the house. There was something about them – apart from the letters he could not decipher – that offended him. He used to tell me that as soon as I was ten he would send me off to work and that I'd better get rid of all my scatterbrained ideas because otherwise I'd end up being a loser, a nobody. I used to hide my books under the mattress and would wait for him to go out or fall asleep so that I could read. Once he caught me reading at night and flew into a rage. He tore the book from my hands and flung it out of the window.

'If I catch you wasting electricity again, reading all this nonsense, you'll be sorry.'

My father was not a miser and, despite the hardships we suffered, whenever he could he gave me a few coins so that I could buy myself some treats like the other children. He was convinced that I spent them on liquorice sticks, sunflower seeds or sweets, but I would keep them in a coffee tin under the bed and, when I'd collected four or five reales, I'd secretly rush out to buy myself a book.

My favourite place in the whole city was the Sempere & Sons bookshop on Calle Santa Ana. It smelled of old paper and dust and it was my sanctuary, my refuge. The bookseller would let me sit on a chair in a corner and read any book I liked to my heart's content. He hardly ever allowed me to pay for the books he placed in my hands but, when he wasn't looking, I'd leave the coins I'd managed to collect on the counter before I left. It was only small change – if I'd had to buy a book with that pittance, I would probably only have been able to afford a booklet of cigarette papers. When it was time for me to leave, I would do so dragging my feet, a weight on my soul. If it had been up to me, I would have stayed there forever.

One Christmas Sempere gave me the best gift I have ever received. It was an old volume, read and experienced to the full.

'*Great Expectations*, by Charles Dickens . . .' I read on the cover.

I was aware that Sempere knew a few authors who frequented his establishment and, judging by the care with which he handled the volume, I thought that perhaps this Mr Dickens was one of them.

'A friend of yours?'

'A lifelong friend. And from now on, he's your friend too.'

That afternoon I took my new friend home, hidden under my clothes so that my father wouldn't see it. It was a rainy winter, with days as grey as lead, and I read *Great Expectations* about nine times, partly because I had no other book at hand, partly because I did not think there could be a better one in the whole world and I was beginning to suspect that Mr Dickens had written it just for me. Soon I was convinced that I didn't want to do anything else in life but learn to do what Mr Dickens had done.

One day I was suddenly awoken at dawn by my father shaking me. He had come back from work early. His eyes were bloodshot and his breath smelled of spirits. I looked at him in terror as he touched the naked bulb that hung from the ceiling.

'It's warm.'

He fixed his eyes on mine and threw the bulb angrily against the wall. It burst into a thousand pieces that fell on my face, but I didn't dare brush them away.

'Where it is?' asked my father, his voice cold and calm.

I shook my head, trembling.

'Where is that fucking book?'

I shook my head once more. In the half-light I hardly saw the blow coming. My sight blurred and I felt myself falling out of bed, with blood in my mouth and a sharp pain like white fire burning behind my lips. When I tilted my head I saw what I imagined to be pieces of a couple of broken teeth on the floor. My father's hand grabbed me by the neck and lifted me up.

'Where it is?'

'Please, father—'

He threw me face-first against the wall with all his might, and the bang on my head made me lose my balance and crash down like a bag of bones. I crawled into a corner and stayed there, curled up in a ball, watching as my father opened my wardrobe, pulled out the few clothes I possessed and threw them on the floor. He looked in drawers and trunks without finding the book until, exhausted, he came back for me. I closed my eyes and pressed myself up against the wall, waiting for another blow that never came. I opened my eyes again and saw my father sitting on the bed, crying with shame and hardly able to breathe. When he saw me looking at him, he rushed off down the stairs. His footsteps echoed as he walked off into the silence of dawn and only when I was sure he was a good distance away did I drag myself as far as the bed and pull my book out of its hiding place under the mattress. I got dressed and went out, clutching the book under my arm.

A sheet of sea mist was descending over Calle Santa Ana as I reached the door of the bookshop. The bookseller and his son lived on the first floor of the same building. I knew that six o'clock in the morning was not a good time to call on anyone, but my only thought at that moment was to save the book, for I was sure that if my father found it when he returned home he would destroy it with all the anger that boiled inside him. I rang the bell and waited. I had to ring two or three times before I heard the balcony door open and saw old Sempere, in his dressing gown and slippers, looking at me in astonishment. Half a minute later he came down to open the front door and when he saw my face all trace of anger disappeared. He knelt down in front of me and held me by my arms.

'God Almighty! Are you all right? Who did this to you?'

'Nobody. I fell.'

I held out the book.

'I came to return it, because I don't want anything to happen to it . . .'

Sempere looked at me but didn't say a word – he simply took me in his arms and carried me up to the apartment. His son, a twelve-year-old boy who was so shy I didn't remember ever having heard his voice, had woken up at the sound of his father going out, and was waiting on the landing. When he saw the blood on my face he looked at his father with fear in his eyes.

'Call Doctor Campos.'

The boy nodded and ran to the telephone. I heard him speak, realising that he was not dumb after all. Between the two of them they settled me into an armchair in the dining room and cleaned the blood off my wounds while we waited for the doctor to arrive.

'Aren't you going to tell me who did this to you?'

I didn't utter a sound. Sempere didn't know where I lived and I was not going to give him any ideas.

'Was it your father?'

I looked away.

33

'No. I fell.'

Doctor Campos, who lived four or five doors away, arrived five minutes later. He examined me from head to toe, feeling my bruises and dressing my cuts as delicately as possible. You could see his eyes burning with indignation, but he made no comment.

'There's nothing broken, but the bruises will last a while and they'll hurt for a few days. Those two teeth will have to come out. They're no good any more and there's a risk of infection.'

When the doctor had left, Sempere made me a cup of warm cocoa and smiled as he watched me drink it.

'All this just to save *Great Expectations*, eh?'

I shrugged my shoulders. Father and son looked at one another with a conspiratorial smile.

'Next time you want to save a book, save it properly; don't risk your life. Just let me know and I'll take you to a secret place where books never die and nobody can destroy them.'

I looked at both of them, intrigued.

'What place is that?'

Sempere gave me a wink and smiled at me in that mysterious manner that seemed to be borrowed from an Alexandre Dumas romance, and which, people said, was a family trait.

'Everything in due course, my friend. Everything in due course.'

My father spent that whole week with his eyes glued to the floor, consumed with remorse. He bought a new light bulb and even told me that I could turn it on, but not for long, because electricity was very expensive. I preferred not to play with fire. On the Saturday he tried to buy me a book and went to a bookshop on Calle de la Palla, opposite the old Roman walls – the first and last bookshop he ever entered – but as he couldn't read the titles on the spines of the hundreds of tomes that were on show, he came out empty-handed. Then he gave me some money, more than usual, and told me to buy whatever I wanted with it. It seemed the perfect moment to bring up something that I'd wanted to say to him for a long time but had never found the opportunity.

'Doña Mariana, the teacher, has asked me whether you could go by the school one day and talk to her,' I said, trying to sound casual.

'Talk about what? What have you done?'

'Nothing, father. Doña Mariana wanted to talk to you about my future education. She says I have possibilities and thinks she could help me win a scholarship for a place at the Escolapios . . .'

'Who does that woman think she is, filling your head with nonsense and telling you she's going to get you into a school for rich kids? Have you any idea what that pack is like? Do you know how they're going to look at you and treat you when they find out where you come from?'

I looked down.

'Doña Mariana only wants to help, father. That's all. Please don't get angry. I'll tell her it's not possible, end of story.'

My father looked at me angrily, but controlled himself and took a few deep breaths with his eyes shut before speaking again.

'We'll manage, do you understand? You and me. Without the charity of those sons-of-bitches. And with our heads held high.'

'Yes, father.'

He put a hand on my shoulder and looked at me as if, for a split second that was never to return, he was proud of me, even though we were so different, even though I liked books that he could not read, even if mother had left us both to face each other. At that moment I thought my father was the kindest man in the world, and that everyone would realise this if only, just for once, life saw fit to deal him a good hand of cards.

'All the bad things you do in life come back to you, David. And I've done a lot of bad things. A lot. But I've paid the price. And our luck is going to change. You'll see . . .'

Doña Mariana was razor sharp and could see what was going on, but despite her insistence I didn't mention the subject of my education to my father again. When my teacher realised there was no hope she told me that every day, when lessons were over, she would devote an hour just to me, to talk to me about books, history and all the things that scared my father so much.

'It will be our secret,' said the teacher.

By then I had begun to understand that my father was ashamed that others might think him ignorant, a residue from a war which, like all wars, was fought in the name of God and country to make a few men, who were already far too powerful when they started it, even more powerful. Around that time I started occasionally to accompany my father on his night shift. We'd take a tram in Calle Trafalgar which left us by the entrance to the Pueblo Nuevo Cemetery. I would stay in his cubicle, reading old copies of the newspaper, and at times I would try to chat with him, a difficult task. By then, my father hardly ever spoke at all, neither about the war in the colonies nor about the woman who had abandoned him. Once I asked him why my mother had left us. I suspected it had been my fault, because of something I'd done, perhaps just for being born.

'Your mother had already left me before I was sent to the front. I was the idiot; I didn't realise until I returned. Life's like that, David. Sooner or later, everything and everybody abandons you.'

'I'm never going to abandon you, father.'

I thought he was about to cry and I hugged him so as not to see his face.

The following day, unannounced, my father took me El Indio, a large store that sold fabrics on Calle del Carmen. We didn't actually go in, but from the windows at the shop entrance my father pointed at a smiling young woman who was serving some customers, showing them expensive flannels and other textiles. 'That's your mother,' he said. 'One of these days I'll come back here and kill her.'

'Don't say that, father.'

He looked at me with reddened eyes, and I knew then that he still loved her and that I would never forgive her for it. I remember that I watched her secretly, without her knowing we were there, and that I only recognised her because of a photograph my father kept in a drawer, next to his army revolver. Every night, when he thought I was asleep, he would take it out and look at it as if it held all the answers, or at least enough of them.

For years I would have to return to the doors of that store to spy on her in secret. I never had the courage to go in or to approach her when I saw her coming out and walking away down the Ramblas, towards a life that I had imagined for her, with a family that made her happy and a son who deserved her affection and the touch of her skin more than I did. My father never knew that sometimes I would sneak round there to see her, or that some days I even followed close behind, always ready to take her hand and walk by her side, always fleeing at the last moment. In my world, great expectations only existed between the pages of a book.

The good luck my father yearned for never arrived. The only courtesy life showed him was not to make him wait too long. One night, when we reached the doors of the newspaper building to start the shift, three men came out of the shadows and gunned him down before my very eyes. I remember the smell of sulphur and the halo of smoke that rose from the holes the bullets had burned through his coat. One of the gunmen was about to finish him off with a shot to the head when I threw myself on top of my father and another one of the murderers stopped him. I remember the eyes of the gunman fixing on mine, debating whether he should kill me too. Then, all of a sudden, the men hurried off and disappeared into the narrow streets trapped between the factories of Pueblo Nuevo.

That night my father's murderers left him bleeding to death in my arms and me alone in the world. I spent almost two weeks sleeping in the workshops of the newspaper press, hidden among Linotype machines that looked like giant steel spiders, trying to silence the excruciating whistling sound that perforated my eardrums when night fell. When I was discovered, my hands and clothes were still stained with dry blood. At first nobody knew who I was, because I didn't speak for about a week and when I did it was only to yell my father's name until I was hoarse. When they asked me about my mother I told them she had died and I had nobody else in the world. My story reached the ears of Pedro Vidal, the star writer at the paper and a close friend of the editor. At his request, Vidal ordered that I should be given a runner's job and be allowed to live in the caretaker's modest rooms, in the basement, until further notice.

Those were years in which blood and violence were beginning to be an everyday occurrence in Barcelona. Days of pamphlets and bombs that left bits of bodies shaking and smoking in the streets of the Raval quarter, of gangs of black figures who prowled about at night shedding blood, of processions and parades of saints and generals who smelled of death and deceit, of inflammatory speeches in which everyone lied and everyone was right. The anger and hatred which, years later, would lead such people to murder one another in the name of grandiose slogans and coloured rags could already be smelled in the poisoned air. The continual haze from the factories slithered over the city and masked its cobbled avenues furrowed by trams and carriages. The night belonged to gaslight, to the shadows of narrow side streets shattered by the flash of gunshots and the blue trace of burned gunpowder. Those were years when one grew up fast, and with childhood slipping out of their hands, many children already had the look of old men.

With no other family to my name but the dark city of Barcelona, the newspaper became my shelter and my world until, when I was fourteen, my salary permitted me to rent that room in Doña Carmen's *pensión*. I had barely lived there a week when the landlady came to my room and told me that a gentleman was asking for me. On the landing stood a man dressed in grey, with a grey expression and a grey voice, who asked me whether I was David Martín. When I nodded, he handed me a parcel wrapped in coarse brown paper then vanished down the stairs, the trace of his grey absence contaminating the world of poverty I had joined. I took the parcel to my room and closed the door. Nobody, except two or three people at the newspaper, knew that I lived there. Intrigued, I removed the wrapping. It was the first package I had ever received. Inside was a wooden case that looked vaguely familiar. I placed it on the narrow bed and opened it. It contained my father's old revolver, given to him by the army, which he had brought with him when he returned from the Philippines to earn himself an early and miserable death. Next to the revolver was a small cardboard box with bullets. I held the gun and felt its weight. It smelled of gunpowder and oil. I wondered how many men my father had killed with that weapon with which he had probably hoped to end his own life, until someone got there first. I put it back and closed the case. My first impulse was to throw it into the rubbish bin, but then I realised that it was all I had left of my father. I imagined it had come from the moneylender who, when my father died, had tried to recoup his debts by confiscating what little we had in the old apartment overlooking the Palau de la Música: he had now decided to send me this gruesome souvenir to welcome me to the world of adulthood. I hid the case on top of my cupboard, against the wall, where filth accumulated and where Doña Carmen would not be able to reach it, even with stilts, and I didn't touch it again for years.

That afternoon I went back to Sempere & Sons and, feeling I was now a man of the world as well as a man of means, I made it known to the bookseller that I intended to buy that old copy of *Great Expectations* I had been forced to return to him years before.

'Name your price,' I said. 'Charge me for all the books I haven't paid you for in the last ten years.'

Sempere, I remember, gave me a wistful smile and put a hand on my shoulder.

'I sold it this morning,' he confessed.

6

Three hundred and sixty-five days after I had written my first story for *The Voice of Industry* I arrived, as usual, at the newspaper offices but found the place almost deserted. There was just a handful of journalists – colleagues who, months ago, had given me affectionate nicknames and even words of encouragement, but now ignored my greeting and gathered in a circle to whisper among themselves. In less than a minute they had picked up their coats and disappeared as if they feared they would catch something from me. I sat alone in that cavernous room, staring at the strange sight of dozens of empty desks. Slow, heavy footsteps behind me announced the approach of Don Basilio.

'Good evening, Don Basilio. What's going on here today? Why has everyone left?'

Don Basilio looked at me sadly and sat at the desk next to mine.

'There's a Christmas dinner for the staff. At the Set Portes restaurant,' he said quietly. 'I don't suppose they mentioned anything to you.'

I feigned a carefree smile and shook my head.

'Aren't you going?' I asked.

Don Basilio shook his head.

'I'm no longer in the mood.'

We looked at each other in silence.

'What if I take you somewhere?' I suggested. 'Wherever you fancy. Can Solé, if you like. Just you and me, to celebrate the success of *The Mysteries of Barcelona*.'

Don Basilio smiled, slowly nodding his head.

'Martín,' he said at last. 'I don't know how to say this to you.'

'Say what to me?'

Don Basilio cleared his throat.

'I'm not going to be able to publish any more instalments of *The Mysteries of Barcelona*.'

I gave him a puzzled look. Don Basilio looked away.

'Would you like me to write something else? Something more like Galdós?'

'Martín, you know what people are like. There have been complaints. I've tried to put a stop to this, but the editor is a weak man and doesn't like unnecessary conflicts.'

'I don't understand, Don Basilio.'

'Martín, I've been asked to be the one to tell you.'

Finally, he shrugged his shoulders.

'I'm fired,' I mumbled.

Don Basilio nodded.

Despite myself, I felt my eyes filling with tears.

'It might feel like the end of the world to you now, but believe me when I say that deep down it's the best thing that could have happened to you. This place isn't for you.'

'And what place is for me?' I asked.

'I'm sorry, Martín. Believe me, I'm very sorry.'

Don Basilio stood up and put a hand affectionately on my shoulder.

'Happy Christmas, Martín.'

That same evening I emptied my desk and left for good the place that had been my home, disappearing into the dark, lonely streets of the city. On my way to the *pensión* I stopped by the Set Portes restaurant under the arches of Casa Xifré. I stayed outside, watching my colleagues laughing and raising their glasses through the window pane. I hoped my absence made them happy or at least made them forget that they weren't happy and never would be.

I spent the rest of that week pacing the streets, sheltering every day in the Ateneo library and imagining that when I returned to the *pensión* I would discover a note from the newspaper editor asking me to rejoin the team. Hiding in one of the reading rooms, I would pull out the business card I had found in my hand when I woke up in El Ensueño, and start to compose a letter to my unknown benefactor, Andreas Corelli, but I always tore it up and tried rewriting it the following day. On the seventh day, tired of feeling sorry for myself, I decided to make the inevitable pilgrimage to my maker's house.

I took the train to Sarriá in Calle Pelayo – in those days it still operated above ground – and sat at the front of the carriage to gaze at the city and watch the streets become wider and grander the further we drew away from the centre. I got off at the Sarriá stop and from there took a tram that dropped me by the entrance to the Monastery of Pedralbes. It was an unusually hot day for the time of year and I could smell the scent of the pines and broom that peppered the hillside. I set off up Avenida Pearson, which at that time was already being developed. Soon I glimpsed the unmistakeable profile of Villa Helius. As I climbed the hill and got nearer, I could see Vidal sitting in the window of his tower in his shirtsleeves, enjoying a cigarette. Music floated on the air and I remembered that Vidal was one of the privileged few who owned a radio receiver. How good life must have looked from up there, and how insignificant I must have seemed.

I waved at him and he returned my greeting. When I reached the villa I met the driver, Manuel, who was on his way to the coach house carrying a handful of rags and a bucket of steaming-hot water.

'Good to see you here, David,' he said. 'How's life? Keeping up the good work?'

'I do my best,' I replied.

'Don't be modest. Even my daughter reads those adventures you publish in the newspaper.'

I swallowed hard, amazed that the chauffeur's daughter not only knew of my existence but had even read some of the nonsense I wrote.

41

'Cristina?'

'I have no other,' replied Don Manuel. 'Don Pedro is upstairs in his study, in case you want to go up.'

I nodded gratefully, slipped into the mansion and went up to the third floor, where the tower rose above the undulating rooftop of polychrome tiles. There I found Vidal, installed in his study with its view of the city and the sea in the distance. He turned off the radio, a contraption the size of a small meteorite which he'd bought a few months earlier when the first Radio Barcelona broadcast had been announced from the studios concealed under the dome of the Hotel Colón.

'It cost me almost two hundred pesetas, and it broadcasts a load of rubbish.'

We sat in chairs facing one another, with all the windows wide open and a breeze that to me, an inhabitant of the dark old town, smelled of a different world. The silence was exquisite, like a miracle. You could hear insects fluttering in the garden and the leaves on the trees rustling in the wind.

'It feels like summer,' I ventured.

'Don't pretend everything is OK by talking about the weather. I've already been told what happened,' Vidal said.

I shrugged my shoulders and glanced over at his writing desk. I was aware that my mentor had spent months, or even years, trying to write what he called a 'serious' novel far removed from the light plots of his crime fiction, so that his name could be inscribed in the more distinguished sections of libraries. I couldn't see many sheets of paper.

'How's the masterpiece going?'

Vidal threw his cigarette butt out of the window and stared into the distance.

'I don't have anything left to say, David.'

'Nonsense.'

'Everything in life is nonsense. It's just a question of perspective.'

'You should put that in your book. *The Nihilist on the Hill.* Bound to be a success.'

'You're the one who is going to need a success. Correct me if I'm wrong, but you'll soon be short of cash.'

'I could always accept your charity.'

'It might feel like the end of the world to you now, but—'

'I'll soon realise that this is the best thing that could have happened to me,' I said, completing the sentence. 'Don't tell me Don Basilio is writing your speeches now. Or is it the other way round?'

Vidal laughed.

'What are you going to do?'

'Don't you need a secretary?'

'I've already got the best secretary I could have. She's more intelligent than me, infinitely more hard-working and when she smiles I even feel that this lousy world still has some future.'

'And who is this marvel?'

'Manuel's daughter.'

'Cristina.'

'At last I hear you utter her name.'

'You've chosen a bad week to make fun of me, Don Pedro.'

'Don't look at me all doe-eyed. Did you think Pedro Vidal was going to allow that mediocre, constipated, envious bunch to sack you without doing anything about it?'

'A word from you to the editor could have changed things.'

'I know. That's why I was the one who suggested he should fire you,' said Vidal.

I felt as if he'd just slapped me on the face.

'Thanks for the push,' I improvised.

'I told him to fire you because I have something much better for you.'

'Begging?'

'Have you no faith? Only yesterday I was talking about you to a couple of partners who have just opened a new publishing house and are looking for fresh blood to exploit. You can't trust them, of course.'

'Sounds marvellous.'

'They know all about *The Mysteries of Barcelona* and are prepared to make you an offer that will get you on your feet.'

'Are you serious?'

'Of course I'm serious. They want you to write a series in instalments in the most baroque, bloody and delirious Grand Guignol tradition – a series that will tear *The Mysteries of Barcelona*

43

to shreds. I think that this is the opportunity you've been waiting for. I told them you'd go and talk to them and that you'd be able to start work immediately.'

I heaved a deep sigh. Vidal winked and then embraced me.

7

That was how, only a few months after my twentieth birthday, I received and accepted an offer to write penny dreadfuls under the name of Ignatius B. Samson. My contract committed me to hand in two hundred pages of typed manuscript a month packed with intrigues, high-society murders, countless underworld horrors, illicit love affairs featuring cruel lantern-jawed landowners and damsels with unmentionable desires, and all sorts of twisted family sagas with backgrounds as thick and murky as the water in the port. The series, which I decided to call *City of the Damned*, was to appear in monthly hardback instalments with full-colour illustrated covers. In exchange I would be paid more money than I had ever imagined could be made doing something that I cared about, and the only censorship imposed on me would be dictated by the loyalty of my readers. The terms of the offer obliged me to write anonymously under an extravagant pseudonym, but it seemed a small price to pay for being able to make a living from the profession I had always dreamed of practising. I would put aside any vanity about seeing my name printed on my work, whilst remaining true to myself, to what I was.

My publishers were a pair of colourful characters called Barrido and Escobillas. Barrido, who was small, squat, and always affected an oily, sibylline smile, was the brains of the operation. He sprang from the sausage industry and although he hadn't read more than three books in his life – and this included the catechism and the telephone directory – he was possessed of a proverbial audacity for cooking the books, which he falsified for his investors, displaying a talent for fiction that any of his authors might have envied. These, as Vidal had predicted, the firm swindled, exploited and, in the end, kicked into the gutter when the winds were unfavourable – something that always happened sooner or later.

Escobillas played a complementary role. Tall, gaunt, with a vaguely threatening appearance, he had gained his experience in the undertaker business and beneath the pungent eau de cologne with which he bathed his private parts there always seemed to be a vague whiff of formaldehyde that made one's hair stand on end. His role was essentially that of the sinister foreman, whip in hand, always ready to do the dirty work, to which Barrido, with his more cheerful nature and less athletic disposition, wasn't naturally inclined. The *ménage à trois* was completed by their secretary, Herminia, who followed them like a loyal dog wherever they went, and whom we all nicknamed Lady Venom because, although she looked as if butter wouldn't melt in her mouth, she was as trustworthy as a rattlesnake on heat.

Social niceties aside, I tried to see them as little as possible. Ours was a strictly commercial relationship and none of the parties felt any great desire to alter the established protocol. I had resolved to make the most of the opportunity and work hard: I wanted to prove to Vidal, and to myself, that I was worthy of his help and his trust. With fresh money in my hands, I decided to abandon Doña Carmen's *pensión* in search of more comfortable quarters. For some time now I'd had my eye on a huge pile of a house at number 30, Calle Flassaders, a stone's throw from Paseo del Borne, which for years I had passed as I went between the newspaper and the *pensión*. Topped by a tower that rose from a facade carved with reliefs and gargoyles, the building had been closed for years, its front door sealed with chains and rusty padlocks. Despite its gloomy and somewhat melodramatic appearance, or perhaps for that very reason, the idea of inhabiting it awoke in me that desire that only comes with ill-advised ideas. In other circumstances I would have accepted that such a place was far beyond my meagre budget, but the long years of abandonment and oblivion to which the dwelling seemed condemned made me hope that, if nobody else wanted it, perhaps its owners might accept my offer.

Asking around in the area, I discovered that the house had been empty for years and was handled by a property manager called Vicenç Clavé who had an office in Calle Comercio, opposite the market. Clavé was a gentleman of the old school who liked to dress in a similar fashion to the statues of mayors or national heroes that greeted you at the various entrances of Ciudadela Park; and if you weren't careful, he would take off on rhetorical flights that encompassed every subject under the sun.

'So you're a writer. Well, I could tell you stories that would make good books.'

'I don't doubt it. Why don't you begin by telling me the story of the house in Flassaders, number 30?'

Clavé adopted the look of a Greek mask.

'The tower house?'

'That's the one.'

'Believe me, young man, you don't want to live there.'

'Why not?'

Clavé lowered his voice. Whispering as if he feared the walls might hear us, he delivered his verdict in a funereal tone.

'That house is jinxed. I visited the place when I went along with the notary to seal it up and I can assure you that the oldest part of Montjuïc Cemetery is more cheerful. It's been empty since then. That place has bad memories. Nobody wants it.'

'Its memories can't be any worse than mine. Anyhow, I'm sure they'll help bring down the asking price.'

'Some prices cannot be paid with money.'

'Can I see it?'

My first visit to the tower house was one morning in March, in the company of the property manager, his secretary and an auditor from the bank who held the title deeds. Apparently, the building had been trapped for years in a labyrinth of legal disputes until it finally reverted to the lending institution that had guaranteed its last owner. If Clavé was telling the truth, nobody had set foot in that house for at least twenty years.

8

Years later, when I read an account about British explorers penetrating the dark passages of a thousand-year-old Egyptian burial place – mazes and curses included – I would recall that first visit to the tower house in Calle Flassaders. The secretary came equipped with an oil lamp because the building had never had electricity installed. The auditor turned up with a set of fifteen keys with which to liberate the countless padlocks that fastened the chains. When the front door was opened, the house exhaled a putrid smell, like a damp tomb. The auditor started to cough, and the manager, who was making an effort not to look too sceptical or disapproving, covered his mouth with a handkerchief.

'You first,' he offered.

The entrance resembled one of those interior courtyards in the old palaces of the area, paved with large flagstones and with a stone staircase that led to the front door of the living quarters. Daylight filtered in through a glass skylight, completely covered in pigeon and seagull excrement, that was set on high.

'There aren't any rats,' I announced once I was inside the building.

'A sign of good taste and common sense,' said the property manager behind me.

We proceeded up the stairs until we reached the landing on the main floor, where the auditor spent ten minutes trying to find the right key for the lock. The mechanism yielded with an unwelcoming groan and the heavy door opened, revealing an endless corridor strewn with cobwebs that undulated in the gloom.

'Holy Mother of God,' mumbled the manager.

No one else dared take the first step, so once more I had to lead the expedition. The secretary held the lamp up high, looking at everything with a baleful air.

The manager and the auditor exchanged a knowing look. When

47

they noticed that I was observing them, the auditor smiled calmly.

'A good bit of dusting and some patching up and the place will look like a palace,' he said.

'Bluebeard's palace,' the manager added.

'Let's be positive,' the auditor corrected him. 'The house has been empty for some time: there's bound to be some minor damage.'

I was barely paying attention to them. I had dreamed about that place so often as I walked past its front door that now I hardly noticed the dark, gloomy aura that possessed it. I walked up the main corridor, exploring rooms of all shapes and sizes in which old furniture lay abandoned under a thick layer of dust and shadow. One table was still covered with a frayed tablecloth on which sat a dinner service and a tray of petrified fruit and flowers. The glasses and cutlery were still there, as if the inhabitants of the house had fled in the middle of dinner.

The wardrobes were crammed with threadbare faded clothes and shoes. There were whole drawers filled with photographs, spectacles, fountain pens and watches. Dust-covered portraits observed us from every surface. The beds were made and covered with a white veil that shone in the half-light. A gramophone rested on a mahogany table. It had a record on it and the needle had slid to the end. I blew on the film of dust that covered it and the title of the recording came into view: W. A. Mozart's *Lacrimosa*.

'The symphony orchestra performing in your own home,' said the auditor. 'What more could one ask for? You'll live like a lord here.'

The manager shot him a murderous look, clearly in disagreement. We went through the apartment until we reached the gallery at the back, where a coffee service lay on a table and an open book on an armchair was still waiting for someone to turn over the page.

'It looks like whoever lived here left suddenly, with no time to take anything with them,' I said.

The auditor cleared his throat.

'Perhaps the gentleman would like to see the study?'

The study was at the top of a tall tower, a peculiar structure at the heart of which was a spiral staircase that led off the main corridor, while its outside walls bore the traces of as many generations as the city could remember. There it stood, like a watchtower suspended over the roofs of the Ribera quarter, crowned by a narrow dome of metal and tinted glass that served as a lantern, and topped by a weathervane in the shape of a dragon. We climbed the stairs, and when we reached the room at the top, the auditor quickly opened the windows to let in air and light. It was a rectangular room with high ceilings and dark wooden flooring. Its four large arched windows looked out on all four sides, giving me a view of the cathedral of Santa María del Mar to the south, the large Borne market to the north, the railway station to the east and to the west the endless maze of streets and avenues tumbling over one another towards Mount Tibidabo.

'What do you say? Marvellous!' proposed the auditor enthusiastically.

The property manager examined everything with a certain reserve and displeasure. His secretary held the lamp up high, even though it was no longer needed. I went over to one of the windows and leaned out, spellbound.

The whole of Barcelona stretched out at my feet and I wanted to believe that when I opened those windows – my new windows – each evening its streets would whisper stories to me, secrets in my ear, that I could catch on paper and narrate to whoever cared to listen. Vidal had his exuberant and stately ivory tower in the most elegant and elevated part of Pedralbes, surrounded by hills, trees and fairytale skies. I would have my sinister tower rising above the oldest, darkest streets of the city, surrounded by the miasmas and shadows of that necropolis which poets and murderers had once called the Rose of Fire.

What finally decided the matter was the desk that dominated the centre of the study. On it, like a great sculpture of metal and light, stood an impressive Underwood typewriter for which, alone, I would have paid the price of the rent. I sat in the plush armchair facing the desk, stroked the typewriter keys, and smiled.

'I'll take it,' I said.

The auditor sighed with relief and the manager rolled his eyes and crossed himself. That same afternoon I signed a ten-year rental agreement. While workmen were busy wiring the house for electricity, I devoted my time to cleaning, tidying and straightening the place up with the help of three servants whom Vidal sent trouping down without first asking me whether or not I wanted any help. I soon discovered that the *modus operandi* of that commando

49

of electrical experts consisted in first drilling holes right, left and centre and then asking. Three days after their deployment, the house did not have a single light bulb that worked, but one would have thought that the place had been infested by a plague of woodworm that devoured plaster and the noblest of minerals.

'Are you sure there isn't a better way of fixing this?' I would ask the head of the battalion, who resolved everything with blows of the hammer.

Otilio, as the talented man was called, would show me the building plans supplied by the property manager when I was handed the keys, and argue that the problem lay with the house, which was badly built.

'Look at this,' he would say. 'I mean, when something is badly made, it's badly made, and there are no two ways about it. Here, for example. Here it says that you have a water tank on the terrace. Well, no, sir, you have a water tank in the back yard.'

'What does it matter? The water tank has nothing to do with you, Otilio. Concentrate on the electrics. Light. Not taps, not water pipes. Light. I need light.'

'But everything is connected. What do you think about the gallery?'

'I think it has no light.'

'According to the plans this should be a supporting wall. Well, my mate Remigio here tapped it ever so slightly and half the wall came crashing down. And you should see the bedrooms. According to this plan, the size of the room at the end of the corridor should be almost forty square metres. Not in a million years! I'd be surprised if it measured twenty. There's a wall where there shouldn't be a wall. And as for the waste pipes, well, best not talk about them. Not one of them is where it's supposed to be.'

'Are you sure you know how to read the plans?'

'Listen, I'm a professional. Mark my words: this house is a jigsaw puzzle. Everybody's grandmother has poked their nose into this place.'

'I'm afraid you're going to have to make do with what there is. Perform a few miracles or do whatever you want, but by Friday I want to see all the walls plastered and painted, and the lights working.'

'Don't rush me; this is precision work. One has to act strategically.'

'So what is your plan?'

'For a start we're off to have our breakfast.'

'You only got here half an hour ago!'

'Señor Martín, we're not going to get anywhere with that attitude.'

The ordeal of building work and botched jobs went on a week longer than expected, but even with the presence of Otilio and his squadron of geniuses making holes where they shouldn't and enjoying two-and-a-half-hour breakfasts, the thrill of being able to live in that old rambling house, which I had dreamed about for so long, would have kept me going for years with candles and oil lamps if need be. I was lucky in that the Ribera quarter was a spiritual home for all kinds of craftsmen: just a stone's throw from my new home I found someone who could put in new locks that didn't look as if they'd been stolen from La Bastille, as well as twentieth-century wall lights and taps. The idea of having a telephone line installed did not appeal to me and, judging by what I'd heard on Vidal's wireless, these 'new mass communication media', as the press called them, were not aimed at people such as myself. I decided that my existence would be one of books and silence. All I took from the *pensión* was a change of clothes and the case containing my father's gun, his only memento. I distributed the remainder of my clothes and personal belongings among the *pensión* residents. Had I also been able to leave behind my memories, even my skin, I would have done so.

The same day as the first instalment of *City of the Damned* was published, I spent my first official and electrified night in the tower house. The novel was an imaginary intrigue I had woven round the story of the fire in El Ensueño in 1903, about a ghostly creature who had bewitched the streets of the Raval quarter ever since. Before the ink had dried on that first edition I had already started work on the second novel of the series. By my reckoning, based on thirty uninterrupted days' work a month, Ignatius B. Samson had to produce an average of 6.66 pages a day to comply with the terms of the agreement, which was crazy but had the advantage of not giving me much time to think about it.

I hardly noticed that, as the days went by, I was beginning to consume more coffee and cigarettes than oxygen. As I gradually poisoned my brain, I had the feeling that it was turning into a steam engine that never cooled down. But Ignatius B. Samson was young and resilient. He worked all night and collapsed from exhaustion at dawn, possessed by strange dreams in which the letters on the page trapped in the typewriter would come unstuck and, like spiders made of ink, would crawl up his hands and face, working their way through his skin and nesting in his veins until his heart was covered in black and his pupils were clouded in pools of darkness. I would barely leave the old rambling house for weeks on end, and would forget what day of the week it was, or what month of the year. I paid no attention to the recurring headaches that would sometimes plague me, arriving all of a sudden as if a metal awl were boring a hole through my skull, burning my eyes with a flash of white light. I had grown accustomed to living with a constant ringing in my ears that only the murmur of wind or rain could mask. Sometimes, when a cold sweat covered my face and I felt my hands shaking on the Underwood keyboard, I told myself that the following day I would go to the doctor. But on that day there was always another scene, and another story to tell.

To celebrate the first year of Ignatius B. Samson's life, I decided to take the day off and reacquaint myself with the sun, the breeze and the streets of a city I had stopped walking through and now only imagined. I shaved, tidied myself up and donned the best and most presentable of my suits. I left the windows open in the study and in the gallery to air the house and let the thick fog that had become its scent be scattered to the four winds. When I went out into the street, I found a large envelope at the bottom of the letter box. Inside was a sheet of parchment, sealed with the angel motif and written on in that exquisite writing. It said:

Dear David,

I wanted to be the first to congratulate you on this new stage of your career. I have thoroughly enjoyed reading the first instalments of *City of the Damned*. I hope you will like this small gift.

I would like to reiterate my admiration for you, and my hope that one day our paths may cross. Trusting that this will come about, please accept the most affectionate greetings from your friend and reader,

Andreas Corelli

The gift was the same copy of *Great Expectations* that Señor Sempere had given me when I was a child, the same copy I had returned to him before my father could find it and the same copy that, years later, when I had wanted to recover it at any price, had disappeared only hours before in the hands of a stranger. I stared at the bundle of paper which to me, in a not so distant past, had seemed to contain all the magic and light of the world. The cover still bore my bloodstained fingerprints.

'Thank you,' I whispered.

9

Señor Sempere put on his reading spectacles to examine the book closely. He placed it on a cloth he had spread out on his desk in the back room and pulled down the reading lamp so that its beam focused on the volume. His examination lasted a few minutes, during which I maintained a reverential silence. I watched him turn over the pages, smell them, stroke the paper and the spine, weigh the book with one hand and then the other, and finally close the cover and examine with a magnifying glass the bloodstained fingerprints left by me twelve or thirteen years earlier.

'Incredible,' he mused, removing his spectacles. 'It's the same book. How did you say you recovered it?'

'I really couldn't tell you, Señor Sempere. Do you know anything about a French publisher called Andreas Corelli?'

'For a start he sounds more Italian than French, although the name Andreas could be Greek . . .'

'The publishing house is in Paris. Éditions de la Lumière.'

Sempere looked doubtful.

'I'm afraid it doesn't ring a bell. I'll ask Barceló. He knows everything; let's see what he says.'

Gustavo Barceló was one of the senior members of the second-hand booksellers' guild in Barcelona and his vast expertise was as legendary as his somewhat abrasive and pedantic manner. There was a saying in the trade: when in doubt, ask Barceló. At that very moment Sempere's son put his head round the door and signalled to his father. Although he was two or three years older than me he was so shy that he could make himself invisible.

'Father, someone's come to collect an order that I think you took.'

The bookseller nodded and handed me a thick, worn volume.

'This is the latest catalogue of European publishers. Why don't you have a look at it and see if you can find anything while I attend to the customer?' he suggested.

I was left alone in the back room, searching in vain for Éditions de la Lumière, while Sempere returned to the counter. As I leafed through the volume, I could hear him talking to a female voice that sounded familiar. I heard them mention Pedro Vidal. Intrigued, I put my head round the door to find out more.

Cristina Sagnier, the chauffeur's daughter and my mentor's secretary, was going through a pile of books which Sempere was noting down in his ledger. When she saw me she smiled politely, but I was sure she did not recognise me. Sempere looked up and when he noticed the silly expression on my face he took a quick X-ray of the situation.

'You do know each other, don't you?' he said.

Cristina raised her eyebrows in surprise and looked at me again, unable to place me.

'David Martín. A friend of Don Pedro's,' I said.

'Oh, of course,' she replied. 'Good morning.'

'How is your father?' I asked.

'Fine, fine. He's waiting for me on the corner with the car.'

Sempere, who never missed a trick, quickly interjected.

'Señorita Sagnier has come to collect some books Señor Vidal ordered. As they are so heavy, perhaps you could help her take them to the car . . .'

'Please don't worry . . .' protested Cristina.

'But of course,' I blurted out, ready to lift the pile of books that turned out to weigh as much as the luxury edition of the *Encyclopædia Britannica*, appendices included.

I felt something go crunch in my back and Cristina gave me an embarrassed look.

'Are you all right?'

'Don't worry, miss. My friend Martín here might be a man of letters, but he's as strong as a bull,' said Sempere. 'Isn't that right, Martín?'

Cristina was looking at me unconvinced. I offered her my 'strong man' smile.

'Pure muscle,' I said. 'This is just a warm-up exercise.'

Sempere's son was about to offer to carry half the books, but his father, in a display of great diplomacy, held him back. Cristina kept the door open for me and I set off to cover the fifteen or twenty metres that separated me from the Hispano-Suiza parked on the corner of Puerta del Ángel. I only just managed to get there, my arms almost on fire. Manuel, the chauffeur, helped me unload the books and greeted me warmly.

'What a coincidence, meeting you here, Señor Martín.'

'Small world.'

Cristina gave me a grateful smile and got into the car.

'I'm sorry about the books.'

'It was nothing. A bit of exercise lifts the spirit,' I volunteered, ignoring the tangle of knots I could feel in my back. 'My regards to Don Pedro.'

I watched them drive off towards Plaza de Cataluña, and when I turned I noticed Sempere at the door of the bookshop, looking at me with a cat-like smile, and gesturing to me to wipe the drool off my chin. I went over to him and couldn't help laughing at myself.

'I know your secret now, Martín. I thought you had a steadier nerve in these matters.'

'Everything gets a bit rusty.'

'I should know! Can I keep the book for a few days?'

I nodded.

'Take good care of it.'

10

A few months later I saw her again, in the company of Pedro Vidal, at the table that was always reserved for him at La Maison Dorée. Vidal invited me to join them, but a quick look from her was enough to tell me that I should refuse the offer.

'How is the novel going, Don Pedro?'

'Swimmingly.'

'I'm pleased to hear it. Bon appétit.'

My meetings with Cristina were always by chance. Sometimes I would bump into her in the Sempere & Sons bookshop, where she often went to collect books for Vidal. If the opportunity arose, Sempere would leave me alone with her, but soon Cristina grew wise to the trick and would send one of the young boys from Villa Helius to pick up the orders.

'I know it's none of my business,' Sempere would say. 'But perhaps you should stop thinking about her.'

'I don't know what you're talking about, Señor Sempere.'

'Come on, Martín, we've known each other for a long time . . .'

The months seemed to slip by in a blur. I lived at night, writing from evening to dawn, and sleeping all day. Barrido and Escobillas couldn't stop congratulating themselves on the success of *City of the Damned*, and when they saw me on the verge of collapse they assured me that after a couple more novels they would grant me a sabbatical so that I could rest or devote my time to writing a personal work, which they would publish with much fanfare and with my real name printed in large letters on the cover. It was always just a couple of novels away. The sharp pains, the headaches and the dizzy spells became more frequent and intense, but I attributed them to exhaustion and treated them with more injections of caffeine, cigarettes and some tablets tasting of gunpowder that contained codeine and God knows what else, supplied on the quiet by a chemist in Calle Argenteria. Don Basilio, with whom I had lunch on alternate Thursdays in an outdoor café in La Barceloneta, urged me to go to the doctor. I always said yes, I had an appointment that very week.

Apart from my old boss and the Semperes, I didn't have much time to see anybody else except Vidal, and when I did see him it was more because he came to see me than through any effort on my part. He didn't like my tower house and always insisted that we go out for a stroll, to the Bar Almirall on Calle Joaquín Costa, where he had an account and held literary gatherings on Friday evenings. I was never invited to them because he knew that all those attending, frustrated poetasters and arse-lickers who laughed at his jokes in the hope of some charity – a recommendation to a publisher or a compliment to soothe their wounded pride – hated me with an unswerving vigour and determination that were quite absent from their more artistic endeavours, which were persistently ignored by the fickle public. There, knocking back absinthe and puffing on Caribbean cigars, he spoke to me about his novel, which was never finished, about his plans for retiring from his life of retirement, and about his romances and conquests: the older he got, the younger and more nubile they became.

'You don't ask after Cristina,' he would sometimes say, maliciously.

'What do you want me to ask?'

'Whether she asks after you.'

'Does she ask after me, Don Pedro?'

'No.'

'Well, there you are.'

'The fact is, she did mention you the other day.'

'And what did she say?'

'You're not going to like it.'

'Go on.'

'She didn't say it in so many words, but she seemed to imply that she couldn't understand how you could prostitute yourself by writing second-rate serials for that pair of thieves; that you were throwing away your talent and your youth.'

I felt as if Vidal had just plunged a frozen dagger into my stomach.

'Is that what she thinks?'

Vidal shrugged his shoulders.

'Well, as far as I'm concerned she can go to hell.'

I worked every day except Sundays, which I spent wandering the streets, always ending up in some bar on the Paralelo where it wasn't hard to find company and passing affection in the arms of another solitary soul like myself. It wasn't until the following morning, when I woke up lying next to a stranger, that I realised they all looked like her: the colour of their hair, the way they walked, a gesture or a glance. Sooner or later, to fill the painful silence of farewells, those one-night stands would ask me how I earned my living, and when, surrendering to my vanity, I explained that I was a writer, they would take me for a liar, because nobody had ever heard of David Martín, although some of them did know of Ignatius B. Samson, and had heard people talk about *City of the Damned*. After a while I began to say that I worked at the customs offices in the port, or that I was a clerk in a solicitors' office called Sayrach, Muntaner and Cruells.

One afternoon I was sitting in the Café de la Ópera with a music teacher called Alicia, helping her get over – or so I imagined – someone who was hard to forget. I was about to kiss her when I saw Cristina's face on the other side of the glass pane. When I reached the street, she had already vanished among the crowds in the Ramblas. Two weeks later Vidal insisted on inviting me to the premiere of *Madame Butterfly* at the Liceo. The Vidal family owned a box in the dress circle and Vidal liked to attend once a week during the opera season. When I met him in the foyer I discovered that he had also brought Cristina. She greeted me with an icy smile and didn't speak to me again or even glance at me until, halfway through the second act, Vidal decided to go down to the adjoining Círculo club to say hello to one of his cousins. We were left alone together in the box, with no other shield than Puccini and the hundreds of faces in the semi-darkness of the theatre. I held back for about ten minutes before turning to look her in the eye.

'Have I done something to offend you?' I asked.

'No.'

'Can we pretend to be friends then, at least on occasions like this?'

'I don't want to be your friend, David.'

'Why not?'

'Because you don't want to be my friend either.'

She was right, I didn't want to be her friend.

'Is it true that you think I prostitute myself?'

'Whatever I think doesn't matter. What matters is what you think.'

I sat there for another five minutes and then stood up and left without saying a word. By the time I reached the wide Liceo staircase I'd already promised myself that I would never give her a second thought, look, or a kind word.

The following afternoon I saw her in front of the cathedral, and when I tried to avoid her she waved at me and smiled. I stood there, glued to the spot, watching her approach.

'Aren't you going to invite me for a drink?'

'I'm a streetwalker and I'm not free for another two hours.'

'Well then, let me invite you. How much do you charge for accompanying a lady for an hour?'

I followed her reluctantly to a chocolate shop on Calle Petritxol. We ordered two cups of hot chocolate and sat facing one another, seeing who would break the silence first. For once, I won.

'I didn't mean to offend you yesterday, David. I don't know what Don Pedro told you, but I've never said such a thing.'

'Maybe you only thought it, which is why he would have told me.'

'You have no idea what I think,' she replied harshly. 'Nor does Don Pedro.'

I shrugged my shoulders.

'Fine.'

'What I said was very different. I said that I didn't think you were doing what you felt inside.'

I smiled and nodded. The only thing I felt at that moment was the need to kiss her. Cristina held my gaze defiantly. She didn't turn her face when I stretched out my hand and touched her lips, sliding my fingers down her chin and neck.

'Not like this,' she said at last.

By the time the waiter brought the steaming cups of chocolate she had already left. Months went by before I even heard her name again.

One day towards the end of September, when I had just finished a new instalment of *City of the Damned*, I decided to take a night off.

59

I could feel the approach of one of those storms of nausea and burning stabs in my brain. I gulped down a handful of codeine pills and lay on my bed in the darkness waiting for the cold sweat and the trembling of my hands to stop. I was on the point of falling asleep when I heard the doorbell. I dragged myself to the hall and opened the door. Vidal, in one of his impeccable Italian silk suits, was lighting a cigarette in a beam of light that seemed painted for him by Vermeer himself.

'Are you alive, or am I speaking to an apparition?' he asked.

'Don't tell me you've come all the way from Villa Helius just to throw that at me.'

'No. I've come because I haven't heard from you in two months and I'm worried about you. Why don't you get a telephone installed in this mausoleum, like normal people would?'

'I don't like telephones. I like to see people's faces when they speak and for them to see mine.'

'In your case I'm not sure that's a good idea. Have you looked at yourself in the mirror recently?'

'That's your department.'

'There are bodies in the mortuary at the Clínico hospital with a rosier face than yours. Go on, get dressed.'

'Why?'

'Because I say so. We're going out for a stroll.'

Vidal would not take no for an answer. He dragged me to the car, which was waiting in Paseo del Borne, and told Manuel to start the engine.

'Where are we going?' I asked.

'Surprise.'

We crossed the whole of Barcelona until we reached Avenida Pedralbes and started the climb up the hillside. A few minutes later we glimpsed Villa Helius, with all its windows lit up, projecting a bubble of bright gold across the twilight. Giving nothing away, Vidal smiled mysteriously at me. When we reached the mansion he told me to follow him and led me to the large sitting room. A group of people was waiting for me there, and as soon as they saw me, they started to clap. I recognised Don Basilio, Cristina, Sempere – both father and son – and my old schoolteacher Doña Mariana; some of the authors who, like me, published their work with Barrido &

Escobillas, and with whom I had established a friendship; Manuel, who had joined the group, and a few of Vidal's conquests. Vidal offered me a glass of champagne and smiled.

'Happy twenty-eighth birthday, David.'

I'd forgotten.

After the meal I excused myself for a moment and went out into the garden for some fresh air. A starry night cast a silver veil over the trees. I'd been there only for a minute or so when I heard footsteps approaching and turned to find the last person I was expecting to see: Cristina Sagnier. She smiled at me, as if apologising for the intrusion.

'Pedro doesn't know I've come out to speak to you,' she said.

She had dropped the 'Don', but I pretended not to notice.

'I'd like to talk to you, David,' she said, 'but not here, not now.'

Even in the shadows of the garden I was unable to hide my bewilderment.

'Can we meet tomorrow somewhere?' she asked. 'I promise I won't take up much of your time.'

'Where shall we meet?'

'Could it be at your house? I don't want anyone to see us, and I don't want Pedro to know I've spoken with you.'

'As you wish . . .'

Cristina smiled with relief.

'Thanks. Will tomorrow be all right? In the afternoon?'

'Whenever you like. Do you know where I live?'

'My father knows.'

She leaned over a little and kissed me on the check.

'Happy birthday, David.'

Before I could say anything, she had vanished across the garden. When I went back to the sitting room she had already left. Vidal glanced at me coldly from one end of the room and only smiled when he realised that I was watching him.

An hour later Manuel, with Vidal's approval, insisted on driving me home in the Hispano-Suiza. I sat next to him, as I did whenever we were alone in the car: the chauffeur would take the opportunity to give me driving tips and, unbeknown to Vidal, would even let me take the wheel for a while. That night Manuel was quieter than usual and did not say a word until we reached the town centre. He looked thinner than the last time I'd seen him and I had the feeling that age was beginning to take its toll.

'Is anything wrong, Manuel?' I asked.

The chauffeur shrugged his shoulders.

'Nothing important, Señor Martín.'

'If there's anything worrying you . . .'

'Just a few health problems. When you get to my age, everything is a worry, as you know. But I don't matter any more. The one who matters is my daughter.'

I wasn't sure how to reply, so I simply nodded.

'I'm aware that you hold a certain affection for her, Señor Martín. For my Cristina. A father can see these things.'

Again I just nodded. We didn't exchange any more words until Manuel stopped the car at the entrance to Calle Flassaders, held out his hand to me, and once more wished me a happy birthday.

'If anything should happen to me,' he said then, 'you would help her, wouldn't you, Señor Martín? You would do that for me?'

'Of course, Manuel. But nothing is going to happen to you!'

The chauffeur bade me farewell. I saw him get into the car and drive away slowly. I wasn't absolutely sure, but I could have sworn that, after a journey in which he had hardly opened his mouth, he was now talking to himself.

11

I spent the whole morning running about the house, straightening things and tidying up, airing the rooms, cleaning objects and corners I didn't even know existed. I rushed down to a florist in the market and when I returned, laden with bunches of flowers, I realised I had forgotten where I'd hidden the vases in which to put them. I dressed as if I was going out to look for work. I practised words and greetings that sounded ridiculous. I looked at myself in the mirror and saw that Vidal was right: I looked like a vampire. Finally I sat down in an armchair in the gallery to wait, with a book in my hands. In two hours I hadn't turned over the first page. At last, at exactly four o'clock in the afternoon, I heard Cristina's footsteps on the stairs and jumped up. By the time she rang the front doorbell I'd been at the door for an eternity.

'Hello, David. Is this a bad moment?'

'No, no, on the contrary. Please come in.'

Cristina smiled politely and stepped into the corridor. I led her to the reading room in the gallery, and offered her a seat. She was examining everything carefully.

'It's a very special place,' she said. 'Pedro did tell me you had an elegant home.'

'He prefers the term "gloomy", but I suppose it's just a question of degrees.'

'May I ask why you came to live here? It's a rather large house for someone who lives alone.'

Someone who lives alone, I thought. You end up becoming what you see in the eyes of those you love.

'The truth?' I asked. 'The truth is that I came to live here because for years I had seen this house almost every day on my way to and from the newspaper. It was always closed up, and I began to think it was waiting for me. In the end I dreamed, literally, that one day I would live in it. And that's what happened.'

'Do all your dreams come true, David?'

The ironic tone reminded me too much of Vidal.

'No,' I replied. 'This is the only one. But you wanted to talk to me about something and I'm distracting you with stories that probably don't interest you.'

I sounded more defensive that I would have wished. The same thing that had happened with the flowers was happening with my longing: once I held it in my hands, I didn't know where to put it.

'I wanted to talk to you about Pedro,' Cristina began.

'Ah.'

'You're his best friend. You know him. He talks about you as if you were his son. He loves you more than anyone. You know that.'

'Don Pedro has treated me like a father,' I said. 'If it hadn't been for him and for Señor Sempere, I don't know what would have become of me.'

'The reason I wanted to talk to you is that I'm very worried about him.'

'Why are you worried?'

'You know that some years ago I started work as his secretary. The truth is that Pedro is a very generous man and we've ended up being good friends. He has behaved very well towards my father, and towards me. That's why it hurts me to see him like this.'

'Like what?'

'It's that wretched book, the novel he wants to write.'

'He's been at it for years.'

'He's been destroying it for years. I correct and type out all his pages. Over the years I've been working as his secretary he's destroyed at least two thousand pages. He says he has no talent. He says he's a fraud. He's constantly at the bottle. Sometimes I find him upstairs in his study, drunk, crying like a child . . .'

I swallowed hard.

'He says he envies you, he wants to be like you, he says people lie and praise him because they want something from him – money, help – but he knows that his book is worthless. He keeps up appearances with everyone else, his smart suits and all that, but I see him every day, and I know he's losing hope. Sometimes I'm afraid he'll do something stupid. It's been going on for some time now. I haven't said anything because I didn't know who to speak to. If he knew I'd come to see you he'd be furious. He always says: don't bother David with my worries. He's got his whole life ahead of him and I'm nothing now. He's always saying things like that. Forgive me for telling you all this, but I didn't know who to turn to . . .'

We sank into a deep silence. I felt an intense cold invading me: the knowledge that while the man to whom I owed my life had plunged into despair, I had been locked in my own world and hadn't paused for one second to notice.

'Perhaps I shouldn't have come . . .'

'No,' I said. 'You've done the right thing.'

Cristina looked at me with a hint of a smile and for the first time I felt that I was not a stranger to her.

'What can we do?' she asked.

'We're going to help him,' I said.

'What if he doesn't let us?'

'Then we'll do it without him noticing.'

12

I will never know whether I did it to help Vidal, as I kept telling myself, or simply as an excuse to spend more time with Cristina. We met almost every afternoon in my tower house. Cristina would bring the pages Vidal had written in longhand the day before, always full of deletions, with whole paragraphs crossed out, notes all over the page and a thousand and one attempts to save what was beyond repair. We would go up to the study and sit on the floor. Cristina would read the pages out loud and then we would discuss them at length. My mentor was attempting to write an epic saga covering three generations of a Barcelona family that was not very different from his own. The action began a few years before the Industrial Revolution with the arrival in the city of two orphaned brothers and developed into a sort of biblical parable in the Cain and Abel mode. One of the brothers ended up becoming the richest and most powerful magnate of his time, while the other devoted himself to the Church and helping the needy, only to end his days tragically during an episode that was quite evidently borrowed from the misfortunes of the priest and poet Jacint Verdaguer. Throughout their lives the two brothers were at loggerheads, and an endless list of characters filed past in torrid melodramas, scandals, murders, tragedies and other requirements of the genre, all of it set against the background of the birth of modern Barcelona and its world of industry and finance. The narrator was a grandchild of one of the two brothers, who reconstructed the story while he watched the city burn from a palatial mansion in Pedralbes during the riots of the Tragic Week of 1909.

The first thing that surprised me was that the story was one that I had suggested to him some years earlier, as a means of getting him started on his most significant work, the novel he always said he would write one day. The second thing was that he had never told me he'd decided to use the idea, or that he'd already spent years on it, and not through any lack of opportunity. The third thing was that the novel, as it stood, was a complete and utter flop: not one of the elements of the book worked, starting with the characters and the structure, passing through the atmosphere and the plot, ending with a language and a style that suggested the efforts of a pretentious amateur with too much spare time on his hands.

'What do you think of it?' Cristina asked. 'Can it be saved?'

I preferred not to tell her that Vidal had borrowed the premise from me, not wishing her to be more worried than she already was, so I smiled and nodded.

'It needs some work, that's all.'

As the day grew dark, Cristina would sit at the typewriter and between us we rewrote Vidal's book, letter by letter, line by line, scene by scene.

The storyline put together by Vidal was so vague and insipid that I decided to recover the one I had invented when I originally suggested it to him. Slowly we brought the characters back to life, rebuilding them from head to toe. Not a single scene, moment, line or word survived the process and yet, as we advanced, I had the impression that we were doing justice to the novel that Vidal carried in his heart and had decided to write without knowing how.

Cristina told me that sometimes, weeks after he remembered writing a scene, Vidal would reread it in its final typewritten version, and was surprised at his craftsmanship and the fullness of a talent in which he had ceased to believe. She feared he might discover what we were doing and told me we should be more faithful to his original work.

'Never underestimate a writer's vanity, especially that of a mediocre writer,' I would reply.

'I don't like to hear you talking like that about Pedro.'

'I'm sorry. Neither do I.'

'Perhaps you should slow down a bit. You don't look well. I'm not worried about Pedro any more – I'm concerned about you.'

'Something good had to come of all this.'

In time I grew accustomed to savouring the moments I shared with her. It wasn't long before my own work suffered the consequences. I found the time to work on *City of the Damned* where there was none, sleeping barely three hours a day and pushing myself to the limit to meet the deadlines in my contract. Both Barrido and Escobillas made it a rule not to read any book – neither the ones they published nor the ones published by the competition – but Lady Venom did read them and soon began to suspect that something strange was happening to me.

'This isn't you,' she would say every now and then.

'Of course it's not me, dear Herminia. It's Ignatius B. Samson.'

I was aware of the risks I was taking, but I didn't care. I didn't care if I woke up every day covered in sweat and with my heart beating so hard I felt as if it was going to crack my ribs. I would have paid that price and much more to retain the slow, secret contact that unwittingly turned us into accomplices. I knew perfectly well that Cristina could read this in my eyes every time she came, and I knew perfectly well that she would never respond to my advances. There was no future, or great expectations, in that race to nowhere, and we both knew it.

Sometimes, when we grew tired of attempting to refloat the leaking ship, we would abandon Vidal's manuscript and try to talk about something other than the intimacy which, from being so hidden, was beginning to weigh on our consciences. Now and then, I would muster enough courage to take her hand. She let me, but I knew it made her feel uncomfortable: she felt that it was not right, that our debt of gratitude to Vidal united and separated us at the same time. One night, shortly before she left, I held her face in my hands and tried to kiss her. She remained motionless and when I saw myself in the mirror of her eyes I didn't dare speak. She stood up and left without saying a word. After that, I didn't see her for two weeks, and when she returned she made me promise nothing like that would ever happen again.

'David, I want you to understand that when we finish working on Pedro's book we won't be seeing one another as we do now.'

'Why not?'

'You know why.'

My advances were not the only thing Cristina didn't approve of. I began to suspect that Vidal had been right when he said she disliked the books I was writing for Barrido & Escobillas, even if she kept quiet about it. It wasn't hard to imagine her thinking that my efforts were strictly mercenary and soulless, that I was selling my integrity for a pittance, thereby lining the pockets of a couple of sewer rats, because I didn't have the courage to write from my heart, with my own name and my own feelings. What hurt me most was that, deep down, she was probably right. I fantasised about ending my contract and writing a book just for her, a book with which I could earn her respect. If the only thing I knew how to do wasn't good enough for Cristina, perhaps I should return to the grey, miserable days of the newspaper. I could always live off Vidal's charity and favours.

I had gone out for a walk after a long night's work, unable to sleep. Wandering about aimlessly, my feet led me uphill until I reached the building site of the Sagrada Familia. When I was small, my father had sometimes taken me there to gaze up at the babel of sculptures and porticoes that never seemed to take flight, as if the building were cursed. I liked going back to visit the place and discover that it had not changed; that although the city was endlessly growing around it, the Sagrada Familia remained forever in a state of ruin.

Dawn was breaking when I arrived: the towers of the Nativity facade stood in silhouette against a blue sky, scythed by red light. An eastern wind carried the dust from the unpaved streets and the acid smell from the factories shoring up the edges of the Sant Martí quarter. I was crossing Calle Mallorca when I saw the lights of a tram approaching through the early morning mist. I heard the clatter of the metal wheels on the rails and the sound of the bell which the driver was ringing to warn people of the tram's advance. I wanted to run, but I couldn't. I stood there, glued to the ground between the rails, watching the lights of the tram leaping towards me. I heard the driver's shouts and saw the plume of sparks that shot out from the wheels as he slammed on the brakes. Even then, with death only a few metres away, I couldn't move a muscle. The smell of electricity invaded the white light that blazed in my eyes, and then the tram's headlight went out. I fell over like a puppet, only conscious for a few more seconds, time enough to see the tram's smoking wheel stop just centimetres from my face. Then all was darkness.

13

I opened my eyes. Thick columns of stone rose like trees in the shadows towards a naked vault. Needles of dusty light fell diagonally, revealing what looked like endless rows of ramshackle beds. Small drops of water fell from the heights like black tears, exploding with an echo as they touched the ground. The darkness smelled of mildew and damp.

'Welcome to purgatory.'

I sat up and turned to find a man dressed in rags who was reading a newspaper by the light of a lantern. He brandished a smile that showed half of his teeth were missing. The front page of the newspaper he was holding announced that General Primo de Rivera was taking over all the powers of the state and installing a gentlemanly dictatorship to save the country from imminent disaster. That newspaper was at least five years old.

'Where am I?'

The man peered over his paper and looked at me curiously.

'At the Ritz. Can't you smell it?'

'How did I get here?'

'Half dead. They brought you in this morning on a stretcher and you've been sleeping it off ever since.'

I felt my jacket and realised that all the money I'd had on me had vanished.

'What a mess the world is in,' cried the man, reading the news in his paper. 'It seems that in the advanced stages of stupidity, a lack of ideas is compensated for by an excess of ideologies.'

'How do I get out of here?'

'If you're in such a hurry . . . There are two ways, the permanent and the temporary. The permanent way is via the roof: one good leap and you can rid yourself of all this rubbish forever. The temporary way is somewhere over there, at the end, where that idiot is holding his fist in the air with his trousers falling off him, making the revolutionary salute to everyone who passes. But if you go out that way you'll come back sooner or later.'

The first man was watching me with amusement and the kind of lucidity that shines occasionally only in madmen.

'Are you the one who stole my money?'

'Your suspicion offends me. When they brought you here you were already as clean as a whistle, and I only accept bonds that can be cashed at a bank.'

I left the lunatic sitting on his bed with his out-of-date newspaper and his up-to-date speeches. My head was still spinning and I was barely able to walk more than four steps in a straight line, but I managed to reach a door that led to a staircase on one of the sides of the huge vault. A faint light seemed to filter down from the top of the stairwell. I went up four or five floors until I felt a gust of fresh air that was coming through a large doorway at the top. I walked outside and at last understood where I was.

Spread out before me was a lake, suspended above the treetops of Ciudadela Park. The sun was beginning to set over Barcelona and the weed-covered water rippled like spilt wine. The Water Reservoir building looked like a crude castle or a prison. It had been built to supply water to the pavilions of the 1888 Universal Exhibition, but in time its vast, cathedral-like interior had ended up as a shelter for the destitute and the dying who had no other refuge from the night or the cold. The huge water basin on the flat rooftop was now a murky stretch of water that slowly bled away through the cracks in the building.

Then I noticed a figure posted on one of the corners of the roof. As if the mere touch of my gaze had alerted him, he turned round sharply and looked at me. I still felt a bit dazed and my vision was blurred, but I thought the figure seemed to be getting closer. He was approaching too fast, as if his feet weren't touching the ground when he walked, and he moved in sudden agile bursts, too quick for the eye to catch. I could barely see his face against the light, but I was able to tell that he was a gentleman with black, shining eyes that seemed too big for his face. The closer he got to me the more his shape seemed to lengthen and the taller he seemed to grow. I felt a shiver as he advanced and took a few steps back without realising that I was moving towards the water's edge. I felt my feet treading air and began to fall backwards into the pond when the stranger suddenly caught me by the arm. He pulled me up gently and led me back to solid ground. I sat on one of the benches that surrounded the water basin and took a deep breath, then looked up and saw him clearly for the first time. His eyes were a normal size, his height similar to mine, and his walk and gestures were like those of any other gentleman. He had a kind and reassuring expression.

'Thank you,' I said.

'Are you all right?'

'Yes. Just a bit dizzy.'

The stranger sat down next to me. He wore a dark, exquisitely tailored three-piece suit with a small silver brooch on his lapel, an angel with outspread wings that looked oddly familiar. It occurred to me that the presence of an impeccably dressed gentleman here on the roof terrace was rather unusual. As if he could read my thoughts, the stranger smiled at me.

'I hope I didn't alarm you,' he ventured. 'I suppose you weren't expecting to meet anyone up here.'

I looked at him in confusion and saw my face reflected in his black pupils as they dilated like an ink stain on paper.

'May I ask what brings you here?'

'The same thing as you: great expectations.'

'Andreas Corelli,' I mumbled.

His face lit up.

'What a great pleasure it is to meet you in person at last, my friend.'

He spoke with a light accent which I was unable to identify. My instinct told me to get up and leave as fast as possible, before the stranger could utter another word, but there was something in his voice, in his eyes, that transmitted calm and trust. I decided not to ask myself how he could have known he would find me there, when even I had not known where I was. He held out his hand and I shook it. His smile seemed to promise redemption.

'I suppose I should thank you for all the kindness you have shown me over the years, Señor Corelli. I'm afraid I'm indebted to you.'

'Not at all. I'm the one who is indebted to you, my friend, and I should excuse myself for approaching you in this way, at so inconvenient a place and time, but I confess that I've been wanting to speak to you for a while and have never found the opportunity.'

'Go ahead then. What can I do for you?' I asked.

'I want you to work for me.'

'I'm sorry?'

'I want you to write for me.'

'Of course. I'd forgotten you're a publisher.'

The stranger laughed. He had a sweet laugh, the laugh of a child who has never misbehaved.

'The best of them all. The publisher you have been waiting for all your life. The publisher who will make you immortal.'

The stranger offered me one of his business cards, which was identical to the one I still had, the one I was holding when I awoke from my dream of Chloé.

ANDREAS CORELLI
Éditeur
Éditions de la Lumière
Boulevard St.-Germain, 69, Paris

'I'm flattered, Señor Corelli, but I'm afraid it's not possible for me to accept your invitation. I have a contract with . . .'

'Barrido & Escobillas, I know. Riff-raff with whom, without wishing to offend you, you should have no dealings whatsoever.'

'It's an opinion shared by others.'

'Señorita Sagnier, perhaps?'

'You know her?'

'I've heard of her. She seems to be the sort of woman whose respect and admiration one would give anything to win, don't you agree? Doesn't she encourage you to abandon those parasites and be true to yourself?'

'It's not that simple. I have an exclusive contract that ties me to them for another six years.'

'I know, but that needn't worry you. My lawyers are studying the matter and I can assure you there are a number of ways in which legal ties can be rendered null and void, should you wish to accept my proposal.'

'And your proposal is?'

Corelli gave me a mischievous smile, like a schoolboy sharing a secret.

'That you devote a year exclusively to working on a book I would commission, a book whose subject matter you and I would discuss when we signed the contract and for which I would pay you, in advance, the sum of one hundred thousand francs.'

I looked at him in astonishment.

'If that sum does not seem adequate I'm open to considering any other sum you might think more appropriate. I'll be frank, Señor Martín: I'm not going to quarrel with you about money. And between you and me, I don't think you'll want to either, because I know that when I tell you the sort of book I want you to write for me, the price will be the least of it.'

I sighed, laughing quietly.

'I see you don't believe me.'

'Señor Corelli, I'm an author of penny dreadfuls that don't even carry my name. My publishers, whom you seem to know, are a couple of second-rate fraudsters who are not worth their weight in manure, and my readers don't even know I exist. I've spent years earning my living in this trade and I have yet to write a single page that satisfies me. The woman I love thinks I'm wasting my life, and she's right. She also thinks I have no right to desire her because we're a pair of insignificant souls whose only reason for existence is the debt of gratitude we owe to a man who pulled us both out of poverty, and perhaps she's right about that too. It doesn't matter. Before I know it, I'll be thirty and I'll realise that every day I look less like the person I wanted to be when I was fifteen. If I reach thirty, that is, because recently my health has been about as consistent as my work. Right now I'm satisfied if I manage one or two decent sentences in an hour. That's the sort of author and the sort of man I am. Not the sort who receives visits from Parisian publishers with blank cheques for writing a book that will change his life and make all his dreams come true.'

Corelli observed me with a serious expression, carefully weighing every word.

'I think you judge yourself too severely, a quality that always distinguishes people of true worth. Believe me when I say that throughout my professional life I've come across hundreds of characters for whom you wouldn't have given a toss and who had an extremely high opinion of themselves. But I want you to know that, even if you don't believe me, I know exactly what sort of author and what sort of man you are. I've been watching you for years, as you are well aware. I've read all your work, from the very first story you wrote for *The Voice of Industry* to *The Mysteries of Barcelona*, and now each of the instalments of the Ignatius B. Samson series. I dare say I know you better than you know yourself. Which is why I'm sure that in the end you will accept my offer.'

'What else do you know?'

'I know we have something, or a great deal, in common. I know you lost your father, and so did I. I know what it is like to lose one's father when you still need him. Yours was snatched from you in tragic circumstances. Mine, for reasons that are neither here nor there, rejected me and threw me out of his house – perhaps that was even more painful. I know that you feel lonely, and believe me when I tell you that this is a feeling I have also experienced. I know that in your heart you harbour great expectations, none of which has come true, and that, although you're not aware of it, this is slowly killing you with every passing day.'

His words brought about a long silence.

'You know a lot of things, Señor Corelli.'

'Enough to think that I would like to be better acquainted with you and become your friend. I don't suppose you have many friends. Neither do I. I don't trust people who say they have a lot of friends. It's a sure sign that they don't really know anyone.'

'But you're not looking for a friend, you're looking for an employee.'

'I'm looking for a temporary partner. I'm looking for you.'

'You seem very sure of yourself.'

'It's a fault I was born with,' Corelli replied, standing up. 'Another is my gift for seeing into the future. That's why I realise that perhaps it's still too soon: hearing the truth from my lips is not enough for you yet. You need to see it with your own eyes. Feel it in your flesh. And, believe me, you'll feel it.'

He held out his hand and waited until I took it.

'Can I at least be reassured that you will think about what I've told you and that we'll speak again?' he asked.

'I don't know what to say, Señor Corelli.'

'Don't say anything right now. I promise that next time we meet you'll see things more clearly.'

With those words he gave me a friendly smile and walked off towards the stairs.

'Will there be a next time?' I asked.

Corelli stopped and turned.

'There always is.'

'Where?'

In the last rays of daylight falling on the city his eyes glowed like embers.

I saw him disappear through the door to the staircase. Only then did I realise that during the entire conversation I had not once seen him blink.

14

The doctor's surgery was on a top floor with a view of the sea gleaming in the distance and the slope of Calle Muntaner, dotted with trams, which slid down to the Ensanche between grand houses and imposing edifices. The place smelled clean. The waiting rooms were tastefully decorated. The paintings were calming, with landscapes full of hope and peace. The shelves displayed books that exuded authority. Nurses moved about like ballet dancers and smiled as they went by. It was a purgatory for people with well-lined pockets.

'The doctor will see you now, Señor Martín.'

Doctor Trías was a man with a patrician air and an impeccable appearance, who radiated serenity and confidence with every gesture. Grey, penetrating eyes behind rimless glasses. A kind, friendly smile, never frivolous. Doctor Trías was a man accustomed to jousting with death, and the more he smiled the more frightening he became. Judging by the way he escorted me to his room and asked me to sit down I got the feeling that, although some days before, when I had begun to undergo medical tests, he had spoken about recent medical breakthroughs in the fight against the symptoms I had described to him, as far as he was concerned, there was no doubt.

'How are you?' he asked, his eyes darting hesitantly between me and the folder on his desk.

'You tell me.'

He smiled faintly, like a good player.

'The nurse tells me you're a writer, although here, on the form you filled in when you arrived, I see you put down that you are a mercenary.'

'In my case there's no difference at all.'

'I believe some of my patients have read your books.'

'I hope it has not caused permanent neurological damage.'

The doctor smiled as if he'd found my comment amusing, and then adopted a more serious expression, implying that the banal and kind preambles to our conversation had come to an end.

'Señor Martín, I notice that you have come here on your own. Don't you have any close family? A wife? Siblings? Parents still alive?'

'That sounds a little ominous,' I ventured.

'Señor Martín, I'm not going to lie to you. The results of the first tests are not as encouraging as we'd hoped.'

I looked at him. I didn't feel fear or unease. I didn't feel anything.

'Everything points to the fact that you have a growth lodged in the left lobe of your brain. The results confirm what I feared from the symptoms you described to me, and there is every indication that it might be a carcinoma.'

For a few seconds I was unable to say anything at all. I couldn't even pretend to be surprised.

'How long have I had it?'

'It's impossible to say for sure, but I presume the tumour has been growing there for some time, which would explain the symptoms you told me about and the difficulties you have recently experienced with your work.'

I took a deep breath and nodded. The doctor observed me patiently, with a kind mien, letting me take my time. I tried to start various sentences that never reached my lips. Finally our eyes met.

'I suppose I'm in your hands, doctor. You'll have to tell me which treatment to follow.'

I saw his despairing look as he realised I had not wanted to understand what he was telling me. I nodded once more, fighting the tide of nausea that was beginning to rise up my throat. The doctor poured me a glass of water from a jug and handed it to me. I drank it in one gulp.

'There is no treatment?' I said.

'There is. There are a lot of things we can do to relieve the pain and ensure maximum comfort and peace . . .'

'But I'm going to die.'

'Yes.'

'Soon.'

'Possibly.'

I smiled to myself. Even the worst news is a relief when all it does is confirm what you already knew without wanting to know.

'I'm twenty-eight,' I said, without quite knowing why.

'I'm sorry, Señor Martín. I'd like to have given you better news.'

I felt as if I had finally confessed to a lie or a minor sin, and the large slab of remorse that had been pressing down on me was instantly removed.

'How much longer do I have?'

'It is difficult to determine exactly. I'd say a year, a year and a half at most.'

His tone clearly implied that this was a more than optimistic prognosis.

'And of that year, or whatever it is, how long do you think I'll still be able to work and cope on my own?'

'You're a writer and you work with your brain. Unfortunately that is where the problem is located and where we will first meet limitations.'

'Limitations is not a medical term, doctor.'

'The most likely outcome is that, as the disease progresses, the symptoms you've been experiencing will become more intense and more frequent and, after a time, you'll have to be admitted to hospital so that we can take care of you.'

'I won't be able to write.'

'You won't even be able to think about writing.'

'How long?'

'I don't know. Nine or ten months. Perhaps more, perhaps less. I'm very sorry, Señor Martín.'

I nodded and stood up. My hands were shaking and I needed some air.

'Señor Martín, I realise you need time to think about all the things I've told you, but it is important that we start your treatment as soon as possible . . .'

'I can't die yet, doctor. Not yet. I have things to do. Afterwards I'll have a whole lifetime in which to die.'

15

That night I went up to the study in the tower and sat at my typewriter, even though I knew that my brain was a blank. The windows were wide open, but Barcelona no longer wanted to tell me anything; I was unable to finish a single page. Anything I did manage to conjure up seemed banal and empty. It was enough to reread my words to understand that they were barely worth the ink with which they'd been typed. I was no longer able to hear the music that issues from a decent piece of prose. Bit by bit, like slow, pleasant poison, the words of Andreas Corelli began to drip into my thoughts.

I still had at least a hundred pages to go for my umpteenth delivery of those comic-book adventures that had provided both Barrido and Escobillas with such bulging pockets, but in that moment I knew I was never going to finish it. Ignatius B. Samson had been left lying on the rails in front of that tram, exhausted, his soul bled dry, poured into too many pages that should never have seen the light of day. But before departing he had conveyed to me his last wishes: that I should bury him without any fuss and that, for once in my life, I should have the courage to use my own voice. His legacy to me was his considerable repertoire of smoke and mirrors. And he asked me to let him go, because he had been born to be forgotten.

I took all the finished pages of his last novel and set fire to them, sensing that a tombstone was being lifted off me with every page I threw into the flames. A moist, warm breeze blew that night over the rooftops and as it came in through my windows it took with it the ashes of Ignatius B. Samson, scattering them through the streets of the old city, where they would always remain – however much his words were lost forever and his name slipped from the memory of even his most devoted readers.

The following day I turned up at the offices of Barrido & Escobillas. The receptionist was new, almost a child, and didn't recognise me.

'Your name?'

'Hugo, Victor.'

The receptionist smiled and connected to the switchboard to let Herminia know.

'Doña Herminia, Señor Hugo Victor is here to see Señor Barrido.'

I saw her nod and disconnect the switchboard.

'She says she'll be right out.'

'Have you been working here long?'

'A week,' the girl replied attentively.

Unless I was mistaken, she was the eighth receptionist Barrido & Escobillas had employed since the start of the year. The firm's employees who reported directly to the artful Herminia didn't last long because as soon as Lady Venom discovered that they had one ounce of common sense more than she had – which happened nine times out of ten – fearing she might be overshadowed, she would accuse them of theft or some other absurd transgression and make one scene after another until Escobillas kicked them out, threatening them with a hired assassin if they let the cat out of the bag.

'How good to see you, David,' said Lady Venom. 'You're looking very handsome. You seem well.'

'That's because I was run over by a tram. Is Barrido in?'

'The things you come out with! He's always in for you. He's going to be very pleased when I tell him you've come to pay us a visit.'

'You can't imagine how pleased.'

Lady Venom took me to Barrido's office, which was decorated like a chancellor's palatial rooms in a comic opera, with a profusion of carpets, busts of emperors, still-lifes and leather-bound volumes bought in bulk which, I imagined, were probably blank inside. Barrido gave me the oiliest of smiles and shook my hand.

'We're all waiting impatiently for the next instalment. I must tell you, we've been reprinting the last two and they're flying out of the window. Another five thousand copies, how about that?'

I thought it was more likely to be at least fifty thousand, but I just nodded enthusiastically. Barrido & Escobillas had perfected what was known among Barcelona publishers as the double print run, and theirs was as neatly arranged as a bunch of flowers. Every title had an official print run of a few thousand copies, on which a ridiculous margin was paid to the author. Then, if the book took off, they would print one or many undercover editions of tens of thousands of copies, which were never declared and for which the author never saw a penny. The latter could be distinguished from the official edition because Barrido had them printed on the quiet in an old sausage plant in Santa Perpètua de Mogoda, and if you leafed through the pages they gave off the unmistakable smell of vintage pork.

'I'm afraid I have bad news.'

Barrido and Lady Venom exchanged looks but kept on grinning. Just then, Escobillas materialised through the door and looked at me with that dry, disdainful air he had, as if he were measuring you up for a coffin.

'Look who has come to see us. Isn't this a nice surprise?' Barrido asked his partner, who replied with a nod.

'What bad news?' asked Escobillas.

'Is there a bit of a delay, Martín, my friend?' Barrido added in a friendly tone. 'I'm sure we can accommodate—'

'No. There's no delay. Quite simply, there's not going to be another book.'

Escobillas took a step forward and raised his eyebrows. Barrido giggled.

'What do you mean, there's not going to be another book?' asked Escobillas.

'I mean that yesterday I burned it, and there's not a single page of the manuscript left.'

A heavy silence fell. Barrido made a conciliatory gesture and pointed to what was known as the visitors' armchair, a black, sunken throne in which authors and suppliers were cornered so that they could meet Barrido's eyes from the appropriate height.

'Martín, sit down and tell me what this is about. There's something worrying you, I can see. You can be open with us – we're like family.'

Lady Venom and Escobillas nodded with conviction, showing the measure of their esteem in a look of spellbound devotion. I decided to remain standing. They all did the same, staring at me as if I were a pillar of salt that was about to start talking. Barrido's face hurt from so much smiling.

'And?'

'Ignatius B. Samson has committed suicide. He left a twenty-page unpublished story in which he dies together with Chloé Permanyer, locked in an embrace after swallowing poison.'

'The author dies in one of his own novels?' asked Herminia, confused.

'It's his avant-garde farewell to the world of writing instalments. A detail I was sure you would love.'

'And could there not be an antidote, or . . .?' Lady Venom asked.

'Martín, I don't need to remind you that it is you, and not the allegedly deceased Ignatius, who has a contract—' said Escobillas.

Barrido raised his hands to silence his colleague.

'I think I know what's wrong, Martín. You're exhausted. You've been overloading your brain for years without a break – something this house values and is grateful for. You just need a breather. I can understand. We do understand, don't we?'

Barrido glanced at Escobillas and at Lady Venom, who nodded and tried to look serious.

'You're an artist and you want to make art, high literature, something that springs from your heart and will engrave your name in golden letters on the steps of history.'

'The way you put it makes it sound ridiculous,' I said.

'Because it is,' said Escobillas.

'No, it isn't,' Barrido cut in. 'It's human. And we're human. I, my partner and Herminia, who, being a woman and a creature of delicate sensitivity, is the most human of all, isn't that right, Herminia?'

'Indeed,' Lady Venom agreed.

'And as we're human, we understand you and want to support you. Because we're proud of you and convinced that your success will be our success and because in this firm, when all's said and done, what matters is the people, not the numbers.'

At the end of his speech, Barrido gave a theatrical pause. Perhaps he expected me to break into applause, but when he saw that I wasn't moved he charged on unimpeded with his exposition.

'That is why I'm going to propose the following: take six months, nine if need be, because after all this is like a birth, and lock yourself up in your study to write the great novel of your life. When you've finished it, bring it to us and we'll publish it under your name, putting all our irons in the fire and all our resources behind you. Because we're on your side.'

I looked at Barrido and then at Escobillas. Lady Venom was about to burst into tears from the emotion.

'With no advance, needless to say.'

Barrido clapped his hands euphorically in the air.

'What do you say?'

I began work that very day. My plan was as simple as it was crazy. During the day I would rewrite Vidal's book and at night I'd work on mine. I would polish all the dark arts Ignatius B. Samson had taught me and place them at the service of what little decency and dignity was left in my heart. I would write out of gratitude, despair and vanity. I would write especially for Cristina, to prove to her that I too was able to pay the debt I had with Vidal and that even if he was about to drop dead, David Martín had earned himself the right to look her in the eye without feeling ashamed of his ridiculous hopes.

I didn't return to Doctor Trías's surgery. I didn't see the point. The day I could no longer write another word, or imagine one, I would be the first to know. My trustworthy and unscrupulous chemist supplied me with as many codeine treats as I requested without asking any questions, as well as the occasional delicacy that set my veins alight, obliterating both pain and consciousness. I didn't tell anyone about my visit to the doctor or about the test results.

My basic needs were covered by a weekly delivery which I ordered from Can Gispert, a wonderful grocer's emporium on Calle Mirallers, behind the cathedral of Santa María del Mar. The order was always the same. It was usually brought to me by the owners' daughter, a girl who stared at me like a frightened fawn when I told her to wait in the entrance hall while I fetched the money to pay her.

'This is for your father, and this is for you.'

I always gave her a ten-céntimo tip, which she accepted without saying a word. Every week the girl rang my doorbell with the delivery, and every week I paid her and gave her a ten-céntimo tip. For nine months and a day, the time it took me to write the only book that would bear my name, that young girl, whose name I didn't know and whose face I forgot every week until I saw her standing in the doorway again, was the person I saw the most.

Without warning, Cristina had stopped coming to our afternoon meetings. I was beginning to fear that Vidal might have got wind of our ploy. Then, one afternoon, when I was waiting for her after about a week's absence, I opened the door thinking it was her, and instead there was Pep, one of the servants at Villa Helius. He brought me a parcel sent by Cristina. It was carefully sealed and contained the whole of Vidal's manuscript. Pep explained that Cristina's father had suffered an aneurysm which had left him practically disabled, and she'd taken him to a sanatorium in Puigcerdà, in the Pyrenees, where apparently there was a young doctor who was an expert in the treatment of such ailments.

'Señor Vidal has taken care of everything,' Pep explained. 'No expense spared.'

Vidal never forgot his servants, I thought, not without some bitterness.

'She asked me to deliver this to you by hand. And not to tell anyone about it.'

The young man handed me the parcel, relieved to be free of the mysterious item.

'Did she leave an address where I could find her if I needed to?'

'No, Señor Martín. All I know is that Señorita Cristina's father has been admitted to a place called Villa San Antonio.'

A few days later, Vidal paid me one of his surprise visits and spent the whole afternoon in my house, drinking my anisette, smoking my cigarettes and talking to me about his chauffeur's misfortune.

'It's hard to believe. A man who was as strong as an ox, and suddenly he's struck down, just like that. He doesn't even know who he is any more.'

'How is Cristina?'

'You can imagine. Her mother died years ago and Manuel is the only family she has left. She took a family album with her and shows him photographs every day to see whether the poor fellow can remember anything.'

While Vidal spoke, his novel – or should I say my novel – rested face down on the table in the gallery, a pile of papers only half a metre away from his hands. He told me that in Manuel's absence he had urged Pep – apparently a good horseman – to get stuck into the art of driving, but so far the young man was proving hopeless.

'Give him time. A motor car isn't a horse. The secret is practice.'

'Now that you mention it, Manuel taught you how to drive, didn't he?'

'A little,' I admitted. 'And it's not as easy as it seems.'

'If the novel you're writing doesn't sell, you can always become my chauffeur.'

'Let's not bury poor Manuel yet, Don Pedro.'

'That comment was in bad taste,' Vidal admitted. 'I'm sorry.'

'How's your novel going, Don Pedro?'

'It's going well. Cristina has taken the final manuscript with her to Puigcerdà so that she can type up a clean copy and get it all shipshape while she's there with her father.'

'I'm glad to see you looking happy.'

Vidal gave me a triumphant smile.

'I think it's going to be something big,' he said. 'After all those months I thought I'd wasted, I reread the first fifty pages Cristina typed out for me and I was quite surprised at myself. I think it will surprise you too. I may still have some tricks to teach you.'

'I've never doubted that, Don Pedro.'

That afternoon Vidal was drinking more than usual. Over the years I'd got to know the full range of his anxieties and reservations, and I guessed that this visit was not a simple courtesy call. When he had polished off my supplies of anis, I served him a generous glass of brandy and waited.

'David, there are things about which you and I have never spoken . . .'

'About football, for example.'

'I'm serious.'

'I'm listening, Don Pedro.'

He looked at me for a while, hesitating.

'I've always tried to be a good friend to you, David. You know that, don't you?'

'You've been much more than that, Don Pedro. I know and you know.'

'Sometimes I ask myself whether I shouldn't have been more honest with you.'

'About what?'

Vidal stared into his glass of brandy.

'There are some things I've never told you, David. Things that perhaps I should have told you years ago . . .'

I let a moment or two go by. It seemed an eternity. Whatever Vidal wanted to tell me, it was clear that all the brandy in the world wasn't going to get it out of him.

'Don't worry, Don Pedro. If these things have waited for years, I'm sure they can wait until tomorrow.'

'Tomorrow I may not have the courage to tell you.'

I realised that I had never seen him look so frightened. Something had got stuck in his heart and I was beginning to feel uncomfortable.

'Here's what we'll do, Don Pedro. When your book and mine are published we'll get together to celebrate and you can tell me whatever it is you need to tell me. Invite me to one of those expensive places I'm not allowed into unless I'm with you, and then you can confide in me as much as you like. Does that sound all right?'

When it started to get dark I went with him as far as Paseo del Borne, where Pep was waiting by the Hispano-Suiza, wearing Manuel's uniform – which was far too big for him, as was the motor car. The bodywork was peppered with unsightly new scratches and bumps.

'Keep at a relaxed trot, eh, Pep?' I advised him. 'No galloping. Slowly but surely, as if it were a draught horse.'

'Yes, Señor Martín. Slowly but surely.'

When he left, Vidal hugged me tightly, and as he got into the car it seemed to me that he was carrying the whole world on his shoulders.

16

A few days after I had put the finishing touches to both novels, Vidal's and my own, Pep turned up at my house unannounced. He was wearing the uniform inherited from Manuel that made him look like a boy dressed up as a field marshal. At first I thought he was bringing me some message from Vidal, or perhaps from Cristina, but his sombre expression spoke of an anxiety that made me rule out that possibility as soon as our eyes met.

'Bad news, Señor Martín.'

'What has happened?'

'It's Señor Manuel.'

While he was explaining what had happened his voice faltered, and when I asked him whether he wanted a glass of water he almost burst into tears. Manuel Sagnier had died three days earlier at the sanatorium in Puigcerdà after prolonged suffering. At his daughter's request he had been buried the day before in a small cemetery at the foot of the Pyrenees.

'Dear God,' I murmured.

Instead of water I handed Pep a large glass of brandy and parked him in an armchair in the gallery. When he was calmer, Pep explained that Vidal had sent him to meet Cristina, who was returning that afternoon on a train due to arrive at five o'clock.

'Imagine how Señorita Cristina must be feeling . . .' he mumbled, distressed at the thought of having to be the one to meet her and comfort her on the journey back to the small apartment above the coach house of Villa Helius, the home she had shared with her father since she was a little girl.

'Pep, I don't think it's a good idea for you to go and meet Señorita Sagnier.'

'Orders from Don Pedro.'

'Tell Don Pedro that I'll do it.'

By dint of alcohol and persuasion I convinced him that he should go home and leave the matter in my hands. I would meet her and take her to Villa Helius in a taxi.

'I'm very grateful, Señor Martín. You're a man of letters so you'll have a better idea of what to say to the poor thing.'

At a quarter to five I made my way towards the recently opened Estación de Francia railway station. That year's International Exhibition had left the city strewn with wonders, but my favourite was that temple-like vault of glass and steel, even if only because it was so close and I could see it from the study in the tower house. That afternoon the sky was scattered with black clouds galloping in from the sea and clustering over the city. Flashes of lightning echoed on the horizon and a charged warm wind smelling of dust announced a powerful summer storm. When I reached the station I noticed the first few drops, shiny and heavy, like coins falling from heaven. By the time I walked down to the platform where the train was due to arrive the rain was already pounding the station's vaulted roof. Night seemed to fall suddenly, interrupted only by flashes of light bursting over the city, leaving a trail of noise and fury.

The train came in almost an hour late, a serpent of steam slithering beneath the storm. I stood by the engine waiting for Cristina to appear among the passengers emerging from the carriages. Ten minutes later everybody had descended and there was still no trace of her. I was about to go back home, thinking that perhaps Cristina hadn't taken that train after all, when I decided to have a last look and walked all the way down to the end of the platform, peering carefully through all the compartment windows. I found her in the carriage before last, sitting with her head against the window, staring into the distance. I climbed into the carriage and walked up to the door of her compartment. When she heard my steps, she turned and looked at me without surprise, smiling faintly. She stood up and hugged me silently.

'Welcome back,' I said.

Cristina's only baggage was a small suitcase. I gave her my hand and we went down to the platform, which by now was deserted. We walked all the way to the main foyer without exchanging a word. When we reached the exit we stopped. It was raining hard and the line of taxis that had been there when I arrived had vanished.

'I don't want to return to Villa Helius tonight, David. Not yet.'

'You can stay at my house if you like, or we can find you a room in a hotel.'

'I don't want to be alone.'

'Let's go home. If there's one thing I have it's too many bedrooms.'

I sighted a porter who had put his head out to look at the storm and was holding an impressive-looking umbrella. I went up to him and offered to buy it for five times its real value. He gave it to me wreathed in an obliging smile.

Protected by that umbrella we ventured out into the deluge and headed towards the tower house, at which we arrived completely drenched ten minutes later, thanks to the gusts of wind and the puddles. The storm had caused a power cut; the streets were buried in a liquid darkness speckled here and there with the light cast by oil lamps or candles from balconies and doors. I had no doubt that the marvellous electrical system in my house must have been one of the first to succumb. We had to fumble our way up the stairs and when we opened the front door of the apartment, a breath of lightning emphasised its gloomiest and most inhospitable aspect.

'If you've changed your mind and you'd rather we looked for a hotel . . .'

'No, it's fine. Don't worry.'

I left Cristina's suitcase in the hall and went to the kitchen in search of a box of assorted candles I kept in the larder. I started to light them, one by one, fixing them on plates, and in tumblers and glasses. Cristina watched me from the door.

'It will only take a minute,' I assured her. 'I have a lot of practice.'

I began to distribute the candles around the rooms, along the corridor and in various corners, until the whole house was enveloped in a flickering twilight of pale gold.

'It looks like a cathedral,' Cristina said.

I took her to one of the rooms that I didn't use but kept clean and tidy because of the few times Vidal, too drunk to return to his mansion, had stayed the night.

'I'll bring you some clean towels. If you don't have anything to change into, I can offer you a wide selection of dreadful belle époque clothes, which the former owners left in the wardrobes.'

My clumsy attempt at humour barely drew a smile from her, and she simply nodded. I left her sitting on the bed while I rushed off to fetch the towels. When I returned she was still sitting there, motionless. I left the towels next to her on the bed and brought over a couple of candles that I'd placed by the door, to give her a bit more light.

'Thanks,' she murmured.

'While you change I'll go and prepare some hot soup for you.'

'I'm not hungry.'

'It will do you good, all the same. If you need anything, let me know.'

I left her alone and went off to my room to remove my sodden shoes. I put water on to boil and sat waiting in the gallery. The rain was still crashing down, angrily machine-gunning the large windows; it poured through the gutters up in the tower and funnelled along the flat roof, sounding like footsteps on the ceiling. Further out, the Ribera quarter was plunged into almost total darkness.

After a while the door of Cristina's room opened and I heard her approaching. She was wearing a white dressing gown and had thrown an ugly woollen shawl over her shoulders.

'I've borrowed this from one of the wardrobes,' she said. 'I hope you don't mind.'

'You can keep it if you like.'

She sat in one of the armchairs and glanced round the room, stopping to look at a pile of paper on the table. She looked at me and I nodded.

'I finished it a few days ago,' I said.

'And yours?'

I thought of both manuscripts as mine, but I just nodded again.

'May I?' she asked, taking a page and bringing it nearer the candlelight.

'Of course.'

I watched her read, a thin smile on her lips.

'Pedro will never believe he's written this,' she said.

'Trust me,' I replied.

Cristina put the sheet back on the pile and looked at me for a long time.

'I've missed you,' she said. 'I didn't want to, but I have.'

'Me too.'

'Some days, before going to the sanatorium, I'd walk to the station and sit on the platform to wait for the train coming from Barcelona, hoping you might be on it.'

I swallowed hard.

'I thought you didn't want to see me,' I said.

'That's what I thought, too. My father often asked after you, you know? He asked me to look after you.'

'Your father was a good man,' I said. 'A good friend.'

Cristina nodded and smiled, but I could see that her eyes were filling with tears.

'In the end he couldn't remember anything. There were days when he confused me with my mother and would ask me to forgive him for the years he spent in prison. Then weeks would go by when he hardly seemed to notice I was there. Over time, loneliness gets inside you and doesn't go away.'

'I'm sorry, Cristina.'

'In the last few days I thought he was better. He was beginning to remember things. I had brought with me one of his albums and I started to show him the photographs again, pointing out who was who. There is one very old picture, taken in Villa Helius, in which you and he are both sitting in the motor car. You're at the steering wheel and my father is teaching you how to drive. You're both laughing. Do you want to see it?'

I hesitated, but didn't dare break that moment.

'Of course . . .'

Cristina went to look for the album in her suitcase and returned with a small book bound in leather. She sat next to me and started turning the pages, which were filled with old snapshots, cuttings and postcards. Manuel, like my father, had barely learned to read and write and his memories were mostly made up of images.

'Look, here you are.'

I looked at the photograph and vividly recalled the summer day when Manuel had let me climb into the first car Vidal ever bought and had taught me the basics of driving. Then we had taken the car out along Calle Panamá and, doing about five kilometres per hour – a dizzying speed to me at the time – had driven as far as Avenida Pearson, returning with me at the wheel.

'You're an ace driver!' Manuel had concluded. 'If you're ever stuck with your stories, you could consider a future in racing.'

I smiled, remembering that moment which I thought I had lost. Cristina handed me the album.

'Keep it. My father would have liked you to have it.'

'It's yours, Cristina. I can't accept it.'

'I would rather you kept it.'

'It's in storage then, until you want to come and collect it.'

I started to turn the pages, revisiting faces I remembered and gazing at others I had never seen. There was the wedding photograph of Manuel Sagnier and his wife Marta, whom Cristina resembled a great deal, studio portraits of Cristina's uncles and grandparents, a picture of a street in the Raval quarter with a procession going by, another of the San Sebastián bathing area on La Barceloneta beach. Manuel had collected old postcards of Barcelona and newspaper cuttings with photos of a very young Vidal – one of him posing by the doors of the Hotel Florida at the top of Mount Tibidabo, and another where he stood arm in arm with a staggering beauty in the halls of La Rabasada casino.

'Your father worshipped Don Pedro.'

'He always said we owed everything to him,' Cristina answered.

I continued to travel through poor Manuel's memories until I came to a page with a photograph that didn't seem to fit in with the rest. It was a picture of a girl of about eight or nine, walking along a small wooden jetty that stretched out into a sheet of luminous sea. She was holding the hand of an adult, a man dressed in a white suit, who was partly cut off by the frame. At the end of the jetty you could make out a small sailing boat and an endless horizon on which the sun was setting. The girl, who was standing with her back to the camera, was Cristina.

'This is my favourite,' murmured Cristina.

'Where was it taken?'

'I don't know. I don't remember that place or that day. I'm not even sure whether that man is my father. It's as if the moment never existed. I found the picture years ago in my father's album and I've never known what it means. It seems to be trying to say something to me.'

I went on turning the pages while Cristina told me who each person was.

'Look, this is me when I was fourteen.'

'I know.'

Cristina looked at me sadly.

'I didn't realise, did I?'

I shrugged my shoulders.

'You'll never be able to forgive me.'

I preferred to go on turning the pages than to look into her eyes.

'There's nothing to forgive.'

'Look at me, David.'

I closed the album and did as she asked.

'It's a lie,' she said. 'I did realise. I realised every day, but I thought I had no right.'

'Why?'

'Because our lives don't belong to us. Not mine, not my father's, not yours . . .'

'Everything belongs to Vidal,' I said bitterly.

Slowly, she took my hand and brought it to her lips.

'Not today,' she murmured.

I knew I was going to lose her as soon as the night was over, and the pain and loneliness that were gnawing at her went away. I knew she was right, not because what she had said was true, but because, deep down, we both believed it and it would always be the same. We hid like two thieves in one of the rooms without daring to light a single candle, without even daring to speak. I undressed her slowly, going over her skin with my lips, conscious that I would never do so again. Cristina gave herself with anger and abandon, and when we were overcome by exhaustion she fell asleep in my arms without feeling the need to say anything. I fought off sleep, enjoying the warmth of her body and thinking that if the following day death should come to take me away, I would go in peace. I caressed Cristina in the dark, listening to the storm outside as it left the city, knowing that I was going to lose her but also knowing that, for a few minutes, we had belonged to one another, and to nobody else.

When the first breath of dawn touched the windows I opened my eyes and found the bed empty. I went out into the corridor and as far as the gallery. Cristina had left the album and had taken Vidal's novel. I went through the whole house, which already smelled of her absence, and one by one blew out the candles I had lit the night before.

17

Nine weeks later I was standing in front of number 17, Plaza de Cataluña, where the Catalonia bookshop had opened its doors two years earlier. I was staring in amazement at what seemed to be an endless display filled with copies of a novel called *The House of Ashes* by Pedro Vidal. I smiled to myself. My mentor had even used the title I had suggested to him years before when I had given him the idea for the story. I decided to go in and ask for a copy. I opened it at random and began to reread passages I knew by heart, for I had only finished going over them a couple of months earlier. I didn't find a single word in the whole book that I hadn't put there myself, except for the dedication: 'For Cristina Sagnier, without whom . . .'

When I handed the book back to the shop assistant he told me not to think twice about buying it.

'We received it two days ago and I've already read it,' he added. 'A great novel. Take my advice and buy it now. I know the papers are praising it to the skies and that's usually a bad sign, but in this case it's the exception that proves the rule. If you don't like it, bring it to me and I'll give you your money back.'

'Thanks,' I replied. Knowing what I knew his recommendation was flattering. 'But I've read it too.'

'May I interest you in something else?'

'You don't have a novel called *The Steps of Heaven*?'

The bookseller thought for a moment.

'That's the one by Martín, isn't it? I heard a rumour he also wrote *City* . . .'

I nodded.

'I've asked for it, but the publishers haven't sent me any copies. Let me have a good look.'

I followed him to the counter, where he consulted one of his colleagues, who shook his head.

'It was meant to arrive yesterday, but the publisher says he has no

93

copies. I'm sorry. If you like, I'll reserve one for you when we get them . . .'

'Don't worry. I'll come back another day. And thank you very much.'

'I'm sorry, sir. I don't know what can have happened. As I say, I should have had it . . .'

When I left the bookshop I went over to a newspaper stand at the top of the Ramblas. There I bought a copy of every newspaper, from *La Vanguardia* to *The Voice of Industry*. I sat down in the Canaletas Café and began delving into their pages. Each paper carried a review of the novel I had written for Vidal, full page, with large headlines and a portrait of Don Pedro looking meditative and mysterious, wearing a new suit and puffing on a pipe with studied disdain. I began to read the headlines and then the first and last paragraphs of the reviews.

The first one I found opened with these words: '*The House of Ashes* is a mature, rich work of great quality which takes its place among the best examples of contemporary literature.' Another paper informed the reader that 'nobody in Spain writes better than Pedro Vidal, our most respected and noteworthy novelist', and a third asserted that this was a 'superlative novel, of masterful craftsmanship and exquisite quality'. A fourth newspaper summed up the great international success of Vidal and his work: 'Europe bows to the master' (although the novel had only come out two days earlier in Spain and, were it to be translated, wouldn't appear in any other country for at least a year). The piece then went into a long-winded ramble about the great international acclaim and huge respect that Vidal's name aroused among 'the most famous international experts', even though, as far as I knew, none of his other books had been translated into any language, except for a novel whose translation into French he himself had financed and which had only sold a hundred and twenty-six copies. Miracles aside, the consensus of the press was that 'a classic has been born', and that the novel marked 'the return of one of the greats, the best pen of our times: Vidal, undisputed master'.

On the opposite page in some of those papers, covering a far more modest space of one or two columns, I also found a few reviews of a novel by someone called David Martín. The most favourable began like this: 'A first novel, written in a pedestrian style, *The Steps of Heaven*, by the novice David Martín, shows the author's lack of skill and talent from the very first page.' The last review I could bring myself to read, published in *The Voice of Industry*, opened succinctly with a short introduction in bold letters that stated: 'David Martín, a completely unknown author, and writer of classified advertisements, surprises us with what is perhaps this year's worst literary debut.'

I left the newspapers and the coffee I had ordered on the table and made my way down the Ramblas to the offices of Barrido & Escobillas. On the way I passed four or five bookshops, all of which were decorated with countless copies of Vidal's novel. In none did I see a single copy of mine. My experience in the Catalonia bookshop was repeated in each place.

'I'm sorry, I don't know what can have happened. It was meant to arrive the day before yesterday, but the publisher says he's run out of stock and doesn't know when he'll be reprinting. If you'd care to leave me your name and a telephone number, I can let you know if it arrives . . . Have you asked in Catalonia? Well, if they don't have it . . .'

The two partners received me with grim, unfriendly expressions: Barrido, behind his desk, stroking a fountain pen, and Escobillas, standing behind him, boring through me with his eyes. Lady Venom, who sat on a chair next to me, was licking her lips with anticipation.

'I can't tell you how sorry I am, my dear Martín,' Barrido was explaining. 'The problem is as follows. The booksellers place their orders based on the reviews that appear in the papers – don't ask me why. If you go into the warehouse next door you'll see that we have three thousand copies of your novel just lying there.'

'With all the expense and the loss which that entails,' Escobillas completed in a clearly hostile tone.

'I stopped by the warehouse before coming here and I saw for myself that there were three hundred copies. The manager told me that's all they printed.'

'That's a lie,' Escobillas proclaimed.

Barrido interrupted him in a conciliatory tone.

'Please excuse my partner, Martín. You must understand that we're just as indignant as you, or even more so, about the disgraceful treatment the press has given a book with which all of us at the firm were so in love. But I beg you to understand that, despite our faith in your talent, our hands are tied because of all the confusion created by the malicious press. However, don't be disheartened. Rome was not built in a day. We're doing everything in our power to give your work the promotion its estimable literary merit deserves—'

'With a three-hundred-copy print run.'

Barrido sighed, hurt by my lack of trust.

'It's a five-hundred-copy print run,' Escobillas specified. 'The other two hundred were collected by Barceló and Sempere in person yesterday. The rest will go out with our next delivery; they couldn't go out with this one because there were too many new titles. If you bothered to understand our problems and weren't so selfish you would recognise this.'

I looked at the three of them in disbelief.

'Don't tell me you're not going to do anything.'

Barrido gave me a mournful look.

'And what would you have us do, my friend? We have bet everything on you. Try to help us a little.'

'If only you'd written a book like the one your friend Vidal has written,' said Escobillas.

'Now that was one hell of a novel,' Barrido asserted. 'Even *The Voice of Industry* says so.'

'I knew this was going to happen,' Escobillas went on. 'You're so ungrateful.'

Lady Venom, sitting by my side, was looking at me sadly. I thought she was going to take my hand to comfort me so I quickly moved it away. Barrido gave me one of his unctuous smiles.

'Maybe it's all for the best, Martín. Maybe it's a sign from Our Lord, who, in his infinite wisdom, wants to show you the way back to the work that has given so much happiness to the readers of *City of the Damned*.'

I burst out laughing. Barrido joined in and, at this signal from him, so did Escobillas and Lady Venom. I watched the choir of hyenas and told myself that, under other circumstances, this would have seemed a moment of delicious irony.

'That's better. I like to see you handling this with a positive attitude,' Barrido proclaimed. 'What do you say? When will we have the next instalment by Ignatius B. Samson?'

The three of them looked at me expectantly. I cleared my throat so I could speak clearly and smiled at them.

'You can go screw yourselves.'

18

On leaving, I wandered aimlessly for hours round the streets of Barcelona. I was finding it difficult to breathe, as if something were pressing down on my chest. A cold sweat covered my forehead and hands. When evening fell, not knowing where else to hide, I started to make my way back home. As I passed Sempere & Sons, I saw the bookseller filling his shop window with copies of my novel. It was already late and the shop was closed, but the light was still on. I tried to rush past, but Sempere noticed me and smiled with a sadness that I had never seen on his face before. He went over to the door and opened it.

'Come in for a while, Martín.'

'Some other day, Señor Sempere.'

'Do it for me.'

He took me by the arm and dragged me into the bookshop. I followed him to the back room and he offered me a chair. He poured two glasses of something that looked thicker than tar and motioned to me to down it in one, as he did.

'I've been glancing through Vidal's book,' he said.

'This season's success story,' I pointed out.

'Does he know you've written it?'

'What does it matter?' I said, shrugging my shoulders.

Sempere looked at me the same way he'd looked at that eight-year-old boy who had come to his house one distant day with a bruised face and broken teeth.

'Are you all right, Martín?'

'I'm fine.'

Sempere shook his head, muttering to himself, and got up to take something from one of the shelves. It was a copy of my novel. He handed it to me with a pen and smiled.

'Please sign it for me.'

When I'd finished writing something for him, Sempere took the book from my hands and placed it carefully in the glass case behind the counter where he displayed first editions that were not for sale. It was his private shrine.

'You don't have to do that, Señor Sempere,' I mumbled.

'I'm doing it because I want to and because the occasion demands it. This book is a piece of your heart, Martín. And it is also a piece of my heart, for the small part I played in it. I'll place you between *Le Père Goriot* and *L'Éducation Sentimentale*.'

'That's a sacrilege.'

'Nonsense. It's one of the best books I've sold in the last ten years, and I've sold a lot,' old Sempere said.

Sempere's kind words could only scratch the surface of the cold, impenetrable calm that was beginning to invade me. I ambled back to my house, in no hurry.

When I walked into the tower house I poured myself a glass of water. As I drank it in the kitchen, in the dark, I burst out laughing.

The following morning I received two courtesy calls. The first one was from Pep, Vidal's new chauffeur. He was bringing a message from his boss, summoning me to a lunch at La Maison Dorée – doubtless the celebration he had promised me some time ago. Pep seemed a little stiff and anxious to leave as soon as possible. The air of complicity he'd once had with me had evaporated. He wouldn't come in, preferring to wait on the landing. Without looking straight at me, he handed me Vidal's written message, and as soon as I told him I would go to the lunch, he left without saying goodbye.

The second visit, half an hour later, brought my two publishers to my door, accompanied by a forbidding-looking gentleman with piercing eyes who identified himself as a lawyer. The formidable trio arrived displaying a mixture of mourning and belligerence, leaving me in no doubt as to the purpose of the occasion. I invited them into the gallery, where they proceeded to sit down on the sofa, lined up from left to right in descending order of height.

'May I offer you anything? A small glass of cyanide?'

I was not expecting a smile and I didn't get one. After a brief preamble from Barrido concerning the terrible losses that the fiasco associated with the failure of *The Steps of Heaven* was going to cause the publishing house, the lawyer went on to give a brief exposition which, in plain language, said that if I didn't return to my work in the guise of Ignatius B. Samson and hand in a manuscript for the

City of the Damned series within a month and a half, they would proceed to sue me for breach of contract, damages and five or six other legal terms that escaped me because by then I wasn't paying attention. It was not all bad news. Despite the aggravations caused by my behaviour, Barrido and Escobillas had found a pearl of generosity in their hearts with which to smooth away our differences and establish a new alliance, a friendship, which would benefit both sides.

'If you want, you can buy all the copies of *The Steps of Heaven* that haven't been distributed at a special rate of 75 per cent of the cover price, since there is clearly no demand for the title and it will be impossible for us to include it in our next delivery,' Escobillas explained.

'Why don't you give me back my rights? After all, you didn't pay a penny for the book and you're not planning on trying to sell a single copy.'

'We can't do that, dear friend,' Barrido pointed out. 'Even if no advance materialised in front of you personally, the edition has required a huge outlay and the agreement you signed with us was for twenty years, automatically renewable under the same terms if our firm decides to exercise its rights. You have to understand that we are also entitled to something. The author can't get everything.'

When he had finished his speech I invited the gentlemen to make their way to the exit, either willingly or with the help of a kick – they could choose. Before I slammed the door in their faces, Escobillas was good enough to cast me one of his evil-eyed looks.

'We demand a reply within a week, or that will be the end of you,' he muttered.

'In a week you and that idiot partner of yours will be dead,' I replied calmly, without quite knowing why I'd uttered those words.

I spent the rest of the morning staring at the walls, until the bells of Santa María reminded me that it would soon be time for my meeting with Pedro Vidal.

He was waiting for me at the best table in the room, toying with a glass of white wine and listening to the pianist, who was playing with velvet fingers a piece by Granados. When he saw me, he stood up and held out his hand.

'Congratulations,' I said

Vidal smiled, waiting for me to sit down before sitting down himself. We let a minute of silence go by, cocooned by the music and the glances of the distinguished people who greeted Vidal from afar or came up to the table to congratulate him on his success, which was the talk of the town.

'David, you can't imagine how sorry I am about what has happened,' he began.

'Don't be sorry, enjoy it.'

'Do you think this means anything to me? The flattery of a few poor devils? My greatest joy would have been to see you succeed.'

'I'm sorry I've let you down once again, Don Pedro.'

Vidal sighed.

'David, it's not my fault if they've gone for you. It's your fault. You were crying out for it. You're quite old enough to know how these things work.'

'You tell me.'

Vidal clicked his tongue, as if my naivety offended him.

'What did you expect? You're not one of them. You never will be. You haven't wanted to be, and you think they're going to forgive you. You lock yourself up in that great rambling house and you think you can survive without joining the church choir and putting on the uniform. Well you're wrong, David. You've always been wrong. This isn't how you play the game. If you want to play alone, pack your bags and go somewhere where you can be in charge of your own destiny, if such a place exists. But if you stay here, you'd better join some parish or other – any one will do. It's that simple.'

'Is that what you do, Don Pedro? Join the parish?'

'I don't have to, David. I feed them. That's another thing you've never understood.'

'You'd be surprised at how quickly I'm learning. But don't worry, the reviews are the least of it. For better or for worse, tomorrow nobody will remember them, neither mine nor yours.'

'What's the problem, then?'

'It doesn't matter.'

'Is it those two sons-of-bitches? Barrido and the corpse-robber?'

'Forget it, Don Pedro. As you say, it's my fault. Nobody else's.'

The head waiter came over to the table with an enquiring look. I hadn't laid eyes on the menu and wasn't going to.

'The usual, for both of us,' Vidal told him.

The head waiter left with a bow. Vidal was observing me as if I were a dangerous animal locked in a cage.

'Cristina was unable to come,' he said. 'I brought this, so you could sign it for her.'

He put on the table a copy of *The Steps of Heaven* wrapped in purple paper with the Sempere & Sons stamp on it, and pushed it towards me. I made no move to pick it up. Vidal had gone pale. After his forceful remarks and his defensive tone, his manner seemed to have changed. Here comes the final thrust, I thought.

'Tell me once and for all whatever it is you want to say, Don Pedro. I won't bite.'

Vidal downed his wine in one gulp.

'There are two things I've been wanting to tell you. You're not going to like them.'

'I'm beginning to get used to that.'

'One is to do with your father.'

The bitter smile left my lips.

'I've wanted to tell you for years, but I thought it wouldn't do you any good. You're going to think I didn't tell you out of cowardice, but I swear, I swear on anything you hold sacred, that—'

'That what?' I cut in.

Vidal sighed.

'The night your father died—'

'The night he was murdered,' I corrected him icily.

'It was a mistake. Your father's death was a mistake.'

I looked at him, confused.

'Those men were not out to get him. They made a mistake.'

I recalled the look in the three gunmen's eyes, in the fog, the smell of gunpowder and my father's dark blood pouring through my hands.

'The person they wanted to kill was me,' said Vidal almost inaudibly. 'An old partner of my father's discovered that his wife and I . . .'

I closed my eyes and listened to a morbid laughter rising up inside me. My father had been riddled with bullets because of one of the great Pedro Vidal's bits of skirt.

'Please say something,' Vidal pleaded.

I opened my eyes.

'What is the second thing you were going to tell me?'

I'd never seen Vidal look so frightened. It suited him.

'I've asked Cristina to marry me.'

A long silence.

'She said yes.'

Vidal looked down. One of the waiters came over with the starters. He left them on the table, wishing us bon appétit. Vidal did not dare look at me again. The starters were getting cold. After a while I took the copy of *The Steps of Heaven* and left.

That afternoon, after leaving La Maison Dorée, I found myself making my way down the Ramblas, carrying the copy of *The Steps of Heaven*. As I drew closer to the corner with Calle del Carmen my hands began to shake. I stopped by the window of the Bagués jewellery shop, pretending to be looking at some gold lockets in the shape of fairies and flowers, dotted with rubies. The baroque and ornate facade of El Indio was just a few metres away; anyone would have thought it was a grand bazaar full of wonders and extraordinary objects, not just a shop selling fabrics and linen. I approached the store slowly and stepped into the entrance hall that led to the main door. I knew she wouldn't recognise me, that I might not recognise her, but even so I stood there for about five minutes before daring to go in. When I did, my heart was beating hard and my hands were sweating.

The walls were lined with shelves full of large rolls of fabric of all types. Shop assistants, armed with tape measures and special scissors tied to their belts, spread the beautiful textiles on the tables and displayed them as if they were precious jewels to well-bred ladies, who were accompanied by their maids and seamstresses.

'Can I help you, sir?'

The words came from a heavily built man with a high-pitched voice, dressed in a flannel suit that looked as if it was about to burst at the seams and fill the shop with floating shreds of cloth. He observed me with a condescending air and a smile midway between forced and hostile.

'No,' I mumbled.

Then I saw her. My mother was coming down a stepladder holding a handful of remnants. She wore a white blouse and I recognised her instantly. Her figure had grown a little fuller and her face, less well-chiselled than it used to be, had that slightly defeated expression that comes with routine and disappointment. The shop assistant was annoyed and kept talking to me, but I hardly heard his voice. I only saw her drawing closer, then walking past me. She looked at me for a second, and when she saw that I was watching her, she smiled meekly, the way one smiles at a customer or at one's boss, and then continued with her work. I had such a lump in my throat that I almost wasn't able to open my mouth to silence the assistant and I hurried off towards the exit, my eyes full of tears. Once I was outside I crossed over the street and went into a café. I sat at a table by the window from which I could see the door of El Indio, and I waited.

Almost an hour and a half had gone by when I saw the shop assistant who had tried to serve me come out and lower the entrance shutter. Soon afterwards the lights started to go out and some of the staff emerged. I got up and went outside. A boy of about ten was sitting by the entrance to the next-door building, looking at me. I beckoned him to come closer, and when he did so, I showed him a coin. He gave me a huge smile – I noticed he was missing a number of teeth.

'See this packet? I want you to give it to a lady who is about to come out right now. Tell her that a gentleman asked you to give it to her, but don't tell her it was me. Understood?'

The boy nodded. I gave him the coin and the book.

'Now we'll wait.'

We didn't have to wait long. Three minutes later I saw her coming out. She was heading for the Ramblas.

'It's that lady, see?'

My mother stopped for a moment by the portico of the church of Belén and I made a sign to the boy, who ran after her. I watched the scene from a short distance away, but could not hear her words. The boy handed her the packet and she gave it a puzzled look, not sure whether to accept it or not. The boy insisted and finally she took the parcel in her hands and watched the boy run away. Disconcerted, she turned to right and left, searching with her eyes. She weighed up the packet, examining the purple wrapping paper. Finally curiosity got the better of her and she opened it.

I watched her take the book out. She held it with both hands, looking at the cover, then turning it over to examine the back. I could hardly breathe and wanted to go up to her and say something, but couldn't. I stood there, only a few metres away from my mother, spying on her without her being aware of my presence, until she set off again, clutching the book, walking towards Colón. As she passed the Palace of La Virreina she went over to a waste bin and threw the book inside. I watched as she headed down the Ramblas until she was lost among the crowd, as if she had never been there at all.

19

Sempere was alone in the bookshop, gluing down the spine of a copy of *Fortunata and Jacinta* that was coming apart. When he looked up, he saw me on the other side of the door. In just a few seconds he realised the state I was in and signalled to me to come in. As soon as I was inside, he offered me a chair.

'You don't look well, Martín. You should go and see a doctor. If you're scared I'll come with you. Physicians make my flesh crawl too, with their white gowns and those sharp things in their hands, but sometimes you've got to go through with it.'

'It's just a headache, Señor Sempere. It's already getting better.'

Sempere poured me a glass of Vichy water.

'Here. This cures everything, except for stupidity, which is an epidemic on the rise.'

I smiled weakly at Sempere's joke, then drank down the water and sighed. I felt a wave of nausea and an intense pressure throbbed behind my left eye. For a moment I thought I was going to collapse and I closed my eyes. I took a deep breath, praying I wouldn't drop dead right there. Destiny couldn't have such a perverse sense of humour as to guide me to Sempere's bookshop so I that could present him with a corpse, after all he'd done for me. I felt a hand holding my head gently. Sempere. I opened my eyes and saw the bookseller and his son, who had just stepped in, watching me as if they were at a wake.

'Shall I call the doctor?' Sempere's son asked.

'I'm better, thanks. Much better.'

'Your way of getting better makes one's hair stand on end. You look grey.'

'A bit more water?'

Sempere's son rushed to fill me another glass.

'Forgive the performance,' I said. 'I can assure you I hadn't rehearsed it.'

'Don't talk nonsense!'

'It might do you good to eat something sweet. Maybe it was a drop in your sugar levels . . .' the boy suggested.

'Run over to the baker's on the corner and get him something,' the bookseller agreed.

When we were left alone, Sempere fixed his eyes on mine.

'I promise I'll go to the doctor,' I said.

A few minutes later the bookseller's son returned with a paper bag full of the most select assortment of buns in the area. He handed it to me and I chose a brioche which, any other time, would have seemed to me as tempting as a chorus girl's backside.

'Bite,' Sempere ordered.

I ate my brioche obediently, and slowly I began to feel better.

'He seems to be reviving,' Sempere's son observed.

'What the corner-shop buns can't cure—'

At that moment we heard the doorbell. A customer had come into the bookshop and, at Sempere's nod, his son left us to serve him. The bookseller stayed by my side, trying to feel my pulse by pressing on my wrist with his index finger.

'Señor Sempere, do you remember, many years ago, when you said that if one day I needed to save a book, really save it, I should come to see you?'

Sempere glanced at the rejected book I had rescued from the bin, which I was still holding in my hands.

'Give me five minutes.'

It was beginning to get dark when we walked down the Ramblas among a crowd who had come out for a stroll on a hot, humid afternoon. There was only the hint of a breeze; balcony doors and windows were wide open, with people leaning out of them, watching the human parade under an amber-coloured sky. Sempere walked quickly and didn't slow down until we sighted an arcade of shadows at the entrance to Calle Arco del Teatro.

Before crossing over he looked at me solemnly and said: 'Martín, you mustn't tell anyone what you're about to see. Not even Vidal. No one.'

I nodded, intrigued by the bookseller's air of seriousness and secrecy. I followed him through the narrow street, barely a gap between bleak and dilapidated buildings that seemed to bend over like willows of stone, attempting to close the narrow strip of sky between the rooftops. Soon we reached a large wooden door that looked as if it might be guarding the entrance to an old basilica that had spent a century at the bottom of a lake. Sempere went up the steps to the door and took hold of the brass knocker shaped like a smiling demon's face. He knocked three times then came down the steps again to wait by my side.

'You can't tell anyone what you're about to see . . . no one. Not even Vidal. No one.'

Sempere nodded severely. We waited for about two minutes until we heard what sounded like a hundred bolts being unlocked simultaneously. With a deep groan, the large door opened halfway and a middle-aged man with thick grey hair, a face like a vulture and penetrating eyes stuck his head round it.

'We were doing just fine and now here's Sempere!' he snapped. 'What are you bringing me today? Another aficionado who hasn't got himself a girlfriend because he'd rather live with his mother?'

Sempere paid no attention to this sarcastic greeting.

'Martín, this is Isaac Monfort, the keeper of this place. His friendliness has no equal. Do everything he says. Isaac, this is David Martín, a good friend, a writer and a trustworthy person.'

The man called Isaac looked me up and down without much enthusiasm and then exchanged a glance with Sempere.

'A writer is never trustworthy. Let's see, has Sempere explained the rules to you?'

'Only that I can never tell anyone what I will see here.'

'That is the first and most important rule. If you don't keep it, I personally will wring your neck. Do you get the idea?'

'One hundred per cent.'

'Come on, then,' said Isaac, motioning me to come in.

'I'll say goodbye now, Martín. You'll find a safe place here.'

I realised that Sempere was referring to the book, not to me. He hugged me and then disappeared into the night. I stepped inside and Isaac pulled a lever on the back of the door. A thousand mechanisms, knotted together in a web of rails and pulleys, sealed it up. Isaac took a lamp from the floor and raised it to my face.

'You don't look well,' he pronounced.

'Indigestion,' I replied.

'From what?'

'Reality.'

'Join the queue.'

We walked down a long corridor, and on either side, through the shadows, I thought I could make out frescoes and marble staircases. We advanced further into the palatial building and shortly there appeared, in front of us, what looked like the entrance to a large hall.

'What have you got there?' Isaac asked.

'*The Steps of Heaven*. A novel.'

'What a tacky title. Don't tell me you're the author.'

'Who, me?'

Isaac sighed, shaking his head and mumbling to himself.

'And what else have you written?'

'*City of the Damned*, volumes one to twenty-seven, among other things.'

Isaac turned round and smiled with satisfaction.

'Ignatius B. Samson?'

'May he rest in peace, and at your service.'

At that point, the mysterious keeper stopped and left the lamp resting on what looked like a balustrade rising in front of a large vault. I looked up and was spellbound. There before me stood a colossal labyrinth of bridges, passages and shelves full of hundreds of thousands of books, forming a gigantic library of seemingly impossible perspectives. Tunnels zigzagged through the immense structure, which seemed to rise in a spiral towards a large glass dome, curtains of light and darkness filtering through it. Here and there I could see isolated figures walking along footbridges, up stairs, or carefully examining the contents of the passageways of that cathedral of books and words. I couldn't believe my eyes and I looked at Isaac Monfort in astonishment. He was smiling like an old fox enjoying his favourite game.

'Ignatius B. Samson, welcome to the Cemetery of Forgotten Books.'

20

I followed the keeper to the foot of the large nave that housed the labyrinth. The floor we were stepping over was sewn with tombstones, their inscriptions, crosses and faces dissolving into the stone. The keeper stopped and lowered the gas lamp so that the light slid over some of the pieces of the macabre puzzle.

'The remains of an old necropolis,' he explained. 'But don't let that give you any ideas about dropping dead here.'

We continued towards an area just before the central structure that seemed to form a kind of threshold. In the meantime Isaac was rattling off the rules and duties, fixing his gaze on me from time to time, while I tried to soothe him with docile assent.

'Article one: the first time somebody comes here he has the right to choose a book, whichever one he likes, from all the books there are in this place. Article two: upon adopting a book you undertake to protect it and do all you can to ensure it is never lost. For life. Any questions so far?'

I looked up towards the immensity of the labyrinth.

'How does one choose a single book among so many?'

Isaac shrugged his shoulders.

'Some like to believe it's the book that chooses the person . . . destiny, in other words. What you see here is the sum of centuries of books that have been lost and forgotten, books condemned to be destroyed and silenced forever, books that preserve the memory and soul of times and marvels that no one remembers any more. None of us, not even the eldest, knows exactly when it was created or by whom. It's probably as old as the city itself, and has been growing with it, in its shadow. We know the building was erected using the remains of palaces, churches, prisons and hospitals that may once have stood here. The origin of the main structure goes back to the beginning of the eighteenth century and has not stopped evolving since then. Before that, the Cemetery of Forgotten Books was hidden under the tunnels of the medieval town. Some say that, during the time of the Inquisition, people who were learned and had free minds would hide forbidden books in sarcophagi, or bury them in ossuaries all over the city to protect them, trusting that future generations would dig them up. In the middle of the last century a long tunnel was discovered leading from the bowels of the labyrinth to the basement of an old library that nowadays is sealed off, hidden in the ruins of an old synagogue in the Jewish quarter. When the last of the old city walls came down, there was a landslide and the tunnel was flooded with water from an underground stream that for centuries has run beneath what is now the Ramblas. It's inaccessible at present, but we imagine that for a long time the tunnel was one of the main entrance routes to this place. Most of the structure you can see was developed during the nineteenth century. Only about a hundred people know about it and I hope Sempere hasn't made a mistake by including you among them . . .'

I shook my head vigorously, but Isaac was looking at me with scepticism.

'Article three: you can bury your own book wherever you like.'

'What if I get lost?'

'An additional clause, from my own stable: try not to get lost.'

'Has anyone ever got lost?'

Isaac snorted.

'When I started here years ago there was a story doing the rounds about Darío Alberti de Cymerman. I don't suppose Sempere has told you this, of course . . .'

'Cymerman? The historian?'

'No, the seal tamer. How many Darío Alberti de Cymermans do you know? What happened is that in the winter of 1889 Cymerman went into the labyrinth and disappeared inside it for a whole week. He was found in one of the tunnels, half dead with fright. He had walled himself up behind a few rows of holy texts so he couldn't be seen.'

'Seen by whom?'

Isaac looked at me for a long while.

'By the man in black. Are you sure Sempere hasn't told you anything about this?'

'I'm sure he hasn't.'

Isaac lowered his voice, adopting a conspiratorial tone.

'Over the years, some members have occasionally seen the man in black in the tunnels of the labyrinth. They all describe him differently. Some even swear they have spoken to him. There was a time when it was rumoured that the man in black was the ghost of an accursed author whom one of the members had betrayed after taking one of his books from here and not keeping the promise to protect it. The book was lost forever and the deceased author wanders eternally along the passages, seeking revenge – well, you know, the sort of Henry James effect people like so much.'

'You're not saying you believe the rumours.'

'Of course not. I have another theory. The Cymerman theory.'

'Which is . . . ?'

'That the man in black is the master of this place, the father of all secret and forbidden knowledge, of wisdom and memory, the bringer of light to storytellers and writers since time immemorial . . . He is our guardian angel, the angel of lies and of the night.'

'You're pulling my leg.'

'Every labyrinth has its Minotaur,' Isaac suggested. He smiled mysteriously and pointed towards the entrance. 'It's all yours.'

I set off along a footbridge then slowly entered a long corridor of books that formed a rising curve. When I reached the end of the curve the tunnel divided into four passages radiating out from a small circle from which a spiral staircase rose, vanishing upwards into the heights. I climbed the steps until I reached a landing that led into three different tunnels. I chose one of them, the one I thought would lead to the heart of the building, and entered. As I walked, I ran my fingers along the spines of hundreds of books. I let myself be imbued with the smell, with the light that filtered through the cracks or from the glass lanterns embedded in the wooden structure, floating among mirrors and shadows. I wandered aimlessly for almost half an hour until I reached a sort of closed chamber with a table and chair. The walls were made of books and seemed quite solid except for a small gap that looked as if someone had removed a book from it. I decided that this would be the new home for *The Steps of Heaven*. I looked at the cover for the last time and reread the first paragraph, imagining the moment when, many years after I was dead and forgotten, someone, if fortune had it, would go down that same route and reach that room to find an unknown book into which I had poured everything I had. I placed it there, feeling that I was the one being left on the shelf. It was then that I felt the presence behind me, and turned to find the man in black, his eyes fixed steadily on mine.

21

At first I didn't recognise my own eyes in the mirror, one of the many that formed a chain of muted light along the corridors of the labyrinth. What I saw in the reflection was my face and my skin, but the eyes were those of a stranger. Murky, dark and full of malice. I looked away and felt the nausea returning. I sat on the chair by the table and took a deep breath. I imagined that even Doctor Trías might be amused at the thought that the tenant lodged in my brain – the tumorous growth as he liked to call it – had decided to deal me the final blow in that place, thereby granting me the honour of being the first permanent citizen of the Cemetery of Forgotten Novelists, buried in the company of his last and most ill-fated work, the one that had taken him to the grave. Someone would find me there in ten months, or ten years, or perhaps never. A grand finale worthy of *City of the Damned*.

I think I was saved by my bitter laughter. It cleared my head and reminded me of where I was and what I'd come to do. I was about to stand up again when I saw it. It was a rough-looking volume, dark, with no visible title on the spine. It lay on top of a pile of four other books at the end of the table. I picked it up. The covers were bound in what looked like leather, some sort of tanned hide, darkened as a result of much handling rather than from dye. The words of the title, which seemed to have been branded onto the cover, were blurred, but on the fourth page the same title could be clearly read:

Lux Aeterna
D. M.

I imagined that the initials, which coincided with mine, were those of the author, but there was no other indication in the book to confirm this. I turned a few pages quickly and recognised at least five different languages alternating through the text. Spanish, German, Latin, French and Hebrew. Reading a paragraph at random, it reminded me of a prayer in the traditional liturgy that I couldn't quite remember. I wondered whether the notebook was perhaps some sort of missal or prayer book. The text was punctuated with numerals and verses, with the first words underlined, as if to indicate episodes or thematic divisions. The more I examined it, the more I realised it reminded me of the Gospels and catechisms of my school days.

I could have left, chosen any other tome from among the hundreds of thousands, and abandoned that place never to return. I almost thought I had done just that, as I walked back through the tunnels and corridors of the labyrinth, until I became aware of the book in my hands, like a parasite stuck to my skin. For a split second the idea crossed my mind that the book had a greater desire to leave the place than I did, that it was somehow guiding my steps. After a few detours, in the course of which I passed the same copy of the fourth volume of LeFanu's complete works a couple of times, I found myself, without knowing how, by the spiral staircase, and from there I succeeded in locating the way out of the labyrinth. I had imagined Isaac would be waiting for me by the entrance, but there was no sign of him, although I was certain that somebody was observing me from the shadows. The large vault of the Cemetery of Forgotten Books was engulfed in a deep silence.

'Isaac?' I called out.

The echo of my voice trailed off into the shadows. I waited in vain for a few seconds and then made my way towards the exit. The blue mist that filtered down from the dome began to fade until the darkness around me was almost absolute. A few steps further on I made out a light flickering at the end of the gallery and realised that the keeper had left his lamp at the foot of the door. I turned to scan the dark gallery one last time, then pulled the handle that kick-started the mechanism of rails and pulleys. One by one, the bolts were released and the door yielded a few centimetres. I pushed it just enough to get through and stepped outside. A few seconds later the door began to close again, sealing itself with a sonorous echo.

22

As I walked away from that place I felt its magic leaving me and the nausea and pain took over once more. Twice I fell flat on my face, first in the Ramblas and the second time when I was trying to cross Vía Layetana, where a boy lifted me up and saved me from being run over by a tram. It was with great difficulty that I managed to reach my front door. The house had been closed all day and the heat – that humid, poisonous heat that seemed to suffocate the town a little more every day – floated on the air like dusty light. I went up to the study in the tower and opened the windows wide. Only the faintest of breezes blew and the sky was bruised by black clouds that moved in slow circles over Barcelona. I left the book on my desk and told myself there would be time enough to examine it in detail. Or perhaps not. Perhaps time was already coming to an end for me. It didn't seem to matter much any more.

At that point I could barely stand and needed to lie down in the dark. I salvaged one of the bottles of codeine pills from the drawer and swallowed two or three in one gulp. I kept the bottle in my pocket and made my way down the stairs, not quite sure whether I would be able to get to my room in one piece. When I reached the corridor I thought I noticed a flickering along the line of light coming from beneath the main door. I walked slowly to the entrance, leaning on the walls.

'Who's there?' I asked.

There was no reply, no sound at all. I hesitated for a moment, then opened the door and stepped out onto the landing. I leaned over to look down the stairs that descended in a spiral, merging into darkness. There was nobody there. When I turned back to face the door I noticed that the small lamp on the landing was blinking. I went back into the house and turned the key to lock the door, something I often forgot to do. Then I saw it. A cream-coloured envelope with a serrated edge. Someone had slipped it under the door. I knelt down to pick it up. The paper was thick, porous. The envelope was sealed and had my name on it. The emblem on the wax was in the shape of an angel with its wings outspread.

I opened it.

Dear Señor Martín,

I'm going to spend some time in the city and it would give me great pleasure to meet up with you and perhaps take the opportunity to revisit the subject of my proposal. I'd be very grateful if, unless you're otherwise engaged, you would care to join me for dinner this coming Friday 13th at 10 o'clock, in a small villa I have rented for my stay in Barcelona. The house is on the corner of Calle Olot and Calle San José de la Montaña, next to the entrance to Güell Park. I trust and hope that you will be able to come.

Your friend,
ANDREAS CORELLI

I let the note fall to the floor and dragged myself to the gallery. There I lay on the sofa, sheltering in the half-light. There were seven days to go before that meeting. I smiled to myself. I didn't think I was going to live seven more days. I closed my eyes and tried to sleep. The constant ringing in my ears seemed more deafening than ever and stabs of white light lit up my mind with every beat of my heart.

You won't even be able to think about writing.

I opened my eyes again and scanned the bluish shadow that veiled the gallery. Next to me, on the table, lay the old photograph album that Cristina had left behind. I hadn't found the courage to throw it away, or even touch it. I reached for the album and opened it, turning the pages until I found the image I was looking for. I pulled it off the page and examined it. Cristina, as a child, walking hand in hand with a stranger along the jetty that stretched out into the sea. I pressed the photograph against my chest and let exhaustion overcome me. Slowly, the bitterness and the anger of that day, of those years, faded and a warm darkness wrapped itself around me, full of voices and hands that were waiting for me. I had an overwhelming desire to surrender to it, but something held me back and a dagger of light and pain wrenched me from that pleasant sleep that promised to have no end.

Not yet – the voice whispered – *not yet.*

*

I sensed the days were passing because there were times when I awoke and thought I could see sunlight coming through the slats in the shutters. Once or twice I was sure I heard someone knocking on the door and voices calling my name, but after a while they stopped. Hours or days later I got up and put my hands on my face and found blood on my lips. I don't know whether I went outside or whether I dreamed that I did, but without knowing how I had got there I found myself making my way up Paseo del Borne, towards the cathedral of Santa María del Mar. The streets were deserted beneath a mercury moon. I looked up and thought I saw the ghost of a huge black storm spreading its wings over the city. A gust of white light split the skies and a mantle woven with raindrops cascaded down like a shower of glass daggers. A moment before the first drop touched the ground, time came to a standstill and hundreds of thousands of tears of light were suspended in the air like specks of dust. I knew that someone or something was walking behind me and could feel its breath on the nape of my neck, cold and filled with the stench of rotting flesh and fire. I could feel its fingers, long and pointed, hovering over my skin, and at that moment the young girl who only lived in the picture I held against my chest seemed to approach through the curtain of rain. She took me by the hand and pulled me, leading me back to the tower house, away from that icy presence that had crept along behind me. When I recovered consciousness, the seven days had passed.

Day was breaking on Friday, 13 July.

23

Pedro Vidal and Cristina Sagnier were married that afternoon. The ceremony took place at five o'clock in the chapel of the Monastery of Pedralbes and only a small section of the Vidal clan attended; the most select members of the family, including the father of the groom, were ominously absent. Had there been any gossip, people would have said that the youngest son's idea of marrying the chauffeur's daughter had fallen on the heads of the dynasty like a jug of cold water. But there was none. Thanks to a discreet pact of silence, the chroniclers of society had better things to do that afternoon, and not a single publication mentioned the ceremony. There was nobody there to relate how a bevy of Vidal's ex-lovers had clustered together by the church door, crying in silence like a sisterhood of faded widows still clinging to their last hope. Nobody was there to describe how Cristina had held a bunch of white roses in her hand and worn an ivory-coloured dress that matched her skin, making it seem as if the bride were walking naked up to the altar, with no other adornment than the white veil covering her face and an amber-coloured sky that appeared to be retreating into an eddy of clouds above the tall bell tower.

There was nobody there to recall how she stepped out of the car and how, for an instant, she stopped to look up at the square opposite the church door, until her eyes found the dying man whose hands shook and who was muttering words nobody could hear, words he would take with him to the grave.

'Damn you. Damn you both.'

Two hours later, sitting in the armchair of my study, I opened the case that had come to me years before and contained the only thing I had left of my father. I pulled out the revolver, which was wrapped in a cloth, and opened the chamber. I inserted six bullets and closed the weapon. I placed the barrel against my temple, drew back the hammer and shut my eyes. At that moment I felt a gust of wind whip against the tower and the study windows burst open, hitting the wall with great force. An icy breeze touched my face, bringing with it the lost breath of great expectations.

24

The taxi slowly made its way up to the outskirts of the Gracia district, towards the solitary, sombre grounds of Güell Park. The hill was dotted with large houses that had seen better days, peering through a grove of trees that swayed in the wind like black water. I spied the large door of the estate high up on the hillside. Three years earlier, when Gaudí died, the heirs of Count Güell had sold the deserted grounds – whose sole inhabitant had been its architect – to the town hall for one peseta. Now forgotten and neglected, the garden of columns and towers looked more like a cursed paradise. I told the driver to stop by the park gates and paid my fare.

'Are you sure you wish to get out here, sir?' the driver asked, looking uncertain. 'If you like, I can wait for you for a few minutes . . .'

'It won't be necessary.'

The murmur of the taxi disappeared down the hill and I was left alone with the echo of the wind among the trees. Dead leaves trailed about the entrance to the park and swirled round my feet. I went up to the gates, which were closed with rusty chains, and scanned the grounds on the other side. Moonlight licked the outline of the dragon that presided over the staircase. A dark shape came slowly down the steps, watching me with eyes that shone like pearls under water. It was a black dog. The animal stopped at the foot of the steps and only then did I realise it was not alone. Two more animals were watching me. One of them had crept through the shadow cast by the guard's house, which stood at one side of the entrance. The other, the largest of the three, had climbed onto the wall and was looking down at me from barely two metres away, steaming breath pouring out between its bared fangs. I drew away very slowly, without taking my eyes off it and without turning round. Step by step I reached the pavement opposite the entrance. Another of the dogs had scrambled up the wall and was following me with its eyes. I quickly surveyed the ground in search of a stick or a stone to use in self-defence if they decided to attack, but all I could see were dry leaves. I knew that if I looked away and started to run, the animals would chase me and I wouldn't have got more than twenty metres before they caught me and tore me to pieces. The largest dog advanced a few steps along the wall and I was sure it was going to pounce on me. The third one, the only one I had seen at first and which had probably acted as a decoy, was beginning to climb the lower part of the wall to join the other two. I'm done for, I thought.

At that moment, a flash lit up the wolfish faces of the three animals, and they stopped in their tracks. I looked over my shoulder and saw the mound that rose about fifty metres from the entrance to the park. The lights in the house had been turned on, the only lights on the entire hillside. One of the animals gave a muffled groan and disappeared back into the park. The others followed it a few moments later.

Without thinking twice, I began to walk towards the house. Just as Corelli had pointed out in his invitation, the building stood on the corner of Calle Olot and Calle San José de la Montaña. It was a slender, angular, three-storey structure shaped like a tower, its roof crowned with sharp gables, that looked down like a sentinel over the city with the ghostly park at its feet.

The house was at the top of a steep slope, with steps leading up to the front door. The large windows exhaled golden haloes of light. As I climbed the stone steps I thought I noticed the outline of a figure leaning on one of the balustrades on the second floor, as still as a spider waiting in its web. I climbed the last step and stopped to recover my breath. The main door was ajar and a sheet of light stretched out towards my feet. I approached slowly and stopped on the threshold. A smell of dead flowers emanated from within. I knocked gently on the door and it opened slightly. Before me was an entrance hall and a long corridor leading into the house. I heard a dry, repetitive sound, like that of a shutter banging against a window in the wind; it came from somewhere inside the house and reminded me of a heart beating. Advancing a few steps into the hall I saw a staircase on my left that led to the upper floors. I thought I heard light footsteps, a child's footsteps, climbing somewhere high above.

'Good evening?' I called out.

Before the echo of my voice had lost itself down the corridor, the percussive sound that was beating somewhere in the house stopped. Total silence now fell all around me and an icy draught kissed my cheek.

'Señor Corelli? It's Martín. David Martín.'

I got no reply, so I ventured forward. The walls were covered with framed photographs of different sizes. From the poses and the clothes worn by the subjects I assumed they were all at least twenty or thirty years old. At the bottom of each frame was a small silver plaque with the name of the person in the photograph and the year it was taken. I studied the faces that were observing me from another time. Children and old people, ladies and gentlemen. They all bore the same shadow of sadness in their eyes, the same silent cry. They stared at the camera with a longing that chilled my blood.

'Does photography interest you, Martín, my friend?' said a voice next to me.

Startled, I turned round. Andreas Corelli was gazing at the photographs next to me with a smile tinged with melancholy. I hadn't seen or heard him approach, and when he smiled at me I felt a shiver down my spine.

'I thought you wouldn't come.'

'So did I.'

'Then let me offer you a glass of wine and we'll drink a toast to our errors.'

I followed him to a large room with wide French windows overlooking the city. Corelli pointed to an armchair and then filled two glasses from a decanter on a table. He handed me a glass and sat on the armchair opposite mine.

I tasted the wine. It was excellent. I almost downed it in one and soon felt the warmth sliding down my throat, calming my nerves. Corelli sniffed at his and watched me with a friendly, relaxed smile.

'You were right,' I said.

'I usually am,' Corelli replied. 'It's a habit that rarely gives me any satisfaction. Sometimes I think that few things would give me more pleasure than being sure I had made a mistake.'

'That's easy to resolve. Ask me. I'm always wrong.'

'No, you're not wrong. I think you see things as clearly as I do and it doesn't give you any satisfaction either.'

Listening to him it occurred to me that the only thing that could give me some satisfaction at that precise moment was to set fire to the whole world and burn along with it. As if he'd read my thoughts, Corelli smiled and nodded, baring his teeth.

'I can help you, my friend.'

To my surprise, I found myself avoiding his eyes, concentrating instead on that small brooch with the silver angel on his lapel.

'Pretty brooch,' I said, pointing at it.

'A family heirloom,' Corelli replied.

I thought we'd exchanged enough pleasantries to last the whole evening.

'Señor Corelli, what am I doing here?'

Corelli's eyes shone the same colour as the wine he was gently swilling in his glass.

'It's very simple. You're here because at last you've realised that this is the place you should be. You're here because I made you an offer a year ago. An offer that at the time you were not ready to accept, but which you have not forgotten. And I'm here because I still think that you're the person I'm looking for, and that is why I preferred to wait twelve months rather than let you go.'

'An offer you never got round to explaining in detail.'

'In fact, the only thing I gave you was the details.'

'One hundred thousand francs in exchange for working for you for a whole year, writing a book.'

'Exactly. Many people would think that was the essential information. But not you.'

'You told me that when you described the sort of book you wanted me to write for you, I'd do it even if you didn't pay me.'

Corelli nodded.

'You have a good memory.'

'I have an excellent memory, Señor Corelli, so much so that I don't recall having seen, read or heard about any book you've published.'

'Do you doubt my solvency?'

I shook my head, trying not to let him notice the longing and greed that gnawed at my insides. The less interest I showed, the more tempted I felt by the publisher's promises.

'I'm simply curious about your motives,' I pointed out.

'As you should be.'

'Anyhow, may I remind you that I have an exclusive contract with Barrido & Escobillas for five more years. The other day I received a very revealing visit from them, and from a litigious-looking lawyer. Still, I suppose it doesn't really matter, because five years is too long, and if there's one thing I'm certain of, it's that I have very little time.'

'Don't worry about lawyers. Mine are infinitely more litigious-looking than the ones that couple of pustules use, and they've never lost a case. Leave all the legal details and litigation to me.'

From the way he smiled when he uttered those words I thought it best never to have a meeting with the legal advisers for Éditions de la Lumière.

'I believe you. I suppose that leaves us with the question of what the other details of your offer are – the essential ones.'

'There's no simple way of saying this, so I'd better get straight to the point.'

'Please do.'

Corelli leaned forward and locked his eyes on mine.

'Martín, I want you to create a religion for me.'

At first I thought I hadn't heard him properly.

'What did you say?'

Corelli held his gaze on mine, his eyes unfathomable.

'I said that I want you to create a religion for me.'

I stared at him for a long moment, thunderstruck.

'You're pulling my leg.'

Corelli shook his head, sipping his wine with relish.

'I want you to bring together all your talent and devote yourself body and soul, for one year, to working on the greatest story you have ever created: a religion.'

I couldn't help bursting out laughing.

'You're out of your mind. Is that your proposal? Is that the book you want me to write?'

Corelli nodded calmly.

'You've got the wrong writer: I don't know anything about religion.'

'Don't worry about that. I do. I'm not looking for a theologian. I'm looking for a narrator. Do you know what a religion is, Martín, my friend?'

'I can barely remember the Lord's Prayer.'

'A beautiful and well-crafted prayer. Poetry aside, a religion is really a moral code that is expressed through legends, myths or any type of literary device in order to establish a system of beliefs, values and rules with which to regulate a culture or a society.'

'Amen,' I replied.

'As in literature or in any other act of communication, what confers effectiveness on it is the form and not the content,' Corelli continued.

'You're telling me that a doctrine amounts to a tale.'

'Everything is a tale, Martín. What we believe, what we know, what we remember, even what we dream. Everything is a story, a narrative, a sequence of events with characters communicating an emotional content. We only accept as true what can be narrated. Don't tell me you're not tempted by the idea.'

'I'm not.'

'Are you not tempted to create a story for which men and women would live and die, for which they would be capable of killing and allowing themselves to be killed, of sacrificing and condemning themselves, of handing over their soul? What greater challenge for your career than to create a story so powerful that it transcends fiction and becomes a revealed truth?'

We stared at each other for a few seconds.

'I think you know what my answer is,' I said at last.

Corelli smiled.

'I do. But I think you're the one who doesn't yet know it.'

'Thank you for your company, Señor Corelli. And for the wine and the speeches. Very stimulating. Be careful who you throw them at. I hope you find your man, and that the pamphlet is a huge success.'

I stood up and turned to leave.

'Are you expected somewhere, Martín?'

I didn't reply, but I stopped.

'Don't you feel anger, knowing there could be so many things to live for, with good health and good fortune, and no ties?' said Corelli behind my back. 'Don't you feel anger when these things are being snatched from your hands?'

I turned back slowly.

'What is a year's work compared to the possibility of having everything you desire come true? What is a year's work compared to the promise of a long and fulfilling existence?'

Nothing, I said to myself, despite myself. Nothing.

'Is that your promise?'

'You name the price. Do you want to set fire to the whole world and burn with it? Let's do it together. You fix the price. I'm prepared to give you what you most want.'

'I don't know what it is that I want most.'

'I think you do know.'

The publisher smiled and winked at me. He stood up and went over to a chest of drawers that had a gas lamp resting on it. He opened the first drawer and pulled out a parchment envelope. He handed it to me but I didn't take it, so he left it on the table that stood between us and sat down again, without saying a word. The envelope was open and inside I could just make out what looked like a few wads of one-hundred franc notes. A fortune.

'You keep all this money in a drawer and leave the door open?' I asked.

'You can count it. If you think it's not enough, name an amount. As I said, I'm not going to argue with you over money.'

I looked at the small fortune for a long moment, and in the end I shook my head. At least I'd seen it. It was real. The offer, and the vanity he had awoken in me in those moments of misery and despair, were real.

'I cannot accept it,' I said.

'Do you think it's dirty money?'

'All money is dirty. If it were clean nobody would want it. But that's not the problem.'

'So?'

'I cannot accept it because I cannot accept your proposal. I couldn't even do so if I wanted to.'

Corelli considered my words carefully.

'May I ask why?'

'Because I'm dying, Señor Corelli. Because I only have a few weeks left to live, perhaps only days. Because I have nothing left to offer.'

Corelli looked down and fell into a deep silence. I heard the wind scratching at the windows and sliding over the house.

'Don't tell me you didn't know,' I added.

'I sensed it.'

Corelli remained seated, not looking at me.

'There are plenty of writers who can write this book for you, Señor Corelli. I am grateful for your offer. More than you can imagine. Goodnight.'

I began to walk away.

'Let's say I was able to help you get over your illness,' he said.

I stopped halfway down the corridor and turned round. Corelli was barely a metre away, staring straight at me. I thought he was a bit taller than when I'd first seen him, there in the corridor, and that his eyes were larger and darker. I could see my reflection in his pupils getting smaller as they dilated.

'Does my appearance worry you, Martín, my friend?'

I swallowed hard.

'Yes,' I confessed.

'Please come back and sit down. Give me the opportunity to

explain some more. What have you got to lose?'

'Nothing, I suppose.'

He put his hand gently on my arm. His fingers were long and pale.

'You have nothing to fear from me, Martín. I'm your friend.'

His touch was comforting. I allowed him to guide me back to the sitting room and sat down meekly, like a child waiting for an adult to speak. Corelli knelt down by my armchair and fixed his eyes on mine. He took my hand and pressed it tightly.

'Do you want to live?'

I wanted to reply but couldn't find the words. I realised that I had a lump in my throat and my eyes were filling with tears. Until then I had not understood how much I longed to keep on breathing, to keep on opening my eyes every morning and be able to go out into the street, to step on stones and look at the sky, and, above all, to keep on remembering.

I nodded.

'I'm going to help you, Martín, my friend. All I ask of you is that you trust me. Accept my offer. Let me help you. Let me give you what you most desire. That is my promise.'

I nodded again.

'I accept.'

Corelli smiled and bent over to kiss me on the cheek. His lips were icy cold.

'You and I, my friend, are going to do great things together. You'll see,' he whispered.

He offered me a handkerchief to dry my tears. I did so without feeling the silent shame of weeping before a stranger, something I had not done since my father died.

'You're exhausted, Martín. Stay here for the night. There are plenty of bedrooms in this house. I can assure you that tomorrow you'll feel better, and that you'll see things more clearly.'

I shrugged my shoulders, though I realised that Corelli was right. I could barely stand up and all I wanted to do was sleep deeply. I couldn't even bring myself to get up from the armchair, the most comfortable and most comforting in the universal history of all armchairs.

'If you don't mind, I'd rather stay here.'

'Of course. I'm going to let you rest. Very soon you'll feel better. I give you my word.'

Corelli went over to the chest of drawers and turned off the gas lamp. The room was submerged in a bluish dusk. My eyelids were pressing down heavily and a sense of intoxication filled my head, but I managed to make out Corelli's silhouette crossing the room and disappearing into the shadows. I closed my eyes and heard the murmur of the wind behind the windowpanes.

25

I dreamed that the house was slowly sinking. At first, little teardrops of dark water began to appear through the cracks in the tiles, in the walls, in the relief on the ceiling, through the holes of the door locks. It was a cold liquid that crept slowly and heavily, like mercury, and gradually formed a layer covering the floor and climbing up the walls. I felt the water going over my feet, rising fast. I stayed in the armchair, watching as the water level rose to my throat and then, in just a few seconds, reached the ceiling. I felt myself floating and could see pale lights rising and falling behind the windows. There were human figures also suspended in that watery darkness. Trapped in the current as they floated by, they stretched their hands out to me, but I could not help them and the water dragged them away inexorably. Corelli's one hundred thousand francs flowed around me, undulating like paper fish. I crossed the room to a closed door at the other end. A thread of light shone through the lock. I opened the door and saw that it led to a staircase descending to the deepest part of the house. I went down.

At the bottom of the stairs an oval room opened up, and in its centre I could distinguish a group of figures gathered in a circle. When they became aware of my presence they turned round and I saw that they were dressed in white and wore masks and gloves. Strong white lights burned over what seemed to be an operating table. A man whose face had no features or eyes was arranging the objects on a tray of surgical instruments. One of the figures stretched out his hand to me, inviting me to draw closer. I went over to them and felt that they were taking hold of me, grabbing my head and my body and lifting me onto the table. The lights were blinding, but I managed to see that all the figures were identical and had the face of Doctor Trías. I laughed to myself. One of the doctors was holding a syringe and injected it into my neck. I didn't feel the prick, just a pleasant, muzzy sensation of warmth spreading through my body. Two of the doctors placed my head in some holding contraption and proceeded to adjust the crown of screws that held a padded plate at one end. I felt them tying down my arms and legs with straps. I put up no resistance. When my whole body had been immobilised from head to toe, one of the doctors handed a scalpel to another of his clones, who then leaned over me. I felt someone take my hand and hold it. It was a boy who looked at me tenderly and had the same face I had on the day my father was killed.

I saw the blade of the scalpel coming down in the liquid darkness and felt the metal making a cut across my forehead. There was no pain. I could feel something issuing out of the cut and saw a black cloud bleeding slowly from the wound and spreading into the water. The blood rose towards the lights in spirals, like smoke, twisting into ever-changing shapes. I looked at the boy, who was smiling at me and holding my hand tightly. Then I noticed it. Something was moving inside me. Something that, until just a minute ago, had been gripping my mind like pincers. I felt it being dislodged, like a thorn stuck right into the marrow that was being pulled out with pliers. I panicked and wanted to get up, but I was immobilised. The boy kept his eyes on mine and nodded. I thought I was going to faint, or wake up, and then I saw it. I saw it reflected in the lights of the operating theatre. Two black filaments were emerging from the wound, creeping over my skin. It was a black spider the size of a fist. It ran across my face and before it could jump onto the table, one of the surgeons skewered it with a scalpel. He lifted it up so that I could see it. The spider kicked its legs and bled, silhouetted against the light. A white stain covered its carapace suggesting the shape of wings spread open. An angel. After a while the spider's legs went limp and its body withered. It was still held aloft, and when the boy reached out to touch it, it crumbled into dust. The doctors undid my ties and loosened the contraption that had gripped my skull. With their help I sat up on the table and put my hand on my forehead. The wound was closing. When I looked around me once more, I realised I was alone.

The lights of the operating theatre went out and the room was dark. I went back to the staircase and ascended the steps that led back to the sitting room. The light of dawn was filtering through the water, trapping a thousand floating particles. I was tired. More than I'd ever been in my whole life. I dragged myself to the armchair and let myself fall into it. My body collapsed, and when I was finally at rest on the chair I could see a trail of tiny bubbles beginning to move around the ceiling. A small air chamber was being formed at the top and I realised that the water level was starting to come down. The water, thick and shiny like jelly, gushed out through the cracks in the windows as if the house were a submarine emerging from the deep. I curled up in the armchair, succumbing to a sense of weightlessness and peace which I hoped would never end. I closed my eyes and listened to the murmur of the water around me. I opened them again and saw drops raining down from on high, slowly, like tears caught in mid-flight. I was tired, very tired, and all that I wanted to do was fall into a deep sleep.

I opened my eyes to the intense brightness of a warm noon. Light fell like dust through the French windows. The first thing I noticed was that the hundred thousand francs were still on the table. I stood up and went over to the window. I drew aside the curtain and an arm of blinding light inundated the room. Barcelona was still there, shimmering like a mirage. I realised that the humming in my ears, which only the sounds of the day used to disguise, had disappeared completely. I heard an intense silence, as pure as crystal water, which I didn't remember ever having experienced before. Then I heard myself laughing. I brought my hands to my head and touched my skin: I felt no pressure whatsoever. I could see clearly and felt as if my five senses had only just awoken. I could even smell the old wood of the coffered ceiling and columns. I looked for a mirror but there wasn't one in the sitting room. I went out in search of a bathroom or another room where I might find a mirror and be able to see that I hadn't woken up in a stranger's body, that the skin I could feel and the bones were my own. All the rooms in the house were locked. I went through the whole floor without being able to open a single door. When I returned to the sitting room I noticed that where I had dreamed there was a door leading to the basement there was only a painting of an angel crouching on a rock that looked out over an endless lake. I went to the stairs that led to the upper floors, but as soon as I'd gone up one flight I stopped. A heavy, impenetrable darkness seemed to reside beyond.

'Señor Corelli?' I called out.

My voice was lost as if it had hit something hard, without leaving an echo or trace. I went back to the sitting room and gazed at the money on the table. One hundred thousand francs. I took the money and felt its weight. The paper begged to be stroked. I put it in my pocket and set off again down the passage that led to the exit. The dozens of faces in the portraits were still staring at me with the intensity of a promise. I preferred not to confront their looks and continued walking towards the door, but just as I was nearing the end of the passage I noticed that among the frames there was an empty one, with no inscription or photograph. I became aware of a sweet scent, a scent of parchment, and realised it was coming from my fingers. It was the perfume of money. I opened the main door and stepped out into the daylight. The door closed heavily behind me. I turned round to look at the house, dark and silent, oblivious to the radiant clarity of the day, the blue skies and brilliant sun. I checked my watch. It was after one o'clock. I had slept more than twelve hours in a row on an old armchair, and yet I had never felt better in all my life. I walked down the hill towards the city with a smile on my face, certain that, for the first time in a long while, perhaps for the first time in my whole life, the world was smiling at me.

Act Two

Lux Aeterna

1

I celebrated my return to the world of the living by paying homage to one of the most influential temples in town: the main offices of the Banco Hispano Colonial on Calle Fontanella. The sight of a hundred thousand francs sent the manager, the auditors and the army of cashiers and accountants into ecstasy, and elevated me to the ranks of clients who inspired a devotion and warmth that was almost saintly. Having sorted out formalities with the bank, I decided to deal with another Horseman of the Apocalypse by walking up to a newspaper stand in Plaza Urquinaona. I opened a copy of *The Voice of Industry* and looked for the local news section, which had once been mine. Don Basilio's expert touch was still apparent in the headlines and I recognised almost all of the bylines, as if not a day had gone by. Six years of General Primo de Rivera's lukewarm dictatorship had brought to the city a poisonous, murky calm that didn't sit well with the reporting of crime and sensational stories. I was about to close the newspaper and collect my change when I saw it. Just a brief news item in a column highlighting four different incidents, on the last page of the section.

MIDNIGHT FIRE IN THE RAVAL QUARTER
ONE DEAD AND TWO BADLY INJURED

Joan Marc Huguet/Barcelona

A serious fire started in the early hours of Friday morning at 6, Plaza dels Àngels, head office of the publishing firm Barrido & Escobillas. The firm's director, Don José Barrido, died in the blaze, and his partner, Don José Luis López Escobillas, was seriously injured. An employee, Don Ramón Guzmán, was also badly injured, trapped by the flames as he attempted to rescue the other two men. Firefighters are speculating that the blaze may have been started by a chemical product that was being used for renovation work in the offices. Other causes are not being ruled out, however, as eyewitnesses claim to have seen a man leaving the building moments before the fire began. The victims were taken to the Clínico hospital, where one was pronounced dead on arrival. The other two remain in a critical condition.

I got there as quickly as I could. The smell of burning reached as far as the Ramblas. A group of neighbours and onlookers had congregated in the square opposite the building, and plumes of white smoke rose from the rubble by the entrance. I saw some of the firm's employees trying to salvage what little remained from the ruins. Boxes of scorched books and furniture bitten by flames were piled up in the street. The facade of the building was blackened and the windows had been blasted out by the fire. I broke through the circle of bystanders and went in. A powerful stench stuck in my throat. Some of the staff from the publishing house who were busy rescuing their belongings recognised me and mumbled a greeting, their heads bowed.

'Señor Martín . . . what a tragedy.'

I crossed what had once been the reception and went into Barrido's office. The flames had devoured the carpets and reduced the furniture to glowing skeletons. In one corner, the coffered ceiling had collapsed, opening a pathway of light towards the rear patio along which floated a bright beam of ashes. One chair had miraculously survived the fire. It was in the middle of the room and sitting on it was Lady Venom, crying, her eyes downcast. I knelt down in front of her. She recognised me and smiled between her tears.

'Are you all right?' I asked.

She nodded.

'He told me to go home, you know? He said it was late and I should get some rest because today was going to be a very long day. We were finishing the monthly accounts . . . If I'd stayed another minute . . .'

'What happened, Herminia?'

'We were working late. It was almost midnight when Señor Barrido told me to go home. The publishers were expecting a gentleman . . .'

'At midnight? Which gentleman?'

'A foreigner, I think. It had something to do with a proposal. I'm not sure. I would happily have stayed on, but Señor Barrido told me—'

'Herminia, that gentleman, do you remember his name?'

She gave me a puzzled look.

'I've already told the inspector who came here this morning everything I can remember. He asked for you.'

'An inspector? For me?'

'They're talking to everyone.'

'Of course.'

Lady Venom looked straight at me, eying me with distrust, as if she were trying to read my thoughts.

'They don't know whether he'll come out of this alive,' she murmured, referring to Escobillas. 'We've lost everything, the archives, the contracts . . . everything. The publishing house is finished.'

'I'm sorry, Herminia.'

A crooked, malicious smile appeared.

'You're sorry? Isn't this what you wanted?'

'How can you think that?'

She looked at me suspiciously.

'Now you're free.'

I was about to touch her arm but Herminia stood up and took a step back, as if my presence scared her.

'Herminia—'

'Go away,' she said.

I left Herminia among the smoking ruins. When I went back outside I bumped into a group of children rummaging through the rubble. One of them had disinterred a book from the ashes and was examining it with a mixture of curiosity and disdain. The cover had been disfigured by the fire and the edges of the pages were charred, but otherwise the book was unspoilt. From the lettering on the spine, I knew that it was one of the instalments of *City of the Damned*.

'Señor Martín?'

I turned to find three men wearing cheap suits that were at odds with the humid, sticky air. One of them, who seemed to be in charge, stepped forward and proffered me the friendly smile of an expert salesman. The other two, who seemed as rigid and unyielding as a hydraulic press, glued their openly hostile eyes on mine.

'Señor Martín, I'm Inspector Víctor Grandes and these are my colleagues Officers Marcos and Castelo from the investigation and security squad. I wonder if you would be kind enough to spare us a few minutes.'

'Of course,' I replied.

The name Víctor Grandes rang a bell from my days as a reporter. Vidal had devoted some of his columns to him, and I particularly recalled one in which he described Grandes as a revelation, a solid figure whose presence in the squad confirmed the arrival of a new generation of elite professionals, better prepared than their predecessors, incorruptible and tough as steel. The adjectives and the hyperbole were Vidal's, not mine. I imagined that Inspector Grandes would have moved up the ranks since then, and his presence was proof that the police were taking the fire at Barrido & Escobillas seriously.

'If you don't mind we can go to a nearby café so that we can talk undisturbed,' said Grandes, his obliging smile not diminishing one inch.

'As you wish.'

Grandes took me to a small bar on the corner of Calle Doctor Dou and Calle Pintor Fortuny. Marcos and Castelo walked behind us, never taking their eyes off me. Grandes offered me a cigarette, which I refused. He put the packet back in his pocket and didn't open his mouth again until we reached the café and I was escorted to a table at the back, where the three men positioned themselves around me. Had they taken me to a dark, damp dungeon the meeting would have seemed more friendly.

'Señor Martín, you must already know what happened early this morning.'

'Only what I've read in the paper. And what Lady Venom told me . . .'

'Lady Venom?'

'I'm sorry. Miss Herminia Duaso, the directors' assistant.'

Marcos and Castelo exchanged glances that were priceless. Grandes smiled.

'Interesting nickname. Tell me, Señor Martín, where were you last night?'

How naive of me; the question caught me by surprise.

'It's a routine question,' Grandes explained. 'We're trying to establish the whereabouts of anyone who might have been in touch with the victims during the last few days. Employees, suppliers, family . . .'

'I was with a friend.'

As soon as I opened my mouth I regretted my choice of words. Grandes noticed it.

'A friend?'

'Well he's really someone connected to my work. A publisher. Last night I'd arranged a meeting with him.'

'Can you tell me until what time you were with this person?'

'Until late. In fact, I ended up sleeping at his house.'

'I see. And this person you describe as being connected to your work, what is his name?'

'Corelli. Andreas Corelli. A French publisher.'

Grandes wrote the name down in a little notebook.

'The surname sounds Italian,' he remarked.

'As a matter of fact, I don't really know what his nationality is.'

'That's understandable. And this Señor Corelli, whatever his citizenship may be, would he be able to corroborate the fact that last night you were with him?'

I shrugged my shoulders.

'I suppose so.'

'You suppose so?'

'I'm sure he would. Why wouldn't he?'

'I don't know, Señor Martín. Is there any reason why you would think he might not?'

'No.'

'That's settled then.'

Marcos and Castelo were looking at me as if I'd done nothing but tell lies since we sat down.

'One last thing. Could you explain the nature of the meeting you had last night with this publisher of indeterminate nationality?'

'Señor Corelli had arranged to meet me because he wanted to make me an offer.'

'What type of offer?'

'A professional one.'

'I see. To write a book, perhaps?'

'Exactly.'

'Tell me, is it usual after a business meeting to spend the night in the house of, how shall I put it, the contracting party?'

'No.'

'But you say you spent the night in this publisher's house.'

'I stayed because I wasn't feeling well and I didn't think I'd be able to get back to my house.'

'The dinner upset you, perhaps?'

'I've had some health problems recently.'

Grandes nodded, looking duly concerned.

'Dizzy spells, headaches . . .' I added.

'But it's reasonable to assume that now you're feeling better?'

'Yes. Much better.'

'I'm glad to hear it. In fact, you're looking enviably well. Don't you agree?'

Castelo and Marcos nodded.

'Anyone would think you've had a great weight taken off your shoulders,' the inspector pointed out.

'I don't understand.'

'I'm talking about the dizzy spells and the aches and pains.'

Grandes was handling this farce with an exasperating sense of timing.

'Forgive my ignorance regarding your professional life, Señor Martín, but isn't it true that you signed an agreement with the two publishers that didn't expire for another six years?'

'Five.'

'And didn't this agreement tie you, so to speak, exclusively to Barrido & Escobillas?'

'Those were the terms.'

'Then why would you need to discuss an offer with a competitor if your agreement didn't allow you to accept it?'

'It was just a conversation. Nothing more.'

'Which nevertheless turned into a soirée at this gentleman's house.'

'My agreement doesn't forbid me to speak to third parties. Or spend the night away from home. I'm free to sleep wherever I wish and to speak to whomever I want.'

'Of course. I wasn't trying to imply that you weren't, but thank you for clarifying that point.'

'Can I clarify anything else?'

'Just one small detail. Now that Señor Barrido has passed away, and supposing that, God forbid, Señor Escobillas does not recover from his injuries and also dies, the publishing house would be dissolved and so would your contract. Am I wrong?'

'I'm not sure. I don't really know how the company was set up.'

'But would you say that it was likely?'

'Possibly. You'd have to ask the publishers' lawyer.'

'In fact, I already have. And he has confirmed that, if what nobody wants to happen does happen and Señor Escobillas passes away, that is exactly how things will stand.'

'Then you already have the answer.'

'And you would have complete freedom to accept the offer of Señor . . .'

'Corelli.'

'Tell me, have you accepted it already?'

'May I ask what this has to do with the cause of the fire?' I snapped.

'Nothing. Simple curiosity.'

'Is that all?' I asked.

Grandes looked at his colleagues and then at me.

'As far as I'm concerned, yes.'

I made as if to stand up, but the three policemen remained glued to their seats.

'Señor Martín, before I forget,' said Grandes. 'Can you confirm whether you remember that a week ago Señor Barrido and Señor Escobillas paid you a visit at your home, at number 30, Calle Flassaders, in the company of the aforementioned lawyer?'

'They did.'

'Was it a social or a courtesy call?'

'The publishers came to express their wish that I should return to my work on a series of books I'd put aside for a few months while I devoted myself to another project.'

'Would you describe the conversation as friendly and relaxed?'

'I don't remember anyone raising his voice.'

'And do you remember replying to them, and I quote, "In a week you and that idiot partner of yours will be dead"? Without raising your voice, of course.'

I sighed.

'Yes,' I admitted.

'What were you referring to?'

'I was angry and said the first thing that came into my head, inspector. That doesn't mean that I was serious. Sometimes one says things one doesn't mean.'

'Thank you for your candour, Señor Martín. You have been very helpful. Good afternoon.'

I walked away from that place with all three sets of eyes fixed like daggers on my back, and with the firm belief that if I'd replied to every one of the inspector's questions with a lie I wouldn't have felt as guilty.

2

The meeting with Víctor Grandes and the couple of basilisks he used as escorts left a nasty taste in my mouth, but it had gone by the time I'd walked in the sun for a hundred metres or so, in a body I hardly recognised: strong, free of pain and nausea, with no ringing in my ears or agonising pinpricks in my skull, no weariness or cold sweats. No recollection of that certainty of death that had suffocated me only twenty-four hours ago. Something told me that the tragedy of the previous night, including the death of Barrido and the very likely demise of Escobillas, should have filled me with grief and anguish, but neither I nor my conscience was able to feel anything other than a pleasant indifference. That July morning, the Ramblas were in party mood and I was their prince.

I took a stroll as far as Calle Santa Ana, with the idea of paying a surprise visit to Señor Sempere. When I walked into the bookshop, Sempere senior was behind the counter settling accounts; his son had climbed a ladder and was rearranging the bookshelves. The bookseller gave me a friendly smile and I realised that for a moment he hadn't recognised me. A second later his smile disappeared, his mouth dropped and he came round the counter to embrace me.

'Martín? Is it really you? Holy Mother of God . . . you look completely different! I was so worried. We went round to your house a few times, but you didn't answer the door. I've even been to the hospitals and police stations.'

His son stared at me in disbelief from the top of the ladder. I had to remind myself that only a week before they had seen me looking like one of the inmates of the local morgue.

'I'm sorry I gave you a fright. I was away for a few days on a work-related matter.'

'But you did listen to me and go to the doctor, didn't you?'

I nodded.

'It turned out to be something very minor, to do with my blood pressure. I took a tonic for a few days and now I'm as good as new.'

'Give me the name of the tonic – I might take a shower in it . . . What a joy it is, and a relief, to see you looking so well!'

These high spirits were soon punctured when he turned to the news of the day.

'Did you hear about Barrido and Escobillas?' he asked.

'I've just come from there. It's hard to believe.'

'Who would have imagined it? It's not as if they aroused any warm feelings in me, but this . . . And tell me, from a legal point of view, how does it all leave you? I don't mean to sound crude.'

'To tell you the truth, I don't know. I think the two partners owned the company. There must be heirs, I suppose, but it's conceivable that, if they both die, the company as such will cease to exist. And, with it, any agreement I had with them. Or at least that's what I think.'

'In other words, if Escobillas, may God forgive me, kicks the bucket too, then you're a free man.'

I nodded.

'What a dilemma . . .' mumbled the bookseller.

'What will be will be . . .' I said.

Sempere nodded, but I noticed that something was bothering him and he wanted to change the subject.

'Anyway. The thing is, it's wonderful that you've dropped by because I wanted to ask you a favour.'

'Say no more: it's already done.'

'I warn you, you're not going to like it.'

'If I liked it, it wouldn't be a favour, it would be a pleasure. And if the favour is for you, it will be.'

'It's not really for me. I'll explain and you decide. No obligation, all right?'

Sempere leaned on the counter and adopted his confidential manner, bringing back childhood memories of times I had spent in that shop.

'There's this young girl, Isabella. She must be seventeen. As bright as a button. She's always coming round here and I lend her books. She tells me she wants to be a writer.'

'Sounds familiar.'

'The thing is, a week ago she left one of her stories with me – just twenty or thirty pages, that's all – and asked for my opinion.'

'And?'

Sempere lowered his tone, as if he were revealing a secret from an official inquiry.

'Masterly. Better than 99 per cent of what I've seen published in the last twenty years.'

'I hope you are including me in the remaining one per cent or I'll consider my self-esteem well and truly trodden on.'

'That's just what I was coming to. Isabella adores you.'

'She adores me?'

'Yes, as if you were the Virgin of Montserrat and the Baby Jesus all in one. She's read the whole *City of the Damned* series ten times over, and when I lent her *The Steps of Heaven* she told me that if she could write a book like that she'd die a peaceful death.'

'You were right. I don't like the sound of this.'

'I knew you'd try to wriggle out of it.'

'I'm not wriggling out. You haven't told me what the favour is.'

'You can imagine.'

I sighed. Sempere clicked his tongue.

'I warned you.'

'Ask me something else.'

'All you have to do is talk to her. Give her some encouragement, some advice . . . Listen to her, read some of her stuff and give her a

140

little guidance. The girl has a mind as quick as a bullet. You're really going to like her. You'll become friends. She could even work as your assistant.'

'I don't need an assistant. Still less someone I don't know.'

'Nonsense. Besides, you do know her. Or at least that's what she says. She says she's known you for years, but you probably don't remember her. It seems that the couple of simple souls she has for parents are convinced that this literature business will consign her to eternal damnation, or at least to a secular spinsterhood. They're wavering between locking her up in a convent or marrying her off to some jerk who will give her eight children and bury her forever among pots and pans. If you do nothing to save her, it's tantamount to murder.'

'Don't pull a *Jane Eyre* on me, Señor Sempere.'

'Look. I wouldn't ask you, because I know that you're as much of a fan of this altruism stuff as you are of dancing *sardanas*, but every time I see her come in here and look at me with those little eyes that seem to be popping with intelligence and enthusiasm, I think of the future that awaits her and it breaks my heart. I've already taught her all I can. The girl learns fast, Martín. She reminds me of you when you were a young lad.'

I sighed.

'Isabella what?'

'Gispert. Isabella Gispert.'

'I don't know her. I've never heard that name in my life. Someone's been telling you a tall story.'

The bookseller shook his head and mumbled under his breath.

'That's exactly what Isabella said you'd say.'

'So, she's talented *and* she's psychic. What else did she say?'

'She suspects you're a much better writer than a person.'

'What an angel, this Isabelita.'

'Can I tell her to come and see you? No obligation?'

I gave in. Sempere smiled triumphantly and wanted to seal the pact with an embrace, but I escaped before the old bookseller was able to complete his mission of trying to make me feel like a good Samaritan.

'You won't be sorry, Martín,' I heard him say as I walked out of the door.

3

When I got home, Inspector Víctor Grandes was sitting on the front doorstep, calmly smoking a cigarette. With the poise of a matinee star he smiled when he saw me, as if he were an old friend on a courtesy call. I sat down next to him and he pulled out his cigarette case. Gitanes, I noticed. I accepted.

'Where are Hansel and Gretel?'

'Marcos and Castelo were unable to come. We had a tip-off, so they've gone to find an old acquaintance in Pueblo Seco who is probably in need of a little persuasion to jog his memory.'

'Poor devil.'

'If I'd told them I was coming here, they would probably have joined me. They think the world of you.'

'Love at first sight, I noticed. What can I do for you, inspector? May I invite you upstairs for a cup of coffee?'

'I wouldn't dare invade your privacy, Señor Martín. In fact, I simply wanted to give you the news personally before you found out from other sources.'

'What news?'

'Escobillas passed away early this afternoon in the Clínico hospital.'

'God. I didn't know,' I said.

Grandes shrugged his shoulders and continued smoking in silence.

'I could see it coming. Nothing anyone could do about it.'

'Have you discovered anything about the cause of the fire?' I asked.

The inspector looked at me, then nodded.

'Everything seems to indicate that somebody spilled petrol over Señor Barrido and then set fire to him. The flames spread when he panicked and tried to get out of his office. His partner and the other employee who rushed over to help him were trapped.'

I swallowed hard. Grandes smiled reassuringly.

'The publishers' lawyer was saying this afternoon that, given the personal nature of your agreement, it becomes null and void with the death of the publishers, although their heirs will retain the rights on all the works published until now. I suppose he'll write to you, but I thought you might like to know in advance, in case you need to take any decision concerning the offer from the other publisher you mentioned.'

'Thank you.'

'You're welcome.'

Grandes had a last puff of his cigarette and threw the butt on the ground. He smiled affably and stood up. Then he patted me on the shoulder and walked off towards Calle Princesa.

'Inspector?' I called.

Grandes stopped and turned round.

'You don't think that . . .'

Grandes gave a weary smile.

'Take care, Martín.'

I went to bed early and woke all of a sudden thinking it was the following day, only to discover that it was just after midnight.

In my dreams I had seen Barrido and Escobillas trapped in their office. The flames crept up their clothes until every inch of their bodies was covered. First their clothes, then their skin began to fall off in strips, and their panic-stricken eyes cracked in the heat. Their bodies shook in spasms of agony until they collapsed among the rubble. Flesh peeled off their bones like melted wax, forming a smoking puddle at my feet, in which I could see my own smiling reflection as I blew out the match I held in my fingers.

I got up to fetch a glass of water and, assuming I'd missed the train to sleep, I went up to the study, opened the drawer in my desk and pulled out the book I had rescued from the Cemetery of Forgotten Books. I turned on the reading lamp and twisted its flexible arm so that it focused directly on the book. I opened it at the first page and began to read:

Lux Aeterna

D. M.

At first glance, the book was a collection of texts and prayers that seemed to make no sense. It was a manuscript, a handful of typed pages bound rather carelessly in leather. I went on reading and after a while thought I sensed some sort of method in the sequence of events, songs and meditations that punctuated the main body of the text. The language possessed its own cadence and what had at first seemed like a complete absence of form or style gradually turned into a hypnotic chant that permeated the reader's mind, plunging him into a state somewhere between drowsiness and forgetfulness. The same thing happened with the content, whereby the central theme did not become apparent until well into the first section, or chant – for the work seemed to be structured in the manner of ancient poems written in an age when time and space proceeded at their own pace. I realised then that *Lux Aeterna* was, for want of a better description, a sort of book of the dead.

After reading the first thirty or forty pages of circumlocutions and riddles, I found myself caught up in a precise, extravagant and increasingly disturbing puzzle of prayers and entreaties, in which death, referred to at times – in awkwardly constructed verses – as a white angel with reptilian eyes, and at other times as a luminous boy, was presented as a sole and omnipresent deity, made manifest in nature, desire and in the fragility of existence.

Whoever the mysterious D. M. was, death hovered over his verses like an all-consuming and eternal force. A Byzantine tangle of references to various mythologies of heaven and hell were knotted together here into a single plane. According to D. M. there was only one beginning and one end, only one creator and one destroyer who presented himself under different names to confuse men and tempt them in their weakness, a sole God whose true face was divided into two halves: one sweet and pious, the other cruel and demonic.

That much I was able to deduce, but no more, because beyond those principles the author seemed to have lost the course of his narrative and it was almost impossible to decipher the prophetic references and images that peppered the text. Storms of blood and fire pouring over cities and peoples. Armies of corpses in uniform running across endless plains, destroying all life as they passed. Babies strung up with torn flags at the gates of fortresses. Black seas where thousands of souls in torment were suspended for all eternity

144

beneath icy, poisoned waters. Clouds of ashes and oceans of bones and rotten flesh infested with insects and snakes. The succession of hellish, nauseating images went on unabated.

As I turned the pages I had the feeling that, step by step, I was following the map of a sick and broken mind. Line after line, the author of those pages had, without being aware of it, documented his own descent into a chasm of madness. The last third of the book seemed to suggest an attempt at retracing his steps, a desperate cry from the prison of his insanity so that he might escape the labyrinth of tunnels that had formed in his mind. The text ended suddenly, midway through an imploring sentence, offering no explanation.

By this time my eyelids were beginning to close. A light breeze wafted through the window. It came from the sea, sweeping the mist off the rooftops. I was about to close the book when I realised that something was trapped in my mind's filter, something connected to the type on those pages. I returned to the beginning and started to go over the text. I found the first example on the fifth line. From then on the same mark appeared every two or three lines. One of the characters, the capital S, was always slightly tilted to the right. I took a blank page from the drawer, slipped it behind the roller of the Underwood typewriter on my desk and wrote a sentence at random:

`'Sometimes I hear the bells of Santa María del Mar.'`

I pulled out the paper and examined it under the lamp.

`'Sometimes...of Santa María...'`

I sighed. *Lux Aeterna* had been written on that very same typewriter and probably, I imagined, at that same desk.

4

The following morning I went out to have my breakfast in a café opposite Santa María del Mar. The Borne district was heaving with carts and people going to the market, with shopkeepers and wholesalers opening their stores. I sat at one of the outdoor tables, asked for a *café con leche* and adopted an orphaned copy of *La Vanguardia* that was lying on the next table. While my eyes slid over the headlines and leads, I noticed a figure walking up the steps to the church door and sitting down at the top to observe me on the sly. The girl must have been about sixteen or seventeen and was pretending to write things down in a notebook while she stole glances at me surreptitiously. I sipped my coffee calmly. After a while I beckoned to the waiter.

'Do you see that young lady sitting by the church door? Tell her to order whatever she likes. It's on me.'

The waiter nodded and went up to her. When she saw him approaching she buried her head in her notebook, assuming an expression of total concentration that made me smile. The waiter stopped in front of her and cleared his throat. She looked up from her notebook and stared at him. He explained what his mission was and then pointed in my direction. The girl looked at me in alarm. I waved at her. She went crimson. She stood up and came over to my table, with short steps, her eyes fixed firmly on the ground.

'Isabella?' I asked.

The girl looked up and sighed, annoyed at herself.

'How did you know?' she asked.

'Supernatural intuition,' I replied.

She held out her hand and I shook it without much enthusiasm.

'May I sit down?' she asked.

She sat down without waiting for a reply. In the next half a minute the girl changed her position about six times until she returned to the original one. I observed her with a calculated lack of interest.

'You don't remember me, do you, Señor Martín?'

'Should I?'

'For years I delivered your weekly order from Can Gispert.'

The image of the girl who for so long had brought my food from the grocer's came into my mind, then dissolved into the more adult and slightly more angular features of this Isabella, a woman of soft shapes and steely eyes.

'The little girl I used to tip,' I said, although there was little or nothing left of the girl in her.

Isabella nodded.

'I always wondered what you did with all those coins.'

'I bought books at Sempere & Sons.'

'If only I'd known . . .'

'I'll go if I'm bothering you.'

'You're not bothering me. Would you like something to drink?'

The girl shook her head.

'Señor Sempere tells me you're talented.'

Isabella shrugged her shoulders and smiled at me sceptically.

'Normally, the more talent one has, the more one doubts it,' I said. 'And vice versa.'

'Then I must be quite something,' Isabella replied.

'Welcome to the club. Tell me, what can I do for you?'

Isabella took a deep breath.

'Señor Sempere told me that perhaps you could read some of my work and give me your opinion and some advice.'

I fixed my eyes on hers for a few seconds before replying. She held my gaze without blinking.

'Is that all?'

'No.'

'I could see it coming. What is chapter two?'

Isabella hesitated only for a split second.

'If you like what you read and you think I have potential, I'd like you to allow me to become your assistant.'

'What makes you think I need an assistant?'

'I can tidy up your papers, type them, correct errors and mistakes . . .'

'Errors and mistakes?'

'I didn't mean to imply that you make mistakes . . .'

'Then what did you mean to imply?'

'Nothing. But four eyes are always better than two. And besides, I can take care of your correspondence, run errands, help with research. What's more, I know how to cook and I can—'

'Are you asking for a post as assistant or cook?'

'I'm asking you to give me a chance.'

Isabella looked down. I couldn't help but smile. Despite myself, I really liked this curious creature.

'This is what we'll do. Bring me the best twenty pages you've written, the ones you think will show me what you are capable of. Don't bring any more because I won't read them. I'll have a good look at them and then, depending on what I think, we'll talk.'

Her face lit up and, for a moment, the veil of tension and toughness that governed her expression disappeared.

'You won't regret it,' she said.

She stood up and looked at me nervously.

'Is it all right if I bring the pages round to your house?'

'Leave them in my letter box. Is that all?'

She nodded vigorously and backed away with those short, nervous steps. When she was about to turn and start running, I called her.

'Isabella?'

She looked at me meekly, her eyes clouded with sudden anxiety.

'Why me?' I asked. 'And don't tell me it's because I'm your favourite author or any of that sort of flattery with which Sempere has advised you to soft-soap me, because if you do, this will be the first and last conversation we ever have.'

Isabella hesitated for a moment. Then, looking at me candidly, she replied with disarming bluntness.

'Because you're the only writer I know.'

She gave me an embarrassed smile and went off with her notebook, her unsteady walk and her frankness. I watched her turn the corner of Calle Mirallers and vanish behind the cathedral.

5

When I returned home an hour later, I found her sitting on my doorstep, clutching what I imagined must be her story. As soon as she saw me she stood up and forced a smile.

'I told you to leave it in my letter box,' I said.

Isabella nodded and shrugged her shoulders.

'As a token of my gratitude I've brought you some coffee from my parents' shop. It's Colombian and really good. The coffee didn't fit through your letter box so I thought I'd better wait for you.'

Such an excuse could only have been invented by a budding novelist. I sighed and opened the door.

'In.'

I went up the stairs, Isabella following like a lapdog a few steps behind.

'Do you always take that long to have your breakfast? Not that it's any of my business, of course, but I've been waiting here for three quarters of an hour, so I was beginning to worry. I said to myself, I hope he hasn't choked on something. It would be just my luck. The one time I meet a writer in the flesh and then he goes and swallows an olive the wrong way and bang goes my literary career,' she rattled on.

I stopped halfway up the flight of steps and looked at her with the most hostile expression I could muster.

'Isabella, for things to work out between us we're going to have to set down a few rules. The first is that I ask the questions and you just answer them. When there are no questions from me, you don't give me answers or spontaneous speeches. The second rule is that I can take as long as I damn well please to have breakfast, an afternoon snack or to daydream, and that does not constitute a matter for debate.'

'I didn't mean to offend you. I understand that slow digestion of food is an aid to inspiration.'

'The third rule is that sarcasm is not allowed before noon. Understood?'

'Yes, Señor Martín.'

'The fourth is that you must not call me Señor Martín, not even at my funeral. I might seem like a fossil to you, but I like to think that I'm still young. In fact, I am young, end of story.'

'How should I call you?'

'By my name: David.'

The girl nodded. I opened the door of the apartment and showed her in. Isabella hesitated for a moment, then slipped in giving a little jump.

'I think you still look quite young for your age, David.'

I stared at her in astonishment.

'How old do you think I am?'

Isabella looked me up and down, assessing.

'About thirty? But a young-looking thirty?'

'Just shut up and go and make some coffee with that concoction you've brought.'

149

'Where is the kitchen?'

'Look for it.'

We shared a delicious Colombian coffee sitting in the gallery. Isabella held her cup and watched me furtively as I read the twenty pages she had brought with her. Every time I turned a page and looked up I was confronted by her expectant gaze.

'If you're going to sit there looking at me like an owl, this will take a long time.'

'What do you want me to do?'

'Didn't you want to be my assistant? Then assist. Look for something that needs tidying and tidy it, for example.'

Isabella looked around.

'Everything is untidy.'

'This is your chance then.'

Isabella agreed and went off, with military determination, to confront the chaos that reigned in my home. I listened as her footsteps retreated down the corridor and then continued reading. The story she had brought me had almost no narrative thread. With a sharp sensitivity and an articulate turn of phrase, it described the feelings and longings that passed through the mind of a girl confined to a cold room in an attic of the Ribera quarter, from which she gazed at the city with its people coming and going along dark, narrow streets. The images and the sad music of her prose spoke of a loneliness that bordered on despair. The girl in the story spent hours trapped in her world; sometimes she would sit facing a mirror and slit her arms and thighs with a piece of broken glass, leaving scars like the ones just visible under Isabella's sleeves. I had almost finished my reading when I noticed that she was looking at me from the gallery door.

'What?'

'I'm sorry to interrupt, but what's in the room at the end of the corridor?'

'Nothing.'

'It smells odd.'

'Damp.'

'I can clean it if you like . . .'

'No. That room is never used. And besides, you're not my maid. You don't need to clean anything.'

'I'm only trying to help.'

'You can help by getting me another cup of coffee.'

'Why? Did the story make you feel drowsy?'

'What's the time, Isabella?'

'It must be about ten o'clock.'

'And what does that mean?'

'No sarcasm before noon,' Isabella replied.

I smiled triumphantly and handed her my empty cup. She took it and headed off towards the kitchen.

When she returned with the steaming coffee, I had just read the last page. Isabella sat down opposite me. I smiled and slowly sipped the delicious brew. The girl wrung her hands and gritted her teeth, glancing now and then at the pages of her story, which I had left face down on the table. She held out for a couple of minutes without saying a word.

'And?' she said at last.

'Superb.'

Her face lit up.

'My story?'

'The coffee.'

She gave me a wounded look and went to gather her pages.

'Leave them where they are.'

'Why? It's obvious that you didn't like them and you think I'm nothing but a poor idiot.'

'I didn't say that.'

'You didn't say anything, which is worse.'

'Isabella, if you really want to devote yourself to writing, or at least to writing something others will read, you're going to have to get used sometimes to being ignored, insulted and despised, and almost always to being considered with indifference. It comes with the territory.'

Isabella looked down and took a deep breath.

'I don't know if I have any talent. I only know that I like to write. Or, rather, that I need to write.'

'Liar.'

She looked up and gazed at me harshly.

'OK. I am talented. And I don't care two hoots if you think that I'm not.'

I smiled.

'That's better; I couldn't agree with you more.'

She looked confused.

'In that I have talent, or in that you think that I don't?'

'What do you think?'

'Then, do you believe I have potential?'

'I think you are talented and passionate, Isabella. More than you think and less than you expect. But there are a lot of people with talent and passion, and many of them never get anywhere. This is only the first step for achieving anything in life. Natural talent is like an athlete's strength. You can be born with more or less ability, but nobody can become an athlete just because he or she was born tall, or strong, or fast. What makes the athlete, or the artist, is the work, the vocation and the technique. The intelligence you are born with is just ammunition. To achieve something with it you need to transform your mind into a high-precision weapon.'

'Why the military metaphor?'

'Every work of art is aggressive, Isabella. And every artist's life is a small war or a large one, beginning with oneself and one's limitations. To achieve anything you must first have ambition and then talent, knowledge, and finally the opportunity.'

Isabella considered my words.

'Do you hurl that speech at everyone, or have you just made it up?'

'The speech isn't mine. It was "hurled" at me, as you put it, by someone to whom I asked the same questions that you're asking me today. It was many years ago, but not a day goes by when I don't realise how right he was.'

'So, can I be your assistant?'

'I'll think about it.'

Isabella nodded, satisfied. On the table, close to where she was sitting, lay the photograph album Cristina had left behind. She opened it at random, starting from the back, and was soon staring at a picture of Señora de Vidal, taken by the gates of Villa Helius two or three years before she was married. I swallowed hard. Isabella closed the album and let her eyes wander around the gallery until they came to rest on me. I was observing her impatiently. She gave me a nervous smile, as if I'd caught her poking around where she had no business.

'Your girlfriend is very beautiful,' she said.

The look I gave her removed the smile in an instant.

'She's not my girlfriend.'

'Oh.'

A long silence ensued.

'I suppose the fifth rule is that I'm not to meddle in anything that doesn't concern me, right?'

I didn't reply. Isabella nodded to herself and stood up.

'Then I'd better leave you in peace and not bother you any more today. If you like, I can come back tomorrow and we'll start then.'

She gathered her pages and smiled shyly. I nodded.

Isabella left discreetly and disappeared down the corridor. I heard her steps as she walked away and then the sound of the door closing. Her absence made me aware, for the first time, of the silence that bewitched that house.

6

Perhaps there was too much caffeine coursing through my veins, or maybe it was just my conscience trying to return, like electricity after a power cut, but I spent the rest of the morning turning over in my mind an idea that was far from comforting. It was hard to imagine that there was no connection between the fire in which Barrido and Escobillas had perished, Corelli's proposal – I hadn't heard a single word from him, which made me suspicious – and the strange manuscript I had rescued from the Cemetery of Forgotten Books, which I suspected had been written within the four walls of my study.

The thought of returning to Corelli's house uninvited, to ask him about the fact that our conversation and the fire should have occurred practically at the same time, was not appealing. My instinct told me that when the publisher decided he wanted to see me again he would do so *motu propio* and I was in no great hurry to pursue our inevitable meeting. The investigation into the fire was already in the hands of Inspector Víctor Grandes and his two bulldogs, Marcos and Castelo, on whose list of favourite people I came highly recommended. The further away I kept from them, the better. This left only the connection between the manuscript and the tower house. After years of telling myself it was no coincidence that I had ended up living here, the idea was beginning to take on a different significance.

I decided to start my own investigation in the place to which I had confined most of the belongings left behind by the previous inhabitants. I found the key to the room at the far end of the corridor in the kitchen drawer, where it had spent many years. I hadn't been in that room since the men from the electrical company had wired up the house. When I put the key into the lock, I felt a draught of cold air from the keyhole brushing across my fingers, and I realised that Isabella was right; the room did give off a strange smell, reminiscent of dead flowers and freshly turned earth.

I opened the door and covered my mouth and nose. The stench was intense. I groped around the wall for the light switch, but the naked bulb hanging from the ceiling didn't respond. The light from the corridor revealed the outline of the boxes, books and trunks I had banished to that room years before. I looked at everything with disgust. The wall at the end was completely covered by a large oak wardrobe. I knelt down by a box full of old photographs, spectacles, watches and other personal items. I began to rummage without really knowing what I was looking for, but after a while I abandoned the undertaking with a sigh. If I was hoping to discover anything I needed a plan. I was about to leave the room when I heard the wardrobe door slowly opening behind my back. A puff of icy, damp air touched the nape of my neck. I turned round slowly. The wardrobe door was half open and I could see the old dresses and suits that hung inside it, eaten away by time, fluttering like seaweed under water. The current of fetid cold air was coming from within. I stood up and walked towards the wardrobe. I opened the doors wide and pulled aside the clothes hanging on the rail. The wood at the back was rotten and had begun to disintegrate. Behind it I noticed what looked like a wall of plaster with a hole in it, a few centimetres wide. I leaned in to see what was on the other side of the wall, but it was almost pitch dark. The faint glow from the corridor cast only a vaporous thread of light through the hole into the space beyond, and all I could perceive was a murky gloom. I put my eye closer, trying to make out some shape, but at that moment a black spider appeared at the mouth of the hole. I recoiled quickly and the spider ran into the wardrobe, disappearing among the shadows. I closed the wardrobe door, left the room, turned the key in the lock and put it safely in the top of a chest of drawers in the corridor. The stench that had been trapped in the room had spread down the passage like poison. I cursed the moment I had decided to open that door and went outside to the street, hoping to forget, if only for a few hours, the darkness that throbbed at the heart of the tower house.

Bad ideas always come in twos. To celebrate the fact that I'd discovered some sort of camera obscura hidden in my home, I went to Sempere & Sons with the idea of taking the bookseller to lunch at La Maison Dorée. Sempere the elder was reading a beautiful edition of Potocki's *The Manuscript Found in Saragossa* and wouldn't even hear of it.

'I don't need to pay to see snobs and halfwits congratulating one another, Martín.'

'Don't be grumpy. I'm buying.'

Sempere declined. His son, who had witnessed the conversation from the entrance to the back room, looked at me, hesitating.

'What if I take your son with me? Will you stop talking to me?'

'It's up to you how you waste your time and money. I'm staying here to read: life's too short.'

Sempere's son was the very model of discretion. Even though we'd known one another since we were children, I couldn't remember having had more than three or four short conversations with him. I didn't know of any vices or weaknesses he might have, but I had it on good authority that among the girls in the quarter he was considered to be quite a catch, the official golden bachelor. More than one would drop by the bookshop with any old excuse and stand sighing by the shop window. But Sempere's son, even if he did notice, never tried to cash in on these promises of devotion and parted lips. Anyone else would have made a brilliant career in seduction with only a tenth of the capital. Anyone but Sempere's son who, one sometimes felt, deserved to be called a saint.

'At this rate, he's going to end up on the shelf,' Sempere complained from time to time.

'Have you tried throwing a bit of chilli pepper into his soup to stimulate the blood flow in key areas?' I would ask.

'You can laugh, you rascal. I'm close to seventy and I don't have a single grandson.'

We were received by the same head waiter I remembered from my last visit, but without the servile smile or welcoming gesture. When I told him we hadn't made a reservation he nodded disdainfully, clicking his fingers to summon a young waiter, who guided us unceremoniously to what I imagined was the worst table in the room, next to the kitchen door and buried in a dark, noisy corner. During the following twenty-five minutes nobody came near our table, not even to offer us the menu or pour us a glass of water. The staff walked past, banging the door and utterly ignoring our presence and our attempts to attract their attention.

'Don't you think we should leave?' Sempere's son said at last. 'I'd be happy with a sandwich in any old place . . .'

He'd hardly finished speaking when I saw them arrive. Vidal and his wife were advancing towards their table escorted by the head waiter and two other waiters who were falling over themselves to offer their congratulations. The Vidals sat down and a couple of minutes later the royal audience began: one after the other, all the diners in the room went over to congratulate Vidal. He received these obeisances with divine grace and sent each one away shortly afterwards. Sempere's son, who had become aware of the situation, was observing me.

'Martín, are you all right? Why don't we leave?'

I nodded slowly. We got up and headed for the exit, skirting the edges of the dining room on the opposite side from the Vidals' table. Before we left the restaurant we passed by the head waiter, who didn't even bother to look at us, and as we reached the main door I saw, in the mirror above the doorframe, that Vidal was leaning over and kissing Cristina on the lips. Once outside, Sempere's son looked at me, mortified.

156

'I'm sorry, Martín.'

'Don't worry. Bad choice. That's all. If you don't mind, I'd prefer it if you didn't tell your father about all this . . .'

'Not a word,' he assured me.

'Thanks.'

'Don't mention it. What do you say if I treat you to something more plebeian? There's an eatery in Calle del Carmen that's a knockout.'

I'd lost my appetite, but I gladly accepted.

'Sounds like a plan.'

The place was near the library and served good homemade meals at inexpensive prices for the people of the area. I barely touched my food, which smelled infinitely better than anything I'd smelled at La Maison Dorée in all the years it had been open, but by the time dessert came round I had already drunk, on my own, a bottle and a half of red wine and my head was spinning.

'Tell me something, Sempere. What have you got against improving the human race? How is it that a young, healthy citizen, blessed by the Lord Almighty with as fine a figure as yours, has not yet taken advantage of the best offers on the market?'

The bookseller's son laughed.

'What makes you think that I haven't?'

I touched my nose with my index finger and winked at him. Sempere's son nodded.

'You will probably take me for a prude, but I like to think that I'm waiting.'

'Waiting for what? For your equipment to get rusty?'

'You sound just like my father.'

'Wise men think and speak alike.'

'There must be something else, surely?' he asked.

'Something else?'

Sempere nodded.

'What do I know?' I said.

'I think you do know.'

'Fat lot of good it's doing me.'

I was about to pour myself another glass when Sempere stopped me.

'Moderation,' he murmured.

'See what a prude you are?'

'We all are what we are.'

'That can be cured. What do you say if you and I go out on the town?'

Sempere looked sorry for me.

'Martín, I think the best thing you can do is go home and rest. Tomorrow is another day.'

'You won't tell your father I got plastered, will you?'

On my way home I stopped in at least seven bars to sample their most potent stock until, for one reason or another, I was thrown out; each time I walked on down the street in search of my next port of call. I had never been a big drinker and by the end of the afternoon I was so drunk I couldn't even remember where I lived. I recall that a couple of waiters from the Hostal Ambos Mundos in Plaza Real took me by the arms and dumped me on a bench opposite the fountain, where I fell into a deep, thick stupor.

I dreamed that I was at Vidal's funeral. A blood-filled sky glowered over the maze of crosses and angels surrounding the large mausoleum of the Vidal family in Montjuïc Cemetery. A silent cortège peopled with black veils encircled the amphitheatre of darkened marble that formed the portico of the tomb. Each figure carried a long white candle. The light from a hundred flames sculpted the contours of a great marble angel on a pedestal overcome with grief and loss. At the angel's feet lay the open grave of my mentor and, inside it, a glass sarcophagus. Vidal's body, dressed in white, lay under the glass, his eyes wide open. Black tears ran down his cheeks. The silhouette of his widow, Cristina, emerged from the cortège; she fell on her knees next to the body, drowning in grief. One by one, the members of the procession walked past the deceased and dropped black roses on his glass coffin, until it was almost completely covered and all one could see was his face. Two faceless gravediggers lowered the coffin into the grave, the base of which was flooded with a thick, dark liquid. The sarcophagus floated on the sheet of blood, which slowly filtered through the cracks in the glass cover, until little by little, it filled the coffin, covering Vidal's dead body. Before his face was completely submerged, my mentor moved his eyes and looked at me. A flock of black birds took to the air and I started to run, losing my way among the paths of the endless city of the dead. Only the sound of distant crying enabled me to find the exit and to avoid the laments and pleadings of the dark, shadowy figures who waylaid me, begging me to take them with me, to rescue them from their eternal darkness.

Two policemen woke me, tapping my leg with their truncheons. Night had fallen and it took me a while to work out whether these were normal policemen on the beat, or agents of the Fates on a special mission.

'Now, sir, go and sleep it off at home, understood?'

'Yes, colonel!'

'Hurry up or you'll spend the night in jail; let's see if you find that funny.'

He didn't have to tell me twice. I got up as best I could and set off towards my house, hoping to get there before my feet led me off into some other seedy dive. The journey, which would normally have taken me ten or fifteen minutes, almost tripled in time. Finally, by some miraculous twist, I arrived at my front door only to find Isabella sitting there, like a curse, this time inside the main entrance of the building, in the courtyard.

'You're drunk,' said Isabella.

'I must be, because in mid delirium tremens I thought I discovered you sleeping in my doorway at midnight.'

'I had nowhere else to go. My father and I quarrelled and he's thrown me out.'

I closed my eyes and sighed. My brain, dulled by alcohol and bitterness, was unable to give any shape to the torrent of denials and curses piling up behind my lips.

'You can't stay here, Isabella.'

'Please, just for tonight. Tomorrow I'll look for a *pensión*. I beg you, Señor Martín.'

'Don't give me that doe-eyed look,' I threatened.

'Besides, it's your fault that I've been thrown out,' she added.

'My fault. I like that! I don't know whether you have any talent for writing, but you certainly have plenty of imagination! For what ill-fated reason, pray tell me, is it my fault that your dear father has chucked you out?'

'When you're drunk you have an odd way of speaking.'

'I'm not drunk. I've never been drunk in my life. Now answer my question.'

'I told my father you'd taken me on as your assistant and that from now on I was going to devote my life to literature and couldn't work in the shop.'

'What?'

'Can we go in? I'm cold and my bum's turned to stone from sitting on the steps.'

My head was going round in circles and I felt nauseous. I looked up at the faint glimmer that seeped through the skylight at the top of the stairs.

'Is this a punishment from above to make me repent my rakish ways?'

Isabella followed my eyes upwards, looking puzzled.

'Who are you talking to?'

'I'm not talking to anyone; I'm giving a monologue. It's the inebriated man's prerogative. But tomorrow morning first thing I'm going to talk to your father and put an end to this absurdity.'

'I don't think that's a good idea. He's sworn to kill you if he sees you. He's got a double-barrelled shotgun hidden under the counter. He's like that. He once killed a mule with it. It was in the summer, near Argentona—'

'Shut up. Not another word. Silence.'

Isabella nodded and looked at me expectantly. I began searching for my key. At that point I couldn't cope with this garrulous adolescent's drama. I needed to collapse onto my bed and lose consciousness, preferably in that order. I continued looking for a couple of minutes, but in vain. Finally, without saying a word, Isabella came over to me and rummaged through the pocket of my jacket, which my hands had already explored a hundred times, and found the key. She showed it to me, and I nodded, defeated.

Isabella opened the door to the apartment, keeping me upright, then guided me to my bedroom as if I were an invalid, and helped me onto my bed. After settling my head on the pillows, she removed my shoes. I looked at her in confusion.

'Don't worry, I'm not going to take your trousers off.'

She loosened my collar, sat down beside me and smiled with a

160

melancholy expression that belied her youth.

'I've never seen you so sad, Señor Martín. It's because of that woman, isn't it? The one in the photograph.'

She held my hand and stroked it, calming me.

'Everything passes, believe me. Everything.'

Despite myself, I could feel my eyes filling with tears and I turned my head so that she couldn't see my face. Isabella turned off the light on the bedside table and stayed there, sitting close to me in the dark, listening to the weeping of a miserable drunk, asking no questions, offering no opinion, offering nothing other than her company and her kindness, until I fell asleep.

7

I was woken by the agony of the hangover – a press clamping down on my temples – and the scent of Colombian coffee. Isabella had set a table by my bed with a pot of freshly brewed coffee and a plate with bread, cheese, ham and an apple. The sight of the food made me nauseous, but I stretched out my hand to reach for the coffee pot. Isabella, who had been watching from the doorway, rushed forward and poured a cup for me, full of smiles.

'Drink it like this, good and strong; it will work wonders.'

I accepted the cup and drank.

'What's the time?'

'One o'clock in the afternoon.'

I snorted.

'How long have you been awake?'

'About seven hours.'

'Doing what?'

'Cleaning, tidying up, but there's enough work here for a few months,' Isabella replied.

I took another long sip of coffee.

'Thanks,' I mumbled. 'For the coffee. And for cleaning up, although you don't have to do it.'

'I'm not doing it for you, if that's what you're worried about. I'm doing it for myself. If I'm going to live here, I'd rather not have to worry about getting stuck to something if I lean on it accidentally.'

'Live here? I thought we'd said that—'

As I raised my voice, a stab of pain scythed through my brain.

'Shhhh,' whispered Isabella.

I nodded, agreeing to a truce. I couldn't quarrel with Isabella now, and I didn't want to. There would be time enough to take her back to her family once the hangover had beaten a retreat. I finished my coffee in one long gulp and got up. Five or six thorns pierced my head. I groaned. Isabella caught hold of my arm.

'I'm not an invalid. I can manage on my own.'

She let go of me tentatively. I took a few steps towards the corridor, with Isabella following close behind, as if she feared I was about to topple over at any moment. I stopped in front of the bathroom.

'May I pee on my own?'

'Mind how you aim,' the girl murmured. 'I'll leave your breakfast in the gallery.'

'I'm not hungry.'

'You have to eat something.'

'Are you my apprentice or my mother?'

'It's for your own good.'

I closed the bathroom door and sought refuge inside. It took a while for my eyes to adjust to what I was seeing. The bathroom was unrecognisable. Clean and sparkling. Everything in its place. A new bar of soap on the sink. Clean towels that I didn't even know I owned. A smell of bleach.

'Good God,' I mumbled.

I put my head under the tap and let the cold water run for a couple of minutes, then went out into the corridor and slowly made my way to the gallery. If the bathroom was unrecognisable, the gallery now belonged to another world. Isabella had cleaned the windowpanes and the floor and tidied the furniture and armchairs. A diaphanous light filtered through the tall windows and the smell of dust had disappeared. My breakfast awaited on the table opposite the sofa, over which the girl had spread a clean throw. The books on the shelves seemed to have been reorganised and the glass cabinets had recovered their transparency. Isabella served me a second cup of coffee.

'I know what you're doing, and it's not going to work.'

'Pouring you a coffee?'

She had tidied up the books that lay scattered around in piles on tables and in corners. She had emptied magazine racks that had been overflowing for a decade or more. In just seven hours she had swept away years of darkness, and still she had the time and energy to smile.

'I preferred it as it was,' I said.

'Of course you did, and so did the hundred thousand cockroaches you had as lodgers. I've sent them packing with the help of some ammonia.'

'So that's the stink I can smell?'

'This "stink" is the smell of cleanliness,' Isabella protested. 'You could be a little bit grateful.'

'I am.'

'It doesn't show. Tomorrow I'll go up to the study and—'

'Don't even think about it.'

Isabella shrugged her shoulders, but she still looked determined and I knew that in twenty-four hours the study in the tower was going to suffer an irreparable transformation.

'By the way, this morning I found an envelope in the corridor. Somebody must have slipped it under the door last night.'

I looked at her over my cup.

'The main door downstairs is locked,' I said.

'That's what I thought. Frankly, I did find it rather odd and, although it had your name on it—'

'You opened it.'

'I'm afraid so. I didn't mean to.'

'Isabella, opening other people's letters is not a sign of good manners. In some places it's even considered a crime that can be punished by a prison sentence.'

'That's what I tell my mother – she always opens my letters. And she's still free.'

'Where's the letter?'

Isabella pulled an envelope out of the pocket of the apron she had donned and handed it to me, averting her eyes. The envelope had serrated edges and the paper was thick, porous and ivory-coloured, with an angel stamped on the red wax – now broken – and my name written in red, perfumed ink. I opened it and pulled out a folded sheet.

Dear David,
I hope this finds you in good health and that you have banked the agreed money without any problems. Do you think we could meet tonight at my house to start discussing the details of our project? A light dinner will be served around ten o'clock. I'll be waiting for you.

Your friend,
ANDREAS CORELLI

I folded the sheet of paper and put it back in the envelope. Isabella looked at me with curiosity.

'Good news?'

'Nothing that concerns you.'

'Who is this Señor Corelli? He has nice handwriting, not like yours.'

I looked at her severely.

'If I'm going to be your assistant, it's only logical that I should know who your contacts are. In case I have to send them packing, that is.'

I grunted.

'He's a publisher.'

'He must be a good one, just look at the writing paper and envelope he uses. What book are you writing for him?'

'It's none of your business.'

'How can I help you if you won't tell me what you're working on? No, don't answer; I'll shut up.'

For ten miraculous seconds, Isabella was silent.

'What's this Señor Corelli like, then?'

I looked at her coldly.

'Peculiar . . .'

'Birds of a feather . . .'

Watching that girl with a noble heart I felt, if anything, more miserable, and understood that the sooner I got her away from me, even at the risk of hurting her, the better it would be for both of us.

'Why are you looking at me like that?'

'I'm going out tonight, Isabella.'

'Shall I leave some supper for you? Will you be back very late?'

'I'll be having dinner out and I don't know when I'll be back, but by the time I return, whenever it is, I want you to have left. I want you to collect your things and go. I don't care where to. There's no place for you here. Do you understand?'

Her face grew pale, and her eyes began to water. She bit her lip and smiled at me, her cheeks lined with falling tears.

'I'm not needed here. Understood.'

'And don't do any more cleaning.'

I got up and left her alone in the gallery. I hid in the study, up in the tower, and opened the windows. I could hear Isabella sobbing down in the gallery. I gazed at the city stretching out under the midday sun then turned my head to look in the other direction, where I thought I could almost see the shining tiles covering Villa Helius. I imagined Cristina, Señora de Vidal, standing by the windows of her tower, looking down at the Ribera quarter. Something dark and murky filled my heart. I forgot Isabella's weeping and wished only for the moment when I would meet Corelli, so that we could discuss his accursed book.

I stayed in the study as the afternoon spread over the city like blood floating in water. It was hot, hotter than it had been all summer, and the rooftops of the Ribera quarter seemed to shimmer like a mirage. I went down to the lower floor and changed my clothes. The house was silent, and in the gallery the shutters were half-closed and the windows tinted with an amber light that spread down the corridor.

'Isabella?' I called.

There was no reply. I went over to the gallery and saw that the girl had left. Before doing so, however, she had cleaned and put in order a collection of the complete works of Ignatius B. Samson. For years they had collected dust and oblivion in a glass cabinet that now shone immaculately. She had taken one of the books and left it open on a lectern. I read a line at random and felt as if I were travelling back to a time when everything seemed simple and inevitable.

'Poetry is written with tears, novels with blood, and history with invisible ink,' said the cardinal, as he spread poison on the knife-edge by the light of a candelabra.

The studied naivety of those lines made me smile and brought back a suspicion that had never really left me: perhaps it would have been better for everyone, especially for me, if Ignatius B. Samson had never committed suicide and David Martín had never taken his place.

8

It was getting dark when I went out. The heat and the humidity had encouraged many of my neighbours to bring their chairs out into the street, hoping for a breeze that never came. I dodged the improvised rings of people sitting around front doors and on street corners, and made my way to the railway station, where there was always a queue of taxis waiting for customers. I got into the first cab in the rank. It took us about twenty minutes to cross the city and climb the hill on whose slopes lay Gaudí's ghostly forest. The lights in Corelli's house could be seen from afar.

'I didn't know anyone lived here,' the driver remarked.

As soon as I'd paid for my ride, including a tip, he sped off, not wasting a second. I waited a few moments, savouring the strange silence that filled the place. Not a single leaf moved in the wood that covered the hill behind me. A starlit sky with wisps of cloud spread in every direction. I could hear the sound of my own breathing, of my clothes rustling as I walked, of my steps getting closer to the door. I rapped with the knocker, then waited.

The door opened a few moments later. A man with drooping eyes and drooping shoulders nodded when he saw me and beckoned me in. His outfit suggested that he was some sort of butler or servant. He made no sound at all. I followed him down the passageway with the portraits on either side, and when we came to the end, he showed me into the large sitting room with its view over the whole city in the distance. He bowed slightly and left me on my own, walking away as slowly as he had when he brought me in. I went over to the French windows and looked through the net curtains, killing time while I waited for Corelli. A couple of minutes had gone by before I noticed that someone was observing me from a corner of the room. He was sitting in an armchair, completely still, half in darkness, the light from an oil lamp revealing only his legs and his hands as they rested on the arms of the chair. I recognised him by the glow of his unblinking eyes and by the angel-shaped brooch he always wore on his lapel. As soon as I looked at him he stood up and came over to me with quick steps – too quick – and a wolfish smile that froze my blood.

'Good evening, Martín.'

I nodded, trying to smile back.

'I've startled you again,' he said. 'I'm sorry. May I offer you something to drink, or shall we go straight to dinner?'

'To tell you the truth, I'm not hungry.'

'It's the heat, I'm sure. If you like, we can go into the garden and talk there.'

The silent butler reappeared and proceeded to open the doors to the garden, where a path of candles placed on saucers led to a white metal table with two chairs facing each other. The flame from the candles burned bright and did not flicker. The moon cast a soft, bluish hue. I sat down, and Corelli followed suit, while the butler poured us two glasses from a decanter of what I thought must be wine or some sort of liqueur I had no intention of tasting. In the light of the waxing moon, Corelli seemed younger, his features sharper. He observed me with an intensity verging on greed.

'Something is bothering you, Martín.'

'I suppose you've heard about the fire.'

'A terrible end, and yet there was poetic justice in it.'

'You think it just that two men should die in such a way?'

'Would a gentler way have seemed more acceptable? Justice is an affectation of perspective, not a universal value. I'm not going to pretend to feel dismayed when I don't, and I don't suppose you will either, however hard you try. But if you prefer, we can have a minute's silence.'

'That won't be necessary.'

'Of course not. It's only necessary when one has nothing valid to say. Silence makes even idiots seem wise for a minute. Anything else worrying you, Martín?'

'The police seem to think I have something to do with what happened. They asked me about you.'

Corelli nodded, unconcerned.

'The police must do their work and we must do ours. Shall we close this matter?'

I nodded. Corelli smiled.

'A while ago, as I was waiting for you, I realised that you and I have a small rhetorical conversation pending. The sooner we get it out of the way, the sooner we can get started. I'd like to begin by asking what faith means to you.'

I pondered for a moment.

'I've never been a religious person. Rather than believe or disbelieve, I doubt. Doubt is my faith.'

'Very prudent and very bourgeois. But you don't win a game by hitting the balls out of court. Why would you say that so many different beliefs have appeared and disappeared throughout history?'

'I don't know. Social, economic or political factors, I suppose. You're talking to someone who left school at the age of ten. History has never been my strong point.'

'History is biology's dumping ground, Martín.'

'I think I wasn't at school the day that lesson was taught.'

'This lesson is not taught in classrooms, Martín. It is taught through reason and the observation of reality. This lesson is the one nobody wants to learn and is therefore the one we must examine carefully in order to be able to do our work. All business opportunities stem from someone else's inability to resolve a simple and inevitable problem.'

'Are we talking about religion or economics?'

'You choose the label.'

'If I understand you correctly, you're suggesting that faith, the act of believing in myths, ideologies or supernatural legends, is the consequence of biology.'

'That's exactly right.'

'A rather cynical view, coming from a publisher of religious texts,' I remarked.

'A dispassionate and professional view,' Corelli explained. 'Human beings believe just as they breathe – in order to survive.'

'Is that your theory?'

'It's not a theory, it's a statistic.'

'It occurs to me that at least three quarters of the world would disagree with that assertion,' I said.

'Of course. If they agreed they wouldn't be potential believers. Nobody can really be convinced of something he or she doesn't *need* to believe in through some biological imperative.'

'Are you suggesting then that it is part of our nature to be deceived?'

'It is part of our nature to survive. Faith is an instinctive response to aspects of existence that we cannot explain by any other means – be it the moral void we perceive in the universe, the certainty of death, the mystery of the origin of things, the meaning of our own lives, or the absence of meaning. These are basic and extremely simple aspects of existence, but our own limitations prevent us from responding in an unequivocal way, and for that reason we generate an emotional response, as a defence mechanism. It's pure biology.'

'According to you, then, all beliefs or ideals are nothing more than fiction.'

'All interpretation or observation of reality is necessarily fiction. In this case, the problem is that man is a moral animal abandoned in an amoral universe and condemned to a finite existence with no other meaning than to perpetuate the natural cycle of the species. It is impossible to survive in a prolonged state of reality, at least for a human being. We spend a good part of our lives dreaming, especially when we're awake. As I said, pure biology.'

I sighed.

'And after all this, you want me to invent a fable that will make the unwary fall on their knees and persuade them that they have seen the light, that there is something to believe in, something to live and die for – even to kill for.'

'Exactly. I'm not asking you to invent anything that hasn't already been invented, one way or another. I'm only asking you to help me give water to the thirsty.'

'A praiseworthy and pious proposition,' I said with irony.

'No, simply a commercial proposition. Nature is one huge free market. The law of supply and demand is a molecular fact.'

'Perhaps you should find an intellectual to do this job. I can assure you that most of them have never seen a hundred thousand francs in their lives. I bet they'd be prepared to sell their soul, or even invent it, for a fraction of that amount.'

The metallic glow in his eyes made me suspect that Corelli was about to deliver another of his hard-hitting pocket sermons. I visualised the credit in my account at the Banco Hispano Colonial and told myself that a hundred thousand francs were well worth the price of listening to a Mass, or a collection of homilies.

'An intellectual is usually someone who isn't exactly distinguished by his intellect,' Corelli asserted. 'He claims that label to compensate for his own inadequacies. It's as old as that saying: tell me what you boast of and I'll tell you what you lack. Our daily bread. The incompetent always present themselves as experts, the cruel as pious, sinners as excessively devout, usurers as benefactors, the small-minded as patriots, the arrogant as humble, the vulgar as elegant and the feeble-minded as intellectual. Once again, it's all the work of nature. Far from being the sylph to whom poets sing, nature is a cruel, voracious mother who needs to feed on the creatures she gives birth to in order to stay alive.'

Corelli and his fierce biological poetics were beginning to make me feel queasy. I was uncomfortable at the barely contained vehemence of the publisher's words, and I wondered whether there was anything in the universe that did not seem repugnant and despicable to him, including myself.

'You should give inspirational talks in schools and churches on Palm Sunday. You'd be a tremendous success,' I suggested.

Corelli laughed coldly.

'Don't change the subject. What I'm searching for is the opposite of an intellectual, in other words, someone intelligent. And I have found that person.'

'You flatter me.'

'Better still, I pay you. And I pay you very well, which is the only real form of flattery in this whorish world. Never accept medals unless they come printed on the back of a cheque. They only benefit those who give them. And since I'm paying you, I expect you to listen and follow my instructions. Believe me when I say that I have no interest at all in making you waste your time. While you're in my pay, your time is also my time.'

His tone was friendly, but his eyes shone like steel and left no room for misunderstandings.

'You don't need to remind me every five minutes.'

'Forgive my insistence, dear Martín. If I'm making your head spin with all these details it's only because I'm trying to get them out of the way sooner rather than later. What I want from you is the form, not the content. The content is always the same and has been in place ever since human life began. It's engraved on your heart with a serial number. What I want you to do is find an intelligent and seductive way of answering the questions we all ask ourselves and you should do so using your own reading of the human soul, putting into practice your art and your profession. I want you to bring me a narrative that awakens the soul.'

'Nothing more . . .'

'Nothing less.'

'You're talking about manipulating feelings and emotions. Would it not be easier to convince people with a rational, simple and straightforward account?'

'No. It's impossible to initiate a rational dialogue with someone about beliefs and concepts if he has not acquired them through reason. It doesn't matter whether we're looking at God, race, or national pride. That's why I need something more powerful than a simple rhetorical exposition. I need the strength of art, of stagecraft. We think we understand a song's lyrics, but what makes us believe in them, or not, is the music.'

I tried to take in all his gibberish without choking.

'Don't worry, there'll be no more speeches for today,' Corelli interjected. 'Now let's discuss practical matters: we'll meet about once a fortnight. You will inform me of your progress and show me the work you've produced. If I have any changes or observations to make, I will point them out to you. The work will continue for twelve months, or whatever fraction of that time you need to complete the job. At the end of that period you will hand in all the work and the documents it generated, with no exceptions: they belong to the sole proprietor and guarantor of the rights, in other words, me. Your name will not appear as the author of the document and you will agree not to claim authorship after delivery, or to discuss the work you have written or the terms of this agreement, either in private or in public, with anybody. In exchange, you will receive the initial payment of one hundred thousand francs, which has already been paid to you, and, upon receipt of the work to my satisfaction, an additional bonus of fifty thousand francs.'

I gulped. One is never wholly conscious of the greed hidden in one's heart until one hears the sweet sound of silver.

'Don't you want to formalise the contract in writing?'

'Ours is a gentleman's agreement, based on honour: yours and mine. It has already been sealed. A gentleman's agreement cannot be broken because it breaks the person who has signed it,' said Corelli in a tone that made me think it might have been better to sign a piece of paper, even if it had to be written in blood. 'Any questions?'

'Yes. Why?'

'I don't follow you, Martín.'

'Why do you want all this material, or whatever you wish to call it? What do you plan to do with it?'

'Problems of conscience, at this stage, Martín?'

'Perhaps you think of me as someone with no principles, but if I'm going to take part in the project you're proposing, I want to know what the objective is. I think I have a right to know.'

Corelli smiled and placed his hand on mine. I felt a shiver at the contact of his skin, which was icy cold and smooth as marble.

'Because you want to live.'

'That sounds vaguely threatening.'

'A simple and friendly reminder of what you already know. You'll help me because you want to live and because you don't care about the price or the consequences. Because not that long ago you saw yourself at death's door and now you have an eternity before you and the opportunity of a life. You will help me because you're human. And because, although you don't want to admit it, you have faith.'

I withdrew my hand from his reach and watched him get up from his chair and walk over to the end of the garden.

'Don't worry, Martín. Everything will turn out all right. Trust me,' said Corelli in a sweet, almost paternal tone.

'May I leave now?'

'Of course. I don't want to keep you any longer than is necessary. I've enjoyed our conversation. I'll let you go now, so you can start mulling over all the things we've discussed. You'll see that, once the indigestion has passed, the real answers will come to you. There is nothing in the path of life that we don't already know before we started. Nothing important is learned, it is simply remembered.'

He signalled to the taciturn butler, who was waiting at the edge of the garden.

'A car will pick you up and take you home. We'll meet again in two weeks' time.'

'Here?'

'It's in the lap of the Gods,' Corelli said, licking his lips as if he'd made a delicious joke.

The butler came over and motioned for me to follow him. Corelli nodded and sat down, his eyes lost once more on the city below.

9

The car – for want of a better word – was waiting by the door of the large, old house. It was not an ordinary automobile, but a collector's item. It reminded me of an enchanted carriage, a cathedral on wheels, its chrome and curves engineered by science, its bonnet topped by a silver angel like a ship's figurehead. In other words, a Rolls-Royce. The butler opened the door for me and took his leave with a bow. I stepped inside: it looked more like a hotel room than a motor car. The engine started up as soon as I settled in the seat, and we set off down the hill.

'Do you know the address?' I asked.

The chauffeur, a dark figure on the other side of a glass partition, nodded vaguely. We crossed Barcelona in the narcotic silence of that metal carriage, barely touching the ground, or so it seemed. Streets and buildings flew past the windows like underwater cliffs. It was after midnight when the black Rolls-Royce turned off Calle Comercio and entered Paseo del Borne. The car stopped on the corner of Calle Flassaders, which was too narrow for it to pass through. The chauffeur got out and opened my door with a bow. I stepped from the car and he closed the door and got in again without saying a word. I watched him leave, the dark silhouette blending into a veil of shadows. I asked myself what I had done, and, choosing not to seek an answer, I set off towards my house feeling as if the whole world was a prison from which there was no escape.

When I walked into the apartment I went straight up to the study. I opened the windows on all four sides and let the humid breeze penetrate the room. I could see people lying on mattresses and sheets on some of the neighbouring flat roofs, trying to escape the suffocating heat and get some sleep. In the distance, the three large chimneys in the Paralelo area rose like funeral pyres spreading a mantle of white ash over Barcelona. Nearer to me, on the dome of La Mercè church, the statue of Our Lady of Mercy, poised for ascension into heaven, reminded me of the angel on the Rolls-Royce and of the one Corelli always sported on his lapel. After many months of silence it felt as if the city were speaking to me again, telling me its secrets.

Then I saw her, curled up on a doorstep in that miserable, narrow tunnel between old buildings they called Fly Alley. Isabella. I wondered how long she'd been there and told myself it was none of my business. I was about to close the window and walk over to the desk when I noticed that she was not alone. Two figures were slowly, perhaps too slowly, advancing towards her from the other end of the street. I sighed, hoping they would pass her by. They didn't. One of them took up a position blocking the exit from the alley. The other knelt down in front of the girl, stretching an arm out towards her. The girl moved. A few moments later the two figures closed in on Isabella and I heard her scream.

It took me about forty-five seconds to get there. When I did, one of the two men had grabbed Isabella by her arms and the other had pulled up her skirt. A terrified expression gripped the girl's face. The second man guffawed as he made his way between her thighs, holding a knife to her throat. Three lines of blood oozed from the cut. I looked around me. A couple of boxes of rubbish and a pile of cobblestones and building materials lay abandoned by the wall. I grabbed what turned out to be a metal bar, solid and heavy, about half a metre long. The first man to notice my presence was the one

174

holding the knife. I took a step forward, brandishing the metal bar. His eyes jumped from the bar to my eyes and his smile disappeared. The other turned and saw me advancing towards them holding the bar up high. A nod from me was enough to make him let go of Isabella and quickly stand behind his companion.

'Come on, let's go,' he whispered.

The other man ignored his words. He was looking straight at me with fire in his eyes, the knife still in his hand.

'Who asked you to stick your oar in, you son-of-a-bitch?'

I took Isabella by the arm, lifting her up from the ground, without taking my eyes off the man with the knife. I searched for the keys in my pocket and gave them to her.

'Go home,' I shouted. 'Do as I say.'

Isabella hesitated for a moment, but soon I heard her running towards Calle Flassaders. The guy with the knife saw her leave and smiled angrily.

'I'm going to slash you, you bastard.'

I didn't doubt his ability or his wish to carry out his threat, but something in his eyes made me think that my opponent was not altogether stupid and if he had not done so already it was because he was wondering how much the metal bar I was holding might weigh and, above all, whether I'd have the strength, the courage and the time to squash his skull with it before he could thrust his blade into me.

'Go on,' I invited him.

The man held my eyes for a few seconds and then laughed. The other one sighed with relief. The first folded his blade and spat at my feet. Then he turned round and walked off into the shadows from which he had emerged, his companion running behind him like a puppy.

I found Isabella curled up at the bottom of the stairs in the inner courtyard of the tower house. She was trembling and held the keys with both hands. When she saw me come in she jumped up.

'Do you want me to call a doctor?'

She shook her head.

'Are you sure?'

'They hadn't managed to do anything to me yet,' she mumbled, fighting away the tears.

'It didn't look that way.'

'They didn't do anything, all right?' she protested.

'All right,' I said.

I wanted to hold her arm as we went up the stairs, but she avoided any contact.

Once in the apartment I took her to the bathroom and turned on the light.

'Have you any clean clothes you can put on?'

Isabella showed me the bag she was carrying and nodded.

'Come on, you wash while I get something ready for dinner.'

'How can you be hungry after what just happened?'

'Well, I am.'

Isabella bit her lower lip.

'The truth is, so am I . . .'

'End of discussion then,' I said.

I closed the bathroom door and waited until I heard the taps running, then returned to the kitchen and put some water on to boil. There was a bit of rice left, some bacon, and a few vegetables that Isabella had brought over the day before. I improvised a dish made from leftovers and waited almost thirty minutes for her to come out of the bathroom, downing almost half a bottle of wine in that time. I heard her crying with anger on the other side of the wall. When she appeared at the kitchen door her eyes were red and she looked more like a child than ever.

'I'm not sure that I'm still hungry,' she murmured.

'Sit down and eat.'

We sat down at the small table in the middle of the kitchen. Isabella examined her plate of rice and chopped-up bits with some suspicion.

'Eat,' I ordered.

She brought a tentative spoonful to her lips.

'It's good,' she said.

I poured her half a glass of wine and topped it up with water.

'My father doesn't let me drink wine.'

'I'm not your father.'

We had dinner in silence, exchanging glances. Isabella finished her plate and the slice of bread I'd given her. She smiled shyly. She didn't realise that the shock hadn't yet hit her. Then I went with her to her bedroom door and turned on the light.

'Try to get some rest,' I said. 'If you need anything, bang on the wall. I'm in the next room.'

Isabella nodded. 'I heard you snoring the other night.'

'I don't snore.'

'It must have been the pipes. Or maybe there's a neighbour with a pet bear.'

'One more word and you're back in the street.'

'Thanks,' she whispered. 'Don't close the door completely, please. Leave it ajar.'

'Goodnight,' I said, turning out the light and leaving Isabella in the dark.

Later, while I undressed in my bedroom, I noticed a dark mark on my cheek, like a black tear. I went over to the mirror and brushed it away with my fingers. It was dried blood. Only then did I realise that I was exhausted and my whole body was aching.

10

The following morning, before Isabella woke up, I walked over to her family's grocery shop on Calle Mirallers. It was just getting light and the security grille over the shop door was only half open. I slipped inside and found a couple of young boys piling up boxes of tea and other goods on the counter.

'We're closed,' one of them said.

'Well, you don't look closed. Go and fetch the owner.'

While I waited, I kept myself busy by examining the family emporium of the ungrateful heiress Isabella, who in her infinite innocence had turned her back on the ambrosia of commerce to prostrate herself before the miseries of literature. The shop was a small bazaar full of marvels brought from every corner of the world. Jams, sweets and teas. Coffees, spices and tinned food. Fruit and cured meats. Chocolates and smoked ham. A Pantagruelian paradise for well-lined pockets. Don Odón, the girl's father and manager of the establishment, appeared shortly afterwards wearing a blue overall, a marshal's moustache and an expression of alarm that seemed to herald a heart attack at any moment. I decided to skip the pleasantries.

'Your daughter says you have a double-barrelled shotgun with which you have sworn to kill me,' I said, stretching my arms out to the sides. 'Well, here I am.'

'Who are you, you scoundrel?'

'I'm the scoundrel who's had to take in a young girl because her pathetic father was unable to keep her under control.'

The shopkeeper's angry expression disappeared and was replaced with a faint-hearted smile.

'Señor Martín? I didn't recognise you . . . How is my child?'

I sighed.

'Your child is safe and sound in my house, snoring like a mastiff, but with her honour and virtue intact.'

The shopkeeper crossed himself twice, much relieved.

'God bless you.'

'Thank you very much, but in the meantime I'm going to ask you to come and collect her today without fail, otherwise I'll smash your face in, shotgun or no shotgun.'

'Shotgun?' the shopkeeper mumbled in confusion.

His wife, a small nervous-looking woman, was spying on us from behind the curtain that concealed the back room. Something told me there would be no shots fired here. Don Odón huffed and puffed and looked as if he was on the point of collapse.

'Nothing would please me more, Señor Martín. But the girl doesn't want to be here,' he argued, devastated.

When I realised the shopkeeper was not the rogue Isabella had painted him as, I was sorry for the way I'd spoken.

'You haven't thrown her out of your house?'

Don Odón opened his eyes wide and looked hurt. His wife stepped forward and took her husband's hand.

'We had an argument,' he said. 'Things were said that shouldn't have been said, on both sides. But that girl has such a temper, you wouldn't believe it . . . She threatened to leave us and said she'd never come back. Her saintly mother nearly passed away from the palpitations. I shouted at her and said I'd stick her in a convent.'

'An infallible argument when reasoning with a seventeen-year-old girl,' I pointed out.

'It was the first thing that came to mind,' the shopkeeper argued. 'As if I would put her in a convent!'

'From what I've seen, you'd need the help of a whole regiment of infantry.'

'I don't know what that girl has told you, Señor Martín, but you mustn't believe her. We might not be very refined, but we're not monsters either. I don't know how to deal with her any more. I'm not the type of man who would pull out a belt and give her forty lashes. And my missus here daren't even shout at the cat. I don't know where the girl gets it from. I think it's all that reading. Mind you, the nuns did warn us. And my father, God rest his soul, used to say it too: the day women are allowed to learn to read and write, the world will become ungovernable.'

'A deep thinker, your father, but that doesn't solve your problem or mine.'

'What can we do? Isabella doesn't want to be with us, Señor Martín. She says we're dim and we don't understand her; she says we want to bury her in this shop . . . There's nothing I'd like more than to understand her. I've worked in this shop since I was seven years old, from dawn to dusk, and the only thing I understand is that the world is a nasty place with no consideration for a young girl who has her head in the clouds,' the shopkeeper explained, leaning on a barrel. 'My greatest fear is that, if I force her to return, she might really run away and fall into the hands of any old . . . I don't even want to think about it.'

'It's true,' his wife said, with a slight Italian accent. 'Believe me, the girl has broken our hearts, but this is not the first time she's gone away. She's turned out just like my mother, who had a Neapolitan temperament . . .'

'Oh, *la mamma*,' said Don Odón, shuddering even at the memory of his mother-in-law.

'When she told us she was going to stay at your house for a few days while she helped you with your work, well, we felt reassured,' Isabella's mother went on, 'because we know you're a good person and basically the girl is nearby, only two streets away. We're sure you'll be able to convince her to return.'

I wondered what Isabella had told them about me to persuade them that yours truly could walk on water.

'Only last night, just round the corner from here, two labourers on their way home were given a terrible beating. Imagine! It seems they were battered with an iron pole, smashed to bits like dogs. One of them might not survive, and it looks like the other one will be crippled for life,' said the mother. 'What sort of world are we living in?'

Don Odón gave me a worried look.

'If I go and fetch her, she'll leave again. And this time I don't know whether she'll end up with someone like you. It's not right for a young girl to live in a bachelor's house, but at least you're honest and will know how to take care of her.'

The shopkeeper looked as if he was about to cry. I would have preferred it if he'd rushed off to fetch the gun. There was still the chance that some Neapolitan cousin might turn up, armed with a blunderbuss, to save the girl's honour. *Porca miseria.*

'Do I have your word that you'll look after her for me until she comes to her senses?'

I grunted. 'You have my word.'

I returned home laden with superb delicacies which Don Odón and his wife had insisted on foisting on me. I promised them I'd take care of Isabella for a few days, until she agreed to reason things out and understand that her place was with her family. The shopkeepers wanted to pay me for her keep, but I refused. My plan was that, before the week was up, Isabella would be back sleeping in her own home, even if, to achieve that, I had to keep up the pretence that she was my assistant. Taller towers had toppled.

When I got home I found her sitting at the kitchen table. She had washed all the dishes from the night before, had made coffee and had dressed and styled her hair so that she resembled a saint in a religious picture. Isabella, who was no fool, knew perfectly well where I'd been and looked at me like an abandoned dog, smiling meekly. I left the bags with the delicacies from Don Odón by the sink.

'Didn't my father shoot you with his gun?'

'He'd run out of bullets and decided to throw all these pots of jam and Manchego cheese at me instead.'

Isabella pressed her lips together, trying to look serious.

'So the name Isabella comes from your grandmother?'

'*La mamma*,' she confirmed. 'In the area they called her Vesuvia.'

'You don't say.'

'They say I'm a bit like her. When it comes to persistence.'

There was no need for a judge to pronounce on that, I thought.

'Your parents are good folk, Isabella. They don't misunderstand you any more than you misunderstand them.'

The girl didn't say anything. She poured me a cup of coffee and waited for the verdict. I had two options: throw her out and give the two shopkeepers a fit; or be bold and patient for two or three more days. I imagined that forty-eight hours of my most cynical and cutting performance would be enough to break the iron deter- mination of the young girl and send her, on her knees, back to her mother's apron strings, begging for forgiveness and full board.

'You can stay here for the time being—'

'Thank you!'

'Not so fast. You can stay here under the following conditions: one, that you go and spend some time in the shop every day, to say hello to your parents and tell them you're well; and two, that you obey me and follow the rules of this house.'

It sounded patriarchal but excessively faint-hearted. I maintained my austere expression and decided to make my tone more severe.

'What are the rules of this house?' Isabella enquired.

'Basically, whatever I damn well please.'

'Sounds fair.'

'It's a deal, then.'

Isabella came round the table and hugged me gratefully. I felt the warmth and the firm shape of her seventeen-year-old body against mine. I pushed her away delicately, keeping my distance.

'The first rule is that this is not *Little Women* and we don't hug one another or burst into tears at the slightest thing.'

'Whatever you say.'

'That will be the motto on which we'll build our coexistence: whatever I say.'

Isabella laughed and rushed off into the corridor.

'Where do you think you're going?'

'To tidy up your study. You don't mean to leave it like that, do you?'

11

I had to find a place where I could think, where I could escape from my new assistant's domestic pride and her obsession with cleanliness. So I went to the library in Calle del Carmen, set in a nave of Gothic arches that had once housed a medieval hospice. I spent the rest of the day surrounded by volumes that smelled like a papal tomb, reading about mythology and the history of religions until my eyes were about to fall out onto the table and roll away along the library floor. After hours of reading without a break, I worked out that I had barely scratched a millionth of what I could find beneath the arches of that sanctuary of books, let alone everything else that had been written on the subject. I decided to return the following day and the day after that: I would spend at least a week filling the cauldron of my thoughts with pages and pages about gods, miracles and prophecies, saints and apparitions, revelations and mysteries – anything rather than think about Cristina, Don Pedro and their life as a married couple.

As I had an obliging assistant at my disposal, I instructed her to find copies of catechisms and school books currently used for religious instruction, and to write me a summary of each one. Isabella did not dispute my orders, but she frowned when I gave them.

'I want to know, in numbing detail, how children are taught the whole business, from Noah's Ark to the Feeding of the Five Thousand,' I explained.

'Why?'

'Because that's the way I am. I have a wide range of interests.'

'Are you doing research for a new version of "Away in a Manger"?'

'No. I'm planning a novel about the adventures of a second lieutenant nun. Just do as I say and don't question me or I'll send you back to your parents' shop to sell quince jelly galore.'

'You're a despot.'

'I'm glad to see we're getting to know one another.'

'Does this have anything to do with the book you're writing for that publisher, Corelli?'

'It might.'

'Well, I get the feeling it's not a book that will have much commercial scope.'

'And what would you know?'

'More than you think. And there's no need to get so worked up, either. I'm only trying to help you. Or have you decided to stop being a professional writer and change into an elegant amateur?'

'For the moment I'm too busy being a nanny.'

'I wouldn't bring up the question of who is the nanny here, because I'd win that debate hands down.'

'So what debate does Your Excellency fancy?'

'Commercial art versus stupid moral idiocies.'

'Dear Isabella, my little Vesuvia: in commercial art – and all art that is worthy of the name is commercial sooner or later – stupidity is almost always in the eye of the beholder.'

'Are you calling me stupid?'

'I'm calling you to order. Do as I say. End of story. Shush.'

I pointed to the door and Isabella rolled her eyes, mumbling some insult or other which I didn't quite hear as she walked off down the passageway.

While Isabella went around schools and bookshops in search of textbooks and catechisms to precis for me, I went back to the library in Calle del Carmen to further my theological education, an endeavour I undertook fuelled by strong doses of coffee and stoicism. The first seven days of that strange creative process only enlightened me with more doubts. One of the few truths I discovered was that the vast majority of authors who had felt a calling to write about the divine, the human and the sacred must have been exceedingly learned and pious, but as writers they were dreadful. For the long-suffering reader forced to skim over their pages it was a real struggle not to fall into a coma induced by boredom with each new paragraph.

After surviving thousands of pages on the subject, I was beginning to get the impression that the hundreds of religious beliefs catalogued throughout the history of the printed letter were all extraordinarily similar. I attributed this first impression to my ignorance or to a lack of adequate information, but I couldn't rid myself of the idea that I'd been going through the storyline of dozens of crime novels in which the murderer turned out to be either one person or another, but the mechanics of the plot were, in essence, always the same. Myths and legends, either about divinities or the formation and history of peoples and races, began to look like pictures on a jigsaw puzzle, slightly different from one another but always built with the same pieces, though not in the same order.

After two days I had already become friends with Eulalia, the head librarian, who picked out texts and volumes from the ocean of paper in her care and from time to time came to see me at my table in the corner to ask whether I needed anything else. She must have been around my age, and had wit coming out of her ears, usually in the form of sharp, somewhat poisonous jibes.

'You're reading a lot of hagiography, sir. Have you decided to become an altar boy now, at the threshold of maturity?'

'It's only research.'

'Ah, that's what they all say.'

The librarian's clever jokes provided an invaluable balm that enabled me to survive those texts that seemed to be carved in stone, and to press on with my pilgrimage. Whenever Eulalia had a free moment she would come over to my table and help me classify all that bilge – pages abounding with stories of fathers and sons; of pure, saintly mothers; betrayals and conversions; prophets and martyrs; envoys from heaven; babies born to save the universe; evil creatures, horrifying to look at and usually taking the form of an animal; ethereal beings with racially acceptable features who acted as agents of good; and heroes subjected to terrible tests to prove their destiny. Earthly existence was always perceived as a temporary rite of passage which invited one to a docile acceptance of one's lot and the rules of the tribe, because the reward was always in the hereafter, a paradise brimming with all the things one had lacked during corporeal life.

On Thursday at midday, Eulalia came over to my table during one of her breaks and asked me whether, apart from reading missals, I ate every now and then. So I asked her to lunch at nearby Casa Leopoldo, which had just opened to the public. While we enjoyed a delicious oxtail stew, she told me she'd been in the same job for over two years and had spent two more years working on a novel that was proving difficult to finish. It was set in the library on Calle del Carmen and the plot was based on a series of mysterious crimes that took place there.

'I'd like to write something similar to those novels that were published some years ago by Ignatius B. Samson,' she said. 'Ever heard of them?'

'Vaguely,' I replied.

Eulalia couldn't quite find a way forward with her writing so I suggested she give it all a slightly sinister tone and focus the story on a secret book possessed by a tormented spirit, with subplots that were apparently supernatural in content.

'That's what Ignatius B. Samson would do, in your place,' I suggested.

'And what are you doing reading all about angels and devils? Don't tell me you're a repentant ex-seminarist.'

'I'm trying to find out what the origins of different religions and myths have in common,' I explained.

'What have you discovered so far?'

'Almost nothing. I don't want to bore you with my lament.'

'You won't bore me. Go on.'

I shrugged my shoulders.

'Well, what I've found most interesting so far is that, generally speaking, beliefs arise from an event or character that may or may not be authentic, and rapidly evolve into social movements that are conditioned and shaped by the political, economic and societal circumstances of the group that accepts them. Are you still awake?'

Eulalia nodded.

'A large part of the mythology that develops around each of these doctrines, from its liturgy to its rules and taboos, comes from the bureaucracy generated as they develop and not from the supposed supernatural act that originated them. Most of the simple, well-intentioned anecdotes are a mixture of common sense and folklore, and all the belligerent force they eventually develop comes from a subsequent interpretation of those principles, or even their distortion, at the hands of bureaucrats. The administrative and hierarchic aspects seem to be crucial in the evolution of belief systems. The truth is first revealed to all men, but very quickly individuals appear claiming sole authority and a duty to interpret, administer and, if need be, alter this truth in the name of the common good. To this end they establish a powerful and potentially repressive organisation. This phenomenon, which biology shows us is common to any social group, soon transforms the doctrine into a means of achieving control and political power. Divisions, wars and break-ups become inevitable. Sooner or later, the word becomes flesh and the flesh bleeds.'

I thought I was beginning to sound like Corelli and I sighed. Eulalia gave a hesitant smile.

'Is that what you're looking for? Blood?'

'It's the caning that leads to learning, not the other way round.'

'I wouldn't be so sure.'

'I have a feeling you went to a convent school.'

'The Sisters of the Holy Infant Jesus. The black nuns. Eight years.'

'Is it true what they say, that girls from convent schools are the ones who harbour the darkest and most unmentionable desires?'

'I bet you'd love to find out.'

'You can put all the chips on "yes".'

'What else have you learned in your crash course on theology?'

'Not much else. My initial conclusions have left an unpleasant aftertaste – it's so banal and inconsequential. All this seemed more or less evident already without the need to swallow whole encyclopedias and treatises on where to tickle angels – perhaps because I'm unable to understand anything beyond my own prejudices or because there is nothing else to understand and the crux of the matter lies in simply believing or not believing, without stopping to wonder why. How's my rhetoric? Are you still impressed?'

'It's giving me goose pimples. A shame I didn't meet you when I was a school girl with dark desires.'

'You're cruel, Eulalia.'

The librarian laughed heartily, looking me in the eye.

'Tell me, Ignatius B., who has broken your heart and left you so angry?'

'I see books aren't the only things you read.'

We sat a while longer at the table, watching the waiters coming and going across the dining room of Casa Leopoldo.

'Do you know the best thing about broken hearts?' the librarian asked.

I shook my head.

'They can only really break once. The rest is just scratches.'

'Put that in your book.'

I pointed to her engagement ring.

'I don't know who the idiot is, but I hope he knows he's the luckiest man in the world.'

Eulalia smiled a little sadly. We returned to the library and to our places: she went to her desk and I to my corner. I said goodbye to her the following day, when I decided that I couldn't, and wouldn't, read another line about revelations and eternal truths. On my way to the library I had bought her a white rose in one of the stalls on the Ramblas and I left it on her empty desk. I found her in one of the passages, sorting out some books.

'Are you abandoning me so soon?' she said when she saw me. 'Who is going to flirt with me now?'

'Who isn't?'

She came with me to the exit and shook my hand at the top of the flight of stairs that led to the courtyard of the old hospital. Halfway down I stopped and turned round. She was still there, watching me.

'Good luck, Ignatius B., I hope you find what you're looking for.'

12

While I was having dinner with Isabella at the gallery table, I noticed my new assistant was casting me sidelong glances.

'Don't you like the soup? You haven't touched it . . .' the girl ventured.

I looked at the plate I had allowed to grow cold, took a spoonful and pretended I was tasting the most exquisite delicacy.

'Delicious,' I remarked.

'And you haven't said a word since you returned from the library,' Isabella added.

'Any other complaints?'

Isabella looked away, upset. I ate some of the cold soup with little appetite, as it gave me an excuse for not speaking.

'Why are you so sad? Is it because of that woman?'

I went on stirring my spoon around in the soup. Isabella didn't take her eyes off me.

'Her name is Cristina,' I said eventually. 'And I'm not sad. I'm pleased for her because she's married my best friend and she's going to be very happy.'

'And I'm the Queen of Sheba.'

'You're a busybody, that's what you are.'

'I prefer you like this, when you're in a foul mood, because you tell the truth.'

'Then let's see how you like this: clear off to your room and leave me in peace, for Christ's sake!'

She tried to smile, but by the time I stretched out my hand towards her, her eyes had filled with tears. She took my plate and hers and fled to the kitchen. I heard the plates falling into the sink and then a few moments later the door of her bedroom slammed shut. I sighed and savoured the glass of red wine left on the table, an exquisite vintage from Isabella's parents' shop. After a while I went along to her bedroom door and knocked gently. She didn't reply, but I could hear her crying. I tried to open the door, but the girl had locked herself in.

I went up to the study, which after Isabella's visit smelled of fresh flowers and looked like the cabin in a luxury cruiser. She had tidied up all the books, dusted and left everything shiny and unrecognisable. The old Underwood looked like a piece of sculpture and the letters on the keys were clearly visible again. A neat pile of paper, containing summaries of religious textbooks and catechisms, lay on the desk next to the day's mail. A couple of cigars on a saucer emitted a delicious scent: Macanudos, one of the Caribbean delicacies supplied to Isabella's father on the quiet by a contact in the state tobacco industry. I took one of them and lit it. It had an intense flavour that seemed to hold all the aromas and poisons a man could wish for in order to die in peace.

I sat at the desk and went through the day's letters, ignoring them all except one: ochre parchment embellished with the writing I would have recognised anywhere. The missive from my new publisher and patron, Andreas Corelli, summoned me to meet him on Sunday, mid-afternoon, at the top of the main tower of the new cable railway that crossed the port of Barcelona.

The tower of San Sebastián stood one hundred metres high amid a jumble of cables and steel that induced vertigo just by looking at it. The service had been launched that same year to coincide with the International Exhibition, which had turned everything upside down and sown Barcelona with wonders. The cable railway crossed the docks from that first tower to a huge central structure reminiscent of the Eiffel Tower that served as the junction. From there the cable cars departed, suspended in mid-air, for the second part of the journey up to Montjuïc, where the heart of the exhibition was located. This technological marvel promised views of the city which until then had been the preserve only of airships, birds with a large wingspan, and hailstones. From my point of view, men and seagulls were not supposed to share the same airspace and as soon as I set foot in the lift that went up the tower I felt my stomach shrink to the size of a marble. The journey up seemed endless, the jolting of that brass capsule an exercise in pure nausea.

I found Corelli gazing through one of the large windows that looked out over the docks, his eyes lost among watercolours of sails and masts as they slid across the water. He wore a white silk suit and was toying with a sugar lump, which he then proceeded to swallow with an animal voracity. I cleared my throat and the boss turned round, smiling with pleasure.

'A marvellous view, don't you think?'

I nodded, white as a sheet.

'You don't like heights?'

'I like to keep my feet on the ground as much as possible,' I replied, maintaining a prudent distance from the window.

'I've gone ahead and bought return tickets,' he informed me.

'What a kind thought.'

I followed him to the footbridge from which one stepped into the cars that departed from the tower and travelled, suspended a sickening height above the ground, for what looked like a horribly long time.

'How did you spend the week, Martín?'

'Reading.'

He glanced at me briefly.

'By your bored expression I suspect it was not Alexandre Dumas.'

'A collection of dandruffy academics and their leaden prose.'

'Ah, intellectuals. And you wanted me to sign one up. Why is it that the less one has to say the more one says it, and in the most pompous and pedantic way possible?' Corelli asked. 'Is it to fool the world or just to fool themselves?'

'Probably both.'

The boss handed me the tickets and signalled to me to go in first. I showed the tickets to the member of staff who held the cable-car door open and entered unenthusiastically. I decided to stand in the centre, as far as possible from the windows. Corelli smiled like an excited child.

'Perhaps part of your problem is that you've been reading the commentators and not the people they were commenting on. A common mistake, but fatal when you're trying to learn something,' Corelli pointed out.

The doors closed and a sudden jerk sent us into orbit. I held onto a metal rail and took a deep breath.

'I sense that scholars and theoreticians are no heroes of yours,' I said.

'I have no heroes, my friend, still less those who cover themselves or each other in glory. Theory is the practice of the impotent. I suggest that you put some distance between yourself and the encyclopedists' accounts and go straight to the sources. Tell me, have you read the Bible?'

I hesitated for a moment. The cable car lurched on into the void. I looked at the floor.

'Fragments here and there, I suppose,' I mumbled.

'You suppose. Like almost everyone. A serious mistake. Everyone should read the Bible. And reread it. Believers or non-believers, it doesn't matter. I read it at least once a year. It's my favourite book.'

'And are you a believer or a sceptic?' I asked.

'I'm a professional. And so are you. What we believe, or don't believe, is irrelevant as far as our work is concerned. To believe or to disbelieve is a faint-hearted act. Either one knows or one doesn't. And that's all there is to it.'

'Then I confess that I don't know anything.'

'Follow that path and you'll find the footsteps of the great philosopher. And along the way read the Bible from start to finish. It's one of the greatest stories ever told. Don't make the mistake of confusing the word of God with the missal industry that lives off it.'

The longer I spent in the company of the publisher, the less I understood him.

'I'm quite lost. We were talking about legends and fables and now you're telling me that I must think of the Bible as the word of God?'

A shadow of impatience and irritation clouded his eyes.

'I'm speaking figuratively. God isn't a charlatan. The word is human currency.'

He smiled at me the way one smiles at a child who cannot understand the most elemental things. As I observed the publisher, I realised that I found it impossible to know when he was talking seriously and when he was joking. As impossible as guessing at the purpose of the extravagant undertaking for which he was paying me such a princely sum. In the meantime the cable car was bobbing about like an apple on a tree lashed by a gale. Never had I thought so much about Isaac Newton.

'You're a yellow-belly, Martín. This machine is completely safe.'

'I'll believe it when I'm back on firm ground.'

We were nearing the midpoint of the journey, the tower of San Jaime that rose up from the docks near the large customs building.

'Do you mind if we get off here?' I asked.

Corelli shrugged his shoulders. I didn't feel at ease until I was inside the tower's lift and felt it touch the ground. When we walked out into the port we found a bench facing the sea and the slopes of Montjuïc. We sat down to watch the cable car flying high above us; me with a sense of relief, Corelli with longing.

'Tell me about your first impressions. What have these days of intensive study and reading suggested to you?'

I proceeded to summarise what I thought I'd learned, or unlearned, during those days. The publisher listened attentively, nodding and occasionally gesticulating with his hands. At the end of my report about the myths and beliefs of human beings, Corelli gave a satisfactory verdict.

'I think you've done an excellent work of synthesis. You haven't found the proverbial needle in the haystack, but you've understood that the only thing that really matters in the whole pile of hay is the damned needle – the rest is just fodder for asses. Speaking of donkeys, tell me, are you interested in fables?'

'When I was small, for about two months I wanted to be Aesop.'

'We all give up great expectations along the way.'

'What did you want to be as a child, Señor Corelli?'

'God.'

He leered like a jackal, wiping the smile off my face.

'Martín, fables are possibly one of the most interesting literary forms ever invented. Do you know what they teach us?'

'Moral lessons?'

'No. They teach us that human beings learn and absorb ideas and concepts through narrative, through stories, not through lessons or theoretical speeches. This is what any of the great religious texts teach us. They're all tales about characters who must confront life and overcome obstacles, figures setting off on a journey of spiritual enrichment through exploits and revelations. All holy books are, above all, great stories whose plots deal with the basic aspects of human nature, setting them within a particular moral context and a particular framework of supernatural dogmas. I was content for you to spend a dismal week reading theses, speeches, opinions and comments so that you could discover for yourself that there is nothing to learn from them, because they're nothing more than exercises in good or bad faith – usually unsuccessful – by people who are trying, in turn, to understand. The professorial conversations are over. From now on I'll ask you to start reading the stories of the Brothers Grimm, the tragedies of Aeschylus, the Ramayana or the Celtic legends. Please yourself. I want you to analyse how these texts work, I want you to distil their essence and find out why they provoke an emotional reaction. I want you to learn the grammar, not the moral. And I want you to bring me something of your own in two or three weeks' time, the beginning of a story. I want you to make me believe.'

'I thought we were professionals and couldn't commit the sin of believing in anything.'

Corelli smiled, baring his teeth.

'One can only convert a sinner, never a saint.'

13

The days passed. Accustomed as I was to years of living alone and to that state of methodical and undervalued anarchy common to bachelors, the continued presence of a woman in the house, even though she was an unruly adolescent with a volatile temper, was beginning to play havoc with my daily routine. I believed in controlled disorder; Isabella didn't. I believed that objects find their own place in the chaos of a household; Isabella didn't. I believed in solitude and silence; Isabella didn't. In just a couple of days I discovered that I was no longer able to find anything in my own home. If I was looking for a paperknife, or a glass, or a pair of shoes, I had to ask Isabella where providence had kindly inspired her to hide them.

'I don't hide anything. I put things in their place. Which is different.'

Not a day went by when I didn't feel the urge to strangle her half a dozen times. When I took refuge in my study, searching for peace and quiet in which to think, Isabella would appear after a few minutes, a smile on her face, bringing me a cup of tea or some biscuits. She would wander around the study, look out of the window, tidy everything I had on my desk and then she would ask me what I was doing there, so quiet and mysterious. I discovered that seventeen-year-old girls have such huge verbal energy that their brain drives them to expend it every twenty seconds. On the third day I decided I had to find her a boyfriend – if possible a deaf one.

'Isabella, how is it that a girl as attractive as you has no suitors?'

'Who says I don't?'

'Isn't there any boy you like?'

'Boys my age are boring. They have nothing to say and half of them seem like complete idiots.'

I was going to say that they didn't improve with age but didn't want to spoil her illusions.

'So what age do you like them?'

'Old. Like you.'

'Do I seem old to you?'

'Well, you're not exactly a spring chicken.'

It was preferable to think she was pulling my leg than to accept the punch below the belt that hurt my vanity. I decided to respond with a few drops of sarcasm.

'The good news is that young girls like old men, and the bad news is that old men, especially decrepit, slobbering old men, like young girls.'

'I know. I wasn't born yesterday.'

Isabella observed me. She was scheming and smiled with a hint of malice.

'Do you like young girls too?'

The answer was on my lips before she had asked the question. I adopted a masterful, impartial tone, like a professor of geography.

'I liked them when I was your age. Now I generally like girls of my own age.'

'At your age they're no longer girls; they're young women or, to be precise, ladies.'

'End of argument. Have you nothing to do downstairs?'

'No.'

'Then start writing. You're not here to wash the dishes and hide my things. You're here because you said you wanted to learn to write and I'm the only idiot you know who can help you.'

'There's no need to get angry. It's just that I lack inspiration.'

'Inspiration comes when you stick your elbows on the table, your bottom on the chair and you start sweating. Choose a theme, an idea, and squeeze your brain until it hurts. That's called inspiration.'

'I have a topic.'

'Hallelujah.'

'I'm going to write about you.'

A long silence as we exchanged glances, like opponents across a game board.

'Why?'

'Because I find you interesting. And strange.'

'And old.'

'And touchy. Almost like a boy of my age.'

Despite myself I was beginning to get used to Isabella's company, to her jibes and to the light she had brought into that house. If things continued this way, my worst fears were going to come true and we'd end up being friends.

'What about you? Have you found a subject with all those whopping great tomes you're consulting?'

I decided that the less I told Isabella about my commission, the better.

'I'm still at the research stage.'

'Research? And how does that work?'

'Basically, you read thousands of pages to learn what you need to know and to get to the heart of a subject, to its emotional truth, and then you shed all that knowledge and start again at square one.'

Isabella sighed.

'What is emotional truth?'

'It's sincerity within fiction.'

'So, does one have to be an honest, good person to write fiction?'

'No. One has to be skilled. Emotional truth is not a moral quality, it's a technique.'

'You sound like a scientist,' protested Isabella.

'Literature, at least good literature, is science tempered with the blood of art. Like architecture or music.'

'I thought it was something that sprang from the artist, just like that, all of a sudden.'

'The only things that spring all of a sudden are unwanted body hair and warts.'

Isabella considered these revelations without much enthusiasm.

'You're saying all this to discourage me and make me go home.'

'I should be so lucky!'

'You're the worst teacher in the world.'

'It's the student who makes the teacher, not the other way round.'

'It's impossible to argue with you because you know all the rhetorical tricks. It's not fair.'

'Nothing is fair. The most one can hope is for things to be logical. Justice is a rare illness in a world that is otherwise a picture of health.'

'Amen. Is that what happens as you grow older? Do people stop

195

believing in things, as you have?'

'No. Most people, as they grow old, continue to believe in nonsense, usually even greater nonsense. I swim against the tide because I like to annoy.'

'Tell me something I don't know! Well, when I'm older I'll go on believing in things,' Isabella threatened.

'Good luck.'

'And what's more, I believe in you.'

She didn't look away as I fixed my eyes on hers.

'Because you don't know me.'

'That's what you think. You're not as mysterious as you imagine.'

'I don't pretend to be mysterious.'

'That was a kind substitute for unpleasant. I also know a few rhetorical tricks.'

'That isn't rhetoric. It's irony. They're two different things.'

'Do you always have to win every argument?'

'When it's as easy as this, yes.'

'And that man, the boss . . .'

'Corelli?'

'Corelli. Does he make it easy for you?'

'No. Corelli knows even more tricks than I do.'

'That's what I thought. Do you trust him?'

'Why do you ask?'

'I don't know. Do you trust him?'

'Why shouldn't I trust him?'

Isabella shrugged her shoulders.

'What exactly has he commissioned you to write? Aren't you going to tell me?'

'I told you. He wants me to write a book for his publishing company.'

'A novel?'

'Not exactly. More like a fable. A legend.'

'A book for children?'

'Something like that.'

'And you're going to do it?'

'He pays very well.'

Isabella frowned.

'Is that why you write? Because they pay you well?'

'Sometimes.'

'And this time?'

'This time I'm going to write the book because I have to.'

'Are in you debt to him?'

'You could put it that way, I suppose.'

Isabella weighed up the matter. She was about to say something, but thought twice about it and bit her lip. Instead, she gave me an innocent smile and one of her angelic looks with which she was capable of changing the subject with a simple batting of her eyelids.

'I'd also like to be paid to write,' she said.

'Anyone who writes would like the same, but it doesn't mean that he or she will achieve it.'

'And how do you achieve it?'

'You begin by going down to the gallery, taking pen and paper—'

'Digging your elbows in and squeezing your brain until it hurts. I know.'

She looked into my eyes, hesitating. She'd been staying in my house for a week and a half and I still showed no signs of sending her home. I imagined she was asking herself when I was going to do it, or why I hadn't done it yet. I also asked myself that very question and could find no answer.

'I like being your assistant, even if you are the way you are,' she said at last.

The girl was staring at me as if her life depended on a kind word. I yielded to temptation. Good words are a vain benevolence that demand no sacrifice and are more appreciated than real acts of kindness.

'I also like you being my assistant, Isabella, even if I am the way I am. And I will like it even more when there is no longer any need for you to be my assistant as you will have nothing more to learn from me.'

'Do you think I have potential?'

'I have no doubt whatsoever. In ten years you'll be the teacher and I'll be the apprentice,' I said, repeating words that still tasted of treason.

'You liar,' she said, kissing me sweetly on the cheek before running off down the stairs.

14

That afternoon I left Isabella sitting at the desk we had set up for her in the gallery, facing her blank pages, while I went over to Gustavo Barceló's bookshop on Calle Fernando hoping to find a good, readable edition of the Bible. All the sets of New and Old Testaments I had in the house were printed in microscopic type on thin, almost translucent onionskin paper and reading them, rather than bringing about fervour and divine inspiration, only induced migraines. Barceló, who among many other things was a persistent collector of holy books and apocryphal Christian texts, had a private room at the back of his shop filled with a formidable assortment of Gospels, lives of saints and holy people, and all kinds of other religious texts.

When I walked into the bookshop, one of the assistants rushed into the back-room office to alert the boss. Barceló emerged looking euphoric.

'Bless my eyes! Sempere told me you'd been reborn, but this is quite something. Next to you, Valentino looks like someone just back from the salt mines. Where have you been hiding, you rogue?'

'Oh, here and there,' I said.

'Everywhere except at Vidal's wedding party. You were sorely missed, my friend.'

'I doubt that.'

The bookseller nodded, implying that he understood my wish not to discuss the matter.

'Will you accept a cup of tea?'

'Or two. And a Bible. If possible, one that is easy to read.'

'That won't be a problem,' said the bookseller. 'Dalmau?'

The shop assistant called Dalmau came over obligingly.

'Dalmau, our friend Martín here needs a Bible that is legible, not decorative. I'm thinking of Torres Amat, 1825. What do you think?'

One of the peculiarities of Barceló's bookshop was that books were spoken about as if they were exquisite wines, catalogued by bouquet, aroma, consistency and vintage.

'An excellent choice, Señor Barceló, although I'd be more inclined towards the updated and revised edition.'

'Eighteen sixty?'

'Eighteen ninety-three.'

'Of course. That's it! Wrap it up for our friend Martín and put it on the house.'

'Certainly not,' I objected.

'The day I charge an unbeliever like you for the word of God will be the day I'm struck dead by lightning, and with good reason.'

Dalmau rushed off in search of my Bible and I followed Barceló into his office, where the bookseller poured two cups of tea and offered me a cigar from his humidor. I accepted it and lit it with the flame of the candle he handed me.

'Macanudo?'

'I see you're educating your palate. A man must have vices, expensive ones if possible, otherwise when he reaches old age he will have nothing to be redeemed of. In fact, I'm going to have one with you. What the hell!'

A cloud of exquisite cigar smoke covered us like high tide.

'I was in Paris a few months ago and took the opportunity to make some enquiries on the subject you talked about with our friend Sempere some time before,' Barceló explained.

'Éditions de la Lumière.'

'Exactly. I wish I'd been able to scratch a little deeper, but unfortunately, after the publishing house closed down, nobody, it seems, bought its backlist, so it was difficult to gather much information.'

'You say it closed? When?'

'In 1914, if I'm not mistaken.'

'There must be some mistake.'

'Not if we're talking about the same Éditions de la Lumière, on Boulevard Saint-Germain.'

'That's the one.'

'In fact, I made a note of everything so I wouldn't forget it when I saw you.'

Barceló looked in the drawer of his desk and pulled out a small notebook.

'Here it is: "Éditions de la Lumière, publishing house specialising in religious texts with offices in Rome, Paris, London and Berlin. Founder and publisher, Andreas Corelli. Date of the opening of the first office in Paris, 1881—"'

'Impossible,' I muttered.

Barceló shrugged his shoulders.

'Of course, I could have got it wrong, but—'

'Did you get a chance to visit the offices?'

'As a matter of fact, I did try, because my hotel was opposite the Panthéon, very close by, and the former offices of the publishing house were on the southern pavement of the boulevard, between Rue Saint-Jacques and Boulevard Saint-Michel.'

'And?'

'The building was empty, bricked up, and it looked as if there'd been a fire or something similar. The only thing that had remained intact was the door knocker, an exquisite object in the shape of an angel. Bronze, I think. I would have taken it, had there not been a *gendarme* watching me disapprovingly. I didn't have the courage to provoke a diplomatic incident – heaven forbid France should decide to invade us again!'

'With the way things are, they might be doing us a favour.'

'Now that you mention it . . . But going back to the subject: when I saw what a state the place was in, I went to the café next door to make some enquiries and they told me the building had been like that for twenty years.'

'Were you able to discover anything about the publisher?'

'Corelli? From what I gathered, the publishing house closed when he decided to retire, although he can't even have been fifty years old. I think he moved to a villa in the south of France, in the Luberon, and died shortly afterwards. They say a snake bit him. A viper. That's what you get for retiring to Provence.'

'Are you sure he died? '

'Père Coligny, an old competitor of Corelli, showed me his death notice – he had it framed and treasures it like a trophy. He said he looks at it every day to remind himself that the damned bastard is dead and buried. His exact words, although in French they sounded much prettier and more musical.'

'Did Coligny mention whether the publisher had any children?'

'I got the impression that Corelli was not his favourite topic, because as soon as he could Coligny slipped away from me. It seems there was some scandal – Corelli stole one of his authors from him, someone called Lambert.'

'What happened?'

'The funniest thing about all this is that Coligny had never actually set eyes on Corelli. His only contact with him was by correspondence. The root of the problem, I think, was that Monsieur Lambert signed an agreement to write a book for Éditions de la Lumière behind Coligny's back, when Coligny had sole rights to his work. Lambert was a terminal opium addict and had accumulated enough debts to pave Rue de Rivoli from end to end. Coligny suspected that Corelli had offered Lambert an astronomical sum and that the poor man, who was dying, had accepted it because he wanted to leave his children well provided for.'

'What sort of book was it?'

'Something with a religious content. Coligny mentioned the title, some fancy Latin expression that was fashionable at the time, but I can't remember it now. As you know, the titles of missals all run in a similar vein. *Pax Gloria Mundi* or something like that.'

'And what happened to the book and Lambert?'

'That's where matters become complicated. It seems that poor Lambert, in a fit of madness, wanted to burn his manuscript, so he set fire to it, and to himself, in the offices of the publishing house. A lot of people thought the opium had frazzled his brains, but Coligny suspected that it was Corelli who had pushed him towards suicide.'

'Why would he want to do that?'

'Who knows? Perhaps he didn't want to pay him the sum he had promised? Perhaps it was all just Coligny's fantasies – I'd say he was a great fan of Beaujolais twelve months a year. He told me that Corelli had tried to kill him in order to release Lambert from his contract and that Corelli only left him in peace when he decided to terminate the agreement with the author and let him go.'

'Didn't you say he'd never seen him?'

'Exactly. I think Coligny must have been raving. When I visited him in his apartment I saw more crucifixes, madonnas and figures of saints than you'd find in a shop selling Christmas mangers. I got the impression that he wasn't all that well in the head. When I left he told me to stay away from Corelli.'

'But hadn't he told you Corelli was dead?'

'*Ecco qua.*'

I fell silent. Barceló looked at me with curiosity.

'I have the feeling that my discoveries aren't a huge surprise to you.'

I gave him a carefree smile, trying to make light of it all.

'On the contrary. Thank you for taking the time to investigate.'

'Not at all. Going to Paris in search of gossip is a pleasure in itself; you know me.'

Barceló tore the page with the information out of his notebook and handed it to me.

'In case it's of any use to you. I've noted down everything I was able to discover.'

I stood up and we shook hands. He came with me to the door, where Dalmau had the parcel ready for me.

'How about a print of the Baby Jesus – one of those where he opens and closes his eyes depending how you look at it? Or one of the Virgin Mary surrounded by lambs: when you move it, they turn into cherubs with rosy cheeks. A wonder of stereoscopic technology.'

'The revealed word is enough for the time being.'

'Amen.'

I was grateful to the bookseller for his attempts to cheer me up, but as I walked away from the shop a cold anxiety began to invade me and I had the feeling that the streets and my destiny were set on nothing but quicksand.

15

On my way home I stopped by a stationer's in Calle Argenteria to look at the shop window. On a sheet of fabric was a case containing a set of nibs, an ivory pen and a matching ink pot engraved with what looked like fairies or muses. There was something melodramatic about the whole set, as if it had been stolen from the writing desk of some Russian novelist, the sort who would bleed to death over thousands of pages. Isabella had beautiful handwriting that I envied, as pure and clear as her conscience, and the set seemed to have been made for her. I went in and asked the shop assistant to show it to me. The nibs were gold-plated and the whole business cost a small fortune, but I decided that it would be a good idea to repay my young assistant's kindness and patience with this little gift. I asked the man to wrap it in bright purple paper with a ribbon the size of a carriage.

When I got home I was looking forward to the selfish satisfaction that comes from arriving with a gift in one's hand. I was about to call Isabella as if she were a faithful pet with nothing better to do than wait devotedly for her master's return, but what I saw when I opened the door left me speechless. The corridor was as dark as a tunnel. The door of the room at the other end was open, casting a square of flickering yellow light across the floor.

'Isabella?' I called out. My mouth was dry.

'I'm here.'

The voice came from inside the room. I left the parcel on the hall table and walked down the corridor. I stopped in the doorway and looked inside. Isabella was sitting on the floor. She had placed a candle inside a tall glass and was earnestly devoting herself to her second vocation after literature: tidying up other people's belongings.

'How did you get in here?'

She smiled at me and shrugged her shoulders.

'I was in the gallery and I heard a noise. I thought it was you coming back, but when I went into the corridor I saw that this door was open. I thought you'd told me it was locked.'

'Get out of here. I don't want you coming into this room. It's very damp.'

'Don't be silly. With all the work there is to do here? Come on. Look at all the things I've found.'

I hesitated.

'Here, come in.'

I stepped into the room and knelt down beside her. Isabella had separated all the items and boxes into categories: books, toys, photographs, clothes, shoes, spectacles. I looked at all the objects with a certain apprehension. Isabella seemed to be delighted, as if she'd discovered King Solomon's mines.

'Is all of this yours?'

I shook my head.

'It belonged to the previous owner.'

'Did you know him?'

'No. It had all been here for years when I moved in.'

Isabella was holding a packet of letters and held it out to me as if it were evidence in a magistrate's court.

'Well, I think I've discovered his name.'

'You don't say.'

Isabella smiled, clearly delighted with her detective work.

'Marlasca,' she announced. 'His name was Diego Marlasca. Don't you think it's odd?'

'What?'

'That his initials are the same as yours: D. M.'

'It's just a coincidence; tens of thousands of people in this town have the same initials.'

Isabella winked at me. She was really enjoying herself.

'Look what else I've found.'

Isabella had salvaged a tin box full of old photographs. They were images from another age, postcards of old Barcelona, of pavilions that had been demolished in Ciudadela Park after the 1888 Universal Exhibition, of large crumbling houses and avenues full of people dressed in the ceremonious style of the time, of carriages and memories the colour of my childhood. Faces with absent expressions stared at me from thirty years back. In some of those photographs I thought I recognised the face of an actress who had been popular when I was a young boy and who had long since disappeared into obscurity. Isabella watched me in silence.

'Do you remember her?' she asked, after a time.

'I think her name was Irene Sabino. She was quite a famous actress in the Paralelo theatres. This was a long time ago. Before you were born.'

'Just look at this, then.'

Isabella handed me a photograph in which Irene Sabino appeared leaning against a window. It didn't take me long to identify that window as the one in my study at the top of the tower.

'Interesting, isn't it?' Isabella asked. 'Do you think she lived here?'

I shrugged my shoulders.

'Maybe she was Diego Marlasca's lover . . .'

'I don't think that's any of our business.'

'Sometimes you're so boring.'

Isabella put the photographs back in the box. As she did so, one of them slipped from her hands. The picture fell at my feet. I picked it up and examined it: Irene Sabino, wearing a dazzling black gown, posed with a group of people dressed for a party in what seemed to be the grand hall of the Equestrian Club. It was just a picture of a social gathering that wouldn't have caught my eye had I not noticed in the background, almost blurred, a gentleman with white hair standing at the top of a staircase. Andreas Corelli.

'You've gone pale,' said Isabella.

She took the photograph from my hand and perused it silently. I stood up and made a sign to Isabella to leave the room.

'I don't want you to come in here again,' I said weakly.

'Why?'

I waited for her to leave the room and closed the door behind us. Isabella looked at me as if I wasn't altogether sane.

'Tomorrow you'll call the Sisters of Charity and tell them to come and collect all this. They're to take everything. What they don't want, they can throw away.'

'But—'

'Don't argue with me.'

I didn't want to face her and went straight to the stairs that led up to the study. Isabella watched me from the corridor.

'Who is that man, Señor Martín?'

'Nobody,' I murmured. 'Nobody.'

16

I went up to the study. Night had fallen, but there was no moon or stars in the sky. I opened the windows and gazed at the city in shadows. Only a light breeze was blowing and the sweat tingled on my skin. I sat on the windowsill and lit the second of the cigars Isabella had left on my desk a few days before, waiting for a breath of fresh air or a more presentable idea than the collection of clichés with which I was supposed to begin work on the boss's commission. I heard the shutters in Isabella's bedroom open on the floor below. A rectangle of light fell across the courtyard, punctured by the profile of her silhouette. Isabella went up to her window and gazed into the darkness without noticing my presence. I watched her slowly undress. I saw her walk over to the mirror and examine her body, stroking her belly with the tips of her fingers and going over the cuts she had made on the inside of her arms and thighs. She looked at herself for a long time, wearing nothing but a defeated air, then turned off the light.

I went back to my desk and sat in front of the pile of notes. I went over sketches of stories full of mystic revelations and prophets who survived extraordinary trials and who returned bearing the revealed truth; of messianic infants abandoned at the doors of humble families with pure souls who were persecuted by evil, godless empires; of promised paradises for those who would accept their destiny and the rules of the game with a sporting spirit; and of idle, anthropomorphic deities with nothing better to do than keep a telepathic watch on the conscience of millions of fragile primates – primates who learned to think just in time to discover that they had been abandoned to their lot in a remote corner of the universe and whose vanity, or despair, made them slavishly believe that heaven and hell were eager to know about their paltry little sins.

I asked myself if this was what the boss had seen in me, a mercenary mind with no qualms about hatching a narcotic story fit for sending small children to sleep, or for convincing some poor hopeless devil to murder his neighbour in exchange for the eternal gratitude of some god who subscribed to the rule of the gun. Some days earlier another letter had arrived, requesting that I meet up with the boss to discuss the progress of my work. Setting aside my scruples, I realised that I had barely twenty-four hours before the meeting, and at the rate I was going I'd arrive with my hands empty but with my head full of doubts and suspicions. Since there was no alternative, I did what I'd done for so many years in similar circumstances. I placed a sheet of paper in the Underwood and, with my hands poised on the keyboard like a pianist waiting for the beat, I began to squeeze my brain to see what would come out.

17

'Interesting,' the boss pronounced when he'd finished the tenth and last page. 'Strange, but interesting.'

We were sitting on a bench in the gilded haze of the Shade House in Ciudadela Park. A vault of wooden strips filtered the sun until it was reduced to a golden shimmer, and all around us a garden of plants shaped the play of light and dark in the peculiar, luminous gloom. I lit a cigarette and watched the smoke rise from my fingers in blue spirals.

'Coming from you, strange is a disturbing adjective,' I noted.

'I meant strange as opposed to vulgar,' Corelli specified.

'But?'

'There are no buts, Martín. I think you've found an interesting route with a lot of potential.'

For a novelist, when someone comments that their pages are interesting and have potential, it is a sign that things aren't going well. Corelli seemed to read my anxiety.

'You've turned the question round. Instead of going straight for the mythological references you've started with the more prosaic. May I ask where you got the idea of a warrior messiah instead of a peaceful one?'

'You mentioned biology.'

'Everything we need to know is written in the great book of nature,' Corelli agreed. 'We only need the courage and the mental and spiritual clarity with which to read it.'

'One of the books I consulted explained that among humans the male attains the plenitude of his fertility at the age of seventeen. The female attains it later and preserves it, and somehow acts as selector and judge of the genes she agrees to reproduce. The male, on the other hand, simply offers himself and wastes away much faster. The age at which he reaches his maximum reproductive strength is also when his combative spirit is at its peak. A young man is the perfect soldier. He has great potential for aggression and a limited critical capacity – or none at all – with which to analyse it and judge how to channel it. Throughout history, societies have found ways of using this store of aggression, turning their adolescents into soldiers, cannon fodder with which to conquer their neighbours or defend themselves against their aggressors. Something told me that our protagonist was an envoy from heaven, but an envoy who, in the first flush of youth, took arms and liberated truth with blows of iron.'

'Have you decided to mix history with biology, Martín?'

'From what you said, I understood them to be one and the same thing.'

Corelli smiled. I don't know whether he was aware of it, but when he smiled he looked like a hungry wolf. I swallowed hard and tried to ignore the goose pimples.

'I've given this some thought,' I said, 'and I realised that most of the great religions were either born or reached their apogee at a time when the societies that adopted them had a younger and poorer demographic base. Societies in which 70 per cent of the population was under the age of eighteen – half of them men with their veins bursting with violence and the urge to procreate – were perfect breeding grounds for an acceptance and explosion of faith.'

'That's an oversimplification, but I see where you're going, Martín.'

'I know. But with these general ideas in mind, I asked myself: why not get straight to the point and establish a mythology around this warrior messiah? A messiah full of blood and anger, who saves his people, his genes, his womenfolk and his patriarchs from the political and racial dogma of his enemies, that is to say, from anyone who does not subject himself to his doctrine.'

'What about the adults?'

'We'll get to the adult by having recourse to his frustration. As life advances and we have to give up the hopes, dreams and desires of our youth, we acquire a growing sense of being a victim of the world and of other people. There is always someone else to blame for our misfortunes or failures, someone we wish to exclude. Embracing a doctrine that will turn this grudge and this victim mentality into something positive provides comfort and strength. The adult then feels part of the group and sublimates his lost desires and hopes through the community.'

'Perhaps,' Corelli granted. 'What about all this iconography of death and the flags and shields? Don't you find it counter-productive?'

'No. I think it's essential. Clothes maketh the man, but above all, they maketh the churchgoer.'

'And what do you say about women, the other half? I'm sorry, but I find it hard to imagine a substantial number of women in a society believing in pennants and shields. Boy Scout psychology is for children.'

'The main pillar of every organised religion, with few exceptions, is the subjugation, repression, even the annulment of women in the group. Woman must accept the role of an ethereal, passive and maternal presence, never of authority or independence, or she will have to take the consequences. She might have a place of honour in the symbolism, but not in the hierarchy. Religion and war are male pursuits. And anyhow, woman sometimes ends up becoming the accomplice in her own subjugation.'

'And the aged?'

'Old age is the lubricant of belief. When death knocks at the door, scepticism flies out of the window. A serious cardiovascular fright and a person will even believe in Little Red Riding Hood.'

Corelli laughed.

'Careful, Martín, I think you're becoming more cynical than I am.'

I looked at him as if I were an obedient pupil anxious for the approval of a demanding teacher. Corelli patted me on the knee, nodding with satisfaction.

'I like it. I like the flair of it. I want you to go on turning things round and finding a shape. I'm going to give you more time. We'll meet in two or three weeks. I'll let you know a few days beforehand.'

'Do you have to leave the city?'

'Business matters concerning the publishing house. I'm afraid I have a few days of travel ahead of me, but I'm going away contented. You've done a good job. I knew I'd found my ideal candidate.'

The boss stood up and put out his hand. I dried the sweat from my palm on my trouser leg and we shook hands.

'You'll be missed,' I began.

'Don't exaggerate, Martín; you were doing very well.'

I watched him leave in the haze of the Shade House, the echo of his steps fading away into the shadows. I remained there a good while, wondering whether the boss had risen to the bait and swallowed the pile of tall stories I'd given him. I was sure that I'd told him exactly what he wanted to hear. I hoped so, and I also hoped that the string of nonsense would keep him satisfied for the time being, convinced that his servant, the poor failed novelist, had become a convert. I told myself that anything that could buy me more time in which to discover what I had got myself into was worth a try. When I stood up and left the Shade House, my hands were still shaking.

18

Years of experience writing thrillers provide one with a set of principles on which to base an investigation. One of them is that all moderately solid plots, including those seemingly about affairs of passion, are born from the unmistakable whiff of money and property. When I left the Shade House I walked to the Land Registry in Calle Consejo de Ciento and asked whether I could consult the records in which the sales, purchase and ownership of my house were listed. Books in the Land Registry archive contain almost as much information on the realities of life as the complete works of the most respected philosophers – if not more.

I began by looking up the section containing the details of my lease of number 30, Calle Flassaders. There I found the necessary data with which to trace the history of the property before the Banco Hispano Colonial took ownership in 1911, as part of the appropriation of the Marlasca family assets – apparently the family had inherited the building upon the death of the owner. A lawyer named S. Valera was mentioned as having represented the family. Another leap into the past allowed me to find information relating to the purchase of the building by Don Diego Marlasca Pongiluppi in 1902 from a certain Bernabé Massot y Caballé. I made a note of all this on a slip of paper, from the name of the lawyer and all those taking part in the transactions to the relevant dates.

One of the clerks announced in a loud voice that there were fifteen minutes to closing time so I got ready to leave, but before that I hurriedly tried to consult the records for Andreas Corelli's house next to Güell Park. After fifteen minutes of searching in vain, I looked up from the register and met the ashen eyes of the clerk. He was an emaciated character, gel shining on moustache and hair, oozing that belligerent apathy of those who turn their job into a platform for obstructing the life of others.

'I'm sorry. I can't find a property,' I said.

'That must be because it doesn't exist or because you don't know how to search properly. We've closed for today.'

I repaid his kindness and efficiency with my best smile.

'I might find it with your expert help,' I suggested.

He gave me a nauseous look and snatched the volume from my hands.

'Come back tomorrow.'

My next stop was the ostentatious building of the Bar Association in Calle Mallorca, only a few streets away. Beneath a series of glass chandeliers, I climbed the wide steps that were guarded by what looked like a statue of Justice but with the bosom and attitude of a Paralelo starlet. When I reached the secretary's office, a small, mousy-looking man welcomed me and asked how he could help.

'I'm looking for a lawyer.'

'You've come to the right place. We don't know how to get rid of them here. There seem to be more every day. They multiply like rabbits.'

'It's the modern world. The one I'm looking for is called, or was called, Valera, S. Valera, with a V.'

The little man disappeared into a labyrinth of filing cabinets, muttering under his breath. I waited, leaning on the counter, my eyes wandering over a decor infused with the inexorable weight of the law. Five minutes later the man returned with a folder.

'I've found ten Valeras. Two with an S. Sebastián and Soponcio.'

'Soponcio?'

'You're very young, but years ago this was a name with a certain cachet, and ideal for the legal profession. Then along came the Charleston and ruined everything.'

'Is Don Soponcio still alive?'

'According to the folder and the date he stopped paying his membership of this association, Soponcio Valera y Menacho was received into the glory of Our Lord in the year 1919. Memento mori. Sebastián is his son.'

'Still practising?'

'Fully, and constantly. I sense you will want the address.'

'If it's not too much trouble.'

The little man wrote it down on a small piece of paper which he handed to me.

'Number 442, Diagonal. It's just a stone's throw away. But it's two o'clock, and by now most top lawyers will be at lunch with rich widows or manufacturers of fabrics and explosives. I'd wait until four o'clock.'

I put the address in my jacket pocket.

'I'll do that. Thank you for your help.'

'That's what we're here for. God bless.'

I had a couple of hours to kill before paying a visit to Señor Valera, so I took a tram down Vía Layetana and got off when it reached Calle Condal. The Sempere & Sons bookshop was just a step away and I knew from experience that – contravening the immutable tradition of local shops – the old bookseller didn't close at midday. I found him, as usual, standing at the counter, cataloguing books and serving a large group of customers who were wandering around the tables and bookshelves hunting for treasure. He smiled when he saw me and came over to say hello. He looked thinner and paler than the last time I'd seen him. He must have noticed my anxiety because he shrugged his shoulders as if to make light of the matter.

'Some win; others lose. You're looking fit and well and I'm all skin and bones, as you can see,' he said.

'Are you all right?'

'Fresh as a daisy. It's the damned angina. Nothing serious. What brings you here, Martín, my friend?'

'I thought I'd take you out to lunch.'

'Thank you, but I can't abandon ship. My son has gone to Sarriá to appraise a collection and business isn't so good that we can afford to close the shop when there are customers about.'

'Don't tell me you're having financial problems.'

'This is a bookshop, Martín, not an investment broker's. The world of letters provides us with just enough to get by, and sometimes not even that.'

'If you need help . . .'

Sempere held up his hand.

'If you want to help me, buy a book or two.'

'You know that the debt I owe you can never be repaid with money.'

'All the more reason not even to think about it. Don't worry about us, Martín. The only way they'll get me out of here is in a pine box. But if you like, you can come and share a tasty meal of bread, raisins and fresh Burgos cheese. With that, and the Count of Montecristo, anyone can live to be a hundred.'

19

Sempere hardly tasted his food. He smiled wearily and pretended to be interested in my comments, but I could see that from time to time he was having trouble breathing.

'Tell me, Martín, what are you working on?'

'It's difficult to explain. A book I've been commissioned to write.'

'A novel?'

'Not exactly. I wouldn't know how to describe it.'

'What's important is that you're working. I've always said that idleness dulls the spirit. We have to keep the brain busy, or at least the hands if we don't have a brain.'

'But some people work more than is reasonable, Señor Sempere. Shouldn't you take a break? How many years have you been here, always hard at work, never stopping?'

Sempere looked around him.

'This place is my life, Martín. Where else would I go? To a sunny bench in the park, to feed pigeons and complain about my rheumatism? I'd be dead in ten minutes. My place is here. And my son isn't ready to take up the reins of the business, even if he thinks he is.'

'But he's a good worker. And a good person.'

'Between you and me, he's too good a person. Sometimes I look at him and wonder what will become of him the day I go. How is he going to cope . . .?'

'All fathers say that, Señor Sempere.'

'Did yours? Forgive me, I didn't mean to . . .'

'Don't worry. My father had enough worries of his own without having to worry about me as well. I'm sure your son has more experience than you think.'

Sempere looked dubious.

'Do you know what I think he lacks?'

'Malice?'

'A woman.'

'He'll have no shortage of girlfriends with all the turtle doves who cluster round the shop window to admire him.'

'I'm talking about a real woman, the sort who makes you become what you're supposed to be.'

'He's still young. Let him have fun for a few more years.'

'That's a good one! If he'd at least have some fun. At his age, if I'd had that chorus of young girls after me, I'd have sinned like a cardinal.'

'The Lord gives bread to the toothless.'

'That's what he needs: teeth. And a desire to bite.'

Something else seemed to be going round his mind. He was looking at me and smiling.

'Maybe you could help . . .'

'Me?'

'You're a man of the world, Martín. And don't give me that expression. I'm sure that if you apply yourself you'll find a good woman for my son. He already has a pretty face. You can teach him the rest.'

I was speechless.

'Didn't you want to help me?' the bookseller asked. 'Well, there you are.'

'I was talking about money.'

'And I'm talking about my son, the future of this house. My whole life.'

I sighed. Sempere took my hand and pressed it with what little strength he had left.

'Promise you'll not allow me to leave this world before I've seen my son set up with a woman worth dying for. And who'll give me a grandson.'

'If I'd known this was coming, I'd have stayed at the Novedades Café for lunch.'

Sempere smiled.

'Sometimes I think you should have been my son, Martín.'

I looked at the bookseller, who seemed more fragile and older than ever before, barely a shadow of the strong, impressive man I remembered from my childhood days, and I felt the world crumbling around me. I went up to him and, before I realised it, did what I'd never done in all the years I'd known him. I gave him a kiss on his forehead, which was spotted with freckles and touched by a few grey hairs.

'Do you promise?'

'I promise,' I said, as I walked to the door.

20

Señor Valera's office occupied the top floor of an extravagant modernist building located at number 442 Avenida Diagonal, just round the corner from Paseo de Gracia. For want of a better description, the building looked like a cross between a giant grandfather clock and a pirate ship, and was adorned with huge French windows and a roof with green dormers. In any other part of the world the baroque and Byzantine structure would have been proclaimed either as one of the seven wonders of the world or as the freakish creation of a mad artist who was possessed by demons. In Barcelona's Ensanche quarter, where similar buildings cropped up everywhere, like clover after rain, it barely raised an eyebrow.

I walked into the hallway and was shown to a lift that reminded me of something a giant spider might have left behind, if it were weaving cathedrals instead of cobwebs. The doorman opened the cabin and imprisoned me in the strange capsule that began to rise through the middle of the stairwell. A severe-looking secretary opened the carved oak door at the top and showed me in. I gave her my name and explained that I had not made an appointment, but that I was there to discuss a matter relating to the sale of a building in the Ribera quarter. Something changed in her expression.

'The tower house?' she asked.

I nodded. The secretary led me to an empty office. I sensed that this was not the official waiting room.

'Please wait, Señor Martín. I'll let Señor Valera know you're here.'

I spent the next forty-five minutes in that office, surrounded by bookshelves that were packed with volumes the size of tombstones, bearing inscriptions on the spines such as '1888–1889, B.C.A. Section One. Second title'. It seemed like irresistible reading matter. The office had a large window looking onto Avenida Diagonal that provided an excellent view over the city. The furniture smelled of fine wood, weathered and seasoned with money. Carpets and leather armchairs were reminiscent of those in a British club. I tried to lift one of the lamps presiding over the desk and guessed that it must weigh at least thirty kilos. A huge oil painting, resting over a hearth that had never been used, portrayed the rotund and expansive presence of none other than Don Soponcio Valera y Menacho. The titanic lawyer sported moustaches and sideburns like the mane of an old lion, and his stern eyes, with the fire and steel of a hanging judge, dominated every corner of the room from the great beyond.

'He doesn't speak, but if you stare at the portrait for a while he looks as if he might do so at any moment,' said a voice behind me.

I hadn't heard him come in. Sebastián Valera was a man with a quiet gait who looked as if he'd spent the best part of his life trying to crawl out from under his father's shadow and now, at fifty-plus, was tired of trying. He had penetrating and intelligent eyes, and that exquisite manner only enjoyed by royal princesses and the most expensive lawyers. He offered me his hand and I shook it.

'I'm sorry to have kept you waiting, but I wasn't expecting your visit,' he said, pointing to a seat.

'Not at all. Thank you for receiving me.'

Valera gave me the smile of someone who knows how much he charges for every minute.

'My secretary tells me your name is David Martín. You're David Martín, the author?'

The look of surprise must have given me away.

'I come from a family of great readers,' he explained. 'How can I help?'

'I'd like to ask you about the ownership of a building in—'

'The tower house?' the lawyer interrupted politely.

'Yes.'

'You know it?' he asked.

'I live there.'

Valera looked at me for a while without abandoning his smile. He straightened up in his chair and seemed to go tense.

'Are you the present owner?'

'Actually I rent the place.'

'And what is it you'd like to know, Señor Martín?'

'If possible, I'd like to know about the acquisition of the building by the Banco Hispano Colonial and gather some information on the previous owner.'

'Don Diego Marlasca,' the lawyer muttered. 'May I ask what is the nature of your interest?'

'Personal. Recently, while I was doing some refurbishment on the building, I came across a number of items that I think belonged to him.'

The lawyer frowned.

'Items?'

'A book. Or, rather, a manuscript.'

'Señor Marlasca was a great lover of literature. In fact, he was the author of a large number of books on law, and also on history and other subjects. A great scholar. And a great man, although at the end of his life there were those who wished to tarnish his reputation.'

My surprise must have been evident.

'I assume you're not familiar with the circumstances surrounding Señor Marlasca's death.'

'I'm afraid not.'

Valera sighed, as if he were debating whether or not to go on.

'You're not going to write about this, are you, or about Irene Sabino?'

'No.'

'Do I have your word?'

I nodded.

'You couldn't say anything that wasn't already said at the time, I suppose,' Valera muttered, more to himself than to me.

The lawyer looked briefly at his father's portrait and then fixed his eyes on me.

'Diego Marlasca was my father's partner and his best friend. Together they founded this law firm. Señor Marlasca was a brilliant lawyer. Unfortunately he was also a very complicated man, subject to long periods of melancholy. There came a time when my father and Señor Marlasca decided to dissolve their partnership. Señor Marlasca left the legal profession to devote himself to his first vocation: writing. They say most lawyers secretly wish to leave the profession and become writers—'

'Until they compare the salaries.'

'The fact is that Don Diego had struck up a friendship with Irene Sabino, quite a popular actress at the time, for whom he wanted to write a play. That was all. Señor Marlasca was a gentleman and was never unfaithful to his wife, but you know what people are like. Gossip. Rumours and jealousy. Anyhow, word got round that Don Diego was having an affair with Irene Sabino. His wife never forgave him for it, and the couple separated. Señor Marlasca was shattered. He bought the tower house and moved in. Sadly, he'd only been living there for a year when he died in an unfortunate accident.'

'What sort of accident?'

'Señor Marlasca drowned. It was a tragedy.'

Valera lowered his eyes and sighed.

'And the scandal?'

'Let's just say there were evil tongues who wanted people to believe that Señor Marlasca had committed suicide after an unhappy love affair with Irene Sabino.'

'And was that so?'

Valera removed his spectacles and rubbed his eyes.

'To tell you the truth, I'm not sure. I don't know and I don't care. What happened, happened.'

'What became of Irene Sabino?'

Valera put his glasses on again.

'I thought you were only interested in Señor Marlasca and the ownership of the house.'

'It's simple curiosity. Among Señor Marlasca's belongings I found a number of photographs of Irene Sabino, as well as letters from her to Señor Marlasca—'

'What are you getting at?' Valera snapped. 'Is it money you want?'

'No.'

'I'm glad, because nobody is going to give you any. Nobody cares about the subject any more. Do you understand?'

'Perfectly, Señor Valera. I had no intention of bothering you or insinuating that anything was out of place. I'm sorry if I offended you with my questions.'

The lawyer smiled and let out a gentle sigh, as if the conversation had already ended.

'It doesn't matter. I'm the one who should apologise.'

Taking advantage of the lawyer's conciliatory tone, I put on my sweetest expression.

'Perhaps his widow . . .'

Valera shrunk into his armchair, visibly uncomfortable.

'Doña Alicia Marlasca? Señor Martín, please don't misunderstand me, but part of my duty as the family lawyer is to preserve their privacy. For obvious reasons. A lot of time has gone by, and I wouldn't like to see old wounds reopened unnecessarily.'

'I understand.'

The lawyer was looking at me tensely.

'And you say you found a book?' he asked.

'Yes . . . a manuscript. It's probably not important.'

'Probably not. What was the work about?'

'Theology, I'd say.'

Valera nodded.

'Does that surprise you?'

'No. On the contrary. Diego was an authority on the history of religion. A learned man. In this firm he is still remembered with great affection. Tell me, what particular aspects of the history of the property are you interested in?'

'I think you've already helped me a great deal, Señor Valera. I wouldn't like to take up any more of your time.'

The lawyer nodded, looking relieved.

'It's the house, isn't it?' he asked.

'A strange place, yes,' I agreed.

'I remember going there once when I was young, shortly after Don Diego bought it.'

'Do you know why he bought it?'

'He said he'd been fascinated with it ever since he was a child and had always thought he'd like to live there. Don Diego was like that. Sometimes he acted like a young boy who would give everything up in exchange for a dream.'

I didn't say anything.

'Are you all right?'

'Yes, fine. Do you know anything about the owner from whom Señor Marlasca bought the house? Someone called Bernabé Massot?'

'He'd made his money in the Americas. He didn't spend more than an hour in the house. He bought it when he returned from Cuba and kept it empty for years. He didn't say why. He lived in a mansion he had built in Arenys de Mar and sold the tower house for tuppence. He didn't want to have anything to do with it.'

'And before him?'

'I think a priest lived there. A Jesuit. I'm not sure. My father was the person who took care of Don Diego's business and when the latter died, he burned all of the files.'

'Why would he do that?'

'Because of all the things I've told you. To avoid rumours and preserve the memory of his friend, I suppose. The truth is, he never told me. My father was not the sort of man to offer explanations, but he must have had his reasons. Good reasons, I'm sure. Diego had been a good friend to him, as well as being his partner, and all of it was very painful for my father.'

'What happened to the Jesuit?'

'I believe he had disciplinary issues with the order. He was a friend of Father Cinto Verdaguer, and I think he was mixed up in some of his problems, if you know what I mean.'

'Exorcisms?'

'Gossip.'

'How could a Jesuit who had been thrown out of the order afford a house like that?'

Valera shrugged his shoulders and I sensed that I was scraping the bottom of the barrel.

'I'd like to be of further help, Señor Martín, but I don't know how. Believe me.'

'Thank you for your time, Señor Valera.'

The lawyer nodded and pressed a bell on the desk. The secretary who had greeted me appeared in the doorway. Valera stretched out his hand and I shook it.

'Señor Martín is leaving. See him to the door, Margarita.'

The secretary inclined her head and led the way. Before leaving the office I turned round to look at the lawyer, who was standing crestfallen beneath his father's portrait. I followed Margarita out to the main door but just as she was about to close it I turned and gave her the most innocent of smiles.

'Excuse me. Señor Valera just gave me Señora Marlasca's address, but now that I think of it I'm not sure I remember the house number correctly . . .'

Margarita sighed, anxious to be rid of me.

'It's 13. Carretera de Vallvidrera, number 13.'

'Of course.'

'Good afternoon,' said Margarita.

Before I was able to say goodbye, the door was slammed in my face with the solemnity of a holy sepulchre.

21

When I returned to the tower house, I looked with different eyes at the building that had been my home and my prison for too many years. I went through the front door feeling as if I was entering the jaws of a being made of stone and shadow, and ascended the wide staircase, penetrating the bowels of this creature; when I opened the door of the main floor, the long corridor that faded into darkness seemed, for the first time, like the antechamber of a poisoned and distrustful mind. At the far end, outlined against the scarlet twilight that filtered through from the gallery, was the silhouette of Isabella advancing towards me. I closed the door and turned on the light.

Isabella had dressed as a refined young lady, with her hair up and a few touches of make-up that made her look ten years older.

'You're looking very attractive and elegant,' I said coldly.

'Like a girl your age, don't you think? Do you like the dress?'

'Where did you find it?'

'It was in one of the trunks in the room at the end. I think it belonged to Irene Sabino. What do you think? Doesn't it fit me well?'

'I told you to get someone to take everything away.'

'And I did. This morning I went to the parish church but they told me they couldn't collect, and we'd have to take it to them ourselves.'

I looked at her but didn't say anything.

'It's the truth,' she added.

'Take that off and put it back where you found it. And wash your face. You look like—'

'A tart?' Isabella completed.

I shook my head and sighed.

'No. You could never look like a tart, Isabella.'

'Of course. That's why you don't fancy me,' she muttered, turning round and heading for her room.

'Isabella,' I called.

She ignored me.

'Isabella,' I repeated, raising my voice.

She threw me a hostile glance before slamming the bedroom door shut. I heard her beginning to move things about. I walked over to the door and rapped with my knuckles. There was no reply. I rapped again. Not a word. I opened the door and found her gathering the few things she'd brought with her and putting them in her bag.

'What are you doing?' I asked.

'I'm leaving, that's what I'm doing. I'm going and I'm leaving you in peace. Or in war, because with you one never knows.'

'May I ask where you're going?'

'What do you care? Is that a rhetorical or an ironic question? It's obvious that you don't give a damn about anything, but as I'm such an idiot I can't tell the difference.'

'Isabella, wait a moment . . .'

'Don't worry about the dress, I'm taking it off right now. And you

222

can return the nibs, because I haven't used them and I don't like them. They're kitsch and childish.'

I moved closer and put a hand on her shoulder. She jumped away as if a snake had brushed against her.

'Don't touch me.'

I withdrew to the doorway in silence. Isabella's hands and lips were shaking.

'Isabella, forgive me. Please. I didn't mean to offend you.'

She looked at me with tears in her eyes and gave a bitter smile.

'You've done nothing but that. Ever since I got here. You've done nothing but insult me and treat me as if I were a poor idiot who didn't understand a thing.'

'I'm sorry,' I repeated. 'Leave your things. Don't go.'

'Why not?'

'Because I'm asking you, please, not to go.'

'If I need pity and charity, I can find it elsewhere.'

'It's not pity, or charity, unless that's what you feel for me. I'm asking you to stay because I'm the idiot here, and I don't want to be alone. I can't be alone.'

'Great. Always thinking of others. Buy yourself a dog.'

She let the bag fall on the bed and faced me, drying her tears as the pent-up anger slowly dissipated.

'Well then, since we're playing at telling the truth, let me tell you that you're always going to be alone. You'll be alone because you don't know how to love or how to share. You're like this house: it makes my hair stand on end. I'm not surprised your lady in white left you, or that everyone else has too. You don't love and you don't allow yourself to be loved.'

I stared at her, crushed, as if I'd just been given a beating and didn't know where the blows had come from. I searched for words but could only stammer.

'Is it true you don't like the pen set?' I managed at last.

Isabella rolled her eyes, exhausted.

'Don't look at me like a beaten dog. I might be stupid, but not that stupid.'

I didn't reply but remained leaning against the doorframe. Isabella observed me with an expression somewhere between suspicion and pity.

'I didn't mean to say what I said about your friend, the one in the photographs. I'm sorry,' she mumbled.

'Don't apologise. It's the truth.'

I left the room, eyes downcast, and took refuge in the study, where I gazed at the dark city buried in mist. After a while I heard her hesitant footsteps on the staircase.

'Are you up there?' she called out.

'Yes.'

Isabella came into the room. She had changed her clothes and washed the tears from her face. She smiled and I smiled back at her.

'Why are you like that?'

I shrugged my shoulders. Isabella came over and sat next to me, on the windowsill. We enjoyed the play of silences and shadows over the rooftops of the old town. After a while, she grinned at me and said, 'What if we were to light one of those cigars my father gives you and share it?'

'Certainly not.'

Isabella sank back into silence, but every now and then she glanced at me and smiled. I watched her out of the corner of my eye and realised that just by looking at her it was easier to believe there might be something good and decent left in this lousy world and, with luck, in myself.

'Are you staying?' I asked.

'Give me a good reason why I should. An honest reason. In other words, coming from you, a selfish one. And it had better not be a load of drivel or I'll leave right away.'

She barricaded herself behind a defensive look, waiting for one of my usual flattering remarks, and for a moment she seemed to be the only person in the world to whom I couldn't and didn't wish to lie. I looked down and for once I spoke the truth, even if it was only to hear it myself.

'Because you're the only friend I have left.'

The hard expression in her eyes disappeared, and before I could discern any pity, I looked away.

'What about Señor Sempere and that pedant, Barceló?'

'You're the only one who has dared tell me the truth.'

'What about your friend, the boss, doesn't he tell you the truth?'

'The boss is not my friend. And I don't think he's ever told the truth in his entire life.'

Isabella looked at me closely.

'You see? I knew you didn't trust him. I noticed it in your face from the very first day.'

I tried to recover some of my dignity, but all I found was sarcasm.

'Have you added face-reading to your list of talents?'

'You don't need any talent to read a face like yours,' Isabella retorted. 'It's like reading *Tom Thumb*.'

'And what else can you read in my face, dearest fortune-teller?'

'That you're scared.'

I tried to laugh without much enthusiasm.

'Don't be ashamed of being scared. To be afraid is a sign of common sense. Only complete idiots are not afraid of anything. I read that in a book.'

'The coward's handbook?'

'You needn't admit it if it's going to undermine your sense of masculinity. I know you men believe that the size of your stubbornness should match the size of your privates.'

'Did you also read that in your book?'

'No, that wisdom's homemade.'

I let my hands fall, surrendering in the face of the evidence.

'All right. Yes, I admit that I do feel a vague sense of anxiety.'

'You're the one who's being vague. You're scared stiff. Admit it.'

'Don't get things out of proportion. Let's say that I have some reservations concerning my publisher, which, given my experience, is understandable. As far as I know, Corelli is a perfect gentleman and our professional relationship will be fruitful and positive for both parties.'

'That's why your stomach rumbles every time his name crops up.'

I sighed. I had no arguments left.

'What can I say, Isabella?'

'That you're not going to work for him any more.'

'I can't do that.'

'And why not? Can't you just give him back his money and send him packing?'

'It's not that simple.'

'Why not? Have you got yourself into trouble?'

'I think so.'

'What sort of trouble?'

'That's what I'm trying to find out. In any case, I'm the only one to blame, so I must be the one to solve it. It's nothing that should worry you.'

Isabella looked at me, resigned for the time being but not convinced.

'You really are a hopeless person. Did you know that?'

'I'm getting used to the idea.'

'If you want me to stay, the rules here must change.'

'I'm all ears.'

'No more enlightened despotism. From now on, this house is a democracy.'

'Liberty, equality and fraternity.'

'Watch it where fraternity is concerned. But no more ordering around, and no more little Mr Rochester numbers.'

'Whatever you say, Miss Eyre.'

'And don't get your hopes up, because I'm not going to marry you even if you go blind.'

I put out my hand to seal our pact. She shook it with some hesitation and then gave me a hug. I let myself be wrapped in her arms and leaned my face on her hair. Her touch was full of peace and welcome, the life light of a seventeen-year-old girl, and I wanted to believe that it resembled the embrace my mother had never had time to give me.

'Friends?' I whispered.

'Till death us do part.'

22

The new regulations of the Isabellian reign came into effect at nine o'clock the following morning, when my assistant turned up in the kitchen and informed me how things were going to be from then on.

'I've been thinking that you need a routine in your life. Otherwise you get sidetracked and act in a dissolute manner.'

'Where did you get that expression from?'

'From one of your books. Dis-so-lute. It sounds good.'

'And it's great for rhymes.'

'Don't change the subject.'

During the day we would both work on our respective manuscripts. We would have dinner together and then she'd show me the pages she'd written that day and we'd discuss them. I swore I would be frank and give her appropriate suggestions, not just empty words to keep her happy. Sundays would be our day off and I'd take her to the pictures, to the theatre or out for a walk. She would help me find documents in libraries and archives and it would be her job to make sure the larder was always well stocked thanks to her connection with the family emporium. I would make breakfast and she'd make dinner. Lunch would be prepared by whoever was free at that moment. We divided up the chores and I promised to accept the irrefutable fact that the house needed to be cleaned regularly. I would not attempt to find her a boyfriend under any circumstances and she would refrain from questioning my motives for working for the boss or from expressing her opinion on the matter unless I asked for it. The rest we would make up as we went along.

I raised my cup of coffee and we toasted my unconditional surrender.

In just a couple of days I had given myself over to the peace and tranquillity of the vassal. Isabella awoke slowly, and by the time she emerged from her room, her eyes half-closed, wearing a pair of my slippers that were much too big for her, I had the breakfast ready, with coffee and the morning paper, a different one each day.

Routine is the housekeeper of inspiration. Only forty-eight hours after the establishment of the new regime, I discovered that I was beginning to recover the discipline of my most productive years. The hours of being locked up in the study crystallised into pages and more pages, in which, not without some anxiety, I began to see the work taking shape, reaching the point at which it stopped being an idea and became a reality.

The text flowed, brilliant, electric. It read like a legend, a mythological saga about miracles and hardships, peopled with characters and scenes that were knotted around a prophecy of hope

for the race. The narrative prepared the way for the arrival of a
warrior saviour who would liberate the nation of all pain and
injustice in order to give it back the pride and glory that had been
snatched away by its enemies – foes who had conspired since time
immemorial against the people, whoever that people might be. The
mechanics of the plot were impeccable and would work equally well
for any creed, race or tribe. Flags, gods and proclamations were the
jokers in a pack that always dealt the same cards. Given the nature
of the work, I had chosen one of the most complex and difficult
techniques to apply to any literary text: the apparent absence of
technique. The language resounded plain and simple, the voice was
honest and clean, a consciousness that did not narrate, but simply
revealed. Sometimes I would stop to reread what I'd written and,
overcome with blind vanity, I'd feel that the mechanism I was
setting up worked with perfect precision. I realised that for the first
time in a long while I had spent whole hours without thinking
about Cristina or Pedro Vidal. Life, I told myself, was improving.
Perhaps for that very reason, because it seemed that at last I
was going to get out of the predicament into which I'd fallen, I did
what I've always done when I've got myself back on the rails: I
ruined it all.

One morning, after breakfast, I donned one of my respectable suits.
I stepped into the gallery to say goodbye to Isabella and saw her
leaning over her desk, rereading pages from the day before.

'Are you not writing today?' she asked without looking up.

'I'm having a day off for meditation.'

I noticed the set of pen nibs and the ink pot decorated with
muses next to her notebook.

'I thought you considered it kitsch,' I said.

'I do, but I'm a seventeen-year-old girl and I have every right in
the world to like kitsch things. It's like you with your cigars.'

The smell of eau de cologne reached her and she looked at me
questioningly. When she saw that I'd dressed to go out she frowned.

'You're off to do some more detective work?' she asked.

'A bit.'

'Don't you need a bodyguard? A Doctor Watson? Someone with a
little common sense?'

228

'Don't learn how to find excuses for not writing before you learn how to write. That's a privilege of professionals and you have to earn it.'

'I think that if I'm your assistant, that should cover everything.'

I smiled meekly.

'Actually, there *is* something I wanted to ask you. No, don't worry. It's to do with Sempere. I've heard that he's hard up and that the bookshop is at risk.'

'That can't be true.'

'Unfortunately it is, but it's all right because we're not going to allow matters to get any worse.'

'Señor Sempere is very proud and he's not going to let you . . . You've already tried, haven't you?'

I nodded.

'That's why I thought we need to be a little shrewder, and resort to something more cunning,' I said.

'Your speciality.'

I ignored her disapproving tone. 'This is what I've planned: you drop by the bookshop, as if you just happened to be passing, and tell Sempere that I'm an ogre, that you're sick of me—'

'Up to now it sounds one-hundred-per-cent credible.'

'Don't interrupt. You tell him all that and also tell him that what I pay you to be my assistant is a pittance.'

'But you don't pay me a penny . . .'

I sighed. This required patience.

'When he says he's sorry to hear it, and he will, make yourself look like a damsel in distress and confess, if possible with a tear or two, that your father has disinherited you and wants to send you to a nunnery. Tell him you thought that perhaps you could work in his shop for a few hours a day, for a trial period, in exchange for a three-per-cent commission on what you sell. That way, you can carve out a future for yourself far from the convent, as a liberated woman devoted to the dissemination of literature.'

Isabella grimaced.

'Three per cent? Do you want to help Sempere or fleece him?'

'I want you to put on a dress like the one you wore the other night, get yourself all spruced up, as only you know how, and pay him a visit while his son is in the shop, which is usually in the afternoons.'

'Are we talking about the handsome one?'

'How many sons does Señor Sempere have?'

Isabella made her calculations and, when she began to understand what was going on, she threw me a sulphurous look.

'If my father knew the kind of perverse mind you have, he'd buy himself that shotgun.'

'All I'm saying is that the son must see you. And the father must see the son seeing you.'

'You're even worse than I imagined. Now you're devoting yourself to the white slave trade.'

'It's pure Christian charity. Besides, you were the first to admit that Sempere's son is good-looking.'

'Good-looking and a bit slow.'

'Don't exaggerate. Sempere junior is just shy in the presence of females, which does him credit. He's a model citizen who, despite being aware of his enticing appearance, exercises extreme self-control out of respect and devotion to the immaculate purity of Barcelona's womenfolk. Don't tell me this doesn't bestow an aura of nobility that appeals to your instincts, both maternal and the rest.'

'Sometimes I think I hate you, Señor Martín.'

'Hold on to that feeling, but don't blame poor young Sempere for my deficiencies as a human being because, strictly speaking, he's a saint.'

'We agreed that you wouldn't try to find me a boyfriend.'

'I've said nothing about a boyfriend. If you'll let me finish, I'll tell you the rest.'

'Go on, Rasputin.'

'When the older Sempere says yes to you, and he will, I want you to spend two or three hours a day at the counter in the bookshop.'

'Dressed like what? Mata Hari?'

'Dressed with the decorum and good taste that is characteristic of you. Pretty, suggestive, but without standing out. As I've said, if necessary you can rescue one of Irene Sabino's dresses, but it must be modest.'

'Two or three of them look fantastic on me,' Isabella commented, licking her lips in anticipation.

'Then wear whichever one covers you the most.'

'You're a reactionary. What about my literary education?'

'What better classroom than Sempere & Sons? You'll be surrounded by masterpieces from which you can learn in bulk.'

'And what should I do? Take a deep breath to see if something sticks?'

'It's just for a few hours a day. After that you can continue your work here, as you have until now, receiving my advice, which is always priceless and will turn you into a new Jane Austen.'

'And where's the cunning plan?'

'The cunning plan is that every day I'll give you a few pesetas, and every time you are paid by a customer and open the till you'll slide them in discreetly.'

'So that's your plan . . .'

'That's the plan. As you can see, there's nothing perverse about it.'

Isabella frowned again.

'It won't work. He'll notice there's something wrong. Señor Sempere is nobody's fool.'

'It will work. And if Sempere seems puzzled, you tell him that when customers see a pretty girl behind the counter, they let go of the purse strings and become more generous.'

'That might be so in the cheap haunts you frequent, not in a bookshop.'

'I beg to differ. If I were to go into a bookshop and come across a shop assistant who is as pretty and charming as you are, then I might even be capable of buying the latest national book award winner.'

'That's because your mind is as filthy as a hen house.'

'I also have – or should I say "we have" – a debt of gratitude towards Sempere.'

'That's a low blow.'

'Then don't make me aim even lower.'

Every self-respecting act of persuasion must first appeal to curiosity, then to vanity, and lastly to kindness or remorse. Isabella looked down and slowly nodded.

'And when were you planning to set this plan of the bounteous goddess in motion?'

'Don't put off for tomorrow what you can do today.'

'Today?'

'This afternoon.'

'Tell me the truth. Is this a strategy for laundering the money the boss pays you, and to purge your conscience, or whatever it is you have where there should be one?'

'You know my motives are always selfish.'

'And what if Señor Sempere says no?'

'Just make sure the son is there and you're dressed in your Sunday best, but not for Mass.'

'It's a degrading and offensive plan.'

'And you love it.'

At last Isabella smiled, cat-like.

'What if the son suddenly grows bold and allows his hands to wander?'

'I can guarantee the heir won't dare lay a finger on you unless it's in the presence of a priest waving a marriage certificate.'

'That sounds a bit extreme.'

'Will you do it?'

'For you?'

'For literature.'

23

When I stepped outside I was greeted by an icy breeze sweeping up the streets, and I knew that autumn was tiptoeing its way into Barcelona. In Plaza Palacio I got on a tram that was waiting there, empty, like a large wrought-iron rat trap. I sat by the window and paid the conductor for my ticket.

'Do you go as far as Sarriá?' I asked.

'As far as the square.'

I leaned my head against the window and soon the tram set off with a jerk. I closed my eyes and succumbed to one of those naps that can only be enjoyed on board some mechanical monstrosity, the sleep of modern man. I dreamed that I was travelling in a train made of black bones, its coaches shaped like coffins, crossing a deserted Barcelona that was strewn with discarded clothes, as if the bodies that had occupied them had simply evaporated. A wasteland of abandoned hats and dresses, suits and shoes that covered the silent streets. The engine gave off a trail of scarlet smoke that spread across the sky like spilt paint. A smiling boss travelled next to me. He was dressed in white and wore gloves. Something dark and glutinous dripped from the tips of his fingers.

'What has happened to all the people?'

'Have faith, Martín. Have faith.'

As I awoke, the tram was gliding slowly into Plaza de Sarriá. I jumped off before it reached the stop and made my way up Calle Mayor de Sarriá. Fifteen minutes later I arrived at my destination.

Carretera de Vallvidrera started in a shady grove behind the red-brick castle of San Ignacio's school. The street climbed uphill, bordered by solitary mansions, and was covered with a carpet of fallen leaves. Low clouds slid down the mountainside, dissolving into puffs of mist. I walked along the pavement and tried to work out the street numbers as I passed garden walls and wrought-iron gates. Behind them, barely visible, stood houses of darkened stone and dried-up fountains beached between paths that were thick with weeds. I walked along a stretch of road beneath a long row of cypress trees and discovered that the numbers jumped from 11 to 15. Confused, I retraced my steps in search of number 13. I was beginning to suspect that Señor Valera's secretary was, in fact, cleverer than she had seemed and had given me a false address, when I noticed an alleyway leading off the pavement. It ran for about fifty metres towards some dark iron railings that formed a crest of spears atop a stone wall.

I turned into the narrow cobbled lane and walked down to the railings. A thick, unkempt garden had crept towards the other side and the branches of a eucalyptus tree passed through the spearheads like the arms of prisoners pleading through the bars of a cell. I pushed aside the leaves that covered part of the wall and found the letters and numbers carved in the stone.

CASA MARLASCA

13

As I followed the railings that ran round the edge of the garden, I tried to catch a glimpse of the interior. Some twenty metres along I

233

discovered a metal door fitted into the stone wall. A large door knocker rested on the iron sheet that was welded together with tears of rust. The door was ajar. I pushed with my shoulder and managed to open it just enough to pass through without tearing my clothes on the sharp bits of stone that jutted out from the wall. The air was infused with the intense stench of wet earth.

A path of marble tiles led through the trees to an open area covered with white stones. On one side stood a garage, its doors open, revealing the remains of what had once been a Mercedes-Benz and now looked like a hearse abandoned to its fate. The house was a three-storey building in the modernist style, with curved lines and a crown of dormer windows coming together in a swirl beneath turrets and arches. Narrow windows, sharp as daggers, opened in its facade, which was peppered with reliefs and gargoyles. The glass panes reflected the silent passing of the clouds. I thought I could see the outline of a face behind one of the first-floor windows.

Without quite knowing why, I raised my arm and smiled faintly. I didn't want to be taken for a thief. The figure remained there watching me, as still as a spider. I looked down for a moment and, when I looked up again, it had disappeared.

'Good morning!' I called out.

I waited for a few seconds and when no reply came I proceeded slowly towards the house. An oval-shaped swimming pool flanked the eastern side, beyond which stood a glass conservatory. Frayed deckchairs surrounded the swimming pool. A diving board, overgrown with ivy, was poised over the sheet of murky water. I walked towards the edge and saw that it was littered with dead leaves and algae rippling over the surface. I was looking at my own reflection in the water when I noticed a dark figure hovering behind me.

I spun round and met a pointed, sombre face, examining me nervously.

'Who are you and what are you doing here?'

'My name is David Martín and Señor Valera, the lawyer, sent me.'

Alicia Marlasca pressed her lips together.

'You're Señora de Marlasca? Doña Alicia?'

'What's happened to the one who usually comes?' she asked.

I realised that Señora Marlasca had taken me for one of the articled clerks from Valera's office and had assumed I was bringing papers to sign or some message from the lawyers. For a moment I considered adopting that identity, but something in the woman's face told me that she'd heard enough lies to last her a lifetime.

'I don't work for the firm, Señora Marlasca. The reason for my visit is a personal matter. I wonder whether you would have a few minutes to speak about one of the old properties belonging to your deceased husband, Don Diego.'

The widow turned pale and looked away. She was leaning on a stick and I noticed a wheelchair in the doorway of the conservatory: I assumed she spent more time in it than she would care to admit.

'None of the properties belonging to my husband remain, Señor . . .'

'Martín.'

'The banks kept everything, Señor Martín. Everything except for this house, which, thanks to the advice of Señor Valera's father, was put in my name. The rest was taken by the scavengers . . .'

'I'm referring to the tower house, in Calle Flassaders.'

The widow sighed. I reckoned she was around sixty to sixty-five years old. The echo of what must once have been a dazzling beauty had scarcely faded.

'Forget that house. It's cursed.'

'Unfortunately I can't. I live there.'

Señora Marlasca frowned.

'I thought nobody wanted to live there. It stood empty for years.'

'I've been renting it for some time. The reason for my visit is that, while I was doing some renovations, I came across a few personal items which I think belonged to your deceased husband and, I suppose, to you.'

'There's nothing of mine in that house. Whatever you've found must belong to that woman . . .'

'Irene Sabino?'

Alicia Marlasca smiled bitterly.

'What do you really want to know, Señor Martín? Tell me the truth. You haven't come all this way to return some old things belonging to my husband.'

We gazed at each other in silence and I knew that I couldn't and didn't want to lie to this woman, whatever the cost.

'I'm trying to find out what happened to your husband, Señora Marlasca.'

'Why?'

'Because I think the same thing may be happening to me.'

Casa Marlasca had the feel of an abandoned mausoleum that characterises large houses sustained on absence and neglect. Far from its days of fortune and glory, when an army of servants kept it pristine and full of splendour, the house was now a ruin. Paint was peeling off the walls; the floor tiles were loose; the furniture was rotten and damp; the ceilings sagged and the large carpets were threadbare and discoloured. I helped the widow sit on her wheelchair and, following her instructions, pushed her to a reading room that contained hardly any books or pictures.

'I had to sell almost everything to survive,' she explained. 'If it hadn't been for Señor Valera, who still sends me a small pension every month on behalf of the firm, I wouldn't have known what to do.'

'Do you live here alone?'

The widow nodded.

'This is my home. The only place where I've been happy, even though that was many years ago. I've always lived here and I'll die here. I'm sorry I haven't offered you anything. It's been so long since I last had visitors that I've forgotten how to treat a guest. Would you like coffee or a tea?'

'I'm fine, thanks.'

Señora Marlasca smiled and pointed to the armchair in which I was sitting.

'That was my husband's favourite. He used to sit by the fire and read until late. I sometimes sat here, next to him, and listened. He liked telling me things, at least he did back then. We were very happy in this house . . .'

'What happened?'

The widow stared at the ashes in the hearth.

'Are you sure you want to hear this story?'

'Please.'

24

'To be honest, I'm not quite certain when my husband, Diego, met her. I just remember that one day he began to mention her in passing, and that soon not a day went by without him saying her name: Irene Sabino. He told me he'd been introduced to her by a man called Damián Roures who organised seances somewhere on Calle Elisabets. Diego was an expert on religions and had gone to a number of seances as an observer. In those days Irene Sabino was one of the most popular actresses in the Paralelo. She was beautiful, I will not deny it. Apart from that, I think she was just about able to count up to ten. People said she'd been born in the shacks of Bogatell beach, that her mother had abandoned her in the Somorrostro shanty town and she'd grown up among beggars and fugitives. At fourteen she started to dance in cabarets and nightclubs in the Raval and the Paralelo. Dancing is one way of putting it. I suppose she began to prostitute herself before she learned to read and write, if she ever did learn, that is . . . For a while she was the main star at La Criolla, or that's what people said. Then she went on to more upmarket venues. I think it was at the Apolo that she met a man called Juan Corbera, whom everyone called Jaco. Jaco was her manager and probably her lover. It was Jaco who invented the name Irene Sabino and the legend that she was the secret offspring of a famous Parisian cabaret star and a prince of the European nobility. I don't know what her real name was, or whether she ever had one. Jaco introduced her to the seances, at Roures's suggestion, I believe, and they shared the benefits of selling her supposed virginity to wealthy, bored men who went along to those shams to kill the monotony. Her speciality was couples, they say.

'What Jaco and his partner Roures didn't suspect was that Irene was obsessed with the sessions and really believed she could make contact with the world of spirits. She was convinced that her mother sent her messages from the other side, and even when she became famous she continued attending the seances to try to establish contact with her. That is where she met my husband Diego. I suppose we were going through a bad patch, like all marriages do. Diego had been wanting to leave the legal profession for some time to devote himself to writing. I admit that he didn't find the support he needed from me. I thought that if he did it, he would be throwing his life away, although probably what I really feared losing was all this, the house, the servants . . . I lost everything anyhow, and my husband too. What ended up separating us was the loss of Ismael. Ismael was our son. Diego was crazy about him. I've never seen a father so dedicated to his son. Ismael was his life, not I. We were arguing in the bedroom on the first floor. I began to reproach him for the time he spent writing, and for the fact that his partner, Valera, tired of having to shoulder Diego's work as well as his own, had sent him an ultimatum and was thinking about dissolving their partnership and setting himself up independently. Diego said he didn't care: he was ready to sell his part in the business so that he could dedicate himself to his vocation. That afternoon we couldn't find Ismael. He wasn't in his room or in the garden. I thought that when he'd heard us arguing he must have been frightened and had left the house. It wasn't the first time he'd done that. Some months earlier he'd been found on a bench in Plaza de Sarriá, crying. We went out to look for him as it was getting dark, but there was no sign of him anywhere. We went to our neighbours' houses, to hospitals . . . When we returned at dawn, after spending all night looking for him, we found his body at the bottom of the pool. He'd drowned the previous afternoon and we hadn't heard his cries for help because we were too busy shouting at each other. He was seven years old. Diego never forgave me, nor himself. Soon we were unable to bear each other's presence. Every time we looked at one another, every time we touched, we saw our dead son's body at the bottom of that damned pool. One day I woke up and knew that Diego had abandoned me. He left the law firm and went to live in a rambling old house in the Ribera quarter which he had been obsessed with for years. He said he was writing and he'd received a very important commission from a publisher in Paris, so I didn't need to worry about money. I knew he was with Irene, even if he didn't admit it. He was a broken man and was convinced that he only had a short time to live. He thought he'd caught some illness, a sort of parasite, that was eating him up. All he ever spoke about was death. He wouldn't listen to anyone. Not to me, not to Valera . . . only to Irene and Roures, who poisoned his mind with stories about spirits and extracted money from him by promising to put him in touch with Ismael. On one occasion I went to the tower house and begged him to open the door. He wouldn't let me in. He told me he was busy, said he was working on something that was going to enable him to save Ismael. I realised then that he was beginning to lose his mind. He believed that if he wrote that wretched book for the Parisian publisher our son would return from the dead. I think that between the three of them – Irene, Roures and Jaco – they managed to get their hands on what little money he had left, we had left . . . He no longer saw anybody and spent his time locked up in that horrible place. Months later they found him dead. The police said it had been an accident, but I never believed it. Jaco had disappeared and there was no trace of the money. Roures maintained he didn't know anything. He declared that he hadn't had any contact with Diego for months because Diego had gone mad, and he scared him. He said that in his last appearances at the seances Diego had frightened his customers with stories of accursed souls so Roures had not allowed him to return. Diego said there was a huge lake of blood under the city; that his son spoke to him in his dreams; that Ismael was trapped by a shadow with a serpent's skin who pretended to be another boy and played with him . . . Nobody was surprised when they found him dead. Irene said Diego had taken his own life because of me; she said that his cold and calculating wife, who had allowed his son to die because she didn't want to give up her life of luxury, had pushed him to his death. She said she was the only one who had truly loved him and that she'd never accepted a penny from him. And I think, at least in that respect, she was telling the truth. I'm sure Jaco used her to seduce Diego in order to rob him of everything. Later, when matters came to a head, Jaco left her behind and fled without sharing a single thing. That's what the police said, or at least some of them. I always felt that they didn't want to stir things up and the suicide version of events turned out to be very convenient. But I don't believe Diego took his own life. I didn't believe it then and I don't believe it now. I think Irene and Jaco murdered him. And not just for the money. There was something else. I remember that one of the policemen assigned to the case, a young man called Salvador, Ricardo Salvador, thought the same. He said there was something that didn't add up in the official version of events and that somebody was covering up the real cause of Diego's death. Salvador tried very hard to establish the facts but he was removed from the case and was eventually thrown out of the police force. Even then he continued to investigate on his own. He came to see me sometimes and we became good friends . . . I was a woman on my own, ruined and desperate. Valera kept telling me I should remarry. He also blamed me for what had happened to my husband and even insinuated that there were plenty of unmarried shopkeepers around who wouldn't mind having a pleasant-looking widow with aristocratic airs warm their beds in their golden years. Eventually even Salvador stopped visiting me. I don't blame him. By trying to help me he had ruined his own life. Sometimes I think that the only thing I've ever managed to do for others is destroy their lives . . . I hadn't told anybody this story until today, Señor Martín. If you want some advice, forget that house; forget me, my husband and this whole story. Go away, far away. This city is damned. Damned.'

25

I left Casa Marlasca in low spirits and wandered aimlessly through the maze of lonely streets that led to Pedralbes. The sky was covered with a mesh of clouds that barely allowed the sun to filter through. Needles of light perforated the grey shroud and swept across the hillside. I followed these lines of light with my eyes and saw how, in the distance, they caressed the enamelled roof of Villa Helius. The windows shone in the distance. Ignoring common sense, I set off in that direction. As I drew near, the sky darkened and a cutting wind lifted the fallen leaves into spirals. I stopped when I reached Calle Panamá. Villa Helius rose before me. I didn't dare cross the road and approach the wall surrounding the garden. Instead, I stood there for God knows how long, unable to leave or to go over to the door and knock. Then I saw her, walking across one of the large windows on the second floor. An intense cold invaded me. I was about to leave when she turned and stopped. She went up to the windowpane and I felt her eyes resting on mine. She raised her hand as if she were about to greet me, but didn't spread out her fingers. I didn't have the courage to hold her gaze; I turned round and walked off down the street. My hands were shaking and I thrust them into my pockets. Before turning the corner I looked back again and saw that she was still there, watching me. I tried to hate her but I couldn't find the strength.

I arrived home feeling chilled to the bone. As I walked through the front door I noticed the top of an envelope peeping out of the letter box. Parchment and sealing wax. News from the boss. I opened it while I dragged myself up the stairs. His elegant handwriting summoned me to a meeting the following day. When I reached the landing, the door was already ajar and Isabella was waiting for me with a smile.

'I was in the study and saw you coming,' she said.

I tried to smile back at her, but can't have been very convincing. She looked me in the eye and her face took on a worried expression.

'Are you all right?'

'It's nothing. I think I've caught a bit of a chill.'

'I have some broth on the stove. It'll work wonders. Come in.'

Isabella took my arm and led me to the gallery.

'I'm not an invalid, Isabella.'

She let go of me and looked down.

'I'm sorry.'

I didn't feel like a confrontation with anybody, still less my obstinate assistant, so I allowed her to guide me to one of the gallery armchairs into which I fell like a sack of bones. Isabella sat opposite me and looked at me with alarm.

'What happened?'

I smiled reassuringly.

'Nothing. Nothing has happened. Weren't you going to give me a bowl of soup?'

'Right away.'

She shot off towards the kitchen and I heard her rushing about. I took a deep breath and closed my eyes until I heard her footsteps approaching.

She handed me a steaming bowl of exaggerated dimensions.

'It looks like a chamber pot,' I said.

'Drink it and don't be so rude.'

I sniffed at the broth. It smelled good, but I didn't want to seem too docile.

'It smells odd,' I said. 'What's in it?'

'It smells of chicken because it's made of chicken, salt and a dash of sherry. Drink it.'

I took a sip and gave the bowl back to Isabella. She shook her head.

'All of it.'

I sighed and took another sip. It was good, whether I wanted to admit it or not.

'So, how was your day?' Isabella asked.

'It had its moments. How did you get on?'

'You're looking at the new star shop assistant of Sempere & Sons.'

'Excellent.'

'By five o'clock I'd already sold two copies of *The Picture of Dorian Gray* and a set of the complete works of Kipling to a very distinguished gentleman from Madrid who gave me a tip. Don't look at me like that; I put the tip in the till.'

'What about Sempere's son? What did he say?'

'He didn't actually say very much. He was like a stuffed dummy the whole time pretending he wasn't looking, but he couldn't take his eyes off me. I can hardly sit down my bum's so sore from him staring at it every time I went up the ladder to bring down a book. Happy?'

I smiled and nodded.

'Thanks, Isabella.'

She looked straight into my eyes.

'Say that again.'

'Thank you, Isabella. From the bottom of my heart.'

She blushed and looked away. We sat for a while in a placid silence, enjoying that camaraderie which doesn't even require words. I drank my broth until I could barely swallow another drop, and then showed her the empty bowl. She nodded.

'You've been to see her, haven't you? That woman, Cristina,' said Isabella, trying not to meet my eyes.

'Isabella, the reader of faces . . .'

'Tell me the truth.'

'I only saw her from a distance.'

Isabella looked at me cautiously, as if she were debating whether or not to say something that was stuck in her conscience.

'Do you love her?' she finally asked.

For a moment there was silence.

'I don't know how to love anybody. You know that. I'm a selfish person and all that. Let's talk about something else.'

Isabella's eyes settled on the envelope sticking out of my pocket.

'News from the boss?'

'The monthly call. His Excellency Señor Andreas Corelli is pleased to ask me to attend a meeting tomorrow at seven o'clock in the morning by the entrance to the Pueblo Nuevo Cemetery. He couldn't have chosen a better place.'

'And you plan to go?'

'What else can I do?'

'You could take a train this very evening and disappear forever.'

'You're the second person to suggest that to me today. To disappear from here.'

'There must be a reason.'

'And who would be your guide through the disasters of literature?'

'I'd go with you.'

I smiled and took her hand in mine.

'With you to the ends of the earth and back, Isabella.'

Isabella withdrew her hand suddenly and looked offended.

'You're making fun of me.'

'Isabella, if I ever decide to make fun of you, I'll shoot myself.'

'Don't say that. I don't like it when you talk like that.'

'I'm sorry.'

My assistant turned to her desk and sank into a deep silence. I watched her going over her day's pages, making corrections and crossing out whole paragraphs with the pen set I had given her.

'I can't concentrate with you looking at me.'

I stood up and went past her desk.

'Then I'll leave you to work, and after dinner you can show me what you've written.'

'It's not ready. I have to correct it all and rewrite it and—'

'It's never ready, Isabella. Get used to it. We'll read it together after dinner.'

'Tomorrow.'

I gave in.

'Tomorrow.'

I walked away, leaving her alone with her words. I was just closing the door when I heard her voice calling me.

'David?'

I stopped on the other side of the door, but didn't say anything.

'It's not true. It's not true that you don't know how to love anyone.'

I took refuge in my bedroom and closed the door. I lay down on the bed, curled up, and closed my eyes.

26

I left the house after dawn. Dark clouds crept over the rooftops, stealing the colour from the streets. As I crossed Ciudadela Park I saw the first drops hitting the trees and exploding on the path like bullets, raising eddies of dust. On the other side of the park a forest of factories and gas towers multiplied towards the horizon, the soot from the chimneys diluted in the black rain that plummeted from the sky like tears of tar. I walked along the uninviting avenue of cypress trees leading to the gates of the cemetery, the same route I had taken so many times with my father. The boss was already there. I saw him from afar, waiting patiently under the rain, at the foot of one of the large stone angels that guarded the main entrance to the graveyard. He was dressed in black and the only thing that set him apart from the hundreds of statues on the other side of the cemetery railings was his eyes. He didn't move an eyelash until I was a few metres away. Not quite sure what to do, I raised my hand to greet him. It was cold and the wind smelled of lime and sulphur.

'Visitors naively think that it's always sunny and hot in this town,' said the boss. 'But I say that sooner or later Barcelona's ancient, murky soul is always reflected in the sky.'

'You should publish tourist guides instead of religious texts,' I suggested.

'It comes to the same thing, more or less. How have these peaceful, calm days been? Have you made progress with the work? Do you have good news for me?'

I opened my jacket and handed him a sheaf of pages. We entered the cemetery in search of a place to shelter from the rain. The boss chose an old mausoleum with a dome held up by marble columns and surrounded by angels with sharp faces and fingers that were too long. We sat on a cold stone bench. The boss gave me one of his canine smiles, his shining pupils contracting to a black point in which I could see the reflection of my own uneasy expression.

'Relax, Martín. You make too much of the props.'

Calmly, the boss began to read the pages I had brought.

'I think I'll go for a walk while you read,' I said.

Corelli didn't bother to look up.

'Don't escape from me,' he murmured.

I got away as fast as I could without making it obvious that I was doing just that, and wandered among the paths with their twists and turns. I skirted obelisks and tombs as I entered the heart of the necropolis. The tombstone was still there, marked by a vase containing only the skeleton of shrivelled flowers. Vidal had paid for the funeral and had even commissioned a pietà from a sculptor of some repute in the undertakers' guild. She guarded the tomb, eyes looking heavenward, her hands on her chest in supplication. I knelt down by the tombstone and cleaned away the moss that had covered the letters chiselled on it.

JOSÉ ANTONIO MARTÍN CLARÉS
1875–1908
Hero of the Philippines War
His country and his friends will never forget him

'Good morning, father,' I said.

I watched the black rain as it slid down the face of the pietà, listened to the sound of the drops hitting the tombstones, and offered a smile to the health of those friends he'd never had and that country that had consigned him to a living death in order to enrich a handful of *caciques* who never knew he existed. I sat on the gravestone and put my hand on the marble.

'Who would have guessed, eh?'

My father, who had lived on the verge of destitution, rested eternally in a bourgeois tomb. As a child I had never understood why the newspaper had decided to give him a funeral with a smart priest and hired mourners, with flowers and a resting place fit for a sugar merchant. Nobody told me it was Vidal himself who paid for the lavish funeral of the man who had died in his place, although I had always suspected as much and had attributed the gesture to that infinite kindness and generosity with which the heavens had blessed my mentor and idol.

'I must beg your forgiveness, father. For years I hated you for leaving me here, alone. I told myself you'd got the death you deserved. That's why I never came to see you. Forgive me.'

My father had never liked tears. He thought a man never cried for others, only for himself. And if he did, he was a coward and deserved no pity. I didn't want to cry for him and betray him yet again.

'I would have liked you to have seen my name in a book, even if you couldn't read it. I would have liked you to have been here with me, to see that your son is managing to get on in life and has been able to do things that you were never allowed to do. I would have liked to have known you, father, and for you to have known me. I turned you into a stranger in order to forget you and now I'm the stranger.'

I didn't hear the boss approaching, but when I raised my head I saw him watching me from just a few metres away. I stood up and went over to him, like a well-trained dog. I wondered whether he knew my father was buried there and whether he had asked me to meet him in the graveyard for that very reason. My expression must have betrayed me, because the boss shook his head and put a hand on my shoulder.

'I didn't know, Martín. I'm sorry.'

I was not going to open that door of friendship to him. I turned away to rid myself of his gesture of sympathy and pressed my eyes shut to contain the tears of anger. I started to walk towards the exit, without him. The boss waited a few seconds and then decided to follow me. He walked beside me in silence until we reached the main gates. There I stopped and glared at him impatiently.

'Well? Any comments?'

The boss ignored my hostile tone and smiled indulgently.

'The work is excellent.'

'But—'

'If I had any observation to make it would be that you've hit the nail on the head by constructing the whole story from the point of view of a witness to the events, someone who feels like a victim and speaks on behalf of a people awaiting the warrior saviour. I want you to continue along those lines.'

'You don't think it sounds forced, contrived . . . ?'

'On the contrary. Nothing makes us believe more than fear, the certainty of being threatened. When we feel like victims, all our actions and beliefs are legitimised, however questionable they may be. Our opponents, or simply our neighbours, stop sharing common ground with us and become our enemies. We stop being aggressors and become defenders. The envy, greed or resentment that motivates us becomes sanctified, because we tell ourselves we're acting in self-defence. Evil, menace, those are always the preserve of the other. The first step towards believing passionately is fear. Fear of losing our identity, our life, our status or our beliefs. Fear is the gunpowder and hatred is the fuse. Dogma, the final ingredient, is only a lighted match. That is where I think your work has a hole or two.'

'Please clarify one thing: are you looking for a faith or a dogma?'

'It's not enough that people should believe. They must believe what we want them to believe. And they must not question it or listen to the voice of whoever questions it. Dogma must form part of identity itself. Whoever questions it is our enemy. He is evil. And it is our right and our duty to confront and destroy him. It is the only road to salvation. Believe in order to survive.'

I sighed and looked away, nodding reluctantly.

'You don't looked convinced, Martín. Tell me what you're thinking. Do you think I'm mistaken?'

'I don't know. I think you are simplifying things in a dangerous way. Your whole speech sounds like a stratagem for generating and channelling hatred.'

'The adjective you were going to use was not "dangerous" but "repugnant", but I won't hold that against you.'

'Why should we reduce faith to an act of rejection and blind obedience? Is it not possible to believe in values of acceptance, of harmony?'

The boss smiled. He was enjoying himself.

'It is possible to believe in anything, Martín, be it the free market or even the tooth fairy. We can even believe that we don't believe in anything, as you do, which is the greatest credulity of them all. Am I right?'

'The customer is always right. What is the other hole you see in the story?'

'I miss having a villain. Whether we realise it or not, most of us define ourselves by opposing rather than by favouring something or someone. To put it another way, it is easier to react than to act. Nothing arouses a passion for dogma more than a good antagonist. And the more unlikely, the better.'

'I thought that role would work better in the abstract. The antagonist would be the non-believer, the alien, the one outside the group.'

'Yes, but I'd you like you to be more specific. It's difficult to hate an idea. That requires a certain intellectual discipline and a slightly obsessive, sick mind. There aren't too many of those. It's much easier to hate someone with a recognisable face whom we can blame for everything that makes us feel uncomfortable. It doesn't have to be an individual character. It could be a nation, a race, a group . . . anything.'

The boss's flawless cynicism could even get the better of me. I gave a despondent sigh.

'Don't pretend to be a model citizen now, Martín. It's all the same to you and we need a villain in this vaudeville. You should know that better than anyone. There is no drama without a conflict.'

'What sort of villain would you like? A tyrant invader? A false prophet? The bogeyman?'

'I'll leave the outfit to you. Any of the usual suspects suits me. One of the functions of our villain must be to allow us to adopt the role of the victim and claim our moral superiority. We project onto him all those things we are incapable of recognising in ourselves, things we demonise according to our particular interests. It's the basic arithmetic of the Pharisees. I keep telling you: you need to read the Bible. All the answers you're looking for are in there.'

'I'm on the case.'

'All you have to do is convince the sanctimonious that they are free of all sin and they'll start throwing stones, or bombs, with gusto. In fact, it doesn't take much, because they can be convinced with the bare minimum of encouragement and excuses. I don't know whether I'm making myself clear.'

'You are making yourself abundantly clear. Your arguments have the subtlety of a blast furnace.'

'I'm not sure I like that condescending tone, Martín. Does this mean you think this project isn't on a par with your moral or intellectual purity?'

'Not at all,' I mumbled faint-heartedly.

'What is it, then, something tickling your conscience, dear friend?'

'The usual thing. I'm not sure I'm the nihilist you need.'

'Nobody is. Nihilism is an attitude, not a doctrine. Place the flame from a candle under the testicles of a nihilist and notice how quickly he sees the light of existence. Something else is bothering you.'

I raised my head and summoned up the most defiant tone I was capable of, looking the boss in the eye.

'Perhaps what's bothering me is that I understand everything you say, but I don't feel it.'

'Do I pay you to have feelings?'

'Sometimes feeling and thinking are one and the same. The idea is yours, not mine.'

The boss smiled, and allowed a dramatic pause, like a schoolteacher preparing the lethal sword thrust with which to silence an unruly pupil.

'And what do you feel, Martín?'

The irony and disdain in his voice encouraged me and I gave vent to the humiliation accumulated during all those months in his shadow. Anger and shame at feeling terrified by his presence and allowing his poisonous speeches. Anger and shame because he had proved to me that, even if I would rather believe the only thing I had in me was despair, my soul was as petty and miserable as his sewer humanism claimed. Anger and shame at feeling, knowing, that he was always right, especially when it hurt to accept that.

'I've asked you a question, Martín. What is it you *feel*?'

'I feel that the best course would be to leave things as they are and give you back your money. I feel that, whatever it is you are proposing with this absurd venture, I'd rather not take part in it. And, above all, I feel regret for ever having met you.'

The boss lowered his eyelids and sank into a long silence. He turned and walked a few steps towards the cemetery gates. I watched his dark silhouette outlined against the marble garden, a motionless shape under the rain. I felt afraid, a murky fear that was beginning to grow inside me, inspiring a childish wish to beg forgiveness and accept any punishment in exchange for not having to bear that silence. And I felt disgust. At his presence and, in particular, at myself.

The boss turned round and came over to me again. He stopped just centimetres from me and put his face close to mine. I felt his cold breath on my skin and drowned in his black, bottomless eyes. This time his voice and his tone were like ice, devoid of that studied humanity that peppered his conversation and his gestures.

'I will only tell you once. You fulfil your obligations and I'll fulfil mine. It's the only thing you can and must feel.'

I was not aware that I was nodding repeatedly until the boss pulled the sheaf of papers from his pocket and handed it to me. He let the pages fall before I was able to catch them and a gust of wind swept them away, scattering them near the cemetery gates. I rushed to recover them from the rain, but some of the pages had fallen into puddles and were bleeding in the water, the words coming off the paper in filaments. I gathered them together in a fistful of wet paper. When I looked up again, the boss had gone.

27

If ever I had needed to see a friendly face, it was then. The old building of *The Voice of Industry* peered over the cemetery walls. I set off in that direction, hoping to find my former master Don Basilio, one of those rare souls immune to the world's stupidity, who always had good advice. When I walked into the newspaper offices I discovered that I still recognised most of the staff. It seemed as if not a minute had passed since I'd left the place so many years ago. Those who, in turn, recognised me gave me suspicious looks and turned their heads to avoid having to greet me. I slipped into the editorial department and went straight to Don Basilio's office, which was at the far end. It was empty.

'Who are you looking for?'

I turned round and saw Rosell, one of the journalists who'd already seemed old to me even when I was working there. Rosell had penned the poisonous review of *The Steps of Heaven* describing me as a 'writer of classified advertisements'.

'Señor Rosell, I'm Martín. David Martín. Don't you remember me?'

Rosell spent a few moments inspecting me, pretending to have great difficulty recognising me, but finally he nodded.

'Where's Don Basilio?'

'He left two months ago. You'll find him at the offices of *La Vanguardia*. If you see him, give him my regards.'

'I'll do that.'

'I'm sorry about your book,' said Rosell with an obliging smile.

I crossed the editorial department, cutting a path between unfriendly looks, twisted smiles and venomous whispers. Time cures all, I thought, except the truth.

Half an hour later, a taxi dropped me off at the door of the main offices of *La Vanguardia* in Calle Pelayo. In contrast to the rather forbidding shabbiness of my old newspaper, everything here spoke of elegance and opulence. I made myself known at the reception and a chirpy young boy who looked like an unpaid trainee, reminding me of myself in my youth, was dispatched to let Don Basilio know he had a visitor. My old friend's leonine presence remained unscathed by the passage of time. If anything, with his new attire matching the exclusive scenery, Don Basilio struck as formidable a figure as he had in his days at *The Voice of Industry*. His eyes lit up with joy when he saw me, and, breaking his iron protocol, he greeted me with an embrace that could easily have lost me two or three ribs had there not been an audience present – happy or not, Don Basilio had to keep up appearances and a certain reputation.

'Getting a little respectable, are we, Don Basilio?'

My old boss shrugged his shoulders, making a gesture to indicate that he was playing down the new decor.

'Don't let it impress you.'

'Don't be modest, Don Basilio; you've ended up with the jewel in the crown. Are you taking them in hand?'

Don Basilio pulled out his perennial red pencil and showed it to me, winking as he did so.

'I get through four a week.'

'Two fewer than at *The Voice*.'

'Give me time. I have one or two experts here who punctuate with a pistol and think that an intro is a starter from the province of Logroño.'

Despite his words, it was obvious that Don Basilio felt comfortable in his new home, and he looked healthier than ever.

'Don't tell me you've come to ask me for work, because I might even give it to you,' he threatened.

'That's very kind of you, Don Basilio, but you know I gave up the cloth and journalism isn't for me.'

'Then let me know how this grumpy old man can be of service.'

'I need some information about an old case for a story I'm working on. The death of a well-known lawyer called Marlasca, Diego Marlasca.'

'What year are we talking about?'

'Nineteen hundred and four.'

Don Basilio sighed.

'That's going back a long way. A lot of water has flowed by since then.'

'Not enough to wash the matter away.'

Don Basilio put a hand on my shoulder and asked me to follow him into the editorial department.

'Don't worry; you've come to the right place. These good people maintain an archive that would be the envy of the Vatican. If there was anything in the press, we'll find it for you. Besides, the archivist is a good friend of mine. Let me warn you that next to him I'm Snow White. Pay no attention to his unfriendly disposition. Deep down – very deep down – he's kindness itself.'

I followed Don Basilio through a wide hall with fine wood

panelling. On one side was a circular room with a large round table and a series of portraits from which we were observed by an illustrious group of frowning members of the aristocracy.

'The room for the witches' sabbaths,' Don Basilio explained. 'All the section heads meet here with the deputy editor, yours truly, and the editor, and like good Knights of the Round Table, we find the Holy Grail every evening at seven o'clock.'

'Impressive.'

'You ain't seen nothing yet,' said Don Basilio, winking at me. 'Look at this.'

Don Basilio stood beneath one of the august portraits and pushed the wooden panel covering the wall. The panel yielded with a creak, leading to a hidden corridor.

'What do you say, Martín? And this is only one of the many secret passages in the building. Not even the Borgias had a set-up like this.'

I followed Don Basilio down the corridor and we reached a large reading room surrounded by glass cabinets, the repository of *La Vanguardia*'s secret library. At one end of the room, under the beam emanating from a lampshade of green glass, a middle-aged man was sitting at a table examining a document with a magnifying glass. When he saw us come in he raised his head and gave us a look that would have made anyone young enough, or sensitive enough, turn to stone.

'Let me introduce you to José María Brotons, lord of the underworld, chief of the catacombs of this holy house,' Don Basilio announced.

Without letting go of the magnifying glass, Brotons observed me with eyes that seemed to go rusty on contact. I went up to him and shook his hand.

'This is my old apprentice, David Martín.'

Brotons reluctantly shook my hand and glanced at Don Basilio.

'Is this the writer?'

'The very one.'

Brotons nodded.

'He's certainly courageous, stepping out into the street after the thrashing they gave him. What's he doing here?'

'He's come to plead for your help, your blessing and advice on an important matter of documental archaeology,' Don Basilio

253

explained.

'And where's the blood sacrifice?' Brotons spat out.

I swallowed.

'Sacrifice?' I asked.

Brotons looked at me as if I were an idiot.

'A goat, a lamb, a capon if pressed . . .'

My mind went blank. For an endless moment Brotons kept his eyes fixed on mine without blinking. Then, just as I started to feel the prickle of sweat down my back, the archivist and Don Basilio roared with laughter. I let them laugh as much as they wanted at my expense, until they couldn't breathe and had to dry their tears. Clearly, Don Basilio had found a soulmate in his new colleague.

'Come this way, young man,' Brotons said, doing away with his fierce countenance. 'Let's see what we can find.'

28

The newspaper archives were located in one of the basements, under the floor that housed the huge rotary press, a product of post-Victorian technology. It looked like a cross between a monstrous steam engine and a machine for making lightning.

'Let me introduce you to the rotary press, better known as Leviathan. Mind how you go: they say it has already swallowed more than one unsuspecting person,' said Don Basilio. 'It's like the story of Jonah and the whale, only what comes out again is mincemeat.'

'Surely you're exaggerating.'

'One of these days we could throw in that new trainee, the smart alec who likes to say that print is dead,' Brotons proposed.

'Set a time and a date and we'll celebrate with a stew,' Don Basilio agreed.

They both laughed like schoolchildren. Birds of a feather, I thought.

The archive was a labyrinth of corridors bordered by three-metre-high shelving. A couple of pale creatures who looked as if they hadn't left the cellar in fifteen years officiated as Brotons's assistants. When they saw him, they rushed over, like loyal pets awaiting instructions. Brotons looked at me inquisitively.

'What is it we're looking for?'

'Nineteen hundred and four. The death of a lawyer called Diego Marlasca. A pillar of Barcelona society, founding member of the Valera, Marlasca y Sentís legal firm.'

'Month?'

'November.'

At a signal from Brotons, the two assistants ran off in search of copies dating back to November 1904. It was a time when each day was so stained with the presence of death that most newspapers ran large obituaries on their front pages. A character as important as Marlasca would probably have generated more than a simple death notice in the city's press and his obituary would have been front-cover material. The assistants returned with a few volumes and placed them on a large desk. We divided up the task between all five present and found Diego Marlasca's obituary on the front page, just as I'd imagined. The edition was dated 23 November 1904. It was Brotons who made the discovery.

'*Habemus* cadaver,' he announced.

There were four obituary notices devoted to Marlasca. One from the family, another from the law firm, one from the Barcelona Bar Association and the last from the cultural association of the Ateneo Barcelonés.

'That's what comes from being rich. You die five or six times,' Don Basilio pointed out.

The announcements were not in themselves very interesting – pleadings for the immortal soul of the deceased, a note explaining that the funeral would be for close friends and family only, grandiose verses lauding a great, erudite citizen, an irreplaceable member of Barcelona society, and so on.

'The type of thing you're interested in probably appeared a day or two earlier, or later,' Brotons said.

We checked through the papers covering the week of Marlasca's death and found a sequence of news items relating to the lawyer. The first reported that the distinguished lawyer had died in an accident. Don Basilio read the text out loud.

'This was written by a chimp,' he pronounced. 'Three redundant paragraphs that don't say anything and only at the end does it explain that the death was accidental, but without saying what sort of accident it was.'

'Here we have something more interesting,' said Brotons.

An article published the following day explained that the police were investigating the circumstances of the accident. The most revealing piece of information was that, according to the forensic evidence, Marlasca had drowned.

'Drowned?' interrupted Don Basilio. 'How? Where?'

'It doesn't say. Perhaps they had to shorten the item to include this urgent and extensive apologia for the *sardana*, a three-column article entitled "To the strains of the *tenora*: spirit and mettle",' Brotons remarked.

'Does it say who was in charge of the investigation?' I asked.

'It mentions someone called Salvador. Ricardo Salvador,' said Brotons.

We went over the rest of the news items related to the death of Marlasca, but there was nothing of any substance. The texts parroted one another, repeating a chorus that sounded too much like the official line supplied by the law firm of Valera & Co.

'This has the distinct whiff of a cover-up,' said Brotons.

I sighed, disheartened. I had hoped to find something more than sugary remembrances and hollow news items that threw no new light on the facts.

'Didn't you have a good contact in police headquarters?' Don Basilio asked. 'What was his name?'

'Víctor Grandes,' Brotons said.

'Perhaps he could put Martín in touch with this person, Salvador.'

I cleared my throat and the two hefty men looked at me with a frown.

'For reasons that have nothing to do with this matter, or perhaps because they're too closely related, I'd rather not involve Inspector Grandes,' I said.

Brotons and Don Basilio exchanged glances.

'Right. Any other names that should be deleted from the list?'

'Marcos and Castelo.'

'I see you haven't lost your talent for making friends,' offered Don

Basilio.

Brotons rubbed his chin.

'Let's not worry too much. I think I might be able to find another way in that will not arouse suspicion.'

'If you find Salvador for me, I'll sacrifice whatever you want, even a pig.'

'With my gout I've given up pork, but I wouldn't say no to a good cigar,' Brotons said.

'Make it two,' added Don Basilio.

While I rushed off to a tobacconist's on Calle Tallers in search of two specimens of the most exquisite and expensive Havana cigars, Brotons made a few discreet calls to police headquarters and confirmed that Salvador had left the police force, or rather that he had been made to leave, and had gone on to work as a corporate bodyguard as well as doing investigative work for various law firms in the city. When I returned to the newspaper offices to present my benefactors with their two cigars, the archivist handed me a note with an address:

Ricardo Salvador
Calle de la Lleona, 21. Top floor.

'May the publisher-in-chief of *La Vanguardia* bless you,' I said. 'And may you live to see it.'

29

Calle de la Lleona, better known to locals as the Street of the Three Beds in honour of the notorious brothel it harboured, was an alleyway almost as dark as its reputation. It started in the shadowy arches of Plaza Real and extended into a damp crevice, far from sunlight, between old buildings piled on top of one another and sewn together by a perpetual web of clothes lines. The crumbling, ochre facades were dilapidated, and the slabs of stone covering the ground had been bathed in blood during the years when the city had been ruled by the gun. More than once I'd used the setting as a backdrop to my stories in *City of the Damned* and even now, deserted and forgotten, it still smelled of crime and gunpowder. The grim surroundings seemed to indicate that Superintendent Salvador's early retirement package from the police force had not been a generous one.

Number 21 was a modest property squeezed between two buildings that held it together like pincers. The main door was open, revealing a pool of shadows from which a steep, narrow staircase rose in a spiral. The floor was flooded with a dark, slimy liquid oozing from the cracks in the tiles. I climbed the steps as best I could, without letting go of the handrail, but not trusting it either. There was only one door on every landing. Judging by the appearance of the building I didn't think that any of the apartments could be larger than forty square metres. A small skylight crowned the stairwell and bathed the upper floors in a tenuous light. The door to the top-floor apartment was at the end of a short corridor and I was surprised to find it open. I rapped with my knuckles, but got no reply. The door opened onto a small sitting room containing an armchair, a table and a bookshelf filled with books and brass boxes. A sort of kitchen-cum-washing area occupied the adjoining room. The saving grace in that cell was a terrace that led to the flat roof. The door to the terrace was also open and a fresh breeze blew through it, bringing with it the smell of cooking and laundry from the rooftops of the old town.

'Is anyone home?' I called out.

Nobody answered, so I walked over to the terrace door and stepped outside. A jungle of roofs, towers, water tanks, lightning conductors and chimneys spread out in every direction. Before I was able to take another step, I felt the touch of cold metal on the back of my neck and heard the metallic click of a revolver as the hammer was cocked. All I could think to do was raise my hands and not move even an eyebrow.

'My name is David Martín. I got your address from police headquarters. I wanted to speak to you about a case you handled.'

'Do you usually go into people's homes uninvited, Señor David Martín?'

'The door was open. I called out but you can't have heard me. Can I put my hands down?'

'I didn't tell you to put them up. Which case?'

'The death of Diego Marlasca. I rent the house that was his last home. The tower house in Calle Flassaders.'

He said nothing. I could still feel the revolver pressing against my back.

'Señor Salvador?' I asked.

'I'm wondering whether it wouldn't be better to blow your head off right now.'

'Don't you want to hear my story first?'

The pressure from the revolver seemed to lessen and I heard the hammer being uncocked. I slowly turned round. Ricardo Salvador was an imposing figure, with grey hair and pale blue eyes that penetrated like needles. I guessed that he must have been about fifty but it would have been difficult to find men half his age who would dare get in his way. I gulped. Salvador lowered the revolver and turned his back to me, returning to the apartment.

'I apologise for the welcome,' he mumbled.

I followed him to the minute kitchen and stopped in the doorway. Salvador left the pistol on the sink and lit the stove with bits of paper and cardboard. He pulled out a coffee pot and looked at me questioningly.

'No, thanks.'

'It's the only good thing I have, I warn you,' he said.

'Then I'll have one with you.'

Salvador put a couple of generous spoonfuls of coffee into the pot, filled it with water and put it on the flames.

'Who has spoken to you about me?'

'A few days ago I visited Señora Marlasca, the widow. She's the one who told me about you. She said you were the only person who had tried to discover the truth and it had cost you your job.'

'That's one way of describing it, I suppose,' he said.

I noticed that at my mention of the widow his expression darkened, and I wondered what might have happened between them during those unfortunate days.

'How is she?' he asked. 'Señora Marlasca.'

'I think she misses you.'

Salvador nodded, his fierce manner crumbling.

'I haven't been to see her for a long time.'

'She thinks you blame her for what happened. I think she'd like to see you again, even though so much time has gone by.'

'Perhaps you're right. Maybe I should go and pay her a visit . . .'

'Can you talk to me about what happened?'

Salvador recovered his severe expression.

'What do you want to know?'

'Marlasca's widow told me that you never accepted the official line that her husband took his own life. She said you had suspicions.'

'More than suspicions. Has anyone told you how Marlasca died?'

'All I know is that people said it was an accident.'

'Marlasca died by drowning. At least, that's what the police report said.'

'How did he drown?'

'There's only one way of drowning, but I'll come back to that later. The curious thing is where he drowned.'

'In the sea?'

Salvador smiled. It was a dark, bitter smile, like the coffee that was brewing.

'Are you sure you want to hear this?'

'I've never been surer of anything in my life.'

He handed me a cup and looked me up and down, assessing me.

'I assume you've visited that son-of-a-bitch Valera.'

'If you mean Marlasca's partner, he's dead. The one I spoke to was his son.'

'Another son-of-a-bitch, except he has fewer guts. I don't know what he told you, but I'm sure he didn't say that between them they managed to get me thrown out of the police force and turned me into a pariah who couldn't even beg for money in the streets.'

'I'm afraid he forgot to include that in his version of events,' I conceded.

'It doesn't surprise me.'

'You were going to tell me how Marlasca drowned.'

'That's where it gets interesting,' said Salvador. 'Did you know that Señor Marlasca, apart from being a lawyer, a scholar and a writer, had, as a young man, won the annual Christmas swim across the port organised by the Barcelona Swimming Club?'

'How can a champion swimmer drown?' I asked.

'The question is where did he drown. Señor Marlasca's body was found in the pond on the roof of the Water Reservoir building in Ciudadela Park. Do you know the place?'

I swallowed and nodded. It was there that I'd first encountered Corelli.

'If you know it, you'll know that, when it's full, it's barely a metre deep. It's essentially a basin. The day the lawyer was found dead, the reservoir was half-empty and the water level was no more than sixty centimetres.'

'A champion swimmer doesn't drown in sixty centimetres of water, just like that,' I observed.

'That's what I said to myself.'

'Were there other points of view?'

Salvador smiled bitterly.

'For a start, it's doubtful whether he drowned at all. The pathologist who carried out the autopsy found water in the lungs, but his report said that death had occurred as a result of heart failure.'

'I don't understand.'

'When Marlasca fell into the pond, or when he was pushed, he was on fire. His body had third-degree burns on the torso, arms and face. According to the pathologist, the body could have been alight for almost a minute before it came into contact with the water. The remains of the lawyer's clothes showed the presence of some type of solvent on the fabrics. Marlasca was burned alive.'

It took me a few minutes to digest all this.

'Why would anyone want to do something like that?'

'A settling of scores? Pure cruelty? You choose. My opinion is that somebody wanted to delay the identification of Marlasca's body in order to gain time and confuse the police.'

'Who?'

'Jaco Corbera.'

'Irene Sabino's agent.'

'Who disappeared the same day Marlasca died, together with the balance from a personal account in the Banco Hispano Colonial which his wife didn't know about.'

'A hundred thousand French francs,' I said.

261

Salvador looked at me, intrigued.

'How did you know?'

'It's not important. What was Marlasca doing on the roof of the reservoir anyway? It's not exactly on the way to anywhere.'

'That's another confusing point. We found a diary in Marlasca's study in which he had written down an appointment there at five in the afternoon. Or that's what it looked like. In the diary he'd only specified a time, a place and an initial. C. Probably for Corbera.'

'Then what do you think happened?' I asked.

'What I think, and what the evidence suggests, is that Jaco fooled Irene into manipulating Marlasca. As you probably know, the lawyer was obsessed with all that mumbo-jumbo about seances, especially since the death of his son. Jaco had a partner, Damián Roures, who was mixed up in that world. A real fraudster. Between the two of them, and with the help of Irene Sabino, they conned Marlasca, promising that they could help him make contact with the boy in the spirit world. Marlasca was a desperate man, ready to believe anything. That trio of vermin had organised the perfect sting but then Jaco became too greedy for his own good. Some think that Sabino didn't act in bad faith, that she genuinely was in love with Marlasca and believed in all that supernatural nonsense, just as he did. It is a possibility but I don't buy it, and seeing how things turned out, it's irrelevant. Jaco knew that Marlasca had those funds in the bank and decided to get him out of the way and disappear with the money, leaving a trail of chaos behind him. The appointment in the diary may well have been a red herring left by Sabino or Jaco. There was no way at all of knowing whether Marlasca himself had noted it down.'

'And where did the hundred thousand francs Marlasca had in the Hispano Colonial come from?'

'Marlasca had paid that money into the account himself, in cash, the year before. I haven't the faintest idea where he could have laid hands on a sum of that size. What I do know is that the remainder was withdrawn, in cash, on the morning of the day Marlasca died. Later, the lawyers said that the money had been transferred to some sort of discretionary fund and had not disappeared; they said Marlasca had simply decided to reorganise his finances. But I find it hard to believe that a man should reorganise his finances, moving almost one hundred thousand francs in the morning, and be discovered, burned alive, in the afternoon, without there being some connection. I don't believe this money ended up in some mysterious fund. To this day, there has been nothing to convince me that the money didn't end up in the hands of Jaco Corbera and Irene Sabino. At least at first, because I doubt that she saw any of it after Jaco disappeared.'

'What happened to Irene?'

'That's another aspect that makes me think Jaco tricked both of his accomplices. Shortly after Marlasca's death, Roures left the afterlife industry and opened a shop selling magic tricks on Calle Princesa. As far as I know, he's still there. Irene Sabino worked for a couple more years in increasingly tawdry clubs and cabarets. The last thing I heard, she was prostituting herself in El Raval and living in poverty. She obviously didn't get a single franc. Nor did Roures.'

'And Jaco?'

'He probably left the country under a false name and is living comfortably somewhere off the proceeds.'

The whole story, far from clarifying things in my mind, only raised more questions. Salvador must have noticed my unease and gave me a commiserating smile.

'Valera and his friends in the town hall managed to persuade the press to publish the story about an accident. He resolved the matter with a grand funeral: he didn't want to muddy the reputation of the law firm, whose client list included many members of the town hall and the city council. Nor did he wish to draw attention to Marlasca's strange behaviour during the last twelve months of his life, from the moment he abandoned his family and associates and decided to buy a ruin in a part of town he had never set his well-shod foot in so that he could devote himself to writing, or at least that's what his partner said.'

'Did Valera say what sort of thing Marlasca wanted to write?'

'A book of poems, or something like that.'

'And you believed him?'

'I've seen many strange things in my work, my friend, but a wealthy lawyer who leaves everything to go and write sonnets is not part of the repertoire.'

'So?'

'So the reasonable thing would have been for me to forget the whole matter and do as I was told.'

'But that's not what happened.'

'No. And not because I'm a hero or an idiot. I did it because every time I saw the suffering of that poor woman, Marlasca's widow, it made my stomach turn, and I couldn't look at myself in the mirror without doing what I was supposedly being paid to do.'

He pointed around the miserable, cold place that was his home.

'Believe me: if I'd known what was coming I would have preferred to be a coward and wouldn't have stepped out of line. I can't say I wasn't warned at police headquarters. With the lawyer dead and buried, it was time to turn the page and put all our efforts into the pursuit of starving anarchists and schoolteachers with suspicious ideologies.'

'You say buried . . . Where is Diego Marlasca buried?'

'In the family vault in San Gervasio Cemetery, I think, not far from the house where the widow lives. May I ask why you are so interested in this matter? And don't tell me your curiosity was aroused just because you live in the tower house.'

'It's hard to explain.'

'If you want a friendly piece of advice, look at me and learn from my mistakes. Let it go.'

'I'd like to. The problem is that I don't think the matter will let *me* go.'

Salvador watched me for a long time. Then he took a piece of paper and wrote down a number.

'This is the telephone number of the downstairs neighbours. They're good people and the only ones who have a telephone in the whole building. You can get hold of me there, or leave me a message. Ask for Emilio. If you need any help, don't hesitate to call. And watch out. Jaco disappeared from the scene many years ago, but there are still people who don't want this business stirred up again. A hundred thousand francs is a lot of money.'

I took the note and put it away.

'Thank you.'

'Not at all. Anyhow, what more can they do to me now?'

'Would you have a photograph of Diego Marlasca? I haven't found one anywhere in the tower house.'

'I don't know . . . I think I must have one somewhere. Let me have a look.'

Salvador walked over to a desk in a corner of the sitting room and pulled out a brass box full of bits of paper.

'I still have things from the case . . . As you see, even after all those years, I haven't learned my lesson. Here. Look. This photograph was given to me by the widow.'

He handed me an old studio portrait of a tall, good-looking man in his forties, who was smiling at the camera, against a velvet backdrop. I tried to read those clear eyes, wondering how they could possibly conceal the dark world I had found in the pages of *Lux Aeterna*.

'May I keep it?'

Salvador hesitated.

'I suppose so. But don't lose it.'

'I promise I'll return it.'

'Promise me you'll be careful and I'd be much happier. And that if you're not, and you get into a mess, you'll call me.'

We shook on it.

'I promise.'

30

The sun was setting as I left Ricardo Salvador on his cold roof terrace and returned to Plaza Real. The square was bathed in a dusty light that tinted the figures of passers-by with a reddish hue. From there I set off walking and ended up at the only place in town where I always felt welcome and protected. When I reached Calle Santa Ana, the Sempere & Sons bookshop was about to close. Twilight was advancing over the city and the sky was breached by a line of blue and purple. I stopped in front of the shop window and saw that Sempere's son was saying goodbye to a customer at the front door. When he saw me he smiled and greeted me with a shyness that spoke of his innate decency.

'I was just thinking about you, Martín. Everything all right?'

'Couldn't be better.'

'It shows in your face. Here, come in, I'll make you some coffee.'

He held the shop door open and showed me in. I stepped into the bookshop and breathed in that perfume of paper and magic that strangely no one had ever thought of bottling. Sempere's son took me to the back room, where he set about preparing a pot of coffee.

'How is your father? He looked fragile the other day.'

Sempere's son nodded, as if appreciative of my concern. I realised that he probably didn't have anyone to talk to about the subject.

'He's seen better times, that's for sure. The doctor says he has to be careful with his angina, but he insists on working more than ever. Sometimes I have to get angry with him, but he seems to think that if he leaves me to look after the shop the business will fail. This morning, when I got up, I asked him to stay in bed and not to come down to work today. Well, would you believe it, three minutes later I found him in the dining room, putting on his shoes.'

'He's a man with fixed ideas,' I agreed.

'He's as stubborn as a mule,' replied Sempere's son. 'Thank goodness we now have a bit of help, otherwise . . .'

I adopted my best expression of surprise and innocence, which always came in handy and needed little practice.

'The girl,' Sempere's son explained. 'Isabella, your apprentice. That's why I was thinking about you. I hope you don't mind if she spends a few hours here each day. The truth is that, with the way things are, I'm very grateful for the help, but if you have any objections . . .'

I suppressed a smile when I noticed how he savoured the double 'l' in Isabella.

'Well, as long as it's only temporary. The truth is, Isabella is a good girl. Intelligent and hard-working,' I said. 'And trustworthy. We get on very well.'

'She says you're a despot.'

'Is that what she says?'

'In fact, she has a nickname for you: Mr Hyde.'

'How charming. Pay no attention to her. You know what women are like.'

'Yes, I do,' said Sempere's son in a tone that made it clear that he might know a lot of things, but certainly hadn't the faintest clue about women.

'Isabella might say that about me, but don't think she doesn't tell me things about you,' I countered.

I noticed a change in his expression, and let my words sink through the layers of his armour. He handed me a cup of coffee with an attentive smile and rescued the conversation using a trick that would have been unworthy even of a second-rate operetta.

'Goodness knows what she says about me.'

I left him to soak in uncertainty for a few moments.

'Would you like to know?' I asked casually, hiding a smile behind my cup.

Sempere's son shrugged his shoulders.

'She says you're a good and generous man; she says that people don't understand you because you're shy and they can't see beyond that, and, I quote, you have the presence of a film star and a fascinating personality.'

Sempere's son looked at me in astonishment.

'I'm not going to lie to you, Sempere, my friend. The truth is I'm glad you've brought up the subject because I've been wanting to talk to you about it and didn't know how.'

'Talk about what?'

I lowered my voice and fixed my eyes on his.

'Between you and me, Isabella wants to work here because she admires you and, I fear, is secretly in love with you.'

Sempere gulped.

'But, pure love, eh? Spiritual. Like the love of a Dickens heroine, if you see what I mean. No frivolities or childish nonsense. Isabella might be young, but she's a real woman. You must have noticed, I'm sure . . .'

'Now that you mention it . . .'

'And I'm not referring to her – if you'll pardon me – exquisitely tender frame, but to her kindness and the inner beauty that is just waiting for the right moment to emerge and make some fortunate man the happiest in the world.'

Sempere didn't know where to look.

'Besides, she has hidden talents. She speaks languages. She plays the piano like an angel. She has a good head for numbers, as good as any Isaac Newton. And to cap it all she's a wonderful cook. Look at me. I've put on a few kilos since she started working for me. Delicacies that even in La Tour d'Argent . . . Don't tell me you haven't noticed?'

'She didn't mention that she could cook . . .'

'I'm talking about love at first sight.'

'Well, really . . .'

'Do you know what the matter is? Deep down, although she gives the impression she's an untamed shrew, the girl is docile and shy to a pathological degree. I blame the nuns: they unhinge them with all those stories of hell and all those sewing lessons. Long live secular education.'

'Well, I would have sworn she took me for a little less than an idiot,' Sempere assured me.

'There you are. Irrefutable proof. Sempere, my friend, when a woman treats you like an idiot it means her hormones are racing!'

'Are you sure about that?'

'As sure as the Bank of Spain. Believe me; I know quite a lot about this subject.'

'That's what my father says. And what am I to do?'

Well, that depends. Do you like the girl?'

'Like her? I don't know. How do you know if—?'

'It's very simple. Do you look at her furtively and feel like biting her?'

'Biting her?'

'On her backside, for example.'

'Señor Martín!'

'Don't be bashful; we're among gentlemen. It's a known fact that we men are the missing link between the pirate and the pig. Do you like her or don't you?'

'Well, Isabella is an attractive girl.'

'What else?'

'Intelligent. Pleasant. Hard-working.'

'Go on.'

'And a good Christian, I think. Not that I'm much of a practising Catholic, but . . .'

'Don't I know it. Isabella almost lives in the church. Those nuns . . . I tell you!'

'But quite frankly, it had never occurred to me to bite her.'

'It hadn't occurred to you until I mentioned it.'

'I must say, I think talking about her like that – or about any other woman – shows a lack of respect. You should be ashamed . . .' protested Sempere's son.

'Mea culpa,' I intoned, raising my hands in a gesture of surrender. 'But never mind: we each show our devotion in our own way. I'm a frivolous, superficial creature, hence my canine focus, but you, with that *aurea gravitas* of yours, are a man of mysterious and profound feelings. The important thing is that the girl adores you and that the feeling is mutual.'

'Well . . .'

'Don't you "well" me. Let's face it, Sempere. You're a respectable and responsible man. Had it been me, what can I say, but you're not a fellow to play fast and loose with the noble, pure feelings of a ripe young girl. Am I mistaken?'

'I suppose not.'

'Well that's it, then.'

'What is?'

'Isn't it obvious?'

'No.'

'It's time to go courting.'

'Excuse me?'

'Courting or, in scientific terms, time for a kiss and a cuddle. Look here, Sempere, for some strange reason, centuries of supposed civilisation have brought us to a situation in which one cannot go sidling up to women on street corners, or asking them to marry us, just like that. First there has to be courtship.'

'Marry? Have you gone mad?'

'What I'm trying to say is that perhaps – and deep down this is your idea even if you're not aware of it – today or tomorrow or the next day, when you get over all this shaking and dribbling over her, you could take Isabella out, when she finishes work at the bookshop. Take her out for afternoon tea somewhere special, and you'll realise once and for all that you were made for one another. You could take her to Els Quatre Gats, where they're so stingy they dim the lights to save on electricity – that always helps in these situations. Ask for some curd cheese for the girl with a good spoonful of honey; that always whets the appetite. Then, casually, you let her have a swig or two of that muscatel that goes straight to the head. At that point, placing a hand on her knee, you stun her with that sweet talk you hide so well, you rascal.'

'But I don't know anything about her, or what interests her, or . . .'

'She's interested in the same things as you. She's interested in books, in literature, in the very smell of the treasures you have here – and in the penny novels with their promise of romance and adventure. She's interested in brushing aside loneliness and in not wasting time trying to understand that in this rotten world nothing is worth a single céntimo if there isn't someone to share it with. Now you know the essentials. The rest you can find out and enjoy as you go along.'

Sempere looked thoughtful, glancing first at his cup of coffee, which he hadn't touched, then at yours truly, who with great difficulty was trying to maintain the smile of a stock-market trader.

'I'm not sure whether to thank you or report you to the police,' he said at last.

Just then, Sempere senior's heavy footsteps were heard in the bookshop. A few seconds later he put his head round the door of the back room and stood there looking at us with a frown.

'What's going on? The shop is left unattended and you're sitting here chattering as if it were a bank holiday. What if a customer had come in? Or some scoundrel trying to make off with our goods?'

Sempere's son sighed, rolling his eyes.

'Don't worry, Señor Sempere. Books are the only things in this world that no one wants to steal,' I said, winking at him.

His face lit up with a knowing smile. Sempere's son took the opportunity to escape from my clutches and slink off back to the bookshop. His father sat next to me and sniffed at the cup of coffee his son had left untouched.

'What does the doctor say about the effects of caffeine on the heart?' I asked.

'That man can't even find his backside with an anatomy book. What could he know about the heart?'

'More than you, I'm sure,' I replied, snatching the cup from him.

'I'm as strong as an ox, Martín.'

'You're a mule, that's what you are. Please go back upstairs and get into bed.'

'It's only worth staying in bed if you're young and in good company.'

'If you want company, I'll find someone for you, but I don't think your heart is up to it right now.'

'Martín, at my age, eroticism is reduced to enjoying caramel

270

custard and looking at widows' necks. The one I'm worried about here is my heir. Any progress in that field?'

'We're fertilising the soil and sowing the seeds. We'll have to see if the weather is favourable and we get a harvest. In two or three days I'll be able to give you an estimate about the first shoots that is sixty to seventy per cent reliable.'

Sempere gave a satisfied smile.

'A masterstroke, sending Isabella to be our shop assistant,' he said. 'But don't you think she's a bit young for my son?'

'He's the one who seems a bit green, if I may be frank. He's got to get his act together or Isabella will eat him alive. Thank goodness he's a decent sort, otherwise . . .'

'How can I repay you?'

'By going upstairs and getting into bed. If you need some spicy company, take a copy of *Moll Flanders*.'

'You're right. Good old Defoe never lets you down.'

'Not even if he tries. Go on, off to bed.'

Sempere stood up. He moved with difficulty and his breathing was laboured, with a hoarse rattle that made one's hair stand on end. I took his arm and noticed that his skin was cold.

'Don't be alarmed, Martín. It's my metabolism; it's a little slow.'

'Today it's as slow as *War and Peace*.'

'A little nap and I'll be as good as new.'

I decided to go up with him to the apartment where father and son lived, above the bookshop, and make sure he got under the blankets. It took us a quarter of an hour to negotiate the stairs. On the way we met one of the neighbours, an affable secondary-school teacher called Don Anacleto, who taught language and literature at the Jesuits' school in Calle Caspe.

'How's life looking today, Sempere, my friend?'

'Rather steep, Don Anacleto.'

With the teacher's help I managed to reach the first floor with Sempere practically hanging from my neck.

'If you will forgive me, I must retire to rest after a long day spent fighting that pack of primates I have for pupils,' the teacher announced. 'I'm telling you, this country is going to disintegrate within one generation. They'll tear each other to pieces like rats.'

Sempere made a gesture to indicate that I shouldn't pay too much attention to Don Anacleto.

'He's a good man,' he whispered, 'but he drowns in a glass of water.'

When I stepped into the apartment I was suddenly reminded of that distant morning when I had arrived there covered in blood, holding a copy of *Great Expectations*. I recalled how Sempere had carried me up to his home and given me a cup of hot cocoa while we were waiting for the doctor, and how he'd whispered soothing words, cleaning the blood off my body with a warm towel and a gentleness that nobody had ever shown me before. At that time Sempere was a strong man and to me he seemed like a giant in every way; without him I don't think I would have survived those years of scant hope. Little or nothing remained of that strength as I held him in my arms to help him into bed and covered him with a couple of blankets. I sat down next to him and took his hand, not knowing what to do.

'Listen, if we're both going to start crying our eyes out you'd better leave,' he said.

'Take care, you hear me?'

'I'll wrap myself in cotton wool, don't worry.'

I nodded and started walking towards the door.

'Martín?'

At the doorway I turned round. Sempere was looking at me with the same anxiety he had shown that morning long ago, when I'd lost a few teeth and much of my innocence. I left before he could ask me what was wrong.

31

One of the first expedients of the professional writer that Isabella had learned from me was the art of procrastination. Every veteran in the trade knows that any activity, from sharpening a pencil to cataloguing daydreams, has precedence over sitting down at one's desk and squeezing one's brain. Isabella had absorbed this fundamental lesson by osmosis and when I got home, instead of finding her at her desk, I surprised her in the kitchen as she was giving the last touches to a dinner that smelled and looked as if its preparation had been a question of a few hours.

'Are we celebrating something?' I asked.

'With that face of yours, I don't think so.'

'What's the smell?'

'Caramelised duck with baked pears and chocolate sauce. I found the recipe in one of your cookery books.'

'I don't own any cookery books.'

Isabella got up and brought over a leather-bound volume, which she placed on the table: *The 101 Best Recipes of French Cuisine* by Michel Aragon.

'That's what you think. On the second row of the library bookshelves I've found all sort of things, including a handbook on marital hygiene by Doctor Pérez-Aguado with some very suggestive illustrations and gems such as "Woman, in accordance with the divine plan, has no knowledge of carnal desire and her spiritual and sentimental fulfilment is sublimated in the natural exercise of motherhood and household chores." You've got a veritable King Solomon's mine there.'

'Can you tell me what you were looking for on the second row of the shelves?'

'Inspiration. Which I found.'

'But of a culinary persuasion. We agreed that you were going to write every day, with or without inspiration.'

'I'm stuck. And it's your fault, because you've got me moonlighting and mixed up in your schemes with the immaculate son of Sempere.'

'Do you think it's right to make fun of the man who's madly in love with you?'

'What?'

'You heard me. Sempere's son confessed to me that you've robbed him of sleep. Literally. He can't sleep, he can't eat and he can't even pee, poor guy, for thinking so much about you all day.'

'You're delirious.'

'The one who is delirious is poor Sempere. You should have seen him. I came very close to shooting him, to put an end to his pain

273

and misery.'

'But he pays no attention to me whatsoever,' Isabella protested.

'Because he doesn't know how to open his heart and find the words with which to express his feelings. We men are like that. Brutish and primitive.'

'He had no trouble finding words to tell me off for not putting a collection of the *National Episodes* in the right order!'

'That's not the same. Administrative procedure is one thing, the language of passion another.'

'Nonsense.'

'There's no nonsense in love, my dear assistant. Changing the subject, are we having dinner or aren't we?'

Isabella had set a table to match her banquet, using a whole arsenal of dishes, cutlery and glasses I'd never seen before.

'I don't know why, if you have all these beautiful things, you don't use them. They were all in boxes, in the room next to the laundry,' said Isabella. 'Typical man!'

I picked up one of the knives and examined it in the light of the candles that Isabella had placed on the table. I realised these household utensils belonged to Diego Marlasca and this made me lose my appetite altogether.

'Is anything the matter?' asked Isabella.

I shook my head. My assistant served the food and stood there looking at me expectantly. I tasted a mouthful and smiled.

'Very good,' I said.

'It's a bit leathery, I think. The recipe said you had to cook it over a low flame for goodness knows how long, but on your stove the heat is either non-existent or scorching, with nothing in between.'

'It's good,' I repeated, eating without appetite.

Isabella kept giving me furtive looks. We continued to eat in silence, the tinkling of the cutlery and plates our only company.

'Were you serious about Sempere's son?'

I nodded, without glancing up from my plate.

'And what else did he say about me?'

'He said you have a classical beauty, you're intelligent, intensely feminine – that's how old-fashioned he is – and he feels there's a spiritual connection between you.'

Isabella threw me a murderous look.

'Swear you're not making this up,' she said.

I put my right hand on the cookery book and raised my left hand.

'I swear on *The 101 Best Recipes of French Cuisine*,' I declared.

'One usually swears with the other hand.'

I changed hands and repeated the performance with a solemn expression.

Isabella puffed.

'What am I going to do?'

'I don't know. What do people do when they're in love? Go for a stroll, go dancing . . .'

'But I'm not in love with this man.'

I went on sampling the caramelised duck, ignoring her insistent stare. After a while, Isabella banged her hand on the table.

'Will you please look at me? This is all your fault.'

I calmly put down my knife and fork, wiped my mouth with the napkin and looked at her.

'What am I going to do?' she asked again.

'That depends. Do you like Sempere or don't you?'

A cloud of doubt crossed her face.

'I don't know. To begin with, he's a bit old for me.'

'He's practically my age,' I pointed out. 'One or two years older, at the most. Maybe three.'

'Or four or five.'

I sighed.

'He's in the prime of his life. Hadn't we decided that you like them mature?'

'Don't tease me.'

'Isabella, who am I to tell you what to do?'

'That's a good one!'

'Let me finish. What I mean is that this is something between Sempere's son and you. If you want my advice, I'd say give him a chance. Nothing else. If one of these days he decides to take the first step and asks you out, let's say, to have tea, accept the invitation. Perhaps you'll get talking and you'll end up being friends, or maybe you won't. But I think Sempere is a good man, his interest in you is genuine and I dare say, if you think about it, deep down you feel something for him too.'

'You're mad.'

'But Sempere isn't. And I think that not to respect the affection and admiration he feels for you would be mean. And you're not mean.'

'This is emotional blackmail.'

'No, it's life.'

Isabella looked daggers at me. I smiled.

'Will you at least finish your dinner?' she ordered.

I bolted down the food on my plate, mopped it up with bread, and let out a sigh of satisfaction.

'What's for pudding?'

After dinner I left a pensive Isabella going over her doubts and anxieties in the reading room and went up to the study in the tower. I pulled out the photograph of Diego Marlasca lent to me by Salvador and left it by the base of the table lamp. Then I looked through the small citadel of writing pads, notes and sheets of paper I had been accumulating for the boss. Still feeling the chill of Diego Marlasca's cutlery in my hands, I did not find it hard to imagine him sitting there, gazing at the same view over the rooftops of the Ribera quarter. I took one of my pages at random and began to read. I recognised the words and sentences because I'd composed them, but the troubled spirit that fed them felt more remote than ever. I let the sheet of paper fall to the floor and looked up only to meet my own reflection in the windowpane, a stranger in the blue darkness burying the city. I knew I was not going to be able to work that night, that I would be incapable of putting together a single paragraph for the boss. I turned off the lamp and stayed there in the dark, listening to the wind scratching at the windows and imagining Diego Marlasca in flames, throwing himself into the water of the reservoir, while the last bubbles of air left his lips and the freezing liquid filled his lungs.

I awoke at dawn, my body aching from being encased in the armchair. As I got up I heard the grinding of two or three cogs in my anatomy. I dragged myself to the window and opened it wide. The flat rooftops in the old town shone with frost and a purple sky wreathed itself around Barcelona. At the sound of the bells of Santa María del Mar, a cloud of black wings took to the air from a dovecote. The smell of the docks and the coal ash issuing from neighbouring chimneys was borne on a biting cold wind.

I went down to the kitchen to make some coffee. I glanced at the larder and was astonished. Since Isabella's arrival in the house, it looked more like the Quílez grocer's in Rambla de Cataluña. Among the parade of exotic delicacies imported by Isabella's father, I found a tin of English chocolate biscuits and decided to have some. Half an hour later, once my veins were pumping with sugar and caffeine, my brain started to work and I had the brilliant idea of beginning the day by complicating my existence even further, if that was possible. As soon as the shops opened, I'd pay a visit to the one selling items for conjurers and magicians in Calle Princesa.

'What are you doing up so early?'

Isabella, the voice of my conscience, was observing me from the doorway.

'Eating biscuits.'

Isabella sat at the table and poured herself a cup of coffee. She looked as if she hadn't slept all night.

'My father says this was the Queen Mother's favourite brand.'

'No wonder she looked so strapping.'

Isabella took one of the biscuits and bit into it distractedly.

'Have you thought about what you're going to do? About Sempere, I mean . . .'

She threw me a venomous look.

'And what are you going to do today? Nothing good, I'm sure.'

'A couple of errands.'

'Right.'

'Right, right? Or "Right, I don't believe you"?'

Isabella set the cup on the table, her face as severe as that of a judge.

'Why do you never talk about whatever it is you're involved in with that man, the boss?'

'Among other things, for your own good.'

'For my own good. Of course. How stupid could I be? By the way, I forgot to mention that your friend, the inspector, came by yesterday.'

'Grandes? Was he on his own?'

'No. He came with two thugs as large as wardrobes with faces like pointers.'

The thought of Marcos and Castelo at my door tied my stomach in knots.

'And what did Grandes want?'

'He didn't say.'

'What *did* he say, then?'

'He asked me who I was.'

'And what did you reply?'

'I said I was your lover.'

'Outstanding.'

'Well, one of the large ones seemed to find it very amusing.'

Isabella took another biscuit and devoured it in two bites. She noticed me looking at her and immediately stopped chewing.

'What did I say?' she asked, projecting a shower of biscuit crumbs.

32

A sliver of light fell through the blanket of clouds, illuminating the red paintwork of the shopfront in Calle Princesa. The establishment selling conjuring tricks stood behind a carved wooden canopy. Its glass doors revealed only the bare outlines of the gloomy interior. Black velvet curtains were draped across cases displaying masks and Victorian-style apparatus: marked packs of cards, weighted daggers, books on magic, and bottles of polished glass containing a rainbow of liquids labelled in Latin and probably bottled in Albacete. The bell tinkled as I came through the door. An empty counter stood at the far end of the shop. I waited a few seconds, examining the collection of curiosities. I was searching for my face in a mirror that reflected everything in the shop except me when I glimpsed, out of the corner of my eye, a small figure peeping round the curtain of the back room.

'An interesting trick, don't you think?' said the little man with grey hair and penetrating eyes.

I nodded.

'How does it work?'

'I don't yet know. It arrived a few days ago from a manufacturer of trick mirrors in Istanbul. The creator calls it refractory inversion.'

'It reminds one that nothing is as it seems,' I said.

'Except for magic. How can I help you, sir?'

'Am I speaking to Señor Damián Roures?'

The little man nodded slowly, without blinking. I noticed that his lips were set in a bright smile which, like the mirror, was not what it seemed. Beneath it, his expression was cold and cautious.

'Your shop was recommended to me.'

'May I ask by whom?'

'Ricardo Salvador.'

Any pretence of a smile disappeared from his face.

'I didn't know he was still alive. I haven't seen him for twenty-five years.'

'What about Irene Sabino?'

Roures sighed, muttering under his breath. He came round the counter and went over to the door. After hanging up the CLOSED sign he turned the key.

'Who are you?'

'My name is Martín. I'm trying to clarify the circumstances surrounding the death of Señor Diego Marlasca, whom I understand you knew.'

'As far as I know, they were clarified many years ago. Señor Marlasca committed suicide.'

'That was not my understanding.'

'I don't know what that policeman has told you. Resentment affects one's memory, Señor . . . Martín. At the time, Salvador tried to peddle a conspiracy for which he had no proof. Everyone knew he was warming the widow Marlasca's bed and trying to set himself up as the hero of the hour. As expected, his superiors made him toe the line and when he didn't, they threw him out of the police force.'

'He thinks there was an attempt to hide the truth.'

Roures scoffed.

'The truth . . . don't make me laugh. What they tried to hide was a scandal. Valera and Marlasca's law firm had its fingers stuck in almost every pie that was being baked in this town. Nobody wanted a story like that to be uncovered. Marlasca had abandoned his position, his work and his marriage to lock himself up in that rambling old house doing God knows what. Anyone with half a

279

brain could see that it wouldn't end well.'

'That didn't stop you and your partner Jaco profiting from his madness by promising him he'd be able to make contact with the hereafter during your seances . . .'

'I never promised him a thing. Those sessions were a simple amusement. Everyone knew. Don't try to saddle me with the man's death – because all I was doing was earning an honest living.'

'And your partner, Jaco?'

'I answer only for myself. What Jaco might have done is not my responsibility.'

'Then he did do something.'

'What do you want me to say? That he went off with the money Salvador insisted Marlasca had in a secret account? That he killed Marlasca and fooled us all?'

'And that's not what happened?'

Roures stared at me.

'I don't know. I haven't seen him since the day Marlasca died. I told Salvador and the rest of the police everything I knew. I never lied. If Jaco did do something, I never knew about it or got anything out of it.'

'What can you tell me about Irene Sabino?'

'Irene loved Marlasca. She would never have plotted anything that might hurt him.'

'Do you know what happened to her? Is she still alive?'

'I think so; I was told she was working in a laundry in the Raval quarter. Irene was a good woman. Too good. That's why she's ended up the way she has. She believed in those things. She believed in them with all her heart.'

'And Marlasca? What was he looking for in that world?'

'Marlasca was involved in something, but don't ask me what. Something that neither Jaco nor I had sold him. All I know is that I once heard Irene say that apparently Marlasca had found someone, someone I didn't know – and, believe me, I knew everyone in the profession – who had promised him that if he did something, I don't know what, he would recover his son Ismael from the dead.'

'Did Irene say who that someone was?'

'She'd never seen him. Marlasca didn't let her. But she knew that he was afraid.'

'Afraid of what?'

Roures clicked his tongue.

'Marlasca thought that he was cursed.'

'Can you explain?'

'I've already told you. He was ill. He was convinced that something had got inside him.'

'Something?'

'A spirit. A parasite. I don't know. Look, in this business you get to know a lot of people who are not exactly in their right mind. A personal tragedy hits them: they lose a lover or a fortune and they fall down the hole. The brain is the most fragile organ in the body. Señor Marlasca was not of sound mind; anyone could see that after talking to him for five minutes. That's why he came to me.'

'And you told him what he wanted to hear.'

'No. I told him the truth.'

'Your truth?'

'The only truth I know. I thought he was seriously unbalanced and I didn't want to take advantage of him. That sort of thing never ends well. In this business there is a line you don't cross, if you know what's good for you. We offer our services to people who come to us looking for a bit of fun, or some excitement and comfort from the world beyond, and we charge accordingly. But anyone who seems to be on the verge of losing their mind, we send home. It is a show like any other. What you want are spectators, not visionaries.'

'Exemplary ethics. So, what did you say to Marlasca?'

'I told him it was all a load of mumbo-jumbo. I told him I was a trickster who made a living organising seances for poor devils who had lost their loved ones and needed to believe that lovers, parents and friends were waiting for them in the next world. I told him there was nothing on the other side, just a giant void, and this world was all we had. I told him to forget about the spirits and return to his family.'

'And he believed you?'

'Obviously not. He stopped coming to the sessions and looked elsewhere for help.'

'Where?'

'Irene had grown up in the shacks of Bogatell beach and although she'd made a name for herself dancing and acting in the clubs on the Paralelo, she still belonged to that place. She told me she'd taken Marlasca to see a woman they called the Witch of Somorrostro, to ask for protection from the person to whom Marlasca was indebted.'

'Did Irene mention the name of that person?'

'If she did I can't remember. As I said, they'd stopped coming to the seances.'

'Andreas Corelli?'

'I've never heard that name.'

'Where can I find Irene Sabino?'

'I've already told you all I know,' Roures replied, exasperated.

'One last question and I'll go.'

'Let's see if that's true.'

'Do you remember ever hearing Marlasca mention something called *Lux Aeterna*?'

Roures frowned, shaking his head.

'Thanks for you help.'

'You're welcome. And if at all possible don't come back.'

I nodded and walked off towards the exit, Roures's eyes following me distrustfully.

'Wait,' he called suddenly.

I turned round. The little man observed me, hesitating.

'I seem to remember that *Lux Aeterna* was the name of some sort of religious pamphlet we sometimes used in the sessions in Calle Elisabets. It was part of a collection of similar books, probably loaned to us by the Afterlife Society, which had a library specialising in the occult. I don't know if that's what you're referring to.'

'Do you remember what the pamphlet was about?'

'The person who was most familiar with it was my partner, Jaco – he managed the seances. But I seem to recall that *Lux Aeterna* was a poem about death and the seven names of the Son of Morning, Bringer of Light.'

'Bringer of Light?'

Roures smiled.

'Lucifer.'

33

When I left the shop I returned home, wondering what to do next. I was approaching the entrance to Calle Moncada when I saw him. Inspector Grandes was leaning against a wall and enjoying a cigarette. He smiled at me and waved and I crossed the street towards him.

'I didn't know you were interested in magic, Martín.'

'Nor did I know that you were following me, inspector.'

'I'm not following you. It's just that you're a difficult man to find and I decided that if the mountain wouldn't come to me, I'd go to the mountain. Do you have five minutes to spare, for a drink? It's on police headquarters.'

'In that case . . . No chaperones today?'

'Marcos and Castelo stayed behind doing paperwork, but if I'd told them I was coming to see you, I'm sure they'd have volunteered.'

We walked through the canyon of old palaces until we reached the Xampañet Tavern, where we found a table at the far end. A waiter, armed with a mop that stank of bleach, stared at us and Grandes asked for a couple of beers and a *tapa* of Manchego cheese. When the beers and the snack arrived, the inspector offered me the plate. I declined.

'Do you mind? I'm always starving at this time of day.'

'Bon appétit.'

Grandes wolfed down the cubes of cheese and licked his lips.

'Didn't anyone tell you that I came by your house yesterday?'

'I didn't get the message until later.'

'I understand. Hey, she's gorgeous, the girl. What's her name?'

'Isabella.'

'You rascal, some people have all the luck. I envy you. How old is the little sweetheart?'

I threw him a toxic look. The inspector smiled, obviously pleased.

'A little bird told me you've been playing at detectives lately.

Aren't you going to leave anything to the professionals?'

'What's your little bird's name?'

'He's more of a big bird. One of my superiors is a close friend of Valera, the lawyer.'

'Are you also on the payroll?'

'Not yet, my friend. You know me. I'm of the old school. Honour and all that shit.'

'A shame.'

'And tell me, how is poor Ricardo Salvador? Do you know? I haven't heard that name for over twenty years. Everyone assumed he was dead.'

'A premature diagnosis.'

'And how is he?'

'Alone, betrayed and forgotten.'

The inspector nodded slowly. 'Makes one think of the future in this job, doesn't it?'

'I bet that in your case things will be different, and your promotion to the top is just a question of a couple of years. I can just imagine you as chief commissioner before the age of forty-five, kissing the hands of bishops and generals during the Corpus parade.'

Grandes ignored my sarcasm.

'Speaking of hand-kissing, have you heard about your friend Vidal?'

Grandes never started a conversation without having an ace hidden up his sleeve. He watched me with a smile, relishing my anxiety.

'What about him?' I mumbled.

'They say his wife tried to kill herself the other night.'

'Cristina?'

'Of course, you know her . . .'

I didn't realise that I'd stood up and my hands were shaking.

'Calm down. Señora de Vidal is all right. Just a fright. It seems that she overdid it with the laudanum. Will you sit down, Martín? Please.'

I sat down. My stomach was a bag of nails.

'When was this?'

'Two or three days ago.'

My mind filled with the image of Cristina in the window of Villa

Helius a few days earlier, waving at me while I avoided her eyes and turned my back on her.

'Martín?' the inspector asked, waving a hand in front of my face as if he feared I'd lost my mind.

'What?'

The inspector seemed to be genuinely worried.

'Have you anything to tell me? I know you won't believe me, but I'd like to help you.'

'Do you still think it was me who killed Barrido and his partner?'

Grandes shook his head.

'I've never believed it was you, but there are others who would like to.'

'Then why are you still investigating me?'

'Calm down. I'm not investigating you, Martín. I never have. The day I do investigate you, you'll know. For the time being I'm only observing you. Because I like you and I'm concerned that you're going to get yourself into a mess. Why won't you trust me and tell me what's going on?'

Our eyes met and for an instant I was tempted to tell him everything. I would have done so, had I known where to begin.

'Nothing is going on, inspector.'

Grandes nodded and looked at me with pity, or perhaps it was only disappointment. He finished his beer and left a few coins on the table. He gave me a pat on the back and got up.

'Look after yourself, Martín. And watch how you go. Not everyone holds you in the same esteem as I do.'

'I'll keep that in mind.'

It was almost midday when I got home, unable to stop thinking about what the inspector had told me. When I reached the tower house I climbed the steps slowly, as if my very soul was weighing me down. I opened the door of the apartment, fearing I'd find Isabella in the mood for conversation. The house was silent. I walked up the corridor until I reached the gallery and there I found her, asleep on the sofa, an open book on her chest – one of my old novels. I couldn't help but smile. The temperature inside the house had dropped considerably during those autumn days and I was afraid Isabella might catch a chill. Sometimes I'd see her wandering about the apartment wrapped in a woollen shawl she wore over her shoulders. I went to her room to find the shawl, so that I could quietly cover her with it. Her door was ajar. Although I was in my own home, I'd rarely entered that room since Isabella had installed herself there and now felt uneasy doing so. I saw the shawl folded over a chair and went to fetch it. The room had Isabella's sweet, lemony scent. The bed was still unmade and I leaned over to smooth out the sheets and blankets. I knew that when I applied myself to these domestic chores my moral standing rose in the eyes of my assistant.

It was then that I noticed there was something wedged between the mattress and the base of the bed. The corner of a piece of paper stuck out from under the folded sheet. When I tugged at it I realised it was a bundle of papers. I pulled it out completely and found that I was holding what looked like about twenty blue envelopes tied together with a ribbon. My whole body felt cold. I untied the knot in the ribbon and took one of the envelopes. It had my name and address on it. Where the return address should have been, it simply said: Cristina.

I sat on the bed with my back to the door and examined the envelopes, one by one. The first letter was a few weeks old, the last had been posted three days ago. All of the envelopes were open. I closed my eyes and felt the letters falling from my hands. I heard her breathing behind me, standing motionless in the doorway.

'Forgive me,' whispered Isabella.

She walked over slowly and knelt down to pick up the letters. When she'd gathered them together she handed them to me with a wounded look.

'I did it to protect you,' she said.

Her eyes filled with tears and she placed a hand on my shoulder.

'Leave,' I said.

I pushed her away and stood up. Isabella collapsed onto the floor, moaning as if something were burning inside her.

'Leave this house.'

I left the apartment without even bothering to close the door behind me. Once outside, I faced a world of buildings and faces that seemed strange and distant. I started to walk aimlessly, oblivious to the cold and the rain-filled wind that was starting to lash the town with the breath of a curse.

34

The tram stopped by the gates of Bellesguard, a mansion standing on the edge of the city, at the foot of the hill. I walked on towards the entrance to San Gervasio Cemetery, following the yellowish beam projected through the rain by the tram lights. The walls of the graveyard rose some fifty metres ahead, a marble fortress from which emerged a mass of statues the colour of the storm. I found a cubicle next to the entrance where a guard, wrapped in a coat, was warming his hands over a brazier. When he saw me appear in the rain he looked startled and stood up. He examined me for a few seconds before opening the cubicle door.

'I'm looking for the Marlasca family vault.'

'It'll be dark in less than half an hour. You'd better come back another day.'

'The sooner you tell me where it is, the sooner I'll leave.'

The guard checked a list and showed me the site by pointing a finger to a map of the graveyard hanging on the wall. I walked off without thanking him.

It wasn't difficult to find the vault among the citadel of tombs and mausoleums crowded together inside the walls of the cemetery. The structure stood on a marble base. Modernist in style, the mausoleum was shaped like an arch formed by two wide flights of steps that spread out like an amphitheatre. The steps led to a gallery held up by columns, inside which was an atrium flanked by tombstones. The gallery was crowned by a dome, and the dome, in turn, by a marble figure sullied by the passage of time. Its face was hidden by a veil, but as I approached I had the impression that this sentinel from beyond the grave was turning its head to watch me. I went up one of the staircases, and when I reached the entrance to the gallery, I stopped to look behind me. The distant city lights were just visible in the rain.

I stepped into the gallery. In the centre stood a statue of a woman in prayer, embracing a crucifix. The face had been disfigured and someone had painted the eyes and lips black, giving her a wolfish aspect. That was not the only sign of desecration in the vault. The tombstones seemed to be covered in what looked like markings or scratches made with a sharp object, and some had been defaced with obscene drawings and words that were almost illegible in the failing light. Diego Marlasca's tomb was at the far end. I went up to it and put my hand on the tombstone. Then I pulled out the photograph of Marlasca Salvador had given me and examined it.

At that moment I heard footsteps on the stairway to the vault. I put the photograph back into my coat pocket and turned, facing the entrance to the gallery. The footsteps stopped and all I could hear now was the rain beating against the marble. I went towards the entrance and looked out. The figure had its back to me and was gazing at the city in the distance. It was a woman dressed in white, her head covered by a shawl. Slowly she turned and looked at me. She was smiling. Despite the years, I recognised her instantly. Irene Sabino. I took a step towards her and only then did I realise there was someone else behind me. The blow to the back of my neck fired off a spasm of white light. I felt myself falling to my knees. A second later I collapsed on the flooded marble. A dark silhouette stood over me in the rain. Irene knelt down beside me; I felt her hands surrounding my head and feeling the place where I'd been hit. I saw her fingers emerging, covered in blood. She stroked my face. The last thing I saw before I lost consciousness was Irene Sabino pulling out a razor and opening it, silvery drops of rain sliding across the blade's edge as it drew towards me.

I opened my eyes to the blinding glare of an oil lamp. The guard's face was watching me impassively. I tried to blink as a flash of pain shot through my skull from the back of my neck.

'Are you alive?' the guard asked, without specifying whether the question was directed at me or was purely rhetorical.

'Yes', I groaned. 'Don't you dare stick me in a hole.'

The guard helped me to sit up. Every time I moved I felt a stab of pain in my head.

'What happened?'

'You tell me. I should have locked this place up over an hour ago, but as I hadn't seen you leave, I came to investigate and found you sleeping it off.'

'What about the woman?'

'What woman?'

'There were two.'

'Two women?'

I sighed, shaking my head.

'Can you help me get up?'

With the guard's assistance I managed to stand. It was then that I felt a burning sensation and noticed that my shirt was open. There were a number of superficial cuts running in lines across my chest.

'Hey, that doesn't look good . . .'

I closed my coat and felt the inside pocket. Marlasca's photograph had disappeared.

'Do you have a telephone in the booth?'

'Sure, it's in the room with the Turkish baths.'

'Can you at least help me reach Bellesguard, so that I can call from there?'

The guard swore and held me by the armpits.

'I did tell you to come back another day,' he said, resigned.

35

A few minutes before midnight I finally reached the tower house. As soon as I opened the door I knew that Isabella had left. The echo of my footsteps down the corridor sounded different. I didn't bother to turn on the light. I went further into the apartment and put my head round the door of what had been her room. Isabella had cleaned and tidied it. The sheets and blankets were neatly folded on a chair and the mattress was bare. Her smell still floated in the air. I went to the gallery and sat at the desk my assistant had used. She had sharpened the pencils and arranged them in a glass. The pile of blank sheets had been carefully stacked in a tray and the pen and nib set I had given her had been left on one side of the table. The house had never seemed so empty.

In the bathroom I removed my wet clothes and put a bandage

with surgical spirit on the nape of my neck. The pain had subsided to a mute throb and a general feeling that was not unlike a monumental hangover. In the mirror, the cuts on my chest looked like lines drawn with a pen. They were clean, superficial cuts, but they stung a great deal. I cleaned them with surgical spirit and hoped they wouldn't become infected.

I got into bed and covered myself up to the neck with two or three blankets. The only parts of my body that didn't hurt were those that the cold and the rain had numbed to the point that I couldn't feel them at all. I lay there slowly warming up, listening to that cold silence, a silence of absence and emptiness that smothered the house. Before leaving, Isabella had left the pile of Cristina's letters on the bedside table. I stretched out my hand and took one at random, dated two weeks earlier.

Dear David,

The days go by and I keep on writing letters to you which I suppose you prefer not to answer – if you even open them, that is. I've started to think that I write them just for myself, to kill the loneliness and to believe for a moment that you're close to me. Every day I wonder what has happened to you, and what you're doing.

Sometimes I think you've left Barcelona, and won't return, and I imagine you in some place surrounded by strangers, beginning a new life that I will never know. At other times I think you still hate me, that you destroy these letters and wish you had never known me. I don't blame you. It's curious how easy it is to tell a piece of paper what you don't dare say to someone's face.

Things are not simple for me. Pedro couldn't be kinder and more understanding, so much so that sometimes his patience and his desire to make me happy irritate me, which only makes me feel miserable. He has shown me that my heart is empty, that I don't deserve to be loved by anyone. He spends most of the day with me and doesn't want to leave me alone.

I smile every day and I share his bed. When he asks me whether I love him I say I do, and when I see the truth reflected in his eyes I feel like dying. He never reproaches me. He talks about you a great deal. He misses you. He misses you so much that sometimes I think you're the person he loves most in this world. I see him growing old, on his own, in the worst possible company – mine. I don't expect you to forgive me, but if there's one thing I wish for in this world, it is for you to forgive him. I'm not worth depriving him of your friendship and company.

Yesterday I finished one of your books. Pedro has them all and I've been reading them because it's the only way I can feel that I'm with you. It was a sad, strange story, about two broken dolls abandoned in a travelling circus that come alive for one night, knowing they are going to die at dawn. As I read it I felt you were writing about us.

A few weeks ago I dreamed that I saw you again: we passed in the street and you didn't remember me. You smiled and asked me what my name was. You didn't know anything about me. You didn't hate me. Every night when Pedro falls asleep next to me, I close my eyes and beg heaven or hell that I might dream the same dream again.

Tomorrow, or perhaps the next day, I'll write again to tell you that I love you, even if it means nothing to you.

CRISTINA

I let the letter fall to the floor, unable to read any more. Tomorrow would be another day, I told myself. It could hardly be worse than this one. Little did I imagine the delights in store. I must have slept for a couple of hours at the most when, all of a sudden, I awoke. It was still long before dawn. Somebody was banging on the door of my apartment. I spent a couple of seconds in a daze, looking for the light switch. Again, the knocking on the door. I must have forgotten to lock the main entrance to the street. I turned on the light, got out of bed and walked along to the entrance hall. I slid open the spyhole. Three faces in the shadows of the landing. Inspector Grandes and, behind him, Marcos and Castelo. All three with their eyes trained on the spyhole. I took two deep breaths before opening.

'Good evening, Martín. I'm sorry about the time.'

'And what time is this supposed to be?'

'Time to move your arse, you son-of-a-bitch,' muttered Marcos, which drew from Castelo a smile so cutting I could have shaved with it.

Grandes looked at them disapprovingly and sighed.

'A little after three in the morning,' he said. 'May I come in?'

I groaned but let him in. The inspector signalled to his men to wait on the landing. Marcos and Castelo agreed reluctantly, throwing me reptilian looks. I slammed the door in their faces.

'You should be more careful with those two,' said Grandes, wandering up the corridor as if he owned the place.

'Please, make yourself at home . . .' I said.

I returned to the bedroom and dressed any old how, putting on the first things I found – dirty clothes piled on a chair. When I came out, there was no sign of Grandes in the corridor.

I went over to the gallery and found him there, gazing through the windows at the low clouds that crept over the flat roofs.

'Where's the sweetheart?'

'In her own home.'

Grandes turned round, smiling.

'Wise man, you don't keep them full board,' he said, pointing at the armchair. 'Sit down.'

I slumped into the chair. Grandes remained standing, his eyes fixed on me.

'What?' I finally asked.

'You don't look so good, Martín. Did you get into a fight?'

'I fell.'

'I see. I understand that today you visited the magic shop owned by Señor Damián Roures in Calle Princesa.'

'You saw me coming out of the shop at lunchtime. What's all this about?'

Grandes was gazing at me coldly.

'Fetch a coat and a scarf, or whatever. It's cold outside. We're off to the police station.'

'What for?'

'Do as I say.'

A car from police headquarters was waiting for us in Paseo del Borne. Marcos and Castelo pushed me unceremoniously into the back, posting themselves on either side.

'Is the gentleman comfortable?' asked Castelo, digging his elbow into my ribs.

The inspector sat in the front, next to the driver. None of them opened their mouths during the five minutes it took to drive up Vía Layetana, deserted and buried in an ochre mist. When we reached the central police station, Grandes got out and went in without waiting. Marcos and Castelo took an arm each, as if they were trying to crush my bones, and dragged me through a maze of stairs, passages and cells until we reached a room with no windows that smelled of sweat and urine. In the centre stood a worm-eaten table and two dilapidated chairs. A naked bulb hung from the ceiling and there was a grating over a drain in the middle of the room, where the two inclines of the floor met. It was bitterly cold. Before I realised what was happening, the door was shut behind me with a bang. I heard footsteps moving away. I walked round that dungeon a dozen times until I collapsed on one of the shaky chairs. For the next hour, apart from my breathing, the creaking of the chair and the echo of water dripping, I didn't hear another sound.

An eternity later I heard footsteps approaching and shortly afterwards the door opened. Marcos stuck his head round and peered into the cell with a smile. He held the door open for Grandes, who came in without looking at me and sat on the chair on the other side of the table. Grandes nodded to Marcos and the latter closed the door, but not without first blowing me a silent kiss. The inspector took a good thirty seconds before deigning to look me in the eye.

'If you were trying to impress me, you've done so, inspector.'

He ignored my irony and fixed his eyes on me as if he'd never seen me before in his life.

'What do you know about Damián Roures?' he asked.

I shrugged my shoulders.

'Not much. He owns a magic shop. In fact, I knew nothing about him until a few days ago, when Ricardo Salvador mentioned him. Today, or yesterday – I've lost track of the time – I went to see him in search of information about the previous occupier of the house in which I live. Salvador told me that Roures and the owner—'

'Marlasca.'

'Yes, Diego Marlasca. As I was saying, Salvador told me that Roures had had dealings with him some years ago. I asked Roures a few questions and he replied as best he could. There's little else.'

Grandes inclined his head.

'Is that your story?'

'I don't know. What's yours? Let's compare and perhaps I'll finally understand what the hell I'm doing here in the middle of the night, freezing to death in a basement that smells of shit.'

'Don't raise your voice to me, Martín.'

'I'm sorry, inspector, but I think you could at least have the courtesy to tell me why I'm here.'

'I'll tell you why you're here. About three hours ago, one of the residents of the apartment block in which Señor Roures's shop is located was returning home late when he found that the door of the shop was open and the lights were on. He was surprised, so he went in, and when he did not see the owner or hear him reply to his calls, he went into the back room, where he found Roures, his hands and feet bound with wire to a chair, over a pool of blood.'

Grandes paused, his eyes boring into me. I imagined there was more to come. Grandes always liked to end on something dramatic.

'Dead?' I asked.

Grandes nodded.

'Quite dead. Someone had amused himself by pulling out the man's eyes and cutting out his tongue with a pair of scissors. The pathologist believes he died by choking on his own blood about half an hour later.'

I felt I needed air. Grandes was walking around. He stopped behind my back and I heard him light a cigarette.

'How did you get that bruise? It looks recent.'

'I slipped in the rain and hit the back of my neck.'

'Don't treat me like an idiot, Martín. It's not advisable. Would you rather I left you for a while with Marcos and Castelo, to see if they can teach you some manners?'

'All right. Someone hit me.'

'Who?'

'I don't know.'

'This conversation is beginning to bore me, Martín.'

'Well, just imagine what it's doing to me.'

Grandes sat down in front of me again and offered a conciliatory smile.

'Surely you don't believe I had anything to do with the death of that man?'

'No, Martín. I don't. What I do believe is that you're not telling me the truth, and that somehow the death of that poor wretch is related to your visit. Like the death of Barrido and Escobillas.'

'What makes you think that?'

'Call it a hunch.'

'I've already told you I don't know anything.'

'And I've already warned you not to take me for an idiot, Martín. Marcos and Castelo are out there waiting for an opportunity to have a private conversation with you. Is that what you want?'

'No.'

'Then help me get you out of this so that I can send you home before your sheets get cold.'

'What do you want to hear?'

'The truth, for example.'

I pushed the chair back and stood up, exasperated. I was chilled to the bone and my head felt as if it was going to burst. I began to walk round the table in circles, spitting out the words as if they were stones.

'The truth? I'll tell you the truth. The truth is I don't know what the truth is. I don't know what to tell you. I don't know why I went to see Roures, or Salvador. I don't know what I'm looking for or what is happening to me. That's the truth.'

Grandes watched me stoically.

'Stop walking in circles and sit down. You're making me giddy.'

'I don't want to.'

'Martín, you're not telling me anything. All I'm asking you to do is to help me so that I can help you.'

'You wouldn't be able to help me even if you wanted to.'

'Then who can?'

I dropped back into the chair.

'I don't know . . .' I murmured.

I thought I saw a hint of pity, or perhaps it was just tiredness, in the inspector's eyes.

'Look, Martín. Let's begin again. Let's do it your way. Tell me a story, and start at the beginning.'

I stared at him in silence.

'Martín. Don't think that because I like you I'm not going to do my work.'

'Do whatever you have to do. Call Hansel and Gretel, if you like.'

At that moment I noticed a touch of anxiety on his face. Footsteps were advancing along the corridor and something told me the inspector wasn't expecting them. I heard voices and nervously Grandes went up to the door. He tapped three times with his knuckles and Marcos, who was on guard, opened up. A man dressed in a camel-hair coat and a matching suit came into the room, looked around him in disgust, and then gave me a sweet smile while he calmly removed his gloves. I watched him in astonishment. It was Valera, the lawyer.

'Are you all right, Señor Martín?' he asked.

I nodded. The lawyer led the inspector over to a corner. I heard them whispering. Grandes gesticulated with suppressed fury. Valera watched him coldly and shook his head. The conversation went on for almost a minute. Finally Grandes huffed and let his hands fall to his sides.

'Pick up your scarf, Señor Martín. We're leaving,' Valera ordered. 'The inspector has finished his questioning.'

Behind him, Grandes bit his lip, looking daggers at Marcos, who shrugged his shoulders. Without losing his expert smile, Valera took me by the arm and led me out of the dungeon.

'I trust that the treatment you received from these police officers has been correct, Señor Martín.'

'Yes,' I managed to stammer.

'Just a moment,' Grandes called out behind us.

Valera stopped and, motioning for me to be quiet, he turned round.

'If you have any more questions for Señor Martín you can direct them to our office and we will be glad to help you. In the meantime, and unless you have a more important reason for keeping Señor Martín on the premises, we shall retire. We wish you a good evening and thank you for your kindness, which I will certainly mention to your superiors, especially to Chief-Inspector Salgado, who, as you know, is a dear friend.'

Sergeant Marcos started to move towards us, but Inspector Grandes stopped him. I exchanged a last glance with him before Valera took me by the arm again and pulled me away.

'Don't wait about,' he whispered.

We walked down the dimly lit passage until we came to a staircase that took us up to another long corridor. At the end of the second corridor a small door opened onto the ground-floor entrance hall and the main exit, where a chauffeur-driven Mercedes-Benz was waiting for us with its engine running. As soon as he saw Valera, the chauffeur jumped out and opened the door for us. I sat down on the back seat. The car was equipped with heating and the leather seats were warm. Valera sat next to me and, with a tap on the glass that separated the back from the driver's compartment, instructed the chauffeur to set off. Once the car was en route and had settled in the central lane of Vía Layetana, Valera smiled at me as if nothing had happened. He pointed at the mist that parted like undergrowth as we drove through it.

'A disagreeable night, isn't it?' he said casually.

'Where are we going?'

'To your home, of course. Unless you'd rather go to a hotel or—'

'No. That's fine.'

The car was rolling along down Vía Layetana. Valera gazed at the deserted streets with little interest.

'What are you doing?' I finally asked.

'What do you think I'm doing? Representing you and looking after your interests.'

'Tell the driver to stop the car,' I said.

The chauffeur looked at Valera's eyes in the mirror. Valera shook his head and gestured to him to continue.

'Don't talk nonsense, Señor Martín. It's late, it's cold and I'm taking you home.'

'I'd rather walk.'

'Be reasonable.'

'Who sent you?'

Valera sighed and rubbed his eyes.

'You have good friends, Señor Martín. It is important in life to have good friends and especially to know how to keep them,' he said. 'As important as knowing when one is stubbornly following the wrong path.'

'Might that path be the one that goes past Casa Marlasca, number 13, Carretera de Vallvidrera?'

Valera smiled patiently, as if he were scolding an unruly child.

'Señor Martín, believe me when I say that the further away you stay from that house and that business, the better for you. Do accept at least this piece of advice.'

When he reached Paseo de Colón, the chauffeur turned and drove up to Calle Comercio and from there to the entrance of Paseo del Borne. The carts with meat and fish, ice and spices were beginning to accumulate opposite the large marketplace. As we drove past, four boys were unloading the carcass of a calf, leaving a trail of blood that could be smelled in the air.

'Your area is charming, full of picturesque scenes, Señor Martín.'

The driver stopped on the corner of Calle Flassaders and got out of the car to open the door for us. The lawyer got out with me.

'I'll come with you to the door,' he said.

'People will think we're lovers.'

We entered the alleyway, a chasm of shadows, and headed towards my house. On reaching the front door, the lawyer offered me his hand with professional courtesy.

'Thanks for getting me out of that place.'

'Don't thank me,' replied Valera, pulling an envelope out of the inside pocket of his coat.

I recognised the wax seal with the angel even in the tenuous light that dripped from the street lamp above our heads. Valera handed me the envelope and, with a final nod, walked back to the waiting car. I opened my front door and went up the steps to the apartment. When I got in I went straight to the study and placed the envelope on the desk. I opened it and pulled out the folded sheet of paper with the boss's writing.

> Martín, dear friend,
>
> I trust this note finds you in good health and good spirits. I happen to be passing through the city and would love the pleasure of your company this Friday at seven o'clock in the evening in the billiard room of the Equestrian Club, where we can talk about the progress of our project.
>
> Until then, please accept my warm regards,
>
> ANDREAS CORELLI

I folded the sheet of paper and put it carefully in the envelope. Then I lit a match and, holding the envelope by one corner, moved it closer to the flame. I watched it burn until the wax turned to scarlet tears that fell on the desk and my fingers were covered in ashes.

'Go to hell,' I whispered. The night, darker than ever, leaned in against the windowpanes.

36

Sitting in the armchair in the study, I waited for a dawn that did not come, until anger got the better of me and I went out into the street ready to defy Valera's warning. A cold, biting wind was blowing, the sort that precedes dawn in wintertime. As I crossed Paseo del Borne I thought I heard footsteps behind me. I turned round for a moment but couldn't see anyone except for the market boys unloading carts so I continued walking. When I reached Plaza Palacio I saw the lights of the first tram of the day waiting in the mist that crept up from the port. Snakes of blue light crackled along the overhead power cable. I stepped into the tram and sat at the front. The same conductor who'd been present on my last trip took the money for my ticket. A dozen or so passengers dribbled in, each one alone. After a few minutes the tram set off and we began our journey. Across the sky stretched a web of red capillaries between black clouds. There was no need to be a poet or a wise man to know that it was going to be a bad day.

By the time we reached Sarriá, dawn had broken with a grey, dull light that robbed the morning of any colour. I climbed the deserted, narrow streets of the district towards the lower slopes of the hillside. Occasionally I thought I again heard footsteps behind me, but each time I stopped and looked back there was nobody there. At last I reached the entrance to the passage leading to Casa Marlasca and made my way through a blanket of dead leaves that crunched underfoot. Slowly, I crossed the courtyard and walked up the stairs to the front door, peering through the large windows of the facade. I rapped with the knocker three times and moved back a few steps. I waited for a moment, but no answer came. I knocked again and heard the echoes fading away inside the house.

'Good morning!' I called out.

The grove surrounding the property seemed to absorb the sound of my voice. I went around the house, past the swimming pool area and then on to the conservatory. Its windows were darkened by closed wooden shutters which made it impossible to see inside, but one of the windows next to the glass door was slightly open. The bolt securing the door was just visible through the gap. I put my arm through the window and slid open the bolt. The door gave way with a metallic creak. I looked behind me once more, to make sure there was nobody there, and went in.

As my eyes adjusted to the gloom, I began to distinguish a few outlines. I went over to the windows and half-opened the shutters. A fan of light cut through the darkness, revealing the full profile of the room.

'Is anyone here?' I called out.

The sound of my voice sank into the bowels of the house like a coin falling into a bottomless well. I walked to the end of the conservatory, where an arch of carved wood led to a dim corridor lined with paintings that were barely visible on the velvet-covered walls. At the end of the corridor there was a large, round sitting room with mosaic floors and a mural of enamelled glass showing the figure of a white angel with one arm extended and fingers pointing like flames. A wide staircase rose in a spiral around the room. I stopped at the foot of the stairs and called out again.

'Good morning! Señora Marlasca?'

The total silence of the house drowned the dull echo of my words. I went up the stairs to the first floor and paused on the landing, looking down on the sitting room and the mural. From there I could see the trail my feet had left on the film of dust covering the ground. Apart from my footsteps, the only other sign of movement I could discern was parallel lines drawn in the dust, about half a metre apart, and a trail of footprints between them. Large footprints. I stared at those marks in some confusion until I understood what I was seeing: the movement of a wheelchair and the marks of the person pushing it.

I thought I heard a noise behind my back and turned. A half-open door at one end of the corridor was gently swinging and I could feel a breath of cold air. I moved slowly towards the door, glancing at the rooms on either side, bedrooms with dust sheets covering the furniture. The closed windows and heavy darkness suggested these rooms had not been used in a long time, except for one, which was larger than the others, the master bedroom. It smelled of that odd mixture of perfume and illness associated with elderly people. I imagined this must be the room of Marlasca's widow, but there was no sign of her.

The bed was neatly made. Opposite it stood a chest of drawers with a number of framed photographs on it. In all of them, without exception, was a boy with fair hair and a cheerful expression. Ismael Marlasca. In some pictures he posed next to his mother or other children. There was no sign of Diego Marlasca in any of them.

The sound of a door banging in the corridor startled me again and I exited the bedroom, leaving the pictures as I'd found them. The door to the room at the end was still swinging back and forth. I walked up to it and stopped for a second before entering, taking a deep breath.

Inside, everything was white. The walls and the ceiling were painted an immaculate white. White silk curtains. A small bed covered with white sheets. A white carpet. White shelves and cupboards. After the darkness that had prevailed throughout the house, the contrast dazzled my vision for a few seconds. The room seemed to be straight out of a fairy tale. There were toys and storybooks on the shelves. A life-size china harlequin sat at a dressing table, looking at himself in the mirror. A mobile of white birds hung from the ceiling. At first sight it looked like the room of a spoilt child, Ismael Marlasca, but it had the oppressive air of a funeral chamber.

I sat on the bed and sighed. Only then did I notice that something in the room seemed out of place. Beginning with the smell. A sickly, sweet stench floated in the air. I stood up and looked around me. On a chest of drawers I saw a china plate with a black candle, its wax melted into a cluster of tears. I turned round. The smell seemed to be coming from the head of the bed. I opened the drawer of the bedside table and found a crucifix broken in three. The stench grew stronger. I walked around the room a few times but was unable to find the source. Then I saw it. There was something under the bed. A tin box, the sort that children use to hold their childhood treasures. I pulled out the box and placed it on the bed. The stench was now more powerful, and penetrating. I ignored my nausea and opened the box. Inside was a white dove, its heart pierced by a needle. I took a step back, covering my mouth and nose, and retreated to the corridor. The harlequin with its jackal smile observed me in the mirror. I ran back to the staircase and hurtled down the stairs, looking for the passage that led to the reading room and the door to the garden. At one point I thought I was lost and the house, like a creature capable of moving its passageways and rooms at will, was trying to prevent me from escaping. At last I sighted the conservatory and ran to the door. Only then, while I was struggling to release the bolt, did I hear malicious laughter behind me and know I was not alone in the house. I turned for an instant and saw a dark figure watching me from the end of the corridor, carrying a shining object in its hand. A knife.

The bolt yielded and I pushed open the door, falling headlong onto the marble tiles surrounding the swimming pool. My face was barely centimetres away from the surface and I could smell the stench of stagnant water. For a moment I peered into the shadows at the bottom of the pool. There was a short break in the clouds and a shaft of sunlight pierced the water, touching the floor with its loose fragments of mosaic. The vision was over in a second: the wheelchair, tilted forward, stranded on the pool floor. The sunlight continued its journey to the deep end and it was there that I saw her: lying against the wall was what looked like a body shrouded in a threadbare white dress. At first I thought it was a doll, with scarlet lips shrivelled by the water and eyes as bright as sapphires. Her red hair undulated gently in the rancid water and her skin was blue. It was Marlasca's widow. A second later the gap in the clouds closed again and the water was once more a clouded mirror in which I could glimpse only my face and a form that appeared in the doorway of the conservatory behind me, holding a knife. I shot up and ran straight into the garden, crossing the grove, scratching my face and hands on the bushes, until I reached the iron door and was out in the alleyway. I didn't stop running until I reached the main road. There I turned, out of breath, and saw that Casa Marlasca was once again hidden down its long alleyway, invisible to the world.

37

I returned home on the same tram, crossing a city that was growing darker by the minute. An icy wind lifted the fallen leaves from the streets. When I got out in Plaza Palacio I heard two sailors, who were walking up from the docks, talking about a storm that was approaching from the sea and would hit the town before nightfall. I looked up and saw a blanket of reddish clouds beginning to cover the sky, spreading over the sea like blood. In the streets surrounding the Borne Market people were rushing to secure doors and windows, shopkeepers were closing early and children came outside to play in the wind, lifting their arms and laughing at the distant roar of thunder. Street lamps flickered and a flash of lightning bathed the buildings in a sudden white light. I hurried to the door of the tower house and rushed up the steps. The rumble of the storm could be felt through the walls, getting closer.

It was so cold indoors that I could see my breath as I stepped into the corridor. I went straight to the room with an old charcoal stove that I had used only four or five times since I'd lived there, and lit it with a wad of old newspapers. I also lit the wood fire in the gallery and sat on the floor facing the flames. My hands were shaking, I didn't know whether from cold or fear. I waited until I had warmed up, staring out at the web of white light traced by lightning across the sky.

The rain didn't arrive until nightfall, and when it did, it plummeted in curtains of furious drops that quickly blinded the night and flooded rooftops and alleyways, hitting walls and windowpanes with tremendous force. Little by little, with the help of the stove and the fireplace, the house started to warm up, but I was still cold. I got up and went to the bedroom in search of blankets to wrap around myself. I opened the wardrobe and started to rummage in the two large drawers at the bottom. The case was still there, hidden at the back. I picked it up and placed it on the bed.

I opened the case and stared at my father's old revolver, the only thing I had left of him. I held it, stroking the trigger with my thumb. I opened the drum and inserted six bullets from the ammunition box in the false bottom of the case. I left the box on the bedside table and took the gun and a blanket back to the gallery. Lying on the sofa wrapped in the blanket, with the gun against my chest, I abandoned myself to the storm behind the windowpanes. I could hear the ticking of the clock on the mantelpiece but didn't need to look at it to realise that there was barely half an hour to go before my meeting with the boss in the billiard room at the Equestrian Club.

I closed my eyes and imagined him travelling through the deserted streets of the city, sitting on the back seat of his car, his golden eyes shining in the dark, the silver angel on the hood of the Rolls-Royce plunging through the storm. I imagined him motionless, like a statue, not breathing or smiling, with no expression at all. I heard the crackle of burning wood and the sound of the rain on the windows; I fell asleep with the weapon in my hands and the certainty that I was not going to keep my appointment.

Shortly after midnight I opened my eyes. The fire was almost out and the gallery was submerged in the flickering half-light projected by the last blue flames in the embers. It continued to rain heavily. The revolver was still in my hands: it felt warm. I remained like that for a few seconds, barely blinking. I knew that there was someone at the door before I heard the knock.

I pushed aside the blanket and sat up. I heard the knock again. Knuckles on the front door. I stood up, holding the gun in my hands, and went into the corridor. Again the knock. I took a few steps towards the door and stopped. I imagined him smiling on the landing, the angel on his lapel gleaming in the dark. I pulled back the hammer on the gun. Once again the sound of a hand, knocking on the door. I tried to turn the light on, but there was no power. I kept walking. I was about to slide the spyhole open, but didn't dare. I stood there stock-still, hardly daring to breathe, with the gun raised and pointing towards the door.

'Go away,' I called out, with no strength in my voice.

Then I heard a sob on the other side of the door, and lowered the gun. I opened the door and found her there in the shadows. Her clothes were soaking and she was shivering. Her skin was frozen.

When she saw me, she almost collapsed into my arms. I could find no words; I just held her tight. She smiled weakly at me and when I put my hand on her cheek she kissed it and closed her eyes.

'Forgive me,' whispered Cristina.

She opened her eyes and gave me a broken look that would have stayed with me even in hell. I smiled at her.

'Welcome home.'

38

I undressed her by candlelight. I removed her shoes and dress, which were soaking wet, and her laddered stockings. I dried her body and her hair with a clean towel. She was still shaking with cold when I put her to bed and lay down next to her, hugging her to give her warmth. We stayed like that for a long time, not saying anything, just listening to the rain. Slowly I felt her body warming up and her breathing become deeper. I thought she had fallen asleep but then I heard her speak.

'Your friend came to see me.'

'Isabella.'

'She told me she'd hidden my letters. She said she hadn't done it in bad faith. She thought she was doing it for your own good. Perhaps she was right.'

I leaned over and searched her eyes. I caressed her lips and for the first time she smiled weakly.

'I thought you'd forgotten me,' she said.

'I tried.'

Her face was marked by tiredness. The months I had not seen her had drawn lines on her skin and her eyes had an air of defeat and emptiness.

'We're no longer young,' she said, reading my thoughts.

'When have we ever been young, you and I?'

I pulled away the blanket and looked at her naked body stretched out on the white sheet. I stroked her neck and her breasts, barely touching her skin with my fingertips. I drew circles on her belly and traced the outline of the bones of her hips. I let my fingers play with the almost transparent hair between her thighs.

Cristina watched me without saying a word, her smile sad and her eyes half open.

'What are we going to do?' she asked.

I bent over her and kissed her lips. She embraced me and we remained like that as the light from the candle sputtered then went out.

'We'll think of something,' she whispered.

I woke up shortly after dawn and discovered I was alone in the bed. I sat up suddenly, fearing that Cristina had left again in the middle of the night. Then I saw her clothes and shoes on the chair and let out a deep sigh. I found her in the gallery, wrapped in a blanket, sitting on the floor by the fireplace, where a breath of blue fire emerged from a smouldering log. I sat down next to her and kissed her on the neck.

'I couldn't sleep,' she said, her eyes fixed on the fire.

'You should have woken me.'

'I didn't dare. You looked as if you were sleeping for the first time in months. I preferred to explore your house.'

'And?'

'This house is cursed with sadness,' she said. 'Why don't you set fire to it?'

'And where would we live?'

'In the plural?'

'Why not?'

'I thought you'd stopped writing fairy tales.'

'It's like riding a bike. Once you learn . . .'

Cristina looked at me.

'What's in that room at the end of the corridor?'

'Nothing. Junk.'

'It's locked.'

'Do you want to see it?'

She shook her head.

'It's only a house, Cristina. A pile of stones and memories. That's all.'

Cristina nodded but looked unconvinced.

'Why don't we go away?' she asked.

'Where to?'

'Far away.'

I couldn't help smiling, but she didn't smile back.

'How far?' I asked.

'Far enough that people won't know who we are, and won't care either.'

'Is that what you want?' I asked.

'Don't you?'

I hesitated for a second.

'What about Pedro?' I asked, almost choking on the words.

She let the blanket fall from her shoulders and looked at me defiantly. 'Do you need his permission to sleep with me?'

I bit my tongue.

Cristina looked at me, her eyes full of tears.

'I'm sorry,' she whispered. 'I had no right to say that.'

I picked up the blanket and tried to cover her, but she moved away, rejecting my gesture.

'Pedro has left me,' she said in a broken voice. 'He went to the Ritz yesterday to wait until I'd gone. He said he knew I didn't love him, that I married him out of gratitude or pity. He said he doesn't want my compassion and that every day I spend with him pretending to love him only hurts him. Whatever I did he would always love me, he said, and that is why he doesn't want to see me again.'

Her hands were shaking.

'He's loved me with all his heart and all I've done is make him miserable,' she murmured.

She closed her eyes and her face twisted in pain. A moment later she let out a deep moan and began to hit her face and body with her fists. I threw myself on her and put my arms around her, holding her still. Cristina struggled and shouted. I pressed her against the floor, restraining her. Slowly she gave in, exhausted, her face covered in tears, her eyes reddened. We remained like that for almost half an hour, until I felt her body relaxing and she fell into a long silence. I covered her with the blanket and embraced her, hiding my own tears.

'We'll go far away,' I whispered in her ear, not knowing whether she could hear or understand me. 'We'll go far away where nobody will know who we are, and won't care either. I promise.'

Cristina tilted her head and looked at me, her face robbed of all expression, as if her soul had been smashed to pieces with a hammer. I held her tight and kissed her on the forehead. The rain was still whipping against the windowpanes. Trapped in that grey, pale light of a dead dawn, it occurred to me for the first time that we were sinking.

39

That same morning I abandoned my work for the boss. While Cristina slept I went up to the study and put the folder containing all the pages, notes and drafts for the project in an old trunk by the wall. My first impulse had been to set fire to it, but I didn't have the courage. I had always felt that the pages I left behind were a part of me. Normal people bring children into the world; we novelists bring books. We are condemned to put our whole lives into them, even though they hardly ever thank us for it. We are condemned to die in their pages and sometimes even to let our books be the ones who, in the end, will take our lives. Among all the strange creatures made of paper and ink that I'd brought into the world, this one, my mercenary offering to the promises of the boss, was undoubtedly the most grotesque. There was nothing in those pages that deserved anything better than to be burned, and yet they were still flesh of my flesh and I couldn't find the courage to destroy them. I abandoned the work in the bottom of that trunk and left the study with a heavy heart, almost ashamed of my cowardice and the murky sense of paternity inspired in me by that manuscript of shadows. The boss would probably have appreciated the irony of the situation. All it inspired in me was disgust.

Cristina slept well into the afternoon. I took advantage of her sleep to go over to the grocer's shop next to the market and buy some milk, bread and cheese. The rain had stopped at last, but the streets were full of puddles and you could feel the dampness in the air, like a cold dust that permeated your clothes and your bones. While I waited for my turn in the shop I had the feeling that someone was watching me. When I went outside again and crossed Paseo del Borne, I turned and saw that a boy was following me. He could not have been more than five years old. I stopped and looked at him. The boy held my gaze.

'Don't be afraid,' I said. 'Come here.'

The boy came closer, until he was standing about two metres away. His skin was pale, almost blue, as if he'd never seen the sunlight. He was dressed in black and wore new, shiny, patent leather shoes. His eyes were dark, with pupils so large they left no space for the whites.

'What's your name?' I asked.

The boy smiled and pointed at me with his finger. I was about to take a step towards him but he ran off, disappearing into Paseo del Borne.

When I got back to my front door I found an envelope stuck in it. The red wax seal with the angel was still warm. I looked up and down the street, but couldn't see anybody. I went in and double-locked the main door behind me. Then I paused at the foot of the staircase and opened the envelope.

> Dear friend,
> I deeply regret that you were unable to come to our meeting last night. I trust you are well and there has been no emergency or setback. I am sorry I couldn't enjoy the pleasure of your company, but I hope that whatever it was that did not allow you to join me is quickly and favourably resolved and that next time it will be easier for us to meet. I must leave the city for a few days, but as soon as I return I'll send word. Hoping to hear from you and to learn about your progress in our joint project, please accept, as always, my friendship and affection,
>
> ANDREAS CORELLI

I crushed the letter in my fist and put it in my pocket, then went quietly into the apartment and closed the door. I peeked into the bedroom and saw that Cristina was still asleep. Then I went to the kitchen and began to prepare coffee and a light lunch. A few minutes later I heard Cristina's footsteps behind me. She was looking at me from the doorway, clad in an old jumper of mine that went halfway down her thighs. Her hair was a mess and her eyes were still swollen. Her lips and cheeks had dark bruises, as if I'd hit her hard. She avoided my eyes.

'I'm sorry,' she whispered.

'Are you hungry?' I asked.

She shook her head, but I ignored the gesture and motioned for her to sit at the table. I poured her a cup of coffee with milk and sugar and gave her a slice of freshly baked bread with some cheese and a little ham. She made no move to touch her plate.

'Just a bite,' I suggested.

She nibbled the cheese and gave me a smile.

'It's good,' she said.

We ate in silence. To my surprise, Cristina finished off half the food on her plate. Then she hid behind the cup of coffee and gave me a fleeting look.

'If you want, I'll leave today,' she said at last. 'Don't worry. Pedro gave me money and—'

'I don't want you to go anywhere. I don't want you to go away ever again. Do you hear me?'

'I'm not good company, David.'

'That makes two of us.'

'Did you mean it? What you said about going far away?'

I nodded.

'My father used to say that life doesn't give second chances.'

'Only to those who never had a first chance. Actually, they're second-hand chances that someone else hasn't made use of, but that's better than nothing.'

She smiled faintly.

'Take me for a walk,' she suddenly said.

'Where do you want to go?'

'I want to say goodbye to Barcelona.'

40

Halfway through the afternoon the sun appeared from behind the blanket of clouds left by the storm. The shining streets were transformed into mirrors, on which pedestrians walked, reflecting the amber of the sky. I remember that we went to the foot of the

Ramblas where the statue of Columbus peered out through the mist. We walked without saying a word, gazing at the buildings and the crowds as if they were a mirage, as if the city were already deserted and forgotten. Barcelona had never seemed so beautiful and so sad to me as it did that afternoon. When it began to grow dark we walked to the Sempere & Sons bookshop and stood in a doorway on the opposite side of the street, where nobody could see us. The shop window of the old bookshop cast a faint light over the damp, gleaming cobblestones. Inside we could see Isabella standing on a ladder, sorting out the books on the top shelf, as Sempere's son pretended to be going through an accounts book, looking furtively at her ankles all the while. Sitting in a corner, old and tired, Señor Sempere watched them both with a sad smile.

'This is the place where I've found almost all the good things in my life,' I said without thinking. 'I don't want to say goodbye.'

When we returned to the tower house it was already dark. As we walked in we were greeted by the warmth of the fire which I had left burning when we went out. Cristina went ahead down the corridor and, without saying a word, began to get undressed, leaving a trail of clothes on the floor. I found her lying on the bed, waiting. I lay down beside her and let her guide my hands. As I caressed her I could feel her muscles going tense. There was no tenderness in her eyes, just a longing for warmth, and an urgency. I abandoned myself to her body, charging at her with anger, feeling her nails dig into my skin. I heard her moan with pain and with life, as if she lacked air. At last we collapsed, exhausted and covered in sweat. Cristina leaned her head on my shoulder and looked into my eyes.

'Your friend told me you'd got yourself into trouble.'

'Isabella?'

'She's very worried about you.'

'Isabella has a tendency to believe she's my mother.'

'I don't think that's what she was getting at.'

I avoided her eyes.

'She told me you were working on a new book, commissioned by a foreign publisher. She calls him the boss. She says he's paying you a fortune but you feel guilty for having accepted the money. She says you're afraid of this man, the boss, and there's something murky about the whole business.'

I sighed with annoyance.

'Is there anything Isabella hasn't told you?'

'The rest is between us,' she answered, winking at me. 'Was she lying?'

'She wasn't lying, she was speculating.'

'And what's the book about?'

'It's a story for children.'

'Isabella told me you'd say that.'

'If Isabella has already given you all the answers, why are you questioning me?'

Cristina looked at me severely.

'For your peace of mine, and Isabella's, I've abandoned the book. *C'est fini*,' I assured her.

Cristina frowned and looked dubious.

'And this man, the boss, does he know?'

'I haven't spoken to him yet. But I suppose he has a good idea. And if he doesn't, he soon will.'

'So you'll have to give him back the money?'

'I don't think he's bothered about the money in the least.'

Cristina fell into a long silence.

'May I read it?' she asked at last.

'No.'

'Why not?'

'It's a draft and it doesn't make any sense yet. It's a pile of ideas and notes, loose fragments. Nothing readable. It would bore you.'

'I'd still like to read it.'

'Why?'

'Because you've written it. Pedro always says that the only way you can truly get to know an author is through the trail of ink he leaves behind him; the person you think you see is only an empty character: truth is always hidden in fiction.'

'He must have read that on a postcard.'

'In fact he took it from one of your books. I know because I've read it too.'

'Plagiarism doesn't prevent it being nonsense.'

'I think it makes sense.'

'Then it must be true.'

'May I read it then?'

'No.'

That evening, sitting opposite one another at the kitchen table, looking up occasionally, we ate the remains of the bread and cheese. Cristina had little appetite, and examined every morsel of bread in the light of the oil lamp before putting it in her mouth.

'There's a train leaving the Estación de Francia for Paris tomorrow at midday,' she said. 'Is that too soon?'

I couldn't get the image of Andreas Corelli out of my mind: I imagined him coming up the stairs and calling at my door at any moment.

'I suppose not,' I agreed.

'I know a little hotel opposite the Luxembourg Gardens where they rent out rooms by the month. It's a bit expensive, but . . .' she added.

I preferred not to ask her how she knew of the hotel.

'The price doesn't matter, but I don't speak French.'

'I do.'

I looked down.

'Look at me, David.'

I raised my eyes reluctantly.

'If you'd rather I left . . .'

I shook my head. She held my hand and brought it to her lips.

'It'll be fine. You'll see,' she said. 'I know. It will be the first thing in my life that will work out all right.'

I looked at her, a broken woman with tears in her eyes, and didn't wish for anything in the world other than the ability to give her back what she'd never had.

We lay down on the sofa in the gallery under a couple of blankets, staring at the embers in the fireplace. I fell asleep stroking Cristina's hair, thinking it was the last night I would spend in that house, the prison in which I had buried my youth. I dreamed that I was running through the streets of a Barcelona strewn with clocks whose hands were turning backwards. Alleyways and avenues twisted as I ran, as if they had a will of their own, creating a living labyrinth that blocked me at every turn. Finally, under a midday sun that burned in the sky like a red-hot metal sphere, I managed to reach the Estación de Francia and was speeding towards the platform where the train was beginning to pull away. I ran after it but the train gathered speed and, despite all my efforts, all I managed to do was touch it with the tips of my fingers. I kept on running until I was out of breath, and when I reached the end of the platform fell into a void. When I glanced up it was too late. The train was disappearing into the distance, Cristina's face staring back at me from the last window.

I opened my eyes and knew that Cristina was not there. The fire was reduced to a handful of ashes. I stood up and looked through the windows. Dawn was breaking. I pressed my face against the glass and noticed a flickering light shining from the windows of the study. I went to the spiral staircase that led up the tower. A copper-coloured glow spilled down over the steps. I climbed them slowly. When I reached the study I stopped in the doorway. Cristina was sitting on the floor with her back to me. The trunk by the wall was open. Cristina was holding the folder containing the boss's manuscript and was untying the ribbon.

When she heard my footsteps she stopped.

'What are you doing up here?' I asked, trying to hide the note of alarm in my voice.

Cristina turned and smiled.

'Nosing around.'

She followed the direction of my gaze to the folder in her hands and adopted a mischievous expression.

'What's in here?'

'Nothing. Notes. Comments. Nothing of any interest . . .'

'You liar. I bet this is the book you've been working on,' she said. 'I'm dying to read it . . .'

'I'd rather you didn't,' I said in the most relaxed tone I could muster.

Cristina frowned. I took advantage of the moment to kneel down beside her and delicately snatch the folder away.

'What's the matter, David?'

'Nothing's the matter,' I assured her with a stupid smile plastered across my lips.

I tied the ribbon again and put the folder back in the trunk.

'Aren't you going to lock it?' asked Cristina.

I turned round, ready to offer some excuse, but Cristina had already disappeared down the stairs. I sighed and closed the lid of the trunk.

I found her in the bedroom. For a moment she looked at me as if I were a stranger.

'Forgive me,' I began.

'You don't have to ask me to forgive you,' she replied. 'I shouldn't have stuck my nose in where I have no business.'

'No, it's not that.'

'It doesn't matter,' she said icily, her tone cutting the air.

I put off a second remark for a more auspicious moment.

'The ticket office at the Estación de Francia will be open soon,' I said. 'I thought I'd go along so that I can buy the tickets first thing. Then I'll go to the bank and withdraw some money.'

'Very good.'

'Why don't you get a bag ready in the meantime? I'll be back in a couple of hours at the most.'

Cristina barely smiled.

'I'll be here.'

I went over to her and held her face in my hands.

'By tomorrow night we'll be in Paris,' I said.

I kissed her on the forehead and left.

41

The large clock suspended from the ceiling of the Estación de Francia was reflected in the shining surface of the vestibule beneath my feet. The hands pointed to seven thirty-five in the morning, but the ticket offices hadn't opened yet. A porter, armed with a large broom and an exaggerated manner, was polishing the floor, whistling a popular folk song and, within the limits imposed by his limp, jauntily moving his hips. As I had nothing better to do, I stood there observing him. He was a small man who looked as if the world had wrinkled him up to such a degree that it had taken everything from him except his smile and the pleasure of being able to clean that bit of floor as if it were the Sistine Chapel. There was nobody else around, but finally he realised that he was being watched. When his fifth pass over the floor brought him to my

315

observation post on one of the wooden benches surrounding the hall, the porter stopped and leaned on his mop with both hands.

'They never open on time,' he explained, pointing towards the ticket offices.

'Then why do they have a notice saying they open at seven?'

The little man sighed philosophically.

'Well, they also have train timetables and in the fifteen years I've been here I haven't seen a single one leave on time,' he remarked.

The porter continued with his cleaning and fifteen minutes later I heard the window of the ticket office opening. I walked over and smiled at the clerk.

'I thought you opened at seven,' I said.

'That's what the notice says. What do you want?'

'Two first-class tickets to Paris on the midday train.'

'For today?'

'If that's not too much trouble.'

It took him almost a quarter of an hour. Once he had finished his masterpiece, he dropped the tickets on the counter disdainfully.

'One o'clock. Platform Four. Don't be late.'

I paid and, as I didn't then leave, he gave me a hostile look.

'Anything else?'

I smiled and shook my head, at which point he closed the window in my face. I turned and crossed the immaculate vestibule, its brilliant shine courtesy of the porter, who waved at me from afar and wished me a bon voyage.

The central offices of the Banco Hispano Colonial on Calle Fontanella were reminiscent of a temple. A huge portico gave way to a nave, which was flanked by statues and extended as far as a row of windows that looked like an altar. On either side of this altar, like side-chapels and confessionals, were oak tables and easy chairs fit for a general, with a small army of auditors and other staff in attendance, neatly dressed and sporting friendly smiles. I withdrew four thousand francs and received instructions on how to take out money at their Paris branch, at the intersection of Rue de Rennes with Boulevard Raspail, near the hotel Cristina had mentioned. With that small fortune in my pocket I said goodbye, disregarding the warning given to me by the manager about the risks of walking the streets with that amount of cash in my pocket.

The sun was rising in a blue sky the colour of good luck, and a clean breeze brought with it the smell of the sea. I was walking briskly as if relieved of a tremendous burden, and I began to think that the city had decided to let me go without any ill feeling. In Paseo del Borne I stopped to buy flowers for Cristina, white roses tied with a red ribbon. I climbed the steps to the apartment, two at a time, with a smile on my lips, bearing the certainty that this would be the first day of a life I thought I had lost forever. I was about to open the door when, as I put the key in the lock, it gave way. It was open.

I stepped into the hall. The house was silent.

'Cristina?'

I left the flowers on a shelf and put my head round the door of the bedroom. Cristina wasn't there. I walked up the corridor to the gallery. There was no sign of her. I went to the staircase that led up to the study and called out in a loud voice.

'Cristina?'

Nothing but an echo. I checked the clock on one of the glass cabinets in the gallery. It was almost nine. I imagined that Cristina must have gone out to get something and, being used to leaving such matters as doors and keys to the servants in Pedralbes, she had left the front door open. While I waited, I decided to lie down on the sofa in the gallery. The sun poured in through the large windows: a clean, bright winter sun that felt like a warm caress. I closed my eyes and tried to think about what I was going to take with me. I'd spent half my life surrounded by all these objects, and now, when it was time to part from them, I felt incapable of making a shortlist of the ones I considered essential. Slowly, without noticing, lying under the warmth of the sun and lulled by tepid hope, I fell asleep.

When I woke up and looked at the clock, it was twelve thirty. There was barely half an hour left before the train was due to leave. I jumped up and ran to the bedroom.

'Cristina?'

This time I went through the whole house, room by room, until I reached the study. There was nobody, but I thought I could smell something odd. Phosphorus. The light from the windows trapped a faint web of blue filaments of smoke suspended in the air. I found a couple of burned matches on the study floor. I felt a pang of anxiety and knelt down by the trunk. I opened it and sighed with relief. The folder containing the manuscript was still there. I was about to close the lid when I noticed something: the red ribbon of the folder was undone. I picked it up and opened it, leafing through the pages, but nothing seemed to be missing. I closed it again, this time tying the ribbon with a double knot, and put it back in its place. After closing the trunk, I went down to the lower floor. I sat on a chair in the gallery, facing the long corridor that led to the front door, and waited. The minutes went by with infinite cruelty.

Slowly, the awareness of what had happened fell upon me, and my desire to believe and to trust turned to bitterness. I heard the bells of Santa María strike two o'clock. The train to Paris had left the station and Cristina had not returned. I realised then that she had gone, that those brief hours we had shared were nothing but a mirage. I went up to the study again and sat down. The dazzling day I saw through the windowpanes was no longer the colour of luck; I imagined her back in Villa Helius, seeking the shelter of Pedro Vidal's arms. Resentment slowly poisoned my blood and I laughed at myself and my absurd hopes. I remained there, incapable of taking a single step, watching the city grow dark as the afternoon went by and the shadows lengthened. Finally I stood up and went over to the window, opened it wide and looked out. Beneath me a sheer drop, sufficiently high. Sufficiently high to crush my bones, to turn them into daggers that would pierce my body and let it die in a pool of blood on the courtyard below. I wondered whether the pain would be as bad as I imagined it, or whether the impact would be enough to numb the senses and offer a quick, efficient death.

Then I heard three knocks on the door. One, two, three. Insistent. I turned, still dazed by my thoughts. The call came again. There was someone knocking on the door. My heart skipped a beat and I rushed downstairs, convinced that Cristina had returned, that something had happened along the way that had detained her, that my miserable, despicable feelings of betrayal were unjustified and that today was, after all, the first day of that promised life. I ran to the door and opened it. She was there in the shadows, dressed in white. I was about to embrace her, but then I saw her face, wet with tears. It was not Cristina.

'David,' Isabella whispered in a broken voice. 'Señor Sempere has died.'

Act Three

The Angel's Game

1

Night had fallen by the time we reached the bookshop. A golden glow broke through the blue of the night outside Sempere & Sons, where about a hundred people had gathered holding candles. Some cried quietly, others looked at each other, not knowing what to do. I recognised some of the faces – friends and customers of Sempere, people to whom the old bookseller had given books as presents, readers who had been initiated into the art of reading through him. As the news spread through the area, more readers and friends arrived, all finding it hard to believe that Señor Sempere had died.

The shop lights were on and I could see Don Gustavo Barceló inside, embracing a young man who could hardly stand. I didn't realise it was Sempere's son until Isabella pressed my hand and led me into the bookshop. When he saw me come in, Barceló looked up and smiled dolefully. The bookseller's son was weeping in his arms and I didn't have the courage to go and greet him. It was Isabella who went over and put her hand on his back. Sempere's son turned round and I saw his distraught face. Isabella led him to a chair and helped him sit down; he collapsed like a rag doll and Isabella knelt down beside him and hugged him. I had never felt as proud of anyone as I was that day of Isabella. She no longer seemed a girl but a woman, stronger and wiser than any of the rest us.

Barceló came over and held out a trembling hand. I shook it.

'It happened a couple of hours ago,' he explained in a hoarse voice. 'He'd been left alone in the bookshop for a moment and when his son returned . . . They say he was arguing with someone . . . I don't know. The doctor said it was his heart.'

I swallowed hard.

'Where is he?'

Barceló nodded towards the door of the back room. I walked over, but before going in I took a deep breath and clenched my fists. Then I walked through the doorway and saw him: he was lying on a table, his hands crossed over his belly. His skin was as white as paper and his features seemed to have sunk in on themselves. His eyes were still open. I found it hard to breathe and felt as if I'd been dealt a strong blow to the stomach. I leaned on the table and tried to steady myself. Then I bent over him and closed his eyelids. I stroked his cheek, which was cold, and looked around me at that world of pages and dreams he had created. I wanted to believe that Sempere was still there, among his books and his friends. I heard steps behind me and turned. Barceló was accompanied by two sombre-looking men, both dressed in black.

'These gentlemen are from the undertaker's,' said Barceló.

They nodded with professional gravitas and went over to examine the body. One of them, who was tall and gaunt, took a brief measurement and said something to his colleague, who wrote down his instructions in a little notebook.

'Unless there is any change, the funeral will be tomorrow afternoon, in the Pueblo Nuevo Cemetery,' said Barceló. 'I thought it best to take charge of the arrangements because his son is devastated, as you can see. And with these things, the sooner . . .'

'Thank you, Don Gustavo.'

The bookseller glanced at his old friend and smiled tearfully.

'What are we going to do now that the old man has left us?' he said.

'I don't know . . .'

One of the undertakers discreetly cleared his throat.

'If it's all right with you, in a moment my colleague and I will go and fetch the coffin and—'

'Do whatever you have to do,' I cut in.

'Any preferences regarding the ceremony?'

I stared at him, not understanding.

'Was the deceased a believer?'

'Señor Sempere believed in books,' I said.

'I see,' he replied as he left the room.

I looked at Barceló, who shrugged his shoulders.

'Let me ask his son,' I added.

I went back to the front of the bookshop. Isabella glanced at me inquisitively and stood up. She left Sempere's son and came over to me and I whispered the problem to her.

'Señor Sempere was a good friend of the local parish priest – from the church of Santa Ana right next door. People say the bigwigs in the diocese have been wanting to get rid of the priest for years, because they consider him a rebel in the ranks, but he's so old they decided to wait for him to die instead. He's too tough a nut for them to crack.'

'Then he's the man we need,' I said.

'I'll speak to him,' said Isabella.

I pointed towards Sempere's son.

'How is he?'

Isabella met my gaze.

'And how are you?' she replied.

'I'm fine,' I lied. 'Who's going to stay with him tonight?'

'I am,' she said, without a moment's hesitation.

I kissed her on the cheek and returned to the back room. Barceló was sitting in front of his old friend, and while the two undertakers took further measurements and debated about suits and shoes, he poured two glasses of brandy and offered one to me. I sat down next to him.

'To the health of our friend Sempere, who taught us all how to read, and even how to live,' he said.

We toasted and drank in silence. We remained there until the undertakers returned with the coffin and the clothes in which Sempere was going to be buried.

'If it's all right with you, we'll take care of this,' the one who seemed to be the brighter of the two suggested. I agreed. Before leaving the room and going back to the front of the shop I picked up the old copy of *Great Expectations,* which I'd never come back to collect, and put it in Sempere's hands.

'For the journey,' I said.

A quarter of an hour later, the undertakers brought out the coffin and placed it on a large table that had been set up in the middle of the bookshop. A multitude had been gathering in the street, waiting in silence. I went over to the door and opened it. One by one, the friends of Sempere & Sons filed through. Some were unable to hold back the tears, and such were the scenes of grief that Isabella took the bookseller's son by the hand and led him up to the apartment above the bookshop, where he had lived all his life with his father.

Barceló and I stayed in the shop, keeping old Sempere company while people came in to say their farewells. Those closest to him stayed on.

The wake lasted the entire night. Barceló remained until five in the morning and I didn't leave until Isabella came down to the shop shortly after dawn and ordered me to go home, if only to change my clothes and freshen up.

I looked at poor Sempere and smiled. I couldn't believe I'd never see him again, standing behind the counter, when I came in through that door. I remembered the first time I'd visited the bookshop, when I was just a child, and the bookseller had seemed tall and strong. Indestructible. The wisest man in the world.

'Go home, please,' murmured Isabella.

'What for?'

'Please . . .'

She came out into the street with me and hugged me.

'I know how fond you were of him and what he meant to you,' she said.

Nobody knew, I thought. Nobody. But I nodded and, after kissing her on the cheek, I wandered off, walking through streets that seemed emptier than ever, thinking that if I didn't stop, if I kept on walking, I wouldn't notice that the world I thought I knew was no longer there.

2

The crowd had gathered by the cemetery gates to await the arrival of the hearse. Nobody dared speak. We could hear the murmur of the sea in the distance and the echo of a freight train rumbling towards the city of factories that spread out beyond the graveyard. It was cold and snowflakes drifted in the wind. Shortly after three o'clock in the afternoon, the hearse, pulled by a team of black horses, turned into Avenida de Icaria, which was lined with rows of cypress trees and old storehouses. Sempere's son and Isabella travelled with it. Six colleagues from the Barcelona booksellers' guild, Don Gustavo among them, lifted the coffin onto their shoulders and carried it into the cemetery. The crowd followed, forming a silent cortège that advanced through the streets and mausoleums of the cemetery beneath a blanket of low clouds that rippled like a sheet of mercury. I heard someone say that the bookseller's son looked as if he'd aged fifteen years in one night. They referred to him as Señor Sempere, because he was now the person in charge of the bookshop; for four generations that enchanted bazaar in Calle Santa Ana had never changed its name and had always been managed by a Señor Sempere. Isabella held his arm – without her support he looked as if he might have collapsed like a puppet with no strings.

The parish priest of Santa Ana, a veteran the same age as the deceased, waited at the foot of the tomb, a sober slab of marble without decorative elements that could almost have gone unnoticed. The six booksellers who had carried the coffin left it resting beside the grave. Barceló noticed me and greeted me with a nod. I preferred to stay towards the rear of the crowd, I'm not sure whether out of cowardice or respect. From there I could see my father's grave, some thirty metres away.

Once the congregation had spread out, the parish priest looked up and smiled.

'Señor Sempere and I were friends for almost forty years, and in all that time we spoke about God and the mysteries of life on only one occasion. Almost nobody knows this, but Sempere had not set foot in a church since the funeral of his wife Diana, to whose side we bring him today so that they might lie next to one another forever. Perhaps for that reason people assumed he was an atheist, but he was truly a man of faith. He believed in his friends, in the truth of things and in something to which he didn't dare put a name or a face because he said as priests that was our job. Señor Sempere believed we are all a part of something, and that when we leave this world our memories and our desires are not lost, but go on to become the memories and desires of those who take our place. He didn't know whether we created God in our own image or whether God created us without quite knowing what he was doing. He believed that God, or whatever brought us here, lives in each of our deeds, in each of our words, and manifests himself in all those things that show us to be more than mere figures of clay. Señor Sempere believed that God lives, to a smaller or greater extent, in books, and that is why he devoted his life to sharing them, to protecting them and to making sure their pages, like our memories and our desires, are never lost. He believed, and he made me believe it too, that as long as there is one person left in the world who is capable of reading them and experiencing them, a small piece of God, or of life, will remain. I know that my friend would not have liked us to say our farewells to him with prayers and hymns. I know that it would have been enough for him to realise that his friends, many of whom have come here today to say goodbye, will never forget him. I have no doubt that the Lord, even though old Sempere was not expecting it, will receive our dear friend at his side, and I know that he will live forever in the hearts of all those who are here today, all those who have discovered the magic of books thanks to him, and all those who, without even knowing him, will one day go through the door of his little bookshop where, as he liked to say, the story has only just begun. May you rest in peace, Sempere, dear friend, and may God give us all the opportunity to honour your memory and feel grateful for the privilege of having known you.'

An endless silence fell over the graveyard when the priest finished speaking. He retreated a few steps, blessing the coffin, his eyes downcast. At a sign from the chief undertaker, the gravediggers moved forward and slowly lowered the coffin with ropes. I remember the sound as it touched the bottom and the stifled sobs among the crowd. I remember that I stood there, unable to move, watching the gravediggers cover the tomb with the large slab of marble on which a single word was written, 'Sempere', the tomb in which his wife Diana had lain buried for twenty-six years.

The congregation shuffled away towards the cemetery gates, where they separated into groups, not quite knowing where to go, because nobody wanted to leave the place and abandon poor Señor Sempere. Barceló and Isabella led the bookseller's son away, one on each side of him. I stayed on until I thought everyone else had left; only then did I dare go up to Sempere's grave. I knelt and put my hand on the marble.

'See you soon,' I murmured.

I heard him approaching and knew who it was before I saw him. I got up and turned round. Pedro Vidal offered me his hand and the saddest smile I have ever seen.

'Aren't you going to shake my hand?' he asked.

I didn't and a few seconds later Vidal nodded to himself and pulled his hand away.

'What are you doing here?' I spat out.

'Sempere was my friend too,' replied Vidal.

'I see. And are you here alone?'

Vidal looked puzzled.

'Where is she?' I asked.

'Who?'

I let out a bitter laugh. Barceló, who had noticed us, was coming over, looking concerned.

'What did you promise her, to buy her back?'

Vidal's eyes hardened.

'You don't know what you're saying, David.'

I drew closer, until I could feel his breath on my face.

'Where is she?' I insisted.

'I don't know,' said Vidal.

'Of course,' I said, looking away.

I was about to walk towards the exit when Vidal grabbed my arm and stopped me.

'David, wait—'

Before I realised what I was doing, I turned and hit him as hard as I could. My fist crashed against his face and he fell backwards. I noticed that there was blood on my hand and heard steps hurrying towards me. Two arms caught hold of me and pulled me away from Vidal.

'For God's sake, Martín . . .' said Barceló.

The bookseller knelt down next to Vidal, who was gasping as blood streamed from his mouth. Barceló cradled his head and threw me a furious look. I fled, passing some of the people who had been present at the graveside and who had stopped to watch the altercation. I didn't have the courage to look them in the eye.

3

I didn't leave the house for several days, sleeping at odd times and barely eating. At night I would sit in the gallery by the open fire and listen to the silence, hoping to hear footsteps outside the door, thinking that Cristina would return, that as soon as she heard about the death of Señor Sempere she'd come back to me, if only out of compassion, which by now would have been enough for me. When almost a week had gone by since the death of the bookseller and I realised that Cristina was not going to return, I began to visit the study again. I rescued the boss's manuscript from the trunk and started to reread it, savouring every phrase, every paragraph. Reading it produced in me both nausea and a dark satisfaction. When I thought of the hundred thousand francs that at first had seemed so much, I smiled and reflected that I'd sold myself to that son-of-a-bitch too cheaply. Vanity papered over my bitterness, and pain closed the door of my conscience. In an act of pure arrogance, I reread my predecessor Diego Marlasca's *Lux Aeterna*, and then threw it into the fire. Where he had failed, I would triumph. Where he had lost his way, I would find the path out of the labyrinth.

I went back to work on the seventh day. I waited until midnight and sat down at my desk. A clean sheet in the old Underwood typewriter and the city black behind the windowpanes. The words and images sprang forth from my hands as if they'd been waiting angrily in the prison of my soul. The pages flowed from me without thought or measure, with nothing more than the desire to bewitch, or poison, hearts and minds. I stopped thinking about the boss, about his reward or his demands. For the first time in my life I was writing for myself and nobody else. I was writing to set the world on fire and be consumed along with it. I worked every night until I collapsed from exhaustion. I banged the typewriter keys until my fingers bled and fever clouded my vision.

One morning in January, when I'd lost all notion of time, I heard someone knocking on the door. I was lying on my bed, my eyes lost in the old photograph of Cristina as a small child, walking hand in hand with a stranger along a jetty that reached out into a sea of light. That image seemed to be the only good thing I had left, the key to all mysteries. I ignored the knocking for a few minutes, until I heard her voice and knew she was not going to give up.

'Open the door, damn you! I know you're there and I'm not leaving until you open it or I knock it down.'

When she saw me Isabella stepped back and looked horrified.

'It's only me, Isabella.'

She pushed me aside and made straight for the gallery, where she flung open the windows. Then she went to the bathroom and started filling the tub. She took my arm and dragged me there, then made me sit on the edge of the bath and examined my eyes, lifting my eyelids with her fingertips and muttering to herself. Without saying a word she began to remove my shirt.

'Isabella, I'm not in the mood.'

'What are all these cuts? But . . . what have you done to yourself?'

'They're just scratches.'

'I want a doctor to see you.'

'No.'

'Don't you dare say no to me,' she replied harshly. 'You're getting into this bathtub right now; you're going to wash yourself with soap and water and you're going to have a shave. You have two options: either you do it, or I will. And don't imagine for one second that I won't.'

I smiled.

'I know.'

'Do as I say. In the meantime I'm going to find a doctor.'

I was about to reply, but she raised her hand to silence me.

'Don't say another word. If you think you're the only person for whom life is painful, you're wrong. And if you don't mind letting yourself die like a dog, at least have the decency to remember that there are those of us who do care – although, to tell the truth, I don't see why.'

'Isabella . . .'

'Into the water. And please remove your trousers and underpants.'

'I know how to take a bath.'

'I'd never have guessed.'

While Isabella went off in search of a doctor, I submitted to her orders and subjected myself to a baptism of cold water and soap. I hadn't shaved since the funeral and when I looked in the mirror I was greeted by the face of a wolf. My eyes were bloodshot and my skin had an unhealthy pallor. I put on clean clothes and went to wait in the gallery. Isabella returned twenty minutes later with a physician I thought I'd seen in the area once or twice.

'This is the patient. Pay no attention whatsoever to anything he says to you. He's a liar,' Isabella announced.

The doctor glanced at me, calibrating the extent of my hostility.

'It's over to you, doctor,' I said. 'Just imagine I'm not here.'

We went to my bedroom and he began the subtle rituals that form the basis of medical science: he took my blood pressure, listened to my chest, examined my pupils and my mouth, and asked me questions of a mysterious nature. When he inspected the razor cuts Irene Sabino had made on my chest, he raised an eyebrow.

'What's this?'

'It's a long story, doctor.'

'Did you do it to yourself?'

I shook my head.

'I'm going to give you an ointment for the cuts, but I'm afraid you'll be left with some scars.'

'I think that was the idea.'

He continued with his examination and I submitted to everything obediently, my eye on Isabella, who was watching anxiously from the doorway. I understood then how much I had missed her and how much I appreciated her company.

'What a fright you gave me,' she mumbled with disapproval.

The doctor frowned when he saw the raw wounds on the tips of my fingers. He proceeded to bandage them one by one.

'When did you last eat?'

I didn't reply. The doctor exchanged glances with Isabella.

'There is no cause for alarm, but I'd like to see him in my surgery tomorrow at the latest.'

'I'm afraid that won't be possible, doctor,' I said.

'He'll be there,' Isabella assured him.

'In the meantime I recommend that he begins by eating something warm, first broth and then solids. A lot of water but no coffee or other stimulants, and above all he must get lots of rest. Let him go out for a little fresh air and sunshine, but he mustn't overexert himself. He is showing the classic symptoms of exhaustion and dehydration and the beginnings of anaemia.'

Isabella sighed.

'It's nothing,' I remarked.

The doctor looked at me, unconvinced, and stood up.

'Tomorrow afternoon in my surgery, at four o'clock. I don't have the correct instruments or environment for a proper examination here.'

He closed his bag and politely said goodbye. Isabella accompanied him to the door and I heard them murmuring on the landing for a few minutes. I got dressed again and waited, like a good patient, sitting on the bed. I heard the front door close and the doctor's steps as he descended the stairs. I knew that Isabella was in the entrance hall, pausing before coming into the bedroom. When at last she did, I greeted her with a smile.

'I'm going to prepare something for you to eat.'

'I'm not hungry.'

'I couldn't care less. You're going to eat and then we're going to go out so that you get some fresh air. End of story.'

Isabella prepared a broth for me, to which I added morsels of bread. I then forced myself to swallow it with a cheerful face, although to me it tasted like grit. Eventually I cleaned my bowl and showed it to Isabella, who had been standing on guard duty while I ate. Next she took me to the bedroom, searched for a coat in the wardrobe, equipped me with gloves and a scarf, and pushed me towards the front door. When we stepped outside a cold wind was blowing, but the sky shone with an evening sun that turned the streets the colour of amber. She put her arm in mine and we set off.

'As if we were engaged,' I said.

'Very funny.'

We walked to Ciudadela Park and into the gardens surrounding the Shade House. When we reached the pond by the large fountain we sat down on a bench.

'Thank you,' I murmured.

Isabella didn't reply.

'I haven't asked you how you are,' I volunteered.

'That's nothing new.'

'So how are you?'

Isabella paused.

'My parents are delighted that I've returned. They say you've been a good influence. If only they knew . . . The truth is, we do get on better than before. Not that I see that much of them. I spend most of my time in the bookshop.'

'How's Sempere? How is he taking his father's death?'

'Not very well.'

'And how are you taking him?'

'He's a good man,' she said.

Isabella fell silent and lowered her eyes.

'He proposed to me,' she said after a while. 'A couple of days ago, in Els Quatre Gats.'

I contemplated her profile, serene and robbed of that youthful innocence I had wanted to see in her and which had probably never been there.

'And?' I finally asked.

'I've told him I'll think about it.'

'And will you?'

Isabella's gaze was lost in the fountain.

'He told me he wanted to have a family, children . . . He said we'd live in the apartment above the bookshop, that somehow we'd make a go of it, despite Señor Sempere's debts.'

'Well, you're still young . . .'

She tilted her head and looked me in the eye.

'Do you love him?' I asked.

She gave a smile that seemed endlessly sad.

'How do I know? I think so, although not as much as he thinks he loves me.'

'Sometimes, in difficult circumstances, one can confuse compassion with love,' I said.

'Don't you worry about me.'

'All I ask is that you give yourself some time.'

We looked at each other, bound by an infinite complicity that needed no words, and I hugged her.

'Friends?'

'Till death us do part.'

4

On our way home we stopped at a grocer's in Calle Comercio to buy some milk and bread. Isabella told me she was going to ask her father to deliver an order of fine foods and I'd better eat everything up.

'How are things in the bookshop?' I asked.

'The sales have gone right down. I think people feel sad about coming to the shop, because they remember poor Señor Sempere. As things stand, it's not looking good.'

'How are the accounts?'

'Below the waterline. In the weeks I've been working there I've gone through the ledgers and realised that Señor Sempere, God rest his soul, was a disaster. He'd simply give books to people who couldn't afford them. Or he'd lend them out and never get them back. He'd buy collections he knew he wouldn't be able to sell just because the owners had threatened to burn them or throw them away. He supported a whole host of second-rate bards who didn't have a penny to their name by giving them small sums of money. You can imagine the rest.'

'Any creditors in sight?'

'Two a day, not counting letters and final demands from the bank. The good news is that we're not short of offers.'

'To buy the place?'

'A couple of sausage merchants from Vic are very interested in the premises.'

'And what does Sempere's son say?'

'He just says that pork can be mightier than the sword. Realism isn't his strong point. He says we'll stay afloat and I should have faith.'

'And do you?'

'I have faith in arithmetic, and when I do the sums they tell me that in two months' time the bookshop window will be full of chorizo and slabs of bacon.'

'We'll find a solution.'

Isabella smiled.

'I was hoping you'd say that. And speaking of unfinished business, please tell me you're no longer working for the boss.'

I showed her my hands were clean.

'I'm a free agent once more.'

She accompanied me up the stairs and was about to say goodbye when she appeared to hesitate.

'What?' I asked her.

'I'd decided not to tell you, but . . . I'd rather you heard it from me than from someone else. It's about Señor Sempere.'

We went into the house and sat down in the gallery by the open fire, which Isabella revived by throwing on a couple of logs. The ashes of Marlasca's *Lux Aeterna* were still visible and my former assistant threw me a glance I could have framed.

'What were you going to tell me about Sempere?'

'It's something I heard from Don Anacleto, one of the neighbours in the building. He told me that on the afternoon Señor Sempere died he saw him arguing with someone in the shop. Don Anacleto was on his way back home and he said that their voices could be heard from the street.'

'Who was he arguing with?'

'It was a woman. Quite old. Don Anacleto didn't think he'd ever seen her around there, though he did say she looked vaguely familiar – but you never know with Don Anacleto, he likes to chatter on more than he likes sugared almonds.'

'Did he hear what they were arguing about?'

'He thought they were talking about you.'

'About me?'

Isabella nodded.

'Sempere's son had gone out for a moment to deliver an order in Calle Canuda. He wasn't away for more than ten or fifteen minutes. When he got back he found his father lying on the floor, behind the counter. Señor Sempere was still breathing but he was cold. By the time the doctor arrived, it was too late . . .'

I felt the whole world collapsing on top of me.

'I shouldn't have told you . . .' whispered Isabella.

'No. You did the right thing. Did Don Anacleto say anything else about the woman?'

'Only that he heard them arguing. He thought it was about a book. Something she wanted to buy and Señor Sempere didn't want to sell to her.'

'And why did he mention me? I don't understand.'

'Because it was your book. *The Steps of Heaven*. It was Señor Sempere's only copy, in his personal collection, and was not for sale . . .'

I was filled with a dark certainty.

'And the book . . . ?' I began.

'It's no longer there. It disappeared,' Isabella explained. 'I checked the sales ledger, because Señor Sempere always made a note of every book he sold, with the date and the price, and this one wasn't there.'

'Does his son know?'

'No. I haven't told anybody except you. I'm still trying to understand what happened that afternoon in the bookshop. And why. I thought perhaps you might know . . .'

'I suspect the woman tried to take the book by force, and in the quarrel Señor Sempere suffered a heart attack. That's what happened,' I said. 'And all over a damned book of mine.'

I could feel my stomach churning.

'There's something else,' said Isabella.

'What?'

'A few days later I bumped into Don Anacleto on the stairs and he told me he'd remembered how he knew that woman. He said that at first he couldn't put his finger on it, but now he was sure he'd seen her, many years ago, in the theatre.'

'In the theatre?'

Isabella nodded.

I was silent for a long while. Isabella watched me anxiously.

'Now I'm not happy about leaving you here. I shouldn't have told you.'

'No, you did the right thing. I'm fine. Honestly.'

Isabella shook her head.

'I'm staying with you tonight.'

'What about your reputation?'

'It's your reputation that's in danger. I'll just go to my parents' store to phone the bookshop and let him know.'

'There's no need, Isabella.'

335

'There would be no need if you'd accepted that we live in the twentieth century and had installed a telephone in this mausoleum. I'll be back in a quarter of an hour. No arguments.'

During Isabella's absence, the death of my old friend Sempere began to weigh on my conscience. I recalled how the old bookseller had always told me that books have a soul, the soul of the person who has written them and of those who have read them and dreamed about them. I realised that until the very last moment he had fought to protect me, giving his own life for a bundle of paper and ink on which, he felt, my soul had been inscribed. When Isabella returned, carrying a bag of delicacies from her parents' shop, she only needed to take one look at me.

'You know that woman,' she said. 'The woman who killed Sempere . . .'

'I think so. Irene Sabino.'

'Isn't she the one in the old photographs we found? The actress?'

I nodded.

'Why would she want your book?'

'I don't know.'

Later, after sampling one or two treats from Can Gispert, we sat together in the large armchair in front of the hearth. We were both able to fit in, and Isabella leaned her head on my shoulder while we stared at the flames.

'The other night I dreamed that I had a son,' she said. 'I dreamed that he was calling to me but I couldn't reach him because I was trapped in a place that was very cold and I couldn't move. He kept calling me and I couldn't go to him.'

'It was only a dream.'

'It seemed real.'

'Maybe you should write it as a story,' I suggested.

Isabella shook her head.

'I've been thinking about that. And I've decided that I'd rather live my life than write about it. Please don't take it badly.'

'I think it's a wise decision.'

'What about you? Are you going to live your life?'

'I'm afraid I've already lived quite a lot of it.'

'What about that woman? Cristina?'

I took a deep breath.

'Cristina has left. She's gone back to her husband. Another wise decision.'

Isabella pulled away and frowned at me.

'What?' I asked.

'I think you're mistaken.'

'What about?'

'The other day Gustavo Barceló came by and we talked about you. He told me he'd seen Cristina's husband, what's his name . . .'

'Pedro Vidal.'

'That's the one. And Señor Vidal had told him that Cristina had gone off with you, that he hadn't seen her or heard from her in over a month. As a matter of fact, I was surprised not to find her here, but I didn't dare ask . . .'

'Are you sure that's what Barceló said?'

Isabella nodded.

'Now what have I said?' she asked in alarm.

'Nothing.'

'There's something you're not telling me . . .'

'Cristina isn't here. I haven't seen her since the day Señor Sempere died.'

'Where is she then?'

'I don't know.'

Little by little we grew silent, curled up in the armchair by the fire, and in the small hours Isabella fell asleep. I put my arm round her and closed my eyes, thinking about all the things she had said and trying to find some meaning. When the light of dawn appeared through the windowpanes of the gallery, I opened my eyes and saw that Isabella was already awake.

'Good morning,' I said.

'I've been meditating,' she declared.

'And?'

'I'm thinking about accepting Sempere's proposal.'

'Are you sure?'

'No.' She laughed.

'What will your parents say?'

'They'll be upset, I suppose, but they'll get over it. They would prefer me to marry a prosperous merchant who sold sausages

337

rather than books, but they'll just have to put up with it.'

'It could be worse,' I remarked

Isabella agreed.

'Yes. I could end up with a writer.'

We looked at one another for a long time, until she extracted herself from the armchair. She collected her coat and buttoned it up, her back turned to me.

'I must go,' she said.

'Thanks for the company,' I replied.

'Don't let her escape,' said Isabella. 'Search for her, wherever she may be, and tell her you love her, even if it's a lie. We girls like to hear that kind of thing.'

She turned round and leaned over to brush my lips with hers. Then she squeezed my hand and left without saying goodbye.

5

I spent the rest of that week scouring Barcelona for anyone who might remember having seen Cristina over the last month. I visited the places I'd shared with her and traced Vidal's favourite route through cafés, restaurants and elegant shops, all in vain. I showed everyone I met a photograph from the album Cristina had left in my house and asked whether they had seen her recently. Somewhere, I forget where, I came across a person who recognised her and remembered having seen her with Vidal some time or other. Other people even remembered her name, but nobody had seen her in weeks. On the fourth day, I began to suspect that Cristina had left the tower house that morning after I went to buy the train tickets, and had evaporated off the face of the earth.

Then I remembered that Vidal's family kept a room permanently reserved at the Hotel España, on Calle Sant Pau, behind the Liceo theatre. It was used whenever a member of the family visited the opera and didn't feel like returning to Pedralbes in the early hours. I knew that Vidal and his father had also used it – at least in their golden years – to enjoy the company of young ladies whose presence in their official residences in Pedralbes would have led to undesirable rumours – due either to the low or the high birth of the lady in question. More than once Vidal had offered the room to me when I still lived in Doña Carmen's *pensión* in case, as he put it, I felt like undressing a damsel somewhere that wasn't quite so alarming. I didn't think Cristina would have chosen the hotel room as a refuge – if she knew of its existence, that is – but it was the only place left on my list and nowhere else had occurred to me.

It was getting dark when I arrived at the Hotel España and asked to speak to the manager, presenting myself as Señor Vidal's friend. When I showed him Cristina's photograph, the manager, a gentleman who mistook frostiness for discretion, smiled politely and told me that 'other' members of Vidal's staff had already been there a few weeks earlier, asking after that same person, and he had told them what he was telling me now: he had never seen that lady in the hotel. I thanked him for his icy kindness and walked away in defeat.

As I passed the glass doors that led into the dining room, I thought I registered a familiar profile. The boss was sitting at one of the tables, the only guest there, eating what looked like lumps of sugar. I was about to make a quick getaway when he turned and waved at me, smiling. I cursed my luck and waved back. He signalled for me to join him. I walked through the dining-room door, dragging my feet.

'What a lovely surprise to see you here, dear friend. I was just thinking about you,' said Corelli.

I shook hands with him reluctantly.

'I thought you were out of town,' I said.

'I came back sooner than planned. Would you care for a drink?'

I declined. He asked me to sit down at his table and I obeyed. The boss wore his usual three-piece suit of black wool and a red silk tie. As always, he was impeccably attired, but something didn't quite add up. It took me a few seconds to notice what it was – the angel brooch was not in his lapel. Corelli followed the direction of my gaze.

'Alas, I've lost it, and I don't know where,' he explained.

'I hope it wasn't too valuable.'

'Its value was purely sentimental. But let's talk about more important matters. How are you, my dear friend? I've missed our conversations enormously, despite our occasional disagreements. It's difficult to find a good conversationalist.'

'You overrate me, Señor Corelli.'

'On the contrary.'

A brief silence followed, those bottomless eyes drilling into mine. I told myself that I preferred him when he embarked on his usual banal conversations – when he stopped speaking his face seemed to change and the air thickened around him.

'Are you staying here?' I asked to break the silence.

'No, I'm still in the house by Güell Park. I had arranged to meet a friend here this afternoon, but he seems to be late. The manners of some people are deplorable.'

'There can't be many people who dare to stand you up, Señor Corelli.'

The boss looked me straight in the eye.

'Not many. In fact, the only person I can think of is you.'

The boss took a sugar lump and dropped it into his cup. A second lump followed, and then a third. He tasted the coffee and added four more lumps. Then he picked up yet another and popped it in his mouth.

'I love sugar,' he said.

'So I see.'

'You haven't told me anything about our project, Martín, dear friend,' he cut in. 'Is there a problem?'

I winced.

'It's almost finished,' I said.

The boss's face lit up with a smile I tried to ignore.

'That is wonderful news. When will I be able to see it?'

'In a couple of weeks. I need to do some revisions. Pruning and finishing touches more than anything else.'

'Can we set a date?'

'If you like . . .'

'How about Friday? That's the twenty-third. Will you accept an invitation to dine and celebrate the success of our venture?'

Friday 23 January was exactly two weeks away.

'Fine,' I agreed.

'That's confirmed, then.'

He raised his sugar-filled cup as if he were drinking a toast and downed the contents in one.

'How about you?' he asked casually. 'What brings you here?'

'I was looking for someone.'

'Someone I know?'

'No.'

'And have you found the person?'

'No.'

The boss savoured my silence.

'I get the impression that I'm keeping you here against your will, dear friend.'

'I'm just a little tired, that's all.'

'Then I won't take up any more of your time. Sometimes I forget that although I enjoy your company, perhaps mine is not to your liking.'

I smiled meekly and took the opportunity to stand up. I saw myself reflected in his pupils, a pale doll trapped in a dark well.

'Take care of yourself, Martín. Please.'

'I will.'

I took my leave with a quick nod and headed for the exit. As I walked away I heard him putting another sugar lump in his mouth and crunching it between his teeth.

When I turned into the Ramblas I noticed that the canopies outside the Liceo were lit up and a long row of cars, guarded by a small regiment of chauffeurs in uniform, was waiting by the pavement. The posters announced *Così fan tutte* and I wondered if Vidal had felt like forsaking his castle to go along. I scanned the circle of drivers that had formed on the central pavement and soon spotted Pep among them. I beckoned him over.

'What are you doing here, Señor Martín?'

'Where is she?'

'Señor Vidal is inside, watching the performance.'

'Not "he". "She". Cristina. Señora de Vidal. Where is she?'

Poor Pep swallowed hard.

'I don't know. Nobody knows.'

He told me that Vidal had spent weeks attempting to find her and that his father, the patriarch of the clan, had even hired various members of the police force to try to discover where she was.

'At first, Señor Vidal thought she was with you . . .'

'Hasn't she called, or sent a letter, a telegram . . .?'

'No, Señor Martín. I swear. We're all very worried, and Señor Vidal, well . . . I've never seen him like this in all the years I've known him. This is the first time he's gone out since Señorita Cristina, I mean Señora Cristina . . .'

'Do you remember whether Cristina said something, anything, before she left Villa Helius?'

'Well . . .' said Pep, lowering his voice to a whisper. 'You could hear her arguing with Señor Vidal. She seemed sad to me. She spent a lot of time by herself. She wrote letters and every day she went to the post office in Paseo Reina Elisenda to post them.'

'Did you ever speak to her alone?'

'One day, shortly before she left, Señor Vidal asked me to drive her to the doctor.'

'Was she ill?'

'She couldn't sleep. The doctor prescribed laudanum.'

'Did she say anything to you on the way there?'

Pep hesitated.

'She asked after you, in case I'd heard from you or seen you.'

'Is that all?'

'She just seemed very sad. She started to cry, and when I asked her what was the matter she said she missed her father – Señor Manuel . . .'

I suddenly understood and cursed myself for not having thought of it sooner. Pep looked at me in surprise and asked me why I was smiling.

'Do you know where she is?' he asked.

'I think so,' I murmured.

I thought I could hear a voice calling from the other side of the street and glimpsed a familiar figure in the Liceo foyer. Vidal hadn't even managed to last the first act. Pep turned to attend to his master's call, and before he had time to tell me to hide, I had already disappeared into the night.

6

Even from afar it looked like bad news: the ember of a cigarette in the blue of the night, silhouettes leaning against a dark wall, the spiralling breath of three figures lying in wait by the main door of the tower house. Inspector Víctor Grandes, accompanied by his two guard dogs Marcos and Castelo, led the welcome committee. It wasn't hard to work out that they'd found Alicia Marlasca's body at the bottom of her pool in Sarriá and that my place on their blacklist had gone up a few points. The minute I caught sight of them I stopped and melted into the shadows, observing them for a few seconds to make sure they hadn't noticed me – I was only some fifty metres away. I could distinguish Grandes's profile in the thin light shed by the street lamp on the wall. Retreating into the darkness, I slipped into the first alleyway I could find, disappearing into the mass of passages and arches of the Ribera quarter.

Ten minutes later I reached the main entrance to the Estación de Francia. The ticket offices were closed, but I could still see a few trains lined up by the platforms under the large vault of glass and steel. I checked the timetables. Just as I had feared, there were no departures scheduled until the following day and I couldn't risk returning home and bumping into Grandes and Co. Something told me that on this occasion my visit to police headquarters would include full board, and not even the good offices of the lawyer Señor Valera would get me out of there as easily as the last time.

I decided to spend the night in a cheap hotel opposite the old Stock Exchange, in Plaza Palacio. Legend had it that the building was inhabited by a number of walking cadavers, one-time speculators whose greed and poor arithmetic skills had exploded in their faces. I chose this dump because I imagined that not even the Fates would come looking for me there. I registered under the name of Antonio Miranda and paid for the room in advance. The receptionist, who looked like a mollusc, seemed to be embedded in

343

his cubbyhole, which also served as a towel rack and souvenir shop. He handed me the key, a bar of El Cid soap that stank of bleach and looked as if it had already been used, and informed me that if I wanted female company he could send up a serving girl nicknamed Cock-Eye as soon as she returned from a home visit.

'She'll make you as good as new,' he assured me.

I turned down the offer, claiming the onset of lumbago, and hurried up the stairs wishing him goodnight. The room had the appearance and shape of a sarcophagus. One quick look was enough to persuade me that I should lie on the old bed fully clothed rather than getting under the sheets to fraternise with whatever was growing there. I covered myself with a threadbare blanket I found in the wardrobe – which at least smelled of mothballs – and turned off the light, trying to imagine that I was actually in the sort of suite that someone with a hundred thousand francs in the bank could afford. I barely slept all night.

I left the hotel halfway through the morning and made my way to the station, where I bought a first-class ticket, hoping I'd be able to sleep on the train to make up for the dreadful night I'd spent in that dive. Seeing that there were still twenty minutes to go before the train's departure, I went over to the row of public telephones. I gave the operator the number Ricardo Salvador had given me – that of his downstairs neighbour.

'I'd like to speak to Don Emilio, please.'

'Speaking.'

'My name is David Martín. I'm a friend of Señor Ricardo Salvador. He told me I could call him at this number in an emergency.'

'Let's see . . . Can you wait a moment while we get him?'

I looked at the station clock.

'Yes. I'll wait. Thanks.'

More than three minutes went by before I heard the sound of footsteps and then Ricardo Salvador's voice.

'Martín? Are you all right?'

'Yes.'

'Thank goodness. I read about Roures in the newspaper and was very concerned about you. Where are you?'

'Señor Salvador, I don't have much time now. I need to leave Barcelona.'

'Are you sure you're all right?'

'Yes. Listen: Alicia Marlasca is dead.'

'The widow? Dead?'

A long silence. I thought I could hear Salvador sobbing and cursed myself for having broken the news to him so bluntly.

'Are you still there?'

'Yes . . .'

'I'm calling to warn you. You must be careful. Irene Sabino is alive and she's been following me. There is someone with her. I think it's Jaco.'

'Jaco Corbera?'

'I'm not sure it's him. I think they know I'm on their trail and they're trying to silence all the people I've been speaking to. I think you were right . . .'

'Why would Jaco return now?' Salvador asked. 'It doesn't make sense.'

'I don't know. I have to go now. I just wanted to warn you.'

'Don't worry about me. If that bastard comes to visit me, I'll be ready for him. I've been ready for twenty-five years.'

The stationmaster blew the whistle: the train was about to leave.

'Don't trust anyone. Do you hear me? I'll call you as soon as I get back.'

'Thanks for calling, Martín. Be careful.'

7

The train was beginning to glide past the platform as I took refuge in my compartment and collapsed on the seat. I abandoned myself to the flow of tepid air from the heating and the gentle rocking of the train. We left the city behind us, crossing the forest of factories and chimneys and escaping the shroud of scarlet light that covered it. Slowly the wasteland of railway depots and trains abandoned on

345

sidings dissolved into an endless plain of fields, woodlands, rivers, and hills crowned with large, run-down houses and watchtowers. The occasional covered wagon or hamlet peered through a bank of mist. Small railway stations slipped by; bell towers and farmhouses appeared like mirages in the distance.

At some point in the journey I fell asleep, and when I woke again the landscape had changed dramatically. We were now passing through steep valleys with rocky crags rising between lakes and streams. The train skirted great forests that climbed the soaring mountains. After a while, the tangle of hills and tunnels cut into the rock gave way to a large open valley with never-ending pastures, where herds of wild horses galloped across the snow and small stone villages appeared in the distance. The peaks of the Pyrenees rose up on the other side, their snow-covered slopes set alight by the amber glow of evening. In front of us was a jumble of houses and buildings clustered around a hill. The ticket inspector put his head through the door of my compartment and smiled.

'Next stop, Puigcerdà,' he announced.

The train stopped and let out a blast of steam that inundated the platform. When I got out I was enveloped in a thick mist that smelled of static. Shortly afterwards, I heard the stationmaster's bell and the train set off again. As the coaches filed past, the shape of the station began to emerge around me like an apparition. I was alone on the platform. A fine curtain of snow was falling, and to the west a red sun peeped below the vault of clouds, scattering the snow with tiny bright embers. I went over to the stationmaster's office and knocked on the glass door. He looked up, opened the door and gazed at me distractedly.

'Could you tell me how to find a place called Villa San Antonio?'

He raised an eyebrow.

'The sanatorium?'

'I think so.'

The stationmaster adopted the pensive air of someone trying to work out how best to offer directions to a stranger. Then, with the help of a whole catalogue of gestures and expressions, he came up with the following:

'You have to walk right through the village, past the church square, until you reach the lake. On the other side of the lake there's a long avenue with large houses on either side that leads to Paseo de la Rigolisa. There, on a corner, you'll find a three-storey house surrounded by a garden. That's the sanatorium.'

'And do you know of anywhere I might find accommodation?'

'On the way you'll pass the Hotel del Lago. Tell them Sebas sent you.'

'Thank you.'

'Good luck . . .'

I walked through the lonely streets of the village beneath the falling snow, looking for the outline of the church tower. On the way I passed a few locals, who bobbed their heads and looked at me suspiciously. When I reached the square, two men who were unloading coal from a cart pointed me in the right direction, and a couple of minutes later I found myself walking down a road that bordered a large, frozen lake surrounded by stately-looking mansions with pointed towers. The great expanse of white was studded with small rowing boats trapped in the ice, and around it, like a ribbon, ran a promenade punctuated by benches and trees. I walked over to the edge and gazed at the frozen lake spread out at my feet. The ice must have been almost twenty centimetres thick and in some places it shone like opaque glass, hinting at the current of black water that flowed under its shell.

The Hotel del Lago, a two-storey house painted dark red, stood at the end of the lake. Before continuing on my way, I stopped to book a room for two nights and paid in advance. The receptionist informed me that the hotel was almost empty and I could take my pick of rooms.

'Room 101 has spectacular views of the sunrise over the lake,' he suggested. 'But if you prefer a room facing north I have—'

'You choose,' I cut in, indifferent to the majestic beauty of the landscape.

'Then room 101 it is. In the summer, it's the honeymooners' favourite.'

He handed me the keys of the nuptial suite and informed me of the hours for dinner. I told him I'd return later and asked if Villa San Antonio was far from there. The receptionist adopted the same expression I had seen on the face of the stationmaster, first shaking his head, then giving me a friendly smile.

'It's quite near, about ten minutes' walk. If you take the promenade at the end of this street, you'll see it a short distance away. You can't miss it.'

Ten minutes later I was standing by the gates of a large garden strewn with dead leaves half-buried in the snow. Beyond the garden, Villa San Antonio rose up like a sombre sentinel wrapped in a halo of golden light that radiated from the windows. As I crossed the garden my heart was pounding and my hands perspired despite the bitter cold. I walked up the stairs to the main door. The entrance hall was covered in black and white floor tiles like a chessboard and led to a staircase at the far end. There I saw a young girl in a nurse's uniform holding the hand of a man who was trembling and seemed to be eternally suspended between two steps, as if his whole life had suddenly become trapped in that moment.

'Good afternoon?' said a voice to my right.

Her eyes were black and severe, her features sharp, without a trace of warmth, and she had the serious air of one who has learned not to expect anything but bad news. She must have been in her early fifties, and although she wore the same uniform as the young nurse, everything about her exuded authority and rank.

'Good afternoon. I'm looking for someone called Cristina Sagnier. I have reason to believe she is staying here . . .'

The woman observed me without batting an eyelid.

'Nobody *stays* here, sir. This place is not a hotel or a guest house.'

'I'm sorry. I've just come on a long journey in search of this person . . .'

'Don't apologise,' said the nurse. 'May I ask you if you are family or a close friend?'

'My name is David Martín. Is Cristina Sagnier here? Please . . .'

The nurse's expression softened and there followed the hint of a smile. I took a deep breath.

'I'm Teresa, the sister in charge of night duty. If you'd be so kind as to follow me, Señor Martín, I'll take you to the office of Doctor Sanjuán.'

'How is Señorita Sagnier? Can I see her?'

Another faint and impenetrable smile.

'This way, please.'

The rectangular room had four blue walls but no windows and was lit by two lamps that hung from the ceiling, giving off a metallic light. The only three objects in the room were an empty table and two chairs. It was cold and the air smelled of disinfectant. The nurse had described the room as an office, but after ten minutes of waiting on my own, anchored to one of the chairs, all I could see was a cell. Even though the door was shut I could hear voices, sometimes isolated shouts, on the other side of the wall. I was beginning to lose all notion of how long I'd been there when the door opened and a man came in. He was in his mid-thirties and wore a white coat. His smile was as cold as the air that filled the room. Doctor Sanjuán, I imagined. He walked round the table and sat on the other chair, planting his hands on the desk and observing me with vague curiosity for a few moments.

'I realise you must be tired after your journey but I'd like to know why Señor Pedro Vidal isn't here,' he said at last.

'He wasn't able to come.'

The doctor kept his gaze fixed on me, waiting. His eyes were cold and he seemed like the type of person who listens but does not hear.

'Can I see her?'

'You can't see anyone unless you tell me the truth about why you're here.'

I surrendered. I hadn't travelled a hundred and fifty kilometres just to lie.

'My name is Martín, David Martín. I'm a friend of Cristina Sagnier.'

'Here we call her Señora de Vidal.'

'I don't care what you call her; I want to see her. Now.'

The doctor sighed.

'Are you the writer?'

I stood up impatiently.

'What sort of place is this? Why can't I see her?'

'Sit down, please. I beg you.'

He pointed to the chair and waited for me to sit down again.

'May I ask when was the last time you saw her or spoke to her?'

'Just over a month ago,' I replied. 'Why?'

'Do you know anyone who might have seen or spoken to her since then?'

'No . . . I don't know. What's going on?'

The doctor put his fingertips to his lips, measuring his words.

'Señor Martín, I'm afraid I have bad news.'

I felt a knot in the pit of my stomach.

'What's wrong with her?'

The doctor did not reply, and for the first time I thought I glimpsed the shadow of a doubt in his eyes.

'I don't know,' he said.

We walked along a short corridor flanked by metal doors. Doctor Sanjuán went in front of me, holding a bunch of keys in his hands. As we passed I thought I could hear voices whispering, suppressed laughter and sobs. The room was at the end of the corridor. The doctor opened the door but stopped at the threshold, his expression unreadable.

'Fifteen minutes,' he said.

I went in and heard the doctor shut the door behind me. Before me lay a room with a high ceiling and white walls reflected in a floor of shining tiles. On one side stood a bed – a metallic frame surrounded by a white gauze curtain. It was empty. Large French windows looked out over the snowy garden, trees, and in the distance the outline of the lake. I didn't notice her until I'd taken a few steps into the room.

She was sitting in an armchair by the window, wearing a white nightdress, her hair up in a plait. I went round in front of her and looked straight at her, but her eyes didn't move. I knelt down next to her, but she didn't even blink. I put my hand over hers, but she didn't move a single muscle. Then I noticed the bandages covering her arms, from her wrists to her elbows, and the straps that tied her to the chair. I stroked her cheek, gathering a tear that trickled down her face.

'Cristina,' I whispered.

Her eyes were blank: she seemed completely unaware of my presence. I brought a chair over and sat opposite her.

'It's David,' I murmured.

For a quarter of an hour we remained like that, not speaking, her hand in mine, her eyes lost and my questions unanswered. At some point I heard the door open again and felt someone taking me gently by the arm and pulling me away. It was Doctor Sanjuán. I let myself be led to the corridor without offering any resistance. The doctor shut the door and took me back to his freezing office. I collapsed into a chair, unable to utter a single word.

'Would you like me to leave you alone for a few minutes?' he asked.

I nodded. The doctor left the room, closing the door behind him. I stared at my right hand, which was shaking, and clenched my fist. I hardly felt the cold of that room, or heard the shouts and voices that filtered through the walls. I only knew that I needed some air and had to get out of that place.

8

Doctor Sanjuán found me in the hotel dining room, sitting by the fire next to a plate of food I hadn't touched. There was nobody else there except for a maid who was going round the deserted tables, polishing the cutlery. Outside it had grown dark and the snow was still falling, like a dusting of powdered blue glass. The doctor walked over to my table and smiled at me.

'I thought I'd find you here,' he said. 'All visitors end up in this hotel. It's where I spent my first night in the village when I arrived ten years ago. What room were you given?'

'It's supposed to be the newly-weds' favourite, with views over the lake.'

'Don't you believe it. That's what they say about all the rooms.'

Away from the sanatorium and without his white coat, Doctor Sanjuán looked more relaxed, even friendly.

'I hardly recognised you without your uniform,' I remarked.

'Medicine is like the army. The cowl maketh the monk,' he replied. 'How are you feeling?'

'I'm all right.'

'I see. I missed you earlier, when I went back to the office to look for you.'

'I needed some air.'

'I understand. I was hoping you wouldn't be affected quite so much.'

'Why?'

'Because I need you. Or rather, Cristina needs you.'

I gave a deep sigh.

'You must think I'm a coward,' I said.

The doctor shook his head.

'How long has she been like this?'

'Weeks. Practically since she arrived here. And she's getting steadily worse.'

'Is she aware of where she is?'

'It's hard to tell,' the doctor replied with a shrug.

'What happened to her?'

Doctor Sanjuán exhaled.

'She was found, four weeks ago, not far from here – in the village graveyard, lying on her father's grave. She was delirious and suffering from hypothermia. They brought her to the sanatorium because one of the Civil Guards recognised her from last year, when she spent a few months here, because of her father. A lot of people in the village knew her. We admitted her and she was kept under observation for a night or two. She was dehydrated and had probably not slept in days. Every now and then she regained consciousness, and when she did, she spoke about you. She said you were in great danger. She made me swear I wouldn't call anyone, not even her husband, until she was capable of doing so herself.'

'Even so, why didn't you let Vidal know what had happened?'

'I would have but . . . You'll think this is absurd.'

'What?'

'I was convinced that she was fleeing from something and thought it was my duty to help her.'

'Fleeing from what?'

'I'm not sure,' he said with an ambiguous expression.

'What is it you're not telling me?'

'I'm just a doctor. There are things I don't understand.'

'What things?'

Doctor Sanjuán smiled nervously.

'Cristina thinks that something, or someone, has got inside her and wants to destroy her.'

'Who?'

'I only know that she thinks it has something to do with you, and that it frightens her. That's why I think nobody else can help her. It's also why I didn't let Vidal know, as I ought to have done. Because I knew that sooner or later you would turn up here.'

He looked at me with a strange mixture of pity and despair.

'I'm fond of her too, Señor Martín. The months Cristina spent visiting her father . . . we ended up being good friends. I don't suppose she talked to you about me – there was no reason why she should. It was a very difficult time for her. She confided a lot of things in me, and I in her, things I've never told anyone else. In fact, I even proposed to her. So you see, even the doctors here are slightly nuts. Of course she refused me. I don't know why I'm telling you this.'

'But she'll be all right again, won't she, doctor? She'll recover . . .'

Doctor Sanjuán turned his head towards the fire.

'I hope so,' he replied.

'I want to take her away from here.'

The doctor raised his eyebrows.

'Take her away? Where to?'

'Home.'

'Señor Martín, let me be frank. Aside from the fact that you're not a relative, nor, indeed, the patient's husband – which is a legal requirement – Cristina is in no fit state to go anywhere.'

'She's better off here with you, locked up in a rambling old house, tied to a chair and full of drugs? Don't tell me you've proposed to her again.'

The doctor observed me carefully, ignoring the offence my words had clearly caused him.

'Señor Martín, I'm glad you're here because I believe that together we can help Cristina. I think your presence will allow her to come out of the place into which she has retreated. I believe it, because the only word she has uttered in the last two weeks is your name. Whatever happened to her, I think it had something to do with you.'

The doctor was watching me as if he expected something from me, something that would answer all his questions.

'I thought she had abandoned me,' I began. 'We were about to run away together, leaving everything behind. I had gone out for a moment to buy the train tickets and do an errand. I wasn't away for more than ninety minutes but when I returned home, Cristina had left.'

'Did anything happen before she left? Did you have an argument?'

I bit my lip.

'I wouldn't call it an argument.'

'What would you call it?'

'I caught her looking through some papers relating to my work and I think she was offended by what she must have taken as a lack of trust.'

'Was it something important?'

'No. Just a manuscript, a draft.'

'May I ask what type of manuscript it was?'

I hesitated.

'A fable.'

'For children?'

'Let's say for a family audience.'

'I see.'

'No, I don't think you do. There was no argument. Cristina was slightly annoyed because I wouldn't let her have a look, but that was all. When I left, she was fine, packing a few things. That manuscript is not important.'

The doctor acquiesced, more out of courtesy than conviction.

'Could it be that while you were out someone else visited her?'

'I was the only one who knew she was there.'

'Can you think of any reason why she would have decided to leave the house before you returned?'

'No. Why?'

'It's only a question, Señor Martín. I'm trying to understand what happened between the moment you last saw her and her appearance here.'

'Did she say what, or who, had got inside her?'

'It's just a manner of speaking, Señor Martín. Nothing has got inside Cristina. It's not unusual for patients who have suffered a traumatic experience to feel the presence of dead relatives or imaginary people, or even to disappear into their own minds and close every door to the outside world. It's an emotional response, a form of self-defence against feelings or emotions that seem unacceptable. But you mustn't worry about that now. What matters and what's going to help is that, if there is anyone who is important to her right now, that person is you. From what Cristina confided in me at the time, I know that she loves you, Señor Martín. She loves you as she's never loved anyone else, and certainly as she'll never love me. That's why I'm asking you to help me. Don't let yourself be blinded by fear or resentment. Help me, because we both want the same thing. We both want Cristina to be able to leave this place.'

I felt ashamed.

'I'm sorry if—'

The doctor raised his hand to silence me. Then he stood up and put on his overcoat.

'I'll see you tomorrow,' he said.

'Thank you, doctor.'

'Thank *you*. For coming here.'

The following morning I left the hotel just as the sun was beginning to rise over the frozen lake. A group of children was playing by the shore, throwing stones at the hull of a small boat wedged in the ice. It had stopped snowing and white mountains were visible in the distance. Large clouds paraded across the sky like monumental cities built of mist. I reached Villa San Antonio shortly before nine o'clock. Doctor Sanjuán was waiting for me in the garden with Cristina. They were sitting in the sun and the doctor held Cristina's hand as he spoke to her. She barely glanced at him. When he saw me crossing the garden, he beckoned me over to join them. He had kept a chair for me opposite Cristina. I sat down and looked at her, her eyes on mine without seeing me.

'Cristina, look who's here,' said the doctor.

I took Cristina's hand and moved closer to her.

'Speak to her,' said the doctor.

I nodded, lost in her absent gaze, but could find no words. The doctor stood up and left us alone. I saw him disappear into the sanatorium, but not without first asking a nurse to keep a close eye on us. Ignoring the presence of the nurse, I pulled my chair even closer to Cristina's. I brushed her hair from her forehead and she smiled.

'Do you remember me?' I asked.

I could see my reflection in her eyes, but didn't know whether she could see me or hear my voice.

'The doctor says you'll get better soon and we'll be able to go home. Or wherever you like. I'll leave the tower house and we'll go far away, just as you wanted. A place where nobody will know us and nobody will care who we are or where we're from.'

Her hands were covered with long woollen gloves that masked the bandages on her arms. She had lost weight and there were deep lines on her skin; her lips were cracked and her eyes dull and lifeless. All I could do was smile and stroke her cheek and her forehead, talking non-stop, telling her how much I'd missed her and how I'd looked for her everywhere. We spent a couple of hours like that, until the doctor returned and Cristina was taken indoors. I stayed there, sitting in the garden, not knowing where else to go, until I saw Doctor Sanjuán reappear at the door. He came over and sat down beside me.

'She didn't say a word,' I said. 'I don't think she was even aware that I was here . . .'

'You're wrong, my friend,' he replied. 'This is a long process, but I can assure you that your presence helps her – a lot.'

I accepted the doctor's meagre reassurance and kind-hearted lie.

'We'll try again tomorrow,' he said.

It was only midday.

'And what am I going to do until tomorrow?' I asked him.

'Aren't you a writer? Then write. Write something for her.'

9

I walked round the lake back to the hotel. The receptionist had told me where to find the only bookshop in the village, and I was able to buy some blank sheets of paper and a fountain pen that must have been there since time immemorial. Thus equipped, I locked myself in my room. I moved the table over to the window and asked for a flask of coffee. I spent almost an hour gazing at the lake and the mountains in the distance before writing a single word. I remembered the old photograph Cristina had given me, that image she had never been able to place, of a girl walking along a wooden jetty that stretched out to sea. I imagined myself walking down that pier, my steps following behind her, and slowly the words began to flow and the outline of a story emerged. I knew I was going to write the story that Cristina could never remember, the story that had led her, as a child, to walk over those shimmering waters holding on to a stranger's hand. I would write the tale of a memory that never was, the memory of a stolen life. The images and the light that began to appear between sentences took me back to the old, shadowy Barcelona that had shaped us both. I wrote until the sun had set and there was not a drop of coffee left in the flask, until the frozen lake was lit up by a blue moon and my eyes and hands were aching. I let the pen drop and pushed aside the sheets of paper lying on the table. When the receptionist came to knock on my door to ask if I was coming down for dinner, I didn't hear him. I had fallen fast asleep, for once dreaming and believing that words, even my own, had the power to heal.

Four days passed with the same rhythm. I rose at dawn and went out onto the balcony to watch the sun tint with scarlet the lake at my feet. I would arrive at the sanatorium around half past eight in the morning and usually found Doctor Sanjuán sitting on the entrance steps, gazing at the garden with a steaming cup of coffee in his hands.

'Do you never sleep, doctor?' I would ask.

'No more than you,' he replied.

Around nine o'clock the doctor would take me to Cristina's room and open the door, then leave us. I always found her sitting in the same armchair facing the window. I would bring over a chair and take her hand. She was barely aware of my presence. Then I would read out the pages I'd written for her the night before. Every day I started again from the beginning. Sometimes, when I interrupted my reading and looked at her, I would be surprised to discover the hint of a smile on her lips. I spent the day with her until the doctor returned in the evening and asked me to leave. Then I would trudge back to the hotel through the snow, eat some dinner and go up to my room to continue writing until I was overcome by exhaustion. The days ceased to have a name.

When I went into Cristina's room on the fifth day, as I did every morning, the armchair in which she was usually waiting for me was empty. I looked around anxiously and found her on the floor, curled up into a ball in a corner, clasping her knees, her face covered with tears. When she saw me she smiled, and I realised that she had recognised me. I knelt down next to her and hugged her. I don't remember ever having been as happy as I was during those miserable seconds when I felt her breath on my face and saw that a glimmer of light had returned to her eyes.

'Where have you been?' she asked.

That afternoon Doctor Sanjuán gave me permission to take her out for an hour. We walked down to the lake and sat on a bench. She started to tell me a dream she'd had, about a child who lived in the dark maze of a town in which the streets and buildings were alive and fed on the souls of its inhabitants. In her dream, as in the story I had been reading to her, the girl managed to escape and came to a jetty that stretched out over an endless sea. She was holding the hand of the faceless stranger with no name who had saved her and who now went with her to the very end of the wooden platform, where someone was waiting for her, someone she would never see, because her dream, like the story I had been reading to her, was unfinished.

Cristina had a vague recollection of Villa San Antonio and Doctor Sanjuán. She blushed when she told me she thought he'd proposed to her a week ago. Time and space seemed to be confused in her mind. Sometimes she thought that her father had been admitted to one of the rooms and she'd come to visit him. A moment later she couldn't remember how she'd got there and at times she ceased to care. She remembered that I'd gone out to buy the train tickets and referred to the morning in which she had disappeared as if it were just the previous day. Sometimes she confused me with Vidal and asked me to forgive her. At others, fear cast a shadow over her face and she began to tremble.

'He's getting closer,' she would say. 'I have to go. Before he sees you.'

Then she would sink into a deep silence, unaware of my presence, unaware of the world itself, as if something had dragged her to some remote and inaccessible place.

After a few days, the certainty that Cristina had lost her mind began to affect me deeply. My initial hope became tinged with bitterness, and on occasions, when I returned at night to my hotel cell, I felt that old pit of darkness and hatred, which I had thought forgotten, opening up inside me. Doctor Sanjuán, who watched over me with the same care and tenacity with which he treated his patients, had warned me that this would happen.

'Don't give up hope, my friend,' he would say. 'We're making great progress. Have faith.'

I nodded meekly and returned day after day to the sanatorium to take Cristina out for a stroll as far as the lake and listen to the dreamed memories she'd already described dozens of times but which she discovered anew every day. Each day she would ask me where I'd been, why I hadn't come back to fetch her, and why I'd left her alone. Each day she looked at me from her invisible cage and asked me to hold her tight. Each day, when I said goodbye to her, she asked me if I loved her and I always gave her the same reply.

'I'll always love you,' I would say. 'Always.'

One night I was woken by the sound of someone knocking on my door. It was three in the morning. I stumbled over, in a daze, and found one of the nurses from the sanatorium standing in the doorway.

'Doctor Sanjuán has asked me to come and fetch you.'

'What's happened?'

Ten minutes later I was walking through the gates of Villa San Antonio. The screams could be heard from the garden. Cristina had apparently locked the door of her room from the inside. Doctor Sanjuán, who looked as if he hadn't slept for a week, and two male nurses were trying to force the door open. Inside, Cristina could be heard shouting and banging on the walls, knocking down furniture as if she were destroying everything she could find.

'Who is in there with her?' I asked, petrified.

'Nobody,' replied the doctor.

'But she's speaking to someone . . .' I protested.

'She's alone.'

An orderly rushed up, carrying a large crowbar.

'It's the only thing I could find,' he said.

The doctor nodded and the orderly levered the crowbar between the door and the frame.

'How was she able to lock herself in?' I asked.

'I don't know . . .'

For the first time I thought I saw fear in the doctor's face, and he avoided my eyes. The porter was about to force the door when suddenly there was silence on the other side.

'Cristina?' called the doctor.

There was no reply. The door finally gave way and flew open with a bang. I followed the doctor into the room. It was dark. The window was open and an icy wind was blowing. The chairs, tables and armchair had been knocked over and the walls were stained with an irregular line of what looked like black ink. It was blood. There was no trace of Cristina.

The male nurses ran out to the balcony and scanned the garden for footprints in the snow. The doctor looked right and left, searching for Cristina. Then we heard laughter coming from the bathroom. I went to the door and opened it. The floor was scattered with bits of glass. Cristina was sitting on the tiles, leaning against the metal bathtub like a broken doll. Her hands and feet were bleeding, covered in cuts and splinters of glass, and her blood still trickled down the cracks in the mirror she had destroyed with her fists. I put my arms around her and searched her eyes. She smiled.

'I didn't let him in,' she said.

'Who?'

'He wanted me to forget, but I didn't let him in,' she repeated.

The doctor knelt down beside me and examined the wounds covering Cristina's body.

'Please,' he murmured, pushing me aside. 'Not now.'

One of the male nurses had rushed to fetch a stretcher. I helped him lift Cristina onto it and held her hand as they wheeled her to a treatment room. There, Doctor Sanjuán injected her with a sedative and in a matter of seconds her consciousness stole away. I stayed by her side, looking into her eyes until they became empty mirrors and one of the nurses led me gently from the room. I stood there, in the middle of a dark corridor that smelled of disinfectant, my hands and clothes stained with blood. I leaned against the wall and then slid to the floor.

Cristina woke up the following morning to find herself lying on a bed, bound with leather straps, locked up in a windowless room with no other light than the pale glow from a bulb on the ceiling. I had spent the night in a corner, sitting on a chair, observing her, with no notion of time passing. Suddenly she opened her eyes, and grimaced at the stabbing pain from the wounds that covered her arms.

'David?' she called out.

'I'm here,' I replied.

When I reached the bed I leaned over so that she could see my face and the anaemic smile I'd rehearsed for her.

'I can't move.'

'They've strapped you down. It's for your own good. As soon as the doctor comes he'll take them off.'

'You take them off.'

'I can't. It must be the doctor—'

'Please,' she begged.

'Cristina, it's better—'

'Please.'

I saw pain and fear in her eyes, but above all a lucidity and a presence that had not been there in all the days I had visited her in that place. She was herself again. I untied the first two straps, which crossed over her shoulders and waist, and stroked her face. She was shaking.

'Are you cold?'

She shook her head.

'Do you want me to call the doctor?'

She shook her head again.

'David, look at me.'

I sat on the edge of the bed and met her gaze.

'You must destroy it,' she said.

'I don't understand.'

'You must destroy it.'

'What must I destroy?'

'The book.'

'Cristina, I'd better call the doctor—'

'No. Listen to me.'

She grabbed my hand.

'The morning you went to buy the tickets, do you remember? I went up to your study again and opened the trunk.'

I took a breath.

'I found the manuscript and began to read it.'

'It's just a fable, Cristina . . .'

'Don't lie to me. I've read it, David. At least enough to know that I had to destroy it . . .'

'You don't need to worry about that now. I told you: I've abandoned the manuscript.'

'But it hasn't abandoned you. I tried to burn it . . .'

For a moment I let go of her hand when I heard those words, repressing the surge of anger I felt when I remembered the burned matches I'd found on the floor of the study.

'You tried to burn it?'

'But I couldn't,' she muttered. 'There was someone else in the house.'

'There was no one in the house, Cristina. Nobody.'

'As soon as I lit the match and held it close to the manuscript, I sensed him behind me. I felt a blow to the back of my neck and then I fell.'

'Who hit you?'

'It was all very dark, as if the daylight had suddenly vanished. I turned round but could only see his eyes. Like the eyes of a wolf.'

'Cristina . . .'

'He took the manuscript from my hands and put it back in the trunk.'

'Cristina, you're not well. Let me call the doctor . . .'

'You're not listening to me.'

I smiled at her and kissed her on the forehead.

'Of course I'm listening to you. But there was no one else in the house.'

She closed her eyes and tilted her head, moaning as if my words were like daggers cutting her inside.

'I'm going to call the doctor.'

I bent over to kiss her again and then stood up. I went towards the door, feeling her eyes on my back.

'Coward,' she said.

When I came back to the room with Doctor Sanjuán, Cristina had undone the last strap and was staggering round the room towards the door, leaving bloody footprints on the white tiles. We laid her back on the bed and held her down. Cristina shouted and fought with such anger it made my blood freeze. The noise alerted the other staff. An orderly helped us restrain her while the doctor tied the straps. Once she was immobilised, the doctor looked at me severely.

'I'm going to sedate her again. Stay here and this time don't even think of untying her straps.'

I was left alone with her for a moment but could not calm her. Cristina went on fighting to escape. I held her face and tried to catch her eye.

'Cristina, please—'

She spat at me.

'Go away.'

The doctor returned with a nurse who carried a metal tray with a syringe, dressings, and a glass bottle containing a yellowish solution.

'Leave the room,' he ordered.

I went to the doorway. The nurse held Cristina against the bed and the doctor injected the sedative into her arm. Cristina's shrieks pierced the room. I covered my ears and went out into the corridor.

Coward, I told myself. Coward.

10

Beyond Villa San Antonio, a tree-lined path led out of the village, following an irrigation channel. The framed map in the hotel dining room bestowed on it the sugary name of Lovers' Lane. That afternoon, after leaving the sanatorium, I ventured down the gloomy path, which was more suggestive of loneliness than romance. I walked for about half an hour without meeting a soul, leaving the village behind, until the sharp outline of Villa San Antonio and the large rambling houses that surrounded the lake were small cardboard cut-outs on the horizon. I sat on one of the benches dotted along the path and watched the sun setting at the other end of the Cerdanya valley. Some two hundred metres from where I sat, I could see the silhouette of a small, isolated country chapel in the middle of a snow-covered field. Without quite knowing why, I got up and made my way towards it. When I was about a dozen metres away, I noticed that the chapel had no door. The stone walls had been blackened by the flames that had devoured the building. I climbed the steps to what had once been the entrance and went in. The remains of burned pews and loose pieces of timber that had fallen from the ceiling were scattered among the ashes. Weeds had crept into the building and grown up around the former altar. The fading light shone through the narrow stone windows. I sat on what remained of a pew in front of the altar and heard the wind whispering through the cracks in the burned-out vault. I looked up and wished I had even a breath of the faith my old friend Sempere had possessed – his faith in God or in books – with which I could pray to God, or to hell, to give me another chance and let me take Cristina away from that place.

'Please,' I murmured, fighting back the tears.

I smiled bitterly, a defeated man pitifully begging a God in whom he had never trusted. I looked around at that holy site filled with nothing but ruins and ashes, emptiness and loneliness, and knew that I would go back to fetch her that very night, with no more miracle or blessing than my own determination to tear her away from the clutches of that faint-hearted, infatuated doctor who had decided to turn her into his own sleeping beauty. I would set fire to the sanatorium rather than allow anyone to touch her again. I would take her home and die by her side. Hatred and anger would light my way.

I left the old chapel at nightfall and crossed the silvery field, which glowed in the moonlight, returning to the tree-lined path. In the dark, I followed the trail of the irrigation channel until I glimpsed the lights of Villa San Antonio in the distance and the citadel of towers and attic windows surrounding the lake. When I reached the sanatorium I didn't bother to ring the bell next to the wrought-iron gates. After jumping over the wall, I crept across the garden, then went round the building to one of the back entrances. It was locked from the inside but I didn't hesitate for a moment before smashing the glass with my elbow and grabbing hold of the door handle. I went down the corridor, listening to the voices and whisperings, catching the aroma of broth that rose from the kitchen, until I reached the room at the end where the good doctor had imprisoned Cristina, his fantasy princess, lying forever in a limbo of drugs and straps.

I had expected to find the door locked, but the handle yielded beneath my hand. I pushed the door open and went into the room. The first thing I noticed was that I could see my own breath floating in front of my face. The second thing was that the white-tiled floor was stained with bloody footprints. The large window that overlooked the garden was open and the curtains fluttered in the wind. The bed was empty. I drew closer and picked up one of the leather straps with which the doctor and the orderly had tied Cristina down. They had all been cleanly cut, as if they were made of paper. I went out into the garden and saw a trail of red footprints across the snow. I followed it to the stone wall surrounding the grounds on which I found yet more blood. I climbed up and jumped over to the other side. The erratic footprints led off towards the village. I remember that I began to run.

I followed the tracks as far as the park that bordered the lake. A full moon burned over the large sheet of ice. That is when I saw her. She was limping over the frozen lake, a line of bloodstained footprints behind her, the nightdress covering her body trembling in the breeze. By the time I reached the shore, Cristina had walked about thirty metres towards the centre of the lake. I shouted her name and she stopped. Slowly she turned and I saw her smile as a cobweb of cracks began to weave itself beneath her feet. I jumped onto the ice, feeling the frozen surface buckle, and ran towards her. Cristina stood still, looking at me. The cracks under her feet were expanding into a mesh of black veins. The ice was giving way and I fell flat on my face.

'I love you,' I heard her say.

I crawled towards her, but the web of cracks was growing and now encircled her. Barely a few metres separated us when I heard the ice finally break. Black jaws snapped open and swallowed her up into a pool of tar. As soon as she disappeared under the surface, the plates of ice began to join up, sealing the opening through which Cristina had plunged.

Caught by the current, her body slid a couple of metres towards me under the ice. I managed to pull myself to the place where she had become trapped and I pounded the ice frantically. Cristina, her eyes open and her hair streaming out around her, watched me from the other side of the translucent sheet. I hammered at the ice until I'd shattered my hands, but in vain. Cristina never let her eyes stray from mine. She placed her hand on the ice and smiled. The last bubbles of air were escaping from her lips and her pupils dilated for the last time. A second later, she began to sink forever into the blackness.

11

I didn't return to my room to collect my things. From where I was hiding among the trees by the lake, I saw the doctor and a couple of Civil Guards approach the hotel then spied them talking to the receptionist through the French windows. I crossed the village, stealing through the deserted streets, until I came to the station, which was buried in fog. Two gas lamps helped me distinguish the shape of a train waiting at the platform, its dark metal skeleton reflecting the red light of the stop signal at the end of the station. The locomotive had been shut down and tears of ice hung from its rails and levers. The carriages were in darkness, the windows veiled with frost. No light shone from the stationmaster's office. The train was not scheduled to leave for several hours, and the station was empty.

I went over to one of the carriages and tried the door but it was bolted shut. I stepped down onto the track and walked round the train. Under cover of darkness I climbed onto the platform linking the guard's van to the rear coach and tried my luck with the connecting door. It was open. I slipped into the coach and stumbled through the gloom until I reached one of the compartments. I went in and bolted the door. Trembling with cold, I collapsed onto the seat. I didn't dare close my eyes, fearing I would see Cristina's face again, looking at me from beneath the ice. Minutes went by, perhaps hours. At some point I asked myself why I was hiding and why I couldn't feel anything.

I cocooned myself in that void and waited, squirrelled away like a fugitive, listening to a thousand groans of metal and wood as they contracted in the cold. I scanned the shadows beyond the windows until finally the beam of a lamp glanced across the walls of the coach and I heard voices on the platform. I cleared a spyhole with my fingers through the film of mist that coated the windowpane and saw the engine driver and a couple of railway workers making their way towards the front of the train. Some ten metres away, the stationmaster was talking to the two Civil Guards I'd seen with the doctor earlier. I saw him nod and extract a bunch of keys, then he walked towards the train followed by the two Guards. I pulled back from the window. A few seconds later I heard the click of the carriage door as it opened, then footsteps approaching. I unbolted the door, leaving the compartment open, and lay down on the floor under one of the rows of seats, pressing my body against the wall. I heard the Civil Guards drawing closer and saw the beam from their torches drawing needles of blue light through the compartment window. When the steps stopped by my compartment I held my breath. The voices subsided. I heard the door being opened and a pair of boots passed within centimetres of my face. The guard remained there for a few seconds, then left and closed the door.

I stayed where I was, motionless, as he moved away down the carriage. A couple of minutes later I heard a rattling and warm air breathed out through the radiator grille by my face. An hour later the first light of dawn crept slowly through the windows. I came out from my hiding place and looked outside. Travellers walked alone or in couples up the platform, dragging their suitcases and bundles. The rumble of the locomotive could be felt through the walls and floor of the coach. After a few minutes the travellers began to climb into the train and the ticket collector turned on the lights. I sat on the seat by the window and acknowledged some of the passengers who walked by my compartment. When the large clock in the station struck eight, the train began to move. Only then did I close my eyes and hear the church bells ringing in the distance, like the echo of a curse.

The return journey was plagued by delays. Some overhead power cables had fallen and we didn't reach Barcelona until the afternoon of that Friday, 23 January. The city was buried under a crimson sky across which stretched a web of black smoke. It was hot, as if winter had suddenly departed, and a dirty, damp smell rose from the sewers. When I opened the front door of the tower house I found a white envelope on the ground. I recognised the wax seal and didn't bother to pick it up because I knew exactly what it contained: a reminder of my meeting with the boss that very evening in his rambling old house by Güell Park, at which I was to hand over the manuscript. I climbed the stairs and opened the main door of the apartment. Without turning on the light I went straight up to the study, where I walked over to one of the windows and stared back at the room touched by the flames of that infernal sky. I imagined her there, just as she had described, kneeling by the trunk. Opening it and pulling out the folder with the manuscript. Reading those accursed pages with the certainty that she must destroy them. Lighting the matches and drawing the flame to the paper.

There was someone else in the house.

I went over to the trunk but stopped a few paces from it, as if I were standing behind her, spying on her. I leaned forward and opened it. The manuscript was still there, waiting for me. I stretched out my hand to touch the folder gently with my fingertips. Then I saw it. The silver shape shone at the bottom of the trunk like a pearl at the bottom of a lake. I picked it up between two fingers and examined it. The angel brooch.

'Son-of-a-bitch,' I heard myself say.

I pulled the box containing my father's old revolver from the back of the wardrobe and opened the cylinder to make sure it was loaded. I put the remaining contents of the ammunition box in the left pocket of my coat, then wrapped the weapon in a cloth and put in into my right-hand pocket. Before leaving I stopped for a moment to gaze at the stranger who looked at me from the mirror in the entrance hall. I smiled, a calm hatred burning in my veins, and went out into the night.

12

Andreas Corelli's house stood out on the hillside against the blanket of dark red clouds. Behind me, the forest of shadows of Güell Park gently swayed. A breeze stirred the branches, making the leaves hiss like snakes. I stopped by the entrance and looked up at the house. There was not a single light on in the whole building and the shutters on the French windows were closed. I could hear the panting of the dogs that prowled behind the walls of the park, following my scent. I pulled the revolver out of my pocket and turned back towards the park gates, where I could make out the shape of animals, liquid shadows watching me from the blackness.

I walked up to the main door of the house and gave three dry raps with the knocker. I didn't wait for a reply. I would have blown it open with a shot, but it wasn't necessary: the door was already open. I turned the bronze handle, releasing the bolt, and the oak door slowly swung inwards under its own weight. The long passage opened up before me, a sheet of dust covering the floor like fine sand. I took a few steps towards the staircase that rose up on one side of the entrance hall, disappearing in a spiral of shadows. Then I walked along the corridor that led to the sitting room. Dozens of eyes followed me from the gallery of old photographs covering the wall. The only sounds I could hear were my own footsteps and breathing. I reached the end of the corridor and stopped. The strange, reddish glow of the night filtered through the shutters in narrow blades of light. I raised the revolver and stepped into the sitting room, my eyes adjusting to the dark. The pieces of furniture were in the same places as before, but even in that faint light I noticed that they looked old and were covered in dust. Ruins. The curtains were frayed and the paint on the walls was peeling off in strips. I went over to one of the French windows to open the shutters and let in some light, but just before I reached it I realised I was not alone. I froze and then turned around slowly.

His silhouette, sitting in the usual armchair in the corner of the room, was unmistakable. The light that bled in through the shutters revealed his shiny shoes and the outline of his suit. His face was buried in shadows, but I knew he was looking at me. And I knew he was smiling. I raised the revolver and pointed it at him.

'I know what you've done,' I said.

Corelli didn't move a muscle. His figure remained motionless, like a spider waiting to jump. I took a step forward, pointing the gun at his face. I thought I heard a sigh in the dark and, for a moment, the reddish light caught his eyes and I was certain he was going to pounce on me. I fired. The weapon's recoil hit my forearm like the blow of a hammer. A cloud of blue smoke rose from the gun. One of Corelli's hands fell from the arm of the chair and swung, his fingernails grazing the floor. I fired again. The bullet hit him in the chest and opened a smoking hole in his clothes. I was left holding the revolver with both hands, not daring to take a single step, transfixed in front of the motionless shape in the armchair. The swaying of his arm gradually came to a halt and the body was still, his nails, long and polished, scraping the oak floor. There was no sound at all, no hint of movement, from the body that had just received two bullet wounds – one in the face, the other in the chest. I moved back a few steps towards the French window and kicked it open, not taking my eyes off the armchair where Corelli lay. A column of hazy light cut a passageway through the room from the balustrade outside to the corner, revealing the face and body of the boss. I tried to swallow, but my mouth was dry. The first shot had ripped open a hole between his eyes. The second had pierced his lapel. Yet there was not a single drop of blood. In its place a fine, shiny dust spilled out down his clothes, like sand slipping through an hourglass. His eyes shone and his lips were frozen in a sarcastic smile. It was a dummy.

I lowered the revolver, my hands still shaking, and edged closer. I bent over the grotesque puppet and tentatively stretched my hand towards its face. For a moment I feared that those glass eyes would suddenly move or those hands with long fingernails would hurl themselves round my neck. I touched the cheek with my fingertips. Enamelled wood. I couldn't help but let out a bitter laugh – one wouldn't expect anything less from the boss. Once again I confronted that mocking grin and I hit the puppet so hard with the gun that it collapsed to the ground and I started kicking it. The wooden frame began to lose its shape until arms and legs were twisted together in an impossible position. I moved back a few steps and looked around me. The large canvas with the figure of the angel was still on the wall: I tore it down with one great tug. Behind the picture was the door that led into the basement – I remembered it from the night I'd fallen asleep there. I tried the handle. It was open. I looked down the staircase, which led into a well of darkness, then went back to the sitting room, to the chest of drawers from which I'd seen Corelli take the hundred thousand francs during our first meeting in that house. In one of the drawers I found a tin with candles and matches. For a moment I wavered, wondering whether the boss had also left those things there on purpose, hoping I would find them just as I had found the dummy. I lit one of the candles and crossed the sitting room to the door. I glanced at the fallen doll one last time and, holding the candle up high, my right hand firmly gripping the revolver, I prepared to go down.

I descended step by step, stopping each time to look back over my shoulder. When I reached the basement I held the candle as far away from me as I could and moved it around in a semicircle. Everything was still there: the operating table, the gas lamps and the tray with surgical instruments. Everything covered with a patina of dust and cobwebs. But there was something else. Other dummies could be seen leaning against the wall, as immobile as the puppet of the boss. I left the candle on the operating table and walked over to the inert bodies. Among them, I recognised the butler who had served us that night and the chauffeur who had driven me home after my dinner with Corelli in the garden. There were other figures I was unable to identify. One of them was turned against the wall, its face hidden. I poked it with the end of the gun, making it spin round, and a second later found myself staring at my own image. I felt a shiver down my spine. The doll that looked like me had only half a face.

The other half was unfinished. I was about to crush it with my foot when I heard a child's laughter coming from the top of the steps.

I held my breath. Then came a few dry, clicking sounds. I ran back up the stairs, and when I reached the sitting room the figure of the boss was no longer where I'd left it. Footprints trailed off towards the corridor that led to the exit. I cocked the gun and followed the tracks, pausing at the entrance to the corridor. The footprints stopped halfway down. I searched for the hidden shape of the boss among the shadows, but saw no sign of him. At the end, the main door was still open. I advanced cautiously towards the point where the trail ran out. It took me a few seconds to notice that the gap I remembered between the portraits on the wall was no longer there. Instead there was a new frame, and in that frame, in a photograph that looked as if it had been taken with the same camera as the rest of the macabre collection, I saw Cristina dressed in white, her gaze lost in the eye of the lens. She was not alone. Two arms enveloped her, holding her up. Their owner smiled for the camera: Andreas Corelli.

13

I set off down the hill towards the tangle of dark streets that formed the Gracia district. There I found a café in which a large group of locals had assembled and were angrily discussing politics or football – it was hard to tell which. I dodged in and out of the crowd, through a cloud of smoke and noise, until I reached the bar. The bartender gave me a vaguely hostile look with which I imagined he received all strangers – anyone living more than a couple of streets beyond his establishment, that is.

'I need to use a phone,' I said.

'The telephone is for customers only.'

'Then get me a brandy. And the telephone.'

The bartender picked up a glass and pointed towards a corridor on the other side of the room with a notice above it saying TOILETS.

At the end of the passage, opposite the entrance to the toilets, I found what was trying to pass for a telephone booth, exposed to the intense stench of ammonia and the noise that filtered through from the café. I took the receiver off the hook and waited until I had a line. A few seconds later an operator from the exchange replied.

'I need to make a call to a law firm. The name of the lawyer is Valera, number 442, Avenida Diagonal.'

The operator took a couple of minutes to find the number and connect me. I waited, holding the receiver with one hand and blocking my left ear with the other. Finally she confirmed that she was putting my call through and moments later I recognised the voice of Valera's secretary.

'I'm sorry, but Señor Valera isn't here right now.'

'It's important. Tell him my name is Martín. David Martín. It's a matter of life and death.'

'I know who you are, Señor Martín. I'm sorry, but I can't put you through because he's not here. It's half past nine at night and he left the office a long time ago.'

'Then give me his home address.'

'I cannot give you that information, Señor Martín. I do apologise. If you wish, you can phone tomorrow morning and—'

I hung up and again waited for a line. This time I gave the operator the number Ricardo Salvador had given me. His neighbour answered the phone and told me he would go up to see whether the ex-policeman was in. Salvador was soon on the line.

'Martín? Are you all right? Are you in Barcelona?'

'I've just arrived.'

'You must be careful. The police are looking for you. They came round here asking questions about you and Alicia Marlasca.'

'Víctor Grandes?'

'I think so. He came with a couple of big guys I didn't like the look of. I think he wants to dump the deaths of Roures and Marlasca's widow on you. You'd better keep your eyes peeled – they're probably watching you. If you like, you could come here.'

'Thanks, Señor Salvador. I'll think about it. I don't want to get you into any more trouble.'

'Whatever you do, watch out. I think you were right: Jaco is back. I don't know why, but he's back. Do you have a plan?'

'I'm going to try to find Valera, the lawyer. I think the publisher for whom Marlasca worked is at the heart of all this, and I think Valera is the only person who knows the truth.'

Salvador paused for a moment.

'Do you want me to come with you?'

'I don't think that will be necessary. I'll call you once I've spoken to Valera.'

'As you wish. Are you armed?'

'Yes.'

'I'm glad to hear that.'

'Señor Salvador . . . Roures spoke to me about a woman in the Somorrostro area whom Marlasca had consulted. Someone he had met through Irene Sabino.'

'The Witch of Somorrostro.'

'What do you know about her?'

'There isn't much to know. I don't think she even exists, the same as this mysterious publisher. What you need to worry about is Jaco and the police.'

'I'll bear that in mind.'

'Call me as soon as you know anything, will you?'

'I will. Thanks.'

I hung up and as I passed the bar I left a few coins to cover the calls and the glass of brandy, which was still there, untouched.

Twenty minutes later I was standing outside number 442, Avenida Diagonal, looking up at the lights that were on in Valera's office, at the top of the building. The porter's lodge was closed, but I banged on the door until the porter peered out and came over with a distinctly unfriendly expression on his face. As soon as he'd opened the door a little to get rid of me, I gave it a push and slipped into the hallway, ignoring his protests. I went straight to the lift. The porter tried to stop me by grabbing hold of my arm, but I threw him a poisonous look that quickly dissuaded him.

When Valera's secretary opened the door, her expression rapidly changed from surprise to fear, especially when I stuck my foot in the gap to make sure she didn't slam the door in my face and went in without being invited.

'Let the lawyer know I'm here,' I said. 'Now.'

The secretary looked at me, her face completely white.

I took her by the elbow and pushed her into the lawyer's office. The lights were on, but there was no trace of Valera. The terrified secretary sobbed, and I realised that I was digging my fingers into her arm. I let go and she retreated a few steps. She was shaking. I sighed and tried to make some sort of calming gesture that only served to reveal the gun tucked into the waistband of my trousers.

'Please, Señor Martín . . . I swear that Señor Valera isn't here.'

'I believe you. Calm down. I only want to talk to him. That's all.'

The secretary nodded. I smiled at her.

'Please be so kind as to pick up the telephone and call him at home,' I said firmly.

The secretary lifted the receiver and murmured the lawyer's number to the operator. When she got a reply she handed me the phone.

'Good evening,' I ventured.

'Martín, what an unfortunate surprise,' said Valera at the other end of the line. 'May I know what you're doing in my office at this time of night, aside from terrorising my employees?'

'My apologies for any trouble I may be causing, Señor Valera, but I urgently need to locate your client, Señor Andreas Corelli, and you're the only person who can help me.'

A long silence.

'I'm afraid you're mistaken, Señor Martín. I cannot help you.'

'I was hoping to resolve this amicably, Señor Valera.'

'You don't understand, Martín. I don't know Señor Corelli.'

'Excuse me?'

'I've never seen him or spoken to him, and I certainly don't know where to find him.'

'Let me remind you that he hired you to get me out of police headquarters.'

'A couple of weeks before that, we received a cheque with a letter explaining that you were an associate of his, that Inspector Grandes was harassing you and that we should take care of your defence if it became necessary to do so. With the letter came the envelope that he asked us to hand to you personally. All I did was pay in the cheque and ask my contact at police headquarters to let me know if you were ever taken there. That's what happened, and you'll remember that I got you out by threatening Grandes with a whole storm of trouble if he didn't agree to expedite your release. I don't think you can complain about our services.'

At that point the silence was mine.

'If you don't believe me, ask Señorita Margarita to show you the letter,' Valera added.

'What about your father?' I asked.

'My father?'

'Your father and Marlasca had dealings with Corelli. He must have known something . . .'

'I can assure you that my father was never directly in touch with this Señor Corelli. All his correspondence, if indeed there was any – because there is absolutely nothing in the files at the office – was dealt with personally by the deceased Señor Marlasca. In fact, and since you ask, I can tell you that my father even doubted the existence of this Señor Corelli, especially during the final months of Señor Marlasca's life, when he began to – how shall I say it – have contact with that woman.'

'What woman?'

'The chorus girl.'

'Irene Sabino?'

I heard him give an irritated sigh.

'Before he died, Señor Marlasca arranged a fund, administered and managed by our firm, from which a series of payments were to be made to an account in the names of Juan Corbera and María Antonia Sanahuja.'

Jaco and Irene Sabino, I thought.

'What was the size of the fund?'

'It was a deposit in foreign currency. I seem to remember it was something like a hundred thousand French francs.'

'Did Marlasca say where he'd obtained that money?'

'We're a law firm, not a detective agency. Our company merely followed the instructions stipulated in Señor Marlasca's last wishes, we did not question them.'

'What other instructions did he leave?'

'Nothing special. Simple payments to third parties that had nothing to do with the office or with his family.'

'Do you remember any one in particular?'

'My father took charge of these matters himself, to avoid any of the office employees having access to information that might be, let us say, awkward.'

'And didn't your father find it odd that his ex-partner should wish to hand over that sum of money to strangers?'

'Of course he thought it was odd. A lot of things seemed odd to him.'

'Do you remember where those payments were sent?'

'How could I possibly remember? It must have been twenty-five years ago.'

'Make an effort,' I said. 'For Señorita Margarita's sake.'

The secretary gave me a terrified look, to which I responded with a wink.

'Don't you dare lay a finger on her,' Valera threatened.

'Don't give me ideas,' I cut in. 'How's your memory? Is it refreshed?'

'I could have a look at my father's private diaries.'

'Where are they?'

'Here, among his papers. But it will take a few hours . . .'

I put down the phone and looked at Valera's secretary, who had burst into tears. I offered her a handkerchief and gave her a pat on the shoulder.

'Come on now, don't get all worked up. I'm leaving. See? I only wanted to talk to him.'

She nodded with a look of terror on her face, her eyes fixed on the revolver. I buttoned up my coat and smiled.

'One last thing.'

She looked up, fearing the worst.

'Write down the lawyer's address for me. And don't try to trick me, because if you lie I'll come back and you can be quite sure that I'll leave all my inherent good nature downstairs in the porter's lodge.'

Before I left I asked Margarita to show me where the telephone cable was and I cut it, saving her from the temptation of warning Valera that I was on my way, or of calling the police to inform them about our small disagreement.

14

Señor Valera lived in a palatial building, situated on the corner of Calle Girona and Calle Ausiàs March, that seemed to have pretensions to being a Norman castle. I imagined he must have inherited the monstrosity from his father, together with the firm, and that every stone in its structure derived from the blood and sweat of entire generations of Barcelona's inhabitants who could never have dreamed of even entering such a palace. I told the porter I was delivering some documents from the lawyer's office on behalf of Señorita Margarita. After a moment's hesitation, he allowed me to go up. I climbed the wide staircase at a leisurely pace, under the porter's attentive gaze. The first-floor landing was larger than most of the homes I remembered from my childhood days in the old Ribera quarter, which was only a short distance away. The door knocker was shaped like a bronze fist. The moment I grasped it I realised that the door was already open. I pushed it gently and looked inside. The entrance hall led to a long passageway, about three metres wide, its walls lined with blue velvet and covered with pictures. I closed the door behind me and scanned the warm half-light that was coming from the other end. Faint music floated in the air, a piano lament in a melancholic and elegant style: Granados.

'Señor Valera?' I called out. 'It's Martín.'

As there was no reply, I ventured down the passage, following the trace of that sad music. I passed paintings and recesses containing statuettes of madonnas and saints and went through a series of arches, each one veiled by net curtains, until I came to the end of the corridor, where a large dark room spread out before me. The room was rectangular, its walls lined with bookshelves from floor to ceiling. At the far end I could make out a half-open door and, through it, the flickering orange shadows of an open fire.

'Valera?' I called again, raising my voice.

A silhouette appeared in the light projected by the flames through the door. Two shining eyes examined me suspiciously. A dog that looked like an Alsatian but whose fur was white padded towards me. I stood still, unbuttoning my coat and looking for the revolver. The animal stopped at my feet and peered up at me, then let out a whine. I stroked its head and it licked my fingers. Then it turned, walked back to the doorway, stopped again and looked back at me. I followed it.

On the other side of the door I discovered a reading room presided over by a large fireplace. The only light came from the flames, casting a dance of flickering shadows over the walls and ceiling. In the middle of the room there was a table with a large gramophone from which the music emanated. Opposite the fire, with its back to the door, stood a large leather armchair. The dog went over to the chair and turned to look at me again. I went closer, close enough to see a hand resting on the arm of the chair. The hand held a burning cigar from which rose a plume of blue smoke.

'Valera? It's Martín. The door was open . . .'

The dog lay down at the foot of the armchair, never taking its eyes off me. Slowly, I walked round in front of the chair. Señor Valera was sitting there, facing the fire, his eyes open and a faint smile on his lips. He was wearing a three-piece suit and his other hand rested on a leather-bound notebook. I drew closer and searched his face. He didn't blink. Then I noticed a red tear, a tear of blood, that was gliding down his cheek. I knelt down and removed the notebook from his hand. The dog gave me a distraught look. I stroked its head.

'I'm sorry,' I whispered.

The book seemed to be some sort of diary, with its entries, each handwritten and dated, separated by a short line. Valera had it open at the middle. The first entry on the page was dated 23 November 1904.

Payment note (356 on 23-11-04), 7,500 pesetas, from D.M. trust account. Sent with Marcel (in person) to the address supplied by D.M. Alleyway behind old cemetery – stonemason's workshop Sanabre & Sons.

I reread that entry a few times, trying to scratch some meaning out of it. I knew the alleyway from my days at *The Voice of Industry*. It was a miserable, narrow street, sunk behind the walls of the Pueblo Nuevo Cemetery, with a jumble of workshops where headstones and memorials were produced. It ended by one of the riverbeds that crossed Bogatell beach and the citadel of shacks stretching down to the sea: the Somorrostro. For some reason, Marlasca had given instructions to pay a considerable amount of money to one of those workshops.

On the same page, under the same date, was another entry relating to Marlasca, showing the start of the payments to Jaco and Irene Sabino.

Bank transfer from D.M. trust to account in Banco Hispano Colonial (Calle Fernando branch) no. 008965-2564-1. Juan Corbera—Maria Antonia Sanahuja. First monthly payment of 7,000 pesetas. Establish payment plan.

I kept on leafing through the notebook. Most annotations concerned expenses and minor operations pertaining to the firm. I had to look over a number of pages full of cryptic reminders before I found another mention of Marlasca. Again, it referred to a cash payment made through a person called Marcel, who was probably one of the articled clerks in the office.

Payment note (279 on 29-12-04), 15,000 pesetas from D.M. trust account. Paid via Marcel. Bogatell beach, next to level crossing. 9 a.m. Contact will give name.

The Witch of Somorrostro, I thought. After his death, Diego Marlasca had been handing out large amounts of money through his partner. This contradicted Salvador's suspicion that Jaco had fled with the money. Marlasca had ordered the payments to be made in person and had left the money in a trust, managed by the law firm. The other two payments suggested that shortly before dying Marlasca had been in touch with a stonemason's workshop and with some murky character from the Somorrostro district, dealings that had translated into a large amount of money changing hands. I closed the notebook feeling more confused than ever.

As I turned to leave, I noticed that one of the walls of the reading room was covered with neatly framed portraits set against a wine-coloured velvet background. I went closer and recognised the dour and imposing face of Valera the elder, whose portrait still presided over his son's office. In most of the pictures the lawyer appeared in the company of the great and the good of Barcelona, at what seemed to be different social occasions and civic events. It was enough to examine a dozen or so of those pictures and identify the array of celebrities who posed, smiling, next to the old lawyer, to understand that the firm of Valera, Marlasca & Sentís was a vital cog in the machinery of this city. Valera's son, much younger but still recognisable, also appeared in some of the photographs, always in the background, always with his eyes buried in the shadow of the patriarch.

I sensed it before I saw him. In the photograph were both Valeras, father and son. The picture had been taken by the door of the law firm, at number 442, Avenida Diagonal. Next to them stood a tall, distinguished-looking man. His face had also been in many of the other photographs in the collection, always close to Valera. Diego Marlasca. I concentrated on those turbulent eyes, that sharp and serene profile staring at me from a picture taken twenty-five years ago. Just like the boss, he had not aged a single day. I smiled bitterly when I understood how easily he'd fooled me. That face was not the one that appeared in the photograph given to me by my friend the ex-policeman.

The man I knew as Ricardo Salvador was none other than Diego Marlasca.

15

The staircase was in darkness when I left the Valera family mansion. I groped my way towards the entrance and, as I opened the door, the street lamps cast a rectangle of blue light back across the hall, at the end of which I spotted the stern eyes of the porter. I hurried away towards Calle Trafalgar, where the tram set out on its journey down to the gates of Pueblo Nuevo Cemetery – the same tram I had taken so many times with my father when I accompanied him on his night shifts at *The Voice of Industry*.

The tram was almost empty and I sat at the front. As we approached Pueblo Nuevo we entered a network of shadowy streets covered in large puddles. There were hardly any street lamps and the tram's headlights revealed the contours of the buildings like a torch shining through a tunnel. At last I sighted the gates of the cemetery, its crosses and sculptures set against an endless horizon of factories and chimneys injecting red and black into the vault of the sky. A group of emaciated dogs prowled around the foot of the two large angels guarding the graveyard. For a moment they stood still, staring into the lights of the tram, their eyes lit up like the eyes of jackals, before they scattered into the shadows.

I jumped from the tram while it was still moving and set off, skirting the walls of the cemetery. The tram sailed away like a ship in the fog and I quickened my pace. I could hear and smell the dogs following behind me in the dark. When I reached the back of the cemetery I stopped on the corner of the alley and blindly threw a stone at them. I heard a sharp yelp and then the sound of paws galloping away into the night. The alley was just a narrow walkway trapped between the wall and the row of stonemasons' workshops, all jumbled together. The notice Sanabre & Sons swung in the dusty light of a street lamp that stood about thirty metres further on. I went to the door, just a grille secured with chains and a rusty lock, and blew it open with one shot.

The echo of the shot was swallowed by the wind as it gusted up the passageway, carrying salt from the breaking waves of the sea only a hundred metres away. I opened the grille and walked into the Sanabre & Sons workshop, drawing back the dark curtain that masked the interior so that the light from the street lamp could penetrate. Beyond was a deep, narrow nave, populated by marble figures seemingly frozen in the shadows, their faces only half-sculpted. I took a few steps past madonnas cradling infants in their arms, white women holding marble roses and looking heavenward, and blocks of stone on which I could just make out the beginnings of an expression. The scent of dust from the stone filled the air.

There was nobody there except for these nameless effigies. I was about to retrace my steps when I saw it. The hand peeped out from behind a tableau of figures covered with a cloth at the back of the workshop. As I walked towards it, the shape gradually revealed itself to me. Finally I stood in front of it and gazed up at that great angel of light, the same angel the boss had worn on his lapel and I had found at the bottom of the trunk in the study. The figure must have been two and a half metres high, and when I looked at its face I recognised the features, especially the smile. At its feet was a gravestone, with an inscription:

DAVID MARTÍN
1900–1930

I smiled. One thing I had to admit about my good friend Diego Marlasca was that he had a sense of humour and a taste for the unexpected. It shouldn't have surprised me, I told myself, that in his eagerness he'd got ahead of himself and prepared such a heartfelt send-off. I knelt down by the gravestone and stroked my name. Behind me I heard light footsteps. I turned and saw a familiar face. The boy wore the same black suit he had worn when he followed me weeks ago in Paseo del Borne.

'The lady will see you now,' he said.

I nodded and stood up. The boy offered me his hand, and I took it.

'Don't be frightened,' he said, as he led me towards the exit.

'I'm not,' I whispered.

The boy took me to the end of the alleyway. From there I could make out the line of the beach, hidden behind a row of run-down warehouses and the remains of a cargo train abandoned on a weed-covered siding. Its coaches were eaten away by rust, and all that was left of the engine was a skeleton of boilers and metal struts waiting for the scrapyard.

Up above, the moon peeped through the gaps in a bank of leaden clouds. Out at sea, the blurred shapes of distant freighters appeared between the waves, and on the sands of Bogatell beach lay the skeletons of old fishing boats and coastal vessels, spewed up by storms. On the other side, like a mantle of rubbish stretching out from the great, dark fortress of industry, stood the shacks of the

Somorrostro encampment. Waves broke only a few metres from the first row of huts made of cane and wood. Plumes of white smoke slithered among the roofs of the miserable hamlet growing between the city and the sea like an endless human dumping ground. The stench of burned rubbish floated in the air. We stepped into the streets of that forgotten city, passages that opened up between structures held together with stolen bricks, mud and driftwood. The boy led me on, unaware of the distrustful stares of the locals. Unemployed day labourers, Gypsies ousted from similar camps on the slopes of Montjuïc or opposite the communal graves of the Can Tunis Cemetery, homeless old men, women and children. They all observed me with suspicion. As we walked by, women of indeterminate age stood by fires outside their shacks, heating up water or food in tin canisters. We stopped in front of a whitish structure, at the door of which we saw a girl with the face of an old woman, limping on a leg withered by polio. She was dragging a bucket with something grey and slimy moving about inside it. Eels. The boy pointed to the door.

'It's here,' he said.

I took a last look at the sky. The moon was hiding behind the clouds again and a veil of darkness advanced towards us from the sea.

I went in.

16

Her face was lined with memories and the look in her eyes could have been ten or a hundred years old. She was sitting by a small fire watching the dancing flames with the fascination of a child. Her hair was the colour of ash and she wore it tied up in a plait. She had a slim, austere figure; her movements were subtle and unhurried. She was dressed in white and wore a silk scarf knotted round her throat. She smiled warmly and offered me a chair next to her. I sat down. We spent a couple of minutes in silence, listening to the crackle of the embers and the murmur of the sea. In her presence time seemed to stop, and the urgency that had brought me to her door had strangely disappeared. Slowly, as I absorbed the heat from the fire, the cold that had gripped my bones melted away. Only then did she turn her eyes from the flames and, holding my hand, she opened her lips.

'My mother lived in this house for forty-five years,' she said. 'It wasn't even a house then, just a hut made of cane and old rubbish washed up by the sea. Even when she had earned herself a reputation and had the chance to get out of this place, she refused. She always said that the day she left the Somorrostro, she would die. She was born here, among the people of the beach, and she would remain here until her last day. Many things were said about her. Many people talked about her, but very few really knew her. Many feared and hated her. Even after her death. I'm telling you all this because I think it's fair that you should know: I'm not the person you're looking for, or you think you're looking for. The one many called The Witch of Somorrostro was my mother.'

I looked at her in confusion.

'When . . .?'

'My mother died in 1905,' she said. 'She was killed a few metres away from here, by the sea; stabbed in the neck.'

'I'm sorry. I thought that—'

'A lot of people do. The wish to believe can even conquer death.'

'Who killed her?'

'You know who.'

It took me a few seconds to reply.

'Diego Marlasca . . .'

She nodded.

'Why?'

'To silence her. To cover his tracks.'

'I don't understand. Your mother had helped him . . . He even gave her a large amount of money in exchange.'

'That's exactly why he wanted to kill her, so that she would take his secret to the grave.'

She watched me, a half-smile playing on her lips as if my confusion amused her and made her pity me at the same time.

'My mother was an ordinary woman, Señor Martín. She grew up

385

in poverty and the only power she possessed was her will to survive. She never learned to read or write, but she knew how to see inside people. She felt what they felt, knew their secrets and their longings. She could read it in their eyes, in their gestures, in their voices, in the way they walked or their mannerisms. She knew what they were going to say or do before they did. That's why a lot of people called her a sorceress, because she was able to see in them what they refused to see themselves. She earned her living selling love potions and enchantments which she prepared with water from the riverbed, herbs and a few grains of sugar. She helped lost souls believe what they wanted to believe. When she gained a certain popularity, a lot of people from well-to-do families began to pay her visits and seek her favours. The rich wanted to become even richer. The powerful wanted more power. The mean wanted to feel like saints, and the pious wanted to be punished for sins they regretted not having had the courage to commit. My mother listened to them all and accepted their coin. With this money she sent me and my siblings to the same schools as the sons of her customers. She bought us another name and another life far from this place. My mother was a good person, Señor Martín. Don't be fooled. She never took advantage of anyone, nor did she make them believe more than they needed to believe. Life had taught her that we all require big and small lies in order to survive, just as much as we need air. She used to say that if during one single day, from dawn to dusk, we could see the naked reality of the world, and of ourselves, we would either take our own lives or lose our minds.'

'But—'

'If you've come here in search of magic, I'm sorry to disappoint you. My mother told me there was no magic; she said there was no more good or evil in this world than we imagine there to be, either out of greed or innocence. Or sometimes madness.'

'That's not what she told Diego Marlasca when she accepted his money,' I objected. 'Seven thousand pesetas in those days must have bought quite a few years of a good name and good schools.'

'Diego Marlasca needed to believe. My mother helped him to do so. That's all.'

'Believe in what?'

'In his own salvation. He was convinced that he had betrayed himself and those he loved. He believed that he had placed his life on a path of evil and falsehood. My mother thought this didn't make him any different from most men who at some point in their lives stop to look at themselves in the mirror. The most despicable humans are the ones who always feel virtuous and look down on the rest of the world. But Diego Marlasca was a man with a conscience, and he was not satisfied with what he saw. That's why he went to my mother. Because he had lost all hope, and probably his mind.'

'Did Marlasca say what he had done?'

'He said he'd handed his life over to a shadow.'

'A shadow?'

'Those were his words. A shadow who followed him and possessed the same shape, face and voice as his own.'

'What did that mean?'

'Guilt and remorse have no meaning. They are feelings, emotions, not ideas.'

It occurred to me that not even the boss could have explained this more clearly.

'And what was your mother able to do for him?' I asked.

'Only comfort him and help him find some peace. Diego Marlasca believed in magic and that's why my mother thought she should convince him that his road to salvation passed through her. She spoke to him of an ancient spell, a fisherman's legend she had heard as a child among the hovels by the sea. When a man lost his way in life and felt that death had put a price on his soul, the legend said that if he found a pure soul who would agree to be sacrificed in order to save him, he would be able to disguise his own black heart with it, and death, which cannot see, would pass him by.'

'A pure soul?'

'Free of sin.'

'And how was this to be carried out?'

'With pain, of course.'

'What sort of pain?'

'A blood sacrifice. One soul in exchange for another. Death in exchange for life.'

A long silence amid the whisper of the sea and the wind swirling among the shacks.

'Irene would have pulled out her own eyes and heart for Marlasca. He was her reason for living. She loved him blindly and, like him, believed that his only salvation lay in magic. At first she wanted to take her own life, offering it to him as a sacrifice, but my mother dissuaded her. She told her what she already knew, that her soul was not free of sin and that her sacrifice would be in vain. She said that to save her. To save them both.'

'From whom?'

'From themselves.'

'But she made a mistake . . .'

'Even my mother couldn't see everything.'

'What did Marlasca do?'

'My mother never wanted to tell me – she didn't want me and my siblings to be a part of it. She separated us and sent each of us far away to different boarding schools so that we would forget where we came from and who we were. She said that now we were the ones who were cursed. She died shortly afterwards, alone. We didn't find out until much later. When they discovered her body nobody dared touch it: they let the sea take it away. Nobody dared speak about her death either. But I knew who had killed her and why. Even today I believe my mother knew she was going to die soon and by whose hand. She knew and she did nothing about it because in the end she too believed. She believed because she was unable to accept what she'd done. She believed that by handing over her soul she would save ours, the soul of this place. That's why she didn't want to flee, because, as the legend says, the soul that sacrifices itself should always remain in the place where the treasonable act was committed, like a bandage over the eyes of death.'

'And where is the soul that saved Diego Marlasca?'

The woman smiled.

'There are no souls or salvations, Señor Martín. That's just an old wives' tale, gossip. Only ashes and memories remain, but if there are any they will be in the place where Marlasca committed his crime, the secret he has hidden all these years to mock his own destiny.'

'The tower house . . . I've lived there for almost ten years and there's nothing . . .'

She smiled again and, with her eyes fixed on mine, leaned towards me and kissed me on the cheek. Her lips were frozen, like the lips of a corpse, and her breath smelled of dead flowers.

'Perhaps you haven't been looking in the right place,' she whispered in my ear. 'Perhaps the trapped soul is your own.'

Then she untied the scarf she wore round her neck and revealed a large scar across her throat. This time her smile was malicious and her eyes shone with a cruel, defiant light.

'Soon the sun will rise. Leave while you can,' said the Witch of Somorrostro, turning her back to me and looking into the flames once more.

The boy in the black suit appeared in the doorway and offered me his hand, an indication that my time was up. I stood and followed him. When I turned I caught my reflection in a mirror hanging on the wall. In it I could see the profile of an old hag, dressed in rags, hunched over by the fire. Her dark, cruel laughter stayed with me until I was out of the door.

17

Dawn was breaking when I arrived at the tower house. The lock on the front door was broken. I pushed it open and stepped into the courtyard. The locking mechanism on the back of the door was smoking and gave off an acrid smell. Acid. I climbed the stairs slowly, convinced that I would find Marlasca waiting for me in the shadows of the landing, or that if I turned around he would be there, behind me, smiling. As I walked up the last flight of stairs I noticed that the keyhole on the apartment door also showed signs of acid. I put in the key and had to struggle with it for a couple of minutes; the lock was damaged but had apparently not yielded. Finally I succeeded and pulled out the key, which was slightly gnawed by the substance, and pushed open the door. I left it open behind me and headed down the corridor without taking off my coat. I pulled the revolver out of my pocket and unlocked the barrel, emptying the cartridges of the bullets I had fired and replacing them with new ones, just as I'd seen my father do so many times when he returned home at dawn.

'Salvador?' I called.

The echo of my voice spread through the house. I cocked the hammer and continued to advance until I reached the room at the end. The door was ajar.

'Salvador?' I asked.

I pointed my gun at the door and kicked it open. There was no trace of Marlasca inside, just the mountain of boxes and old objects piled up in a corner. Again I noticed the odd smell that seemed to filter through the walls. I went over to the wardrobe that covered the back wall and opened its doors wide, removing all the old clothes from the hangers. The cold, damp draught that came from the hole behind it caressed my face. Whatever it was that Marlasca had hidden in the house, it was on the other side of that wall.

I put the weapon in my pocket and removed my coat. Standing by a rear corner of the wardrobe, I put my arm into the space between the frame and the wall. I managed to grab the back of the wardrobe with my hand and I pulled it forward hard. The first pull allowed me to gain a few centimetres and secure my hold. I pulled it forward again. The wardrobe now moved almost a hand's width. I kept on pulling the end of the wardrobe until the wall behind it became visible and there was enough room for me to slip in. Once I was behind the wardrobe I pushed it with my shoulder, moving it right away against the adjacent wall. I stopped to recover my breath and examine my work. The wall was painted an ochre colour, different from the rest of the room. Beneath the paint I could feel some sort of clay-like mass. I rapped on it with my knuckles. The echo left no room for doubt. This was not a supporting wall. There was something on the other side. I leaned my head against it and listened carefully. Then I heard a noise. Steps along the corridor, approaching . . . I moved away and stretched out my hand towards the coat I had left on a chair, in order to grab the gun. A shadow filled the doorway. I held my breath. It peered into the room.

'Inspector . . .' I whispered.

Víctor Grandes smiled at me coldly. I imagined he must have spent hours waiting for me, hiding in some doorway in the street.

'Are you refurbishing the house, Martín?'

'Just tidying up.'

The inspector looked at the pile of clothes and boxes thrown on the floor and the displaced wardrobe.

'I've asked Marcos and Castelo to wait downstairs. I was going to knock, but the door was open so I took the liberty of coming straight in. I said to myself: this must mean that my friend Martín is expecting me.'

'What can I do for you, inspector?'

'Come along with me to the police station, if you'd be so kind.'

'Am I being arrested?'

'I'm afraid so. Are you going to make it easy for me or are we going to have to do this the hard way?'

'No, I'll come,' I assured him.

'I appreciate that.'

'May I get my coat?'

Grandes stared straight at me for a moment. Then I picked up the coat and he helped me put it on. I felt the weight of the revolver against my thigh. Before leaving the room, the inspector cast a last glance at the wall that had been revealed. Then he told me to go on out into the corridor. Marcos and Castelo had come up to the landing and were waiting for me with triumphant smiles. Just as we were about to leave I stopped for a second to look back inside the house, which seemed to withdraw into a well of shadows. I wondered if I would ever see it again. Castelo pulled out some handcuffs, but Grandes stopped him.

'That won't be necessary, will it, Martín?'

I shook my head. Grandes closed the door and pushed me gently but firmly towards the stairs.

18

This time there were no dramatic effects, no sinister setting, no echoes of damp, dark dungeons. The room was large and full of light, with a high ceiling. It reminded me of a classroom in an exclusive religious school, crucifix on the wall included. It was on the first floor of police headquarters, with large French windows that offered views of people and trams beginning their morning procession along Vía Layetana. In the middle of the room were two chairs and a metal table that looked tiny stranded in such a large, empty space. Grandes led me to the table and ordered Marcos and Castelo to leave us. The two policemen took their time following the order. I could practically smell their anger in the air. Grandes waited for them to leave and then relaxed.

'I thought you were going to throw me to the lions,' I said.

'Sit down.'

I did as I was told. Had it not been for the expression on the faces of Marcos and Castelo as they left, the metal door and the iron bars on the other side of the windowpanes, nobody would have guessed that my situation was grave. What finally convinced me was the Thermos flask of hot coffee and the packet of cigarettes that Grandes left on the table, but above all his warm, confident smile. This time the inspector was deadly serious.

He sat opposite me, opened a file, and produced a few photographs which he proceeded to place on the table, one next to the other. The first picture was of Valera, the lawyer, seated in the armchair in his sitting room. Next to that was a photograph of the dead body of Marlasca's widow, or what remained of it, shortly after they pulled it out of the swimming pool at her house on Carretera de Vallvidrera. A third picture showed a little man, with his throat slit open, who looked like Damián Roures. The fourth picture was of Cristina Sagnier, taken on the day she married Pedro Vidal. The last two were studio portraits of my former publishers, Barrido and Escobillas. Once he had neatly lined up all six photographs, Grandes gave me an inscrutable look and let a couple of minutes go by, studying my reaction to the images, or the absence of one. Then he calmly poured two cups of coffee and pushed one towards me.

'Before we begin I'd like to give you the opportunity to tell me the whole story, Martín. In your own way, and no rush,' he said at last.

'It won't be any use,' I replied. 'It won't change anything.'

'Would you prefer us to interview the other people we think might be implicated? Your assistant, for example? What was her name? Isabella?'

'Leave her alone. She doesn't know anything.'

'Convince me.'

I turned my head towards the door.

'There's only one way of getting out of this room, Martín,' said the inspector, showing me a key.

Once again, I felt the weight of the gun in my coat pocket.

'Where would you like me to start?'

'You're the narrator. All I ask of you is that you tell me the truth.'

'I don't know what the truth is.'

'The truth is what hurts.'

For a little over two hours, Víctor Grandes didn't once open his mouth. He listened attentively, nodding every now and then and jotting down words in his notebook. At first I looked at him, but soon I forgot he was there and realised that I was telling the story to myself. The words made me travel to a time I had thought lost, to the night when my father was murdered at the gates of the newspaper building. I remembered my days in the offices of *The Voice of Industry*, the years I'd survived by writing stories through the night and that first letter signed by Andreas Corelli promising me great expectations. I remembered my first meeting with the boss in the Water Reservoir building, and the days in which the certainty of imminent death was the only horizon before me. I spoke to him about Cristina, about Vidal and about a story whose end anyone might have guessed but me. I spoke to him about the two books I had written, one under my own name and the other using Vidal's, of the loss of those miserable expectations and of the afternoon when I saw my mother drop into a waste bin the one good thing I thought I'd done in my life. I wasn't looking for pity or understanding from the inspector. It was enough for me to try to trace an imaginary map of the events that had led me to that room, to that moment of complete emptiness. I returned to the house next to Güell Park and the night when the boss had made me an offer I could not refuse. I confessed my first suspicions, my discoveries about the history of the tower house, the strange death of Diego Marlasca and the web of deceit in which I'd become embroiled – or which I had chosen in order to satisfy my vanity, my greed, and my desire to live at any price. To live so that I could tell the story.

I left nothing out. Nothing except the most important part, the part I did not even dare tell myself. In the account I gave Grandes, I returned to the sanatorium to look for Cristina but all I found was a trail of footsteps lost in the snow. Perhaps, if I repeated those words over and over again, even I would end up believing that was what had happened. My story ended that very morning, when I returned from the Somorrostro shacks to discover that Diego Marlasca wanted to add my portrait to the line-up the inspector had placed on the table.

When I finished my tale I fell into a deep silence. I had never felt as tired in all my life. I wanted to go to sleep and never wake again. Grandes was observing me from the other side of the table. He seemed confused, sad, angry and above all lost.

'Say something,' I said.

Grandes sighed. He got up from his chair and went over to the window, turning his back on me. I pictured myself pulling the gun out of my coat, shooting him in the back of the neck and getting out of there with the key he kept in his pocket. In sixty seconds I could be back on the street.

'The reason we're talking is because a telegram arrived yesterday from the Civil Guard barracks in Puigcerdà, stating that Cristina Sagnier has disappeared from the sanatorium and you're the main suspect. The doctor in charge of the centre said that you'd wanted to take her away and that he'd refused to discharge her. I'm telling you all this so that you understand exactly why we're here, in this room, with hot coffee and cigarettes, talking like old friends. We're here because the wife of one of the richest men in Barcelona has disappeared and you're the only person who knows where she is. We're here because the father of your friend Pedro Vidal, one of the most powerful men in this town, has taken a personal interest in the case. It appears that he's an old acquaintance of yours and has politely asked my superiors that we obtain the information we need before laying a finger on you, leaving other considerations for later. Had it not been for that, and for my insistence that I wanted to try to clarify the matter in my own way, right now you'd be in a dungeon in Campo de la Bota. And instead of speaking to me you'd be talking directly to Marcos and Castelo, who, for your information, think any course of action that doesn't start with breaking your knees with a hammer is a waste of time and might put Señora de Vidal's life in danger. This is an opinion that my superiors, who think I'm giving you too much leeway, are endorsing more heartily with every passing minute.'

Grandes turned and looked at me, restraining his anger.

'You haven't listened to me,' I said. 'You haven't listened to anything I said.'

'I've listened to you perfectly well, Martín. I've listened to how, when you were a desperate, dying man, you entered into a pact with a mysterious Parisian publisher, whom nobody has ever heard of, in order to invent, in your own words, a new religion in exchange for a hundred thousand French francs, only to discover that in fact you had fallen into a sinister plot – involving a lawyer who faked his own death twenty-five years ago to escape a destiny which is now your own, and his lover, a chorus girl who had known better days. I have listened to how this destiny led you to fall into the trap of an accursed old house which had already trapped your predecessor, Diego Marlasca; and how you found proof in that house that somebody was following you and murdering anyone who might reveal the secret of a man who, judging from your own words, is almost as mad as you. The man in the shadows, who adopted the identity of a former policeman in order to hide the fact that he is alive, has been committing a number of crimes with the help of his lover, and that includes provoking the death of Señor Sempere, for some strange motive that not even you are able to explain.'

'Irene Sabino killed Sempere when she was trying to steal a book from him. A book which she thought contained my soul.'

Grandes hit his forehead with the palm of his hand as if he'd just stumbled on the nub of the matter.

'Of course. How stupid of me. That explains it all. Like that business about the terrible secret revealed to you by a sorceress on Bogatell beach. The Witch of Somorrostro. I like that. Very typical of you. Let's see whether I've understood this correctly. This Señor Marlasca has imprisoned a soul in order to mask his own soul and thus escape from some sort of curse. Tell me, did you get that out of *City of the Damned* or have you just invented it?'

'I haven't invented anything.'

'Put yourself in my position and tell me whether you would have believed a single word you've said.'

'I suppose I wouldn't. But I've told you everything I know.'

'Of course. You've given me information and specific details so that I can check the truth of your story, from your visit to Doctor

Trías, your account at the Banco Hispano Colonial, your own gravestone waiting for you in a Pueblo Nuevo workshop and even a legal connection between the man you call *the boss* and Valera's law firm, together with many other clues that are not unworthy of your skill in creating detective novels. The only thing you have not told me and which, in all frankness, for your good and mine, I was hoping to hear, is where I can find Cristina Sagnier.'

I realised that the only thing that could save me at that moment was a lie. The moment I told him the truth about Cristina, my hours were numbered.

'I don't know where she is.'

'You're lying.'

'I told you that telling you the truth wouldn't be of any use,' I answered.

'Except to make me look like an idiot for wanting to help you.'

'Is that what you're trying to do, inspector? Help me?'

'Yes.'

'Then check out everything I've said. Find Marlasca and Irene Sabino.'

'My superiors have given me twenty-four hours to question you. If by then I don't hand them Cristina Sagnier safe and sound, or at least alive, I'll be removed from the case and it will be passed on to Marcos and Castelo, who have been looking forward to a chance to prove themselves and are certainly not going to waste it.'

'Then don't lose any time.'

Grandes snorted.

'I hope you know what you're doing, Martín.'

19

I worked out that it must have been nine o'clock in the morning when Inspector Víctor Grandes left me locked up in that room with no other company than a Thermos flask of cold coffee and his packet of cigarettes. He posted one of his men by the door and I heard the inspector ordering the man not to let anyone in under any circumstances. Five minutes after his departure I heard someone knocking and recognised Sergeant Marcos's face through the glass. I couldn't hear his words, but the movement of his lips made his meaning crystal clear:

Get ready, you bastard.

I spent the rest of the morning sitting on the windowsill watching people who thought themselves free walking past the iron bars, smoking, even eating sugar lumps with the same relish I'd seen the boss do on more than one occasion. Tiredness, or perhaps it was just the final wave of despair, hit me by noon and I lay down on the floor, my face towards the wall. I fell asleep in less than a minute. When I woke up, the room was in darkness. Night had fallen and the street lamps along Vía Layetana cast shadows of cars and trams on the ceiling. I stood up, feeling the cold of the floor in every muscle, and walked over to a radiator in one corner of the room. It was even icier than my hands.

At that moment, I heard the door open behind me and I turned to find the inspector watching me. At a signal from Grandes, one of his men turned on the light and closed the door. The harsh, metallic light blinded me for a moment. When I opened my eyes again, I saw that the inspector looked almost as bad as I did.

'Do you need to go to the bathroom?' he asked.

'No. Taking advantage of the circumstances, I decided to wet myself and practise for when you send me off to the chamber of horrors with those inquisitors Marcos and Castelo.'

'I'm glad to see you haven't lost your sense of humour. You're going to need it. Sit down.'

We resumed our earlier positions.

'I've been checking the details of your story.'

'And?'

'Where would you like me to begin?'

'You're the policeman.'

'My first visit was to Doctor Trías's surgery in Calle Muntaner. It was brief. Doctor Trías died twelve years ago and the surgery has belonged to a dentist called Bernat Llofriu for eight. Needless to say, he's never heard of you.'

'Impossible.'

'Wait, it gets better. On my way from there I went by the main offices of the Banco Hispano Colonial. Impressive decor and impeccable service. I felt like opening a savings account. There, I was able to find out that you've never held an account with that bank, that they've never heard of anyone called Andreas Corelli and that there is no customer who at this time holds a foreign currency account with them to the tune of one hundred thousand French francs. Shall I continue?'

I pressed my lips together, but let him go on.

'My next stop was the law firm of the deceased, Señor Valera. There I discovered that you do have a bank account, not with the Hispano Colonial but with the Banco de Sabadell, from which you transferred two thousand pesetas to the lawyers' account about six months ago.'

'I don't understand.'

'Very simple. You hired Valera anonymously, or that's what you thought, because banks have total recall and once they've seen a penny fly away they never forget it. I confess that, by this point, I was beginning to enjoy myself and decided to pay a visit to the stonemasons' workshop, Sanabre & Sons.'

'Don't tell me you didn't see the angel . . .'

'I saw it. Impressive. Like the letter signed in your own handwriting, dated three months ago, when you commissioned the work, and the receipt for the advance payment which good old Sanabre had kept in his account books. A charming man, very proud of his work. He told me it was his masterpiece. He said he'd received divine inspiration.'

'Didn't you ask about the money Marlasca paid him twenty-five years ago?'

'I did. He had also kept those receipts. They were for works to improve, maintain and alter the family mausoleum.'

'Someone is buried in Marlasca's tomb who isn't Marlasca.'

'That's what you say. But if you want me to desecrate a grave, you must understand that you have to provide me with a more solid argument. Anyway, let me continue with my revision of your story.'

I swallowed.

'Since I was there, I decided to walk over to Bogatell beach, where for one *real* I found at least ten people ready to reveal the huge secret of the Witch of Somorrostro. I didn't tell you this morning when you were narrating your story so as not to ruin the drama, but in fact the big, stout woman who called herself by that name died years ago. The old woman I saw this morning doesn't even frighten children, and is laid up in a chair. And there's a detail you will love: she's dumb.'

'Inspector—'

'I haven't finished. You can't say I don't take my work seriously. So much so that from there I went to the large old mansion you described to me next to Güell Park, which has been abandoned for at least ten years and in which I'm sorry to say there were no pictures or prints or anything else but cat shit. What do think?'

I didn't reply.

'Tell me, Martín. Put yourself in my position. What would you have done?'

'Given up, I suppose.'

'Exactly. But I'm not you and, like an idiot, after such a worthwhile journey, I decided to follow your advice and look for the fearsome Irene Sabino.'

'Did you find her?'

'Give the police some credit, Martín. Of course we found her. A complete wreck in a miserable *pensión* in the Raval, where she's lived for years.'

'Did you speak to her?'

Grandes nodded.

'At length.'

'And?'

'She hasn't the faintest idea who you are.'

'Is that what she told you?'

'Among other things.'

'What things?'

'She told me that she met Diego Marlasca at a session organised by Roures in an apartment on Calle Elisabets, where a spiritualist group called the Afterlife Society held meetings in the year 1903. She told me she met a man who took refuge in her arms, a man who was destroyed by the loss of his son and trapped in a marriage that no longer made any sense. She told me that Marlasca was kind-hearted but disturbed. He believed that something had got inside

399

him and was convinced that he was soon going to die. She told me that before he died he left some money in a trust, so that she and the man she had abandoned to be with Marlasca – Juan Corbera, aka Jaco – would receive something once he was gone. She told me that Marlasca took his own life because he couldn't bear the pain that was consuming him. She told me that she and Juan Corbera had lived off Marlasca's charity until the trust ran out, and soon afterwards the man you call Jaco dumped her. People say he died alone, an alcoholic, working as a nightwatchman in the Casaramona factory. She told me that she did take Marlasca to see the woman they called the Witch of Somorrostro, because she thought the woman might comfort him and make him believe he would be reunited with his son in the next life . . . Shall I continue?'

I unbuttoned my shirt and showed him the cuts Irene Sabino had engraved on my chest the night she and Marlasca had attacked me in the San Gervasio Cemetery.

'A six-pointed star. Don't make me laugh, Martín. You could have made those cuts yourself. Irene Sabino is just a poor woman who earns her living in a laundry in Calle Cadena, not a sorceress.'

'And what about Ricardo Salvador?'

'Ricardo Salvador was thrown out of the police force in 1906, after spending two years stirring up the case of Diego Marlasca's death while having an illicit relationship with the widow of the deceased. The last thing anyone knew about him was that he'd decided to take a ship to the Americas and start a new life.'

I couldn't help but burst out laughing at the enormity of the deceit.

'Don't you realise, inspector? Don't you realise you're falling into the same trap that was laid for me by Marlasca?'

Grandes looked at me with pity.

'You're the one who doesn't realise, Martín. The clock is ticking, and instead of telling me what you did with Cristina Sagnier, you persist in trying to convince me with a story that sounds like something from *City of the Damned*. There's only one trap here: the one you've laid for yourself. And every moment that goes by without you telling me the truth makes it more difficult for me to get you out of it.'

Grandes waved his hand in front of my eyes a couple of times, as if he wanted to make sure that I could still see.

'No? Nothing? As you wish. Let me finish telling you what the day had to offer. After my visit to Irene Sabino I was beginning to feel rather tired, so I returned for a while to police headquarters, where I still found the time, and the energy, to call the Civil Guard barracks in Puigcerdà. They've confirmed that you were seen leaving Cristina Sagnier's hospital room on the night she disappeared, that you never returned to your hotel to collect your baggage, and that the head of the sanatorium told them you'd cut the straps that held down the patient. I then called an old friend of yours, Pedro Vidal, who was kind enough to come over to police headquarters. The poor man is devastated. He told me that the last time you two met you hit him. Is that true?'

I nodded.

'I must tell you that he doesn't hold it against you. In fact, he almost tried to persuade me to let you go. He says there must be an explanation for all this. That you've had a difficult life. That it was his fault you lost your father. That he feels responsible. All he wants is to recover his wife and he has no intention of retaliating against you in any way.'

'You've told Vidal the whole thing?'

'I had no option.'

I hid my face in my hands.

'What did he say?' I asked.

Grandes shrugged.

'He thinks you've lost your mind. He thinks you must be innocent and he doesn't want anything to happen to you, whether you're innocent or not. His family is another matter. I know for certain that Vidal's father has secretly offered Marcos and Castelo a bonus if they extract a confession from you in less than twelve hours. They've assured him that in one morning they'll get you to recite the entire *Canigó* epic.'

'And what do you think?'

'The truth? The truth is that I'd like to believe Pedro Vidal is right and you've lost your mind.'

I didn't tell him that, at that very moment, I was beginning to believe it too. Then I looked at Grandes and noticed something in his expression that didn't add up.

'There's something you haven't told me,' I remarked.

'I'd say I've told you more than enough,' he retorted.

'What haven't you told me?'

Grandes observed me attentively and then tried to hide his laughter.

'This morning you told me that the night Señor Sempere died he was overheard arguing with someone in the bookshop. You suspected that the person in question wanted to buy a book, a book of yours, and when Sempere refused to sell it, there was a fight and the bookseller suffered a heart attack. According to you, this item was almost unique, one of a handful of copies in existence. What was the book called?'

'*The Steps of Heaven.*'

'Exactly. That is the book which, according to you, was stolen the night Sempere died.'

I nodded. The inspector pulled a cigarette out of the packet and lit it. He took a couple of long drags, then put it out.

'This is my dilemma, Martín. On the one hand you've told me a pile of cock and bull stories that either you've invented, thinking I'm an idiot, or – and I'm not sure if this is worse – you've started to believe yourself from repeating them so often. Everything points to you, and the easiest thing for me would be to wash my hands of all this and pass you over to Marcos and Castelo.'

'But—'

'But, and it's a tiny, insignificant but, a but that my colleagues would have no problem at all dismissing altogether. And yet it bothers me like a speck of dust in my eye and makes me wonder whether, perhaps – and what I'm about to say contradicts everything I've learned in twenty years doing this job – what you've told me is not the truth, but is not false either.'

'All I can say is that I've told you what I remember, inspector. You may or may not believe me. The truth is that at times I don't even believe myself. But it's what I remember.'

Grandes stood up and began to walk around the table.

'This afternoon, when I was talking to María Antonia Sanahuja, or Irene Sabino, in her *pensión*, I asked her if she knew who you were. She said she didn't. I explained that you lived in the tower house where she and Marlasca spent a few months. I asked her again if she remembered you. She said she didn't. A while later I told her you'd visited the Marlasca family tomb and that you were sure you'd seen her there. For the third time that woman denied ever having seen you. And I believed her. I believed her until, as I was leaving, she told me she was feeling a bit cold and she opened her wardrobe to take out a woollen shawl and put it around her shoulders. I then noticed that there was a book on the table. It caught my eye because it was the only book in the room. While she had her back to me, I opened it and I read a handwritten inscription on the first page.'

'*To Señor Sempere, the best friend a book could ever have: you opened the doors to the world for me and showed me how to go through them,*' I quoted from memory.

'Signed by David Martín,' Grandes completed.

The inspector stopped in front of the window.

'In half an hour they'll come for you and I'll be taken off the case,' he said. 'You'll be handed over to Sergeant Marcos, and I'll no longer be able to help you. Have you anything else to tell me that might allow me to save your neck?'

'No.'

'Then grab that ridiculous revolver you've been hiding for hours in your coat and, taking great care not to shoot yourself in the foot, threaten that if I don't hand you the key that opens this door, you'll blow my head off.'

I turned towards the door.

'In exchange I ask only that you tell me where Cristina Sagnier is, if she's still alive, that is.'

I looked down. I couldn't find my voice.

'Did you kill her?'

I let a long silence go by.

'I don't know.'

Grandes came over and handed me the key to the door.

'Get the hell out of here, Martín.'

I hesitated for a second before taking it.

'Don't use the main staircase. At the end of the corridor, to your left, there's a blue door that only opens from the inside and will take you to the fire escape. The exit is on the back alley.'

'How can I thank you?'

'You can start by not wasting time. You have around thirty

minutes before the whole department will be hot on your heels. Don't waste them.'

I took the key and walked to the door. Before leaving I turned round briefly. Grandes had sat down at the table and was looking at me, his expression blank.

'That brooch with the angel,' he said, touching his lapel.

'Yes?'

'I've seen you wearing it on your lapel ever since I met you,' he said.

20

The streets of the Raval quarter were tunnels of shadows dotted with flickering street lamps that barely grazed the darkness. It took me a little over the thirty minutes granted to me by Inspector Grandes to discover that there were two laundries in Calle Cadena. The first, scarcely a cave behind a flight of stairs that glistened with steam, employed only children with violet-stained hands and yellow eyes. The second was an emporium of filth that stank of bleach, and it was hard to believe that anything clean could ever emerge from there. It was run by a large woman who, at the sight of a few coins, wasted no time in admitting that María Antonia Sanahuja worked there six afternoons a week.

'What has she done now?' the matron asked.

'It's an inheritance. Tell me where I can find her and perhaps some of it will come your way.'

The matron laughed, but her eyes shone with greed.

'As far as I know she lives in Pensión Santa Lucía, in Calle Marqués de Barberá. How much has she inherited?'

I dropped the coins on the counter and got out of that grimy hole without bothering to reply.

The *pensión* where Irene Sabino lived languished in a sombre building that looked as if it had been assembled with disinterred bones and stolen headstones. The metal plates on the letter boxes inside the entrance hall were covered in rust. There were no names on the ones for the first two floors. The third floor housed a dressmaking workshop pompously entitled the Mediterranean Textile Company. The fourth floor was occupied by Pensión Santa Lucía. A narrow staircase rose in the gloom, and the dampness from the sewers filtered through the walls, eating away at the paint like acid. After walking up four floors I reached a sloping landing with just one door. I banged on it with my fist. A few minutes later the door was opened by a tall, thin man, seemingly escaped from an El Greco nightmare.

'I'm looking for María Antonia Sanahuja,' I said.

'Are you the doctor?' he asked.

I pushed him to one side and went in. The apartment was a jumble of dark, narrow rooms clustered either side of a corridor that ended in a large window overlooking the inner courtyard. The air was rank with the stench rising from the drains. The man who had opened the door was still standing on the threshold, looking at me in confusion. I assumed he must be one of the residents.

'Which is her room?' I asked.

He gave me an impenetrable look. I pulled out the revolver and showed it to him. Without losing his calm, the man pointed to the last door in the passage. When I got there I realised that it was locked and began to struggle with the handle. The other residents had stepped out into the corridor, a chorus of forgotten souls who looked as if they hadn't seen the sun for years. I recalled my miserable days in Doña Carmen's *pensión* and it occurred to me that my old home looked like the new Ritz Hotel compared to this purgatory, which was only one of many in the maze of the Raval quarter.

'Go back to your rooms,' I said.

No one seemed to have heard me. I raised my hand, showing my weapon. They all darted back into their rooms like frightened rodents, except for the tall Knight of the Doleful Countenance. I concentrated on the door once again.

'She's locked the door from the inside,' the resident explained. 'She's been there all afternoon.'

A smell that reminded me of bitter almonds seeped under the

door. I knocked a few times, but got no reply.

'The landlady has a master key,' suggested the resident. 'If you can wait . . . I don't think she'll be long.'

My only reply was to take a step back and hurl myself with all my might against the door. The lock gave way after the second charge. As soon as I found myself in the room, I was overwhelmed by that bitter, nauseating smell.

'My God,' mumbled the resident behind my back.

The ex-star of the Paralelo lay on a ramshackle bed, pale and covered in sweat. Her lips were black and when she saw me she smiled. Her hands clutched the bottle of poison; she had swallowed it down to the last drop. The stench from her breath filled the room. The resident covered his nose and mouth with his hand and went outside. I gazed at Irene Sabino writhing in pain while the poison ate away at her insides. Death was taking its time.

'Where's Marlasca?'

She looked at me through tears of agony.

'He no longer needed me,' she said. 'He's never loved me.'

Her voice was harsh and broken. A dry cough seized her, a piercing sound ripping from her chest, and a second later a dark liquid trickled through her teeth. Irene Sabino observed me as she clung to the last breath of life. She took my hand and pressed it hard.

'You're damned, like him.'

'What can I do?'

She shook her head. A new coughing fit seized her. The capillaries in her eyes were breaking and a web of bleeding lines spread towards her pupils.

'Where is Ricardo Salvador? Is he in Marlasca's grave, in the mausoleum?'

Irene Sabino shook her head. Her lips formed a soundless word: *Jaco.*

'Where is Salvador, then?'

'He knows where you are. He can see you. He'll come for you.'

I thought she was becoming delirious. Her grip weakened.

'I loved him,' she said. 'He was a good man. A good man. He changed him. He was a good man . . .'

The terrible sound of disintegrating flesh emerged from her lips, and her body was racked by spasms. Irene Sabino died with her eyes fixed on mine, taking the secret of Diego Marlasca with her.

I covered her face with a sheet. In the doorway, the resident made the sign of the cross. I looked around me, trying to find something that might help, some clue to indicate what my next step should be. Irene Sabino had spent her last days in a cell four metres deep by two wide. There were no windows. The metal bed on which her corpse lay, a wardrobe on the other side and a small table against the wall were the only furniture. A suitcase sat under the bed, next to a chamber pot and a hatbox. On the table lay a plate with a few breadcrumbs, a jug of water and a pile of what looked like postcards but turned out to be images of saints and memorial cards given out at funerals. Folded in a white cloth was something shaped like a book. I unwrapped it and found the copy of *The Steps of Heaven* that I had dedicated to Señor Sempere. The compassion awoken in me by the woman's suffering evaporated in an instant. This wretched woman had killed my good friend, and all because she wanted to take this lousy book from him. Then I remembered what Sempere told me the very first time I went into his bookshop: that every book has a soul, the soul of the person who wrote it and of those who read it and dream about it. Sempere had died believing in those words and I could see that, in her own way, Irene Sabino had also believed in them.

I turned the pages and reread the dedication. I found the first mark on the seventh page. A brownish line, in the shape of a six-pointed star, identical to the one she had engraved on my chest with the razor edge some weeks earlier. I realised that the line had been drawn with blood. I went on turning the pages and finding new motifs. Lips. A hand. Eyes. Sempere had given his life for some paltry fortune-teller's mumbo-jumbo.

I put the book in the inside pocket of my coat and knelt down by the bed. I pulled out the suitcase and emptied its contents on the floor: nothing but old clothes and shoes. In the hatbox I found a leather case containing the razor with which Irene Sabino had made the marks on my chest. Suddenly I noticed a shadow crossing the floor and I spun round, aiming the revolver. The tall thin resident looked at me in surprise.

'I think you have company,' he said.

I went out of the room and headed for the front door. As I stepped onto the landing I heard heavy footsteps climbing the stairs. A face appeared in the stairwell, squinting up, and I found myself looking straight into the eyes of Sergeant Marcos two floors down. He moved out of sight and his steps quickened. He was not alone. I closed the door and leaned against it, trying to think. My accomplice observed me expectantly.

'Is there any other way out of here?' I asked.

He shook his head.

'What about the roof terrace?'

He pointed to the same door I had just shut. Three seconds later I felt the impact of Marcos and Castelo's bodies as they tried to knock it down. I moved away, backing along the corridor with my gun pointed towards the door.

'I think I'll go to my room,' the resident said. 'It's been a pleasure.'

'Same here.'

I fixed my eyes on the door, which was shuddering with every blow. The old wood around the hinges and the lock began to crack. By now I was at the end of the corridor and I opened the window overlooking the inner courtyard. A vertical shaft approximately one metre square plunged into the shadows below. The edge of the flat roof was just visible some three metres above the window. On the other side of the shaft a drainpipe was secured to the wall by means of round metal bands, all corroded by rust, with black tears of damp oozing down the spattered surface of the pipe. Behind me, Marcos and Castelo continued to thunder at the door. I turned round and saw that it was almost off its hinges. I reckoned I had only a few seconds left: there was no alternative but to climb onto the windowsill and jump.

I managed to grab hold of the drainpipe and rest a foot on one of the bands that supported it. I stretched up, reaching for the upper section of the pipe, but as soon as I seized it, it came away in my hand and a whole metre of the pipe tumbled down the shaft. I almost fell with it too, but managed to hold on to a piece of metal that attached one of the bands to the wall. The drainpipe on which I had hoped to climb up to the flat roof was now impassable. There were only two ways out of my current situation: to return to the corridor that Marcos and Castelo were about to enter at any moment, or to descend into the black gorge. I heard the door being flung against the inside wall of the apartment and let myself begin to slide, holding on to the drainpipe as best I could, tearing off quite a bit of skin in the process. I had managed to descend about a metre and a half when I saw the shape of the two policemen in the beam of light cast by the window onto the darkness of the shaft. Marcos's face was the first to appear as he leaned out. He smiled. I asked myself whether he was going shoot me right there and then. Castelo popped up next to him.

'Stay here. I'll go down to the apartment below,' Marcos ordered.

Castelo nodded. They wanted me alive, at least for a few hours. I heard Marcos running away. It wouldn't be long before I saw him looking out of the window scarcely a metre below. I glanced down and saw that there was light at the windows of the second and first floors, but the third floor was in darkness. Carefully I lowered myself until I felt my foot touching the next band. The third-floor window was now in front of me, with an empty corridor leading from it towards the door at the far end. I could hear Marcos knocking. By that time of day the dressmakers had already closed and nobody was there. The knocking stopped and I realised that Marcos had gone down to the second floor to try his luck there. I looked up and saw that Castelo was still watching me, licking his lips like a cat.

'Don't fall – we're going to have some fun when we catch you,' he said.

I heard voices on the second floor and knew that Marcos had succeeded in getting into the apartment. Without thinking twice, I threw myself with all the strength I could muster against the window of the third floor. I smashed through the windowpane, keeping my face and neck covered with my coat, and landed in a pool of broken glass. I hauled myself up and, as I did so, noticed a dark stain spreading across my left arm. A shard of glass, sharp as a dagger, protruded just above my elbow. I caught hold of it and pulled. The cold sensation gave way to a blaze of pain that made me fall to my knees. From the floor I saw that Castelo had started to climb down the drainpipe. Before I was able to pull out the gun, he leaped towards the window. I saw his hands grabbing hold of the outer frame. Instinctively, I jumped up and started hammering at the frame with all my might, putting the whole weight of my body behind every blow. I heard the bones in his fingers break with a dry snapping sound, and Castelo howled in pain. I pulled out the gun and pointed it at his face, but his hands had already begun to slip. A second of terror in his eyes, and then he fell down the shaft, his body ricocheting against the walls, leaving a trail of blood in the patches of light that filtered through from the lower windows.

I dragged myself towards the front door. The wound on my arm was throbbing and I noticed that I also had a few cuts on my legs, but I kept moving. On either side of the passageway there were rooms in semi-darkness full of sewing machines, bobbins of thread and tables topped with large rolls of material. I reached the main door and took hold of the handle. A tenth of a second later I felt it turn. Marcos was on the other side, attempting to force the lock. I retreated a few steps. A huge roar suddenly shook the door and part of the lock shot out in a cloud of sparks and blue smoke. Marcos was going to blast the lock away. I took shelter in the nearest room, which was filled with motionless figures, some with arms or legs missing: shop-window mannequins all piled up together. I slipped in between the torsos just as I heard a second shot. The front door opened with a bang. A halo of gunpowder floated in the hazy yellow light that seeped in from the landing. I heard Marcos fumbling with the door, then the sound of his heavy footsteps in the hallway. Glued to the wall, hiding behind the dummies, I clutched the revolver in trembling hands.

'Martín, come out,' Marcos said calmly as he advanced. 'I'm not going to hurt you. I have orders from Grandes to take you to the police station. We've found that man Marlasca. He's confessed to everything. You're clean. Don't go and do something stupid now. Come on, let's talk about this at police headquarters.'

I saw him walk past the doorway of the room where I was hiding.

'Martín, listen to me. Grandes is on his way. We can clear this up without any need to complicate matters further.'

I cocked the hammer. Marcos's footsteps came to a halt. There was a slight scraping sound on the tiles. He was on the other side of the wall. He knew perfectly well that I was in that room, and that I couldn't get out without going past him. I saw his profile slink through the doorway and melt into the liquid darkness of the room;

410

the gleam of his eyes was the only trace of his presence. He was barely four metres away from me. I began to slide down against the wall until I reached the floor. I could see Marcos's shoes behind the legs of the dummies.

'I know you're here, Martín. Stop being childish.'

He stopped and didn't move. Then I saw him kneel down and touch the trail of blood I had left with his fingertips. He brought a finger to his mouth. I imagined he was smiling.

'You're bleeding a lot, Martín. You need a doctor. Come out and I'll take you to a surgery.'

I kept quiet. Marcos stopped in front of a table and picked up a shining object that was lying among scraps of material. Large textile scissors.

'It's up to you, Martín.'

I heard the shearing sound made by the edge of the scissor blades as he opened and closed them. A stab of pain gripped my arm and I bit my lip to stifle the groan. Marcos turned his face in my direction.

'Speaking of blood, you'll be pleased to hear that we have your little whore, that Isabella girl. Before we start with you we'll have some fun with her . . .'

I raised the weapon and pointed it at his face. The sheen of the metal gave me away. Marcos jumped at me, knocking down the dummies and dodging the shot. I felt his weight on my body and his breath on my face. The scissor blades closed only a centimetre from my left eye. I butted my forehead against his face with all the strength I could muster and he fell to one side. Then I lifted my gun and pointed it at him. Marcos, his lip split, sat up and fixed his eyes on mine.

'You don't have the guts,' he whispered.

He placed his hand on the barrel and smiled at me. I pulled the trigger. The bullet blew off his hand, flinging his arm back. Marcos fell to the floor, holding his mutilated, smoking wrist, while his face, splattered with gunpowder burns, dissolved into a grimace of pain, a silent howl. I got up and left him there, bleeding to death in a pool of his own urine.

21

Somehow I managed to crawl through the narrow streets of the Raval as far as the Paralelo, where a row of taxis had formed outside the Apolo theatre. I slipped into the first one I could find. When he heard the door, the driver turned round; he took one look at me and pulled a face. I fell onto the back seat, ignoring his protests.

'Listen, you're not going to die on me back there, are you?'

'The sooner you take me where I want to go, the sooner you'll get shot of me.'

The driver cursed under his breath and started the engine.

'Where do you want to go?'

I don't know, I thought.

'Just drive and I'll let you know.'

'Drive where?'

'Pedralbes.'

Twenty minutes later I glimpsed the lights of Villa Helius. I pointed them out to the driver, who couldn't get rid of me fast enough. He left me at the entrance to the mansion and almost forgot to charge me the fare. I staggered up to the large front door and rang the bell, then collapsed on the steps and leaned my head against the wall. I heard footsteps approaching and at some point thought I saw the door open and heard someone saying my name. I felt a hand on my forehead and I seemed to recognise Vidal's eyes.

'I'm sorry, Don Pedro,' I begged. 'I had nowhere else to go . . .'

I heard him call out and after a while I felt various hands taking my legs and arms and lifting me. When I opened my eyes again I was in Don Pedro's bedroom, lying on the same bed he had shared with Cristina during the two short months of their marriage. I sighed. Vidal was watching me from the end of the bed.

'Don't speak now,' he said. 'The doctor is on his way.'

'Don't believe them, Don Pedro,' I moaned. 'Don't believe them.'

'Of course not.'

Vidal picked up a blanket and covered me with it.

'I'll go downstairs to wait for the doctor,' he said. 'Get some rest.'

After a while I heard footsteps and voices coming into the bedroom. I could feel my clothes being removed and glimpsed the dozens of cuts covering my body like bloodstained ivy. I felt tweezers poking into my wounds, pulling out needles of glass that brought with them bits of skin and flesh. I felt the heat of antiseptic and the pricks of the needle as the doctor sewed up my wounds. There was no longer any pain, only tiredness. Once I had been bandaged, sewn up and mended like a broken puppet, the doctor and Vidal covered me with a sheet and placed my head on the sweetest, softest pillow I had ever come across. I opened my eyes to see the doctor's face, an aristocratic-looking gentleman with a reassuring smile. He was holding a hypodermic syringe.

'You've been lucky, young man,' he said as he plunged the needle into my arm.

'What's that?' I mumbled.

Vidal's face appeared next to the doctor's.

'It will help you rest.'

A cold mist spread up my arm and across my chest. I felt myself falling into a chasm of black velvet while Vidal and the doctor watched me from on high. Gradually, the world closed until it was reduced to a single drop of light that evaporated in my hands. I sank into that warm, chemical peace from which I would have preferred never to escape.

I remember a world of black water under the ice. Moonlight touched the frozen vault, breaking into thousands of dusty beams that swayed in the current as it pulled me away. The white mantle draped around her body undulated, the silhouette of her body just visible in the translucent waters. Cristina stretched out a hand towards me and I fought against that cold, heavy current. When our fingers were only a hair's breadth apart, a sombre mass unfolded its wings behind her, enveloping her like an explosion of ink. Tentacles of black light surrounded her arms, her throat and her face, dragging her inexorably towards a dark void.

22

I awoke to hear Víctor Grandes saying my name. I sat bolt upright, not recognising where I was – if anything, the place looked like a suite in a luxury hotel. The shooting pain from the dozens of cuts that streaked my torso brought me back to reality. I was in Vidal's bedroom in Villa Helius. Through the closed shutters, a hint of mid-afternoon light. A fire was blazing in the grate and the room was warm. The voices came from the floor below. Pedro Vidal and Víctor Grandes.

Ignoring the stinging of my skin, I got out of bed. My dirty, bloodstained clothes had been thrown onto an armchair. I looked for the coat. The gun was still in the pocket. I drew back the hammer and left the room, following the trail of voices as far as the stairs. I went down a few steps, keeping close to the wall.

'I'm very sorry about your men, inspector,' I heard Vidal saying. 'Rest assured that if David gets in touch with me, or if I hear of his whereabouts, I'll let you know immediately.'

'I'm grateful for your help, Señor Vidal. I'm sorry to bother you in the circumstances, but the situation is extremely serious.'

'I understand. Thank you for your visit.'

The sound of the front door closing. Vidal's laboured breathing at the foot of the staircase. I went down a few more steps and found him leaning his forehead against the door. When he heard me he opened his eyes and turned round.

He didn't say anything, just looked at the gun I held in my hands. I put it down on the small table at the bottom of the stairs.

'Come on, let's see if we can find you some clean clothes,' he said.

I followed him to a huge dressing room that looked more like a costume museum. All the exquisite suits I remembered from Vidal's years of glory were there. Dozens of ties, shoes, and cufflinks in red velvet boxes.

'This is all from when I was young. It should fit you.'

Vidal chose for me. He handed me a shirt that was probably

414

worth as much as a small plot of land, a three-piece suit made to measure in London and a pair of Italian shoes that would not have disgraced the boss's wardrobe. I dressed in silence while Vidal observed me with a pensive look.

'A bit wide on the shoulders, but you'll have to make do,' he said, handing me a pair of sapphire cufflinks.

'What did the inspector tell you?'

'Everything.'

'And you believed him?'

'What does it matter?'

'It matters to me.'

Vidal sat on a stool by a wall that was covered in mirrors from ceiling to floor.

'He says you know where Cristina is,' he said.

I did not deny it.

'Is she alive?'

I looked him in the eye and, very slowly, nodded my head. Vidal gave a weak smile, eluding my eyes. Then he burst into tears, emitting a deep groan that came from his very soul. I sat down next to him and hugged him.

'Forgive me, Don Pedro, forgive me . . .'

Later, as the sun began to drop over the horizon, Vidal gathered my old clothes and threw them into the fire. Before he abandoned my coat to the flames he pulled out the copy of *The Steps of Heaven* and handed it to me.

'Of the two books you wrote last year, this was the good one,' he said.

I watched him poking my clothes about in the fire.

'When did you realise?'

Vidal shrugged.

'Even a conceited idiot can't be fooled forever, David.'

I couldn't make out whether there was resentment in his tone, or just sadness.

'I did it because I thought I was helping you, Don Pedro.'

'I know.'

He smiled.

'Forgive me,' I murmured.

'You must leave the city. There's a cargo ship moored in the San

Sebastián dock that sets sail tonight. It's all arranged. Ask for Captain Olmo. He's expecting you. Take one of the cars from the garage. You can leave it at the port. Pep will fetch it tomorrow. Don't speak to anyone. Don't go back to your house. You'll need money.'

'I have enough money,' I lied.

'There's never enough. When you disembark in Marseilles, Olmo will go with you to a bank and will give you fifty thousand francs.'

'Don Pedro—'

'Listen to me. Those two men that Grandes says you've killed . . .'

'Marcos and Castelo. I think they worked for your father, Don Pedro.'

Vidal shook his head.

'My father and his lawyers only ever deal with the top people, David. How do you think those two knew where to find you thirty minutes after you left the police station?'

A cold feeling of certainty washed over me.

'Through my friend, Inspector Víctor Grandes.'

Vidal agreed.

'Grandes let you go because he didn't want to dirty his hands in the police station. As soon as he got you out of there, his two men were on your trail. Your death was to read like a telegram: escaping murder suspect dies while resisting arrest.'

'Just like the old days on the news,' I said.

'Some things never change, David. You should know better than anyone.'

He opened his wardrobe and handed me a brand new coat. I accepted it and put the book in the inside pocket. Vidal smiled at me.

'For once in your life you're well dressed.'

'It suited you better, Don Pedro.'

'That goes without saying.'

'Don Pedro, there are a lot of things—'

'They don't matter any more, David. You don't owe me an explanation.'

'I owe you much more than an explanation . . .'

'Then tell me about her.'

Vidal looked at me with desperate eyes that begged me to lie to him. We sat in the sitting room, facing the French windows with their view over the whole of Barcelona, and I lied to him with all my heart. I told him that Cristina had rented a small attic in Rue de

Soufflot, under the name of Madame Vidal, and had said that she'd wait for me every day, in the middle of the afternoon, by the fountain in the Luxembourg Gardens. I told him that she spoke about him constantly, that she would never forget him and that I knew that however many years I spent by her side I'd never be able to fill the void he had left. Don Pedro's gaze was lost in the distance.

'You must promise me you'll look after her, David. That you'll never leave her. Whatever happens, you'll stay by her side.'

'I promise, Don Pedro.'

In the pale light of evening all I could see was a defeated old man, sick with memories and guilt; a man who had never believed and whose only balm now was to believe.

'I wish I'd been a better friend to you, David.'

'You've been the best of friends, Don Pedro. You've been much more than that.'

Vidal stretched out his arm and took my hand. He was trembling.

'Grandes spoke to me about that man, the one you call the boss . . . He says you are in debt to him and you think the only way of paying him back is by giving him a pure soul . . .'

'That's nonsense, Don Pedro. Don't pay any attention.'

'Would a dirty, tired soul like mine be of any use to you?'

'I know of no purer soul than yours, Don Pedro.'

Vidal smiled.

'If I could have changed places with your father, I would have, David.'

'I know.'

He stood up and gazed at the evening swooping over the city.

'You should be on your way,' he said. 'Go to the garage and take a car. Whichever you like. I'll see if I have some cash.'

I picked up the coat, then went into the garden and walked over to the coach house. The Villa Helius garage was home to two automobiles that gleamed like royal carriages. I chose the smaller, more discreet car, a black Hispano-Suiza that looked as if it had not been used more than two or three times and still smelled new. I sat at the steering wheel and started the engine, then drove the car out of the garage and waited in the yard. A minute went by, and still Vidal hadn't come out. I got out of the car, leaving the engine running. I went back into the house to say goodbye to him and tell him not to worry about the money, I would manage. As I walked across the entrance hall I remembered I'd left the gun on the table. When I went to pick it up it wasn't there.

'Don Pedro?'

The door to the sitting room was ajar. I looked in and could see him standing in the middle of the room. He raised my father's revolver to his chest, placing the barrel at his heart. I rushed towards him but the roar of the shot drowned my shouts. The weapon fell from his hands. His body slumped over and he fell to the floor, leaving a scarlet trail on the marble tiles. I dropped to my knees beside him and supported him in my arms. Dark, thick blood gushed from the hole where the bullet had pierced his clothes. Don Pedro's eyes locked on mine while his smile filled with blood, and his body stopped trembling, and he collapsed. The room was filled with the scent of gunpowder and misery.

23

I returned to the car and sat down, my bloodstained hands on the steering wheel. I could hardly breathe. I waited a minute and then released the handbrake. The lights of the city throbbed under the shroud of the evening sky. I set off down the street, leaving the silhouette of Villa Helius behind me. When I reached Avenida Pearson I stopped and looked through the rear-view mirror. A car had just turned into the street from a hidden alleyway and positioned itself some fifty metres behind me. Its lights were not on. Víctor Grandes.

I continued down Avenida de Pedralbes until I passed the large wrought-iron dragon guarding the entrance to Finca Güell. Inspector Grandes's car was still following about a hundred metres behind. When I reached Avenida Diagonal I turned left towards the centre of town. There were barely any cars around so Grandes had no difficulty following me until I decided to turn right, hoping to lose him through the narrow streets of Las Corts. By then the inspector was aware that his presence was no secret and had turned on his headlights. For about twenty minutes we dodged through a knot of streets and trams. I slipped in between omnibuses and carts, with Grandes's headlights relentlessly at my back. After a while the hill of Montjuïc rose before me. The large palace of the International Exhibition and the remains of the other pavilions had been closed for just two weeks, but in the twilight mist they looked like the ruins of some great, forgotten civilisation. I took the large avenue to the cascade of ghostly lights that illuminated the Exhibition fountains, accelerating as quickly as the engine would allow. As we ascended the road that snaked its way up the mountain towards the Great Stadium, Grandes was gaining ground until I could clearly distinguish his face in the rear-view mirror. For a moment I was tempted to take the road leading to the military fortress on the summit, but I knew that if there was one place with no way out, it was there. My only hope was to make it to the other side of the mountain, the side that looked down onto the sea, and disappear into one of the docks at the port. To do that I needed to put some time between us, but the inspector was now about fifteen metres behind me. The large balustrades of Miramar opened up before us, with the city spread out at our feet. I pulled at the handbrake with all my strength and let Grandes smash into the Hispano-Suiza. The impact pushed us both along almost twenty metres, raising a spray of sparks across the road. I let go of the brake and went forward a short distance while Grandes was still struggling to regain control, then I put my car into reverse and accelerated hard.

By the time Grandes realised what I was doing it was already too late. Thanks to one of the most select makes in town, I charged at him with the all the power of a bodywork and an engine that were far more robust than those protecting him. The force of the crash shook Grandes from his seat and his head banged against the windscreen, smashing it to smithereens. Steam surged from the bonnet of his car and the headlights went out. I put my car into gear and accelerated away, heading for the Miramar viewpoint. After a few seconds I realised that in the collision the back mudguard had been crushed against the tyre, which now rubbed on the metal as it turned. The smell of burning rubber filled the car. Twenty metres further on the tyre burst and the car began to zigzag until it came to a halt, wreathed in a cloud of black smoke. I abandoned the Hispano-Suiza and glanced back at where Grandes's car still sat –

the inspector was dragging himself out of the driver's seat. I looked around me. The stop for the cable cars that crossed over the port and the town from Montjuïc to the tower of San Sebastián was about fifty metres away. I could make out the shape of the cars dangling from their wires as they slid through the dusk, and I ran towards them.

One of the staff was getting ready to close the doors to the building when he saw me hurrying up the road. He held the door open and pointed inside.

'Last trip of the evening,' he warned. 'You'd better hurry.'

The ticket office was about to close but I scurried in, bought the last ticket on sale, and rushed over to join a group of four people waiting by the cabin. I didn't notice their clothes until the employee opened the door. Priests.

'The cable railway was built for the International Exhibition and is equipped with the latest technology. Its safety is guaranteed at all times. From the start of the journey this security door, which can only be opened from the outside, will remain locked to avoid accidents, or, heaven forbid, a suicide attempt. Of course, with Your Eminences on board, there is no danger of—'

'Young man,' I interrupted. 'Can you speed up the ceremony? It's getting late.'

The employee threw me a hostile glance. One of the priests noticed my bloodstained hands and crossed himself. The young man continued with his long-winded speech.

'You'll be travelling through the Barcelona sky at a height of some seventy metres above the waters of the port, enjoying spectacular views over the city until now only available to swallows, seagulls and other creatures endowed with feathers by the Almighty. The trip lasts ten minutes and makes two stops, the first at the central tower in the port, or as I like to call it Barcelona's Eiffel Tower, or the tower of San Jaime, and the second and last at the tower of San Sebastián. Without further delay, I wish Your Eminences a happy journey, and on behalf of the company I hope we will see you again on board the Port of Barcelona Cable Railway in the not-too-distant future.'

I was the first person to enter the cable car. The employee held out his hand as the four priests went by, hoping for a tip that never graced his fingertips. Visibly disappointed, he slammed the door shut and turned round, ready to operate the lever. Inspector Víctor Grandes was waiting there for him, in a sorry state but smiling and holding out his badge. The employee opened the door and Grandes strode into the cable car, greeting the priests with a nod and winking at me. Seconds later we were floating out into the void.

The cabin lifted off from the terminal towards the mountain edge. The priests had all clustered on one side, ready to enjoy the evening views over Barcelona and ignore whatever murky business had brought Grandes and me together in that place. The inspector sidled over and showed me the gun he had in his hand. Large reddish clouds hung over the water of the port. The cable car sank into one of them and for a moment it felt as if we had plunged into a lake of fire.

'Have you ever been on this before?' Grandes asked.

I nodded.

'My daughter loves it. Once a month she asks me to take her on a return trip. A bit expensive, but it's worth it.'

'With the amount of money old Señor Vidal is paying you for my head, I'm sure you'll be able to bring your daughter here every day, if you feel like it. Simple curiosity: what price did he put on me?'

Grandes smiled. The cable car emerged from the crimson cloud and we found ourselves suspended over the port, with the lights of the city spilling over its dark waters.

'Fifteen thousand pesetas,' he replied, patting a white envelope that peeped out of his coat pocket.

'I suppose I should feel flattered. Some people would kill for two duros. Does that include the price of betraying your two men?'

'Let me remind you that the only person who has killed anyone here is you.'

By now the four priests were watching us, filled with shock and concern, oblivious to the delights of the vertiginous flight over the city. Grandes gave them a cursory look.

'When we reach the first stop, if it's not too much to ask, I'd be grateful if Your Eminences would get off and allow us to discuss a few mundane matters.'

The tower on the docks of Barcelona port rose before us like a cupola of steel with great metal threads wrenched from a mechanical cathedral. The cable car entered the dome and stopped by the platform. When the door opened, the four priests hastened out. Grandes, gun in hand, told me to go to the far end of the cabin. As he got out, one of the priests gave me an anxious look.

'Don't worry, young man, we'll call the police,' he said, just before the door closed.

'Yes, please do!' replied Grandes.

Once the door was locked, the cable car resumed its journey. We emerged from the tower and started on the last stage of the crossing. Grandes went over to the window and gazed at the view of the city, a fantasy of lights and mist, cathedrals and palaces, alleyways and wide avenues woven into a labyrinth of shadows.

'The city of the damned,' said Grandes. 'The further away you are, the prettier it looks.'

'Is that my epitaph?'

'I'm not going to kill you, Martín. I don't kill people. You're going to do that for me. As a favour. For me and for yourself. You know I'm right.'

Saying no more, the inspector fired three shots at the locking mechanism of the door and kicked it open. The door was left hanging in the air and a blast of damp wind filled the cabin.

'You won't feel anything, Martín. Believe me. The impact will only take a tenth of a second. It's instant. And then, peace.'

I gazed at the door. A fall of over seventy metres into the void opened up before me. I looked at the tower of San Sebastián and reckoned there were still a few minutes to go before we would arrive. Grandes read my thoughts.

'Soon it will all be over, Martín. You should be grateful to me.'

'Do you really think I killed all those people, inspector?'

Grandes raised his revolver and pointed it at my heart.

'I don't know, and I don't care.'

'I thought we were friends.'

He muttered in disagreement.

'You don't have any friends, Martín.'

I heard the roar of the shot and felt a blow to my chest, as if I'd been hit in the ribs with a jackhammer. I fell on my back, unable to breathe, a spasm of pain spreading through my body like petrol on fire. Grandes had grabbed my feet and was pulling me towards the door. The top of the tower of San Sebastián appeared between veils of cloud. Grandes stepped over my body and knelt down behind me, then started pushing me by my shoulders towards the door. I felt the cold air on my legs. Grandes gave another push and my waist slid over the edge. The pull of gravity was instant. I was beginning to fall.

I stretched out my arms towards the policeman and dug my fingers into his neck. Anchored by the weight of my body, the inspector was trapped and couldn't move from the doorway. I pressed with all my might, pushing on his windpipe, squashing the arteries in his neck. He struggled to free himself from my grip with one hand while the other groped about for his gun. Finally his fingers found the trigger. The shot grazed my temple and hit the doorframe, but the bullet bounced back into the cabin and went clean through his hand. I sunk my nails further into his neck, feeling his skin yield. Grandes groaned. Using all the strength I had left, I managed to get more than half my body back inside the car. Once I was able to grab hold of the metal walls, I let go of Grandes and threw myself away from him.

I touched my chest and found the hole left by the inspector's shot. I opened my coat and pulled out the copy of *The Steps of Heaven*. The bullet had pierced the front cover and the four hundred pages of the book, so that it peeped out, like the tip of a silver finger, through the back cover. Next to me, Grandes was writhing on the ground, grabbing at his neck with despair. His face was purple and the veins on his forehead and temples stood out like tensed cables. He looked at me, pleading. A cobweb of broken blood vessels spread across his eyes and I realised I had squashed his windpipe and that he was suffocating. I watched him as he lay shaking on the floor in agony. I pulled the white envelope from his pocket, opened it and counted fifteen thousand pesetas. The price of my life. I put the envelope in my pocket. Grandes was dragging himself across the floor towards the gun. I stood up and kicked it out of reach. He grabbed my ankle, begging for mercy.

'Where's Marlasca?' I asked.

His throat emitted a dull moan. I fixed my eyes on his and realised that he was laughing. The cable car had already entered the tower of San Sebastián when I pushed him through the doorway and saw his body plunge eighty metres through a maze of rails, cables, cogwheels and steel bars that tore him to pieces as he fell.

24

The tower house was buried in darkness. I groped my way up the stone staircase until I reached the landing and found the front door ajar. I pushed it open and waited on the threshold, scanning the shadows that filled the long corridor. I took a few steps then stopped, not moving a muscle. I felt the wall until I found the light switch. I tried it four times but without success. The first door to the right, three metres away, led into the kitchen. I remembered that I kept an oil lamp in the larder and there I found it, among unopened coffee tins from the Can Gispert emporium. I put the lamp on the kitchen table and lit it. A faint amber light suffused the kitchen walls. I picked it up and stepped out into the corridor.

As I advanced, the flickering light held high, I expected to see something or someone emerge at any moment from one of the doors on either side. I knew I was not alone; I could smell it. A sour stench, of anger and hatred, floated in the air. I reached the end of the corridor and stopped in front of the last room. The lamp cast its soft glow over the wardrobe that had been pulled away from the wall and the clothes thrown on the floor – exactly as I had left them when Grandes had come to arrest me two nights ago. I continued towards the foot of the spiral staircase and warily mounted the stairs, peering behind my shoulder every two or three steps, until I reached the study. The ruby aura of twilight flooded in through the windows. I hurried across the room to the wall where the trunk stood and opened it. The folder with the boss's manuscript had disappeared.

I crossed the room again, heading back to the stairs. As I walked past my desk I noticed that the keyboard of my old typewriter had been destroyed – as if someone had been punching it. Gingerly, I went down the steps, entered the corridor, and put my head round the entrance to the gallery. Even in the half-light I could see that all my books had been hurled onto the floor and the leather of the armchairs was in tatters. I turned round to examine the twenty metres of corridor that separated me from the front door. The light from the lamp only reached half that distance, beyond which the shadows rolled on like black water.

I remembered I'd left the door to the apartment open when I came in. Now it was closed. I walked on a couple of metres, but something stopped me as I passed the last room in the corridor. When I'd walked past it the first time I hadn't noticed, because the door to that room opened to the left and I hadn't looked in far enough to see. But now, as I drew closer, I saw it clearly. A white dove, its wings spread out like a cross, was nailed to the door. Drops of blood dripped down the wood. Fresh blood.

I entered the room. I looked behind the door, but there wasn't anyone there. The wardrobe was still pulled to one side. The cold, damp air that emanated from the hole in the wall permeated the room. I left the lamp on the floor and placed my hands on the softened filler around the hole. I started to scratch with my nails and felt it crumble beneath my fingers. I looked around and found an old paperknife in a drawer of one of the small tables piled up in a corner. I dug the knife-edge into the filler. The plaster came away easily; it was only about three centimetres thick. On the other side I discovered wood.

A door.

I searched for the edges using the knife, and the shape of the door began to emerge. By then I'd already forgotten the close presence that was poisoning the house, lurking in the shadows. The door had no handle, just a lock that had rusted away from being covered by damp plaster for years. I plunged the paperknife into it and struggled in vain, then began to kick the lock until the filler that held it in place was slowly dislodged. I finished freeing it with the paperknife and, once it was loose, the door opened with a simple push.

A gust of putrid air burst from within, impregnating my clothes and my skin. I picked up the lamp and entered. The room was a rectangle about five or six metres deep. The walls were covered with pictures and inscriptions that looked as if they had been made with someone's fingers. The lines were brownish and dark. Dried blood. The floor was covered with what at first I thought was dust, but when I lowered the lamp turned out to be the remains of small bones. Animal bones broken up into a layer of ash. Numerous objects hung from a piece of black string suspended from the ceiling. I recognised religious figures, images of saints, madonnas with their faces burned and their eyes pulled out, crucifixes knotted with barbed wire, and the remains of tin toys and dolls with glass eyes. The silhouette was at the far end, almost invisible.

A chair facing the corner. On the chair I saw a figure. It was dressed in black. A man. His hands were cuffed behind his back. Thick wire bound his arms and legs to the frame. An icy coldness took hold of me.

'Salvador?'

I advanced slowly towards him. The figure did not move. I paused a step away and stretched out my hand. My fingers skimmed over the man's hair and rested on his shoulder. I wanted to turn his body round, but felt something give way under my fingers. A second later I thought I heard a whisper and the corpse crumbled into dust that spilled through his clothes and the wire bonds, then rose in a dark cloud that remained suspended between the walls of the prison where for years this man's body had remained hidden. I looked at the film of ash on my hands and brought them to my face, spreading the remains of Ricardo Salvador's soul on my skin. When I opened my eyes I saw that Diego Marlasca, his jailer, was waiting in the doorway, with the boss's manuscript in his hand and fire in his eyes.

'I've been reading it while I waited for you, Martín,' said Marlasca. 'A masterpiece. The boss will know how to reward me when I give it to him on your behalf. I admit that I was never able to solve the puzzle. I fell by the wayside. I'm glad to see the boss found a more talented successor.'

He put the manuscript on the floor.

'Get out of my way.'

'I'm sorry, Martín. Believe me. I'm sorry. I was starting to like you,' he said, pulling out what looked like an ivory handle from his pocket. 'But I can't let you out of this room. It's time for you to take the place of poor Salvador.'

He pressed a button on the handle and a double-edged blade shone in the gloom.

He threw himself at me, shouting angrily. The blade sliced my cheek open and would have gouged out my left eye if I hadn't jumped to one side. I fell backwards onto the bones and dust covering the floor. Marlasca grabbed the knife with both hands and crashed down on top of me, putting all his weight on the blade. The knifepoint stopped only centimetres from my chest, while my right hand held Marlasca's throat.

He twisted to bite me on the wrist and I punched him hard in the face with my free hand. He seemed unperturbed, driven by an anger that went beyond reason and pain, and I knew he wouldn't let me out of that cell alive. He charged at me with incredible strength. I felt the tip of the knife cut through my skin. I hit him again as hard as I could. My fist collided with his face and I heard the bones of his nose crack. Marlasca gave another shout, ignoring the pain, and plunged the knife a centimetre into my flesh. A sharp pain seared through my chest. I hit him once more, searching out his eye sockets with my fingertips, but Marlasca raised his chin and I could only dig my nails into his cheek. This time I felt his teeth on my fingers.

I plunged my fist into his mouth, splitting his lips and knocking out a few teeth. I heard him howl and then he hesitated for a second before coming at me again. I pushed him to one side and he fell to the floor, dropping the knife, his face a mask of blood. I stepped away from him, praying that he wouldn't get up again. A moment later he had crawled over to the knife and was getting to his feet.

He grasped the blade and threw himself on me with a deafening shriek, but this time he didn't catch me by surprise. I reached for the handle of the lamp and swung it at him with all my might. The lamp smashed against his face, spreading oil over his eyes, his lips, his throat and his chest. It caught fire immediately. In just a few seconds a blanket of flames covered his entire body. His hair shrivelled. I saw a look of hatred through the tongues of fire that were devouring his eyelids. I picked up the manuscript and fled.

Marlasca still held the knife in his hands as he tried to follow me out of that accursed room and fell face down on the pile of old clothes, which then burst into flames. The fire leaped at the wood of the wardrobe and the furniture that was piled up against the wall. I rushed towards the corridor but still he pursued me, arms outstretched, trying to catch me. As I reached the door I turned round and saw Diego Marlasca being consumed by the blaze, furiously punching the walls, which caught alight at his touch. The fire spread to the books scattered in the gallery and then the curtains. It writhed across the ceiling like bright orange snakes, licking the frames of doors and windows, creeping up the steps to the study. The last image I recall is of a doomed man falling to his knees at the end of the corridor, the vain hopes of his madness lost and his body reduced to a human torch by a storm of flames that spread relentlessly through the tower house. I opened the front door and ran down the stairs.

Some of the neighbours had assembled in the street when they saw the first flames in the windows of the tower. Nobody noticed me as I slipped away. Shortly afterwards, I heard the windowpanes in the study shatter. I turned to see the fire embracing the dragon-shaped weathervane. Soon I was making my way towards Paseo del Borne, walking against a tide of local residents who were all staring upwards, their eyes captivated by the brightness of the pyre that rose into the black sky.

25

That night I returned, for the last time, to the Sempere & Sons bookshop. The CLOSED sign was hanging on the door, but as I drew closer I noticed there was still a light on inside and that Isabella was standing behind the counter, alone, engrossed in a thick accounts ledger. Judging from the expression on her face, it predicted the end of the old bookshop's days. But as I watched her nibbling the end of her pencil and scratching the tip of her nose with her forefinger, I was certain that as long as she was there the place would never disappear. Her presence would save it, as it had saved me. I didn't dare break that moment so I stayed where I was, smiling to myself, watching her unawares. Suddenly, as if she'd read my thoughts, she looked up and saw me. I waved at her and saw that, despite herself, her eyes were filled with tears. She closed the book and came running out from behind the counter to open the door. She was staring at me as if she couldn't quite believe I was there.

'That man said you'd run away . . . He said we'd never see you again.'

I presumed Grandes had paid her a visit before he died.

'I want you to know that I didn't believe a word of what he told me,' said Isabella. 'Let me call—'

'I don't have much time, Isabella.'

She looked at me, crestfallen.

'You're leaving, aren't you?'

I nodded. Isabella gulped nervously.

'I told you I don't like farewells.'

'I like them even less. That's why I haven't come to say goodbye. I've come to return a couple of things that don't belong to me.'

I pulled out the copy of *The Steps of Heaven* and handed it to her.

'This should never have left the glass case containing Señor Sempere's personal collection.'

Isabella took it and when she saw the bullet still trapped in its pages she looked at me in silence. I then pulled out the white envelope that held the fifteen thousand pesetas with which old Vidal had tried to buy my death, and left it on the counter.

'And this goes towards all the books that Sempere gave me over the years.'

Isabella opened it and counted the money in astonishment.

'I don't know whether I can accept it . . .'

'Consider it my wedding present, in advance.'

'And there was I, still hoping you'd lead me to the altar one day, even if only to give me away.'

'Nothing would have pleased me more.'

'But you have to go.'

'Yes.'

'Forever.'

'For a while.'

'What if I come with you?'

I kissed her on the forehead, then hugged her.

'Wherever I go, you'll always be with me, Isabella. Always.'

'I have no intention of missing you.'

'I know.'

'Can I at least come with you to the train or whatever?'

I hesitated too long to refuse those last few minutes of her company.

'To make sure you're really going, and I've finally got rid of you,' she added.

'It's a deal.'

*

We strolled down the Ramblas, Isabella's arm in mine. When we reached Calle Arco del Teatro, we crossed over towards the dark alleyway that ran deep into the Raval quarter.

'Isabella, you mustn't tell anyone what you're about to see tonight.'

'Not even Sempere junior?'

I sighed.

'Of course you can tell him. You can tell him everything. We can hardly keep any secrets from him.'

When the doors opened, Isaac, the keeper, smiled at us and stepped aside.

'It's about time we had an important visit,' he said, bowing to Isabella. 'Am I right in supposing you'd rather be the guide, Martín?'

'If you don't mind . . .'

Isaac stretched out his hand and I shook it.

'Good luck,' he said.

The keeper withdrew into the shadows, leaving me alone with Isabella. My ex-assistant – now the new manager of Sempere & Sons – observed everything with a mixture of astonishment and apprehension.

'What sort of a place is this?' she asked.

I took her hand and led her the remaining distance to the large hall that housed the entrance.

'Welcome to the Cemetery of Forgotten Books, Isabella.'

Isabella looked up towards the glass dome and became lost in that impossible vision of white rays of light that criss-crossed a babel of tunnels, footbridges and bridges, all leading into a cathedral made of books.

'This place is a mystery. A sanctuary. Every book, every volume you see, has a soul. The soul of the person who wrote it and the soul of those who read it and lived and dreamed with it. Every time a book changes hands, every time someone runs his eyes down its pages, its spirit grows and strengthens. In this place, books no longer remembered by anyone, books that are lost in time, live forever, waiting for the day when they will reach a new reader's hands, a new spirit . . .'

*

Later I left Isabella waiting by the entrance to the labyrinth and set off alone through the tunnels, clutching that accursed manuscript I had not had the courage to destroy. I hoped my feet would guide me to the place where I was to bury it forever. I turned a thousand corners until I thought I was lost. Then, when I was convinced I'd followed the same path a dozen times, I discovered I was standing at the entrance to the small chamber where I'd seen my own reflection in the mirror in which the eyes of the man in black were ever-present. I found a gap between two spines of black leather and there, without thinking twice, I buried the boss's folder. I was about to leave the chamber when I turned and went back to the shelf. I picked up the volume next to the slot in which I had confined the manuscript and opened it. I'd only read a couple of sentences when I heard that dark laughter again behind me. I returned the book to its place and picked another at random, flicking through the pages. I took another, then another, and went on in this way until I had examined dozens of the volumes that populated the room. I realised that they all contained different arrangements of the same words, that the same images darkened their pages and the same fable was repeated in them like a pas de deux in an infinite hall of mirrors. *Lux Aeterna.*

When I emerged from the labyrinth Isabella was waiting for me, sitting on some steps, holding the book she had chosen. I sat down next to her and she leaned her head on my shoulder.

'Thank you for bringing me here,' she said.

I suddenly understood that I would never see that place again, that I was condemned to dream about it and to sculpt what I remembered of it into my memory, considering myself lucky to have been able to walk through its passages and touch its secrets. I closed my eyes for a moment so that the image might become engraved in my mind. Then, without daring to look back, I took Isabella's hand and made my way towards the exit, leaving the Cemetery of Forgotten Books behind me forever.

Isabella came with me to the dock, where the ship was waiting to take me far away from that city, from everything I knew.

'What did you say the captain was called?'

'Charon.'

431

'I don't think that's funny.'

I hugged her for the last time and looked into her eyes. On the way we had agreed there would be no farewells, no solemn words, no promises to fulfil. When the midnight bells rang in Santa María del Mar, I went on board. Captain Olmo greeted me and offered to take me to my cabin. I said I would rather wait. The crew cast off and gradually the hull moved away from the dock. I positioned myself at the stern, watching the city fade in a tide of lights. Isabella remained there, motionless, her eyes fixed on mine, until the dock was lost in the night and the great mirage of Barcelona sank into the black waters. One by one the lights of the city went out, and I realised that I had already begun to remember.

Epilogue

1945

Fifteen long years have passed since the night I fled the city of the damned. For a long time mine has been an existence filled with absences, with no other name or presence than that of a travelling stranger. I've had a hundred names and a hundred trades, none of them my own.

I have disappeared into huge cities and villages so small that nobody had a past or a future. In no place did I linger more than was necessary. Sooner rather than later I would flee again, without warning, leaving behind me only a couple of old books and second-hand clothes in sombre rooms where time showed no pity and memory burned. Uncertainty has been my only recollection. The years have taught me to live in the body of a stranger who does not know whether he committed those crimes he can still smell on his hands, or whether he has indeed lost his mind and is condemned to roam a world in flames which he dreamed up in exchange for a few coins and the promise of evading a death that now seems to him like the sweetest of rewards. I have often asked myself whether the bullet that Inspector Grandes fired at my heart went right through the pages of the book, whether I was the one who died in the cabin suspended in the sky.

During my years of pilgrimage I've seen how the inferno promised in the pages I wrote for the boss has taken on a life of its own. I have fled from my own shadow a thousand times, always looking over my shoulder, always expecting to find it round a corner, on the other side of the street or at the foot of my bed in the endless hours that precede dawn. I've never allowed anyone to know me long enough to ask why I never grow old, why no lines appear on my face, why my reflection is the same as the night I left Isabella in the port of Barcelona, and not a minute older.

There came a time when I believed I had exhausted all the hiding places of the world. I was so tired of being afraid, of living and dying from my memories, that I stopped where the land ended and an ocean began – an ocean which, like me, looks the same every morning – and, worn out, I collapsed.

It is a year to the day since I came to this place and recovered my name and my trade. I bought this old hut on the beach, just a shed that I share with the books left behind by the previous owner and a typewriter which I like to think might be the same one on which I wrote hundreds of pages that perhaps nobody remembers – I will never know. From my window I see a small wooden jetty that stretches out into the sea and, moored at the end, the boat that came with the house, a simple rowing boat in which I sometimes go out as far as the reef, at which point the coast almost disappears from view.

I had not written again until I got here. The first time I slipped a page into the typewriter and placed my hands on the keyboard, I was afraid I'd be unable to write a single line. I began writing this story during my first night in the hut. I wrote until dawn, just as I did years ago, without yet knowing who I was writing it for. During the day I walked along the beach or sat on the jetty opposite the hut – a gangway between sky and sea – reading through the piles of old newspapers I found in one of the cupboards. Their pages brought me stories of the war, of the world in flames that I had dreamed up for the boss.

It was while I was reading those chronicles about the war in Spain, and then in Europe and the world, that I decided I no longer had anything to lose; all I wanted to know was whether Isabella was all right and if perhaps she still remembered me. Or maybe I only wanted to know whether she was still alive. I wrote that letter, addressed to the old Sempere & Sons bookshop in Calle Santa Ana in Barcelona, which would take weeks or months to arrive at its destination, if it ever did arrive. For the sender's name I wrote *Mr Rochester*, knowing that if the letter did reach her hands, Isabella would know who it was from. If she wished, she could leave it unopened and forget me forever.

For months I continued writing this story. I saw my father's face again, and I walked through the offices of *The Voice of Industry*, dreaming that I might be able, one day, to emulate the great Pedro Vidal. Once more, I saw Cristina Sagnier for the first time, and I went into the tower house to dive into the madness that had consumed Diego Marlasca. I wrote from midnight until dawn without resting, feeling alive for the first time since I had fled from the city.

The letter arrived one day in June. The postman had slipped the envelope under my door while I slept. It was addressed to *Mr Rochester* and the return address read simply: *Sempere & Sons Bookshop, Barcelona.* For a few minutes I walked in circles round the hut, not daring to open it. Finally I went out and sat by the edge of the sea. In the letter I found a single page and a second, smaller, envelope. The second envelope, which looked worn, just had my name on it, *David*, in a handwriting I had not forgotten despite all the years that had flowed by since I last saw it.

In the letter, Sempere's son told me that after a few years of tempestuous and intermittent courting, he and Isabella had married on 18 January 1935 in the church of Santa Ana. The ceremony, against all odds, had been conducted by the ninety-year-old priest who had delivered the eulogy at Señor Sempere's funeral and who, contrary to the bishop's eagerness to see the back of him, refused to die and went on doing things his own way. A year later, only days before the Civil War broke out, Isabella had given birth to a boy whose name would be Daniel Sempere. The terrible years of the war brought with them all manner of hardships, and shortly after the end of the conflict Isabella contracted cholera and died in her husband's arms, in the apartment they shared above the bookshop. She was buried in Montjuïc on Daniel's fourth birthday, during rain that lasted two days and two nights, and when the little boy had asked him if heaven was crying, his father couldn't bring himself to reply.

The envelope with my name on it contained a letter that Isabella had written to me during her final days, which she'd made her husband swear he would send to me if he ever discovered my whereabouts.

Dear David,

Sometimes I think I began to write this letter to you years ago and still haven't been capable of finishing it. A lot of time has passed since I last saw you and a lot of terrible, miserable things have happened, and yet not a day goes by when I don't think of you and wonder where you are, whether you have found peace, whether you are writing, whether you've become a grumpy old man, whether you're in love or whether you still remember us, the small bookshop of Sempere & Sons, and the worst assistant you ever had.

I'm afraid you left without teaching me how to write and I don't even know where to begin to put into words all the things I would like to say to you. I would like you to know that I have been happy, that thanks to you I found a man whom I've loved and who has loved me. Together we've had a child, Daniel. I always talk to him about you and he has given my life a meaning that all the books in the world wouldn't be able to explain.

Nobody knows this, but sometimes I still go back to that dock where I saw you leave and I sit there a while, alone, waiting, as if I believe that some day you'll return. If you do, you will see that despite all the things that have happened the bookshop is still there, the plot of land on which the tower house once stood is still empty and all the lies that were said about you have been forgotten. So many people in these streets have blood on their souls that they no longer dare to remember, and when they do they lie to themselves because they cannot look at their own reflection in the mirror. In the bookshop we still sell your books, but under the counter, because they have been declared immoral. This country is filled with more people who are intent on destroying and burning books than with those who want to read them. These are bad times and I often think that there are worse times to come.

My husband and the doctors think they are fooling me, but I know that I have little time left. I know I will die soon and that by the time you receive this letter I will no longer be here. That is why I wanted to write to you, because I wanted you to know that I'm not afraid, that my only sorrow is that I'll leave behind a good man who has given me his life, and my Daniel, alone in a world that every day seems to me more as you said it was and not as I wanted to believe it could be.

I wanted to write to you so that you know that despite everything I have experienced, I'm grateful for the time I have spent here, grateful for having met you and for having been your friend. I wanted to write to you because I'd like you to remember me and, one day, if you have someone as I have my little Daniel, I'd like you to talk to that someone about me and, through your words, make me live forever.

From one who loves you,

ISABELLA

Two days after I received that letter I realised I was not alone on the beach. I felt his presence in the first breath of dawn but I would not, and could not, flee again. It happened one afternoon after I sat down to write by the window, while I waited for the sun to sink into the horizon. I heard the footsteps on the wooden planks of the jetty and I saw him.

The boss, dressed in white, was walking down the jetty, holding the hand of a girl of about seven or eight years old. I recognised the image instantly, the old photograph Cristina had always treasured without knowing where it came from. The boss reached the end of the jetty and knelt down beside the girl. Together they watched the sun spill over the ocean in an endless sheet of molten gold. I stepped out of the hut and walked along the wooden gangway. When I reached the end, the boss turned and smiled at me. There was no threat or resentment on his face, only a hint of melancholy.

'I've missed you, dear friend,' he said. 'I've missed our conversations, even our small arguments . . .'

'Have you come to settle a score?'

The boss smiled and shook his head.

'We all make mistakes, Martín. I was the first. I stole what you loved the most. I didn't do it to hurt you. I did it out of fear. Out of fear that she might drive you away from me, from our work. I was wrong. I've taken a long time to admit it, but if there is anything I do have, it is time.'

I observed him carefully. The boss, like me, had not grown a day older.

'Why have you come here, then?'

The boss shrugged his shoulders.

'I came to say goodbye.'

His eyes concentrated on the girl whose hand he was holding and who was looking at me curiously.

'What's your name?' I asked.

'Her name's Cristina,' said the boss.

I looked into her eyes and she nodded. I felt my blood freeze. I could only guess at the features, but the look was unmistakable.

'Cristina, say hello to my friend David. From now on you're going to live with him.'

I exchanged glances with the boss but didn't say a word. The girl stretched out her hand to me, as if she had practised that movement a thousand times, and then laughed in embarrassment. I leaned down towards her and shook it.

'Hello,' she said in a quiet voice.

'Very good, Cristina,' said the boss approvingly. 'And what else?'

The girl looked as if she'd suddenly remembered something.

'I was told you're a maker of stories and fairy tales.'

'One of the best,' the boss added.

'Will you make one for me?'

I hesitated a few seconds. The girl looked anxiously at the boss.

'Martín?' the boss whispered.

'Of course,' I said at last. 'I'll make you as many stories as you want.'

The girl smiled and, drawing closer to me, kissed me on the cheek.

'Cristina, why don't you go down to the beach and wait there while I say goodbye to my friend?' the boss asked.

Cristina nodded and walked away, looking back and smiling with every step. Next to me, the boss's voice sweetly whispered his eternal curse.

'I've decided to give you back what you loved the most, what I stole from you. I've decided that for once you will walk in my shoes and will feel what I feel – you won't age a single day and you will see Cristina grow; you will fall in love with her again and one day you will see her die in your arms. That is my blessing, and my revenge.'

I closed my eyes, saying no to myself.

'That is impossible. She will never be the same person.'

'That will depend on you, Martín. I'm giving you a blank sheet. This story no longer belongs to me.'

I heard his steps fade away, and when I opened my eyes the boss was no longer there. At the foot of the jetty, Cristina was looking at me intently. I smiled at her and she hesitated, then came over.

'Where's the gentleman?' she asked.

'He's gone.'

Cristina looked around her, at the endless, deserted beach.

'Forever?'

'Forever.'

She smiled and sat down beside me.

'I dreamed that we were friends,' she said.

I looked at her and nodded.

'And we are friends. We always have been.'

She laughed and took my hand. I pointed in front of us, at the sun dipping into the sea, and Cristina watched it with tears in her eyes.

'Will I remember one day?'

'One day.'

I knew then that I would devote every minute we had left together to making her happy, to repairing the pain I had caused her and returning to her what I had never known how to give her. These pages will be our memory until she draws her last breath in my arms and I take her with me to the open sea, where the deep currents flow, to sink with her forever, and escape at last to a place where neither heaven nor hell will ever be able to find us.